THE BANE CHRONICLES

THE SHADOWHUNTER CHRONICLES

THE LAST HOURS

Chain of Gold

THE SHADOWHUNTER'S CODEX

With Joshua Lewis

TALES FROM THE SHADOWHUNTER ACADEMY

With Sarah Rees Brennan, Maureen Johnson

and Robin Wasserman

THE INFERNAL DEVICES

Clockwork Angel

Clockwork Prince

Clockwork Princess

THE MORTAL INSTRUMENTS

City of Bones

City of Ashes

City of Glass

City of Fallen Angels

City of Lost Souls

City of Heavenly Fire

***e*Book**
available

The Bane Chronicles

CASSANDRA CLARE

SARAH REES BRENNAN

MAUREEN JOHNSON

WALKER
BOOKS

First published in Great Britain 2014 by Walker Books Ltd
87 Vauxhall Walk, London SE11 5HJ

This edition published 2015

8 10 9

This book has been typeset in Dolly

Printed and bound by CPI Group (UK) Ltd, Croydon CR0 4YY

British Library Cataloguing in Publication Data:
a catalogue record for this book is available from the British Library

ISBN 978-1-4063-6058-5

www.walker.co.uk

FSC
www.fsc.org
MIX
Paper from responsible sources
FSC® C020471

This is for the people—they know who they are—who write letters and e-mails, and come up at signings, and say Magnus and Alec mean a lot to them.

Like Magnus, you are magical and you are heroes.

CONTENTS

What Really Happened in Peru

By Cassandra Clare and Sarah Rees Brennan

So he kept at it with the charango, *despite the fact that he was forbidden to play it in the house. He was also discouraged from playing it in public places by a crying child, a man with papers talking about city ordinances, and a small riot.*

As a last resort he went up to the mountains and played there. Magnus was sure that the llama stampede he witnessed was a coincidence. The llamas could not be judging him.

—What Really Happened in Peru

It was a sad moment in Magnus Bane's life when he was banned from Peru by the High Council of Peruvian warlocks. It was not just because the posters with a picture of him that were passed around Downworld in Peru were so wildly unflattering. It was because Peru was one of his favorite places. He had had many adventures there, and had many wonderful memories, starting with the time in 1791 when he had invited Ragnor Fell to join him for a festive sightseeing escape in Lima.

1791

Magnus awoke in his roadside inn just outside Lima, and once he had arrayed himself in an embroidered waistcoat, breeches, and shining buckled shoes, he went in search of breakfast. Instead he found his hostess, a plump woman whose long hair was covered with a black mantilla, in a deep, troubled conference with one of the serving girls about a recent arrival to the inn.

"I think it's a sea monster," he heard his hostess whisper. "Or a merman. Can they survive on land?"

"Good morning, ladies," Magnus called out. "Sounds like my guest has arrived."

Both women blinked twice. Magnus put the first blink down to his vivid attire, and the second, slower blink down to what he had just said. He gave them both a cheery wave and wandered out through wide wooden doors and across the courtyard into the common room, where he found his fellow warlock Ragnor Fell skulking in the back of the room with a mug of *chicha de molle*.

"I'll have what he's having," Magnus said to the serving lady. "No, wait a moment. I'll have three of what he's having."

"Tell them I'll have the same," said Ragnor. "I achieved this drink only through some very determined pointing."

Magnus did, and when he returned his gaze to Ragnor, he saw that his old friend was looking his usual self: hideously dressed, deeply gloomy, and deeply green of skin. Magnus often gave thanks that his own warlock's mark was not so obvious. It was sometimes inconvenient to have the gold-green, slit-pupilled eyes of a cat, but this was usually easily hidden with a small glamour, and if not, well, there were quite a few ladies—and men—who didn't find it a drawback.

"No glamour?" Magnus inquired.

"You said that you wanted me to join you on travels that would be a ceaseless round of debauchery," Ragnor told him.

Magnus beamed. "I did!" He paused. "Forgive me. I do not see the connection."

"I have found I have better luck with the ladies in my natural state," Ragnor told him. "Ladies enjoy a bit of variety. There was a woman in the court of Louis the Sun King who said none could compare to her 'dear little cabbage.' I hear it's become quite a popular term of endearment in France. All thanks to me."

He spoke in the same glum tones as usual. When the six drinks arrived, Magnus seized on them.

"I'll be needing all of these. Please bring more for my friend."

"There was also a woman who referred to me as her sweet peapod of love," Ragnor continued.

Magnus took a deep restorative swallow, looked at the sunshine outside and the drinks before him, and felt better about the entire situation. "Congratulations. And welcome to Lima, the City of Kings, my sweet peapod."

* * *

After breakfast, which was five drinks for Ragnor and seventeen for Magnus, Magnus took Ragnor on a tour of Lima, from the golden, curled, and carved facade of the archbishop's palace to the brightly colored buildings across the plaza, with their practically mandatory elaborate balconies, where the Spanish had once executed criminals.

"I thought it would be nice to start in the capital. Besides, I've been here before," Magnus said. "About fifty years ago. I had a lovely time, aside from the earthquake that almost swallowed the city."

"Did you have something to do with that earthquake?"

"Ragnor," Magnus reproached his friend. "You cannot blame me for every little natural disaster that happens!"

"You didn't answer the question," Ragnor said, and sighed. "I am relying on you to be ... more reliable and less like you than you usually are," he warned as they walked. "I don't speak the language."

"So you don't speak Spanish?" Magnus asked. "Or you don't speak Quechua? Or is it that you don't speak Aymara?"

Magnus was perfectly aware he was a stranger everywhere he went, and he took care to learn all the languages so he could go anywhere he chose. Spanish had been the first language that he had learned to speak, after his native language. That was the one tongue he did not speak often. It reminded him of his mother, and his stepfather—reminded him of the love and the prayer and despair of his childhood. The words of his homeland rested a little too heavily on his tongue, as if he had to mean them, had to be serious, when he spoke.

(There were other languages—Purgatic and Gehennic and Tartarian—that he had learned so that he could communicate with those from the demon realms, languages he was forced to use often in his line of work. But those reminded him of his blood father, and those memories were even worse.)

Sincerity and gravity, in Magnus's opinion, were highly overrated, as was being forced to relive unpleasant memories. He would much rather be amused and amusing.

"I don't speak any of the things that you just said," Ragnor told him. "Although, I must speak Prattling Fool, since I can understand you."

"That is hurtful and unnecessary," Magnus observed. "But of course, you can trust me completely."

"Just don't leave me here without guidance. You have to swear, Bane."

Magnus raised his eyebrows. "I give you my word of honor!"

"I will find you," Ragnor told him. "I will find whatever chest of absurd clothes you have. And I will bring a llama into the place where you sleep and make sure that it urinates on everything you possess."

"There is no need to get nasty about this," Magnus said. "Don't worry. I can teach you every word that you need to know right now. One of them is '*fiesta*.'"

Ragnor scowled. "What does that mean?"

Magnus raised his eyebrows. "It means 'party.' Another important word is '*juerga*.'"

"What does that word mean?"

Magnus was silent.

"Magnus," said Ragnor, his voice stern. "Does that word also mean 'party'?"

Magnus could not help the sly grin that spread across his face. "I would apologize," he said. "Except that I feel no regret at all."

"Try to be a little sensible," Ragnor suggested.

"We're on holiday!" said Magnus.

"You're always on holiday," Ragnor pointed out. "You've been on holiday for thirty years!"

It was true. Magnus had not been settled anywhere since his lover died—not his first lover, but the first one who had lived by his side and died in his arms. Magnus had thought of her often enough that the mention of her did not hurt him, her remembered face like the distant familiar beauty of stars, not to be touched but to shine in front of his eyes at night.

"I can't get enough adventure," Magnus said lightly. "And adventure cannot get enough of me."

He had no idea why Ragnor sighed again.

Ragnor's suspicious nature continued to make Magnus very sad and disappointed in him as a person, such as when they visited Lake Yarinacocha and Ragnor's eyes narrowed as he demanded: "Are those dolphins *pink?*"

"They were pink when I got here!" Magnus exclaimed indignantly. He paused and considered. "I am almost certain."

They went from *costa* to *sierra* seeing all the sights of Peru. Magnus's favorite was perhaps the city of Arequipa, a piece of the moon, made of sillar rock that when touched by the sun blazed as dazzling and scintillating a white as moonlight striking water.

There was a very attractive young lady there too, but in the end she decided she preferred Ragnor. Magnus could have lived his whole long life without becoming involved in a warlock love triangle, or hearing the endearment "adorable pitcher plant of a man" spoken in French, which Ragnor did understand. Ragnor, however, seemed very pleased and for the first time did not seem to regret that he'd come when Magnus had summoned him to Lima.

In the end Magnus was able to persuade Ragnor away from Arequipa only by introducing him to another lovely young lady, Giuliana, who knew her way in the rain forest and assured them both that she would be able to lead them to *ayahuasca*, a plant with remarkable magical properties.

Later Magnus had cause to regret choosing this particular lure as he pulled himself through the green swathes of the Manu rain forest. It was all green, green, green, everywhere he looked. Even when he looked at his traveling companion.

"I don't like the rain forest," Ragnor said sadly.

"That's because you are not open to new experiences in the same way I am!"

"No, it is because it is wetter than a boar's armpit and twice as smelly here."

Magnus pushed a dripping frond out of his eyes. "I admit you make an excellent point and also paint a vivid picture with your words."

It was not comfortable in the rain forest, that much was true, but it was wonderful there all the same. The thick green of the undergrowth was different from the delicate leaves on trees higher up, the bright feathery shapes of some plants gently waving at the rope-like strands of others. The green all around was broken up by sudden bright interruptions: the vivid splash of flowers and the rush of movement that meant animals instead of leaves.

Magnus was especially charmed by the sight of the spider monkeys above, dainty and glossy with long arms and legs spread out in the trees like stars, and the shy swift spring of squirrel monkeys.

"Picture this," said Magnus. "Me with a little monkey friend. I could teach him tricks. I could dress him in a cunning jacket. He could look just like me! But more monkey-shaped."

"Your friend has gone mad and giddy with the altitude sickness," Giuliana announced. "We are many feet above sea level here."

Magnus was not entirely sure why he had brought a guide, except that it seemed to calm Ragnor down. Other people probably dutifully followed their guides in unfamiliar and potentially dangerous places, but Magnus was a warlock and fully prepared to have a magical battle with a jaguar demon if that was required. It would be an excellent story, which might impress some of the ladies who were not inexplicably allured by Ragnor. Or some of the gentlemen.

Lost in picking fruit and in the contemplation of jaguar demons, Magnus looked around at one point and found himself separated from his companions—lost in the green wilderness.

He paused and admired the bromeliads, huge iridescent flower-like bowls made out of petals, shimmering with color and water. There were frogs inside the jewel-bright recesses of the flowers.

Then he looked up into the round brown eyes of a monkey.

"Hello, companion," said Magnus.

The monkey made a terrible sound, half snarl and half hiss.

"I begin to rather doubt the beauty of our friendship," said Magnus.

Giuliana had told them not to back down when approached by monkeys, but to stay still and preserve an air of calm authority. This monkey was much larger than the other monkeys Magnus had seen, with broader bunched shoulders and thick, almost black fur—a howler monkey, Magnus remembered they were called.

Magnus threw the monkey a fig. The monkey took the fig.

"There," said Magnus. "Let us consider the matter settled."

The monkey advanced, chewing in a menacing fashion.

"I rather wonder what I am doing here. I enjoy city life, you know," Magnus observed. "The glittering lights, the constant companionship, the liquid entertainment. The lack of sudden monkeys."

He ignored Giuliana's advice and took a smart step back, and also threw another piece of fruit. The monkey did not take the bait this time. He coiled and rattled out a growl, and Magnus took several more steps back and into a tree.

Magnus flailed on impact, was briefly grateful that nobody was watching him and expecting him to be a sophisticated warlock, and had a monkey assault launched directly to his face.

He shouted, spun, and sprinted through the rain forest. He did not even think to drop the fruit. It fell one by one in a bright cascade as he ran for his life from the simian menace. He heard it in hot pursuit and fled faster, until all his fruit was gone and he ran right into Ragnor.

"Have a care!" Ragnor snapped.

"In my defense, you are quite well camouflaged," Magnus pointed out, and then he detailed his terrible monkey adventure twice, once for Giuliana in Spanish, and again for Ragnor in English.

"But of course you should have retreated at once from the dominant male," Giuliana said. "Are you an idiot? You are extremely lucky he was distracted from ripping out your throat by the fruit. He thought you were trying to steal his females."

"Pardon me, but we did not have the time to exchange that kind of personal information," Magnus said. "I could not have known! Moreover, I wish to assure both of you that I did not make any amorous advances on female monkeys." He paused and winked. "I didn't actually see any, so I never got the chance."

Ragnor looked very regretful about all the choices that had led to his being in this place and especially in this company. Later he stooped and hissed, low enough so Giuliana could not hear and in a way that reminded Magnus horribly of his monkey nemesis: "Did you forget that you can do *magic*?"

Magnus spared a moment to toss a disdainful look over his shoulder.

"I am not going to ensorcel a monkey! Honestly, Ragnor. What do you take me for?"

Life could not be entirely devoted to debauchery and monkeys. Magnus had to finance all the drinking somehow. There was always a Downworlder network to be found, and he had made sure to make the right contacts as soon as he'd set foot in Peru.

When his particular expertise was called for, he brought Ragnor with him. They boarded the ship in the Salaverry harbor together, both dressed in their greatest finery. Magnus was wearing his largest hat, with an ostrich feather plume.

Edmund García, one of the richest merchants in Peru, met them on the foredeck. He was a man with a florid complexion, dressed in an expensive-looking cassock, knee breeches, and a powdered wig. An engraved pistol hung from his leather belt. He squinted at

Ragnor. "Is that a sea monster?" he demanded.

"He is a highly respected warlock," said Magnus. "You are, in fact, getting two warlocks for the price of one."

García had not made his fortune by turning his nose up at bargains. He was instantly and forevermore silent on the subject of sea monsters.

"Welcome," he said instead.

"I dislike boats," Ragnor observed, looking around. "I get vilely seasick."

The turning green joke was too easy. Magnus was not going to stoop to make it.

"Would you care to elaborate on what this job entails?" he asked instead. "The letter I received said you had need of my particular talents, but I must confess that I have so many talents that I am not sure which one you require. They are all, of course, at your disposal."

"You are strangers to our shores," said Edmund. "So perhaps you do not know that the current state of prosperity in Peru rests on our chief export—guano."

"What's he saying?" Ragnor asked.

"Nothing you would like, so far," Magnus said. The boat lurched beneath them on the waves. "Pardon me. You were talking about bird droppings."

"I was," said García. "For a long time the European merchants were the ones who profited most from this trade. Now laws have been passed to ensure that Peruvian merchants will have the upper hand in such dealings, and the Europeans will have to make us partners in their enterprises or retire from the guano business. One of my ships, bearing a large quantity of guano as cargo, will be one of the first sent out now that the laws have been passed. I fear attempts may be made on the ship."

"You think pirates are out to steal your bird droppings?" Magnus asked.

"What's going on?" Ragnor moaned piteously.

"You don't want to know. Trust me." Magnus looked at García. "Varied though my talents are, I am not sure they extend to guarding, ah, guano."

He was dubious about the cargo, but he did know something about Europeans swooping in and laying claim to everything they saw as if it were unquestionably theirs, land and lives, produce and people.

Besides which, he had never had an adventure on the high seas before.

"We are prepared to pay handsomely," García offered, naming a sum.

"Oh. Well, in that case, consider us hired," said Magnus, and he broke the news to Ragnor.

"I'm still not sure about any of this," Ragnor said. "I'm not even sure where you got that hat."

Magnus adjusted it for maximum jauntiness. "Just a little something I picked up. Seemed appropriate for the occasion."

"Nobody else is wearing anything even remotely like it."

Magnus cast a disparaging look around at all the fashion-challenged sailors. "I feel sorry for them, of course, but I do not see why that observation should alter my current extremely stylish course of action."

He looked from the ship deck across to the sea. The water was a particularly clear green, with the same shading of turquoise and emerald as in a polished green tourmaline. Two ships were visible on the horizon—the ship that they were on their way to join, and a second, which Magnus suspected strongly was a pirate ship intent on attacking the first.

Magnus snapped his fingers, and their own ship swallowed the horizon at a gulp.

"Magnus, don't magic the ship to go faster," Ragnor said.

"Magnus, why are you magicking the ship to go faster?"

Magnus snapped his fingers again, and blue sparks played along the weather-worn and storm-splintered side of the ship. "I spy dread pirates in the distance. Ready yourself for battle, my greenish friend."

Ragnor was loudly sick at that and even more loudly unhappy about it, but they were gaining on the two ships, so Magnus was overall pleased.

"We are not hunting pirates. Nobody is a pirate! We are safeguarding cargo and that's all. And what is this cargo, anyway?" Ragnor asked.

"You're happier not knowing, my sweet little peapod," Magnus assured him.

"Please stop calling me that."

"I never shall, never," Magnus vowed, and he made a swift economical gesture, with his rings catching the sunshine and painting the air in tiny bright brushstrokes.

The ship Magnus insisted on thinking of as the enemy pirate ship noticeably listed to one side. It was possible Magnus had gone slightly too far there.

García seemed extremely impressed that Magnus could disable ships from a distance, but he wanted to be absolutely sure the cargo was safe, so they drew their vessel alongside the larger ship—the pirate ship was by now lagging far, far behind them.

Magnus was perfectly happy with this state of affairs. Since they were hunting pirates and adventuring on the high seas, there was something that he had always wanted to try.

"You do it too," he urged Ragnor. "It will be dashing. You'll see."

Then he seized a rope and swung, dashingly, across fathoms of shining blue space and over a stretch of gleaming deck.

Then he dropped, neatly, into the hold.

Ragnor followed him a few moments later.

"Hold your nose," Magnus counseled urgently. "Do not breathe in. Obviously someone was checking on the cargo, and left the hold open, and we both just jumped directly in."

"And now here we are, all thanks to you, in the soup."

"If only," said Magnus.

There was a brief pause for them both to evaluate the full horror of the situation. Magnus, personally, was in horror up to his elbows. Even more tragically, he had lost his jaunty hat. He was simply trying not to think of what substance they were mostly buried in. If he thought very hard of anything other than the excrement of tiny winged mammals, he could imagine that he was stuck in something else. Anything else.

"Magnus," Ragnor said. "I can see that the cargo we're guarding is some very unpleasant substance, but could you tell me exactly what it *is*?"

Seeing that concealment and pretense were useless, Magnus told him.

"I hate adventures in Peru," Ragnor said at last in a stifled voice. "I want to go home."

It was not Magnus's fault when the ensuing warlock tantrum managed to sink the boat full of guano, but he was blamed just the same. Even worse, he was not paid.

Magnus's wanton destruction of Peruvian property was not, however, the reason he was banned from Peru.

1885

The next time Magnus was back in Peru, he was on a job with his friends Catarina Loss and Ragnor Fell. This proved Catarina had, besides magic, supernatural powers of persuasion, because Ragnor had sworn that he would never set foot in Peru again and certainly never in Magnus's company. But the two had had some adventures together in England during the 1870s, and Ragnor had grown better disposed toward Magnus. Still, the whole time they were walking into the valley of the Lurín River with their client, Ragnor was sending Magnus suspicious little glances out of the corner of his eye.

"This constant air of foreboding that you have when you're around me is hurtful and unwarranted, you know," Magnus told Ragnor.

"I was airing the smell out of my clothes for years! Years!" Ragnor replied.

"Well, you should have thrown them out and bought clothes that were both more sweetly scented and more stylish," Magnus said. "Anyway, that was decades ago. What have I done to you lately?"

"Don't fight in front of the client, boys," Catarina implored in her sweet voice, "or I will knock your heads together so hard, your skulls will crack like eggs."

"I can speak English, you know," said Nayaraq, their client, who was paying them extremely generously.

Embarrassment descended on the entire group. They reached Pachacamac in silence. They beheld the walls of piled rubble, which looked like a giant, artful child's sculpture made of sand.

There were pyramids here, but it was mostly ruins. What remained was thousands of years old, though, and Magnus could feel magic thrumming even in the sand-colored fragments.

"I knew the oracle who lived here seven hundred years ago," Magnus announced grandly. Nayaraq looked impressed.

Catarina, who knew Magnus's actual age perfectly well, did not.

Magnus had first started putting a price on his magic when he was less than twenty years old. He'd still been growing then, not yet fixed in time like a dragonfly caught in amber, iridescent and everlasting but frozen forever and a day in the prison of one golden instant. When he was growing to his full height and his face and body were changing infinitesimally every day, when he was a little closer to human than he was now.

You could not tell a potential customer, expecting a learned and ancient magician, that you were not even fully grown. Magnus had started lying about his age young, and had never dropped the habit.

It did get a little embarrassing sometimes when he forgot what lie he'd told to whom. Someone had once asked him what Julius Caesar was like, and Magnus had stared at him for much too long and said, "Not tall?"

Magnus looked around at the sand lying close to the walls, and at the cracked crumbling edges of those walls, as if the stone were bread and a careless hand had torn a piece away. He carefully maintained the blasé air of one who had been here before and had been incredibly well dressed that time too.

"Pachacamac" meant "Lord of Earthquakes." Fortunately, Nayaraq did not want them to create one. Magnus had never created an earthquake on purpose and preferred not to dwell on unfortunate accidents in his youth.

What Nayaraq wanted was the treasure that her mother's mother's mother's mother, a beautiful noble girl living in the Acllahausi—the house of the women chosen by the sun—had hidden when the conquerors had come.

Magnus was not sure why she wanted it, as she seemed to have money enough, but he was not being paid to question her. They walked for hours in sun and shadow, by the ruined walls that bore the marks of time and the faint impressions of frescoes, until they found what she was looking for.

When the stones were removed from the wall and the treasure was dug out, the sun struck the gold and Nayaraq's face at the same time. That was when Magnus understood that Nayaraq had not been searching for gold but for truth, for something real in her past.

She knew of Downworlders because she had been taken by the faeries, once. But this was not illusion or glamour, this gold shining in her hands as it had once shone in her ancestor's hands.

"Thank you all very much," she said, and Magnus understood and for a moment almost envied her.

When she was gone, Catarina let her own glamour fall away to reveal blue skin and white hair that dazzled in the dying sunlight.

"Now that that's settled, I have something to propose. I have been jealous for years about all the adventures you two had in Peru. What do you say to continuing on here for a while?"

"Absolutely!" said Magnus.

Catarina clapped her hands together.

Ragnor scowled. "Absolutely not."

"Don't worry, Ragnor," Magnus said carelessly. "I am fairly certain nobody who remembers the pirate misunderstanding is still alive. And the monkeys definitely aren't still after me. Besides, you know what this means."

"I do not want to do this, and I will not enjoy it," Ragnor said. "I would leave at once, but it would be cruel to abandon a lady in a foreign land with a maniac."

"I am so glad we are all agreed," said Catarina.

"We are going to be a dread triumvirate," Magnus informed Catarina and Ragnor with delight. "That means thrice the adventure."

Later they heard that they were wanted criminals for desecrating a temple, but nevertheless, that was not the reason, nor the time, that Magnus was banned from Peru.

1890

It was a beautiful day in Puno, the lake out the window a wash of blue and the sun shining with such dazzling force that it seemed to have burned all the azure and cloud out of the sky and left it all a white blaze. Carried on the clear mountain air, out over the lake water and through the house, rang Magnus's melody.

Magnus was turning in a gentle circle under the windowsill when the shutters on Ragnor's bedroom window slammed open.

"What—what—what are you doing?" he demanded.

"I am almost six hundred years old," Magnus claimed, and Ragnor snorted, since Magnus changed his age to suit himself every few weeks. Magnus swept on. "It does seem about time to learn a musical instrument." He flourished his new prize, a little stringed instrument that looked like a cousin of the lute that the lute was embarrassed to be related to. "It's called a *charango*. I am planning to become a *charanguista*!"

"I wouldn't call that an instrument of music," Ragnor observed sourly. "An instrument of torture, perhaps."

Magnus cradled the *charango* in his arms as if it were an easily offended baby. "It's a beautiful and very unique instrument! The sound box is made from an armadillo. Well, a dried armadillo shell."

"That explains the sound you're making," said Ragnor. "Like a lost, hungry armadillo."

"You are just jealous," Magnus remarked calmly. "Because you do not have the soul of a true artiste like myself."

"Oh, I am positively green with envy," Ragnor snapped.

"Come now, Ragnor. That's not fair," said Magnus. "You know I love it when you make jokes about your complexion."

Magnus refused to be affected by Ragnor's cruel judgments. He regarded his fellow warlock with a lofty stare of superb indifference, raised his *charango*, and began to play again his defiant, beautiful tune.

They both heard the staccato thump of frantically running feet from within the house, the swish of skirts, and then Catarina came rushing out into the courtyard. Her white hair was falling loose about her shoulders, and her face was the picture of alarm.

"Magnus, Ragnor, I heard a cat making a most unearthly noise," she exclaimed. "From the sound of it, the poor creature must be direly sick. You have to help me find it!"

Ragnor immediately collapsed with hysterical laughter on his windowsill. Magnus stared at Catarina for a moment, until he saw her lips twitch.

"You are conspiring against me and my art," he declared. "You are a pack of conspirators."

He began to play again. Catarina stopped him by putting a hand on his arm.

"No, but seriously, Magnus," she said. "That noise is appalling."

Magnus sighed. "Every warlock's a critic."

"Why are you doing this?"

"I have already explained myself to Ragnor. I wish to become proficient with a musical instrument. I have decided to devote myself to the art of the *charanguista*, and I wish to hear no more petty objections."

"If we are all making lists of things we wish to hear no more...," Ragnor murmured.

Catarina, however, was smiling.

"I see," she said.

"Madam, you do not see."

"I do. I see it all most clearly," Catarina assured him. "What is her name?"

"I resent your implication," Magnus said. "There is no woman in the case. I am married to my music!"

"Oh, all right," Catarina said. "What's his name, then?"

His name was Imasu Morales, and he was gorgeous.

The three warlocks were staying near the harbor, along the shoreline of Lake Titicaca, but Magnus liked to see and be part of life in a way that Ragnor and Catarina, familiar with quiet and solitude from childhood on account of their unusual complexions, did not quite understand. He went walking about the city and up into the mountains, having small adventures. On a few occasions that Ragnor and Catarina kept hurtfully and unnecessarily reminding him of, he had been escorted home by the police, even though that incident with the Bolivian smugglers had been a complete misunderstanding.

Magnus had not been involved in any dealings with smugglers

that night, though. He had simply been walking through the Plaza Republicana, skirting around artfully sculpted bushes and artfully sculpted sculptures. The city below shone like stars arranged in neat rows, as if someone were growing a harvest of light. It was a beautiful night to meet a beautiful boy.

The music had caught Magnus's ear first, and then the laughter. Magnus had turned to look and saw sparkling dark eyes and rumpled hair, and the play of the musician's fingers. Magnus had a list of favored traits in a partner—black hair, blue eyes, honest—but in this case what drew him in was an individual response to life. Something he hadn't seen before, and which made him want to see more.

He moved closer, and managed to catch Imasu's eye. Once both were caught, the game could begin, and Magnus began it by asking if Imasu taught music. He wanted to spend more time with Imasu, but he wanted to learn as well—to see if he could be absorbed in the same way, create the same sounds.

Even after a few lessons, Magnus could tell that the sounds he made with the *charango* were slightly different from the sounds Imasu made. Possibly more than slightly. Ragnor and Catarina both begged him to give the instrument up. Random strangers on the street begged him to give the instrument up. Even cats ran from him.

But: "You have real potential as a musician," Imasu said, his voice serious and his eyes laughing.

Magnus made it his policy to listen to people who were kind, encouraging, and extremely handsome.

So he kept at it with the *charango*, despite the fact that he was forbidden to play it in the house. He was also discouraged from playing it in public places by a crying child, a man with papers talking about city ordinances, and a small riot.

As a last resort he went up to the mountains and played there. Magnus was sure that the llama stampede he witnessed was a coincidence. The llamas could not be judging him.

Besides, the *charango* was definitely starting to sound better. He was either getting the hang of it or succumbing to auditory hallucinations. Magnus chose to believe it was the former.

"I think I really turned a corner," he told Imasu earnestly one day. "In the mountains. A metaphorical, musical corner, that is. There really should be more roads up there."

"That's wonderful," Imasu said, eyes shining. "I can't wait to hear it."

They were in Imasu's house, as Magnus was not allowed to play anywhere else in Puno. Imasu's mother and sister were both sadly prone to migraines, so many of Magnus's lessons were on musical theory, but today Magnus and Imasu were in the house alone.

"When can we expect your mother and sister back?" Magnus asked, very casually.

"In a few weeks," Imasu replied. "They went to visit my aunt. Um. They didn't flee—I mean, leave the house—for any particular reason."

"Such charming ladies," Magnus remarked. "So sad they're both so sickly."

Imasu blinked.

"Their headaches?" Magnus reminded him.

"Oh," Imasu said. "Oh, right." There was a pause, then Imasu clapped his hands together. "You were about to play something for me!"

Magnus beamed at him. "Prepare," he intoned, "to be astounded."

He lifted the instrument up in his arms. They had come to understand each other, he felt, his *charango* and he. He could make music flow from the air or the river or the curtains if he so chose, but this was different, human and strangely touching. The stumble and screech of the strings were coming together, Magnus thought, to form a melody. The music was almost there, in his hands.

When Magnus looked at Imasu, he saw Imasu had dropped his head into his hands.

"Er," Magnus said. "Are you quite all right?"

"I was simply overcome," Imasu said in a faint voice.

Magnus preened slightly. "Ah. Well."

"By how awful that was," Imasu said.

Magnus blinked. "Pardon?"

"I can't live a lie any longer!" Imasu burst out. "I have tried to be encouraging. Dignitaries of the town have been sent to me, asking me to plead with you to stop. My own sainted mother begged me, with tears in her eyes—"

"It isn't as bad as all that—"

"Yes, it is!" It was like a dam of musical critique had broken. Imasu turned on him with eyes that flashed instead of shining. "It is worse than you can possibly imagine! When you play, all of my mother's flowers lose the will to live and expire on the instant. The quinoa has no flavor now. The llamas are migrating because of your music, and llamas are not a migratory animal. The children now believe there is a sickly monster, half horse and half large mournful chicken, that lives in the lake and calls out to the world to grant it the sweet release of death. The townspeople believe that you and I are performing arcane magic rituals—"

"Well, that one was rather a good guess," Magnus remarked.

"—using the skull of an elephant, an improbably large mushroom, and one of your very peculiar hats!"

"Or not," said Magnus. "Furthermore, my hats are extraordinary."

"I will not argue with that." Imasu scrubbed a hand through his thick black hair, which curled and clung to his fingers like inky vines. "Look, I know that I was wrong. I saw a handsome man, thought that it would not hurt to talk a little about music and strike up a common interest, but I don't deserve this. You are going to get stoned in the town square, and if I have to listen to you play again, I will drown myself in the lake."

"Oh," said Magnus, and he began to grin. "I wouldn't. I hear there is a dreadful monster living in that lake."

Imasu seemed to still be brooding about Magnus's *charango* playing, a subject that Magnus had lost all interest in. "I believe the world will end with a noise like the noise you make!"

"Interesting," said Magnus, and he threw his *charango* out the window.

"Magnus!"

"I believe that music and I have gone as far as we can go together," Magnus said. "A true artiste knows when to surrender."

"I can't believe you did that!"

Magnus waved a hand airily. "I know, it is heartbreaking, but sometimes one must shut one's ears to the pleas of the muse."

"I just meant that those are expensive and I heard a crunch."

Imasu looked genuinely distressed, but he was smiling, too. His face was an open book in glowing colors, as fascinating as it was easy to read. Magnus moved from the window into Imasu's space and let one hand curl around Imasu's callused fingers, the other very lightly around his wrist. He saw the shiver run through Imasu's whole body, as if he were an instrument from which Magnus could coax any sound he pleased.

"It desolates me to give up my music," Magnus murmured. "But I believe you will discover I have many talents."

That night when he came home and told Ragnor and Catarina that he had given up music, Ragnor said, "In five hundred years I have never desired the touch of another man, but I am suddenly possessed with a desire to kiss that boy on the mouth."

"Hands off," said Magnus, with easy, pleased possessiveness.

The next day all of Puno rose and gathered together in a festival. Imasu told Magnus he was sure the timing of the festival was entirely unrelated. Magnus laughed. The sun came through in slants across Imasu's eyes, in glowing strips across his brown skin, and Imasu's mouth curled beneath Magnus's. They did not make it outside in time to see the parade.

* * *

Magnus asked his friends if they could stay in Puno for a while, and was not surprised when they agreed. Catarina and Ragnor were both warlocks. To them, as to Magnus, time was like rain, glittering as it fell, changing the world, but something that could also be taken for granted.

Until you loved a mortal. Then time became gold in a miser's hands, every bright year counted out carefully, infinitely precious, and each one slipping through your fingers.

Imasu told him about his father's death and about his sister's love for dancing that had inspired Imasu to play for her, and that this was the second time he had ever been in love. He was both *indígena* and Spanish, more mingled even than most of the mestizos, too Spanish for some and not Spanish enough for others. Magnus talked a little with Imasu about that, about the Dutch and Batavian blood in his own veins. He did not talk about demonic blood or his father or magic, not yet.

Magnus had learned to be careful about giving his memories with his heart. When people died, it felt like all the pieces of yourself you had given to them went as well. It took so long, building yourself back up until you were whole again, and you were never entirely the same.

That had been a long, painful lesson.

Magnus had still not learned it very well, he supposed, as he found himself wanting to tell Imasu a great deal. He did not only wish to talk about his parentage, but about his past, the people he had loved—about Camille; and about Edmund Herondale and his son, Will; and even about Tessa and Catarina and how he had met her in Spain. In the end he broke down and told the last story, though he left out details like the Silent Brothers and Catarina's almost being burned as a witch. But as the seasons changed, Magnus began to think that he should tell Imasu about magic at least, before he suggested that Magnus stop living with Catarina and Ragnor, and Imasu stop living with his mother and sister, and that they find a place together that Imasu could fill with music and Magnus with magic. It was time to settle down, Magnus thought, for a short while at least.

It came as a shock when Imasu suggested, quite quietly: "Perhaps it is time for you and your friends to think of leaving Puno."

"What, without you?" Magnus asked. He had been lying sunning himself outside Imasu's house, content and making his plans for a little way into the future. He was caught off guard enough to be stupid.

"Yes," Imasu answered, looking regretful about the prospect of making himself clearer. "Absolutely without me. It's not that I have not had a wonderful time with you. We have had fun together, you and I, haven't we?" he added pleadingly.

Magnus nodded, with the most nonchalant air he could manage, and then immediately ruined it by saying, "I thought so. So why end it?"

Perhaps it was his mother, or his sister, some member of Imasu's family, objecting to the fact that they were both men. This would not be the first or the last time that happened to Magnus, although Imasu's mother had always given Magnus the impression he could do anything he liked with her son just so long as he never touched a musical instrument in her presence ever again.

"It's you," Imasu burst out. "It is the way you are. I cannot be with you any longer because I do not want to be."

"Please," Magnus said after a pause. "Carry on showering me with compliments. This is an extremely pleasant experience for me, by the way, and precisely how I was hoping my day would go."

"You are just..." Imasu took a deep, frustrated breath. "You seem always ... ephemeral, like a glittering shallow stream that passes the whole world by. Not something that will stay, not something that will last." He made a small, helpless gesture, as if letting something go, as if Magnus had wanted to be let go. "Not someone permanent."

That made Magnus laugh, suddenly and helplessly, and he threw his head back. He'd learned this lesson a long time ago: Even in the midst of heartbreak, you could still find yourself laughing.

Laughter had always come easily to Magnus, and it helped, but not enough.

"Magnus," said Imasu, and he sounded truly angry. Magnus wondered how many times when Magnus had thought they were simply arguing, Imasu had been leading up to this moment of parting. "This is exactly what I was talking about!"

"You're quite wrong, you know. I am the most permanent person that you will ever meet," said Magnus, his voice breathless with laughter and his eyes stung a little by tears. "It is only that it never makes any difference."

It was the truest thing he had ever told Imasu, and he never told him any more truth than that.

Warlocks lived forever, which meant they saw the intimate, terrible cycle of birth, life, and death over and over again. It also meant that they had all been witness to literally millions of failed relationships.

"It's for the best," Magnus informed Ragnor and Catarina solemnly, raising his voice to be heard above the sounds of yet another festival.

"Of course," murmured Catarina, who was a good and loyal friend.

"I'm surprised it even lasted this long; he was much better looking than you," mumbled Ragnor, who deserved a cruel and terrible fate.

"I'm only two hundred years old," said Magnus, ignoring his friends' mutual snort at the lie. "I can't settle down yet. I need more time to devote myself to debauchery. And I think—" He finished his drink and looked speculatively around. "I think I am going to ask that charming young lady over there to dance."

The girl he was eyeing, he noted, was eyeing him back. She had lashes so long they were almost sweeping her shoulders.

It was possible Magnus was a little bit drunk. *Chicha de molle* was famous for both its swift effects and the horrible hangovers that followed.

Ragnor twitched violently and made a sound like a cat whose tail has been stepped on. "Magnus, please, no. The music was bad enough!"

"Magnus is not as bad at dancing as he is at the *charango*," Catarina remarked thoughtfully. "Actually, he dances quite well. Albeit with a certain, er, unique and characteristic flair."

"I do not feel even slightly reassured," Ragnor said. "Neither of you are reassuring people."

After a brief heated interlude, Magnus returned to the table breathing slightly hard. He saw that Ragnor had decided to amuse himself by hitting his own forehead repeatedly against the tabletop.

"What did you think you were doing?" Ragnor demanded between gloomy thumps.

Catarina contributed, "The dance is a beautiful, traditional dance called El Alcatraz, and I thought Magnus performed it—"

"Brilliantly," Magnus suggested. "Dashingly? Devastatingly attractively? Nimbly?"

Catarina pursed her lips in thought before selecting the appropriate word. "Spectacularly."

Magnus pointed at her. "That's why you're my favorite."

"And traditionally the man gyrates—"

"You did gyrate spectacularly," Ragnor observed in a sour voice.

Magnus made a little bow. "Why, thank you."

"—and attempts to set fire to his partner's skirts with a candle," Catarina continued. "It's a wonderful, vibrant, and rather gorgeous dance."

"Oh, 'attempts,' is it?" Ragnor asked. "So it is not traditional for someone to utilize magic, actually set the woman's skirts and his own ostentatious coat on fire, and keep dancing even though both the dance partners involved are now actually spinning towers of flame?"

Catarina coughed. "Not strictly traditional, no."

"It was all under control," Magnus declared loftily. "Have a little faith in my magic fingers."

Even the girl he'd danced with had thought it was some marvelous trick. She had been enveloped in real, bright fire and she had tipped back her head and laughed, the tumble of her black hair becoming a crackling waterfall of light, the heels of her shoes striking sparks like glittering leaping dust all over the floor, her skirt trailing flame as if he were following a phoenix tail. Magnus had spun and swung with her, and she'd thought he was marvelous for a single moment of bright illusion.

But, like love, fire didn't last.

"Do you think that eventually our kind becomes far enough removed from humanity that we transform into creatures that are untouchable and unlovable by humanity?" Magnus asked.

Ragnor and Catarina stared at him.

"Don't answer that," Magnus told them. "That sounded like the question of a man who doesn't need answers. That sounded like the question of a man who needs another drink. Here we go!"

He lifted a glass. Ragnor and Catarina did not join him, but Magnus was happy to make the toast on his own.

"To adventure," he said, and drank.

Magnus opened his eyes and saw brilliant light, felt hot air drag across his skin like a knife scraping across burned bread. His whole brain throbbed and he was promptly, violently sick.

Catarina offered him a bowl. She was a muddle of white and blue in his blurred vision.

"Where am I?" Magnus croaked.

"Nazca."

So Magnus was still in Peru. That indicated that he had been rather more sensible than he'd feared.

"Oh, so we went on a little trip."

"You broke into a man's house," Catarina said. "You stole a carpet and enchanted it to fly. Then you sped off into the night air. We pursued you on foot."

"Ah," said Magnus.

"You were shouting some things."

"What things?"

"I prefer not to repeat them," Catarina said. She was a weary shade of blue. "I also prefer not to remember the time we spent in the desert. It is a mammoth desert, Magnus. Ordinary deserts are quite large. Mammoth deserts are so called because they are larger than ordinary deserts."

"Thank you for that interesting and enlightening information," Magnus croaked, and tried to bury his face in his pillow, like an ostrich trying to bury its head in the sand of a mammoth desert. "It was kind of you both to follow me. I'm sure I was pleased to see you," he offered weakly, hoping that this would lead to Catarina's bringing him more liquids and perhaps a hammer with which he could smash in his skull.

Magnus felt too weak to move in quest of a liquid, himself. Healing magic had never been his specialty, but he was almost certain that moving would cause his head to topple from his shoulders. He could not allow that to happen. He had confirmation from many witnesses that his head looked superb where it was.

"You told us to leave you in the desert, because you planned to start a new life as a cactus," Catarina said, her voice flat. "Then you conjured up tiny needles and threw them at us. With pinpoint accuracy."

Magnus chanced another look up at her. She was still very blurry. Magnus thought this was unkind. He'd believed they were friends.

"Well," he said with dignity. "Considering my highly intoxicated state, you must have been impressed with my aim."

"'Impressed' is not the word to use to describe how I felt last night, Magnus."

"I thank you for stopping me there," Magnus said. "It was for the best. You are a true friend. No harm done. Let's say no more about it. Could you possibly fetch me—"

"Oh, we couldn't stop you," Catarina interrupted. "We tried, but you giggled, leaped onto the carpet, and flew away again. You kept saying that you wanted to go to Moquegua."

Magnus really did not feel at all well. His stomach was sinking and his head was spinning.

"What did I do in Moquegua?"

"You never got there," Catarina said. "But you were flying about and yelling and trying to, ahem, write messages for us with your carpet in the sky."

Magnus had a sudden vivid memory, wind and stars in his hair, of the things he had been trying to write. Fortunately, he didn't think Ragnor or Catarina spoke the language he had been writing in.

"We then stopped for a meal," Catarina said. "You were most insistent that we try a local specialty that you called *cuy*. We actually had a very pleasant meal, even though you were still very drunk."

"I'm sure I must have been sobering up at that point," Magnus argued.

"Magnus, you were trying to flirt with your own plate."

"I'm a very open-minded sort of fellow!"

"Ragnor is not," Catarina said. "When he found out that you were feeding us guinea pigs, he hit you over the head with your plate. It broke."

"So ended our love," Magnus said. "Ah, well. It would never have worked between me and the plate anyway. I'm sure the food did me good, Catarina, and you were very good to feed me and put me to bed—"

Catarina shook her head. She seemed to be enjoying this, like a nightmare nurse telling a child she did not especially like a terrifying bedtime story. "You fell down on the floor. Honestly, we thought it best to leave you sleeping on the ground. We thought you would remain there for some time, but we took our eyes off you for one minute, and then you scuttled off. Ragnor claims he saw you making for the carpet, crawling like a huge demented crab."

Magnus refused to believe he had done any such thing. Ragnor was not to be trusted.

"I believe him," Catarina said treacherously. "You were having a great deal of difficulty walking upright even before you were hit with the plate. Also, I believe the food did not do you much good at all, because then you flew all over the place exclaiming that you could see great big monkeys and birds and llamas and kitty cats drawn on the ground."

"Gracious," Magnus said. "I progressed to full hallucinations? It's official. That sounds like ... almost the most drunk I have ever been. Please don't ask questions about the most drunk I have ever been. It's a very sad story involving a birdcage."

"You were not hallucinating, actually," Catarina said. "Once we stood on the hills yelling 'Get down, you idiot,' we could see the vast drawings in the ground as well. They're very grand and beautiful. I think they were part of an ancient ritual to summon water from the earth. Seeing them at all was worth coming to this country."

Magnus still had his head sunk deep in the pillow, but he preened slightly.

"Always happy to enrich your life, Catarina."

"It was not grand or beautiful," Catarina said reminiscently, "when you were sick all over those mystical and immense designs from a civilization long gone by. From a height. Continuously."

He briefly felt regret and shame. Then he mostly felt the urge to get sick again.

Later, when he was soberer, Magnus would go to see the Nazca Lines, and commit to memory the trenches where gravel had been cut away to show naked clay in sprawling, specific patterns: a bird with its wings outstretched in soaring flight, a monkey with a tail whose curves Magnus thought positively indecent—obviously, he approved—and a shape that might have been a man.

When scientists discovered and spent the 1930s and 1940s investigating the Nazca Lines, Magnus was a little annoyed, as if shapes scored in stone were his own personal property.

But then he accepted it. That was what humans did: They left one another messages through time, pressed between pages or carved into rock. Like reaching out a hand through time, and trusting in a phantom hoped-for hand to catch yours. Humans did not live forever. They could only hope what they made would endure.

Magnus supposed he could let the humans pass their message on.

But his acceptance came much, much later. Magnus had other things to do the day after he first saw the Nazca Lines. He had to be sick thirty-seven times.

After the thirtieth time Magnus was ill, Catarina became concerned.

"I really think you might have a fever."

"I have told you again and again that I am most vilely unwell, yes," Magnus said coldly. "Probably dying, not that either of you ingrates will care."

"Shouldn't have had the guinea pig," said Ragnor, and he cackled. He seemed to be bearing a grudge.

"I feel far too faint to help myself," Magnus said, turning to the person who cared for him and did not take unholy joy in his suffering. He did his best to look pathetic and suspected that right now his best was really excellent. "Catarina, would you—"

"I'm not going to waste magic and energy that could save lives to cure the ill effects of a night spent drinking excessively and spinning at high altitudes!"

When Catarina looked stern, it was all over. It would be more use to throw himself on Ragnor's tender green mercies.

Magnus was just about to try that when Catarina announced

thoughtfully, "I think it would be best if we tried out some of the local mundane medicines."

The way mundanes in this part of Peru practiced medicine, it appeared, was to rub a guinea pig all over the afflicted sufferer's body.

"I demand that you stop this!" Magnus protested. "I am a warlock and I can heal myself, and also I can blast your head clean off!"

"Oh, no. He's delirious, he's crazed, don't listen to him," Ragnor said. "Continue applying the guinea pig!"

The lady with the guinea pigs gave them all an unimpressed look and continued to go about her guinea pig business.

"Lie back, Magnus," said Catarina, who was extremely open-minded and always interested in exploring other fields of medicine, and apparently willing to have Magnus serve as a hapless pawn in her medical game. "Let the magic of the guinea pig flow through you."

"Yes indeed," put in Ragnor, who was not very open-minded at all, and giggled.

Magnus did not find the whole process as inherently hilarious as Ragnor did. As a child he'd taken *djamu* many times. There was bile of goat in that (if you were lucky—bile of alligator if you weren't). And guinea pigs and *djamu* were both better than the bloodletting someone had tried on him in England once.

It was just that he generally found mundane medicine very trying, and he wished they would wait until he felt better to inflict these medical procedures on him.

Magnus tried to escape several times, and had to be forcibly restrained. Later Catarina and Ragnor liked to act out the time he tried to take the guinea pigs with him, reportedly shouting "Freedom!" and "I am your leader now."

There was a distinct possibility that Magnus was still a tiny bit drunk.

At the end of the whole horrific ordeal, one of the guinea pigs was cut open and its entrails examined to see if the cure had been effected. At the sight of it Magnus was promptly sick again.

Some days later in Lima, after all the trauma and guinea pigs, Catarina and Ragnor finally trusted Magnus enough to let him have one—just one, and they were watching him insultingly closely—drink.

"What you were saying before, on That Night," said Catarina.

Catarina and Ragnor both called it that, and in both cases Magnus could hear them using the capitals for emphasis.

"Don't fret," Magnus said airily. "I no longer want to go be a cactus and live in the desert."

Catarina blinked and winced, visibly having a flashback. "Not what I was referring to, but good to know. I meant about humans, and love."

Magnus did not particularly want to think about whatever he had been babbling piteously about on the night when he'd gotten his heart broken. There was no point in wallowing. Magnus refused to wallow. Wallowing was for elephants, depressing people, and depressing elephants.

Catarina continued despite the lack of encouragement. "I was born this color. I did not know how to wear a glamour as a newborn. There was no way to look like anything but what I was then, all the time, even though it was not safe. My mother saw me and knew what I was, but she hid me from the world. She raised me in secret. She did everything she could to keep me safe. A great wrong was done to her, and she gave back love. Every human I heal, I heal in her name. I do what I do to honor her, and to know that when she saved my life she saved countless lives through the centuries."

She turned a wide, serious gaze to Ragnor, who was sitting at the table and looking at his hands uncomfortably, but who responded to the cue.

"My parents thought I was a faerie child or something, I think,"

Ragnor said. "Because I was the color of springtime, my mother used to say," he added, and blushed emerald. "Obviously it all came out as a bit more complicated than that, but by then they'd gotten fond of me. They were always fond of me, even though I was unsettling to have around the place, and Mother told me that I was grouchy as a baby. I outgrew that, of course."

A polite silence followed this statement.

A faerie child would be easier to accept, Magnus thought, than that demons had tricked or hurt a woman—or, more rarely, a man—and now there was a marked child to remind the parent of their pain. Warlocks were always born from that, from pain and demons.

"It is something to remember, if we feel distant from humans," Catarina said. "We owe a great deal to human love. We live forever by the grace of human love, which rocked strange children in their cradles and did not despair and did not turn away. I know which side of my heritage my soul comes from."

They were sitting outside their house, in a garden surrounded by high walls, but Catarina was always the most cautious of them all. She looked around in the dark before she lit the candle on the table, light springing from nothing between her cupped hands and turning her white hair to silk and pearls. In the sudden light Magnus could see her smile.

"Our fathers were demons," said Catarina. "Our mothers were heroes."

That was true, of course, for them.

Most warlocks were born wearing unmistakable signs of what they were, and some warlock children died young because their parents abandoned or killed what they saw as unnatural creatures. Some were raised as Catarina and Ragnor had been, in love that was greater than fear.

Magnus's warlock's mark was his eyes, the pupils slit, the color lucent and green-gold at the wrong angles, but these features had not developed immediately. He had not been born with Catarina's blue or Ragnor's green skin, had been born a seemingly human baby with unusual amber eyes. Magnus's mother had not realized his father was a demon for some time, not until she had gone to the cradle one morning and seen her child staring back at her with the eyes of a cat.

She knew, then, what had happened, that whatever had come to her in the night in the shape of her husband had not been her husband. When she had realized that, she had not wanted to go on living.

And she hadn't.

Magnus did not know if she had been a hero or not. He had not been old enough to know about her life, or fully comprehend her pain. He could not be sure in the way Ragnor and Catarina looked sure. He did not know if, when his mother knew the truth, she had still loved him or if all love had been blotted out by darkness. A darkness greater than the one known by his friends' mothers, for Magnus's father was no ordinary demon.

"And I saw Satan fall," Magnus murmured into his drink, "like lightning from Heaven."

Catarina turned to him. "What was that?"

"Rejoice that your names are written in Heaven, my dear," said Magnus. "I am so touched that I laugh and have another drink so that I may not weep."

After that he took another walk outside.

He remembered now why he had told them, on that dark drunken night, that he wanted to go to Moquegua. Magnus had been to that town only once before, and had not stayed long.

Moquegua meant "quiet place" in Quechua, and that was exactly what the town was, and exactly why Magnus had felt uneasy there. The peaceful cobbled streets, the plaza with its wrought-iron fountain where children played, were not for him.

Magnus's life philosophy was to keep moving, and in places like Moquegua he understood why it was necessary to keep moving. If he did not, someone might see him as he really was. Not that he thought he was so very dreadful, but there was still that voice in his head like a warning: *Keep in bright constant motion, or the whole illusion will collapse in on itself.*

Magnus remembered lying in the silver sand of the night desert and thinking of quiet places where he did not belong, and how sometimes he believed, as he believed in the passage of time and the joy of living and the absolute merciless unfairness of fate, that there was no quiet place in the world for him, and never would be. *Thou shalt not tempt the Lord thy God.*

Nor was it wise to tempt angels, even of the fallen sort.

He shook the memory off. Even if that were true, there would always be another adventure.

You might think that Magnus's spectacular night of drunken debauchery and countless crimes must be the reason he was banned from Peru, but that is not in fact the case. Amazingly, Magnus was allowed back into Peru. Many years later he went back, this time alone, and he did indeed find another adventure.

1962

Magnus was strolling through the streets of Cuzco, past the convent of La Merced and down the Calle Mantas, when he heard the man's voice. The first thing he noticed was how nasal said voice was. The next thing he noticed was that he was speaking English.

"I don't care what you say, Kitty. I maintain that we could have gotten a bus to Machu Picchu."

"Geoffrey, there are no buses to Machu Picchu from New York."

"Well, really," said Geoffrey after a pause. "If the National Geographic Society is going to put the wretched place in their paper, they might at least have arranged a bus."

Magnus was able to spot them then, wending their way through the arches that lined the street once you were past the bell tower.

Geoffrey had the nose of a man who never shut up. It was peeling in the hot sun and arid air, and the once-crisp edges of his white trousers were wilting like a sad, dying flower.

"Another thing here is the natives," said Geoffrey. "I had hoped we could get some decent pictures. I expected them to be so much more colorful, don't you know?"

"It's almost as if they are not here for your entertainment," said Magnus in Spanish.

Kitty turned around at the sound, and Magnus saw a small mocking face and red hair curling underneath the brim of a very large straw hat. Her lips were curling too.

Geoffrey turned when she turned.

"Oh, well spotted, old girl," he said. "Now, he's what I call colorful."

That much was true. Magnus was wearing more than a dozen scarves all in different colors and carefully arrayed to swirl about him like a fantastic rainbow. He was not too impressed by Geoffrey's powers of observation, however, since Geoffrey was apparently unable to imagine that anyone with brown skin could possibly be a visitor like himself.

"I say, fellow, do you want to have your picture taken?" asked Geoffrey.

"You're an idiot," Magnus told him, smiling brightly.

Magnus was still speaking in Spanish. Kitty choked on a laugh and turned it into a cough.

"Ask him, Kitty!" said Geoffrey, with the air of one prompting a dog to do a trick.

"I apologize for him," she said in halting Spanish.

Magnus smiled and offered his arm with a flourish. Kitty skipped over the flagstones, worn so smooth by time that the stone was like water, and seized his arm.

"Oh, charming, charming. Mother will love to see these shots," said Geoffrey enthusiastically.

"How do you put up with him?" Magnus inquired.

Kitty and Magnus beamed like actors, toothy, ecstatic, and entirely insincere.

"With some difficulty."

"Let me offer an alternate proposition," Magnus said between the locked teeth of his smile. "Run away with me. Right now. It will be the most amazing adventure, I promise you that."

Kitty stared at him. Geoffrey turned around, in quest of someone who could take shots of them all together. Behind Geoffrey's back Magnus saw Kitty begin, slowly and delightedly, to smile.

"Oh, all right. Why not?"

"Excellent," said Magnus.

He spun and seized her hand, and they ran, laughing, together down the sunlit street.

"We'd better go pretty quickly!" Kitty shouted, voice breathless as they rushed. "He's bound to notice soon that I stole his watch."

Magnus blinked. "Pardon?"

There was a noise behind them. It sounded disturbingly like a ruckus. Magnus was, through hardly any fault of his own, somewhat familiar with the sound of the police being summoned and also the sounds of a hot pursuit.

He pulled Kitty into an alleyway. She was still laughing, and undoing the buttons of her blouse.

"It will probably take them a little longer," she murmured, the mother-of-pearl buttons parting enough to show the sudden rich flash of emeralds and rubies, "to realize that I also stole all his mother's jewels."

She gave Magnus a little saucy smile. Magnus burst out laughing.

"Do you con a lot of annoying rich men?"

"And their mothers," said Kitty. "I could probably have taken them for the whole family fortune, or at least the silver, but a handsome man asked me to run away with him, and I thought, *What the hell.*"

The sound of pursuit was closer now.

"You are about to be very glad you did," Magnus told her. "Since you showed me yours, I believe it's only fair I show you mine."

He snapped his fingers, making sure to trail blue sparks to impress the lady. Kitty was clever enough to realize what was going on as soon as one of the first pursuers glanced down the alleyway and ran on.

"They can't see us," she breathed. "You turned us invisible."

Magnus raised his eyebrows and made a gesture of display. "As you see," he said. "And they don't."

Magnus had seen humans shocked and scared and amazed by his power. Kitty flung herself into his arms.

"Tell me, handsome stranger," she said. "How do you feel about a life of magical crime?"

"Sounds like an adventure," said Magnus. "But promise me something. Promise we will always steal from the irritating and spend the cash on booze and useless trinkets."

Kitty pressed a kiss to his mouth. "I swear."

They fell in love, not even for a mortal lifetime but for a mortal summer, a summer of laughing and running and being wanted by the law in several different countries.

In the end Magnus's favorite memory of that summer was an image he had never seen: that last picture on Geoffrey's camera, of a man trailing bright colors and a woman hiding them beneath a white blouse, both smiling because they knew a joke he did not.

Magnus's sudden turn to a life of crime, shockingly enough, was not the reason he was banned from Peru either. The High Council of Peruvian warlocks met in secret, and a letter was sent to Magnus several months later announcing that he had been banned from Peru, on pain of death, for "crimes unspeakable." Despite his inquiries, he never received an answer to the question of what he had been banned for. To this day, whatever it is that actually got him banned from Peru is—and perhaps must always remain—a mystery.

The Runaway Queen

By Cassandra Clare and Maureen Johnson

On the word "Axel," she froze. This was all he needed. He shoved her backward out the window. The balloon, bumped back by the force, shifted a foot or so away from the window—so she landed half in, half out.

—The Runaway Queen

THUMP
THMP
THUMP
WAK
YOUR MAJESTY, YOU MUST STOP. YOU MUST LISTEN TO ME.
AXEL–
gasp
...
PUSH
EEEK!

Paris, June 1791

There was a smell to Paris in the summer mornings that Magnus enjoyed. This was surprising, because on summer mornings Paris smelled of cheese that had sat in the sun all day, and fish and the less desirable parts of fish. It smelled of people and all the things that people produce (this does not refer to art or culture but to the baser things that were dumped out of windows in buckets). But these were punctuated by other odors, and the odors would shift rapidly from street to street, or building to building. That heady whiff of a bakery might be followed by an unexpected flush of gardenias in a garden, which gave way to the iron-rich pong of a slaughterhouse. Paris was nothing if not alive—the Seine pumping along like a great artery, the vessels of the wider streets, narrowing down to the tiniest alleys ... and every inch of it had a smell.

It all smelled of *life*—life in every form and degree.

The smells today, however, were a bit strong. Magnus was taking an unfamiliar route, one that took him through quite a rough patch of Paris. The road here was not as smooth. It was brutally hot inside his cabriolet as it bumped its way along. Magnus had animated one of his magnificent Chinese fans, and it flapped ineffectively at him, barely stirring the breeze. It was, if he was completely honest with himself (and he did not want to be), a bit too hot for this new striped blue-and-rose-colored coat, made of taffeta and satin, and the silk faille waistcoat embroidered with a scene of birds and cherubs. The wing collar, and the wig, and the silk breeches, the wonderful new gloves in the most delicate lemon yellow ... it was all a bit *warm*.

Still. If one could look this fabulous, one had an obligation to. One should wear *everything*, or one should wear nothing at all.

He settled back into his seat and accepted the sweat proudly, glad that he lived by his principles, principles which were widely embraced in Paris. In Paris people were always after the latest fashion. Wigs that hit the ceiling and had miniature boats in them; outrageous silks; white paint and high, blushed cheeks on the men and the women; the decorative beauty spots; the tailoring; the colors... In Paris one could have the eyes of a cat (as he did) and tell people it was a trick of fashion.

In a world such as this, there was much work for an enterprising warlock. The aristocracy loved a bit of magic and were willing to pay for it. They paid for luck at the faro table. They paid him to make their monkeys speak, to make their birds sing their favorite arias from the opera, to make their diamonds glow in different colors. They wanted beauty spots in the shapes of hearts, champagne glasses, and stars to spontaneously appear on their cheeks. They wanted to dazzle their guests by having fire shoot from their fountains, and then to amuse those same guests by having their chaise longues wander across the room. And their lists of requests for the bedroom—well, he kept careful notes on those. They were nothing if not imaginative.

In short, the people of Paris and the neighboring royal town of Versailles were the most decadent people Magnus had ever met, and for this he revered them deeply.

Of course, the revolution had put a damper on some of this. Magnus was daily reminded of that fact—even now, as he pulled back the blue silk curtains of the carriage. He received a few penetrating looks from the *sans-culottes* pushing their carts or selling their cat meat. Magnus kept apartments in the Marais, on the rue

Barbette, quite near the Hôtel de Soubise, home of his old (and recently deceased) friend the Prince of Soubise. Magnus had an open invitation to wander the gardens or entertain himself there anytime he chose. In fact, he could walk into any number of great houses in Paris and be warmly greeted. His aristocratic friends were silly but mostly harmless. But now it was problematic to be seen in their company. Sometimes it was problematic to be seen at all. It was no longer a good thing to be very rich or well connected. The unwashed masses, producers of the stink, had taken over France, overturning everything in their unwashed path.

His feelings about the revolution were mixed. People *were* hungry. The price of bread was still very high. It did not help that the queen, Marie Antoinette, when told that her people could not afford bread, had suggested that they eat cake instead. It was sensible to him that the people should demand and receive food, and firewood, and all the basic needs of life. Magnus always felt for the poor and the wretched. But at the same time, never had there been a society quite as wonderful as that of France at its dizzying heights and excesses. And while he liked excitement, he also liked to have some sense of what was going on, and that feeling was in short supply. No one quite knew who was in charge of the country. The revolutionaries squabbled all the time. The constitution was always being written. The king and queen were alive and supposedly still somewhat in power, but they were controlled by the revolutionaries. Periodically there would be killings, fires, or attacks, all in the name of liberation. Living in Paris was like living in a powder keg that was stacked on top of several other powder kegs, which were in a ship tossing blindly at sea. There was always the feeling that one day the people—the undefined *people*—just might decide to kill everyone who could afford a hat.

Magnus sighed and leaned back out of the range of prying eyes and put a jasmine-scented cloth to his nose. Enough stink and bother. He was off to see a balloon.

* * *

Of course, Magnus had flown before. He'd animated carpets and rested upon the backs of migrating flocks of birds. But he'd never flown by a human hand. This ballooning thing was new and, frankly, a little alarming. Just shooting up into the air in a fabulous and garish creation, with the whole of Paris staring at you...

This, of course, was why he had to try it.

The hot air balloon craze had largely passed him by when it had first been the rage of Paris, almost ten years before. But just the other day, when Magnus had had perhaps a little too much wine, he'd looked up and seen one of the sky-blue, egg-shaped wonders drifting past, with its gold illustrations of zodiacal signs and fleurs-de-lis, and all at once he'd been overcome with the desire to get into its basket and ride over the city. It had been a whim, and there was nothing Magnus attached more importance to than a whim. He'd managed to track down one of the Montgolfier brothers that very day and had paid far too many *louis d'or* for a private ride.

And now that Magnus was on his way to take said ride on this hot afternoon, he reflected back on just how much wine he had drunk on the afternoon when he had set this all up.

It had been quite a lot of wine.

His carriage finally came to a stop near the Château de la Muette, once a beautiful little palace, now falling apart. Magnus stepped out into the swampy afternoon and walked into the park. There was a heavy, oppressive feel to the air that made Magnus's wonderful clothes hang heavily. He walked along the path until he came to the meeting spot, where his balloon and its crew awaited him. The balloon was deflated on the grass—the silk just as beautiful as ever, but the overall effect not as impressive as he had hoped. He had better dressing gowns, when it came down to it.

One of the Montgolfiers (Magnus could not remember which one he had hired) came rushing up to him with a flushed face.

"Monsieur Bane! *Je suis désolé*, monsieur, but the weather ... today it will not cooperate. It is most annoying. I have seen a flash of lightning in the distance."

Sure enough, as soon as these words were spoken, there was a distant rumble. And the sky did have a greenish cast.

"Flight is not possible today. Tomorrow, perhaps. Alain! The balloon! Move it at once!"

And with that, the balloon was rolled up and carried to a small gazebo.

Dismayed, Magnus decided to have a turn around the park before the weather deteriorated. One could see the most fetching ladies and gentlemen walking there, and it did seem to be a place that people came to when they were feeling ... amorous. No longer a private wooded area and park, the Bois de Boulogne was now open to the people, who used the wonderful grounds for growing potatoes for food. They also wore cotton and proudly called themselves *sans-culottes*, meaning "without knee breeches." They wore long, workmanlike pants, and they cast long, judgmental looks at Magnus's own exquisite breeches, which matched the rose-colored stripe in his jacket, and his faintly silver stockings. It really was getting difficult to be wonderful.

Also, the park seemed singularly devoid of handsome, lovestruck persons. It was all long trousers and long looks and people mumbling about the latest revolutionary craze. The more noble sorts all looked nervous and turned their gazes to the path whenever a member of the Third Estate walked by.

But Magnus did see someone he knew, and he wasn't happy about it. Coming toward him at great speed was Henri de Polignac, dressed in black and silver. Henri was a darkling of Marcel Saint Cloud's, who was the head of the most powerful clan of vampires in Paris. Henri was also a terrible bore. Most subjugates were. It was hard to have a conversation with someone who was always saying, "Master says this" and "Master says that." Always groveling. Always lingering about, waiting to be bitten. Magnus had to wonder what

Henri was doing out in the park during the day—the answer was certainly something bad. Hunting. Recruiting. And now, bothering Magnus.

"Monsieur Bane," he said, with a short bow.

"Henri."

"It's been some time since we've seen you."

"Oh," Magnus said airily. "I've been quite busy. Business, you know. Revolution."

"Of course. But Master was just saying how long it's been since he's seen you. He was wondering if you'd fallen off the face of the earth."

"No, no," Magnus said. "Just keeping busy."

"As is Master," Henri said with a twisted little smile. "You really must come by. Master is having a party on Monday evening. He would be very cross with me if I did not invite you."

"Would he?" Magnus said, swallowing down the slightly bitter taste that had risen in his mouth.

"He would indeed."

One did not turn down an invitation from Saint Cloud. At least, one didn't if one wanted to continue living contentedly in Paris. Vampires took offense *so* easily—and Parisian vampires were the worst of all.

"Of course," Magnus said, delicately peeling one of his lemon-yellow gloves from his hand, simply for something to do. "Of course. I would be delighted. Most delighted."

"I will tell Master you will be in attendance," Henri replied.

The first drops of rain began to fall, landing heavily on Magnus's delicate jacket. At least this allowed him to say his good-byes quickly. As he hurried across the grass, Magnus put up his hand. Blue sparks webbed between his fingers, and instantly the rain no longer struck him. It rolled off an invisible canopy he had conjured just over his head.

Paris. It was problematic sometimes. So political. (Oh, his shoes

... his shoes! Why had he worn the silk ones with the curled toes today? He had *known* he'd be in a park. But they were new and pretty and by Jacques of the rue des Balais and could not be resisted.) Perhaps it was best, in the current climate, to consider retiring to somewhere simpler. London was always a good retreat. Not as fashionable, but not without its charms. Or he could go to the Alps... Yes, he did love the clean, fresh air. He could frolic through the edelweiss and enjoy the thermal baths of Schinznach-Bad. Or farther afield. It had been too long since he'd been to India, after all. And he could never resist the joys of Peru...

Perhaps it was best to stay in Paris.

He got inside the cabriolet just as the skies truly opened and the rain drummed down so hard on the roof that he could no longer hear his thoughts. The balloon-maker's assistants hurriedly covered the balloon works, and the people scurried for cover under trees. The flowers seemed to brighten in the splash of the rain, and Magnus took a great, deep breath of the Paris air he loved so well.

As they drove off, a potato hit the side of his carriage.

The day, in a very literal sense, appeared to be a wash. There was only one thing for it—a long, cool bath with a cup of hot lapsang souchong. He would bathe by the window and drink in the smoky tea, and watch the rain drench Paris. Then he would recline and read *Le Pied de Fanchette* and Shakespeare for several hours. Then, some violet champagne and an hour or two to dress for the opera.

"Marie!" Magnus called as he entered the house. "Bath!"

He kept as staff an older couple, Marie and Claude. They were extremely good at their jobs, and years of service in Paris had left them completely unsurprised by anything.

Of the many places he had lived, Magnus found his Paris house to be one of the most pleasing abodes. Certainly there were places of greater natural beauty—but Paris had *unnatural* beauty, which was arguably better. Everything in the house gave him pleasure. The silk wallpaper in yellow and rose and silver and blue, the ormolu tables and giltwood armchairs, the clocks and mirrors and porcelains... With every step he took farther into the house, to his main salon, he was reminded of the good of the place.

Many Downworlders stayed away from Paris. There were certainly many werewolves in the country, and every wooded glen had its fey. But Paris, it seemed, was the terrain of the vampire. It made sense, in many ways. Vampires were courtly creatures. They were pale and elegant. They enjoyed darkness and pleasure. Their hypnotic gazes—the *encanto*—enchanted many a noble. And there was nothing quite as pleasurable, decadent, and dangerous as letting a vampire drink your blood.

It had all gotten a bit out of hand during the vampire craze of 1787, though. That's when the blood parties had started. That's when all the children had gone missing and some other young people first returned home pale and with the absent look of the subjugate. Like Henri, and his sister, Brigitte. They were the nephew and niece of the Duke de Polignac. Once beloved members of one of the great families of France, they now lived with Saint Cloud and did his bidding. And Saint Cloud's bidding could be a strange thing indeed. Magnus didn't mind a little decadence—but Saint Cloud was evil. Classic, straightforward evil of the most old-fashioned type. The Shadowhunters of the Paris Institute seemed to have little effect on the goings-on, possibly because in Paris there were many places to hide. There were miles of catacombs, and it was extremely easy to snatch someone from the street and drag them below. Saint Cloud had friends in places high and low, and it would have been very difficult to go after him.

Magnus did all he could to avoid the Parisian vampires and the vampires who appeared on the edges of the court at Versailles. No good ever came of an encounter.

But enough of that. Time for the bath, which Marie was already filling. Magnus kept a large tub in his main salon, right by the window, so he could watch the street below as he bathed. When the water was ready, he submerged himself and began reading. An hour or so later he had dropped his book bathside and was watching some clouds pass overhead while absently thinking about the story of Cleopatra dissolving an invaluable pearl in a glass of wine. There was a knock on his chamber door, and Claude entered.

"There is a man here to see you, Monsieur Bane."

Claude understood that in Magnus's business it was not necessary to take names.

"All right," Magnus said with a sigh. "Show him in."

"Will monsieur be receiving his visitor in the bath?"

"Monsieur is considering it," Magnus said, with an even deeper sigh. It was annoying, but professional appearances had to be kept. He stepped out, dripping, and put on a silk dressing gown embroidered on the back with the picture of a peacock. He threw himself petulantly into a chair by the window.

"Claude!" he yelled. "Now! Send him in!"

A moment later the door opened again, and there stood a very attractive man with black hair and blue eyes. He wore clothes of an obviously fine quality. The tailoring was absolutely delicious. This was the sort of thing Magnus wanted to happen more often. How generous the universe could be, when she wanted to be! After denying him his balloon ride and giving him such an unpleasant encounter with Henri.

"You are Monsieur Magnus Bane," the man said with certainty. Magnus was rarely misidentified. Tall, golden-skinned, cat-eyed men were rare.

"I am," Magnus replied.

Many nobles Magnus had met had the absentminded air of people who had never had to take care of any matters of importance. This man was different. He had a very erect bearing, and a look of purpose. Also, he spoke French with a faint accent, but what kind of accent, Magnus could not immediately place.

"I have come to speak to you on a matter of some urgency. I wouldn't normally ... I..."

Magnus knew this hesitation well. Some people were nervous in the presence of warlocks.

"You are uncomfortable, monsieur," Magnus said with a smile. "Allow me to make you comfortable. I have a great talent in these matters. Please sit. Have some champagne."

"I prefer to stand, monsieur."

"As you wish. But may I have the pleasure of learning your name?" Magnus asked.

"My name is Count Axel von Fersen."

A count! Named Axel! A military man! With black hair and blue eyes! And in a state of distress! Oh, the universe had outdone herself. The universe would be sent flowers.

"Monsieur Bane, I have heard of your talents. I can't say whether I believe what I've heard, but rational, intelligent, sensible people swear to me that you are capable of wonderful things beyond my understanding."

Magnus spread his hands in false modesty.

"It's all true," he said. "As long as it was wonderful."

"They say you can alter a person's appearance by some sort of ... conjuring trick."

Magnus allowed this insult to pass.

"Monsieur," von Fersen said, "what are your feelings on the revolution?"

"The revolution will happen regardless of my feelings on the matter," Magnus said coolly. "I am not a native son of France, so I do not presume to have opinions on how the nation conducts itself."

"And I am not a son of France either. I am from Sweden. But I do have feelings on this, very strong feelings..."

Magnus liked it when von Fersen talked about his very strong feelings. He liked it very much.

"I come here because I must, and because you are the only person who can help. By coming here today and telling you what I am going to tell you, I put my life in your hands. I also risk lives much more valuable than mine. But I do not do so blindly. I have learned much about you, Monsieur Bane. I know you have many aristocratic friends. I know you have been in Paris for six years, and you are well liked and well known. And you are said to be a man of your word. Are you, monsieur, a man of your word?"

"It really depends upon the word," Magnus said. "There are so many wonderful words out there..."

Magnus silently cursed himself on his poor knowledge of Swedish. He could have added another witty line. He tried to learn seductive phrases in all languages, but the only Swedish he had ever really needed was, "Do you serve anything aside from pickled fish?" and "If you wrap me in furs, I can pretend to be your little fuzzy bear."

Von Fersen visibly steadied himself before speaking again.

"I need you to save the king and queen. I need you to preserve the royal family of France."

Well. That was certainly an unexpected turn. As if in reply, the sky darkened again and there was another rumble of thunder.

"I see," Magnus replied after a moment.

"How does that statement make you feel, monsieur?"

"Quite the same as always," Magnus replied, making sure to keep his calm demeanor. "With my hands."

But he felt anything but calm. The peasant women had broken into the palace of Versailles and thrown out the king and queen, who now lived at the Tuileries, that broken-down old palace in the middle of Paris. The people had produced pamphlets detailing the supposed crimes of the royal family. They seemed to focus quite heavily on Queen Marie Antoinette, accusing her of the most terrible things—often sexual. (There was no way possible she could have done all of the things the pamphleteers claimed. The crimes were too gross, too immoral, and far too physically challenging.

Magnus himself had never attempted half of them.)

Anything relating to the royal family was bad and dangerous to know.

Which made it as appealing as it was frightening.

"Obviously, monsieur, I've just taken a great risk in saying that much to you."

"I realize that," Magnus said. "But save the royal family? No one has harmed them."

"It is only a matter of time," von Fersen said. His emotion brought a flush to his cheeks that made Magnus's heart flutter a bit. "They are prisoners. Kings and queens who are imprisoned are generally not freed to rule again. No ... no. It is only a matter of time before the situation grows very dire. It is already intolerable, the conditions under which they are forced to live. The palace is dirty. The servants are cruel and mocking. Every day their possessions and natural entitlements are diminished. I am certain ... I am quite, quite certain ... if they are not freed, they shall not live. And I cannot live with that knowledge. When they were dragged from Versailles, I sold everything and followed them to Paris. I will follow them anywhere."

"What is it you want me to do?" Magnus said.

"I am told you can alter a person's appearance through ... some kind of ... marvel."

Magnus was happy to accept *that* description of his talents.

"Whatever price you wish, it shall be paid. The royal family of Sweden will also be informed of your great service."

"With all due respect, monsieur," Magnus said, "I do not live in Sweden. I live here. And if I do this..."

"If you do this, you do the greatest service to France. And when the family is restored to their proper place, you will be honored as a great hero."

Again, this made little difference. But what did make a difference was von Fersen himself. It was the blue eyes and the dark hair and the passion and the obvious courage. It was the way he stood, tall and strong...

"Monsieur, will you stand with us? Do we have your word, monsieur?"

It was also a very bad idea.

It was a terrible idea.

It was the worst idea he had ever heard.

It was irresistible.

"Your word, monsieur," Axel said again.

"You have it," Magnus said.

"Then I will come again tomorrow night and lay the plan out in front of you," von Fersen said. "I will show you what must happen."

"I insist we dine together," Magnus said. "If we are to undertake this great adventure together."

There was a momentary pause, and then Axel gave a sharp nod.

"Yes," he said. "Yes. I agree. We will dine together."

When von Fersen left, Magnus looked at himself in the mirror for a long time, looking for signs of madness. The actual magic involved was very simple. He could easily get himself in and out of the palace and cast a simple glamour. No one would ever know.

He shook his head. This was Paris. Everyone knew everything, somehow.

He took a long sip of the now warm violet champagne and swished it round his mouth. Any logical doubts he had were drowned out by the beating of his heart. It had been so long since he'd felt the rush. In his mind now there was only von Fersen.

The next night, Magnus had dinner brought in, courtesy of the chef at the Hôtel de Soubise. Magnus's friends permitted his use of the kitchen staff and their excellent foodstuffs when he needed to set an especially fine table. Tonight he had a delicate pigeon bisque, turbot, Rouen duckling with orange, spit-roasted veal, green beans au jus, artichokes, and a table full of cream puffs, fruit, and tiny cakes.

The meal was simple enough to arrange—getting dressed, however, was not. Absolutely nothing was right. He needed something that was flirtatious and fetching, yet businesslike and serious. And at first it seemed that the lemon-yellow coat and breeches with the purple waistcoat fit the bill precisely, but these were discarded for the lime-green waistcoat, and then the violet breeches. He settled on an entire ensemble in a simple cerulean blue, but not before he had emptied out the entire contents of his wardrobe.

Waiting was a delicious agony. Magnus could only pace, looking out the window, waiting for von Fersen's carriage to appear. He made countless trips to the mirror, and then to the table Claude and Marie had so carefully laid before he'd sent them away for the evening. Axel had insisted on privacy, and Magnus was happy to oblige.

At precisely eight o'clock a carriage stopped in front of Magnus's door, and out he stepped. Axel. He even looked up, as if he knew that Magnus would be looking down, waiting for him. He smiled a greeting, and Magnus felt a pleasant kind of sickness, a panic...

He hurried down the steps to admit Axel himself.

"I've dismissed my staff for the evening, as you asked," he said, trying to regain his composure. "Do come in. Our dinner is ready for us. You'll excuse the informality of my service."

"Of course, monsieur," Axel said.

But Axel did not linger over his food, or allow himself the pleasures of sipping his wine and taking in Magnus's charms. He launched right into the business at hand. He even had maps, which he unrolled on the sofa.

"The escape plan has been developed over several months," he said, picking an artichoke from a silver dish. "By me, some friends of the cause, and the queen herself."

"And the king?" Magnus asked.

"His Majesty has ... removed himself from the situation somewhat. He is very despondent over the state of things. Her Majesty has assumed much responsibility."

"You seem to be very ... fond of Her Majesty," Magnus noted carefully.

"She is to be admired," Axel said, dabbing at his lips with his napkin.

"And clearly she trusts you. You must be very close."

"She has graciously allowed me into her confidence."

Magnus could read between the lines. Axel didn't kiss and tell, which made him only more attractive.

"The escape is to be made on Sunday," Alex went on. "The plan is simple, but exacting. We have arranged it so the guards have seen certain people leaving by certain exits at certain times. On the night of the escape, we will substitute the family for these people. The children will be woken at ten thirty. The dauphin will be dressed as a young girl. He and his sister will be removed from the palace by the royal governess, the Marquise de Tourzel, and will walk to meet me at the Grand Carrousel. I will be driving the traveling carriage. We will then wait for Madame Elisabeth, sister of the king. She shall leave by the same door as the children. When His Majesty finishes his *coucher* for the evening and is left alone, he will leave as well, disguised as the Chevalier de Coigny. Her Majesty ... will escape last."

"Marie Antoinette will leave *last*?"

"It was her decision," von Fersen said quickly. "She is extremely courageous. She demands to go last. If the others are discovered missing, she wishes to sacrifice herself in order to aid their escape."

There was that frisson of passion in his voice again. But this time when he looked at Magnus, his gaze stayed there for a moment, fixed on the catlike pupils.

"So why do you want only the queen glamoured?"

"Partially it has to do with timing," Axel said. "The order in which people must be seen coming and going. His Majesty will be with people right up until his *coucher*, and he departs instantly after that. Only Her Majesty will be alone in the palace for some time. She is also more recognizable."

"Than the king?"

"But of course! His Majesty is not ... a handsome man. Gazes do not linger on his face. What people recognize are his clothes, and carriage, all the external signs of his royal status. But Her Majesty ... her face is known. Her face is studied and drawn and painted. Her style is copied. She is beautiful, and her face has been committed to many a memory."

"I see," Magnus said, wanting to move away from the subject of the queen's beauty. "And what will happen to you?"

"I will drive the carriage as far as Bondy," he said, his gaze still fixed on Magnus. He continued to list details—troop movements, stations to change the horses, things of that nature. Magnus had no interest in these details. They could not hold his attention like the way the elegant ruff of shirt fabric brushed Axel's chin as he spoke. The heavy plumpness of his lower lip. No king or queen or palace or work of art had anything that could compare with that lower lip.

"As for your payment..."

These words drew Magnus back in.

"The matter of payment is quite simple," Magnus said. "I require no money—"

"Monsieur," Axel said, leaning forward, "you do this as a true patriot of France!"

"I do this," Magnus continued calmly, "to develop our friendship. I ask only to see you again when the thing is done."

"To see me?"

"To see you, monsieur."

Axel's shoulders drew back a bit, and he looked down at his plate. For a moment Magnus thought it was all for nothing, that he had made the wrong move. But then Axel looked back up, and the candlelight flickered in his blue eyes.

"Monsieur," he said, taking Magnus's hand across the table, "we shall be the closest of friends evermore."

This was precisely what Magnus wanted to hear.

* * *

On Sunday morning, the day of the escape, Magnus woke to the usual clamor of church bells ringing all over Paris. His head was a bit thick and clouded from a long evening with the Count de —— and a group of actors from the Comédie-Italienne. It seemed that during the night he had also acquired a monkey. It sat on the footboard of his bed, happily eating Magnus's morning bread. It had already tipped over the pot of tea that Claude had brought in, and there was a pile of shredded ostrich feathers in the middle of the floor.

"Hello," Magnus said to the monkey.

The monkey did not reply.

"I shall call you Ragnor," Magnus added, leaning back against the pillows gently. "Claude!"

The door opened, and Claude came in. He did not appear in the least bit surprised about Ragnor's presence. He just immediately set to work cleaning up the spilled tea.

"I'll need you to get a leash for my monkey, Claude, and also a hat."

"Of course, monsieur."

"Do you think he needs a little coat as well?"

"Perhaps not in this weather, monsieur."

"You're right," Magnus said with a sigh. "Make it a simple dressing gown, just like mine."

"Which one, monsieur?"

"The one in rose and silver."

"An excellent choice, monsieur," Claude said, getting to work on the feathers.

"And take him to the kitchen and get him a proper breakfast, will you? He'll need fruit and water, and perhaps a cool bath."

By this point Ragnor had hopped down from the foot of the bed and was making his way toward an exquisite Sevres porcelain vase, when Claude plucked him up like he'd been monkey-plucking all his life.

"Ah," Claude added, reaching into his coat, "a note came for you this morning."

He made his quiet exit with the monkey. Magnus tore open the note. It read:

There is a problem. It is to be delayed until tomorrow.
—Axel

Well, that was the evening's plans ruined.

Tomorrow was Saint Cloud's party. Both of these obligations needed to be met. But it could be done. He would take his carriage to the edge of the Tuileries palace, attend to the business with the queen, get back into the carriage, and get to the party. He'd had busier nights.

And Axel was worth it.

Magnus spent far more of the next day and evening worrying about Saint Cloud's party than about his business with the royal family. The glamour would be easy. The party would likely be fraught and uncomfortable. All he had to do was put in an appearance, smile, and chat for a bit, and then he could be on his way. But he couldn't escape the feeling that somehow this evening was going to go wrong.

But first, the small matter of the queen.

Magnus took his bath and dressed after dinner, and then quietly left his apartments at nine, instructing his driver to take him to the vicinity of the Tuileries garden and return at midnight. This was a familiar enough trip. Many people went to the garden for a "chance encounter" amongst the topiaries. He walked around for a bit, making his way through the shadowy garden, listening to the snuffling noises of lovers in the shrubbery, occasionally peeking through the leaves to have a little look.

At ten thirty he made his way, by following Axel's map, to the outside of the apartments of the long-departed Duc de Villequier. If all went to plan, the young princess and dauphin would be exiting those unguarded doors soon, with the dauphin disguised as a little girl. If they did not exit, the plan was already foiled.

But only a few minutes later than expected, the children came out with their nurses, all in the disguises. Magnus followed them quietly as they walked through the north-facing courtyard, down the rue de l'Échelle, and to the Grand Carrousel. And there, with a plain carriage, was Axel. He was dressed as a rough Parisian coachman. He was even smoking a pipe and making jokes, all in a perfect low Paris accent, all traces of his Swedishness gone. There was Axel in the moonlight, lifting the children into the carriage— Magnus was struck speechless for a moment. Axel's bravery, his talent, his gentleness ... it tugged on Magnus's heart in a way that was slightly unfamiliar, and it made it very difficult to be cynical.

He watched them drive away, and then returned to his task. He would enter through that same door. Even though the door was unguarded, Magnus needed his glamour to protect him, so that anyone looking over would see only a large cat sneaking into the palace through a door that seemed to blow open.

With thousands of people coming in and out—and no royal staff of hundreds of cleaners—the floors were grimy, with clumps of dried mud and footprints. There was a musty smell about the place, a mix of damp, smoke, mold, and a few unemptied chamber pots, some of which sat in the halls. There was no light, save what was reflected from windows, off mirrors, and weakly amplified with crystal chandeliers that were thick with spiderwebs and dimmed by soot.

Axel had given Magnus a hand-drawn map with very clear instructions on how to get through the seemingly endless series of arches and largely empty grand rooms, their gilded furnishings either absent or having been roughly appropriated by guards. There were a few secret doors hidden in the paneling, which Magnus quietly passed through. As he went deeper into the palace, the rooms grew a bit cleaner, the candles a bit more frequent. There were smells of cooking food and pipe smoke and more people passing by.

And then he arrived at the royal chambers. At the door he'd been instructed to enter, a guard sat by, idly whistling and kicking back on his chair. Magnus sent up a small spark in the corner of the room, and the guard got up to examine it. Magnus slipped the key into the lock and entered. These rooms had a velvety silence about them that felt unnatural and uncomfortable. He smelled smoke from a recently extinguished candle. Magnus was not cowed by royalty, but his heart began to beat a bit more quickly as he reached for the second key Axel had given him. Axel had a key to the queen's private rooms. The fact was both exciting and unsettling.

And there she was—Queen Marie Antoinette. He'd seen her image many times, but now she was in front of him, and altogether human. That was the shock of it. The queen was a human, in her sleeping dress. There was a loveliness about her. One part, no doubt, was simply the training she had had—her regal bearing and small, delicate footsteps. The pictures had never done justice to her eyes, though, which were large and luminous. Her hair had been carefully coiffed in a halo of light curls, over which she wore a light linen cap. Magnus remained in the shadows and watched her pace her room, going from bed to window and back to bed again, clearly terrified about the fate of her family.

"You notice nothing, madame," he said quietly. The queen turned as he said this and looked at the corner of the room in confusion, then returned to her pacing. Magnus drew closer, and as he did so, he could see how the strain of things had taken its toll on the woman. Her hair was thin, and pale, turning brittle and gray at points. Still, her face had a fierce, determined glow that Magnus quite admired. He could see why Axel felt for her—there was a strength there he never would have expected.

He wiggled his fingers, and blue flames crackled between them.

Again the queen turned in confusion. Magnus passed his hand by her face, changing her visage from the familiar and royal to the familiar and ordinary. Her eyes diminished in size and grew dark, her cheeks became plumper and heavily flushed with red, her nose increased in size, and her chin receded. Her hair became more limp and darkened to a chestnut brown. He went a little further than was absolutely necessary, even altering her cheekbones and ears a bit until no one could mistake the woman in front of him for the queen. She looked as she was supposed to look—like a Russian noblewoman of a different age, a different life altogether.

He created a noise near the window to draw her attention away, and when her back was turned, he exited. He left the palace through a heavily trafficked exit behind the royal apartments, where the queen kept a gate open for Axel's nightly entrances and exits.

It was altogether simple and elegant, and a good night's work. Magnus smiled to himself, looked up at the moon hanging over Paris, and thought of Axel, driving around in his coach. Then he thought of Axel doing other things. And then he hurried on. There were vampires to see.

It was a fortunate thing that vampire parties always started so late. Magnus's carriage drew up to Saint Cloud's door after midnight. The footmen, all vampires, helped him from his carriage, and Henri greeted him by the door.

"Monsieur Bane," he said, with his creepy little smile. "Master will be so very pleased."

"I'm so glad," Magnus said, barely concealing his sarcasm. Henri's eyebrow flicked just a bit. Then he turned and put his arm out to a girl of similar age and appearance—blond, glassy-eyed, dull of expression, and very beautiful.

"You know my sister, Brigitte?"

"Of course. We've met several times, mademoiselle, in your ... previous life."

"My previous life," Brigitte said with a little, tinkling laugh. "My previous life."

Brigitte's previous life was an idea that continued to entertain her, as she kept giggling and smiling to herself. Henri put his arm around her in a way that was not entirely brotherly.

"Master has very generously allowed us to keep our names," he said. "And I was most pleased when he permitted me to return to my former home and bring my sister back here to live. Master is most generous in this way, as he is in all ways."

This caused Brigitte to have another fit of giggles. Henri gave her a playful pat on the bottom.

"I'm absolutely parched," Magnus said. "I think I'll find some champagne."

Unlike the dreary and poorly lit Tuileries, Saint Cloud's house was spectacular. It didn't quite qualify as a palace, in terms of size, but it had all of the opulence of the décor. It was a veritable jungle of patterns, with paintings packed frame to frame up to the ceilings. And all of Saint Cloud's chandeliers sparkled and were full of black candles, dripping black wax onto the floor. The wax was then instantly scraped up by a small army of darklings. A few mundane hangers-on were draped over the furniture, most holding wineglasses—or bottles. Most slumped with their necks exposed, just waiting, begging to be bitten. The vampires stayed on their own side of the room, laughing amongst themselves and pointing, as if choosing what to eat from a table laden with delicacies.

In mundane Parisian society the large powdered wig had recently gone out of fashion, in favor of more natural styles. In vampire society the wigs were bigger than ever. One female vampire wore a wig that was at least six feet high, powdered a light pink, and supported by a delicate latticework of what Magnus suspected was the bones of children. She had a bit of blood at the corner of her mouth, and Magnus could not figure out if the slashes of red on her cheeks were blood or extreme streaks of blush. (Like the wigs, the Paris vampires also favored the slightly passé makeup styles, such as the sharp spots of blush on the cheeks, possibly in mockery of the humans.)

He passed an ashen-faced harpist who had—Magnus noted grimly—been shackled to the floor by his ankle. If he played well enough, he might be kept alive for a while to play again. Or he could be a late-night snack. Magnus was tempted to sever the harpist's chain, but just at that moment there was a voice from above.

"Magnus! Magnus Bane, where have you been?"

Marcel Saint Cloud was leaning over the rail and waving down. Around him, a cluster of vampires peered at Magnus over their fans of feather and ivory and bone.

Saint Cloud was, though it pained Magnus to admit it, strikingly beautiful. The old ones all had a very special look about them—a luster that came with age. And Saint Cloud was old, possibly one of Vlad's very first vampire court. He was not as tall as Magnus, but was very finely boned, with jutting cheekbones and long fingers. His eyes were utterly black, but caught the light like mirrored glass. And his clothes ... well, he used the same tailor as Magnus, so of course they were wonderful.

"Always busy," Magnus said, managing a smile as Saint Cloud and his cluster of followers descended the steps. They clung to his heels, altering their pace to fall in line with his. Sycophants.

"You've just missed de Sade."

"What a shame," Magnus replied. The Marquis de Sade was a decidedly eerie mundane, with the most perverse imagination Magnus had ever come across since the Spanish Inquisition.

"There are some things I want to show you," Saint Cloud said, putting a cold arm around Magnus's shoulders. "Absolutely wonderful things!"

One thing Saint Cloud and Magnus had in common was a rich appreciation for mundane fashion, furniture, and art. Magnus tended to buy his, or receive them as payment. Marcel traded with the revolutionaries—or with the street people who had raided great houses and taken the pretty things from inside. Or his darklings handed over their possessions. Or things just arrived in his house. It was best not to ask too many questions but simply to admire, and admire loudly. Marcel would take offense if Magnus didn't praise every item.

Suddenly, a chorus of voices from an outside courtyard was calling for Saint Cloud.

"Something seems to be going on," Marcel said. "Perhaps we should investigate."

The voices were high, excited, and giddy—all tones Magnus didn't want to hear at a vampire party. Those tones meant very bad things.

"What is it, my friends?" Marcel said, walking toward the front hall.

There was a tangle of vampires standing at the foot of the front steps, with Henri at the head. A few of them were holding a struggling figure. She made high-pitched squeals from a mouth that sounded covered, though it was impossible to see her in the throng.

"Master..." Henri's eyes were wide. "Master, we have found ... You will not believe, Master..."

"Show me. Bring it forward. What is it?"

The vampires ordered themselves a bit and threw the human into the cleared space on the ground. It was all Magnus could do not to make a sound of alarm, or give away anything at all.

It was Marie Antoinette.

Of course, the glamour he had applied did not affect the vampires. The queen was exposed, her face white with shock.

"You ...," she said, addressing the crowd in a shaky voice, "what you have done... You will—"

Marcel raised a silencing hand, and to Magnus's surprise, the queen stopped speaking.

"Who brought her?" he asked. "How did this happen?"

"It was I, monsieur," said a voice. A dapper vampire named Coselle stepped to the front. "I was on my way here, coming down the rue du Bac, and I absolutely could not believe my eyes. She must have gotten out of the Tuileries. She was just on the street, monsieur, looking panicked and lost."

Of course. The queen would not have been accustomed to being out on the streets on her own. And in the dark it was easy to go the wrong way. She had made a wrong turn and crossed the Seine somehow.

"Madame," Marcel said, walking down the stairs. "Or should I say 'Your Majesty'? Do I have the pleasure of addressing our beloved and most ... illustrious queen?"

A low snicker from around the room, but aside from that no noise at all.

"I am she," the queen said, rising to her feet. "And I demand—"

Marcel put up his hand again, indicating silence. He descended the rest of the steps and walked to the queen, stood in front of her, and examined her closely. Then he gave a small bow.

"Your Majesty," he said. "I am thrilled beyond words that you could attend my party. We are all thrilled beyond words, are we not, my friends?"

By now, all the vampires who could fit had crowded into the doorway. Those who could not were leaning out of the windows. There were nods and smiles, but no reply. The silence was terrible. Outside Marcel's courtyard wall, even Paris itself seemed to have fallen silent.

"My dear Marcel," Magnus said, forcing a laugh. "I do *hate* to disappoint you, but this is not the queen. This is the mistress of one of my clients. Her name is Josette."

As this statement appeared to be plainly and glaringly false, Marcel and the others remained silent, waiting to hear more. Magnus walked down the steps, trying to look like he was amused by this turn of events.

"She's very good, isn't she?" he said. "I cater to many tastes, much like you. And I happen to have a client who wishes to do to the queen what she has been doing to the French people for many years. I was hired to do a complete transformation. And I must say, at the risk of sounding immodest, that I have done an excellent job of it."

"I have never known you to be modest," Marcel said without a hint of a smile.

"It's an overrated quality," Magnus replied with a shrug.

"Then how do you explain the fact that this woman claims she is, in fact, Queen Marie Antoinette?"

"I am the queen, you monster!" she said, her voice now hysterical. "I am the queen. I am the queen!"

Magnus got the impression that she was saying this not as a way of impressing her captors but as a way of assuring herself of her own identity and sanity. He stepped calmly in front of her and snapped his fingers in front of her face. She fell unconscious at once, slumping gently into his arms. "Why," he said, calmly turning toward Marcel, "would the queen of France be wandering down this street, unattended, in the middle of the night?"

"A fair question."

"Because she wasn't. Josette was. She had to be complete in every way. At first my client wanted her only to look like the queen, but then he insisted on the entire package, as it were. Appearance, personality, all of it. Josette absolutely believes she is Marie Antoinette. In fact, I was doing a bit of work on her in this very regard when she became afeared and escaped from my apartments. Perhaps she followed me here. Sometimes my talents get the better of me."

He set the queen gently on the ground.

"It also appears she has a light glamour on her," Marcel added.

"For mundanes," Magnus said. "You can't have a woman who looks exactly like the queen passing through the streets. It's quite a light one, like a summer shawl. She was not supposed to leave the house. I was still working."

Marcel squatted down and took the queen's face in his hand, turning it from side to side, sometimes looking at the face itself, sometimes at the neck. A long minute or two passed in which the entire assembled group waited for his next utterance.

"Well," Marcel said at last, standing back up. "I must congratulate you on an excellent piece of work."

Magnus had to brace himself in order that his sigh of relief would not be seen.

"All of my work is excellent, but I accept your congratulations," he said, flicking a careless hand in Marcel's direction.

"A marvel such as this, it would be such a success at one of my gatherings. So I really must insist that you sell her to me."

"Sell her?" Magnus said.

"Yes." Marcel leaned down and traced his finger down the queen's jawline. "Yes, you must. Whatever your client paid you, I'll double it. But I really must have her. Quite stunning. Whatever you like, I will pay."

"But, Marcel..."

"Now, now, Magnus." Marcel slowly waggled a finger. "We all have our weaknesses, and our weaknesses must be indulged if they are to flourish. I will have her."

It wouldn't do to imply that this fictional client was more important than Marcel.

Think. He had to *think*. And he knew that Marcel was watching him think."If you insist," Magnus replied. "But, as I said, I was still working. I just had a few finishing touches left to do. She still has a few unfortunate habits left over from her previous life. All of those Versailles mannerisms—there are so many of them—they all had to be stitched in like fine embroidery. And I hadn't yet signed the work. I do like to sign my work."

"How long would this take?"

"Oh, not long at all. I could bring her back tomorrow..."

"I would prefer she stayed here. After all, how long does it take you to sign your work?" Marcel asked with a light smile.

"It can take time," Magnus said, responding with his own knowing smile. "I have an exquisite signature."

"While I deal in used goods, I do prefer ones in pristine condition. Don't be long about it. Henri, Charles ... take Madam upstairs and put her in the blue room. Let Monsieur Bane complete his signature. We are looking forward to seeing the final product shortly."

"Of course," Magnus said.

Slowly he followed the prostrate queen and the darklings back inside.

After Henri and Charles put the queen on the bed, Magnus locked the door and slid a large wardrobe to block it. Then he threw open the shutters. The blue room was a third-floor room, a sheer drop down to the receiving courtyard. That was the only way out.

Magnus allowed himself a few moments of swearing before shaking his head and taking stock of his situation again. He could probably get himself out of this, but to get both himself and the queen ... *and* to return the queen to Axel...

He looked out the window again, to the ground below. Most of the vampires had gone back inside. A few servants and darklings remained to greet the carriages, though. Down would not work, but *up*...

Up, in a balloon, for instance.

Magnus was certain of one thing—this work was going to be very difficult. The balloon itself was on the other side of Paris. He reached out with his mind and found what he was looking for. It was rolled up still, in the gazebo in the Bois de Boulogne. He rolled it to the grass, he willed it to inflate, glamoured it invisible, and then he lifted it from the ground. He felt it lift, and he guided it up, over the trees of the park, over the houses and the streets, carefully avoiding the spires of the churches and cathedrals, over the river. It was strongly buoyant and was pulled easily by the wind. It wanted to go straight up into the sky, but Magnus held on.

At some point he would run dry of power, and then he would

lose consciousness. He could only hope that this would happen late enough in the process, but there was really no telling. As the balloon drew nearer, he did his best to glamour it completely, making it invisible to even the vampires just below. He watched it come to the window, and as carefully as he could, he guided it close. He leaned out as far as he could and caught hold of it. The basket had a small door, which he managed to get open.

When one steals a flying balloon and animates it to fly over Paris, one should, ideally, have some idea how said balloon normally works. Magnus had never been interested in the mechanics of the balloon—his only interest was that the mundanes could now fly in a colorful piece of silk. So when he discovered that the basket contained a fire, he was dismayed.

Also, the queen herself was probably not heavy, but her dress—and whatever she had concealed or sewn into the dress for her escape—certainly was, and Magnus had no energy to spare. He snapped his fingers, and the queen woke. Just in time he drew a finger across her lips and silenced the scream that was about to come from her mouth.

"Your Majesty," he said, the exhaustion weighing his voice. "There is no time to explain, and no time for introductions. What I need you to do is—as quickly as possible—step out of that window. You cannot see it, but there is something out there that will catch you. But we must be quick."

The queen opened her mouth and, finding that she could not speak, began to run around the room, picking up objects and hurling them at Magnus. Magnus cringed as vases hit the wall next to him. He managed to lash the balloon to the window with the curtain and grabbed the queen. She began to pummel Magnus. Her fists were small and she was clearly unused to this sort of activity, but her blows were not entirely ineffective. He had very little strength left, and she seemed to be running on raw fear, which quicksilvered her veins.

"Your Majesty," he hissed. "You must stop. You must listen to me. Axel—"

On the word "Axel," she froze. This was all he needed. He shoved her backward out the window. The balloon, bumped back by the force, shifted a foot or so away from the window—so she landed half in, half out. She hung there, terrified and grasping at something she could feel but not see, her slippered feet kicking into the air and smacking into the side of the building. Magnus had to accept a few flurried kicks in the chest and face before he was able to roll her over into the basket. Her skirts tumbled over her head, and the Queen of France was reduced to a pile of cloth and two flailing legs. He jumped into the basket himself, closed the basket door, and released the hold on the basket with a deep sigh. The balloon went straight up, shooting above the rooftops. The queen had managed to flip herself over and scramble to her knees. She touched the basket, her eyes wide with a childlike wonder. She drew herself up slowly and peered over the side of the basket, took one look at the view below, and fainted dead away.

"Someday," Magnus said, looking at the crumpled royal person at his feet, "I must write my memoirs."

This was not the balloon ride Magnus had hoped for.

For a start, the balloon was low and suicidally slow, and seemed to like nothing more than dropping suddenly onto roofs and chimneys. The queen was shifting and groaning on the floor of the basket, causing it to sway back and forth in a nausea-inducing way. An owl made a sudden assault. And the sky was dark, so dark that Magnus had largely no idea where he was going. The queen moaned a bit and lifted her head.

"Who *are* you?" she asked weakly.

"A friend of a friend," Magnus replied.

"What are we—"

"It's best if you don't ask, Your Majesty. You really don't want the answer. And I think we're being blown south, which is the completely wrong direction."

"Axel..."

"Yes." Magnus leaned over and tried to make out the streets below. "Yes, Axel ... but here's a question... If you were trying to find, say, the Seine, where would you look?"

The queen put her head back down.

He managed to find enough strength to restore the glamour on the balloon, rendering it invisible to the mundanes. He did not have the energy to completely glamour himself in the process, so some people were treated to the view of Magnus's upper half sailing past their third-story window in the dark. Some people didn't spare the candles, and he got one or two very interesting views.

Eventually he caught sight of a shop he knew. He pulled the balloon down the street, until more and more looked familiar, and then he caught sight of Notre Dame.

Now the question was ... where to put the balloon *down*? You couldn't just land a balloon in the middle of Paris. Even an invisible one. Paris was just too ... spiky.

There was only one thing for it, and Magnus already hated it.

"Your Majesty," he said, prodding the queen with his foot. "Your Majesty, *you must wake up*."

The queen stirred again.

"Now," Magnus said, "you won't like what I am about to say, but trust me when I say it is the best of several terrible alternatives..."

"Axel..."

"Yes. Now, in a minute we are going to land in the Seine—"

"What?"

"And it would be very good if you perhaps held your nose. And I'm guessing your dress is full of jewels, so..."

The balloon was dropping fast, and the water was coming up. Magnus carefully navigated them to a spot between two bridges.

"You may get—"

The balloon simply dropped like a stone. The fire went out, and the silk immediately came down on Magnus and the queen. Magnus was almost out of strength, but he managed to find enough to rend the silk in two so it didn't trap them. He swam on his own power, pulling her under his arm to the bank. They were, as he'd hoped, quite close to the Tuileries and its dock. He got her over to the steps and threw her down.

"Stay here," he said, dripping wet and panting.

But the queen was unconscious again. Magnus envied her.

He trudged up the steps and back up onto the streets of Paris. Axel would probably have been circling the area. They had agreed that if anything went wrong, Magnus was to send a blue flash into the sky, like a firework. He did it. Then he sank to the ground and waited.

About fifteen minutes later a carriage pulled up—not the simple, plain one from before but a massive one, in black and green and yellow. One that could easily carry half a dozen or more people for several days, in the grandest of possible styles. Axel hopped down from the driver's seat and rushed to Magnus.

"Where is she? Why are you wet? What has happened?"

"She's fine," Magnus said, putting up a hand. "*This* is the carriage? A *berline de voyage*?"

"Yes," von Fersen said. "Their Majesties insist. And it would be unseemly for them to arrive in something less grand."

"And impossible not to be noticed!"

For the first time von Fersen looked uncomfortable. He had clearly hated this idea and had fought it.

"Yes, well ... this is the carriage. But..."

"She's on the steps. We had to land in the river."

"Land?"

"It's a long story," Magnus said. "Let's just say things got complicated. But she is alive."

Axel got to his knees in front of Magnus.

"You will never be forgotten for this," Axel said in a low voice.

"France will remember. Sweden will remember."

"I don't care if France or Sweden remembers. I care if you remember."

Magnus was genuinely shocked when it was Axel who instigated the kiss—how sudden it was, how passionate, how all of Paris, and all the vampires, and the Seine and the balloon and everything fell away and it was just the two of them for one moment. One perfect moment.

And it was Magnus who broke it.

"Go," he whispered. "I need you to be safe. Go."

Axel nodded, looking a bit shocked at his own action, and ran to the dock steps. Magnus got up, and with one last look started to walk.

Going home was not an option. Saint Cloud's vampires were probably at his apartments right now. He had to get inside until dawn. He spent the night at the *petite maison* of Madame de ——, one of his more recent lovers. At dawn he returned to his apartments. The front door was ajar. He made his way inside cautiously.

"Claude!" he called, carefully staying in the pool of sunlight by the door. "Marie! Ragnor!"

"They are not here, monsieur," said a voice.

Henri. Of course. He was sitting on the staircase.

"Did you hurt them?"

"We took the ones called Claude and Marie. I don't know who Ragnor is."

"Did you *hurt* them?" Magnus said again.

"They are beyond hurt now. My master asked me to send his compliments. He said they made for excellent feasting."

Magnus felt sick. Marie and Claude had been good to him, and now...

"Master would like very much to see you," Henri said. "Why don't we go there together, now, and you can speak when he wakes this evening."

"I think I'll decline the invitation," Magnus said.

"If you do, I think you will find Paris a most inhospitable place to live. And who is that new gentleman of yours? We'll find his name eventually. Do you understand?"

Henri stood, and tried to look menacing, but he was a mundane, a darkling of seventeen.

"What I think, little darkling," Magnus said, stepping closer, "is that you forget who you're dealing with."

Magnus allowed some blue sparks to flick between his fingers. Henri backed up a step.

"Go home and tell your master that I've gotten his message. I have given offense that I did not mean to give. I will leave Paris at once. The matter can be considered closed. I accept my punishment."

He stepped away from the door and extended his arm, indicating that Henri should exit.

As he'd expected, everything was a shambles—furniture overturned, burn marks up the walls, art missing, books shredded. In his bedchamber wine had been poured onto his bed and his clothes... At least he thought it was wine.

Magnus didn't take long to pick through the wreckage. With the flick of his hand, the marble fireplace moved away from the wall. He retrieved a sack heavy with *louis d'or*, a thick roll of *assignats*, and a collection of wonderful rings in citrine, jade, ruby, and one magnificent blue topaz.

This was his insurance policy, should the revolutionaries have raided his house. Vampires, revolutionaries ... it was all the same now. The rings went on his fingers, the *assignats* into his coat, and the *louis d'or* into a handsome leather satchel, which had also been stored inside the wall for this very purpose. He reached back farther into the opening and produced one last item—the Gray Book, bound in green velvet. This he carefully placed in the satchel.

He heard a tiny noise behind him, and Ragnor crawled out from under the bed.

"My little friend," Magnus said, picking up the frightened monkey. "At least you survived. Come. We'll go together."

When Magnus heard the news, he was high in the Alps, resting by a stream, crushing some edelweiss under his thumb. Magnus had tried to avoid all things French for weeks—French people, French food, French news. He had given himself over to pork and pounded veal, thermal bathing, and reading. For most of this time he had passed his days alone—with little Ragnor—and in the quiet. But just that morning an escaped nobleman from Dijon had come to stay at the inn where Magnus was living. He looked like a man who liked to talk at length, and Magnus was in no mood for such company, so he'd gone to sit by the stream. He was not surprised when the man followed him there.

"You! Monsieur!" he called to Magnus as he puffed and huffed up the hillside.

Magnus flicked some edelweiss from his fingernail.

"Yes?"

"The innkeeper says you recently came from Paris, monsieur! Are you my countryman?"

Magnus wore a light glamour at the inn, so he could pass as a random noble French refugee, one of hundreds that were flowing over the border.

"I came from Paris," Magnus said noncommittally.

"And you have a monkey?"

Ragnor was scampering around. He had taken to the Alps extremely well.

"Ah, monsieur, I am so glad to find you! For weeks I have not spoken to anyone from my land." He wrung his hands together. "I hardly know what to think or do these days. Such terrible times! Such horrors! You have heard about the king and queen, no doubt?"

"What about them?" Magnus said, keeping his face impassive.

"Their Majesties, God protect them! They tried to escape Paris!

They made it as far as the town of Varennes, where it is said a postal worker recognized the king. They were captured and sent back to Paris. Oh, terrible times!"

Without a word Magnus got up, scooped up Ragnor, and returned to the inn.

He had not wanted to think of this matter. In his mind Axel and the family had been safe. That was how he'd needed it to be. But now.

He paced his room, and finally wrote a letter to Axel's address in Paris. Then he waited for the reply.

It took three weeks, and came in an unfamiliar hand, from Sweden.

> *Monsieur,*
> *Axel wishes you to know he is well, and returns the depth of feeling. The King and Queen, as you know, are now imprisoned in Paris. Axel has been moved to Vienna to plead their case to the Emperor, but I fear he is determined to return to Paris, at the risk of his life. Monsieur, as Axel seems to hold you in high esteem, won't you please write to him and discourage this enterprise? He is my beloved brother, and I worry for him constantly.*

There was an address in Vienna given, and the note was signed simply "Sophie."

Axel would return to Paris. Of that, Magnus was sure.

Vampires, fey folk, werewolves, Shadowhunters, and demons—these things made sense to Magnus. But the mundane world—it seemed to have no pattern, no form. Their quicksilver politics. Their short lives...

Magnus thought once again of the blue-eyed man standing in his parlor. Then he lit a match and burned the note.

Vampires, Scones, and Edmund Herondale

By Cassandra Clare and Sarah Rees Brennan

It was then that the fair-haired Shadowhunter that Magnus had spotted at the Institute somersaulted from the top of a wall and landed gracefully in the street before him.

—Vampires, Scones, and Edmund Herondale

AFTER ALL,
ATTRACTIVE AND INTERESTING PERSONS DO NOT SIMPLY DROP OUT OF THE SKY.
!!
DEVASTATING ENSEMBLES MADE ON BOND STREET WITH RED BRO-CADE WAISTCOATS DO NOT SIMPLY DROP OUT OF THE SKY!
I BEG YOUR PARDON?

London, 1857

Ever since the unfortunate events of the French Revolution, Magnus had nursed a slight prejudice against vampires. The undead were always killing one's servants and endangering one's pet monkey. The vampire clan in Paris was still sending Magnus rude messages about their small misunderstanding. Vampires bore a grudge longer than any technically living creatures, and whenever they were in a bad temper, they expressed themselves through murder. Magnus generally wished his companions to be somewhat less—no pun intended—bloodthirsty.

There was also the fact that sometimes vampires committed crimes worse than murder. They committed crimes against fashion. When one was immortal, one tended to forget the passing of time. Still, that was no excuse for wearing a bonnet last fashionable in the era of Napoléon I.

Magnus was beginning, however, to feel as if he might have been a trifle hasty in dismissing *all* vampires.

Lady Camille Belcourt was a terribly charming woman. She was also attired in the absolute height of fashion. Her dress had a darling hoop skirt, and the fall of blue taffeta in seven narrow flounces about her chair made it appear as if she were rising from a cascade of gleaming blue water. There was not very much material at all around her bosom, which was as pale and curved as a pearl. All that broke the perfect pallor of the curve of bosom and the column of neck was a black velvet ribbon and the thick shining ringlets clustered about her face. One gold ringlet was long enough so that it rested in the delicate curve of her collarbone, which led Magnus's eyes back once again to—

Really, all roads led back to Lady Camille's bosom.

It was a wonderfully designed dress. It was also a wonderfully designed bosom.

Lady Camille, as observant as she was beautiful, noticed Magnus noticing, and smiled.

"The marvelous thing about being a creature of the night," she confided in a low voice, "is that one need never wear anything but evening clothes."

"I had never considered that point before," said Magnus, much struck.

"Of course I adore variety, so I do seize any opportunity to change costumes. I find there are many occasions during an adventurous night for a lady to divest herself of her garments." She leaned forward, one pale, smooth elbow resting against the Shadowhunters' mahogany table. "Something tells me that you are a man who knows something about adventurous nights."

"My lady, with me, every night is an adventure. Pray continue your discourse on fashion," Magnus urged her. "It is one of my favorite subjects."

Lady Camille smiled.

Magnus lowered his voice discreetly. "Or if you choose, pray continue your discourse on disrobing. I believe that is my most favorite subject of all."

They sat side by side at a long table in the Shadowhunters' London Institute. The Consul, a dreary Nephilim heading up the proceedings, was droning on about all the spells they wished warlocks to make available to them at cut-rate prices, and about their notions of proper behavior for vampires and werewolves.

Magnus had not heard a single way in which these "Accords" could conceivably benefit Downworlders, but he could certainly see why the Shadowhunters had developed a passionate desire to ratify them.

He began regretting his agreement to make the voyage to London and its Institute so that the Shadowhunters could waste his valuable time. The Consul, who Magnus believed was called Morgwhatsit, seemed passionately in love with his own voice.

Though, actually he had stopped talking.

Magnus glanced away from Camille to find the far less pleasant sight of the Consul—his disapproval writ across his face, as stark as the runes on his skin—staring at him. "If you and the—the vampire woman could cease your flirtation for a moment," he said in acid tones.

"Flirting? We were merely indulging in a little risqué conversation," Magnus said, offended. "When I begin to flirt, I assure you the entire room will know. My flirtations cause sensations."

Camille laughed. "What a clever rhyme."

Magnus's joke seemed to liberate the restless discontent of all Downworlders at the table.

"What else are we to do but talk amongst ourselves?" asked a werewolf stripling, still young but with the intense green eyes of a fanatic and the thin determined face of a fanatic who was actually competent. His name was Ralf Scott. "We have been here for three hours and have not been given the chance to speak at all. You Nephilim have done all the talking."

"I cannot believe," put in Arabella, a charming mermaid with charmingly placed seashells, "that I swam up the Thames, and consented to be hauled out by pulleys and put in a large glass aquarium, for *this*."

She spoke quite loudly.

Even Morgwhatsit looked taken aback. *Why*, Magnus wanted to know, were Shadowhunter names so long, when warlocks gave themselves elegant family names of one syllable? The long names were sheer self-importance.

"You wretches should be honored to be in the London Institute," snarled a silver-haired Shadowhunter by the name of Starkweather. "I wouldn't allow any of you in my Institute, unless I was carrying one of your filthy heads on a pike. Silence, and let your betters speak for you."

An extremely awkward pause ensued. Starkweather glared around, and his eyes dwelled on Camille, not as if she were a beautiful woman but as if she might be a fine trophy for his wall. Camille's eyes went to her leader and friend, the pale-haired vampire Alexei de Quincey, but he did not respond to her mute appeal. Magnus put out his hand and took hers.

Her skin was cool, but her fingers fit his very neatly. He saw Ralf Scott glance over at them and blanch. He was even younger than Magnus had thought. His eyes were huge and glass green, transparent enough for all his emotions to shine through, in his thin face. They were fixed on Camille.

Interesting, Magnus thought, and filed the observation away.

"These are meant to be peace accords," Scott said, deliberately slowly. "Which means we are all meant to have a chance to have our voices heard. I have heard how peace will benefit Shadowhunters. I wish now to discuss how it will benefit Downworlders. Will we be given seats on the Council?"

Starkweather began to choke. One of the Shadowhunter women stood up hastily. "Gracious, I think my husband was so excited by the chance to deliver a speech that he did not offer refreshments," she said loudly. "I am Amalia Morgenstern." *Oh, that's it*, Magnus thought. *Morgenstern. Awful name.* "And is there anything I can offer you?" the woman continued. "I will ring for the maid in a trice."

"No raw meat for the dog, mind," Starkweather said, and sniggered. Magnus saw another Shadowhunter woman titter silently behind her hand. Ralf Scott sat, pale and still. He had been the moving force behind assembling Downworlders here today, and had been the only werewolf willing to come. Even his own young brother, Woolsey, had stayed away, parting from Ralf on the front steps of the Institute with an insouciant toss of his blond head and a wink at Magnus. (Magnus had thought, *Interesting*, about that, too.)

The faeries had flatly refused to attend, the queen having set herself against the idea. Magnus was the only warlock who had come, and Ralf had been forced to hunt him down, knowing his connections to the Silent Brothers. Magnus himself had not had high hopes about this attempt to forge a peace with Shadowhunters, but it was a shame to see the boy's airy dreams come to this.

"We are in England, are we not?" asked Magnus, and he bent a charming smile on Amalia Morgenstern, who looked rather flustered. "I would be delighted if we could have some scones."

"Oh, certainly," said Amalia. "With clotted cream, of course."

Magnus gazed upon Camille. "Some of my fondest memories include lashings of cream and beautiful women."

Magnus was enjoying scandalizing the Shadowhunters. Camille rather looked as if she were enjoying it too. Her green eyes were heavy-lidded for a moment with amused satisfaction, as if she were a cat who had already had her fill of cream.

Amalia rang the bell. "While we wait for scones, we can hear the rest of dear Roderick's speech!"

There was an appalled silence, and in the stillness the mutter outside the door rang out, loud and clear.

"Merciful Angel, give me strength to endure..."

Roderick Morgenstern, who Magnus thought truly deserved to have a name that sounded like a goat chewing gravel, stood up happily to continue his speech. Amalia attempted to rise unobtrusively from her seat—Magnus could have told her that hoop skirts and stealth together were a lost cause—and made her way to the door, which she threw open.

Several young Shadowhunters tumbled into the room like puppies falling over one another. Amalia's eyes rounded in comic surprise. "What on earth—"

Despite Shadowhunters having the swiftness of angels, only one managed to land with grace. It was a boy, or rather a young man, who ended his fall on one knee before Amalia, like Romeo proposing to Juliet.

He had hair the color of a coin that was pure gold, no base metal, and the lines of his face were as clean and elegant as a profile etched on one of those princely coins. His shirt had become disarranged at some point during the eavesdropping, the collar pulled open to reveal the edge of a rune drawn on his white skin.

The most remarkable thing about him were his eyes. They were laughing eyes, at once both joyous and tender: they were the radiant pale blue of a sky slipping toward evening in Heaven, when angels who had been sweet all day found themselves tempted to sin.

"I could not bear to be parted from you a moment longer, dear, dearest Mrs. Morgenstern," said the young man, possessing himself of Amalia's hand. "I yearn for you."

He made play with his long golden eyelashes, and Amalia Morgenstern was forthwith reduced to blushes and smiles.

Magnus had always had a decided preference for black hair. It appeared as though fate were determined that he should broaden his horizons. Either that or the blonds of the world had formed some sort of conspiracy to be good-looking all of a sudden.

"Excuse me, Bane?" said Roderick Morgenstern. "Are you attending?"

"I'm so sorry," Magnus said politely. "Somebody incredibly attractive just came into the room, and I ceased to pay attention to a word you were saying."

It was perhaps an ill-judged remark. The Shadowhunter elders, representatives from the Clave, all appeared horrified and dismayed at any Downworlder expressing interest in one of their youths. The

Nephilim also had very decided opinions on the subject of inverts and deviant behavior, since as a group their chief occupations were waving large weaponry about and judging everybody they met.

Camille, meanwhile, looked as if she found Magnus even more interesting than she had before. She looked back and forth between him and the young blond Shadowhunter boy, and covered her smile with a gloved hand.

"He *is* delightful," she murmured to Magnus.

Magnus was watching as Amalia shooed out the young Shadowhunters—the blond boy; an older young man with thick brown hair and significant eyebrows; and a dark-eyed, birdlike little girl, barely more than a toddler, who looked over her shoulder and said, "Papa?" in a clear questioning voice to the head of the London Institute, a grave dark man called Granville Fairchild.

"Go, Charlotte. You know your duty," said Fairchild. Duty before all; that was the warrior's way, Magnus reflected. Certainly duty before love.

Little Charlotte, already a dutiful Shadowhunter, trotted obediently away.

Camille's low voice recalled Magnus to attention. "I don't suppose you'd like to share him?"

Magnus smiled back at her. "Not as a meal, no. Was that what you meant?"

Camille laughed. Ralf Scott made an impatient noise, but was shushed by de Quincey, who muttered at him in annoyance; while over that noise rose the discontented grumblings of Roderick Morgenstern, a man who clearly wished to continue with his speech—and then finally the refreshments arrived, carried in on silver tea trays by a host of maids.

Arabella the mermaid lifted a hand, sloshing energetically in her aquarium.

"If you please," she said. "I would like a scone."

* * *

When Morgenstern's interminable speech was finally done, everybody had lost all will to converse and simply wished to go home. Magnus parted from Camille Belcourt with deep reluctance and from the Shadowhunters with deep relief.

It had been some time since Magnus was last in love, and he was beginning to feel the effects. He remembered the glow of love as brighter and the pain of loss as gentler than they had actually been. He found himself looking into many faces for potential love, and seeing many people as shining vessels of possibility. Perhaps this time there would be that indefinable something that sent hungry hearts roving, longing and searching for something, they knew not what, and yet could not give up the quest. Every time a face or a look or a gesture caught Magnus's eye these days, it woke to life a refrain in Magnus's breast, a song in persistent rhythm with his heartbeat. *Perhaps this time, perhaps this one.*

As he walked down Thames Street, he began to plot ways in which to see Camille again. He should pay a call upon the vampire clan in London. He knew de Quincey lived in Kensington.

It was only civil.

"After all," Magnus remarked aloud to himself, swinging his monkey-headed cane, "attractive and interesting persons do not simply drop out of the sky."

It was then that the fair-haired Shadowhunter that Magnus had spotted at the Institute somersaulted from the top of a wall and landed gracefully in the street before him.

"Devastating ensembles made on Bond Street with red brocade waistcoats do not simply drop out of the sky!" Magnus proclaimed experimentally to the Heavens.

The young man frowned. "I beg your pardon?"

"Oh, nothing, nothing at all," said Magnus. "May I help you? I do not believe I have had the pleasure of making your acquaintance."

The Nephilim stooped and picked up his hat, which had fallen onto the cobblestones when he'd made his leap. He then took it off in order to flourish it in Magnus's direction. The effect of the smile and the eyelashes together was like a small earthquake of attractiveness. Magnus could not blame Amalia Morgenstern for her giggling, even if the boy was far too young for her.

"No fewer than four of my esteemed elders told me I was on no account to ever converse with you, so I vowed that I would know you. My name is Edmund Herondale. May I ask your name? They referred to you only as 'that disgraceful one-warlock show.'"

"I am deeply moved by that tribute," Magnus told Edmund, and made his own bow. "Magnus Bane, at your service."

"Now we are acquainted," Edmund said. "Capital! Do you frequent any low dens of sin and debauchery?"

"Oh, now and then."

"The Morgensterns said you did, while they were throwing away the plates," Edmund said, with every sign of enthusiasm. "Shall we go?"

Throwing away the plates? It took Magnus a moment to comprehend, and when he did, he felt cold inside. The Shadowhunters had thrown away the very plates Downworlders had touched, afraid their china would be corrupted.

On the other hand, that was not Edmund's fault. The only other place Magnus had to go was the mansion he had perhaps rashly purchased in Grosvenor Square. A recent adventure had caused him to become temporarily wealthy (a state he despised; he usually tried to get rid of his money as soon as he had it), so he had decided to live in style. The *ton* of London were referring to him, he believed, as "Bane the nabob." This meant a great many people in London were anxious to make his acquaintance, and a great many of them seemed tiresome. Edmund, at least, did not.

"Why not?" Magnus decided.

Edmund glowed. "Excellent. Very few people are willing to have real adventures. Haven't you found that out, Bane? Isn't it sad?"

"I have very few rules in life, but one of them is to never decline an adventure. The others are: to avoid becoming romantically entangled with sea creatures; to always ask for what you want, because the worst thing that can happen is embarrassment but the best thing that can happen is nudity; to demand ready money up front; and to never play cards with Catarina Loss."

"What?"

"She cheats," Magnus explained. "Never mind that one."

"I would like to meet a lady who cheats at cards," Edmund said wistfully. "Aside from Granville's aunt Millicent, who is a terror at piquet."

Magnus had never truly considered that the high-and-mighty Shadowhunters ever played cards, let alone cheated at them. He supposed he had imagined that their leisure activities consisted of weapons training and having discussions about their infinite superiority over everyone else.

Magnus ventured to give Edmund a hint. "Mundane clubs do generally frown upon patrons who have, purely for random example, an abundance of weaponry about their person. So that might be an impediment."

"Absolutely not," Edmund promised him. "Why, I have the most paltry assortment of weapons on me. Only a few miserable daggers, a single stiletto knife, a couple of whips—"

Magnus blinked. "Hardly an armory," he said. "Though, it sounds like a most amusing Saturday."

"Capital!" said Edmund Herondale, apparently taking this for approval of his company on Magnus's excursion. He looked delighted.

White's club, on St. James's Street, had not changed outwardly at all. Magnus regarded the pale stone facade with pleasure: the Greek columns and the arched frames to the higher windows, as if each window were a chapel unto itself; the cast-iron balcony, which bore an intricate swirling pattern that had always made Magnus think of a procession of snail shells; the bow window out of which a famous man had once looked, and bet on a race between raindrops. The club had been established by an Italian, had been the haunt of criminals, and had been the irresistible bane of English aristocrats for more than a hundred years.

Whenever Magnus heard anything described as a "bane," he felt sure he would like it. It was why he had chosen that particular last name for himself, and also why he had joined White's several years before on a flying visit to London, in the main because his friend Catarina Loss had bet him that he could not do it.

Edmund swung around one of the black cast-iron lamps set before the door. The leaping flame behind the glass was dim compared to his eyes.

"This used to be a place where highwaymen drank hot chocolate," Magnus told Edmund carelessly as they walked inside. "The hot chocolate was very good. Being a highwayman is chilly work."

"Did you ever ask someone to stand and deliver?"

"I'll just say this," said Magnus. "I look dashing in a tasteful mask and a large hat."

Edmund laughed again—he had an easy and delighted laugh, like a child. His gaze was roving all over the room, from the ceiling—constructed to look as if they stood in a vast stone barrel—to the chandelier dripping glittering jewels like a duchess; to the green baize-covered tables that clustered on the right side of the room, where men were playing cards and losing fortunes.

Edmund's quality of bright wonder and surprise made him seem younger than he was; it lent a fragile air to his beauty. Magnus did not wonder why he, one of the Nephilim, was not warier of a Downworlder. He doubted Edmund Herondale was wary of anything in life. He was eager to be entertained, ready to be thrilled, essentially trusting of the world.

Edmund pointed to where two men stood, one making an entry in a large book with a defiant flourish of his pen.

"What's afoot there?"

"I presume they are recording a wager. There is a betting book here in White's that is quite celebrated. All sorts of bets are taken—whether a gentleman could manage to ravish a lady in a balloon a thousand feet off the ground, whether a man could live underwater for a day."

Magnus found them a pair of chairs near a fire, and made a gesture indicating that he and his companion were sorely in need of a drink. Their thirst was supplied the next instant. There were advantages to a truly excellent gentlemen's club.

"Do you think one could?" Edmund inquired. "Not live underwater; I know mundanes cannot. The other thing."

"My experiences in a balloon with a lady were not very pleasant," Magnus said, wincing at the memory. Queen Marie Antoinette had been an exciting but not comfortable traveling companion. "I would be disinclined to indulge in carnal delights in a balloon with a lady or a gentleman. No matter how delightful they were."

Edmund Herondale did not seem in the least surprised by the mention of a gentleman in Magnus's romantic speculations.

"It would be a lady in the balloon for me," he said.

"Ah," said Magnus, who had suspected as much.

"But I am always flattered to be admired," said Edmund, with an engaging grin. "And I am always admired."

He said it with that easy smile and another golden flutter of eyelashes, in the same way he had wound Amalia Morgenstern around his finger. It was clear he knew he was outrageous, and he expected people to like it. Magnus suspected they all did.

"Ah, well," Magnus said, giving up the matter gracefully. "Any particular lady?"

"I am not perfectly certain I believe in marriage. Why have just one bonbon when you can have the box?"

Magnus raised his eyebrows and took a swallow of his excellent brandy. The young man had a way with words and the naïve delight of someone who had never had his heart broken.

"No one's ever really hurt you, have they?" said Magnus, who saw no point in beating about the bush.

Edmund looked alarmed. "Why, are you about to?"

"With all those whips on your person? Hardly. I merely meant that you seem like someone who has never had his heart broken."

"I lost my parents as a child," said Edmund candidly. "But rare is the Shadowhunter with an intact family. I was taken in by the Fairchilds and raised in the Institute. Its halls have ever been my home. And if you mean love, then no, my heart has never been broken. Nor do I foresee that it will be."

"Don't you believe in love?"

"Love, marriage, the whole business is extremely overrated. For instance, this chap I know called Benedict Lightwood recently got leg-shackled, and the affair is hideous—"

"Your friends moving forward into a different era of their lives can be difficult," Magnus said sympathetically.

Edmund made a face. "Benedict is not my friend. It's the poor young lady I feel sorry for. The man is peculiar in his habits, if you see what I'm trying to say."

"I don't," Magnus said flatly.

"Bit of a deviant, is what I'm getting at."

Magnus regarded him with a cold air.

"Bad News Benedict, we call him," said Edmund. "Mostly due to his habit of consorting with demons. The more tentacles, the better, if you catch my meaning."

"Oh," Magnus said, enlightened. "I know who you mean. I have a friend from whom he bought some most unusual woodcuts. Also a couple of engravings. Said friend is simply an honest tradesman, and I have never bought anything from him myself, mind you."

"Also Benedict Lightworm. And Bestial Benedict," Edmund continued bitterly. "But he sneaks about while the rest of us get up to honest larks, and the Clave all think that he's superlatively well behaved. Poor Barbara. I'm afraid she acted hastily because of her broken heart."

Magnus leaned back in his chair. "And who broke her heart, might I ask?" he asked, amused.

"Ladies' hearts are like bits of china on a mantelpiece. There are so many of them, and it is so easy to break them without noticing." Edmund shrugged, a little rueful but mostly amused, and then a man in an unfortunate waistcoat walked into his armchair.

"I beg your pardon," said the gentleman. "I believe I am somewhat foxed!"

"I am prepared to charitably believe you were drunk when you got dressed," Magnus said under his breath.

"Eh?" said the man. "The name's Alvanley. You ain't one of those Indian nabobs, are you?"

Though he never much felt like explaining his origins to white-skinned Europeans who didn't care to know the difference between Shanghai and Rangoon, given the troubles in India, it was not actually a good idea for Magnus to be taken for Indian. He sighed and disclaimed, made his introduction and his bow.

"Herondale," said Edmund, bowing too. Edmund's golden assurance and open smile did their work.

"New to the club?" Alvanley asked, suddenly benevolent. "Well, well. It's a celebration. May I offer you both another drink?"

Alvanley's friends, some at the card table and some milling about, raised a discreet cheer. Queen Victoria had, so the happy report went, risen safe from childbed, and both mother and daughter were doing admirably.

"Drink to the health of our new Princess Beatrice, and to the queen!"

"Doesn't the poor woman have nine children?" asked Magnus. "By the ninth I would think she would be too exhausted to think of a new name, and certainly too fatigued to rule a country. I will drink to her health by all means."

Edmund was very ready to be plied with more drinks, though at one point he slipped up and referred to the queen as Vanessa rather than Victoria.

"Ahahaha," said Magnus. "He is on the ran-tan, and no mistake!"

Edmund was flushed with drink and almost immediately got absorbed in a card game. Magnus joined in playing Macao as well, but he found himself observing the Shadowhunter with some concern. People who blithely believed that the world owed them good luck could be dangerous at the gaming table. Add to that the fact that Edmund clearly craved excitement, and his kind of temperament was the very one most suited for disaster at play. There was something unsettling about the glitter of the boy's eyes suddenly, changed by the light of the club's wax candles, from being like a sky to being like a sea an instant before a storm.

Edmund, Magnus decided, put him in mind of nothing so much as a boat—a shining beautiful thing, buffeted by the whims of the water and winds. Only time would tell if he would find anchor and harbor, or if all that beauty and charm would be reduced to a wreck.

All imaginings aside, there was no need for Magnus to play nursemaid to Shadowhunters. Edmund was a man full-grown and able to care for himself. It was Magnus who grew bored in the end, and coaxed Edmund out of White's for a sobering walk in the night air.

They had not wandered far from St. James's Street when Magnus paused in his retelling of a certain incident in Peru because he felt Edmund come to attention next to him, every line of that angelic athlete's body suddenly tensed. He brought to mind forcibly a pointer dog hearing an animal in the undergrowth.

Magnus followed the line of Edmund's sight until he saw what the Shadowhunter was seeing: a man in a bowler hat, his hand set firmly on a carriage door, having what appeared to be an altercation with the occupants of the carriage.

It was shockingly uncivil, and but a moment later it became worse. The man had hold of a woman's arm, Magnus saw. She was dressed plainly, as befit an abigail or lady's maid. The man tried to wrench her from the carriage by main force.

He would have succeeded but for the interference of the other occupant of the carriage, a small dark lady, this one in a gown that rustled like silk as her voice rang out like thunder.

"Unhand her, you wretch!" said the lady, and she belabored the man about the head with her bonnet.

The man started at the unexpected onslaught and let go of the woman, but turned his attention to the lady and grasped the hand holding the bonnet instead. The woman gave a shout that seemed more outrage than terror, and struck him in the nose. The man's face turned slightly at the blow, and Magnus and Edmund were both able to see his eyes.

There was no mistaking the void behind those brilliant poison-green eyes. *Demon,* Magnus thought. A demon, and a hungry one, to be trying to abduct women from carriages in a London street.

A demon, and a very unlucky one, to do so in front of a Shadowhunter.

It did occur to Magnus that Shadowhunters generally hunted in groups, and that Edmund Herondale was inebriated.

"Very well," Magnus said. "Let us pause for a moment and consider— Oh, you have already run off. Splendid."

He found himself addressing Edmund's coat, wrenched off and left in a heap upon the cobblestones, and his hat, spinning gently beside it.

Edmund jumped and somersaulted in midair, vaulting neatly onto the roof of the carriage. As he did so, he drew weapons from the concealing folds of his garments: the two whips he had spoken of before, arcs of sizzling light against the night sky. He wielded them with cutting precision, their light waking golden fire in his tousled hair and casting a glow on his carved features, and by that light Magnus saw his face change from a laughing boy's to the stern countenance of an angel.

One whip curled around the demon's waist like a gentleman's hand around a lady's waist during a waltz. The other wrapped as tight as wire about his throat. Edmund twisted one hand, and the demon spun, crashing to the ground.

"You heard the lady," said Edmund. "Unhand her."

The demon, his teeth suddenly much more numerous than before, snarled and lunged for the carriage. Magnus raised his hand and made the carriage door fly shut and the carriage jolt forward a few paces, despite the fact that the carriage driver was missing—presumed eaten—and despite the Shadowhunter who was still standing atop it.

Edmund did not lose his balance. As surefooted as a cat, he simply leaped down to the ground and struck the Eidolon demon a blow across the face with his whip, sending him flying backward again. Edmund landed a foot upon the demon's throat, and Magnus saw the creature begin to writhe, its outlines blurring into a changing shape.

He heard the creak of a carriage door being opened and saw the lady who had punched the demon essaying to emerge from relative safety to the demon-haunted street.

"Ma'am," Magnus said, advancing. "I must counsel you not to exit the carriage while a demon-slaying is in progress."

She looked him full in the face. She had large dark blue eyes, the color of the sky immediately before night turned it black, and the hair slipping from her elaborate coiffure was black, as if night had come with no stars. Though her beautiful eyes were very wide, she did not look frightened, and the hand that had struck the demon was still clenched in a fist.

Magnus made a silent vow to come to London far more often in the future. He was meeting the most delightful people.

"We must render assistance to that young man," said the lady, in a lilting musical accent.

Magnus glanced over to Edmund, who was at present being thrown against a wall and who was bleeding rather profusely, but grinning and sliding a dagger from his boot with one hand as he choked the demon with the other.

"Do not be alarmed, dear lady. He has the matter well in hand," he said as Edmund slid the dagger home. "So to speak."

The demon gurgled and thrashed in its death throes. Magnus made the decision to ignore the furor behind him, and made the two women a superb bow. It did not seem to console the maidservant, who shrank into the shadowed recesses of the carriage and attempted to crawl into a pocket handkerchief, face foremost.

The lady of the shining ebony hair and pansy eyes let go her hold on the carriage door and gave Magnus her hand instead. Her hand was small, soft, and warm; she was not even trembling.

"I am Magnus Bane," said Magnus. "Call on me for aid at any time of mortal danger, or if in urgent need of an escort to a flower show."

"Linette Owens," said the lady, and dimpled. She had delicious dimples. "I heard the capital held many dangers, but this seems excessive."

"I am aware that all this must seem very strange and frightening to you."

"Is that man an evil faerie?" Miss Owens inquired. She met Magnus's startled look with her own steady gaze. "I am from Wales," she said. "We still believe in the old ways and the fey folk there."

She tipped her head back to scrutinize Magnus. Her crown of midnight-colored plaits seemed like it had to be too massive for such a small head, on such a slender neck.

"Your eyes...," she said slowly. "I believe you must be a good faerie, sir. What your companion is, I cannot tell."

Magnus glanced over his shoulder at his companion, who he had almost forgotten was there. The demon was darkness and dust at Edmund's feet, and with his foe well and truly vanquished, Edmund had turned his attention to the carriage. Magnus observed the spark of Edmund's golden charm kindle at the sight of Linette, blooming from candle to sun in an instant.

"What am I?" he asked. "I am Edmund Herondale, and, my lady, I am always and forever at your service. If you will have me."

He smiled, and the smile was slow and devastating. In the dark narrow street long past midnight, his eyes were high summer.

"I do not mean to seem indelicate or ungrateful," said Linette Owens, "but are you a dangerous lunatic?"

Edmund blinked.

"I fear I must point out that you are walking the streets armed to the teeth. Did you expect to do battle with a monstrous creature this night?"

"Not 'expect' exactly," said Edmund.

"Then are you an assassin?" asked Linette. "Are you an overzealous soldier?"

"Madam," said Edmund. "I am a Shadowhunter."

"I am not familiar with the word. Can you do magic?" Linette asked, and placed her hand on Magnus's sleeve. "This gentleman can do magic."

She bestowed an approving smile on Magnus. Magnus was extremely gratified.

"Honored to be of assistance, Miss Owens," he murmured.

Edmund looked as if he had been struck about the face with a fish.

"Of course—of course I can't do magic!" he managed to splutter out, sounding in true Shadowhunter fashion appalled by the very idea.

"Oh, well," said Linette, clearly rather disappointed. "That is not your fault. We all make do with what we have. I am indebted to you, sir, for saving me and my friend from an unspeakable fate."

Edmund preened, and in his pleasure spoke incautiously. "Think nothing of it. It would be my honor to escort you to your home, Miss Owens. The streets about Mall Pall can be very treacherous for women at night."

There was a silence.

"Do you mean Pall Mall?" Linette asked, and smiled slightly. "I am not the one overset by strong liquor. Should you like me to escort you home instead, Mr. Herondale?"

Edmund Herondale was left at a loss for words. Magnus suspected it was a novel experience, and one that would probably be good for him.

Miss Owens turned slightly from Edmund back to Magnus.

"My abigail, Angharad, and I were traveling from my estate in Wales," she explained. "We are to spend the London season with a distant relative of mine. We have had a long and tiring journey, and I wished to believe that we might reach London before nightfall. It was very stupid and reckless of me, and it has caused Angharad great distress. Your aid was invaluable."

Magnus could discern a great deal more from what Linette Owens had told him than what the lady had actually said. She had referred not to her papa's estate but to her own, in a casual manner, as one accustomed to ownership. That combined with the costly material of her dress and a certain something about her bearing confirmed it for Magnus—the lady was an heiress, and not simply the heiress of a fortune but of an estate. The way she spoke of Wales made Magnus think the lady would not wish to have her lands cared for by some steward at a remove. Society would think it a scandal and a shame for an estate to be in the hands of a woman, especially one so young and so pretty. Society would expect her to contract a marriage so that her husband could administer the estate, take possession of both the land and the lady.

She must have come to London because she'd found the suitors available in Wales not to her taste, and was on a quest to find a husband to take back to Wales with her.

She had come to London in search of love.

Magnus could sympathize with that. He was aware that love was not always part of the bargain in high-society marriages, but

Linette Owens seemed to have a mind of her own. He thought it likely she had a purpose—the right marriage, to the right man—and that she would accomplish it.

"Welcome to London," Magnus told her.

Linette dropped a small curtsy in the open carriage. Her eyes traveled over Magnus's shoulder and softened. Magnus looked around, and Edmund was standing there, one whip curled around his wrist as if he were comforting himself with it. Magnus had to admit it was a feat to look so gloriously handsome and yet so woebegone.

Linette visibly yielded to a charitable impulse and stepped out of the carriage. She made her way across the cobblestones and stood before the forlorn young Shadowhunter.

"I am sorry if I was uncivil, or if I in any way implied I thought you were a ... *twpsyn*," said Linette, tactfully not translating the word.

She put her hand out, and Edmund offered his, palm up and whip still curled around his shirt-sleeved wrist. There was a sudden hungry openness to his face; the moment had a sudden weight. Linette hesitated and then placed her hand in his.

"I am very much obliged to you for saving me and Angharad from a dreadful fate. Truly I am," said Linette. "Again, I apologize if I was ungracious."

"I will give you leave to be as ungracious as you choose," Edmund said. "If I can see you again."

He looked down at her, not making play with his eyelashes. His face was naked and open.

The moment turned. Edmund's serious, humble honesty did what eyelashes and swagger had not, and made Linette Owens hesitate.

"You can pay a call at 26 Eaton Square, at Lady Caroline Harcourt's," she said. "If you still wish to in the morning."

She drew her hand away, and after a single uncertain instant, Edmund let her.

Linette touched Magnus's arm before she ascended into the carriage. She was just as pretty and amiable as before, but something in her manner had changed. "Please come pay a call on me as well, if you care to, Mr. Bane."

"Sounds delightful."

He took her hand and helped her into the carriage, giving her away in one light graceful movement.

"Oh, and Mr. Herondale," said Miss Owens, putting her lovely laughing head through the carriage window. "Please leave your whips at home."

Magnus made a small shooing gesture, minuscule cerulean sparks dancing between his fingers. The carriage set off driverless in the dark, down the London streets.

It was some time before Magnus attended another meeting about the proposed Accords, in the main because there had been disagreements about the choice of venue. Magnus himself had voted that they meet somewhere other than the section of the Institute that had been built off sacrosanct ground. He felt that the place had the air of the servants' quarters. Mainly because Amalia Morgenstern had mentioned that the area used to be the Fairchilds' servants' quarters.

The Shadowhunters had resisted the idea of frequenting any low den of Downworlders (direct quote from Granville Fairchild), and the suggestion of staying outdoors and going to the park was vetoed because it was felt that the dignity of a conclave would be much impaired if some oblivious mundanes had a picnic in their midst.

Magnus did not believe a word of it.

After weeks of wrangling, their group finally capitulated and trailed dispiritedly back to the London Institute. The only bright spot was a literal bright spot—Camille was wearing an extremely fascinating red hat, and dainty red lace gloves.

"You look foolish and frivolous," said de Quincey under his

breath as the Shadowhunters found their places around the table in the large dim room.

"De Quincey is quite right," said Magnus. "You look foolish, frivolous, and fabulous."

Camille preened, and Magnus found it delightful and sympathetic, the way a small compliment could please a woman who had been beautiful for centuries.

"Exactly the effect I was attempting to produce," said Camille. "Shall I tell you a secret?"

"Pray do." Magnus leaned in toward her, and she inclined toward him.

"I wore it for you," Camille whispered.

The dim, stately room, its walls cloaked in tapestries emblazoned with swords, stars, and the runes the Nephilim wore on their own skin, brightened suddenly. All of London seemed to brighten.

Magnus had been alive hundreds of years himself, and yet the simplest things could turn a day into a jewel, and a succession of days into a glittering chain that went on and on. Here was the simplest thing: a pretty girl liked him, and the day shone.

Ralf Scott's thin pale face turned paler still, and was set in lines of pain now, but Magnus did not know the boy and was not bound to care overmuch for his broken heart. If the lady preferred Magnus, Magnus was not inclined to argue with her.

"How pleased we are to receive you all here again," said Granville Fairchild, as stern as ever. He folded his hands before him on the table. "At long last."

"How pleased we are that we could come to an agreement," said Magnus. "At long last."

"I believe Roderick Morgenstern has prepared a few words," said Fairchild. His face was set, and his deep voice rang hollow. There was a slight suggestion of a kitten crying all alone in a large cave.

"I believe I have heard enough from Shadowhunters," said Ralf Scott. "We have already heard the terms of the Nephilim for the preservation of peace between our kind and yours—"

"The list of our requirements was by no means complete," interrupted a man called Silas Pangborn.

"Indeed it was not," said the woman at his side, as stern and beautiful as one of the Nephilim's statues. Pangborn had introduced her as "Eloisa Ravenscar, my *parabatai*" with the same proprietary air as he might have said "my wife."

Evidently, they stood united against Downworlders.

"We have terms of our own," said Ralf Scott.

There was utter silence from the Shadowhunters. From their faces, Magnus did not think they were preparing themselves to listen attentively. Instead they seemed stunned by Downworlder impudence.

Ralf persisted, despite the utter lack of encouragement for him to do so. The boy was valiant even in a lost cause, Magnus thought, and despite himself he felt a little pang.

"We will want guarantees that no Downworlder whose hands are clean of mundane blood will be slaughtered. We want a law that states that any Shadowhunter who does strike down an innocent Downworlder will be punished." Ralf bore the outbreak of protest, and shouted it down. "You people live by laws! They are all you understand!"

"Yes, our laws, passed down to us by the Angel!" thundered Fairchild.

"Not rules that demon scum try to impose on us," sneered Starkweather.

"Is it too much to ask, to have laws to defend us as well as laws to defend the mundanes and the Nephilim?" Ralf demanded. "My parents were slain by Shadowhunters because of a terrible misunderstanding, because my parents were in the wrong place at the wrong time and presumed guilty because they were werewolves. I am raising my young brother alone. I want my people to be protected, to be strong, and not to be driven into corners until they either become killers or are killed!"

Magnus looked over to Camille, to share the spark of sympathy and indignation for Ralf Scott, so terribly young and terribly hurt and terribly in love with her. Camille's face was untouched, more like a porcelain doll's face than a person's, her skin porcelain that could not redden or pale, her eyes cold glass.

He felt a qualm and dismissed it out of hand. It was a vampire's face, that was all—no reflection of how she actually felt. There were many who could not read anything but evil in Magnus's own eyes.

"What a terrible shame," said Starkweather. "I would have thought you might have more siblings to share the burden. You people generally have litters, do you not?"

Ralf Scott jumped up and hit the table with an open palm. His fingers grew claws and scored the surface of the table.

"I think we need scones!" exclaimed Amalia Morgenstern.

"How dare you?" bellowed Granville Fairchild.

"That table is mahogany!" cried Roderick Morgenstern, looking appalled.

"Good Lord, you people are stupid," said Ralf darkly. "Many, many things are made out of mahogany."

"I would very much like a scone," said Arabella the mermaid. "Also possibly some cucumber sandwiches."

"I like egg and cress," contributed Rachel Branwell.

"I will not stand to be so insulted!" said a Shadowhunter called Waybread, or some such thing.

"You will not be insulted, and yet you will insist on murdering us," Camille remarked, her cool voice cutting the air. Magnus felt almost unbearably proud of her, and Ralf threw her a passionately grateful look. "It seems hardly fair."

"Do you know that, last time, they threw away the plates that our very touch had profaned, once we were gone?" Magnus asked softly. "We can come to an agreement only if we begin at a position of some mutual respect."

Starkweather barked a laugh. Magnus actually did not hate Starkweather; at least he was no hypocrite. No matter how foul, Magnus did appreciate honesty.

"Then we won't come to an agreement."

"I fear I must agree," Magnus murmured. He pressed a hand over his heart and his new peacock-blue waistcoat. "I strive to find some respect in my heart for you, but alas! It seems an impossible quest."

"Damned insolent magical libertine!"

Magnus inclined his head. "Just so."

When the refreshments tray arrived, the pause in hurling insults in order to consume scones was so excruciatingly awkward that Magnus excused himself under the pretext that he had to use the conveniences.

There were only a few chambers in the Institute into which Downworlders were permitted to venture. Magnus had simply intended to creep off into a shadowed corner, and he was rather displeased to find that the first shadowed corner he came upon was occupied.

There was an armchair and a small table. Slumped on the tabletop that depicted filigree gold angels was a seated man, cradling a small box in his hands. Magnus recognized the shining hair and broad shoulders immediately.

"Mr. Herondale?" he inquired.

Edmund started badly. For a moment Magnus thought he might fall from his chair, but Shadowhunter grace saved him. He stared at Magnus with blurred, wounded surprise, like a child slapped from sleep. Magnus doubted he had been doing much sleeping; his face was marked with sleepless nights.

"Had a night of it, did we?" Magnus asked, a little more gently.

"I had a few glasses of wine with the duck a l'orange," Edmund said, with a pallid smile that vanished as soon as it was born. "I shall never eat duck again. I cannot believe I used to like duck. The duck betrayed me." He was silent, then admitted, "Perhaps more than a few glasses. I have not seen you in Eaton Square."

Magnus wondered why on earth Edmund had thought he would, and then he recalled. It was the beautiful young Welsh girl's address.

"You went to Eaton Square?"

Edmund looked at him as if Magnus were dull-witted.

"Pardon me," said Magnus. "I simply find it hard to imagine one of the mundanes' glorious invisible protectors paying a social call."

This time Edmund's grin was the old one, brilliant and engaging, even though it did not last. "Well, they did ask me for a card, and I had not the faintest idea what they meant by that. I was turned away with vast contempt by her butler."

"I take it you did not give the matter up there."

"No indeed," said Edmund. "I simply lay in wait, and after a mere few days had the opportunity to follow Li—Miss Owens, and caught up with her riding in Rotten Row. I have seen her every day since then."

"'Follow' her? I wonder that the lady did not alert a constable."

The glow returned to Edmund's face, rendering him in gold and blue and pearl again. "Linette says I am fortunate she did not." He added, a little shyly, "We are engaged to be married."

That was news indeed. The Nephilim generally married among themselves, an aristocracy based on their belief in their own sanctity. Any prospective mundane bride or bridegroom would be expected to drink from the Mortal Cup and be transformed through dangerous alchemy into one of the Angel's own. It was not a transformation that all survived.

"Congratulations," said Magnus, and he kept his concerns locked in his own bosom. "I presume Miss Owens will soon Ascend?"

Edmund took a deep breath. "No," he said. "She will not."

"Oh," said Magnus, understanding at last.

Edmund looked down at the box he held in his hands. It was a simple wooden affair, with the symbol for infinity drawn upon the side in what looked like burned match. "This is a Pyxis," he said. "It holds within it the spirit of the first demon I ever slew. I was fourteen years old, and it was the day when I knew what I was born to do, what I was born to be—a Shadowhunter."

Magnus looked at Edmund's bowed head, his scarred warrior's hands clenched on the small box, and could not help the sympathy kindling within him.

Edmund spoke, in a confessional stream to his own soul and to the only person he knew who might listen and not think Edmund's love was blasphemy. "Linette thinks it her duty and her calling to care for the people on her estate. She does not wish to be a Shadowhunter. And I—I would not wish it, or ask it of her. Men and women perish in attempts to Ascend. She is brave and beautiful and unwavering, and if the Law says she is not worthy exactly as she is, then the Law is a lie. I cannot believe the unfairness of it, that I have found the one woman in all the world whom I could love, and what does the Law say to this feeling that I know is sacred? In order to be with her, either I am meant to ask my dearest love to risk her life, a life that is worth more to me than my own. Or I am meant to cut away the other part of my soul—burn away my life's purpose and all the gifts the Angel gave me."

Magnus remembered how Edmund had looked in that gorgeous leap to attack the demon, how his whole body had changed from restless energy to absolute purpose when he saw a demon: when he threw himself into the fray with the simple, natural joy of one who was doing what he was made for.

"Did you ever want to be anything else?"

"No," said Edmund. He stood and put a hand against the wall and raked the other hand through his hair, an angel brought to his knees, wild and bewildered by pain.

"But what of your dim view of marriage?" Magnus demanded. "What of having only one bonbon when you could have the box?"

"I was very stupid," Edmund said, almost violently. "I thought of love as a game. It is not a game. It is more serious than death. Without Linette, I might as well be dead."

"You speak of giving up your Shadowhunter nature," said Magnus softly. "One can give up many things for love, but one should not give up oneself."

"Is that so, Bane?" Edmund whirled on him. "I was born to be a warrior, and I was born to be with her. Tell me how to reconcile the two, because I cannot!"

Magnus made no answer. He was looking at Edmund and remembering when he had drunkenly thought of the Shadowhunter as a lovely ship, that might sail straight out to sea or wreck itself upon the rocks. He could see the rocks now, dark and jagged on the horizon. He saw Edmund's future without Shadowhunting, how he would yearn for the danger and the risk. How he would find it at the gaming tables. How fragile he would always be once his sense of purpose was gone.

And then there was Linette, who had fallen in love with a golden Shadowhunter, an avenging angel. What would she think of him when he was just another Welsh farmer, all his glory stripped away?

Yet love was not something to be thrown aside lightly. It came so rarely, only a few times in a mortal life. Sometimes it came but once. Magnus could not say Edmund Herondale was wrong to seize love when he had found it.

He could think Nephilim Law was wrong for making him choose.

Edmund exhaled. He looked drained. "I beg your pardon, Bane," he said. "I am simply being a child, screaming and kicking against fate, and it is time to stop being a stupid boy. Why struggle against a choice that is already made? If I were asked to choose between sacrificing my life or sacrificing Linette's every day for the rest of eternity, I would sacrifice my own every time."

Magnus looked away, so as not to see the wreckage. "I wish you luck," he said. "Luck and love."

Edmund made a small bow. "I bid you good day. I think we will not meet again."

He walked away, into the inner reaches of the Institute. A few feet away, he wavered and paused, light from one of the narrow church windows turning his hair rich gold, and Magnus thought he would turn. But Edmund Herondale never looked back.

Magnus returned with a heavy heart to the room where the Shadowhunters and Downworlders were still fighting a war of words. Neither side seemed inclined to give way. Magnus was inclined to give the matter up as hopeless.

Through the stained-glass windows the curtains of night began to show the signs of drawing down to reveal the day, and the vampires had to leave.

"It seems to me," said Camille, drawing on her scarlet gloves, "that another meeting will prove just as futile as these have been."

"If Downworlders continue to be insolent wretches," said Starkweather.

"If Shadowhunters continue to be sanctimonious murderers," snapped Scott. Magnus could not quite look at his face, not after Edmund Herondale's. He did not want to watch as another boy's dreams died.

"Enough!" said Granville Fairchild. "Madam, do not ask me to believe that you have never harmed a human soul. I am not a fool. And what kills Shadowhunters have made, they have made in the cause of justice and in the defense of the helpless."

Camille smiled a slow, sweet smile. "If you believe that," she murmured, "then you are a fool."

Cue another dreary, wearying burst of outrage from the assembled Shadowhunters. It warmed Magnus to see Camille defending the boy. She was fond of Ralf Scott, he thought. Perhaps more than fond. Magnus might hope that she would choose him, but he found he could not begrudge Scott her affection. He offered her his arm as they left the room, and she took it. They went out into the street together.

And there on the very doorstep of the Institute, the demons descended. Achaieral demons, their teeth razors and their wide wings scorched-black leather like the aprons of blacksmiths. They blanketed the night, blotting out the moon and wiping away the stars, and Camille shuddered at Magnus's side, her fangs out. At the sign of Camille's fear, Ralf Scott lunged at the enemy, transforming as he went, and brought one down in a bloody tangle onto the cobbles.

The Shadowhunters rushed out too, weapons sliding out of sheaths and garments alike. Amalia Morgenstern, it emerged, had been hiding a small tasteful axe under her hoop skirt. Roderick Morgenstern ran out into the street and stabbed the demon Ralf Scott was wrestling with.

From the small cart that contained her aquarium, Arabella gave a scream of real fear, and ducked down to the bottom of her woefully inadequate tank.

"To me, Josiah!" thundered Fairchild, and Josiah Waybread—no, Magnus thought it was Wayland, actually—joined him. They ranged themselves in front of Arabella's cart and stood to defend her, letting no demon past the bright line of their blades.

Silas Pangborn and Eloisa Ravenscar moved to the street, fighting back-to-back, their weapons bright blurs in their hands and their movements in perfect synchronization, as if the pair of them had melded into a single fierce creature. De Quincey followed and fought with them.

The presence at Magnus's side was gone suddenly. Camille left him and went running to help Ralf Scott. One demon leaped onto her from behind and seized her up in its bladelike talons. Ralf howled despair and grief. Magnus blasted the demon out of the sky. Camille went tumbling onto the ground, and Magnus knelt and gathered her, shaking, into his arms. He was amazed to see the gleam of tears in her green eyes, was amazed at how fragile she felt.

"I beg your pardon. I am not generally so easily overset. A mundane fortune-teller once told me that death would come to me as a surprise," Camille said, her voice trembling. "A foolish superstition, is it not? Yet I always wish to be warned. I fear nothing, if only I am told that danger is coming."

"I would be entirely overset myself, if my ensemble had been spoiled by demons who know nothing of fashion," said Magnus, and Camille laughed.

Her eyes looked like grass under the dew, and she was brave and beautiful and would fight for their kind and yet rest against him. It was in that moment that Magnus felt as if he had stopped searching for love.

Magnus looked up from Camille's enchanting face to see that the Shadowhunters and Downworlders were, for a wonder, not arguing. Instead they were all observing one another, standing in the suddenly-quiet street with the bodies of their foes around them, vanquished because they had stood together. There was a certain wonder in the air, as if the Nephilim could not see the Downworlders as demonic when they had fought alongside them against true demons. The Shadowhunters were warriors; the bonds of war meant a great deal to them.

Magnus was no warrior, but he remembered how the Shadowhunters had moved to protect a mermaid and a werewolf. That meant something to him, too. Perhaps there was something to be salvaged here this night. Perhaps they could make this wild idea of the Accords work after all.

Then he felt Camille move in his arms, and saw where she was looking. She was gazing at Ralf Scott, and he was looking back at her. There was a world of hurt in his eyes.

The boy climbed to his feet, and vented his ire on the Shadowhunters.

"You people did this," he raged. "You want us all dead. You lured us here—"

"Are you *mad?*" Fairchild demanded. "We are Nephilim. If we wanted you dead, you would be dead. We do not require demons to do our killing for us, and we certainly do not wish for them to befoul our very doorstep. My daughter lives here. I would not put her in danger for anything you care to name, and certainly not for Downworlders."

Magnus had to admit he had a point.

"It is you people who brought that filth to us!" Starkweather bellowed.

Magnus opened his mouth to argue, and then he recalled how excessively vehement the queen of the faeries had been when she argued against an agreement with Shadowhunters, and yet how strangely curious she had been about the details thereof, such as the time and place of their meetings. He closed his mouth.

Fairchild gave Magnus a condemning glance, as if the Shadowhunter could read the guilt of all Downworlders on his countenance. "If what Starkweather says is true, you have lost any opportunity to forge an agreement between our people."

It was done, then, and Magnus saw the rage pass from Ralf Scott's face as he visibly gave up his struggle. Ralf looked up at Fairchild with clear eyes, and spoke in a calm, ringing voice.

"You will not give us aid? Very well. We do not need it. Werewolves will take care of their own. I will see it done."

The werewolf boy evaded de Quincey's detaining hand and paid no heed to Fairchild's sharp reply. The only one he paid attention to was Camille. He looked at her for a moment. Camille lifted her hand, then dropped it, and Ralf whirled and walked away from both Shadowhunters and his fellow Downworlders. Magnus saw him square his thin shoulders as he went, a boy accepting a heavy burden and accepting that he had lost what he loved best. Magnus was reminded of Edmund Herondale.

Magnus did not see Edmund Herondale again, but he heard him once more.

The Shadowhunters decided that Magnus and Camille were the most reasonable among the Downworlders that they had assembled. Given that the other choices were intemperate werewolves and Alexei de Quincey, Magnus could not feel himself flattered by the preference.

The Nephilim asked Magnus and Camille to come for a private meeting, to exchange information so that they could continue to correspond, independent of Ralf Scott. Implicit in their request was the promise that the Shadowhunters might offer their protection if Magnus and Camille needed it at some future time. In exchange, of course, for magic or Downworlder information.

Magnus went to the meeting to see Camille, and for no other reason. He told himself that he was not thinking at all of that fight against the demons, and how they had been united.

When he stepped into the Institute, however, he was pulled up short by the sounds. The noises came from the depths of the building, and they were the rattling, tormented sounds of someone being flayed alive. They sounded like the screams of a soul in Hell, or a soul being ripped from Heaven.

"What is that?" Magnus asked.

There were only a few Shadowhunters present at this unofficial meeting, instead of the mass of Clave representatives. Only Granville Fairchild, Silas Pangborn, and Josiah Wayland were in attendance. The three Shadowhunters stood in the small hall, cries of agony reverberating from the tapestry-covered walls and the domed ceiling, and all three Nephilim appeared entirely indifferent.

"A young Shadowhunter by the name of Edmund Herondale has disgraced his family name and forsaken his calling so that he might fling himself into the arms of a mundane chit," Josiah Wayland answered, with no sign of emotion. "He is being stripped of his Marks."

"And being stripped of your Marks," Magnus said slowly. "It is like that?"

"It is being remade, into a baser thing," said Granville Fairchild, his voice cold, though his face was pale. "It is against the will of the Angel. Of course it hurts."

There was a shuddering scream of agony to underlie his words. He did not turn his head.

Magnus felt cold with horror. "You're barbarians."

"Do you want to rush to his aid?" inquired Wayland. "If you try, every one of us will move to strike you down. Do not dare to question our motives or our way of life. You speak of that which is higher and nobler than you can possibly understand."

Magnus heard another scream, and this one broke off into desperate sobbing. The warlock thought of the bright boy he had spent one night at a club with, his face radiant and untouched by pain. This was the price Shadowhunters set on love.

Magnus started forward, but the Shadowhunters drew together with bared blades and stern faces. An angel with a flaming sword, proclaiming that Magnus should not pass, could not have expressed more conviction of his own righteousness. He heard the echoes of his stepfather's voice in his mind: *devil's child, Satan's get, born to be damned, forsaken by God.*

The long lonely cry of a suffering boy he could not help chilled Magnus through to the bone, like cold water seeping through to find a grave. Sometimes he thought they were all forsaken, every soul on this earth.

Even the Nephilim.

"There is nothing to be done, Magnus. Come away," said Camille's voice in his ear in an undertone. Her hand was small but held Magnus's arm in a firm grip. She was strong, stronger than Magnus was, perhaps in all ways. "Fairchild raised the boy from a child, I believe, and yet he is throwing him away like refuse into the street. The Nephilim have no pity."

Magnus allowed her to draw him away, into the street and away from the Institute. He was impressed that she was still so calm. Camille had fortitude, Magnus thought. He wished she could teach him the trick of being less foolish, and less easily hurt.

"I hear you are leaving us, Mr. Bane," Camille said. "I shall be sorry to see you go. De Quincey hosts the most famous parties, and I hear you are quite the life and soul of any party you attend."

"I am sorry to go, indeed," said Magnus.

"If I might ask why?" said Camille, her lovely face upturned, her green eyes glittering. "I had rather thought that London had caught your fancy, and that you might stay."

Her invitation was almost irresistible. But Magnus was no Shadowhunter. He could have pity on someone who was suffering, and young.

"That young werewolf, Ralf Scott," Magnus said, abandoning pretense. "He is in love with you. And it seemed to me you looked at him with some interest as well."

"And if that is true?" Camille asked, laughing. "You do not strike me as the sort of man to step aside and renounce a claim for the benefit of another!"

"Ah, but I am not a man. Am I? I have years, and so do you," he added, and that was glorious too, the idea of loving someone and not fearing they would soon be lost. "But werewolves are not immortals. They age and die. The Scott boy has but one chance for your love, where I—I might go and return, and find you here again."

She pouted prettily. "I might forget you."

He bent to her ear. "If you do, I shall have to recall myself forcibly to your attention." His hands spanned her waist, the silk of her dress smooth under the pads of his fingertips. He could feel the swell and rise of her under his touch. His lips brushed her skin, and he felt her jump and shudder. He whispered, "Love the boy. Give him his happiness. And when I return, I shall devote an age to admiring you."

"An entire age?"

"Perhaps," said Magnus, teasing. "How does Marvell's poem go?

"An hundred years should go to praise
Thine eyes and on thy forehead gaze;
Two hundred to adore each breast,
But thirty thousand to the rest;
An age at least to every part,
And the last age should show your heart..."

Camille's eyebrows had lifted at the reference to her bosom, but her eyes were sparkling. "And how do you know that I have a heart?"

Magnus raised his own eyebrows, conceding the point. "I have heard it said that love is faith."

"Whether your faith is justified," Camille said, "time will tell."

"Before time tells us anything more," Magnus said, "I humbly beg of you to accept a small token of my regard."

He reached inside his coat, which was made of blue superfine fabric and which he hoped Camille found dashing, and produced the necklace. The ruby glinted in the light of a nearby streetlamp, its heart the rich color of blood.

"It is a pretty thing," said Magnus.

"Very pretty." She sounded amused at the understatement.

"Not worthy of your beauty, of course, but what could be? There is one small thing besides prettiness to recommend it. There is a spell on the jewel, to warn you when demons are near."

Camille's eyes went very wide. She was an intelligent woman, and Magnus saw she knew the full value of the jewel and of the spell.

Magnus had sold the house in Grosvenor Square, and what else had he to do with the proceeds? He could think of nothing more valuable than purchasing a guarantee that would keep Camille safe, and cause her to remember him kindly.

"I will think of you when I am far away," Magnus promised, fastening the pendant about her white throat. "I would like to think of you fearless."

Camille's hand fluttered, a white dove, to the sparkling heart of the necklace and away again. She looked up into Magnus's eyes.

"In all justice, I must give you a token to remember me by," she said, smiling.

"Oh, well," said Magnus as she drew close. His hand settled on the small silk circle of her waist. Before his lips met hers, he murmured, "If it is in the cause of justice."

Camille kissed him. Magnus spared a thought to making the streetlamp burn more brightly, and the flame within the iron and glass case filled the whole street with soft blue light. He held her and the promise of possible love, and in that warm instant all the narrow streets of London seemed to expand, and he could even think kindly of Shadowhunters, and one more than the rest.

He spared a moment to hope that Edmund Herondale would find comfort in the arms of his beautiful mundane love, that he would live a life that made all he had lost and all he had suffered seem worthwhile.

Magnus's ship would sail that night. He left Camille so that she might search out Ralf Scott, and he boarded his steamship, a glorious iron-hulled thing called the *Persia* that had been made with the latest of mundane inventiveness. His interest in the ship and his thoughts of an adventure to come made him regret his departure less, but even so, he stood at the rail as the ship departed into night waters. He looked his last on the city he was leaving behind.

Years later Magnus would return to London and Camille Belcourt's side, and find it not all that he had dreamed. Years later another desperate Herondale boy with blue, blue eyes would come to his door, shaking with the cold of the rain and his own wretchedness, and this one Magnus would be able to help.

Magnus knew none of that then. He only stood on the deck of the ship and watched London and all its light and shadows slide away out of sight.

The Midnight Heir

By Cassandra Clare and Sarah Rees Brennan

A loud explosion caused him to look up. There was a boy standing in the middle of the room, a cocked silver pistol in his hand. He was surrounded by broken glass, having just shot off one arm of the chandelier.

—The Midnight Heir

BANG

It took Magnus nearly twenty minutes to notice the boy shooting out all the lights in the room, but to be fair, he had been distracted by the décor.

It had been nearly a quarter century since Magnus had been in London. He had missed the place. Certainly New York had an energy at the turn of the century that no other city could match. Magnus loved being in a carriage rattling into the dazzling lights of Longacre Square, pulling up outside the Olympia Theatre's elaborate French Renaissance facade, or rubbing elbows with a dozen different kinds of people at the hot dog festival in Greenwich Village. He enjoyed traveling on the elevated railways, squealing brakes and all, and he was much looking forward to traveling through the vast underground systems they were building below the very heart of the city. He had seen the construction of the great station at Columbus Circle just before he had left, and hoped to return to find it finished at last.

But London was London, wearing its history in layers, with every age contained in the new age. Magnus had history here too. Magnus had loved people here, and hated them. There had been one woman whom he had both loved and hated, and he had fled London to escape that memory. He sometimes wondered if he had been wrong to leave, if he should have endured the bad memories for the sake of the good, and suffered, and stayed.

Magnus slouched down in the tufted velvet chair—shabby at

the arms, worn by decades of sleeves rubbing away the fabric—and gazed around the room. There was a gentility to English places that America, in all her brash youthfulness, could not match. Glimmering chandeliers dripped from the ceiling—cut glass, of course, not crystal, but it shed a pretty light—and electric sconces lined the walls. Magnus still found electricity rather thrilling, though it was duller than witchlight.

Groups of gentlemen sat at tables, playing rounds of faro and piquet. Ladies who were no better than they should be, whose dresses were too tight and too bright and too all the things Magnus liked most, lounged on velvet-covered benches along the walls. Gentlemen who had done well at the tables approached them, flushed with victory and pound notes; those whom Lady Luck had not smiled on drew on their coats at the door and slunk off silently into the night, bereft of money and companionship.

It was all very dramatic, which Magnus enjoyed. He had not yet grown tired of the pageantry of ordinary life and ordinary people, despite the passage of time and the fact that people were all very much the same in the end.

A loud explosion caused him to look up. There was a boy standing in the middle of the room, a cocked silver pistol in his hand. He was surrounded by broken glass, having just shot off one arm of the chandelier.

Magnus was overwhelmed with the feeling the French called déjà vu, the feeling that *I have been here before*. He had, of course, been in London before, twenty-five years past.

This boy's face was a face to recall the past. This *was* a face from the past, one of the most beautiful faces Magnus could ever recall seeing. It was a face so finely cut that it cast the shabbiness of this place into stark relief—a beauty that burned so fiercely that it put the glare of the electric lights to shame. The boy's skin was so white and clear that it seemed to have a light shining behind it. The lines of his cheekbones, his jaw, and his throat—exposed by a linen shirt open at the collar—were so clean and perfect that he almost would have looked like a statue were it not for the much disheveled and slightly curling hair falling into his face, as black as midnight against his lucent pallor.

The years drew Magnus back again, the fog and gaslight of a London more than twenty years lost rising to claim Magnus. He found his lips shaping a name: Will. Will Herondale.

Magnus stepped forward instinctively, the movement feeling as if it were not of his own volition.

The boy's eyes went to him, and a shock passed through Magnus. They were not Will's eyes, the eyes Magnus remembered being as *blue as a night sky in Hell*, eyes Magnus had seen both despairing and tender.

This boy had shining golden eyes, like a crystal glass filled brimful with crisp white wine and held up to catch the light of a blazing sun. If his skin was luminous, his eyes were radiant. Magnus could not imagine these eyes as tender. The boy was very, very lovely, but his was a beauty like that Helen of Troy might have had once, disaster written in every line. The light of his beauty made Magnus think of cities burning.

Fog and gaslight receded into memory. His momentary lapse into foolish nostalgia was over. This was not Will. That broken, beautiful boy would be a man now, and this boy was a stranger.

Still, Magnus did not think that such a great resemblance could be a coincidence. He made his way toward the boy with little effort, as the other denizens of the gaming hell seemed, perhaps understandably, reluctant to approach him. The boy was standing alone as though the broken glass all around him were a shining sea and he were an island.

"Not precisely a Shadowhunter weapon," Magnus murmured. "Is it?"

Those golden eyes narrowed into bright slits, and the long-fingered hand not holding the pistol went to the boy's sleeve, where

Magnus presumed his nearest blade was concealed. His hands were not quite steady.

"Peace," Magnus added. "I mean you no harm. I am a warlock the Whitelaws of New York will vouch for as being quite—well, mostly—harmless."

There was a long pause that felt somewhat dangerous. The boy's eyes were like stars, shining but giving no clue to his feelings. Magnus was generally good at reading people, but he found it difficult to predict what this boy might do.

Magnus was truly surprised by what the boy said next.

"I know who you are." His voice was not like his face; it had gentleness to it.

Magnus managed to hide his surprise and raised his eyebrows in silent inquiry. He had not lived three hundred years without learning not to rise to every bait offered.

"You are Magnus Bane."

Magnus hesitated, then inclined his head. "And you are?"

"I," the boy announced, "am James Herondale."

"You know," Magnus murmured, "I rather thought you might be called something like that. I am delighted to hear that I am famous."

"You're my father's warlock friend. He would always speak of you to my sister and me whenever other Shadowhunters spoke slightingly of Downworlders in our presence. He would say he knew a warlock who was a better friend, and more worth trusting, than many a Nephilim warrior."

The boy's lips curled as he said it, and he spoke mockingly but with more contempt than amusement behind the mockery, as if his father had been a fool to tell him this, and James himself was a fool to repeat it.

Magnus found himself in no mood for cynicism.

They had parted well, he and Will, but he knew Shadowhunters. The Nephilim were swift to judge and condemn a Downworlder for ill deeds, acting as if every sin were graven in stone for all time, proving that Magnus's people were evil by nature. Shadowhunters' conviction of their own angelic virtue and righteousness made it easy for them to let a warlock's good deeds slip their minds, as if they were written in water.

He had not expected to see or hear of Will Herondale on this journey, but if Magnus had thought of it, he would have been unsurprised to be all but forgotten, a petty player in a boy's tragedy. Being remembered, and remembered so kindly, touched him more than he would have thought possible.

The boy's star-shining, burning-city eyes traveled across Magnus's face and saw too much.

"I would not set any great store by it. My father trusts a great many people," James Herondale said, and laughed. It was quite clear suddenly that he was extremely drunk. Not that Magnus had imagined he was firing at chandeliers while stone-cold sober. "Trust. It is like placing a blade in someone's hand and setting the very point against your own heart."

"I have not asked you to trust me," Magnus pointed out mildly. "We have just met."

"Oh, I'll trust you," the boy told him carelessly. "It hardly matters. We are all betrayed sooner or later—all betrayed, or traitors."

"I see that a flair for the dramatic runs in the blood," Magnus said under his breath. It was a different kind of dramatics, though. Will had made an exhibition of vice in private, to drive away those nearest and dearest to him. James was making a public spectacle.

Perhaps he loved vice for vice's own sake.

"What?" James asked.

"Nothing," said Magnus. "I was merely wondering what the chandelier had done to offend you."

James looked up at the ruined chandelier, and down at the shards of glass at his feet, as if he were noticing them only now.

"I was bet," he said, "twenty pounds that I would not shoot out all the lights of the chandelier."

"And who bet you?" said Magnus, not divulging a hint of what he thought—that anyone who bet a drunk seventeen-year-old boy that he could wave around a deadly weapon with impunity ought to be in gaol.

"That fellow there," James announced, pointing.

Magnus looked in the general direction James was gesturing toward, and spied a familiar face at the faro table.

"The green one?" Magnus inquired. Coaxing drunken Shadowhunters into making fools of themselves was a favorite occupation among the Downworlders, and this performance had been a tremendous success. Ragnor Fell, the High Warlock of London, shrugged, and Magnus sighed inwardly. Perhaps gaol would be a bit extreme, though Magnus still felt his emerald friend could use taking down a peg or two.

"Is he *really* green?" James asked, not seeming to care overmuch. "I thought that was the absinthe."

Then James Herondale, son of William Herondale and Theresa Gray, the two Shadowhunters who had been the closest of their kind to friends that Magnus had ever known—though Tessa had not been quite a Shadowhunter, or not entirely—turned his back on Magnus, set his sights on a woman serving drinks to a table surrounded by werewolves, and shot her down. She collapsed on the floor with a cry, and all the gamblers sprang from their tables, cards flying and drinks spilling.

James laughed, and the laugh was clear and bright, and it was then that Magnus began to be truly alarmed. Will's voice would have shaken, betraying that his cruelty had been part of his playacting, but his son's laugh was that of someone genuinely delighted by the chaos erupting all around him.

Magnus's hand shot out and grasped the boy's wrist, the hum and light of magic crackling along his fingers like a promise. "That's enough."

"Be easy," James said, still laughing. "I am a very good shot, and

Peg the tavern maid is famous for her wooden leg. I think that is why they call her Peg. Her real name, I believe, is Ermentrude."

"And I suppose Ragnor Fell bet you twenty pounds that you couldn't shoot her without managing to draw blood? How very clever of you both."

James drew his hand back from Magnus's, shaking his head. His black locks fell around a face so like his father's that it prompted an indrawn breath from Magnus. "My father told me you acted as a sort of protector to him, but I do not need your protection, warlock."

"I rather disagree with that."

"I have taken a great many bets tonight," James Herondale informed him. "I must perform all the terrible deeds I have promised. For am I not a man of my word? I want to preserve my honor. And I want another drink!"

"What an excellent idea," Magnus said. "I have heard alcohol only improves a man's aim. The night is young. Imagine how many barmaids you can shoot before dawn."

"A warlock as dull as a scholar," said James, narrowing his amber eyes. "Who would have thought such a thing existed?"

"Magnus has not always been so dull," said Ragnor, appearing at James's shoulder with a glass of wine in hand. He gave it to the boy, who took it and downed it in a distressingly practiced manner. "There was a time, in Peru, with a boat full of pirates—"

James wiped his mouth on his sleeve and set down his glass. "I should love to sit and listen to old men reminiscing about their lives, but I have a pressing appointment to do something that is actually interesting. Another time, chaps."

He turned upon his heel and left. Magnus made to follow him.

"Let the Nephilim control their brat, if they can," Ragnor said, always happy to see chaos but not be involved in it. "Come have a drink with me."

"Another night," Magnus promised.

"Still such a soft touch, Magnus," Ragnor called after him.

"Nothing you like better than a lost soul or a bad idea."

Magnus wanted to argue with that, but it was difficult when he was already forsaking warmth and the promise of a drink and a few rounds of cards, and running out into the cold after a deranged Shadowhunter.

Said deranged Shadowhunter turned on him, as if the narrow cobbled street were a cage and he some wild, hungry animal held there too long.

"I wouldn't follow me," James warned. "I am in no mood for company. Especially the company of a prim magical chaperone who does not know how to enjoy himself."

"I know perfectly well how to enjoy myself," remarked Magnus, amused, and he made a small gesture so that for an instant all the iron streetlamps lining the street rained down varicolored sparks of light. For an instant he thought he saw a light that was softer and less like burning in James Herondale's golden eyes, the beginnings of a childlike smile of delight.

The next moment, it was quenched. James's eyes were as bright as the jewels in a dragon's hoard, and no more alive or joyful. He shook his head, black locks flying in the night air, where the magic lights were fading.

"But you do not wish to enjoy yourself, do you, James Herondale?" Magnus asked. "Not really. You want to go to the devil."

"Perhaps I think I will enjoy going to the devil," said James Herondale, and his eyes burned like the fires of Hell, enticing, and promising unimaginable suffering. "Though I see no need to take anyone else with me."

No sooner had he spoken than he vanished, to all appearances softly and silently stolen away by the night air, with no one but the winking stars, the glaring streetlamps, and Magnus as witnesses.

Magnus knew magic when he saw it. He spun, and at the same moment heard the click of a decided footstep against a cobblestone. He turned to face a policeman walking his beat, truncheon swinging at his side, and a look of suspicion on his stolid face as he surveyed Magnus.

It was not Magnus the man had to watch out for.

Magnus saw the buttons on the man's uniform cease their gleaming, even though he was under a streetlamp. Magnus was able to discern a shadow falling where there was nothing to cast it, a surge of dark within the greater darkness of the night.

The policeman gave a shout of surprise as his helmet was whisked away by unseen hands. He stumbled forward, hands fumbling blindly in the air to retrieve what was long gone.

Magnus gave him a consoling smile. "Cheer up," he said. "You can find far more flattering headgear at any shop in Bond Street."

The man fainted. Magnus considered pausing to help him, but there was being a soft touch, and then there was being ridiculous enough to not pursue a most enticing mystery. A Shadowhunter who could turn into a shadow? Magnus turned and bolted after the bobbing policeman's helmet, held aloft only by a taunting darkness.

They ran down street after street, Magnus and the darkness, until the Thames barred their path. Magnus heard the sound of its rushing swiftness rather than saw it, the dark waters at one with the night.

What he did see was white fingers suddenly clenched on the brim of the policeman's helmet, the turn of James Herondale's head, darkness replaced with the tilt of his slowly appearing grin. Magnus saw a shadow coalescing once more into flesh.

So the boy had inherited something from his mother as well as his father, then. Tessa's father had been a fallen angel, one of the kings of demons. The boy's lambent golden eyes seemed to Magnus like his own eyes suddenly, a token of infernal blood.

James saw Magnus looking, and winked before he hurled the helmet up into the air. It flew for a moment like a strange bird, spinning gently around in the air, then hit the water. The darkness was disrupted by a silver splash.

"A Shadowhunter who knows magic tricks," Magnus observed. "How novel."

A Shadowhunter who attacked the mundanes it was his mandate to protect—how delighted the Clave would be by that.

"We are but dust and shadows, as the saying goes," said James. "Of course, the saying does not add, 'Some of us also turn into shadows occasionally, when the mood takes us.' I suppose nobody predicted that I would come to pass. It's true that I have been told I am somewhat unpredictable."

"May I ask who bet you that you could steal a policeman's helmet, and why?"

"Foolish question. Never ask about the last bet, Bane," James advised him, and reached casually to his belt, where his gun was slung, and then he drew it in one fluid, easy motion. "You should be worrying about the next one."

"There isn't any chance," Magnus asked, without much hope, "that you are rather a nice fellow who believes he is cursed and must make himself seem unlovable to spare those around him from a terrible fate? Because I have heard that happens sometimes."

James seemed amused by the question. He smiled, and as he smiled, his waving black locks blended with the night, and the glow of his skin and his eyes grew as distant as the light of the stars until they became so pale, they diffused. He was nothing but a shadow among shadows again. He was an infuriating Cheshire cat of a boy, nothing left of him but the impression of his smile.

"My father was cursed," James said from the darkness. "Whereas I? I'm damned."

The London Institute was exactly as Magnus remembered it, tall and white and imposing, its tower cutting a white line against the dark sky. Shadowhunter Institutes were built as monuments to withstand the ravages of demons and time. When the doors opened, Magnus beheld again the massive stone entryway and the two flights of stairs.

A woman with wildly curling red hair, whom Magnus was sure he should remember but didn't, answered the door, her face creased with sleep and crossness. "What d'you want, warlock?" she demanded.

Magnus shifted the burden in his arms. The boy was tall, and Magnus had had a long night besides. Annoyance made his tone rather sharp as he answered:

"I want you to go tell Will Herondale that I have brought his whelp home."

The woman's eyes widened. She gave an impressed sort of whistle and vanished abruptly. A handful of moments later Magnus saw a white figure come softly down one of the staircases.

Tessa was like the Institute: hardly changed at all. She had the same smooth youthful face that she had worn twenty-five years before. Magnus thought she must have stopped aging no more than three or four years after he had last seen her. Her hair was in a long brown plait, hanging over one shoulder, and she was holding a witchlight in one hand and had a small sphere of light shining in her palm in the other.

"Been taking magic lessons, have we, Tessa?" Magnus asked.

"Magnus!" Tessa exclaimed, and her grave face lit with a welcoming smile that sent a pang of sweetness through Magnus. "But they said— Oh, no. Oh, where did you find Jamie?"

She reached the bottom of the steps, went over to Magnus, and cradled the boy's damp head in her hand in an almost absentminded gesture of affection. In that gesture Magnus saw how she had changed, saw the ingrained habit of motherhood, love for someone she had created and whom she cherished.

No other warlock would ever have a child of their own blood. Only Tessa could have that experience.

Magnus turned his head away from Tessa at the sound of a new footfall on the stairs.

The memory of Will the boy was so fresh that it was something of a shock to see Will himself now, older, broader of shoulder, but still with the same tousled black hair and laughing blue eyes. He looked just as handsome as he had ever been—more so perhaps, since he seemed so much happier. Magnus saw more marks of laughter than of time on his face, and found himself smiling. It was true what Will had said, he realized. They were friends.

Recognition crossed Will's face, and with it pleasure, but almost instantly he saw the burden Magnus carried, and worry erased all else.

"Magnus," he said. "What on earth happened to James?"

"What happened?" Magnus asked musingly. "Well, let me see. He stole a bicycle and rode it, not using his hands at any point, through Trafalgar Square. He attempted to climb Nelson's Column and fight with Nelson. Then I lost him for a brief period of time, and by the time I caught up with him, he had wandered into Hyde Park, waded into the Serpentine, spread his arms wide, and was shouting, 'Ducks, embrace me as your king!'"

"Dear God," said Will. "He must have been vilely drunk. Tessa, I can bear it no longer. He is taking awful risks with his life and rejecting all the principles I hold most dear. If he continues making an exhibition of himself throughout London, he will be called to Idris and kept there away from the mundanes. Does he not realize that?"

Magnus shrugged. "He also made inappropriate amorous advances to a startled grandmotherly sort selling flowers, an Irish wolfhound, an innocent hat stand in a dwelling he broke into, and myself. I will add that I do not believe his admiration of my person, dazzling though I am, to be sincere. He told me I was a beautiful, sparkling lady. Then he abruptly collapsed, naturally in the path of an oncoming train from Dover, and I decided it was well past time to take him home and place him in the bosom of his family. If you had rather I put him in an orphanage, I fully understand."

Will was shaking his head, shadows in his blue eyes now. "Bridget," he shouted, and Magnus thought, *Oh, yes, that was the maid's name*. "Call for the Silent Brothers," Will finished.

"You mean call for Jem," Tessa said, dropping her voice, and she and Will shared a look—what Magnus could describe only as a *married* look, the look of two people who understood each other completely and yet found each other adorable all the same.

It was quite sickening.

He cleared his throat. "Still a Silent Brother, then, is he?"

Will gave Magnus a withering look. "It does tend to be a permanent state. Here, give me my son."

Magnus let Will take James from his arms, which were left lighter if more damp, and Magnus followed Will's and Tessa's lead up the stairs. Inside the Institute it was clear they had been redecorating. Charlotte's dark drawing room now held several comfortable-looking sofas, and the walls were covered in light damask. Tall shelves were lined with books, volumes with the gilt rubbed off their spines and, Magnus was sure, the pages much thumbed. It appeared both Tessa and Will remained great readers.

Will deposited James onto one of the sofas. Tessa rushed to find a blanket as Magnus turned toward the door, only to find his hand caught in Will's grasp.

"It was very good of you to bring Jamie home," Will said. "But you were always so good to me and mine. I was little more than a boy then, and not as grateful or as gracious as I should have been."

"You were well enough, Will," said Magnus. "And I see you have grown to be better. Also, you are not bald, and neither have you grown fat. All that dashing about and fighting evil you people do is at least useful for keeping a trim figure in middle age."

Will laughed. "It's very good to see you, too." He hesitated. "About Jamie..."

Magnus tensed. He had not wanted to distress Will and Tessa too much. He had not told them that James had fallen when he was in the Serpentine, and made very little effort to rescue himself from drowning. He had not seemed to want to be taken from the cold depths of the water: had fought Magnus as he dragged him out, then laid his pale cheek against the dank earth of the riverbank and hid his face in his arms.

For a moment Magnus had thought he was crying, but as he stooped down to check on the boy, he found he was barely conscious. With his cruel golden eyes closed, he once again reminded Magnus of the lost boy Will had been. Magnus touched his damp hair gently and said "James," in as kind a voice as he could.

The boy's pale hands were splayed against the dark earth. The glimmer of the Herondale ring shone against his skin, and the edge of something metallic shone under his sleeve as well. His eyes were shut, the black lashes ink-dark crescents against the lines of his cheekbones. Sparkling drops of water were caught in the curling ends of those lashes, which made him look unhappy in a way he did not when awake.

"*Grace*," James had whispered in his sleep, and was silent.

Magnus had not been angry: he had found himself wishing for a benevolent grace many times himself. He bent and gathered the boy up in his arms. His head lolled against Magnus's shoulder. In sleep James had looked peaceful and innocent, and wholly human.

"This just isn't like him," Will was saying now as Tessa drew a blanket up over the boy, tucking him in firmly.

Magnus raised an eyebrow. "He's *your* son."

"What are you trying to imply?" Will demanded, and for a moment Magnus saw his eyes flash, and saw the boy with messy black hair and glaring blue eyes standing in his drawing room, furious at the whole world and at no part of it more than himself.

"It isn't like him," Tessa agreed. "He's always been so quiet, so studious. Lucie was the impetuous one, but they are both kind, good-hearted children. At parties Jamie could most often be found curled up in a corner with his Latin, or laughing at a private joke with his *parabatai*. He always kept Matthew out of trouble as well as himself. He was the only one who could make that indolent boy attend to his studies," she remarked, with a slight smile that betokened she was fond of her son's *parabatai*, no matter what his faults. "Now he is out at all hours, doing the most disgraceful things, and he will not listen to reason. He will not listen to anybody. I understand what you mean about Will, but Will was lonely and wretched in the days when he behaved badly. James has been wrapped in love all his life."

"Betrayed!" Will muttered. "Cruelly maligned by my friend and now by my own cherished wife, scorned, my name blackened—"

"I see you are still fond of histrionics, Will," said Magnus. "As well as still handsome."

They had grown up. Neither of them looked startled at all. Tessa raised her eyebrows, and Magnus saw something of her son in her then. They both had the same expressive, arched brows, giving their faces a look of both inquiry and amusement, though in James's face the amusement was bitter.

"Do stop flirting with my husband," said Tessa.

"I shall not," Magnus declared, "but I will pause briefly so that I may catch up on your news. I have not heard from you since you sent word the baby had arrived and both he and his lovely mother were thriving."

Will looked surprised. "But we sent you several letters in care of the Morgensterns, who were going to visit the Whitelaws at the New York Institute. It was you who proved to be a shocking correspondent."

"Ah," said Magnus. He himself was not even slightly surprised. This was typical behavior from Shadowhunters. "The Morgensterns must have forgotten to deliver them. How careless."

Tessa, he saw, did not look too surprised either. She was both warlock and Shadowhunter, and yet not quite either. The Shadowhunters believed that Shadowhunter blood trumped all else, but Magnus could well believe that many of the Nephilim might be unkind to a woman who could do magic and whom the years did not touch.

He doubted any of them dared be unkind in front of Will, though.

"We will be more careful about whom we entrust with our letters in future," Tessa said decisively. "We have been out of touch for far too long. How fortunate that you are here in London, both for us and for Jamie. What brings you here, business or pleasure?"

"I wish it were the business of pleasure," Magnus told her. "But no, it is very dull. A Shadowhunter I believe you know sent for me—Tatiana Blackthorn? The lady used to be a Lightwood, did she not?" Magnus turned to Will. "And your sister Cecily married her brother. Gilbert. Gaston. I have a shocking memory for Lightwoods."

"I begged Cecily not to throw herself away on a Lightworm," Will muttered.

"Will!" said Tessa. "Cecily and Gabriel are very happy together."

Will threw himself dramatically into an armchair, touching his son's wrist as he passed by, with a light, careful caress that spoke volumes.

"At least you must admit, Tess, that Tatiana is as mad as a mouse trapped in a teapot. She refuses to speak to any of us, and that includes her brothers, because she says we had a hand in her father's death. Actually, she says we pitilessly slew him. Everybody tries to point out that at the time of the pitiless slaying her father was a giant worm who had eaten her husband and followed up his meal with a palate-cleansing servant sorbet, but she insists on lurking about the manor house and sulking with all the curtains drawn."

"She has lost a great deal. She lost her child," Tessa said. "And she did speak to us that once, in Idris." She stroked back her son's hair, her face troubled. Will looked to James and fell silent.

"Mrs. Blackthorn has come from Idris to her family manor in England specifically so I might visit her, and she sent me a message through the usual Downworlder channels promising me a princely sum if I would come and cast a few spells to increase the attractions of her young ward," Magnus said, attempting to strike a lighter note. "I gather she wishes to marry her off."

Tatiana would not be the first Shadowhunter to seek a warlock's spells to make her life easier and more pleasant. She was, however, the Shadowhunter offering the best price.

"Did she?" Will asked. "It's not as if the girl looks like a toad in a bonnet."

Tessa laughed and stifled the laugh against her hand, and Will grinned, looking pleased with himself, as he always had when he'd managed to amuse Tessa.

"I suppose I should not be casting aspersions on anybody else's children, since my son is all about in his wits. He shoots things, you know."

"I did know that he shoots things," Magnus said tactfully. "Yes."

Will sighed. "The Angel grant me patience so I do not strangle him, and wisdom so I can talk some sense into his great fat head."

"I do wonder where he gets it from," said Magnus pointedly.

"It is not the same," said Tessa. "When Will was Jamie's age, he tried to drive everyone he loved away. Jamie is as loving as ever to us, to Lucie, to Matthew, his *parabatai*. It is himself he wishes to destroy."

"And yet there is no reason for it," Will said, striking the arm of his chair with his clenched fist. "I know my son, and he would not behave this way unless he felt he had no other choice. Unless he was trying to achieve a goal, or punish himself in some way, because he felt he had done some wrong—"

You called for me? I am here.

Magnus looked up to see Brother Zachariah standing in the doorway. He was a slender outline, the hood of his robe down, baring his face. The Silent Brothers rarely bared their faces, knowing how most Shadowhunters reacted to the scars and disfigurement of their skin. It was a sign of trust that Jem showed himself to Will and Tessa in this way.

Jem was still Jem—like Tessa, he had not aged. The Silent Brothers were not immortal but aged incredibly slowly. The powerful runes that gave them knowledge and allowed them to speak with their minds also slowed their bodies' aging, turning the Brothers to living statues. Jem's hands were pale and slender under the cuffs of his robe, still musician's hands after all this time. His face seemed carved out of marble, his eyes shuttered crescents, the dark runes of the Brothers standing out on his high cheekbones. His hair waved around his temples, darkness shot with silver.

A great sadness welled up in Magnus at the sight of him. It was human to age and die, and Jem stood outside that humanity now, outside the light that burned so brightly and so briefly. It was cold outside that light and fire. No one had greater cause to know that cold than Magnus did.

On seeing Magnus, Jem inclined his head. *Magnus Bane. I did not know you would be here.*

"I—" Magnus began, but Will was already on his feet, striding across the room to Jem. He had lit up at the sight of him, and Magnus could feel Jem's attention move from himself to Will, and catch there. Those two boys had been so different, yet at times they had seemed so wholly one that it was strange for Magnus to see Will changed as all humans changed, while Jem was set apart, to see that both had gone somewhere the other could not follow. He imagined it must be even stranger for them.

And yet. There was still about them what had always reminded Magnus of an old legend he'd heard of the red thread of fate: that an invisible scarlet thread bound certain people, and however tangled it became, it could not and would not break.

The Silent Brothers moved the way one imagined a statue would move if it could. Jem had moved the same way coming in, but as Will neared him, Jem took a step toward his former *parabatai*, and the step was swift, eager, and human, as if being close to the people whom he loved made him feel made of flesh and racing blood once more.

"You're here," said Will, and implicit in the words was the sense that Will's contentment was complete. Now Jem was there, all was right with the world.

"I knew you would come," said Tessa, rising from her son's side to go after her husband, toward Jem. Magnus saw Brother Zachariah's face glow at the sound of her voice, runes and pallor no longer mattering. He was a boy again for an instant, his life just beginning, his heart full of hope and love.

How they loved each another, these three, how they had suffered for each another, and yet how much joy they clearly took from simply being in the same room. Magnus had loved before, many times, but he did not ever recall feeling the peace that radiated out from these three only from being in the others' presence. He had craved peace sometimes, like a man wandering for centuries in the desert never seeing water and having to live with the want of it.

Tessa, Will, and their lost Jem stood together in a tight knot. Magnus knew that for a few moments nothing existed in the world but the three of them.

He looked at the sofa where James Herondale lay, and saw that he was awake, his gold eyes like watchful flames teaching the candles to burn brightly. James was the young one, the boy with his whole life ahead of him, but there was no hope or joy in his face. Tessa, Will, and Jem looked natural being together, but even in this room with those who loved him better than life, James looked utterly alone. There was something desperate and desolate about his face. He tried to lean up on one elbow, and collapsed back against the cushions of the sofa, his black head tipped back as if it were too heavy for him to bear. A Herondale ring glittered on his finger, a silver bracelet on his wrist.

Tessa, Will, and Jem were murmuring together, Will's hand on Jem's arm. Magnus had never seen anyone touch a Silent Brother like that, in simple friendship. It made him ache inside, and he saw that hollow ache reflected on the face of the boy on the sofa.

Obeying an impetuous impulse, Magnus crossed the room and knelt down by the couch, close to Will's son, who looked at him with tired golden eyes. "You see them," James said. "The way they all love one another. I used to think everyone loved that way. The way it is in fairy tales. I used to think that love was giving and generous and good."

"And now?" Magnus asked.

The boy turned his face away. Magnus found himself facing the back of James's head, seeing his mop of black hair so like his father's, and the edge of his *parabatai* rune just under his collar. It must be on his back, Magnus thought, above the blade of his shoulder, where an angel's wing would be.

"James," said Magnus in a low, hurried voice. "Once your father had a terrible secret that he thought he could not tell to a soul in the world, and he told me. I can see that there is something gnawing at you, something you are keeping hidden. If there is anything you want to tell me, now or at any time, you have my word that I will keep your secrets, and that I will help you if I can."

James shifted to look at Magnus. In his face Magnus thought he caught a glimpse of softening, as if the boy were releasing his relentless grip on whatever was tormenting him. "I am not like my father," he said. "Do not mistake my despair for nobility in disguise, for it is not that. I suffer for myself, not for anyone else."

"But *why* do you suffer?" Magnus said in frustration. "Your mother was correct when she said you have been loved all your life. If you would just let me help you—"

The boy's expression shut like a door. He turned his face away from Magnus again, and his eyes closed, the light falling on the fringe of his eyelashes.

"I gave my word I would never tell," he said. "And there is not a living soul on this earth who can help me."

"James," Magnus said, honestly surprised by the despair in the boy's tone, and the alarm in Magnus's voice caught the attention of the others in the room. Tessa and Will looked away from Jem and to their son, the boy who bore Jem's name, and as one they all moved over to where he lay, Will and Tessa hand in hand.

Brother Zachariah bent over the back of the sofa and touched James's hair tenderly with those musician's fingers.

"Hello, Uncle Brother Zachariah," James said without opening his eyes. "I would say that I'm sorry to bother you, but I'm sure this is the most excitement you've had all year. Not so lively in the City of Bones, now is it?"

"James!" Will snapped. "Don't talk to Jem like that."

As if I am not used to badly behaved Herondales, Brother Zachariah said, in the way Jem had always tried to make peace between Will and the world.

"I suppose the difference is that Father always cared what you thought about him," said James. "And I don't. But don't take it personally, Uncle Jem. I do not care what anybody thinks."

And yet he made a habit of making an exhibition of himself, as Will had put it, and Magnus had no doubt it was deliberate. He must care what someone thought. He must be doing all this for a purpose. *But what purpose could it be?* Magnus wondered.

"James, this is so unlike you," Tessa said worriedly. "You have always cared. Always been kind. What is troubling you?"

"Perhaps nothing is troubling me. Perhaps I have simply realized I was rather boring before. Don't you think I was boring? All that studying, and the Latin." He shuddered. "Horrible."

There is nothing boring about caring, or about an open, loving heart, said Jem.

"So say all of you," replied James. "And it is easy to see why, the three of you, falling over yourself to love one another—each more than the other. And it *is* kind of you to trouble yourselves about me." His breath caught a little, and then he smiled, but it was a smile of great sadness. "I wish I did not trouble you so."

Tessa and Will exchanged looks of despair. The room was thick with worry and parental concerns. Magnus was beginning to feel bowed under by the weight of humanity.

"Well," he announced. "As educational and occasionally damp as this evening has been, I do not wish to intrude on a family reunion, and I really do not wish to experience any family drama, as I find with Shadowhunters that it tends to be extensive. I must be on my way."

"But you could stay here," Tessa offered. "Be our guest. We would be delighted to have you."

"A warlock in the hallowed chambers of a Shadowhunter Institute?" Magnus shuddered. "Only think."

Tessa gave him a sharp look. "Magnus—"

"Besides, I have an appointment," Magnus said. "One I should not be late for."

Will looked up with a frown. "At this time of night?"

"I have a peculiar occupation, and keep peculiar hours," said Magnus. "I seem to recall you coming to me for assistance quite a few times at odd hours of the night." He inclined his head. "Will. Tessa. Jem. Good evening."

Tessa moved to his side. "I will show you out."

"Good-bye, whoever you are," said James sleepily, closing his eyes. "I cannot recall your name."

"Don't mind him," Tessa said in a low voice as she moved with Magnus toward the exit. She paused in the doorway for a moment, looking back at her son and the two men who stood with him. Will and Jem were shoulder to shoulder, and from across the room it was impossible to miss Jem's slighter frame, the fact that he had not aged, as Will had. Though, there was in Will's voice all the eagerness of a boy when he said, in answer to a question Magnus did not hear, "Why, yes, of course you can play it before you go. It is in the music room as always, kept ever the same for you."

"His violin?" Magnus murmured. "I did not think the Silent Brothers cared for music."

Tessa sighed softly and moved out into the corridor, Magnus beside her. "Will does not see a Silent Brother when he looks at James," she said. "He sees only Jem."

"Is it ever difficult?" he asked.

"Is what difficult?"

"Sharing your husband's heart so entirely with someone else," he said.

"If it were different, it would not be Will's heart," Tessa said. "He knows he shares my heart with Jem as well. I would have it no other way—and he would have it no other way with me."

So much a part of one another that there was no way to be untangled, even now, and no wish to be so. Magnus wanted to ask if Tessa was ever afraid of what would happen to her when Will was gone, when their bond was finally severed, but he did not. It would with luck be a long time until Tessa's first death, a long time before she entirely realized the burden of being immortal and yet loving that which was not.

"Very beautiful," Magnus said instead. "Well, I wish you all the best with your little hellion."

"We shall see you again before you leave London, of course," said Tessa in that tone of hers she had had even as a girl, that brooked no contradiction.

"Indeed," Magnus said. He hesitated. "And, Tessa, if you ever need me—and I hope if you do, it will be many long, happy years from now—send me a message, and I will be with you at once."

They both knew what he meant.

"I will," said Tessa, and she gave him her hand. Hers was small and soft, but her grip was surprisingly strong.

"Believe me, dear lady," Magnus told her with an assumption of lightness. He released her hand and bowed with a flourish. "Call me and I come!"

As Magnus turned to walk away from the church, he heard the sound of violin music carried to him on the cloudy London air, and remembered another night, a night of ghosts and snow and Christmas music, and Will standing on the steps of the Institute, watching Magnus as he went. Now it was Tessa who stood at the door with her hand lifted in farewell until Magnus was at the gate with its ominous lettered message: WE ARE DUST AND SHADOWS. He looked back and saw her slight pale figure at the Institute threshold and thought again, *Yes, perhaps I was wrong to leave London.*

It was not the first time Magnus had made his way from London to Chiswick to visit Lightwood House. Benedict Lightwood's home had often been thrown open to Downworlders who'd been amenable to his idea of a good time.

It had been a grand manor once, the stone brilliant white and adorned with Greek statuary and too many pillars to count. The Lightwoods were proud and ostentatious people, and their home, in all its neoclassical glory, had reflected that.

Magnus knew what had become of all that pride. The patriarch, Benedict Lightwood, had contracted a disease from consorting with demons and had transformed into a murderous monster that his own sons had been forced to slay, with the assistance of a host of other Shadowhunters. Their manor had been taken away by the Clave as punishment, their monies confiscated, and their family had become a laughingstock, a byword for sin and a betrayal of all that the Shadowhunters held dear.

Magnus had little time for the Shadowhunters' overweening arrogance, and usually enjoyed seeing them taken down a peg, but even he had rarely seen a family fall so far so terribly fast. Gabriel and Gideon, Benedict's two sons, had managed to claw their way back to respectability through good behavior and the graces of the Consul, Charlotte Branwell. Their sister, however, was another matter entirely.

How she had managed to get Lightwood House back into her clutches, Magnus did not know. *As mad as a mouse trapped in a teapot*, Will had said of her, and knowing of the family's disgraced state,

Magnus hardly expected the grandeur of Benedict's time. Doubtless the place would be shabby now, dusty with time, only a few servants left to keep it up and in order—

The carriage Magnus had hired came to a stop. "The place looks abandoned," opined the driver, casting a doubtful eye over at the iron gates, which looked rusted shut and bound with vines.

"Or haunted," Magnus suggested brightly.

"Well, I can't get in. Them gates won't open," said the driver gruffly. "You'll have to get out and walk, if you're that determined."

Magnus was. His curiosity was alight now, and he approached the gates like a cat, ready to scale them if need be.

A tweak of magic, a bit of an opening spell, and the gates burst wide with a shower of rusted metal flakes, onto a long, dark overgrown drive that led up to a ghostly manor house in the distance, glimmering like a tombstone under the full moon.

Magnus closed the gates and went forward, listening to the sound of night birds in the trees overhead, the rustle of leaves in the night wind. A forest of blackened tangles loomed all about him, the remains of the famous Lightwood gardens. Those gardens had been lovely once. Magnus distantly recalled overhearing Benedict Lightwood drunkenly saying that they had been his dead wife's joy.

Now the high hedges of the Italian garden had formed a maze, a twisted one from which there was clearly no escape. They had killed the monster Benedict Lightwood had become in these gardens, Magnus remembered hearing, and the black ichor had seeped from the monster's veins into the earth in a dark unstoppable flood.

Magnus felt a scratch against one hand and looked down to see a rosebush that had survived but gone wild. It took him a moment to identify the plant, for though the shape of the blooms was familiar, the color was not. The roses were as black as the blood of the dead serpent.

He plucked one. The flower crumbled in his palm as if it were made of ash, as if it had already been dead.

Magnus passed on toward the house.

The corruption that had claimed the roses had not spared the manor. What had once been a smooth white facade was now gray with years, streaked with the black of dirt and the green of rot. The shining pillars were twined about with dying vines, and the balconies, which Magnus remembered as like the hollows of alabaster goblets, were now filled with the dark snarls of thorns and the debris of years.

The door knocker had been an image of a shining golden lion with a ring held in its mouth. Now the ring lay rotted on the steps, and the gray lion's mouth hung open and empty in a hungry snarl. Magnus knocked briskly on the door. He heard the sound echo through the inside of the house as if all were the heavy silence of a tomb therein and ever would be, as if any noise was a disturbance.

The conviction that everyone in this house must be dead had gained such a hold on Magnus that it was a shock when the woman who had summoned him here opened the door.

It was, of course, rather odd for a lady to be opening her own front door, but from the look of the place, Magnus assumed the entire staff of servants had been given the decade off.

Magnus had a dim recollection of seeing Tatiana Lightwood at one of her father's parties: a glimpse of a perfectly ordinary girl with wide green eyes, behind a hastily closing door.

Even after seeing the house and the grounds, he was not prepared for Tatiana Blackthorn.

Her eyes were still very green. Her stern mouth was bracketed with lines of bitter disappointment and grave pain. She looked like a woman in her sixties, not her forties. She was wearing a gown of a fashion decades past—it hung from her wasted shoulders and fluttered around her body like a shroud. The fabric bore dark brown stains, but in patches it was a faded pastel bordering on white, while other spots remained what Magnus thought must have been its original fuchsia.

She should have looked ridiculous. She was wearing a silly bright pink dress for a younger woman, someone who was almost a girl, in love with her husband and going on a visit to her papa.

She did not look ridiculous. Her stern face forbade pity. She, like the house, was awe-inspiring in her ruin.

"Bane," Tatiana said, and held the door open wide enough that Magnus could pass through. She said no word of welcome.

She shut the door behind Magnus, the sound as final as the closing of a tomb. Magnus paused in the hall, waiting for the woman behind him, and as he waited, he heard another footstep above their heads, a sign there was someone else alive in the house.

Down the wide curving staircase toward them came a girl. Magnus had always found mortals to be beautiful, and had seen many mortals whom anybody would have described as beautiful.

This was extraordinary beauty, beauty unlike the beauty of most mortals.

In the stained and filthy ruin the house had become, she shone like a pearl. Her hair was the color of a pearl too, palest ivory with a sheen of gold on it, and her skin was the luminous pink and white of a seashell. Her lashes were thick and dark, veiling eyes of deep unearthly gray.

Magnus drew in a breath. Tatiana heard him and looked over, smiling a triumphant smile. "She's glorious, isn't she? My ward. My Grace."

Grace.

The realization struck Magnus like a blow. Of course James Herondale had not been calling out for something as inchoate and distant as a benediction, the soul's yearning for divine mercy and understanding. His desperation had been centered on something far more flesh-and-blood than that.

But why is it a secret? Why can no one help him? Magnus struggled to keep his face a blank as the girl moved toward him and offered her hand.

"How do you do," she murmured.

Magnus stared down at her. Her face was a porcelain cup, upturned; her eyes held promises. The combination of beauty, innocence, and the promise of sin was staggering. "Magnus Bane," she said, in a breathy, soft voice. Magnus couldn't help staring at her. Everything about her was so perfectly constructed to appeal. She was beautiful, yes, but it was more than that. She seemed shy, yet all her attention was focused on Magnus, as if he were the most fascinating thing she had ever seen. There was no man who did not want to see himself reflected like that in a beautiful girl's eyes. And if the neckline of her dress was a shade low, it did not seem scandalous, for her gray eyes were full of an innocence that said that she did not know of desire, not yet, but there was a lushness to the curve of her lip, a dark light in her eyes that said that under the right hands she would be a pupil who yielded the most exquisite result...

Magnus took a step back from her as if she were a poisonous snake. She did not look hurt, or angry, or even startled. She turned a look on Tatiana, a sort of curious inquiry. "Mama?" she said. "What is wrong?"

Tatiana curled her lip. "This one is not like others," she said. "I mean, he likes girls well enough, and boys as well, I hear, but his taste does not run to Shadowhunters. And he is not mortal. He has been alive a long time. One cannot expect him to have the normal—reactions."

Magnus could well imagine what the normal reactions would be—the reactions of a boy like James Herondale, sheltered and taught that love was gentle, love was kind, that one should love with all one's heart and give away all one's soul. Magnus could imagine the normal reactions to this girl, a girl whose every gesture, every expression, every line, cried, *Love her, love her, love her.*

But Magnus was not that boy. He reminded himself of his manners, and bowed.

"Charmed," he said. "Or whatever effect would please you best, I'm sure."

Grace regarded him with cool interest. Her reactions were muted, Magnus thought, or rather, carefully gauged. She seemed a creature made to attract everyone and express nothing real, though it would take a master observer, like Magnus, to know it.

She reminded Magnus suddenly not of any mortal but of the vampire Camille, who had been his latest and most regrettable real love.

Magnus had spent years imagining there was fire behind Camille's ice, that there were hopes and dreams and love waiting for him. What he had loved in Camille had been nothing but illusion. Magnus had acted like a child, fancying there were shapes and stories to be made of the clouds in the sky.

He turned away from the sight of Grace in her trim white-and-blue dress, like a vision of Heaven in the gray hell of this house, and looked to Tatiana. Her eyes were narrowed with contempt.

"Come, warlock," she said. "I believe we have business to discuss."

Magnus followed Tatiana and Grace up the stairs and down a long corridor that was almost pitch black. Magnus heard the crack and crunch of broken glass beneath his feet, and in the dim, hardly-there light he saw something scuttling away from his approach. He hoped it was something as harmless as a rat, but something about its movements suggested a shape far more grotesque.

"Do not try to open any doors or drawers while you are here, Bane." Tatiana's voice floated back to him. "My father left behind many guardians to protect what is ours."

She opened the door, and Magnus beheld the room within. There were an upturned desk and heavy curtains sagging in the windows like bodies from a gibbet, and on the wooden floor were splinters and streaks of blood, the marks of a long-ago struggle nobody had cleaned up.

There were many picture frames hanging askew or with the glass broken. A great many of them seemed to contain nautical adventures—Magnus had been put off the sea by his ill-fated attempt to live a piratical life for a day—but even the pictures that were whole were clouded with gray. The painted ships appeared to be sinking in seas of dust.

There was only one portrait that was whole and clean. It was an oil painting, with no glass covering it, but there was not a speck of dust on its surface. It was the only clean thing, besides Grace, in the entire house.

The portrait was of a boy, about seventeen years old. He was sitting in a chair, his head resting against the back as if he did not have the strength to support it on his own. He was terribly thin and as white as salt. His eyes were a deep, still green, like a woodland pool hidden under the overhanging leaves of a tree, never exposed to sun or wind. He had dark hair falling, as fine-spun and straight as silk, across his brow, and his long fingers were curled over the arms of the chair, almost clinging to it, and the desperate clutch of those hands told a silent story of pain.

Magnus had seen portraits like this before, the last images of the lost. He could tell even across the years how much effort it had cost the boy to sit for that portrait, for the comfort of loved ones who would live after he was gone.

His pallid face had the distant look of one who had already taken too many steps along the path to death for him to be recalled. Magnus thought of James Herondale, burning up with too much light, too much love, too much, too much—while the boy in the portrait was as lovely as a dying poet, with the fragile beauty of a candle about to gutter out.

On the ragged wallpaper that might once have been green and that had mutated to a grayish-green color, like a sea flooded with waste, were words written in the same dark brown as the stains on Tatiana's dress. Magnus had to admit to himself what that color was: blood that had been spilled years since and yet never washed clean.

The wallpaper was hanging off the walls in tatters. Magnus could make out only a word here and there on the remaining pieces: PITY, REGRET, INFERNAL.

The last sentence in the series was still legible. It read, MAY GOD HAVE MERCY ON OUR SOULS. Beneath this, written not in blood but cut through the wallpaper into the wall by what Magnus suspected was a different hand, were the words, GOD HAS NO MERCY AND NOR WILL I.

Tatiana sank into an armchair, its upholstery worn and stained by the years, and Grace knelt at her adoptive mother's side on the grimy floor. She knelt daintily, delicately, her skirts billowing around her like the petals of a flower. Magnus supposed that it must have been a habit with her to come to rest in filth, and rise from it to all outward appearance radiantly pure.

"To business, then, madam," said Magnus, and he added silently to himself, *To leaving this house as soon as possible.* "Tell me exactly why you have need of my fabulous and unsurpassed powers, and what you would have me do."

"You can already see, I trust," said Tatiana, "that my Grace is in no need of spells to enhance her natural charms."

Magnus looked at Grace, who was gazing at her hands linked in her lap. Perhaps she was already using spells. Perhaps she was simply beautiful. Magic or nature, they were much the same thing to Magnus.

"I'm sure she is already an enchantress in her own right."

Grace said nothing, only glanced up at him from under her lashes. It was a demurely devastating look.

"I want something else from you, warlock. I want you," Tatiana said, slowly and distinctly, "to go out into the world and kill me five Shadowhunters. I will tell you how it is to be done, and I will pay you most handsomely."

Magnus was so astonished, he honestly believed he must have heard her incorrectly. "Shadowhunters?" he repeated. "Kill?"

"Is my request so very strange? I have no love for the Shadowhunters."

"But, my dear madam, you *are* a Shadowhunter."

Tatiana Blackthorn folded her hands in her lap. "I am no such thing."

Magnus stared at her for a long moment. "Ah," he said. "I beg your pardon. Uh, would it be terribly uncivil of me to inquire what you do believe yourself to be? Do you think that you are a lamp shade?"

"I do not find your levity amusing."

Magnus's tone was hushed as he said, "I beg your pardon again. Do you believe yourself to be a pianoforte?"

"Hold your tongue, warlock, and do not talk of matters about which you know *nothing*." Tatiana's hands were clenched suddenly, curled as tight as claws in the skirt of her once-bright dress. The note of real agony in her voice was enough to silence Magnus, but she continued. "A Shadowhunter is a warrior. A Shadowhunter is born and trained to be a hand of God upon this earth, wiping it free of evil. That is what our legends say. That is what my father taught me, but my father taught me other things too. He decreed that I would not be trained as a Shadowhunter. He told me that was not my place, that my place in life was to be the dutiful daughter of a warrior, and in time the helpmeet of a noble warrior and the mother of warriors who would carry on the glory of the Shadowhunters for another generation."

Tatiana made a sweeping gesture to the words on the walls, the stains on the floor.

"Such glory," she said, and laughed bitterly. "My father and my family were disgraced, and my husband was torn apart in front of my eyes—torn apart. I had one child, my beautiful boy, my Jesse, but he could not be trained to be a warrior. He was always so weak, so sickly. I begged them not to put the runes on him—I was certain that would kill him—but the Shadowhunters held me back and held him down as they burned the Marks into his flesh. He screamed and screamed. We all thought he would die then, but he did not. He held on for me, for his mama, but their cruelty damned him. Each year he grew sicker and weaker until it was too late. He was sixteen when they told me he could not live."

Her hands moved restlessly as she spoke, from her gesture at the walls to plucking at her gown dyed with old, old blood. She touched her arms as if they still hurt where she had been held back by the Shadowhunters, and she toyed with a large ornate locket that hung around her neck. She opened and closed it, the tarnished metal gleaming between her fingers, and Magnus thought he saw a glimpse of a ghastly portrait. Her son again?

He looked toward the picture on the wall, the pale young face, and calculated how old a child of Rupert Blackthorn's must have been when the man had died twenty-five years before. If Jesse Blackthorn had died when he was sixteen then the boy must have been dead for nine years, but perhaps a mother's mourning never ended.

"I am aware that you have suffered greatly, Mrs. Blackthorn," said Magnus, as gently as he was able. "But instead of some plot of vengeance through the senseless slaughter of Shadowhunters, consider that there are many Shadowhunters who desire nothing more than to help you, and to ease your pain."

"Indeed? Of whom do you speak? William Herondale"—and in Tatiana's mouth hatred dripped from every syllable of Will's name—"sneered at me because all I did was scream as my beloved died, but tell me, what else could I have done? What else had I ever been taught to do?" Tatiana's eyes were huge and poison-green, eyes with enough pain in them to eat away at a world and devour a soul. "Can you tell me, warlock? Could William Herondale tell me? Can anyone tell me what I should have done, when I did everything I was ever asked to do? My husband is dead, my father is dead, my brothers are lost, my home was stolen, and the Nephilim had no power to save my son. I was everything I was ever asked to be, and as my reward my life was burned to ash. Do not speak to me of easing my pain. My pain is all that I have left. Do not speak to me of being a Shadowhunter. I am not one of them. I refuse to be."

"Very well, madam. You have made your anti-Shadowhunter position amply clear," said Magnus. "What I do not know is why you think I will help you get what you want."

Magnus was many things, but he had never been a fool. The death of a few Shadowhunters was not an aim in itself. If that were all she wanted, she would not have needed to go to Magnus.

The only reason she could have to go to a warlock was if she wanted to use those deaths, to alchemize Shadowhunter lives into magic for a spell. It would be the darkest of dark spells, and the fact that Tatiana knew of it told Magnus this was not the first time she had turned to dark magic.

What Tatiana Blackthorn, whose pain had eaten away at her like a wolf inside her breast, wanted from dark magic, Magnus did not know. He did not want to know what she had done with power in the past, and he certainly did not want her to have power that could be cataclysmic now.

Tatiana frowned a little puzzled frown that made her look like Benedict Lightwood's spoiled and cosseted daughter again.

"For money, of course."

"You imagine I would kill five people, and leave untold power in your hands," said Magnus, "for money?"

Tatiana waved a hand. "Oh, don't try to drive the price up by aping your betters and pretending that you have any morals or tender feelings, demon spawn. Name a higher sum and be done with it. The hours of the night are precious to me, and I wish to waste no further time on one such as you."

It was the casualness with which she spoke that was so chilling. Mad though Tatiana might have been, here she was not raving or bitter. She was simply working from the facts as Shadowhunters knew them: that a Downworlder must be so entirely corrupt that she did not even dream he had a heart.

Of course, of course, the vast majority of the Shadowhunters thought of him as something less than human, and as far below the children of the Angel as apes were below men. He might sometimes be useful, but he was a creature to be despised, used but then discarded, his touch avoided because it was unclean.

He had been very useful to Will Herondale, after all. Will had not come to him searching for a friend but a convenient source of magic. Even the best Shadowhunters were not so different from the rest.

"Let me say to you what I said once, in an entirely different context, to Catherine the Great," Magnus declared. "My dear lady, you cannot afford me, and also, please leave that horse alone. Good night."

He made a bow and then made his way, with some speed, out of the room. As the door shut with a snap, he heard Tatiana's voice snapping to match it: "Go after him!"

He was not surprised to hear soft footsteps pattering after him down the stairs. Magnus turned from the front door and met Grace's eyes.

Her footfalls were as light as a child's, but she did not look like a child. In that porcelain-pure face her eyes were gray hollows, deep alluring lakes with sirens in their depths. She met Magnus's eyes with a level gaze, and Magnus was reminded once again of Camille.

It was remarkable that a girl who looked no more than sixteen could rival a centuries-old vampire for self-possession. She had not had time to freeze past caring. *There must*, Magnus thought, *be something behind all this ice.*

"You will not return upstairs, I see," Grace said. "You want no part of Mama's plan."

It was not a question, and she did not sound shocked or curious. It did not seem unthinkable to her, then, that Magnus might have scruples. Perhaps the girl had qualms of conscience herself, but she was shut up here in this dark house with a madwoman, nothing but bitterness poured into her ears from dusk to daybreak. Little wonder if she was different from other girls.

Magnus felt regret suddenly for the way he had shuddered back from Grace. She was not much more than a child, after all, and nobody knew better than he what it was like to be judged and shunned. He reached out to touch her arm. "Do you have somewhere else to go?" Magnus asked her.

"Somewhere else?" said Grace. "We reside mainly in Idris."

"What I mean is, would she let you leave? Do you need help?"

Grace moved with such speed that it was as if she were a bolt of lightning wrapped in muslin, the long gleaming blade flying from her skirts to her hand. She held the glittering point against Magnus's chest, over his heart.

Here was a Shadowhunter, Magnus thought. Tatiana had learned something from the mistakes of her father. She'd had the girl trained.

"I am no prisoner here."

"No?" Magnus asked. "Then what are you?"

Grace's awful, awe-inspiring eyes narrowed. They were glittering like the steel, and were, Magnus was sure, no less deadly. "I am my mother's blade."

Shadowhunters often died young, and left children behind to be raised by others. That was nothing unusual. It was natural that such a ward, taken into a Shadowhunter's home, would think of and speak to their guardian as a parent. Magnus had thought nothing of it. Yet now it occurred to him that a child might be so grateful to be taken in that her loyalty would be fierce, that a girl raised by Tatiana Blackthorn might not wish for rescue. She might wish for nothing more than the fulfillment of her mother's dark plans.

"Are you threatening me?" Magnus said softly.

"If you do not intend to help us," she said, "then leave this house. Dawn is coming."

"I am not a vampire," Magnus said. "I shall not disappear with the light."

"You will if I kill you before the sun comes up," said Grace. "Who would miss one warlock?"

And she smiled, a wild smile that reminded him again of Camille. That potent blend of beauty and cruelty. He had fallen victim to it himself. He could only imagine again, with growing horror, what the effect would have been on James Herondale, a gentle boy who had been reared to believe that love, too, was gentle. James had given his heart to this girl, Magnus thought, and Magnus knew well enough from Edmund and Will what it meant when a Herondale gave his heart away. It was not a gift that could be returned.

Tessa, Will, and Jem had raised James in love, and had surrounded him with love and the goodness it could produce. But they had given him no armor against the evil. They had wrapped his heart in silks and velvet, and then he had given it to Grace Blackthorn, and she had spun for it a cage of razor wire and broken glass, burned it to bits, and blown away the remains, another layer of ashes in this place of beautiful horrors.

Magnus waved a hand behind his back, then stepped away from Grace's blade, away through the magically open door.

"You will tell no one of what my mother asked of you tonight," said Grace. "Or I will ensure your destruction."

"I believe you think you could," Magnus breathed. She was terrible and brilliant, like the light shining off the edge of a razor. "Oh, and by the way? I suspect that if James Herondale had known I was coming here, he would have sent his regards."

Grace lowered her sword, nothing more. Its point rested gently on the ground. Her hand did not shake, and her lashes screened her eyes. "What do I care for James Herondale?" she asked.

"I thought you might. After all, a blade does not get to choose where it is pointed."

Grace looked up. Her eyes were still, deep pools, entirely unruffled.

"A blade does not care," she told him.

Magnus turned and made his way past tangles of black roses and undergrowth down toward the rusted gates. He looked back at the manor only once, saw the wreck of what had been grand and gracious, and saw a curtain fluttering in a window high above, and the suggestion of a face. He wondered who was watching him go.

He could warn Downworlders to steer clear of Tatiana and her endeavors. No matter what the price offered, no Downworlder would fail to listen to a warning against one of the Nephilim. Tatiana would raise no dark magic.

Magnus could do that much, but he did not see a way to help James Herondale. Grace and Tatiana might have cast a spell on him, Magnus supposed. He would not put it past either of them, but he could not see why they would. What possible role could James Herondale have to play in whatever dark plot they were hatching? More likely the boy had simply fallen prey to her charms. Love was love; there was no spell to cure a broken heart that did not also destroy that heart's capacity for love forever.

And there was no reason for Magnus to tell Will and Tessa what he had learned. James's feelings for Grace were his secret to keep. Magnus had told the boy he would never betray his secrets; he had sworn it. He had never betrayed Will's confidence, and he would not betray James's now. What good would it do Will and Tessa, to know the name of their son's pain and still have no remedy for it?

He thought once more of Camille, and how it had hurt him to learn the truth about her, how he had struggled like a man crawling over knives not to know it, and finally, with even greater pain, had been forced to accept it.

Magnus did not take such suffering lightly, but even mortals did not die of broken hearts. No matter how cruel Grace had been, he told himself, James would heal. Even though he was a Herondale.

He opened the gates with his hands, thorns scratching his flesh, and he remembered again his first sight of Grace and the feeling he'd had of being faced with a predator. She was very different from Tessa, who had always steadied and anchored Will, softened his eyes into humor and his lips to gentleness.

It would be ironic, Magnus thought, terribly and cruelly ironic, for one Herondale to be saved by love, and another Herondale damned by it.

He tried to shake off both the memory of Tessa and Will and the echo of Tatiana's condemning words. He had promised Tessa that he would return, but now he found all he wanted to do was escape. He did not want to care what Shadowhunters thought of him. He did not want to care what would become of them or their children.

He had offered help to three Shadowhunters this night. One of them had replied that he was beyond help, one had asked him to commit murder, and one had pointed a blade at him.

His relationship of mutual distant tolerance with the Whitelaws of the New York Institute seemed suddenly alluring. He was part of Downworld New York, and would have it no other way. He was glad he had left London. He discovered in himself a pang for New York and its brighter lights, and fewer broken hearts.

"Where to?" asked the driver.

Magnus thought of the ship from Southampton to New York, of standing on the deck of the boat, letting the sea air wash him clean of the musty air of London. He said, "I believe I am going home."

The Rise of the Hotel Dumort

By Cassandra Clare and Maureen Johnson

The arrow made a kind of singing noise as it cut through the air. It entered Aldous's chest like a knife sliding easily into an apple. Aldous sat upright for a moment, looking at it; then he slumped to the side, dead.

Magnus watched his blood hit the granite.

—The Rise of the Hotel Dumort

SHUNK
STAY OR GO. DECIDE NOW, AS I AM GOING TO OPEN THE POR–
RUN!
KRAK
BRRRM

Late September 1929

Magnus spotted the little vamp vampire right away. She was winding her way through the crowd, pausing for a moment for a quick shimmy by the band. She had perfectly bobbed hair, shiny black with a straight bang, just like Louise Brooks. She wore an electric-blue dress with delicate, dripping beadwork that skimmed her knees.

In most ways, she looked exactly like a normal customer at Magnus's speakeasy, and she easily blended in with the three or four dozen people who packed onto his small dance floor. But there was something *separate* about her, something dreamy and strange. The music was fast, but she danced at a sultry middle pace. Her skin was stark white, but not the dusty white from cosmetic powder. And as she did her lonely little snake dance right in front of the saxophone player, she turned herself and made direct eye contact with Magnus. When she did so, two little half fangs appeared against a bright red lip. Realizing they were out, she giggled and clapped a hand to her mouth. A moment later, they had retracted.

Meanwhile, Alfie, who was by now clinging to the bar for support, forged on with a story.

"I tole him ... Magnus, you listenin'?"

"Of course, Alfie," Magnus said. Alfie was a very handsome and entertaining regular with excellent taste in suits and a love of strong cocktails. He told very good stories and smiled very good smiles. He was a banker or something. Stockbroker maybe. Everyone had something to do with money these days.

"... I tole him, you can't take a boat up to your hotel room. And he said, ''Course I can. I'm a *captain*!' I said, I said to him, I said—"

"One moment, Alfie. Something I need to attend to."

"I'm just gettin' to the bes' part..."

"Just one moment," Magnus said again, patting his friend's arm. "I'll be right back."

Alfie followed the track of Magnus's gaze and arrived at the girl.

"Now that's a tasty tomato," he said, nodding. "But I didn't think that was your taste."

"My tastes are universal," Magnus replied with a smile.

"Well, getta wiggle on. She won't be here all night. I'll watcha bar for you." Alfie slapped the bar. "You can trust me."

Magnus nodded to Max, his excellent bartender, and Max immediately made another South Side for Alfie. "To keep your whistle wet while I'm gone."

"Ver' kind," Alfie said, nodding. "You're an egg, Dry."

Magnus called his bar Mr. Dry's. America was technically now all "dry," alcohol being illegal everywhere. But the truth was, most places were "wet"—awash with the stuff. New York especially. Everyone in New York drank, and the fact that they now did so illegally only made it better. The speakeasy, as far as Magnus was concerned, was one of mankind's greatest achievements. Intimate, celebratory, illegal without being immoral—a frisson of danger without any real peril.

Mr. Dry's was not a large place—speakeasies rarely were. By nature, they were secret. His was concealed behind the facade of a wig store on West 25th Street. To get in, you needed to say the password to his very efficient doorman, who viewed the prospective guest through a small slit panel in a reinforced door in the back wall of the shop. Once inside, you squeezed through a narrow hallway and entered Magnus's proud domain—ten tables and a marble bar (imported from Paris) backed by a mahogany display of every elusive bottle of things exotic Magnus had been able to get his hands on.

Most of the space went to his stage and dance floor. It pulsated under the pounding of dancing feet. In the morning, it would be cleaned and waxed, and the scuff marks of a thousand blows of dance shoes would be wiped away. He gently slipped through the dancers, most so intense and inebriated that they were unaware he was there. He enjoyed the soft (and occasionally not so soft) pummeling of flying limbs and kicking heels. He enjoyed feeling the body heat and being carried by the movement and the surge of the dancers as they more or less became one solid, pulsating mass.

The little vampire was young—no more than sixteen—and she only came up to Magnus's chest height. He leaned down and spoke into her ear.

"Perhaps I can buy you a drink?" he said. "A private one? In the back?"

The tips of the fangs popped out again when she smiled.

Magnus already felt somewhat reassured—the half-fanged smile probably wasn't from hunger. Drunkenness could cause fangs to poke out a bit. But vampires, like mundanes, often sought after salty foods and amorous encounters when inebriated.

"This way," he said, pushing back a curtain and revealing a short hallway leading to a single door. Right behind the main club, Magnus had constructed a small and intensely private room with a zinc bar. This room was lined in large stained-glass panels, illuminated from behind with electric lights, portraying Dionysus, the Greek god of wine. This was where he kept the very best and the very worst of his stock, and this was where he conducted his most private business.

"I don't believe we've met before," he said as she plopped happily onto a bar stool and spun around.

"Oh, I know who *you* are. You're Magnus Bane."

She had one of those New York accents that Magnus was still getting used to, even though he had been here for several months. It was brassy and big, like a blinking neon sign. Her kid-leather dancing shoes had scuffed toes, and there was a mud stain halfway up the base of the heel, plus flecks of other substances that Magnus didn't want to know anything about. These were shoes for dancing *and* shoes for hunting.

"And what may I call you?"

"Call me Dolly," she said.

Magnus pulled a bottle of cold champagne out of the large tub of ice that contained at least sixty identical bottles.

"I like this place," Dolly said. "It's got class."

"I'm glad you think so."

"Lotsa places are classy," Dolly said, reaching into a jar on the bar and helping herself to some maraschino cherries, plucking them up with her long (and probably dirty) fingernails. "But they're fake classy, you know? This seems real classy. You got good wine. Like that stuff."

She indicated the cut-rate champagne Magnus was holding and pouring into a glass for her. The bottle, like the others in the tub, was certainly nice, but they'd all been filled with fizzed-up cheap wine and cunningly recorked. Vampires could drink quite a lot and could be expensive to have around, and he felt certain she would not be able to tell the difference. He was right. She drained half the glass in the first sip and held it out for a top-up.

"Well, Dolly," Magnus said, refilling her glass, "I certainly don't care what you get up to on the street or anywhere else, but I do like my clientele. I consider it a matter of good service to make sure vampires don't eat them under my roof."

"I didn't come here to eat," she said. "We go down to the Bowery for that. I was told to come down here and ask about you."

The shoes did bear out the Bowery story. Those downtown streets could be filthy.

"Oh? And who is so kind as to inquire about little me?"

"Nobody," the girl said.

"Nobody," Magnus said, "is one of my favorite names."

This caused the vampire girl to giggle and spin on her stool. She drained off the glass and held it out for more. Magnus refilled it once again.

"My friend..."

"Nobody."

"Nobody, yeah. I just met h—this person, but this person is one of mine, ya know?"

"A vampire."

"Right. Anyways, they want to tell you something," she said. "They said you gotta get out of New York."

"Oh really? And why is that?"

In reply, she giggled and half slid, half fell from the stool and broke into a shuffling and drunken private Charleston to the music that came pounding through the wall.

"See," she said, as she did her little dance, "things are about to get dangerous. Something about the mundie money and how it's an omen. See, it's all going to break, or something. All the money. And when it does, it means that the world is going to end..."

Magnus sighed internally.

The New York Downworld was one of the most ridiculous places he had ever been, which was partly the reason he now spent his time serving illegal alcohol to mundanes. And still, he couldn't avoid this nonsense. People came to bars to talk, and so did Downworlders. The werewolves were paranoid. The vampires were gossips. Everyone had a story. Something was always *about to happen*, something big. It was just part of the mood of the time. The mundanes were making absurd amounts of money on Wall Street and spending it on fripperies and moving pictures and booze. These were things Magnus could respect. But the Downworld dealt in half-baked omens and pointless rivalries. Clans were fighting one another for control of small, inconsequential patches of ground. The fey kept to themselves as ever, occasionally snatching the stray human from outside the Central Park Casino and luring them down to their world with the promise of a party they would never forget.

At least a pretty flapper vampire talking nonsense was better than a slobbering drunk werewolf. Magnus nodded as if listening and mentally counted the bottles of brandy and rum in the storage shelves below the bar.

"These mundies, see, they're trying to raise a demon..."

"Mundanes do that all too frequently," Magnus said, moving a misplaced bottle of gold rum that had been put in with the spiced. "Right now, they also enjoy sitting on the top of flagpoles and walking on the wings of airborne biplanes. This is the age of stupid hobbies."

"Well, these mundies mean business."

"They always mean business, Dolly," Magnus said. "It always ends messily. I've seen enough mundanes splattered on walls to last me—"

Suddenly a bell on the wall started ringing feverishly. This was followed by a loud, deep call from the main room.

"RAID!"

This was followed by a lot of screaming.

"Excuse me a moment," Magnus said. He set the bottle of cheap champagne on the bar and indicated that Dolly should help herself, as he was sure she would even without permission. He went back through into the main bar, where an atmosphere of general madness had taken over. The band didn't pack up, but they had stopped playing. Some people were gulping back drinks, others running for the door, still others crying and panicking.

"Ladies and gentlemen!" he called. "Please simply set your drinks on the tables. All will be well. Remain seated."

Magnus had enough regulars now that there was somewhat of an established routine. These people were sitting down and cheerfully lighting cigarettes, barely turning to look at the axes that were already picking their way through the door.

"Lights!" Magnus called dramatically.

At once, the bar staff turned off all the lights and the speakeasy was thrown into darkness, save for the glowing orange tips of cigarettes.

"Now, please, everyone," Magnus said, over the yells of police and the banging of the axe and the splintering of the wood. "If we could all count to three together. One!"

They joined in nervously for "two" and "three." There was a flash of blue, then a final crack as the door came down and the police tumbled inside. Then all at once, the lights came up again. But the speakeasy was gone. All the patrons found in front of them were porcelain teapots and cups of tea. The jazz band had been replaced by a string quartet, who immediately began playing soothing music. The bottles behind the bar were gone, replaced by a well-stocked bookshelf. Even the décor had changed—the walls were lined with bookshelves and velvet draperies, all concealing the bar and the stock of alcohol.

"Gentlemen!" Magnus threw open his arms. "Welcome to our tea and book circle. We were just about to discuss tonight's book, *Jude the Obscure*. You're just in time! I may have to ask you to pay for the door, but I understand the impulse. One simply mustn't be late to the discussion!"

The crowd began to fall about laughing. They waggled their teacups at the police and waved copies of the books.

Magnus tried to vary this routine every time. Once, when the lights came back up, he had transformed the bar into an apiary, with buzzing beehives all around the room. Another time it became a prayer circle, with many of the guests wearing the garb of nuns and ministers.

Usually, this confused the police so much that the raids were brief and relatively nonviolent. But each time, he sensed their frustration growing. Tonight the group was led by McMantry, as crooked a cop as Magnus had ever met. Magnus had refused to pay him off on principle, and now he was coming down on Mr. Dry's Bar. They had come prepared this time. Every officer had a tool—at least a dozen axes, just as many sledgehammers, crowbars, and even a shovel or two.

"Take them all," McMantry said. "Everyone goes in the wagon. And then take this joint apart."

Magnus waggled his fingers behind his back to conceal the blue light that webbed between them. At once, four panels fell away from the walls, revealing hallways and escape routes. His customers ran for them. They would come out in four different locations, some blocks away. Just a bit of gentle, protective magic. No one deserved to go to jail for having a cocktail. A few officers tried to follow, only to find the passages were suddenly blind.

Magnus let the heavy glamour drop, and the speakeasy regained its normal appearance. This stunned the police long enough to allow him to slip behind a nearby curtain and glamour himself invisible. He walked right out of the bar, past the officers. He paused only for a moment to watch them pull back the curtain and study the wall behind, looking for the way to access the escape hatch they assumed had to be there.

Back out on the street, it was a thick September night. New York often stayed hot this time of year, and New York humidity had its own special quality. The air was viscous, full of the murk of the East River and the Hudson and the sea and the swamp, full of smoke and ash, full of the smell of every kind of cooking food, and the raw smell of gas.

He walked down to one of the exit points, where an excited cluster of customers stood laughing and talking about what had just happened. This group was made up of some of his favorite regulars, including the handsome Alfie.

"Come on!" Magnus said. "I think we should continue this at my place, don't you?"

A dozen people agreed that this was an excellent idea. Magnus hailed a taxi, and some of the others did the same. Soon there was a merry little chain of taxis ready to go. Just as one more person was squeezing into the backseat with Magnus, Dolly leaned in the window and spoke into his ear.

"Hey, Magnus!" she said. "Don't forget. Watch the money!"

Magnus gave her a polite, *yes, whatever* nod, and she giggled and tripped off. She was such a tiny thing. Very pretty indeed. And very drunk. She would probably go off to the Bowery now and eat her fill of the city's less fortunate.

Then the train of taxis began to move, and the entire party (which, from a glance out the back window, looked to have expanded by another dozen) made its way uptown to the Plaza Hotel.

When Magnus woke the next morning, the first thing he noticed was the fact that it was much, much, much too bright. Someone really needed to get rid of the sun.

Magnus quickly worked out that the excessive brightness was due to the fact that all the curtains seemed to be missing from the bedroom of his suite. He then noted the four fully dressed (*sigh*) people sleeping around him on the bed, all oblivious to the sunlight and dead to the world.

The third thing he noticed, perhaps the most puzzling, was the pile of car tires at the foot of the bed.

It took Magnus a few moments and a number of strange contortions to get over the sleepers and out of his bed. There were easily twenty more sleeping and passed-out people all over the living room. The curtains were also missing from the windows of this room, but he could see where they'd all gone. People were using them as blankets and improvised tenting. Alfie alone was awake, sitting on the sofa and looking out at the sunny day miserably.

"Magnus," he groaned. "Kill me, won't you?"

"Why, that's *illegal*!" Magnus replied. "And you know how I feel about breaking the law. And who are all these people? There weren't this many when I fell asleep."

Alfie shrugged, indicating that the universe was mysterious and nothing would ever be fully understood.

"I mean it," Alfie said. "If you don't want to use that voodoo whatever, just hit me on the head with something. You gotta kill me."

"I'll get you a bracer," Magnus said. "Iced tomato juice and Tabasco, sliced grapefruits, and a plate of scrambled eggs, that's what we need. I'll have room service send up two dozen of each."

He stumbled over a few people to the phone, only to find that he had actually reached for a large, decorative cigarette dispenser. It was possible he was not quite at his best either.

"And coffee," he added, setting this down and picking up the telephone receiver with tremendous dignity. "I will order some of that as well."

Magnus placed the order with room service, who had by now stopped questioning Mr. Bane's unusual needs for things like twenty-four plates of scrambled eggs and "enough coffee to fill one of your larger bathtubs." He joined Alfie on the sofa and watched a few of his new guests turn and groan in their slumber.

"I gotta stop this," Alfie said. "I can't go on like this."

Alfie was clearly one of those people who turned maudlin after a good night out. Somehow, this only made him more attractive.

"It's just a hangover, Alfie."

"It's more than that. See, there's this girl..."

"Ah," Magnus said, nodding. "You know, the quickest way to mend a broken heart is to get right back on the wagon..."

"Not for me," Alfie said. "She was the only one. I make good money. I got everything I want. But I lost her. See..."

Oh no. A story. This was perhaps too maudlin and too much for the early hour, but handsome and heartbroken young men could occasionally be indulged. Magnus tried to look attentive. It was hard to do so over the glare of the sun and his desire to go back to sleep, but he tried. Alfie recounted a story about a girl named Louisa, something about a party, and some confusion over a letter, and there was something about a dog and possibly a speedboat. It was either a speedboat or a mountain cabin. Those things are hard to mix up, but it really was *much too early* for this. Anyway, there was definitely a dog and a letter, and it all ended in disaster and Alfie coming to Magnus's bar every night to drink away his sorrows. As the story lurched to its conclusion, Magnus saw the first of the sleepers on his floor start to show signs of life. Alfie did too, and he leaned in to speak to Magnus more privately.

"Listen, Magnus," Alfie said. "I know you can ... do things."

This sounded promising.

"I mean..." Alfie struggled for a moment. "You can do things that aren't natural..."

This sounded very promising *indeed*, at least at first. However, Alfie's saucer-eyed expression indicated that this was not an amorous inquiry.

"What do you mean?" Magnus asked.

"I mean..." Alfie lowered his voice further. "You do ... those things you do. They're ... they're magic. I mean, they have to be. I don't believe in the stuff, but..."

Magnus had maintained the premise that he was nothing but a showman. It was a premise that made sense, and most people were happy to accept it. But Alfie—an otherwise down-to-earth mundie—appeared to have seen through it.

Which was attractive. And worrying.

"What exactly are you asking me, Alfie?"

"I want her back, Magnus. There has to be a way."

"Alfie..."

"Or help me forget. I bet you could do that."

"Alfie..." Magnus didn't really want to lie, but this was not a discussion he was going to get into. Not now, and not here. Yet it seemed like he needed to say *something*.

"Memories are important," he said.

"But it *hurts*, Magnus. Thinking about her makes me ache."

Magnus didn't really want this kind of thing this early in the morning—this talk of aching memories and wanting to forget. This conversation needed to end, now.

"I need a quick splash in the bath to restore myself. Let room service in, won't you? You'll feel better once you eat something."

Magnus patted Alfie on the shoulder and made his way to the bathroom. He had to eject two more sleepers from the bathtub and the bathroom floor in order to engage in his ablutions. By the time he emerged, room service had produced six rolling tables laden with pitchers of tomato juice and all the eggs and grapefruit and coffee needed to make the morning bright again. Some of the near dead sleeping around the suite had risen and were now noisily eating and drinking and comparing notes to see who was feeling the worst.

"Did you get our presents, Magnus?" one of the men said.

"I did, thank you. I'd been needing some spare tires."

"We got them off a police car. To get them back for ruining your place."

"Very kind of you. Speaking of, I suppose I should go check on what's left of my establishment. The police didn't look happy last night."

No one paid much attention when he left. They continued to eat and drink and talk and laugh over their suffering, and occasionally run to the bathroom to be ill. It was this way more or less every night and every morning. Strangers appeared in his hotel room, always a wreck after the previous night. In the morning, they stuck themselves back together again. They rubbed at raccoon-eyed faces full of smeared makeup, looked for lost hats and feathers and beads and phone numbers and shoes and hours. It wasn't a bad life. It wouldn't last, but nothing ever did.

They would all be like Alfie in the end, crying on his sofa at dawn and regretting it all. Which was why Magnus stayed away from those kinds of problems. Keep moving. Keep dancing.

Magnus whistled as he closed the door to his suite, and he doffed his hat to a very disapproving-looking older lady in the hall who heard the ruckus inside. By the time he had taken the elevator down to the lobby, he was in a good enough mood to tip the elevator operator five dollars.

Magnus's good mood lasted only a few minutes. This taxi ride was considerably less merry than the last one. The sun was being obstinately bright, the taxi choked and sputtered, and the streets were more full of traffic than usual—six cars across, all honking at once, all blowing noxious fumes through the window. Every police car he saw reminded him of the indignities he had suffered last night.

When he reached 25th Street, the full extent of the destruction was immediately made clear. The door to the wig shop was broken and had been replaced (not very carefully) with a wooden board and a chain. Magnus opened this with a quick shot of blue light from his fingers and pulled the wood away. The wig shop had sustained fairly serious damage—displays overturned, wigs all over the floor in a shallow wash of beer and wine, looking like strange sea life. The hidden door had been ripped completely off its hinges and was thrown across the room. He sloshed his way through the tight hallway, which had about three inches of mixed and souring alcohol pooled on the recessed floor. The head of this stream came trickling down the three steps that led up to the bar. This door was completely gone, reduced to splinters. Beyond that, Magnus saw only destruction—shattered glass, broken tables, piles of debris. Even the innocent chandelier had been beaten down from its perch and lay in pieces on what was left of the dance floor.

But this was not the worst of it. Sitting in the wreckage on one of three unbroken chairs was Aldous Nix, the High Warlock of Manhattan.

"Magnus," he said. "Finally. I've been waiting for an hour."

Aldous was old—even by warlock standards. He predated the calendar. Based on his recollections of things, the general consensus was that he was probably just under two thousand years old. He had the appearance of a man maybe in his late fifties, with a fine white beard and a neatly trimmed head of white hair. His mark was his clawed hands and feet. The feet were disguised by specially made boots, the hands by the fact that he almost always kept one pocketed and the other wrapped around the silver ball handle of a long black cane.

That Aldous sat there in the middle of the wreckage was a sort of accusation.

"What have I done to deserve this honor?" Magnus said, carefully stepping onto the mess on the floor. "Or have you always wanted to see a deconstructed bar? It is something of a spectacle."

Aldous knocked a bit of broken bottle away with his cane.

"There's better business to be done, Magnus. Do you really want to spend your time selling illegal liquor to mundanes?"

"Yes."

"Bane..."

"*Aldous...*," Magnus said. "I've been involved in so many problems and battles. There's nothing wrong with wanting to live simply for a while and avoid trouble."

Aldous waved his hand at the wreckage.

"This isn't trouble," Magnus said. "Not real trouble."

"But it's also not a serious endeavor."

"There's nothing wrong with wanting to enjoy life a little. We have forever. Should we really spend all of it working?"

It was a stupid question to ask. Aldous probably would spend all of eternity working.

"Magnus, you can't have failed to notice that things are changing. Things are afoot. The Great Mundane War..."

"They always get into wars," Magnus said, picking up the bases of a dozen shattered wineglasses and setting them in a row.

"Not like that. Not so global. And they are approaching magic. They make light and sound. They communicate over distances. It doesn't worry you?"

"No," Magnus said. "It doesn't."

"So you don't see it coming?"

"Aldous, I've had a long night. What are you talking about?"

"It comes, Magnus." Aldous's voice was suddenly very deep. "You can feel it all around. It's coming, and everything will break apart."

"*What's* coming?"

"The break, and the fall. The mundanes put their faith in their paper money, and when that turns to ash, the world will turn upside down."

Being a warlock certainly didn't preclude you from going a little funny in the head. In fact, being a warlock could easily *make* you go a little funny in the head. When the true weight of eternity really settled on you—usually in the middle of the night when you were alone—the weight could be unbearable. The knowledge that all would die and you would live on and on, into some vast unknown future populated by who knew what, that everything would always keep falling away and you would go on and on...

Aldous had been thinking about it. He had the look.

"Have a drink, Aldous," Magnus said compassionately. "I keep a few special bottles hidden in a safe under the floor in the back. I have a Château Lafite Rothschild from 1818 that I've been saving for a sunny day."

"You think that's the solution to everything, don't you, Bane? Drinking and dancing and making love ... but I tell you this, something is coming, and we'd be fools to ignore it."

"When have I *ever* claimed not to be a fool?"

"Magnus!" Aldous stood suddenly and slammed the tip of his walking stick down, sending a flood of purple bolts crackling along the wreckage of the floor. Even when he was talking crazy, Aldous was a powerful warlock. Stick around for two thousand years—you're bound to pick up a thing or two.

"When you decide to be serious, come and find me. But don't wait too long. I have a new residence, at the Hotel Dumont, on 116th Street."

Magnus was left in the dripping remains of his bar. One Downworlder coming in and talking a load of nonsense about omens and disaster was to be ignored. But having that followed by a visit from Aldous, who seemed to be saying much the same thing ...

... unless those two rumors were one and the same, and they had both originated with Aldous, who was not sounding like the voice of complete reason.

That made sense, actually. The High Warlock of Manhattan gets a little strange, starts talking about doom and mundane money and disaster ... someone would pick that story up and carry it along, and like all stories, it would find its way to Magnus.

Magnus tapped his fingers on the cracked marble of his once-pristine bar. Time, he had noticed, moved more quickly these days. Aldous wasn't completely wrong about that. Time was like water, sometimes glacial and slow (the 1720s ... *never again*), sometimes a still pond, sometimes a gentle brook, and then a rushing river. And sometimes time was like vapor, vanishing even as you passed through it, draping everything in mist, refracting the light. That had been the 1920s.

Even in fast times like these, Magnus could not instantly reopen his bar. He had to keep up some pretense of normalcy. A few days, maybe a week. Maybe he would even clean it up the mundie way, by hiring people to come with buckets and wood and nails. Maybe he would even do it himself. It would probably do him good.

So Magnus rolled up his sleeves and set to work, collecting

broken glass, throwing broken chairs and tables into a pile. He got a mop and pushed along puddles of mixed booze and dirt and splinters. After a few hours of this, he grew tired and bored and snapped his fingers, setting the whole place to rights.

Aldous's words still preyed on his mind. Something should be done. Someone should be told. Someone more responsible and interested than him should take over this concern. Which, of course, meant only one group of people.

Shadowhunters would not come to speakeasies. They respected the mundane law against alcohol (always so tedious with their "The law is hard but it is the law"). This meant that Magnus had to take a trip to the Upper East Side, to the Institute.

The grandeur of the Institute never failed to impress him—the way it towered high and mighty above everything else, timeless and unmoving in its Gothic disapproval of all that was modern and changeable. Downworlders could not normally enter the Institute through the main door—the Sanctuary was their entrance. But Magnus was no ordinary Downworlder, and his connection to the Shadowhunters was long and well-known.

This didn't mean that he got a warm reception. The housekeeper, Edith, said nothing as she admitted him except, "Wait here." He was left in the foyer, where he eyed the fusty decorations with a critical eye. The Shadowhunters did love their burgundy wallpaper and their rose-shaped lamps and their heavy furnishings. Time would never move quickly here.

"Come on," Edith said, returning.

Magnus followed her down the hall to a reception room, where Edgar Greymark, the head of the Institute, stood in front of a bookstand.

"Edgar," Magnus said, nodding. "I see you've bowed to the pressure and installed a telephone."

Magnus pointed to a telephone sitting on a small table in a dark corner, as if it was being punished for existing.

"It's a dammed nuisance. Have you heard the noise it makes? But you can speak to the other Institutes easily and get ice delivered, so..."

He let the book he was reading close heavily.

"What brings you to see us, Magnus?" he said. "I understand you've been running a drinking establishment. Is that correct?"

"Quite correct," Magnus said with a smile. "Though it currently might be more useful as a pile of kindling."

Edgar didn't ask for an explanation of that remark, and Magnus didn't offer one.

"You are aware that the sale of liquor is currently against the law," Edgar went on, "but I suppose that's why you enjoy it."

"Everyone should have a hobby or two," Magnus said. "Mine just happen to include illegal trade, drinking, and carousing. I've heard of worse."

"We tend not to have time for hobbies."

Shadowhunters. Always better than you.

"I'm here because I've heard things in this drinking establishment of mine, things about the Downworld that you might want to know about."

Magnus recounted everything he could think of—everything Aldous had said, including his odd demeanor. Edgar listened, his expression never changing.

"You're basing this on the ramblings of Aldous Nix?" he said, when Magnus had finished. "Everyone knows Aldous isn't himself these days."

"I've lived longer than you," Magnus said. "My experience is wide, and I've learned to trust my instincts."

"We do not act on instinct," Edgar said. "Either you have information, or you do not."

"Considering our long history, Edgar, I think that perhaps you should act on what I am saying."

"What would you have us do?"

Magnus resented having to spell everything out. He had come to the Shadowhunters with information. It wasn't up to him to explain precisely how they should interpret it.

"Speak to him, perhaps?" Magnus said. "Do what you do best—keep an eye out."

"We are always watchful, Magnus." There was a slight edge of sarcasm to Edgar's tone that Magnus really did not appreciate. "We will bear all of this in mind. Thank you for coming to see us. Edith will show you out."

He rang a bell, and the sour-faced Edith appeared in an instant to take the Downworlder out of her house.

Before going to the Institute, Magnus had been resolved to do nothing. Just pass on the information and get on with his endless life. But Edgar's dismissal of his concerns motivated him. Aldous said the Hotel Dumont was on 116th Street, which wasn't far at all. That was just up in Italian Harlem, perhaps a twenty-minute walk away. Magnus set his course northward. New York was a place that changed very abruptly from neighborhood to neighborhood. The Upper East Side was moneyed and dignified to the point of pain. But as he went up, the houses got smaller, the driving more aggressive, and the horse carts more frequent. Above 100th Street, the children got more boisterous, playing stickball in the street and chasing one another as mothers shouted through windows.

The feeling on these streets was altogether more pleasant. There was more of a family atmosphere, with good smells coming from the windows. And it was nice to see a neighborhood where not everyone had white skin. Harlem was the center of black culture and the best music in the entire world. It was the hottest, most cutting-edge place to be.

Which, he supposed, was why someone had plopped down this grand monstrosity of a hotel. The Dumont didn't quite fit in with the brownstones and the shops and restaurants, but the Dumont didn't look like the kind of place that cared if its neighbors liked it or not. It sat back a bit, on a small side street that may very well have been custom-made for it. It had a great colonnaded front with dozens of sash windows, all with drawn curtains. A pair of heavy metal doors were firmly closed.

Magnus sat in the soda fountain across the street and decided to watch and wait. What he was waiting for, he wasn't sure. Something. Anything. He wasn't really sure that anything would happen at all, but he was now set on his course. The first hour or so was deadly dull. He read a newspaper to kill time. He ate a sardine sandwich and had some coffee. He used his power to retrieve a lost ball for some kids across the street, who had no idea he was doing so. He was almost ready to give up when a parade of extremely expensive automobiles began to roll up to the front of the hotel. It was like seeing a showing of the grandest cars in the world—a Rolls-Royce, a Packard, a few Pierce-Arrows, an Isotta Fraschini, three Mercedes-Benzes, and a Duesenberg—all polished to such a high degree that Magnus could hardly see them in the dazzling glow of the sunset. He blinked his watering eyes and observed driver after driver opening doors and releasing the cars' passengers.

These were most certainly wealthy people. The rich bought wonderful clothes you recognized. The *richest* had their people go to Paris and buy the entire new collection that no one outside of the fashion house had seen. These people belonged to the latter group. They were all, Magnus noted, between forty and sixty years of age. The men were all bearded and hatted, the women not quite young or free enough for the petal-pink Chanels and the ethereal chiffon Vionnets they had acquired. They all walked quickly into the hotel, without conversing or stopping to admire the sunset. They looked sufficiently self-important and grim to suggest that they could probably have come together to try to raise a demon. (People who tried to raise demons always looked like that.) But what troubled

Magnus the most was that they were clearly seeking Aldous's help in this. Aldous had powers and knowledge that Magnus couldn't even begin to guess at.

And so Magnus waited. About an hour passed. The chauffeurs brought the cars around in a row, and one by one, the group got into them and rolled back into the New York night. There were no demons. Nothing. Magnus left his stool and began walking back down to the Plaza, trying to make sense of it all.

Maybe it had all been nothing. Aldous took a dim view of mundanes. Perhaps he was simply playing with this group of supposedly important people. There were worse amusements than toying with a bunch of deluded and stupid millionaires, taking their money and telling them you were going to do magic for them. You could make a fortune in no time at all and make your way to the French Riviera and not lift a finger again for ten years. Maybe twenty.

But Aldous was not the kind of warlock who played those games, and ten or twenty years—those weren't even measures of time he counted.

Maybe Aldous had simply gotten weird. It happened. Magnus wondered if, hundreds of years from now, the same thing would happen to him. Maybe he would also hole himself up in a hotel and spend time with some rich people, doing who knew what. Was that really so different from what he was doing now? Hadn't he spent the morning clearing garbage from his mundane bar?

It was time to go home.

October 1929

Magnus had lost interest in his bar somewhat. His planned closure of a few days stretched into a week, then two, then three. With Mr. Dry's temporarily closed, a few of Magnus's regulars found themselves with nowhere to go. So, of course, they simply came to Magnus's hotel room every night. First it was just one or two, but within a week there was a constant stream of people. This included the hotel management, who politely suggested that Mr. Bane "might like to take his friends and associates elsewhere." Magnus replied, equally politely, that these were not friends or associates. Usually they were strangers. This did not make the management very happy.

And this wasn't entirely true, either. Alfie was there from the start, and now had taken up permanent residence on Magnus's sofa. He had grown only more morose as time wore on. He went off to wherever he worked during the day, came back drunk, and stayed that way. Then he stopped going to work.

"It's getting bad, Magnus," he said one afternoon, waking from a whiskey-induced stupor.

"I'm sure it is," Magnus said, not looking up from his copy of *War and Peace*.

"I mean it."

"I'm sure you do."

"Magnus!"

Magnus lifted his head wearily.

"It's getting bad. It can't last. It's already starting to crumble. See?"

He rattled a newspaper in Magnus's direction.

"Alfie, you need to be a bit more specific. Unless you are talking about that newspaper, which seems fine."

"I mean"—Alfie pulled himself up and looked over the back of the sofa—"that the entire financial structure of the United States could fall down at any second. Everybody said it could happen and I never believed them, but now it seems like it could really happen."

"These things do."

"How can you not care?"

"Practice," Magnus said, looking back to his book and turning the page.

"I don't know." Alfie slid down a bit. "Maybe you're right. Maybe it will all be fine. It has to be, right?"

Magnus didn't bother to point out that that wasn't what he had said. Alfie seemed appeased, and that was good enough. But now Magnus had lost the flow of what he was reading and no longer felt like continuing. These visitors were getting annoying.

After a few days, Magnus was completely tired of the company, but he was not inclined to throw them out. That would have been unseemly. He simply took a second suite on a different floor and stopped coming home. His guests seemed aware of this, but no one minded as long as the door to Magnus's old suite was open and no one cut off the room service account.

Magnus tried to fill the time with ordinary pursuits—reading, walks in Central Park, a talking picture or a show, some shopping. The heat broke, and a mellow October settled over the city. One day he hired a boat and spent the day drifting around Manhattan, looking at the skeletons of the many new skyscrapers and wondering what actually would happen if it all fell apart, and wondering how much he currently cared. He had seen governments and economies fall before. But these people ... they made big things and had a long way to fall.

So he opened some champagne.

He noticed that many people spent their days huddled around the stock tickers that graced every club and hotel, many restaurants, even some bars and barbershops. It amazed Magnus how these silly little clockworks under glass could fascinate some people. People gathered around them, sitting hour after hour, just watching the machine spit out a long tongue of paper full of symbols. Someone would catch the paper as it unscrolled and read the magic it contained.

The twenty-fourth of October brought the first scare, with the market tumbling and regaining a bit of footing. Everyone had an uneasy weekend; then the next week came, and everything got much worse. Then came Tuesday the twenty-ninth, and it all came down, just like everyone had apparently predicted, yet never really believed would happen. Magnus couldn't avoid the shock wave, not even in the peace of his room at the Plaza. The telephone began to ring. There were voices in the hall, even a scream or two. He went down to the lobby, where a full-on panic was in progress, people running out with their suitcases, every telephone cabinet occupied, a man crying in the corner.

Out on the street it was worse. A group of people outside were in fevered conversation.

"They're jumping out of buildings downtown," one man said. "I heard it. My friend works down there, and he says they're just opening the windows and throwing themselves out."

"So it's really happening?" another man said, grabbing his hat off his head and holding it over his heart, as if for protection.

"Happening? It's happened! The banks are starting to board up the doors!"

Magnus decided it was probably best to go back upstairs, lock the door, and get out a good bottle of wine.

He did get upstairs, and he did get into his room, but the moment he arrived, one of the recent strangers from his other room appeared in the doorway.

"Magnus," he said, his breath reeking of booze, "you gotta come. Alfie's trying to jump out the window."

"Well, that craze took hold fast," Magnus said with a sigh. "Where?"

"In your old room."

There was no time for Magnus to inquire how long they had known about his new room. He followed the man as he stagger-ran through the halls of the Plaza. They took the back stairs up three floors to the old suite, where the door was hanging open and several people were gathered around the door to Magnus's old bedroom.

"He's locked himself in there and put something against the

door," one of the men said. "We looked out of this window and saw him on the ledge."

"All of you, get out," Magnus said. "Now."

When they were gone, Magnus extended his hand and sent the bedroom door flying open. The bedroom window, once the source of a beautiful view of Central Park and too much sunlight, now framed the crouching figure of Alfie. He was perched on the thin concrete lip just outside, nervously smoking a cigarette.

"Don't come any closer, Magnus!" he said.

"I don't plan on it," Magnus said, sitting on the bed. "But could you share your cigarettes? This is my room you plan on defenestrating from, after all."

This puzzled Alfie for a moment, but he carefully reached into his pocket, produced a pack of cigarettes, and threw them inside.

"So," Magnus said, picking them up off the floor and pulling one from the pack, "before you go, why don't you tell me what this is all about?"

He snapped his fingers and the cigarette caught flame. This was entirely for Alfie's benefit, and definitely caught his attention.

"You ... you know what this is about ... what did you just do?"

"I lit a cigarette."

"I mean, what did you just *do?*"

"Oh, that." Magnus crossed his legs and sat back a bit. "Well, I think you've guessed by now, Alfie, that I'm not like the other children."

Alfie squat-bounced on his heels for a moment, considering this. His gaze was clear, and Magnus thought this was probably the first time in weeks that he had been completely sober.

"So it's true," he said.

"So it's true."

"So, what are you?"

"What I am is someone who doesn't want you to jump out of the window. The rest are details."

"Give me one good reason not to jump," Alfie said. "Everything is gone. Louisa. Everything I owned, everything I made."

"Nothing is permanent," Magnus said. "I know this from experience. But you can get new things. You can meet new people. You can go on."

"Not when I remember what I had," Alfie said. "So if you are ... whatever you are, you can do something, can't you?"

Magnus drew on the cigarette for a moment in thought.

"Come inside, Alfie," he finally said. "And I will help you."

The actual process of altering memory was tricky. The mind is a complex web, and memory is important to learning. Pull the wrong memory and you might make someone who forgets that fire burns. But memories can be softened, or shortened. A talented warlock—and Magnus was nothing if not talented—can embroider the past into something quite different in shape and tone.

But it was not easy work.

Why Magnus was doing this for no money for a mundane who had been freeloading off him for weeks was unclear. Maybe it was because this day was a day of great suffering, and this was the part of the suffering Magnus could end.

An hour later Alfie walked out of his suite not quite remembering a girl named Louisa, who was a bus fare collector or something. Perhaps a librarian in his hometown? He couldn't have told you why he even had thought of her name. He also had no clear recollection of his brief fortune.

It was tiring, and when it was done, Magnus leaned against the sill of the window and looked over the darkening city, over the great expanse of Central Park.

That was when he noticed the strange light in the sky, right over the uptown area. It was a cone-shaped light, smaller toward the skyline and widening into the clouds, and it had a faintly greenish cast.

It was right over the Hotel Dumont.

* * *

There was no getting a cab. Every cab in the city was taken, and they were all speeding. Everybody was going somewhere, trying to ditch stocks or sell something, or they were just moving in total panic, zigzagging the city in a frenzy. So Magnus ran up the east side of the park, all the way to 116th Street. The Hotel Dumont looked exactly the same as it had when Magnus had last seen it. All the curtains were still drawn, the doors still closed. It was cold, quiet, and unwelcoming. But when Magnus tried the front door, he found it unlocked.

The first odd thing was that the hotel seemed to be completely vacant. There was no one at the desk, no one in the lobby, no one anywhere. It was certainly a magnificent setting, with a graceful and gilded grand staircase. And it was all very plush and padded. A rich red-and-gold carpet covered the floor, and the windows were covered with heavy drapes that stretched from floor to ceiling. It was cool, shaded, muffled, and disturbingly quiet. Magnus looked up and around, right up to the frescoed ceiling with its fat-faced cherubs pointing at one another and gleefully swinging on vine swings in gardens.

Just to the left, there was a wide archway flanked by pillars covered in a floral pattern. This clearly led to one of the hotel's grander rooms and seemed as likely a place as any to look. Magnus opened this door. It led to a ballroom—an utterly magnificent one—with a white marble floor and a lacing of gilded balconies all around the room, broken by gilded mirrors that reflected the room back on itself over and over.

They also reflected the pile of human bodies scattered at the far end of the floor, around what appeared to be a highly polished granite slab. That these were the same people Magnus had seen getting out of the many expensive cars, he was fairly certain. There were some faces left, some bits of fine clothing scattered around the room in strips and ribbons, sometimes still attached to a loose arm or torso. The floor on that end of the room was entirely blackish-red, the blood having spread and pooled evenly over the marble like a fine glaze.

"By the Angel..."

Magnus turned and found Edgar Greymark standing behind him, in full Shadowhunter battle black, his seraph blade drawn.

"Good of you to come," Magnus said. The remark was meant to be sarcastic but came out flat. It *was* good of them to come. Whatever was happening, help would be required.

"Did you think we would just ignore your warning?" Edgar asked.

Magnus decided not to reply to that. They probably had ignored his warning and, like him, seen the light in the sky.

"Who are these people?" Edgar asked.

"I believe these are some mundanes who came here to see Aldous."

"And where is Aldous?"

"I haven't seen him. I've only arrived myself."

Edgar raised his hand, and a half-dozen more Shadowhunters appeared and went to the bodies and examined them.

"Looks like a Behemoth attack to me," one girl said as she examined a pile of blood and fleshy bits and some shredded crepe de chine. "Messy. Disorganized. And these are probably double rows of teeth marks, but it's hard to tell..."

Behind them, there was a massive bang, and they all turned as a young man yelled and dropped something to the ground, which smoked and hissed.

"My Sensor exploded," he growled.

"I think we can assume some very serious demonic activity," Edgar said. "Search the hotel. Find Aldous Nix and bring him here."

The Shadowhunters ran off, and Edgar and Magnus remained with the pile of bodies.

"Do you have any idea what might be happening here?" Edgar asked.

"I told you all I knew," Magnus said. "I came because I saw something in the sky. I found this."

"What is Aldous capable of?"

"Aldous is two thousand years old. He's capable of *anything*."

"Aldous Nix is two thousand years old?"

"So I've heard. He doesn't invite me to his birthday parties."

"He seemed a bit dotty to me, but I never thought ... well, it doesn't matter what I thought. We clearly have several demons in the area. That's our first concern. And Nix..."

"Is here," said a voice.

Aldous stepped out from behind one of the heavy wall hangings. He leaned heavily on his cane, walking slowly to the granite slab, where he sat. Edgar raised his weapon a bit, but Magnus steadied his arm.

"What happened here, Aldous?" Magnus asked.

"It was merely a test," Aldous said. "For the benefit of my sponsors, who have kindly engaged this entire hotel to allow me to do my work in peace."

"Your sponsors," Magnus said. "These people here, on the floor, in pieces."

"What is this work?" Edgar asked.

"The work? Ah. Now that is an interesting subject. But not for your ears. I will speak to him." He pointed to Magnus. "The rest of you can go and keep busy. You Shadowhunters always keep busy. There must be ten demons out there. I didn't make note of them all, but as the girl said, they looked to be mostly Behemoths. Nasty things. Go kill them."

Edgar Greymark was not the kind of man who liked to be dismissed, but Magnus gave him a look and tried to encourage him to back away.

"Yes," Edgar growled. "We do have some work. But do not leave, Nix. We will be back to discuss this."

Magnus nodded, and Edgar left the ballroom, shutting the

doors loudly behind him. Aldous regarded his gnarled hands for a moment before speaking.

"Magnus, we don't belong here. We never have belonged here. I've lived in this world longer than anyone I know, and that is the only truth I can rely on. I'm sure you've come to that conclusion as well."

"Not exactly," Magnus said. He stepped a bit closer but avoided the great sea of blood and bodies that lay between them.

"Not exactly?"

"I sometimes feel a bit out of place, but I very much consider myself of this world. Where else would I be from?"

"You may have been born here, but you originate in another dimension."

"You mean the Void?"

"I mean that exactly. I intend to go where I do belong. I want to go to the only place I feel I can truly call my home. I want to go to Pandemonium. I was opening up a Portal to allow me to get there."

"And these people?"

"These people believed they ran the world. They believed that their money entitled them to control. They heard about me, they came to me seeking a way to gain that control without war, without force. And I told them that I would expose them to a power they never knew possible if they gave me what I needed. So they gave me this hotel. I've been working here for some months, preparing the way. This entire building is now a latticework of spells and enchantments. The walls are spun with electrum and demon metal. It is a channel now. It will be the perfect and strongest Portal."

"And they came here..."

"For a demonstration. I did tell them there were risks. Perhaps I wasn't clear enough. I thought I was..."

He smiled a bit at this.

"They were monsters, Magnus. They could not be allowed to live. Stupid mundanes, thinking they could rule their world by harnessing *our* power? No. They died quickly."

"And, I would imagine, in great pain and terror."

"Perhaps. But their sufferings have ended. And now, so have mine. Come with me."

"Come with you? To Pandemonium? To the *Void*? And here I thought that my invitation to summer in New Jersey was the worst I had ever received."

"This isn't the time for jokes, Bane."

"Aldous," Magnus said, "you are talking about going to the demon realm. You do not come back from there. And you know what horrors you would face."

"We don't know what it's like. We don't know anything. I wish to know. My final wish is for knowledge of that most mysterious place, my true home. The final step to finish the spell," he said, pulling up on the balled head of his cane and revealing a knife. "A few drops of warlock blood. Just a bit will do. A slice across the palm."

Aldous looked at the knife thoughtfully, then at Magnus.

"If you stay here, the Portal will open, and you will come with me. If you do not wish to come, leave now."

"Aldous, you can't—"

"I most certainly can, and I'm about to. Make your choice, Magnus. Stay or go, but if you go, go now."

What was now extremely clear to Magnus was that Aldous was insane. You did not plan trips to the Void if you were compos mentis. Going to the Void was an act greater and more terrible than suicide—it was sending yourself to Hell. But it was also very, very hard to talk to people who had gone insane. Alfie could be talked off the window with reason. It would not be so easy with Aldous. Physical force was just as difficult an approach. Any move Magnus made here would likely be predicted and met with equal or greater strength.

"Aldous..."

"You stay then? You come with me?"

"No. I just—I—"

"You worry for me," Aldous said. "You think I don't know what I'm doing."

"I wouldn't put it like that, exactly..."

"I have considered this for a long time, Magnus. I know what I am doing. So please. Stay or go. Decide now, as I am going to open the Por—"

The arrow made a kind of singing noise as it cut through the air. It entered Aldous's chest like a knife sliding easily into an apple. Aldous sat upright for a moment, looking at it; then he slumped to the side, dead.

Magnus watched his blood hit the granite.

"RUN," he yelled.

The young Shadowhunter was still proudly looking at his work, how perfectly he had hit his mark. He didn't notice the web of cracks spreading from the altar and across the floor, splintering the white marble into hundreds and thousands of pieces with a sound like breaking ice.

Magnus ran. He ran in a way he wasn't aware he could run, and when he reached the Shadowhunter, he grabbed him and dragged him along. They had just reached the door and jumped out when one great belch of fire exploded into the foyer, filling the room with fire from floor to ceiling. Just as quickly, the fire was suctioned back into the ballroom. The doors of the hotel pulled themselves shut. The very building shook as if an enormous vacuum had appeared just over it and was sucking it up.

"What's happening?" said the Shadowhunter.

"He's opened some kind of channel to the Void," Magnus said, staggering to his feet.

"What?"

Magnus shook his head. There was no time to explain.

"Was everyone out of the building?" he asked.

"I'm not sure. The demons were both inside and out. We caught a half dozen of them in the street, but..."

The building shuddered and seemed to stretch just an inch or two, as if it was being pulled upward.

"Get back from here," Magnus said. "I have no idea what happens next, but it looks like this whole thing could ... just get back!"

In all his years, in all his studies, Magnus had never encountered anything that had prepared him for this—a building turned into a perfect Portal, a warlock who wanted to go home to the Void, using his own blood as a key. This was not in the lesson books. This would require guesswork. And a lot of luck. And probably some stupidity.

If he was wrong at any point, which he likely would be, he would be sucked into the Void. Into Hell itself. Which was where the stupidity came in.

Magnus pulled open the door. The Shadowhunter behind him cried out, but Magnus just yelled for him to stay back.

This is a terrible idea, Magnus thought as he found himself in the lobby again. *This may be the worst idea I've ever had.*

The fire that had blasted into the heart of the building had scorched every surface, blackening the ceiling, destroying the furnishings, exposing the floor under the carpet, and charring the great staircase. The doors to the ballroom, however, were completely unharmed.

Magnus stepped back inside the ballroom carefully.

Still not sucked into the Void, he thought. *Good. Definitely good.*

The bodies were now smoldering skeletons, and the white marble floor was completely fractured. The blood had evaporated and left a dark stain. The granite slab, however, was fine. It was also levitating, about six feet from the ground, bathed in the faint green light Magnus had seen earlier. Aldous was nowhere to be seen.

What are you?

The voice came from nowhere. It was in the room. It was outside. It was in Magnus's head.

"A warlock," Magnus answered. "And what are you?"

We are many.

"Please don't say you are legion. Someone's taken that."

Do you make mirth from the mundane scriptures, warlock?

"Just breaking the ice," Magnus said to himself.

Ice?

"Where is Aldous?" Magnus said, more loudly.

He is with us. Now you will come with us. Come to the altar.

"I think I'll pass," Magnus said. "I've got a place here I like a lot."

This was interesting. It didn't seem that the demons could come out. If they could, they would have. This was what demons did. But a connection had been opened. A one-way connection, but still a connection.

Magnus stepped just a tiny bit closer, trying to look for any markings on the floor, anything to tell him how large the Portal was. There was nothing.

Warlock, do you not tire of your life?

"That's a very philosophical question for a nameless and faceless voice from a Void," Magnus replied.

Do you not tire of eternity? Do you not wish to end your suffering?

"By leaping into the Void? Not really."

You are like us. You have our blood. You are one of us. Come and be welcome. Come and be with your own.

Blood...

If warlock blood opened the Portal ... well, warlock blood might be able to close it.

... or not.

It was as good a guess as any.

"Why would you want that?" Magnus asked. "Pandemonium has to be a pretty crowded place, considering you're always trying to leave it."

Would you not know your father?

"My father?"

Yes, warlock. Your father. Would you not know him?

"My father never took much interest in me," Magnus said.

Would you not know your father, even if you spoke to him?

Magnus stopped on that one.

"No," he said. "I don't suppose I would. Unless you are trying to tell me that what I am hearing now is the voice of my father."

You hear your own blood, warlock.

Magnus regarded the levitating slab, the destruction, the remains of the bodies. He also became dimly aware of a presence behind him. Some of the Shadowhunters had come inside and were looking at the slab, but seemed to hear nothing.

"Magnus?" one of them asked.

"Keep back," Magnus replied.

Why do you protect them? They would not protect you.

Magnus went to the closest Shadowhunter, grabbed a blade, and cut himself.

"You." He pointed to the Shadowhunter who had shot Aldous. "Give me an arrow. Now."

The arrow was handed over, and Magnus tipped it in his blood. Then he rubbed some more blood down the shaft for good measure. He didn't need the bow. He directed the arrow at the slab with all his might, casting every Portal-closing spell he knew.

It felt like he was locked in place, his entire body concrete, time stretched and slow. Magnus was no longer certain where, or maybe even what, he was, only that he was still spell-casting, only that the altar remained, and the voices in his mind were yelling. Hundreds of voices. Thousands of them.

Magnus...

Magnus, come to me...

Magnus, come...

But Magnus held on. And then the slab fell to the ground, breaking into countless pieces.

There was a figure leaning against Magnus's hotel door when he returned home that night.

"You got the message then, huh?" Dolly said. "About the mundie money? Guess it all went bust, huh?"

"It does appear to have all gone bust," Magnus said.

"I didn't think you believed me."

Magnus leaned against the opposite wall and sighed heavily. There was no noise from any of the rooms on the hall, except for some distant, muffled yelling at the far end. He got the feeling that many people were probably leaving the hotel now that they had no money to pay the bill, or they were sitting behind their doors in stunned silence. And yet they had no idea that the crash was really the least of their worries, and the real danger had been averted. They would never know. They never did.

"You look tired," Dolly said. "Like you need a pick-me-up."

"I just closed a Portal to the Void. I need sleep. About three days' worth."

Dolly let out a low whistle.

"My friend said you're a hot potato. She wasn't joking, huh?"

"She?"

Dolly slapped a hand over her mouth, nicking her nose with her long, lacquered nails.

"Oops!"

"Who sent you?" Magnus asked.

Dolly lowered her hand and flashed a smile.

"A good friend of yours."

"I'm not sure I have any good friends."

"Oh, you do." Dolly swung her tiny beaded purse in a loop. "You do. See ya around, Magnus."

She made her way down the hall with a swinging step, turning around every once in a while to look back at him. Magnus slid down the wall a few inches, feeling the exhaustion hanging over his entire body. But with one massive effort, he pulled himself up and hurried after Dolly. He watched from around the corner as she got into an elevator, and he immediately pushed the button for the next one.

This elevator was quite full of grim-looking people, visibly shattered by the day's news. So what he was going to do next was very unfortunate for them.

Magnus flicked his fingers and took over the control of the elevator from the operator, sending it on a very fast, somewhat uncontrolled descent. He'd tipped the operator very well the other day, so he felt he had a pass to take over if he liked. He had no such pass for the other passengers, who all started screaming as the elevator dropped floor after floor.

He made it to the lobby before Dolly, pushing past the still-traumatized (and several praying) people in his elevator. He ducked through the lobby, staying off to the side, behind columns and potted palms and groups of people. He slipped inside a telephone cabinet and watched Dolly pass by, her heels clicking lightly on the marble floor. He followed her, as quietly and inconspicuously as possible, to the front door, glamouring himself to slip past the doorman. There was a car just outside, a massive red Pierce-Arrow, with silver curtains over the windows of the passenger area, concealing the inhabitant's face. The door, however, was open. A driver stood by, at attention. Through the opening, Magnus could see a foot and an ankle, both very handsome, and a little silver shoe, and a bit of stockinged leg. Dolly bounced over to the car and leaned into the open door. They had a conversation Magnus couldn't hear, and then Dolly proceeded to climb inside the car, giving all the people in front of the Plaza a nice look at her rear end. Then the passenger leaned forward to speak to the driver, and Magnus caught her face in profile. There was no mistaking the face.

It was Camille.

Saving Raphael Santiago

By Cassandra Clare and Sarah Rees Brennan

He uncoiled, as swift as a snake, and sprang.

It was only because Magnus had seen where the vampire was looking and because he knew how Raphael felt, the exact exquisitely cold feeling of being an outcast, so alone that he barely seemed to exist, that he moved fast enough.

—Saving Raphael Santiago

THEY'RE ALL DEAD
AND I AM DEAD TOO.
GRAB

It was a violent heat wave in the late summer of 1953. The sun was viciously pummeling the pavement, which seemed to have become flatter than usual in submission, and some Bowery boys were opening a fire hydrant to make a fountain in the street and gain a few minutes of relief.

It was the sun getting to him, Magnus thought later, that had filled him with the desire to be a private eye. That and the Raymond Chandler novel he had just completed.

Still, there was a problem with the plan. On the covers of books and in films, most detectives looked like they were dressed up in Sunday suits for a small-town jamboree. Magnus wished to wash away the stain of his newly adopted profession and dress in a way that was both suitable to the profession, pleasing to the eye, and on the cutting edge of fashion. He ditched the trench coat and added some green velvet cuffs to his gray suit jacket, along with a curly-brimmed bowler hat.

The heat was so awful that he had to take off his jacket as soon as he set foot out of doors, but it was the thought that counted, and besides, he was wearing emerald-green suspenders.

Becoming a detective wasn't really a decision based wholly on his wardrobe. He was a warlock, and people—well, not everyone thought of them as people—often came to him for magical solutions to their problems, which he gave them, for a fee. Word had spread throughout New York that Magnus was the warlock who would get you out of a jam. There was a Sanctuary, too, up in Brooklyn, if you needed to hide, but the witch who ran it didn't solve your problems. Magnus solved problems. So why not get paid for it?

Magnus had not thought that simply deciding to become a private eye would cause a case to land in his lap the moment he painted the words MAGNUS BANE, PRIVATE DETECTIVE onto his window in bold black letters. But as if someone had whispered his private conviction into Fate's ear, a case arrived.

Magnus arrived back at his apartment building after getting an ice-cream cone, and when he saw her, he was glad that he'd finished it. She was clearly one of those mundanes who knew enough about the Shadow World to come to Magnus for magic.

He tipped his hat to her and said, "Can I help you, ma'am?"

She wasn't a blonde to make a bishop kick a hole through a stained-glass window. She was a small dark woman and though she was not beautiful, she had a bright, intelligent charm about her, powerful enough so that if she wanted any windows smashed, Magnus would see what he could do. She was wearing a slightly worn but still very becoming plaid dress, belted at her small waist. She looked to be in her late thirties, the same age as Magnus's current lady companion, and under black curling hair she had a small heart-shaped face, and eyebrows so thin that they gave her a challenging air that made her both more attractive and more intimidating.

She shook his hand, her hand small but her grip firm. "I am Guadalupe Santiago," she said. "You are a—" She waved her hand. "I do not know the word for it precisely. A sorcerer, a magic maker."

"You can say 'warlock,' if you like," said Magnus. "It doesn't matter. What you mean is, someone with the power to help you."

"Yes," said Guadalupe. "Yes, that's what I meant. I need you to help me. I need you to save my son."

Magnus ushered her in. He thought he understood the situation now that she had mentioned help for a relative. People would often come to him for healing, not as often as they came to Catarina Loss but often enough. He would much rather heal a young mundane boy than one of the haughty Shadowhunters who came to him so often, even if there was less money in it for him.

"Tell me about your son," he said.

"Raphael," said Guadalupe. "His name is Raphael."

"Tell me about Raphael," said Magnus. "How long has he been sick?"

"He is not sick," said Guadalupe. "I fear he may be dead." Her voice was firm, as if she were not voicing what must assuredly be the most horrible fear of every parent.

Magnus frowned. "I don't know what people have told you, but I can't help with that."

Guadalupe held up a hand. "This is not about ordinary sickness or anything that anyone in my world can cure," she told him. "This is about your world, and how it has touched mine. This is about the monsters from whom God has turned his face away, those who watch in the darkness and prey on innocents."

She took a turn about his living room, her plaid skirt belling about her brown legs.

"*Los vampiros*," she whispered.

"Oh God, not the bloody vampires again," said Magnus. "No pun intended."

The dread words spoken, Guadalupe regained her courage and proceeded with her tale. "We have all heard whispers of such creatures," she said. "Then there were more than whispers. There was one of the monsters, creeping around our neighborhood. Taking little girls and boys. One of my Raphael's friends, his small brother was taken and found almost on his own doorstep, his little body drained of blood. We prayed, we mothers all prayed, every family prayed, that the scourge would be lifted. But my Raphael, he had started hanging around with a crowd of boys who were a little older than him. Good boys, you understand, from good families, but a little—rough, wanting a little too much to show that they were men before they truly were men at all, if you know what I mean?"

Magnus had stopped making jokes. A vampire hunting children for sport—a vampire who had the taste for it and no inclination to stop—was no joke. He met Guadalupe's eyes with a level, serious gaze, to show that he understood.

"They formed a gang," said Guadalupe. "Not one of the street gangs, but—well, it was to protect our streets from the monster, they said. They tracked him to his lair once, and they were all talking about how they knew where he was, how they could go get him. I should have— I was not paying attention to the boys' talk. I was afraid for my younger boys, and it all seemed like a game. But then Raphael, and all his friends ... they disappeared, a few nights ago. They'd stayed out all night before, but this—this is too long. Raphael would never make me worry like this. I want you to find out where the vampire is, and I want you to go after my son. If Raphael is alive, I want you to save him."

If a vampire had already killed human children, a gang of teenagers coming after him would seem like bonbons delivered to his door. This woman's son was dead.

Magnus bowed his head. "I will try to find out what happened to him."

"No," said the woman.

Magnus found himself looking up, arrested by her voice.

"You don't know my Raphael," she said. "But I do. He is with older boys, but he is not the tagalong. They all listen to him. He is only fifteen, but he is as strong and as quick and as clever as a grown man. If only one of them has survived, he will be that one. Do not go looking for his body. Go and save Raphael."

"You have my word," Magnus promised her, and meant it.

He was in a hurry to leave. Before he visited the Hotel Dumont, the place which had been abandoned by mortals and haunted by vampires since the 1920s, the place where Raphael and his friends had gone, he had other inquiries to make. Other Downworlders would know about a vampire who was breaking the Law that flagrantly, even if they had been hoping the vampires would work it out among themselves, even if the other Downworlders had not yet decided to go to the Shadowhunters.

Guadalupe grasped Magnus's hand before he went, though, and her fingers clung to him. Her challenging look had turned beseeching. Magnus had the feeling she would never have begged for herself, but she was willing to beg for her boy.

"I gave him a cross to wear around his throat," she said. "The padre at Saint Cecilia's gave it to me with his own hands, and I gave it to Raphael. It is small and made of gold; you will know him by it." She took a shaking breath. "I gave him a cross."

"Then you gave him a chance," said Magnus.

Go to faeries for gossip about vampires, to werewolves for gossip about faeries, and do not gossip about werewolves, because they try to bite your face off: that was Magnus's motto.

He happened to know a faerie who worked in Lou Walters's Latin Quarter nightclub, on the seedier and nakeder side of Times Square. Magnus had gone to see Mae West here a time or two and had spotted a chorus girl with a glamour that covered up her faerie wings and pale amethyst skin. He and Aeval had been friendly ever since—as friendly as you could be when both you and the dame were in it only for information.

She was sitting on the steps, already in costume. There was a great deal of delicate lilac flesh on display.

"I'm here to see a faerie about a vampire," he said in a low voice, and she laughed.

Magnus couldn't laugh back. He had the feeling that he would not be able to shake off the memory of Guadalupe's face or her hold on his arm anytime soon. "I'm looking for a boy. Human. Taken by one of the Spanish Harlem clan, most likely."

Aeval shrugged, one graceful fluid motion. "You know

vampires. Could be any one of them."

Magnus hesitated, and then added, "The word is, this vampire likes them very young."

"In that case..." Aeval fluttered her wings. Even the most hardened Downworlders didn't like the thought of preying on children. "I might have heard something about a Louis Karnstein."

Magnus motioned for her to go on, leaning in and tipping back his hat so she could speak into his ear.

"He was living in Hungary until very recently. He's old and powerful, which is why the Lady Camille has welcomed him. And he has a particular fondness for children. He thinks their blood is the purest and sweetest, as young flesh is the tenderest. He was chased out of Hungary by mundanes who found his lair ... who found all the children in it."

Save Raphael, Magnus thought. It seemed a more and more impossible mission.

Aeval looked at him, her huge oval eyes betraying a faint flicker of worry. When the fey were worried, it was time to panic.

"Get it done, warlock," she said. "You know what the Shadowhunters will do if they find out about someone like that. If Karnstein is up to his old tricks in our city, it will be the worse for us all. The Nephilim will kill every vampire they see. It will be seraph blades first and questions later for everybody."

Magnus did not like to go near the Hotel Dumont if he could help it. It was decrepit and unsettling, it held bad memories, and it also occasionally held his evil former lady love.

But today it seemed like the hotel was his inescapable destination.

The sun was scalding in the sky, but it would not be for long. If Magnus had vampires to fight, he wanted to do it when they were at their weakest.

The Hotel Dumont was still beautiful, but barely so, Magnus thought as he walked inside. It was being buried by time, thick clusters of spiderwebs forming curtains on every arch. Ever since the twenties the vampires had considered it their private property and had hung around there. Magnus had never asked how Camille and the vampires had been involved in the tragedy of the 1920s, or what right they felt they now had to the building. Possibly the vampires simply enjoyed the allure of a place that was both decadent and abandoned. Nobody else came near it. The mundanes whispered that it was haunted.

Magnus had not let go of the hope that mundanes would come back, claim and restore it, and chase the vampires away. It would annoy Camille so much.

A young vampire hurried toward Magnus across the foyer, the colors of her red-and-green cheongsam and her henna-dyed hair vivid in the gray gloom.

"You are not welcome here, warlock!" she said.

"Am I not? Oh dear, what a social faux pas. I do apologize. Before I go, may I ask one thing? What can you tell me about Louis Karnstein?" Magnus asked conversationally. "And the children he has been bringing into the hotel and murdering?"

The girl shrank back as if Magnus had brandished a cross in her face.

"He's a guest here," she said, low. "And the Lady Camille said we were to show him every honor. We didn't know."

"No?" Magnus asked, and disbelief colored his voice like a drop of blood in water.

The vampires of New York were careful, of course. There was a minimum of human bloodshed, and any "accidents" were covered up fast, under the nose of Shadowhunters as they were. Magnus could easily believe, however, that if Camille had reason to please a guest, she would let him get away with murder. She would do it as easily as she would have the guest plied with luxurious surroundings: silver, velvet, and human lives.

And Magnus did not believe for a second that once Louis

Karnstein had brought the succulent morsels home, carrying all the blame but willing to share some of the blood, that they had not feasted. He looked at the delicate girl and wondered how many people she had killed.

"Would you rather," he said very gently, "that I go away and come back with the Nephilim?"

The Nephilim—the bogeyman for monsters, and all those who could be monsters. Magnus was sure this girl could be a monster if she wanted. He knew that he could be a monster himself.

He knew something else. He did not intend to leave a young boy in the monsters' lair.

The girl's eyes widened. "You're Magnus Bane," she said.

"Yes," Magnus said. It was sometimes good to be recognized.

"The bodies are upstairs. In the blue room. He likes to play with them ... after." She shuddered and stepped out of his way, disappearing back into the shadows.

Magnus squared his shoulders. He assumed the conversation had been overheard, since no challenge was offered to him and no other vampires arrived as he made his way up the curving staircase, the gold and scarlet of it lost under a carpet of gray but the shape intact. He went higher and higher to the apartments, where he knew that the vampire clan of New York would entertain their valued guests.

He found the blue room easily enough: it was one of the largest and had probably been the most grand of the hotel's apartments. If this had still been a hotel in any normal sense of the word, the guest in these quarters would have had to pay substantial damages. A hole had been staved in the high ceiling. The arched ceiling had been painted baby blue, robin's egg blue, the delicate blue that artists imagined the summer sky to be.

The true summer sky showed through the hole in the roof, a blazing unforgiving white, as relentless as the hunger that drove Karnstein, burning as brightly as a torch wielded by someone going to face a monster.

Magnus saw dust all over the floor, dust that he did not think was simply an indication of the accumulation of time. He saw dust, and he saw bodies: humped-up, tossed aside like rag dolls, sprawled like crushed spiders upon the ground and against the walls. There was no grace in death.

There were the bodies of teenage boys, the ones who had come in an eager fearless bevy to hunt the predator who was stalking their streets, who had innocently thought good would triumph. And there were other bodies, the older bodies of younger children. The children that Louis Karnstein had seized off Raphael Santiago's streets, and killed, and kept.

There was no saving these children, Magnus thought. There was nothing in this room but blood and death, and the echo of fear, the loss of all possibility of redemption.

Louis Karnstein was mad, then. It happened sometimes, with age and distance from humanity. Magnus had seen it happen with a fellow warlock thirty years before.

Magnus hoped if he ever went mad like that himself, so mad that he poisoned the very air around him and hurt everyone he came into contact with, that there would be someone who loved him enough to stop him. To kill him, if it came to that.

Arterial spray and bloody handprints decorated the dingy blue walls, and on the floor there were dark pools. There was human and vampire blood: vampire blood a deeper red, a red that stayed red even when it dried, red forever and always. Magnus edged around the spots, but in one pool of human blood he saw something glittering, submerged almost past hope but with a stubborn shine that caught his eye.

Magnus stooped and plucked the shining thing out of that dark pool. It was a cross, small and golden, and he thought that he could return this to Guadalupe at least. He put it in his pocket.

Magnus took a step forward, and then another step. He was not sure the floor would hold him, he told himself, but he knew that was only an excuse. He did not want to step out amid all that death.

But suddenly he knew that he had to.

He had to because at the farthest corner of the room, in the deepest shadows, he heard ugly, greedy sucking sounds. He saw a boy in the arms of a vampire.

Magnus lifted his hand, and the force of his magic flung the vampire through the air into one of the blood-streaked walls. Magnus heard a crack and saw the vampire slump to the ground. He would not stay down long.

Magnus ran across the room, stumbling over the bodies and sliding on the blood, to fall to his knees beside the boy, to gather him into his arms. He was young, fifteen or sixteen, and he was dying.

Magnus could not magic blood into a body, especially not one already shutting down from the lack of it. He cradled the boy's lolling dark head in one hand, watched his fluttering eyelids, and waited to see if there might be a moment in which the boy could focus. In which Magnus could tell him good-bye.

The boy never looked at him and never spoke. He clutched at Magnus's hand. Magnus thought he was reaching out by reflex, as a baby might, but Magnus held on and tried to give the boy what comfort he could.

The boy breathed once, twice, three times, and then his grip went slack.

"Did you know his name?" Magnus demanded roughly of the vampire who had killed him. "Was it Raphael?"

He did not know why he asked. He did not want to know that the boy Guadalupe had sent him to find had just died in his arms, that the last member of that gallant, doomed mission to save innocents had almost survived long enough—but not quite. He could not forget the imploring look on Guadalupe Santiago's face.

He looked over at the vampire, who had not moved to attack. He was sitting down, slumped against the wall where Magnus had thrown him.

"Raphael," the vampire answered slowly. "You came here looking for Raphael?" He gave a short, sharp, almost incredulous laugh.

"Why is that funny?" Magnus demanded. A dark fury was rising in his chest. It had been a long time since he had killed a vampire, but he was willing to do it again.

"Because I am Raphael Santiago," said the boy.

Magnus stared at the vampire boy—at Raphael. He had his knees pulled up to his chest, his arms wrapped around them. Under his head of loose curls was a delicate heart-shaped face like his mother's, big dark eyes that would have enchanted women—or men—when he was grown, and a soft, childish mouth stained with blood. Blood masked the lower half of his face, and Magnus could see the white gleam of teeth against Raphael's lower lip, like diamonds in the darkness. He was the only thing moving in that whole room full of terrible stillness. He was shaking, fine tremors running all along his thin frame, shaking so hard that Magnus could see it, so hard that it looked violent, the teeth-rattling chill of someone so cold, they were about to slip into stillness and death. It was as hot as the mundanes imagined Hell to be in this room full of death, but the boy shook as though he were so cold, he could never be warm again.

Magnus stood up, moved carefully around dust and the dead until he was close to the vampire boy, and then said gently, "Raphael?"

Raphael lifted his face to the sound of Magnus's voice. He had seen many other vampires with skin as white as salt. Raphael's skin was still brown, but it did not have the warm tone of his mother's skin. It was not the flesh of a living boy any longer.

There was no saving Raphael.

His hands were covered in dirt and blood, as though he had crawled out of his grave very recently. His face was streaked with grave dirt too. He had black hair, a soft-looking curly mass of it that his mother must have loved to run her fingers through, that she must have stroked when he had nightmares and called for her, touched with light fingers when he was sleeping in his bed and she did not want to wake him, hair that she might have kept a baby curl of. That hair was full of grave dust.

There were red tear tracks on his face, shining darkly. There was blood on his neck, but Magnus knew the wound had closed over.

"Where's Louis Karnstein?" Magnus asked.

When Raphael spoke, this time in low, soft Spanish, he said, "The vampire thought I would help him with the others if he turned me into one of his own kind." He laughed suddenly, a bright, mad sound. "But I did not," he added. "No. He wasn't expecting that. He's dead. He turned to ashes and they blew away on the wind." He gestured toward the hole in the roof.

Magnus was startled into silence. It was extremely unusual for a new vampire to rise and overcome the hunger enough to think, or do anything else besides feed. Magnus wondered if Raphael had killed more than one of his friends.

He would not ask, and not only because it would have been cruel to ask. Even if Raphael had killed and then turned on his master and overcome Karnstein, he had to have a will of iron.

"They're all dead," said Raphael, seeming to master himself. His voice was clear suddenly. His dark eyes were clear too as he stared at Magnus, and then he deliberately turned away from Magnus, dismissing him as unimportant.

Raphael, Magnus saw with an ever-growing sense of unease, was looking at that blazingly bright hole in the ceiling, the one he had gestured to when he said that Karnstein had turned to ashes.

"They're all dead," Raphael repeated slowly. "And I am dead too."

He uncoiled, as swift as a snake, and sprang.

It was only because Magnus had seen where the vampire was looking and because he knew how Raphael felt, the exact exquisitely cold feeling of being an outcast, so alone that he barely seemed to exist, that he moved fast enough.

Raphael sprang for the spot of lethal light on the floor, and

Magnus sprang at Raphael. He knocked the boy to the floor just before he reached the sunlight.

Raphael gave an incoherent scream like a bird of prey, a vicious cry that was nothing but rage and hunger, that echoed in Magnus's head and made his flesh creep. Raphael thrashed and crawled for the sun, and when Magnus would not let him go, Raphael used every bit of his fledgling vampire strength to struggle free, clawing and twisting. He had no hesitation, no remorse, and none of the usual vampire fledgling's discomfort with his new power. He tried to bite Magnus's throat out. He tried to tear him limb from limb. Magnus had to use magic to fasten his limbs to the floor, and even with Raphael's whole body pinned, Magnus had to evade his snapping fangs and only just managed it.

"Let me go!" shouted the boy at last, his voice breaking.

"Hush, hush," Magnus whispered. "Your mother sent me, Raphael. Be still. Your mother sent me to find you." He drew the gold cross he had found from his pocket and held it gleaming in front of Raphael's face. "She gave me this, and she told me to save you."

Raphael flinched away from the cross, and Magnus put it away hastily, but not before the boy stopped fighting and began to sob, sobs that racked his whole body, as if he could wrench himself, his hated new self, apart from the inside out if he shook and raged enough.

"Are you stupid?" he gasped out. "You *can't* save me. Nobody can do that."

Magnus could taste his despair as if it were blood. Magnus believed him. He held on to the boy, newborn in grave dirt and blood, and he wished that he had found him dead.

The sobbing had rendered Raphael worn enough that he was docile. Magnus brought him to his own home because he had not the faintest idea what else to do with him.

Raphael sat, a small tragic bundle on Magnus's sofa.

Magnus would have felt painfully sorry for him, but he had stopped in a phone booth on his way home to ring up Etta at the small jazz club where she was singing tonight, to tell her not to come around to his place for a while because he had a baby vampire to deal with.

"A baby vampire, huh?" Etta had asked, laughing, the same way a wife might laugh at her husband who always brings home the strangest items from a local antiques market. "I don't know any exterminator in the city you could call to deal with that."

Magnus had smiled. "I can deal with it myself. Trust me."

"Oh, I usually do," Etta had said. "Though my mama tried to teach me better judgment."

Magnus had been on the phone gabbing with Etta for only a couple of minutes, but when he'd gotten out, it had been to find Raphael crouched on the pavement. He'd hissed, fangs white and needle-sharp in the night, like a cat protective of his prey when Magnus had approached. The man in his arms, the crisp white collar of his shirt dyed crimson, had been already unconscious; Magnus wrenched him away from the hissing vampire and propped him in an alley, hoping he'd think he'd been mugged.

When he came back to the sidewalk, Raphael was still sitting there, hands curled into claws and pressed to his chest. There was still a trace of blood on his mouth. Magnus felt despair hollow his heart. Here was not simply a suffering child. Here was a monster with the face of a Caravaggio angel.

"You should have let me die," Raphael said in a small, hollow voice.

"I couldn't."

"Why not?"

"Because I promised your mother I would bring you home," said Magnus.

Raphael went still at the mention of his mother, as he had back at the hotel. Magnus could see his face in the glow of the streetlights. He had the blankly hurt look of a child who had been slapped: pain and bewilderment and no way to handle either of those feelings.

"And do you think she would want me home?" Raphael asked. "L-like *this?*"

His voice trembled, and his lower lip, still stained with a man's blood, wobbled. He swiped a vicious hand across his face, and Magnus saw it again: the way he pulled himself together in an instant, the stern control he exerted over himself.

"Look at me," he said. "Tell me she would invite me in."

Magnus could not tell him that. He remembered how Guadalupe had talked about monsters, those who walked in the darkness and preyed on innocents. He thought of how she might react—the woman who had given her son a cross—to a son with blood on his hands. He remembered his stepfather forcing him to repeat prayers until once-holy words tasted bitter in his mouth, remembered his mother and how she had not been able to touch him once she'd known, and how his stepfather had held him down under the surface of the water. Yet they had loved him once, and he had loved them.

Love did not overcome everything. Love did not always endure. All you had could be taken away, love could be the last thing you had, and then love could be taken too.

Magnus knew, though, how love could be a last hope and a star to steer by. Light that went out had still shone once.

Magnus could not promise Raphael his mother's love, but since Raphael still loved his mother, Magnus wanted to help him and thought he might know how.

He prowled forward, over his own rug, and saw Raphael's dark eyes flash, startled, at his sudden purposeful movement.

"What if she never had to know?"

Raphael blinked slowly, almost reptilian in his hesitation. "What do you mean?" he asked warily.

Magnus reached into his pocket and produced the glittering thing inside it, held cupped in the palm of his hand.

"What if you came to her door," Magnus asked, "wearing the cross that she gave you?"

He dropped the cross, and reflexively Raphael caught it in his open hand. The cross hit Raphael's palm, and he saw Raphael wince, saw the wince become a shudder that ran all through his thin body and made his face go tight with pain.

"All right, Raphael," Magnus said gently.

Raphael opened his eyes and glared at Magnus, which was not what Magnus had been expecting. The smell of burning flesh filled Magnus's room. He was going to have to invest in some potpourri.

"Well done, Raphael," Magnus said. "Bravely done. You can put it down now."

Raphael held Magnus's gaze, and very slowly he closed his fingers over the cross. Tiny wisps of smoke filtered out through the spaces between his fingers.

"Well done?" echoed the vampire boy. "Bravely done? I'm just getting started."

He sat there on Magnus's sofa, his whole body an arch of pain, and he held on to his mother's cross. He did not let go.

Magnus reassessed the situation.

"A good start," Magnus told him in a condescending tone. "But it's going to take a lot more than that."

Raphael's eyes narrowed, but he did not respond.

"Of course," Magnus added casually, "maybe you can't do it. It's going to be a lot of work, and you're just a kid."

"I know it's going to be a lot of work," Raphael told him, biting off the end of every word. "I have only you to help me, and you're not terribly impressive."

It dawned on Magnus that Raphael's question in the vampires' hotel—*Are you stupid?*—had been not only an expression of despair but also an expression of Raphael's personality.

He was soon to learn that it was also Raphael's favorite question.

In the nights that followed, Raphael acquired a good deal of horribly monochrome clothing, chased off several of Magnus's clients with caustic and unkind remarks, devoted his unlife to rattling Magnus's cage, and remained sternly unimpressed by any magic Magnus displayed. Magnus warned him about Shadowhunters, the Angel's children who would try to chase him down if he broke any of their Laws, and told him about all that there was to offer and all the people he could meet. The whole of Downworld was laid out before him, faeries and werewolves and enchantment, and the only thing Raphael seemed interested in was how long he could hold the cross for, how much longer he could hold it for each night.

Etta's verdict was that nothing razzed that kid's berries.

Etta and Raphael were distant with each other. Raphael was openly and insultingly surprised that Magnus had a lady friend, and Etta, though she knew of Downworld, was wary around all Downworlders but Magnus. Chiefly Raphael stayed out of the way when Etta came by.

They had met at a club fifteen years before, Etta and Magnus. He had convinced her to dance with him, and she said she had been in love by the end of the song. He told her he had been in love before the beginning.

It was their tradition that when Etta came in after a late night during which Magnus had not been able to join her—and Magnus was missing many nights, because of Raphael—Etta would kick off her high heels, feet aching from a long night, but keep her fancy beaded dress on, and they would dance together, murmuring bebop into each other's ears and competing as to which tune they would dance to the longest.

The first time Etta encountered Raphael, she was a little quiet afterward.

"He was made a vampire only a few days ago," she said eventually, when they were dancing. "That's what you said. Before that he was just a boy."

"If it helps, I have a suspicion that he was a menace."

Etta did not laugh. "I always thought of vampires as so old," she said. "I never thought about how people can become them. I guess it makes sense. I mean—Raphael, the poor kid, he's too young. But I can see how people might want to stay young forever. The same way you do."

Etta had been talking about age more and more in the last few months. She had not mentioned the men who came to hear her sing at clubs, who wanted to take her away and have children with her. She had not had to.

Magnus understood, could read the signs like a sailor knew which clouds in the sky would bring a storm. He had been left before, for many reasons, and this one was not unusual.

Immortality was something you paid for, and those you loved paid for, over and over again. There had been a precious few who had stayed with Magnus until death had parted them, but come death or a new stage of their lives where they felt he could not follow, they were all parted from him by something.

He could not blame Etta.

"Would you want it?" Magnus asked at last, after a long time swaying together. He did not make the offer, but he thought it, that he could have it arranged. There were ways. Ways one might pay a terrible price for. Ways his father knew of, and Magnus hated his father. But if she could stay with him always—

There was another silence. All Magnus heard was the click of his shoes, and the soft shuffle of her bare feet, on his wooden floors.

"No," said Etta, her cheek pressed against his shoulder. "No. If I could have it all my own way, I'd want a little more time with you. But I wouldn't stop the clock for it."

* * *

Strange and painful reminders came to Magnus every now and then, when he had become accustomed to Raphael as the always irritated and irritating housemate who had been wished upon him. He would be surprised with a reminder of what he already knew: that Raphael's clock had been stopped, that his human life had been viciously wrenched away from him.

Magnus was constructing a new hairstyle with the aid of Brylcreem and a dash of magic when Raphael came up behind him and surprised him. Raphael often did that, since he had the silent tread of his vampire kind. Magnus suspected that he did it on purpose, but since Raphael never cracked a smile, it was hard to tell.

"You're very frivolous," Raphael remarked disapprovingly, staring at Magnus's hair.

"And you're very fifteen," Magnus shot back.

Raphael usually had a retort for whatever Magnus threw at him, but instead of a reply Magnus received a long silence. When Magnus looked up from his mirror, he saw that Raphael had moved over to the window and was looking out onto the night.

"I would be sixteen by now," said Raphael, voice as distant and cold as the light of the moon. "If I had lived."

Magnus remembered the day when he had realized that he was no longer aging, looking in a mirror that seemed colder than all other mirrors had before, as if he had been viewing his reflection in a shard of ice. As if the mirror had been responsible for holding his image so utterly frozen and so utterly distant.

He wondered how different it was to be a vampire, to know down to the precise day, the hour, the minute when you stopped belonging to the common warm and changing course of humanity. When you stood still, and the world whirled on and never missed you.

He did not ask.

"You people," said Raphael, which was how he referred to warlocks, because he was quite the charmer. "You stop aging randomly, don't you? You're born like a human is born, and you're always what you are, but you age like a human does, until you don't anymore."

Magnus wondered if Raphael had read those same thoughts on Magnus's face.

"That's right."

"Do you think your people have souls?" Raphael asked. He was still staring out the window.

Magnus had known people who thought he did not. He believed he did, but that did not mean he had never doubted.

"Doesn't matter," Raphael continued before Magnus could answer. His voice was flat. "Either way I envy you."

"Why so?"

The moonlight poured in on Raphael, bleaching his face so he looked like a marble statue of a saint who had died young.

"Either you still have your souls," said Raphael, "or you never had them, and you do not know what it is to wander the world damned, exiled, and missing them forever."

Magnus put his hairbrush down. "All Downworlders have souls," he said. "It's what makes us different from demons."

Raphael sneered. "That is a Nephilim belief."

"So what?" Magnus said. "Sometimes they're right."

Raphael said something unkind in Spanish. "They think they are such saviors, the *cazadores de sombras*," he said. "The Shadowhunters. Yet they have never come to save me."

Magnus looked at the boy silently. He had never been able to argue against his stepfather's convictions regarding what God wanted or God judged. He did not know how to convince Raphael that he might still have a soul.

"I see you're trying to distract me from the real point here," Magnus said instead. "You had a birthday—a perfect excuse for me to throw one of my famous parties—and you didn't even tell me about it?"

Raphael stared at him silently, then turned and walked away.

Magnus had often thought of getting a pet, but he had never

considered acquiring a sullen teenage vampire. Once Raphael was gone, he thought, he was getting a cat. And he would always throw his cat a birthday party.

It was soon afterward that Raphael wore a cross around his neck, all night, without crying out or exhibiting any visible signs of discomfort. At the end of the night, when he removed it, there was a faint mark against his chest, as of a long-healed burn, but that was all.

"So that's it," Magnus said. "That's great. You're done! Let's go visit your mother."

He had sent her a message telling her not to worry and not to visit, that he was using all the magic he could to save Raphael and could not be disturbed, but he knew it would not keep her away forever.

Raphael's expression was blank as he fiddled with the chain in one hand, his only sign of uncertainty. "No," he said. "How many times are you going to underestimate me? I'm not done. I'm not even close."

He explained to Magnus what he wanted to do next.

"You are doing a good deal to help me," Raphael said the next night as they approached the graveyard. His voice was almost clinical.

Magnus thought but did not say, *Yes, because there were times when I was as desperate as you, and as miserable, and as convinced that I had no soul.* People had helped him when he'd needed it, because he had needed it and for no other reason. He remembered the Silent Brothers coming for him in Madrid, and teaching him that there was still a way to live.

"You don't need to be grateful," Magnus said instead. "I'm not doing it for you."

Raphael shrugged, a fluid easy gesture. "All right, then."

"I mean, you could be grateful occasionally," Magnus said. "You could tidy up the apartment once in a while."

Raphael considered this. "No, I don't think I will."

"I think your mother should have beaten you," said Magnus. "Frequently."

"My father hit me once, back in Zacatecas," Raphael said casually.

Raphael had not mentioned a father before, and Guadalupe had not mentioned a husband, though Magnus knew there were several brothers.

"He did?" Magnus tried to make his voice both neutral and encouraging, in case Raphael wanted to confide in him.

Raphael, not the confiding type, looked amused. "He didn't hit me twice."

It was a small graveyard, secluded and far away in Queens, hemmed in by tall and dark buildings, one warehouse and one abandoned Victorian home. Magnus had arranged for the area to be sprinkled with holy water, blessed, and made sacred. Churches were hallowed ground but graveyards not so. All vampires had to be buried somewhere, and had to rise.

It would not provide a barrier like the Institute of the Shadowhunters, but it would be hard enough for Raphael to rest his foot on the ground.

It was another test. Raphael had promised not to do more than touch his foot to the ground.

Raphael had promised.

When Raphael lifted his chin, like a horse taking a bit between its teeth, and charged right onto the holy ground, running and burning and screaming, Magnus wondered how he could ever have believed him.

"Raphael!" he shouted, and ran after him, into the darkness and onto the sacred earth.

Raphael sprang onto a gravestone, landed balanced on it. His curly hair was blown back from his thin face, his body arched, his fingers clawed against the marble edge. His teeth were bared from vicious tip to gum, and his eyes were black and lifeless. He looked like a revenant, a nightmare rearing up from a grave. Less human, with less of a soul, than any savage beast.

He leaped. Not at Magnus but at the perimeter of the graveyard. He came out on the other side.

Magnus chased after him. Raphael was swaying, leaning against the low stone wall as if he could barely stay on his feet. The skin on his arms was visibly bubbling. He looked as if he wanted to claw off the rest of his skin in agony but did not have the strength.

"Well, you did it," Magnus remarked. "By which I mean you almost gave me a heart attack. Don't stop now. The night is young. What are you going to do to upset me next?"

Raphael glanced up at him and grinned. It was not a nice expression.

"I am going to do the same thing again."

Magnus supposed he had asked for that.

When Raphael had run through the holy ground again not once but ten times, he leaned against the wall looking worn and spent, and while he was too weak to run, he leaned against the wall and murmured to himself, choking at first and then getting the word out, the name of God.

He choked up blood as he said it, coughed, and kept murmuring. "*Dios.*"

Magnus bore the sight of him, too weak to stand and still hurting himself, as long as he could.

"Raphael, don't you think you've done enough?"

Predictably, Raphael glared at him. "No."

"You have forever to learn how to do this and how to control yourself. You have—"

"But *they don't!*" Raphael burst out. "*Dios*, do you understand nothing? The only thing I have left is the hope of seeing them, of not breaking my mother's heart. I need to convince her. I need to do it perfectly, and I need to do it soon, while she still hopes that I am alive."

He had spoken "*Dios*" almost without flinching that time.

"You're being very good."

"It is no longer possible for me to be good," Raphael said, his voice steely. "If I were still good and brave, I would do what my mother would want if she knew the truth. I would walk out into the sun and end my own life. But I am a selfish, wicked, heartless beast, and I do not want to burn in the fires of Hell yet. I want to go see my m-mother, and I will. I will. I will!"

Magnus nodded. "What if God could help you?" he asked gently.

It was as close as he could get to saying, *What if everything you believe is wrong and you could still be loved and still be forgiven?*

Raphael shook his head stubbornly.

"I am one of the Night Children. I am no longer a child of His, no longer under His watchful eye. God will not help me," Raphael said, his voice thick, speaking through a mouthful of blood. He spat the blood out again. "And God will not stop me."

Magnus did not argue with him again. Raphael was still so young in so many ways, and his whole world had shattered around him. All he had left to make sense of the world were his beliefs, and he would cling to them even if his very beliefs told him that he was hopelessly lost, damned, and dead already.

Magnus did not even know if it would be right to try to take those beliefs away.

That night when Magnus was sleeping, he woke and heard the low, fervent murmur of Raphael's voice. Magnus had heard people praying many times and recognized the sound. He heard the names, unfamiliar names, and wondered if they had been Raphael's friends. Then he heard the name Guadalupe, the name of Raphael's mother, and he knew the other names had to be the names of Raphael's brothers.

As mortals called on God, on angels and saints, as they chanted while telling their rosary, Raphael was pronouncing the only names that were sacred to him and would not burn his tongue to utter. Raphael was calling on his family.

* * *

There were many drawbacks to having Raphael as a roommate that did not concern Raphael's conviction that he was a damned lost soul, or even the fact that Raphael used up so much soap in the shower (even though he never sweated and hardly needed to shower so often) and never did the washing up. When Magnus pointed this out, Raphael responded that he never ate food and was therefore not creating any washing up, which was just like Raphael.

One more drawback became apparent the day that Ragnor Fell, High Warlock of London and perpetual enormous green thorn in Magnus's side, came by to pay an unexpected visit.

"Ragnor, this is a welcome surprise," said Magnus, flinging the door open wide.

"I was paid by some Nephilim to make the trip," said Ragnor. "They wished for a spell."

"And my waiting list was too long." Magnus nodded sadly. "I am in great demand."

"And you constantly give the Shadowhunters lip, so they all dislike you, save a few wayward rebellious souls," said Ragnor. "How many times have I told you, Magnus? Behave professionally in a professional setting. Which means no being rude to Nephilim, and also no getting attached to Nephilim."

"I never get attached to Nephilim!" Magnus protested.

Ragnor coughed, and in the midst of the cough said something that sounded like "blerondale."

"Well," said Magnus. "Hardly ever."

"No getting attached to the Nephilim," Ragnor repeated sternly. "Speak respectfully to your clients and give them the service they wish for as well as the magic. And save incivility for your friends. Talking of which, I have not seen you in this age, and you look even more of a horror than you usually do."

"That's a filthy lie," said Magnus.

He knew he looked extremely sharp. He was wearing an amazing brocade tie.

"Who is at the door?" Raphael's imperious voice drifted from the bathroom, and the rest of Raphael came with it, dressed in a towel but looking just as critical as ever. "I told you that you have to start keeping regular business hours, Bane."

Ragnor squinted over at Raphael. Raphael looked balefully back at Ragnor. There was a certain tension in the air.

"Oh, Magnus," said Ragnor, and he covered his eyes with one large green hand. "Oh no, no."

"What?" said Magnus, puzzled.

Ragnor abruptly lowered his hand. "No, you're right, of course. I'm being silly. He's a vampire. He only looks fourteen. How old are you? I bet you're older than either of us, ha-ha."

Raphael looked at Ragnor as if he were mad. Magnus found it quite refreshing to have someone else looked at that way for a change.

"I'd be sixteen by now," he said slowly.

"Oh, Magnus!" Ragnor wailed. "That's disgusting! How could you? Have you lost your mind?"

"What?" Magnus asked again.

"We agreed eighteen was the cutoff age," said Ragnor. "You, I, and Catarina made a vow."

"A v— Oh, wait. You think I'm dating Raphael?" Magnus asked. "Raphael? That's ridiculous. That's—"

"That's the most revolting idea I've ever heard."

Raphael's voice rang out to the ceiling. Probably people in the street could hear him.

"That's a little strong," said Magnus. "And, frankly, hurtful."

"And if I did wish to indulge in unnatural pursuits—and let me be clear, I certainly do not," Raphael continued scornfully, "as if I would choose *him*. Him! He dresses like a maniac, acts like a fool, and makes worse jokes than the man people throw rotten eggs at outside the Dew Drop every Saturday."

Ragnor began to laugh.

"Better men than you have begged for a chance to win all this," Magnus muttered. "They have fought duels in my honor. One man fought a duel *for* my honor, but that was a little embarrassing since it is long gone."

"Do you know he spends hours in the bathroom sometimes?" Raphael announced mercilessly. "He wastes actual magic on his hair. On his hair!"

"I love this kid," said Ragnor.

Of course he did. Raphael was filled with grave despair about the world in general, was eager to insult Magnus in particular, and had a tongue as sharp as his teeth. Raphael was obviously Ragnor's soul mate.

"Take him," Magnus suggested. "Take him far, far away."

Instead Ragnor took a chair, and Raphael got dressed and joined him at the table.

"Let me tell you another thing about Bane," Raphael began.

"I'm going out," Magnus announced. "I'd describe what I'm going to do when I go out, but I find it hard to believe that either of you would understand the concept of 'enjoying a good time with a group of entertaining companions.' I do not intend to return until you people are done insulting your charming host."

"So you're moving out and giving me the apartment?" Raphael asked. "I accept."

"Someday that smart mouth is going to get you into a lot of trouble," Magnus called darkly over his shoulder.

"Look who's talking," said Ragnor.

"Hello?" said Raphael, as laconic as usual. "Damned soul."

Worst roommate ever.

Ragnor stayed for thirteen days. They were the longest thirteen days of Magnus's life. Every time Magnus tried to have a little fun, there they were, the short one and the green one, shaking their heads in tandem and then saying snotty things. On one occasion Magnus turned his head very quickly and saw them exchanging a fist bump.

"Write to me," Ragnor said to Raphael when he was leaving. "Or call me on your telephone if you want. I know the youths like that."

"It was great to meet you, Ragnor," said Raphael. "I was beginning to think all warlocks were completely useless."

It was not long after Ragnor left that Magnus tried to recall the last time Raphael had drunk blood. Magnus had always avoided thinking about how Camille got her meals, even when he'd loved her, and he did not want to see Raphael kill again. But he saw Raphael's skin tone change, saw the strained look about his mouth, and thought about getting this far and having Raphael shrivel up out of sheer despair.

"Raphael, I don't know quite how to put this, but are you eating right?" Magnus asked. "Until recently you were a growing boy."

"*El hambre agudiza el ingenio*," said Raphael.

Hunger sharpens the wit.

"Good proverb," said Magnus. "However, like most proverbs, it sounds wise and yet does not actually clarify anything."

"Do you think I would permit myself to be around my mother—around my small brothers—if I were not sure beyond a shadow of a doubt that I could control myself?" Raphael said. "I want to know that if I were trapped in a room with one of them, if I had not tasted blood in days, I could control myself."

Raphael almost killed another man that night, in front of Magnus's eyes. He proved his point.

Magnus did not have to worry about Raphael starving himself out of pity, or mercy, or any softer feeling for the rest of humanity. Raphael did not consider himself a part of humanity anymore and thought he could commit any sin in the world because he was already damned. He had simply been abstaining from drinking blood to prove to himself that he could, to test his own limits, and to exercise the absolute self-control that he was determined to achieve.

The next night Raphael ran over sacred ground and then calmly drank blood from a tramp sleeping on the street who might never wake up, despite the healing spell Magnus whispered over him. They were walking through the night, Raphael calculating out loud how much longer it would take him to become as strong as he needed to be.

"I think you're fairly strong," said Magnus. "And you have quite a lot of self-control. Look how you sternly repress all the hero worship you are longing to show me that you feel."

"It is sometimes an exercise of real self-control not to laugh in your face," Raphael said gravely. "That much is true."

It was then that Raphael stiffened, and when Magnus made an inquiring sound, Raphael hushed him sharply. Magnus looked down at Raphael's dark eyes and followed the direction in which they were fixed. He didn't know what Raphael was casting an eyeball at, but he figured it was no harm to follow him when Raphael moved.

There was an alley stretching behind an abandoned Automat. In the shadows there was a rustling that could have been rats in garbage, but as they drew closer, Magnus could hear what had attracted Raphael: the sound of giggling, and the sound of sucking, and the whimpers of pain.

He was not sure what Raphael was doing, but he had no plans to abandon him now. Magnus clicked his fingers, and there was light—radiating from his hand, filling the alleyway with brightness, and falling onto the faces of the four vampires in front of him, and their victim.

"What do you people think you're doing?" Raphael demanded.

"What does it look like?" said the only girl of the group. Magnus recognized her as the lone brave soul who had accosted him at the

Hotel Dumont. "We're drinking blood. What, are you new?"

"Is that what you were doing?" Raphael asked in a voice of exaggerated surprise. "So sorry. That must have escaped my attention, since I was preoccupied with how incredibly stupid you were all being."

"Stupid?" echoed the girl. "Do you mean 'wrong'? Are you lecturing us on—"

Raphael clicked his fingers impatiently at her. "Do I mean 'wrong'?" he said. "We're all dead and damned already. What would 'wrong' even mean to beings like us?"

The girl tilted her head and looked thoughtful.

"I mean *stupid*," said Raphael. "Not that I consider hunting down a slow-witted child honorable, mind you. Consider this: you kill her, you bring the Shadowhunters down on all of us. I don't know about you people, but I do not wish for the Nephilim to come and cut my life short with a blade because someone was a little too peckish and a lot dumb."

"So you're saying, 'Oh, spare her life,'" sneered one of the boys, though the girl elbowed him.

"But even if you don't kill her," Raphael continued relentlessly, as if nobody had interrupted him at all, "well, then, you've already drunk from her, under uncontrolled and frenzied conditions that would make it easy for her to accidentally taste some of your blood. Which will leave her with a compulsion to follow you about. Do this to enough victims and you'll either be snowed under with subjugates—and frankly they are not the best conversationalists—or you'll make them into more vampires. Which, mathematically speaking, eventually leaves you with a blood supply problem because there are no humans left. Humans can waste resources knowing that at least they will not be around to deal with the consequences, but you chumps don't even have that excuse. *Goodness me*, you nosebleeds are going to think when a seraph blade cuts your head off or you stare around at a bleak landscape while starving to death, *if only I'd been a smart cookie and listened to Raphael when I had the chance.*"

"Is he serious?" another vampire asked, sounding awed.

"Almost invariably," Magnus said. "It's what makes him such tedious company."

"Is that your name? Raphael?" asked the vampire girl. She was smiling, her black eyes dancing.

"Yes," said Raphael irritably, immune to flirtation the same way he was immune to all things that were fun. "What is the point of being immortal if you do nothing with it but be irresponsible and unacceptably stupid? What's your name?"

The vampire girl's smile spread, showing her fangs sparkling behind her lipsticked mouth. "Lily."

"Here lies Lily," said Raphael. "Killed by vampire hunters because she was murdering people and then not even having the intelligence to cover her tracks."

"What, now you're telling us to be afraid of mundanes?" another vampire said, laughing, this one a man with silver at his temples. "Those are old stories told to frighten the youngest of us. I assume you're pretty young yourself, but—"

Raphael smiled, fangs bared, though his expression had nothing to do with humor. "I am rather young," he said. "And when I was alive, I was a vampire hunter. I killed Louis Karnstein."

"You're a vampire vampire hunter?" asked Lily.

Raphael swore in Spanish. "No, of course I'm not a vampire vampire hunter," he said. "Exactly what kind of treacherous weasel would I be then? Additionally, what a stupid thing to be. I would instantly be killed by all the other vampires, who would come together over a common threat. At least I hope they would. Maybe they would all be too stupid. I am someone who talks sense," Raphael informed them all severely, "and there is *very little* job competition."

The vampire with graying hair was almost pouting. "Lady Camille lets us do what we want."

Raphael was not a fool. He was not going to insult the leader of the vampire clan in his own city.

"Lady Camille clearly has enough to do without running around after you idiots, and she assumes you have more sense than you have. Let me give you something to think about it, if you are capable of thinking."

Lily sidled over to Magnus, her eyes still on Raphael.

"I like him," she said. "He's kind of bossy, even though he's such an oddball. You know what I mean?"

"Sorry. I went deaf with sheer amazement that anyone could like Raphael."

"And he isn't afraid of anything," Lily continued, grinning. "He's talking to Derek like a schoolteacher talking to a naughty child, and I personally have seen Derek rip people's heads off and drink from the stem."

They both looked at Raphael, who was giving a speech. The other vampires were cowering away slightly.

"You are already dead. Do you wish to be crushed out of existence completely?" Raphael asked. "Once we leave this world, all we have to look forward to is torment in the eternal fires of Hell. Do you want your damned existence to count for nothing?"

"I think I need a drink," Magnus murmured. "Does anyone else want a drink?"

Every vampire who was not Raphael silently raised their hand. Raphael looked accusing and judgmental, but Magnus believed his face was stuck that way.

"Very well. I'm prepared to share," said Magnus, taking his gold-embossed flask out from its specially designed place on his gold-embossed belt. "But I'm warning you, I'm all out of blood of the innocent. This is Scotch."

After the other vampires were drunk, Raphael and Magnus sent the mundane girl on her way, a little dizzy from lack of blood but otherwise fine. Magnus was not surprised when Raphael performed the *encanto* on her perfectly. He supposed Raphael had been practicing that, too. Or possibly it just came extremely naturally to Raphael to impose his will on others.

"Nothing happened. You will go tuck yourself up in your bed and remember nothing. Do not go wandering in these areas at night. You will meet unsavory men and bloodsucking fiends," Raphael told the girl, his eyes on hers, unwavering. "And go to church."

"Do you think your calling might be telling everyone in the world what to do?" Magnus asked as they were walking home.

Raphael regarded him sourly. He had such a sweet face, Magnus thought—the face of an innocent angel, and the soul of the crankiest person in the entire world.

"You should never wear that hat again."

"My point exactly," said Magnus.

The Santiagos' house was in Harlem, on 129th Street and Lenox Avenue.

"You don't have to wait around for me," Raphael told Magnus as they walked. "I was thinking that after this, however it ends up, I will go to Lady Camille Belcourt and live with the vampires. They could use me there, and I could use—something to do. I'm ... sorry if that offends you."

Magnus thought about Camille, and all that he suspected about her, remembered the horror of the twenties and that he still did not know quite how she had been involved in that.

But Raphael could not stay as Magnus's guest, a temporary guest in Downworld with nowhere to belong to, nothing to anchor him in the shadows and keep him away from the sun.

"Oh no, Raphael, please don't leave me," Magnus said in a monotone. "Where would I be without the light of your sweet smile? If you go, I will throw myself upon the ground and weep."

"Will you?" asked Raphael, raising one thin eyebrow. "Because if you do, I will stay and watch the show."

"Get out," Magnus told him. "Out! I want you out. I'm going to throw a party when you leave, and you know you hate those. Along with fashion, and music, and fun as a concept. I will never blame you for going and doing what suits you best. I want you to have a purpose. I want you to have something to live for, even if you don't think you're alive."

There was a brief pause.

"Well, excellent," said Raphael. "Because I was going anyway. I am sick of Brooklyn."

"You are an insufferable brat," Magnus informed him, and Raphael smiled one of his rare, shockingly sweet smiles.

His smile faded quickly as they approached his old neighborhood. Magnus could see that Raphael was fighting back panic. Magnus remembered his stepfather's and his mother's faces. He knew how it felt when family turned away from you.

He would rather have the sun taken away from him, as it had already been for Raphael, than have love taken away. He found himself praying, as he seldom had in years, like the man who had raised him used to, like Raphael did, that Raphael would not have to bear both being taken.

They approached the door of the house, a stoop with weathered green latticework. Raphael stared at it with mingled longing and fear, as a sinner might stare at the gates of Heaven.

It was up to Magnus to knock on the door, and wait for the answer.

When Guadalupe Santiago answered the door and saw her son, the time for prayer was over.

Magnus could see her whole heart in her eyes as she looked at Raphael. She had not moved, had not flung herself upon him. She was staring at him, at his angel's face and dusky curls, at his slight frame and flushed cheeks—he had fed before he came, so that he would look more alive—and more than anything else, at the gold chain gleaming around his neck. Was it the cross? He could see her wondering. Was it her gift, meant to keep him safe?

Raphael's eyes were shining. It was the one thing they had not planned for, Magnus realized in sudden horror. The one thing they had not practiced—preventing Raphael from weeping. If he shed tears in front of his mother, those tears would be blood, and the whole game would be over.

Magnus started talking as fast as he could.

"I found him for you, as you asked," he said. "But when I reached him, he was very close to death, so I had to give him some of my own power, make him like me." Magnus caught Guadalupe's eyes, though that was difficult since her entire attention was on her son. "A magic maker," he said, as she'd said to him once. "An immortal sorcerer."

She thought vampires were monsters, but she had come to Magnus for help. She could trust a warlock. She could believe a warlock was not damned.

Guadalupe's whole body was tense, but she gave a tiny nod. She recognized the words, Magnus knew, and she wanted to believe. She wanted so badly to believe what they were saying that she could not quite bring herself to trust them.

She looked older than she had a few months ago, worn by the time her son had been gone. She looked older but no less fierce, and she stood with her arm blocking the doorway, children peering in around her but protected by her body.

But she did not shut the door. She listened to the story, and she gave her absolute attention to Raphael, her eyes tracing the familiar lines of his face whenever he spoke.

"All this time I have been in training so I could come home to you and make you proud. Mother," Raphael said, "I assure you, I beg you will believe me. I still have a soul."

Guadalupe's eyes were still fixed on the thin, glittering chain around his neck. Raphael's shaking fingers pulled the cross free from his shirt. The cross danced as it dangled from his hand, gold and shining, the brightest thing in all the nighttime city.

"You wore it," Guadalupe whispered. "I was so afraid that you would not listen to your mother."

"Of course I did," said Raphael, his voice trembling. But he did not cry, not Raphael of the iron will. "I wore it, and it kept me safe. It saved me. You saved me."

Guadalupe's whole body changed then, from enforced stillness to movement, and Magnus realized that more than one person in this conversation had been exercising iron self-control. He knew where Raphael got it from.

She stepped over the threshold and held out her arms. Raphael ran into them, gone from Magnus's side more quickly than a human could move, and clasped one arm tight around her neck. He was shaking in her arms, shaking all over as she stroked his hair.

"Raphael," she murmured into his black curls. First Magnus and Raphael had not been able to stop talking, and now it seemed she could not. "Raphael, *mijo*, Raphael, my Raphael."

At first Magnus knew in the jumble of words of love and comfort only that she was inviting Raphael in, that they were safe, that they had succeeded, that Raphael could have his family and his family would never have to know. All the words she said were both endearments and statements, love and laying claim: my son, my boy, my child.

The other boys crowded up around Raphael, given their mother's blessing, and Raphael touched them with gentle hands, touched the little ones' hair, tugging with affection that looked careless, though it was so very careful, and shoved the older boys in rough but never too rough greeting.

Playing his role as Raphael's benefactor and teacher, Magnus hugged Raphael too. As prickly as he was, Raphael did not invite embraces. Magnus had not been so close to him since the day he'd fought to stop Raphael from going into the sun. Raphael's back felt thin under Magnus's hands—fragile, though he was not.

"I owe you, warlock," Raphael said, a cool whisper against

Magnus's ear. "I promise you I won't forget."

"Don't be ridiculous," said Magnus, and then because he could get away with it, when he drew back, he ruffled Raphael's curly hair.

The indignant look on Raphael's face was hilarious.

"I will leave you to be alone with your family," Magnus told him, and he went.

Before he did, though, he paused and created a few blue sparks from his fingers that formed tiny play houses and stars, that made magic something fun that the children did not fear. He told them all that Raphael was not quite as accomplished or fabulously talented as he himself was, and would not be able to perform such tiny miracles for years. He made a flourishing bow that had the little ones laughing and Raphael rolling his eyes.

Magnus did leave, walking slowly. The winter was coming but was not quite there yet, and he was happy to simply walk and enjoy the little things in life, the crisp winter air, the few stray golden leaves still curling under his feet, the bare trees above him waiting to be reborn in glory. He was going home to an apartment that he suspected would feel slightly too empty, but soon he would invite Etta over, and she would dance with him and fill the rooms with love and laughter, as she would fill his life with love and laughter, for a little while yet before she left him.

He heard steps thundering after him and thought it was Raphael for a moment, the masquerade in ruins around them suddenly, when they'd thought they were victorious.

But it was not Raphael. Magnus did not see Raphael again for several months, and by then Raphael was Camille's second-in-command, calmly ordering around vampires hundreds of years older than himself as only Raphael could. Raphael spoke to Magnus then as one important Downworlder to another, with perfect professionalism, but Magnus knew Raphael had not forgotten anything. Relations had always been strained between Magnus and the vampires of New York, Camille's clan, but suddenly they were less strained. New York vampires came to his parties, though Raphael did not, and came to him for magical aid, though Raphael never would again.

The footsteps chasing Magnus's in the cool winter night were not Raphael's but Guadalupe's. She was panting from how hard she had been running, her dark hair slipping free of its pins, forming a cloud about her face. She almost ran into him before she could stop herself.

"Wait," she said. "I haven't paid you."

Her hands were shaking, spilling over with bills. Magnus closed her fingers around the money and closed his hands around hers.

"Take it," she urged him. "Take it. You earned it; you earned more. You brought him back to me, my oldest boy, the sweetest of them all, my dear heart, my brave boy. You saved him."

She was still shaking as Magnus held her hands, so Magnus rested his forehead against hers. He held her close enough to kiss, close enough to whisper the most important secrets in the world, and he spoke to her as he would have wanted some good angel to speak to his family, to his own shivering young soul, long ago and in a land far away.

"No," he murmured. "No, I didn't. You know him better than anyone else ever has or ever will. You made him, you taught him to be all he is, and you know him down to his bones. You know how strong he is. You know how much he loves you. If I gave you anything, give me your faith now. Teach one thing to all your children. I have never told you anything more true than this. Believe this, if you believe nothing else. Raphael saved himself."

The Fall of the Hotel Dumort

By Cassandra Clare and Maureen Johnson

Her silver-blond hair was long and down, looking wild. She patted the end of the bed. This was not the greeting he'd been expecting. This was not the Camille he remembered, or even the one he had seen in passing.

—The Fall of the Hotel Dumort

MAGNUS! MAGNUS! MAGNUS! COME HERE! COME! SIT DOWN!

July 1977

"What do *you* do?" the woman asked.

"This and that," Magnus said.

"Are you in fashion? You look like you're in fashion."

"No," he said. "I *am* fashion."

It was a bit of a twee remark, but it seemed to delight his seat companion on the plane. The comment had been a bit of a test, actually. Everything seemed to delight his companion—the seat back in front of her, her nails, her glass, her own hair, everyone else's hair, the barf bag...

The plane had been in the air for only an hour, but Magnus's companion had gotten up to use the restroom four times. Each time she'd emerged moments later, furiously rubbing her nose and visibly twitching. Now she was leaning over him, her winged blond hair dipping into his champagne glass, her neck reeking of Eau de Guerlain. The faint trace of white powder still clung to her nose.

He could have done this trip in seconds by stepping through a Portal, but there was something pleasant about aircraft. They were charming, intimate, and slow. You got to meet people. Magnus liked meeting people.

"But your *outfit*?" she said. "What *is* it?"

Magnus looked down at his red-plaid-and-black-vinyl oversize suit with a shredded T-shirt underneath. It was au courant for the

London punk set, but New York wasn't quite there yet.

"I do PR," the woman said, apparently forgetting the question. "For discos and clubs. The best clubs. Here. Here."

She dug around in her massive purse—and stopped for a moment when she found her cigarettes. She shoved one of these between her lips, lit it, and continued digging until she produced a small tortoiseshell card case. She popped this open and picked out one card, which read: *ELECTRICA*.

"Come," she said, tapping the card with a long, red nail. "Come. It's just opening. It's going to be smashing. *Soooo* much better than Studio 54. Oh. Excuse me a second. You want?"

She showed him a small vial in the palm of her hand.

"No, thank you."

And then she was fumbling out of the seat again, her purse bumping into Magnus's face as she went back to the bathroom.

The mundanes had gotten very interested in drugs again. They went through these phases. Now it was cocaine. He hadn't seen this much of the stuff since the turn of the century, when they'd been putting it in everything—tonics and potions and even Coca-Cola. He thought for a while that they'd put this drug behind them, but it was back again, in full force.

Drugs had never interested Magnus. A good wine, absolutely, but he steered clear of potions and powders and pills. You didn't take drugs and do magic. Also, people who did drugs were boring. Hopelessly, relentlessly boring. Drugs made them either too slow or too fast, and mostly they talked about drugs. And then they either quit—a gruesome process—or they died. There was never a step in between.

Like all mundane phases, this too would pass. Hopefully soon. He closed his eyes and decided to sleep his way across the Atlantic. London was behind him. Now it was time to go home.

Stepping outside at JFK, Magnus got his first reminder of why he'd summarily left New York two summers before. New York was *too damn hot* in the summer. It was just touching a hundred degrees, and the smell of jet fuel and exhaust fumes mixed with the swampy gasses that hung around this far tip of the city. The smell, he knew, would only get worse.

With a sigh he joined a taxi line.

The cab was as comfortable as any metal box in the sun, and his sweating driver added to the general perfume in the air.

"Where to, buddy?" he asked, taking in Magnus's outfit.

"Corner of Christopher and Sixth Avenue."

The cabbie grunted and hit the meter, and then they pulled out into traffic. The smoke from the driver's cigar streamed back directly into Magnus's face. He lifted a finger and redirected it out the window.

The road from JFK to Manhattan was a strange one, weaving through family neighborhoods, and desolate stretches, and past sprawling graveyards. It was an age-old tradition. Keep the dead out of the city—but not too far. London, where he had just been, was ringed with old graveyards. And Pompeii, which he'd visited a few months back, had an entire avenue of the dead, tombs leading right up to the city wall. Past all of the New York neighborhoods and graveyards, at the end of the crowded expressway, shimmering in the distance—there was Manhattan—its spires and peaks just lighting up for the night. From death to life.

He hadn't meant to be away from the city for so long. He had just been going to take the briefest trip to Monte Carlo ... but then, these things can go on. A week in Monte Carlo turns into two on the Riviera, which turns into a month in Paris, and two months in Tuscany, and then you end up on a boat headed for Greece, and then you wind up back in Paris again for the season, and then you go to Rome for a bit, and London...

And sometimes you accidentally go for two years. It happens.

"Where you from?" the cabbie asked, eyeing Magnus in the rear-view mirror.

"Oh, around. Here mostly."

"You're from here? You been away? You look like you been away."

"For a while."

"You hear about these murders?"

"Haven't read a paper in a while," Magnus said.

"Some loony-tune. Calls himself Son of Sam. They called him the forty-four-caliber killer too. Goes around shooting couples on lovers' lanes, you know? Sick bastard. Real sick. Police haven't caught him. They don't do nothing. Sick bastard. City's full of them. You shouldn'ta come back."

New York cabdrivers—always little rays of sunshine.

Magnus got out on the tree-lined corner of Sixth Avenue and Christopher Street, in the heart of the West Village. Even at nightfall the heat was stifling. Still, it seemed to encourage a party atmosphere in the neighborhood. The Village had been an interesting place before he'd left. It seemed that in his absence things had taken on a whole new level of festivity. Costumed men walked down the street. The outdoor cafés were swarming. There was a carnival atmosphere that Magnus found instantly inviting.

Magnus's apartment was a walk-up, on the third story of one of the brick houses that lined the street. He let himself in and sprang lightly up the steps, full of high spirits. His spirits fell when he reached his landing. The first thing he noticed, right by his door, was a strong and bad smell—something rotten, mixed with something like skunk, mixed with other things he had no desire to identify. Magnus did not live in a stinky apartment. His apartment smelled of clean floors, flowers, and incense. He put the key into the lock, and when he tried to push the door open, it stuck. He had to shove it hard to get it to open. The reason was immediately clear—there were boxes of empty wine bottles on the other side. And, much to his surprise, the television was on. Four vampires were crashed on his sofa, blankly watching cartoons.

He knew they were vampires at once. The draining of the color behind the skin, the languid pose. Also, these vampires hadn't even bothered to wipe the blood from the corners of their mouths. All of them had dried bits of the stuff around their faces. There was a record spinning on the player. It had reached the end and was stuck on the blank end strip, hissing gently in disapproval.

Only one of the vampires even turned to look at him.

"Who are you?" she asked.

"Magnus Bane. I live here."

"Oh."

She turned back to the cartoon.

When Magnus had left two years before, he'd left his apartment in the care of a housekeeper, Mrs. Milligan. He'd sent money every month for the bills and the cleaning. Clearly she had paid the bills. The electricity was still on. But she hadn't cleaned, and Mrs. Milligan probably hadn't invited these four vampires to come and stay and generally trash the place. Everywhere Magnus looked there were signs of destruction and decay. One of the kitchen chairs had been broken and was in pieces on the floor. The others were piled with magazines and newspapers. There were overflowing ashtrays, and makeshift ashtrays, and then just trails of ash and plates full of cigarette butts. The living room curtains were cockeyed and torn. Everything was askew, and some things were simply missing. Magnus had many lovely pieces of art that he'd collected over the years. He looked for a favorite piece of Sevres porcelain that he'd kept on a table in the hall. That, of course, was gone. As was the table.

"I don't want to be rude," Magnus said, unhappily eyeing a pile of stinking garbage on the corner of one of his best Persian carpets, "but may I ask why you're in my house?"

This got a bleary look.

"We live here," said the girl at the end, the spunky one who could actually turn her head.

"No," Magnus said. "I think I just explained that I live here."

"You weren't here. So we lived here."

"Well, I'm back. So you're going to need to make other arrangements."

No response.

"Let me be more clear," he said, standing in front of the television. Blue light crackled between his fingers. "If you're here, you may know who I am. You may know what I'm capable of. Perhaps you'd like me to summon up someone to help you out? Or perhaps I could open a Portal and send you to the far side of the Bronx? Ohio? Mongolia? Where would you like to be dropped?"

The vampires on the sofa said nothing for a minute or two. Then they managed to look at one another. There was a grunt, a second grunt, and then they pulled themselves up from the sofa with tremendous difficulty.

"Don't worry about your things," Magnus said. "I'll send them along. To the Dumont?"

The vampires had long ago claimed the doomed old Hotel Dumont. It was the general address of all New York vampires.

Magnus looked at them more closely. He had never quite seen vampires like these. They appeared to be—sick? Vampires didn't really get sick. They got hungry, but they didn't get sick. And these vampires had eaten. The evidence was all over their faces. Also, they were twitching a bit.

Considering the state of the place, he didn't feel like worrying over their health.

"Come on," one of them said. They shuffled out onto the landing and then down the stairs. Magnus shut the door firmly and, with a swoop of his hand, moved a marble-topped dry sink to block the door from the inside. At least that had been too heavy and sturdy to break or remove, but it was full of old dirty clothes that seemed to be covering up something he instinctively knew he never wanted to see.

The smell was terrible. That had to go first. One crack of blue hit the air, and the funk was replaced with the light smell of night-blooming jasmine. He took the record off the record player. The vampires had left behind a pile of albums. He had a look through this and picked out the new Fleetwood Mac album that everyone was playing. He liked them. There was a light magical sound to the music. Magnus swept his hand through the air again, and slowly the apartment began to right itself. As a thank-you, he sent the garbage and the various disgusting little piles over to the Dumont. He had promised to send them their things, after all.

Despite the magic he used on his window air-conditioning unit, despite the cleaning, despite everything he had done—the apartment still felt sticky and dirty and unpleasant. Magnus slept poorly. He gave up at around six in the morning and went out in search of coffee and breakfast. He was still on London time anyway.

Out on the street some people were clearly just coming home for the night. There was a woman hopping along in one high heel and one bare foot. There were three people covered in glitter and sweat, all wearing flopping feather boas, emerging from a cab by his corner. Magnus settled down in the corner booth of a diner across the street. It was the only thing open. It was surprisingly full. Again, most of the people seemed to be at the end of their day, not the start, and were gobbling pancakes to soak up the alcohol in their stomachs.

Magnus had purchased a paper by the cash register. The cabbie hadn't been lying—the news in New York was bad. He'd left a troubled city and returned to a broken one. The city was broke. Half the buildings in the Bronx had burned down. Trash piled up on the streets because there was no money for collection. Muggings, murders, robbery ... and yes, someone calling himself the Son of Sam and claiming to be an agent of Satan was running around with a gun and shooting people at random.

"I thought that was you," said a voice. "Magnus. Where you been, man?"

A young man slid into the other side of the booth. He wore jeans, a leather vest with no shirt, and a gold cross on a chain around his neck. Magnus smiled and folded his paper away.

"Greg!"

Gregory Jensen was an extremely handsome young werewolf with shoulder-length blond hair. Blond was not Magnus's favorite hair color, but Greg certainly carried his well. Magnus had had a bit of a crush on Greg for a while, a crush he'd eventually let go of when he'd met Greg's wife, Consuela. Werewolf love was intense. You didn't get near it.

"I'm telling you"—Greg pulled the ashtray from under the table's jukebox and lit up a cigarette—"things have been messed up recently. I mean, *messed up*."

"Messed up how?"

"The vampires, man." Greg took a long drag. "There's something wrong with them."

"I found a few in my apartment last night when I got home," Magnus said. "They didn't seem right. They were disgusting, for a start. And they looked sick."

"They are sick. They're feeding like crazy. It's getting bad, man. It's getting bad. I'm telling you..."

He leaned in and lowered his voice.

"Shadowhunters are going to be *all over us* if the vampires don't get it under control. Right now I'm not sure the Shadowhunters know what's going on. The murder rate in the city is so high, maybe they can't tell. But it won't be long before they figure it out."

Magnus leaned back in his seat.

"Camille usually keeps things under control."

Greg gave a heavy shrug. "I can only tell you that the vamps started coming around to all the clubs and discos. They love that stuff. But then they just started attacking people all the time. In the clubs, on the streets. The NYPD thinks the attacks are weird muggings, so it's been kept quiet so far. But when the Shadowhunters find out, they're going to come down on us. They're getting trigger-happy. Any excuse."

"The Accords prohibit—"

"The Accords my ass. I'm telling you, it won't be long before they start ignoring the Accords. And the vampires are so in violation that anything can happen. I'm telling you, it's all so *messed up*."

A plate of pancakes was deposited in front of Magnus, and he and Greg stopped speaking for a moment. Greg stubbed out his barely smoked cigarette.

"I gotta go," he said. "I was out patrolling to see if anyone had been attacked, and I saw you through the window. Wanted to say hi. It's nice to see you back."

Magnus dropped five dollars onto the table and pushed the pancakes away.

"I'll come with you. I want to see this for myself."

The temperature had shot up in the hour or so he'd been in the diner. This amplified the pong of the overflowing trash—spilling out of metal trash cans (which only cooked it and intensified the scent), bags of it piled up on the curbs. Trash just thrown down onto the street itself. Magnus stepped over the hamburger wrappers and cans and newspapers.

"Two basic areas to patrol," Greg said, lighting up a new cigarette. "This area and midtown west. We go street by street. I'm working west from here. There are a lot of clubs over by the river, in the Meatpacking District."

"It's quite warm."

"This heat, man. I guess it could be the heat making them freak out. It gets to everyone."

Greg pulled off his vest. There were certainly worse things than taking a walk with a handsome, shirtless man on a summer morning. Now that it was more of a civilized hour, people were out. Gay couples walking hand in hand, in the open, during the day. That was fairly new. Even as the city seemed to be falling apart, something good was happening.

"Has Lincoln spoken to Camille?" Magnus asked.

Max Lincoln was the head of the werewolves. Everyone just called him by his last name, which fit with his tall and gaunt frame and bearded face—and because, like the more famous Lincoln, he was a famously calm and resolute leader.

"They don't talk," Greg said. "Not anymore. Camille comes down here for the clubs, and that's it. You know what she's like."

Magnus knew all too well. Camille had always been a bit aloof, at least to strangers and acquaintances. She had the air of royalty. The private Camille was a different beast entirely.

"What about Raphael Santiago?" Magnus asked.

"He's gone."

"Gone?"

"Rumor is that he's been sent away. I heard that from one of the fey. They claim to have overheard it from some vamps walking through Central Park. He must have known about what was happening and had some words with Camille. Now he's just gone."

This didn't bode well.

They walked through the Village, past the shops and cafés, up toward the Meatpacking District, with its cobbled streets and disused warehouses. Many of these were now clubs. There was a desolate feel here in the morning—just the remains of the abandoned parties and the river slugging along below. Even the river seemed to resent the heat. They checked everywhere—in the alleys, next to the trash. They looked under vans and trucks.

"Nothing," Greg said as they peered into and poked the last pile of trash in the last alley. "Guess it was a quiet night. Time to check in. It's late."

This required a quick walk in the ever-increasing heat. Greg couldn't pay for a cab and refused to allow Magnus to do so, so Magnus unhappily joined in the jog all the way down to Canal Street. The werewolves' den was concealed behind the facade of a take-out-only restaurant in Chinatown. One werewolf stood behind the counter, under the menu and the stock photos of various Chinese dishes. She looked Magnus over. When Greg nodded, she let them pass through a beaded curtain to the back.

There was no kitchen behind the back wall. Instead there was a door that led to a much larger facility—the old Second Precinct police station. (The cells came in handy during the full moon.) Magnus followed Greg down the dimly lit hallway to the main room of the station, which was already full. The pack had gathered, and Lincoln stood at the head of the room, listening to a report and nodding gravely. When he saw Magnus, he raised a hand in greeting.

"All right," Lincoln said. "Looks like everyone is here. And we have a guest. Many of you know Magnus Bane. He's a warlock, as you see, and a friend to this pack."

This was accepted at once, and there were nods and greetings all around. Magnus leaned against a file cabinet near the back to watch the proceedings.

"Greg," Lincoln said, "you're the last in. Anything?"

"Nope. My patch was clean."

"Good. But unfortunately, there was an incident. Elliot? Want to explain?"

Another werewolf stepped forward.

"We found a body," he said. "In midtown, near Le Jardin. Definitely a vampire attack. Clear marking on the neck. We slit the throat so the puncture marks were hidden."

There was a general groan around the room.

"That will keep the words 'vampire killer' out of the papers for a while," Lincoln said. "But clearly things have gotten worse, and now someone is dead."

Magnus heard various remarks in low voices about vampires,

and some in louder voices. All of the remarks contained profanity.

"Okay." Lincoln put his hands up and silenced the general sounds of dismay. "Magnus, what do you think about this?"

"I don't know," Magnus said. "I only just got back."

"Ever seen anything like this? Mass, random attacks?"

All heads turned in his direction. He steadied himself against the file cabinet. He wasn't quite ready to give a presentation on the ways of vampires at this hour of the morning.

"I've seen bad behavior," Magnus said. "It really depends. I've been in places where there was no police force and no Shadowhunters nearby, so sometimes it can get out of hand. But I've never seen anything like it here, or in any developed area. *Especially* not near an Institute."

"We need to take care of this," a voice called out.

Various voices of assent echoed around the room.

"Let's talk outside," Lincoln said to Magnus.

He nodded at the door, and the werewolves parted so that Magnus could pass. Lincoln and Magnus got some burned coffee at the corner deli and sat on a stoop in front of an acupuncturist's shop.

"Something's wrong with them," Lincoln said. "Whatever it is, it hit fast, and it hit hard. If we have diseased vampires around causing this kind of bloodshed ... eventually we'll have to act, Magnus. We can't let it go on. We can't let murders happen, and we can't run the risk of bringing the Shadowhunters down here. We can't have problems like that starting up again. It will end badly for all of us."

Magnus examined the crack in the step below. "Have you contacted the Praetor Lupus?" he asked.

"Of course. But we can't identify who is doing this. It doesn't seem like the work of one rogue fledgling. This is multiple attacks in multiple locations. The only luck for us is that all of the victims have been on various substances, so they can't articulate what happened to them. If one of them says vampire, the police will think it's because they're high. But eventually the story will take shape. The press will get wind of it, and the Shadowhunters will get wind of it, and the whole thing will escalate rapidly."

Lincoln was right. If this went on, the werewolves would be well within their rights to act. And then there would be blood.

"You know Camille," Lincoln said. "You could talk to her."

"I *knew* Camille. You probably know her better than I do at this point."

"I don't know how to talk to Camille. She's a difficult person to communicate with. I would have spoken to her already if I knew how. And our relationship isn't quite the same as the relationship you had."

"We don't really get along," Magnus said. "We haven't spoken for several decades."

"But everyone knows that you two were..."

"*That* was a long time ago. A hundred years ago, Lincoln."

"For you two does that kind of time even matter?"

"What would you want me to say to her? It's hard to walk in after that long a time and just say, 'Stop attacking people. Also, how have you been since the turn of the century?'"

"If there's something wrong, maybe you could help them. If they're just overfeeding, then they need to know that we're prepared to act. And if you care for her, which I think you do, she deserves this warning. It would be for the good of us all."

He put his hand on Magnus's shoulder.

"Please," Lincoln said. "It's possible we can still fix this. Because if this goes on, we'll all suffer."

Magnus had many exes. They were strewn throughout history. Most of them were memories, long dead. Some were now very old. Etta, one of his last loves, was now in a nursing home and no longer recognized him. It had become too painful to visit her.

Camille Belcourt was different. She'd come into Magnus's life under the light of a gas lamp, looking regal. That had been in

London, and it had been a different world. Their romance had happened in fog. It had happened in carriages bumping along cobbled streets, on settees covered in damson-colored silk. They'd loved in the time of the clockwork creatures, before the mundane wars. There seemed to be more time then, time to fill, time to spend. And they'd filled it. And they'd spent it.

They had parted badly. When you love someone that intensely and they do not love you in the same way, it is impossible to part well.

Camille had arrived in New York at the end of the 1920s, just as the Crash had been happening and everything had been falling apart. She had a great sense of drama, and a good nose for places that were in crisis and in need of a guiding hand. In no time at all she'd become the head of the vampires. She had a place inside the famous Eldorado building on the Upper West Side. Magnus knew where she was, and she knew where Magnus was. But neither of them contacted the other. They had passed each other, purely by accident, at various clubs and events over the years. They'd exchanged only a quick nod. That relationship was over. It was a live wire, not to be touched. It was the one temptation in life Magnus knew to leave alone.

And yet here he was, just twenty-four hours back in New York, stepping into the Eldorado. This was one of New York's great art deco apartment buildings. It sat right on the west side of Central Park, overlooking the reservoir. It was notable for its two matching square towers jutting up like horns. The Eldorado was the home of the old money, the celebrities, the people who simply *had*. The uniformed doorman was trained not to take notice of anyone's attire or mien as long as they looked like they had come to the building for a legitimate reason. For the occasion Magnus had decided to skip his new look. There would be no punk here—no vinyl or fishnet. Tonight was a Halston suit, black, with wide satin lapels. This passed the test, and he got a nod and a light smile. Camille lived on the twenty-eighth floor of the north tower, a silent oak-paneled and brass-railed elevator ride up into some of the most expensive real estate in Manhattan.

The towers made for some very small, very intimate floors. Some had only one or two inhabitants. There were two in this case. Camille lived in 28C. Magnus could hear music seeping out from under the door. There was a strong smell of smoke and the leftover perfume of whoever had just passed this way. Despite the fact that there was activity inside, it took about three minutes of knocking before someone answered.

He was surprised to find that he recognized this person at once. It was a face from long ago. At the time the woman had had a little black bob and had worn a flapper dress. She'd been young then, and while she had retained the basic youth (vampires didn't really age), she looked world-worn. Now her hair was bleached blond and formed into heavy, long curls. She wore a skin-tight gold dress that skimmed her knees, and a cigarette dangled from the side of her mouth.

"Well, well, well. It's everyone's favorite warlock! I haven't seen you since you were running that speakeasy. It's been a long time."

"It has," Magnus said. "Daisy?"

"Dolly." She pushed the door open wider. "Look who it is, everyone!"

The room was full of vampires, all of whom were dressed extremely well. Magnus had to give them that. The men wore the white suits that were so popular this season. The women all had fantastic disco dresses, mostly in white or gold. The mix of hair spray, cigarette smoke, incense, and colognes and perfumes took his breath away for a moment.

Aside from the strong smells, there was a tension in the air that had no real basis. Magnus was no stranger to vampires, yet this group was *uptight*, looking to one another. Shifting around. Waiting for something.

There was no invitation to enter.

"Is Camille in?" Magnus finally asked.

Dolly cocked a hip against the door.

"What brings you here tonight, Magnus?"

"I've just gotten back from an extended vacation. It just felt right to pay a visit."

"Did it?"

In the background someone turned down the record player until the music was barely audible.

"Someone go talk to Camille," Dolly said without turning around. She remained where she was, blocking the doorway with her tiny body. She closed the door a bit to reduce the space she had to fill. She continued smiling up at Magnus in a way that was a bit unnerving.

"Just a minute," she said.

In the background someone moved into the hallway.

"What's this?" Dolly said, plucking something from Magnus's pocket. "Electrica? I've never heard of this club."

"It's new. They claim to be better than Studio 54. I've never been to either, so I don't know. Someone gave me the passes."

Magnus had stuck the passes into his pocket as he'd been walking out the door. After all, he had gone to the effort of dressing up. Should this errand end as badly as he thought it would, it would be nice to have somewhere to go afterward.

Dolly twisted the passes into a fan and waved it lightly in front of her face.

"Take them," Magnus said. It was evident that Dolly had already taken them and was not giving them back, so it seemed polite to make it official.

The vampire emerged from the hallway and conferred with some others on the sofa and around the room. Then a different vampire came over to the door. Dolly stepped behind the door for a moment, closing it farther. Magnus heard a mumbling. Then the door opened again, wide enough to admit him.

"It's your lucky night," she said. "This way."

The white wall-to-wall carpet was so shaggy and thick that Dolly wobbled on her high heels as she traversed it. The carpet had stains all over it—spilled drinks, ash, and puddles of things he supposed were blood. The white sofas and chairs were in similar condition. The many large plants and potted palms and fronds were all dry and sagging. Several pictures on the walls were askew. There were bottles and empty glasses with dried-up wine at the bottom everywhere. It was the same kind of disarray Magnus had found in his apartment.

More disturbing was the silence from all the vampires in the room who watched him being led along by Dolly to the hallway. And then there was the sofa full of unmoving humans—subjugates, no doubt, all dazed and slumped, their mouths hanging open, the bruises and wounds on their necks and arms and hands looking quite ugly. The glass table in front of them had a fine coating of white powder and a few razor blades. The only noise was the muted music and a low rumble of thunder outside.

"This way," Dolly said, taking Magnus by the sleeve.

The hall was dark, and there were clothes and shoes all over the floor. Muffled noises came from the three doors along the hall. Dolly walked right to the end, to a double door. She rapped on this once and pushed it open.

"Go ahead," she said, still smiling her weird little smile.

In stark contrast to the whiteness of everything in the living room, this room was the dark side of the apartment. The carpet was an indigo black, like a nighttime sea. The walls were covered in deep silver wallpaper. The lamp shades were all covered by gold and silver shawls and throws. The tables were all mirrored, reflecting the view back and forth again. And in the middle of it all was a massive black lacquer bed with black sheets and a heavy gold cover. And on it was Camille, in a peach silk kimono.

And a hundred years seemed to vanish. Magnus felt himself unable to speak for a moment. It might as well have been London again, the whole twentieth century rolled up into a ball and tossed aside.

But then the present moment came crashing back when Camille began an ungainly crawl in his direction, slipping on the satin sheets.

"Magnus! Magnus! Magnus! Come here! Come! Sit down!"

Her silver-blond hair was long and down, looking wild. She patted the end of the bed. This was not the greeting he'd been expecting. This was not the Camille he remembered, or even the one he had seen in passing.

As he made to step over what he thought was a lump of clothing, he realized there was a human on the floor, facedown. He bent down and gently reached into the mass of long black hair to turn the person's face upward. It was a woman, and there was still some warmth in her, and a faint pulse beating in her neck.

"That's Sarah," Camille said, flopping onto the bed and hanging her head off the end to watch.

"You've been feeding from her," Magnus said. "Is she a willing donor?"

"Oh, she loves it. Now, Magnus... You look marvelous, by the way. Is that Halston...? We're just about to go out. And *you* are coming with us."

She slid from the bed and tripped her way into a massive closet. Magnus heard hangers being scraped along rails. Magnus examined the girl on the floor again. She had punctures all over her neck—and now she was smiling weakly at Magnus and pushing back her hair, offering him a bite.

"I'm not a vampire," he said, resting her head gently on the floor again. "And you should get out of here. Do you want my help?"

The girl made a sound that was just between a laugh and a whimper.

"Which one of these?" Camille said as she came stumbling back out of the closet, holding two almost identical black evening dresses.

"This girl is weak," he said. "Camille, you've taken too much blood from her. She needs a hospital."

"She's fine. Leave her alone. Help me pick a dress."

Everything about this exchange was wrong. This was not how the reunion should have gone. It should have been coy; it should have had many strange pauses and moments of double meaning. Instead Camille was acting like she'd just seen Magnus yesterday. Like they were simply friends. It was enough of an entry to allow him to get to the point.

"I'm here because there's a problem, Camille. Your vampires are killing people and leaving bodies on the street. They're overfeeding."

"Oh, Magnus." Camille shook her head. "I may be in charge, but I don't control them. You have to allow for a certain amount of freedom."

"This includes killing mundanes and leaving their bodies out on the sidewalk?"

Camille was no longer listening. She had dropped the dresses onto the bed and was picking though a pile of earrings. Meanwhile Sarah was attempting to crawl in Camille's direction. Without even looking at her, Camille set a mirror full of white powder down on the floor. Sarah went right for it and began sniffing it up.

And then Magnus understood.

While human drugs didn't quite work on Downworlders, there was no telling what would happen when that drug was run through a human circulatory system *and then ingested* through the human blood.

It all made sense. The disarray. The confused behavior. The frenzied feeding in the clubs. The fact that they all looked so ill, that their personalities seemed to have changed. He'd seen this a thousand times in mundanes.

Camille was looking at him now, her gaze unwavering.

"Come out with us tonight, Magnus," she cooed. "You are a man who knows a good time. I am a woman who provides a good time. Come out with us."

"Camille, you have to stop. You have to know how dangerous this is."

"It's not going to kill me, Magnus. That's quite impossible. And you don't understand how it *feels*."

"The drug can't kill you, but other things can. If you continue like this, you know there are people out there who can't let you go on murdering mundanes. Someone will act."

"Let them try," she said. "I could take on ten Shadowhunters once I've had some of this."

"It may not be—"

Camille dropped to the floor before he could finish and buried her face into Sarah's neck. Sarah flailed once and groaned, then became silent and motionless. He heard the sickening sound of the drinking, the sucking. Camille lifted her head, blood all around her mouth, running down her chin.

"Are you coming or not?" she said. "I would simply love to take you to Studio 54. You've never had a night out like one of our nights out."

Magnus had to force himself to keep looking at her like this.

"Let me help you. A few hours, a few days—I could get this out of your system."

Camille dragged the back of her hand across her mouth, smearing the blood onto her cheek.

"If you're not coming along, then stay out of our way. Consider this a polite warning, Magnus. Dolly!"

Dolly was already at the door. "Think you're done here," she said.

Magnus watched Camille sink her teeth into Sarah again.

"Yes," he said. "I think I am."

Outside, a downpour was in progress. The doorman held an umbrella over Magnus's head and hailed him a cab. The incongruity of the

civility downstairs and what he'd seen upstairs was...
It wasn't to be thought about. Magnus got into the cab, gave his destination, and closed his eyes. The rain drummed onto the cab. It felt like the rain was beating directly onto his brain.

Magnus wasn't surprised to find Lincoln sitting on the steps by his door. Wearily he waved him inside.

"Well?" Lincoln said.

"It's not good," Magnus replied, pulling off his wet jacket. "It's the drugs. They're feeding on the blood of people who are taking drugs. It must be escalating their need and lowering their impulse control."

"You're right," Lincoln said. "That isn't good. I thought it might have something to do with the drugs, but I thought they were immune to things like addiction."

Magnus poured them each a glass of wine, and they sat and listened to the rain for a moment.

"Can you help her?" Lincoln asked.

"If she lets me. But you can't cure an addict who doesn't want to be cured."

"No," Lincoln said. "I've seen that myself with our own. But you understand ... we can't let this behavior continue."

"I know you can't."

Lincoln finished his wine and set the glass down gently.

"I'm sorry, Magnus. I really am. But if it happens again, you need to leave it to us."

Magnus nodded. Lincoln gave him a squeeze on the shoulder, then let himself out.

For the next several days Magnus kept to himself. The weather was brutal, flicking between heat and storm. He tried to forget about the scene in Camille's apartment, and the best way to forget was to keep busy. He hadn't really kept up with his work for the last two years. There were clients to call. There were spells to study and translations to do. Books to read. The apartment needed redecorating. There were new restaurants and new bars and new people...

Every time he stopped, he flashed back to the sight of Camille squatting on the carpet, the girl limp in her arms, the mirror full of drugs, Camille's face covered in blood. The mess. The stink. The horror. The blank looks.

When you lost someone to addiction—and he had lost many—you lost something very precious. You watched them fall. You waited for them to hit the bottom. It was a terrible wait. He would have nothing to do with it. What happened now was not his problem. He had no doubt that Lincoln and the werewolves would take care of things, and the less he knew the better.

It kept him awake at night. That, and the thunder.

Sleeping alone was Hell, so he decided not to sleep alone.

He still woke up.

It was the night of July thirteenth—lucky thirteen. The thunderstorm outside was incredibly loud, louder than the air conditioner, louder than the radio. Magnus was just finishing up a translation and was about to go out to dinner, when the lights flickered. The radio faded in and out. Then everything went very bright as power surged through the wires. Then...

Out. Air conditioner, lights, radio, everything. Magnus flicked his hand absently and lit a candle on his desk. Power outages were not uncommon. It was a moment before he realized that things had grown very quiet and very dark indeed, and there were voices shouting outside. He went to the window and opened it.

Everything was dark. The streetlights. Every building. Everything except the headlights of the cars. He took the candle and carefully walked down the two flights to the street and joined the excited masses of people. The rain had stopped—it was just thunder grumbling in the background.

New York ... was off. Everything was off. There was no skyline.

There was no glow of the Empire State Building. It was utterly, utterly dark. And one word was being yelled from window to window, from street to car to doorway...

"BLACKOUT."

The parties started almost at once. It was the ice cream shop on the corner that kicked it off, selling anything they had for a dime a cone, and then just giving away the ice cream to anyone who came by with a bowl or a cup. Then the bars started passing around cocktails in paper cups to passersby. Everyone poured out onto the streets. People propped battery-powered radios in the windows, so there was a mix of music and news reports. The outage had been caused by a lightning strike. All of New York was down. It would be hours—days?—before service was restored.

Magnus returned to his apartment, got a bottle of champagne from his refrigerator, and returned to his front stoop to drink it, sharing it with a few people who walked past. It was too hot to stay inside, and the outside was far too interesting to miss. People started dancing on the sidewalk, and he joined in for a while. He accepted a martini from a nice young man with a beautiful smile.

Then there was a hissing. People gathered around one of the radios, one playing news. Magnus and his new friend, who was named David, joined them.

"*... fires throughout the five boroughs. More than a hundred fires have been reported in the last hour. And we have multiple reports of lootings. Gunfire is being exchanged. Please—if you are out tonight, use extreme caution. Though all police have been called in to duty, there are not enough officers to ...*"

Another radio a few yards away, on a different station, gave a similar report.

"*... hundreds of stores have been broken into. There are reports of total breakdowns in some areas. You are strongly advised to stay indoors. If you cannot get home, seek shelter in a ...*"

In the short silence, Magnus could hear sirens in the distance.

The Village was a tight community, so it celebrated. But clearly this was not the case all over the city.

"Magnus!"

Magnus turned to find Greg breaking through the group. He pulled Magnus away from the crowd, into a quiet space between two parked cars.

"I thought that was you," he said. "It's all happening. They've gone nuts. The blackout... The vampires are going crazy at this club. I can't even explain it. It's on Tenth Ave and down a block. No cabs in this blackout. You have to run."

Now that Magnus was trying to get somewhere, he realized the pure madness of the blacked-out streets. Since there were no traffic lights, normal people were trying to guide traffic. Cars were either frozen in place or moving far too fast. Some were parked and turned inward, their headlights being used to illuminate stores and restaurants. Everyone was out—the Village had poured out of every building, and there was no room anywhere. Magnus and Greg had to weave through the people, through the cars, tripping in the dark.

The crowds thinned somewhat the closer they got to the river. The club was in one of the old meatpacking warehouses. The brick industrial facade had been painted silver, and the word ELECTRICA, along with a lightning bolt, was above the old service doors. Two werewolves stood by these, holding flashlights, and Lincoln waited off to the side. He was deep in conversation with Consuela, who was his second-in-command. When they saw Magnus, Consuela stepped aside to a waiting van, and Lincoln came over.

"This is what we feared," Lincoln said. "We waited too long."

The werewolves guarding the entrance parted, and Lincoln pushed open the doors. Inside the club it was entirely pitch black, save for the beams from the werewolves' flashlights. There was a strong smell of spilled, mixed liquor and something unpleasantly tangy and sharp.

Magnus raised his hands. The neon lights around the room

buzzed and glowed. The overhead work lights—unflattering fluorescents—sputtered on. And the disco ball crept to life, slowly spinning, sending a thousand points of colored reflected light around the room. The dance floor, made of large squares of colored plastic, was also illuminated from below.

Which made the scene all the more terrible.

There were four bodies, three women and one man. All looked like they had been running for various points of exit. Their skin was the color of ash, marked everywhere with greenish-purple bruises and dozens of marks, and garishly lit by the red, yellow, and blue lights below them. There was very little blood. Just a few small puddles here and there. Not nearly as much blood as there should have been.

One of the dead women, Magnus noticed, had familiar long blond hair. He'd last seen her on the plane, handing him the passes...

Magnus had to turn away quickly.

"They were all drained," Lincoln said. "The club hadn't opened for the night yet. They were having trouble with their sound system even before the power went out, so the only people here were the employees. Two there..."

He pointed to the raised DJ platform with its piles of turntables and speakers. Some werewolves were up there examining the scene.

"Two behind the bar," he continued. "Another one ran and hid in the bathroom, but the door was broken down. And these four. Nine total."

Magnus sat down on one of the nearby chairs and put his head in his hands for a moment to gather himself. No matter how long you lived, you never got used to seeing terrible things. Lincoln gave him a moment to collect himself.

"This is my fault. When I went to see Camille, one of them took the passes to this place from my pocket."

Lincoln pulled over a chair and sat next to Magnus.

"That doesn't make it your fault. I asked you to speak to Camille.

If Camille came here because of you ... it doesn't put the blame on either of us, Magnus. But you can see now, it can't go on."

"What do you plan on doing?" Magnus said.

"There are fires tonight. All over the city. We take this opportunity. We burn this place down. I think it would spare the victims' families for them to think their loved ones died in a fire, rather than..."

He indicated the terrible scene just behind them.

"You're right," Magnus said. "No good could come of anyone seeing their loved one like that."

"No. And no good would come of the police seeing this. It would send the city into a complete panic, and the Shadowhunters would be forced to come down here. We keep this quiet. We deal with it."

"And the vampires?"

"We're going to go and get them, and lock them in here while it burns. We have permission from the Praetor Lupus. The entire clan is to be treated as infected, but we'll try to be judicious. The first one we'll be getting, though, is Camille."

Magnus exhaled slowly.

"Magnus," Lincoln said, "what else can we do? She's the clan leader. We need this to end now."

"Give me an hour," Magnus said. "One hour. If I can get them off the streets in an hour—"

"There's already a group headed up to Camille's apartment. Another will go to the Hotel Dumont."

"How long ago did they leave?"

"About a half hour."

"Then I'm going now." Magnus stood. "I have to try to do something."

"Magnus," Lincoln said, "if you stand in the way, the pack will remove you from the situation. Do you understand that?"

Magnus nodded.

"I'll come up when we're done here," Lincoln said. "I'll go to the Dumont. That's where they'll end up anyway."

* * *

A Portal was required. Given the situation on the streets, there was every chance that the werewolves hadn't gotten to Camille's apartment yet—if that was even where she was. He would just need to get to her. But before he could even start to draw the runes, he heard a voice in the dark.

"You're here."

Magnus turned on his heel and threw up a hand to illuminate the alley.

Camille was moving toward him, unsteady. She wore a long, black dress—rather, it was a dress that was now colored black from the sheer quantity of blood on it. It was still wet and heavy, and it stuck to her legs as she made her way forward.

"Magnus..."

Her voice was thick. Smears of blood covered Camille's face, her arms, her silver-blond hair. She held one hand against a wall for support as she moved toward him in a series of heavy, toddler-like steps.

Magnus approached her slowly. As soon as he got close enough, she gave up the effort of standing and fell forward. He caught her halfway to the ground.

"I knew you'd come," she said.

"What have you done, Camille?"

"I was looking for you... Dolly said you were ... you were here."

Magnus gently lowered her to the ground.

"Camille ... do you know what's happened? Do you know what you did?"

The smell coming from her was nauseating. Magnus breathed sharply through his nose to steady himself. Camille's eyes were rolling back into her head. He gave her a shake.

"You need to listen to me," he said. "Try to stay awake. You need to summon all of them."

"I don't know where they are... They're everywhere. It's so *dark*.

It's our night, Magnus. For my little ones. For us."

"You must have grave dirt," Magnus said.

This got a loose nod.

"Okay. We get the grave dirt. You use it to summon them. Where is the grave dirt?"

"In the vault."

"And where is the vault?"

"Green-Wood ... Cemetery. Brooklyn..."

Magnus stood and began to draw the runes. When he was finished and the Portal began to open, he picked Camille up from the ground and held on to her tightly.

"Think of it now," he said. "Get it clearly in your mind. The vault."

Considering Camille's state, this was a risky proposition. Holding her closer, feeling the blood on her clothing seep through his shirt ... Magnus stepped through.

There were trees here. Trees and a bit of moonlight cutting through the cloudy night sky. Absolutely no people, no voices. Just the distant rumble of the stuck traffic. And hundreds of white slabs jutting up from the ground.

Magnus and Camille were standing in front of a mausoleum that resembled a folly—the front piece of a tiny colonnaded temple. It was built directly into the side of a low hill.

Magnus looked down and saw that Camille had found the strength to wrap her slender arms around him. She was shuddering a bit.

"Camille?"

She tipped her head upward. She was crying. Camille did not cry. Even under these circumstances, Magnus was moved. He still wanted to console her, wanted to take the time to tell her everything would be all right. But all he could say was, "Do you have the key?"

She shook her head. There hadn't been much chance of that. Magnus put his hand on the lock securing the wide metal doors, closed his eyes, and concentrated until he felt the light click under his fingertips.

The vault was about eight-foot square and was made of concrete. The walls were lined with wooden shelves, floor to ceiling. And those shelves were filled with small glass vials of earth. The vials varied quite a bit—some were thick green, or yellow blown glass with visible bubbles. There were thinner bottles, some extremely small bottles, a few tiny brown bottles. The oldest ones were stopped up with corks. Some had glass stoppers. The newest had screw-on caps. The age was also seen in the layers of dust, the grime, the amount of webbing running between them. In the back, you wouldn't have been able to lift some of the bottles from the shelves, so thick was the accumulated residue. There was a history of New York vampirism here that would probably have interested many, that was probably worth studying...

Magnus put out his hands, and with one great blast of blue light, all the vials burst at once. There was a great cough of dirt and glass powder.

"Where will they go?" he asked Camille.

"The Dumont."

"Of course," Magnus said. "Them and everyone else. We're going there, and you're going to do as I say. We need to make this right, Camille. You have to try. Do you understand?"

She nodded once.

This time Magnus was in control of the Portal. They emerged on 116th Street, in the middle of what appeared to be a full-scale riot. There were fires here. The echoes of screams and breaking glass went from one end of the street to the other. No one took any notice of the fact that Magnus and Camille were suddenly in their midst. It was too dark, and far too crazy. The heat was much worse in this area, and Magnus felt his entire body dripping with sweat.

There were two vans parked directly in front of the Dumont, and an unmistakable crowd of werewolves was already gathered. They had baseball bats and chains. That was all that was visible. There were undoubtedly some containers of holy water. There was already plenty of fire around.

Magnus pulled Camille down behind the cover of a parked Cadillac that had already had all its windows smashed. He reached around inside and popped open the door.

"Get in," he said to Camille. "And stay down. They're after you. Let me go and talk to them."

Even as Magnus was making his way around the car, Camille found the strength to crawl across the glass-strewn front seat and was falling out through the driver's side door. When Magnus tried to get her back inside, she pushed him away.

"Get out of the way, Magnus. It's me they want."

"They'll *kill* you, Camille."

But she had been seen. The werewolves crossed the street, bats at the ready. Camille held up a hand. Several vampires had just arrived in front of the hotel. Several others had already fought, and several others were lying, still, on the sidewalk. A few more were being restrained.

"Go inside the hotel," she ordered.

"Camille—they'll burn us," one said. "*Look* at them. Look at what's happening."

Camille looked to Magnus, and he understood. She was leaving this to him.

"Get inside," she said again. "That is not a request."

One by one over the course of the next hours, every vampire in New York—no matter what condition they were in—appeared on the steps of the Dumont. Camille, leaning against the doors for support, ordered them inside. They passed through the phalanx of werewolves with their bats and chains, looking wary. It was almost dawn when the last groups appeared.

Lincoln arrived at the same time.

"Some are missing," Camille said as he got out of his car.

"Some are dead," Lincoln replied. "You have Magnus to thank that more aren't dead."

Camille nodded once, then went inside the hotel and shut the doors.

"And now?" Lincoln said.

"You can't cure them without their consent—but you can dry them out. They stay locked in there until they are clean," Magnus said.

"And if this doesn't work?"

Magnus looked at the broken-down facade of the Dumont. Someone, he noticed, had changed the *n* to an *r*. Dumort. Hotel of the dead.

"Let's see what happens," Magnus said.

For three days, Magnus kept the wards on the Dumont. He went by several times a day. Werewolves patrolled the perimeter all hours, making sure no one got out. On the third day, just after sunset, Magnus released the ward on the front door and went inside, and sealed it again behind him.

Clearly there had been an organizing principle at work inside the hotel. The vampires who had not been affected by the drug were littered throughout the lobby and on the balconies and steps. They were mostly sleeping. The werewolves now permitted them to rise and leave.

With Lincoln and his aides by his side, Magnus retraced the steps he had taken almost fifty years before, to the ballroom of the Dumont. Once again the doors were sealed—this time with a chain.

"Get the cutters from the van," Lincoln said.

There was a truly terrible smell coming from under the door.

Please, Magnus thought. *Be empty.*

Of course the ballroom would not be empty. It was a silly wish that all the events of the last three days simply hadn't happened.

Because in the end nothing is worse than seeing the fall of one you loved. It was somehow worse than losing a love. It made everything seem questionable. It made the past bitter and confused.

The werewolf returned with the bolt cutters, and the chain was snapped, and landed on the floor with a hollow clank. A few of the unaffected vampires had remained behind to watch, and they were gathered at the werewolves' backs.

Magnus pushed the door open.

The white marble floor of the ballroom was splintered. Had that really been fifty years ago, right here, where Aldous had opened the Portal to the Void?

The vampires were scattered in every part of the room, maybe thirty in all. These were the sick, and they were all in a profound state of suffering. The smell alone was enough to gag anyone. And the werewolves lifted their hands to their faces to block it out.

The vampires made no move and gave no greeting. Only a few lifted their faces to see what was happening. Magnus stepped over them, looking at each one. He found Dolly near the center of the room, not moving. He found Camille sprawled behind one of the long curtains that hung at the far end of the ballroom. Like the others, she was surrounded by a number of foul pools of regurgitated blood.

Her eyes were open.

"I want to walk," she said. "Help me, Magnus. Help me walk a bit. I need to look strong."

There was a steadiness to her voice, despite the fact that she was too weak to get up on her own. Magnus bent down and lifted her to her feet, then supported her as she walked, with as much dignity as she could, over the slumped bodies of her clan. He sealed the doors again when they had left.

"Up," she said. "Around. I need to walk. Upstairs."

He could feel the strain as she took each step. Sometimes he was mostly carrying her.

"Do you remember?" she said. "Old Aldous opening the Portal here ... remember? I had to warn you about what he was doing."

"I remember."

"Even the mundanes knew to stay away from the place and let it rot. I hate that some of my little ones live in rotten places, but it's dark. It's safe."

It was too difficult to talk and walk, so she fell silent again and leaned against Magnus's chest. When they reached the top floor, they stood against the rail and looked down at the wreckage of the hotel lobby.

"It never really went away for us, did it?" she said. "There's really never been another—not like you. Is it the same for you?"

"Camille..."

"I know we can't go back. I know. Just tell me there's never been another like me."

In truth there had been many others. And while Camille was certainly in a class by herself, there had been much love—at least on Magnus's part. Yet there was a hundred years of pain in that question, and Magnus had to wonder if maybe he had not been so alone in his feeling.

"No," Magnus said. "There's never been another like you."

She seemed to gain some strength from that.

"It was never meant to happen," she said. "There was a club downtown where some of the mundanes enjoyed getting bitten. They had the drugs in their system. They are quite powerful, these substances. It just took hold. I was given some of the infected blood to drink as a gift. I didn't know what I was drinking—I only knew what effect it had. I didn't know we were capable of addiction. We didn't know."

Magnus looked at the char on the ceiling. Old wounds. Nothing ever *really* went away.

"I will ... I will make the command," she said. "What happened here will never happen again. You have my word."

"It's not me you have to tell."

"Tell the Praetor," she replied. "Tell the Shadowhunters if you must. It will not happen again. I'll forfeit my life before I allow it."

"It's probably best you speak to Lincoln."

"Then I will speak to him."

The mantle of dignity had returned to her shoulders. Despite all that had happened, she was still Camille Belcourt.

"You should leave now," she said. "This isn't for you anymore."

Magnus wavered for a moment. Something—some part of him wanted to remain. But he found that he was already walking down the steps.

"Magnus," Camille called.

He turned.

"Thank you for lying to me. You have always been kind. I never have been. That was why we couldn't be, wasn't it?"

Without replying, Magnus turned and continued down the stairs. Raphael Santiago passed him on the way up.

"I am sorry," Raphael said.

"Where have you been?"

"When I saw what was happening, I tried to stop them. Camille attempted to make me drink some of the blood. She wanted everyone in her inner circle to participate. She was sick. I have seen such things before and knew how they would end. So I went away. I returned when a vial of my grave soil was broken."

"I never saw you enter the hotel," Magnus said.

"I entered through a broken basement window. I thought it was best to remain hidden for a while. I have been caring for the sick. It has been very unpleasant, but..."

He looked up, past Magnus's shoulder, in Camille's direction.

"I must go now. We have much to do here. Go, Magnus. There's nothing for you here."

Raphael had always been able to read Magnus a little too well.

* * *

Magnus made his decision when he was in the cab going home. Once he got inside his apartment, he prepared without hesitation, gathering everything he would need. He would need to be very specific. He would write it all down.

Then he called Catarina. He drank some wine while he waited for her to arrive.

Catarina was perhaps Magnus's truest and closest friend, aside from Ragnor (and that relationship was often in a state of flux). Catarina was the only one who'd gotten any letters or calls while he'd been on his two-year trip. He hadn't, however, actually told her he was home.

"Really?" she said when he opened the door. "*Two years*, and then you come back and don't even call for two weeks? And then it's, 'Come over, I need you'? You didn't even *tell* me you were home, Magnus."

"I'm home," he said, giving what he considered to be his most winning smile. The smiling took a bit of effort, but hopefully it looked genuine.

"Don't even try that face with me. I am not one of your conquests, Magnus. I am your friend. We are supposed to get pizza, not do the nasty."

"The nasty? But I—"

"Don't." She held up a warning finger. "I mean it. I almost didn't come. But you sounded so pathetic on the phone that I had to."

Magnus examined her rainbow T-shirt and pair of red overalls. Both of these stood out strongly against her blue skin. The contrast hurt Magnus's eyes. He decided not to comment on her attire. The red overalls were very popular. It was just that most people weren't blue. Most people did not *live* the rainbow.

"Why are you looking at me like that? Seriously, Magnus—"

"Let me explain," he said. "Then yell at me if you want."

So he explained. And she listened. Catarina was a nurse, and a good listener.

"Memory spells," she said, shaking her head. "Not really my thing. I'm a healer. You're the one who handles all this kind of stuff. If I do it wrong..."

"You won't."

"I might."

"I trust you. Here."

He handed Catarina the folded piece of paper. On it was a list of every time he'd seen Camille in New York. Every time in the entire twentieth century. These were the things that had to go.

"You know, there's a reason we can remember," she said more softly.

"That's much easier when your life has an expiration date."

"It may be more important for us."

"I loved her," he said. "I can't take what I saw."

"Magnus..."

"Either you do this or I attempt to do it on myself."

Catarina sighed and nodded. She examined the paper for several moments, then took hold of Magnus's temples very gently.

"You remember you're lucky to have me, right?" she said.

"Always."

Five minutes later Magnus was puzzled to find Catarina sitting beside him on the sofa.

"Catarina? What—"

"You were sleeping," she said. "You left the door open. I let myself in. You have to lock your door. This city is nuts. You may be a warlock, but that doesn't mean you won't get your stereo stolen."

"I usually lock it," Magnus said, rubbing his eyes. "I didn't even realize I fell asleep. How did you know I was—"

"You called me and said you were home and wanted to go out for pizza."

"I did? What time is it?"

"Time for pizza," she replied.

"I called you?"

"Uh-huh." She stood and put out a hand to help him up. "And you've been back for two weeks and just called me tonight, so you're in trouble. You sounded sorry on the phone but not sorry enough. More groveling will be needed."

"I know. I'm sorry. I was..."

Magnus struggled for the words. What had he been doing the last couple of weeks? Working. Calling clients. Dancing with handsome strangers. Something else too, but he couldn't quite think of it. It didn't matter.

"Pizza," she said again, pulling him to his feet.

"Pizza. Sure. Sounds good."

"Hey," she said as he was locking the door. "Have you heard anything about Camille recently?"

"*Camille?* I haven't seen her in at least ... eighty years? Something like that? Why are you asking about Camille?"

"No reason," she said. "Her name just popped into my mind. By the way, you're buying."

What to Buy the Shadowhunter Who Has Everything

(And Who You're Not Officially Dating Anyway)

By Cassandra Clare and
Sarah Rees Brennan

"Is Alec your lover?" asked Elyaas the tentacle demon.

Magnus stared. He was not ready for anyone to say "lover" to him with an oozing note of slime beneath the word. He felt he would never be ready.

—What to Buy the Shadowhunter Who Has Everything (And Who You're Not Officially Dating Anyway)

YOU SHOULD GET HIM A MIXED TAPE. KIDS LOVE MIXED TAPES.
THEY'RE THE COOL 'IN' THING RIGHT NOW.
WAS THE LAST TIME YOU WERE SUMMONED THE 80'S?
IT MIGHT HAVE BEEN
THINGS HAVE CHANGED.
DO PEOPLE STILL LISTEN TO FLEETWOOD MAC?
I LOVE THE MAC.

Magnus woke up with the slow golden light of midday filtering through his window, and his cat sleeping on his head.

Chairman Meow sometimes expressed his affection in this unfortunate way. Magnus gently but very firmly disentangled the cat from his hair, tiny claws doing even more damage as the Chairman was dislodged with a long sad cry of feline discomfort.

Then the cat jumped onto the pillow, apparently fully recovered from his ordeal, and leaped from the bed. He hit the floor with a soft thump and dashed with a rallying cry to the food bowl.

Magnus rolled over in bed so that he was lying across the mattress sideways. The window overlooking his bed was stained glass. Diamonds of gold and green drifted over his sheets, resting warmly against his bare skin. He lifted his head from the pillow he was clutching and then realized what he was doing: searching the air for a trace of the smell of coffee.

It had happened a few times in the last several weeks, Magnus stumbling out into the kitchen toward the rich scent of coffee, pulling on a robe from his wide and varied selection, and finding Alec there. Magnus had bought a coffeemaker because Alec had consistently seemed mildly distressed by Magnus's magicking-slash-slightly-stealing cups of coffee and tea from The Mudd Truck. The machine was extra bother, but Magnus was glad he had bought it. Alec had to know the coffeemaker was for him and his delicate moral sensibilities, and Alec seemed to feel a sense of comfort around the machine that he felt about nothing else, making coffee without asking if he could, bringing Magnus a cup when he was working. Everywhere else in Magnus's loft Alec was still careful, touching things as if he had no right to them, as if he were a guest.

And of course he was a guest. It was only that Magnus had an irrational desire for Alec to feel at home in his loft, as if that would mean something, as if that would give Magnus a claim on Alec or indicate that Alec wanted a claim on him. Magnus supposed that was it. He badly wanted Alec to want to be here, and to be happy when he was here.

He could not kidnap the Lightwoods' eldest born and keep him as a decoration about the house, however. Alec had fallen asleep twice—on the sofa, not the bed. Once after a long slow night of kissing; and once when Alec had come over for a brief coffee, clearly exhausted after a long day of demon-hunting, and he had slid into unconsciousness almost instantly. Magnus had also taken to leaving his front door open, since nobody was going to rob the High Warlock of Brooklyn, and Alec would sometimes come by in the early mornings.

Every time Alec had dropped by—or in the mornings after Alec had fallen asleep there—Magnus had woken to the sounds and smells of Alec's making him coffee, even though Alec knew that Magnus could magic coffee out of the air. Alec had done it only a few times, had been there for only a handful of mornings. It was not something Magnus should be getting used to.

Of course Alec wasn't here today, because it was his birthday, and he was going to be with his family. And Magnus wasn't exactly the kind of boyfriend you could bring to family outings. In fact, speaking of family outings, the Lightwoods didn't even know Alec had a boyfriend—much less one that was also a warlock—and Magnus had no idea if they ever would. It wasn't something he pushed Alec about. He could tell by Alec's carefulness that it was too early.

There was no reason for Magnus to slide out of bed, amble out through the living space into the kitchen space, and picture Alec kneeling at the counter, making coffee and wearing an ugly sweater, his face intent on the simple task. Alec was even conscientious about coffee. *And he wears truly awful sweaters,* Magnus thought, and was dismayed when the thought brought with it a rush of affection.

It was not the Lightwoods' fault. They obviously provided Alec's sister, Isabelle, and Jace Wayland with plenty of money to dress themselves in flattering outfits. Magnus suspected that Alec's mother bought his clothes, or Alec bought them himself on the basis of pure practicality—*Oh, look, how nice; gray won't show the ichor too much*—and then he wore the ugly functional clothes on and on without even seeming to notice that age was fraying them, or wear and tear causing holes.

Against his will, Magnus found a smile curving his lips as he rummaged around for his big blue coffee cup that said BETTER THAN GANDALF across the front in sparkly letters. He was besotted; he was officially revolted by himself.

He might have been besotted, but he had other things to think of besides Alec today. A mundane company had hired him to summon up a cecaelia demon. For the amount of money they were paying, and considering that cecaelia demons were lesser demons who could scarcely cause all that much fuss, Magnus had agreed to not ask questions. He sipped his coffee and contemplated his demon-summoning outfit for the day. Demon summoning was not something Magnus did often, on account of it being technically extremely illegal. Magnus did not have enormous respect for the Law, but if he was breaking it he wanted to look good doing it.

His thoughts were interrupted by the sound of the buzzer. He had not left his door open for Alec today, and he raised his eyebrows at the sound. Ms. Connor was twenty minutes early.

Magnus deeply disliked people who were early to business meetings. It was just as bad as being late, since it put everyone out, and even worse, people who were early always acted terribly superior about their bad timekeeping skills. They acted as though it were morally more righteous to get up early than to stay up late, even if you got the same amount of work done in the exact same amount of time. Magnus found it to be one of the great injustices of life.

It was possible that he was a bit cranky about not getting to finish his coffee before he had to deal with work.

He buzzed in the company representative. Ms. Connor turned out to be a woman in her midthirties whose looks bore out her Irish name. She had thick red hair done up in a twist, and the kind of impenetrable white skin that Magnus was prepared to bet never tanned. She was wearing a boxy but expensive-looking blue suit, and she looked extremely askance at Magnus's outfit.

This was Magnus's home, she had arrived early, and Magnus felt entirely within his rights to be dressed in nothing but black silk pajama bottoms decorated with a pattern of tigers and flamingos dancing. He did realize that the pants were sliding down his hips a fraction, and pulled them up. He saw Ms. Connor's disapproving gaze slip down his bare chest and fasten on the smooth brown skin where a belly button should have been. Devil's mark, his stepfather had called it, but he'd said the same thing about Magnus's eyes. Magnus was long past caring whether mundanes judged him.

"Caroline Connor," said the woman. She did not offer a hand. "CFO and vice president of marketing for Sigblad Enterprises."

"Magnus Bane," said Magnus. "High Warlock of Brooklyn and Scrabble champion."

"You come highly recommended. I have heard you are an extremely powerful wizard."

"Warlock," said Magnus, "actually."

"I expected you to be..."

She paused like someone hovering over a selection of chocolates, all of which she was extremely doubtful about. Magnus wondered which she would choose, which marker of a trustworthy magic user she had been imagining or hoping for—elderly, bearded, white.

Magnus had encountered many people in the market for a sage. He had very little time for it.

Still, he had to admit that this was perhaps not the most professional he had ever been.

"Did you expect me to be, perhaps," he suggested gently, "wearing a shirt?"

Ms. Connor lifted her shoulders in a slight shrug.

"Everybody told me that you make eccentric fashion choices, and I'm sure that's a very fashionable hairstyle," she said. "But frankly, it looks like a cat has been sleeping on your head."

Magnus offered Caroline Connor a coffee, which she declined. All she would accept was a glass of water. Magnus was becoming more and more suspicious of her.

When Magnus emerged from his room wearing maroon leather pants and a glittering cowl-neck sweater, which had come with a jaunty little matching scarf, Caroline looked at him with a cool distance that suggested she did not find it to be a huge improvement on his pajama pants. Magnus had already accepted the fact that there would never be an eternal friendship between them, and did not find himself heartbroken.

"So, Caroline," he said.

"I prefer 'Ms. Connor,'" said Ms. Connor, perched on the very edge of Magnus's gold velvet sofa. She was looking around at the furniture as disapprovingly as she had looked at Magnus's bare chest, as if she thought that a few interesting prints and a lamp with bells were somewhat equivalent to Roman orgies.

"Ms. Connor," Magnus amended easily. The customer was always right, and that would be Magnus's policy until the job was completed, at which point he would decline to ever be employed by this company again.

She produced a file from her briefcase, a contract in a dark green binder, which she passed over to Magnus to flip through. Magnus had signed two other contracts in the past week, one graven into a tree trunk in the depths of a German forest under the light of a new moon, and one in his own blood. Mundanes were so quaint.

Magnus scanned through it. Summon minor demon, mysterious purpose, obscene sums of money. Check, check, and check. He signed it with a flourish and handed it back.

"Well," said Ms. Connor, folding her hands in her lap. "I would like to see the demon now, if you please."

"It takes a little while to set up the pentagram and the summoning circle," Magnus said. "You might want to get comfortable."

Ms. Connor looked startled and displeased. "I have a lunch meeting," she noted. "Is there no way to expedite the process?"

"Er, no. This is dark magic, Ms. Connor," said Magnus. "It is not quite the same as ordering a pizza."

Ms. Connor's mouth flattened like a piece of paper being folded in half. "Would it be possible for me to come back in a few hours?"

Magnus's conviction that people who arrived early to meetings had no respect for other people's time was being confirmed. On the other hand, he did not really wish for this woman to remain in his house for any longer than necessary.

"Off you go," Magnus said, keeping his voice urbane and charming. "When you return, there will be a cecaelia demon in place for you to do with as you wish."

"Casa Bane," Magnus muttered as Ms. Connor left, his voice not quite low enough to be sure she wouldn't hear him. "Hot- and cold-running demons, at your service."

He didn't have time to sit around being annoyed. There was work to be done. Magnus set about arranging his circle of black candles. Inside the circle he scratched a pentagram, using a rowan stick freshly cut by faerie hands. The whole process took a couple of hours before he was ready to begin his chant.

"*Iam tibi impero et praecipio, maligne spiritus!* I summon you, by the power of bell, book, and candle. I summon you from the airy void, from the darkest depths. I summon you, Elyaas who swims in the midnight seas of eternally drowning souls, Elyaas who lurks in the shadows that surround Pandemonium, Elyaas who bathes in tears and plays with the bones of lost sailors."

Magnus drawled the words, tapping his nails on his cup and examining his chipped green nail polish. He took pride in his work, but this was not his favorite part of his job, not his favorite client, and not the day for it.

The golden wood of his floor began to smoke, and the smoke rising had the smell of sulfur. But the smoke rose in sullen wisps. Magnus felt a resistance as he pulled the demon dimension closer to him, like a fisherman drawing on a line and getting a fish who put up a fight.

It was too early in the afternoon for this. Magnus spoke in a louder voice, feeling the power rise in him as he spoke, as if his blood were catching on fire and sending sparks from the center of his being out into the space between worlds.

"As the destroyer of Marbas, I summon you. I summon you as the demon's child who can make your seas dry to desert. I summon you by my own power, and by the power of my blood, and you know who my father is, Elyaas. You will not, you dare not, disobey."

The smoke rose higher and higher, became a veil, and beyond the veil for an instant Magnus glimpsed another world. Then the smoke became too thick to see through. Magnus had to wait until it dwindled and coalesced into a shape—not quite the shape of a man.

Magnus had summoned many disgusting demons in his life. The amphisbaena demon had the wings and the trunk of a vast chicken. Mundane stories claimed it had the head and tail of a snake, but that was not in fact true. Amphisbaena demons were covered in tentacles, with one very large tentacle containing an eye, and a mouth with snapping fangs. Magnus could see how the confusion had arisen.

The amphisbaena demons were the worst, but cecaelia demons

were not Magnus's favorites either. They were not aesthetically pleasing, and they left slime all over the floor.

Elyaas's shape was more blob than anything else. His head was something like a man's, but with his green eyes set close together in the center of his face, and a triangular slit serving as both nose and mouth. He had no arms. His torso was abruptly truncated, and his lower parts resembled those of a squid, the tentacles thick and short. And from head to stubby tentacles, he was coated in greenish-black slime, as if he had arisen from a fetid swamp and was sweating out putrefaction from every pore.

"Who summons Elyaas?" he asked in a voice that sounded like a normal, rather jolly, man's voice, with the slight suggestion that it was being heard underwater. It was possible that this was simply because he had a mouthful of slime. Magnus saw the demon's tongue—like a human's but green and ending in a thick point—flicker between his sharp slime-stained teeth as he spoke.

"I do," said Magnus. "But I rather believe we covered that when I was summoning you and you proved recalcitrant."

He spoke cheerfully, but the blue-white flame of the candles responded to his mood and contracted, forming a cage of light around Elyaas that made him yelp. His slime had no effect upon their fire whatsoever.

"Oh, come on!" Elyaas grumbled. "Don't be like that! I was on my way. I was held up by some personal business."

Magnus rolled his eyes. "What were you doing, demon?"

Elyaas looked shifty, insofar as you could tell under the slime. "I had a thing. So how have you been, Magnus?"

"What?" Magnus asked.

"You know, since the last time you summoned me. How have you been keeping?"

"What?" Magnus asked again.

"You don't remember me?" said the tentacle demon.

"I summon a lot of demons," Magnus said weakly.

There was a long pause. Magnus stared into the bottom of his coffee cup and desperately willed more coffee to appear. This was something a lot of mundanes did too, but Magnus had one up on those suckers. His mug did slowly fill again, until it was brimming with rich dark liquid. He sipped and looked at Elyaas, who was shifting uncomfortably from tentacle to tentacle.

"Well," said Elyaas. "This is awkward."

"It's nothing personal," said Magnus.

"Maybe if I jogged your memory," Elyaas suggested helpfully. "You summoned me when you were searching for a demon who cursed a Shadowhunter? Bill Herondale?"

"Will Herondale," said Magnus.

Elyaas snapped his tentacles as if they were fingers. "I knew it was something like that."

"You know," Magnus said, enlightened, "I think I do remember. I'm sorry about that. I realized right away that you weren't the demon I was looking for. You looked kind of blue in one of the drawings, but obviously you are not blue, and I was wasting your time. You were pretty understanding about it."

"Think nothing of it." Elyaas waved a tentacle. "These things happen. And I can look blue. You know, in the right light."

"Lighting's important, it's true," said Magnus.

"So whatever happened with Bill Herondale and that curse a blue demon put on him?" The cecaelia demon's interest seemed genuine.

"*Will* Herondale," Magnus said again. "It's actually rather a long story."

"You know, sometimes we demons pretend we're cursing people and we don't really do it," said Elyaas chattily. "Like, just for kicks? It's kind of a thing with us. Did you know that?"

"You could have mentioned it a century or two ago," Magnus observed frostily.

Elyaas shook his head, smiling a slime-bedecked smile. "The old pretend-to-curse. It's a classic. Very funny." He appeared to notice

Magnus's unimpressed expression for the first time. "Not from your perspective, of course."

"It wasn't funny for Bill Herondale!" said Magnus. "Oh, damn it. Now you've got me doing it."

Magnus's phone buzzed on the counter where he had left it. Magnus made a dive for it, and was delighted when he saw that it was Catarina. He had been expecting her call.

Then he realized the demon was looking at him curiously.

"Sorry," Magnus said. "Mind if I take this?"

Elyaas waved a tentacle. "Oh no, go right ahead."

Magnus pressed the answer button on the phone and walked toward the window, away from the demon and the sulfur fumes.

"Hello, Catarina!" said Magnus. "I am so pleased that you finally called me back."

He might have laid a slight pointed emphasis on the "finally."

"I only did because you said it was urgent," said his friend Catarina, who was a nurse first and a warlock second. Magnus did not think she'd had a date in fifteen years. Before that she'd had a fiancé whom she had kept meaning to marry, but she'd never found the time, and eventually he'd died of old age, still hoping that one day she would set a date.

"It is urgent," said Magnus. "You know that I've been, ah, spending time with one of the Nephilim at the New York Institute."

"A Lightwood, right?" Catarina asked.

"Alexander Lightwood," said Magnus, and he was mildly horrified to hear how his own voice softened on the name.

"I wouldn't have thought you'd have time, with all the other things going on."

It was true. The night when Magnus had met Alec, he had just wanted to throw a party, have some fun, act the part of a warlock filled with joie de vivre until he could feel it. He remembered how in the past, every few years, he used to feel a restless craving for love, and would start to search for the possibility of love in beautiful strangers. Somehow this time around it hadn't happened. He had spent the eighties in a strange cloud of misery, thinking of Camille, the vampire he had loved more than a century before. He had not loved anyone, not really loved them and had them love him back, since Etta in the fifties. Etta had been dead for years and years, and had left him before she'd died. Since then there had been affairs, of course, lovers who'd let him down or whom he'd let down, faces he now barely remembered, glimpses of brightness that had flickered and gone out even as he'd approached.

He hadn't stopped wanting love. He had simply, somehow, stopped looking.

He wondered if you could be exhausted without knowing it, if hope could be lost not all at once but could slip away gradually, day by day, and vanish before you ever realized.

Then Clary Fray had appeared at his party, the girl whose mother had been hiding Clary's Shadowhunter heritage from her all her life. Clary had been brought to Magnus so that he could ensorcel her memory and cloud her sight, over and over again as she'd been growing up, and Magnus had done it. It was not a terribly kind thing to do to a girl, but her mother had been so afraid for her, and it had not felt like Magnus's place to refuse. Yet Magnus had not been able to stop himself from taking a personal interest. Seeing a child grow up, year after year, had been new to him, as had feeling the weight of her memories in his hands. He had started to feel a little responsible, had wanted to know what would become of her and had begun to want the best for her.

Magnus had been interested in Clary, the little redheaded scrap who had grown into a—slightly bigger little redheaded scrap, but had not thought he would be terribly interested in the companions she had found for herself. Not the nondescript mundane boy; not golden-eyed Jace Wayland, who reminded Magnus of too much of a past that he would rather forget; and certainly not either of the

Lightwood siblings, the dark boy and girl whose parents Magnus had good reason to dislike.

It made no sense that his eyes had been drawn to Alec, over and over again. Alec had hung to the back of their little group, had made no effort to attract the eye. He had striking coloring, the rare combination of black hair and blue eyes that had always been Magnus's favorite, and Magnus supposed that was why he had looked in Alec's direction at first. Strange to see the coloring that had so distinguished Will and his sister, so many miles and years gone by, and on someone with an entirely different last name...

Then Alec had smiled at one of Magnus's jokes, and the smile had lit a lamp in his solemn face, making his blue eyes brilliant, and briefly taking Magnus's breath away. And when Magnus's attention had been held, he'd seen a flicker of returned interest in Alec's eyes, a mixture of guilt, intrigue, and pleasure at Magnus's attention. Shadowhunters were old-fashioned about such matters, which was to say bigoted and hidebound, as they were about everything. Magnus had been approached by male Shadowhunters before, of course, but always in a hole-and-corner way, always as if they were doing Magnus some huge favor and as if Magnus's touch, though desired, might sully them. (Magnus had always turned them down.) It had been a shock to see such feelings open and innocent on a beautiful boy's face.

When Magnus had winked at Alec and told him to call him, it had been a reckless impulse, little more than a whim. He had certainly not expected the Shadowhunter on his doorstep a few days later, asking for a date. Nor had he expected the date to go so spectacularly bizarrely, or expected to like Alec quite so much afterward.

"Alec took me by surprise," said Magnus to Catarina at last, which was a massive understatement and so true that it felt like revealing too much.

"Well, it seems like a mad idea to me, but those usually work out for you," said Catarina. "What's the problem?"

That was the million-dollar question. Magnus resolved to sound casual about it. This was not something that he should be worrying about as much as he was, and he wanted advice but did not want to let anyone, not even Catarina, see how much it mattered.

"I'm glad you asked. Here's the thing," said Magnus. "It's Alec's birthday today. He's eighteen. And I'd like to get him a present, because the celebration of one's birth is a traditional time for the giving of gifts, and it indicates your affection for them. But—and at this point I'd like to say that I wish you had returned my call sooner—I don't really have any idea what to get him, and I would appreciate some advice. The thing is, he doesn't really seem to care about material goods, including clothes, which I don't understand, though I find it strangely charming. He is impossible to buy for. The only new things I ever see him with are weapons, and nunchakus are not a romantic gift. Also, I wondered if you thought that getting a present at all might make me seem too keen and chase him off. I've been seeing him for only a little while, and his parents don't even know he likes boys, let alone likes degenerate warlocks, and so I want to be subtle. Maybe getting a gift at all would be a mistake. It's possible that he will think I am being too intense. And as you know, Catarina, I am not intense. I am laissez-faire. I am a jaded sophisticate. I don't want him to get the wrong idea about me or think the present means more than it should. Maybe just a token gift. What do you think?"

Magnus took a deep breath. That had come out a little less cool, calm, well-reasoned, and sophisticated than he had been hoping for.

"Magnus," said Catarina, "I have lives to save."

Then she hung up on him.

Magnus stared at the phone in disbelief. He would never have thought Catarina would do this to him. It seemed like wanton cruelty. He had not sounded that bad on the telephone.

"Is Alec your lover?" asked Elyaas the tentacle demon.

Magnus stared. He was not ready for anyone to say "lover" to him with an oozing note of slime beneath the word. He felt he would never be ready.

"You should get him a mixed tape," said Elyaas. "Kids love mixed tapes. They're the cool 'in' thing right now."

"Was the last time you were summoned the eighties?" Magnus asked.

"It might have been," Elyaas said defensively.

"Things have changed."

"Do people still listen to Fleetwood Mac?" asked the tentacle demon. There was a plaintive note in his voice. "I love the Mac."

Magnus ignored the demon, who had softly begun to sing a slimy song to himself. Magnus was contemplating his own dark fate. He had to accept it. There was no way around it. There was no one else he could turn to.

He was going to have to call Ragnor Fell and ask for advice about his love life.

Ragnor was spending a lot of time lately in Idris, the Shadowhunters' city of glass, where phones, television, and the Internet did not work, and where Magnus imagined the Angel's chosen ones had to resort to pornographic woodcuts when they wanted to unwind after a long day's demon-hunting. Ragnor had used his magic to install a single telephone, but he could not be expected to hang around it all the livelong day. So Magnus was deeply thankful when Ragnor's phone actually rang and the warlock actually picked up.

"Ragnor, thank goodness," he said.

"What is it?" asked Ragnor. "Is it Valentine? I'm in London, and Tessa's in the Amazon and there's no way to contact her. All right. Let me wrap this up fast. You call Catarina, and I will be with you in—"

"Ah," said Magnus. "There's no need for that. Though thank you for your immediate leaping to my rescue, my sweet emerald prince."

There was a pause. Then Ragnor said, in a much less intent and much more grumpy voice, "Why are you bothering me, then?"

"Well, I'd like some advice," said Magnus. "So I turned to you, as one of my oldest and dearest friends, as a fellow warlock and a trusted comrade, as the former High Warlock of London in whom I have implicit confidence."

"Flattery from you makes me nervous," said Ragnor. "It means you want something. Doubtless something awful. I am not becoming a pirate with you again, Magnus. I don't care how much you pay me."

"I wasn't going to suggest it. My question for you is of a more ... personal nature. Don't hang up. Catarina was already extremely unsympathetic."

There was a long silence. Magnus fiddled with his window catch, gazing out at the line of warehouses-turned-apartments. Lace curtains were fluttering in a summer breeze in an open window across the street. He tried to ignore the reflection of the demon in his own window.

"Wait," said Ragnor, and he started to snigger. "Is this about your Nephilim *boyfriend*?"

"Our relationship is as yet undefined," said Magnus with dignity. Then he clutched the phone and hissed, "And how do you know private details about my personal life with Alexander?"

"Ooooh, *Alexander*," Ragnor said in a singsong voice. "I know all about it. Raphael called and told me."

"Raphael Santiago," said Magnus, thinking darkly of the current leader of the New York vampire clan, "has a black ungrateful heart, and one day he will be punished for this treachery."

"Raphael calls me every month," said Ragnor. "Raphael knows that it is important to preserve good relations and maintain regular communication between the different Downworlder factions. I might add, Raphael always remembers important occasions in my life."

"I forgot your birthday one time sixty years ago!" said Magnus. "You need to let that go."

"It was fifty-eight years ago, for the record. And Raphael knows we need to maintain a united front against the Nephilim and not, for instance, sneak around with their underage sons," Ragnor continued.

"Alec is eighteen!"

"Whatever," said Ragnor. "Raphael would never date a Shadowhunter."

"Of course, why would he, when you two are in loooove?" Magnus asked. "'Oooh, Raphael is always so professional.' 'Oooh, Raphael brought up the most interesting points in that meeting you forgot to attend.' 'Oooh, Raphael and I are planning a June wedding.' Besides, Raphael would never date a Shadowhunter because Raphael has a policy of never doing anything that is awesome."

"Stamina runes are not the only things that matter in life," said Ragnor.

"So says someone who is wasting his life," Magnus told him. "And anyway, it's not like ... Alec is..."

"If you tell me about your gooey feelings for one of the Nephilim, I will go double green and be sick," said Ragnor. "I'm warning you now."

Double green sounded interesting, but Magnus did not have time to waste. "Fine. Just advise me on this one practical matter," said Magnus. "Should I buy him a birthday present, and if so, what should it be?"

"I just remembered that I have some very important business to attend to," said Ragnor.

"No," said Magnus. "Wait. Don't do this. I trusted you!"

"I'm sorry, Magnus, but you're breaking up."

"Maybe a cashmere sweater? What do you think about a sweater?"

"Oops, tunnel," said Ragnor, and a dial tone echoed in Magnus's ear.

Magnus did not know why all of his immortal friends had to be so callous and horrible. Ragnor's important business was probably getting together to write a burn book with Raphael. Magnus could see them now, sharing a bench and scribbling happily away about Magnus's stupid hair.

Magnus was drawn from this dark private vision by the actual dark vision currently happening in his loft. Elyaas was generating more and more slime. It was steadily filling the pentagram. The cecaelia demon was wallowing in the stuff.

"I think you should buy him a scented candle," Elyaas proposed, his voice stickier by the minute. He waved his tentacles enthusiastically to illustrate his point. "They come in many exciting scents, like bilberry and orange blossom. It will bring him serenity and he'll think about you when he goes to sleep. Everybody likes scented candles."

"I need you to shut up," said Magnus. "I have to think."

He threw himself onto his sofa. Magnus should have expected that Raphael, filthy traitor and total priss that he was, would have reported back to Ragnor.

Magnus remembered the night when he took Alec to Taki's. Usually they went to places frequented by mundanes. The haunts of Downworld, crawling with faeries, werewolves, warlocks, and vampires who might pass on word to his parents, clearly made Alec nervous. Magnus did not think Alec understood how much Downworld preferred to keep apart from Shadowhunter business.

The café was bustling, and the center of attention was a peri and a werewolf having some kind of territorial dispute. Nobody paid Alec and Magnus any attention at all, except Kaelie, the little blond waitress, who had smiled when they'd come in and who'd been very attentive.

"Do you know her?" asked Magnus.

"A little," said Alec. "She's part nixie. She likes Jace."

She wasn't the only one who liked Jace, Magnus knew that. He didn't see what all the fuss was about, personally. Other than the fact that Jace had a face like an angel's and abs for days.

Magnus started to tell Alec a story about a nixie nightclub he'd been to once. Alec was laughing, and then Raphael Santiago came in the door of the café with his most faithful vampire followers, Lily and Elliott. Raphael spotted Magnus and Alec, and then his thin arched eyebrows hit his hairline.

"Nope, nope, nope, and also no," Raphael said, and he actually took several steps back toward the door. "Turn around, everybody. I do not wish to know this. I refuse to be aware of this."

"One of the Nephilim," said Lily, bad girl that she was, and she drummed on the table of their booth with shining blue fingernails. "My, my."

"Hi?" said Alec.

"Wait a minute," said Raphael. "Are you Alexander Lightwood?"

Alec looked more panicked by the minute. "Yes?" he said, as if he were uncertain on the subject. Magnus thought he might be considering changing his name to Horace Whipplepool and fleeing the country.

"Aren't you twelve?" Raphael demanded. "I distinctly recall you being twelve."

"Uh, that was a while ago," said Alec.

He looked even more freaked out. Magnus supposed it must have been unsettling to be accused of being twelve by someone who looked like a boy of fifteen.

Magnus might have found the situation funny at another time, but he looked at Alec. Alec's shoulders were tense.

He knew Alec well enough by now to know what he was feeling, the conflicting impulses that warred in him. He was conscientious, the kind of person who believed that the others around him were so much more important than he was, who already believed that he was letting everybody down. And he was honest, the kind of person who was naturally open about all he felt and all he wanted. Alec's virtues had made a trap for him: these two good qualities had collided painfully. He felt he could not be honest without disappointing everybody he loved. It was a hideous conundrum for him. It was as if the world had been designed to make him unhappy.

"Leave him alone," Magnus said, and reached for Alec's hand over the table. For a moment Alec's fingers relaxed under Magnus's, began to curl around them, holding his hand back. Then he glanced at the vampires and snatched his hand away.

Magnus had known a lot of men and women over the years who'd been afraid of who they were and what they wanted. He had loved many of them, and had hurt for them all. He had loved the times in the mundane world when people had had to be a little less afraid. He loved this time in the world, when he could reach out in a public place and take Alec's hand.

It did not make Magnus feel any more kindly toward the Shadowhunters to see one of their Angel-touched warriors made afraid by something like this. If they had to believe they were so much better than everyone else, they should at least be able to make their own children feel good about who they were.

Elliott leaned against Alec's seat, shaking his head so his thin dreadlocks whipped about his face. "What would your parents think?" he asked with mock solemnity.

It was funny to the vampires. But it wasn't funny to Alec.

"Elliott," said Magnus. "You're boring. And I don't want to hear that you've been telling any tedious tales around the place. Do you understand me?"

He played with a teaspoon, blue sparks traveling from his fingers to the spoon and back again. Elliott's eyes said that Magnus would not be able to kill him with a spoon. Magnus's eyes invited Elliott to test him.

Raphael ran out of patience, which admittedly was like a desert running out of water.

"*Dios*," snapped Raphael, and the other two vampires flinched. "I am not interested in your sordid encounters or constantly deranged life choices, and I am certainly not interested in prying into the affairs of Nephilim. I meant what I said. I don't want to know about this. And I won't know about this. This never happened. I saw nothing. Let's go."

So now Raphael had gone running off to report to Ragnor. That was vampires for you: always going for the jugular, both literally and metaphorically. They were messing up his love life as well as being inconsiderate party guests who had got blood in Magnus's stereo system at his last party and turned Clary's idiot friend Stanley into a rat, which was just bad manners. Magnus was never inviting any vampires to his parties ever again. It was going to be all werewolves and faeries all the time, even if it was hell getting fur and faerie dust out of the sofa.

Magnus and Alec sat in brief silence after the vampires departed, and then something else happened. The fight between the peri and the werewolf got out of hand. The werewolf's face changed, snarling, and the peri turned the table upside down. A crash rang out.

Magnus started slightly at the sound, and Alec acted. He leaped to his feet, palming a throwing knife with one hand, his other hand going to a weapon in his belt. He moved faster than any other being in the room—werewolf, vampire, or faerie—could have moved.

And he moved automatically in front of the booth where Magnus was sitting, placed his body between Magnus and the threat without even thinking about it. Magnus had seen how Alec acted with his fellow Shadowhunters, with his sister and his *parabatai*, closer than a brother. He guarded their backs, watched out for them, behaved at all times as if their lives were more precious than his own.

Magnus was the High Warlock of Brooklyn, and for centuries had been powerful beyond the dreams of not only mundanes but most of Downworld. Magnus certainly did not need protection, and nobody had ever even thought to offer it, certainly not a Shadowhunter.

The best one could hope for from Shadowhunters, if you were a Downworlder, was to be left alone. Nobody had tried to protect him, that he could remember, since he was very young. He had never wanted anybody to do so, not since he'd been a child who'd had to run to the cold mercy of the Silent Brothers' sanctuary. That had been long ago in a country far away, and Magnus had never wanted to be so weak ever again. Yet seeing Alec spring to defend him caused Magnus to feel a pang in the center of his chest, at once sweet and painful.

And the customers in Taki's café shrank back from Alec, from angelic power revealed in a sudden blaze of fury. In that moment nobody doubted that he could lay waste to them all.

The peri and the werewolf slunk to opposite corners of the café, and then hastily made their retreat from the building. Alec subsided into the booth opposite Magnus, and sent him an embarrassed smile.

It was strange and startling and terribly endearing, like Alec himself.

Magnus then dragged Alec outside, pushed him up against the brick wall of Taki's under the sparking upside-down sign, and kissed him. Alec's blue eyes that had blazed with angelic fury were tender suddenly, and darker with passion. Magnus felt Alec's strong lithe body strain against Magnus's, felt his gentle hands slide up Magnus's back. Alec kissed him back with shattering enthusiasm, and Magnus thought, *Yes, this one, this one fits, after all the stumbling around and searching, and here it is.*

"What was that for?" Alec asked a long time later, eyes shining.

Alec was young. Magnus had never been old, had never known how the world reacted to you when you were old, and had not been allowed to be really young for long either. Being immortal meant being apart from such concerns. All the mortals Magnus had loved had seemed younger and older than him, both at once. But Magnus was keenly aware that this was Alec's first time dating, doing anything at all. He had been Alec's first kiss. Magnus wanted to be good to him, not burden him with the weight of feelings that Alec might not return.

"Nothing," Magnus lied.

Thinking about that night at Taki's, Magnus realized what the perfect present for Alec would be. He also realized that he had no idea how to give it to him.

In the only piece of luck in a terrible day filled with slime and cruel friends, at that very moment the buzzer rang.

Magnus crossed the floor in three easy strides and boomed into the intercom: "WHO DARES DISTURB THE HIGH WARLOCK AT WORK?"

There was a pause.

"Seriously, if you are Jehovah's Witnesses..."

"Ah, no," said a girl's voice, light, self-confident, and with the slight, odd inflection of Idris. "This is Isabelle Lightwood. Mind if I come up?"

"Not at all," said Magnus, and he pressed the button to let her in.

Isabelle Lightwood walked straight for the coffee machine and got herself a cup without asking if she could have any. She was that kind of girl, Magnus thought, the kind who took what she wanted and assumed you would be delighted that she'd taken a fancy to it. She studiously ignored Elyaas as she went: she had taken one look at him when she'd come into Magnus's apartment and apparently decided that asking questions about the presence of the tentacle demon would be impolite and probably boring.

She looked like Alec, had his high cheekbones, porcelain-pale skin, and black hair, though she wore hers long and carefully styled. Her eyes were different, though, glossy and black, like lacquered ebony: both beautiful and indestructible. She seemed as if she could be as cold as her mother, as if she might be as prone to corruption as so many of her ancestors had been. Magnus had known a lot of

Lightwoods, and he had not been terribly impressed by most of them. Not until one.

Isabelle hopped up onto the counter, stretching out her long legs. She was wearing tailored jeans and boots with spike heels, and a deep red silk tank top that matched the ruby necklace at her throat, which Magnus had bought for the price of a London town house more than a hundred years before. Magnus rather liked seeing her wear it. It felt like watching Will's niece, brash, laughing, cheroot-smoking Anna Lightwood—one of the few Lightwoods he had liked—wearing it a hundred years before. It charmed him, made him feel as if he had mattered in that space of time, to those people. He wondered how horrified the Lightwoods would be if they knew that the necklace had once been a dissolute warlock's love gift to a murderous vampire.

Probably not as horrified as they would be if they learned Magnus was dating their son.

He met Isabelle's bold black eyes, and thought that she might not be horrified to learn where her necklace had come from. He thought she might get a bit of a kick out of it. Maybe someday he would tell her.

"So it's Alec's birthday today," Isabelle announced.

"I'm aware," said Magnus.

He said nothing more. He didn't know what Alec had told Isabelle, knew how painfully Alec loved her and wanted to shield her, not to let her down, as he wanted not to let any of them down and passionately feared he would. Secrecy did not sit well with Magnus, who had winked at Alec the first night he'd met him, when Alec had been simply a deliriously good-looking boy glancing at Magnus with shy interest. But it was all more complicated now, when he knew how Alec could be hurt, when Magnus knew how much it would matter to him if Alec were hurt.

"I know you two are ... seeing each other," said Isabelle, picking her words carefully but still meeting Magnus's eyes dead-on. "I don't care. I mean, it doesn't matter to me. At all."

She flung the words defiantly at Magnus. There was no need to be defiant with him, but he understood why she was, understood that she must have practiced the defiant words that she might have to say to her parents one day, if she stood by her brother.

She would stand by him. She loved her brother, then.

"That's good to know," said Magnus.

He had known Isabelle Lightwood was beautiful, and had thought she seemed strong, and funny—had known that she was someone he would not mind having a drink with or having at a party. He had not known that there were depths of loyalty and love in her.

He was not adept at reading Shadowhunter hearts, behind their smooth angelically arrogant facades. He thought that might be why Alec had surprised him so much, had wrong-footed him so that Magnus had stumbled into feelings he had not planned to have. Alec had no facade at all.

Isabelle nodded, as if she understood what Magnus was telling her. "I thought—it seemed important to tell someone that, on his birthday," she said. "I can't tell anyone else, even though I would. It's not like my parents or the Clave would listen to me." Isabelle curled her lip as she spoke of both her parents and the Clave. Magnus was liking her more and more. "He can't tell anyone. And you won't tell anyone, right?"

"It is not my secret to tell," said Magnus.

He might not enjoy sneaking around, but he would not tell anybody's secret. Least of all would he risk causing Alec pain or fear.

"You really like him, right?" Isabelle asked. "My brother?"

"Oh, did you mean Alec?" Magnus retorted. "I thought you meant my cat."

Isabelle laughed and kicked at one of Magnus's cabinet doors with one spike heel, careless and radiant. "Come on, though," she said. "You do."

"Are we going to talk about boys?" Magnus inquired. "I didn't realize, and I am honestly not prepared. Can't you come over another time, when I'm in my jammies? We could do homemade facials and braid each other's hair, and then and only then will I tell you that I think your brother is totally dreamy."

Isabelle looked pleased, if a little mystified. "Most people go for Jace. Or me," she added blithely.

Alec had said as much to Magnus once, seeming stunned that Magnus might hope to see him instead of Jace.

Magnus was not planning on talking about why he preferred Alec. The heart had its reasons, and they were seldom all that reasonable. You might as well have asked why Clary hadn't created a hilarious love triangle by getting a crush on Alec, since he was—in Magnus's admittedly biased opinion—extremely handsome, and had been consistently sullen in her direction, which some girls liked. You liked the people you liked.

For all that, Magnus had many reasons. Nephilim were guarded, Nephilim were arrogant, Nephilim were to be avoided. Even the Shadowhunters Magnus had met and liked had been, every one, a trouble sundae with dark secret cherries on top.

Alec was not like any Shadowhunter Magnus had met before.

"May I see your whip?" asked Magnus.

Isabelle blinked, but to do her justice, she did not demur. She unlooped the electrum whip and tangled its silvery-gold length around her hands for a moment, like a child playing cat's cradle.

Magnus took the whip carefully, laid across his palms like a snake, and he carried it to his closet door, which he opened. He drew out a special potion, one that he had paid an exorbitant price for and that he had been saving for something special. Shadowhunters had their runes to protect them. Warlocks had magic. Magnus had always liked his magic better than theirs. Only a Shadowhunter could bear runes, but he could give magic to anyone. He tipped the potion—faerie dust and blood taken in one of the old rituals, hematite and hellebore and more besides—onto the whip.

In the last extremity this weapon will not fail you; in the darkest hour this weapon will bring your enemy low.

Magnus carried the whip back to Isabelle when he was done.

"What did you do to it?" Isabelle asked.

"I gave it a little extra kick," said Magnus.

Isabelle regarded him with narrowed eyes. "And why would you do that?"

"Why did you come to tell me that you knew about me and Alec?" asked Magnus. "It's his birthday. That means the people who care about him want to give him what he wishes for most. In your case, acceptance. In mine, I know that the most important thing to him in the world is that you be safe."

Isabelle nodded, and their eyes met. Magnus had said far too much, and he worried that Isabelle could see more.

She launched herself off the counter, toward Magnus's small alabaster-topped coffee table, and scrawled on his notepad. "Here's my number."

"May I ask why you're giving it to me?"

"Well, wow, Magnus. I knew you were hundreds of years old and all, but I hoped you were keeping up with modern technology." Isabelle held out her phone to illustrate her point, and waggled it about. "So that you can call me, or text me. If you ever need Shadowhunter help."

"Me need Shadowhunter help?" Magnus inquired, incredulous. "Over the—you're right, hundreds of years—let me tell you that I've found it is almost invariably the other way around. I presume you'll be wanting my number in return, and I'm also prepared to bet, based on nothing more than a passing acquaintance with your circle of friends, that you are going to get into trouble and need my expert magical assistance rather a lot."

"Yeah, maybe," said Isabelle with a rakish grin. "I've been known to be a troublemaker. But I didn't give you my number because I want magical help, and okay, I understand that the High Warlock of Brooklyn probably doesn't need an assist from a bunch of underage

Nephilim. I was thinking that, if you're going to be important to my brother, we should be able to get in touch. And I was thinking that you might want to have it if—if you need to contact me about Alec. Or if I need to contact you."

Magnus understood what the girl meant. His number was easy enough to get—the Institute had it—but in giving him her own, Isabelle was offering the free exchange of information about Alec's safety. The Nephilim led dangerous lives, chasing after demons, stalking the Downworld for lawbreakers, their rune-Marked, angel-swift bodies the last line of defense for the mundane world. The second time Magnus had ever seen Alec, he had been dying of demon poison.

Alec could die at any time, in any of the battles to come. Isabelle would be the only one of the Shadowhunters who knew for sure that there was anything between Magnus and Alec. She would be the only one who knew that if Alec died, Magnus would be someone who needed to be told.

"All right," he said slowly. "Thank you, Isabelle."

Isabelle winked. "No need to thank me. I'll be driving you mad before long."

"I'll be expecting it," said Magnus as she clattered out on her high, weaponized heels. He admired anyone who made beauty and utility work together.

"By the way, that demon is dripping slime all over your floor," said Isabelle, poking her head back around the door.

"Hi," said Elyaas, and he waved a tentacle at her.

Isabelle regarded him with disdain, then raised an eyebrow in Magnus's direction. "Just thought I'd point it out," she said, and closed the door.

"I don't underssssstand the point of your present," said Elyaas. "He isn't even going to know about it? You should have just gone with flowers. Red rossssses are very romantic. Or perhaps tulips if you think that roses say you just want him for ssssssex."

Magnus lay upon his golden sofa and contemplated the ceiling. The sun was low in the sky, a flash of golden paint inscribed with a careless hand over the New York skyline. The demon's shape had become more and more gelatinous as the day had progressed, until he seemed like nothing more than a lurking pile of slime. Possibly Caroline Connor would never come back. Possibly Elyaas was going to live with Magnus now. Magnus had always thought Raphael Santiago was the worst possible roommate he could ever have. Possibly he was about to be proven wrong.

He wished, with a profundity of longing that surprised him, that Alec were here.

Magnus remembered a town in Peru whose Quechua name meant "quiet place." He recalled even more vividly being obscenely drunk and unhappy over his heartbreak of that time, and the maudlin thoughts that had recurred to him over the years, like an unwanted guest slipping in through his doors: that there was no peace for such as he, no quiet place, and there never would be.

Except he found himself remembering lying in bed with Alec—all of their clothes on, lounging on the bed on a lazy afternoon, Alec laughing, head thrown back, the marks Magnus had left on his throat very plain to see.

Time was something that moved in fits and starts for Magnus, dissipating like mist or dragging like chains, but when Alec was here, Magnus's time seemed to fall into an easy rhythm with Alec's, like two heartbeats falling into sync. He felt anchored by Alec, and his whole self felt restless and mutinous when Alec was not there, because he knew how different it would be when Alec *was* there, how the tumultuous world would quiet at the sound of Alec's voice.

It was part of the dichotomy of Alec that had caught Magnus unaware and left him fascinated—that Alec seemed old for his age, serious and responsible, and yet that he approached the world with a tender wonder that made all things new. Alec was a warrior who brought Magnus peace.

Magnus lay on the sofa and admitted it to himself. He knew why he had been acting demented and pestering his friends over a birthday present. He knew why, on an ordinary unpleasant workday, his every thought had been punctuated with a thought of Alec, with insistent longing for him. This was love, new and bright and terrifying.

He had been through a hundred heartbreaks, but he found himself afraid when he thought of Alexander Lightwood breaking his heart. He did not know how this boy with the messy black hair and the worried blue eyes, with his steady hands and his rare sweet smile that was less rare in Magnus's presence, had acquired such power over him. Alec hadn't tried to get it, had never seemed to realize that he had it or tried to do anything with it.

Maybe he didn't want it. Perhaps Magnus was being a fool, as he had been so many times before. He was Alec's first experience, not a boyfriend. Alec was still nursing his first crush, on his best friend, and Magnus was a cautious experimentation, a step away from the safety that golden and much-beloved Jace represented. Jace, who looked like an angel: Jace, who, like an angel, like God himself, would never love Alec back.

Magnus might simply be a walk on the wild side, a rebellion by one of Idris's most careful sons before Alec retreated back into secrecy, circumspection. Magnus remembered Camille, who had never taken him seriously, who had never loved him at all. How much more likely was a Shadowhunter to feel that way?

His gloomy thoughts were interrupted by the sound of the buzzer.

Caroline Connor offered no explanation for her lateness. Indeed, she breezed by Magnus as if he were the doorman, and began immediately to explain her problem to the demon.

"I am part of Pandemonium Enterprises, which caters to a certain subsection of the wealthy."

"Those who have used their money and influence to purchase knowledge of the Shadow World," said Magnus. "I'm aware of your organization. It's been around quite a long time."

Ms. Conner inclined her head. "My particular area is in providing entertainment for our customers in a nautical environment. While there are other cruises in New York Harbor, we provide our customers with a gourmet meal served on a yacht with a view of the more magical denizens of the city—nixies, kelpies, mermaids, various and sundry water sprites. We make it a very exclusive experience."

"Sounds classy," gurgled Elyaas.

"However, we do not want to make it a very exclusive experience in which rebellious mermaids drag our wealthy customers to the bottom of the river," said Ms. Connor. "Unfortunately some of the mermaids do not like being stared at, and this has been occurring. I simply want you to use your infernal powers to dispatch this threat to my company's economic growth."

"Wait a second. You want to *curse* the *mermaids?*" Magnus demanded.

"I could curse some mermaids," Elyaas said agreeably. "Sure."

Magnus glared at him.

Elyaas shrugged his tentacles. "I'm a demon," he said. "I'll curse a mermaid. I'll curse a cocker spaniel. I don't care about *anything*."

"I cannot believe that I have spent a whole day watching slime rise for no reason at all. If you had told me that the problem was angry mermaids, I could have fixed it without summoning demons to curse them," said Magnus. "I have several contacts in the mermaid community, and failing that, there are always the Shadowhunters."

"Oh, yeah. Magnus is dating a Shadowhunter," Elyaas put in.

"That's personal information I'd thank you not to repeat," Magnus said. "And we're not officially dating!"

"My orders were to summon a demon," Ms. Connor said crisply. "But if you can solve the problem in a more efficient way, warlock, I am all for it. I'd prefer not to curse the mermaids; the customers like looking at them. Perhaps some monetary recompense can be arranged. Do we need to amend your contract, warlock, or are the same terms agreeable to you?"

Magnus felt somewhat tempted to argue for a pay raise, but he was already charging them a satisfyingly outrageous sum of money, and he did want to avoid having a curse fall upon all the mermaids of New York. That seemed like it could get really complicated really fast.

He agreed to sign the amended contract, he and Ms. Connor shook hands, and she departed. Magnus hoped that he would never have to see her again. Another day, another dollar. (Well, another huge pile of dollars. Magnus's special skills did not come cheap.)

Elyaas was looking extremely sulky around the tentacles about being denied the opportunity to cause chaos in Magnus's city.

"Thank you for being totally useless all day," said Magnus.

"Good luck with one of the Angel's chosen, demon's son," said Elyaas, his voice suddenly considerably sharper and less slimy. "You think he will ever do anything but despise you, in his heart of hearts? He knows where you belong. We all know it too. Your father will have you in the end. Someday your life here will seem like a dream, like a stupid child's game. Someday the Great Dark One will come and drag you down and down, with usssss..."

His sibilant voice trailed off into a shriek as every candle flame streaked higher and higher, until they licked the ceiling. Then he vanished, with his last cry hanging on the air.

"Should have bought a sssscented candle..."

Magnus proceeded to open every window in the loft. The lingering smell of sulfur and slime had barely begun to clear when the phone in his pocket rang. Magnus pulled it out, not without difficulty—his pants were tight because he felt a responsibility to the world to be gorgeous, but it meant there was not a lot of room in the pocket region—and his heart missed a beat when he saw who the call was from.

"Hey," said Alec when Magnus answered, his voice deep and diffident.

"Why are you calling?" Magnus asked, assailed by a sudden fear that his birthday present had been immediately discovered in some way and the Lightwoods were shipping Alec to Idris because of spells cast on whips by heedless warlocks, which Alec could not explain.

"Um, I can call another time," said Alec, sounding worried. "I'm sure you have better things to do—"

He didn't say it in the way some of Magnus's past lovers would have said it, accusing or demanding reassurance. He said it quite naturally, as if he accepted that was the way of the world, that he would not be anyone's top priority. It made Magnus want to reassure him ten times as much as he would have, had Alec seemed to even slightly expect it.

"Of course I don't, Alexander," he said. "I was just surprised to hear from you. I imagined that you would be with your family on the big day."

"Oh," said Alec, and he sounded shy and pleased. "I didn't expect you to remember."

"It might have crossed my mind once or twice during the day," said Magnus. "So have you been having a wonderful Shadowhunting time? Did someone give you a giant axe in a cake? Where are you, off to celebrate?"

"Er," said Alec. "I'm kind of ... outside your apartment?"

The buzzer rang. Magnus pressed the button to let him enter, speechless for a moment because he had wanted Alec there, so badly, and here he was. It felt more like magic than anything he could do.

Then Alec was there, standing in the open doorway.

"I wanted to see you," said Alec with devastating simplicity. "Is this okay? I can go away if you're busy or anything."

It must have been raining a little outside. There were sparkling drops of water in Alec's messy black hair. He was wearing a hoodie that Magnus thought he might have found in a Dumpster, and sloppy jeans, and his whole face was lit up just because he was looking at Magnus.

"I think," said Magnus, pulling Alec in by the strings on his awful gray hoodie, "that I could be persuaded to clear my schedule."

Then Alec was kissing him, and Alec's kisses were uninhibited and utterly sincere, all of his lanky warrior's body focused on what it wanted, all of his open heart in it as well. For a long wild euphoric moment Magnus believed that Alec did not want anything more than to be with him, that they would not be parted. Not for a long, long time.

"Happy birthday, Alexander," Magnus murmured.

"Thanks for remembering," Alec whispered back.

The Last Stand of the New York Institute

By Cassandra Clare, Sarah Rees Brennan, and Maureen Johnson

Magnus felt for a moment as if he had become a storm, black curling clouds, the slam of thunder and slash of lightning, and all the storm wanted was to leap at Valentine's throat. Magnus's magic lashed out almost of its own volition, leaped from both hands. It looked like lightning, burning so blue that it was almost white. It knocked Valentine off his feet and into a wall. Valentine hit the wall so hard that a crack rang out, and he slid to the floor.

—The Last Stand of the New York Institute

VRAK

New York City, 1989

The man was far too close. He lingered by the postbox about six feet away from Magnus and ate a sloppy Gray's Papaya hot dog covered in chili. When he was done, he crumpled the chili-stained wrapper and threw it onto the ground in Magnus's general direction, then tugged at a hole in his denim jacket and did not look away. It was like the look some animals gave their prey.

Magnus was used to a certain amount of attention. His clothing invited it. He wore silver Doc Martens, artfully torn jeans so huge that only a narrow shining silver belt prevented them from slipping entirely off, and a pink T-shirt so big that it exposed collarbones and quite a slice of chest—the kind of clothing that made people think about nakedness. Small earrings rimmed one ear, ending in a larger one swinging from his earlobe, an earring shaped like a large silver cat wearing a crown and a smirk. A silver ankh necklace rested at the point over his heart, and he had shrugged on a tailored black jacket with jet bead trimming, more to complement the ensemble than to protect against the night air. The look was completed by a Mohawk boasting a deep pink stripe.

And he was leaning against the outside wall of the West Village clinic long after dark. That was enough to bring out the worst in some people. The clinic was for AIDS patients. The modern plague house. Instead of showing compassion, or good sense, or care, many people regarded the clinic with hate and disgust. Every age thought they were so enlightened, and every age was stumbling around in much the same darkness of ignorance and fear.

"Freak," the man finally said.

Magnus ignored this and continued reading his book, Gilda Radner's *It's Always Something*, under the dim fluorescent light of the clinic entrance. Now annoyed by the lack of reply, the man began to mumble a string of things under his breath. Magnus couldn't hear what he was saying, but he could take an educated guess. Slurs about Magnus's perceived sexuality, no doubt.

"Why don't you move along?" Magnus said, calmly flipping a page. "I know an all-night salon. They can fix up that monobrow of yours in no time."

It wasn't the right thing to say, but sometimes these things came out. You could take only so much blind, stupid ignorance without cracking around the edges a bit.

"*What* did you say?"

Two cops walked by at that moment. They cast their eyes in the direction of Magnus and the stranger. There was a look of warning for the man, and a look of thinly veiled disgust for Magnus. The look hurt a bit, but Magnus was sadly used to this treatment. He had sworn long ago that no one would ever change him—not the mundanes who hated him for one thing, or the Shadowhunters currently hunting him for another.

The man walked off, but there were backward looks.

Magnus shoved his book into his pocket. It was almost eight o'clock and really too dark to be reading, and now he was distracted. He looked around. Only a few years before, this had been one of the most vibrant, celebratory, and creative corners of the city. Good food on every corner, and couples strolling along. Now the cafés seemed sparsely populated. The people walked quickly. So many had died, so many wonderful people. From where he was standing Magnus could see three apartments formerly occupied by friends and lovers. If he turned the corner and walked for five minutes, he'd pass a dozen more dark windows.

Mundanes died so easily. No matter how many times he saw it, it never got easier. He had lived for centuries now, and he was still waiting for death to get easier.

Normally he avoided this street for this very reason, but tonight he was waiting for Catarina to finish her shift at the clinic. He shifted from foot to foot and pulled his jacket tighter around his chest, regretting for a moment that he had chosen based on fashionable flimsiness rather than actual warmth and comfort. Summer had stayed late, and then the trees had turned their leaves quickly. Now those leaves were dropping fast and the streets were bare and unsheltered. The only bright spot was the Keith Haring mural on the clinic wall—bright cartoon figures in primary colors dancing together, a heart floating above them all.

Magnus's thoughts were interrupted by the sudden reappearance of the man, who had clearly just walked around the block and gotten himself into a total state over Magnus's comment. This time the man walked right up to Magnus and stood directly in front of him, almost toe to toe.

"Really?" Magnus said. "Go away. I'm not in the mood."

In reply the man pulled out a jackknife and flicked it open. Their close stance meant that no one else could see it.

"You realize," Magnus said, not looking at the point of the knife just below his face, "that by standing as you are, everyone will think we are kissing. And that is terribly embarrassing for me. I have *much* better taste in men."

"You think I won't do it, *freak*? You—"

Magnus's hand went up. A hot flash of blue spread between his fingers, and in the next second his assailant was flying backward across the sidewalk, then falling and striking his head against a fire hydrant. For one moment, when the man's prone form didn't move right away, Magnus was worried that he had killed the man by accident, but then Magnus saw him stir. He peered up at Magnus with his eyes narrowed, a combination of terror and fury plain on his face. He was clearly a little stunned by what had just happened. A trickle of blood ran down his forehead.

At that moment Catarina emerged. She appraised the situation quickly, went right to the fallen man, and passed her hand over his head, stopping the blood.

"Get off me!" he yelled. "You came from in there! Get off me! You got the *thing* all over you!"

"You idiot," Catarina said. "That's not how you contract HIV. I'm a nurse. Let me—"

The stranger shoved Catarina away and scrabbled to his feet. Across the street some passersby watched the exchange with mild curiosity. But when the man stumbled off, they lost interest.

"You're welcome," she said to the retreating figure. "Jackass."

She turned to Magnus. "Are you all right?"

"I'm fine," he said. "He was the one bleeding."

"Sometimes I wish I could just *let* someone like that bleed," Catarina said, taking out a tissue and wiping her hands. "What are you doing here, anyway?"

"I came here to see you home."

"You don't need to do that," she said with a sigh. "I'm fine."

"It's not safe. And you're exhausted."

Catarina was listing slightly to one side. Magnus grabbed her hand. She was so tired that Magnus saw her glamour fade for a moment, saw a wash of blue on the hand he was holding.

"I'm fine," she said again, but without much heart.

"Yes," Magnus said. "Obviously. You know, if you don't start taking care of yourself, you'll force me to come to your house and make my magically disgusting tuna soup until you feel better."

Catarina laughed. "Anything but the tuna soup."

"Then we'll eat something. Come on. I'll take you to Veselka. You need some goulash and a big piece of cake."

They walked east in silence, over slick piles of wet, crushed leaves.

Veselka was quiet, and they got a table by the window. The only people around them spoke quietly in Russian and smoked, and ate cabbage rolls. Magnus had some coffee and rugelach. Catarina made it through a large bowl of borscht, a large plate of fried pierogi with onions and applesauce, a side of Ukrainian meatballs, and a few cherry lime rickeys. It wasn't until she had finished these and ordered a dessert plate of cheese blintzes that she found the energy to speak.

"It's bad in there," she said. "It's hard."

There was little Magnus could say, so he just listened.

"The patients need me," she said, poking her straw into the ice in her otherwise empty glass. "Some of the doctors—people who should *know* better—won't even touch the patients. And it's so horrible, this disease. The way they just waste away. Nobody should die like that."

"No," Magnus said.

Catarina poked at the ice a moment longer and then leaned back in the booth and sighed deeply.

"I can't believe the *Nephilim* are causing trouble now, of all times," she said, rubbing her face with one hand. "Nephilim kids, no less. How is this even happening?"

This was the reason Magnus had waited by the clinic to walk Catarina home. It wasn't because the neighborhood was bad—the neighborhood wasn't bad. He'd waited for Catarina because it was no longer completely safe for Downworlders to be alone. He could hardly believe that Downworld was in a state of chaos and fear over the actions of a gang of stupid Shadowhunter youths.

When he had first heard the murmurings, just a few months before, Magnus had rolled his eyes. A pack of Shadowhunters, barely twenty years old, barely more than children, were rebelling against their parents' laws. Big deal. The Clave and Covenant and respected-elders shtick had always seemed to Magnus the ideal recipe for a youth revolt. This group called themselves the Circle, one Downworlder report had said, and they were led by a charismatic youth named Valentine. The group comprised some of the brightest and best of their generation.

And the Circle members were saying that the Clave did not deal harshly enough with Downworlders. That was how the wheel turned, Magnus supposed, one generation against the next—from Aloysius Starkweather, who'd wanted werewolf heads on the wall, to Will Herondale, who had tried and never quite succeeded in hiding his open heart. Today's youth thought that the Clave's policy of cold tolerance was too generous, apparently. Today's youth wanted to fight monsters, and had conveniently decided that Magnus's people were monsters, every one. Magnus sighed. This seemed like a season of hatred for all the world.

Valentine's Circle had not done much yet. Perhaps they never would do much. But they had done enough. They had roamed Idris, had gone through Portals and visited other cities on missions to aid the Institutes there, and in every city they'd visited, Downworlders had died.

There were always Downworlders who broke the Accords, and Shadowhunters made them pay for it. But Magnus had not been born yesterday, or even this century. He did not think it was a coincidence that wherever Valentine and his friends went, death followed. They were finding any excuse to rid the world of Downworlders.

"What does this Valentine kid even *want?*" Catarina asked. "What's his plan?"

"He wants death and destruction for all Downworld," said Magnus. "His plan is possibly to be a huge jerk."

"And what if they *do* come here?" Catarina asked. "What would the Whitelaws even do?"

Magnus had lived in New York for decades now, and had known the Shadowhunters of the New York Institute all that time. For the last several decades the Institute had been led by the Whitelaws.

They had always been dutiful and distant. Magnus had never liked any of them, and none of them had ever liked Magnus. Magnus had no proof that they would betray an innocent Downworlder, but Shadowhunters thought so much of their own kind and their own blood that Magnus wasn't sure what the Whitelaws would do.

Magnus had gone to meet with Marian Whitelaw, the head of the Institute, and had told her of the reports from Downworld that Valentine and his little helpers were killing Downworlders who were not breaking the Accords, and then the Circle members were lying about it to the Clave afterward.

"Go to the Clave," Magnus had said to her. "Tell them to control their unruly brats."

"Control your unruly tongue," Marian Whitelaw had said coldly, "when you speak of your betters, warlock. Valentine Morgenstern is considered a most promising Shadowhunter, as are his young friends. I knew his wife, Jocelyn, when she was a child; she is a sweet and lovely girl. I will not doubt their goodness. Certainly not with no proof and based on the malicious gossip of Downworld alone."

"They are killing my people!"

"They are killing Downworlder criminals, in full compliance with the Accords. They are showing zeal in the pursuit of evil. Nothing bad can come from that. I would not expect you to understand."

Of course the Shadowhunters would not believe that their best and brightest had become just a little bit too bloodthirsty. Of course they would accept the excuses Valentine and the others gave them, and of course they would believe that Magnus and any other Downworlder who complained simply wanted criminals to escape justice.

Knowing they could not turn to the Shadowhunters, Downworlders had tried to put their own safeguards in place. A safe house had been set up in Chinatown, through an amnesty between the constantly feuding vampires and werewolves, and everybody was on the watch.

Downworlders were on their own. But then, hadn't they always been on their own?

Magnus sighed and eyed Catarina over their plates.

"Eat," he said. "Nothing's happening right now. It's possible nothing *will* happen."

"They killed a 'rogue vampire' in Chicago last week," she said, chopping into a blintz with a fork. "You know they'll want to come here."

They ate in silence, pensive on Magnus's side and exhausted on Catarina's. The check came, and Magnus paid. Catarina didn't think much about things like money. She was a nurse at a clinic with few resources, and he had ample cash on hand.

"Gotta get back," she said. She scrubbed a hand over her weary face, and Magnus saw cerulean trails in the wake of her fingertips, her glamour faltering even as she spoke.

"You are going home and sleeping," Magnus said. "I'm your friend. I know you. You deserve a night off. You should spend it indulging in wanton luxuries such as sleep."

"What if something happens?" she asked. "What if *they* come?"

"I can get Ragnor to help me."

"Ragnor's in Peru," said Catarina. "He says he finds it very peaceful without your accursed presence, and that's a direct quote."

Ragnor was wily enough that Magnus did not worry about him too much. He would never let his guard down anywhere that he did not feel completely safe.

"So it's just us," Catarina said.

Magnus knew that Catarina's heart lay with mortals, and that she was involved more for friendship's sake than because she wanted to fight Shadowhunters. Catarina had her own battles to fight, her own ground to stand on. She was more of a hero than any Shadowhunter that Magnus had ever met. The Shadowhunters had been chosen by an angel. Catarina herself had chosen to fight.

"It's looking like a quiet night," he said. "Come on. Finish up and let me take you home."

"Is this chivalry?" Catarina said with a smile. "Thought that was dead."

"Like us, it never dies."

They walked back the way they had come. It was fully dark now, and the night had taken a decidedly cold turn. There was a suggestion of rain. Catarina lived in a simple, slightly run-down walk-up off West Twenty-First Street, not too far from the clinic. The stove never worked, and the trash cans out front were always overflowing, but she never seemed to care. It had a bed and a place for her clothes. That was all she needed. She led a simpler life than Magnus.

Magnus made his way home, to his apartment farther down in the Village, off Christopher Street. His apartment was also a walk-up, and he took the steps two at a time. Unlike Catarina's, his place was extremely habitable. The walls were bright and cheerful shades of rose and daisy yellow, and the apartment was furnished in some of the items he had collected over the years—a marvelous little French table, a few Victorian settees, and an amazing art deco bedroom set entirely in mirrored glass.

Normally, on a crisp early fall night like this, Magnus would pour himself a glass of wine, put a Cure album into his CD player, crank up the volume, and wait for business to start. Night was often his working time; he had many walk-in clients, and there was always research to do or reading to catch up on.

Tonight he made a pot of strong coffee, sat in the window seat, and looked down on the street below. Tonight, like every other night since the dark murmurs of the bloodthirsty young Shadowhunters had started, he would sit and watch and think. If the Circle did come here, as it seemed that they would do eventually, what would happen? Valentine had a special hatred for werewolves, they said, but he had killed a warlock in Berlin for summoning demons. Magnus had been known to summon a demon himself a time or twenty.

It was extremely likely that if they came to New York, they would come for Magnus. The sensible thing would probably be to leave, disappear into the country. He'd gotten himself a little house in the Florida Keys to while away the brutal New York winters. The house was on one of the smaller, less inhabited islands, and he had a fine boat there as well. If anything happened, he could get in it and speed off into the sea, head for the Caribbean or South America. He'd packed a bag several times, and unpacked it right after.

There was no point in running. If the Circle continued their campaign of so-called justice, they would make the entire world unsafe for Downworlders. And there was no way Magnus could live with himself if he ran away and his friends, such as Catarina, were left to try to defend themselves. He did not like the idea of Raphael Santiago or any of his vampires being killed either, or any of the faeries he knew who worked on Broadway, or the mermaids who swam in the East River. Magnus had always thought of himself as a rolling stone, but he had lived in New York a long time now. He found himself wanting to defend not only his friends but his city.

So he was staying, and waiting, and trying to be ready for the Circle when they came.

The waiting was hardest. Maybe that was why he had engaged the man by the clinic. Something in Magnus wanted the fight to come. He wiggled and flexed his fingers, and blue light webbed between them. He opened the window and breathed in some of the night air, which smelled like a mix of rain, leaves, and pizza from the place on the corner.

"Just do it already," he said to no one.

The kid appeared under his window at around one in the morning, just when Magnus had finally been able to distract himself and start translating an old Greek text that had been on his desk for weeks. Magnus happened to look up and noticed the kid pacing confusedly outside. He was nine, maybe ten years old—a little East Village street punk in a Sex Pistols shirt that probably belonged to an older sibling, and a baggy pair of gray sweatpants. He had a ragged, home-done haircut. And he wore no coat.

All of these things added up to a kid in trouble, and the general streetwise appearance plus a certain fluidity to the walk suggested werewolf. Magnus pushed open the window.

"You looking for someone?" he called.

"Are you Magnificent Bane?"

"Sure," said Magnus. "Let's go with that. Hang on. Open the door when it buzzes."

He slid off the window seat and went to the buzzer by the door. He heard the rapid footfalls on the steps. This kid was in a hurry. Magnus had no sooner opened the door than the kid was inside. Once inside and in the light, the true extent of the boy's distress was clear. His cheeks were highly flushed and stained with dried tear trails. He was sweating despite the cold, and his voice was shaking and urgent.

"You gotta come," he said as he stumbled in. "They have my family. They're here."

"Who are here?"

"The crazy Shadowhunters everyone's freaking about. They're here. They *have my family*. You gotta come *now*."

"The Circle?"

The kid shook his head, not in disagreement but in confusion. Magnus could see he didn't know what the Circle was, but the description fit. The kid had to be talking about the Circle.

"Where are they?" Magnus asked.

"In Chinatown. The safe house." The kid almost shook with impatience. "My mom heard those freaks were here. They already killed a whole buncha vampires up in Spanish Harlem earlier tonight, they said for killing mundanes, but nobody heard of any dead mundanes, and a faerie said they were coming down to Chinatown to get us. So my mom brought all of us to the safe house, but then they broke in. I got out through a window. My mom said to come to you."

The entire story was delivered in such a jumbled, frantic rush that Magnus had no time to unpick it.

"How many are you?" he asked.

"My mom and my brother and sister and six others from my pack."

So nine werewolves in danger. The test had come, and come so quickly that Magnus had no time to really go through his feelings or think through a plan.

"Did you hear anything the Circle said?" Magnus asked. "What did the Circle accuse your family of doing?"

"They said our old pack did something, but we don't know anything about that. It doesn't matter, does it? They kill them anyway, that's what everybody's saying! You *gotta come*."

He grabbed Magnus's hand and made to pull him. Magnus detached the boy and reached for a pad and paper.

"You," he said, scrawling down Catarina's address, "you go here. You go nowhere else. You stay there. There's a nice blue lady there. I will go to the safe house."

"I'm coming with you."

"Either you do as I say or I don't go," Magnus snapped. "There's no time to argue. You decide."

The boy teetered on the edge of tears. He wiped his eyes roughly with the back of his hand.

"You'll get them?" he asked. "You promise?"

"I promise," Magnus said.

How he was going to do that, he had no idea. But the fight had come. At last the fight had come.

The last thing Magnus did before he left was write down the details: where the safe house—a warehouse—was, what he feared the Circle was planning to do to the werewolves inside it. He folded up the piece of paper into the shape of a bird and sent it, with a flick of his fingers and a burst of blue sparks. The frail little paper bird tumbled in the wind like a pale leaf, flying out into the night and toward the towers of Manhattan, which cut the darkness like glittering knives.

He didn't know why he had bothered to send a message to the Whitelaws. He didn't think they would come.

Magnus ran through Chinatown, under neon signs that flickered and sizzled, through the yellow smog of the city that clung like begging ghosts to passersby. He ran by a huddle of people freebasing on a street corner, and then finally reached the street where the warehouse stood, its tin roof rattling in the night wind. A mundane would have seen it as smaller than it really was, shabby and dark, its windows boarded. Magnus saw the lights: Magnus saw the broken window.

There was a small voice in Magnus's head calling for caution, but Magnus had heard tell in great detail of what Valentine's Circle did to vulnerable Downworlders when they found them.

Magnus ran toward the safe house, almost stumbling in his Doc Martens over the cracked pavement. He reached the double doors, spray-painted with halos, crowns, and thorns, and flung them open wide.

In the main room of the safe house, their backs to the wall, stood a cluster of werewolves, still in human form, most of them, though Magnus could see claws and teeth on some crouching in defensive positions.

Surrounding them was a crowd of young Shadowhunters.

Everybody turned around and looked at Magnus.

Even if the Shadowhunters had been expecting an interruption, and the werewolves had been hoping for a savior, apparently nobody had been expecting all the hot pink.

The reports about the Circle were true. So many of them were heartbreakingly young, a brand-new generation of Shadowhunters, shining new warriors who had just reached adulthood. Magnus was not surprised, but he found it sad and infuriating, that they should throw the bright beginnings of their lives away on this senseless hate.

At the front of the Shadowhunter crowd stood a little cluster of people who, though they were young, had an air of authority about them—the inner circle of Valentine's Circle. Magnus did not recognize anyone who matched the description he'd heard of the ringleader.

Magnus was not certain, but he thought the current leader of the group was either the beautiful boy with the golden hair and the deep sweet blue eyes, or the young man beside him with the dark hair and narrow, intelligent face. Magnus had lived a long time, and could tell which members of a group were the leaders of the pack. Neither of these two looked imposing, but the body language of all the others deferred to them. These two were flanked by a young man and a woman, both with black hair and fierce hawklike faces, and behind the black-haired man stood a handsome curly-haired youth. Behind those stood about six more. At the other end of the room was a door, a single door rather than double doors like the ones Magnus had burst in through, an inside door that led to another chamber. A stocky young Shadowhunter stood in front of it.

There were too many of them to fight, and they were all so young and so fresh from the schoolrooms of Idris that Magnus would never have met them before. Magnus had not taught in the academy of the Shadowhunters for decades, but he remembered the rooms, the lessons of the Angel, the upturned young faces drinking in every word about their sacred duty.

And these newly adult Nephilim had come out of their schoolrooms to do this.

"Valentine's Circle, I presume?" he said, and he saw them all jolt at the words, as if they thought Downworlders did not have their own ways of passing along information when they were being hunted. "But I don't believe I see Valentine Morgenstern. I hear he has charisma enough to draw birds out of trees and convince them to live under the sea, is tall, is devastatingly handsome, and has white-blond hair. None of you fit that description."

Magnus paused.

"And you don't have white-blond hair either."

They all looked shocked to be spoken to in that manner. They were of Idris, and no doubt if they knew warlocks at all, they knew warlocks like Ragnor, who made certain to be professional and civil in all his dealings with the Nephilim. Marian Whitelaw might have told Magnus to control his unruly tongue, but she had not been shocked by his speaking out. These stupid children were content to hate from a distance, to fight and never speak to Downworlders, to never risk for a moment seeing their designated enemies as anything like people.

They thought they knew it all, and they knew so little.

"I am Lucian Graymark," said the young man with the thin clever face at the front of the group. Magnus had heard the name before—Valentine's *parabatai*, his second-in-command, dearer than a brother. Magnus disliked him as soon as he spoke. "Who are you to come here and interfere with us in the pursuit of our sworn duty?"

Graymark held his head high and spoke in a clear, authoritative voice that belied his years. He looked every inch the perfect child of the Angel, stern and merciless. Magnus looked back over his shoulder at the werewolves, huddled at the very back of the room.

Magnus lifted a hand and painted a line of magic, a shimmering barrier of blue and gold. He made the light blaze as fiercely as any angel's sword might have, and barred the Shadowhunters' way.

"I am Magnus Bane. And you are trespassing in my city."

That got a little laugh. "*Your* city?" said Lucian.

"You need to let these people go."

"Those *creatures*," said Lucian, "are part of a wolf pack that killed my *parabatai*'s parents. We tracked them down here. We can now exact Shadowhunter justice, as is our right."

"We didn't kill any Shadowhunters!" the only woman among the werewolves said. "And my children are innocent. Killing my children would be murder. Bane, you have to make him let my children go. He has my—"

"I would hear no more of your whining like a mongrel dog," said the young man with the hawklike face, the one standing beside the black-haired woman. They looked like a matched set, and the expressions on their faces were identically ferocious.

Valentine was not famed for his mercy, and Magnus did not have any confidence in his Circle's sparing the children.

The werewolves might have been partially shifted from human to wolf form, but they did not look ready to fight, and Magnus did not know why. There were too many Shadowhunters for Magnus to be sure he could fight them off successfully on his own. The best he could hope for was to stall them with conversation, and hope that he could inspire doubt in some of the Circle, or that Catarina would come or that the Whitelaws would come, and that they might stand with Downworlders and not their own kind.

It seemed a very slim hope, but it was all he had.

Magnus could not help but look again toward the golden-haired youth at the front of the group. There was something terribly familiar about him, as well as a suggestion of tenderness about his mouth, and hurt in the deep blue wells of his eyes. There was something that made Magnus look toward him as the one chance to get the Circle to turn from their purpose.

"What's your name?" Magnus asked.

Those blue eyes narrowed. "Stephen Herondale."

"I used to know the Herondales very well, once upon a time," said Magnus, and he saw it was a mistake by the way Stephen Herondale flinched. The Shadowhunter knew something, had heard some dark whisper about his family tree, then, and was desperate to prove it was not true. Magnus did not know how desperate Stephen Herondale might be, and he had no wish to find out. Magnus went on, genially addressing them all: "I have always been a friend to Shadowhunters. I know many of your families, going back for hundreds of years."

"There is nothing we can do to correct the questionable judgments of our ancestors," Lucian said.

Magnus hated this guy.

"Also," Magnus went on, pointedly ignoring Lucian Graymark, "I find your story suspect. Valentine is ready to hunt down any Downworlder on any vague pretext. What had the vampires he killed in Harlem done to him?"

Stephen Herondale frowned, and glanced at Lucian, who looked troubled in turn, but said, "Valentine told me he went hunting some vampires who broke the Accords there."

"Oh, the Downworlders are all so guilty. And that is so very convenient for you, isn't it? What about their children? The boy who came to collect me was about nine. Has he been dining on Shadowhunter flesh?"

"The pups gnaw on whatever bones their elders drag in," muttered the black-haired woman, and the man beside her nodded.

"Maryse, Robert, please. Valentine is a noble man!" Lucian said, his voice rising as he turned to address Magnus. "He would not hurt a child. Valentine is my *parabatai*, my best beloved swordbrother. His fight is mine. His family has been destroyed, the Accords have been broken, and he deserves and will have his vengeance. Stand aside, warlock."

Lucian Graymark did not have his hand on his weapon, but Magnus saw that the black-haired woman, Maryse, behind him had a blade shining between her fingers. Magnus looked again at Stephen and realized exactly why his face was so familiar. Gold hair and blue eyes—he was a more ethereal and slender version of a young Edmund Herondale, as though Edmund had come back from heaven, twice as angelic. Magnus had not known Edmund for long, but Edmund had been the father of Will Herondale, who had been one of the very few Shadowhunters that Magnus had ever thought of as a friend.

Stephen saw Magnus looking. Stephen's eyes had narrowed so much now that the sweet blue of them was lost, and they seemed black.

"Enough of this byplay with demonspawn!" said Stephen. He sounded as if he were quoting somebody, and Magnus bet that he knew who.

"Stephen, don't—" Lucian ordered, but golden-haired Stephen had already flung a knife in the direction of one werewolf.

Magnus flicked his hand and sent the knife dropping to the ground. He glared at the werewolves. The woman who had spoken before stared intensely back at him, as if trying to convey a message with her eyes alone.

"This is what the modern young Shadowhunter has become, is it?" Magnus asked. "Let me see, how does your little bedtime story about how super-duper extra special you all are go again...? Ah, yes. Through the ages your mandate has been to protect mankind, to fight against evil forces until they are finally vanquished and the world can live in peace. You don't seem terribly interested in peace or protecting anybody. What is it that you're fighting for, exactly?"

"I am fighting for a better world for myself and my son," said the woman called Maryse.

"I have no interest in the world you want," Magnus told her. "Or in your doubtless repellent brat, I might add."

Robert drew a dagger from his sleeve. Magnus was not prepared to waste all his magic deflecting daggers. He lifted a hand into the air, and all the light in the room was quenched. Only the noise and neon glow of the city spilled in, not providing enough illumination to see by, but Robert threw the dagger just the same. That was when the glass of the windows broke and dark forms came flooding in: young Rachel Whitelaw landed in a roll on the floor in front of Magnus, and took the blade meant for him in her shoulder.

* * *

Magnus could see better in the dark than most. He saw that, past all hope, the Whitelaws had come. Marian Whitelaw, the head of the Institute; her husband, Adam; and Adam's brother; and the young Whitelaw cousins whom Marian and Adam had taken in after their parents' deaths. The Whitelaws had already been fighting tonight. Their gear was bloodstained and torn, and Rachel Whitelaw was clearly wounded. There was blood in Marian's gray bob of hair, but Magnus did not think it was hers. Marian and Adam Whitelaw, Magnus happened to know, had not been able to have their own children. The word was that they adored the young cousins who lived with them, that they always made a fuss over any young Shadowhunters who came to their Institute. The Circle members must have been peers of the Whitelaw cousins, brought up together in Idris. The Circle was exactly designed to win the Whitelaws' sympathy.

The Circle was, however, in a panic. They could not see as Magnus could. They did not know who was attacking them, only that somebody had come to Magnus's aid. Magnus saw the swing and heard the clash of blades meeting, so loud it was almost impossible to hear Marian Whitelaw's shouted commands for the Circle to stop and drop their weapons. He wondered which of the Circle even realized who they were fighting. He conjured a small light in his palm and searched for the werewolf woman. He had to know why the werewolves would not attack.

Someone knocked into him. Magnus stared into the eyes of Stephen Herondale.

"Do you never have doubts about all this?" Magnus breathed.

"No," Stephen panted. "I have lost too much—I have sacrificed too much to this great cause ever to turn my back on it now."

As he spoke, he swung his knife up toward Magnus's throat. Magnus turned the hilt hot in the young man's hand until he dropped it.

Magnus suddenly did not care what Stephen had sacrificed,

or about the pain in his blue eyes. He wanted Stephen gone from this earth. Magnus wanted to forget he had ever seen Stephen Herondale's face, so full of hate and so reminiscent of faces Magnus had loved. The warlock summoned a new spell into his hand and was about to hurl it at Stephen, when a thought arrested him. He did not know how he could face Tessa again if he killed one of her descendants.

Then Marian Whitelaw stepped into the light from the spell shimmering in Magnus's palm, and Stephen's face went blank with surprise.

"Ma'am, it's you! We shouldn't— We're Shadowhunters. We shouldn't be fighting over them. They are *Downworlders*," Stephen hissed. "They will turn on you like the treacherous dogs they are. That's their nature. They are not worth fighting for. What do you say?"

"I don't have any proof these werewolves broke the Accords."

"Valentine said," began Stephen, but Magnus heard the uncertainty in his voice. Lucian Graymark might believe they only hunted Downworlders who had broken the Accords, but Stephen at least knew they were acting as vigilantes rather than Law-abiding Shadowhunters. Stephen had been doing it, just the same.

"I do not care what Valentine Morgenstern says. I say that the Law is hard," Marian Whitelaw replied. She drew her blade, swung, and met Stephen's.

Their eyes met, glittering, over their blades.

Marian continued softly, "But it is the Law. You will not touch these Downworlders while I or any of my blood live."

Chaos erupted, but Magnus's darkest imaginings had been proved wrong. When the fight was joined, there were Shadowhunters on his side, fighting with him against Shadowhunters, fighting for Downworlders and the Accords of peace they had all agreed to.

The first fatality was the youngest Whitelaw. Rachel Whitelaw lunged at the woman called Maryse, and the sheer ferocity of the attack took Maryse aback so much that Rachel almost had her. Maryse stumbled and collected herself, fumbling for a new blade. Then the black-haired man, Robert, who Magnus thought was her husband, lunged at Rachel in his turn, and ran her through.

Rachel sagged, the point of the man's blade like a pin piercing her, as if she were a butterfly.

"Robert!" said Maryse softly, as if she could not believe this was happening.

Robert unsheathed his sword from Rachel's chest, and Rachel tumbled to the floor.

"Rachel Whitelaw was just killed by a Shadowhunter," shouted Magnus, and even then he thought Robert might cry out that he had been defending his wife. Magnus thought that the Whitelaws might put away their blades rather than spill more Nephilim blood.

But Rachel had been the baby of the family, everyone's special pet. The Whitelaws as one roared a challenge and hurled themselves into the fray with redoubled ferocity. Adam Whitelaw, a stolid white-haired old man who had always seemed to simply follow his wife's lead, charged at Valentine's Circle, whirling a shining axe over his head, and cut down all those who stood before him.

Magnus edged toward the werewolves, to the woman who was the only one who remained human, even though her teeth and claws were growing apace.

"Why aren't you fighting?" he demanded.

The werewolf woman glared at him as if he were impossibly stupid.

"Because Valentine's here," she snapped. "Because he has my daughter. He took her through there, and they said if we moved to follow her, they would kill her."

Magnus did not have an instant to reflect on what Valentine might do to a helpless Downworlder child. He lifted a hand and blasted from his feet the stocky Shadowhunter at the single door at the far end of the room, and then Magnus ran toward the door.

He heard the cries behind him, of the Whitelaws demanding, "Bane, where are you—" and a shout, Magnus thought from Stephen, saying, "He's going after Valentine! Kill him!"

Behind the door Magnus heard a low, awful sound. He pushed the door open.

On the other side of the door was a small ordinary room, the size of a bedroom, though there was no bed, only two people and a single chair. There was a tall man with a fall of white-blond hair, wearing Shadowhunter black. He was stooped over a girl who looked about twelve. She was fastened to the chair with silver cord, and was making a terrible low sound, a cross between a whine and a moan.

Her eyes were shining, Magnus thought for a moment, the moonlight turning them into mirrors.

His mistake lasted for the briefest of instants. Then Valentine moved slightly and the gleam of the girl's eyes resolved in Magnus's vision. The gleam was not her eyes. The moonlit shine was silver coins pressed to the girl's eyes, tiny wisps of smoke escaping from beneath the bright discs as the tiny sounds escaped from between her lips. She was trying to suppress the sound of her pain, because she was so scared of what Valentine would do to her next.

"Where did your brother go?" demanded Valentine, and the girl's sobbing continued, but she said nothing.

Magnus felt for a moment as if he had become a storm, black curling clouds, the slam of thunder and slash of lightning, and all the storm wanted was to leap at Valentine's throat. Magnus's magic lashed out almost of its own volition, leaped from both hands. It looked like lightning, burning so blue that it was almost white. It knocked Valentine off his feet and into a wall. Valentine hit the wall so hard that a crack rang out, and he slid to the floor.

That one act also used up far too much of Magnus's power, but he could not think of that now. He ran over to the girl's chair and wrenched the chain off her, then touched her face with painful gentleness.

She was crying now, more freely, shuddering and sobbing beneath his hands.

"Hush, hush. Your brother sent me. I'm a warlock; you're safe," he murmured, and clasped the back of her neck.

The coins were hurting her. They had to come off. But would removing them do more damage? Magnus could heal, but it had never been his specialty as it was Catarina's, and he had not had to heal werewolves often. They were so resilient. He could only hope she would be resilient now.

He lifted the coins as gently as he could, and threw them against the wall.

It was too late. It had been too late before he'd ever entered the room. She was blind.

Her lips parted. She said, "Is my brother safe?"

"As safe as can be, sweetheart," said Magnus. "I'll take you to him."

No sooner had he said the word "him" than he felt the cold blade sink into his back and his mouth fill with hot blood.

"Oh, will you?" asked Valentine's voice in his ear.

The blade slid free, hurting as much on the way out as it had on the way in. Magnus gritted his teeth and gripped the back of the chair harder, kept himself arched over and protecting the child, and turned his head to face Valentine. The white-haired man looked older than the other leaders, but Magnus was not sure if he was actually older or if cold purpose simply made his face seem carved from marble. Magnus wanted to smash it.

Valentine's hand moved, and Magnus only just managed to catch Valentine's wrist before he found Valentine's blade in his heart.

Magnus concentrated and made the clasp of his hand burn, blue electricity circling his fingers. He made the contact burn as the touch of silver had burned the girl, and he grinned as he heard Valentine's hiss of pain.

Valentine did not ask his name as the others had, did not treat

Magnus as that much of a person. Valentine simply stared at Magnus with cold eyes, the same way anyone might stare at a loathsome animal in their path and impeding their progress. "You are interfering in my business, warlock."

Magnus spat blood into his face. "You are torturing a child in my city. Shadowhunter."

Valentine used his free hand to deal Magnus a blow that sent Magnus staggering back. Valentine wheeled and followed him, and Magnus thought, *Good*. It meant that he was moving away from the girl.

She was blind, but she was a werewolf, smell and sound as important to her as sight. She could run, and find her way back to her family.

"I thought we were playing a game where we said what the other person was and what we were doing," Magnus told him. "Did I get it wrong? Can I guess again? Are you breaking your own sacred Laws, asshole?"

He glanced at the girl, hoping she would run, but she seemed frozen to the spot with terror. Magnus did not dare call out to her in case it attracted Valentine's attention.

Magnus lifted a hand, sketching a spell in the air, but Valentine saw the spell coming and dodged it. He leaped into the air and then bounded off the wall, Nephilim-swift, to lunge at Magnus. He scythed Magnus's legs out from under him, and when Magnus landed, Valentine kicked him brutally hard. He drew a sword and brought it down. Magnus rolled so that it caught him a glancing blow along the ribs, cutting through shirt and skin but not hitting vital organs. Not this time.

Magnus dearly hoped he was not going to die here, in this cold warehouse, far from anyone he loved. He tried to rise from the floor, but it was slippery with his own blood, and the scraps of magic he had were not enough to heal or fight, let alone both.

Marian Whitelaw stood in front of him, her blades drawn and

new runes shining on her arms. Her hair shone silver in his blurred vision.

Valentine swung his sword, and cut her almost in half.

Magnus gasped, salvation lost as quickly as it had been found, then turned his head toward the sound of more footsteps on the stone.

He was a fool to have hoped for another rescue. He saw one of Valentine's Circle, standing in the doorway with his eyes fixed on the werewolf girl.

"Valentine!" Lucian Graymark shouted. He ran for the girl, and Magnus tensed, coiled himself for a leap, and then froze as he saw Lucian pick the girl up and wheel on his master. "How could you do this? She's a child!"

"No, Lucian. She's a monster in the shape of a child."

Lucian was holding the girl, his hand in her hair, soothing and stroking. Magnus was starting to think he might have really misjudged Lucian Graymark. Valentine's face was as white as bone. He resembled a statue more than ever.

Valentine said slowly, "Did you not promise me unconditional obedience? Tell me, what use have I for a second-in-command who undermines me like this?"

"Valentine, I love you and I share your grief," said Lucian. "I know you are a good man. I know if you stop and think, you will see that this is madness."

When Valentine took a step toward him, Lucian took a step back. He curved his hand protectively over the werewolf girl's head as she clung to him with her small legs locked around his waist, and his other hand wavered as if he might go for his weapon.

"Very well," Valentine said gently, at last. "Have it your way."

He stood aside to let Lucian Graymark pass through the door and out into the corridor, and back into the room where the werewolves had thought they might be safe. He let Lucian bring the werewolves' daughter back to them, and followed him at a distance.

Magnus did not trust Valentine for an instant. He would not believe the girl was safe until she was in her mother's arms.

Lucian Graymark had bought Magnus enough time to gather up his magic. Magnus concentrated, felt his skin knit even as his power drained away.

He pulled himself up from the floor, and ran after them.

The fight in the room they had left was quieter, because there were so many dead. Someone had managed to turn the lights back on. There was a wolf lying dead on the ground, transforming inch by inch into a pale young man. Another young man lay dead beside him, one of the Circle, and in death they did not look so different.

Many of the Shadowhunters in Valentine's Circle were still standing. None of the Whitelaws were. Maryse Lightwood had her face in her hands. Some of the others were visibly shaken. Now the shadows and the frenzy of battle had receded, and they were left in the light to look at what they had done.

"Valentine," Maryse said, her voice imploring as her leader approached. "Valentine, what have we done? The Whitelaws are dead… Valentine…"

They all looked to Valentine as he approached, clustered up to him like frightened children rather than adults. Valentine must have gotten hold of them very young, Magnus thought, but he found himself unable to care if they were brainwashed or deluded, not after what they had done. It seemed like there was no pity left in him.

"You have done nothing but try to uphold the Law," said Valentine. "You know that all traitors to our kind must pay one day. If they had chosen to step aside, to trust us, their fellow children of the Angel, all would have been well."

"What about the Clave?" said the curly-haired man, a note of challenge in his voice.

"Michael," murmured Maryse's husband.

"What of them, Wayland?" Valentine asked, his voice sharp. "The

Whitelaws died because of rogue werewolves. It is the truth, and we will tell the Clave so."

The only one of Valentine's Circle not desperately listening was Lucian Graymark. He made his way to the werewolf woman, and placed the little girl into her arms. Magnus heard the woman's indrawn breath as she saw her daughter's eyes. He heard her begin to cry softly. Lucian stood beside the mother and daughter, looking deeply distressed, then crossed the floor with a suddenly determined tread.

"Let's go, Valentine," he said. "All this with the Whitelaws was ... was a terrible accident. We can't have our Circle suffering for it. We should go now. These creatures aren't worth your time, not any of them. These werewolves are just strays who broke off from their pack. You and I will go hunting in the werewolf encampment where the real threat lies tonight. We will bring down the pack leader together."

"Together. But tomorrow night. Come back to the house tonight?" Valentine asked in a low voice. "Jocelyn has something to tell you."

Lucian clasped Valentine's arm, clearly relieved. "Of course. Anything for Jocelyn. Anything for either of you. You know that."

"My friend," said Valentine, "I do."

Valentine clasped Lucian's arm in return, but Magnus saw the look Valentine gave Lucian. There was love in that look, but hate as well, and the hate was winning. It was as clear as a silvery shark's fin in the dark waters of Valentine's black eyes. There was death in those eyes.

Magnus was not surprised. He had seen many monsters who could love, but only a few who had let that love change them, who had been able to alchemize love for one person into kindness for many.

He remembered Valentine's face as the Circle's leader had cut Marian Whitelaw into bloody halves, and Magnus wondered what it would be like, living with someone like Valentine, wondered what it was like for his wife, who Marian had described as lovely. You could share your bed with a monster, lay your head on the same pillow next to a head filled with murder and madness. Magnus had done it himself.

But love that blind did not last. One day you lifted your head from the pillow and saw you were living in a nightmare.

Lucian Graymark might be the only one of the lot worth bothering with, and Magnus would bet he was as good as dead.

Magnus had been so terribly wrong to let the past deceive him; he'd been wrong to think that the one with depths of goodness in him was Stephen Herondale. Magnus looked at Stephen, at his beautiful face and his weak mouth. Magnus had a sudden impulse to tell the Shadowhunter that Magnus knew and loved his ancestor, that Tessa would be so disappointed in him. But he did not want Valentine's Circle to remember or go after Tessa.

Magnus said nothing. Stephen Herondale had chosen his side, and Magnus had chosen his.

Valentine's Circle withdrew from the warehouse, marching like a little army.

Magnus ran to where old Adam Whitelaw lay in a pool of blood, his shining axe lying, dull and still, in the same dark pool.

"Marian?" Adam asked. Magnus went to his knees in the pool, hands searching to find and close the worst of the wounds. There were so many—too many.

Magnus looked at Adam's eyes, where the light was going out, and knew Adam read the answer on his face before Magnus could think to lie to him.

"My brother?" Adam asked. "The—the children?"

Magnus looked around the room at the dead. When he looked back, Adam Whitelaw had turned his face away and set his mouth so that he would not betray either pain or grief. Magnus used all the magic he had left to ease the man's pain, and in the end Adam lifted a hand and stilled Magnus's, rested his head against Magnus's arm.

"Enough, warlock," he said, his voice rasping. "I would not—I would not live if I could." He coughed, a wet terrible sound, and shut his eyes.

"*Ave atque vale*, Shadowhunter," Magnus whispered. "Your angel would be proud."

Adam Whitelaw did not seem to hear. It was only a very short time later that the last of the Whitelaws died in Magnus's arms.

The Clave believed that the Whitelaws had been killed by rogue werewolves, and nothing Magnus said made any difference. He had not expected them to believe him. He hardly knew why he spoke out, except that the Nephilim so clearly preferred that he be silent.

Magnus waited for the Circle to return.

The Circle did not come to New York again, but Magnus did see them one more time. He saw them at the Uprising.

Not long after the night in the warehouse, Lucian Graymark disappeared as if he had died, and Magnus assumed he had. Then a year later Magnus had word of Lucian again. Ragnor Fell told Magnus there was a werewolf who had once been a Shadowhunter, and that he was spreading word that the time had come, that Downworld had to be ready to fight the Circle. Valentine unveiled his plan and armed his Circle at the time when the Accords of peace between Nephilim and Downworlders were to be signed again. His Circle cut down Shadowhunters and Downworlders alike in the Great Hall of the Angel.

Thanks to Lucian Graymark's warning, Downworlders were able to rush into the Hall and surprise Valentine's Circle. They'd been forewarned and also heavily forearmed.

The Shadowhunters surprised Magnus then, as the Whitelaws had surprised him before. The Clave did not abandon the Downworlders and turn to join with the Circle. The vast majority of them, the Clave and the Institute leaders, made the choice the Whitelaws had made before them. They fought for their sworn allies and for peace, and Valentine's Circle was defeated.

But once the battle was done, the Shadowhunters blamed Downworlders for the deaths of so many of their people, as if the battle had been Downworld's idea. The Shadowhunters prided themselves on their justice, but their justice for Magnus's kind was always bitter.

Relations between the Nephilim and Downworld did not improve. Magnus despaired that they ever would.

Especially when the Clave sent the last remaining members of the Circle, the Lightwoods and another Circle member called Hodge Starkweather, to Magnus's city, to atone for their crimes by running the New York Institute as exiles from the Glass City. The Shadowhunters were scarce enough after the massacre, and could not be replenished without the Mortal Cup, which seemed to have been lost with Valentine. The Lightwoods knew that they had been treated mercifully due to their high connections in the Clave, and that if they slipped up once, the Clave would crush them.

Raphael Santiago of the vampires, who owed Magnus a favor or twenty, reported that the Lightwoods were distant but scrupulously fair with every Downworlder they came into contact with. Magnus knew that sooner or later he would have to work with them, would learn to be civil to them, but he preferred that it be later. The whole bloody tragedy of Valentine's Circle was over, and Magnus would rather not look back on the darkness but look forward and hope for light.

For more than two years after the Uprising, Magnus didn't see any of Valentine's Circle again. Until he did.

New York City, 1993

The life of warlocks was one of immortality, magic, glamour, and excitement through the ages.

Sometimes, though, Magnus wanted to stay in and watch

television on the sofa like everyone else. He was curled up on the sofa with Tessa, and they were watching a video of *Pride and Prejudice*. Tessa was complaining at some length about how the book was better.

"This is not what Jane Austen would have wanted," Tessa told him. "If she could see this, I am certain she would be horrified."

Magnus uncurled from the sofa and went to stand by the window. He was expecting some Chinese to be delivered, and he was starving from a long day of idleness and debauchery. He did not see a deliveryman, though. The only person on the street was a young woman carrying a baby wrapped up tight against the cold. She was walking fast, no doubt on her way home.

"If Jane Austen could see this," Magnus said, "I assume she would be screaming, 'There are tiny demons in this little box! Fetch a clergyman!' and hitting the television with her parasol."

The doorbell rang, and Magnus turned away from the window.

"Finally," Magnus said, grabbing a ten-dollar bill from a table near the door, and he buzzed the deliveryman in. "I need some beef and broccoli before I face any more Mr. Darcy. It's a truth universally acknowledged that if you watch too much television on an empty stomach, your head falls off."

"If your head fell off," Tessa said, "the hairdressing industry would go into an economic meltdown."

Magnus nodded and touched his hair, which was now in a chin-length sweep. He opened the door, still in his pose, and found himself staring at a woman with a crown of red curls. She was holding a child. She was the woman he had seen on the street moments ago. Magnus was startled to see someone at his door who looked so ... mundane.

The young woman was dressed in sloppy jeans and a tie-dyed T-shirt. She lowered her hand, which had been raised as if to knock on the door, and Magnus saw the flicker of faded, silvery scars on her arm. Magnus had seen far too many of those to ever be mistaken.

She bore Covenant Marks, carried the remnants of old runes on her skin like mementos. She was not mundane in the least, then. She was a Shadowhunter, but a Shadowhunter bearing no fresh Marks, not dressed in gear.

She was not here on official Shadowhunter business. She was trouble.

"Who are you?" Magnus demanded.

She swallowed, and replied, "I am—I was Jocelyn Morgenstern."

The name conjured up memories years old. Magnus remembered the blade going into his back and the taste of blood. It made him want to spit.

The monster's bride at his door. Magnus could not stop staring.

She was staring too. She seemed transfixed by his pajamas. Magnus was frankly offended. He had not invited any wives of crazed hate-cult leaders to come around and pass judgment on his wardrobe. If he wished to forgo a shirt and wear scarlet drawstring pajamas patterned with black polar bears, and a black silk bed jacket, he could do so. None of the others who had been lucky enough to see Magnus in his bedroom attire had ever complained.

"I don't remember ordering the bride of an evil maniac," said Magnus. "It was definitely beef and broccoli. What about you, Tessa? Did *you* order the bride of an evil maniac?"

He swung the door open wider so Tessa could see who was there. Nothing else was said for a moment. Then Magnus saw the blanket-covered lump in Jocelyn's arms stir. It was in that moment that he remembered there was a child.

"I have come here, Magnus Bane," Jocelyn said, "to beg your aid."

Magnus gripped the edge of the door until his knuckles went white.

"Let me think," he said. "No."

He was stopped by Tessa's voice, soft. "Let her in, Magnus," she said.

Magnus wheeled around to look at Tessa. "Seriously?"

"I want to speak with her."

Tessa's voice had taken on a strange tone. Also, the delivery person had just appeared in the hall carrying their bag of food. Magnus nodded Jocelyn inside, handed over the ten dollars, and shut the door on the confused man's face before he had a chance to hand over the food.

Now Jocelyn stood awkwardly by the door. The tiny person in her arms kicked its feet and stretched its legs.

"You have a baby," Magnus said, pointing out what was now obvious.

Jocelyn shifted uncomfortably and clutched the baby to her chest.

Tessa padded toward them silently and stood by Jocelyn. Even though she wore black leggings and an oversize gray T-shirt that read WILLIAM WANTS A DOLL, she still always carried an air of formality and authority about her. The shirt, as it happened, was a feminist statement that boys liked to play with dolls and girls with trucks, but Magnus suspected she had chosen it partly because of the name. Tessa's husband had been dead for long enough that his name brought back happy, faded memories instead of the raw agony she had felt for years after his passing. Other warlocks had loved and lost, but few were as hopelessly faithful as Tessa. Decades later she had not allowed anyone else to even come close to winning her heart.

"Jocelyn Fairchild," Tessa said. "Descended from Henry Branwell and Charlotte Fairchild."

Jocelyn blinked as if she had not been expecting a lecture on her own genealogy.

"That's right," she said cautiously.

"I knew them, you see," Tessa explained. "You have a great look of Henry."

"*Knew* them? Then you must be..."

Henry had been dead for the better part of a century, and Tessa looked no older than twenty-five.

"Are you a warlock too, then?" Jocelyn asked suspiciously. Magnus saw her eyes drift from the top of Tessa's head to her feet, searching for a demon's mark, the sign that would indicate to Shadowhunters that she was unclean, inhuman, and to be despised. Some warlocks could hide their marks under their clothes, but Jocelyn could look at as much of Tessa as she wished and never find a mark.

Tessa did not draw herself up obtrusively, but it was clear suddenly that Tessa was taller than Jocelyn was, and her gray eyes could be very cold.

"I am," said Tessa. "I am Theresa Gray, daughter of a Greater Demon and Elizabeth Gray, who was born Adele Starkweather, one of your kind. I was the wife of William Herondale, who was the head of the London Institute, and I was the mother of James and Lucie Herondale. Will and I raised our Shadowhunter children to protect mundanes, to live by the Laws of Clave and Covenant, and to keep to the Accords."

She spoke in the way she well knew how, in the manner of the Nephilim.

"Once, I lived among the Shadowhunters," Tessa said softly. "Once I might almost have seemed like a person to you."

Jocelyn looked lost, in the way that people did when they learned something so strange that the whole world seemed unfamiliar.

"I understand if you find my crimes against Downworlders unforgivable," Jocelyn said, "but I—I have nowhere else to go. And I need help. My daughter needs your help. She is a Shadowhunter and Valentine's daughter. She cannot live among her own kind. We can never go back. I need a spell to shield her eyes from all but the mundane world. She can grow up safe and happy in the mundane world. She never needs to know what her father was." Jocelyn almost choked, but she lifted her chin and added, "Or what her mother did."

"So you come begging to us," Magnus said. "The monsters."

"I have no quarrel with Downworlders," Jocelyn said at last. "I ... my best friend is a Downworlder, and I do not believe he is so changed from the person I always loved. I was wrong. I'll have to live forever with what I did. But please, my daughter did nothing."

Her best friend, the Downworlder. Magnus supposed that Lucian Graymark was still alive, then, though nobody had seen him since the Uprising. Magnus thought a little better of Jocelyn for claiming him as her best friend. People did say she and Lucian had planned to defeat Valentine together, though Jocelyn had not been there to confirm the rumor after the battle. Magnus had not seen Jocelyn during the Uprising. He had not known whether to believe the claim or not.

Magnus had often considered that Shadowhunter justice was more like cruelty, and he did not want to be cruel. He looked at the woman's weary desperate face and the bundle in her arms, and he could not be cruel. He believed in redemption, the inchoate grace in every person he met. It was one of the few things he had to believe in, the possibility of beauty when faced with the reality of so much ugliness.

"You said you were married to a Herondale." Jocelyn appealed to Tessa, voice as faint as if she could already see the weakness of this argument but she had none other to make. "Stephen Herondale was my friend—"

"Stephen Herondale would have killed me if he'd ever met me," said Tessa. "I would not have been safe living among people like you, or like him. I am the wife and mother of warriors who fought and died and never dishonored themselves as you have. I have worn gear, wielded blades, and slain demons, and all I wished was to overcome evil so that I could live and be happy with those I loved. I'd hoped I had made this a better, safer world for my children. Because of Valentine's Circle, the Herondale line, the line that was my son's children's children, is finished. That happened through you and your Circle and your husband. Stephen Herondale died with hate in his heart and the blood of my people on his hands. I can imagine no more horrible way for mine and Will's line to end. I will have to carry for the rest of my life the wound of what Valentine's Circle has done to me, and I will live forever."

Tessa paused, and looked at Jocelyn's white despairing face, and then said, more gently, "But Stephen Herondale made his own choices, and you have made other choices besides the one to hate. I know that Valentine could not have been defeated without your help. And your child has done no wrong to anybody."

"That does not mean she has a right to our help," Magnus interrupted. He didn't want to reject Jocelyn, but there was still a nagging voice inside him that told him she was an enemy. "Besides which, I am not a Shadowhunter charity, and I doubt she has the money to pay for my help. Fugitives are so seldom well funded."

"I'll find the money," said Jocelyn. "I am not a charity case, and I am not a Shadowhunter any longer. I want nothing more to do with the Shadowhunters. I want to be someone else. I want to raise my daughter to be someone else, not bound to the Clave or led astray by anybody. I want her to be braver than I was, stronger than I was, and to let nobody decide her fate but herself."

"Nobody could ask for more than that for their child," Tessa said, and edged closer. "May I hold her?"

Jocelyn hesitated for a moment, holding the tightly wrapped bundle of the child close. Then slowly, reluctantly, her movements almost jerky, she leaned forward and placed her baby with enormous care into the arms of a woman she had just met.

"She's beautiful," Tessa murmured. Magnus did not know if Tessa had held a baby in decades, but she moved the child to her hip, held fast in the circle of her arm, with the instinctive loving and casual air of a parent. Magnus had seen her once, holding one of her grandchildren in just this way. "What's her name?"

"Clarissa," said Jocelyn, looking at Tessa intently, and then, as if she were telling them a secret, she said, "I call her Clary."

Magnus looked over Tessa's shoulder and into the child's face. The girl was older than Magnus had thought, small for her age, but her face had lost the roundness of babyhood: she must be almost two, and already looked like her mother. She looked like a Fairchild. She had red curls, the same color Henry's had been, clustering on her small head, and green eyes, glass-clear and jewel-bright and blinking around curiously at her surroundings. She did not seem to object to being handed to a stranger. Tessa tucked the baby's blanket more securely around her, and Clary's small fat fist closed determinedly around Tessa's finger. The child waved Tessa's finger back and forth, as if to display her new possession.

Tessa smiled down at the baby, a slow bright smile, and whispered, "Hello, Clary."

It was clear that Tessa at least had made up her mind. Magnus leaned in, his shoulder resting lightly against Tessa's, and peered into the child's face. He waved to catch her attention, moving his fingers so all his rings sparkled in the light. Clary laughed, all pearly teeth and the purest joy, and Magnus felt the knot of resentment in his chest ease.

Clary wriggled in a clear and imperious signal that she wanted to be let down, but Tessa handed her to Jocelyn so that Clary's mother could decide whether she should be put down or not. Jocelyn might not want her child roaming a warlock's home.

Jocelyn did look around apprehensively, but either she decided it was safe or small, intently squirming Clary was stubborn and her mother knew she would have to let her go free. She put Clary down, and Clary went toddling determinedly off on her quest. They stood and watched her bright little head bob as she grabbed up, in turn, Tessa's book, one of Magnus's candles (which Clary chewed on thoughtfully for a moment), and a silver tray Magnus had left under the sofa.

"Curious little thing, isn't she?" Magnus asked. Jocelyn glanced toward Magnus. Her eyes had been anxiously fastened on her child. Magnus found himself smiling at her. "Not a bad quality," he assured her. "She could grow up to be an adventurer."

"I want her to grow up to be safe and happy," said Jocelyn. "I don't want her to have adventures. Adventures happen when life is cruel. I want her to have a mundane life, quiet and sweet, and I hoped she would be born not able to see the Shadow World. It is no world for a child. But I've never had much luck with hope. I saw her trying to play with a faerie in a hedge this afternoon. I need you to help me. I need you to help her. Can you blind her to all that?"

"Can I tear away an essential part of your child's nature, and twist her into a shape that would suit you better?" Magnus asked her. "If you want her mad by the end of it."

He regretted the words as soon as he had spoken. Jocelyn stared at him, white-faced, as if she had just been hit. But Jocelyn Morgenstern was not the kind of woman who wept, not the kind of woman who broke, or Valentine would have broken her long since. She held herself tall and asked, her voice level, "Is there anything else you can do?"

"There is ... something else I could try," said Magnus.

He did not say that he would. He kept his eyes on the little girl, and thought of the young werewolf girl Valentine had blinded, of Edmund Herondale stripped of his Marks centuries ago, and of Tessa's Jamie and Lucie and all they had borne. He would not give up a child to the Shadowhunters, for whom the Law came before mercy.

Clary espied Magnus's poor cat. The Great Catsby, who was getting on in years, lay prone upon a velvet cushion, his fluffy gray tail spilling over it.

The adults all saw that disaster was imminent. They took a step forward, as one, but Clary had already firmly pulled the Great Catsby's tail, with the regal assured air of a countess reaching for the bellpull to summon her maid.

The Great Catsby gave a piteous meow to protest the indignity, turned, and scratched Clary, and Clary began to scream. Jocelyn was on her knees beside Clary the next instant, her red hair like a veil over her child, as if she could somehow screen Clary from all the world.

"Is she part banshee?" Magnus asked over the piercing wail. Clary sounded like a police siren. Magnus felt as if he were going to be arrested for the twenty-seventh time. Jocelyn glared at him through her hair, and Magnus lifted his hands in mock surrender. "Oh, pardon me for implying that the bloodlines of Valentine's child are anything less than pure."

"Come on, Magnus," Tessa said quietly. She had loved so many more Shadowhunters than Magnus ever had. She went and stood beside Jocelyn. She put a hand against Jocelyn's shoulder, and Jocelyn did not shake her hand off.

"If you want the child safe," said Magnus, "she doesn't need only a spell to hide her own Sight. She needs to be protected from the supernatural as well, from any demons who might come crawling to her."

"And what Iron Sister and Silent Brother will do that ceremony for me without turning Clary and me over to the Clave?" Jocelyn demanded. "No. I can't risk it. If she knows nothing of the Shadow World, she will be safe."

"My mother was a Shadowhunter who knew nothing of the Shadow World," said Tessa. "That didn't keep her safe."

Jocelyn stared at Tessa in open horror, obviously able to infer the story of what had happened: that a demon had gained access to an unprotected Shadowhunter woman, and Tessa had been the result.

There was a silence. Clary had turned curiously to Tessa as Tessa had approached, her screams forgotten. Now she lifted her chubby little arms out to Tessa. Jocelyn let Tessa take Clary again, and this time Clary did not try to wriggle away from her. Clary wiped her small tearstained face against Tessa's T-shirt. It seemed to be a gesture of affection. Magnus hoped nobody would offer Clary to him in her current sticky condition.

Jocelyn blinked and began, slowly, to smile. Magnus noticed for the first time that she was beautiful. "Clary never goes to strangers. Maybe—maybe she can tell that you're not a stranger to the Fairchilds."

Tessa gazed at Jocelyn, her gray eyes clear. Magnus thought, in this case, Tessa was seeing more than he did. "Maybe. I will help you with the ceremony," she promised. "I know a Silent Brother who will keep any secret, if I ask him to."

Jocelyn bowed her head. "Thank you, Theresa Gray."

It occurred to Magnus how outraged Valentine would have been, to see his wife beseeching Downworlders, to think of his child in a warlock's arms. Magnus's thought of responding to Jocelyn's appeal with cruelty receded even further. This seemed the kind of revenge worth getting—to prove, even after Valentine's death, how wrong Valentine had been.

He walked over to the two women and the child, and he glanced at Tessa, and he saw her nod.

"Well, then," Magnus said, "it seems we are going to help you, Jocelyn Morgenstern."

Jocelyn flinched. "Don't call me that. I'm—I'm Jocelyn Fairchild."

"I thought you weren't a Shadowhunter anymore," Magnus said. "If you don't want them to find you, changing your last name seems a fairly elementary first step. Trust me, I'm an expert. I've watched a lot of spy movies."

Jocelyn looked skeptical, and Magnus rolled his eyes.

"I was also not born with the name 'Magnus Bane,'" he said. "I came up with that one all on my own."

"I actually was born Tessa Gray," Tessa said. "But you should choose whatever name seems right to you. I've always said there is a great deal of power in words, and that means names, too. A name you choose for yourself could tell you the story of what your destiny will be, and who you intend to become."

"Call me Fray. Let me join together the names of the Fairchilds, my lost family, and the Grays. Because you are ... a family friend," said Jocelyn, speaking with sudden firmness.

Tessa smiled at Jocelyn, looking surprised but pleased, and Jocelyn smiled down at her daughter. Magnus saw the determination in her face. Valentine had wanted to crush the world as Magnus knew it. But this woman had helped crush him instead, and now she was looking at her daughter as if she would make another world, shining and brand new, just for Clary, so Clary would never be touched by any of the darkness of the past. Magnus knew what it was to want to forget as badly as Jocelyn did, knew the passionate urge to protect that came with love.

Perhaps none of the children of the new generation—not this small stubborn redheaded scrap, or half-faerie Helen and Mark Blackthorn at the Los Angeles Institute, or even Maryse Lightwood's children growing up in New York far from the Glass City—would ever have to learn the full truth about the ugliness of the past.

Jocelyn stroked her little girl's face, and they all watched as the baby smiled, lit up with the sheer joy of living. She was a story in herself, sweet and full of hope, just beginning.

"Jocelyn and Clary Fray," said Magnus. "It's nice to meet you."

The Course of True Love (And First Dates)

By Cassandra Clare

Alec's eyes were a little wide. Magnus suspected that he had been acting on reflex and had not actually intended to use force meant for demon foes against a mundane.

The redheaded guy squawked, revealing braces, and flapped his hands in what seemed to be either urgent surrender or a very good panicked duck impression.

—The Course of True Love (And First Dates)

DUDE! I'M SORRY! SERIOUSLY! I DIDN'T KNOW YOU WERE A NINJA!
I'M NOT A NINJA.

M

It was [illegible] ooligan, and the city [illegible]
ing [illegible] clouds pressing [illegible]
the [illegible] between the page [illegible] that the
walls [illegible] apartment alone [illegible]
[illegible] it the [illegible]
[illegible]

[illegible]

[illegible] day [illegible]
[illegible]

[illegible]

[illegible] tongue [illegible]
[illegible] ve thought of do[illegible]
[illegible] right [illegible] whatever [illegible]
[illegible] conveniences of [illegible]. Most [illegible]
[illegible] have thought of them [illegible]
[illegible]

It was Friday night in Brooklyn, and the city lights were reflect-ing off the sky: orange-tinted clouds pressing summer heat against the sidewalks like a flower between the pages of a book. Magnus walked the floor of his loft apartment alone and wondered, with what amounted to only mild interest, if he was about to be stood up.

Being asked out by a Shadowhunter had been among the top ten strangest and most unexpected things that had ever happened to Magnus, and Magnus had always endeavored to live a very unexpected life.

He had surprised himself by agreeing.

This past Tuesday had been a dull day at home with the cat and an inventory list that included horned toads. Then Alec Lightwood, eldest son of the Shadowhunters who ran the New York Institute, had turned up on Magnus's doorstep, thanked him for saving his life, and asked him out while turning fifteen shades between puce and mauve. In response Magnus had promptly lost his mind, kissed him, and made a date for Friday.

The whole thing had been extremely odd. For one thing, Alec had come and said thank you to Magnus for saving his life. Very few Shadowhunters would have thought of doing such a thing. They thought of magic as their right, due whenever they needed it, and regarded warlocks as either conveniences or nuisances. Most of the Nephilim would as soon have thought of thanking an elevator for arriving at the right floor.

Then there was the fact that no Shadowhunter had ever asked Magnus out on a date before. They had wanted favors of several kinds, magical and sexual and strange. None of them had wanted to spend time with him, go out to a movie, and share popcorn. He wasn't even sure Shadowhunters *watched* movies.

It was such a simple thing, such a straightforward request—as if no Shadowhunter had ever broken a plate because Magnus had touched it, or spat "warlock" as if it were a curse. As if all old wounds could be healed, made as though they had never been, and the world could become the way it looked through Alec Lightwood's clear blue eyes.

At the time, Magnus had said yes because he wanted to say yes. It was quite possible, however, that he had said yes because he was an idiot.

After all, Magnus had to keep reminding himself, Alec wasn't even all that into Magnus. He was simply responding to the only male attention he'd ever had. Alec was closeted, shy, obviously insecure, and obviously hung up on his blond friend Trace Wayland. Magnus was fairly certain that was the name, but Wayland had reminded Magnus inexplicably of Will Herondale, and Magnus didn't want to think about Will. He knew the best way to spare himself heartbreak was not to think about lost friends and not to get mixed up with Shadowhunters again.

He had told himself that this date would be a bit of excitement, an isolated incident in a life that had become a little too routine, and nothing more.

He tried not to think of the way he'd given Alec an out, and how Alec had looked at him and said with devastating simplicity, *I like you*. Magnus had always thought of himself as someone who could wrap words around people, trip them up or pull the wool over their eyes when he had to. It was amazing how Alec could just cut through it all. It was more amazing that he didn't even seem to be trying.

As soon as Alec had left, Magnus had called Catarina, sworn her to secrecy, and then told her all about it.

"Did you agree to go out with him because you think the Lightwoods are jerks and you want to show them you can corrupt their baby boy?" asked Catarina.

Magnus balanced his feet on Chairman Meow. "I do think the Lightwoods are jerks," he admitted. "And that does sound like something I'd do. *Damn* it."

"No, it doesn't really," said Catarina. "You're sarcastic twelve hours a day, but you're almost never spiteful. You have a good heart under all the glitter."

Catarina was the one with the good heart. Magnus knew exactly whose son he was, and where he came from.

"Even if it was spite, no one could blame you, not after the Circle, after all that happened."

Magnus looked out the window. There was a Polish restaurant across the street from his house, its flashing lights advertising twenty-four-hour borscht and coffee (hopefully not mixed together). He thought of the way Alec's hands had trembled when he'd asked Magnus if he wanted to go out, about how glad and astounded he had seemed when Magnus said yes.

"No," he said. "It's probably a bad idea—it's probably my worst idea this decade—but it had nothing to do with his parents at all. I said yes because of him."

Catarina was quiet for a few moments. If Ragnor was around he would have laughed, but Ragnor had disappeared to a spa in Switzerland for a series of complicated facials meant to bring out the green in his complexion. Catarina had the instinct of a healer: she knew when to be kind.

"Good luck on your date, then," she said at last.

"Much appreciated, but I don't need good luck; I need assistance," said Magnus. "Just because I'm going on this date does not mean it will go well. I'm very charming, but it does take two to tango."

"Magnus, remember what happened the last time you tried to tango. Your shoe flew off and nearly killed someone."

"It was a metaphor. He's a Shadowhunter, he's a Lightwood, and he's into blonds. He's a dating hazard. I need an escape strategy. If the date is a complete disaster, I'll text you. I'll say 'Blue Squirrel, this is Hot Fox. Mission to be aborted with extreme prejudice.' Then you call me and you tell me that there is a terrible emergency that requires my expert warlock assistance."

"This seems unnecessarily complicated. It's your phone, Magnus; there's no need for code names."

"Fine. I'll just text 'Abort.'" Magnus reached out and drew his fingers from Chairman Meow's head to his tail; Chairman Meow stretched and purred his enthusiastic approval of Magnus's taste in men. "Will you help me?"

Catarina dragged in a long, annoyed breath. "I will help you," she promised. "But you've called in all your dating favors for this century, and you owe me."

"It's a bargain," said Magnus.

"And if it all works out," said Catarina, cackling, "I want to be best woman at your wedding."

"I'm hanging up now," Magnus informed her.

He had made a bargain with Catarina. He had done more than that: he had called and made reservations at a restaurant. He had selected a date outfit of red Ferragamo pants, matching shoes, and a black silk waistcoat that Magnus wore without a shirt because it did amazing things for his arms and shoulders. And it had all been for nothing.

Alec was half an hour late. The probability was that Alec's nerve had broken—that he had weighed his life, complete with his precious Shadowhunter duty, against a date with a guy he didn't even like that much—and he was not coming at all.

Magnus shrugged philosophically, and with a casualness he did not quite feel, padded over to his drinks cabinet and made himself an exciting concoction with unicorn tears, energizing potion, cranberry juice, and a twist of lime. He'd look back on this and laugh one day. Probably tomorrow. Well, maybe the day after. Tomorrow he'd be hungover.

He might have jumped when the buzzer sounded through the loft, but there was nobody but Chairman Meow there to see. Magnus was perfectly composed by the time Alec ran up the stairs and hurtled through the door.

Alec could not have been described as perfectly composed. His black hair was going in every direction, like an octopus that had been dropped in soot; his chest was rising and falling hard under his pale-blue T-shirt; and there was a light sheen of perspiration on his face. It took a lot to make Shadowhunters sweat. Magnus wondered exactly how fast he had been running.

"Well, this is unexpected," said Magnus, raising his eyebrows. Still holding his cat, he had flung himself lightly on the sofa, his legs hooked over one of the carved wooden arms. Chairman Meow was draped over his stomach and meowing in perplexity about the sudden change in his situation.

Magnus might have been trying a bit too hard to appear louche and unconcerned, but judging by Alec's crestfallen expression, he was really pulling it off.

"I'm sorry I'm late," Alec panted. "Jace wanted to do some weapons training, and I didn't know how to get away—I mean, I couldn't tell him—"

"Oh, Jace, that's it," said Magnus.

"What?" said Alec.

"I briefly forgot the blond one's name," Magnus explained, with a dismissive flick of his fingers.

Alec looked staggered. "Oh. I'm—I'm Alec."

Magnus's hand paused mid-dismissive-flick. The gleam of city lights through the window reflected off the blue jewels on his fingers, casting bright blue sparks that caught fire and then tumbled and drowned in the deep blue of Alec's eyes.

Alec had made an effort, Magnus thought, though it took a trained eye to spot it. The light-blue shirt fit him considerably better than the unholy gray sweatshirt that Alec had been wearing on Tuesday. He smelled vaguely of cologne. Magnus felt unexpectedly touched.

"Yes," said Magnus slowly, and then he smiled slowly as well. "Your name I remember."

Alec smiled. Maybe it didn't matter if Alec did have a little thing for Apparently-Jace. Apparently-Jace *was* beautiful, but he was the sort of person that knew it, and they were often more trouble than they were worth. If Jace was gold, catching the light and the attention, Alec was silver: so used to everyone else looking at Jace that that was where he looked too, so used to living in Jace's shadow that he didn't expect to be seen. Maybe it was enough to be the first person to tell Alec that he was worth being seen ahead of anyone in a room, and of being looked at longest.

And silver, though few people knew it, was a rarer metal than gold.

"Don't worry about it," said Magnus, swinging himself easily off the couch and pushing Chairman Meow gently onto the sofa cushions, to the Chairman's plaintively voiced dismay. "Have a drink."

He pushed his own drink hospitably into Alec's hand; he hadn't even taken a sip, and he could make himself a new one. Alec looked startled. He was obviously far more nervous than Magnus had thought, because he fumbled and then dropped the glass, spilling crimson liquid all over himself and the floor. There was a crash as the glass hit the wood and splintered.

Alec looked like he had been shot and was extremely embarrassed about it.

"Wow," said Magnus. "Your people are really overselling your elite Nephilim reflexes."

"Oh, by the Angel. I am so—I am so sorry."

Magnus shook his head and gestured, leaving a trail of blue sparks in the air, and the puddle of crimson liquid and broken glass vanished.

"Don't be sorry," he said. "I'm a warlock. There's no mess I can't clean up. Why do you think I throw so many parties? Let me tell you, I wouldn't do it if I had to scrub toilets myself. Have you ever seen a vampire throw up? Nasty."

"I don't really, uh, know any vampires socially."

Alec's eyes were wide and horrified, as if he was picturing debauched vampires throwing up the blood of the innocent. Magnus was prepared to bet he didn't know any Downworlders socially. The Children of the Angel kept to their own kind.

Magnus wondered what exactly Alec was doing here in Magnus's apartment. He bet Alec was wondering the same thing.

It might be a long night, but at least they could both be well-dressed. The T-shirt might show Alec was trying, but Magnus could do a lot better.

"I'll get you a new shirt," Magnus volunteered, and made his way to his bedroom while Alec was still faintly protesting.

Magnus's closet took up half his bedroom. He kept meaning to enlarge it. There were a lot of clothes in it that Magnus thought would look excellent on Alec, but as he riffled through them, he realized that Alec might not appreciate Magnus imposing his unique fashion sense on him.

He decided to go for a more sober selection and chose the black T-shirt that he had been wearing Tuesday. That was perhaps a little sentimental of Magnus.

The shirt admittedly had BLINK IF YOU WANT ME written on it in sequins, but that was about as sober as Magnus got. He tugged the shirt off its hanger and waltzed back into the main room to find that Alec had already taken his own shirt off and was standing around somewhat helplessly, his stained shirt clenched in his fist.

Magnus stopped dead.

The room was illuminated only by a reading lamp; all the other light came from outside the windows. Alec was painted with streetlights and moonlight, shadows curling around his biceps and the slender indentations of his collarbones, his torso all smooth, sleek, bare skin until the dark line of his jeans. There were runes on the flat planes of his stomach and the silvery scars of old Marks snaked around his ribs, with one on the ridge of his hip. His head was bowed, his hair black as ink, his luminously pale skin white as paper. He looked like a piece of art, chiaroscuro, beautifully and wonderfully made.

Magnus had heard the story of how the Nephilim were created many times. They had all left out the bit that said: *And the Angel descended from on high and gave his chosen ones fantastic abs.*

Alec looked up at Magnus, and his lips parted as if he was going to speak. He watched Magnus with wide eyes, wondering at being watched.

Magnus exercised heroic self-control, smiled, and offered the shirt.

"I'm—sorry about being a lousy date," Alec muttered.

"What are you talking about?" Magnus asked. "You're a fantastic date. You've only been here ten minutes, and I already got half of your clothes off."

Alec looked equal parts embarrassed and pleased. He'd told Magnus he was new to all this, so anything more than mild flirting might scare him off. Magnus had a very calm and normal date planned: no surprises, nothing unexpected.

"Come on," said Magnus, and grabbed a red leather duster. "We're going to dinner."

The first part of Magnus's plan, getting the subway, had seemed so simple. So foolproof.

It had not occurred to him that a Shadowhunter boy was not used to being visible and having to interact with the mundanes.

The subway was crowded on a Friday night, which was not surprising but did seem to be alarming to Alec. He was peering around at the mundanes as if he had found himself in a jungle surrounded by menacing monkeys, and he was still looking traumatized by Magnus's shirt.

"Can't I use a glamour rune?" he asked, as they boarded the F train.

"No. I'm not looking like I'm alone on a Friday night just because you don't want mundanes staring at you."

They were able to grab two seats, but it didn't appreciably improve the situation. They sat awkwardly side by side, other people's chatter rushing all around them. Alec was utterly silent. Magnus was fairly sure he wanted nothing more than to go home.

There were purple and blue posters staring down at them, showing elderly couples looking sadly at one another. The posters bore the words WITH THE PASSING YEARS COMES ... IMPOTENCE! Magnus found himself staring at the posters with a sort of absent horror. He looked at Alec and found that Alec could not tear his eyes away either. He wondered if Alec was aware that Magnus was three hundred years old and whether Alec was considering exactly how impotent one might become after that much time.

Two guys came onto the train at the next stop and cleared a space right in front of Magnus and Alec.

One of them began to dance by swinging himself dramatically around the pole. The other sat cross-legged and started beating time on a drum he'd carried in with him.

"Hello, ladies and gentlemen and whatever else you got!" the dude with the drum called out. "We're gonna perform now for your entertainment. I hope you'll enjoy it. We call it ... the Butt Song."

Together they began to rap. It was quite obviously a song they had written themselves.

"Roses are red, and they say love's not made to last,
But I know I'll never get enough of that sweet, sweet ass.
All that jelly in your jeans, all that junk in your trunk,
I just gotta have it—one look and I was sunk.
If you ever wonder why I had to make you mine,
It's 'cause no other lady has a tush so fine.
They say you're not a looker, but I don't mind.
What I'm looking at is the view from behind.
Never been romantic, don't know what love means,
But I know I dig the way you're wearing those jeans.
Hate to see you leave but love to watch you go.
Turn back, then leave again—baby do it slow.
I'm coming right after, gonna make a pass,
Can't get enough of that sweet, sweet ass."

Most of the commuters seemed stunned. Magnus was not sure if Alec was just stunned or if he was also deeply scandalized and privately commending his soul to God. He was wearing an extremely peculiar expression on his face and his lips were very tightly shut.

Under normal circumstances Magnus would have laughed and laughed and given the buskers a lot of money. As it was, he was profoundly grateful when they reached their stop. He did fish out a few dollars for the singers as he and Alec left the train.

Magnus was reminded again of the extreme disadvantages to mundane visibility when a skinny freckled guy slipped by them. Magnus was just thinking that he might have felt a hand snaking into his pocket when the guy gave a combination howl and screech.

While Magnus had idly wondered if he was being pickpocketed, Alec had reacted like a trained Shadowhunter: he grabbed the guy's arm and threw him up in the air. The thief flew, outstretched arms limply wagging, like a cotton-stuffed doll. He landed with a crack on the platform, with Alec's boot on his throat. Another train rattled by, all lights and noise; the Friday night commuters ignored it, forming a knot of bodies in tight shiny clothes and artful hair around Magnus and Alec.

Alec's eyes were a little wide. Magnus suspected that he had been acting on reflex and had not actually intended to use force meant for demon foes against a mundane.

The redheaded guy squawked, revealing braces, and flapped his hands in what seemed to be either urgent surrender or a very good panicked duck impression.

"Dude!" he said. "I'm sorry! Seriously! I didn't know you were a ninja!"

Alec removed his boot, and cast a hunted glance around at the fascinated stares of the bystanders.

"I'm not a ninja," he muttered.

A pretty girl with butterfly clips in her dreadlocks put her hand on his arm. "You were amazing," she told him, her voice fluting. "You have the reflexes of a striking snake. You should be a stuntman. Really, with your cheekbones, you should be an actor. A lot of people are looking for someone as pretty as you who'd do his own stunts."

Alec threw Magnus a terrified and beseeching look. Magnus took pity on him, putting a hand on the small of Alec's back and leaning against him. His attitude and the glance he shot at the girl clearly communicated *my date*.

"No offense," said the girl, rapidly removing her hand so she could dig in her bag. "Let me give you my card. I work in a talent agency. You could be a star."

"He's foreign," Magnus told the girl. "He doesn't have a social security number. You can't hire him."

The girl regarded Alec's bowed head wistfully. "That's a shame. He could be *huge*. Those eyes!"

"I realize he's a knockout," Magnus said. "But I am afraid I have to whisk him away. He is wanted by Interpol."

Alec shot him a strange look. "Interpol?"

Magnus shrugged.

"Knockout?" Alec said.

Magnus raised an eyebrow at him. "You had to know I thought so. Why else would I agree to go on a date with you?"

Apparently Alec had not known for sure, even though he'd said Isabelle and Jace had both commented on it. Maybe the vampires had all gone home and gossiped about the fact Magnus thought one of the Shadowhunters was a dreamboat. Magnus possibly needed to learn subtlety, and Alec possibly was not allowed access to mirrors at the Institute. He looked startled and pleased.

"I thought maybe—you know you said you weren't unsympathetic—"

"I don't do charity," said Magnus. "In any area of my life."

"I'll give the wallet back," piped up a helpful voice.

The red-haired mugger interrupted what might have become a nice moment by scrambling to his feet, digging out Magnus's wallet, and then dropping Magnus's wallet on the ground with a pained yelp.

"That wallet bit me!"

That'll show you not to steal warlocks' wallets, Magnus thought, bending down to retrieve the wallet from a forest of sparkling high heels on the concrete.

Aloud he said, "This just isn't your lucky night, is it?"

"Your wallet bites people?" Alec asked.

"This one bites people," said Magnus, pocketing it. He was glad to have it back, not only because he liked money but because the wallet matched his red crocodile-skin pants. "The John Varvatos wallet bursts into flames."

"Who?" said Alec.

Magnus gazed at Alec sadly.

"Totally cool designer," chipped in the girl with butterfly clips. "You know, they give you designer stuff free when you're a movie star."

"I can always flog a Varvatos wallet," agreed the red-haired mugger. "Not that I'd steal and sell anything belonging to anyone on this platform. Specially not you guys." He shot Alec a look that bordered on hero worship. "I didn't know gay dudes could fight like that. Like, no offense. It was badass."

"You have been taught two important lessons about tolerance and honesty," Magnus informed him severely. "And you still have all your fingers after trying to mug me on a first date, so this was the best outcome you could expect."

There was a murmur of sympathy. Magnus stared around and saw Alec looking a little wild-eyed and everyone else looking concerned. Apparently the crowd they had gathered truly believed in their love.

"Aw, man, I'm really sorry," said the mugger. "I wouldn't want to mess up anybody's first date with a ninja."

"WE ARE LEAVING NOW," said Magnus, in his best High Warlock voice. He was worried that Alexander was planning to fling himself into the path of an oncoming train.

"Have fun on your date, boys," said Butterfly Clips, stuffing her card into the pocket of Alec's jeans. Alec jumped like a startled hare. "Call me if you change your mind about wanting fame and fortune!"

"Sorry again!" said their former mugger, waving a cheerful good-bye.

They left the platform amid a chorus of well-wishers. Alec looked as if he wished only for the sweet release of death.

The restaurant was on East 13th and 3rd, near an American Apparel store and among a row of tired-looking redbrick buildings. It was an Ethiopian and Italian fusion restaurant run by Downworlders. It was on the shady, shabby side, so Shadowhunters did not frequent it. Magnus had strongly suspected that Alec would not want to risk any Nephilim seeing them together.

He'd also brought many mundane dates there, as a way of easing them into his world. The restaurant wanted mundane custom but in the main the clientele were Downworlders, so glamours were used but fairly minimal.

There was a large graffitied dinosaur obscuring the sign. Alec squinted at it, but he followed Magnus inside the restaurant readily enough.

The moment Magnus stepped into the restaurant, he realized he'd made a terrible mistake.

The second the door closed behind them a terrible silence fell around the big, low-lit room. There was a crash as one diner, an ifrit with flaming eyebrows, dove behind a table.

Magnus looked at Alec and realized what they saw: even if he wasn't wearing gear, his arms bore runes, and his clothes showed signs that he was wearing weapons. *Nephilim*. Magnus might as well have walked into a Prohibition-era speakeasy flanked by police officers holding tommy guns.

God, dating sucked.

"Magnus Bane!" hissed Luigi, the owner, as he scurried over. "You brought a Shadowhunter here! Is this a raid? Magnus, I thought we were friends! You could at least have given me a heads-up!"

"We're here socially," said Magnus. He held his hands up, palms out. "I swear. Just to talk and eat."

Luigi shook his head. "For you, Magnus. But if he makes any moves toward my other customers..." He gestured at Alec.

"I won't," Alec said, and cleared his throat. "I'm ... off-duty."

"Shadowhunters are never off-duty," said Luigi darkly, and dragged them to a table in the remotest part of the restaurant, the corner near the swinging doors that led to the kitchen.

A werewolf waiter with a wooden expression that indicated either boredom or constipation wandered over.

"Hello, my name is Erik and I will be your server this eve— Oh my God, you're a Shadowhunter!"

Magnus closed his eyes for a pained moment. "We can leave," he told Alec. "This may have been a mistake."

But a stubborn light had come into Alec's blue eyes. Despite his porcelain looks, Magnus could see the steel underneath. "No, that's fine, this seems ... fine."

"You're making me feel very threatened," said Erik the waiter.

"He's not doing anything," Magnus snapped.

"It's not about what he's doing, it's about how he's making me *feel*," sniffed Erik. He slammed down the menus as if they had personally offended him. "I get stress ulcers."

"The myth that ulcers are caused by stress was debunked years ago," said Magnus. "It's actually some kind of bacteria."

"Um, what are the specials?" Alec asked.

"I can't remember them while my emotions are under this kind of strain," said Erik. "A Shadowhunter killed my uncle."

"I've never killed anyone's uncle," said Alec.

"How would you know?" demanded Erik. "When you're about to kill someone, do you stop and ask them if they have nephews?"

"I kill *demons*," Alec said. "Demons don't have *nephews*."

Magnus knew this to be only technically true. He cleared his throat loudly. "Maybe I should just order for both of us, and we can share?"

"Sure," said Alec, throwing his menu down.

"Do you want a drink?" the waiter asked Alec pointedly, adding *sotto voce*, "Or do you want to stab someone? If you absolutely have to, maybe you could stab the guy in the corner wearing the red shirt. He tips terribly."

Alec opened and shut his mouth, then opened it again. "Is this a trick question?"

"Please go," said Magnus.

Alec was very quiet, even after Erik the annoying waiter was gone. Magnus was fairly sure he was having a horrifying time, and could not blame him. Several of the other customers had left, casting panicked glances over their shoulders as they paid hurriedly.

When the food arrived, Alec's eyes widened when he saw Magnus had ordered their *kitfo* raw. Luigi had put in an effort: there were also luscious *tibs*, *doro wat*, a spicy red onion stew dish, mashed lentils and collards, and all of it laid out atop the thick spongy Ethiopian bread known as *injera*. The Italian part of Luigi's heritage was represented by a heap of *penne*. Alec did make short work of the food, and seemed to know he was supposed to eat with his fingers without being told. He was a New Yorker, Magnus thought, even if he was a Shadowhunter too.

"This is the best Ethiopian I've ever had. Do you know a lot about food?" Alec asked. "I mean, obviously you do. Never mind. That was a dumb thing to say."

"No, it wasn't," Magnus said, frowning.

Alec reached for a bite of *penne arrabiata*. He immediately began to choke on it. Tears streamed from his eyes.

"Alexander!" said Magnus.

"I'm fine!" Alec gasped, looking horrified. He snatched at his piece of bread first and only realized that it was bread when he tried to dab his eyes with it. He dropped the bread hastily and grabbed his napkin up instead, hiding both streaming eyes and scarlet face.

"You are obviously not fine!" Magnus told him, and tried a very tiny bite of the *penne*. It burned like fire: Alec was still wheezing into his napkin. Magnus made a peremptory gesture for the waiter that might have included a few blue sparks snapping and crackling onto other people's tablecloths.

The people eating near them were edging their tables subtly away.

"This *penne* is much too *arrabiata*, and you did it on purpose," said Magnus when the surly werewolf waiter hove into view.

"Werewolf rights," Erik grumped. "Crush the vile oppressors."

"Nobody has ever won a revolution with pasta, Erik," said Magnus. "Now go get a fresh dish, or I'll tell Luigi on you."

"I—" Erik began defiantly. Magnus narrowed his cat's eyes. Erik met Magnus's gaze and decided not to be a waiter hero. "Of course. My apologies."

"What a pill," Magnus remarked loudly.

"Yeah," said Alec, tearing off a new strip of *injera*. "What have the Shadowhunters ever done to him?"

Magnus lifted an eyebrow. "Well, he did mention a dead uncle."

"Oh," said Alec. "Right."

He went back to gazing fixedly at the tablecloth.

"He's still a total pill, though," Magnus offered. Alec mumbled something that Magnus could not make out.

It was then that the door opened and a handsome human man with deep-set green eyes came in. His hands were in the pockets of his expensive suit, and he was surrounded by a group of gorgeous young faeries, male and female.

Magnus slunk down in his chair. Richard. Richard was a mortal who the faeries had adopted in the way they did sometimes, especially when the mortals were musical. He was also something else.

Magnus cleared his throat. "Quick warning. The guy who just walked in is an ex," he said. "Well. Barely an ex. It was very casual. And we parted very amicably."

At that moment, Richard caught sight of him. Richard's whole face spasmed; then he crossed the floor in two steps.

"You are scum!" Richard hissed, and then picked up Magnus's glass of wine and dashed it in his face. "Get out while you can," he continued to Alec. "Never trust a warlock. They'll enchant the years from your life and the love from your heart!"

"Years?" Magnus spluttered. "It was barely twenty minutes!"

"Time means different things to those who are of faerie," said Richard, the pretentious idiot. "You wasted the best twenty minutes of my life!"

Magnus grabbed hold of his napkin and began to clean off his face. He blinked through the red blurriness at Richard's retreating back and Alec's startled face.

"All right," he said. "It's possible I was mistaken about the amicable parting." He tried to smile suavely, which was difficult with wine in his hair. "Ah well. You know exes."

Alec studied the tablecloth. There was art in museums given less attention than this tablecloth.

"Not really," he said. "You're my first ever date."

This wasn't working. Magnus didn't know why he had thought it might work. He had to get out of this date and not hurt Alec Lightwood's pride too much. He wished he could feel satisfaction that he had a plan in place for this, but as he texted Catarina under the table what he felt was a sense of enveloping gloom.

Magnus sat there silently, waited for Catarina to call, and tried to work out a way to say, "No hard feelings. I like you more than any Shadowhunter I've met in more than a century, and I hope you find a nice Shadowhunter boy ... if there are any nice Shadowhunter boys besides you."

His phone rang while Magnus was still mentally composing, the sound harsh in the silence between them. Magnus hastily answered. His hands were not entirely steady, and he was afraid for a moment that he would drop the phone as Alec had dropped his glass, but he managed to answer it. Catarina's voice filtered down the line, clear and unexpectedly urgent. Catarina was clearly a method actor.

"Magnus, there's an—"

"An emergency, Catarina?" Magnus asked. "That's terrible! What's happened?"

"An actual emergency happened, Magnus!"

Magnus appreciated Catarina's commitment to her role but wished that she would not shout so loudly right into his ear.

"That's so awful, Catarina. I mean, I'm really busy, but I suppose if there are lives at stake I can't say n—"

"There are lives at stake, you blithering idiot!" Catarina yelled.

"Bring the Shadowhunter!"

Magnus paused.

"Catarina, I don't think you fully understand the point of what you're meant to do here."

"Are you drunk already, Magnus?" Catarina asked. "Are you off debauching and getting one of the Nephilim—one of the Nephilim who is under twenty-one—*drunk?*"

"The only alcohol that has passed my lips is the wine that was thrown in my face," said Magnus. "And I was totally blameless in that matter as well."

There was a pause. "Richard?" said Catarina.

"Richard," Magnus confirmed.

"Look, never mind him. Listen carefully, Magnus, because I am working, and one of my hands is covered in fluid, and I'm only going to say this once."

"Fluid," said Magnus. "What kind of fluid?"

Alec goggled at him.

"Only going to say this once, Magnus," Catarina repeated firmly. "There is a young werewolf in the Beauty Bar downtown. She went out on the night of a full moon because she wanted to prove to herself that she could still have a normal life. A vampire called this in and the vampires are not going to be of any help because the vampires never are. The werewolf is changing, she is in an unfamiliar and crowded place, and she will probably lose control and kill somebody. I cannot leave the hospital. Lucian Graymark has his phone off, and the word from his pack is that he is in a hospital with a loved one. You are not in a hospital: you are out on a stupid date. If you went to the restaurant you told me that you were going to, then you are the closest person I know who can help. Will you help, or will you continue to waste my time?"

"I'll waste your time another time, darling," said Magnus.

Catarina said, and he could hear the wry smile in her voice, "I bet."

She hung up. Catarina was often too busy to say good-bye. Magnus realized he did not have all that much time himself, but he did waste a moment looking at Alec.

Catarina had said to bring the Shadowhunter, but Catarina did not have a great deal to do with the Nephilim. Magnus did not want to see Alec cut off some poor girl's head for breaking the Law: he did not want someone else to suffer if he made a mistake in judgment, and he didn't want to find himself hating Alec as he had hated so many of the Nephilim.

He also did not want mundanes to be killed.

"I'm so sorry about this," he said. "It's an emergency."

"Um," Alec said, hunching his shoulders, "it's okay. I understand."

"There's an out-of-control werewolf in a bar near here."

"Oh," said Alec.

Something inside Magnus cracked. "I have to go and try to get her under control. Will you come and help me?"

"Oh, this is a real emergency?" Alec exclaimed, and brightened immeasurably. For a moment Magnus felt pleased that a maddened werewolf was ravaging downtown Manhattan, if it made Alec look like that. "I figured it was one of those things where you arranged to have a friend call you so that you could get out of a sucky date."

"Ha ha," said Magnus. "I didn't know people did that."

"Uh-huh." Alec was already standing up, shrugging his jacket on. "Let's go, Magnus."

Magnus felt a burst of fondness in his chest; it felt like a small explosion, pleasant and startling at the same time. He liked how Alexander said the things that other people thought and never said. He liked how Alec called him Magnus, and not "warlock." He liked how Alec's shoulders moved under his jacket. (Sometimes he was shallow.)

And he was cheered that Alec wanted to come. He'd assumed that Alec might be delighted for the pretext to exit an uncomfortable date, but perhaps he'd read the situation wrong.

Magnus threw money down on the table; when Alec made a

demurring noise, he grinned. "Please," he said. "You have no idea how much I overcharge Nephilim for my services. This is only fair. Let's go."

As they went out the door they heard the waiter yell "Werewolf rights!" at their backs.

The Beauty Bar was usually crowded at this time on a Friday night, but the people spilling out of the door were not doing it with the casual air of those who had meandered outside to smoke or hook up. They were lingering under the shining white sign that had BEAUTY written in spiky red letters and what seemed like a picture of a golden Medusa's head underneath. The whole crowd had the air of people who were desperate to escape, yet who hovered, pinned in place by a horrified fascination.

A girl clutched Magnus's sleeve and gazed up at him, her false lashes dusted with silver glitter.

"Don't go in," she whispered. "There's a monster in there."

I am a monster, Magnus thought. *And monsters are* his *specialty*.

He didn't say it. Instead he said, "I don't believe you," and walked in. He meant it, too: the Shadowhunters, even Alec, might believe Magnus was a monster, but Magnus didn't believe it himself. He'd taught himself not to believe it even though his mother, the man he'd called his father, and a thousand others had told him it was true.

Magnus would not believe the girl in there was a monster either, no matter what she might look like to mundanes and Nephilim. She had a soul, and that meant she could be saved.

It was dark in the bar, and contrary to Magnus's expectations, there were still people inside. On a normal night the Beauty Bar was a kitschy little place full of happy people getting manicures from the staff, perched in the chairs that looked like old-fashioned hairdresser's chairs with massive hairdryers set up on the chair backs, or dancing on the black-and-white tiled floor that suggested a chessboard.

Tonight nobody was dancing, and the chairs were abandoned. Magnus squinted at a stain on the chessboard floor and saw that the black and white tiles were smeared with bright red blood.

He glanced toward Alec to see if Alec had noticed this too and found him shifting from foot to foot, obviously nervous.

"You all right?"

"I always do this with Isabelle and Jace," said Alec. "And they're not here. And I can't call them."

"Why not?" Magnus asked.

Alec blushed just as Magnus realized what he meant. Alec couldn't call his friends because he didn't want them to know he was on a date with Magnus. He especially did not want Jace to know. It was not a particularly pleasant thing to think about, but it was Alec's business.

It was also true that Magnus certainly didn't want any more Shadowhunters in the mix intent on dealing out their rough justice, but he saw Alec's problem. From what he'd seen of Jace and Alexander's showy sister, he was sure that Alec was used to protecting them, shielding them from their own rash actions, and that meant Alec was used to defending and not attacking.

"You'll do great without them," Magnus encouraged. "I can help you."

Alec looked skeptical about that, which was ridiculous since Magnus could do actual magic, something Shadowhunters liked to forget when they were deep in contemplation of how superior they were. To Alec's credit, though, he nodded and moved forward. Magnus noted, with slight puzzlement, that whenever Magnus tried to edge ahead, Alec put out an arm or moved slightly faster, staying in front of Magnus in a protective stance.

The people still in the bar were flattened against the walls as if pinned there, unmoving with terror. Someone was sobbing.

There was a low, rattling growl coming from the back lounge of the bar.

Alec crept toward the sound, Shadowhunter-soft and swift, and Magnus followed.

The lounge was decorated with black-and-white pictures of women from the 1950s and a disco ball that obviously provided no useful light. There was an empty stage made of boxes and a reading lamp that provided the only real illumination. There were couches in the center of the room, chairs at the back, and shadows all around.

There was a shadow moving and growling among all the other shadows. Alec prowled forward, hunting it, and the werewolf gave a growl of challenge.

And there was suddenly a slender girl with her hair in long dark coils, trailing ribbons and blood, dashing straight at them. Magnus leaped forward and caught her in his arms before she could distract or be attacked by Alec.

"Don't let him hurt her!" she screamed while at the same time Magnus asked, "How badly did she hurt you?"

Magnus paused and said, "We may be at somewhat of an impasse. Yes or no questions now: Are you badly hurt?"

He took hold of her shoulders gently and looked her over. She had a long, deep scratch all the way up one smooth brown arm. It was welling with blood, falling in fat drops to the floor as they spoke; she was the source of the blood on the floor outside.

She glared at him and lied, "No."

"You're a mundane, aren't you?"

"Yes—or I'm not a werewolf or anything else, if that's what you mean."

"But you know she's a werewolf."

"Yes, dumbass!" snapped the girl. "She told me. I know all about it. I don't care. It's my fault. I encouraged her to go out."

"I'm not the one encouraging werewolves to go out at the full moon and attack people on the dance floor," Magnus said. "But perhaps we can settle which of us is the dumbass at a better time when there are not lives at stake."

The girl clutched his arm. She could see Alec, visible as Shadowhunters almost never were to the mundanes. She could see his weapons. She was bleeding too much, and yet her fear was all for someone else.

Magnus held on to the girl's arm. He would have done better with ingredients and potions, but he sent blue crackling power twining around her arm to soothe the pain and stop the bleeding. When he opened his eyes he saw the girl's gaze fixed on him, her lips parted and her face wondering. Magnus wondered if she had even known that there were people who could do magic, that anything but werewolves existed in the world.

Over her shoulder he saw Alec lunge and join battle with the wolf.

"One last question," said Magnus, speaking rapidly and softly. "Can you trust me to see your friend safe?"

The girl hesitated, and then said, "Yes."

"Then go wait outside," said Magnus. "Outside the bar, not this room. Go wait outside and clear out everyone that you can. Tell people it's a stray dog that wandered in—give people the excuse they will all want to dismiss this. Tell them you're not badly hurt. What's your friend's name?"

She swallowed. "Marcy."

"Marcy will want to know you're safe, once we've got through to her," said Magnus. "Go for her sake."

The girl nodded, a sharp jerky movement, and then fled from Magnus's grip. He heard her platform heels hitting the tiles as she went. He was able, finally, to turn back to Alec.

He saw teeth flash in the dark and did not see Alec, because Alec was a blur of motion, rolling away, then coming back at the wolf.

At Marcy, Magnus thought, and at the same time he saw that Alec hadn't forgotten that Marcy was a person, or at least that Magnus had asked him to help her.

He wasn't using his seraph blades. He was trying not to hurt someone who had fangs and claws. Magnus did not want Alec to get scratched—and he definitely did not want to risk Alec getting bitten.

"Alexander," Magnus called, and realized his mistake when Alec turned his head and then had to back up hurriedly out of the way of the werewolf's vicious swipe at him. He tucked and rolled, landing in a crouch in front of Magnus.

"You have to stay back," he said, breathlessly.

The werewolf, taking advantage of Alec's distraction, growled and sprang. Magnus threw a ball of blue fire at her, knocking her back and sending her spinning. Some yells rose up from the few people still left in the bar, all of whom were hurrying toward the exits. Magnus didn't care. He knew Shadowhunters were meant to protect civilians, but Magnus was emphatically not one.

"You have to remember I'm a warlock."

"I know," Alec said, scanning the shadows. "I just want—" He wasn't making any sense, but the next sentence he spoke unfortunately made perfect sense. "I think," he said clearly, "I think you made her mad."

Magnus followed Alec's gaze. The werewolf was back on her feet and was stalking them, her eyes lit with unholy fire.

"Those are some excellent observational skills you have there, Alexander."

Alec tried to push Magnus back. Magnus caught hold of his black T-shirt and pulled Alec back with him. They moved together slowly out of the back lounge.

The werewolf's friend had been as good as her word: the bar was empty, a glittering shadowy playground for the werewolf to stalk them through.

Alec surprised Magnus and the werewolf both by breaking away and lunging at Marcy. Whatever he had been planning, it didn't work: this time the werewolf's swipe caught him full in the chest.

Alec went flying into a hot pink wall decorated with gold glitter. He hit a mirror set into the wall and decorated with curling gold fretwork with enough force to crack the glass across.

"Oh, stupid Shadowhunters," Magnus moaned under his breath. But Alec used his own body hitting the wall as leverage, rebounding off the wall and up, catching a sparkling chandelier and swinging, then dropping down as lightly as a leaping cat and crouching to attack again in one smooth movement. "Stupid, sexy Shadowhunters."

"Alec!" Magnus called. Alec had learned his lesson: he didn't look around or risk getting distracted. Magnus snapped his fingers, a dancing blue flame appearing from them as if he had snapped on a lighter. That caught Alec's attention. "Alexander. Let's do this together."

Magnus lifted his hands and cast a web of lucent blue lines from his fingers, to baffle the wolf and protect the mundanes. Each of the shimmering strings of light would give off enough of a magical charge to make the wolf hesitate.

Alec wove around them, and Magnus wove the light around him at the same time. He was surprised at the ease with which Alec moved with his magic. Almost every other Shadowhunter he had known had been a little wary and taken aback.

Maybe it was the fact that Magnus had never wished to help and protect in quite this way before, but the combination of Magnus's magic and Alec's strength worked, somehow.

The wolf snarled and ducked and whimpered, her world filled with blinding light, and everywhere she went, there Alec was. Magnus kind of knew how the wolf felt.

The wolf flagged and whimpered, a line of blue light cutting across her brindled fur, and Alec was on it. His knee pressed into the wolf's flank, and his hand went to his belt. Despite everything, fear flashed cold up Magnus's spine. He could picture the knife, and Alec cutting the werewolf's throat.

What Alec drew out was a rope. He wrapped it around the werewolf's neck as he held her pinned down with his body. She struggled and bucked and snarled. Magnus let the lines of magic drop and murmured, the magic words falling from his lips in fading puffs of blue smoke, spells of healing and soothing, illusions of safety and calm.

"Come on, Marcy," Magnus said clearly. "Come *on*!"

The werewolf shuddered and changed, bones popping and fur flowing away, and in a few long, agonizing moments Alec found himself with his arms wrapped around a girl dressed only in the torn ribbons of a dress. She was very nearly naked.

Alec looked more uncomfortable than he had when she was a wolf. He let go quickly, and Marcy slid to a sitting position, her arms clutched around herself. She was whimpering under her breath. Magnus pulled off his long red leather coat and knelt to wrap it around her. Marcy clutched at the lapels.

"Thank you so much," said Marcy, looking up at Magnus with big beseeching eyes. She was a fetching little blonde in human form, which made her giant, angry wolf form seem funnier in retrospect. Then her face tightened with anguish, and nothing seemed funny at all. "Did I ... please, did I hurt anybody?"

"No," said Alec, his voice strong, confident as it only very rarely was. "No, you didn't hurt anyone at all."

"There was someone with me..." Marcy began.

"She was scratched," Magnus said, keeping his voice steady and reassuring. "She's fine. I healed her."

"But I hurt her," Marcy said, and put her face in her blood-stained hands.

Alec reached out and touched Marcy's back, rubbing it gently as if this werewolf stranger was his own sister.

"She's fine," he said. "You didn't—I *know* you didn't want to hurt her, that you didn't want to hurt anyone. You can't help being what you are. You're going to figure it all out."

"She forgives you," Magnus told Marcy, but Marcy was looking at Alec.

"Oh my God, you're a Shadowhunter," she whispered, just as Erik the werewolf waiter had, but with fear in her voice instead of scorn. "What are you going to do to me?" She shut her eyes. "No. I'm sorry. You stopped me. If you hadn't been here—whatever you do to me, I deserve it."

"I'm not going to do anything to you," said Alec, and Marcy opened her eyes and looked up into Alec's face. "I meant what I said. I'm not going to tell anyone. I promise."

Alec had looked the same when Magnus had spoken of his childhood at the party when they had first met. It was something Magnus hardly ever did, but he had felt spiky and defensive about the advent of all these Shadowhunters in his house, at Jocelyn Fray's daughter, Clary, showing up without her mother and with so many questions she deserved answers to. He had not expected to look into a Shadowhunter's eyes and see sympathy.

Marcy sat up, gathering the coat around her. She looked suddenly dignified, as if she had realized she had rights in this situation. That she was a person. That she was a soul, and that soul had been respected as it should have been.

"Thank you," she said calmly. "Thank you both."

"Marcy?" said her friend's voice from the door.

Marcy looked up. "Adrienne!"

Adrienne dashed inside, almost skidding on the tiled floor, and threw herself to the ground and enveloped Marcy in her arms.

"Are you hurt? Show me," Marcy whispered into her shoulder.

"It's fine, it's nothing, it's absolutely all right," said Adrienne, stroking Marcy's hair.

"I'm so sorry," said Marcy, cupping Adrienne's face. They kissed, heedless of the fact that Alec and Magnus were standing right there.

When they broke apart, Adrienne rocked Marcy in her arms and whispered, "We'll figure this out so it never happens again. We will."

Other people followed Adrienne's lead and came in by twos and threes.

"You're pretty snappily dressed for a dogcatcher," said a man Magnus thought was the bartender.

Magnus inclined his head. "Thank you very much."

More people swirled back in, cautiously at first and then in far greater numbers. Nobody was asking where exactly the dog had gone. A great many of them seemed to want drinks.

Perhaps some of them would ask questions later, when the shock had worn off, and this night's work would become a situation that needed clearing up. But Magnus decided that was a problem for later.

"That was nice, what you said to her," said Magnus, when the crowd had completely hidden Marcy and Adrienne from their sight.

"Uh ... it was nothing," said Alec, shifting and looking embarrassed. The Shadowhunters did not see much to approve of in kindness, Magnus supposed. "I mean, that's what we're here for, aren't we? Shadowhunters, I mean. We have to help anyone who needs help. We have to protect people."

The Nephilim Magnus had known had seemed to believe the Downworlders were created to help *them*, and to be disposed of if they didn't help enough.

Magnus looked at Alec. He was sweaty and still breathing a little hard, the scratches on his arms and face healing quickly thanks to the *iratzes* on his skin.

"I don't think we're going to get a drink in here; there's much too long a line," said Magnus slowly. "Let's have a nightcap back at my place."

They walked home. Though it was a long way, it was a nice walk on a summer night, the air warm on Magnus's bare arms and the moon turning the Brooklyn Bridge into a highway of shining white.

"I'm really glad your friend called you to help that girl," Alec confessed as they walked. "I'm really glad you asked me along. I was—I was surprised you did, after how things were going before."

"I was worried you were having a terrible time," Magnus told him. It felt like putting a lot of power in Alec's hands, but Alec was honest with him and Magnus found himself possessed by the strange impulse to be honest back.

"No," said Alec, and went red. "No, that's not it at all. Did I seem— I'm sorry."

"Don't be sorry," Magnus told him softly.

Words seemed to explode out of Alec in a rush, though judging by his expression he wished he could hold them back. "It was my fault. I got everything wrong even before I showed up, and you knew how to order at the restaurant and I had to stop myself laughing at that song on the subway. I have no idea what I'm doing and you're, um, glamorous."

"What?"

Alec looked at Magnus, stricken, as if he thought he'd got everything wrong again.

Magnus wanted to say, *No, I was the one who brought you to a terrible restaurant and treated you like a mundane because I didn't know how to date a Shadowhunter and almost bailed on you even though you were brave enough to ask me out in the first place.*

What Magnus actually ended up saying was, "I thought that terrible song was *hilarious*," and he threw back his head and laughed. He glanced over at Alec and found him laughing too. His whole face changed when he laughed, Magnus thought. Nobody had to be sorry for anything, not tonight.

When they reached Magnus's home, Magnus laid a hand on the front door and it swung open.

"I lost my keys maybe fifteen years ago," Magnus explained.

He really should get around to getting more keys cut. He didn't really need them, though, and it had been a long time since there was anyone he wanted to have his keys—to have ready access to his home because he wanted them there anytime they wanted to come. There had been nobody since Etta, half a century ago.

Magnus gave Alec a sidelong look as they climbed the rickety stairs. Alec caught the glance, and his breathing quickened; his blue eyes were bright. Alec bit his lower lip, and Magnus stopped walking.

It was only a momentary hesitation. But then Alec reached out and caught his arm, fingers tight above his elbow.

"Magnus," he said in a low voice.

Magnus realized that Alec was mirroring the way Magnus had taken hold of Alec's arms on Tuesday: on the day of Alec's first kiss.

Magnus's breath caught in his throat.

That was apparently all the encouragement Alec needed. He leaned in, expression open and ardent in the darkness of the stairs, in the hush of this moment. Alec's mouth met Magnus's, soft and gentle. Getting his breath back was an impossibility, and no longer a priority.

Magnus closed his eyes and unbidden images came to him: Alec trying not to laugh on the subway, Alec's startled appreciation at the taste of new food, Alec glad not to be ditched, Alec sitting on the floor with and telling a werewolf that she could not help what she was. Magnus found himself almost afraid at the thought of what he had nearly done in almost leaving Alec before the evening was over. Leaving Alec was the last thing he wanted to do right now. He pulled in Alec by the belt loops of his jeans, closed all distance between their bodies and caught Alec's tiny needful gasp with his mouth.

The kiss caught fire and all he could see behind his closed eyes were gold sparks; all he was aware of was Alec's mouth, Alec's strong gentle hands that had held down a werewolf and tried not to hurt her, Alec pressing him against the banister so the rotten wood creaked alarmingly and Magnus did not even care—Alec here, Alec now, the taste of Alec in his mouth, his hands pushing aside the fabric of his own worn T-shirt to get at Alec's bare skin underneath.

It took an embarrassingly long time before they both remembered that Magnus had an apartment, and tumbled toward it without disentangling from each other. Magnus blew the door open without looking at it: the door banged so hard against the wall that Magnus cracked an eye open to check that he had not absentmindedly made his front door explode.

Alec kissed a sweet careful line down Magnus's neck, starting from just below his ear to the hollow at the base of his throat. The door was fine. Everything was great.

Magnus pulled Alec down to the sofa, Alec collapsing bonelessly on top of him. Magnus fastened his lips to Alec's neck. He tasted of sweat and soap and skin, and Magnus bit down, hoping to leave a mark on the pale skin there, wanting to. Alec gave a breathy whimper and pushed his body into the contact. Magnus's hands slid up under Alec's rumpled shirt, learning the shape of Alec's body. He ran his fingers over the swell of Alec's shoulders and down the long lean curve of his back, feeling the scars of his profession and the wildness of his kisses. Shyly, Alec undid the buttons on Magnus's waistcoat, laying skin bare and slipping inside to touch Magnus's chest, his stomach, and Magnus felt cool silk replaced by warm hands, curious and caressing. He felt Alec's fingers shaking against his skin.

Magnus reached up and pressed his hand against Alec's cheek, his brown bejeweled fingers a contrast to Alec's moonlight-pale skin: Alec turned his face into the curve of Magnus's palm and kissed it, and Magnus's heart broke.

"Alexander," he murmured, wanting to say more than just "Alec," to call him by a name that was longer than and different from the name everybody else called him, a name with weight and value to it. He whispered the name as if making a promise that he would take his time. "Maybe we should wait a second."

He pushed Alec, just slightly, but Alec took the hint. He took it much further than Magnus had meant it. He scrambled off the sofa and away from Magnus.

"Did I do something wrong?" Alec asked, and his voice was shaking too.

"No," Magnus said. "Far from it."

"Are you sending me home?"

Magnus held up his hands. "I have no interest in telling you what to do, Alexander. I don't want to persuade you to do anything or convince you not to do anything. I'm just saying that you might want to stop and think for a moment. And then you can decide—whatever you want to decide."

Alec looked frustrated. Magnus could sympathize.

Then he scrubbed both hands through his hair—it was already a wreck thanks to Magnus; there was no ruining it any further; it had reached maximum ruination—and paced the floor. He was thinking, Magnus saw, and tried not to wonder what he was thinking of: Jace, Magnus, his family or his duty, how to be kind to himself.

He stopped pacing when he reached Magnus's doorway.

"I should probably go home," said Alec eventually.

"Probably," said Magnus, with great regret.

"I don't want to," Alec said.

"I don't want you to," said Magnus. "But if you don't..."

Alec nodded, quickly. "Good-bye, then," he said, and leaned down for a quick kiss. At least Magnus suspected it was supposed to be quick. He wasn't entirely sure what happened after that, but somehow he was wrapped around Alec entirely and they were on the floor. Alec was gasping and clutching at him, and somebody's hands were on someone else's belt buckle and Alec kissed Magnus so hard he tasted blood, and Magnus said, "Oh, *God*," and then—

And then Alec was back up on his feet and had hold of the doorframe, as if the air had become a tide that might rush him back to Magnus if he didn't grab at some support. He seemed to be struggling with something, and Magnus wondered whether he was going to ask to stay after all or say the whole night had been a mistake. Magnus felt more fear and more anticipation than he was entirely able to play off, and he realized it mattered more than it should, so soon.

He waited, tense, and Alec said, "Can I see you again?"

The words tumbled out in a rush, shy and eager and entirely uncertain of what Magnus would answer, and Magnus felt the headlong rush of adrenaline and excitement that came from the start of a new adventure.

"Yes," said Magnus, still lying on the floor. "I'd like that."

"Um," said Alec, "so—next Friday night?"

"Well..."

Alec looked instantly worried, as if he thought Magnus was going to take it all back and say that actually he had changed his mind. He was beautiful and hopeful and hesitant, a heartbreaker who wore his heart on his sleeve. Magnus found himself wanting to show his hand, to take a risk and be vulnerable. He recognized and accepted this strange new feeling: that he would rather be hurt himself than hurt Alec.

"Friday night would be fine," Magnus said, and Alec smiled his brilliant, light-up-the-world smile and backed out of the apartment, still looking at Magnus. He backed up all the way to the top of the stairs. There was a yell, but Magnus had already risen and closed the door before he could see Alec fall down the steps, as that was the sort of thing a man had to do in private.

He did lean on the windowsill, though, and watch Alec emerge from his building's front door, tall and pale and messy-haired, and walk off down Greenpoint Avenue, whistling off-key. And Magnus found himself hoping.

He had been taught so many times that hope was foolish, but he could not help it, as heedless as a child straying close to the fire and stubbornly refusing to learn from experience. Maybe this time was different—maybe this love was different. It felt so different; surely that had to mean something. Maybe the year to come would be a good year for both of them. Maybe this time things would work out the way Magnus wanted them to.

Maybe Alexander Lightwood would not break his heart.

The Voicemail of Magnus Bane

By Cassandra Clare, Sarah Rees Brennan, and Maureen Johnson

"Hi, Magnus. It's Alec. Alexander. Well, you know that. I'm just calling because I think we need to talk. I guess you're busy. Call me back, okay?"

Beep

—The Voicemail of Magnus Bane

RIIIING
RIIIIIIIING
RIIIIIIING
RIIIIIING
CLICK
SWEET CHEEKS
slide to answer
BEEP
HI, MAGNUS. IT'S ALEC. ALEXANDER. . .

The Voicemail of Magnus Bane, High Warlock of Brooklyn, in the Days Following a Certain Incident in *City of Lost Souls*

Today 2:00 a.m.

"Hi, Magnus. It's Alec. Alexander. Well, you know that. I'm just calling because I think we need to talk. I guess you're busy. Call me back, okay?"

Beep

Today 2:10 a.m.

"Hi, Magnus. This is Isabelle Lightwood. There seems to have been a small misunderstanding. My brother came home under an impression I'm sure is totally mistaken. Call me or else, and let's get this cleared up! I don't know why I said 'or else.' We're all friends here."

Beep

Today 2:35 a.m.

"Isabelle speaking. Maybe there hasn't been a misunderstanding. Maybe you just made a terrible error. That's okay! People make mistakes. All they have to do is grovel and beg for forgiveness, and then all is well. That's how it can be. I'm prepared to let it go this once, Magnus."

Beep

Today 3:00 a.m.

"Isabelle. Let me just follow up by describing what a big mistake you would be making if you broke up with Alec. The Lightwoods are a seriously hot people. Some people say the Herondales used to be hot, but think about it—not only do we outnumber them, but we took their last hottie and we made him ours. Obviously, we won the victory.

"I have looked back on portraits of our ancestors. Gabriel Lightwood was notably smoking. It is rumored that one Consul agreed with everything my great-great aunt Felicia Lightwood ever said, because when she spoke all he heard was 'Foxy foxy foxy.' If you break up with Alec, you will not only be losing one stone cold fox, but a family of foxes. I will pass down the word to my children's children. No Lightwood is ever going to so much as wink at you in a bar. Think about that. Think about being Lightwoodless and lonely five hundred years from now, in a sad and chilly nightclub on the moon."

Beep

Today 11 a.m.

"Hi, it's Alec. I guess you're still busy. That's okay. I know you have a lot of things to do. Just—call me back when you're free? Whenever you're free, it doesn't matter what time. I'll be awake. I really want to talk to you."

Beep

Today 2:30 p.m.

"Hello, Mr. Bane, this is Hadrian Industries. We're calling to engage your services for a simple ritual, in the same vein as the one you performed for us last February. We would like you to bring a crate of horned toads with you. We shall of course amply compensate you for the toads."

Beep

Today 5:14 p.m.

"Mrrrrrowl. Mrrrrrowl."

"Ow! Ow, stupid cat! Ahem. You told me, 'stop calling, Isabelle,' but I'm not the one calling you. Church is calling you. Mine are merely the fingers that work the phone.

"See, here's something you may not have known before you committed your recent rash acts. Our cat, Church, and your cat, Chairman Meow? They're in love. I've never seen such love before. I never knew such love could exist in the heart of a ... cat. Some people say that love between two dude cats is wrong, but I think it's beautiful. Love makes Church happier than I've ever seen him. Nothing makes him happy like Chairman Meow. Not tuna. Not shredding centuries-old tapestries. Nothing. Please don't keep these cats apart. Please don't take the joy of love away from Church.

"Look, this is really just a warning for your own good. If you keep Church and Chairman Meow apart, Church will start to get angry.

"You wouldn't like Church when he's angry."

Beep

Today 6:00 p.m.

"Hi, Magnus. This is Clary. Nobody told me to make this phone call.

"Isabelle did ask me to call you, but I said no, and she doesn't know I'm making this one.

"Honestly, when I first met Alec, I thought he was really horrible. Admittedly, I was a little off my game, what with finding out about magic worlds and Mom being kidnapped. That was a bad time, but Alec still was really not my favorite person.

"He was a jerk, but he wasn't a jerk because he's a bad guy. He was a jerk because he was unhappy, and he felt like he had to pretend to be someone he wasn't. I guess he learned that he had to hide things all the time, when he was growing up—that he had to keep secrets or lose people. He's a lot better when he's with you. He's better because he's happier.

"I don't really know how relationships work. Jace is the only boyfriend I've ever had, and I'm told our relationship has not gone along traditional lines. But I guess that's what a relationship seems like to me: that no matter what else is going on, you're happiest when you're together.

"I'm not just calling because I'm worried about Alec. You seemed really happy with him, too.

"I was wondering how you are. I hope you're doing okay."

Beep

Today 8:26 p.m.

"Hi, Magnus. This is Alec. Alexander. I guess you don't want to talk to me. I can understand that. But I really think if we were together ... if I could just explain...

"I'm so bad with words. I'm sorry. But you always seemed to know what I meant. I don't want to lose that. I don't want to lose you. I want to talk to you so badly, but if I can't, I guess I'm calling to say...

"I'm really sorry. I just called to say that."

Beep

Today 9:39 p.m.

"Hi, Magnus. It's Simon. You know me. Well, you called me Soames last time we spoke, but we've hung out. I'm calling to, uh ... to—sorry if this is out of line—suggest that you maybe take Alec back.

"I think it would be good for morale. Honestly, Alec was really horrible to Clary when they first met, and if he turns all cranky again, I don't know what Clary's going to do. In those days, Clary had way fewer weapons and way fewer brothers.

"This time it's different. Her boyfriend is on fire. She's got enough problems. I guess what I'm saying is that we'd all appreciate it if you took one for the team.

"Not that I'm part of a Shadowhunter team.

"Shadowhunters don't let vampires join the team.

"This message probably seems selfish, and also crazy. I honestly do feel bad for Alec. He's a good guy. Much less annoying than Jace. I've always felt like, given the opportunity, we could be friends. Maybe bros. Maybe we could be bros who shoot arrows together.

"It may at this point be obvious that Isabelle forced me to make this phone call. I'm not really sure what I'm supposed to say.

"Here's the thing. Alec looks really bad.

"Ow, Isabelle! I mean, he's looking fine, he's a very handsome guy. Much better-looking than Jace, if you ask me. But he's obviously really down. Anyone can see it.

"I don't really notice how guys look most of the time, but even I can see it. He has black rings under his eyes, and his sweaters seem to be coming apart with despair. His mom is worried because he's not eating, and I heard Jace hinting about hairbrushes yesterday. Of course, for a badass warrior, Jace is kind of prissy.

"I don't know what happened between you guys, but I know when someone is sorry. I can tell you, whatever he did, Alec is sorry.

"If you could give him a break, that would be great. Okay. I guess that's it.

"Please don't ever tell Jace I said he was a badass."

Beep

Today 11:48 p.m.

"No, you listen, with your not-calling-back face! You're making a big mistake! I was the best thing that ever happened to you!

"Uh. Okay, statistically, that's not very likely.

"A lot of stuff has happened to you. A lot of people have happened to you.

"I think that was what made me do what I did. I just wanted to know that I wasn't, you know, low down on a long list. I didn't want to be a pretty mediocre footnote in the story of your life.

"Oh, God.

"Jace. Jace, wake up. Jace, how do you delete messages on someone else's phone?"

Beep

Today 8:11 a.m.

"Mr. Bane, I am authorized to contact you on behalf of my client. It is my opinion, and I consider it will be the opinion of the judge, that your actions vis-à-vis terminating your relationship with one Alexander Gideon Lightwood, Esquire, were unlawful. I have in my office witnesses and documentation to prove that you were in fact common law married, and Mr. Lightwood could claim half of your freehold in Brooklyn.

"All right, fine, it's Isabelle again.

"All right, my lawyer is Church. But I truly believe that we have a case. And Church has never lost a lawsuit.

"Answer the phone, Magnus!"

Beep

Today 10:31 a.m.

"Mr. Bane, I am calling to leave a message on an urgent business matter. One of our representatives called about the matter of the horned toads delivery. He described your manner of answering the telephone as 'curt' and 'extremely harsh,' and your tone as 'wild, not to say maddened.' Is there a problem with the toads? We are very concerned."

Beep

Today 7:52 p.m.

"Listen up, buddy: nobody breaks up with a Lightwood. Nobody! Meliorn thought that he could tell his faerie buddies over cups of mead that he'd broken up with me, and all I'm saying is that Meliorn hasn't seen his faerie steed in a while.

"Once a guy visited the Institute and thought he could leave a 'Dear Jane' letter for me as he walked out the door. Jace found the letter. Ten minutes later that guy had a broken wrist and a concussion. And then I let Jace at him.

"This is Isabelle, by the way."

Beep

Today 8:01 p.m.

"Hello, Bane. I mean, ah, Magnus. Greetings, Magnus Bane, High Warlock of Brooklyn, from Maryse Lightwood of the New York Institute. Um … head of the New York Institute. I'm totally the head, and I am calling on Shadowhunter business. Because I am in charge of all Shadowhunter business. The matter on which I am calling is a complex one. Too complex to be discussed over the phone. I think, upon consideration, that it would be best if you visited the Institute so we could discuss this in person.

"Please do not misunderstand me. This is a professional phone call about a purely business matter. I am simply intent on important Shadowhunter business.

"You would naturally be welcome to stay for tea and social conversation with whatever members of the Institute might happen to be present at the time of your visit. After we conclude our business, of course."

Beep

Today 10:29 p.m.

"Greetings to High Warlock Magnus Bane from the New York werewolf clan. This is Maia Roberts. Um, Luke would have called, but he's, uh, in the bathroom.

"What? Shut up! He's been in the bathroom for a really long time, okay? We think it might be food poisoning. He's been in the bathroom for so long that we believe that he is no longer our leader.

"Anyway, the werewolves would like to visit with you. You know, just one of those friendly werewolf on warlock visits. And whoever else happens to show up at the meeting.

"I just want to state for the record that this is stupid and he's never going to buy it!"

Beep

Today 1:06 a.m.

"I'm outside your door, Magnus! I'm going to break it down!"

(pause)

"I would have already broken it down if you hadn't put up stupid warlock spells like a stupid warlock cheater! Answer the door right now or I'll kill you! I know you're in there. I know you broke my brother's heart. I'm not going to stand for it.

"Answer the door right now so I can kill you!"

Beep

Today 2:33 a.m.

"Greetings, Magnus Bane, High Warlock of Brooklyn, from Raphael Santiago of the New York vampire clan, loyal servant of our glorious Queen Maureen, forever may she reign in dark glory, and the future Prince Consort Simon, babelicious rock god.

"We have to begin all our telephone calls in this manner now. Including our nightly call to a place called Hot Topic.

"It would be needless to state, after this introduction, that I consider myself a damned soul.

"I am contacting you because our queen wished to send a summons to 'the shiny man who is Simon's friend.' That is a quote. She adds that she supports you and she is a fan of much 'yaoi manga.' I have no idea what that means, and I never wish to know.

"While I am on the telephone, Lily happened to overhear some not terribly interesting conversation at Taki's between several melodramatic teenagers of your acquaintance. Imagine my surprise when I learned that the ill-advised relationship between yourself and an excessively young male Shadowhunter has been abruptly and unpleasantly concluded.

"I wanted to inform you that your esteemed colleague Ragnor Fell now owes me ten dollars due to a small bet that we made amongst ourselves on the subject of how that absurd liaison would end.

"Of course, Ragnor will never pay me my ten dollars, because he was murdered by the Nephilim, due to a conflict between Nephilim that Downworlders were for some reason embroiled in. Just like the conflict we are currently having, so I suppose you could say that Ragnor died for nothing.

"Shadowhunters. Could their new motto be something like 'Not Worth the Bother'?"

Beep

Today 11:23 a.m.

"Hi, Magnus. This is Isabelle. I'm calling to apologize for attempting to break down your door, for the phone calls and visits that I've been told might have counted as harassment, and for describing you to all your neighbors as a filthy Downworlder love weasel. Though I realize some of the things I said might have seemed threatening, of course as a Shadowhunter I would never inflict physical harm on anyone not engaged in evil or at least being totally annoying.

"I feel I was being pretty reasonable the entire time, and playing it pretty cool, but I'm told that from an outside perspective it looks like I might have slightly lost my head.

"I admit I do get a bit protective of my big brother. He always protects me.

"The truth is, I don't have to threaten you with anything worse than you've already done to yourself.

"Alec is brave, and he's good, and he's loyal, and like all Lightwoods he has cheekbones you could use to slice salami. You're never going to find anyone as great as my brother or anyone who loves you as much.

"He's one of the best things in my life, and I'm prepared to bet he's one of the best things in yours. You're going to be so sorry when you wake up and realize what you threw away.

"In exchange for my promise to be cool in future, I'd appreciate it if you deleted this sappy message. I have a reputation in this town to keep up."

Beep

Today 4:02 p.m.

"Hi, Magnus. This is Alec. I'm just calling to say that I might have asked a couple of people who you were actually talking to if they could possibly put in a good word for me with you. And it, uh, has now been brought to my attention that a couple of people might have taken things slightly too far.

"So I guess this is me calling to tell you that I'm really sorry. Again.

"I won't call again. I won't text. I'm sorry about all the texts. Especially about the one I sent at three fifteen in the morning on Wednesday. You know the one. Yeah. I'm very sorry about that.

"You can call me or text me, though, if you ever want to.

"I don't expect you will. But I really hope you do. I won't give up hoping."

Beep

Today 5:06 p.m.

"Mr. Bane, this is Hadrian Industries calling to inform you that you are extremely late for the appointment we made. We have been waiting for over an hour. There is no sign of you. There is no sign of the toads. We want to—"

(message cut off)

These records were obtained, with some difficulty, from a cell phone which appeared to have been broken and burned with intense magical fire.

READ ALL THE BOOKS IN THE BREATHTAKING

THE MORTAL INSTRUMENTS

Clary Fray is seeing things: vampires in Brooklyn and werewolves in Manhattan. Irresistibly drawn to the Shadowhunters, a secret group of warriors dedicated to ridding the earth of demons, Clary encounters the dark side of New York City – and the dangers of forbidden love...

www.ukshadowhunters.com

eBook
available

BEFORE THE MORTAL INSTRUMENTS,

THERE WERE

THE INFERNAL DEVICES

When sixteen-year-old Tessa Gray arrives in England during the reign of Queen Victoria, something terrifying is waiting for her in London's Downworld, where vampires, warlocks and other supernatural folk stalk the gaslit streets. Friendless and hunted, Tessa seeks refuge with the Shadowhunters and finds herself fascinated by – and torn between – two best friends and quickly realizes that love may be the most dangerous magic of all...

www.ukshadowhunters.com

eBook
available

TALES FROM THE SHADOWHUNTER ACADEMY

After living as a mundane and a vampire, Simon Lewis never thought he would become a Shadowhunter, but now he begins his training at Shadowhunter Academy...

Follow the adventures of Simon Lewis, star of the internationally bestselling series The Mortal Instruments, as he trains to become a Shadowhunter. Tales From the Shadowhunter Academy features characters from Cassandra Clare's Mortal Instruments, Infernal Devices and the upcoming Dark Artifices and Last Hours series.

www.ukshadowhunters.com

eBook
available

TALES FROM THE SHADOWHUNTER ACADEMY

Also by Cassandra Clare

THE LAST HOURS

Chain of Gold

THE SHADOWHUNTER'S CODEX

With Joshua Lewis

TALES FROM THE SHADOWHUNTER ACADEMY

With Sarah Rees Brennan, Maureen Johnson and Robin Wasserman

THE INFERNAL DEVICES

Clockwork Angel

Clockwork Prince

Clockwork Princess

THE MORTAL INSTRUMENTS

City of Bones

City of Ashes

City of Glass

City of Fallen Angels

City of Lost Souls

City of Heavenly Fire

e**Book**
available

Tales from the Shadowhunter Academy

CASSANDRA CLARE

SARAH REES BRENNAN

MAUREEN JOHNSON

ROBIN WASSERMAN

WALKER
BOOKS

This is a work of fiction. Names, characters, places and incidents are either the product of the author's imagination or, if real, used fictitiously. All statements, activities, stunts, descriptions, information and material of any other kind contained herein are included for entertainment purposes only and should not be relied on for accuracy or replicated as they may result in injury.

First published 2016 by Walker Books Ltd
87 Vauxhall Walk, London SE11 5HJ

This edition published 2017

6 8 10 9 7

This book has been typeset in Dolly

Printed and bound by CPI Group (UK) Ltd, Croydon CR0 4YY

British Library Cataloguing in Publication Data:
a catalogue record for this book is available from the British Library

ISBN 978-1-4063-7358-5

www.walker.co.uk

MIX
Paper from responsible sources
FSC® C020471

For all those looking for or looking to be a hero like Simon:
Here's to you, saving entire worlds (and maybe the galaxy)

CONTENTS

Welcome to Shadowhunter Academy

By Cassandra Clare and Sarah Rees Brennan

Simon looked at her for a long moment.
She was so overwhelmingly beautiful and impressive,
he found it too much to handle.

—Welcome to Shadowhunter Academy

I'M GOING TO COME BACK.
NO DOUBT.
YOU ALWAYS DO SEEM TO TURN UP.
WHEN I DO, I'M GOING TO BE AWESOME.
DON'T THINK I'LL BE WAITING AROUND, SIMON LEWIS.
OKAY. WELL, I'LL MISS YOU.
IF YOU NEED ME, I'LL COME.
!
OKAY.

The problem was that Simon did not know how to pack like a badass.

For a camping trip, sure; to stay at Eric's or overnight at a weekend gig, fine; or to go on a vacation in the sun with his mom and Rebecca, no problem. Simon could throw together a jumble of suntan lotion and shorts, or appropriate band T-shirts and clean underwear, at a moment's notice. Simon was prepared for normal life.

Which was why he was so completely unprepared to pack for going to an elite training ground where demon-fighting half-angel beings known as Shadowhunters would try to shape him into a member of their own warrior race.

In books and movies, people were either whisked away to a magical land in the clothes they were standing up in, or they glossed over the packing part entirely. Simon now felt he had been robbed of critical information by the media. Should he be putting the kitchen knives in his bag? Should he bring the toaster and rig it up as a weapon?

Simon did neither of those things. Instead, he went with the safe option: clean underwear and hilarious T-shirts. Shadowhunters had to love hilarious T-shirts, right? Everyone loved hilarious T-shirts.

"I don't know how they feel about T-shirts with dirty jokes on them in military academy, sport," said his mom.

Simon turned, too quickly, his heart lurching up into his throat. His mom was standing in the doorway, arms folded. Her always-worried face was crumpled slightly with extra worry, but mostly she was looking at him with love. As she always had.

Except that in a whole other set of memories Simon barely had access to, he'd become a vampire and she'd thrown him out of their house. That was one of the reasons Simon was going to the Shadowhunter Academy, why he'd lied to his mom through his teeth that he desperately wanted to go. He'd had Magnus Bane—a warlock with cat eyes; Simon actually knew a warlock with actual cat eyes—fake papers to convince her that he had a scholarship to this fictitious military academy.

He'd done it all so he would not have to look at his mom every day and remember how she had looked at him when she was afraid of him, when she hated him. When she betrayed him.

"I think I've judged my T-shirts pretty well," Simon told her. "I'm a pretty judicious guy. Nothing too sassy for the military. Just good, solid class-clown material. Trust me."

"I trust you, or I wouldn't be letting you go," said his mom. She walked over to him and planted a kiss on his cheek, and looked surprised and hurt when he flinched, but she did not comment, not on his last day. She put her arms around him instead. "I love you. Remember that."

Simon knew he was being unfair: His mother had thrown him out thinking he was not really Simon anymore but an unholy monster wearing her son's face. Yet he still felt she should have recognized him and loved him in spite of everything. He could not forget what she had done.

Even though she had forgotten it, even though as far as she or almost anybody else in the world was concerned, it had never happened.

So he had to go.

Simon tried to relax in her embrace. "I've got a lot on my plate," he said, curling his hand around his mom's arm. "But I'll try to remember that."

She pulled back. "So long as you do. You sure you're okay getting a lift with your friends?"

She meant Simon's Shadowhunting friends (who he pretended were the military academy buds who had inspired him to join up too). Simon's Shadowhunting friends were the other reason he was going.

"I'm sure," said Simon. "Bye, Mom. I love you."

He meant it. He'd never stopped loving her, in this life or any other.

I love you unconditionally, his mom had said, once or twice, when he was younger. *That's how parents love. I love you no matter what.*

People said things like that, without thinking of potential nightmare scenarios or horrific conditions, the whole world changing and love slipping away. None of them ever dreamed love would be tested, and fail.

Rebecca had sent him a card that said: *GOOD LUCK,*

SOLDIER BOY! Simon remembered, even when he'd been locked out of his home, door barred to him in every way it could be, his sister's arm around him and her soft voice in his ear. She had loved him, even then. So there was that. It was something, but it wasn't enough.

He could not stay here, caught between two worlds and two sets of memories. He had to escape. He had to go and become a hero, the way he had been once. Then all of this would make sense, all of this would mean something. Surely it would not hurt anymore.

Simon paused before he shouldered his bag and departed for the Academy. He put his sister's card in his pocket. He left home for a strange new life and carried her love with him, as he had once before.

Simon was meeting up with his friends, even though none of them were going to the Academy. He'd agreed he would come to the Institute and say good-bye before he left.

There was a time when he could have seen through glamours on his own, but Magnus had to help him do it now. Simon looked up at the strange, imposing bulk of the Institute, remembering uneasily that he had passed this place before and seen an abandoned building. That was another life, though. He remembered some kind of Bible passage about how children saw through smudged glass, but growing up meant you could view things clearly. He could see the Institute quite plainly: an impressive structure rising high above him. The sort of building designed to make humans feel like ants. Simon pushed open the filigreed gate, walked down the narrow path that snaked around the Institute, and crossed through to the grounds.

The walls that surrounded the Institute enclosed a

garden that struggled to thrive given its proximity to a New York avenue. There were impressive stone paths and benches and even a statue of an angel that gave Simon nervous fits, since he was a *Doctor Who* fan. The angel wasn't weeping, exactly, but it looked too depressed for Simon's liking.

Sitting on the stone bench in the middle of the garden were Magnus Bane and Alec Lightwood, a Shadowhunter who was tall and dark and fairly strong and silent, at least around Simon. Magnus was chatty, though, had the aforementioned cat eyes and magic powers, and was currently wearing a clinging T-shirt in a zebra-stripe pattern with pink accents. Magnus and Alec had been dating for some time; Simon guessed Magnus could talk for both of them.

Behind Magnus and Alec, leaning against a stone wall, were Isabelle and Clary. Isabelle was leaning against the garden wall, looking over it and into the distance. She looked as if she were in the middle of posing for an unbelievably glamorous photo shoot. Then again, she always did. It was her talent. Clary, however, was staring stubbornly up into Isabelle's face and talking to her. Simon thought Clary would get her way and get Isabelle to pay attention to her eventually. That was *her* talent.

Looking at either of them caused a pang in his chest. Looking at both of them started a dull, steady ache.

So instead Simon looked for his friend Jace, who was kneeling by himself in the overgrown grass and sharpening a short blade against a stone. Simon assumed Jace had his reasons for this; or possibly he just knew he looked cool doing it. Possibly he and Isabelle could do a joint photo shoot for *Badass Monthly*.

Everyone was assembled. Just for him.

Simon would have felt both honored and loved, except

mostly he felt weird, because he had only a few broken fragments of memory that said he knew these people at all, and a whole lifetime of memories that said they were armed, overly intense strangers. The kind you might avoid on public transportation.

The adults of the Institute and the Clave, Isabelle and Alec's mother and father and the other people, were the ones who had suggested that if Simon wanted to become a Shadowhunter, he should go to the Academy. It was opening its doors for the first time in decades to welcome trainees who could restore the Shadowhunters' ranks that the recent war had decimated.

Clary hadn't liked the idea. Isabelle had said absolutely nothing on the subject, but Simon knew she hadn't liked it either. Jace had argued that he was perfectly capable of training Simon in New York, had even offered to do it all himself and catch Simon up with Clary's training. Simon had thought that was touching, and he and Jace must be closer than he actually remembered them being, but the awful truth was that he didn't want to stay in New York.

He didn't want to stay around *them*. He didn't think he could bear the constant expression on their faces—on Isabelle's and Clary's most of all—of disappointed expectation. Every time they saw him, they recognized him and knew him and expected things of him. And every time he came up blank. It was like watching someone digging where they knew they'd buried something precious, digging and digging and realizing that whatever it was—was gone. But they kept digging just the same, because the idea of losing it was so terrible and because maybe.

Maybe.

He was that lost treasure. He was that maybe. And he

hated it. That was the secret he was trying to keep from them, the one he was always fearing he would betray.

He just had to get through this one last good-bye, and then he would be away from them until he was better, until he was closer to the person they all actually wanted to see. Then they would not be disappointed in him, and he would not be strange to them. He would belong.

Simon did not try to alert the whole group to his presence at once. Instead he sidled up to Jace.

"Hey," he said.

"Oh," Jace said carelessly, as if he hadn't been waiting out here for the express purpose of seeing Simon off. He looked up, golden gaze casual, then looked away. "You."

Being too cool for school was Jace's thing. Simon supposed he must have understood and been fond of it, once.

"Hey, I figured I wasn't going to get the chance to ask this again. You and me," Simon said. "We're pretty tight, aren't we?"

Jace looked at him for a moment, face very still, and then bounded to his feet and said: "Absolutely. We're like this." He crossed two of his fingers together. "Actually, we're more like this." He tried to cross them again. "We had a little bit of initial tension, as you may later recall, but that was all cleared up when you came to me and confessed that you were struggling with your feelings of intense jealousy over my—these were your words—stunning good looks and irresistible charm."

"Did I," said Simon.

Jace clapped him on the shoulder. "Yeah, buddy. I remember it clearly."

"Okay, whatever. The thing is ... Alec's always really quiet around me," Simon said. "Is he just shy, or did I tick him off and I don't remember it? I wouldn't like to go away without trying to make things right."

Jace's expression took on that peculiar stillness again. "I'm glad you asked me that," he said finally. "There is something more going on. The girls didn't want me to tell you, but the truth is—"

"Jace, stop monopolizing Simon," said Clary.

She spoke firmly, as she always did, and Jace turned and answered to it, as he always did, responding to her call as he did to no one else's. Clary came walking toward both of them, and Simon felt that pang in his chest again as her red head drew near. She was so small.

During one of their ill-fated training sessions, in which Simon had been relegated to an observer after a sprained wrist, Simon had seen Jace throw Clary into a wall. She'd come right back at him.

Despite that, Simon kept feeling as if she needed to be protected. Feeling this way was a particular kind of horror, having the emotions without the memories. Simon felt like he was insane to have all these feelings about strangers, without having them properly backed up by familiarity and experiences he could actually recall. At the same time, he knew he wasn't feeling or expressing enough. He knew he wasn't giving them what they wanted.

Clary didn't need to be protected, but somewhere within Simon was the ghost of a boy who had always wanted to be the one to protect her, and he was only hurting her by staying around unable to be that guy.

Memories came, sometimes in an overwhelming and terrifying rush, but mostly in tiny shards, jigsaw pieces Simon could hardly make sense of. One piece was a flash of walking to school with Clary, her hand so little and his barely bigger. He'd felt big then, though, big and proud and responsible for her. He had been determined not to let her down.

"Hey, Simon," she said now. Her eyes were bright with tears, and Simon knew they were all his fault.

He took Clary's hand, small but calloused from both weapons and art. He wished he could find a way back to believing, even though he knew better, that she was his to protect.

"Hey, Clary. You take care of yourself," he said. "I know you can." He paused. "And take care of Jace, that poor, helpless blond."

Jace made an obscene gesture, which actually did feel familiar to Simon, so he knew that was their thing. Jace hastily lowered his hand when Catarina Loss walked around the side of the Institute.

She was a warlock like Magnus, and a friend of his, but instead of having cat eyes she was blue all over. Simon got the feeling she did not like him very much. Maybe warlocks only liked other warlocks. Though Magnus did seem to like Alec quite a lot.

"Hello there," said Catarina. "Ready to go?"

Simon had been dying to go for weeks, but now that the time had come he felt panic clawing at his throat. "Almost," he said. "Just a second."

He nodded to Alec and Magnus, who both nodded to him. Simon felt he had to clear up whatever was weird between himself and Alec before he ventured much more.

"Bye, guys, thanks for everything."

"Believe me, even partially releasing you from a fascist spell was my pleasure," said Magnus, lifting a hand. He wore many rings, which glittered in the spring sunshine. Simon thought he must dazzle his enemies with his magical prowess, but also his glitter.

Alec just nodded.

Simon leaned down and hugged Clary, even though it

made his chest hurt more. The way she felt and smelled was both strange and familiar, conflicting messages running through his brain and his body. He tried not to hug her too hard, even though she was kind of hugging him too hard. In fact, she was pretty much crushing his rib cage. He didn't mind, though.

When he let go of Clary, he turned and hugged Jace. Clary watched, tears running down her face.

"Oof," said Jace, sounding extremely startled, but he patted Simon quickly on the back.

Simon supposed they usually fist-bumped or something. He did not know the warrior way of being bros: Eric was a big hugger. He decided it would probably be good for Jace, and ruffled his hair a little for emphasis before stepping away.

Then Simon gathered up his courage, turned, and walked over to Isabelle.

Isabelle was the last person he had to say good-bye to; she would be the hardest. She wasn't like Clary, openly tearful, or like any of the others, sorry to see him go but basically all right. She seemed more indifferent than anyone, so indifferent Simon knew it was not real.

"I'm going to come back," said Simon.

"No doubt," Isabelle said, staring off into the distance beyond his shoulder. "You always do seem to turn up."

"When I do, I'm going to be awesome."

Simon made the promise, not sure if he could keep it. He felt as if he had to say something. He knew it was what she wanted, for him to return to her the way he had been, better than he was now.

Isabelle shrugged. "Don't think I'll be waiting around, Simon Lewis."

Just like her pretense of indifference, that sounded like

a promise of the complete opposite. Simon looked at her for a long moment. She was so overwhelmingly beautiful and impressive, he found it too much to handle. He could barely believe any of his new memories, but the idea that Isabelle Lightwood had been his girlfriend seemed more unbelievable than the fact that vampires were real and Simon had been one. He didn't have the faintest idea how he had made her feel that way about him once, and so he didn't have the faintest idea how to make her feel that way about him again. It was like asking him to fly. He'd asked her to dance once, to have coffee with him twice in the months since she and Magnus had come to him and given back as much of his memory as they could, but not enough. Each time Isabelle had watched him carefully, expectantly, waiting for some miracle he knew he could not perform. It meant he was tongue-tied around her all the time, so sure he was going to say the wrong thing and shatter everything that he could scarcely say anything.

"Okay," he said. "Well, I'll miss you."

Isabelle's hand shot out, grasping his arm. She still wasn't looking at him.

"If you need me, I'll come," she said, and released him as abruptly as she had grabbed him.

"Okay," Simon said again, and retreated to Catarina Loss's side as she made the Portal to go through to Idris, the country of the Shadowhunters. This parting was so painful and awkward and welcome that he could not quite appreciate how awesome it was to have magic done right in front of him.

He waved good-bye to all these people he barely knew and somehow loved anyway, and he hoped they could not tell how relieved he was to be going.

* * *

Simon had remembered snatches about Idris, towers and a prison and stern faces and blood in the streets, but all of it was from the city of Alicante.

This time, he found himself outside the city. He was standing in the lush countryside, on one side a valley and on the other meadows. There was nothing to be seen for miles but different shades of green. There were the jade-green stretches of meadows upon meadows right down to the crystalline dazzle on the horizon that was the City of Glass, its towers blazing in the sunlight. On the other side, there were the emerald depths of a forest, dark green abundance cloaked in shadows. The tops of the trees ruffled in the wind like viridescent feathers.

Catarina looked around, then took one step, so she was standing right on the lip of the valley. Simon followed her, and in that one step the shadows of the forest lifted, as if shadows could become a veil.

Suddenly there were what Simon recognized as training grounds, stretches of clear ground cut into the earth with fences around them, markings indicating where Shadowhunters would run or throw etched so deep in the earth Simon could see them from where he stood. At the center of the grounds and in the very heart of the forest, the jewel to which all the rest was background setting, was a tall gray building with towers and spires. Simon was suddenly searching for architectural words like "buttress" to describe how stone could carry the shape of a swallow's wings and support a roof. The Academy had a stained-glass window set in its very center. In the window, darkened with age and years, an angel wielding a sword could still be seen, celestial and fierce.

"Welcome to Shadowhunter Academy," said Catarina Loss, her voice gentle.

They began their descent together. At one point Simon's sneakers slid in the soft, crumbling earth of the steep slope, and Catarina had to grab hold of his jacket to steady him.

"I hope you brought some hiking boots, city boy."

"I did not bring hiking boots even slightly," said Simon. He'd known he was packing wrong. His instincts had not led him astray. Nor had they been at all helpful.

Catarina, probably disappointed by Simon's demonstrable lack of intelligence, was silent as they walked under the shadow of the boughs, in the green dusk created by the trees, until the trees became sparse and the sunlight flooded back into the space around them and Shadowhunter Academy loomed in the distance before them. As they drew closer, Simon began to notice certain small flaws with the Academy that he had not observed when he was awestruck and far away. One of the tall, skinny towers was leaning at an alarming angle. There were large bird nests in the arches, and cobwebs hanging as long and thick as curtains fluttered in a few of the windows. One of the panes in the stained-glass window was gone, leaving a black space where the angel's eye should have been so that he looked like an angel turned to piracy.

Simon did not feel good about any of these observations.

There were people walking in front of the Academy, under the gaze of the pirate angel. There was a tall woman with a mane of strawberry-blond hair, and behind her two girls who Simon figured were Academy students. They both looked about his age.

A twig snapped under Simon's clumsy foot and all three of the strolling women looked around. The strawberry blonde leaped into action, running full tilt toward them and falling on Catarina as if she was a long-lost blue sister.

She seized Catarina by the shoulders and Catarina looked extremely discomposed.

"Ms. Loss, thank the Angel you're here," she exclaimed. "Everything is chaos, absolute chaos!"

"I don't believe I've had the ... pleasure," Catarina observed, with a significant pause.

The woman collected herself and released Catarina, nodding so her bright hair flew around her shoulders. "I'm Vivianne Penhallow. The, ah, dean of the academy. Delighted to make your acquaintance."

She might speak formally, but she was awfully young to be spearheading the effort to reopen the Academy and prepare all the new, desperately needed trainees for the Shadowhunter forces. Then again, Simon supposed that was what happened when you were second-cousins-in-law with the Consul. Simon was still trying to work out how Shadowhunter government and also Shadowhunter family trees worked. They all seemed to be related to each other and it was very disturbing.

"What seems to be the problem, Dean Penhallow?"

"Well, not to put too fine a point on it, the weeks allotted to renovating the Academy seem to have been, ah ... 'wildly insufficient' are the words that perhaps best describe the situation," said Dean Penhallow, her words rushing out. "And some of the teachers have already—er—left abruptly. I do not believe they intend to return. In fact some of them informed me of this in very strong language. Also, the Academy is a trifle chilly and, to be perfectly honest, more than a trifle structurally unsound. Moreover, in the interest of thoroughness I must tell you there is a problem with the food supplies."

Catarina raised an ivory eyebrow. "What's the problem with the food supplies?"

"There aren't any food supplies."

"That *is* a problem."

The dean's shoulders sagged and her chest deflated somewhat, as if holding all that in had been confining her in an invisible corset of distress. "These girls with me are two of the older students and of good Shadowhunter families—Julie Beauvale and Beatriz Velez Mendoza. They arrived yesterday and have really been proving themselves invaluable. And this must be young Simon," she said, favoring him with a smile.

Simon was briefly startled and not sure why, until he dimly recalled that very few adult Shadowhunters had ever shown any signs of pleasure at having a vampire in their midst. Of course, she had no reason to hate him on sight now. She'd also seemed eager to meet Catarina, Simon thought; maybe she was all right. Or maybe she was just eager to have Catarina help her.

"Right," said Catarina. "Well, what a surprise that the building left vacant after an upheaval almost two decades ago isn't running entirely smoothly after a few weeks. You'd best show me some of the worst trouble spots. I can shore them up so we don't have all the fuss of a baby Shadowhunter breaking their little neck."

Everyone stared at Catarina.

"The inestimable tragedy, I meant," Catarina amended, and smiled brightly. "Can one of the girls be spared to show Simon to his room?"

She seemed eager to get rid of Simon. She really did not like him. Simon could not think what he could possibly have done to her.

The dean stared at Catarina for a moment longer, and then snapped out of it. "Oh yes, yes, of course. Julie, would you please see to it? Put him in the tower room."

Julie's eyebrows shot up. "Really?"

"Yes, really. The first room as you enter the east wing," the dean said, her voice strained, and turned back to Catarina. "Ms. Loss, I am once again most thankful you have arrived. Can you truly fix some of these irregularities?"

"There is a saying: *It takes a Downworlder to clear up a Shadowhunter mess*," Catarina observed.

"I ... hadn't heard that saying," said Dean Penhallow.

"How odd," said Catarina, her voice fading as they walked away. "Downworlders say it often. Very often."

Simon was left abandoned and staring at the remaining girl, Julie Beauvale. He'd liked the look of the other girl better. Julie was very pretty, but her face and nose and mouth were all oddly narrow, giving the impression that her entire head was pursed with disapproval.

"Simon, was it?" she asked, and her prepursed mouth seemed to purse further. "Follow me."

She turned, her movements sharp as a drill sergeant's, and Simon followed her slowly across the threshold of the Academy into an echoing hall with a vaulted ceiling. He tilted his head and tried to make out if the greenish cast of the ceiling was bad lighting from the stained-glass window or actual moss.

"Please keep up," said Julie's voice, floating from one of the six dark, small doorways cut into the stone wall. Its owner had already vanished, and Simon plunged into the darkness after her.

The darkness turned out to be only a dim stone stairway, which led up into a dim stone corridor. There was still hardly any light, because the windows were tiny slits in the stone. Simon remembered reading about windows like that, made so nobody could fire in at you but so you could fire arrows out.

Julie led him down one passage, down another, up a short flight of stairs, down still another passage, made her way through a small circular room, which was nice for a change but which led to yet another passage. All the dark, close stone and the funny smell, combined with all the corridors, were making Simon think the words "passage tomb." He was trying not to think of the words, but there they were.

"So you're a demon hunter," said Simon, shifting his bag on his shoulders and hurrying after Julie. "What's that like?"

"Shadowhunter, and that's what you're here to find out," the girl told him, and then stopped at one of many doors, stained oak with black iron fittings, the handle carved to look like an angel's wing. She clasped the handle, and Simon saw that it must have been turned so often over the centuries that the details of the angel's wing had been worn almost smooth.

Inside was a small stone room, containing two narrow beds—a suitcase open on one—with carved wooden bedposts, a diamond-paned window blurred with dust, and a large wardrobe tilted to one side as if missing a leg.

There was also already a boy in there, standing on a stool. He revolved slowly on the stool to face them, regarding them from on high as if he were a statue on a plinth.

He did not look unlike a statue, if someone had dressed a statue up in jeans and a colorful red-and-yellow rugby shirt. The lines of his face were clean and statue-reminiscent, and he was broad-shouldered and athletic-looking, as most Shadowhunters were. Simon suspected the Angel did not choose the asthmatic or anyone who had ever gotten hit in the face by a volleyball in gym. The boy had a golden summer tan, dark brown eyes, and curly light-brown hair tumbling over his brow. The boy smiled at the sight of them, a dimple creasing one cheek.

Simon did not consider himself much of a judge of male beauty. But he heard a small sound behind him and glanced over his shoulder.

The small sound had been a sigh bursting in an irrepressible gust from Julie, who also, as Simon watched, performed a simultaneous sigh and slow, involuntary wriggle. Simon thought the siggle was probably an indication that this guy was something out of the ordinary when it came to looks.

Simon rolled his eyes. Apparently, all Shadowhunter dudes were underwear models, including his new roommate. His life was a joke.

Julie seemed occupied regarding the dude on the stool. Simon had several questions, like "who is that?" and "why is he on a stool?" but he didn't want to be a bother.

"I'm really glad you guys are here. Now ... don't panic," the guy on the stool whispered.

Julie backed up a step.

"What's wrong with you?" Simon demanded. "Saying 'don't panic' is guaranteed to make everyone panic! Be specific about the problem."

"Okay, I get what you're saying and you make a fair point," continued the new boy. He had an accent, his voice light yet rumbling over certain syllables. Simon was fairly sure he was Scottish. "It's just that I think there's a demon possum in the wardrobe."

"By the Angel!" said Julie.

Simon said: "That's ridiculous."

There was a sound from within the wardrobe. A dragging, grunting, hissing sound that raised the hairs on the back of Simon's neck.

Quick as a flash and with Shadowhunter grace, Julie leaped onto the bed that did not have an open suitcase on it. Simon supposed that was his bed. The fact that he'd been here only two minutes and already had a girl hurling herself onto his bed would have been thrilling, except that of course she was fleeing infernal rodents.

"Do something, Simon!"

"Yes, Simon—are you Simon? Hi, Simon—please do something about the demonic possum," said the guy on the stool.

"I'm sure it's not a demonic possum."

The sound of scuffling within the wardrobe was very loud, and Simon did not feel entirely sure. It did sound like there was something enormous lurking in there.

"I was born in the City of Glass," said Julie. "I am a Shadowhunter and I can handle the demonic. But I was also raised in a nice house that was not infested with filthy wildlife!"

"Well, I'm from Brooklyn," said Simon, "and not to badmouth my beloved city or call it a verminous garbage heap with good music or anything, but I know rodents. Also, I believe I was a rodent, but that was only for a little while—I don't remember it clearly and I don't want to discuss it. I think I can handle a possum ... which again, I'm sure is not demonic."

"I saw it and you guys didn't!" exclaimed the guy on the stool. "I'm telling you, it was suspiciously large! *Fiendishly* large."

There was another rustle, and some menacing snuffling. Simon sidled over to the open suitcase on the other bed. There were a lot more rugby shirts in there, but on top of them was something else.

"Is that a weapon?" Julie asked.

"Uh, no," said Simon. "It's a tennis racket."

The Shadowhunters needed more extracurricular activities.

He suspected the racket was going to be a truly terrible weapon, but it was what he had. He edged back toward the wardrobe, and threw the door open. There, in the splintered, gnawed-on recesses of the wardrobe, was a possum. Its red eyes shone and its small mouth opened, hissing at Simon.

"How disgusting," said Julie. "Kill it, Simon!"

"Simon, you're our only hope!" said the boy on the stool.

The possum made a movement, as if to dart forward. Simon brought the racket down with a thwack against the stone. The possum hissed again and moved in a different direction. Simon had the wild idea that it was feinting, just before it actually ran between his legs. Simon let out a sound that was too close to a squawk, stumbled back, and hit wildly in several directions, striking flagstones every time. The other two screamed. Simon spun to try to locate the possum, seeing a flash of fur out of the corner of his eye and spinning again. The boy on the stool—either looking for reassurance or in a misguided effort to be helpful—grabbed at Simon's shoulders and tried to turn him, using a handful of his shirt for leverage.

"There!" he yelled in Simon's ear, and Simon whirled of his own accord, was turned against his will, and walked backward into the stool.

He felt the stool tip and tilt against his legs, and the boy on it snatched at Simon's shoulders again. Simon, already dizzy, lurched and then saw the possum's furry little body creeping over his own sneaker and made a fatal mistake. He hit his own foot with the racket. Very hard.

Simon, the stool, the boy on the stool, and the racket all went tumbling onto the stone floor.

The possum streaked out of the doorway. Simon thought it cast him a red-eyed look of triumph as it went.

Simon was in no condition to give chase, since he was in a jumble of chair legs and human legs, and had knocked his head against the bedpost.

He was trying to sit up, rubbing his head and feeling a little dizzy, when Julie jumped off the bed. The bedpost swayed with the force of her movement, and knocked against the back of Simon's head once more.

"Well, I'll leave you guys before the creature returns to his nest!" Julie announced. "Er ... I mean, I'll leave you guys ... to it." She paused in the doorway, staring in the direction the possum had gone. "Bye now," she added, and bolted in the opposite direction.

"Ow," Simon said, giving up on sitting up straight and leaning back on his hands. He grimaced. "Very ow. Well ... that was..."

He gestured to the stool, the open doorway, the disgusting wardrobe, and his supine self.

"That was...," he continued, and found himself shaking his head and laughing. "Just *such* an impressive display from three future awesome demon hunters."

The boy no longer on the stool looked startled, no doubt because he thought his new roommate was deranged and giggled over possums. Simon could not help it. He could not stop laughing.

Any of the Shadowhunters he knew back in New York would have dealt with the situation without blinking an eye. He was sure Isabelle would have cut off the possum's head with a sword. But now he was surrounded by people who panicked and screamed and stood on stools, flailing disasters of human beings who could not cope with a single rodent, and Simon was one of them. They were all just normal kids.

It was such a relief, Simon felt dizzy with it. Or maybe that was because he'd hit his head.

He kept laughing, and when he looked over at his roommate again, the other boy met his eyes.

"What a shame our teachers didn't see that awesome performance," Simon's new roommate said seriously. Then he burst out laughing too, hand against his mouth, laugh lines fanning out from the corners of his eyes, as if he laughed all the time and his face had just grown used to it. "We are gonna slay."

After the slight burst of possum-related hysterics, Simon and his new roommate got up off the floor and got to unpacking and introducing themselves.

"Sorry about all that. I'm not great with scuttling little things. I'm hoping to fight demons a bit higher off the ground. I'm George Lovelace, by the way," said the boy, sitting on the bed beside his open suitcase.

Simon stared at his own bag, full of its many hilarious T-shirts, and then suspiciously at the wardrobe. He didn't know if he trusted the possum wardrobe with his T-shirts.

"So you're a Shadowhunter, then?"

He'd worked out how Shadowhunter names were constructed by now, and he'd already figured George for a Shadowhunter at first sight. Only that had been before Simon thought George might be cool. Now he was disappointed. He knew what Shadowhunters thought of mundanes. It would have been nice to have someone new to all this to go through school with.

It would be nice to have a cool roommate again, Simon thought. Like Jordan. He could not remember Jordan, his roommate when he was a vampire, all that well, but what he remembered was good.

"Well, I'm a Lovelace," said George. "My family quit Shadowhunting due to laziness in the 1700s, then went and settled outside Glasgow to become the best sheep thieves in the land. The only other branch of the Lovelaces gave up Shadowhunting in the 1800s—I think they had a daughter who came back, but she died, so we were all that was left. Shadowhunters used to come knocking to past generations, and my brave ancestors were all like, 'Nope, think we'll stick with the sheep,' until finally the Clave stopped coming around because they were tired of our layabout ways. What can I tell you? The Lovelaces are quitters."

George shrugged and made a *what can you do?* gesture with his tennis racket. The strings were broken. It was still their only weapon in case the possum returned.

Simon checked his phone. Idris had no reception, big surprise, and he tossed it in the suitcase among his T-shirts. "That's a noble legacy."

"Can you believe, I didn't know anything about it until a few weeks ago? The Shadowhunters came to find us again, telling us they needed new, uh, demon hunters in the fight against evil because a bunch of them had died in a war. Can I just say, the Shadowhunters, man, they really know how to win over hearts and minds."

"They should make flyers," Simon suggested, and George grinned. "Just a bunch of them looking very cool and wearing black. The flyer could say 'READY TO BE A

BADASS?' Put me in touch with the Shadowhunter marketing department, I have more gems where that came from."

"I have some bad news to break to you about most Shadowhunters and their abilities with a photocopier," George told him. "Anyway, it turned out my parents had known the whole time and just not informed me. Because why would I be interested in a little thing like that? They said my grandma was insane when she talked about dancing with the faeries! I made myself very clear on the subject of keeping intensely cool secrets from me before I left. Dad said, in fairness, that Gran *is* completely out of her tree. It's just that faeries are also real. Probably not her four-inch-tall faerie lover called Bluebell, though."

"I'd bet against it," said Simon, thinking over all he remembered about faeries. "But I wouldn't bet a lot."

"So, you're from New York?" said George. "Pretty glam."

Simon shrugged: He didn't know what to say, when he had been casually comfortable with New York his whole life, and then found that the city and his own soul had turned traitor. When he had been so painfully eager to leave.

"How did you find out about all this? Do you have the Sight?"

"No," Simon said slowly. "No, I'm just ordinary, but my best friend found out she was a Shadowhunter, and the daughter of this really bad guy. And the sister of this other really bad guy. She has the worst luck with relatives. I got mixed up in it, and to tell you the truth, I don't really remember everything, because—"

Simon paused and tried to think of some way to explain demon-related amnesia that would not convince George that Simon had the same problems as George's grandma. Then he saw George was looking at him, his brown eyes wide.

"You're Simon," he breathed. "Simon *Lewis*."

"Right," Simon said. "Hey. Is my name on the door, or—is there some sort of register I'm meant to be signing—"

"The vampire," said George. "Mary Morgenstern's best friend!"

"Uh, Clary," said Simon. "Uh, yeah. I like to think of myself as the ex-undead."

The way George was looking at him, as if he was seriously impressed rather than disappointed or expectant, was a little embarrassing. Simon had to admit, it was also a little nice. It was so different from the way anyone else had looked at him, in his old life or his new one.

"You don't understand. I arrived in this freezing hellhole full of slime and rodents, and the whole Academy was buzzing with people talking about these heroes who are my age and actually went to a hell dimension. It gave real perspective to the fact that the toilets don't work here."

"The toilets don't work? But what do we—how do we—"

George coughed. "We commune with nature, if you know what I'm saying."

George and Simon looked out of their casement window to the forest below, leaves gently swaying in the wind beyond the diamond-shaped panes of glass. George and Simon looked, darkly, sadly, back at each other.

"Seriously, you and your hero group is all anybody talks about," George said, returning to a more cheerful subject. "Well, that and the fact we have pigeons living in the ovens. You saved the world, didn't you? And you don't remember it. That's got to be weird."

"It is weird, George, thanks for mentioning that."

George laughed, tossed his broken racket on the floor, and kept looking at Simon as if he was someone amazing.

"Wow. Simon Lewis. I guess I have someone at Spinechilling Academy to thank for getting the cool roommate."

George led Simon down to dinner, for which Simon was deeply grateful. The dining hall looked a lot like all the other square stone rooms in the Academy, except on one end it had a massive carved mantelpiece, displaying crossed swords and a motto so worn that Simon could not read it.

There were several round tables, with wooden chairs of varying sizes assembled around them. Simon was starting to genuinely believe they had furnished the Academy from an old person's garage sale. The tables were crowded with kids. Most of them were at least two years younger than Simon. Quite a few were younger than that. Simon had not realized he was on the elderly side for a trainee demon hunter, and it made him nervous. He was deeply relieved when he saw some mildly familiar faces his own age.

Julie of the pursed face, Beatriz, and another boy saw them and waved them over. Simon assumed the wave was for George, but when he sat down Julie actually leaned into him.

"I can't believe you didn't say you were Simon *Lewis*," she said. "I thought you were just a mundane."

Simon leaned slightly away. "I am just a mundane."

Julie laughed. "You know what I mean."

"She means we all owe you a debt, Simon," said Beatriz Mendoza, smiling at him. She had a great smile. "We don't forget that. It's a pleasure to meet you, and it's a pleasure to have you here. We might even be able to get sensible conversation out of a boy for once. No chance of that with Jon here."

The boy, who had biceps the size of Simon's head, reached across the table and offered a hand. Despite his extreme arm intimidation, Simon shook it.

"I'm Jonathan Cartwright. Pleasure."

"Jonathan," Simon repeated.

"It's a very common name for Shadowhunters," said Jon. "After Jonathan Shadowhun—"

"Er, no, I know, I have my copy of the *Codex*," said Simon. Clary had given him hers, actually, and he'd had fun reading the scribbling of practically everybody in the Institute on the pages. He'd felt he was getting to know them, safely away from them where they could not see him fail and expose his gaps of knowledge. "It's just ... I know some people called Jonathan. Not that any of them call themselves Jonathan. Called themselves Jonathan."

He did not remember much about Clary's brother, but he knew his name. He did not particularly want to remember more.

"Oh, right, Jonathan Herondale," said Jon. "Of course you know him. I'm actually pretty good friends with him myself. Taught him a trick or two that probably helped you all out in the demon realms, am I right?"

"Do you mean—Jace?" Simon asked dubiously.

"Yeah, obviously," said Jon. "He's probably mentioned me."

"Not that I recall...," said Simon. "But I do have demon amnesia. So there's that."

Jon nodded and shrugged. "Right. Bummer. He's probably mentioned me and you forgot, on account of the demon amnesia. Not to brag, but we're pretty close, me and Jace."

"I wish I was close to Jace Herondale," Julie sighed. "He is *so* gorgeous."

"He is foxier than a fox fur in a fox hole on fox hunting day," Beatriz agreed dreamily.

"Who's this?" asked Jon, squinting at George, who was leaning back in his chair and looking rather amused.

"Speaking of people being foxy, do you mean? I'm George Lovelace," said George. "I say my surname without shame, because I am secure in my masculinity like that."

"Oh, a Lovelace," said Jon, his brow clearing. "Yeah, you can sit with us."

"I've got to say, my surname has never actually been a selling point before, though," George remarked. "Shadowhunters, go figure."

"Well, you know," said Julie. "You're going to want to hang out with people in your own stream."

"Come again?" Simon asked.

"There are two different streams in the Academy," Beatriz explained. "The stream for mundanes, where they inform the students more fully about the world and give them badly needed basic training, and the stream for real Shadowhunter kids, where we're taught from a more advanced curriculum."

Julie's lip curled. "What Beatriz's saying is, there's the elite and there's the dregs."

Simon stared at them, with a sinking feeling. "So ... I'm going to be in the dregs course."

"No, Simon, no!" Jon exclaimed, looking shocked. "Of course you won't be."

"But I'm a mundane," Simon said again.

"You're not a regular mundane, Simon," Julie told him. "You're an exceptional mundane. That means exceptions are going to be made."

"If anyone tried to put you in with the mundanes, I'd have words with them," Jon continued loftily. "Any friend of Jace Herondale's is, naturally, a friend of mine."

Julie patted Simon's hand. Simon stared at his hand as if it did not belong to him. He did not want to be put in the stream for losers, but he didn't feel comfortable about being assured he would not be either.

But he did think he remembered Isabelle, Jace, and Alec saying some sketchy things about mundanes, now and then. Isabelle, Jace, and Alec weren't so bad. It was just the way they were brought up: They didn't mean what it seemed like they meant. Simon was pretty sure.

Beatriz, who Simon had liked on sight, leaned in across Julie and said: "You've more than earned your place."

She smiled shyly at him. Simon could not help smiling back.

"So ... I'm going to be in the dregs course?" George asked slowly. "I don't know anything about Shadowhunters and Downworlders and demons."

"Oh no," said Jon. "You're a Lovelace. You'll find it will all come very easily to you: It's in your blood."

George bit his lip. "If you say so."

"Most students in the Academy will be in the elite course," Beatriz said hastily. "Our new recruits are mostly like you, George. Shadowhunters are searching all over the world for lost and scattered people with Shadowhunter blood."

"So it's Shadowhunter blood that gets you into the elite stream," George clarified. "And not knowledge at all."

"It's perfectly fair," Julie argued. "Look at Simon. Of course he's in the elite stream. He has proven himself worthy."

"Simon had to save the world, and the rest of us get in because we have the right surname?" George asked lightly. He winked at Simon. "Hard luck on you, mate."

There was an uncomfortable silence around the table, but Simon suspected nobody felt as uncomfortable as he did.

"Sometimes those of Shadowhunter blood are put in the dregs stream, if they disgrace themselves," Julie said shortly. "Mainly, yes, it is reserved for mundanes. That's the way the Academy always worked in the past; it's how it will work in the future. We take some mundanes, those with the Sight or with remarkable athletic promise, into the Academy. It's a wonderful opportunity for them, a chance to become more than they could have ever dreamed. But they cannot keep up with real Shadowhunters. It would hardly be fair to expect them to. They can't all be Simon."

"Some of them simply will not have the aptitude," Jon remarked in a lofty tone. "Some of them won't live through Ascension."

Simon opened his mouth, but before he could ask any further questions he was interrupted by the sound of a lone clap.

"My dear students, my present and future Shadowhunters," said Dean Penhallow, rising from her chair. "Welcome, welcome! To Shadowhunter Academy. It is such a joy to see you all here at the auspicious official opening of the Academy, where we will be training a whole new generation to obey the Law laid down by the Angel. It is an honor to have been chosen to come here, and a joy for us to have you."

Simon looked around. There were about two hundred students here, he thought, uncomfortably crammed around rickety tables. He noticed again that several of them were very young, and grubby and desolate. Simon's heart went out to them, even as he wondered exactly what the running water situation at the Academy was.

Nobody looked as if they felt honored to be here. Simon

found himself wondering again about the Shadowhunters' recruiting methods. Julie talked about them as if they were noble, searching for lost Shadowhunter families and offering mundanes amazing opportunities, but some of these kids looked about twelve. Simon had to wonder what your life must be like, if you were ready to leave it all and go fight demons at twelve.

"There have been a few unexpected losses from the staff, but I'm certain we will do splendidly with the excellent personnel we have remaining," Dean Penhallow continued. "May I introduce Delaney Scarsbury, your training master."

The man sitting next to her got up. He made Jon Cartwright's biceps look like grapes held up to a grapefruit, and he actually had an eye patch, like the angel in the stained-glass window.

Simon turned slowly and looked at George, who he hoped would feel him on this one. He mouthed: *No way.*

George, who obviously did feel him on this one, nodded and mouthed: *Pirate Shadowhunter!*

"I look forward to crushing you all into a pulp and molding that pulp into ferocious warriors," announced Scarsbury.

George and Simon exchanged another speaking glance.

A girl at the table behind Simon began to cry. She looked about thirteen.

"And this is Catarina Loss, a very estimable warlock who will be teaching you a great deal about—history and so on!"

"Yay," said Catarina Loss, with a desultory wave of her blue fingers, as if she'd decided to try clapping without bothering to lift both hands.

The dean soldiered on. "In past years at the Academy,

because Shadowhunters come from all over the globe, every day of the week we would serve a delicious dish from a different nation. We certainly intend to keep up that tradition! But the kitchens are in a slight state of disrepair and for now we have—"

"Soup," said Catarina flatly. "Vats and vats of murky brown soup. Enjoy, kids."

Dean Penhallow continued her one-woman applause. "That's right. Enjoy, everyone. And again, welcome."

There really was nothing on offer but huge metal vats full of very questionable soup.

Simon lined up for food, and peered into the greasy depths of the dark liquid. "Are there alligators in there?"

"I won't make you any promises," said Catarina, inspecting her own bowl.

Simon was exhausted and still starving when he crawled into bed that night. He tried to cheer himself up thinking again about how lately a girl had been on the bed. A girl on his bed for the first time ever, Simon thought, but then memories came like a wisp of cloud over the moon, dimming all certainty. He remembered Clary sleeping in his bed, when they were so little their pajamas had trucks and ponies on them. He remembered kissing Clary, and how she had tasted like fresh lemonade. And he remembered Isabelle, her dark hair flowing over his pillow, her throat bared to him, her toenails scratching his leg, like a sexy vampire movie aside from the bit about the toenails. The other Simon had been not only a hero but a lady-killer. Well, more of a lady-killer than Simon was now.

Isabelle. Simon's mouth moved to form the shape of her name, pressing it into his pillow. He'd told himself he wasn't going to think about her, not until he was really getting somewhere in the Academy. Not until he was on his way to being better, being the person she wanted him to be.

He turned so he was flat on his back and stared up at the stone ceiling.

"Are you awake?" George whispered. "Me too. I keep worrying that the possum will come back. Where did it even come from, Simon? Where did it go?"

The trials of transforming himself into a Shadowhunter became apparent to Simon the very next day.

First, because Scarsbury was measuring them for their gear, which was a terrifying experience on its own. Second, because it involved hurtful personal comments about Simon's physique.

"You have such narrow shoulders," Scarsbury said thoughtfully. "Like a lady."

"I'm lithe," Simon informed him, with dignity.

He looked bitterly over at George, who was lounging on a bench waiting for Simon to finish being measured. George's gear was sleeveless; Julie had already come over to compliment him on how good the fit was and touch his arms.

"Tell you what," said Scarsbury. "I have some gear here meant for a girl—"

"Fine," said Simon. "I mean, terrible, but fine! Give it to me."

Scarsbury shoved the folded black material into Simon's arms. "It's meant for a tall girl," he said in a voice that was possibly intended to be comforting, and definitely too loud.

Everyone looked around and stared at them. Simon prevented himself from taking a sarcastic bow, and stomped off to put on his gear.

After they got gear, they were given weapons. Mundane

students could not wear runes or use steles or most Shadowhunter weapons, so they were all given mundane weapons; it was meant to broaden the Shadowhunter kids' weapons knowledge. Simon feared his own weapons knowledge was as broad as spaghetti.

Dean Penhallow brought around giant boxes of terrifying knives, which seemed very strange in an academic setting, and asked them to select a dagger that suited them.

Simon picked a dagger completely at random, then sat at his desk waggling it about.

Jon nodded to it. "Nice."

"Yeah," Simon said, nodding back and gesturing with it. "That's what I thought. Nice. Very stabby."

He stabbed the dagger into the desk, where it got stuck and Simon had to pry it out of the wood.

Simon thought being trained could not possibly be as bad as being prepared to be trained, but as it turned out it was much worse.

The Academy days were half physical activity. It was like half the day was gym. Stabby, stabby gym.

When they were learning the basics of swordplay, Simon was paired up with the girl he'd noticed in the dining hall, the one who had cried when Scarsbury was introduced.

"She's from the dregs stream, but I understand you're not particularly experienced with swordplay," Scarsbury told him. "If she's not enough of a challenge, let me know."

Simon stared at Scarsbury instead of doing what he wanted to do, which was saying he could not believe an adult was calling someone "dregs" to their face.

He looked at the girl, her dark head bowed, her sword shining in her trembling hand.

"Hey. I'm Simon."

"I know who you are," she muttered.

Right, apparently Simon was a celebrity. If he had all his memories, maybe this would seem normal to him. Maybe he would know that he deserved it, instead of knowing he did not.

"What's your name?" he asked.

"Marisol," she told him reluctantly. She was not shaking anymore, he noted, now that Scarsbury had retreated.

"Don't worry," he said encouragingly. "I'll go easy on you."

"Hmm," said Marisol. She did not look like she was going to cry now; her eyes were narrowed.

Simon was not used to much younger kids, but they were both mundanes. Simon had an awkward fellow feeling. "You settling in okay? Do you miss your parents?"

"I don't have parents," Marisol said in a small, hard voice.

Simon stood stricken. He was such an idiot. He'd thought about it, why mundane kids might come to the Academy. Mundanes would have to choose to give up their parents, their families, their former lives. Unless, of course, they already had no parents and no families. He'd thought about that, but he'd forgotten, obsessing about his own memories and how he would fit in, thinking only about himself. He had a home to go back to, even though it wasn't perfect. He'd had a choice.

"What did the Shadowhunters tell you, when they came to recruit you?"

Marisol stared at him, her gaze clear and cold. "They told me," she said, "that I was going to fight."

She had been taking fencing classes since she could walk, as it turned out. She cut him off at the knees and left him literally in the dust, stumbling as a tiny, swordy whirlwind came at him across the practice grounds, and falling.

He also stabbed himself in the leg with his own sword as he fell, but that was a very minor injury.

"Went a little too easy on her," Jon said, passing by and helping Simon up. "The dregs won't learn if they're not taught, you know."

His voice was kind; his glance at Marisol was not.

"Leave her alone," Simon muttered, but he did not say that Marisol had beaten him fairly. They all thought he was a hero.

Jon grinned at him and walked on. Marisol did not even look at him. Simon studied his leg, which stung.

It was not all stabbing. Some of it was regular stuff, like running, but as Simon tried to run and keep up with people a lot more athletic than he had ever been, he was constantly plagued by memories of how his lungs had never burned for lack of air, how his heart had never pounded from overexertion. He had been fast, once, faster than any of these Shadowhunter trainees, cold and predatory and powerful.

And dead, he reminded himself as he fell behind the others yet again. He didn't want to be dead.

Running was still a lot better than horseback riding. The Academy introduced them to horseback riding on their first Friday there. Simon thought it was supposed to be a treat.

Everyone else acted as if it was a treat. Only those of the elite stream were allowed to go riding, and at mealtimes they had been mocking the dregs for missing out. It seemed to cheer Julie and Jon up, in the face of the endless terrible soup.

Simon, precariously balanced on top of a huge beast that was both rolling its eyes and apparently trying to tap-dance, did not feel this was any sort of treat. The dregs had been sent off to learn elementary facts about Shadowhunting. They had most of their classes apart from the elite, and Jon assured Simon they were boring. Simon felt he could really do with being bored, right about now.

"Si," said George in an undertone. "Quick tip. Riding works better if you keep your eyes open."

"My previous riding experience is the carousel at Central Park," Simon snapped. "Forgive me for not being Mr. Darcy!"

George was, as several of the ladies were remarking, an excellent horseman. He barely had to move for the horse to respond to him, both of them moving smoothly together, sunlight rippling off his stupid curls. He looked right, made it all look easy and graceful, like a knight in the movies. Simon remembered reading books about magic horses that read their rider's every thought, books about horses born of the North Wind. It was all part of being a magical warrior, having a noble steed.

Simon's horse was defective, or possibly a genius that had worked out that Simon could not possibly control it. It went off for a wander in the woods, with Simon on its back alternately pleading, threatening, and offering bribes. If Simon's horse could read his every thought, then Simon's horse was a sadist.

As night drew in and the evening grew cold, the horse wandered back to its stall. Simon had no choice in the matter, but he did manage to tumble off the horse and stagger into the Academy, his fingers and knees gone entirely numb.

"Ah, there you are," said Scarsbury. "George Lovelace was beside himself. He wanted to assemble a search party for you."

Simon regretted his spiteful thoughts about George's horsemanship.

"Let me guess," said Simon. "Everyone else said, 'Nah, being left for dead builds character.'"

"I was not concerned you were going to be eaten by bears in the deep dark woods," said Scarsbury, who did not look as if he had ever been concerned about anything in his life, ever.

"Of course you weren't, that would be abs—"

"You had your dagger," added Scarsbury casually, and walked away, leaving Simon to call after him.

"My—my *bear-killing* dagger? Do you really think me killing bears with a dagger is a plausible scenario? What information do you have about bears in these woods? I think it's your responsibility as an educator to tell me if there are bears in the woods."

"See you at javelin practice bright and early, Lewis," said Scarsbury, and marched on without looking back.

"Are there bears in the woods?" Simon repeated to himself. "It's a simple question. Why are Shadowhunters so bad at simple questions?"

The days passed in a blur of horrible violent activity. If it wasn't javelin practice, Simon was getting thrown around a room (George was very apologetic later, but that did not help). If it wasn't dagger work, it was more swordplay and humiliating defeat before the blades of tiny, evil trainee Shadowhunters. If it wasn't swordplay, it was the obstacle course, and Simon refused to speak of the obstacle course. Julie and Jon were growing noticeably cool at mealtimes, and a few comments about mundies were passed.

At last Simon staggered wearily to the next exercise in futility and sharp objects, and Scarsbury placed a bow in his hands.

"I want everyone to try to hit the targets," said Scarsbury.

"And, Lewis, I want you to try not to hit any of the other trainees."

Simon felt the weight of the bow in his hands. It had a nice balance, he thought, easy to lift and manipulate. He nocked the arrow, and felt the tautness of the string, ready to release, primed to let it fly along the path Simon wanted.

He drew his arm back, and it was that easy: bull's-eye. He fired once more, and then again, arrows flying to find their targets, and his arms burned and his heart pounded with something like joy. He was glad to be able to feel his muscles working and his heart thumping. He was so glad to be alive again, and able to feel every moment of this.

Simon lowered his bow to find everybody staring at him.

"Can you do that again?" asked Scarsbury.

He'd learned to shoot arrows in summer camp, but standing here holding a bow, he remembered something else. He remembered breathing, his heart beating, Shadowhunters watching him. He'd still been human then, a mundane they all despised, but he'd killed a demon. He remembered: He'd seen something had to be done, and he'd done it.

A guy not so different from who he was now.

Simon felt a smile spread across his face, hurting his cheeks. "Yeah. I think I can."

Julie and Jon were both much more friendly over dinner than they had been for the last few days. Simon told them about killing the demon, what he remembered, and Jon offered to teach him some swordplay tricks.

"I would really love to hear more about your adventures," said Julie. "Whatever you can remember. Especially if they involve Jace Herondale. Do you know how he got that sexy scar on his throat?"

"Ah," said Simon. "Actually ... yes. Actually ... that was me."

Everybody stared at him.

"I might have bitten him. A tiny bit. It was more like a nibble, really."

"Was he delicious?" asked Julie, after a thoughtful pause. "He *looks* like he would be delicious."

"Um," said Simon. "He's not a juice box."

Beatriz nodded earnestly. Both the girls seemed very interested in this discussion. Too interested. Their eyes were glazed.

"Did you maybe climb on top of him slowly and then lower your head to his tender, pulsing throat?" Beatriz said. "Could you feel the heat radiating off his body and into yours?"

"Did you lick his throat before you bit him?" Julie asked. "Oh, and did you get a chance to feel his biceps?" She shrugged. "I'm just curious about, you know, vampire techniques."

"I imagine Simon was both gentle and commanding during his special moment with Jace," said Beatriz dreamily. "I mean, it was special, wasn't it?"

"No!" said Simon. "I can't stress that enough. I've bitten several Shadowhunters. I bit Isabelle Lightwood and Alec Lightwood; biting Jace was not a tender and unique moment!"

"You bit Isabelle and Alec Lightwood?!" asked Julie, who was starting to sound freaked-out. "What did the Lightwoods ever do to you?"

"Wow," said George. "I imagined the demon realms were fearsome and terrifying, but seems like it was pretty much nonstop nom nom nom."

"That is not how it was!" Simon said.

"Can we stop talking about this?" Jon demanded, his

voice sharp. "I'm sure you all did what you had to do, but the idea of Shadowhunters being prey for a Downworlder is disgusting."

Simon did not love the way Jon said "Downworlder," as if the words "Downworlder" and "disgusting" were more or less the same thing. But maybe it was natural for Jon to be disturbed. Simon could remember being disturbed about it himself. Simon hadn't wanted to make his friends into his prey either.

Today had gone pretty well. Simon didn't want to ruin it. He decided he was in a good enough mood to let it go.

Simon felt better about the Academy until that night, when he woke from a doze to a deluge of memory.

The memories hit like that sometimes, not in sharp tiny jabs but in an insistent and terrible cascade. He had thought of his former roommate before. He'd known he'd had a friend, a roommate, named Jordan, and that Jordan had been killed. But he hadn't recalled the *feelings* of it—the way Jordan had taken him in when his mother had barred her door, talking about Maia with Jordan, hearing Clary laugh that Jordan was cute, talking to Jordan, patient and kind and always seeing Simon as more than a job, more than a vampire. He remembered seeing Jordan and Jace snarl at each other and then play video games like idiots, and Jordan finding him sleeping in a garage, and Jordan looking at Maia with such regret.

And he remembered holding Jordan's Praetor Lupus pendant in his hands, in Idris, after Jordan was dead. Simon had held that pendant again since then, once he had regained some of his memories, feeling the weight of it and wondering what the Latin motto meant.

He had known Jordan was his roommate, and known he

was one of the many casualties of the war.

He had never truly felt the weight of it, until now.

The sheer weight of memory made him feel as if stones were being piled on his chest, crushing him. Simon couldn't breathe. He erupted from his sheets, swinging his legs over the side of the bed, his feet hitting the stone floor with a shock of cold.

"Wuzz—wuzzit?" mumbled George. "Did the possum come back?"

"Jordan's dead," Simon said bleakly, and put his face in his hands.

There was a silence.

George did not ask him who Jordan had been, or why he suddenly cared. Simon would not have known how to explain the tangle of grief and guilt in his chest: how he hated himself for forgetting Jordan, even though he could not have helped it, how this was like finding out Jordan was dead for the first time and like having a scarred-over wound reopened, both at once. There was a bitter taste in Simon's mouth, like old, old blood.

George reached out and put a hand on Simon's shoulder. He kept it there, grip firm, hand warm and steady, something to anchor Simon in the cold, dark night of memory.

"I'm sorry," he whispered. Simon was sorry too.

At dinner the next day, it was soup again. It had been soup for every meal for many days now. Simon did not remember a life before soup, and he despaired of ever achieving a life after soup. Simon wondered if the Shadowhunters had runes to protect against scurvy.

Their usual group was clustered around their usual table, chatting, when Jon said: "I wish we were being taught about demons by someone with less of an agenda, if you know what I mean."

"Uh," said Simon, who mostly sat through their classes on demons through the ages in deep relief that he was not being asked to move. "Don't we all have the same ... demon-hunting ... agenda?"

"You know what I mean," Jon said. "We've got to be taught about the past crimes of warlocks as well. We have to fight the Downworlders, too. It's naive to pretend they're all tame."

"The Downworlders," Simon repeated. The soup turned to ashes in his mouth, which was actually an improvement. "Like vampires?"

"No!" said Julie hastily. "Vampires are great. They have, you know, class. Compared to the other Downworlders. But if you're talking about creatures like werewolves, Simon, you must see they're not exactly our kind of people. If you can call them people at all."

She said "werewolves" and Simon could not help but think of Jordan, flinching as if he'd been struck and unable to keep his mouth shut a moment longer.

Simon pushed his bowl of soup away and shoved his chair back.

"Don't tell me about what I must, Julie," he said coldly. "I must inform you there are werewolves worth a hundred of your and Jon's Shadowhunter asses. I must say that I am sick to the teeth of you insulting mundanes and telling me I'm your special pet exception, as if I want to be the pet of people who bully kids younger and weaker than they are. And I must tell you, you'd better hope this Academy works out and mundanes like me Ascend, because from all I can see of you, the next generation of Shadowhunters is going to be nothing without us."

He looked toward George, the way he looked to George to share jokes in class and over meals, to see if George agreed with him at all.

George was staring at his plate.

"Come on, man," he muttered. "Don't—don't do this. They'll make you move rooms. Just sit down, and everybody can apologize, and we can go on as we were."

Simon took a deep breath, absorbed the disappointment, and said: "I don't want things to go on as they were. I want things to change."

He turned away from the table, from all of them, marched over to where the dean and Scarsbury were sitting, and announced at the top of his voice: "Dean Penhallow, I want to be placed in the stream for mundanes."

"What?" Scarsbury exclaimed. "The dregs?"

The dean dropped her spoon into her soup with a noisy splash. "The mundane course, Mr. Scarsbury, if you please! Do not refer to our students in that manner. I'm glad you came to me with this, Simon," she said after a moment of hesitation. "I understand you may be having difficulties with the course, given your mundane nature, but—"

"It's not that I'm having difficulty," said Simon. "It's that I'd rather not associate with the elite Shadowhunter families. I just don't think they're my kind of people."

His voice rang out against the stone ceiling. There were a lot of young kids staring at him. One was little Marisol, regarding him with a startled, thoughtful expression. Nobody said anything. They just looked.

"Okay, I've said all I had to say, I'm feeling bashful, and I'm gonna go now," Simon said, and fled the room.

He almost walked right into Catarina Loss, who had been watching from the doorway.

"Sorry," he mumbled.

"Don't be," Catarina said. "In fact, I'm going to come with you. I'll help you pack."

"What?" Simon asked, hurrying after her. "I actually have to move?"

"Yeah, they put the dregs in the underground level," Catarina said.

"They put some kids in the dungeons, and nobody has ever pointed out that this is a disgusting system before now?"

"Is it?" asked Catarina. "Do tell me more about the Shadowhunters, and their occasional tendency to be unfair. I will find it fascinating and surprising. Their excuse is that the lower levels are easier to defend, for the kids who cannot fight as well as their fellow students."

She strode into Simon's room and looked around for his things.

"I actually haven't unpacked very much," Simon said. "I was afraid of the possum in the wardrobe."

"The what?"

"George and I found it very mysterious too," Simon told her earnestly, picking up his bag and stuffing in the few things he had left lying out. He wouldn't want to forget his lady gear.

"Well," Catarina said. "Whatever about possums. The point I want to make is ... I may have gotten you wrong, Simon."

Simon blinked. "Oh?"

Catarina smiled at him. It was astonishing, like a blue sunrise. "I was not looking forward to coming to teach here. Shadowhunters and Downworlders do not get along, and I try to keep myself more separated from the Nephilim even than most others of my kind. But I had a dear friend called Ragnor Fell, who used to live in Idris and taught in the Academy for decades before it was closed. He never had the greatest opinion of Shadowhunters, but he was fond of this place. I—lost him recently, and I knew this place could not operate without teachers. I wanted to do something in memory of him, even though I hated the idea of teaching a pack of arrogant Nephilim brats. But I loved my friend more than I hate Shadowhunters."

Simon nodded. He thought of his remembrance of Jordan, thought of how it hurt to even look at Isabelle and Clary. Without memory, they were lost. And nobody wanted someone they loved to be lost.

"So I may have been a little cranky about coming," Catarina admitted. "I may have been a little cranky about you, because—from all I know, you didn't think much of being a vampire. And now you're cured, what a miracle, and the Shadowhunters are so quick to pull you into the fold. You truly get to be one of them, what you always wanted. You had the stain of being one of us wiped away."

"I didn't...," Simon said, and swallowed. "I can't remember it all. So it's like defending the actions of someone else sometimes."

"Must be frustrating."

Simon laughed. "You have no idea. I don't—I didn't want to be a vampire, I don't think. I wouldn't want to be made one again. Being stuck at age sixteen when all my friends and my family would've grown up without me; having the urge to—to hurt people? I didn't want any of that. But—look, I don't remember much, but I remember enough. I remember I was a person back then, just as much as I am now. Becoming a Shadowhunter won't change that, if I ever do become a Shadowhunter. I've forgotten enough. I will not forget that."

He lifted his bag onto his shoulder, and gestured for Catarina to lead the way to his new room. She did, descending down stone steps Simon had figured were to the basement. He had not figured they kept kids in the basement.

It was dark on the stairs. Simon put a hand to the wall to steady himself, and then snatched it back.

"Oh, disgusting!"

"Yes, most of the subterranean surfaces are coated in black slime," said Catarina, in a matter-of-fact tone. "Watch yourself."

"Thank you. Thanks for that warning."

"You're welcome," said Catarina, a hint of a laugh in her voice. For the first time, it occurred to Simon that Catarina might actually be nice. "You said—if you ever do become a Shadowhunter. Are you thinking about leaving?"

"Now that I've touched the slime, I am," Simon muttered. "No. I don't know what I want, except that I don't want to give up yet."

He almost reconsidered when Catarina led him to his room. It was much darker than the last room, though laid out in the same way. The wooden bedposts of the two narrow beds looked decayed, and in the corners of the room the black slime had grown almost viscous, turning into tiny black slime waterfalls.

"I don't remember hell all that well," Simon said. "But I think I recall it was nicer than this."

Catarina laughed, then shocked Simon by leaning in and giving him a peck on the cheek. "Good luck, Daylighter," she told him, laughing at his expression. "And whatever you do, don't use the bathrooms on this floor. Not on any floor, obviously, but especially on this one!"

Simon did not ask her to explain, because he was terrified. He sat down on his new bed, and then stood hastily back up at the resulting long creak and cloud of dust. Hey, at least this time he didn't have a roommate—he was king of this claustrophobic, slimy domain. He set his mind to unpacking. The wardrobe in this room was actually clean and empty, which was a definite improvement. Simon might go live in the wardrobe with his funny T-shirts.

He was long finished unpacking by the time George sauntered in, dragging his suitcase behind him and bearing his broken racket on his shoulder like a sword. "Hey, man."

"Hey," Simon said cautiously. "Er, what—what are you doing here?"

George dumped his suitcase and his racket on the slimy floor, and threw himself down on the bed. He stretched luxuriously, ignoring the ominous creak of the bed beneath him.

"The thing is, the advanced course is actually pretty hard," George said, as Simon started to smile. "And you may have heard: Lovelaces are quitters."

Simon was even more relieved to have George the next day, so they could sit together rather than at one of the tables of thirteen-year-old mundanes, who were all giving them the side-eye when they were not whispering brokenly about their phones.

The day brightened further when Beatriz plopped down at their new table as well.

"I'm not going to drop out of advanced training to follow you around like Curlytop here," Beatriz announced, "but we can still be friends, right?"

She pulled George's hair affectionately.

"Be careful," George said in a tired, humble voice. "I

did not sleep in our small, slimy room. There is, I believe, a creature living in our walls. I hear it. Scuttling. I have to admit, I may not have made the brightest decision in following Simon. It's possible I'm not that bright. It's possible that looks are all I have."

"Actually ... even though I'm not willing to follow you into boring classes and the endless disrespect of my classmates ... I think it was a very cool thing you did, Simon," said Beatriz.

She smiled, teeth flashing white against her brown skin, and her smile was warm and admiring—about the nicest thing Simon had seen all day.

"You're right, our morals are sound even though our walls are infested. And we'll still have some interesting classes, Si," George said. "Plus, don't worry, we still get sent on missions to fight demons and rogue Downworlders."

Simon choked on his soup. "I was not worrying about that. Are any of our teachers at all worried that sending out people with no superpowers to fight demons might prove just a teeny bit, not to put too fine a point on it, fatal?"

"They have to face trials of courage before they must face Ascension," said Beatriz. "Better for them to drop out because they are scared, or even because a demon ate their leg, than to have them try to Ascend without being suitable, and die in the attempt."

"That's a cool, cheerful, and normal thing to say," Simon said. "Shadowhunters are great at saying normal things."

"Well, I'm looking forward to the missions," said George. "And tomorrow a Shadowhunter is coming in to give a guest lecture on the lesser-utilized weapons. I hope there'll be a practical demonstration."

"Not in a classroom," said Beatriz. "Think of what one

heavy-duty crossbow could do to the walls."

That was all the warning Simon got before he clattered happily into class the next day, George on his heels, and found Dean Penhallow already there, talking with nervous good cheer. The classroom was very full—both the regular stream and the mundane stream were in attendance.

"—despite her tender years, a Shadowhunter of some renown and noted expertise with less-used weapons such as the whip. May I welcome to Shadowhunter Academy our first guest lecturer: Isabelle Lightwood!"

Isabelle turned, sleek black hair flaring around her shoulders and black skirt flaring around her pale legs. She was wearing glittery plum lipstick, so dark it looked almost black. Her eyes did look black, but another small knife of memory pierced Simon, of course at the worst time possible: He remembered the colors of her eyes from close up, very dark brown, like brown velvet, so close to black as to make no difference, but with paler rings of color...

He stumbled over to his desk, and folded into his chair with a thump.

When the dean left, Isabelle turned and regarded her class with absolute contempt.

"I am not actually here to instruct any of you idiots," she told them, walking up and down the rows of desks. "If you want to use a whip, train with one, and if you lose an ear, don't be a big whiny baby."

Several of the boys nodded, as if hypnotized. Almost all the boys were watching Isabelle as if they were a nest of snakes intent on being charmed. Some of the girls were watching her that way too.

"I am here," Isabelle announced, finishing her prowl of

the perimeter and turning to face them all again with snapping eyes, "to determine my relationship."

Simon goggled. She couldn't be talking about him. Could she?

"Do you see that man?" Isabelle asked, pointing at Simon. Apparently she *was* talking about him. "That's Simon Lewis, and he is *my boyfriend.* So if any of you think about trying to hurt him because he's a mundie or—may the Angel have mercy on your soul—pursuing him romantically, I will come after you, I will hunt you down, and I will crush you to powder."

"We're just bros," said George hastily.

Beatriz edged her desk away from Simon's.

Isabelle lowered her hand. The flush of excitement was receding from her face as well, as though she had come to say what she had said, and now that she was out of adrenaline she was actually processing what had come out of her mouth.

"I am going to go now," Isabelle announced. "Thank you for your attention. Class dismissed."

She turned and walked out of the room.

"I have to—" Simon began, rising from his desk on legs that felt a little unsteady. "I have to go."

"Yeah, you do," George said.

Simon went out the door, and ran down the stone corridors of the Academy. He knew Isabelle was fast, so he ran, faster than he'd ever run on the training grounds, and he caught up to her in the hall. She stopped in the dim light of the stained-glass window as he called her name.

"Isabelle!"

She stood waiting for him. Her lips parted and gleamed, like plums under a winter frost, ready to be tasted. Simon could see himself running up to her, catching her in his arms, and kissing her mouth, knowing what it had taken for her to do that—his brave, brilliant Isabelle—and carried away in a whirl of love and joy, but he saw it as if through a pane of glass, as if looking into another dimension, one he could see but not quite touch.

Simon felt a hot pang of grief through his whole body, not just through his chest, as if he had been struck by lightning. But he had to say it.

"I'm not your boyfriend, Isabelle," he called out.

She went white. Simon was horrified by how badly his words had come out.

"I mean, I can't be your boyfriend, Isabelle," he said. "I'm not him—that guy who was your boyfriend. That guy you want."

He almost said: *I wish I could be.* He had wished he could be. That was why he had come to the Academy, to learn how to be that guy they all wanted back. He'd wanted to be that way, be an awesome hero like in a game or a movie. He'd been so sure, at first, that was what he wanted.

Except wishing he could be that guy was like wishing to obliterate the guy he was now: the normal, happy guy in a band, who could still love his mother, who did not wake up in the coldest, darkest hour of the night weeping for dead friends.

And he did not know if he could be that guy she wanted, whether he wished it or not.

"You remember everything, and I—I don't remember enough," Simon went on. "I hurt you when I don't mean to, and I thought I could come to the Academy and come back better, but it's not looking good. The whole game has changed. My skill level has decreased and the difficulty level has been jacked up to impossible—"

"Simon," Isabelle interrupted, "you're talking like a nerd."

She said it almost fondly, but it freaked Simon out more. "And I don't know how to be smooth, sexy vampire Simon for you, either!"

Isabelle's perfect mouth curved, like a dark half-moon in her pale face. "You were never that smooth, Simon."

"Oh," said Simon. "Oh, thank God. I know you've had a lot of boyfriends. I remember there was a faerie, and"—another flash of memory, this time most unwelcome—"a ... Lord Montgomery? You dated a member of the nobility? How am I ever going to compete with that?"

Isabelle still looked fond, but it was diluted with a good deal of impatience. "You're Lord Montgomery, Simon!"

"I don't understand," said Simon. "When you're made a vampire, are you also given a title?"

Maybe that made sense. Vampires were aristocratic.

Isabelle put her fingers up to touch her brow. It was a gesture that seemed like disdainful weariness, like Isabelle was tired of all this, but Simon saw the way her eyes closed, as if she could not look at him when she spoke. "It was just a joke between you and me, Simon."

Simon was tired of all this: of knowing pieces of her so well and others not at all, of knowing he was not what she wanted.

"No," he said. "It was a joke between you and him."

"You are him, Simon!"

"I'm not," Simon told her. "I don't—I don't know how to be, that's what I've been realizing all this time. I thought I could learn to be him, but since I got to the Academy I learned that I can't. I can't experience everything we did over again. I'm never going to be the guy who did all that. I'm going to do different things. I'm going to be a different guy."

"Once you Ascend, you'll get all your memories back!" Isabelle shouted at him.

"If I Ascend, it will be in two years. I'm not going to be the same guy in two years, even if I do get all the memories back, because there will be so many other memories. You're not going to be the same girl. I know you believed in me, Isabelle, I know you believed because you—you cared about him. That means more than I can tell you. But, Isabelle, Isabelle, it isn't fair of me to take advantage of your belief. It isn't fair to keep you waiting for him, when he isn't ever coming back."

Isabelle had her arms crossed, fingers curled into the dark plum velvet of her own jacket as if she was offering herself comfort. "None of this is fair. It isn't fair that part of your life was ripped from you. It's not fair that you were ripped away from me. I'm so angry, Simon."

Simon took a step toward her and took one of her hands, uncurling her fingers from her jacket. He did not take her in his arms but he stood a little distance away from her, their hands linked across the distance. Her trembling mouth sparkled, and so did her eyelashes. He did not know if this was indomitable Isabelle crying, or whether it was sparkly mascara. All he knew was that she shone, like a constellation in the shape of a girl.

"Isabelle," he said. "Isabelle."

She was so much herself, and he had scarcely any idea who he was.

"Do you know why you're here?" she demanded.

He just looked at her. There were so many things that question could mean, and so many ways to answer.

"I mean at the Academy," she said. "Do you know why you want to be a Shadowhunter?"

He hesitated. "I wanted to be that guy again," he said.

"That hero that you all remember ... and this seems like a training school for heroes."

"It's not," Isabelle said flatly. "It's a training school for Shadowhunters. And yeah, I think that's a pretty cool thing, and yeah, I think protecting the world is pretty heroic. But there are cowardly Shadowhunters and evil Shadowhunters and hopeless Shadowhunters. If you're going to get through the Academy, you have to figure out why *you* want to be a *Shadowhunter* and what that means to *you*, Simon. Not just why you want to be special."

He winced, but it was true. "You're right. I don't know. I know that I want to be here. I know I need to be here. Believe me, if you'd seen the bathrooms, you'd know I didn't make this decision lightly."

She gave him a withering look.

"But," he said, "I don't know why. I don't know myself well enough yet. I know what I said to you, at first, and I know what you hoped. That I could turn back into who I was before. I was really wrong and I am really sorry."

"*Sorry?*" Isabelle demanded. "Do you know what a big deal it was for me to come here, to make a fool of myself in front of all these people? Do you know—of course you don't. You don't want me to believe in you? You don't want me to choose you?"

Isabelle pulled her hands away from him, turned her face away as she had in the garden of the Institute that was her home. This time Simon knew it was absolutely his fault.

She was already leaving as she said:

"Have it your way, Simon Lewis. I won't."

Simon was so depressed after Isabelle had gone—after he had driven her away—that he didn't think he'd ever move off his cot bed again. He lay there, listening to George chatter and scrub the walls. He'd removed an impressive amount of the slime.

Simon retreated to where he believed nobody would ever find him. He went and sat in the bathroom. The stone flags were cracked in the bathrooms; there was something dark in one of the toilets. Simon hoped it was just a result of people throwing away the soup.

He had half an hour of peace in the bathroom, alone with the horrible toilets, until George poked his head around the door.

"Hey, buddy," said George. "Do not use these bathrooms. I cannot stress that enough."

"I'm not going to use the bathroom," Simon said drearily. "I'm a mess, but I'm not an idiot. I just wanted to be alone and think depressing thoughts. You want to know a secret?"

George was silent for a moment. "If you want to tell me. You don't have to. We all have secrets."

"I chased away the most amazing girl I have ever met, because I'm too much of a loser to manage being myself. That's my secret: I want to be a hero, but I'm not one. Everybody thinks I'm some amazing warrior who summoned angels and rescued Shadowhunters and saved the world, but it's a joke. I can't even remember what I did. I can't imagine how I did it. I'm no one special, and no one's going to be fooled for long, and I don't even know what I'm doing here. So. You have a secret that can beat that?"

There was a low gurgle from one of the toilets. Simon did not even look toward it. He was not interested in investigating that sound.

"I'm not a Shadowhunter at all," George said in a rush.

Sitting on a bathroom floor was not an ideal way to

receive monumental revelations. Simon frowned. "You're not a Lovelace?"

"No, I'm a Lovelace." George's normally lighthearted voice was stern. "But I'm not a Shadowhunter. I'm adopted. The Shadowhunters who came to recruit me didn't even think of that—of people with Shadowhunter blood wanting mundane children, giving them Shadowhunter names and thinking of them as their own. I was always planning to tell the truth, but I figured it would be easier when I got here—less trouble to decide to let me stay than to work out whether they wanted to bring me. And then I met the others, and I started the course, and I figured out I could keep up with them pretty easily. I saw what they thought of mundanes. I figured it wouldn't do any harm to keep the secret and stay in the elite class and be like the rest of the guys, just for a while."

George shoved his hands in his pockets, and stared at the floor.

"But I'd met you, too, and you didn't have any special powers, and you'd already done more than all the rest of them put together. You do things now, like transfer to the mundane class when you didn't have to, and that made me man up and tell the dean I was a mundie and get transferred too. You did that. The way you are now, okay? So stop talking about what a loser you are, because I wouldn't follow a loser into a slime-covered bedroom or a slime-covered bathroom, and I've followed you into both." George paused and said aggressively: "And I would really like to change the phrasing of that last sentence, because it sounded so bad, but I'm not sure how."

"I'll take it in the spirit it was meant," said Simon. "And I—I'm really glad you told me. I was hoping for a cool mundie roommate from the start."

"Wanna know another secret?" George asked.

Simon was slightly terrified of another revelation, and worried George was a secret agent, but he nodded anyway.

"Everybody in this academy, Shadowhunters and mundanes, people with the Sight and without it, every one of them is looking to be a hero. We are all hoping for it, and trying for it, and soon we will be bleeding for it. You're just like the rest of us, Si. Except there's one thing about you that's different: We all want to be heroes, but you know you can be one. You know in another life, in an alternate universe, however you want to think of it, you were a hero. You can be one again. Maybe not the same hero, but you have it in you to make the right choices, to make the big sacrifices. That's a lot of pressure. But it's a lot more hope than any of the rest of us have. Think about it that way, Simon Lewis, and I think you're pretty lucky."

Simon had not thought about it that way. He'd just kept thinking that a switch was going to be flipped, and he was going to be special again. But Isabelle was right: This could not just be about being special. He remembered seeing the Academy for the first time, how glamorous and impressive it had looked from a distance, and how different it had looked close up. He was starting to think the process of becoming a Shadowhunter was the same way. He was starting to believe it would all be cutting himself with a sword and having his horse run away with him, eating terrible soup and scraping slime off the walls, and figuring out slowly and awkwardly who he really wanted to be, this time around.

George leaned against the bathroom wall, which was an obviously rash and dangerous move, and grinned at him. Seeing that grin, seeing George refuse to be serious for more than a second, reminded Simon of something else about his first day at the Academy. It reminded him of hope.

"Speaking of luck, Isabelle Lightwood is a total babe. Actually, she's better than a babe: She's a hero. She came all the way here to tell the world you were hers. You're telling me she doesn't know another hero when she sees one? You're going to figure out what you're doing here. Isabelle Lightwood believes in you, and for what it's worth, I do too."

Simon stared up at George.

"It's worth a lot," he said finally. "Thanks for saying all that."

"You're welcome. Now please get up off the floor," George implored. "It is so nasty."

Simon did get up off the floor. He left the bathroom, George ahead of him, and both of them almost plowed into Catarina Loss, who was dragging a huge covered tureen over the flagstones with a scraping sound.

"Ms. Loss...," said Simon. "Can I ask you—what you're doing?"

"Dean Penhallow has decided that she is not going to order fresh food supplies until all this delicious, nutritious soup has been consumed. So I am going to bury this soup in the woods," announced Catarina Loss. "Grab the other handle."

"Huh. Okay, good plan," said Simon, grabbing the other handle of the tureen and falling in with Catarina. George followed them as they went, unsteadily balancing the soup tureen between them. As they walked through the drafty, echoing corridors of the Academy, Simon added: "I just have one quick question about the woods. And bears."

The Lost Herondale

By Cassandra Clare and Robin Wasserman

Simon was about to argue, again, when a shining whip lashed out of the shadows and wrapped around the girl's neck. It yanked her off her feet and she landed hard, head cracking against the cement floor.

—The Lost Herondale

KRAK
ISABELLE?
WHY-
YOU'RE WELCOME.

There was a time, not long ago, when Simon Lewis had been convinced that all gym teachers were actually demons escaped from some hell dimension, nourishing themselves on the agonies of uncoordinated youth.

Little did he know he'd been almost right.

Not that Shadowhunter Academy had *gym* class, not exactly. And his physical trainer, Delaney Scarsbury, wasn't so much a demon as a Shadowhunter who probably thought lopping the heads off a few multiheaded hellbeasts comprised an ideal Saturday night—but as far as Simon was concerned, these were technicalities.

"Lewis!" Scarsbury shouted, looming over Simon, who lay flat on the ground, trying to will himself to do another push-up. "What are you waiting for, an engraved invitation?"

Scarsbury's legs were as thick as tree trunks, and his biceps were no less depressingly huge. This, at least, was one difference between the Shadowhunter and Simon's mundane gym teachers, most of whom could barely have bench-pressed a bag of potato chips. Also, none of Simon's gym teachers had worn an eye patch or carried a sword carved with runes and blessed by angels.

But in all the ways that counted, Scarsbury was exactly the same.

"Everyone get a look at Lewis!" he called to the rest of the class, as Simon levered himself into a shaky plank position, willing himself not to do a belly flop into the dirt. Again. "Our hero here might just defeat his evil spaghetti arms after all."

Gratifyingly, only one person laughed. Simon recognized the distinctive snicker of Jon Cartwright, eldest son of a distinguished Shadowhunter family (as he'd be the first to tell you). Jon believed he was born for greatness and seemed especially irritated that Simon—a hapless mundane—had managed to get there first. Even if he could no longer remember doing it. Jon, of course, was the one who'd started calling Simon "our hero." And like all evil gym teachers before him, Scarsbury had been only too happy to follow the popular kid's lead.

Shadowhunter Academy had two tracks, one for the Shadowhunter kids who'd grown up in this world and whose blood destined them for demon-fighting, and one for the mundanes, clueless, lacking in genetic destiny, and scrambling to catch up. They spent most of the day in separate classes, the mundanes studying rudimentary martial arts and memorizing the finer points of the Nephilim Covenant, the Shadowhunters focusing on more advanced skills: juggling throwing stars and studying Chthonian and Marking themselves up with runes of obnoxious superiority and who knew what else. (Simon was still hoping that somewhere in the Shadowhunter manual was the secret of the Vulcan death grip. After all, as his instructors kept reminding them: All the stories are true.) But the two tracks began every day together: Every student, no matter how inexperienced or advanced, was expected to report to the training field at sunrise for a grueling hour of calisthenics. *Divided we stand*, Simon thought, his stubborn biceps refusing to bulge. *United we do push-ups.*

When he'd told his mother he wanted to go to military school so he could toughen up, she'd given him a strange look. (Not as strange as if he'd said he wanted to go to demon-fighting school so he could drink from the Mortal Cup, Ascend to the ranks of Shadowhunter, and just maybe get back the memories that had been stolen from him in a nearby hell dimension, but close.) The look said: *My son, Simon Lewis, wants to sign up for a life where you have to do a hundred push-ups before breakfast?*

He knew this, because he could read her pretty well—but also because once she'd regained the ability to speak, she'd said, "My son, Simon Lewis, wants to sign up for a life where you have to do a hundred push-ups before breakfast?" Then she'd asked him teasingly if he was possessed by some evil creature, and he'd pretended to laugh, trying for once to ignore the tendrils of memory from that other life, his *real* life. The one where he'd been turned into a vampire and his mother had called him a monster and barricaded him from the house. Sometimes, Simon thought he would do anything to get back the memories that had been taken from him—but there were moments when he wondered whether some things were better left forgotten.

Scarsbury, more demanding than any drill sergeant, made his young charges do *two hundred* push-ups every morning ... but he did, at least, let them eat breakfast first.

After the push-ups came the laps. After the laps came the lunges. And after the lunges—

"After you, hero," Jon sneered, offering Simon first shot at the climbing wall. "Maybe if we give you a head start, we won't have to wait around so long for you to catch up."

Simon was too exhausted for a snarky comeback. And definitely too exhausted to claw his way up the climbing wall, one impossibly distant handhold at a time. He made it up a few feet, at least, then paused to give his shrieking muscles a rest. One by one, the other students scrambled up past him, none of them seeming even slightly out of breath.

"Be a hero, Simon," Simon muttered bitterly, remembering the life Magnus Bane had dangled before him in their first meeting—or at least, the first one Simon could remember. "Have an adventure, Simon. How about, turn your life into one long agonizing gym class, Simon."

"Dude, you're talking to yourself again." George Lovelace, Simon's roommate and only real friend at the Academy, hoisted himself up beside Simon. "You losing your grip?"

"I'm talking to myself, not little green men," Simon clarified. "Still sane, last I checked."

"No, I mean"—George nodded toward Simon's sweaty fingers, which had gone pale with the effort of holding his weight—"your grip."

"Oh. Yeah. I'm peachy," Simon said. "Just giving you guys a head start. I figure in battle conditions, it's always the red shirts who go in first, you know?"

George's brow furrowed. "Red shirts? But our gear is black."

"No, *red shirts*. Cannon fodder. *Star Trek?* Any of this ringing a..." Simon sighed at the blank look on George's face. George had grown up in an isolated rural pocket of Scotland, but it wasn't like he'd lived without Internet and cable TV. The problem, as far as Simon could tell, was that the Lovelaces watched nothing but soccer and used their Wi-Fi almost exclusively to monitor Dundee United stats and occasionally to buy sheep feed in bulk. "Forget it. I'm fine. See you at the top."

George shrugged and returned to his climb. Simon watched his roommate—a tan, muscled Abercrombie-model type—swing himself up the plastic rock handholds as effortlessly as Spider-Man. It was ridiculous: George wasn't even a Shadowhunter, not by blood. He'd been adopted by a Shadowhunting family, which made him just as much a mundane as Simon. Except that, like most of the other mundanes—and very *un*like Simon—he was a near-perfect specimen of humanity. Repulsively athletic, coordinated, strong and swift, and as close to a Shadowhunter as you could get without the blood of the angels running through your veins. In other words: a jock.

Life at Shadowhunter Academy was lacking in a lot of things Simon had once believed he couldn't survive without: computers, music, comic books, indoor plumbing. Over the past couple of months, he'd gotten mostly used to doing without, but there was one glaring absence he still couldn't wrap his head around.

Shadowhunter Academy had no nerds.

Simon's mother had once told him that the thing she loved most about being Jewish was that you could step into a synagogue anywhere on earth and feel like you'd come home. India, Brazil, New Zealand, even Mars—if you could rely on *Shalom, Spacemen!*, the homemade comic book that had been the highlight of Simon's third-grade Hebrew school experience. Jews everywhere prayed with the same language, the same melodies, the same words. Simon's mother had told her son that as long as he could always find people who spoke the language of his soul, he would never be alone.

And she'd turned out to be right. As long as Simon could find people who spoke his language—the language of Dungeons & Dragons and World of Warcraft, the language of *Star Trek* and manga and indie rockers with songs like "Han Shot First" and "What the Frak"—he felt like he was among friends.

These Shadowhunters in training, on the other hand? Most of them probably thought manga was some kind of demonic athlete's foot. Simon was doing his best to educate them to the finer things in life, but guys like George Lovelace had about as much aptitude for twelve-sided dice as Simon did for ... well, anything more physically complex than walking and chewing gum at the same time.

As Jon had predicted, Simon was the last one left on the climbing wall. By the time the others had ascended, rung the tiny bell at the top, and rappelled to the ground again, he'd made it only ten meters off the ground. The last time that had happened, Scarsbury, who had an impressive flair for sadism, had made the entire class sit and watch as Simon painstakingly made his way to the top. This time, their trainer cut the torture session mercifully short.

"Enough!" Scarsbury shouted, clapping his hands together. Simon wondered whether there was such a thing as a runed whistle. Maybe he could get Scarsbury one for Christmas. "Lewis, put us all out of our misery and get down from there. The rest of you, hit the weapons room, pick yourself out a sword, then pair up for scrimmage." His iron grip closed over Simon's shoulder. "Not so fast, hero. You stay behind."

Simon wondered whether this was it, the moment that his heroic past was finally overpowered by his hapless present, and he was about to be kicked out of school. But then Scarsbury called out other names—among them Lovelace, Cartwright, Beauvale, Mendoza—most of them Shadowhunters, all of them the best students in the class, and Simon let himself relax, just a little. Whatever it was Scarsbury had to say, it couldn't be that bad, not if he was also saying it to Jon Cartwright, gold medalist in sucking up.

"Sit," Scarsbury boomed.

They sat.

"You're here because you're the twenty most promising students in the class," Scarsbury said, pausing to let the compliment settle over them. Most of the students beamed. Simon willed himself to disappear. More like the nineteen most promising students and the one still coasting on the achievements of his past self. He felt like he was eight years old again, overhearing his mother bully the Little League coach into letting him take a turn at bat. "We've got a Downworlder that broke the Law and needs taking care of," Scarsbury continued, "and the powers that be have decided it's the perfect opportunity for you boys to become men."

Marisol Rojas Garza, a scrawny thirteen-year-old mundane with a permanent *I will kick your ass* expression, cleared her throat loudly.

"Er ... men and women," Scarsbury clarified, looking none too happy about it.

Murmurs rippled across the students, excitement mixed with alarm. None of them had expected a real training mission this soon. Behind Simon, Jon faked a yawn. "Boring. I could kill a rogue Downworlder in my sleep."

Simon, who actually *did* kill rogue Downworlders in his sleep, along with the terrifying tentacled demons and Endarkened Shadowhunters and other bloodthirsty monsters that crawled through his nightmares, didn't feel much like yawning. He felt more like throwing up.

George raised his hand. "Uh, sir, some of us here are still"—he swallowed, and, not for the first time, Simon wondered whether he regretted admitting the truth about himself; the Academy was a much easier place to be when you were on the elite Shadowhunter track, and not just because the elites didn't have to sleep in the dungeon—"mundanes."

"I noticed that myself, Lovelace," Scarsbury said dryly. "Imagine my surprise when I discovered some of you dregs are worth something after all."

"No, I mean..." George hesitated, substantially more easily intimidated than any six-foot-five Scottish sex god (Beatriz Velez Mendoza's description, according to her big-mouthed best friend) had a right to be. Finally, he squared his shoulders and plowed forward. "I mean we're *mundanes*. We can't be Marked, we can't use seraph blades or witchlight or anything, we don't have, like, superspeed and angelic reflexes. Going after a Downworlder when we've only had a couple months of training ... isn't that dangerous?"

A vein in Scarsbury's neck began to throb alarmingly, and his good eye bulged so far out of his head Simon feared it might pop. (Which, he thought, could finally explain the mysterious eye patch.) "Dangerous? *Dangerous?*" he boomed. "Anyone else here afraid of a little *danger?*"

If they were, they were even more afraid of Scarsbury, and so kept their mouths shut. He let the silence hang, thick and angry, for an agonizing minute. Then he scowled at George. "If you're afraid of dangerous situations, boy, you're in the wrong place. And as for the rest of you dregs, best you find out now whether you've got what it takes. If you don't, then drinking from the Mortal Cup will kill you, and trust me, mundies, getting bled dry by a bloodsucker would be a much kinder way to go." He'd fixed his gaze on Simon, maybe because Simon had once *been* a bloodsucker, or maybe because he now seemed the most likely to get drained by one.

It occurred to Simon that Scarsbury could be hoping for that outcome—that he'd selected Simon for this mission in hopes of getting rid of his biggest problem student. Though surely no Shadowhunter, even a Shadowhunting gym teacher, would stoop so low?

Something in Simon, some ghost of a memory, warned him not to be so sure.

"Is that understood?" Scarsbury said. "Is there anyone here who wants to go running to mommy and daddy crying 'please save me from the big, bad vampire'?"

Dead silence.

"Excellent," Scarsbury said. "You have two days to train. Then just keep reminding yourself how impressed all your little friends will be when you come back." He chuckled. "If you come back."

The student lounge was dark and musty, lit by flickering candlelight and watched over by the glowering visages of Shadowhunters past, Herondales and Lightwoods and even the occasional Morgenstern peering down from heavy gilt frames, their bloody triumphs preserved in fading oil paint. But it had several obvious advantages over Simon's bedroom: It wasn't in the dungeon, it wasn't splattered with black slime, it didn't carry the faint whiff of what might have been moldy socks but might have been the bodies of former students decaying under the floorboards, it didn't have what sounded like a large and boisterous family of rats scrabbling behind the walls. But the one notable advantage of his room, Simon was reminded that night, while camped out in a corner playing cards with George, was the guarantee that Jon Cartwright and his Shadowhunter-track groupies would never, ever deign to cross the threshold.

"No sevens," George said, as Jon, Beatriz, and Julie swept into the lounge. "Go fish."

As Jon and the two girls approached, Simon suddenly got *very* interested in the card game. Or, at least, he did his best. At a normal boarding school, there'd be a TV in the lounge, instead of a gigantic portrait of Jonathan Shadowhunter, his eyes blazing as bright as his sword. There'd be music leaking out of the dorm rooms and mingling in the corridor, some of it good, some of it Phish; there'd be e-mail and texting and Internet porn. At the Academy, after-hours options were more limited: There was studying the *Codex*, and there was sleep. Playing cards was about as close as he could get to gaming, and when he went too long without gaming, Simon got a little itchy. It turned out that when you spent all day training to defeat actual, real-world monsters, Dungeons & Dragons questing lost a bit of its luster—or at least, so claimed George and every other student Simon had tried to recruit for a campaign—which left him with old half-forgotten summer camp standards: Hearts, Egyptian Ratscrew, and, of course, Go Fish. Simon stifled a yawn.

Jon, Beatriz, and Julie stood beside them, waiting to be acknowledged. Simon hoped if he waited long enough, they'd just go away. Beatriz wasn't so bad, at least not on her own. But Julie could have been carved out of ice. She had suspiciously few physical flaws—the silky blond hair of a Barbie doll, the porcelain skin of a cosmetics model, better curves than any of the bikini-girl posters papering Eric's garage—and wore the hawkish expression of someone on a search-and-destroy mission for any weakness whatsoever. All that, and she carried a sword.

Jon, of course, was Jon.

Shadowhunters didn't practice magic—that was a fundamental tenet of their beliefs—so it was unlikely that the Academy would teach Simon a way to make Jon Cartwright vanish into another dimension. But a guy could dream.

They didn't go away. Finally, George, congenitally incapable of being rude, set down his cards.

"Can we help you?" George asked, a sliver of ice cooling his Scottish brogue. Jon's and Julie's friendliness had melted away once they learned the truth about George's mundane blood, and though George never said anything about it, he clearly had neither forgiven nor forgotten.

"Actually, yes," Julie said. She nodded at Simon. "Well, *you* can."

Finding out about the imminent vampire-killing mission hadn't exactly tied a bright yellow ribbon around Simon's day; he wasn't in the mood. "What do you want?"

Julie looked awkwardly at Beatriz, who stared down at her feet. "You ask," Beatriz murmured.

"Better if you do," Julie shot back.

Jon rolled his eyes. "Oh, by the Angel! I'll do it." He pulled himself up to his full, impressive height, rested his hands on his hips, and peered down his regal nose at Simon. It had the look of a pose practiced in the mirror. "We want you to tell us about vampires."

Simon grinned. "What do you want to know? Scariest is Eli in *Let the Right One In*, cheesiest is late-era Lestat, most underrated is David Bowie in *The Hunger*. Sexiest is definitely Drusilla, though if you ask a girl, she'll probably say Damon Salvatore or Edward Cullen. But..." He shrugged. "You know girls."

Julie's and Beatriz's eyes were wide. "I didn't think you'd know so many!" Beatriz exclaimed. "Are they ... are they your friends?"

"Oh, sure, Count Dracula and I are like this," Simon said, crossing his fingers to demonstrate. "Also Count Chocula. Oh, and my BFF Count Blintzula. He's a real charmer..." He trailed off as he realized no one else was laughing. In fact, no one seemed to realize he was joking. "They're from TV," he prompted them. "Or, uh, cereal."

"What's he talking about?" Julie asked Jon, perfect nose wrinkling up in confusion.

"Who cares?" Jon said. "I told you this was a waste of time. Like he cares about anyone but himself?"

"What's that supposed to mean?" Simon asked, starting to get irritated.

George cleared his throat, visibly uncomfortable. "Come on, if he doesn't want to talk about it, that's his business."

"Not when it's *our* lives at stake." Julie was blinking hard, like she had something in her eye or—Simon caught his breath. Was she blinking back *tears*?

"What's going on?" he asked, feeling more clueless than usual, which was saying a lot.

Beatriz sighed and gave Simon a shy smile. "We're not asking you for anything personal or, you know, painful. We just want you to tell us what you know about vampires from, um..."

"From being a bloodsucker," Jon filled in for her. "Which, as you may recall, you were."

"But I *don't* recall," Simon pointed out. "Or have you not been paying attention?"

"That's what you say," Beatriz argued, "but..."

"But you think I'm *lying*?" Simon asked, incredulous. The black hole at the center of his memories was such a central fact of his existence, it had never even occurred to him someone might question it. What would be the point of lying about that—and what kind of person would do so? "You all think that? Really?"

One by one, they began to nod ... even George, though at least he had the grace to look sheepish.

"Why would I pretend not to remember?" Simon asked.

"Why would they let someone like *you* in here, if you really didn't have a clue?" Jon retorted. "It's the only thing that makes sense."

"Well, I guess it's a mad, mad, mad world," Simon snapped. "Because what you see is what you get."

"A whole lot of nothing, then," Jon said.

Julie elbowed him, sounding uncharacteristically angry—usually she was happy to go along with whatever Jon said. "You said you'd be *nice*."

"What's the point? Either he doesn't know anything or he doesn't want to tell us. And who cares, anyway? It's just one Downworlder. What's the worst that could happen?"

"You really don't know, do you?" Julie said. "Have you ever even been in battle? Have you ever seen anyone get hurt? Die?"

"I'm a Shadowhunter, aren't I?" Jon said, though Simon noticed that wasn't much of an answer.

"You weren't in Alicante for the war," Julie said darkly. "You don't know how it was. You didn't lose anything."

Jon reared on her. "Don't you tell me what I've lost. I don't know about you, but I'm here to learn how to *fight*, so that next time—"

"Don't say that, Jon," Beatriz pleaded. "There won't be a next time. There can't be."

Jon shrugged. "There's always a next time." He sounded almost hopeful about it, and Simon understood that Julie was probably right. Jon talked like someone who'd been kept very far away from death of any kind.

"I've seen dead sheep," George said brightly, clearly trying to lighten the mood. "That's about it."

Beatriz frowned. "I don't really want to have to fight a vampire. Maybe if it were a faerie..."

"You don't know anything about faeries," Julie snapped.

"I know I wouldn't mind killing a couple of them," Beatriz said.

Julie deflated abruptly as if someone had pricked her and let all the air out. "Me neither. If it were that easy..."

Simon didn't know much about Shadowhunter-Downworlder relations, but he'd figured out pretty quickly that faeries were public enemy number one in Shadowhunterland these days. The *actual* enemy number one, Sebastian Morgenstern, who'd started the Dark War and Turned a bunch of Shadowhunters into evil Sebastian-worshipping zombies, was long dead. Which left his secret allies, the Fair Folk, to bear his consequences. Even Shadowhunters like Beatriz, who seemed to honestly believe that werewolves were like anyone else, if a little hairier, and had a bit of a fangirl crush on the infamous warlock Magnus Bane, talked about the faeries like they were a roach infestation and the Cold Peace like it was merely a pit stop to extermination.

"You were right this morning, George," Julie said. "They shouldn't be sending us out like this, not any of us. We're not ready."

Jon snorted. "Speak for yourself."

As they bickered among themselves about exactly how hard it would be to kill one vampire, Simon stood up. Bad enough that they all thought he was a liar—even worse that, in a way, he sort of was. He couldn't remember anything about being a vampire—nothing useful, at least—but he remembered enough to be extremely uncomfortable with the idea of killing one.

Or maybe it was just the idea of killing *anything*. Simon was a vegetarian, and the only violence he'd ever committed was on-screen, blowing up pixelated dragons and sea slugs.

That's not true, a voice in his head reminded him. *There's plenty of blood on your hands*. Simon shrugged it off. Not remembering something might not mean it never happened, but sometimes pretending that made things easier.

George grabbed his arm before he could leave. "I'm sorry about—you know," he told Simon. "I should have believed you."

"Yeah. You should have." Simon sighed, then assured his roommate there were no hard feelings, which was mostly true. He was halfway down the shadowed corridor when he heard footsteps chasing after him.

"Simon!" Julie cried. "Wait a second."

In the last few months, Simon had discovered the existence of magic and demons, he'd learned that his memories of the past were as flimsy and fake as his sister's old paper dolls, and he'd given up everything he'd ever known to move to a magically invisible country and study demon-hunting. And still, nothing surprised him quite as much as the ever-increasing list of hot girls who urgently wanted something from him. It wasn't nearly as much fun as it should have been.

Simon stopped to let Julie catch up. She was a few inches taller and had the kind of gold-flecked hazel eyes that changed in every light. Here in the dim corridor, they flashed amber in the candelabra's glow. She moved with an easy grace, like a ballet dancer, if ballet dancers habitually sliced people to ribbons with a silver runed dagger. In other words, she moved like a Shadowhunter, and from what Simon had seen of her on the training field, she was going to be a very good one.

And like any good Shadowhunter, she had no inclination to bond with mundanes, much less mundanes who used to be Downworlders—even mundanes who, in a life they could no longer remember, had saved the world. But ever since Isabelle Lightwood had descended on the Academy to stake her claim on Simon, Julie had looked at him with special fascination. Less like someone she wanted to throw into bed and more like someone she wanted to examine under a microscope as she plucked off his limbs, excavated his interior, and sought some glimmer of what might possibly attract a girl like Isabelle Lightwood.

Simon didn't mind letting her look. He liked the sharp curiosity in her gaze, the lack of expectation. Isabelle, Clary, Maia, all those girls back in New York, they claimed to know and love him, and he believed them—but he also knew they didn't love *him*, they loved some bizarro-world version of him, some Simon-shaped doppelgänger, and when they looked at Simon, all they saw, all they wanted to see, was that other guy. Julie may have hated him—okay, clearly hated him—but she also *saw* him.

"It's really true?" she asked him now. "You don't remember any of it? Being a vampire? The demon dimension? The Dark War? None of it?"

Simon sighed. "I'm tired, Julie. Can we just pretend that you asked me that a million more times and I gave you the same answer, and call it a day?"

She brushed at her eye, and Simon wondered again whether it was possible that Julie Beauvale had actual human feelings and, for whatever reason, was blinking back actual human tears. It was too dark in the corridor to see anything but the smooth lines of her face, the glint of gold where her necklace disappeared into her cleavage.

Simon pressed a hand to his collarbone, suddenly remembering the weight of a stone, the flash of a ruby, the steady pulse so like a heartbeat, the look on her face when she'd given it to him for safekeeping, said good-bye, shards of confused memory impossible to piece together, but even as he asked himself *whose* face, *whose* frightened farewell, his mind offered up the answer.

Isabelle.

It was always Isabelle.

"I believe you," Julie said. "I don't get it, but I believe you. I guess I was just hoping..."

"What?" There was an unfamiliar note in her voice, something gentle and uncertain, and she looked almost as surprised as he did to hear it.

"I thought you, of all people, might understand,"

Julie said. "What it's like, to fight for your life. To fight Downworlders. To think you're going to die. To"—her voice didn't waver and her expression didn't change, but Simon could almost feel her blood turn to ice as she forced the words out—"see other people fall."

"I'm sorry," Simon said. "I mean, I know about what happened, but..."

"But it's not the same as being there," Julie said.

Simon nodded, thinking about the hours he'd spent sitting beside his father's bed, long after the heart monitor had flatlined, knowing he'd never wake up. He'd thought: *Okay, I know how this goes.* He'd seen plenty of movies where the hero's father dies; he'd pictured the look on Luke Skywalker's face, returning to find his aunt's and uncle's bodies smoldering in the Tatooine ruins, and thought he understood grief. "There are some things you can't understand unless you've been through them yourself."

"Did you ever wonder why I was here?" Julie asked him. "Training at the Academy, rather than in Alicante or some Institute somewhere?"

"Actually ... no," Simon admitted, but maybe he should have. The Academy had been shut down for decades, and he knew in that time, Shadowhunter families had gotten used to training their children themselves. He also knew that most of them, in the wake of the Dark War, were still doing so, not wanting to let their loved ones too far out of their sight.

She looked away from him then, and her fingers knit together, needing something to hold on to. "I'm going to tell you something now, Simon, and you won't repeat it."

It wasn't a question.

"My mother was one of the first Shadowhunters to be

Turned," she said, her voice deadened. "So she's gone now. After, we evacuated to Alicante, just like everyone else. And when they attacked Alicante ... they locked all the children up in the Accords Hall. They thought we'd be safe there. But there wasn't anywhere safe that day. The faeries got in, and the Endarkened—they would have killed us all, Simon, if it weren't for you and your friends. My sister, Elizabeth. She was one of the last to die. I saw him, this faerie with silver hair, and he was so beautiful, Simon, like liquid mercury, that's what I was thinking when he brought down his sword. That he was beautiful." She shook herself all over. "Anyway. My father's useless now. So that's why I'm here. To learn to fight. So next time..."

Simon didn't know what to say. *I'm sorry* felt so inadequate. But Julie seemed to have run out of words.

"Why are you telling me this?" he asked gently.

"Because I want someone to understand that it *is* a big deal, what they're sending us out to do. Even if it's just one vampire against all of us. I don't care what Jon says. Things happen. People—" She nodded sharply, like she was dismissing not just him but everything that had passed between them. "Also, I wanted to thank you for what you did, Simon Lewis. And for your sacrifice."

"I really don't remember doing anything," Simon said. "You shouldn't thank me. I know what happened that day, but it's like it all happened to someone else."

"Maybe that's how it seems," Julie said. "But if you're going to be a Shadowhunter, you have to learn to see things how they *are*."

She turned away then, and started to head for her room. He was dismissed.

"Julie?" he called softly after her. "Is that why Jon and

Beatriz are at the Academy too? Because of the people they lost in the war?"

"You'll have to ask them," she said, without turning back. "We all have our own story of the Dark War. All of us lost something. Some of us lost everything."

The next day, their history lecturer, the warlock Catarina Loss, announced that she was handing the class over to a special guest.

Simon's heart stopped. The last guest lecturer to honor the students with her presence had been Isabelle Lightwood. And the "*lecture*" had consisted of a stern and humiliating warning that every female in a ten-mile radius should keep her grubby little hands off Simon's hot bod.

Fortunately, the tall, dark-haired man who strode to the front of the classroom looked unlikely to have any interest in Simon or his bod.

"Lazlo Balogh," he said, his tone implying that he should have needed no introduction—but that perhaps Catarina should have done him the honor of supplying one.

"Head of the Budapest Institute," George whispered in Simon's ear. In spite of his self-proclaimed laziness, George had memorized the name of every Institute head—not to mention every famous Shadowhunter in history—before arriving at the Academy.

"I have come to tell you a story," Balogh said, eyebrows angling into a sharp, angry V. Between the pale skin, dark widow's peak, and faint Hungarian accent, Balogh looked more like Dracula than anyone Simon had ever met.

He suspected Balogh wouldn't have appreciated the comparison.

"Several of you in this classroom will soon face your

first battle. I have come to inform you what is at stake."

"We're not the ones who need to be worrying about *stakes*," Jon said, and snickered from the back row.

Balogh lasered a furious glare at him. "Jonathan Cartwright," he said, his accent giving the syllables a sinister shadow. "Were I the son of your parents, I would hold my tongue in the presence of my betters."

Jon went sheet white. Simon could feel the hatred radiating from him, and thought that it was likely Balogh had just made an enemy for life. Possibly everyone in the classroom had, too, because Jon wasn't the type to appreciate an audience to his humiliation.

He opened his mouth, then shut it again in a thin, firm line. Balogh nodded, as if agreeing that, *yes*, it was right that he should shut up and burn with silent shame.

Balogh cleared his throat. "My question for you, children, is this. What is the worst thing a Shadowhunter can do?"

Marisol raised her hand. "Kill an innocent?"

Balogh looked like he'd smelled something bad. (Which—given that the classroom had a bit of a stinkbug infestation—wasn't entirely unlikely.) "You're a mundane," he said.

She nodded fiercely. It was Simon's favorite thing about the tough thirteen-year-old: She never once apologized for who or what she was. To the contrary, she seemed proud of it.

"There was a time when no mundane would have been allowed in Idris," Balogh said. He glanced at Catarina, who was hovering at the edge of the classroom. "And no Downworlders, for that matter."

"Things change," Marisol said.

"Indeed." He scanned the classroom, which was filled with mundanes and Shadowhunters alike. "Would any of the ... more informed students like to hazard a guess?"

Beatriz's hand rose slowly. "My mother always said the worst thing a Shadowhunter could do was forget her duty, that she was here to serve and protect mankind."

Simon caught Catarina's lips quirking up into a half smile.

Balogh's turned noticeably in the other direction. Then, apparently deciding that the Socratic method wasn't all it was cracked up to be, he answered his own question. "The worst thing any Shadowhunter can do is betray his fellows in the heat of battle," he intoned. "The worst thing any Shadowhunter can *be* is a coward."

Simon couldn't help but feel like Balogh was speaking directly to him—that Balogh had peered inside his head and knew exactly how reluctant Simon was to wield his weapon in battle conditions, against an actual living thing.

Well, not exactly *living*, he reminded himself. He'd fought demons before, he knew that, and he didn't think he'd lost sleep over it. But demons were just monsters. Vampires were still people; vampires had souls. Vampires, unlike the creatures in his video games, could hurt and bleed and die—and they could also fight back. In English class the year before, Simon had read *The Red Badge of Courage*, a tedious novel about a Civil War soldier who'd gone AWOL in the heat of battle. The book, which at the time had seemed even more irrelevant than calculus, had put him to sleep, but one line had burrowed itself into his brain: "He was a craven loon." Eric was in the class too, and for a few weeks they'd decided to call their band the Craven Loons, before forgetting all about it. But lately Simon couldn't drive the phrase out of his head. "Loon" as in: nuts for ever thinking he could be a warrior or a hero. "Craven" as in: Spineless. Frightened. Timid. A big fat coward.

"The year was 1828," Balogh declaimed. "This was before the Accords, mind you, before the Downworlders were brought into line and taught to be civilized."

Out of the corner of his eye, Simon saw their history lecturer stiffen. It didn't seem wise to offend a warlock, even one as seemingly unflappable as Catarina Loss, but Balogh continued unheeded.

"Europe was in chaos. Unruly revolutionaries were fomenting discord across the continent. And in the German states, a small cabal of warlocks took advantage of the political situation to visit the most unseemly miseries upon the local population. Some of you mundanes may be familiar with this time of tragedy and havoc from the tales told by the Brothers Grimm." At the surprised look on several students' faces, Balogh smiled for the first time. "Yes, Wilhelm and Jacob were in the thick of it. Remember, children, all the stories are true."

As Simon tried to wrap his head around the idea that, somewhere in Germany, someone's dear old grandmother might actually be a wolf in a hat, Balogh continued his story. He told the class of the small band of Shadowhunters that had been dispensed to "deal with" the warlocks. Of their journey into a dense German forest, its trees alive with dark magic, its birds and beasts enchanted to defend their territory against the forces of justice. In the dark heart of the forest, the warlocks had summoned a Greater Demon, planning to unleash its might on the people of Bavaria.

"Why?" one of the students asked.

"Warlocks don't need a reason," Balogh said, with

another look at Catarina. "The summons of dark magic is always heeded by the weak and easily tempted."

Catarina murmured something. Simon found himself hoping it was a curse.

"There were five Shadowhunters," Balogh continued, "which was more than enough might to take on three warlocks. But the Greater Demon came as a surprise. Even then, right would have triumphed, were it not for the cowardice of the youngest of their party, a Shadowhunter named Tobias Herondale."

A murmur rippled across the classroom. Every student, Shadowhunter and mundane alike, knew the name Herondale. It was Jace's last name. It was the name of heroes.

"Yes, yes, you've all heard of the Herondales," Balogh said impatiently. "And perhaps you've heard good things—of William Herondale, for instance, or his son James, or Jonathan Lightwood Herondale today. But even the strongest tree can have a weak branch. Tobias's brother and sister-in-law died noble deaths in battle before the decade was out. For some, that was enough to wipe away the stain on the name Herondale. But no amount of Herondale glory or sacrifice will make us forget what Tobias did—nor should it. Tobias was inexperienced and distracted, on the mission under duress. He had a pregnant wife at home, and labored under the delusion that this should excuse him from his duties. And when the demon launched its attack, Tobias Herondale, may his name be blackened for the rest of time, turned on his heel and ran away." Then Balogh repeated that last, cracking his hand against the desk with each word. *"Ran. Away."*

He went on to describe, in gruesome, painful detail, what happened next: How three of the remaining Shadowhunters were slaughtered by the demon—one disemboweled, one burned alive, one doused with acidic blood that dissolved him into dust. How the fourth survived only by the intercession of the warlocks, who returned him—disfigured by demonic burns that would never fade—to his people as a warning to stay away.

"Of course, we returned in even greater force, and repaid the warlocks tenfold for what they'd done to the villagers. But the far greater crime, that of Tobias Herondale, still called for vengeance."

"The greater crime? Greater than slaughtering a bunch of Shadowhunters?" Simon said before he could stop himself.

"Demons and warlocks can't help what they are," Balogh said darkly. "Shadowhunters are held to a higher standard. The deaths of those three men sit squarely on the shoulders of Tobias Herondale. And he would have been punished in kind, had he ever been foolish enough to show his face again. He never did, but debts need repaying. A trial was held in absentia. He was judged guilty, and punishment was carried out."

"But I thought you said he never came back?" Julie said.

"Indeed. So the punishment was carried out on his wife, in his stead."

"His *pregnant* wife?" Marisol said, looking like she was about to be sick.

"Sed lex, dura lex," Balogh said. The Latin phrase had been hammered into them from the first day at the Academy, and Simon was coming to hate the sound of it—so often was it used as an excuse for acting like monsters. Balogh steepled his fingers and contemplated the classroom, watching in satisfaction as his message came clear. This was how the Clave treated cowardice on the battlefield; this was justice

under the Covenant. "The Law is hard," Balogh translated for the hushed students. "But it is the Law."

"Choose wisely," Scarsbury warned, watching the students sift through the many pointy options the weapons room had to offer.

"How are we supposed to choose wisely when you won't even tell us what we're going up against?" Jon complained.

"You know it's a vampire," Scarsbury said. "You'll learn more when you arrive on site."

Simon slung a bow over his shoulders and selected a dagger for melee fighting; it seemed the weapon he was least likely to accidentally stab himself with. As the Shadowhunter students Marked themselves with runes of strength and agility and tucked witchlights into their pockets, Simon hooked a slim flashlight to one side of his belt and a portable flamethrower to the other. He touched the Star of David hanging on the same chain as Jordan's pendant around his neck—it wouldn't help much unless this vampire happened to be Jewish, but it made him feel just a little better. Like someone was looking out for him.

There was an electric charge of anticipation in the air that reminded Simon of being a little kid, preparing to go on a field trip. Of course, a visit to the Bronx Zoo or the sewage treatment center carried with it less chance of disembowelment, and instead of lining up to board a school bus, the students assembled themselves in front of a magical Portal that would transdimensionally carry them thousands of miles in the blink of an eye.

"You ready for this?" George asked him, grinning. Decked out in full gear with a longsword slung over his shoulder, Simon's roommate looked every inch the warrior.

For a brief moment, Simon imagined himself saying no. Raising his hand, asking to be excused. Admitting that he didn't know what he was doing here, that every fighting tactic he'd been taught had evaporated from his mind, that he would like to pack up his suitcase, Portal home, and pretend none of this had ever happened.

"As I'll ever be," he said—and stepped through the Portal.

From what Simon remembered, traveling by school bus was a filthy, undignified experience, rife with foul smells, spitballs, and the occasional embarrassing bout of motion sickness.

Traveling by Portal was significantly worse.

Once he'd regained his balance and his breath, Simon looked around—and gasped. No one had mentioned where they were Portaling *to*, but Simon recognized the block immediately. He was back in New York City—and not just New York but Brooklyn. Gowanus, to be specific, a thin stretch of industrial parks and warehouses lining a toxic canal that was less than a ten-minute walk from his mother's apartment.

He was home.

It was exactly as he'd remembered it—and yet, wholly different. Or maybe it was just that he was wholly different, that after only two months in Idris, he'd forgotten the sounds and smells of modernity: the low, steady hum of electricity and the thick haze of car exhaust, the honking trucks and pigeon crap and piles of garbage that had for sixteen years formed the fabric of his daily life.

On the other hand, maybe it was because now that he could see through glamours, he could see the mermaids swimming in the Gowanus.

It was home and not home all at the same time, and Simon felt the same disorientation he had after his summer in the mountains at Camp Ramah, when he'd found himself unable to fall asleep without the sound of cicadas and Jake Grossberg's snoring in the upper bunk. Maybe, he thought, you couldn't know how much going away had changed you until you tried to go home.

"Listen up, men!" Scarsbury shouted, as the final student came through the Portal. They were assembled in front of an abandoned factory, its walls streaked with graffiti and its windows boarded up tight.

Marisol cleared her throat, loudly, and Scarsbury sighed. "Listen up, men and *women*. Inside this building is a vampire who's broken the Covenant and killed several mundanes. Your mission is to track her down, and execute her. And I suggest you do so before sunset."

"Shouldn't the vampires be allowed to deal with this themselves?" Simon asked. The *Codex* had made it pretty clear that Downworlders were trusted to police themselves. Simon wondered whether that involved giving alleged rogue vampires a trial before they were executed.

How did I get here? he wondered—he didn't even believe in the death penalty.

"Not that it's any of your concern," Scarsbury said, "but her clan has handed her over to us, so that you children can get a little blood on your hands. Think of it as a gift, from the vampires to you."

Except "it" wasn't an *it* at all, Simon thought.

"Sed lex, dura lex," George murmured beside him, with an uneasy look, as if he was trying to convince himself.

"There's twenty of you and one of her," Scarsbury said, "and in case even those odds are too much for you, experienced Shadowhunters will be watching, ready to step in when you screw up. You won't see them, but they'll see you, and ensure that you come to no harm. Probably. And if any of you are tempted to turn tail and run, remember what you've learned. Cowardice has its price."

When they were standing on the curb in the bright sunlight, the mission had sounded more than a little unsporting. Twenty Shadowhunters in training, all of them armed to the gills; one captured vampire, trapped in the building by steel walls and sunshine.

But inside the old factory, in the dark, imagining the flicker of motion and the glimmer of fangs behind every shadow, was a different story. The game no longer felt rigged in their favor—it no longer felt like much of a game at all.

The students split up into pairs, prowling through the darkness. Simon volunteered to guard one of the exits, hoping very much that this would prove similar to those gym class soccer games, where he'd spent hours guarding the goal and only a handful of times had to fend off a well-aimed kick.

Of course, each of those times, the ball had sailed over his head and into the net, losing the game for his team. But he tried not to think about that.

Jon Cartwright was stationed at the door beside him, a witchlight stone glowing in his hand. Time passed; they did their best to ignore each other.

"Too bad you can't use one of these," Jon said finally, holding up the stone. "Or one of these." He tapped the seraph blade hanging from his belt. The students hadn't been taught how to fight with them yet, but several of the

Shadowhunter kids had brought their own weapons from home. "Don't worry, hero. If the vamp shows up, I'm here to protect you."

"Great, I can hide behind your massive ego."

Jon wheeled on him. "You want to watch yourself, mundane. If you're not careful, you'll…" Jon's voice trailed off. He backed up until he was pressed against the wall.

"I'll what?" Simon prompted him.

Jon made a noise that sounded suspiciously like a whimper. His hand floundered at his belt, fingers stretching for the seraph blade but coming nowhere near it. His eyes were riveted on a spot just over Simon's shoulder. "Do something!" he squeaked. "She's going to get us!"

Simon had seen enough horror movies to get the picture. And the picture was enough to make him want to bolt for the door, slip through it into the daylight, and keep running until he was back home, doors locked, safely under the bed, where he'd once hidden from imaginary monsters.

Instead, slowly, he turned around.

The girl who melted out of the shadows looked to be about his age. Her brown hair was pulled back into a high ponytail, her glasses were dark pink and horn-rimmed vintage, and her T-shirt featured a bloody, crimson-shirted *Star Trek* officer and read, LIVE FAST, DIE RED. She was, in other words, exactly Simon's type—except for the fangs glinting in his flashlight beam and the inhuman speed with which she streaked across the room and kicked Jon Cartwright in the head. He crumpled to the ground.

"And then there were two," the girl said, and smirked.

It had never occurred to Simon that the vampire would be his age, or at least look it.

"You want to be careful with that thing, Daylighter,"

she said. "I hear you're alive again. Presumably you want to keep it that way."

Simon looked down to realize he had taken the dagger into his hand.

"You going to let me out of here, or what?" she asked.

"You can't go out there."

"No?"

"Sunshine, remember? Makes vampires go poof?" Simon couldn't believe his voice wasn't shaking. Honestly, he couldn't believe he hadn't peed his pants. He was alone with a *vampire*. A cute, girl vampire ... that he was supposed to kill. Somehow.

"Check your watch, Daylighter."

"I don't wear a watch," Simon said. "And I'm not a Daylighter anymore."

She stepped closer to him, close enough to stroke his face. Her finger was cold, her skin as smooth as marble. "Is it true you don't remember?" she said, peering curiously at him. "You don't even remember me?"

"Did I ... do I know you?"

She brushed her fingertips across her lips. "The question is, how *well* did you know me, Daylighter? I'll never tell."

Clary and the others had said nothing about Simon having vampire friends, or ... more-than-friends. Maybe they'd wanted to spare him the details of that part of his life, the part where he'd thirsted for blood and walked in the shadows. Maybe he'd been so embarrassed that he'd never told them.

Or maybe she was lying.

Simon hated this, the not knowing. It made him feel like he was walking on quicksand, every unanswered question, every new discovery about his past sucking him farther down into the muck.

"Let me go, Daylighter," she whispered. "You would never have hurt one of your own."

He'd read in the *Codex* that vampires had the ability to mesmerize; he knew he should be guarding himself against it. But her gaze was magnetic. He couldn't look away.

"I can't do that," he said. "You broke the Law. You killed someone. Many someones."

"How do you know?"

"Because..." He stopped, realizing how feeble it would sound: *because someone told me so.*

She guessed at the answer anyway. "You always do what you're told, Daylighter? You never think for yourself?"

Simon's hand tightened on the dagger. He'd been so worried about discovering he was a coward, too frightened to fight. But now that he was here, facing the supposed monster, he wasn't afraid—he was reluctant.

Sed lex, dura lex.

Except maybe it wasn't so simple; maybe she'd just made a mistake, or someone else had, maybe he'd gotten the wrong information. Maybe she was a cold-blooded killer—but even so, who was he to punish her?

She angled past him toward the door. Without thinking, Simon moved to block her. His dagger swung up, slicing a dangerous arc through the air and whistling past her ear. She danced backward, laughing as she lunged for him, fingers curled like claws. Simon felt it then, for the first time, the adrenaline surge he'd been promised, the clarity of battle. He stopped thinking in terms of techniques and moves, stopped thinking at all, and simply acted, blocking and ducking her attack, aiming a kick at her ankles to sweep her legs out from under her, slashing the dagger across pale skin, drawing blood, and as his mind kicked into gear again, a step behind his body, he thought, *I'm doing it. I'm fighting. I'm* winning.

Until she wrapped a hand around his wrist in an iron grip, flipped him over onto his back as if he were a small child, and straddled him. She'd been playing with him, he realized. Pretending to fight, until she got bored.

She lowered her face toward his, close enough that he would have felt her breath—if she'd been breathing.

He remembered, suddenly, how cold he had been, when he was dead. He remembered the stillness in his chest, where his heart no longer beat.

"I could give it all back to you, Daylighter," she whispered. "Eternal life."

He remembered the hunger, and the taste of blood.

"That wasn't life," he said.

"It wasn't death, either." Her lips were cold on his neck. Everything about her was cold. "I could kill you now, Daylighter. But I'm not going to. I'm not a monster. No matter what they told you."

"I told you, I'm not a Daylighter anymore." Simon didn't know why he was arguing with her, especially now, but it seemed important to say it out loud, that he was alive, that he was human, that his heart beat again. Especially now.

"You were a Downworlder once," she said, rising over him. "That will always be a part of you. Even if you forget, they never will."

Simon was about to argue, again, when a shining whip lashed out of the shadows and wrapped around the girl's neck. It yanked her off her feet and she landed hard, head cracking against the cement floor.

"Isabelle?" Simon said in confusion, as Isabelle Lightwood charged at the vampire, blade gleaming.

He'd never before realized what a horrible crime against nature it was that he had lost his memories of Isabelle in action. It was clear that it was her natural state. Isabelle standing still was beautiful; Isabelle leaping through the air, carving death into cold flesh, was unworldly, burning as brightly as her golden whip. She was like a goddess, Simon thought, and then silently corrected himself—she was like an avenging angel, her vengeance swift and deadly. Before he could lever himself off the ground, the vampire girl's throat was split wide open, her undead eyes rolling back in her head, and like that, it was over. She was dust; she was gone.

"You're welcome." Isabelle extended her hand.

Simon ignored it, rising to his feet without her help. "Why did you do that?"

"Um, because she was about to kill you?"

"No, she wasn't," he said coldly.

Isabelle gaped at him. "You're not seriously mad at me? For saving your ass?"

It wasn't until she asked that he realized he was. Angry at her for killing the vampire girl, angry at her for assuming he *needed* his ass saved and being pretty much right, angry at her for hiding in the dark, waiting to save him, even though he'd made it painfully clear that there couldn't be anything between them anymore. Angry that she was a supernaturally sexy, raven-haired warrior goddess and apparently against all odds still in love with him—and he was apparently going to have to break up with her, *again*.

"She didn't want to hurt me. She just wanted to *go*."

"And what? I should have *let* her? Is that what you were planning to do? There are more people in the world than you, Simon. She killed children. She ripped out their throats."

He couldn't answer. He didn't know what to feel or think. The vampire girl had been a murderer. A cold-blooded murderer, in every sense of the word. But he'd felt a kinship with her as she'd embraced him, a sort of whispering in the back of his mind that said *we are lost children together.*

He wasn't sure there was a place in Isabelle's life for someone lost.

"Simon?" Isabelle was like a tightly coiled spring. He could see how much effort it was taking her just to keep her voice steady, her face free of emotion.

How can I know that? Simon wondered. Looking at her was like seeing double: one Isabelle a stranger he barely knew, one Isabelle the girl that other, better Simon loved so much he would have sacrificed everything for her. There was a part of him—a part beneath memories, beyond rationality—desperate to close the space between them, to take her in his arms, smooth back her hair, lose himself in her bottomless eyes, her lips, her fierce, protective, overwhelming love.

"You can't keep doing this!" he shouted, unsure whether he was yelling at her or himself. "It's not your job to choose for me anymore, to decide what I should do or how I should live. Who I should be. How many times do I have to tell you before you hear me? *I'm not him.* I will never be him, Isabelle. He belonged to you, I get that. But *I don't.* I know you Shadowhunters are used to having everything your way—you set the rules, you know what's best for the rest of us. But not this time, okay? Not with me."

With deliberate calm, Isabelle coiled her whip around her wrist. "Simon, I think you've mistaken me for someone who cares."

It wasn't the emotion in her voice that cracked his heart,

but the lack of it. Behind the words was nothing: no pain, no suppressed anger, only a void. Hollow and cold.

"Isabelle—"

"I didn't come here for you, Simon. This is my job. I thought you wanted it to be your job too. If you still feel that way, I'd suggest you reconsider some things. Like how you speak to your superiors."

"My ... *superiors?*"

"And for the record, since you brought it up? You're right, Simon. I don't know this version of you at all. And I'm pretty sure I don't want to." She stepped past Simon, her shoulder brushing against his for the briefest of moments, then slipped out of the building.

Simon stared after her, wondering if he should follow, but he couldn't seem to make his feet move. At the sound of the door slamming shut, Jon Cartwright blinked his eyes open and woozily eased himself upright. "We got her?" he asked Simon, catching sight of the small pile of dust where the vampire girl had been.

"Yeah," he said wearily. "You could say that."

"Oh yeah, that's right, bloodsucker!" Jon pumped his fist in the air, then made devil fingers. "You mess with a Cartwright bull—you get the horns."

"I'm not saying she *didn't* break the Law," Simon explained, for what seemed like the hundredth time. "I'm just saying, even if she did, why did we have to kill her? I mean—what about, I don't know, *jail?*"

By the time they'd Portaled back to the Academy, dinner was long over. But as a reward for their labors, Dean Penhallow had opened up the dining hall and the kitchen for the twenty returning students. They huddled around a couple of the long tables, gnawing hungrily at stale egg rolls and mercifully flavorless shawarma. The Academy had returned to its traditional policy of serving international food—but unfortunately, all of these foods were prepared by a single chef, who Simon suspected was a warlock, because nearly everything they ate seemed enchanted to taste like dog food.

"Because that's what we do," Jon said. "A vampire—any Downworlder—violates the Covenant, someone has to kill it. Have you not been paying attention?"

"So why isn't there a Downworlder jail?" Simon said. "Why aren't there Downworlder trials?"

"That's not how it *works*, Simon," Julie said. He'd thought she might be friendlier after their conversation in the corridor the other night, but if anything, her edges had gotten sharper, more liable to draw blood. "This isn't your stupid mundane law. This is the Law. Handed down from the Angel. Higher than everything else."

Jon nodded proudly. *"Sed lex, dura lex."*

"Even if it's wrong?" Simon asked.

"How could it be wrong, if it's the Law? That's an oxymoron."

Takes one to know one, he thought childishly, but stopped himself before saying it out loud. Anyway, Jon was more of your garden-variety moron.

"You realize you all sound like you're in some kind of cult," Simon complained. He touched the star that was still hanging at his neck. His family had never been particularly religious, but his father had always loved helping him try to figure out the Jewish perspective on questions of right and wrong. "There's always a little wiggle room," he'd told Simon, "a little space to figure these things out yourself." He'd taught

Simon to ask questions, to challenge authority, to understand and believe in rules before he followed them. There was a noble Jewish heritage of arguing, his father liked to say, even when it came to arguing with God.

Simon wondered now what his father would think of him, at this school for fundamentalists, swearing fealty to a higher Law. What did it even mean to be Jewish in a universe where angels and demons walked the earth, practiced miracles, carried swords? Was thinking for yourself an activity better suited to a world without any evidence of the divine?

"The Law is hard, but it's the Law," Simon added in disgust. "So freaking what? If the Law is wrong, why not change it? Do you know what the world would look like if we were all still following the laws made up back in the Dark Ages?"

"You know who else used to talk like that?" Jon asked ominously.

"Let me guess: Valentine." Simon scowled. "Because apparently in all of Shadowhunter history only one guy has bothered to ask any questions. Yeah, that's me, charismatic, evil supervillain about to lead a revolution. Better report me."

George shook his head warningly. "Simon, I don't think—"

"If you hate it so much, why are you even here?" Beatriz cut in, an uncharacteristically hostile note in her voice. "*You* get to pick the life you want to live." She stopped abruptly, leaving something unspoken hanging in the silence. Something, Simon suspected, like: *Unlike the rest of us.*

"Good question." Simon set down his fork and pushed his chair back.

"Come on, you didn't even finish your..." George waved toward the plate, as if he couldn't bring himself to actually describe it as *food*.

"I just lost my appetite."

Simon was halfway to the dungeons when Catarina Loss stopped him in the hallway.

"Simon Lewis," she said. "We need to talk."

"Can we do it in the morning, Ms. Loss?" he asked. "It's been a long day, and—"

She shook her head. "I know about your day, Simon Lewis. We talk now."

The sky was bright with stars. Catarina's blue skin glowed in the moonlight, and her hair burned silver. The warlock had insisted that they both needed some fresh air, and Simon had to admit she was right. He felt better already, just breathing in the grass and trees and sky. Idris had seasons, but so far, at least, they weren't like the seasons he was used to. Or rather, they were like the best possible versions of themselves: each fall day crisp and bright, the air rich with the promise of bonfires and apple orchards, the approach of winter marked by only a startlingly clear sky and a new sharp bite to the air that was almost pleasurable in its icy pain.

"I heard what you said at dinner, Simon," Catarina said as they strolled across the grounds.

He looked at his teacher with surprise and a bit of alarm. "How could you?"

"I'm a warlock," she reminded him. "I *can* a lot of things."

Right. Magic school, he thought in despair, wondering if he'd ever have any privacy again.

"I want to tell you a story, Simon," she said. "It's something I've told a very few, trusted people, and I hope that you'll choose to keep it to yourself."

It seemed like a strange thing for her to risk on a student she barely knew—but then, she was a warlock. Simon had no idea what they were capable of, but he was getting better at imagining. If he broke her confidence, she'd probably know it.

And act accordingly.

"You were listening in class to the story of Tobias Herondale?"

"I always listen in class," Simon said, and she laughed.

"You're very good at evasive answers, Daylighter. You'd make a good faerie."

"I'm guessing that's not a compliment."

Catarina offered him a mysterious smile. "I'm no Shadowhunter," she reminded him. "My opinions on faeries are my own."

"Why do you still call me Daylighter?" Simon asked. "You know that's not what I am anymore."

"We are all what our pasts have made us," Catarina said. "The accumulation of thousands of daily choices. We can change ourselves, but never erase what we've been." She held up a finger to silence him, as if she knew he was about to argue. "Forgetting those choices doesn't unmake them, Daylighter. You'd do well to remember that."

"Is that what you wanted to tell me?" he asked, his irritation more visible than he'd intended. Why did everyone in his life feel the need to tell him who he was, or who he should be?

"You're impatient with me," Catarina observed. "Fortunately, I don't care. I'm going to tell you another story of

Tobias Herondale now. Listen or not—that's your decision."

He listened.

"I knew Tobias, knew his mother before he was born, watched him as a child struggling to fit into his family, find his place. The Herondales are a rather infamous line, as you probably know. Many of them heroes, some of them traitors, so many of them brash, wild creatures consumed by their passions, whether it be love or hate. Tobias was ... different. He was mild, sweet, the kind of boy who did as he was told. His older brother, William—now, *there* was a Shadowhunter fit to be a Herondale, just as brave and twice as headstrong as the grandson who later bore his name. But not Tobias. He had no special talent for Shadowhunting, and not much love for it either. His father was a hard man, his mother a bit of a hysteric, though few could blame her with a husband like that. A bolder boy might have turned from his family and its traditions, decided he was unfit for the Shadowhunter life and struck out on his own. But for Tobias? That was unthinkable. His parents taught him the Law, and he knew only to follow it. Not so unusual among humans, even when their blood is mixed with the Angel's. Unusual for a Herondale, maybe, but if anyone thought that, Tobias's father made sure they kept their mouths shut. And so he grew up. He married, a match that surprised everyone, for Eva Blackthorn was the opposite of mild. A raven-haired spitfire, somewhat like your Isabelle."

Simon bristled. She wasn't *his* Isabelle, not anymore. He wondered if she ever truly had been. Isabelle didn't seem like the type of girl to *belong* to someone. It was one of the things he liked best about her.

"Tobias loved her more than he'd loved anything—his family, his duty, even himself. There, perhaps, the

Herondale blood ran true. She was carrying her first child when he was called to the mission in Bavaria—you've heard how that story ended."

Simon nodded, heart clenching all over again at the thought of the punishment visited on Tobias's wife. Eva. And her unborn child.

"Lazlo Balogh knows only the version of this story as it's been handed down to him by generations of Shadowhunters. Tobias is no longer a person to them, or an ancestor. He's nothing but a cautionary tale. There are few of us left to remember him as the kind boy he once was."

"How did you know him so well?" Simon asked. "I thought back then, warlocks and Shadowhunters weren't exactly ... you know. On speaking terms." Actually, Simon had thought it was more like killing terms; from what he'd learned from the *Codex* and his history classes, the Shadowhunters of the past had gone after warlocks and other Downworlders the way big-game hunters went after elephants. Sportingly and with bloodthirsty abandon.

"That's a different story," Catarina chided him. "I'm not telling you my story, I'm telling you Tobias's. Suffice it to say, he was a kind boy, even to Downworlders, and his kindness was remembered. What you know, what all Shadowhunters today think they know, is that Tobias was a coward who abandoned his fellows in the heat of battle. The truth is never so simple, is it? Tobias hadn't wanted to leave behind his wife when she was ill and pregnant, but he went anyway, doing as he was told. Deep in those Bavarian woods, he encountered a warlock who knew his greatest fear, and used it against him. He found the chink in Tobias's armor, found a way into his mind by convincing him his wife was in terrible danger. He showed him a vision of Eva, bloody and dying and screaming for Tobias to save her. Tobias was held spellbound and stricken, and the warlock hurled vision after vision of all the horrors in the world Tobias could not bear. Yes, Tobias ran away. His mind broke. He abandoned his fellows and fled into the woods, blinded and tormented by waking nightmares. Like all Herondales, his ability to love without measure, without end, was both his great gift and his great curse. When he thought Eva was dead, he shattered. I know who I blame for the destruction of Tobias Herondale."

"They can't have known he was driven mad!" Simon protested. "No one could punish him for that!"

"They did know," Catarina told him. "That didn't matter. What mattered was his treason against his duty. Eva was never in danger, of course—at least, not until Tobias abandoned his post. That was the last cruel irony of Tobias's life: that he doomed the woman he would have died to save. The warlock had shown him a glimpse of the future, a future that would never have come to pass if Tobias had been able to resist him. He could not resist. He could not be found. The Clave came for Eva."

"You were there," Simon guessed.

"I was," she agreed.

"And you didn't try to stop them?"

"I did not waste my time trying, no. The Nephilim do not pay heed to interfering Downworlders. Only a fool would try to get between the Shadowhunters and their Law."

There was something about the way she said it, wry and sorrowful at the same time, that made him ask, "You're a fool, aren't you?"

She smiled. "It's dangerous to call a warlock names like that, Simon. But ... yes. I tried. I looked for Tobias Herondale, using ways the Nephilim do not have access to, and found him wandering mad in the forest, not even knowing his own name." She lowered her head. "I couldn't save him or Eva. But I saved the baby. I managed that much."

"But how? Where—?"

"I used a certain amount of magic and cunning to make my way into the prison of the Shadowhunters, where you were held once," said Catarina, nodding to him. "I made the baby come early, and cast a spell to make it seem as if she was still carrying the child. Eva was steel that night, relentless and bright in the darkness that had come upon her. She did not falter and she did not flinch and she did not betray herself by any sign as she walked to meet her death. She kept our secret to the very end, and the Shadowhunters who killed her never suspected a thing. After that, it was almost easy. The Nephilim seldom have any interest in the doings of Downworlders—and Downworlders often find their blindness very convenient. They never noticed when I sailed away to the New World with a baby. I stayed there for twenty years, before I went back to my people and my work, and raised the child until he was grown. He has been dust for years, but I can close my eyes and see his face when he was as young as you are now. Tobias and Eva's child. He was a sweet boy, kind as his father and fierce as his mother. The Nephilim believe in living by hard laws and paying high prices, but their arrogance means they do not fully understand the cost of what they do. The world would have been poorer without that boy in it. He had a mundane love, and a mundane life filled with small acts of grace, which would have meant very little to a Shadowhunter. They did not deserve him. I left him as a gift to the mundane world."

"So you're saying there's another Herondale out there

somewhere? Maybe generations of Herondales that no one knows anything about?" There was a line from the Talmud Simon's father had always liked to quote: *He who saves a single life, it is as if he has saved an entire world.*

"It's possible," Catarina said. "I made sure the boy never knew what he was—it was safest that way. If indeed his line lives on, his descendants surely believe themselves mundane. It's only now, with the Shadowhunters so depleted, that the Clave might welcome their lost sons or daughters back to the fold. And perhaps there are those of us who might help that along. When the time is right."

"Why are you telling me this, Ms. Loss? Why now? Why ever?"

She stopped walking and turned to him, silver-white hair billowing in the wind. "Saving that child, that's the biggest crime I've ever committed. At least, according to Shadowhunter Law. If anyone knew, even now..." She shook her head. "But it's also the bravest choice I've ever made. The one I'm most proud of. I'm bound by the Accords just like everyone else, Simon. I do my best to live by the rule of Law. But I make my own decisions. There's always a higher law."

"You say that like it's so easy to know what it *is*," Simon said. "To be so sure of yourself, that you're right, no matter what the Law says."

"It's not easy," Catarina corrected him. "It's what it means to be alive. Remember what I said, Simon. Every decision you make, makes *you*. Never let other people choose who you're going to be."

When he returned to his room, his mind spinning, George was sitting on the ground in the hallway, studying his *Codex*.

"Um, George?" Simon peered down at his roommate.

"Wouldn't it be easier to do that inside? Where there's light? And no disgusting slime on the ground? Well..." He sighed. "Less slime, at least."

"She said I have to wait out here," George said. "That you two need your privacy."

"Who said?" But the question was superfluous, because who else? Before George could answer, he was already opening the door and charging inside. "Isabelle, you can't just throw my roommate—"

He stopped short, so suddenly that he nearly tripped over himself.

"It's not Isabelle," said the girl perched on his bed. Her fire-red hair was pulled into a messy bun and her legs were folded beneath her; she looked utterly at home, as if she'd spent half her life lounging around in his bed. Which, according to her, she had.

"What are you doing here, Clary?"

"I Portaled in," she said.

He nodded, waiting. He was glad to see her, but it also hurt. Just as it always did. He wondered when the pain would go and he would be able to feel the joy of friendship that he knew was still there, like a plant under frozen ground, waiting to grow again.

"I heard what happened today. With the vampire. And Isabelle."

Simon lowered himself onto George's bed, across from her. "I'm fine, okay? No bite marks or anything. It's nice of you to worry about me, but you can't just Portal in and—"

Clary snorted. "I can see your ego's unharmed. I'm not here because I'm worried about you, Simon."

"Oh. Then...?"

"I'm worried about *Isabelle*."

"I'm pretty sure Isabelle can take care of herself."

"You don't know her, Simon. I mean, not anymore. And if she knew I was here, she'd murder me, but ... can you just try to be a little nicer to her? Please?"

Simon was appalled. He knew that he'd disappointed Isabelle, that his very existence was a constant disappointment to her, that she wanted him to be someone else. But it had never occurred to him that he, the non-vampire, non-heroic, non-sexy iteration of Simon Lewis, could have the power to hurt her.

"I'm sorry," he blurted. "Tell her I'm sorry!"

"Are you kidding me?" Clary said. "Did you not hear the part about how she'd murder me if she knew I was talking to you about this? I'm not telling her anything. I'm telling *you*. Be careful with her. She's more fragile than she seems."

"She seems like the strongest girl I've ever met," Simon said.

"She's that, too," Clary allowed. She shifted uncomfortably then, and hopped to her feet. "Well, I should ... I mean, I know you don't really want me around here, so..."

"It's not that, I just—"

"No, I get it, but—"

"I'm sorry—"

"I'm sorry—"

They both laughed, and Simon felt something loosening in his chest, a muscle he hadn't even known was clenched.

"It didn't used to be like this, huh?" he asked. "Awkward?"

"No." She gave him a sad smile. "It was a lot of things, but it was never awkward."

He couldn't imagine it, feeling so at ease with a girl, much less a girl like her, pretty and confident and so filled with light. "I bet I liked that."

"I hope so, Simon."

"Clary—" He didn't want her to leave, not yet, but he wasn't sure what to say to her if she stayed. "Do you know the story of Tobias Herondale?"

"Everyone knows that story," she said. "And, obviously, because of Jace..."

Simon blinked, remembering: *Jace* was a Herondale. The last of the Herondales. Or so he thought.

If he had family out there, lost for generations, he would want to know, wouldn't he? Was Simon supposed to tell him? Tell Clary?

He imagined a lost Herondale out there, some golden-eyed girl or boy who didn't know anything about the Shadowhunters or their sordid legacy. Maybe they would welcome finding out who they really were—but maybe, if Clary and Jace came knocking at their door, telling them stories of angels and demons and a noble tradition of death-defying insanity, they would run screaming in the opposite direction.

Sometimes, Simon wondered what would have happened if Magnus had never found him, never offered him the chance to reenter the Shadowhunter world. He would have been living a lie, sure ... but it would have been a happy lie. He would have gone to college, kept playing with his band, flirted with some non-terrifying girls, lived on the surface of things, never guessing at the darkness that lay beneath.

He guessed that in his other life, telling Clary what he knew wouldn't even have been a question; he guessed that they were the kind of friends who told each other everything.

They weren't any kind of friends now, he reminded himself. She was a stranger who loved him, but she was still a stranger.

"What do you think of it?" he asked her. "What the

Clave did to Tobias's wife and child?"

"What do you *think* I think?" Clary asked. "Given who my father was? Given what happened to Jace's parents, and how he survived it? Isn't it obvious?"

It may have been obvious to someone who knew them and their stories, but not to Simon.

Her face fell. "Oh."

His confusion must have been visible. As was her disappointment—like she was remembering all over again who he was, and who he wasn't.

"It doesn't matter. Let's just say that I do think the Law matters—but it's not the only thing that matters. I mean, if we followed the Law without thinking, would you and I ever have—"

"What?"

She shook her head. "No, I promised myself I wasn't going to keep doing this. You don't need a bunch of stories about what happened to us, who you used to be. You have to figure out who you are *now*, Simon. I want that for you, that freedom."

It amazed him, how well she understood. How she knew what he wanted without him having to ask.

It gave him the nerve to ask her something he'd been wondering ever since he got to the Academy. "Clary, back when we were friends, before you knew about Shadowhunting or anything, were you and I ... the same?"

"The same how?"

He shrugged. "You know, into weird music and comics and, like, really *not* into gym."

"You mean, were we both klutzy nerds?" Clary asked, laughing again. "That's affirmative."

"But now you're—" He waved a hand at her, indicating

the taut biceps, the graceful, coordinated way she moved, everything he knew of her past and present. "You're like this Amazon warrior."

"Thanks? I think? Jace is a good trainer. And, you know, there was incentive to get up to speed pretty quick. Fending off the apocalypse and all. Twice."

"Right. And I guess it's in your blood. I mean, it makes sense that you'd be good at all this stuff."

"Simon—" She narrowed her eyes, suddenly seeming to understand what he was getting at. "You do realize Shadowhunting isn't just about how big your muscles are, right? They don't call it Bodybuilding Academy."

He rubbed his aching biceps ruefully. "Maybe they should."

"Simon, you wouldn't be here if the people in charge didn't think you had what it takes."

"They think *he* had what it takes," Simon corrected her. "The guy with the vampy superstrength and—whatever else it is vampires bring to the table."

Clary got close enough to poke him in the chest, and then she did. Hard. "No, *you*. Simon, do you know how we got as far as we did in that demon dimension? How we managed to get ourselves close enough to Sebastian to take him down?"

"No, but I'm guessing it involved a lot of demon killing?" Simon asked.

"Not as much as there might have been, because *you* came up with a better strategy," Clary said. "Something you figured out from all those years playing D&D."

"Wait, seriously? Are you telling me that stuff actually worked in real life?"

"I'm telling you that. I'm telling you that you saved us, Simon. You did it more than once. Not because you were a vampire, not because of anything you've lost. Because of who you were. Who you still are." She stepped away then and took a deep breath. "I promised myself I wouldn't do this," she said fiercely. "I promised."

"No," he said. "I'm glad you did. I'm glad you came."

"I should get out of here," Clary said. "But try to remember about Izzy, okay? I know you can't understand this, but every time you look at her like she's a stranger, it's like ... it's like someone pressing a hot iron to her flesh. It hurts that much."

She sounded so certain, like she *knew*.

Like maybe they weren't just talking about Isabelle anymore.

Simon felt it then, not the twinge of fondness he often experienced when Clary smiled at him, but a forceful rush of love that nearly swept him off his feet and into her arms. For the first time, he looked at her, and she wasn't a stranger, she was *Clary*—his friend. His family. The girl he'd sworn always to protect. The girl he loved as fiercely as he loved himself.

"Clary—" he said. "When we were friends, it was great, right? I mean, I'm not just imagining things, feeling like this is where we belong? We got each other, we supported each other. We were good together, right?"

Her smile turned from sad to something else, something that glowed with the same certainty that he felt, that there was something real between them. It was as if he'd switched on a light inside her. "Oh, Simon," she said. "We were absolutely amazing."

The Whitechapel Fiend

By Cassandra Clare and Maureen Johnson

She lunged for the fire; Will caught her and hauled her back. Everything seemed to have gone dark and silent in Tessa's ears. All she could think about was her baby. His soft laugh, his storm-black hair like his father's, his sweet disposition, the way he put his arms around her neck, his lashes against his cheeks.

Somehow, she had fallen to the floor. It was hard against her knees. James, *she thought desperately.*

—The Whitechapel Fiend

JAMES.
IT'S ALL RIGHT.
I AM HERE.
TESS—
TESSA—

"I spy," George said, "with my little eye, something that begins with *S*."

"It's slime, isn't it?" Simon said. He was lying on his back on the cot in his dorm room. His roommate, George, was lying on the opposite cot. Both of them were staring up thoughtfully into the darkness, which involved staring at the ceiling, which was unfortunate because the ceiling was gross. "It's always slime."

"Not so," George said. "One time it was mold."

"I'm not sure we can really make the distinction between slime and mold, and I hate that I have to care about that."

"It wasn't 'slime,' anyway."

Simon considered for a moment.

"Is it ... a snake? Please tell me it's not a snake."

Simon curled up his legs involuntarily.

"It's not a snake, but now that's all I will be able to think about. Are there snakes in Idris? It seems like the kind of place where they'd drive the snakes out."

"Isn't that Ireland?" Simon said.

"I don't think there are limitations on snake driving. Surely they got rid of the snakes. Must have done. Oh God, this place has to have snakes..."

There was a faint tremor to George's soft Scottish brogue now.

"Are there raccoons here in Idris?" Simon said, trying to change the subject. He adjusted himself on the hard, narrow bed. There was no point in adjusting. Every position was just as uncomfortable as the last. "We have raccoons in New York. They can get in anywhere. They can open doors. I read online that they even know how to use keys."

"I don't like snakes. Snakes don't need keys."

Simon paused for a moment to recognize the fact that "Snakes don't need keys" was a good album name: It sounded deep for a second, but then completely shallow and obvious, which made you go back to the first thought and think it might be deep.

"So what was it?" Simon asked.

"What was what?"

"What did you spy that begins with *S*?"

"Simon."

This was the kind of game you played when you lived in a sparsely decorated room located in the basement of the Shadowhunter Academy—or, as they had started to refer to it—the floor of ultimate moisture. George had commented many times how it was a shame they weren't slugs, because it was perfectly set up for the slug lifestyle. They had come to an uneasy acceptance of the fact that many creatures had made the Academy their home after it was closed down. They no longer panicked when they heard skittering noises in the wall or under the bed. If the noises were *in* the bed, they allowed themselves some panic. This had happened more than once.

In theory, the mundanes (or dregs, as they were often called) were down in the basement because it was the most secure floor. Simon was sure there was probably some truth to that. But there was probably a lot more truth to the fact that Shadowhunters tended to have a natural snobbery that ran in the blood. But Simon had asked to be here, both with the dregs and in Shadowhunter Academy itself, so there was no point in complaining. With no Wi-Fi, no phones, no television—nights could be long. Once the lights went out, Simon and George often talked to each other across the darkness like this. Sometimes they lay in their respective beds in a companionable silence, each knowing the other was there. It was something. It was everything, really, just to have George in the room. Simon wasn't sure if he would be able to bear it otherwise. And it wasn't just the cold or the rats or anything else about the place physically—it was what was in his head, the ever-increasing noises, slices of memories. They came to him like bits of forgotten songs, tunes he couldn't place. There were remembrances of tremendous joys and fears, but he often couldn't connect them to events or people. They were just feelings, batting him around in the dark.

"Do you ever notice," George said, "how even the blankets feel wet, when you know they're dry? And I come from Scotland. I know wool. I know sheep. But *this* wool? There's something demonic about this wool. I cut my knuckles on it making the bed the other morning."

Simon *mmm*'ed a reply. There was no need for any real attention. He and George had these same conversations every night. The slime and the mold and the creatures in the walls and the rough blankets and the cold. Every night, these were the topics. Simon's thoughts drifted. He'd had two visitors recently, and neither of the visits had gone well.

Isabelle and Clary, two of the most important people in his life (as far as he could tell), had both come to the Academy. Isabelle had appeared to stake her claim on Simon, and Simon—in a move that astonished him still—told her to back off. It couldn't just go back to the way it was. Not like this, not when he couldn't remember what *it* was. And then in the training exercise, Isabelle had shown up and slain a vampire that was about to take Simon down, but she had done so coolly. There was a distressing deadness to the way she spoke. Then Clary had popped up. *Be careful with her,* Clary had said. *She's more fragile than she seems.*

Isabelle—with her whip and her ability to slice a demon in half—was more fragile than she seemed.

The guilt had been keeping him awake at night.

"Isabelle again?" George asked.

"How did you know?"

"Educated guess. I mean, she showed up and threatened to cut anyone to ribbons who got near you, and now you don't seem to be talking, and your friend Clary showed up to talk to you about her, and you also mumble her name when you sleep."

"I do?"

"On occasion. You're either saying 'Isabelle' or 'fishy smell.' Could be either, to be fair."

"How do I fix this?" Simon asked. "I don't even know what I'm fixing."

"I don't know," George said. "But morning comes early. Best try to sleep."

There was a long pause and then...

"There must be snakes," George said. "Isn't this place everything a snake could want? Cool, made of stone, lots of holes to slither in and out of, lots of mice to eat... Why am I still talking? Simon, make me stop talking..."

But Simon let him go on. Even talk of possible nearby snakes was better than what was currently going through his head.

Idris did its seasons properly, in general. It was like New York in that manner—you got each one, distinct and clear. But Idris was more pleasant than New York. The winter wasn't just frozen garbage and slush; the summer wasn't just boiling garbage and air-conditioner drippings that always felt like spit coming from overhead. Idris was greenery in the warm weather, crisp and tranquil in the cold, the air always smelling of freshness and burning log fires.

Mostly. Then there were mornings like the ones this week, which were all bluster. Winds with little fishhooks at the end of every gust. Cold that got inside the clothes. Shadowhunter gear, while practical, wasn't necessarily very warm. It was light, easy to move in, like fighting gear should be. It was not made for standing outside on a boggy stretch at seven in the morning when the sun was barely up. Simon thought of his puffy jacket from home, and his bed, and heating in general. Breakfast, which had been a glue substitute under the banner of porridge, sat heavily in his stomach.

Coffee. That's what this morning needed. Idris had no coffee places, nowhere to pop in and get a cup of the hot, steaming, and awake-making. The breakfast drink at the Academy was a thin tea that Simon suspected was not tea at all, but the watery runoff of one of the many noxious soups that emerged from the back of the kitchen. He swore he'd found a bit of potato skin in his mug that morning. He *hoped* it was potato skin.

One cup from Java Jones. Was that so much to want from life?

"Do you see this tree?" shouted Delaney Scarsbury, pointing at a tree.

Of the many questions their physical trainer had put to them over the last few months, this was one of the most logical and direct and yet confusing. Everyone could clearly see the tree. It was the only tree in this particular patch of field. It was tall, slightly tilted to the left.

Mornings with Scarsbury sounded like the name of a call-in radio show for cranks, but it was, in reality, just physical punishment designed to condition and train them to fight. And to be fair, Simon was more in shape now than he had been when he arrived.

"Do you see this tree?"

The question had been so weirdly obvious that no one had replied. Now they all mumbled a yes, they saw the tree.

"Here is what you are going to do," Scarsbury said. "You are going to climb this tree, walk along that branch"—he pointed to one heavy main branch, maybe fifteen feet from the ground—"and jump off."

"No, I'm not," Simon muttered. Similar sounds of discontent rumbled around the class. No one seemed excited about the prospect of climbing up a tree and then deliberately falling out of it.

"Morning," said a familiar voice.

Simon turned to see Jace Herondale behind him, all smiles. He looked relaxed and rested and utterly comfortable in his gear. Shadowhunters could draw runes for warmth. They didn't need hypoallergenic down-substitute puffy coats. Jace wasn't wearing a hat, either, which allowed his perfectly tousled golden hair to wave attractively in the breeze. He was keeping back and had not yet been noticed by the others, who were still listening to Scarsbury yelling over the wind while pointing at the tree.

"How did you get roped into this?" Simon asked, blowing into his hands to warm them.

Jace shrugged. "Just lending a graceful and athletic hand," he said. "It would be remiss of me to deny the newest generation of Shadowhunters a glimpse of what they could become if they were very, very, very lucky."

Simon closed his eyes for a moment. "You're doing this to impress Clary," he said. "Also checking up on me."

"By the Angel, he's gone telepathic," Jace said, pretending to stagger back. "Basically, everyone's pitching in since all your teachers ran away. I'm assisting with training. Like it or not."

"Hmm," said Simon. "Not."

"Come on now," Jace said, clapping him on the arm. "You used to love doing this."

"Did I?"

"Maybe," Jace said. "You didn't scream. Wait. No. Yes, you did. My mistake. But it's easy. This is just a training exercise."

"The last training exercise involved killing a vampire. In the training exercise before that, I watched someone get an arrow in the knee."

"I've seen worse. Come on. This is a fun exercise."

"There is no fun here," Simon said. "This is not Fun Academy. I should know. I was in a band once called Fun Academy."

"To assist you this morning," Scarsbury yelled, "we have an expert and highly physically able Shadowhunter—Jace Lightwood Herondale."

There was an audible gasp and titters of nervous laughter as every head turned in Jace's direction. There were suddenly a lot of female sighs from the class, and some male ones too. It reminded Simon of standing in line for a rock concert—at any moment, he felt, the crowd might burst into a squeeing noise most unbecoming to future demon hunters.

Jace smiled wider and stepped forward to lead the group. Scarsbury nodded his greeting and stepped back, arms folded. Jace eyed the tree for a moment and then leaned casually against it.

"The trick to falling is not to fall," Jace said.

"Wonderful," Simon said under his breath.

"You are not falling. You are choosing to descend using the most direct means possible. You remain in control of your decent. A Shadowhunter doesn't fall—a Shadowhunter drops. You've been trained in the basic mechanics of how to do this..."

Simon recalled Scarsbury shouting a few things over the wind several days before that may have been training instructions on falls. Phrases like "avoid rocks" and "not on your back" and "unless you're a complete idiot, which some of you are."

"... so now we'll take the theory and put it into practice."

Jace took hold of the tree and scampered up it with the ease of a monkey, then made his way to the branch, where he stood freely and easily.

"Now," he called down to the group, "I look at the ground. I choose my landing site. Remember—protect the head. If there's any way to break momentum, any other surface you can use to lessen the length of the fall, use it—unless it's dangerous. Don't aim for sharp rocks or branches that could pierce or break you. Bend the knees. Keep relaxed. If your hands take the impact, be sure to make contact with the entire palm, but avoid this. Feet down, then roll. Keep that momentum going. Spread out the force of the impact. Like so..."

Jace delicately stepped off the branch and dropped to the ground, striking with a subdued thud. He instantly rolled and was up on his feet again in a moment.

"Like that."

He gave his hair a little shake. Simon watched several people flush as he did so. Marisol had to cover her face with her hands for a moment.

"Excellent," said Scarsbury. "That's what you will do. Jace will assist."

Jace took this as his cue to climb the tree again. He made it look so simple, so elegant—just hand over hand, feet firmly gripped the entire way up. At the top, he took a casual seat in the nook of the branch and swung his legs.

"Who's first?"

There was no movement for a moment.

"Might as well get it over with," George said in a low voice, before holding up his hand and stepping forward.

Though George was not as nimble as Jace, he did make it up the tree. He used a lot of clutching, and his feet slipped several times. Some of the phrases he used were lost to the wind, but Simon was pretty sure they were obscene. Once George reached the branch, Jace leaned back dangerously to make room. George considered the branch for a moment—the lone, unsupported beam stretching over the ground.

“Come on, Lovelace!” Scarsbury shouted.

Simon saw Jace lean in and offer a few words of advice to George, who was still gripping the trunk of the tree. Then, with Jace nodding, George released the tree and took a few careful steps out onto the branch. He hesitated again, teetering a bit in the wind. Then he looked down, and with a pained expression, he stepped off the branch and fell heavily to the ground. The thud he made was much louder than Jace’s, but he did roll and manage to get back on his feet.

“Not bad,” Scarsbury said as George hobbled back to Simon. He was rubbing his arm.

“You do not want to do that,” he said to Simon as he approached.

Simon had already worked that out. The confirmation didn’t help his spirits.

Simon watched his classmates go up the tree one by one. For some, that took up to ten minutes of grunting and clawing and occasionally falling off halfway up. This got a loud “I told you, not on your back” from Scarsbury. Jace stayed in the tree the entire time, like some kind of rakish bird, at points smiling at the students below. Sometimes he looked elegantly bored and walked up and down the branch for fun.

When there was simply no avoiding it anymore, Simon approached for his turn. Jace smiled at him from above.

“It’s easy,” Jace said. “You probably did it all the time as a child. Just do that.”

“I’m from Brooklyn,” Simon replied. “We don’t climb trees.”

Jace shrugged, suggesting that these things were not to be helped.

The first thing Simon learned about the tree was that while it appeared to lean to the side, it was really just straight up. And while the bark was rough and cut into the meat of the hands, it was also slippery, so every time he tried to get a foothold, he lost it. He tried to do it the way he'd seen Jace and George do it—they seemed to grip the tree very lightly. Simon tried this, realized it was futile, and grabbed the tree in a hug so intimate, he wondered if they were now dating. Using this awkward clutching method and some froglike leg pushes, he managed to get up the trunk, scraping his face along the way. About three-quarters of the way up, he felt his palms slick with sweat and he started to lose his grip. The falling feeling filled him with a sudden panic and he gripped harder.

"You're doing fine," Jace said in a voice that suggested Simon was not doing fine, but that was the kind of thing Jace was supposed to say.

Simon made it to the branch using a few desperate moves he knew looked very bad from below. There was almost definitely a moment or two when his butt must have been on display in a less-than-flattering manner. But he made it. Standing up was the next trick, which he accomplished with more fevered gripping of the trunk.

"Good," Jace said, giving a quirky little smile. "Now just walk to me."

Jace walked backward down the branch. *Backward.*

Now that Simon was on the branch, it didn't look like it was fifteen feet off the ground. It looked like it was in the sky. It was round and uneven and slippery as ever and it wasn't meant to be walked on, especially not in the sneakers Simon had chosen to wear that morning.

But he'd gotten this far and he wasn't going to let Jace just do his magic backward walk while he clung to the trunk. He had gotten up there. Climbing down was a bad prospect, so there was really just the one option, and at least it was quick.

Simon took his first step. His body immediately began to shake.

"Look up," Jace said sharply. "Look at me."

"I need to see—"

"You need to look up to keep your balance. *Look at me.*"

Jace had stopped smirking. Simon looked at him.

"Now step again. Don't look down. Your feet will find the branch. Arms out for balance. Don't worry about down yet. Eyes on me."

Somehow, this worked. Simon made it six steps out onto the branch and was amazed to find himself standing there, arms rigid and out like airplane wings, the wind blowing hard. Just out on a tree branch with Jace.

"Now turn to face the Academy. Keep looking out. Use it as a horizon. That's how you stay balanced—you choose a fixed point to concentrate on. Keep your weight forward—you don't want to go over backward."

No. Simon really didn't want to do that. He moved one foot to meet the other, and then he was standing facing the pile of rocks that formed the Academy, and his fellow students below, all looking up. Most did not look impressed, but George gave him a thumbs-up.

"Now," Jace said, "bend a bit at the knees. And then I want you to just step off in one large stepping motion. Don't jump with both feet. Just step. And as you go down, bring your legs together and keep yourself relaxed."

This should not have been the hardest thing he'd ever done. Simon knew he'd done more. He knew he'd fought demons and come back from the dead. Jumping out of a tree should not have felt this terrifying.

He stepped into the air. He felt his brain react to this new information—*There's nothing there, don't do it, there's nothing there*—but momentum had already pulled his other leg off the branch and then...

The good thing that could be said about the experience was that it was quick. Points to gravity on that one. A few seconds of almost blissful fear and confusion and then a hammering feeling as his feet met the earth. His skeleton juddered, his knees buckled in submission, his aching skull lodged a formal complaint, and he fell over sideways in what would have been a roll if he had rolled and not, in fact, just remained there on the ground in a shrimp position.

"Get up, Lewis!" Scarsbury yelled.

Jace landed beside him, like a large killer butterfly, barely making a noise.

"The first one is always the hardest," he said, offering Simon a hand. "The first few dozen, really. I can't remember."

It hurt, but he didn't appear to *be* hurt. The wind was knocked out of his lungs, and he needed a moment to take a few deep breaths. He staggered back to where George was waiting, a sympathetic look on his face. The last two students completed the task, each looking as miserable as Simon, and then they were free to go for lunch. Most of the group was limping as they made their way back across the field.

Since Catarina had buried the soup in the woods, the kitchens of the Academy had been forced to try to come up with some other kind of foodstuff. As usual, an attempt was made to feature food from around the world, to reflect the many nations the students had come from. Today, Simon was informed, featured Swedish cuisine. There were meatballs, a vat of lingonberry sauce, mashed potatoes, smoked salmon, fish balls, beet salad, and at the very end, a strong-smelling item that Simon was informed was a special pickled herring from the Baltic region. Simon got the sense that, prepared by people who knew what they were doing, everything on offer would have looked a lot more delicious—except possibly the pickled herring from the Baltic region. In terms of what a vegetarian could eat, there wasn't much. He got some potatoes and lingonberry sauce and scraped one portion's worth of beet salad out of the practically empty container. Some kind Shadowhunter from Alicante had clearly taken pity on the students and provided bread rolls, which were eagerly snatched up. By the time Simon limped up to the basket, it was empty. He turned to make his way to a table and found Jace in his path. He had a roll in his hand and had already taken a bite.

"How about you sit with me?"

The Academy cafeteria looked less like a school dining hall and more like a terrible, cheap restaurant that had gotten its furnishings out of Dumpsters. There were big tables, and tiny, intimate ones. Simon, still too sore to make jokes about lunch dates, followed Jace to one of the small, rickety tables on the side of the room. He was aware of everyone watching them go. He gave George a nod, hoping to convey that he just had to do this—no offense in not sitting with him. George nodded back.

Jon, Julie, and the others in the elite course, who had been devastated to miss Falling Out of Trees with Jace Herondale 101, all stared over as if ready to leap up and save Jace from the bad company he'd fallen into, carry him away in a litter made of chocolate and roses, and bear his children.

Once they sat, Jace tucked into his lunch and didn't say

a word. Simon watched him eat and waited, but Jace was all about the food. He had taken large helpings of most things, including the pickled Baltic herring. Now that he was even closer to it, Simon began to suspect that this fish had not been pickled at all. Someone at the famed Shadowhunter Academy kitchens had *attempted* to pickle fish—something that took skill and precise adherence to instructions—and had probably just invented a new form of botulism. Jace shoveled it back. Then again, Jace was the sort of *Man vs. Wild* guy who would probably be happy to fish a trout out of a stream with his bare hands and eat it while it was still flopping.

"Did you want to talk to me about something?" Simon finally asked.

Jace forked up a meatball and looked at Simon meditatively. "I've been doing research," he said. "Into my family."

"The Herondales?" Simon supplied, after a short pause.

"You might not remember, but I have kind of a complicated family history," Jace said. "Anyway, I only found out I was a Herondale a little while ago. It took me a while to adjust to the idea. They're kind of a legendary family."

Back to the food for a few minutes. When his plates and bowls were empty, Jace sat back and regarded Simon for a moment. Simon considered asking if Jace was kind of a big deal, but decided he wouldn't get the joke.

Jace went on. "Anyway, the whole thing, it started to remind me—well, of you. It's like there are these important things in my history but I don't know all of them, and I'm trying to pull together an identity that has all these holes in it. The Herondales—some of them were good people, and some of them were monsters."

"None of that needs to affect you," Simon said. "The

choices you make are what matter, not your bloodline. But I imagine you have a lot of people in your life to tell you that. Clary. Alec." He looked at Jace sideways. "Isabelle."

Jace's eyebrows went up. "You want to talk about Isabelle? Or Alec?"

"Alec hates me and I do not know why," Simon said. "Isabelle hates me and I do know why, which is almost worse. So no, I do not want to talk about the Lightwoods."

"It's true you have a Lightwood problem," Jace said, and his golden eyes glinted. "It started with Alec. As you astutely observed, you two have a history. But I shouldn't get in the middle of that."

"Please tell me what's going on with Alec," Simon said. "You are really freaking me out."

"No," Jace said. "There are so many deep feelings involved. There's so much hurt. It wouldn't be right. I didn't come here to stir up trouble. I came here to show potential Shadowhunters how to drop from heights without breaking their necks."

Simon stared at Jace. Jace stared back with wide, innocent golden eyes.

Simon decided that the next time he saw Alec, he would have to ask Alec himself about the secrets that lay between them. This was obviously something he and Alec had to work out on their own.

"But I will say this about your Lightwood problem," Jace said, very casually. "Isabelle and Alec both have difficulty showing when they feel pain. But I can see it in both of them, especially when they try to hide it. She's in pain."

"And I made it worse," Simon said, shaking his head. "This is my fault. Me, with my memory wiped out by some kind of demon king. Me, with no concept of what happened in my life. Me, the guy with no special abilities who's probably going to get killed *in school*. I'm a monster."

"No," Jace said evenly. "No one blames you for not being able to remember. You offered yourself as a sacrifice. You were brave. You saved Magnus. And you saved Isabelle. You saved me. You need to bend your knees more."

"What?"

Jace was standing up now.

"When you first step off. Bend the knees right away. Otherwise you did pretty well."

"But what about Isabelle?" Simon asked. "What do I do?"

"I have no idea," Jace said.

"So you just came here to torture me and talk about yourself?" Simon demanded.

"Oh, Simon, Simon, Simon," said Jace. "You may not remember, but that's kind of our thing."

With that, he walked away, clearly aware of the admiring glances that followed his every step.

After lunch they had a history lecture. Usually they met in a classroom, but today everyone was assembled in the main hall. There was no grandeur to the hall—just some crooked benches, and not enough of them. The chairs from the cafeteria were dragged in to supplement, but there still weren't enough seats. So some students (the elites) had chairs and benches, and the dregs sat on the floor at the front, like the little kids in middle school. After this morning, though, a few hours of sitting on a bare, cold, stone floor was luxury.

Catarina took her place at the wobbly lectern.

"We have a special guest lecturer today," she said. "She is visiting us to talk about the role Shadowhunters play in writing history. As you are likely aware, though I don't want to make any overly optimistic assumptions, Shadowhunters have been involved in many prominent moments in mundane history. Because Shadowhunters must also guard mundanes from knowing about our world, you must also sometimes take control of the writing of that history. By this I mean you have to cover things up. You need to provide a plausible explanation for what's happened—one that does not involve demons."

"Like *Men in Black*," Simon whispered to George.

"So please give your full attention to our esteemed guest," Catarina went on. She stepped aside, and a tall young woman took her place.

"I am Tessa Gray," she said in a low, clear voice. "And I believe in the importance of stories."

The woman at the front of the room looked like she might be a sophomore in college. She was elegantly dressed in a short black skirt, cashmere sweater, and paisley scarf. Simon had seen this woman once before—at Jocelyn and Luke's wedding. Clary had said she had played a very important role in Clary's life when she was a child. She had also informed Simon that Tessa was about a hundred and fifty years old, though she certainly didn't look it.

"For you to understand this story, you have to understand who and what I am. Like Catarina, I am a warlock—however, my mother was not human but a Shadowhunter."

A murmur from around the room, which Tessa glossed over.

"I am not able to bear Marks, but I once lived among Shadowhunters—I was a Shadowhunter's wife, and my children were Shadowhunters. I was witness to much that no other Downworlder ever saw, and now I am almost the only person alive who recalls the truth behind the stories mundanes made up to explain away the times their world brushed ours. I am many things. One is a living record of Shadowhunter history. Here is one story you may have heard of—Jack the Ripper. What can you tell me about that name?"

Simon was ready for this one. He'd read *From Hell* six times. He'd been waiting all his life for someone to ask him an Alan Moore question. His hand shot up.

"He was a murderer," Simon burst out. "He killed prostitutes in London in the late 1800s. He was probably Queen Victoria's doctor, and the whole thing was a royal cover-up to hide the fact that the prince had had an illegitimate child."

Tessa smiled at him. "You are right that Jack the Ripper is the name given to a murderer—or at least, to a series of murders. What you refer to is the royal conspiracy, which has been disproven. I believe it is also the plot of a graphic novel and film called *From Hell*."

Simon's love life was complicated, but there was a pang, just for a moment, for this woman talking graphic novels with him. Ah, well. Tessa Gray, foxy nerd, was probably dating someone already.

"I will give you the simple facts," Tessa said. "Once, I was not called Tessa Gray but Tessa Herondale. In that time, in 1888, in East London, there was a string of terrible murders..."

London, October 1888

"It's not appropriate," Tessa said to her husband, Will.

"He likes it."

"Children like all sorts of things, Will. They like sweets

and fire and trying to stick their head up the chimney. Just because he likes the dagger..."

"Look how steadily he holds it."

Little James Herondale, age two, was in fact holding a dagger quite well. He stabbed it into a sofa cushion, sending out a burst of feathers.

"Ducks," he said, pointing at the feathers.

Tessa swiftly removed the dagger from his tiny hand and replaced it with a wooden spoon. James had recently become very attached to this wooden spoon and carried it with him everywhere, often refusing to go to sleep without it.

"Spoon," James said, tottering off across the parlor.

"Where did he find the dagger?" Tessa asked.

"It's possible I took him to the weapons room," Will said.

"Is it?"

"It is, yes. It's possible."

"And it's possible he somehow got a dagger from where it is secured on the wall, out of his reach," Tessa said.

"We live in a world of possibilities," Will said.

Tessa fixed a gray-eyed stare on her husband.

"He was never out of my sight," Will said quickly.

"If you could manage it," Tessa said, nodding to the sleeping figure of Lucie Herondale in her little basket by the fire, "perhaps you won't give Lucie a broadsword until she's actually able to stand? Or is that asking too much?"

"It seems a reasonable request," Will said, with an extravagant bow. "Anything for you, my pearl beyond price. Even withholding weaponry from my only daughter."

Will knelt down, and James ran to him to show off his spoon. Will admired the spoon as if it were a first edition, his scarred hand large and gentle against James's tiny back.

"Spoon," James said proudly.

"I see, Jamie *bach*," murmured Will, who Tessa had caught singing Welsh lullabies to the children on their most sleepless nights. To his children, Will showed the same love he had always shown to her, fierce and unyielding. And the same protectiveness he had only ever showed to one other person: the person James had been named after. Will's *parabatai*, Jem.

"Uncle Jem would be so impressed," she told Jamie with a smile. It was what she and Will called James Carstairs around their children, though between the two of them he was just Jem, and in public he was Brother Zachariah, a feared and respected Silent Brother.

"Jem," echoed James, quite clearly, and her smile grew. Will and James both tilted up their heads as one to look at her, their storm-cloud-black hair framing their faces. Jamie's was small and round, baby fat obscuring the bones and angles of a face that would one day be as like Will's as his hair. Two pairs of eyes, one darkly brilliant blue and one celestial gold, looked up at her with absolute trust and more than a little mischief. Her boys.

The long, long London summer days that Tessa was still getting used to, even after several years, were now starting to shorten rather rapidly. No more sunlight at ten at night—now the night was gathering at six, and the fog was heavy, and faintly yellow, and it pressed against the windows. Bridget had drawn the curtains, and the rooms were dim but cozy.

It was a strange thing, being a Shadowhunter and a parent. She and Will had been living lives that constantly involved danger, and then suddenly, two very small children had joined them. Yes, they were two very small children who occasionally got hold of daggers and would one day start training to become warriors—if they wished to do so. But now they were simply two very small children. Little James, wobbling around the Institute with his spoon. Little Lucie napping in her cradle or basket or in one of many pairs of willing arms.

These days Will was, Tessa was glad to note, a bit more careful about taking risks. (Usually. She would really have to make sure there were no more daggers for the children.) Bridget could usually keep the children well in hand, but Tessa and Will liked to be at home as much as they could. Cecily and Gabriel's little Anna was a year older than James, and had already blazed her way through the Institute. She sometimes made attempts to go for walks on her own in London, but was always blocked by Auntie Jessamine, who stood guard by the door. Whether or not Anna knew that Auntie Jessamine was a ghost was unclear. She was simply the loving, ethereal force by the doorway who shooed her back inside and told her to stop taking her father's hats. Anna's younger brother, Christopher, James's age, was a quiet boy, more given to taking apart the clocks in the parlor than to talking.

It was a good life. There was a feeling of safety about it that reminded Tessa of a more peaceful time, back when she was in New York, back before she knew all the truths about herself and the world she lived in. Sometimes, when she sat with her children by the fire, it all felt so ... normal. Like there were no demons, no creatures in the night.

She allowed herself these moments.

"What are we having this evening?" Will asked, tucking the dagger into a drawer. "It smells a bit like lamb stew."

Before Tessa could answer, she heard the door open and Gabriel Lightwood came hurrying in, the smell of the cold fog trailing in his wake. He didn't bother to remove his coat. From the way he was walking and the look on his face, Tessa could tell that this little moment of domestic tranquility was over.

"Something wrong?" Will asked.

"This," Gabriel said. He held up a broadsheet newspaper called the *Star*. "It's awful."

"I agree," Will said. "Those halfpenny rags are terrible. But you seem to be more upset about them than is appropriate."

"They may be halfpenny rags, but listen to this."

He stepped under a gaslight, unfolded the paper, and snapped it once to straighten it.

"*The terror of Whitechapel,*" he read.

"Oh," Will said. "That."

Everyone in London knew about the terror in Whitechapel. The murders had been extraordinarily horrible. News of the killings now filled every paper.

"*... has walked again, and this time has marked down two victims, one hacked and disfigured beyond discovery, the other with her throat cut and torn. Again he has got away clear; and again the police, with wonderful frankness, confess that they have not a clue. They are waiting for a seventh and an eighth murder, just as they waited for a fifth, to help them to it. Meanwhile, Whitechapel is half mad with fear. The people are afraid even to talk with a stranger. Notwithstanding the repeated proofs that the murderer has but one aim, and seeks but one class in the community, the spirit of terror has got fairly abroad, and no one knows what steps a practically defenceless community may take to protect itself or avenge itself on any luckless wight who may be taken for the enemy. It is the duty of journalists to keep their heads cool, and not inflame men's passions when what is wanted is cool temper and clear thinking; and we shall try and write calmly about this new atrocity.*"

"Very lurid," said Will. "But the East End is a violent place for mundanes."

"I do not think this is a mundane."

"Wasn't there a letter? The killer sent something?"

"Yes, a very odd letter. I have that as well."

Gabriel went over to a desk in the corner and opened it, revealing a neat stack of newspaper cuttings.

"Yes, here it is. *Dear Boss, I keep on hearing the police have caught me but they won't fix me just yet. I have laughed when they look so clever and talk about being on the right track. That joke about Leather Apron gave me real fits. I am down on whores and I shan't quit ripping them till I do get buckled. Grand work the last job was. I gave the lady no time to squeal. How can they catch me now. I love my work and want to start again. You will soon hear of me with my funny little games. I saved some of the proper red stuff in a ginger beer bottle over the last job to write with but it went thick like glue and I can't use it. Red ink is fit enough I hope. Ha. Ha. The next job I do I shall clip the lady's ears off and send to the police officers just for jolly wouldn't you. Keep this letter back till I do a bit more work, then give it out straight. My knife's so nice and sharp I want to get to work right away if I get a chance. Good luck. Yours truly, Jack the Ripper.*"

"That's quite a name he's given himself," Tessa said. "And quite horrific."

"And almost certainly false," Gabriel said. "A bit of nonsense made up by newspapermen to keep selling the story. And good for us as well, as it gives a human face—or at least the appearance of a human hand—to it. But come, I'll show you."

He waved them over to the table in the middle of the room and removed a map from inside his coat. He spread this out.

"I have just come from the East End," he said. "Something about the stories disturbed me, for more than the obvious reasons. I went there to have a look about for myself. And what happened last night proves my theory. There have been many murders recently—all of women, women who..."

"Prostitutes," Tessa said.

"Quite," Gabriel said.

"Tessa has such an extensive vocabulary," Will said. "It is one of the most attractive things about her. Shame about yours, Gabriel."

"Will, listen to me." Gabriel allowed himself a long sigh.

"Spoon!" James said, running at his uncle Gabriel and jabbing him in the thigh. Gabriel mussed the boy's hair affectionately.

"You're such a good boy," he said. "I often wonder how you could possibly be Will's."

"Spoon," James said, leaning against his uncle's leg lovingly.

"No, Jamie," Will urged. "Your honorable father has been impugned. Attack, attack!"

"Bridget," Tessa said. "Could you take James to have his supper?"

James was ushered from the room, caught up in Bridget's skirts.

"The first murder," Gabriel said, "was here. Buck's Row. That occurred on August the thirty-first. Very vicious, with a number of long cuts to the abdomen. The second was on Hanbury Street on September eighth. Her name was Annie Chapman, and she was found in the courtyard behind a house. This murder had a very similar set of incisions, but was very much worse. The contents of the abdomen were simply removed. Some organs were placed on her shoulder.

Some organs were simply gone. All of the work was done with a surgical precision, and would have taken a skilled surgeon some time to do. This was done in minutes, outdoors, without much light to work by. This was the work that got my attention. And now the last murders, which were only a few nights ago—these were fiendish works indeed. Now, observe closely. The first murder of that night took place here."

He pointed to a spot on the map marked Dutfield's Yard.

"This is right off of Berner Street, you see? This was Elizabeth Stride, and she was found at one in the morning. Similar injuries, but seemingly incomplete. Just forty-five minutes later, the body of Catherine Eddowes is found in Mitre Square."

Gabriel traced his finger along the route from Berner Street to Mitre Square.

"It's a distance of over half a mile," he said. "I've just walked it several times. This second murder was much more terrible in nature. The body was utterly dismembered and organs were removed. The work was very delicate in nature, very skilled. And it was done in darkness, in no more than a few minutes. Work that would have taken a surgeon much more time and certainly some light. It's simply not possible, and yet, it happened."

Tessa and Will considered the map in front of them for a moment while the fire crackled gently behind them.

"He could have had a carriage," Will said.

"Even with a carriage, there would simply not be time to commit these acts. And they are most certainly acts committed by the same being."

"Not the work of werewolves?"

"Definitely not," Gabriel said. "Nor vampires. The bodies have not been drained. They haven't been consumed or torn. They have been cut, with organs removed and arranged, as if by design. This"—Gabriel tapped the map for emphasis—"is demonic in nature. And it has set London into a panic."

"But why would a demon target only these poor women?" Will asked.

"There must be something they require. The fiend does seem to take ... childbearing organs. I propose we patrol the East End, beginning at once. This area."

Gabriel drew a circle around Spitalfields with his finger.

"This is the center of the activity. This is where it must be. Are we agreed?"

"Where's Cecily?" Will asked.

"She has already started the work. She is there now, speaking to some of the women on the street. They find it easier speaking to her. We must start at once."

Will nodded.

"I have one further suggestion. As the beast seems to be attracted to a certain class of woman, we should use glamours ..."

"Or shape-shifters," Tessa said.

"... to attract the demon."

Will's eyes caught blue fire. "You are suggesting using my wife and my sister to lure the thing out?"

"It is the best way," Gabriel said. "And your sister is *my* wife. Both Tessa and Cecily are more than capable, and we would be there as well."

"It is a good plan," Tessa said, forestalling Will and Gabriel's next argument. (They would always have time for another one.)

Gabriel nodded. "Again, are we agreed?"

Tessa looked into her husband's bright blue eyes.

"Agreed," she said.

"Agreed," said Will. "On one condition."

"And what condition is—" Gabriel broke off with a sigh. "Ah," he said. "Brother Zachariah."

"This monster is violent," said Will. "We might need a healer. Someone with the power of a Silent Brother. This is a special situation."

"I cannot recall a situation you did *not* think was special and required his presence," said Gabriel dryly. "You have been known to call upon Brother Zachariah for a broken toe."

"It was turning green," said Will.

"He's right," said Tessa. "Green doesn't suit him. Makes him look bilious." She smiled at Gabriel. "There is no reason for Jem not to accompany us. We may yet need him and it does no harm to have him there."

Gabriel opened his mouth and then closed it again with a click. He hadn't known Jem Carstairs that well before Jem had become a Silent Brother, but he had liked him. Still, unlike his wife, Gabriel was one of the people who (clearly) thought it odd that even though Tessa had once been engaged to Jem, she and Will considered him part of their family and tried to include him in everything they did.

There were few people in the world who understood how much Will and Jem had loved each other, *did* love each other, and how much Will missed him. But Tessa did.

"If we might be able to save one of these poor women, we must try," said Tessa. "If Jem can help, that would be wonderful. If not, Cecily and I will do all we can. I hope you do not think either of us lack the courage."

Will stopped glaring at Gabriel, and turned to Tessa. He looked at her and his face softened: The traces of the wild, broken boy he had been vanished, replaced with the expression often worn by the man he was now, who knew what it was to love and be loved. "Dear heart," he said. He took her hand and kissed it. "Who knows your courage better than I?"

"That October," Tessa Gray said, "there were no Ripper murders reported. The London Institute made sure to patrol every evening, right through until sunrise. It was believed that this kept the demon at bay."

It had gotten dark outside, even though it was only around three in the afternoon. The hall had gotten considerably colder as the sun had faded, and all of the students were hunkered down in the seats, arms wrapped around themselves to keep warm, but utterly alert. Tessa had been talking for some time, showing maps of London, describing truly horrific murders. It was the kind of thing that kept you awake.

"I think," she said, rubbing her hands together, "that it is time for a short break. We'll resume in half an hour."

During long lecture classes, the Academy was merciful enough to allow one bathroom break every few hours, along with some more of the murky tea, which was put out in one of the large halls in steaming, ancient urns. Simon was cold enough to take a cup. Again, some benevolent Shadowhunter had provided a tray of small cakes. Simon was able to get a fleeting look at them before they were snatched up by elites, who were excused first. Some sad little biscuits were left on the side. They looked like they were made of packed sand.

"Good stuff today," George said, picking up a dry biscuit. "Well, not good, but more interesting than usual. I like the new teacher as well. You wouldn't think she was—how old is she?"

"I think a hundred and fifty or something. Maybe older," said Simon. His mind was elsewhere. Tessa Gray had mentioned two names: *Jem Carstairs* and *Brother Zachariah*. Apparently they were the same person. Which was interesting, because somewhere in Simon's shifting memories, he knew those names. And he remembered Emma Carstairs, facing Jace—he couldn't remember why, but he knew it had happened—and saying, *The Carstairs owe the Herondales.*

Simon glanced over at Jace, who was seated in an armchair, being waited on hand and foot by students.

"Miss Gray looks very good for a hundred and fifty," said George, looking over at where Tessa was examining the tea suspiciously. As she moved away from the table, she cast a quick glance toward Jace. There was a wistful sadness in her expression.

At that moment Jace stood up from his chair, scattering hangers-on. The elites all moved to make way for him, and there was a quiet chorus of "Hi, Jace" and a few wheezing sighs as he made his way over to Simon and George.

"You did really well today," he said to George, who was flushed and appeared speechless.

"I … oh. Right. Yeah. Thanks, Jace. Thanks."

"Are you still sore?" Jace asked Simon.

"Mostly my pride."

"That's supposed to goeth before a fall anyway."

Simon winced at the joke. "Really?"

"I've been waiting to say that for a while."

"That's not possible." Jace's expression showed that it was indeed possible. Simon sighed. "Look, Jace, if I could talk to you for a second—"

"Anything you want to tell me can be said around my good buddy George here."

You're going to regret that, Simon thought. "Fine," he said. "Go talk to Tessa."

Jace blinked. "Tessa Gray? The warlock?"

"She used to be a Shadowhunter," said Simon carefully. "Look, she was telling us a story—more a piece of history, really—and do you remember what Emma said? About the Carstairs owing the Herondales?"

Jace put his hands in his pockets. "Sure, I remember. I'm surprised *you* remember."

"I think you should talk to Tessa," said Simon. "I think she could tell you about the Herondales. Things you don't know already."

"Hm," Jace said. "I'll think about it."

He walked off. Simon looked after him, frustrated. He wished he could remember enough about how he and Jace interacted normally to know whether this meant Jace was going to ignore his advice or not.

"He treats you like a friend," George said. "Or an equal. You really did know each other. I mean, I knew that, but..."

Unsurprisingly, Jonathan Cartwright sidled up to them.

"Just talking to Jace, huh?" he said.

"Are you a detective?" Simon replied. "Your powers of observation are amazing."

Jonathan acted like Simon had never spoken.

"Yeah—Jace and I will catch up later."

"Are you really going to keep up the pretense that you know Jace?" Simon asked. "Because you know that's not going to work now, right? Eventually Jace will just come over and say he doesn't know you."

Jonathan looked glum. Before he could say anything, though, the signal was given for everyone to return to the hall, and Simon shuffled in with the others. They took their seats again, and settled in to listen to Tessa.

"We continued to do nightly patrols of the area," Tessa began. "Our duty as Shadowhunters is to protect the mundane world from the influence of demons. We walked, we watched, and we warned all those we could. As much as it was possible, women working in the East End tried to take more care and not walk alone as much. But for women in that profession, safety was rarely a consideration. I had always assumed their lives were hard, but I had no idea..."

London, November 9, 1888

Tessa Herondale certainly knew what poverty was, that it existed. In the time when her aunt had died and she was a young girl left friendless and defenseless in New York, she had felt the cold breath of poverty like a monster stalking at her back. But in the month she and Cecily spent walking the streets of East London under the guise of prostitutes, she knew what it would have been if poverty had caught her and torn at her with its claws.

They dressed the part—old, tattered clothes, heavy rouge on the cheeks. They had to use glamours for the rest, for the true mark of the prostitute was want. Missing teeth. Jaundiced skin. Bodies tight from malnourishment and bent from disease. Women who walked and walked all night long because there was nowhere to sleep, nowhere to sit. They sold themselves for pennies to buy gin because the gin kept them warm, took away the pain for an hour, numbed them to the terrible, brutal reality of their lives. If these women could get the money to have a place to sleep for the night, that didn't mean a bed. It could mean a spot on a floor, or even just a bit of wall to sit against, with a rope run around the room to keep the sleepers from falling over. By the crack of dawn, they'd be tossed out on the street again.

Walking among them, Tessa felt dirty. She felt the remains of her supper in her belly. She knew that her bed in the Institute was warm and contained someone who loved her and would protect her. These women had bruises and cuts. They fought over corners and bits of cracked mirror and scraps of cloth.

And there were children as well. They sat in the fetid streets, no matter their age. Their skin was so dirty as to never be clean. She wondered how many of them had ever had a hot meal in their lives, served on a plate. Had they ever known a home?

Over it all, the smell. The smell was what really ground itself into Tessa's soul. The tang of urine, the night soil, the vomit.

"I'm getting tired of this," said Cecily.

"I think everyone here is tired," Tessa replied.

Cecily sighed sadly.

"One carriage ride away and the streets are quiet and spotless. It's a different world in the West End."

A drunken man approached them and made an overture. Since they had to play the part, Cecily and Tessa smiled and led him to an alley, where they inserted him into an empty oyster barrel and left him.

"A month of this and no sign," Tessa said as they walked away from the flailing, upturned legs of the man. "Either we're keeping it away, or..."

"Or this simply isn't working."

"Magnus Bane would be useful at a time like this."

"Magnus Bane is enjoying New York," Cecily replied. "You're a warlock."

"I don't have Magnus's experience. Anyway, it's nearly dawn. Another hour and we can go home."

Will and Gabriel had taken to posting themselves in the Ten Bells pub, which seemed to be the central place for news of the killer. Indeed, many locals said they had seen him there with the victims before the murders. Sometimes Jem would come by with news from the Silent City. It wasn't unusual for Cecily and Tessa to return exhausted to the pub at the crack of dawn, and find Gabriel gone and Will asleep, wrapped up in Brother Zachariah's parchment robes, head on the table.

Jem would be reading a book, or quietly looking out the window. He could see, in his own fashion, despite his closed eyes. He was glamoured, so that his appearance would not shock the tavern's denizens. Tessa could always feel Cecily tense when she first saw Jem: black runes scored his cheeks, and there was a single white streak in his dark hair.

Sometimes, after Cecily and Gabriel left, Tessa would sit with her hand in Jem's and Will sleeping against her shoulder, listening to the rain on the windows. It never did last for long, though, since she did not like leaving the children alone so much, though Bridget was an excellent nurse.

It was hard on both families. The children would wake to find four exhausted parents who drew endless runes for wakefulness and yet still could barely keep up with Anna, running about in her uncle's waistcoat, or James, waving his spoon and trying to find the dagger he had seen and loved. Lucie woke at all hours needing milk and embraces.

And here it was, another dawn walking the streets of the East End, and for what? And the dawn was coming later and later. The nights were so very long. As the sun rose over

Christ Church in Spitalfields, Cecily turned to Tessa again.

"Home," she said.

"Home," Tessa replied wearily.

They had arranged for a carriage to come for them that morning on Gun Street. They met Will and Gabriel there. They looked a bit worse for wear, as they often had to drink gin all night in order to blend in with the locals. There had been no Jem that night, and Will seemed restless.

"Did you find out anything?" Tessa asked.

"The same as usual," Gabriel said, slurring a little. "All the victims were seen with *a man*. He varies in stature and all manner of appearance."

"So likely an Eidolon," Will said. "It's so generic that it might even be a Du'sien, but I don't think a Du'sien could get that close and convince a woman he was an actual human male, no matter how drunk she was."

"But that tells us nothing," Cecily said. "If it's an Eidolon, it could be anyone."

"It's being remarkably consistent, though," Will said. "It always comes as a man and it always takes women. We're getting nowhere with this."

"Or we're getting everywhere," Gabriel replied. "It hasn't come back."

"We can't do this *forever*."

They'd been having this same conversation every night for the past week. This one ended as it usually did, with the two couples leaning against each other in the back of the carriage and falling asleep until they reached the Institute. They greeted their children, who were having their breakfast with Bridget, and they listened with half-closed eyes as Anna rambled on about her many plans for the day and James banged his spoon.

Tessa and Will started the climb up the steps to their bedroom. Cecily waited for Gabriel, who was lingering in the front parlor.

"I'll be up shortly," he said, his eyes bloodshot. "I just want to read the morning papers."

Gabriel always did this—always checked, every morning. So Tessa, Will, and Cecily returned to bed. Once in their bedroom, Tessa cleaned her face in the basin with the hot water Bridget had left. Their fire was burning, and the bed was turned back, waiting for them. They fell into it gratefully.

They had barely fallen asleep when Tessa heard a fevered banging at the door and Gabriel admitted himself.

"It's happened again," he said, breathless. "By the Angel, this is the worst one yet."

The carriage was recalled, and within the hour, they were on their way back to the East End, this time dressed in gear.

"It happened in a place called Miller's Court, off Dorset Street," Gabriel said.

Of all the terrible streets in East London, Dorset Street was the worst. It was a short road, just off Commercial Street. Tessa had learned much of the goings-on of Dorset Street in the last few weeks. A pair of abusive slum landlords controlled much of the street. There was so much screaming, so much poverty and stench crowded into a small space that it felt like it could push the air out of the lungs. The houses there were subdivided into tiny rooms, each little space rented away. This was a street where everyone had an empty stare, where the prevailing feeling was of desperation.

On the way, Gabriel told them what he'd managed to

find out from the morning papers—the address (number thirteen), the victim's name (Mary Kelly). There was a parade moving through the city for Lord Mayor's Day. News of the crime had spread, though, and was making its way along the parade route. Newspaper boys were chanting about the murder and selling papers like mad. Cecily peered out from the curtain of the carriage.

"They seem to be celebrating it," she said. "They're smiling and running to buy the newspapers. My God, how can people celebrate such a thing?"

"It's interesting," Will said, with a dark grin. "Danger is appealing. Especially to those with nothing to lose."

"It's going to be madness down there," Gabriel said.

Indeed, crowds had already gathered all along the road to Dorset Street. The residents were all out watching the police. The police were attempting to hold people back from a small, dark doorway halfway up the road.

"There," Gabriel said. "Miller's Court. We won't be able to get near it unless you can get in, Tessa. There's a detective down there called Abberline from Scotland Yard. If we can get him over here, or one of the constables working inside the room..."

"I'll get one of them," Will said, breaking through the crowd.

He returned a few minutes later with a man of middling age, with a kindly appearance. He did appear to be very busy, and his forehead was creased with consternation. Whatever Will had told him, it was enough to lure him away from the place of the crime.

"Where is it?" he said, following Will. "You're quite sure..."

"Quite sure."

It was hard to keep people from following them, so Cecily, Tessa, and Gabriel had to block the way while Will led the inspector down an alley. He whistled a few moments later. He was standing in the doorway of a cheap rented room.

"In here," Will said. The inspector was in the corner, looking quite asleep. His clothes were missing. "He'll be fine, but he'll likely wake up soon. Put these on."

While Tessa took the clothes and changed herself into the form of Abberline, Will filled her in on a few more facts he had gotten from people in the street. Mary Kelly was probably last seen at two thirty in the morning, but one person claimed to have seen her as late as eight thirty. No matter what, whatever had killed her had probably long since vanished.

Once Tessa was ready, Will helped her push her way back through the crowd, down Dorset Street, to the small entryway that was Miller's Court. Tessa stepped through the dark passageway into a very small courtyard, barely wide enough to turn around in. There were several houses here, cheaply whitewashed. Dozens of faces peered at her from dirty, broken windows.

Room thirteen was barely a room—it was clearly part of a larger space in which a cheap partition had been constructed. It was mostly empty, containing only a few pieces of broken furniture. It was very, very hot, as if a fire had blazed all night.

In all her time fighting demons, Tessa had never seen anything like this.

There was blood.

It was in such a large amount that Tessa wondered how one small body could contain so much. It had turned part of the floor black, and the bed, on which the woman rested, was utterly stained. There was no other color. As for the woman herself—she was no more. Her body was destroyed in a way that could barely be comprehended. This had taken time. Her face—there was nothing much left to speak of. Many parts of her were removed. They could be seen in many places, around her on the bed. Some parts of her were on a table.

A man was leaning over her. There was a doctor's bag on the floor, so Tessa steadied herself and then spoke.

"Well, doctor?"

The doctor turned.

"I think we'll have to move her soon. They're trying to break in. We'll have to move her carefully."

"Summarize for me the general situation. I need a concise report."

The doctor stood and wiped his bloodstained hands on his trousers.

"Well, a very deep cut across the throat. The head is nearly off. You can see the nose is gone, much of the skin. There are so many slashes and incisions in the abdomen I barely know where to start. The abdominal cavity is empty and her hands have been placed inside the opening. You can see he's left some of the contents here in this room, but some are missing. The heart is gone. The skin on the table I believe to be from the thighs..."

Tessa could not really take in much more of the information. This was enough.

"I see," she said. "There's someone I have to speak to."

"Make the arrangements for her to be moved," the doctor said. "We can't keep her here. They're going to get in. They want to see."

"Constable," Tessa said to a policeman by the door, "see to it that a cart is brought."

Tessa walked away quickly, back down through the crowd, breathing in as deeply as she could to get the smell of blood and entrails out of her nose. She felt a queasiness she had not experienced since her pregnancies. Will took one look at her and embraced her. Cecily came forward and put smelling salts under her nose. They had learned that smelling salts were necessary.

"Bring out the detective," Tessa said, when she had recovered. "He's needed."

The inspector was retrieved and dressed. The smelling salts were applied, and he slowly came around. Once they had him on his feet and assured him that he had simply fainted, they left the area quickly and walked toward White's Row.

"Whatever it was," Gabriel said, "it's likely long gone. It happened hours ago. By having the body indoors, it went unnoticed for some time."

He took out his Sensor, but it showed no activity.

"I suggest we return to the Institute," he said. "We've learned what we can here. It's time to apply ourselves to the problem in a different way. We have to look at the clues it leaves behind."

"The people," Tessa said.

"The people," Gabriel corrected himself.

They were more awake now. Tessa wondered if she would ever sleep again. She found the transition from East to West London more repugnant this time—the clean buildings, the space, the trees, the parks, the lovely carriages, and the lovely clothes and shops. And just a mile or so away...

"What is done cannot be undone," Will said, taking her hand.

"You didn't see her."

"But we will catch the thing that attacked her."

As soon as they turned onto Fleet Street, Tessa felt something wasn't right. She couldn't figure out what it was. The street was utterly quiet. One of the servants from a neighboring property was sweeping leaves from the step. There was a coal cart and a wagon from a greengrocer delivering vegetables. She sat upright, every nerve tense, and when the carriage stopped, she swung the door open quickly and bounded out. Seeing her reaction, the other three followed in a similar fashion.

The first thing that confirmed her fears was that Bridget did not greet them at the door.

"Bridget?" Tessa called.

Nothing.

She looked up at their windows—clean, unbroken, dark. The curtains had been drawn. Will pushed open the door.

They found Bridget at the foot of the staircase. Cecily rushed to her.

"Unconscious," she said. "But breathing. The children! Who is with the children?"

As one, they raced up the stairs. Every light was out, every door closed, every curtain drawn. They all went in separate directions, running to the nursery, to the bedrooms, to every room on the upper floors. Nothing.

"Shadowhunters..."

The voice was neither male nor female, and it seemed to come from everywhere. Will and Tessa met in the corridor, and Will held a witchlight high.

"What are you?" he yelled. "Where are the children?"

"Shadowhunters..."

"Where are the children? You can't have an interest in them. Show yourself."

"Shadowhunters..."

Gabriel and Cecily appeared, seraph blades ready. Will and Tessa reached for theirs. They walked down the steps, watching in every direction.

"I follow you," hissed the voice, which now seemed to come from below them. *"Shadowhunters. I follow you home. Play my game."*

"What is your game?" Will called back. "I'll play any game you like if you show yourself."

"The game is to hide. I like to hide. I like to take ... the pieces. I hide. I take the pieces."

"I know you have form," Will said. "You've been seen. *Show yourself.*"

"Spoon!"

The cry came from the direction of the dining room. All four ran toward the voice. When they opened the door, they found James standing at the far end of the room, spoon held aloft.

"James!" Tessa cried. "Come to Mama! Come now, James!"

James laughed and, instead of running to Tessa, turned in the direction of the great fireplace, within which a tremendous fire burned high. He ran directly into it.

"James!"

Will and Tessa both ran for him, but halfway there, the fire flared up in a multitude of colors: blue and green and black. Heat poured from it, sending them stumbling back.

It subsided as quickly as it had arisen. They dashed again for the fireplace, but there was no sign of James.

"No, *no*!" Tessa screamed. *"Jamie!"*

She lunged for the fire; Will caught her and hauled her back. Everything seemed to have gone dark and silent in Tessa's ears. All she could think about was her baby. His soft laugh, his storm-black hair like his father's, his sweet disposition, the way he put his arms around her neck, his lashes against his cheeks.

Somehow, she had fallen to the floor. It was hard against her knees. *James*, she thought desperately.

A cool hand closed about her wrist. There were words in her head, soft and silent, cool as water. *I am here.*

Her eyes flew open. Jem was kneeling over her. The hood of his robes was thrown back, his black-and-silver hair disarrayed. *It's all right. That was not James. That was the demon itself, tricking you. James is in the house.*

Tessa gasped. "My God! Is that the truth?"

Strong arms were suddenly around her, hugging her tight. "It's true. Jem's had a tracking spell on Lucie and James since they were born. They're alive, they just need us to find them. Tess—Tessa—" She felt Will's tears against her shoulder.

Jem was still holding her hand. *I called for James*, she thought, *and he came.*

Tessa stayed where she was. It was the first time in her life, she thought, that her legs had felt so weak that she couldn't rise. Will had his arms around her and her hand was in Jem's. That was enough to keep her breathing. *The Silent City believes the demon to be a sort of trickster. It means for you to chase it around the Institute. Its motives are unclear, but they seem to be those of a child.*

"If it is a child...," Tessa began, almost to herself.

The others turned to her.

"If it's a child, it thinks it's playing a game. It plays with women. I think it wants ... a mother."

Suddenly it was as if a great wind shook the room.

"I will play," called a different voice.

"Jessamine!" Will said. "She's inside the house."

"I will play with you," said Jessamine's voice, louder now. It seemed to come from every room. "I have toys. I have a dollhouse. Play with *me*."

There was a long silence. Then all of the gas jets flared, sending columns of blue flame almost to the ceiling. Just as quickly, they were sucked back down to the jets and the room was dark again. The fire went out.

"My dollhouse is wonderful," Jessamine's voice went on. "It is very small."

"Very small?" came the reply.

"Bring the children and we shall play."

There was another great whoosh of wind through the room.

"Jessamine's room," Will said.

They made their way carefully to Jessamine's room, where the door stood open. There was Jessamine's dollhouse, her pride and joy, and next to it, the transparent, gossamer figure of Jessamine. A moment later, something came down the chimney, a kind of fog that splintered into pieces and floated about the room like bits of cloud. Jessamine was busy moving about the dolls in one of the rooms and paid attention to no one.

"We need more of us to play," she said.

"It is very small. So many pieces."

The fog drifted toward the dollhouse, but Jessamine suddenly flared. She became like a web, wrapping herself around the dollhouse.

"We need more of us to play," Jessamine hissed. "The children."

"They are in the walls."

"In the walls?" Gabriel said. "How can they..."

"The chimneys," Cecily said. "It uses the chimneys."

They ran from room to room. Each child was found, sound asleep, tucked up into a chimney. Anna was in one of the empty Shadowhunter rooms. James was in the kitchen, Christopher in the parlor. Lucie was in Cecily and Gabriel's bedroom. Once they were secured, along with Bridget, the two sets of parents returned to Jessamine's room, where the shimmering figure of Jessamine was playing with a small girl. Jessamine appeared to be utterly engrossed in the game until she saw the others, who nodded to her.

"Now we will play a new game," Jessamine said.

The small girl turned toward Jessie, and Tessa caught sight of her face. It was pale and smooth, a child's face, but her eyes were entirely black, with no whites to them at all. They looked like specks of ash. *"No. This game."*

"You must close your eyes. It is a very good game. We are going to hide."

"Hide?"

"Yes. We shall play hide-and-seek. You must close your eyes."

"I like to hide."

"But first you must seek. Close your eyes."

The demon child, a small girl, barely five years of age in appearance, closed her eyes. As she did, Will brought the seraph blade down on her and the room was splattered with ichor.

"And it was gone," Tessa said. "The problem, of course, was that the rest of London couldn't be told that it was over. Jack the Ripper had been conjured up out of thin air, and now there was no Jack the Ripper to put in the dock. There would be no capture, no trial, no public hanging. The killings simply stopped. We considered trying to stage something, but there was so much scrutiny by that point that we felt this might complicate matters. But as it turned out, we didn't need to do anything. The public and the newspapers carried the story. New things were published every day, even though we knew there was nothing to report. It turned out people were willing to make up many theories of their own, and they've continued to do so since 1888. Everyone wants to catch the uncatchable killer. Everyone wants to be the hero of the story. And this has remained true in many cases since. In the absence of facts, the media will often make up stories of their own. It can save us a lot of work. In many ways, modern media is one of our greatest assets when it comes to covering up the truth. Do not discount mundanes. They weave their own stories, to make sense of their world. Some of you mundanes will help us make better sense of ours. Thank you for your attention this afternoon," Tessa finished. "I wish you all the luck in the world as you continue your training. What you do is brave and important."

"A round of applause for our esteemed guest," Catarina said.

This was given, and Tessa stepped down and went over to a man, who kissed her lightly on the cheek. He was slender, and very elegant, dressed in black and white. His black hair had one single white streak in it, completing the dichromatic look.

Memories assailed Simon, some easy to access, some hidden behind the frustrating web of forgetfulness. Jem had been at Luke and Jocelyn's wedding as well. The way that he smiled at Tessa, and she back at him, made it clear what their relationship was—they were in love, of the realest, truest kind.

Simon thought of Tessa's story, of the Jem who had been a Silent Brother, and had been a part of her life so long ago. Silent Brothers did live a long time, and Simon's foggy memory did recall something about one who had been returned to normal mortal life by heavenly fire. Which meant that Jem had lived in the Silent City for more than a hundred years, until his service was over. He had returned to life to live with his immortal love.

Now that was a complicated relationship. It made a little memory loss and former vampire status seem almost normal.

Dinner that night was a new culinary terror: Mexican food. There were roast chickens, or *pollo asado*, with the feathers still on, and square tortillas.

Jace didn't appear. Simon didn't have to look around for him, as the entire cafeteria was on alert. Had there been a sighting of his mighty blond head, Simon would have heard the intake of breath. Dinner was followed by two hours of mandatory study in the library. After all that, Simon and George returned to their room, only to find Jace standing by the door.

"Evening," he said.

"Seriously," Simon said. "How long have you been lurking here?"

"I wanted to talk to you." Jace had his hands stuffed in his pockets and was leaning against the wall, looking like an advertisement for a fashion magazine. "Alone."

"People will say we're in love," Simon said.

"You could come into our room," George said. "If you

want to talk. If it's private, I can put earplugs in."

"I'm not going in there," Jace said, glancing in the open doorway. "That room is so damp you could probably hatch frogs on the walls."

"Ah, that'll be in my head now," George said. "I hate frogs."

"So what do you want?" Simon said.

Jace smiled lightly.

"George, go inside the room," Simon said, a bit apologetically. "I'll be right in."

George ducked into their bedroom and shut the door behind him. Simon was now alone with Jace in a long corridor, which was a situation he felt like he'd been in before.

"Thank you," Jace said, surprisingly directly. "You were right about Tessa."

"She's related to you?"

"I went to talk to her." Jace looked shyly pleased, as if a small light inside him had been turned on. It was the sort of expression that would, Simon suspected, have slain adolescent girls in their tracks. "She's my great-great-great-something-grandmother. She was married to Will Herondale. I've learned about him before. He was part of stopping a massive demon invasion into Britain. She and Will were the first Herondales to run the London Institute. I mean, it isn't anything I didn't know, historically, but it's— Well, as far as I know, there isn't anyone alive who shares blood with me. But Tessa does."

Simon leaned back against the wall of the corridor. "Did you tell Clary?"

"Yeah, I was on the phone with her for a couple of hours. She said Tessa hinted at some of this stuff during Luke and Jocelyn's wedding, but she didn't come right out and say it.

She didn't want me to feel burdened."

"Do you?" Simon said. "Feel burdened, that is."

"No," Jace said. "I feel like there's someone else who understands what it means to be a Herondale. Both the good parts and the bad. I worried because of my father—that maybe being a Herondale meant I was weak. And then I learned more and thought maybe I was expected to be some kind of hero."

"Yeah," Simon said. "I know what that's like."

They shared a small moment of bizarre, companionable silence—the boy who'd forgotten everything about his history, and the boy who'd never known it.

Simon broke the silence. "Are you going to see her again? Tessa?"

"She says she's going to take me and Clary on a tour of the Herondale house in Idris."

"Did you meet Jem, too?"

"We've met before," said Jace. "In the Basilias, in Idris. You don't remember, but I—"

"Stopped him being a Silent Brother," said Simon. "I do remember that."

"We talked in Idris," said Jace. "A lot of what he said makes more sense to me now."

"So you're happy," Simon said.

"I'm happy," said Jace. "I mean, I've been happy, really, since the Dark War ended. I've got Clary, and I've got my family. The only dark spot's been you. Not remembering Clary, or Izzy. Or me."

"So sorry to mess up your life with my inconvenient amnesia," Simon muttered.

"I didn't mean it that way," Jace said. "I meant I wish you remembered me because—" He sighed. "Forget it."

"Look, Herondale, you owe me one now. Wait out here."

"For how long?" Jace looked aggrieved.

"As long as it takes." Simon ducked into his room and shut the door. George, who had been lying in bed studying, looked glum when Simon informed him that Jace was lurking in the hall.

"He's making *me* nervous now," George said. "Who'd want Jace Herondale following them around, being all mysterious and taciturn and blond... Oh, right. Probably loads of people. Still, I wish he wouldn't."

Simon didn't bother to lock the bedroom door, partially because there were no locks at Shadowhunter Academy, and partially because if Jace decided to come in and stand over Simon's bed all night, he was going to do that, lock or no.

"He must want something?" George said, stripping off his rugby shirt and throwing it into the corner of the room. "Is this a test? Are we going to have to fight Jace in the middle of the night? Si, not to bag on our awesome demon-fighting prowess, but I do not think that is a fight we can win."

"I don't think so," Simon said, dropping down onto his bed, which dropped much farther than it should have. That was definitely at least two springs breaking.

They got ready for bed. As usual, in the dark, they talked about the mold and the many zoological possibilities crawling around them in the dark. He heard George turn toward the wall, the signal that he was about to sleep and the nightly chat was over.

Simon was awake, hands behind his head, body still achingly sore from the fall out of the tree.

"Do you mind if I turn on a light?" he asked.

"Nae, go ahead. I can barely see it anyway."

They still said "turn on a light" like they were flicking a switch. They had candles at the Academy—nubby little candles that seemed to have been specially made to produce as little light as possible. Simon fumbled around on the small stand next to his bed and found his matches and lit his candle, which he pulled into the bed with him, balancing it on his lap in a way that was probably unsafe. One good thing about the floor of ultimate moisture was that it was unlikely to catch fire. He could still be burned, if the candle overturned in his lap, but it was the only way he would be able to see to write. He reached again for some paper and a pen. No texting here. No typing. Real pen to paper was required. He made a makeshift desk out of a book and began to write:

Dear Isabelle...

Should he start with "dear"? It was the way you started letters, but now that he saw it, it looked weird and old-fashioned and maybe too intimate.

He got a new piece of paper.

Isabelle...

Well, that looked stark. Like he was angry, just saying her name like that.

Another paper.

Izzy,

Nope. Definitely not. They were not at pet names yet. How the hell did you start a letter like this? Simon considered a casual "Hey..." or maybe just forgetting the salutation and getting right to the message. Texting was *so much easier* than this.

He picked up the paper that started with "Isabelle" again. It was the middle choice. He would have to go with that.

Isabelle,

I fell out of a tree today.

I'm thinking of you while I'm in my moldy bed.

I saw Jace today. He may develop food poisoning. Just wanted you to know.

I'm Batman.

I'm trying to figure out how to write this letter.

Okay. That was a possible start, and true.

Let me tell you something you already know—you're amazing. You know it. I know it. Anyone can see that. Here's the problem—I don't know what I am. I have to figure out who I am before I can accept that I'm someone who deserves someone like you. It's not something I can accept just because I've heard it. I need to know that guy. And I know I <u>*am*</u> *that guy you loved—I just have to meet him.*

I'm trying to figure out how that happens. I guess it happens here, in this school where they try to kill you every day. I think it takes time. I know things that take time are annoying. I know it's hard. But I have to get there the hard way.

This letter is probably stupid. I don't know if you're still reading. I don't know if you're going to rip this up or slice it in half with your whip or what.

All of that came out in one solid flow. He tapped the pen against his forehead for a minute.

I'm going to give this to Jace to give to you. He's been trailing me around all day like some kind of Jacey shadow. He's either here to make sure I don't die, or to make sure I die, or maybe because of you. Maybe you sent him.

I don't know. He's Jace. Who knows what he's doing? I'm going to give this to him. He may read it before it gets to you. Jace, if you're reading this, I'm pretty sure you're going to get food poisoning. <u>Do not use the bathrooms.</u>

It wasn't romantic, but he decided to leave it in. It might make Isabelle laugh.

If you are reading this, Jace, stop now.

Izzy—I don't know why you would wait for me, but if you do, I promise to make myself worth that wait. Or I'll try. I can promise I am going to try.

—Simon

Simon opened the door and was not surprised to find Jace standing outside of it.

"Here," Simon said, handing him the letter.

"Took you long enough," Jace said.

"Now we're even," said Simon. "Go party in the Herondale house with your weird family."

"I plan to," said Jace, and smiled a sudden, strangely endearing smile. He had a chipped tooth. The smile made him seem like he was Simon's age, and maybe they were friends after all. "Good night, Wiggles."

"Wiggles?"

"Yes, *Wiggles*. Your nickname? It's what you always made us call you. I almost forgot your name was Simon, I'm so used to calling you Wiggles."

"*Wiggles?* What does that ... even mean?"

"You would never explain," Jace said with a shrug. "It was the big mystery about you. As I said, good night, Wiggles. I'll take care of this."

He held up the letter and used it to make a salute.

Simon shut the door. He knew most people on the hall had probably done everything they could to make sure they heard that exchange. He knew that in the morning he would be called Wiggles and there was nothing he would ever be able to do about it.

But it was a small price to pay to get a letter to Isabelle.

Nothing but Shadows

By Cassandra Clare and Sarah Rees Brennan

The world transformed into sliding grayness, everything still moving slower than James was. Everything was sliding and insubstantial: The battering ram came at him and through him, unable to hurt him; it was like being splashed with water. James lifted a hand and saw the gray air full of stars.

—Nothing but Shadows

KRSH
JAMES!

I knew nothing but shadows,
and I thought them to be real.
—Oscar Wilde

Shadowhunter Academy, 2008

The afternoon sunlight was streaming warm through the arrow-slit windows of their classroom, painting the gray stone walls yellow. The elites and the dregs alike were sleepy from a long morning of training with Scarsbury, and Catarina Loss was giving them a history lesson. History applied to both the elites and the dregs, so they could all learn of the glory of the Shadowhunters and aspire to be a part of that glory. In this class, Simon thought, none of them seemed that different from each other—not that they were all united in aspiring to glory, but they were all equally glazed with boredom.

Until Marisol answered a question correctly, and Jon Cartwright kicked the back of her chair.

"Awesome," Simon hissed behind his book. "That's really cool behavior. Congratulations, Jon. Every time a mundie answers a question wrong, you say it's because they can't rise to the level of Shadowhunters. And every time one of us answers a question right, you punish them. I have to admire your consistency."

George Lovelace leaned back in his chair and grinned, feeding Simon his next line. "I don't see how that's consistent, Si."

"Well, he's consistently a jackass," Simon explained.

"I can think of a few other words for him," George remarked. "But some of them cannot be used around ladies, and some of them are Gaelic and cannot be understood by you mad foreigners."

Jon looked upset. Possibly he was upset that their chairs were too far away to kick.

"I just think she shouldn't speak out of turn," he said.

"It's true that if you mundies listened to us *Shadowhunters*," said Julie, "you might learn something."

"If you Shadowhunters ever listened," said Sunil, a mundie boy who lived down the (slimy) hall from George and Simon, "you might learn a few things yourself."

Voices were rising. Catarina was beginning to look very annoyed. Simon gestured to Marisol and Jon to be quiet, but they both ignored him. Simon felt the same way as when he and Clary had set a fire in his kitchen by trying to toast grapes and create raisins when they were six: amazed and appalled that things had gone wrong so fast.

Then he realized that was a new memory. He grinned

at the thought of Clary with exploded grape in her red hair, and let the classroom situation escalate.

"I'll teach you some lessons down in the training grounds," Jon snapped. "I could challenge you to a duel. Watch your mouth."

"That's not a bad idea," remarked Marisol.

"Oh, hey now," said Beatriz. "Duels with fourteen-year-olds *are* a bad idea."

Everyone looked with scorn upon Beatriz, the voice of reason.

Marisol sniffed. "Not a duel. A challenge. If the elites beat us in a challenge, then they get to speak out first in class for a week. If we beat them, then they hold their tongues."

"I'll do it, and you'll be sorry you ever suggested it, mundie. What's the challenge?" Jon asked. "Staff, sword, bow, dagger work, a horse race, a boxing match? I'm ready!"

Marisol smiled sweetly. "Baseball."

Cue mass puzzlement and panicked looks among the Shadowhunters.

"I'm not ready," George whispered. "I'm not American and I don't play baseball. Is it like cricket, Si? Or more like hurling?"

"You have a sport called hurling in Scotland?" Simon whispered back. "What do you hurl? Potatoes? Small children? Weird."

"I'll explain later," said George.

"I'll explain baseball," said Marisol with a glint in her eye.

Simon had the feeling Marisol was going to be a terrifying, tiny expert on baseball, the same way she was at fencing. He also had the feeling the elite stream was in for a surprise.

"And I will explain how a demonic plague almost wiped out the Shadowhunters," said Catarina loudly from the front of the class. "Or I would, if my students would stop bickering and listen for one minute!"

Everybody went very quiet, and listened meekly about the plague. It was only when the lesson ended that everyone started talking about the baseball game again. Simon had at least played before, so he was hurrying to put away his books and go outside when Catarina said: "Daylighter. Wait."

"Really, 'Simon' would be fine," Simon told her.

"The elite kids are trying to replicate the school they have heard about from their parents," Catarina said. "Mundie students are meant to be seen and not heard, to soak up the privilege of being among Shadowhunters and prepare for their Ascension or death in a spirit of humility. Except you really have been stirring up trouble among them."

Simon blinked. "Are you telling me not to be so hard on the Shadowhunters, because it's just the way they were raised?"

"Be as hard on the smug little idiots as you like," said Catarina. "It's good for them. I'm just telling you so you realize what an effect you're having—and what an effect you could have. You're in an almost unique position, Daylighter. I only know of one other student who dropped from the elites to the dregs—not counting Lovelace, who would have been in the dregs from the beginning if the Nephilim didn't make smug assumptions. But then, smug assumptions are their favorite thing."

That had the effect Catarina must have known it would. Simon stopped trying to fit his copy of *The Shadowhunter's Codex* into his bag and sat down. The rest of the class would take some time to prepare before they actually had the baseball game. Simon could spare a little while.

"Was he a mundane too?"

"No, he was a Shadowhunter," Catarina said. "He went to the Academy more than a century ago. His name was James Herondale."

"A Herondale? Another Herondale?" Simon asked. "Herondales without cease. Do you ever get the feeling you are being chased around by Herondales?"

"Not really," Catarina said. "Not that I'd mind. Magnus says they tend to be a good-looking lot. Of course, Magnus also says they tend to be strange in the head. James Herondale was a bit of a special case."

"Let me guess," Simon said. "He was blond, smug, and adored by the populace."

Catarina's ivory eyebrows rose. "No, he had dark hair and spectacles. There was another boy at school, Matthew Fairchild, who did answer to that description. They did not get along particularly well."

"Really?" said Simon, and reconsidered. "Well then, Team James Herondale. I bet that Matthew guy was a jackass."

"Oh, I don't know," said Catarina. "I always thought he was a charmer, myself. Most people did. Everybody liked Matthew."

This Matthew guy *must* have been a charmer, Simon thought. Catarina rarely spoke about any Shadowhunters with anything like approval, but here she was smiling fondly over a boy from a hundred years ago.

"Everybody except James Herondale?" Simon asked. "The Shadowhunter who got thrown out of the Shadowhunter course. Did Matthew Fairchild have anything to do with that?"

Catarina stepped out from behind her teacher's desk and went to an arrow-slit window. The rays of the dying sun struck through her hair in brilliant white lines, almost giving her a halo. But not quite.

"James Herondale was the son of angels and demons," she said softly. "He was always fated to walk a difficult and painful path, to drink bitter water with sweet, to tread where there were thorns as well as flowers. Nobody could save him from that. People did try."

Shadowhunter Academy, 1899

James Herondale told himself that he was feeling sick only because of the jolting of the carriage. He was really very excited to be going to school.

Father had borrowed Uncle Gabriel's new carriage so he could take James from Alicante to the Academy, just the two of them.

Father had not asked if he could borrow Uncle Gabriel's carriage.

"Don't look so serious, Jamie," Father said, murmuring a Welsh word to the horses that made them trot faster. "Gabriel would want us to have the carriage. It's all between family."

"Uncle Gabriel mentioned last night that he had recently had the carriage painted. Many times. And he has threatened to summon the constabulary and have you arrested," said James. "Many times."

"Gabriel will stop fussing about it in a few years." Father winked one blue eye at James. "Because we will all be driving automobiles by then."

"Mother says you can never drive an automobile," said James. "She made me and Lucie promise that if you ever did, we would not climb into it."

"Your mother was just joking."

James shook his head. "She made us swear on the Angel."

He grinned up at his father. Father shook his head at Jamie, the wind catching at his black hair. Mother said Father and Jamie had the same hair, but Jamie knew his own hair was always untidy. He had heard people call his father's hair *unruly*, which meant being untidy with charisma.

The first day of school was not a good day for James to be thinking about how very different he was from his father.

During their drive from Alicante, several people stopped them on the road, calling out the usual exclamation: "Oh, Mr. Herondale!"

Shadowhunter ladies of many ages said that to his father: three words that were both sigh and summons. Other fathers were called "Mister" without the "Oh" prefix.

With such a remarkable father, people tended to look for a son who would be perhaps a lesser star to Will Herondale's blazing sun, but still someone shining. They were always subtly but unmistakably disappointed to find James, who was not very remarkable at all.

James remembered one incident that made the difference between him and his father starkly apparent. It was always the tiniest moments that came back to James in the middle of the night and mortified him the very most, like it was always the almost invisible cuts that kept stinging.

A mundane lady had wandered up to them at Hatchards bookshop in London. Hatchards was the nicest bookshop in the city, James thought, with its dark wood and glass front, which made the whole shop look solemn and special, and its secret nooks and hidey-holes inside where one could curl up with a book and be quite quiet. James's family often went to Hatchards all together, but when James and his father went alone ladies quite often found a reason to wander over to them and strike up a conversation.

Father told the lady that he spent his days hunting evil and rare first editions. Father could always find something to say to people, could always make them laugh. It seemed a strange, wondrous power to James, as impossible to achieve as it would be for him to shape-shift like a werewolf.

James did not worry about the ladies approaching Father. Father never once looked at any woman the way he looked at Mother, with joy and thanksgiving, as if she was a living wish, granted past all hope.

James did not know many people, but he was good at being quiet and noticing. He knew that what lay between his parents was something rare and precious.

He worried only because the ladies approaching Father were strangers James would have to talk to.

The lady in the bookshop had leaned down and asked: "And what do you like to do, little man?"

"I like—books," James had said. While standing in the bookshop, with a parcel of books under his arm. The lady had given him a pitying look. "I read—erm—rather a lot," James went on, dreary master of the obvious. King of the obvious. Emperor of the obvious.

The lady was so unimpressed that she wandered off without another word.

James never knew what to say to people. He never knew how to make them laugh. He had lived thirteen years of his life, mainly at the Institute in London, with his parents and his little sister, Lucie, and a great many books. He had never had a friend who was a boy.

Now he was going to Shadowhunter Academy, to learn to be as great a warrior as his father, and the warrior bit was not half as worrying as the fact he was going to have to talk to people.

There were going to be a lot of people.

There was going to be a lot of talking.

James wondered why the wheels did not fall right off Uncle Gabriel's carriage. He wondered why the world was so cruel.

"I know that you are nervous about going to school," Father said at length. "Your mother and I were not sure about sending you."

James bit his lip. "Did you think I would be a disaster?"

"What?" Father said. "Of course not! Your mother was simply worried about sending away the only other person in the house who has any sense."

James smiled.

"We've been very happy, having our little family all together," Father said. "I never thought I could be so happy. But perhaps we have kept you too isolated in London. It would be nice for you to find some friends your own age. Who knows, you might meet your future *parabatai* at the Academy."

Father could say what he liked about it being his and Mother's fault for keeping them isolated; James knew it was not true. Lucie had gone to France with Mother and met Cordelia Carstairs, and in two weeks they had become what Lucie described as bosom companions. They sent each other letters every week, reams and reams of paper crossed out and containing sketches. Lucie was as isolated as James was. James had gone on visits too, and never made a bosom companion. The only person who liked him was a girl, and nobody could know about Grace. Perhaps even Grace would not like him, if she knew any other people.

It was not his parents' fault that he had no friends. It was some flaw within James himself.

"Perhaps," Father went on casually, "you and Alastair Carstairs will take a liking to each other."

"He's older than me!" James protested. "He won't have any time for a new boy."

Father smiled a wry little smile. "Who knows? That is the wonderful thing about making changes and meeting strangers, Jamie. You never know when, and you never know who, but someday a stranger will burst through the door of your life and transform it utterly. The world will be turned upside down, and you will be happier for it."

Father had been so happy when Lucie befriended Cordelia Carstairs. Father's *parabatai* had once been called James Carstairs, though his official name now that he belonged to the Silent Brothers—the order of blind, runed monks that aided the Shadowhunters in the darkness—was Brother Zachariah. Father had told James a thousand times about meeting Uncle Jem, how for years Uncle Jem had been the only one who believed in him, who saw his true self. Until Mother came.

"I have spoken to you often of your mother and your uncle Jem and all they did for me. They made me a new person. They saved my soul," Father said, serious as he rarely was. "You do not know what it is, to be saved and transformed. But you will. As your parents, we must give you opportunities to be challenged and changed. That was why we agreed to send you to school. Even though we will miss you terribly."

"Terribly?" James asked, shyly.

"Your mother says she will be brave and keep a stiff upper lip," said Father. "Americans are heartless. I will cry into my pillow every night."

James laughed. He knew he did not laugh often, and Father looked particularly pleased whenever he could make James do it. James was, at thirteen, a little old for such displays, but since it would be months and months until he saw Father again and he was a little frightened to be going to school, he nestled up against Father and took his hand. Father held the reins in one hand and put his own and James's linked hands into the deep pocket of his driving coat. James rested with his cheek against Father's shoulder, not minding the jolting of the carriage as they went down the country roads of Idris.

He did want a *parabatai*. He wanted one badly.

A *parabatai* was a friend who had chosen you to be their best friend, who had made their friendship permanent. They were that sure about how much they liked you, that sure they would never want to take it back. Finding a *parabatai* seemed to James the key to everything, the essential first step to a life where he could be as happy as his father was, be as brilliant a Shadowhunter as his father was, find a love as great as the love his father had found.

Not that he had any particular girl in mind, James told himself, and crushed all thoughts of Grace, the secret girl; Grace, who needed to be rescued.

He wanted a *parabatai*, and that made the Academy a thousand times more terrifying.

James was safe for this little time, resting against his father, but all too soon they reached the valley where the school rested.

The Academy was magnificent, a gray building that

shone among the gathered trees like a pearl. It reminded James of the Gothic buildings from books like *The Mysteries of Udolpho* and *The Castle of Otranto*. Set in the gray face of the building was a huge stained-glass window shining with a dozen brilliant colors, showing an angel wielding a blade.

The angel was looking down on a courtyard teeming with students, all talking and laughing, all there to become the best Shadowhunters they could possibly be. If James could not find a friend here, he knew, he would not be able to find a friend in all the world.

Uncle Gabriel was already in the courtyard. His face had turned an alarming shade of puce. He was shouting something about thieving Herondales.

Father turned to the dean, a lady who was unquestionably fifty years old, and smiled. She blushed.

"Dean Ashdown, would you be so very kind as to give me a tour of the Academy? I was raised in the London Institute with just one other pupil." Father's voice softened, as it always did when he spoke of Uncle Jem. "I never had the privilege of attending myself."

"Oh, Mr. Herondale!" said Dean Ashdown. "Very well."

"Thank you," said Father. "Come on, Jamie."

"Oh no," said James. "I'll—I'll stay here."

He felt uneasy as soon as Father was out of his sight, sailing off with the dean on his arm and a wicked smile at Uncle Gabriel, but James knew he had to be brave, and this was the perfect opportunity. Among the crowd of students in the courtyard, James had seen two boys he knew.

One was tall for almost-thirteen, with an untidy shock of light brown hair. He had his face turned away, but James knew the boy had startling lavender eyes. He had heard girls at parties saying those eyes were wasted on a boy, especially a boy as strange as Christopher Lightwood.

James knew his cousin Christopher better than any other boy at the Academy. Aunt Cecily and Uncle Gabriel had spent a lot of time in Idris over the past few years, but before that both families had been together often: They had all gone down to Wales together for a few holidays, before Grandma and Grandpa died. Christopher was slightly odd and extremely vague, but he was always nice to James.

The boy standing beside Christopher was small and thin as a lath, his head barely coming up to Christopher's shoulder.

Thomas Lightwood was Christopher's cousin, not James's, but James called Thomas's mother Aunt Sophie because she was Mother's very best friend. James liked Aunt Sophie, who was so pretty and always kind. She and her family had been living in Idris for the past few years as well, with Aunt Cecily and Uncle Gabriel—Aunt Sophie's husband was Uncle Gabriel's brother. Aunt Sophie came to London on visits by herself, though. James had seen Mother and Aunt Sophie walk out of the practice rooms giggling together as if they were girls as little as his sister, Lucie. Aunt Sophie had once called Thomas her shy boy. That had made James think he and Thomas might have a lot in common.

At the big family gatherings when they were all together, James had sneaked a few glances at Thomas, and found him always hanging quiet and uneasy on the fringes of a bigger group, usually looking to one of the older boys. He'd wanted to go over to Thomas and strike up a conversation, but he had not been sure what to say.

Two shy people would probably be good friends, but

there was the small problem of how to reach that point. James had no idea.

Now was James's chance, though. The Lightwood cousins were his best hope for friends at the Academy. All he had to do was go over and speak to them.

James pushed his way through the crowd, apologizing when other people elbowed him.

"Hullo, boys," said a voice behind James, and someone pushed past James as if he could not see him.

James saw Thomas and Christopher both turn, like flowers toward the sun. They smiled with identical radiant welcome, and James stared at the back of a shining blond head.

There was one other boy James's age at the Academy who he knew a little: Matthew Fairchild, whose parents James called Aunt Charlotte and Uncle Henry because Aunt Charlotte had practically raised Father, when she was the head of the London Institute and before she became Consul, the most important person a Shadowhunter could be.

Matthew had not come to London the few times Aunt Charlotte and his brother, Charles, had visited. Uncle Henry had been wounded in battle years before any of them were born, and he did not leave Idris often, but James was not sure why Matthew did not come visit. Perhaps he enjoyed himself too much in Idris.

One thing James was certain of was that Matthew Fairchild was *not* shy.

James had not seen Matthew in a couple of years, but he remembered him very clearly. At every family gathering where James hung on the edges of crowds or went off to read on the stairs, Matthew was the life and soul of the party. He would talk with grown-ups as if he were a grown-up.

He would dance with old ladies. He would charm parents and grandparents, and stop babies from crying. Everybody loved Matthew.

James did not remember Matthew dressing like a maniac before today. Matthew was wearing knee breeches when everyone else was wearing the trousers of the sane, and a mulberry-colored velvet jacket. Even his shining golden hair was brushed in a way that struck James as more complicated than the way other boys brushed their hair.

"Isn't this a bore?" Matthew asked Christopher and Thomas, the two boys James wanted for friends. "Everybody here looks like a dolt. I am already in frightful agony, contemplating my wasted youth. Don't speak to me, or I shall break down and sob uncontrollably."

"There, there," said Christopher, patting Matthew's shoulder. "What are you upset about again?"

"Your face, Lightwood," said Matthew, and elbowed him.

Christopher and Thomas both laughed, drawing in close to him. They were all so obviously already friends, and Matthew was so clearly the leader. James's plan for friends was in ruins.

"Er," said James, the sound like a tragic social hiccup. "Hello."

Christopher gazed at him with amiable blankness, and James's heart, which had already been around his knees, sank to his socks.

Then Thomas said, "Hello!" and smiled.

James smiled back, grateful for an instant, and then Matthew Fairchild turned around to see who Thomas was addressing. He was taller than James, his fair hair outlined by the sun as he looked down on him. Matthew gave the impression that he was looking down from a much greater height than he actually was.

"Jamie Herondale, right?" Matthew drawled.

James bristled. "I prefer James."

"I'd prefer to be in a school devoted to art, beauty, and culture rather than in a ghastly stone shack in the middle of nowhere filled with louts who aspire to nothing more than whacking demons with great big swords," said Matthew. "Yet here we are."

"And *I* would prefer to have intelligent students," said a voice behind them. "Yet here I am teaching at a school for the Nephilim."

They turned and then started, as one. The man behind them had snowy-white hair, which he looked too young to have, and horns poking out among the white locks. The most notable thing about him, however, the thing James noted right away, was that he had green skin the color of grapes.

James knew this must be a warlock. In fact, he knew who it must be: the former High Warlock of London, Ragnor Fell, who lived part-time in the countryside outside Alicante, and who had agreed this year that he would teach in the Academy as a diversion from his magical studies.

James knew warlocks were good people, the allies of the Shadowhunters. Father often talked about his friend Magnus Bane, who had been kind to him when he was young.

Father had never mentioned whether Magnus Bane was green. James had never thought to inquire. Now he was rather urgently wondering.

"Which one of you is Christopher Lightwood?" Ragnor Fell asked in a stern voice. His gaze swept them all, and landed on the most guilty-looking person in the group. "Is it you?"

"Thank the Angel, no," Thomas exclaimed, and went red under his summer tan. "No offense, Christopher."

"Oh, none taken," said Christopher airily. He blinked up at Ragnor, as if the tall, scary green man had entirely escaped his notice up until this moment. "Hello, sir."

"Are you Christopher Lightwood?" Ragnor asked, somewhat menacingly.

Christopher's wandering attention became focused on a tree. "Hm? I think so."

Ragnor glared down at Christopher's flyaway brown hair. James was beginning to be afraid he would erupt like a green volcano.

"Are you not certain, Mr. Lightwood? Did you perhaps have an unfortunate encounter when you were an infant?"

"Hm?" said Christopher.

Ragnor's voice rose. "Was the encounter between your infant head and a floor?"

That was when Matthew Fairchild said, "Sir," and smiled.

James had forgotten about The Smile, even though it was often broken out to great effect at family parties. The Smile won Matthew extra time before bed, extra Christmas pudding, extra anything he wanted. Adults were helpless to resist The Smile.

Matthew gave his all to this particular smile. Butter melted. Birds sang. People slipped about dazed amid the butter and birdsong.

"Sir, you will have to forgive Christopher. He's a trifle absentminded, but he is definitely Christopher. It would be very difficult to mistake Christopher for anyone else. I vouch for him, and he can't deny it."

The Smile worked on Ragnor, as it worked on all adults. He unbent a tiny bit. "Are you Matthew Fairchild?"

Matthew's smile became more playful. "I could deny it if I liked. I could deny anything if I liked. But my name certainly is Matthew. It has been Matthew for years."

"What?" Ragnor Fell looked as if he had fallen into a pit of lunatics and could not get out.

James cleared his throat. "He's quoting Oscar Wilde, sir."

Matthew glanced over at him, his dark eyes suddenly wide. "Are you a devotee of Oscar Wilde?"

"He's a good writer," James said coldly. "There are a lot of good writers. I read rather a lot," he added, making it clear that he was certain Matthew did not.

"Gentlemen," Ragnor Fell put in, his voice a dagger. "If you could tear yourselves away from your fascinating literary conversation for a moment and listen to one of the instructors in the establishment where you have supposedly come to learn? I have a letter here about Christopher Lightwood and the unfortunate incident that caused the Clave such concern."

"Yes, that was a very unfortunate accident," said Matthew, nodding earnestly as if he was sure of Ragnor's sympathy.

"And that was not the word I used, Mr. Fairchild, as I am sure you are aware. The letter says that you have volunteered to take full responsibility for Mr. Lightwood, and that you solemnly promise to keep any and all potential explosives out of his reach for the duration of his time at the Academy."

James looked from the warlock to Matthew to Christopher, who was regarding a tree with dreamy benevolence. In desperation, he looked to Thomas.

Explosives? he mouthed.

"Don't ask," said Thomas. "Please."

Thomas was older than James and Christopher, but much smaller. Aunt Sophie had kept him at home an extra year because he was sickly. He did not look sickly now, but he was still rather undersized. His tan, combined with his brown hair and brown eyes and his short stature, made him look like a small, worried horse chestnut. James found himself wanting to pat Thomas on the head.

Matthew patted Thomas on the head.

"Mr. Fell," he said. "Thomas. Christopher. Jamie."

"James," James corrected.

"Do not worry," Matthew said with immense confidence. "I mean, certainly, worry that we are trapped in an arid warrior culture with no appreciation for the truly important things in life. But do not worry about things exploding, because I will not permit anything to explode."

"That was all you needed to say," Ragnor Fell told him. "And you could have said it in far fewer words."

He walked off, in a swirl of green skin and bad temper.

"He was green!" Thomas whispered.

"Really," said Matthew, very dry.

"Oh, really?" asked Christopher brightly. "I didn't notice."

Thomas gazed sadly at Christopher. Matthew ignored him superbly. "I rather liked the unique hue of our teacher. It reminded me of the green carnations that Oscar Wilde's followers wear to imitate him. He had one of the actors in, um, a play of his wear a green carnation onstage."

"It was *Lady Windermere's Fan*," James said.

Matthew was clearly showing off, trying to sound superior and special, and James had no time for it.

Matthew turned The Smile on him. James was

unsurprised to find he was immune to its deadly effects.

"Yes," he said. "Of course. Jamie, I can see that as a fellow admirer of Oscar Wilde—"

"Uh," said a voice to James's left. "You new boys have barely been here five minutes, and all you can find to talk about is some *mundane* who got sent to prison for indecency?"

"So you know Oscar Wilde too, Alastair?" Matthew asked.

James looked up at the taller, older boy. He had light hair but dark brows, strongly marked, like very judgmental black brushstrokes.

So this was Alastair Carstairs, the brother of Lucie's best friend, whom Father hoped James would make friends with. James had pictured someone more friendly, more like Cordelia herself.

Perhaps Alastair would be more friendly if he did not associate James with snotty Matthew.

"I know of many mundane criminals," Alastair Carstairs said in chilly tones. "I read the mundane newspapers to find hints of demonic activity. I certainly don't bother reading plays."

The two boys he was with nodded in good Shadowhunter solidarity.

Matthew laughed in their faces. "Naturally. What use do sad, unimaginative little people have for plays?" he asked. "Or paintings, or dancing, or anything that makes life interesting. I am so glad to be at this dank little school where they will try to squeeze down my mind until it is almost as narrow as yours."

He patted Alastair Carstairs on the arm. James was amazed that he was not immediately struck in the face.

Thomas was staring at Alastair with as much panic as James felt.

"Run along now," Matthew suggested. "Do. Jamie and I were talking."

Alastair laughed, his laugh sounding angrier than a sharp word would have. "I was only trying to give you young ones a little guidance about the way we do things in the Academy. If you're too stupid to take heed, that is not my fault. At least you have a tongue in your head, unlike this one."

He turned and glared daggers at James. James was so surprised and dismayed at this turn of events—he hadn't done *anything*!—that he simply stood and stared with his mouth open.

"Yes, you, the one with the peculiar eyes," Alastair snapped. "What are you gawping at?"

"I—" said James. "I—"

He did have peculiar eyes, he knew. He did not truly need eyeglasses, except for reading, but he wore them all the time in order to conceal his eyes. He could feel himself blushing, and Alastair's voice became as sharp as his laugh. "What's your name?"

"H-Herondale," James stammered out.

"By the Angel, his eyes *are* awful," said the boy to Alastair's right.

Alastair laughed again, this time with more satisfaction. "Yellow. Just like a goat's."

"I don't—"

"Don't strain yourself, Goatface Herondale," Alastair said. "Don't try to speak. You and your friends could perhaps cease obsessing about mundanes and try to think about little matters like saving lives and upholding the Law while you're here, all right?"

He strolled on, his friends laughing with him. James heard the word spreading through the tightly knit crowd with laughter following it, like the ripples from a stone thrown into a pond.

Goatface. Goatface. Goatface.

Matthew laughed. "Well. What an—"

"Thanks so much for dragging me into that," James snapped. He turned on his heel and walked away from the two friends he had hoped for at the Academy, and heard his new name whispered as he went.

James did what he had promised himself he absolutely would not do. He dragged his heavy bag through the courtyard, through the hall, and up several sets of stairs until he found a staircase that seemed private. Then he sat down and opened a book. He told himself that he was only going to read a few pages before he went down again. The Count of Monte Cristo was just descending on his enemies in a balloon.

James emerged hours later, to the sinking realization that the sky had gone dark gray and the sounds from the courtyard had faded away. His mother and Lucie were still in London, far away, and now he was sure his father was gone too.

He was trapped in this Academy full of strangers. He did not even know where he was supposed to sleep tonight.

He wandered around trying to find the bedrooms. He did not discover any, but he did find himself enjoying exploring such a big new place on his own. The Academy was a splendid building, the stone walls shining as if they had been polished. The chandeliers seemed made of jewels, and as James wandered in search of the dining hall, he found many beautiful tapestries depicting Shadowhunters through the ages. He stood looking at an intricate, colorful weaving of Jonathan Shadowhunter fighting during the Crusades, until it occurred to him that dinner must be soon and he did not want to draw any further attention to himself.

The sound of hundreds of strange voices alerted James to where the dining room must be. He fought the impulse to run away, steeled himself, and walked through the doors instead. To his relief, people were still assembling, the older students milling around and chatting to each other with the ease of long familiarity. The new students were hovering, much like James himself.

All except Matthew Fairchild, who was surveying the shining mahogany tables with disdain.

"We have to select a very small table," he told Thomas and Christopher, his satellites. "I am here under protest. I will not break bread with the kind of violent ruffians and raving imbeciles who would attend the Academy willingly."

"You know," James said loudly, "Alastair Carstairs was right."

"That seems very unlikely to me," Matthew responded, then turned. "Oh, it's you. Why are you still carrying your bag?"

"I don't have to answer to you," said James, which he was aware was a bizarre thing to say. Thomas blinked at him in distress, as if he had trusted James not to say bizarre things.

"All right," Matthew said agreeably. "Alastair Carstairs was right about what?"

"People are attending the Academy because they hope to become better Shadowhunters, and save lives. That is a noble and worthy goal. You do not have to sneer at everybody you meet."

"But how else am I going to amuse myself in this place?" Matthew protested. "*You* can sit with us, if you want."

There was an amused glint in his brown eyes. James was certain from the way Matthew was looking at him that he was being made fun of, though he could not quite work out how.

"No thanks," James said shortly.

He looked around at the tables, and saw that the first-year Shadowhunters were now settled around tables in careful, friendly patterns. There were other boys and even a few girls, though, who James could tell were mundanes. It was not so much clothing or build as the way they held themselves: as if they were afraid they might be attacked. Shadowhunters, in contrast, were always ready to attack.

There was one boy in shabby clothes sitting by himself. James crossed the dining room to sit at his table.

"Can I sit here?" he asked, desperate enough to be blunt.

"Yes!" said the other boy. "Oh yes, please. The name's Smith. Michael Smith. Mike."

James reached across the table and shook Mike Smith's hand. "James Herondale."

Mike's eyes widened, clearly recognizing it as a Shadowhunter name. "My mother grew up in the mundane world," James told him quickly. "In America. New York City."

"Your mother was a mundane?" said a girl, coming over and sitting at his table. "Esme Philpott," she added, shaking hands briskly. "I shan't keep it when I Ascend. I'm thinking of changing the Esme too."

James did not know what to say. He did not wish to insult a lady's name by agreeing with her or insult a lady by arguing with her. He was not prepared to be approached by a strange girl. Very few girls were sent to the Academy: of course girls could be just as fine warriors as boys, but not everybody thought that way, and many Shadowhunter families wanted to keep their girls close. Some people thought the Academy had far too many rules, and some far too few. Thomas's sisters, who were very proper, had not come to the Academy. Family legend reported that his cousin Anna Lightwood, who was the least proper person imaginable, had said if they sent her to the Academy, she would run away and become a mundane bullfighter.

"Mmm," said James, a silver-tongued devil with the ladies.

"Did your mother Ascend with no trouble?" Mike asked eagerly.

James bit his lip. He was accustomed to everyone knowing the history of his mother: the child of a stolen Shadowhunter and a demon. Any child of a Shadowhunter was a Shadowhunter. Mother belonged to the Shadowhunter world as much as any of the Nephilim. Only, her skin could not bear Marks, and there had never before been anyone like her in the world. James did not quite know how to explain to people who did not know already. He was afraid he would explain wrong, and the explanation would reflect badly on Mother.

"I know a lot of people who Ascended with no trouble," James said at last. "My aunt Sophie—Sophie Lightwood now—she was a mundane. Father says there never was anyone so brave, before or after Ascension."

"What a relief!" said Esme. "Tell me, I think I've heard of Sophie Lightwood—"

"What a fearful comedown," said one of the boys James had seen with Alastair Carstairs earlier. "Goatface Herondale is actually reduced to sitting with the *dregs*."

Alastair and his other friend laughed. They went to sit at a table with other, older Shadowhunters, and James was certain he heard the word "Goatface" whispered more than once. He felt he was boiling from the inside out with shame.

As for Matthew Fairchild, James looked over at him only once or twice. After James had left him standing in the middle of the dining hall, Matthew had tossed his stupid blond head and chosen a very large table to sit at. He clearly had not meant a word about being so select. He sat with Thomas and Christopher on either side of him like a prince holding court, calling out jokes and summoning people to his side, and soon his table was crowded. He charmed several of the Shadowhunter students away from their tables. Even some of the older students came over to listen to one of Matthew's apparently terribly amusing stories. Even Alastair Carstairs came over for a few minutes. Obviously he and Matthew were great friends now.

James caught Mike Smith looking over at Matthew's table longingly, his face that of an outsider barred from all the fun, doomed to always be at the less exciting table with the less interesting people.

James had wanted friends, but he had not wanted to be the kind of friend who people settled for, because they could not get any better. Except he was, as he had always secretly feared, tedious and poor company. He did not know why books had not taught him how to talk so other people wanted to listen.

James eventually approached the teachers for help finding his bedroom. He found Dean Ashdown and Ragnor Fell in deep conversation.

"I am so terribly sorry," said Dean Ashdown. "This is the

first time we have ever had a warlock teacher—and we are delighted to have you! We should have thoroughly cleaned out the Academy and made sure there were no remnants of a less peaceful time."

"Thank you, Dean Ashdown," Ragnor said. "The removal of the mounted warlock's head from my bedroom will be sufficient."

"I am so terribly sorry!" said Dean Ashdown again. She lowered her voice. "Were you acquainted with the—er, deceased gentleman?"

Ragnor eyed her with disfavor. Though that might just be the way Mr. Fell looked. "If you were to happen upon the grotesquely severed head of one of the Nephilim, would you have to be acquainted with him to feel you might perhaps not fancy sleeping in the room where part of his desecrated corpse remained?"

James coughed in the middle of the dean's third frantic apology. "I do apologize," he said. "Could someone direct me to my room? I—got lost and missed all that."

"Oh, young Mr. Herondale." The dean looked quite happy to be interrupted. "Of course, let me show you the way. Your father entrusted me with a message for you that I can relay as we go."

She left Ragnor Fell scowling after them. James hoped he had not made another enemy.

"Your father said—what a charming language Welsh is, isn't it? So romantic!—*Pob lwc, caraid*. What does it mean?"

James blushed, because he was much too old for his father to be calling him by pet names. "It just means—it means good luck."

He could not help smiling as he trailed the dean down the halls. He was sure nobody else's father had charmed the dean into giving a student a secret message. He felt warm, and watched over.

Until Dean Ashdown opened the door of his new room, bid him a cheerful good-bye, and left him to his horrible fate.

It was a very nice room, airy, with walnut bedposts and white linen canopies. There was a carved wardrobe and even a bookcase.

There was also a distressing amount of Matthew Fairchild.

He was standing in front of a table that had about fifteen hairbrushes on it, several mysterious bottles, and a strange hoard of combs.

"Hullo, Jamie," he said. "Isn't it splendid that we are sharing a room? I am certain we will get along swimmingly."

"James," James said. "What are all those hairbrushes for?"

Matthew looked at him pityingly. "You don't think all this"—he indicated his head with a sweeping gesture—"happens on its own?"

"*I* only use one hairbrush."

"Yes," Matthew observed. "I can tell."

James dragged his trunk over to the foot of his bed, took out *The Count of Monte Cristo*, and made his way back to the door.

"Jamie?" Matthew asked.

"James!" James snapped.

Matthew laughed. "All right, all right. James, where are you going?"

"Somewhere else," said James, and slammed the door behind him.

He could not believe the bad luck that had randomly

assigned him to share a room with Matthew. He found another staircase and read in it until he judged that it was late enough that Matthew would certainly be asleep, and he crept back, lit a candle, and resumed reading in bed.

James might have read a little too long into the night. When he woke up, Matthew was clearly long gone—on top of everything else, he was an early riser—and James was late for his first day of class.

"What else can you expect from Goatface Herondale," said a boy James had never seen before in his life, and several more people sniggered. James grimly took his seat next to Mike Smith.

The classes in which the elites were separated from the dregs were the worst. James had nobody to sit with then.

Or perhaps the first class of every day was the worst, because James always stayed up late into the night reading to forget his troubles, and was late every day. No matter what time he rose, Matthew was always gone. James assumed Matthew did this to mock him, since he could not imagine Matthew doing anything useful early in the morning.

Or perhaps the training courses were the worst, because Matthew was at his most annoying during the training courses.

"I must regretfully decline to participate," he told their teacher once. "Consider me on strike like the coal miners. Except far more stylish."

The next day, he said: "I abstain on the grounds that beauty is sacred, and there is nothing beautiful about these exercises."

The day after that, he merely said: "I object on aesthetic principles."

He kept saying ridiculous things, until a couple of weeks in, when he said: "I won't do it, because Shadowhunters are idiots and I do not want to be at this idiot school. Why does an accident of birth mean you have to either get ripped away from your family, or you have to spend a short, horrible life brawling with demons?"

"Do you want to be expelled, Mr. Fairchild?" thundered one teacher.

"Do what you feel you must," said Matthew, folding his hands and smiling like a cherub.

Matthew did not get expelled. Nobody seemed quite sure what to do with him. His teachers began calling in sick out of despair.

He did only half the work and insulted everyone in the Academy on a daily basis, and he remained absurdly popular. Thomas and Christopher could not be pried away from him. He wandered the halls surrounded by adoring throngs who wanted to hear another amusing anecdote. His and James's room was always completely crowded.

James spent a good deal of time in the stairwells. He spent even more time being called Goatface Herondale.

"You know," Thomas said shyly once, when James had not managed to escape his own room fast enough, "you could pal around with us a little more."

"I could?" James asked, and tried not to sound too hopeful. "I'd ... like to see more of you and Christopher."

"And Matthew," Thomas said.

James shook his head silently.

"Matthew's one of my best friends," Thomas said, almost pleadingly. "If you spent some time with him, I am sure you would come to like him."

James looked over at Matthew, who was sitting on his

bed telling a story to eight people who were sitting on the floor and gazing up at him worshipfully. He met Matthew's eyes, trained in his and Thomas's direction, and looked away.

"I feel I have to decline any more of Matthew's company."

"It makes you stand out, you know," Thomas said. "Spending your time with the mundanes. I think it's why the—the nickname for you has stuck. People are afraid of anybody who is different: It makes them worry everyone else is different too, and just pretending to be all the same."

James stared at him. "Are you saying I should avoid the mundanes? Because they are not as good as we are?"

"No, that's not—" Thomas began, but James was too angry to let him finish.

"The mundanes can be heroes too," James said. "You should know that better than I. Your mother was a mundane! My father told me about all she did before she Ascended. Everyone here knows people who were mundanes. Why should we isolate people who are brave enough to try to become like us—who want to help people? Why should we treat them as if they're less than us, until they prove their worthiness or die? I won't do it."

Aunt Sophie was just as good as any Shadowhunter, and she had been brave long before she Ascended. Aunt Sophie was Thomas's mother. They should know this better than James did.

"I didn't mean it that way," said Thomas. "I didn't think of it that way."

It was as if people didn't think at all, living in Idris.

"Maybe your fathers don't tell you stories like mine does," James said.

"Maybe not everyone listens to stories like you do," Matthew said from across the room. "Not everyone learns."

James glanced at him. It was an unexpectedly nice thing for Matthew, of all people, to say.

"I know a story," Matthew went on. "Who wants to hear it?"

"Me!" said the chorus from the floor.

"Me!"

"Me!"

"Not me," said James, and left the room.

It was another reminder that Matthew had what James would have given anything for, that Matthew had friends and belonged here at the Academy, and Matthew did not care at all.

Eventually there were so many teachers calling in with an acute overdose of Matthew Fairchild that Ragnor Fell was left to supervise the training courses. James wondered why he was the only one who could see this was absurd, and Matthew was ruining classes for everyone. Ragnor could do magic, and was not at all interested in war.

Ragnor let Esme braid ribbons in her horse's mane so it would look like a noble steed. He agreed to let Christopher build a battering ram to knock down trees, because it would be good practice in case they ever had to lay siege to a castle. He watched Mike Smith hit himself over the head with his own longbow.

"Concussions are nothing to be worried about," said Ragnor placidly. "Unless there is severe bleeding of the brain, in which case he may die. Mr. Fairchild, why are you not participating?"

"I think that violence is repulsive," Matthew said firmly. "I am here against my will and I refuse to participate."

"Would you like me to magically strip you and put you

in gear?" Mr. Fell asked. "In front of everybody?"

"That would be a thrill for everybody, I'm sure," said Matthew. Ragnor Fell wiggled his fingers, and green sparks spat from his fingertips. James was pleased to see Matthew actually take a step back. "Might be too thrilling for a Wednesday," Matthew said. "I'll go put on my gear then, shall I?"

"Do," said Ragnor.

He had set up a deck chair and was reading a book. James envied him very much.

He also admired his teacher very much. Here was someone who could control Matthew, at last. After all Matthew's lofty talk about abstaining for the sake of art and beauty, James was looking forward to seeing Matthew make an absolute fool of himself on the practice grounds.

"Anyone volunteer to catch Matthew up on what you have all been learning?" Ragnor asked. "As I have not the faintest idea what that might be."

Just then Christopher's team of students actually hit a tree with their battering ram. The crash and the chaos meant there was not the rush of volunteers to spend time with Matthew that there would otherwise have been.

"I'd be happy to teach Matthew a lesson," said James.

He was quite good with the staff. He had beat Mike ten times out of ten, and Esme nine times out of ten, and he had been holding back with them. It was possible he would also have to hold back with Matthew.

Except that Matthew came out wearing gear, and looking—for a change—actually like a real Shadowhunter. More like a real Shadowhunter than James did, truth be told, since James was ... not as short as Thomas, but not tall yet, and what his mother described as wiry. Which was a kind way to say "no real evidence of muscles in view." Several girls, in fact, turned to look at Matthew in gear.

"Mr. Herondale has volunteered to teach you how to staff fight," Ragnor Fell said. "If you plan to murder each other, go farther down the field where I cannot see you and won't have to answer awkward questions."

"James," said Matthew, in the voice that everyone else liked to listen to so much and that struck James as constantly mocking. "This is so kind of you. I think I do remember a few moves with the staff from training with my mama and my brother. Please be patient with me. I may be a little rusty."

Matthew strolled down the field, the sun brilliant on green grass and his gold hair alike, and weighed the staff in one hand. He turned to James, and James had the sudden impression of narrowed eyes: a look of real and serious intent.

Then Matthew's face and the trees both went sailing by, as Matthew's staff scythed James's legs out from under him and James went tumbling to the ground. He lay there dazed.

"You know," said Matthew thoughtfully. "I may not be so terribly rusty after all."

James scrambled to his feet, clutching at both his staff and his dignity. Matthew moved into position to fight him, the staff as light and easily balanced in his hand as if he were a conductor gesturing with his baton. He moved with easy grace, like any Shadowhunter would, but somehow as if he was playing, as if at any moment he might be dancing.

James realized, to his overwhelming disgust, that this was yet another thing Matthew was good at.

"Best of three," he suggested.

Matthew's staff was a blur between his hands, suddenly.

James did not have time to shift position before a jarring blow landed on the arm that was holding his staff, then his left shoulder so he could not defend. James blocked the staff when it came toward his midsection, but that turned out to be a feint. Matthew scythed him off at the knees again and James wound up flat on his back in the grass. Again.

Matthew's face came into view. He was laughing, as usual. "Why stop at three?" he asked. "I can stand around and beat you all day."

James hooked his staff behind Matthew's ankles and tripped him up. He knew it was wrong, but in the moment he did not care.

Matthew landed on the grass with a surprised "Oof!" which James found briefly satisfying. Once there, he seemed happy enough to lie in the grass. James found himself being regarded by one brown eye amid the greenery.

"You know," Matthew said slowly, "most people like me."

"Well ... congratulations!" James snapped, and scrambled to his feet.

It was the exact wrong moment to stand up.

It should have been the last moment of James's life. Perhaps because he thought it would be the last, it seemed to stretch out, giving James time to see it all: how the battering ram had flown through the hands of Christopher's team in the wrong direction. He saw the horrified faces of the whole team, even Christopher paying attention for once. He saw the great wooden log, sailing directly at him, and heard Matthew scream a warning much too late. He saw Ragnor Fell jump up, his deck chair flying, and lift his hand.

The world transformed into sliding grayness, everything still moving slower than James was. Everything was sliding and insubstantial: The battering ram came at him and through him, unable to hurt him; it was like being splashed with water. James lifted a hand and saw the gray air full of stars.

It was Ragnor who had saved him, James thought as the world tipped from bright, strange grayness into black. This was warlock magic.

He did not know until later that the Academy class had all watched, expecting to see a scene of carnage and death, and instead seen a black-haired boy dissolve and change from one of their own into a shadow cast by nothing, a wicked cutout into the abyss behind the world, dark and unmistakable in the afternoon sun. What had been inevitable death, something the Shadowhunters were used to, became something strange and more terrible.

He did not know until later how right he was. It was warlock magic.

When James woke up, it was night, and Uncle Jem was there.

James reared up from his bed and threw himself into Uncle Jem's arms. He had heard some people found the Silent Brothers frightening, with their silent speech and their stitched eyes, but to him the sight of a Silent Brother's robe always meant Uncle Jem, always meant steadfast love.

"Uncle Jem!" he gasped out, arms around his neck, face buried in his robe, safe for a moment. "What happened? Why do I—I felt so strange, and now you're here, and—"

And the presence of a Silent Brother in the Academy meant nothing good. Father was always inventing excuses for Uncle Jem to come to them—once he had claimed a flowerpot was possessed by a demon. But this was Idris, and a Silent Brother would be summoned to Shadowhunter children only in a time of need.

"Am I—hurt?" asked James. "Is Matthew hurt? He was with me."

Nobody is hurt, said Uncle Jem. *Thanks be to the Angel. It is only that there is now a heavy burden for you to bear, Jamie.*

And the knowledge spilled out from Uncle Jem to James, silent and cold as a grave opening, and yet with Uncle Jem's watchful care mingled with the chill. James shuddered away from the Silent Brother and clung to Uncle Jem at the same time, face wet with tears, fists clutching his robes.

This was his mother's heritage, was what came from mingling the blood of a Shadowhunter with that of a demon, and then with a Shadowhunter again. They had all thought because James's skin could bear Marks that he was a Shadowhunter and nothing else, that the blood of the Angel had burned away all else.

It had not. Even the blood of the Angel could not burn away a shadow. James could perform this strange warlock trick, a trick no warlock Uncle Jem knew could perform. He could transform into a shadow. He could make himself something that was not flesh or blood—certainly not the blood of the Angel.

"What—what *am* I?" James gasped out, his throat raw with sobs.

You are James Herondale, said Uncle Jem. *As you always were. Part your mother, part your father, part yourself. I would not change any part of you if I could.*

James would. He would have burned away this part of himself, wrenched it out, done anything he could to be rid of it. He was meant to be a Shadowhunter, he had always known he was, but would any Shadowhunter fight alongside him, with this horror about him revealed?

"Am I—are they throwing me out of school?" he whispered in Uncle Jem's ear.

No, said Uncle Jem. A feeling of sorrow and anger touched James and then was pulled back. *But James, I do think you should leave. They are afraid that you will—contaminate the purity of their children. They wish to banish you to where the mundane children live. They apparently do not care what happens to the mundane students, and care even less what happens to you. Go home, James. I will bring you home now if you wish it.*

James wanted to go home. He wanted it more than he could remember wanting anything, with an ache that made him feel as if every bone in his body were broken and could not be put back together until he was home. He was loved there, safe there. He would be instantly surrounded in affection and warmth.

Except...

"How would my mother feel," James whispered, "if she knew I had been sent home because of—she'll think it's because of her."

His mother, with her grave gray eyes and her flower-tender face, as quiet as James and yet as ready with words as Father. James might be a stain upon the world, might be something that would contaminate good Shadowhunter children. He was ready to believe it. But not Mother. Mother was kind, Mother was lovely and loving, Mother was a wish come true and a blessing on the earth.

James could not bear to think how Mother would feel if she thought she had hurt him in any way. If he could get through the Academy, if he could make her believe there was no real difference to him, that would spare her pain.

He wanted to go home. He did not want to face anybody

at the Academy. He was a coward. But he was not enough of a coward that he would run away from his own suffering, and let his mother suffer for him.

You are not a coward at all, said Uncle Jem. *I remember a time, when I was still James Carstairs, when your mother learned—as she thought then—that she could not have children. She was so hurt by that. She thought herself so changed, from all she had thought she was. I told her the right man would not care, and of course your father, the best of men, the only one fit for her, did not. I did not tell her ... I was a boy and did not know how to tell her, how her courage in bearing uncertainty of her very self touched me. She doubted herself, but I could never doubt her. I could never doubt you now. I see the same courage in you now, as I saw in her then.*

James wept, scrubbing his face against Uncle Jem's robes as if he were littler than Lucie. He knew Mother was brave, but surely courage did not feel like this; he had thought it would be something fine, not a feeling that could tear you into pieces.

If you saw humanity as I can see it, Uncle Jem said, a whisper in his mind, a lifeline. *There is very little brightness and warmth in the world for me. I am very distant from you all. There are only four points of warmth and brightness, in the whole world, that burn fiercely enough for me to feel something like the person I was. Your mother, your father, Lucie, and you. You love, and tremble, and burn. Do not let any of them tell you who you are. You are the flame that cannot be put out. You are the star that cannot be lost. You are who you have always been, and that is enough and more than enough. Anyone who looks at you and sees darkness is blind.*

"Blinder than a Silent Brother?" James asked, and hiccupped.

Uncle Jem had been made a Silent Brother very young, and strangely: He bore runes on his cheeks, but his eyes, though shadowed, were not stitched shut. Still, James was never sure what he saw.

There was a laugh in James's mind, and he had not laughed, so it must have been Uncle Jem. James clung to him for an instant longer and told himself he could not ask Uncle Jem to take him home after all, or to the Silent City, or anywhere so long as Uncle Jem did not leave him in this academy full of strangers who had never liked him and would hate him now.

They would have to be even blinder than a Silent Brother, Uncle Jem agreed. *Because I can see you, James. I will always look to you for light.*

If James had known how life would be at the Academy from then on, he would have asked Uncle Jem to take him home.

He had not expected Mike Smith to leap to his feet in stark horror when James approached his table.

"Come sit with us," called Clive Cartwright, one of Alastair Carstairs's friends. "You might be a mundie, but at least you're not a *monster.*"

Mike had fled gratefully. James had seen Esme flinch once when he walked by her in the hall. He did not inflict his presence on her again.

It would not have been so bad, James believed, if it had been anywhere but the Academy. These were hallowed halls: This was where children were molded to Ascend or grew up learning to serve the Angel.

And this was a school, and this was how schools worked. James had read books about schools before, had read about someone being sent to Coventry, so nobody talked to them at all. He knew how hate could run like wildfire through a group, and that was only among mundanes facing mundane strangeness.

James was stranger than any mundane could ever dream, stranger than any Shadowhunter had believed possible.

He moved out of Matthew's room, and down into the dark. He was given his own room, because even the mundanes were too scared to sleep in the same room as him. Even Dean Ashdown seemed afraid of him. Everybody was.

They acted as if they wanted to cross themselves when they saw him, but they knew he was worse than a vampire and it would do no good. They shuddered when his eyes rested on them, as if his yellow demon's eyes would burn a hole clear through their souls.

Demon's eyes. James heard it whispered again and again. He had never thought he would long to be called Goatface.

He never spoke to anyone, sat at the back of class, ate as quickly as he could, and then ran away so people did not have to look at him while they ate their meals. He crept around the Academy like a loathed and loathsome shadow.

Uncle Jem had been changed into a Silent Brother because he would have died otherwise. Uncle Jem had a place in the world, had friends and a home, and the horror was that he could not be in the place where he belonged. Sometimes after his visits James would find his mother standing at the window, looking out at the street Uncle Jem had long disappeared from, and he would find his father in the music room staring at the violin nobody but Uncle Jem was allowed to touch.

That was the tragedy of Uncle Jem's life; it was the tragedy of his parents' lives.

But how would it be if there was nowhere in the world that you belonged? If you could get nobody to love you? What if you could not be a Shadowhunter or a warlock or anything else?

Maybe then you were worse than a tragedy. Maybe you were nothing at all.

James was not sleeping very well. He kept slipping into sleep and then startling awake, worried he was slipping into that other world, a world of shadows, where he was nothing but an evil shade among shades. He did not know how he had done it before. He was terrified it was going to happen again.

Maybe everyone else was hoping it would, though. Maybe they were all praying he would become a shadow, and simply slip away.

James woke one morning and could not bear the darkness and the feeling of stone above his head, pressing down all around him, for a moment longer. He staggered up the stairs and out onto the grounds.

He was expecting it to still be night, but the sky was bleached by morning, the stars turned invisible against the near-white of the sky. The only color to be found in the sky was the dark gray of clouds, curling like ghosts around the fading moon. It was raining a little, cold pinpricks against James's skin. He sat down on the stone step of the Academy's back door, lifted a palm to the sky, and watched the silvery rain dash down into the hollow of his hand.

He wished the rain would wash him away, before he had to face yet another morning.

He was watching his hand as he wished that, and he saw it happen then. He felt the change creeping over him and saw his hand grow darkly transparent. He saw the raindrops pass through the shadow of his palm as if it was not there.

He wondered what Grace would think, if she could see him now.

Then he heard the crunch of feet running, pounding against the earth, and his father's training made James's head jerk up to see if anyone was being chased, if anyone was in danger.

James saw Matthew Fairchild running as if he was being chased.

Astonishingly, he was wearing gear that he had not, as far as James knew, been threatened into. Even more astonishingly, he was participating in degrading physical exercise. He was running faster than James had seen anyone run in training—maybe faster than James had ever seen anyone run ever—and he was running grimly, face set, in the rain.

James watched him run, frowning, until Matthew glanced up at the sky, stopped, and then began trudging back to the Academy. James thought he would be discovered for a moment, thought of jumping up and racing around to another side of the building, but Matthew did not make for the door.

Instead he went and stood against the stone wall of the Academy, strange and solemn in his black gear, blond hair wild with wind and wet with rain. He tipped his face up to the sky, and he looked as unhappy as James felt.

It made no sense. Matthew had everything, had always had everything, while James now had less than nothing. It made James furious.

"What's wrong with you?" James demanded.

Matthew's whole body jerked with shock. He swung

to face James, and stared. "What?"

"You might have noticed life is less than ideal for me at this time," James said between his teeth. "So give up making a tragic spectacle of yourself over nothing, and—"

Matthew was not leaning against the wall any longer, and James was not sitting on the step. They were both standing up, and this was not a practice on the training grounds. James thought they were really going to fight; he thought they might really hurt each other.

"Oh, I'm terribly sorry, James Herondale," Matthew sneered. "I forgot nobody could do a single thing like speak or breathe in this place without incurring your extremely judgmental judgment. I must be making a spectacle over nothing, if *you* say so. By the Angel, I'd trade places with you in a second."

"You'd trade places with me?" James shouted. "That's rubbish, that's absolute swill, you would never. Why would you do that? Why would you even say it?"

"Maybe it's the fact you have everything I want," Matthew snarled. "And you don't even seem to want it."

"What?" James asked blankly. He was living in opposites land, in which the sky was the earth and the name of every day started with Y. It was the only explanation. "*What?* What do I have that you could possibly want?"

"They will send you home any time you like," Matthew said. "They're trying to drive you away. And no matter what I do, they won't chuck me out. Not the Consul's son."

James blinked. Rain slithered down his cheeks and down the neck of his shirt, but he hardly felt it. "You want ... to be chucked out?"

"I want to go *home*, all right?" Matthew snapped. "I want to be with my father!"

"What?" James said blankly, one more time.

Matthew might insult the Nephilim, but no matter what he said, he always seemed to be having a marvelous time. James had believed he was enjoying himself at the Academy, as James himself could not. James had never thought he might really be unhappy. He'd never even considered Uncle Henry.

Matthew's face twisted as if he was going to cry. He stared off determinedly into the distance, and when he spoke his voice was hard.

"You think Christopher's bad, but my father is so much worse," Matthew said. "A hundred times as bad as Christopher. A thousand. He's been practicing being terrible for much longer than Christopher. He's so absent-minded, and he can't—he can't walk. He could be working on some new device, or writing a letter to his warlock friend in America about a new device, or working out why some old device literally exploded, and he would not notice if his own hair was on fire. I'm not exaggerating, I'm not making a joke—I have put out fires on my own father's head. My mother is always busy, and my brother, Charles Buford, is always running after her and acting superior. I'm the one who takes care of my father. I'm the one who listens to him. I didn't want to go away to school and leave him, and I've been doing all I can to get chucked out and go back."

I don't take care of my father. My father takes care of me, James wanted to say, but he feared it might be cruel to say that, when Matthew had never had that unquestioning security.

It occurred to James that one day there might be a time when his father did not seem all-knowing, able to solve everything and be anything. The thought made him uncomfortable.

"You've been trying to get expelled?" James asked. He spoke slowly. He *felt* slow.

Matthew made an impatient gesture, as if chopping invisible carrots with an invisible knife. "That is what I've been trying to tell you, yes. But they won't. I have been doing the best impression of the worst Shadowhunter in the world, and yet they won't. What is wrong with the dean, I ask you? Does she want blood?"

"The best impression of the worst Shadowhunter," James repeated. "So you don't—believe in all that stuff about violence being repulsive, and truth and beauty and Oscar Wilde?"

"No, I do," Matthew said hastily. "I really like Oscar Wilde. And beauty and truth. I do think it's nonsense that because we are born what we are, we cannot be painters or poets or create anything—that all we do is kill. My father and Christopher are geniuses, do you know that? Real geniuses. Like Leonardo da Vinci. He was a mundane who—"

"I know who Leonardo da Vinci is."

Matthew glanced at him and smiled: it was The Smile, gradual and illuminating as sunrise, and James had the sinking feeling that he might not be immune after all.

"'Course you do, James," said Matthew. "Forgot who I was talking to for a moment there. Anyway, Christopher and my father are truly brilliant. Their inventions have already changed the way Shadowhunters navigate the world, the way they battle demons. And all Shadowhunters everywhere will always look down on them. They will never see what they do as valuable. And someone who wanted to write plays, to make beautiful art, they would throw away like refuse from the streets."

"Do you—want that?" James asked hesitantly.

"No," said Matthew. "I can't draw for toffee, actually. I certainly can't write plays. The less said about my poetry the better. I do appreciate art, though. I'm an excellent spectator. I could spectate for England."

"You could, um, be an actor," James suggested. "When you talk, everyone listens. Especially when you tell stories."

Also there was Matthew's face, which would probably—go over well onstage or something.

"That's a nice thought," said Matthew. "But I think I would rather not get thrown out of my home and still see my father occasionally. Also, I do think violence is terrible and pointless, but—I'm really good at it. In fact, I enjoy it. Not that I'm letting on to our teachers. I wish I was good at something that could add beauty to the world rather than painting it with blood, I really do, but there you have it."

He shrugged.

James did not think they were going to fight after all, so he sat back down on the step. He felt he wanted a sit-down. "I think Shadowhunters can add beauty to the world," he said. "I mean, for one thing—we save lives. I know I said it before, but it's really important. The people we save, any one of them could be the next Leonardo da Vinci, or Oscar Wilde, or just someone who is really kind, who spreads beauty that way. Or they might just be someone who—someone else loves, like you love your father. Maybe you're right that Shadowhunters are more limited, that we do not get the full range of possibilities mundanes get, but—we get to make the mundanes' lives possible. That's what we're born to. It is a privilege. I'm not going to run away from the Academy. I'm not running away from anything. I can bear Marks, and that makes me a Shadowhunter, and that's what I will be whether the Nephilim want me or not."

"You can be a Shadowhunter without going to the Academy, though," said Matthew. "You can be trained in an Institute, like Uncle Will was. That's what I wanted, so I could stay with Father."

"I could. But—" James hesitated. "I didn't want to be sent home. Mother would have to know why."

Matthew was silent for a little while. There was nothing but the sound of the falling rain.

"I like Aunt Tessa," he said. "I never came to London because I worried about leaving Father. I always wished—she could come to Idris more often."

James had received several shocks this morning that were actually not so bad, but this revelation was unwelcome and inevitable. Of course Mother and Father scarcely ever went to Idris. Of course James and Lucie had been raised in London, a little apart from their families.

Because there were people in Idris, there were arrogant Shadowhunters who thought Mother was not worthy to walk among them, and Father would never have let her be insulted.

Now it would be worse, now people would whisper that she had passed on the taint to her children. People would say horrible things about Lucie, James knew—about his scribbling, laughing little sister. Lucie could never be allowed to come to the Academy.

Matthew cleared his throat. "I suppose I can understand all that. Maybe I will stop being so jealous that you are able to get chucked out of school. Maybe I can understand that your aims are noble. However, I still do not understand why you must make it so clear you detest the sight of me. I know, I know, you're aloof and you wish to be alone with literature all the time, but it's particularly horrible with me. It's very lowering. Most people like me. I told you that. I don't even have to try."

"Yes, you're very good at Shadowhunting and everybody likes you, Matthew," said James. "Thanks for clarifying that."

"You don't like me!" Matthew exclaimed. "I did try with you! And you still don't."

"The thing is," said James, "I tend to like very modest people? Humble, you know."

Matthew paused, considered James for a moment, and then burst out laughing. James was amazed by how gratifying that was. It made him feel like he could let out the humiliating truth.

He closed his eyes and said: "I was jealous of you."

When he opened his eyes, Matthew looked wary, as if expecting a trick. "Of what?"

"Well, you're not considered an unholy abomination upon this earth."

"Yes, but—no offense, James—nobody but you is," Matthew pointed out. "You are our unique feature in the school, like a sculpture of a warrior chicken. If we had one of those. You disliked me before anybody knew you were an unholy abomination, anyway. Well, I suppose you are simply trying to spare my feelings. Decent of you. I under—"

"I'm not aloof," said James. "I don't know where you got that idea."

"All the aloofness, I think," Matthew speculated.

"I'm a swot," said James. "I read books all the time and I do not know how to talk to people. If I was a girl living in olden times, people would call me a bluestocking. I wish I could talk to people like you do. I wish I could smile at people and make them like me. I wish I could tell a story and have everybody listen, and have people follow me around wherever

I went. Well, no, I don't, because I am slightly terrified by people, but I wish I could do all that you can do, just the same. I wanted to be friends with Thomas and Christopher, because I liked them and I thought maybe they were—similar to me, and they might like me back. You were jealous I could get kicked out of school? I was jealous of you first. I was jealous of everything about you, and I still am."

"Wait," said Matthew. "Wait, wait, wait. You don't like me because I am *so very charming*?"

He threw his head back and laughed. He kept laughing. He laughed so much that he had to come and sit beside James on the step, and then he laughed some more.

"Stop it, Matthew," James grumbled. "Stop laughing. I am sharing my innermost feelings with you. This is very hurtful."

"I've been in a bad mood this whole time," said Matthew. "You think I'm charming now? You have *no* idea."

James punched him in the arm. He could not help smiling. He saw Matthew noticing, and looking very pleased with himself.

Sometime later, Matthew ushered James firmly into breakfast and to their table, which James noticed was only Christopher and Thomas, and a rather select table after all.

Christopher and Thomas, in another surprise for James in a morning full of surprises, seemed pleased to see him.

"Oh, have you decided not to detest Matthew any longer?" Christopher asked. "I'm so glad. You were really hurting his feelings. Though we are not supposed to talk about that to you." He gazed dreamily at the bread basket, as if it were a wonderful painting. "I forgot that."

Thomas put his head down on the table. "Why are you the way that you are?"

Matthew reached over and patted Thomas on the back, then rescued Christopher from setting his own sleeves on fire with a candle. He gave James the candle and a smile.

"If you ever see Christopher near an open flame, take him away from it, or take it away from him," Matthew said. "Fight the good fight with me. I must be eternally watchful."

"That must be difficult, when surrounded by, um, your adoring public," said James.

"Well," said Matthew, and paused, "it's possible," he said, and paused again, "I may have been ... slightly showing off? 'Look, if you don't want to be friends with me, everybody else does, and you are making a big mistake.' I may have been doing that. Possibly."

"Is that over?" Thomas asked. "Thank the Angel. You know large crowds of people make me nervous! You know I can never think of anything to say to them! I am not witty like you or aloof and above it all like James or living in cloud cuckoo land like Christopher. I came to the Academy to get away from being bossed by my sisters, but my sisters make me much less nervous than battering rams flying through the air and parties all the time. Can we please have some peace and quiet occasionally!"

James stared at Thomas. "Does everybody think I'm aloof?"

"No, mostly people think you're an unholy abomination upon this earth," Matthew said cheerfully. "Remember?"

Thomas looked ready to put his head back on the table, but he cheered up when he saw James had not taken offense.

"Why would that be?" Christopher asked politely.

James stared. "Because I can turn from flesh and blood into a ghastly shadow?"

"Oh," said Christopher. His dreamy lavender eyes

focused for a moment. "That's very interesting," he told James, his voice clear. "You should let me and Uncle Henry perform many experiments on you. We could do an experiment right now."

"No, we could not," said Matthew. "No experiments at breakfast time. Add it to the list, Christopher."

Christopher sighed.

And just like that, as if it could always have been that easy, James had friends. He liked Thomas and Christopher as much as he'd always known he would.

Of all his new friends, though, he liked Matthew the best. Matthew always wanted to talk about the books James had read, or tell James a story as good as a book. He made obvious efforts to find James when James was not there, and obvious efforts to protect James when he was there. James did not have many nice things to write letters home about: He ended up writing letters that were full of Matthew.

James knew Matthew probably only felt sorry for him. Matthew was always looking after Christopher and Thomas, with the same painstaking care he must have looked after his father. Matthew was kind.

That was all right. James would absolutely have wanted to share a room with Matthew, now it was out of the question.

"Why do people call you Demon Eyes, James?" Christopher asked one day when they were sitting around a table studying Ragnor Fell's account of the First Accords.

"Because I have golden eyes as if lit by eldritch infernal fires," James said. He had heard a girl whispering that and thought it sounded rather poetic.

"Ah," said Christopher. "Do you look at all like your grandfather aside from that? The demonic one, I mean."

"You cannot simply ask whether people look like their

demon grandfather!" Thomas wailed. "Next you will ask Professor Fell if he looks like his demon parent! Please, please do not ask Professor Fell if he looks like his demon parent. He has a cutting tongue. Also, he might cut you with a knife."

"Fell?" Christopher inquired.

"Our teacher," said Matthew. "Our green teacher."

Christopher looked genuinely astonished. "We have a teacher who is green?"

"James looks like his father," said Matthew unexpectedly, then narrowed his laughing dark eyes in James's direction in a musing fashion. "Or he will, when he grows into his face and it stops being angles pointing in all different directions."

James slowly raised his open book to hide his face, but he was secretly pleased.

Matthew's friendship made other friends creep forward too. Esme cornered James and told him how sorry she was that Mike was being an idiot. She also told him that she hoped James did not take this expression of friendly concern in a romantic way.

"I have rather a *tendresse* for Matthew Fairchild, actually," Esme added. "Please put in a good word for me there."

Life was much, much better now that he had friends, but that did not mean anything was perfect, or even mended. People were still afraid of him, still hissing *"Demon Eyes"* and muttering about unclean shadows.

"Pulvis et umbra sumus," said James once, out loud in class, after hearing too many whispers. "My father says that sometimes. We are but dust and shadows. Maybe I'm just—getting a head start on all of you."

Several people in the classroom were looking alarmed.

"What did he say?" Mike Smith whispered, clearly agitated.

"It's not a demon language, buffoon," Matthew snapped. "It's Latin."

Despite everything Matthew could do, the whispers rose and rose. James kept expecting a disaster.

And then the demons were let loose in the woods.

"I'll be partners with Christopher," said Thomas at their next training exercise, sounding resigned.

"Excellent. I will be partners with James," said Matthew. "He reminds me of the nobility of the Shadowhunter way of life. He keeps me right. If I am parted from him I will become distracted by truth and beauty. I know I will."

Their teachers seemed extremely pleased that Matthew was actually participating in training courses now, aside from the courses only for the elites, in which Thomas reported that Matthew was still determined to be hopeless.

James did not know why the teachers were so worried. It was obvious that as soon as anyone was actually in danger, Matthew would leap to their defense.

James was glad to be so sure of that, as they walked through the woods. It was a windy day, and it seemed as if every tree was stooping down to howl in his ear, and he knew that Pyxis boxes had been placed throughout the woods by older students—Pyxis boxes with the smallest and most harmless of demons inside, but still real Pyxis boxes with real demons inside, who they were meant to fight. Pyxis boxes were a little outmoded these days, but they were still sometimes used to transport demons safely. If demons could ever be said to be safe.

James's aunt Ella, who he had never seen, had been

killed by a demon from a Pyxis box when she was younger than James was now.

All the trees seemed to be whispering about demons.

But Matthew was at his side, and both of them were armed. He could trust himself to kill a small, almost powerless demon, and if he could trust himself, he could trust Matthew more.

They waited, and walked, then waited. There was a rustle among the trees: It turned out to be a combination of wind and a single rabbit.

"Maybe the upper years forgot to lay out our demon buffet," Matthew suggested. "It is a beautiful springtime day. At such times as these, one's thoughts are filled with love and blossoms, not demons. Who am I to judge—"

Matthew was abruptly quiet. He clutched James's arm, fingers tight, and James stared down at what Matthew had discovered in the heather.

It was Clive Cartwright, Alastair's friend. He was dead.

His eyes were open, staring into nothing, and in one hand he was clutching an empty Pyxis box.

James grabbed Matthew's arm and turned him in a circle, looking around, waiting. He could tell what had happened: Let's give Demon Eyes a scare, a demon won't hurt its own kind, let's chase him away once and for all with a demon larger than he was expecting.

He could not tell what kind of demon it was, but that question was answered when the demon came toward them through the wild woods.

It was a Vetis demon, its shape almost human but not quite, dragging its gray, scaly body through the fallen leaves. James saw the eel-like heads on its arms lifting, like the heads of pointer dogs out hunting.

James slipped from skin to shadow without a thought, like plunging into water to rescue someone, as easy as that. He ran unseen at the Vetis demon and, raising his sword, cleaved one questing head from its arm. He turned to face the head on the other arm. He was going to call to Matthew, but when he glanced back he saw Matthew clearly, despite the sparkling grayness of the world. Matthew already had his bow out, strung and raised. He could see Matthew's narrowed eyes, the determined focus that always lay behind the laughter, and remained when his laughter was stripped away.

Matthew shot the Vetis demon in the red-eyed, sharp-toothed face that sat atop its neck, just as James cut the other head from its remaining arm. The demon lurched, then fell over sideways, twitching.

And James raced through the trees, through the wind and the whispering, afraid of nothing, with Matthew running behind him. He found Alastair and his remaining friend, hiding behind a tree. He crept up to them, a shadow among the whirling shadows of wind-tossed trees, and held his sword to Alastair's throat.

While James was touching the sword, nobody could see it. But Alastair felt the sharpness of the blade and gasped.

"We didn't mean for any of this to happen!" cried Alastair's friend, looking around wildly. Alastair was wise enough to stay quiet. "It was Clive's idea—he said he would finally get you to leave—he only meant to scare you."

"Who's scared?" James whispered, and the whisper came from nowhere. He heard the older boys gasp in fear. "I'm not the one who's scared. If you come after me again, I won't be the one who suffers. Run!"

The pair that had once been a trio stumbled away. James pressed one hand around the hilt of his sword, against the bark of the tree, and willed himself back into a world of solidity and sunshine. He found Matthew looking at him. Matthew had known, all the time, exactly where he was.

"Jamie," Matthew said, sounding unsettled but impressed. "That was terrifying."

"It's James, for the last time," said James.

"No, I'm calling you Jamie for a little while, because you just displayed arcane power and calling you Jamie makes me feel better."

James laughed, shakily, and that made Matthew smile. It did not occur to them until later that a student was dead, and the Shadowhunters feared and distrusted the demonic—that somebody would be blamed. James did not discover until the next day that his parents had been informed of everything that had transpired, and that he, James Herondale, was now officially expelled.

They kept him in the infirmary until his father came. They did not say this was because the infirmary had bars on its doors.

Esme came and gave James a hug, and promised to look him up when she Ascended.

Ragnor Fell entered, his tread heavy, and for a moment James thought he was going to be asked for his homework. Instead Ragnor stood over his bed and shook his horned head slowly from side to side.

"I waited for you to ask me for help," Ragnor told him. "I thought perhaps you might make a warlock."

"I never wanted to be anything but a Shadowhunter," James said helplessly.

Ragnor said, sounding disgusted as usual: "You Shadowhunters never do."

Christopher and Thomas visited. Christopher brought a fruit basket, under the mistaken impression that James was in the infirmary because he was unwell. Thomas apologized for Christopher several times.

James did not see Matthew, however, until his father arrived. Father did not come on a mission to charm the dean. His face was grim as he escorted James through the shining gray walls of the Academy, under the flaming colors of the stained-glass angel, for the last time. He stalked down stairs and through halls as if defying someone to insult James.

James knew nobody ever would, not in front of Father. They would whisper behind his back, whisper in James's ear, his whole life long.

"You should have told us, Jamie," said Father. "But Jem explained to us why you did not."

"How is Mother?" James whispered.

"She cried when Jem told her, and said you were her sweet boy," said Father. "I believe she may be planning to strangle you and then bake you a cake afterward."

"I like cake," James said at last.

All that suffering, all that nobly trying to spare her, and for what? James thought, as he walked out the door of the Academy. He had saved her only a month or two of pain. He hoped that did not mean he was a failure: He hoped Uncle Jem would still think it was worthwhile.

He saw Matthew standing in the courtyard, hands in his pockets, and brightened up. Matthew had come to say good-bye, after all. It did feel worthwhile to have stayed, after all, to have made a friend like this.

"Are you expelled?" Matthew asked, which James thought was slightly obtuse.

"Yes?" he said, indicating his father and his trunk.

"I thought you were," said Matthew, nodding vigorously so his much-brushed hair went tumbling every which way. "So I had to act. But I wanted to make absolutely certain. You see, James, the thing is—"

"Isn't that Alastair Carstairs?" asked Father, perking up.

Alastair did not meet James's eyes as he slunk toward him. He definitely did not respond to Father's beaming smile. He seemed very interested in the flagstones of the courtyard.

"I just wanted to say ... sorry for everything," he mumbled. "Good luck."

"Oh," said James. "Thanks."

"No hard feelings, old sport," said Matthew. "As a bit of a jolly prank, I put all your belongings in the south wing. I don't know why I did that! Boyish high spirits, I suppose."

"You did *what?*" Alastair gave Matthew a harried look, and departed at speed.

Matthew turned to James's father and dramatically clasped his hand.

"Oh, Mr. Herondale!" he said. "Please take me with you!"

"It's Matthew, isn't it?" Father asked. He tried to disengage his hand. Matthew clung to it with extreme determination.

James smiled. He could have told Father about Matthew's determination.

"You see," Matthew proceeded, "I am also expelled from Shadowhunter Academy."

"You got expelled?" James asked. "When? Why?"

"In about four minutes," Matthew said. "Because I broke my solemn word, and exploded the south wing of the Academy."

James and his father both looked at the south wing. It

stood, looking as if it would stand for another century.

"I hoped it would not come to this, but it has. I gave Christopher certain materials that I knew he could turn into explosives. I measured them very carefully, I made sure they were slow acting, and I made Thomas swear to bring Christopher away. I have left a note explaining that it was all my fault, but I do not wish to explain this to Mother. Please take me with you to the London Institute, so I can be taught how to be a Shadowhunter with James!"

"Charlotte will cut off my head," said Father.

He sounded tempted, though. Matthew was sparkling wickedly up at him, and Father enjoyed wickedness. Besides which, he was no more immune to The Smile than anyone else.

"Father, please," James said in a quiet voice.

"Mr. Herondale, please!" said Matthew. "We cannot be parted." James braced himself for the explanation about truth and beauty, but instead Matthew said, with devastating simplicity: "We are going to be *parabatai*."

James stared.

Father said: "Oh, I see."

Matthew nodded encouragingly, and smiled encouragingly.

"Then nobody should come between you," said Father.

"Nobody." Matthew shook his head as he said "nobody," then nodded again. He looked seraphic. "Exactly."

"Very well," said Father. "Everybody get into the carriage."

"Father, you did not steal Uncle Gabriel's carriage again," said James.

"This is your time of trouble. He would want me to have it, and he would have given it to me if I asked him, which as it happens I did not," said Father.

He helped James and Matthew up, then swung himself up to sit on James's other side. He grasped the reins and they were off.

"When the south wing collapses, there could be flying debris," Father remarked. "Any one of us could be injured." He sounded very cheerful about this. "Best to stop on our way home and see the Silent Brothers."

"That seems excessi—" Matthew began, but James elbowed him. Matthew would learn how Father was about the Silent Brothers soon enough.

Anyway, James did not feel Matthew had a right to characterize anyone else's behavior as excessive, now that he had blown up the Academy.

"I was thinking we could split our training time between the London Institute and my house," Matthew went on. "The Consul's house. Where people cannot insult you, and can get used to seeing you."

Matthew had really meant it about being trained together, James thought. He had worked it all out. And if James was in Idris more often, he could perhaps see Grace more often too.

"I'd like that," said James. "I know you'd like to see more of your father."

Matthew smiled. Behind them, the Academy exploded. The carriage jolted slightly with the force of the impact.

"We don't ... have to be *parabatai*," Matthew said, his voice quiet under the sound of the blast. "I said it to make your father take me with you, so I could execute my new plan, but we don't ... have to. I mean, unless you ... maybe want to be."

James had thought he wanted a friend like himself, a *parabatai* who was shy and quiet and would enter in on

James's feelings about the terror of parties. Instead here was Matthew, who was the life and soul of every party, who made dreadful hairbrush decisions, who was unexpectedly and terribly kind. Who had tried to be his friend and kept trying, even though James did not know what trying to be a friend looked like. Who could see James, even when he was a shadow.

"Yes," James said simply.

"What?" said Matthew, who always knew what to say.

"I'd like that," said James. He curled his hands, one around his father's coat sleeve, and one around Matthew's. He held on to them, all the way home.

Shadowhunter Academy, 2008

"So James found a *parabatai* and everything worked out great," Simon said. "That's awesome."

James was Tessa Gray's son, Simon had realized, a long way into the story. It was strange to think of that: It seemed to bring that lost boy very close, he and his friend. Simon liked the sound of James. He'd liked Tessa, too.

And though he was starting to get the feeling, even without his memories, that he hadn't always liked Jace Herondale—he liked him now.

Catarina rolled her eyes so hard Simon thought he could hear them roll, like tiny, exasperated bowling balls.

"No, Simon. The Academy drove James Herondale out for being different, and all the people who loved him could do was follow him out. The people who drove them out did have to rebuild part of their precious Academy, mind you."

"Uh," said Simon. "Sorry, is the message I'm meant to be learning 'get out, get out as fast as you can'?"

"Maybe," Catarina said. "Maybe the message is to trust your friends. Maybe the message is not that people in the past did badly but that now we must all strive to do better. Maybe the message is you have to work these things out for yourself. You think all lessons have easy conclusions? Don't be a child, Daylighter. You're not immortal anymore. You don't have much time to waste."

Simon took that as the dismissal it was, scooping up his books. "Thanks for the story, Ms. Loss."

He ran down the stairs and out of the Academy, but he was too late, as he'd known he would be.

He was barely out of the door when he saw the dregs, filthy and tired, arm in arm, lurching up from the training grounds. Marisol was in front, her arm looped with George's. It looked as if someone had tried to pull out all her hair.

"Where were you, Lewis?" she called. "We could have used you cheering for us as we won!"

Some way behind them were the elites. Jon was looking very unhappy, which filled Simon with a deep sense of peace.

Trust your friends, Catarina had said.

Simon might speak up for mundies in class, but it mattered more that George and Marisol and Sunil spoke up too. Simon didn't want to change things by being the special one, the exceptional mundane, the former Daylighter and former hero. They had all chosen to come try to be heroes. His fellow dregs could win without him.

There was one more motive Catarina might have had that she had not announced, Simon thought.

She had heard this story from her dead friend Ragnor Fell.

Catarina had listened to her friend's stories, the way James Herondale had listened to his father's stories. Being able to tell the stories over again, having someone to listen and learn, meant her friend was not lost.

Maybe he could write to Clary, Simon thought, as well as Isabelle. Maybe he could trust her to love him despite how often he might fail her. Maybe he was ready to be told stories about himself and about her. He didn't want to lose his friend.

Simon was writing his letter to Clary when George came in, toweling his hair. He had taken his life in his hands and risked the showers in one of the dregs' bathroom.

"Hey," Simon said.

"Hey, where were you while the game was happening?" George asked. "I thought you were never coming back and I'd have to be pals with Jon Cartwright. Then I thought about being pals with Jon, was overwhelmed with despair, and decided to find one of the frogs I know are living in here, give it little frog glasses, and call it Simon 2.0."

Simon shrugged, not sure how much he was supposed to tell. "Catarina kept me after class."

"Careful, or someone might start rumors about you two," said George. "Not that I would judge. She's obviously ... ceruleanly charming."

"She was telling me a long story about Shadowhunters being jerks and about *parabatai*. What do you think about the whole *parabatai* thing, anyway? The *parabatai* rune is like a friendship bracelet you can never take back."

"I think it sounds nice," said George. "I'd like that, to have someone who would always watch my back. Someone who I could count on at the times when this scary world gets the scariest."

"Makes it sound like there's someone you'd ask."

"I'd ask you, Si," said George, with an awkward little smile. "But I know you wouldn't ask me. I know who you would ask. And that's okay. I've still got Frog Simon," he added thoughtfully. "Though I'm not sure he's exactly Shadowhunter material."

Simon laughed at the joke, as George had meant him to, smoothing over the awkward moment.

"How were the showers?"

"I have one word for you, Si," said George. "A sad, sad word. Gritty. I had to shower, though. I was gross. Our victory was amazing but hard-won. Why are Shadowhunters so bendy, Simon? Why?"

George kept complaining about Jon Cartwright's enthusiastic if unskilled attempts at playing baseball, but Simon was not listening.

I know who you would ask.

A flash of memory came to Simon, as it did sometimes, cutting like a knife. *I love you*, he'd told Clary. He'd said it believing he was going to die. He'd wanted those to be his last words before he died, the truest words he could speak.

He'd been thinking all this time about his two possible lives, but he didn't have two possible lives. He had a real life, with real memories and a real best friend. He had his childhood as it had actually been, holding hands with Clary as they crossed the street, and the last year as it had actually been, with Jace saving his life and with him saving Isabelle's and with Clary there, Clary, always Clary.

The other life, the so-called normal life without his best

friend, was a fake. It was like a giant woven tapestry portraying his life, scenes shown in threads that were all the colors of the rainbow, except it had one color—one of the brightest colors—ripped out.

Simon liked George, he liked all his friends at the Academy, but he was not James Herondale. He had already had friends before he came here.

Friends to live and die for, to have entangled with every memory. The other Shadowhunters, especially Clary, were a part of him. She was the color that had been ripped out, the bright thread woven through his first memories to his last. Something was missing from the pattern of Simon's life, without Clary, and it would never be right again, unless she was restored.

My best friend, Simon thought. Another thing worth living in this world for, worth being a Shadowhunter for. Maybe she wouldn't want to be his *parabatai*. God knew Simon was no prize. But if he got through this school, if he managed to become a Shadowhunter, he would have all the memories of his best friend back.

He could try for the bond between Jace and Alec, between James Herondale and Matthew Fairchild. He could ask if she would perform the ritual and speak the words that told the world what was between you, and that it was unbreakable.

He could at least ask Clary.

The Evil We Love

By Cassandra Clare and Robin Wasserman

It seemed suddenly very important to have space between him and Michael. As much space as possible.

"You're what?"

He hadn't meant to shout.

—The Evil We Love

THAT'S NOT FUNNY.
IT'S NOT A JOKE. I'M IN–
DON'T YOU SAY THAT AGAIN. YOU WILL NEVER SAY THAT AGAIN.
I KNOW YOU PROBABLY . . .
I KNOW YOU DON'T FEEL THE SAME WAY, THAT YOU COULDN'T . . .
NOTHING HAS TO CHANGE.

There were, Simon Lewis thought, so many ways to destroy a letter. You could shred it into confetti. You could light it on fire. You could feed it to a dog—or a Hydra demon. You could, with the help of your friendly neighborhood warlock, Portal it to Hawaii and drop it into the mouth of a volcano. And given all the letter-destroying options available, Simon thought, maybe the fact that Isabelle Lightwood had returned *his* letter intact was of significance. Maybe it was actually a good sign.

Or at least a not-entirely-terrible sign.

That, at least, was what Simon had been telling himself for the last few months.

But even he had to admit that when the letter in question was a sort-of-maybe love letter, a letter that included heartfelt, humiliating phrases like "you're amazing" and "I know I am that guy you loved"—and when said letter was returned unopened, "RETURN TO SENDER" scrawled across it in red lipstick—"not-entirely-terrible" might be overly optimistic.

At least she had referred to him as "sender." Simon was pretty sure that Isabelle had devised some other choice names for him, none quite so friendly. A demon had sucked out all of his memories, but his observational faculties were intact—and he'd observed that Isabelle Lightwood wasn't the kind of girl who liked to be rejected. Simon, in defiance of all laws of nature and common sense, had rejected her twice.

He'd tried to explain himself in the letter, apologize for pushing her away. He'd confessed how much he wanted to fight his way back to the person he once was. *Her* Simon. Or at least, a Simon worthy of her.

Izzy—I don't know why you would wait for me, but if you do, I promise to make myself worth that wait, he'd written. *Or I'll try. I can promise I am going to try.*

One month to the day after he sent it, the letter came back unread.

As the dorm room door creaked open, Simon hastily shoved the letter back into his desk drawer, careful to avoid the cobwebs and pockets of mold that coated every piece of furniture no matter how diligently he cleaned. He didn't move hastily enough.

"Not the letter *again?*" Simon's roommate at the Academy, George Lovelace, groaned. He flung himself down on his bed, sweeping an arm melodramatically across his forehead. "Oh, Isabelle, my darling, if I stare at this letter long enough, maybe I'll telepathically woo you back to my weeping bosom."

"I don't have a bosom," Simon said, with as much dignity as he could muster. "And I'm pretty sure if I did, it wouldn't be weeping."

"Heaving, then? That's what bosoms do, isn't it?"

"I haven't spent much time around them," Simon admitted. Not much that he could remember, at least. There had been that aborted attempt at groping Sophie Hillyer back in the ninth grade, but her mother busted him before he could even find the clasp on her bra, much less master it. There had, presumably, been Isabelle. But Simon tried very hard these days not to think about that. The clasp on Isabelle's bra; his hands on Isabelle's body; the taste of—

Simon shook his head violently, almost hard enough to clear it. "Can we stop talking about *bosoms*? Like, forever?"

"Didn't mean to interrupt your very important moping-about-Izzy time."

"I'm not moping," Simon lied.

"Excellent." George grinned triumphantly, and Simon realized he'd fallen into some kind of trap. "So then you'll come out to the training field with me, help break in the new daggers. We're sparring, mundies versus elites—losers have to eat extra helpings of soup for a week."

"Oh yeah, Shadowhunters really know how to party." His heart wasn't in the sarcasm. The truth was, his fellow students *did* know how to party, even if their idea of fun usually involved pointy weapons. With exams behind them and only one more week before the end-of-year party and summer vacation, Shadowhunter Academy felt more like camp than school. Simon couldn't believe he'd been here the whole school year; he couldn't believe he'd *survived* the year. He'd learned Latin, runic writing, and a smattering of Chthonian; he'd fought tiny demons in the woods, endured a full moon night with a newborn werewolf, ridden (and nearly been trampled by) a horse, eaten his weight in soup, and in all that time, he'd been neither expelled nor exsanguinated. He'd even bulked up enough to trade in his ladies'-size gear for a men's size, albeit the smallest one available. Against all odds, the Academy had come to feel like home. A slimy, moldy, dungeonlike home without working toilets, maybe, but home nonetheless. He and George had even named the rats that lived behind their walls. Every night, they left Jon Cartwright Jr., III, and IV a piece of stale bread to nibble, in hopes they'd prefer the crumbs to human feet.

This last week was a time for celebration, late-night carousing, and petty wagering over dagger fights. But Simon couldn't quite find the will for fun. Maybe it was the looming shadow of summer vacation—the prospect of going home to a place that didn't feel much like home anymore.

Or maybe it was, as it always was, Isabelle.

"Definitely you'll have much more fun here, sulking," George said as he changed into his gear. "Silly of me to suggest otherwise."

Simon sighed. "You wouldn't understand."

George had a movie-star face, a Scottish accent, a sun-kissed tan, and the kind of muscles that made girls—even the Shadowhunter Academy girls, who until they met Simon had apparently never encountered a human male without a six-pack—giggle and swoon. Girl trouble, particularly the brand involving humiliation and rejection, was beyond his comprehension.

"Just to be clear," George said, in the rich brogue that even Simon couldn't help but find charming, "you don't remember anything about dating this girl? You don't remember being in love with her, you don't remember what it was like when the two of you—"

"That's right," Simon cut him off.

"Or even *if* the two of you—"

"Again, correct," Simon said quickly. He hated to admit it, but this was one of the things about demon amnesia that bothered him the most. What kind of seventeen-year-old guy doesn't know whether or not he's a virgin?

"Because you're apparently running low on brain cells, you *tell* this gorgeous creature that you've forgotten all about her, reject her publicly, and yet when you pledge your love to her in some goopy romantic letter, you're surprised when she's not having it. Then you spend the next two months mooning over her. Is that about right?"

Simon dropped his head into his hands. "Okay, so when you put it that way, it makes no sense."

"Oh, I've *seen* Isabelle Lightwood—it makes all the sense in the world." George grinned. "I just wanted to get my facts straight."

He bounded out the door before Simon could clarify that it wasn't about how Isabelle looked—although it was true that she looked, to Simon, like the most beautiful girl in the world. But it wasn't about her curtain of silky black hair or the bottomless dark brown of her eyes or the deadly liquid grace with which she swung her electrum whip. He couldn't have explained what it *was* about, since George was right, he didn't remember anything about her or what the two of them had been like as a couple. He still had some trouble believing they ever *were* a couple.

He just knew, on a level beneath reason and memory, that some part of him belonged with Isabelle. Maybe even belonged *to* Isabelle. Whether he could remember why, or not.

He'd written Clary a letter too, telling her how much he wanted to remember their friendship—asking for her help. Unlike Isabelle, she'd written back, telling him the story of how they first met. It was the first of many letters, all of them adding episodes to the epic, lifelong story of Clary and Simon's Excellent Adventure. The more Simon read, the more he remembered, and sometimes he even wrote back with stories of his own. It felt safe, somehow, corresponding by letter; there was no chance that Clary could expect anything of him, and no chance that he would fail her, see the pain in her eyes when she realized all over again that *her* Simon was gone. Letter by letter, Simon's memories of Clary were beginning to knit themselves together.

Isabelle was different. It felt like his memories of Isabelle were buried inside a black hole—something dangerous and ravenous, threatening to consume him if he got too close.

Simon had come to the Academy, in part, to escape his painful and confusing double vision of the past, the cognitive dissonance between the life he remembered and the one he'd actually lived. It was like that cheesy old joke his father had loved. "Doctor, my arm hurts when I move like this," Simon would say, setting him up. His father would answer in an atrocious German accent, his version of "doctor voice": "Then ... *don't move like that.*"

As long as Simon didn't think about the past, the past couldn't hurt him. But, increasingly, he couldn't help himself. There was too much pleasure in the pain.

Classes may have been over for the year, but the Academy faculty was still finding new ways to torture them.

"What do you think it is this time?" Julie Beauvale asked as they settled onto the uncomfortable wooden benches in the main hall. The entire student body, Shadowhunters and mundanes alike, had been summoned first thing Monday morning for an all-school meeting.

"Maybe they finally decided to kick out all the dregs," Jon Cartwright said. "Better late than never."

Simon was too tired and too uncaffeinated to think up a clever retort. So he simply said, "Suck it, Cartwright."

George snorted.

Over the last several months of classes, training, and demon-hunting disasters, their class had grown pretty close—especially the handful of students who were around Simon's age. George was George, of course; Beatriz Mendoza was surprisingly sweet for a Shadowhunter; and even Julie had turned out to be slightly less snotty than she pretended to be. Jon Cartwright, on the other hand... The moment they met, Simon had decided that if looks matched personalities, Jon Cartwright would look like a horse's ass. Unfortunately, there was no justice in the world, and he looked instead like a walking Ken doll. Sometimes first impressions were misleading; sometimes they peered straight through to a person's inner soul. Simon was as sure now as he'd ever been: Jon's inner soul was a horse's ass.

Jon gave Simon a patronizing pat on the shoulder. "I'm going to miss your witty repartee this summer, Lewis."

"I'm going to hope you get eaten by a spider demon this summer, Cartwright."

George slipped an arm around both of them, grinning maniacally and humming "Can You Feel the Love Tonight?"

George had, perhaps, embraced the spirit of celebration a little too enthusiastically of late.

Up at the front of the hall, Dean Penhallow cleared her throat loudly, looking pointedly in their direction. "If we could have some silence, please?"

The room continued chattering, Dean Penhallow continued clearing her throat and asking nervously for order, and things could have gone on like that all morning had Delaney Scarsbury, their training master, not climbed up on a chair. "We'll have silence, or we'll have one hundred push-ups," he boomed. The room hushed immediately.

"I suppose you've all been wondering how you would keep busy now that exams are past?" Dean Penhallow said, her voice rising at the end of her sentence. The dean had a way of turning almost everything into a question. "I think you'll all recognize this week's guest speaker?"

An intimidating barrel-chested man in gray robes strode onto the makeshift stage. The room gasped.

Simon gasped too, but it wasn't the appearance of the Inquisitor that had blown his mind. It was the girl trailing after him, glaring fiercely at his robes like she hoped to set them on fire with her mind. A girl with a curtain of silky black hair and bottomless brown eyes: the Inquisitor's daughter. Known to friends, family, and humiliatingly rejected ex-boyfriends as Isabelle Lightwood.

George elbowed him. "You seeing what I'm seeing?" he whispered. "You want a tissue?"

Simon couldn't help remembering the last time Izzy had shown up at the Academy, for the express purpose of warning every girl in school away from him. He'd been horrified. Right about now, he couldn't imagine anything better.

But Isabelle didn't look inclined to say anything to the class. She simply sat beside her father, arms crossed, glowering.

"She's even prettier when she's angry," Jon whispered.

In a miraculous triumph of restraint, Simon didn't spear him in the eye with a pen.

"You've nearly completed your first year at the Academy," Robert Lightwood told the assembled students, somehow making it sound less like a congratulations than it did like a threat. "My daughter tells me that one of the mundanes' great heroes has a saying, 'With great power comes substantial responsibility.'"

Simon gaped. There was only one way Isabelle Lightwood, as far from a comics nerd as a person could get, would know a line—even a mangled one—from Spider-Man. She'd been quoting Simon.

That had to mean something ... right?

He tried to catch her eye.

He failed.

"You've learned a lot about power this year," Robert Lightwood continued. "This week I'm going to talk to you about responsibility. And what happens when power runs unchecked, or is freely given to the wrong person. I'm going to talk to you about the Circle."

At those words, a hush fell across the room. The Academy faculty, like most Shadowhunters, were very careful to avoid the subject of the Circle—the group of rogue Shadowhunters that Valentine Morgenstern had led in the Uprising. The students knew about Valentine—*everyone* knew about Valentine—but they learned quickly not to ask too many questions about him. Over the last year, Simon had come to understand that the Shadowhunters preferred to believe their choices were perfect, their laws infallible. They didn't like to think about the time they'd been nearly destroyed by a group of their own.

It explained, at least, why the dean was hosting this

session, rather than their history teacher, Catarina Loss. The warlock seemed to tolerate most Shadowhunters—*barely*. Simon suspected that when it came to former members of the Circle, "barely" was too much to hope for.

Robert cleared his throat. "I'd like all of you to ask yourselves what you would have done, were you a student here in Valentine Morgenstern's day. Would you have joined the Circle? Would you have stood by Valentine's side at the Uprising? Raise your hand, if you think it's possible."

Simon was unsurprised to see not a single hand in the air. He'd played this game back in mundane school, every time his history class covered World War II. Simon knew no one ever thought they would be a Nazi.

Simon also knew that, statistically, most of them were wrong.

"Now I'd like you to raise your hand if you think you're an exemplary Shadowhunter, one who would do anything to serve the Clave," Robert said.

Unsurprisingly, many more hands shot up this time, Jon Cartwright's the highest.

Robert smiled mirthlessly. "It was the most eager and loyal of us who were first to join Valentine's ranks," he told them. "It was those of us most dedicated to the Shadowhunter cause who found ourselves the easiest prey."

There was a rustling in the crowd.

"Yes," Robert said. "I say *us*, because I was among Valentine's disciples. I was in the Circle."

The rustling burst into a storm. Some of the students looked unsurprised, but many of them looked as if a nuclear bomb had just gone off inside their brains. Clary had told Simon that Robert Lightwood used to be a member of the Circle, but it was obviously hard for some people to reconcile that with the position of the Inquisitor, which this tall, fearsome man now held.

"The *Inquisitor*?" Julie breathed, eyes wide. "How could they let him...?"

Beatriz looked stunned.

"My father always said there was something off about him," Jon murmured.

"This week, I will teach you about the misuses of power, about great evil and how it can take many forms. My able daughter, Isabelle Lightwood, will be assisting with some of the classwork." Here he gestured to Isabelle, who glanced briefly at the crowd, her impossibly fierce glare somehow growing even fiercer. "Most of all, I will teach you about the Circle, how it began and why. If you listen well, some of you might even learn something."

Simon wasn't listening at all. Simon was staring at Isabelle, willing her to look at him. Isabelle studiously stared at her feet. And Robert Lightwood, Inquisitor of the Clave, arbiter of all things lawful, began to tell the story of Valentine Morgenstern and those who had once loved him.

1984

Robert Lightwood stretched out on the quad, trying not to think about how he'd spent this week the year before. The days after exams and before the summer break were, traditionally, a bacchic release of pent-up energy, faculty looking the other way as students pushed the Academy rules to their limits. A year ago, he and Michael Wayland had snuck off campus and taken a boldly illicit midnight skinny-dip in Lake Lyn. Even with their lips firmly sealed shut, the water had taken its hallucinogenic effect, turning the sky electric. They had lain on their backs side by side, imagining falling stars carving neon tracks across the clouds and dreaming themselves into a stranger world.

That was a year ago, when Robert had still imagined himself young, free to waste his time with childish delights. Before he had understood that, young or not, he had responsibilities.

That was a year ago, before Valentine.

The members of the Circle had co-opted this quiet, shady corner of the quad, where they would be safe from prying eyes—and where they, in turn, would be spared the sight of their classmates having their pointless, meaningless fun. Robert reminded himself that he was lucky to be huddled here in the shade, listening to Valentine Morgenstern declaim.

It was a special privilege, he reminded himself, to be a member of Valentine's coterie, privy to his revolutionary ideas. A year ago, when Valentine had inexplicably befriended him, he'd felt nothing but intense gratitude and a desire to hang on Valentine's every word.

Valentine said the Clave was corrupt and lazy, that these days it cared more about maintaining the status quo and fascistically suppressing dissent than it did carrying out its noble mission.

Valentine said the Shadowhunters should stop cowering in the darkness and walk proudly through the mundane world they lived and died to protect.

Valentine said the Accords were useless and the Mortal Cup was built to be used and the new generation was the hope of the future and the Academy classes were a waste of time.

Valentine made Robert's brain buzz and his heart sing; he made Robert feel like a warrior for justice. Like he was a *part* of something, something extraordinary—like he and the others had been chosen, not just by Valentine, but by the hand of destiny, to change the world.

And yet, very occasionally, Valentine also made Robert feel uneasy.

Valentine wanted the Circle's unquestioning loyalty. He wanted their belief in him, their conviction in the cause, to suffuse their souls. And Robert wanted desperately to give that to him. He didn't want to question Valentine's logic or intent; he didn't want to worry that he believed too little in the things that Valentine said. Or that he believed too much. Today, showered in sunlight, the infinite possibility of summer opening up before him, he didn't want to worry at all. So, as Valentine's words washed over him, Robert let his focus drift, just for a moment. Better to tune out than to doubt. Just for now, his friends could do his listening for him, fill him in later. Wasn't that what friends were for?

There were eight of them today, the Circle's innermost circle, all sitting in hushed silence as Valentine ranted about the Clave's kindness to Downworlders: Jocelyn Fairchild, Maryse Trueblood, Lucian and Amatis Graymark, Hodge Starkweather, and, of course, Michael, Robert, and Stephen. Though Stephen Herondale was the most recent addition to the crowd—and the most recent addition to the Academy, arriving from the London Institute at the beginning of the year—he was also the most devoted to the cause, and to Valentine. He'd arrived at the Academy dressed like a mundane: studded leather jacket, tight acid-washed jeans, blond hair gelled into preposterous spikes like the mundane rock stars who postered his dorm room walls. Only a month later, Stephen had adopted not only Valentine's simple, all-black aesthetic but also his mannerisms, so that the only major difference between them was Valentine's shock of white-blond hair and Stephen's blue eyes. By first frost, he'd sworn off all things mundane and destroyed his beloved Sex Pistols poster in a sacrificial bonfire.

"Herondales do nothing halfway," Stephen said whenever Robert teased him about it, but Robert suspected that something lay beneath the lighthearted tone. Something darker—something hungry. Valentine, he had noticed, had a knack for picking out disciples, homing in on those students with some kind of lack, some inner emptiness that Valentine could fill. Unlike the rest of their gang of misfits, Stephen was ostensibly whole: a handsome, graceful, supremely skilled Shadowhunter with a distinguished pedigree and the respect of everyone on campus. It made Robert wonder ... what was it that only Valentine could see?

His thoughts had wandered so far astray that when Maryse gasped and said, in a hushed voice, "Won't that be dangerous?" he wasn't sure what she was talking about. Nonetheless, he squeezed her hand reassuringly, as this was what boyfriends were meant to do. Maryse was lying with her head in his lap, her silky black hair splayed across his jeans. He smoothed it away from her face, a boyfriend's prerogative.

It had been nearly a year, but Robert still found it difficult to believe that this girl—this fierce, graceful, bold girl with a mind like a razor blade—had chosen *him* as her own. She glided through the Academy like a queen, granting favor, indulging her fawning subjects. Maryse wasn't the most beautiful girl in their class, and certainly not the sweetest or the most charming. She didn't care for things like sweetness or charm. But when it came to the battlefield, no one was more ready to charge the enemy, and certainly no one was better with a whip. Maryse was more than a girl, she was a *force*. The other girls worshipped her; the guys *wanted* her—but only Robert had her.

It had changed everything.

Sometimes, Robert felt like his entire life was an act. That it was only a matter of time before his fellow students saw through him, and realized what he really was, beneath all that brawn and bluster: Cowardly. Weak. Worthless. Having Maryse by his side was like wearing a suit of armor. No one like *her* would choose someone worthless. Everyone knew that. Sometimes, Robert even believed it himself.

He loved the way she made him feel when they were in public: strong and safe. And he loved even more the way she made him feel when they were alone together, when she pressed her lips to the nape of his neck and traced her tongue down the arc of his spine. He loved the curve of her hip and the whisper of her hair; he loved the gleam in her eye when she strode into combat. He loved the taste of her. So why was it that whenever she said, "I love you," he felt like such a liar for saying it back? Why was it that he occasionally—maybe more than occasionally—found his thoughts straying to other girls, to how *they* might taste?

How could he love the way Maryse made him feel ... and still be so uncertain that what he felt was love?

He'd taken to surreptitiously watching the other couples around him, trying to figure out whether they felt the same way, whether their declarations of love masked the same confusion and doubt. But the way Amatis's head nestled comfortably against Stephen's shoulder, the way Jocelyn carelessly threaded her fingers through Valentine's, even the way Maryse idly played with his jeans' fraying seams, as if his clothing, his body, were her property ... all of them seemed so certain of themselves. Robert was certain only of how good he'd gotten at faking it.

"We should glory in the danger, if it means a chance to take down a filthy, rogue Downworlder," Valentine said, glowering. "Even if this wolf pack doesn't have a lead on the monster that—" He swallowed, hard, and Robert knew what he was thinking, because it seemed like these days, it was all Valentine was ever thinking, the fury of it radiating off him as if the thought were written in fire, *the monster that killed my father*. "Even if it doesn't, we'll be doing the Clave a favor."

Ragnor Fell, the green-skinned warlock who'd taught at the Academy for nearly a century, paused halfway across the quad and peered over at them, almost as if he could hear their discussion. Robert assured himself that was impossible. Still, he didn't like the way the warlock's horns angled toward them, as if marking his target.

Michael cleared his throat. "Maybe we shouldn't talk like that about, uh, Downworlders out here."

Valentine snorted. "I hope the old goat does hear me. It's a disgrace, them letting him teach here. The only place a Downworlder has at the Academy is on the dissection table."

Michael and Robert exchanged a glance. As always, Robert knew exactly what his *parabatai* was thinking—and Robert was thinking the same. Valentine, when they first met him, had cut a dashing figure with his blinding white hair and blazing black eyes. His features were smooth and sharp at once, like sculpted ice, but beneath the intimidating veneer was a surprisingly kind boy roused to anger only by injustice. Valentine had always been intense, yes, but it was an intensity bent toward doing what he believed was right, what was *good*. When Valentine said he wanted to correct the injustices and inequities imposed on them by the Clave, Robert believed him, and still did. And while Michael may have had a bizarre soft spot for Downworlders, Robert didn't like them any more than Valentine did; he couldn't imagine why, in this day and age, the Clave was still allowing warlocks to meddle in Shadowhunter affairs.

But there was a difference between clear-eyed intensity and irrational anger. Robert had been waiting a long time now for Valentine's grief-fueled rage to simmer down. Instead, it had sparked an inferno.

"So you won't tell us where you got your intel from," Lucian said, the only one other than Jocelyn who could question Valentine with impunity, "but you want us to sneak off campus and hunt down these werewolves ourselves? If you're so sure the Clave would want them taken care of, why not leave it to them?"

"The Clave is useless," Valentine hissed. "You know that better than anyone, Lucian. But if none of you are willing to risk yourselves for this—if you'd rather stay here and go to a *party*..." His mouth curled as if even speaking the word repelled him. "I'll go myself."

Hodge pushed his glasses up on his nose and leaped to his feet. "I'll go with you, Valentine," he said, too loud. It was Hodge's way—always a little too loud or too quiet, always misreading the room. There was a reason he preferred books to people. "I'm always at your side."

"Sit down," Valentine snapped. "I don't need *you* getting in the way."

"But—"

"What good does your loyalty do me when it comes with a big mouth and two left feet?"

Hodge paled and dropped back to the ground, eyes blinking furiously behind thick lenses.

Jocelyn pressed a hand to Valentine's shoulder—ever so gently, and only for a moment, but it was enough.

"I only mean, Hodge, that your particular skills are wasted on the battlefield," Valentine said, more kindly. The shift in tone was abrupt, but sincere. When Valentine favored you with his warmest smile, he was impossible to resist. "And I couldn't forgive myself if you were injured. I can't ... I can't lose anyone else."

They were all silent then, for a moment, thinking of how quickly it had happened, the dean pulling Valentine off the training field to deliver the news, the way he'd taken it, silent and steady, like a Shadowhunter should. The way he'd looked when he returned to campus after the funeral, his hollow eyes, his sallow skin, his face aging years in a week. Their parents were all warriors, and they knew: What Valentine had lost, any of them could lose. To be a Shadowhunter was to live in the shadow of death.

They couldn't bring his father back, but if they could help him avenge the loss, surely they owed him that much.

Robert, at least, owed him everything.

"Of course we'll come with you," Robert said firmly. "Whatever you need."

"Agreed," Michael said. Where Robert went, he would always follow.

Valentine nodded. "Stephen? Lucian?"

Robert caught Amatis rolling her eyes. Valentine never treated the women with anything less than respect, but when it came to battle, he preferred to fight with men by his side.

Stephen nodded. Lucian, who was Valentine's *parabatai* and the one he relied on most, shifted uncomfortably. "I promised Céline I would tutor her tonight," he admitted. "I could cancel it, of course, but—"

Valentine waved him off, laughing, and the others followed suit.

"Tutoring? Is that what they're calling it these days?" Stephen teased. "Seems like she's already aced her O levels in wrapping you around her little finger."

Lucian blushed. "Nothing's happening there, trust me," he said, and it was presumably the truth. Céline, younger than the rest of the Circle, with the fragile, delicately pretty features of a porcelain doll, had been trailing their group like a lost puppy. It was obvious to anyone with eyes that she'd fallen hard for Stephen, but he was a lost cause, pledged to Amatis for life. She'd picked Lucian as her consolation prize, but it was just as obvious that Lucian had no romantic interest in anyone but Jocelyn Fairchild. Obvious, that is, to everyone except Jocelyn.

"We don't need you for this one," Valentine told Lucian. "Stay and *enjoy* yourself."

"I should be with you," Lucian said, the merriment faded from his voice. He sounded pained at the thought of Valentine venturing into dangerous territory without him, and Robert understood. *Parabatai* didn't always fight side by side—but knowing your *parabatai* was in danger, without you there to support and protect him? It caused an almost physical pain. And Lucian and Valentine's *parabatai* bond was even more intense than most. Robert could almost feel the current of power flowing between them, the strength and love they passed back and forth with every glance. "Where you go, I go."

"It's already decided, my friend," Valentine said, and that simply, it was. Lucian would stay on campus with the others. Valentine, Stephen, Michael, and Robert would slip away from campus after dark and venture into Brocelind Forest in pursuit of a werewolf encampment that, supposedly, could lead them to Valentine's father's killer. They'd make up the rest as they went along.

As the others hurried off to the dining hall for lunch, Maryse grabbed Robert's hand and pulled him close.

"You'll be careful out there, yes?" she said sternly. Maryse said everything sternly—it was one of the things he liked best about her.

She pressed her lithe body against his, kissed his neck, and he felt, in that moment, a passing sense of supreme confidence, that this was where he belonged ... at least, until she whispered, "Come home to me in one piece."

Come home to me. As if he belonged to her. As if, in her mind, they were already married, with a house and children and a lifetime of togetherness, as if the future was already decided.

It was the appeal of Maryse, as it was the appeal of Valentine, the ease with which they could be so sure of what should be, and what was to come. Robert continued hoping that one day it would rub off on him. In the meantime, the less certain he was, the more certain he acted—there was no need for anyone to know the truth.

Robert Lightwood wasn't much of a teacher. He gave them a neatly sanitized account of the early days of the Circle, laying out Valentine's revolutionary principles as if they were a list of ingredients for baking a particularly bland cake. Simon, fruitlessly devoting most of his energy to telepathic communication with Isabelle, was barely listening. He found himself cursing the fact that Shadowhunters were so haughty about the whole we-don't-do-magic thing. If he were a warlock, he'd probably be able to command Isabelle's attention with the flick of a finger. Or, if he were still a vampire, he could have used his vampy powers to enthrall her—but that was something Simon preferred not to think about, because it raised some unsettling questions about how he'd managed to enthrall her in the first place.

What he did hear of Robert's tale didn't much interest him. Simon had never liked history much, at least as it was relayed to him in school. It sounded too much like a brochure, everything neatly laid out and painfully obvious in retrospect. Every war had its bullet-pointed causes; every megalomaniac dictator was so cartoonishly evil you wondered how stupid the people of the past had to be, not to notice. Simon didn't remember much of his own history-making experiences, but he remembered enough to know it wasn't so clear when it was happening. History, the way teachers liked it, was a racetrack, a straight shot from start to finish line; life itself was more of a maze.

Maybe the telepathy worked after all. Because when the speech ended and the students were given permission to disperse, Isabelle hopped off the stage and strolled right up to Simon. She gave him a sharp nod hello.

"Isabelle, I, uh, maybe we could—"

She flashed him a brilliant smile that, for just a moment, made him think all his worrying had been for nothing. Then she said, "Aren't you going to introduce me to your friends? Especially the handsome ones?"

Simon turned to see half the class crowding in behind him, eager for a brush with the famous Isabelle Lightwood. At the front of the pack were George and Jon, the latter practically drooling.

Jon elbowed past Simon and thrust out a hand. "Jon Cartwright, at your service," he said in a voice that oozed charm like a blister oozed pus.

Isabelle took his hand—and instead of jujitsuing him to the ground with a humiliating thump or slicing his hand off at the wrist with her electrum whip, she let him turn her hand over and bring it to his lips. Then she *curtsied*. She *winked*. Worst of all, she *giggled*.

Simon thought he might puke.

Unendurable minutes of torment passed: George blushing and making goofy attempts at jokes, Julie struck speechless, Marisol pretending to be above it all, Beatriz engaging in wan but polite small talk about mutual acquaintances, Sunil bouncing in the back of the crowd, trying to make himself seen, and through it all, Jon smirking and Isabelle beaming and batting her eyes in a display that could only be meant to make Simon's stomach churn.

At least, he desperately hoped it was meant for that. Because the other option—the possibility that Isabelle was smiling at Jon simply because she wanted to, and that she accepted his invitation to squeeze his rock-hard biceps because she wanted to feel his muscles contract beneath her delicate grip—was unthinkable.

"So what do you people do around here for fun?" she asked finally, then narrowed her eyes flirtatiously at Jon. "And don't say 'me.'"

Am I already dead? Simon thought hopelessly. *Is this hell?*

"Neither the circumstances nor the population here have proven themselves conducive to fun," Jon said pompously, as if the bluster in his voice could disguise the fire in his cheeks.

"That all changes tonight," Isabelle said, then turned

on her spiky heel and strode away.

George shook his head, letting out an appreciative whistle. "Simon, your girlfriend—"

"*Ex*-girlfriend," Jon put in.

"She's magnificent," Julie breathed, and from the looks on the others' faces, she was speaking for the group.

Simon rolled his eyes and hurried after Isabelle—reaching out to grab her shoulder, then thinking better of it at the last moment. Grabbing Isabelle Lightwood from behind was probably an invitation to amputation.

"Isabelle," he said sharply. She sped up. So did he, wondering where she was headed. "Isabelle," he said again. They burrowed deeper into the school, the air thick with damp and mold, the stone floor increasingly slick beneath their feet. They hit a fork, corridors branching off to the left and right, and she paused before choosing the one on the left.

"We don't go down this one, generally," Simon said.

Nothing.

"Mostly because of the elephant-size slug that lives at the end of it." This was not an exaggeration. Rumor had it that some disgruntled faculty member—a warlock who'd been fired when the tide turned against Downworlders—had left it behind as a parting gift.

Isabelle kept walking, slower now, picking her way carefully over seeping puddles of slime. Something skittered loudly overhead. She didn't flinch—but she did look up, and Simon caught her fingers playing across the coiled whip.

"Also because of the rats," he added. He and George had gone on an expedition down this corridor in search of the supposed slug ... they gave up after the third rat dropped from the ceiling and somehow found its way down George's pants.

Isabelle breathed a heavy sigh.

"Come on, Izzy, hold up."

Somehow, he'd stumbled on the magic words. She spun around to face him. "Don't call me that," she hissed.

"What?"

"My friends call me Izzy," she said. "You lost that right."

"Izzy—Isabelle, I mean. If you'd read my letter—"

"No. You don't call me Izzy, you don't send me letters, you don't follow me into dark corridors and try to save me from rats."

"Trust me, we see a rat, it's every man for himself."

Isabelle looked like she wanted to feed him to the giant slug. "My point, Simon Lewis, is that you and I are strangers now, just like you wanted it."

"If that's true, then what are you doing here?"

Isabelle looked incredulous. "It's one thing for Jace to believe the world revolves around him, but come on. I know you love fantasy, Simon, but the suspension of disbelief can only go so far."

"This is my school, Isabelle," Simon said. "And you're my—"

She just stared at him, as if defying him to come up with a noun that would justify the possessive.

This wasn't going the way he'd planned.

"Okay, then, why are you here? And why are you being so nice to all my, uh, friends?"

"Because my father's *forcing* me to be here," she said. "Because I guess he thinks some delightful father-daughter bonding time in a slime-covered pit will make me forget that he's a deadbeat adulterer who ditched his family. And I'm being nice to your friends because I'm a nice person."

Now it was Simon who looked incredulous.

"Okay, I'm not," she admitted. "But I've never actually been to school, you know. I figured if I have to be here, I might as well make the best of it. See what I'm missing. Is that enough information for you?"

"I get that you're mad at me, but—"

She shook her head. "You *don't* get it. I'm not mad at you. I'm not anything at you, Simon. You asked me to accept that you were a different person now, someone who I don't know. So I've accepted that. I loved someone—he's gone now. You're nobody I know, and, as far as I can tell, nobody I need to know. I'll only be here a few days, and then we never need to see each other again. How about we don't make it harder than it has to be?"

He couldn't quite catch his breath.

I loved someone, she'd said, and it was the closest she—or any girl—had ever come to saying *I love you* to Simon.

Except that it wasn't close at all, was it?

It was a world away.

"Okay." It was the only word he could force out, but she was already walking on down the corridor. She didn't need his permission to be a stranger; she didn't need anything from him. "You're going the wrong way!" he called after her. He didn't know where she wanted to go, but there seemed little chance she wanted to go slug-ward.

"They're all wrong," she called back, without turning around.

He tried to sense some subtext in her words, a glimmer of pain. Something that would give the lie to her claim, betray the feelings she still harbored for him—prove this was as hard and confusing for her as it was for him.

But the suspension of disbelief could only go so far.

✱ ✱ ✱

Isabelle had said she wanted to make the best of her time at the Academy, and she'd proposed they not make it any harder than it needed to be. Unfortunately, Simon soon discovered, these two things were mutually exclusive. Because Isabelle's version of making the best of things involved Isabelle stretched out like a cat on one of the student lounge's musty leather couches, surrounded by sycophants, Isabelle partaking in George's illicit supply of scotch and inviting the others to do so as well, so that soon all of Simon's friends and enemies were drunk and giddy and in much too good a mood for his liking. Making the best of things apparently meant encouraging Julie to flirt with George and teaching Marisol how to smash statuary with a whip and, worst of all, agreeing to "maybe" be Jon Cartwright's date for the end-of-year party later in the week.

Simon wasn't sure whether any of this was harder than it needed to be—who knew what qualified as *needed to be?*—but it was excruciating.

"So, when does the real fun start?" Isabelle finally said.

Jon waggled his eyebrows. "Just say the word."

Isabelle laughed and touched his shoulder.

Simon wondered whether the Academy would expel him for murdering Jon Cartwright in his sleep.

"Not that kind of fun. I mean, when do we sneak off campus? Go party in Alicante? Go swimming in Lake Lyn? Go..." She trailed off, finally noticing that the others were gaping at her like she was speaking in tongues. "Are you telling me you don't do *any* of that?"

"We're not here to have fun," Beatriz said, somewhat stiffly. "We're here to learn to be Shadowhunters. There are rules for a reason."

Isabelle rolled her eyes. "Haven't you ever heard that rules are meant to be broken? Students are *supposed* to get into a little trouble at the Academy—at least the best students are. Why do you think the rules are so strict? So that only the best can get around them. Think of it like extra credit."

"How would you know?" Beatriz asked. Simon was surprised by her tone. Usually, she was the quietest among them, always willing to go with the flow. But there was an edge in her voice now, something that reminded him that, gentle as she seemed, she was a born warrior. "It's not like you went here."

"I come from a long line of Academy graduates," Isabelle said. "I know what I need to know."

"We're not all interested in following in your *father's* footsteps," Beatriz said, then stood up and walked out of the room.

There was silence in her wake, everyone tensely waiting for Isabelle to react.

Her smile didn't waver, but Simon could feel the heat radiating from her and understood it was taking a great deal of energy for her not to explode—or collapse. He didn't know which it would be; he didn't know how she felt about her father once being one of Valentine's men. He didn't know anything about her, not really. He admitted that.

But he still wanted to scoop her into his arms and hold her until the storm passed.

"No one has ever accused my father of being fun," Isabelle said flatly. "But I assume *my* reputation precedes me. If you meet me here at midnight tomorrow, I'll show you what you've been missing." She took Jon's hand in her own and allowed him to pull her off the couch. "Now. Will you show me to my room? This place is simply impossible to navigate."

"My pleasure," Jon said, winking at Simon.

Then they were gone.

Together.

The next morning the hall echoed with yawning and the groan of hangovers in (fruitless) search of grease and coffee. As Robert Lightwood launched into his second lecture, some tedious disquisition on the nature of evil and a point-by-point analysis of Valentine's critique of the Accords, Simon had to keep pinching himself awake. Robert Lightwood was possibly the only person on the planet who could make the story of the Circle drop-dead boring. It didn't help that Simon had stayed up till dawn, tossing and turning on the lumpy mattress, trying to drive nightmare images of Isabelle and Jon out of his head.

There was something going on with her, Simon was sure of it. Maybe it wasn't about him—maybe it was about her father or some residual homeschooling issues or just some girl thing he couldn't fathom, but she wasn't acting like herself.

She's not your girlfriend, he kept reminding himself. Even if something was wrong, it was no longer his job to fix it. *She can do what she wants.*

And if what she wanted was Jon Cartwright, then obviously she wasn't worth losing a night of sleep over in the first place.

By sunrise he'd almost managed to convince himself of this. But there she was again, up onstage beside her father, her fierce and fiercely intelligent gaze evoking all those annoying *feelings* again.

They weren't memories, exactly. Simon couldn't have named a single movie they watched together; he didn't know any of Isabelle's favorite foods or inside jokes; he didn't know what it felt like to kiss her or twine his fingers with hers. What he felt whenever he looked at her was deeper than that, dwelling in some nether region of his mind. He felt like he *knew* her, inside and out. He felt like he had Superman vision and could x-ray her soul. He felt sorrow and loss and joy and confusion; he felt a cavemanlike urge to slaughter a wild boar and lay it at her feet; he felt the need to do something extraordinary and the belief that, in her presence, he could.

He felt something he'd never felt before—but he had a sinking sensation that he recognized it anyway.

He was pretty sure he felt like he was in love.

1984

Valentine made it easy for them. He'd induced permission from the dean for an "educational" camping trip in Brocelind Forest—two days and nights free to do as they pleased, as long as it resulted in a few scribbled pages on the curative powers of wild herbs.

By all rights, with his uncomfortable questions and rebellious theories, Valentine should have been the black sheep of Shadowhunter Academy. Ragnor Fell certainly treated him like a slimy creature who'd crawled out from under a rock and should be hastily returned there. But the rest of the faculty seemed blinded by Valentine's personal magnetism, unable or unwilling to see through to the disrespect that lay beneath. He was endlessly dodging deadlines and ducking out of classes, excusing himself with nothing more than the flash of a smile. Another student might have been grateful for the latitude, but it only made

Valentine loathe his teachers more—every loophole the faculty opened for him was only more evidence of weakness.

He had no qualms about enjoying its consequences.

The werewolf pack, according to Valentine's intel, was holed up in the old Silverhood manor, a decrepit ruin at the heart of the forest. The last Silverhood had died in battle two generations before, and was used as a name to spook young Shadowhunter children. The death of a soldier was one thing: regrettable, but the natural order of things. The death of a line was a tragedy.

Maybe they were all secretly apprehensive about it, this illicit mission that seemed to cross an invisible line. Never before had they struck against Downworlders without the express permission and oversight of their elders; they had broken rules, but never before had they strayed so close to breaking the Law.

Maybe they just wanted to spend a few more hours like normal teenagers, before they went so far they couldn't turn back.

For whatever reason, the four of them made their way through the woods with a deliberate lack of speed, setting up camp for the night a half mile from the Silverhood estate. They would, Valentine decided, spend the next day staking out the werewolf encampment, gauging its strengths and weaknesses, charting the rhythms of the pack, and attack at nightfall, once the pack had dispersed to hunt. But that was tomorrow's problem. That night, they sat around a campfire, roasted sausages over leaping flames, reminisced about their pasts, and rhapsodized about their futures, which still seemed impossibly far away.

"I'll marry Jocelyn, of course," Valentine said, "and we'll

raise our children in the new era. They'll never be warped by the corrupt laws of a weak, sniveling Clave."

"Sure, because by that time, we'll run the world," Stephen said lightly. Valentine's grim smile made it seem less like a joke than a promise.

"Can't you just see it?" Michael said. "Daddy Valentine, knee deep in diapers. A busload of kids."

"However many Jocelyn wants." Valentine's expression softened, as it always did when he said her name. They'd only been together a couple of months—since his father died—but no one questioned that they were together for good. The way he looked at her ... like she was a different species than the rest of them, a *higher* species. "Can't you see it?" Valentine had confided once, early on, when Robert asked him how he could be so sure of love, so soon. "There's more of the Angel in her than in the rest of us. There's greatness in her. She shines like Raziel himself."

"You just want to flood the gene pool," Michael said. "I imagine you think the world would be better off if every Shadowhunter had a little Morgenstern in them."

Valentine grinned. "I'm told false modesty doesn't suit me, so ... no comment."

"While we're on the subject," Stephen said, a blush rising in his cheeks. "I've asked Amatis. And she said yes."

"Asked what?" Robert said.

Michael and Valentine only laughed, as Stephen's cheeks took fire. "To marry me," he admitted. "What do you think?"

The question was ostensibly directed to all of them, but his gaze was fixed on Valentine, who hesitated an impossibly long time before answering.

"Amatis?" he said finally, furrowing his brow as if he'd

have to give the matter some serious thought.

Stephen caught his breath, and in that moment, Robert almost thought it was possible that he needed Valentine's approval—that despite proposing to Amatis, despite loving her so deeply and desperately that he nearly vibrated with emotion whenever she came near, despite writing her that abominable love song Robert had once found crumpled under his bed, Stephen would cast her aside if Valentine commanded it.

In that moment, Robert almost thought it was possible that Valentine *would command* it, just to see what happened.

Then Valentine's face relaxed into a wide smile, and he threw an arm around Stephen, saying, "It's about time. I don't know what you were waiting for, you idiot. When you're lucky enough to have a Graymark by your side, you do whatever you can to make sure it's forever. I should know."

Then everyone was laughing and toasting and plotting bachelor party schemes and teasing Stephen about his short-lived attempts at songwriting, and it was Robert who felt like the idiot, imagining even for a second that Stephen's love for Amatis could waver, or that Valentine had anything but their best interests at heart.

These were his friends, the best he would ever have, or anyone could ever have.

These were his comrades in arms, and nights like these, bursts of joy beneath starry skies, were their reward for the special obligation they'd taken upon themselves.

To imagine otherwise was only a symptom of Robert's secret weakness, his inveterate lack of conviction, and he resolved not to let himself do so again.

"And you, old man?" Valentine asked Robert. "As if I

even have to ask. We all know Maryse does what she wants."

"And inexplicably, she seems to want you," Stephen added.

Michael, who had fallen unusually silent, caught Robert's eye. Only Michael knew how little Robert liked to think about the future, especially this part of it. How much he dreaded being forced into marriage, parenting, responsibility. If it were up to Robert, he would stay at the Academy forever. It made little sense. Because of what had happened when he was a kid, he was a couple of years older than his friends—he should have been chafing at the restrictions of youth. But maybe—because of what had happened—part of him would always feel cheated and want that time back. He'd spent so long wanting the life he had now. He wasn't ready to let go of it quite yet.

"Well, this old man is exhausted," Robert said, dodging the question. "I think my tent is calling."

As they extinguished the fire and tidied up the site, Michael shot him a grateful smile, having been spared his own interrogation. The only one of them still single, Michael disliked this line of conversation even more than Robert did. It was one of the many things they had in common: They both enjoyed each other's company more than that of any girl. Marriage seemed like such a misguided concept, Robert sometimes thought. How could he care for any wife more than he did for his *parabatai*, the other half of his soul? Why should he possibly be expected to?

He couldn't sleep.

When he emerged from the tent into the silent predawn, Michael was sitting by the ashes of the campfire. He turned toward Robert without surprise, almost as if he'd been waiting for his *parabatai* to join him. Maybe he had.

Robert didn't know whether it was an effect of the bonding ritual or simply the definition of a best friend, but he and Michael lived and breathed in similar rhythms. Before they were roommates, they'd often run into each other in the Academy corridors, sleeplessly roaming the night.

"Walk?" Michael suggested.

Robert nodded.

They traipsed wordlessly through the woods, letting the sounds of the sleeping forest wash over them. Screeches of night birds, skitters of insects, the hush of wind through fluttering leaves, the soft crunch of grass and twigs beneath their feet. There were dangers lurking here, they both knew that well enough. Many of the Academy's training missions took place in Brocelind Forest, its dense trees a useful refuge for werewolves, vampires, and even the occasional demons, though most of those were unleashed by the Academy itself, an ultimate test for particularly promising students. This night the forest felt safe. Or maybe it was simply that Robert felt invincible.

As they walked, he thought not of the mission to come but of Michael, who had been his first true friend.

He'd had friends when he was young, he supposed. The kids growing up in Alicante all knew each other, and he had vague memories of exploring the Glass City with small bands of children, their faces interchangeable, their loyalties nonexistent. As he discovered for himself the year he turned twelve and got his first Mark.

This was, for most Shadowhunter children, a proud day, one they looked forward to and fantasized about the way mundane children inexplicably fixated on birthdays. In some families, the first rune was applied in a quick, businesslike fashion, the child Marked and sent on his way;

in others, there was great festivity, presents, balloons, a celebratory feast.

And, of course, in a very small number of families, the first rune was the last rune, the touch of the stele burning the child's skin, sending him into shock or madness, a fever so intense that only cutting through the Mark would save the life. Those children would never be Shadowhunters; those families would never be the same.

No one ever thought it would happen to them.

At twelve Robert had been scrawny but sure-footed, quick for his age, strong for his size, sure of the Shadowhunting glory that awaited him. As his extended family looked on, his father carefully traced the Voyance rune across Robert's hand.

The stele's tip carved its graceful lines across his pale skin. The completed Mark blazed bright, so bright Robert shut his eyes from the glare of it.

That was the last thing he remembered.

The last he remembered clearly, at least.

After that there was everything he'd tried so hard to forget.

There was pain.

There was the pain that seared through him like a lightning strike and the pain that ebbed and flowed like a tide. There was the pain in his body, lines of agony radiating from the Mark, burrowing from his flesh to his organs to his bones—and then, so much worse, there was the pain in his mind, or maybe it was his soul, an ineffable sensation of *hurt*, as if some creature had burrowed into the depths of his brain and gotten hungrier with the firing of every neuron and synapse. It hurt to think, it hurt to feel, it hurt to remember—but it felt necessary to do these things, because, even in the heart of this agony, some dim part of Robert stayed alert enough to know that if he didn't hang on, didn't feel the hurt, he would slip away forever.

Later he would use all these words and more to try to describe the pain, but none of them captured the experience. What had happened, what he had felt, that was beyond words.

There were other torments to endure, through that eternity he lay in bed, insensible to all around him, imprisoned by his Mark. There were visions. He saw demons, taunting and torturing him, and worse, he saw the faces of those he loved, telling him he was unworthy, telling him he was better off dead. He saw charred, barren plains and a wall of fire, the hell dimension awaiting him if he let his mind slip away, and so, through it all, somehow, he held on.

He lost all sense of himself and the world around him, lost his words and his name—but he held on. Until finally, one month later, the pain abated. The visions faded. Robert awoke.

He learned—once he'd recovered himself enough to understand and care—that he'd been semiconscious for several weeks while a battle had been raging around him, members of the Clave warring with his parents over his treatment as two Silent Brothers did their best to keep him alive. They had all wanted to strip him of the Mark, his parents told him, the Silent Brothers warning daily that this was the only way to ensure his survival and spare him further pain. Let him live out his life as a mundane: This was the conventional treatment for Shadowhunters who couldn't bear Marks.

"We couldn't let them do that to you," his mother told him.

"You're a Lightwood. You were born to this life," his father told him. "This life and no other."

What they didn't say, and didn't need to: *We would rather see you dead than mundane.*

Things were different between them, after that. Robert was grateful to his parents for believing in him—he too would rather be dead. But it changed something, knowing his parents' love for him had a limit. And something must have changed for them, too, discovering that a part of their son couldn't handle the Shadowhunter life, being forced to bear that shame.

Now Robert could no longer remember what his family had been like before the Mark. He remembered only the years since, the coldness that lived between them. They acted their parts: loving father, doting mother, dutiful son. But it was in their presence that Robert felt most alone.

He was, in those months spent recovering, frequently alone. The kids he'd thought of as his friends wanted nothing to do with him. When forced into his presence, they shied away, as if he were contagious.

There was nothing wrong with him, the Silent Brothers said. Having survived the ordeal with the Mark intact, there was no risk of future danger. His body had teetered on the edge of rejection, but his will had turned the tide. When the Silent Brothers examined him for the last time, one of them spoke somberly inside his head, with a message for Robert alone.

You will be tempted to think this ordeal marks you as weak. Instead, remember it as proof of your strength.

But Robert was twelve years old. His former friends were tracing themselves with runes, shipping off to the Academy, doing everything normal Shadowhunters were supposed to do—while Robert hid away in his bedroom, abandoned by his friends, cold-shouldered by his family, and afraid of his own stele. In the face of so much evidence for weakness, even a Silent Brother couldn't make him feel strong.

In this way, nearly a year passed, and Robert began to imagine this would be the shape of the rest of his life. He would be a Shadowhunter in name only; a Shadowhunter afraid of the Marks. Sometimes, in the dark of night, he wished his will hadn't been so strong, that he'd let himself be lost. It would have to be better than the life he'd returned to.

Then he met Michael Wayland, and everything changed.

They hadn't known each other very well, before. Michael was a strange kid, allowed to tag along with the others, but never quite accepted. He was prone to distraction and strange flights of fancy, pausing in the middle of a sparring session to consider where Sensors had come from, and who had thought to invent them.

Michael had shown up at the Lightwoods' manor one day asking if Robert might like to go for a horseback ride. They'd spent several hours galloping through the countryside, and once it was over, Michael said, "See you tomorrow," as if it were a foregone conclusion. He kept coming back. "Because you're interesting," Michael said, when Robert finally asked him why.

That was another thing about Michael. He always said exactly what was in his head, no matter how tactless or peculiar.

"My mother made me promise not to ask about what happened to you," he added.

"Why?"

"Because it would be rude. What do you think? Would it be rude?"

Robert shrugged. No one ever asked him about it or referred to it, not even his parents. It had never occurred to him to wonder why, or whether this was preferable. It was simply the way things were.

"I don't mind being rude," Michael said. "Will you tell me? What it was like?"

Strange, that it could be that simple. Strange, that Robert could be burning to tell someone without even realizing it. That all he needed was someone to ask. The floodgates opened. Robert talked and talked, and when he trailed off, afraid he was going too far, Michael would jump in with another question.

"Why do you think it happened to *you*?" Michael asked. "Do you think it was genetic? Or, like, some part of you just isn't meant to be a Shadowhunter?"

It was, of course, Robert's greatest, most secret fear—but to hear it tossed off so casually like this defused it of all its power.

"Maybe?" Robert said, and instead of shunning him, Michael's eyes lit up with a scientist's curiosity.

He grinned. "We should find out."

They made it their mission: They probed libraries, pored over ancient texts, asked questions that no adult wanted to hear. There was very little written record of Shadowhunters who'd experienced what Robert had—this kind of thing was meant to be a shameful family secret, never spoken of again. Not that Michael cared how many feathers he ruffled or which traditions he overturned. He wasn't particularly brave, but he seemed to have no fear.

Their mission failed. There was no rational explanation for why Robert had reacted so strongly to the Mark, but by the end of that year, it didn't matter. Michael had turned a nightmare into a puzzle—and had turned himself into Robert's best friend.

They performed the *parabatai* ritual before leaving for the Academy, swearing the oath without hesitation. By then they were fifteen years old, a physically unlikely pairing: Robert had finally hit his growth spurt, and loomed over his peers, his muscles thick, his shadow of a beard growing in thicker every day. Michael was slim and wiry, his unruly curls and dreamy expression making him look younger than his age.

"Entreat me not to leave thee,
Or return from following after thee—
For whither thou goest, I will go,
And where thou lodgest, I will lodge.
Thy people shall be my people, and thy God my God.
Where thou diest, will I die, and there will I be buried.
The Angel do so to me, and more also,
If aught but death part thee and me."

Robert recited the words, but they were unnecessary. Their bond had been cemented the day he turned fourteen, when he finally got up the nerve to Mark himself again. Michael was the only one he told, and as he held the stele over his skin, it was Michael's steady gaze that gave him the courage to bear down.

Unthinkable that they had only one last year together before they'd be expected to part. Their *parabatai* bond would remain after the Academy, of course. They'd always be best friends; they'd always charge into battle side by side. But it wouldn't be the same. They'd each marry, move into houses of their own, refocus their attention and their love.

They would always have a claim on each other's souls. But after next year, they would no longer be the most important person in each other's lives. This, Robert knew, was simply how life worked. This was growing up. He just couldn't imagine it, and he didn't want to.

As if listening in on Robert's thoughts, Michael echoed the question he'd dodged earlier. "What really is going on with you and Maryse?" he asked. "Do you think it's for real? Like, for good?"

There was no need to put on a show for Michael. "I don't know," he said honestly. "I don't even know what that would feel like. She's perfect for me. I love spending time with her, I love ... *you know*, with her. But does that mean I love her? It should, but..."

"Something's missing?"

"Not between us, though," Robert said. "It's like there's something missing in me. I see how Stephen looks at Amatis, how Valentine looks at Jocelyn—"

"How *Lucian* looks at Jocelyn," Michael added with a wry grin. They both liked Lucian, despite his irritating tendency to act like Valentine's favor had given him insight beyond his years. But after all these years of watching him pine away for Jocelyn, it was hard to take him entirely seriously. The same went for Jocelyn, who somehow managed to remain oblivious. Robert didn't understand how you could be the center of someone's world without even realizing it.

"I don't know," he admitted, wondering if any girl would ever be the center of his world. "Sometimes I worry there's something wrong with me."

Michael clapped a hand to his shoulder and fixed him with an intense gaze. "There's *nothing* wrong with you,

Robert. I wish you could finally see that."

Robert shook off the hand, along with the weight of the moment. "How about you?" he said with forced gaiety. "It's been, what, three dates with Eliza Rosewain?"

"Four," Michael admitted.

He'd sworn Robert to secrecy about her, saying he didn't want the other guys to know until he was sure it was real. Robert suspected he didn't want *Valentine* to know, as Eliza was a particular thorn in Valentine's side. She asked nearly as many disrespectful questions as he did, and harbored a similar disdain for the current policies of the Clave, but she wanted nothing to do with the Circle or its goals. Eliza thought that a new, united front with mundanes and Downworlders was the key to the future. She argued—loudly, and to the disgust of most of the faculty and students—that the Shadowhunters should be addressing the problems of the mundane world. She could often be found in the quad, shoving unwanted leaflets in students' faces, ranting about nuclear testing, Middle East oil tyrants, some trouble no one understood in South Africa, some disease no one wanted to acknowledge in America... Robert had heard every lecture in full, because Michael always insisted on staying to listen.

"She's very odd," Michael said. "I like it."

"Oh." It was a surprise, a not entirely pleasant one. Michael never liked *anyone*. Until this moment, Robert hadn't realized how much he had counted on that. "Then you should go for it," he said, hoping he sounded sincere.

"Really?" Michael looked rather surprised himself.

"Yes. Definitely." Robert reminded himself: *The less certain you feel, the more certain you act.* "She's perfect for you."

"Oh." Michael stopped walking and settled under the shadow of a tree. Robert dropped to the ground beside him.

"Can I ask you something, Robert?"

"Anything."

"Have you ever been in love? For real?"

"You know I haven't. Don't you think I would have mentioned it?"

"But how can you know for sure, if you don't know what it would feel like? Maybe you have without even realizing it. Maybe you're holding out for something you already have."

There was a part of Robert that hoped this was the case, that what he felt for Maryse *was* the kind of eternal, soul-mate love that everyone talked about. Maybe his expectations were simply too high. "I guess I don't know for sure," he admitted. "What about you? Do you think you know what it would feel like?"

"Love?" Michael smiled down at his hands. "Love, real love, is being seen. Being *known*. Knowing the ugliest part of someone, and loving them anyway. And ... I guess I think two people in love become something else, something more than the sum of their parts, you know? That it must be like you're creating a new world that exists just for the two of you. You're gods of your own pocket universe." He laughed a little then, as if he felt foolish. "That must sound ridiculous."

"No," Robert said, the truth dawning over him. Michael didn't talk like someone who was guessing—he talked like someone who *knew*. Was it possible that after four dates with Eliza, he'd actually fallen in love? Was it possible that his *parabatai*'s entire world had changed, and Robert hadn't even noticed? "It sounds ... nice."

Michael turned his head up to face Robert, his face crinkled with an unusual uncertainty. "Robert, there's something I've been meaning to tell you ... needing to tell you, maybe."

"Anything."

It wasn't like Michael to hesitate. They told each other everything; they always had.

"I..."

He stopped, then shook his head.

"What is it?" Robert pressed.

"No, it's nothing. Forget it."

Robert's stomach cramped. Is this what it would be like now that Michael was in love? Would there be a new distance between them, important things left unsaid? He felt like Michael was leaving him behind, crossing the border into a land where his *parabatai* couldn't follow—and though he knew he shouldn't blame Michael, he couldn't help himself.

Simon was dreaming he was back in Brooklyn, playing a gig with Rilo Kiley to a club full of screaming fans, when suddenly his mother wandered onto the stage in her bathrobe and said, in a flawless Scottish accent, "You're going to miss all the fun."

Simon blinked himself awake, confused, for a moment, why he was in a dungeon that smelled of dung rather than his Brooklyn bedroom—then, once he got his bearings, confused all over again about why he was being awoken in the middle of the night by a wild-eyed Scotsman.

"Is there a fire?" Simon asked. "There better be a fire. Or a demon attack. And I'm not talking about some puny lower-level demon, mind you. You want to wake me up in the middle of a dream about rock superstardom, it better be a Greater Demon."

"It's Isabelle," George said.

Simon leaped out of bed—or gallantly tried to, at least. He got a bit tangled in his sheets, so it was more like he tumbled-twisted-*thudded* out of bed, but eventually he made it to his feet, ready to charge into action. "What happened to Isabelle?"

"Why would anything have happened to Isabelle?"

"You said—" Simon rubbed his eyes, sighing. "Let's start over again. You're waking me up because...?"

"We're meeting Isabelle. Having an adventure. Ring a bell?"

"Oh." Simon had done his best to forget about this. He climbed back into bed. "You can tell me about it in the morning."

"You're not coming?" George asked, as if Simon had said he was going to spend the rest of the night doing extra calisthenics with Delaney Scarsbury, just for fun.

"You guessed it." Simon tugged the blanket over his head and pretended to be asleep.

"But you're going to miss all the fun."

"That is precisely my intention," Simon said, and squeezed his eyes shut until he was asleep for real.

This time he was dreaming of a VIP room backstage at the club, filled with champagne and coffee, a gaggle of groupies trying to break down the door so that—in the dream, Simon somehow knew this was their intent—they could tear off his clothes and ravish him. They pounded at the door, screaming his name, *Simon! Simon! Simon—*

Simon opened his eyes to creeping tendrils of gray, predawn light, a rhythmic pounding at his door, and a girl screaming his name.

"Simon! Simon, wake up!" It was Beatriz, and she didn't sound much in the mood for ravishing.

Sleepily, he padded to the door and let her in. Female

students were most definitely not allowed in male students' rooms after curfew, and it was unlike Beatriz to break a rule like that, so he gathered it must be something important. (If the pounding and shouting hadn't already tipped him off.)

"What's wrong?"

"What's wrong? What's wrong is it's nearly five a.m. and Julie and the others are still off somewhere with your stupid girlfriend and what do you think is going to happen if they don't come back before the morning lecture starts and who knows what could have happened to them out there?"

"Beatriz, breathe," Simon said. "Anyway, she's not my girlfriend."

"Is that all you have to say for yourself?" She was nearly vibrating with fury. "She talked them into sneaking out—for all I know, they drank their weight of Lake Lyn and they've all gone *mad*. They could be *dead* for all we know. Don't you care?"

"Of course I care," Simon said, noting that he was alone in the room. George also had not returned. His brain, muddled with sleep, was functioning below optimal speeds. "Next year I'm bringing a coffeemaker," he mumbled.

"Simon!" She clapped her hands sharply, inches from face. "Focus!"

"Don't you think you're being a little alarmist about this?" Simon asked, though Beatriz was one of the most levelheaded girls he'd ever met. If she was alarmed, there was probably a good reason—but he couldn't see what it might be. "They're with Isabelle. Isabelle Lightwood—she's not going to let anything bad happen."

"Oh, they're with *Isabelle*." Her voice dripped with sarcasm. "I feel oh so relieved."

"Come on, Beatriz. You don't know her."

"I know what I see," Beatriz said.

"And what's that?"

"An entitled rich girl who doesn't have to follow the rules, and doesn't have to worry about consequences. What does she care if Julie and Jon get kicked out of here?"

"What do *I* care if Julie and Jon get kicked out?" Simon muttered, too loudly.

"You care about George," Beatriz pointed out. "And Marisol and Sunil. They're all out there somewhere, and they trust Isabelle as much as you seem to. But I'm telling you, Simon, it doesn't seem right to me. What she said about the Academy wanting us to screw up and get into trouble. More like *she* wants us to get in trouble. Or she wants *something*. I don't know what it is. But I don't like it."

Something about what she said rang true more than he would have liked—but Simon wouldn't let himself go there. It felt disloyal, and he'd been disloyal enough. This week was his chance to prove himself to Isabelle, show her that they belonged in each other's lives. He wasn't going to screw that up by doubting her, even if she wasn't here to see it.

"I trust Isabelle," Simon told Beatriz. "Everyone will be fine, and I'm sure they'll be back before anyone knows they were gone. You should stop worrying about it."

"That's it? That's all you're going to do?"

"What do *you* want to do?"

"I don't know. Something!"

"Well, I am doing something," Simon said. "I'm going to go back to bed. I'm going to dream of coffee and a shiny new Fender Stratocaster and if George still isn't back by morning, I'm going to tell Dean Penhallow that he's sick, so he won't get in trouble. And *then* I'll start worrying."

Beatriz snorted. "Thanks for nothing."

"You're welcome!" Simon called. But he waited until the door had slammed shut behind her to do it.

Simon was right.

When Robert Lightwood began his lecture that morning, every member of the student body was there to hear it, including a very bleary-eyed George.

"How was it?" Simon whispered when his roommate slid into the seat beside him.

"Bloody amazing," George murmured. When Simon pressed him for details, George only shook his head and pressed his finger to his lips.

"Seriously? Just tell me."

"I'm sworn to secrecy," George whispered. "But it's only going to get better. You want in, come along with me tonight."

Robert Lightwood cleared his throat loudly. "I'd like to begin today's lecture, assuming that's all right with the peanut gallery."

George looked around wildly. "They're serving peanuts today? I'm starving."

Simon sighed. George yawned.

Robert began again.

1984

The pack was small, only five wolves. In their deceptively human form: two men, one even bigger than Robert, with muscles the size of his head, and another stooped and aged with scraggly hair spurting from his nose and ears as if his inner wolf were gradually encroaching. One child in blond pigtails. The girl's young mother, her glossy lips and undulating curves prompting thoughts Robert knew better than to say aloud, at least where Valentine could hear. And finally, one sinewy woman with a deep tan and deeper frown who seemed to be in charge.

It was disgusting, Valentine said, werewolves stinking up a distinguished Shadowhunter mansion. And although the manor was decrepit and long abandoned—vines snaking up its walls, weeds sprouting from its foundation, a once noble estate reduced to rust and rubble—Robert saw his point. The house had a lineage, had been home to a line of intrepid warriors, men and women who risked and eventually gave their lives to the cause of humanity, to saving the world from demons. And here were these creatures, infected by their demonic strain—these rogue creatures who'd violated the Accords and killed with abandon, taking refuge in the home of their enemy? The Clave refused to deal with it, Valentine said. They wanted more evidence—not because they weren't sure that these wolves were filthy, violent criminals, but because they didn't want to deal with Downworlder complaints. They didn't want to have to explain themselves; they didn't have the nerve to say: *We knew they were guilty, and so we dealt with it.*

They were, in other words, weak.

Useless.

Valentine said they should be proud to do the job the Clave was unwilling to get done, that they were serving their people, even as they skirted the Law, and with his words, Robert felt that pride bloom. Let the other Academy students have their parties and their petty school melodramas. Let them think growing up meant graduating, marrying, attending meetings. *This* was growing up, just like Valentine said. Seeing an injustice and doing something about it, no matter the risk. No matter the consequences.

The wolves had a keen sense of smell and sharp instincts, even in their human bodies, so the Shadowhunters were careful. They crept around the decaying mansion, peered in windows, waited, watched. Planned. Five werewolves and four young Shadowhunters—those were odds even Valentine didn't want to play. So they were patient, and they were careful.

They waited until dark.

It was disconcerting to watch the wolves in human form, impersonating a normal human family, the younger man washing dishes while the elder one made himself a pot of tea, the child sitting cross-legged on the floor racing her model cars. Robert reminded himself that these trespassers were claiming a home and a life they didn't deserve—that they'd killed innocents and may even have helped slaughter Valentine's father.

Still, he was relieved when the moon rose and they reverted to monstrous form. Robert and the others clung to the shadows while three members of the pack sprouted fur and fangs, leaping through a broken window and into the night. They went out to hunt—leaving, as Valentine suspected they would, their most vulnerable behind. The old man and the child. These were odds more to Valentine's liking.

It wasn't much of a fight.

By the time the two remaining werewolves registered attack, they were surrounded. They didn't even have time to transform. It was over in minutes, Stephen knocking the older one unconscious with a blow to the head, the child cowering in a corner, inches from the tip of Michael's sword.

"We'll take them both for interrogation," Valentine said.

Michael shook his head. "Not the kid."

"They're both criminals," Valentine argued. "Every member of the pack is culpable for—"

"She's a little kid!" Michael said, turning to his *parabatai* for support. "Tell him. We're not dragging some child into the woods to throw her at the mercy of the Clave."

He had a point ... but then, so did Valentine. Robert said nothing.

"We're *not* taking the child," Michael said, and the look on his face suggested he was willing to back up his words with action.

Stephen and Robert tensed, waiting for the explosion. Valentine didn't take well to being challenged; he had very little experience with it. But he only sighed, and offered up a charmingly rueful smile. "Of course not. Don't know what I was thinking. Just the old man, then. Unless you've got some objection to that as well?"

No one had any objections, and the unconscious old man was skin and bones, his weight barely noticeable on Robert's broad shoulders. They locked the child up in a closet, then carried the old man deep into the woods, back to the campsite.

They tied him to a tree.

The rope was woven with silver filament—when the old man woke up, he would wake to pain. It probably wouldn't be enough to bind him in wolf form, not if he was determined to escape. But it would slow him down. Their silver daggers would do the rest.

"You two, patrol a half-mile perimeter," Valentine told Michael and Stephen. "We don't want any of its grubby little friends catching its stench. Robert and I will guard the prisoner."

Stephen nodded sharply, eager as ever to do as Valentine willed.

"And when he wakes up?" Michael asked.

"When *it* wakes up, Robert and I will question it on the subject of its crimes, and what it knows about the crimes of its fellows," Valentine said. "Once we've secured its confession, we'll deliver it to the Clave for its punishment. Does that satisfy you, Michael?"

He didn't sound like he much cared about the answer, and Michael didn't give him one.

"So now we wait?" Robert asked, once they were alone.

Valentine smiled.

When he wanted it to, Valentine's smile could worm its way into the most well-fortified heart, melt it from the inside out.

This one wasn't designed for heat. This was a cold smile, and it chilled Robert to the core.

"I'm tired of waiting," Valentine said, and drew out a dagger. Moonlight glinted off the pure silver.

Before Robert could say anything, Valentine pressed the flat side of the blade against the old man's bare chest. There was a sizzle of flesh, then a howl, as the prisoner woke to agony.

"I wouldn't," Valentine said calmly, as the old man's features began to take on a wolfish cast, fur sprouting across his naked body. "I'm going to hurt you, yes. But change back into a wolf, and I promise, I will kill you."

The transformation stopped as abruptly as it had begun.

The old man issued a series of racking coughs that shook his skinny body from head to toe. He was skinny, so skinny that ribs protruded from pale flesh. There were hollows beneath his eyes and only a few sorry strands of gray hair crossing his liver-spotted skull. It had never occurred to Robert that a werewolf could go bald. Under other circumstances, the thought of it might have amused him.

But there was nothing amusing about the sound the man made as Valentine traced the dagger's tip from jutting collarbone to belly button.

"Valentine, he's just an old man," Robert said hesitantly. "Maybe we should—"

"Listen to your friend," the old man said in a pleading, warbling voice. "I could be your own grandfather."

Valentine struck him across the face with the hilt of the dagger.

"It's not any kind of man," he told Robert. "It's a monster. And it's been doing things it shouldn't be doing, isn't that true?"

The werewolf, apparently concluding that playing aged and weak wouldn't get him out of this one, drew himself up straight and bared sharp teeth. His voice, when he spoke, had lost its tremble. "Who are you, *Shadowhunter*, to tell me what I should and shouldn't be doing?"

"So you admit it, then," Robert said eagerly. "You've violated the Accords."

If he confessed this easily, they could be done with this whole sordid affair, turn the prisoner in to the Clave, go home.

"I don't give my accord to killers and weaklings," the werewolf spat.

"Fortunately, I don't need your accord," Valentine said. "I need only information. You tell me what I need to know, and we'll let you go."

This wasn't what they'd discussed, but Robert held his tongue.

"Two months ago, a pack of werewolves killed a Shadowhunter at the western edge of these woods. Where can I find them?"

"And exactly how would I know that?"

Valentine's icy smile returned. "You better hope that you do, because otherwise you'll be of no use to me."

"Well then, on second thought, maybe I have heard tell of this dead Shadowhunter you're talking about." The wolf barked a laugh. "Wish I could have been there to see him die. To taste of his sweet flesh. It's the fear that gives the meat its taste, you know. Best of all when they cry first, a little salty with the sweet. And rumor has it your doomed Shadowhunter wept buckets. Cowardly, that one was."

"Robert, hold its mouth open." Valentine's voice was steady, but Robert knew Valentine well enough to sense the fury roiling beneath.

"Maybe we should take a moment to—"

"*Hold its mouth open.*"

Robert gripped the man's feeble jaws and pried them open.

Valentine pressed the flat side of the dagger to the man's tongue and held it there as the man's shriek turned into a howl, as his scrawny muscles bulged and fur bloomed across his flesh, as the tongue bubbled and blistered, and then, just as the fully transformed wolf snapped its bindings, Valentine sliced off its tongue. As its mouth gushed blood, Valentine slashed a sharp line across the wolf's midsection. The cut was sure and deep, and the wolf dropped to the ground, intestines spilling from its wound.

Valentine leaped upon the writhing creature, stabbing and slicing, tearing through its hide, flaying flesh to pearly bone, even as the creature flailed and spasmed helplessly beneath him, even as the fight drained out of it, even as its gaze went flat, even as its broken body reclaimed human form, lay still on bloody earth, an old man's face bled pale and turned lifelessly to the night sky.

"That's enough," Robert kept saying, quietly, uselessly. "Valentine, that's enough."

But he did nothing to stop it.

And when his friends returned from their patrol to find Valentine and Robert standing over the disemboweled corpse, he didn't counter Valentine's version of events: The werewolf had slipped free of its bonds and tried to escape. They had endured a fierce battle, killed in self-defense.

The outline of this story was, technically, true.

Stephen clapped Valentine on the back, commiserating with him that he'd lost the potential lead to his father's killer. Michael locked eyes with Robert, his question clear as if he'd spoken it aloud. *What really happened*?

What did you let *happen?*

Robert looked away.

Isabelle was avoiding him. Beatriz was fuming at him. Everyone else was buzzing with too much excitement about the previous night's adventure and the secret one to come. Julie and Marisol only echoed George's cryptic promise—that something *good* was on the horizon, and if Simon wanted to know about it, he would have to join them.

"I don't think Isabelle would want me there," he told Sunil as they picked warily through the steamed heap of vaguely vegetable-shaped objects that passed for lunch.

Sunil shook his head and grinned. The smile fit his face poorly; Sunil with a grin was like a Klingon in a tutu. He was an unusually somber boy who seemed to consider good cheer as a sign of unseriousness, and treated people accordingly. "She told us to convince you to show up. She said 'whatever it takes.' So, you tell me, Simon." The unsettling smile grew. "What's it going to take?"

"You don't even know her," Simon pointed out. "Why are you suddenly so willing to do whatever she tells you to do?"

"We are talking about the same girl here, yes? Isabelle Lightwood?"

"Yes."

Sunil shook his head in wonder. "And you even have to ask?"

So that was the new order: the cult of Isabelle Lightwood. Simon had to admit, he could completely understand how a roomful of otherwise rational people could fall completely under her spell and give themselves to her entirely.

But why would she want them to?

He decided he was going to have to see this for himself. Simply to understand what was going on and make sure it was all on the up-and-up.

Not at all because he desperately wanted to be near her. Or impress her. Or please her.

Come to think of it, maybe Simon understood the cult of Isabelle better than he wanted to admit.

Maybe he'd been its charter member.

"You intend to do *what*?" On the last word, Simon's voice jumped two octaves above normal.

Jon Cartwright snickered. "Simmer down, Mom. You heard her."

Simon looked around the lounge at his friends (and Jon). Over the past year, he'd come to know them inside and out, or at least, he thought that he did. Julie bit her nails bloody when she was nervous. Marisol slept with a sword under her pillow, just in case. George talked in his sleep, usually about sheep-shearing techniques. Sunil had four pet rabbits that he talked about constantly, always worried that little Ringo was getting picked on by his bigger, fluffier brothers. Jon had covered one wall of his room with his little cousin's finger paintings, and wrote her a letter every week. They'd all pledged themselves to the Shadowhunter cause; they'd gone through hell to prove themselves to their instructors and one another. They'd almost finished out the year without a single fatal injury or vampire bite ... and now *this?*

"Ha-ha, very funny," Simon said, hoping he was doing an acceptable job of keeping the desperation out of his tone. "Nice joke on me, get me back for wussing out last night. Utterly hilarious. What's next? You want to convince me they're making another crap *Last Airbender* movie? You want to see me freak out, there are easier ways."

Isabelle rolled her eyes. "No one wants to see you freak out, Simon. Frankly, I could take or leave seeing you at all."

"So this is serious," Simon said. "You're seriously, not at all jokingly, actually, for real planning to *summon a demon?* Here, in the middle of the Shadowhunter Academy? In the middle of the end-of-year party? Because you think it will be ... *fun?*"

"We're obviously not going to summon it in the middle of the party," Isabelle said. "That would be rather foolish."

"Oh, of course," Simon drawled. "*That* would be foolish."

"We're going to summon it here in the lounge," Isabelle clarified. "Then *bring* it to the party."

"Then kill it, of course," Julie put in.

"Of course," Simon echoed. He wondered if maybe he was having a stroke.

"You're making it sound like a bigger deal than it is," George said.

"Yeah, it's just an imp demon," Sunil said. "No biggie."

"Uh-huh." Simon groaned. "Totally. No biggie."

"Imagine the look on everyone's faces when they see what we can do!" Marisol was nearly glowing at the thought of it.

Beatriz wasn't there. If she had been, maybe she could have talked some reason into them. Or helped Simon tie them up and stuff them in the closet until the end of the semester had safely passed and Isabelle was back in New York where she belonged.

"What if something goes wrong?" Simon pointed out. "You've never faced off against a demon in combat conditions, not without the teachers watching your back. You don't know—"

"Neither do you," Isabelle snapped. "At least, you don't remember, isn't that right?"

Simon said nothing.

"Whereas *I* took down my first imp when I was six years old," Isabelle said. "Like I told your friends, it's no big deal. And *they* trust me."

I trust you—that's what he was meant to say. He knew she was waiting for it. They all were.

He couldn't.

"I can't talk you out of this?" he asked instead.

Isabelle shrugged. "You can keep trying, but you'd be wasting all our time."

"Then I'll have to find another way to stop you," Simon said.

"You gonna tell on us?" Jon sneered. "You gonna go be a crybaby and tattle to your favorite warlock?" He snorted. "Once a teacher's pet, always a teacher's pet."

"Shut up, Jon." Isabelle whacked him softly on the arm. Simon probably should have been pleased, but whacking still required touching, and he preferred that Isabelle and Jon never come into physical contact of any sort. "You could try to tell on us, Simon. But I'll deny it. And then who will they believe—someone like me, or someone like you? Some mundane."

She said "mundane" exactly like Jon always did. Like it was a synonym for "nothing."

"This isn't you, Isabelle. This isn't what you're like." He wasn't sure whether he was trying to convince her or himself.

"You don't know what I'm like, remember?"

"I know enough."

"Then you know that you should trust me. But if you don't, go ahead. Tell," she said. "Then everyone will know what *you're* like. What kind of friend you are."

He tried.

He knew it was the right thing to do.

At least, he thought it was the right thing to do.

The next morning, before the lecture, he went to Catarina Loss's office—Jon was right, she was his favorite warlock and his favorite faculty member, and the only one he would trust with something like this.

She welcomed him in, offered him a seat and a mug of something whose steam was an alarming shade of blue. He passed.

"So, Daylighter, I take it you have something to tell me?"

Catarina intimidated him somewhat less than she had at the beginning of the year—which was a bit like saying Jar Jar Binks was "somewhat less" annoying in *Star Wars: Episode II* than he'd been in *Star Wars: Episode I*.

"It's possible I know something that..." Simon cleared his throat. "I mean, if something were happening that..."

He hadn't let himself think through what would happen once the words were out. What would happen to his friends? What would happen to Isabelle, their ringleader? She couldn't exactly get expelled from an Academy where she wasn't enrolled ... but Simon had learned enough about the Clave by now to know there were far worse punishments than getting expelled. Was summoning a minor demon to use as a party trick a violation of the Law? Was he about to ruin Isabelle's life?

Catarina Loss wasn't a Shadowhunter; she had her own secrets from the Clave. Maybe she'd be willing to keep one more, if it meant helping Simon and protecting Isabelle from punishment?

As his mind spun through dark possibilities, the office door swung open and Dean Penhallow poked her blond head in. "Catarina, Robert Lightwood was hoping to chat with you before his session—oh, sorry! Didn't realize you were in the middle of something?"

"Join us," Catarina said. "Simon was just about to tell me something interesting."

The dean stepped into the office, furrowing her brow at Simon. "You look so serious," she told him. "Go ahead, spit it out. You'll feel better. It's like throwing up."

"What's like throwing up?" he asked, confused.

"You know, when you're feeling ill? Sometimes it just helps to get everything out."

Somehow, Simon didn't think vomiting up his confession straight to the dean would make him feel any better.

Hadn't Isabelle proven herself enough—not just to him, but to the Clave, to everyone? She had, after all, pretty much saved the world. How much more evidence would anyone need that she was one of the good guys?

How much evidence did *he* need?

Simon stood up and said the first thing that popped into his mind. "I just wanted to tell you that we all really enjoyed that beet stew they served for dinner. You should serve that again."

Dean Penhallow gave him an odd look. "Those weren't beets, Simon."

This didn't surprise him, as the stew had had an oddly grainy consistency and a taste reminiscent of dung.

"Well ... whatever it was, it was delicious," he said quickly. "I better get going. I don't want to miss the beginning of Inquisitor Lightwood's final lecture. They've been so interesting."

"Indeed," Catarina said dryly. "They've been almost as delicious as the stew."

1984

For most of his time at the Academy, Robert had watched Valentine from a distance. Even though Robert was older, he looked up to Valentine, who was everything Robert wanted to be. Valentine excelled at his training without visible effort. He could best anyone with any weapon. He was careless with his affection, or at least seemed to be, and he was beloved. Not many people noticed how few he truly loved back. But Robert noticed, because when you're watching from the sidelines, invisible, it's easy to see clearly.

It never occurred to him that Valentine was watching him, too.

Not until the day, toward the beginning of this year, that Valentine caught him alone in one of the Academy's dark, underground corridors and said quietly, "I know your secret."

Robert's secret, that he told nobody, not even Michael: He was still afraid of the Marks.

Every time he drew a rune on himself, he had to hold his breath, force his fingers not to tremble. He always hesitated. In class, it was barely noticeable. In battle, it could be the split-second difference between life and death, and Robert knew it. Which made him hesitate even more, at everything. He was strong, smart, talented; he was a *Lightwood.* He should have been among the best. But he couldn't let himself go and act on instinct. He couldn't stop his mind from racing toward potential consequences. He couldn't stop being afraid—and he knew, eventually, it would be the end of him.

"I can help you," Valentine said then. "I can teach you what to do with the fear." As if it were as simple as that—and under Valentine's careful instruction, it was.

Valentine had taught him to retreat to a place in his mind that the fear couldn't touch. To separate himself from the Robert Lightwood who knew how to be afraid—and then to tame that weaker, loathed version of himself. "Your weakness makes you furious, as it should," Valentine had told him. "Use the fury to master it—and then everything else."

In a way Valentine had saved Robert's life. Or at least, the only part of his life that mattered.

He owed Valentine everything.

He at least owed Valentine the truth.

"You don't agree with what I did," Valentine said quietly as the sun crept above the horizon. Michael and Stephen were still asleep. Robert had passed the hours of darkness staring at the sky, sifting through what had happened, and what he should do next.

"You think I was out of control," Valentine added.

"That wasn't self-defense," Robert said. "That was torture. Murder."

Robert was seated on one of the logs around the remains of their campfire. Valentine lowered himself beside him.

"You heard the things it said. You understand why it had to be silenced," Valentine said. "It had to be taught its lesson, and the Clave couldn't have mustered the will. I know the others wouldn't understand. Not even Lucian. But you ... we understand each other, you and I. You're the only one I can really trust. I need you to keep this to yourself."

"If you're so sure you did the right thing, then why keep it a secret?"

Valentine laughed gently. "Always so skeptical, Robert. It's what we all love most about you." His smile faded. "Some of the others are starting to have doubts. About the cause, about me—" He waved away Robert's denials before they could be voiced. "Don't think I can't tell. Everyone wants to be loyal when it's easy. But when things get difficult..." He shook his head. "I can't count on everyone I would like to count on. But I believe I can count on you."

"Of course you can."

"Then you'll keep what passed this night a secret from the others," Valentine said. "Even from Michael."

Much later—too late—it would occur to Robert that

Valentine probably had some version of this conversation with each member of the Circle. Secrets bound people together, and Valentine was smart enough to know it.

"He's my *parabatai*," Robert pointed out. "I don't keep secrets from him."

Valentine's eyebrows shot sky-high. "And you think he keeps no secrets from you?"

Robert remembered the night before, whatever it was Michael had been trying so hard not to say. That was one secret—who knew how many more there were?

"You know Michael better than anyone," Valentine said. "And yet, I imagine there are things I know about him that might surprise you..."

A silence hung between them as Robert considered it.

Valentine didn't lie, or issue empty boasts. If he said he knew something about Michael, something secret, then it was true.

And it was temptation, dangling here before Robert.

He needed only to ask.

He wanted to know; he didn't want to know.

"We all have competing loyalties," Valentine said, before Robert could give in to temptation. "The Clave would like to make these things simple, but it's just another example of their obtuseness. I love Lucian, my *parabatai*. I love Jocelyn. If those two loves were ever to come into conflict..."

He didn't have to complete the thought. Robert knew what Valentine knew, and understood that Valentine loved his *parabatai* enough to allow it. Just as Lucian loved Valentine enough never to act on it.

Maybe some secrets were a mercy.

He held out his hand to Valentine. "You have my word. My oath. Michael will never know about this."

As soon as the words were out, he wondered if he'd made a mistake. But there was no going back.

"I know your secret too, Robert," Valentine said.

At this, an echo of the first words Valentine had ever said to him, Robert felt the ghost of a smile.

"I think we covered that," Robert reminded him.

"You're a coward," Valentine said.

Robert flinched. "How can you say that after everything we've been through? You know I would never shy away from a battle or—"

Valentine shook his head, silencing him. "Oh, I don't mean physically. We've taken care of that, haven't we? When it comes to taking on physical risk, you're the bravest there is. Overcompensating, perhaps?"

"I don't know what you're talking about," Robert said stiffly—afraid he knew all too well.

"You're not afraid of death or injury, Robert. You're afraid of *yourself* and your own weakness. You lack faith—you lack *loyalty*—because you lack the strength of your own convictions. And it's my own fault for expecting more. After all, how can you be expected to believe in anything or anyone if you don't believe in yourself?"

Robert felt suddenly transparent, and didn't much like it.

"I once tried to teach you to master your fear and your weakness," Valentine said. "I see now that was a mistake."

Robert hung his head, waiting for Valentine to cast him out of the Circle. Exile him from his friends and his duty. Ruin his life.

Ironic that it was his own cowardice that had made his worst fears come true.

But Valentine surprised him. "I've given the matter

some thought, and I have a proposition for you," Valentine said.

"What is it?" He was afraid to hope.

"Give up," Valentine said. "Stop trying to pretend away your cowardice, your doubt. Stop trying to ignite some unshakable passion in yourself. If you can't find the courage of your convictions, why not simply accept the courage of mine?"

"I don't understand."

"My proposition is this," Valentine said. "Stop worrying so much about whether or not you're sure. Let me be sure for you. Rely on my certainty, on *my* passion. Let yourself be weak, and lean on me, because we both know I can be strong. Accept that you're doing the right thing because *I* know it to be the right thing."

"If only it were that easy," Robert said, and couldn't deny a stab of longing.

Valentine looked mildly amused, as if Robert had betrayed a childlike misunderstanding of the nature of things. "It's only as hard as you make it," he said gently. "It's as easy as you let it be."

Isabelle brushed past Simon on his way out of the lecture.

"Nine p.m., Jon's room," she whispered in his ear.

"What?" It was like she was informing him of the exact time and place of his death—which, if he was forced to imagine what she might be doing in Jon Cartwright's dorm room, would be imminent.

"Demon o'clock. You know, in case you're still determined to ruin our fun." She gave him a wicked grin. "Or join it."

There was an implied dare on her face, a certainty

that he wouldn't have the nerve to do either. Simon was reminded that though he might have forgotten ever knowing Isabelle, she'd forgotten nothing about him. In fact, it could be argued that she knew him better than he knew himself.

Not anymore, he told himself. A year at the Academy, a year of study and battle and caffeine withdrawal had changed him. It had to.

The question was: Changed him into what?

She'd given him the wrong time.

Of course she had. By the time Simon burst into Jon Cartwright's room, they were nearly ready to complete the ritual.

"You can't do this," Simon told them. "All of you, stop and think."

"Why?" Isabelle said. "Just give us one good reason. Persuade us, Simon."

He wasn't good at speeches. And she knew it.

Simon found himself suddenly furious. This was *his* school; these were *his* friends. Isabelle didn't care what happened here. Maybe there was no deeper story, no hidden pain. Maybe she was exactly what she seemed, and no more: a frivolous person who cared only for herself.

Something at his core revolted against this thought, but he silenced it. This wasn't about his nonrelationship with his nongirlfriend. He couldn't let it be about that.

"It's not just that it's against the rules," Simon said. How were you supposed to explain something that seemed so obvious? It was like trying to persuade someone that one plus one equaled two: It just *did*. "It's not just that you could get expelled or even taken before the Clave. It's *wrong*. Someone could get hurt."

"Someone's always getting hurt," George pointed out, ruefully rubbing his elbow, which, just a couple of days before, Julie had nearly sliced off with a broadsword.

"Because there's no other way to learn," Simon said, exasperated. "Because it's the best of all bad options. This? This is the opposite of necessary. Is this the kind of Shadowhunter you want to be? The kind that toys with the forces of darkness because you think you can handle it? Have you never seen a movie? Read a comic book? That's always how it starts—just a little temptation, just a little taste of evil, and then *bam*, your lightsaber turns red and you're breathing through a big black mask and slicing off your son's hand just to be mean."

They looked at him blankly.

"Forget it."

It was funny, Shadowhunters knew more than mundanes about almost everything. They knew more about demons, about weapons, about the currents of power and magic that shaped the world. But they didn't understand temptation. They didn't understand how easy it was to make one small, terrible choice after another until you'd slid down the slippery slope into the pit of hell. *Dura lex*—the Law is hard. So hard that the Shadowhunters had to pretend it was possible to be perfect. It was the one thing Simon had taken from Robert's lectures about the Circle. Once Shadowhunters started to slide, they didn't stop. "The point is, this is a no-win situation. Either your stupid imp gets out of control and eats a bunch of students—or it *doesn't*, and so you decide next time you can summon a bigger demon. And that one eats you. That is the definition of a lose-lose situation."

"He makes a fair point," Julie said.

"Not as dumb as he looks," Jon admitted.

George cleared his throat. "Maybe—"

"Maybe we should get on with things," Isabelle said, and tossed her silky black hair and blinked her large, bottomless eyes and smiled her irresistible smile—and as if she'd cast some witchy spell over the room, everyone forgot Simon existed and busied themselves with the work of raising a demon.

He'd done everything he could do here. There was only one option left.

He ran away.

1984

Michael let a week pass before he asked the question Robert had been dreading. Maybe he was waiting for Robert to bring it up himself. Maybe he'd tried to convince himself he didn't need to know the truth, that he loved Robert enough not to care—but apparently he had failed.

"Walk with me?" Michael said, and Robert agreed to take one last stroll through Brocelind Forest, even though he'd hoped to stay away from the woods until the next semester. By then, maybe, the memory of what happened there would have faded. The shadows wouldn't seem so ominous, the ground so soaked in blood.

Things had been strange between them this week, quiet and stiff. Robert was keeping his secret about what they'd done to the werewolf, and mulling over Valentine's suggestion, that he be Robert's conscience and Robert's strength, that it would be easier that way. Michael was...

Well, Robert couldn't guess what Michael was thinking—about Valentine, about Eliza, about Robert himself.

And that's what made things so strange. They were *parabatai*; they were two halves of the same self. Robert wasn't supposed to have to *guess*. Before, he'd always known.

"Okay, so what's the real story?" Michael asked, once they were deep enough in the woods that the sounds of campus had long since faded away. The sun was still in the sky, but here in the trees, the shadows were long and the dark was rising. "What did Valentine do to that werewolf?"

Robert couldn't look at his *parabatai*. He shrugged. "Exactly what I told you."

"You've never lied to me before," Michael said. There was sadness in his voice, and something else, something worse—there was a hint of finality in it, like they were about to say good-bye.

Robert swallowed. Michael was right: Before this, Robert had never lied.

"And I suppose you've never lied to me?" he charged Michael. His *parabatai* had a secret, he knew that now. Valentine said so.

There was a long pause. Then Michael spoke. "I lie to you every day, Robert."

It was like a kick in the stomach.

That wasn't just a secret, that wasn't just a *girl*. That was ... Robert didn't even know what it was.

Unfathomable.

He stopped and turned to Michael, incredulous. "If you're trying to shock me into telling you something—"

"I'm not trying to shock you. I'm just ... I'm trying to tell you the truth. Finally. I know you're keeping something from me, something important."

"I'm *not*," Robert insisted.

"You are," Michael said, "and it hurts. And if that

hurts *me*, then I can only imagine—" He stopped, took a deep breath, forced himself on. "I couldn't bear it, if I've been hurting you like that all these years. Even if I didn't realize it. Even if *you* didn't realize it."

"Michael, you're not making any sense."

They reached a fallen log, thick with moss. Michael sank onto it, looking suddenly weary. Like he'd aged a hundred years in the last minute. Robert dropped beside him and put a hand on his friend's shoulder. "What is it?" He knocked softly at Michael's head, trying to smile, to tell himself this was just Michael being Michael. Weird, but inconsequential. "What's going on in that nuthouse you call a brain?"

Michael lowered his head.

He looked so vulnerable like that, the nape of his neck bare and exposed, Robert couldn't bear it.

"I'm in love," Michael whispered.

Robert burst into laughter, relief gushing through him. "Is that all? Don't you think I figured that out, idiot? I told you, Eliza's great—"

Then Michael said something else.

Something that Robert must have misheard.

"What?" he said, though he didn't want to.

This time, Michael lifted his head, met Robert's eyes, and spoke clearly. "I'm in love with *you*."

Robert was on his feet before he'd even processed the words.

It seemed suddenly very important to have space between him and Michael. As much space as possible.

"You're what?"

He hadn't meant to shout.

"That's not funny," Robert added, trying to modulate his voice.

"It's not a joke. I'm in—"

"Don't you say that again. You will *never* say that again."

Michael paled. "I know you probably… I know you don't feel the same way, that you couldn't…"

All at once, with a force that nearly swept him off his feet, Robert was flooded by a rush of memories: Michael's hand on his shoulder. Michael's arms around him in an embrace. Michael wrestling with him. Michael gently adjusting his grip on a sword. Michael lying in bed a few feet away from him, night after night. Michael stripping down, taking his hand, pulling him into Lake Lyn. Michael, chest bare, hair soaked, eyes shining, lying in the grass beside him.

Robert wanted to throw up.

"Nothing has to change," Michael said, and Robert would have laughed, if it wouldn't so surely have led to puking. "I'm still the same person. I'm not asking anything of you. I'm just being honest. I just needed you to know."

This is what Robert knew: That Michael was the best friend he'd ever had, and probably the purest soul he'd ever know. That he should sit beside Michael, promise him that this was okay, that nothing needed to change, that the oath they'd sworn to each other was true, and forever. That there was nothing to fear in Michael's—Robert's stomach turned at the word—*love*. That Robert was arrow straight, that it was *Maryse's* touch that made his body come alive, the memory of *Maryse's* bare chest that made his pulse race—and that Michael's confession didn't call any of this into doubt. He knew he should say something reassuring to Michael, something like, "I can't love you that way, but I will love you forever."

But he also knew what people would think.

What they would think about Michael … what they would assume about Robert.

People would talk, they would gossip, they would *suspect* things. *Parabatai* couldn't date each other, of course. And couldn't ... anything else. But Michael and Robert were so *close*; Michael and Robert were so *in sync*; surely people would want to know if Michael and Robert were *the same*.

Surely people would *wonder*.

He couldn't take it. He'd worked too hard to become the man he was, the Shadowhunter he was. He couldn't stand to have people looking at him like that again, like he was different.

And he couldn't stand to have Michael looking at him like *this*.

Because what if he started wondering too?

"You'll never say that again," Robert said coldly. "And if you insist on it, that will be the last thing you ever say to me. Do you understand me?"

Michael just gaped at him, eyes wide and uncomprehending.

"And you will never speak of it to anyone else, either. I won't have people thinking that about us. About *you*."

Michael murmured something unintelligible.

"What?" Robert said sharply.

"I said, what will they think?"

"They'll think you're disgusting," Robert said.

"Like you do?"

A voice at the back of Robert's mind said, *Stop*.

It said, *This is your last chance*.

But it said so very quietly.

It wasn't sure.

"Yes," Robert said, and he said it firmly enough that there would be no question that he meant it. "I think you're disgusting. I swore an oath to you, and I will honor it. But make no mistake: Nothing between us will ever be the same. In fact, from now on, nothing is between us, period."

Michael didn't argue. He didn't say anything. He simply turned, fled into the trees, and left Robert alone.

What he'd said, what he'd done ... it was unforgivable. Robert knew that. He told himself: It was Michael's fault, Michael's decision.

He told himself: He was only doing what he needed to do to survive.

But he saw the truth now. Valentine was right. Robert wasn't capable of absolute love or loyalty. He'd thought Michael was the exception, the proof that he could be certain of someone—could be *steady*, no matter what.

Now that was gone.

Enough, Robert thought. Enough struggling, enough doubting his own choices, enough falling prey to his own weakness and lack of faith. He would accept Valentine's offer. He would let Valentine choose for him, let Valentine *believe* for him. He would do whatever he needed to hang on to Valentine, and to the Circle, and to its cause.

It was all he had left.

Simon ran through the dingy corridors, skidded across slimy floors, and raced down dented stairways, the whole way cursing the Academy for being such a labyrinthine fortress with no cell reception. His feet pounded against worn stone, his lungs heaved, and though the journey seemed endless, only a few minutes passed before he threw himself into Catarina Loss's office.

She was always there, day or night, and that night was no different.

Well, slightly different: That night she wasn't alone.

She stood behind her desk with her arms crossed, flanked by Robert Lightwood and Dean Penhallow, the three of them looking so somber it was almost like they were waiting for him. He didn't let himself hesitate or think of the consequences.

Or think of Izzy.

"There's a group of students trying to raise a demon," Simon panted. "We have to stop them."

No one seemed surprised.

There was a soft throat clearing—Simon turned to discover Julie Beauvale creeping out from behind the door he'd flung open in her face.

"What are you doing here?"

"Same thing you are," Julie said. Then she blushed and gave him an embarrassed little shrug. "I guess you made a good case."

"But how did you get here before me?"

"I took the east stairwell, obviously. Then that corridor behind the weapons room—"

"But doesn't that dead-end at the dining hall?"

"Only if you—"

"Perhaps we can table this fascinating cartographic discussion until later," Catarina Loss said mildly. "I think we have more important business at hand."

"Like teaching your idiot students a lesson," Robert Lightwood growled, and stormed out of the office. Catarina and the dean strode after him.

Simon exchanged a nervous glance with Julie. "You, uh, think we're supposed to follow them?"

"Probably," she said, then sighed. "We might as well let them expel all of us in one shot."

They traipsed after their teachers, letting themselves fall more and more behind.

As they neared Jon's room, Robert's shouts were audible from halfway down the corridor. They couldn't quite make out his words through the thick door, but the volume and cadence made the situation quite clear.

Simon and Julie eased the door open and slipped inside.

George, Jon, and the others were lined up against the wall, faces pale, eyes wide, all of them looking steeled for a firing squad. While Isabelle was standing by her father's side ... *beaming?*

"Failures, all of you!" Robert Lightwood boomed. "You lot are supposed to be the best and brightest this school has to offer, and this is what you have to show for yourselves? I *warned* you about the dangers of charisma. I *told* you of the need to stand up for what's right, even if it hurts the ones you love most. And *all of you* failed to listen."

Isabelle coughed pointedly.

"All of you except two," Robert allowed, jerking his head at Simon and Julie. "Well done. Isabelle was right about you."

Simon was reeling.

"It was all a stupid *test?*" Jon yelped.

"A rather clever test, if you ask me?" Dean Penhallow said.

Catarina looked as if she had some things to say on the subject of foolish Shadowhunters playing cat-and-mouse games with their own, but as usual, she bit her tongue.

"What percentage of our grades will this be?" Sunil asked.

With that, there was a lot of yelling. Quite a bit of ranting about sacred responsibilities and carelessness and how unpleasant a night in the dungeons of the Silent City could be. Robert thundered like Zeus, Dean Penhallow did her best not to sound like a babysitter scolding her charges for stealing an extra cookie, while Catarina Loss put in the occasional sarcastic remark about what happened to Shadowhunters who thought it would be fun to slum it in warlock territory. At one point, she interrupted Robert Lightwood's tirade to add a pointed comment about Darth Vader—and a sly look at Simon that made him wonder, not for the first time, just how closely she was watching him, and why.

Through it all, Isabelle watched Simon, something unexpected in her gaze. Something almost like ... pride.

"In conclusion, next time, you'll listen when your elders talk," Robert Lightwood shouted.

"Why would anyone listen to anything you had to say about doing the right thing?" Isabelle snapped.

Robert's face went red. He turned to her slowly, fixing her with the kind of icy Inquisitor glare that would have left anyone else whimpering in a fetal ball. Isabelle didn't flinch.

"Now that this sordid business is concluded, I'd ask you all to give me and my dutiful daughter here some privacy. I believe we have some things to settle," Robert said.

"But this is my room," Jon whined.

Robert didn't need to speak, just turned that Inquisitor glare on him; Jon flinched.

He fled, along with everyone else, and Simon was about to follow suit when Isabelle's fingers snatched for his wrist.

"He stays," she told her father.

"He most certainly does not."

"Simon stays with me, or I leave with him," Isabelle said. "Those are your choices."

"Er, I'm happy to go—" Simon began, "happy" being his polite substitute for "desperate."

"*You stay*," Isabelle commanded.

Robert sighed. "Fine. You stay."

That ended the discussion. Simon dropped down onto the edge of Jon's bed, trying to wish himself invisible.

"It's obvious to me that you don't want to be here," Robert told his daughter.

"What gave it away? The fact that I told you a million times that I didn't want to come? That I didn't want to play your stupid game? That I thought it was cruel and manipulative and a total waste of time?"

"Yes," Robert said. "That."

"And yet you made me come with you anyway."

"Yes," he said.

"Look, if you thought enforced bonding time was going to fix anything or make up for what you—"

Robert sighed heavily. "I've told you before, what happened between your mother and me has nothing to do with you."

"It has *everything* to do with me!"

"Isabelle..." Robert glanced at Simon, then lowered his voice. "I would really prefer to do this without an audience."

"Too bad."

Simon tried even harder to fade into the background, hoping maybe if he tried hard enough, his skin would take on the same pattern as Jon Cartwright's surprisingly flowered sheets.

"You and I, we've never talked about my time in the Circle, or why I followed Valentine," Robert said. "I hoped you kids would never have to know that part of me."

"I heard your lecture, just like everyone else," she said sullenly.

"We both know that the story tailored for public

consumption is never the whole truth." Robert frowned. "What I didn't tell those students—what I've never told anyone—is that unlike most of the Circle, I wasn't what you'd call a true believer. The others, they thought they were Raziel's sword in human form. You should have seen your mother, blazing with righteousness."

"So now it's all Mom's fault? Nice, Dad. Really nice. Am I supposed to think you're some awesome guy for seeing through Valentine but going along with him anyway? Because your girlfriend *said so*?"

He shook his head. "You're missing my point. *I* was the most to blame. Your mother, the others, they thought they were doing what was right. They loved Valentine. They loved the cause. They *believed*. I could never muster that faith ... but I went along anyway. Not because I thought it was right. Because it was *easy*. Because Valentine seemed so sure. Substituting his certainty for my own seemed like the path of least resistance."

"Why are you telling me this?" Some of the venom had drained from her voice.

"I didn't understand then, what it would mean to be truly certain of something," Robert said. "I didn't know how it felt to love something, or someone, beyond all reservation. Unconditionally. I thought maybe, with my *parabatai*, but then—" He swallowed whatever he'd been about to say. Simon wondered how it could be worse than what he'd already confessed to. "Eventually, I assumed I just didn't have it in me. That I wasn't built for that kind of love."

"If you're about to tell me that you found it with your *mistress*..." Isabelle shuddered.

"Isabelle." Robert took his daughter's hands in his own. "I'm telling you that I found it with Alec. With you. With..."

He looked down. "With Max. Having you kids, Isabelle—it changed everything."

"Is that why you spent years treating Alec like he had the plague? Is that how you show your kids that you love them?"

At that, if possible, Robert looked even *more* ashamed of himself. "Loving someone doesn't mean you're never going to make mistakes," he said. "I've made more than my share. I know that. And some of them I will never have the chance to make up for. But I'm trying my best with your brother. He knows how much I love him. How proud I am of him. I need you to know it too. You kids, you're the one thing I'm certain of, the one thing I'll always be certain of. Not the Clave. Not, unfortunately, my marriage. *You*. And if I have to, I'll spend the rest of my life trying to prove to you that you can be certain of me."

It was a lame party, the kind that even Simon had to admit might have been livened up by a demon or two. The decorations—a few sad streamers, a couple of underinflated helium balloons, and a hand-drawn poster that (mis) spelled out "*CONGRATULATONS*"—looked as if they'd been grudgingly thrown together at the last minute by a bunch of fifth graders in detention. The refreshment table was crowded with whatever food had been left over at the end of the semester, including stale croissants, a casserole dish filled with orange Jell-O, a vat of stew, and several plates heaped with unidentifiable meat products. As electricity didn't work in Idris and no one had thought to hire a band, there was no music, but a handful of faculty members had taken it upon themselves to improvise a barbershop quartet. (This, in Simon's mind, didn't qualify as music.) Isabelle's posse of demon summoners had been let off with a stern warning, and even allowed to attend the party, but none of them seemed much in the mood for revelry—or, understandably, for Simon.

He was lingering alone by the punch bowl—which smelled enough like fish to preclude him actually pouring himself any punch—when Isabelle joined him.

"Avoiding your friends?" she asked.

"Friends?" He laughed. "I think you mean 'people who hate my guts.' Yeah, I tend to avoid those."

"They don't hate you. They're embarrassed, because you were right and they were stupid. They'll get over it."

"Maybe." It didn't seem likely, but then, not much that had happened this year fell into the category of "likely."

"So, I guess, thanks for sticking around for that whole thing with my dad," Isabelle said.

"You didn't exactly give me much of a choice," he pointed out.

Isabelle laughed, almost fondly. "You really have no idea how a social encounter is supposed to work, do you? I say 'thank you'; you say 'you're welcome.'"

"Like, if I said, thank you for fooling all my friends into thinking you were a wild-and-crazy demon summoner so that they could get in trouble with the dean, you would say...?"

"You're welcome for teaching them all a valuable lesson." She grinned. "One that, apparently, you didn't need to learn."

"Yeah. About that." Even though it had all been a test—even though, apparently, Isabelle had *wanted* him to report her, he still felt guilty. "I'm sorry I didn't figure out what you were doing. Trust you."

"It was a game, Simon. You weren't supposed to trust me."

"But *I* shouldn't have fallen for it. Of all people—"

"You can't be expected to know me." There was an impossible gentleness in Isabelle's voice. "I do understand that, Simon. I know things have been ... difficult between us, but I'm not deluded. I may not like reality, but I can't deny it."

There were so many things he wanted to say to her.

And yet, right at this high-pressure moment, his mind was blank.

The uncomfortable silence sat heavily between them. Isabelle shifted her weight. "Well, if that's all, then..."

"Back to your date with Jon?" Simon couldn't help himself. "Or ... was that just part of the game?"

He hoped she wouldn't catch the pathetic note of hope in his voice.

"That was a different game, Simon. Keep up. Did it ever occur to you I just enjoy torturing you?" There was that wicked smile again, and Simon felt like it had the power to light him on fire; he felt like he was already burning.

"So, you and he, you never—"

"Jon's not exactly my type."

The next silence was slightly more comfortable. The kind of silence, Simon thought, where you gazed googly-eyed at someone until the tension could only be broken with a kiss.

Just lean in, he told himself, because even though he couldn't actually *remember* ever making the first move on a girl like this, he'd obviously done so in the past. Which meant he had it in him. Somewhere. *Stop being such a coward and freaking LEAN IN.*

He was still mustering up his courage when the moment passed. She stepped back. "So ... what was in that letter, anyway?"

He had it memorized. He could recite it to her right now, tell her that she was amazing, that even if his brain didn't remember loving her, his soul was permanently molded to fit hers, like some kind of Isabelle-shaped cookie cutter had stamped his heart. But writing something down was different from saying it out loud—in public, no less.

He shrugged. "I don't really remember. Just apologizing for yelling at you that time. And that other time. I guess."

"Oh."

Did she look disappointed? Relieved? Irritated? Simon searched her face for clues, but it was impervious.

"Well ... apology accepted. And stop staring at me like I have a bug on my nose."

"Sorry. Again."

"And ... I guess ... *I'm* sorry I returned it without reading it."

Simon couldn't remember whether she'd ever apologized to him before. She didn't seem the type to apologize to anyone.

"If you wrote me another one sometime, I might even read it," she said, with studied indifference.

"School's over for the semester, remember? This weekend I go back to Brooklyn." It seemed unimaginable.

"They don't have mailboxes in Brooklyn?"

"I guess I could send you a postcard of the Brooklyn

Bridge," Simon allowed—then took a deep breath, and went for it. "Or I could hand deliver one. To the Institute, I mean. If you wanted me to. Sometime. Or something."

"Sometime. Something..." Isabelle mulled it over, letting him twist in the wind for a few endless, agonizing seconds. Then her smile widened so far that Simon thought he might actually self-combust. "I guess it's a date."

Pale Kings and Princes

By Cassandra Clare and Robin Wasserman

This morning Mayhew ceded the classroom to a girl a few years older than Simon. Her white-blond hair fell in ringlets around her shoulders, her blue-green eyes sparkled, and her mouth was set in a grim line that suggested she'd rather be anywhere else. Professor Mayhew stood beside her, but Simon noticed the way he kept his distance and was careful not to turn his back on her. Mayhew was afraid.

—Pale Kings and Princes

TELL THEM YOUR NAME.
Helen Blackthorn...
LOUDER!
HELEN BLACKTHORN.
DAUGHTER OF ANDREW & ELEANOR BLACKTHORN.
LIAR! TRY AGAIN.

What I Did on My Summer Vacation
By Simon Lewis

This summer, I lived in Brooklyn. Every morning I ran through the park. One morning, I met a nixie who lived in the dog pond. She had—

Simon Lewis paused to consult his Chthonian/English dictionary for the word for "blond"—there was no entry. Apparently words relating to hair color were a nonissue for creatures of the demon dimensions. Much like, he'd discovered, words relating to family, friendship, or watching TV. He chewed his eraser, sighed, then bent over the page again. Five hundred words on how he spent his summer were due to his Chthonian teacher by morning, and after an hour of work he had written approximately ... thirty.

She had hair. And—
—an enormous rack.

"Just trying to help," Simon's roommate, George Lovelace, said, reaching over Simon's shoulder to scrawl in an ending to the sentence.

"And failing miserably," Simon said, but he couldn't suppress a grin.

He'd missed George this summer, more than he had expected to. He'd missed all of it more than he'd expected—not just his new friends, but Shadowhunter Academy itself, the predictable rhythms of the day, all the things he'd spent months complaining about. The slime, the dank, the morning calisthenics, the chittering of creatures trapped in the walls ... he'd even missed the soup. Simon had spent most of his first year at the Academy worrying that he was out of place—that, any minute, someone important would realize they'd made a terrible mistake and send him back home.

It wasn't until he was back in Brooklyn, trying to sleep beneath Batman sheets with his mother snoring in the next room, that he realized home wasn't home anymore.

Home, unexpectedly, inexplicably, was Shadowhunter Academy.

Park Slope wasn't quite the same as he remembered, not with the werewolf cubs frolicking in the Prospect Park dog run, the warlock selling artisanal cheese and love potions at the Grand Army farmers' market, the vampires lounging on the banks of the Gowanus, flicking cigarette butts at strolling hipsters. Simon had to keep reminding himself that they'd been there all along—Park Slope hadn't changed; Simon had. Simon was the one who now had the Sight. Simon was the one who flinched at flickering shadows and, when Eric had the misfortune of sneaking up behind him, instinctively yanked his old friend off his feet and slammed him to the ground with an effortless judo flip.

"Dude," Eric gasped, goggling up at him from the parched August grass, "stand down, soldier."

Eric, of course, thought he'd spent the year at military school—as did the rest of the guys, as did Simon's mother and sister. Lying to almost everyone he loved: That was another thing different about his Brooklyn life now, and maybe the thing that made him most eager for escape. It was one thing to lie about where he'd been all year, to make up half-assed stories about demerits and drill sergeants, most of them cribbed from bad eighties movies. It was another thing altogether to lie about who he was. He had to pretend to be the guy they remembered, the Simon Lewis who thought demons and warlocks were confined to the pages of comic books, the one whose closest brush with death involved aspirating a chocolate-covered almond. But he wasn't that Simon anymore, not even close. Maybe he wasn't a Shadowhunter, not yet—but he wasn't exactly a mundane anymore either, and he was tired of pretending to be.

The only person he didn't have to pretend with was Clary, and as the weeks passed, he'd spent more and more time with her, exploring the city and listening to stories of the boy he used to be. Simon still couldn't quite remember what they'd been to each other in that other life, the one he'd been magicked into forgetting—but the past seemed to matter less and less.

"You know, I'm not the person I used to be either," Clary had said to him one day, as they nursed their fourth coffee at Java Jones. Simon was doing his best to turn his blood into caffeine, in preparation for September. The Academy was a coffee-free zone. "Sometimes, that old Clary feels just as far away from me as the old Simon must from you."

"Do you miss her?" Simon asked, but he meant: *Do you miss* him? The old Simon. The other Simon. The better, braver Simon, who he was always worried he no longer had it in himself to be.

Clary had shaken her head, fiery red curls bouncing at her shoulders, green eyes glinting with certainty. "And I don't miss you anymore, either," she'd said, with that uncanny knack to know what was going on in his head. "Because I have you back. At least, I hope..."

He'd squeezed her hand. It was answer enough for both of them.

"Speaking of what you did on your summer vacation," George said now, flopping back on his sagging mattress, "are you ever going to tell me?"

"Tell you what?" Simon leaned back in his chair—then, at the ominous sound of cracking wood, abruptly leaned forward again. As second-years, Simon and George had been offered the opportunity to claim a room above-ground, but they'd both decided to stay in the dungeon. Simon had gotten rather attached to the gloomy damp—and he'd discovered there were certain advantages to being far from the prying eyes of the faculty. Not to mention the judgmental glares of the elite-track students. While the Shadowhunter kids in his class had, for the most part, come around to the slim possibility that their mundane peers could have something to offer, there was a whole new class now, and Simon didn't relish teaching them the lesson all over again. Still, as his desk chair decided whether or not to split in half and something furry and gray scampered past his feet, he wondered if it was too late to change his mind.

"Simon. Mate. Toss me a bone here. Do you know how I spent *my* summer vacation?"

"Shearing sheep?" George had sent him a handful of postcards over the last two months. The front of each of them had borne a photograph of the idyllic Scottish countryside. And on the back, a series of messages circling a single theme:

Bored.
So bored.
Kill me now.
Too late, already dead.

"Shearing sheep," George confirmed. "Feeding sheep. Herding sheep. Mucking about in sheep muck. While you were ... who-knows-what-ing with a certain raven-haired superwarrior. You're not going to let me live vicariously?"

Simon sighed. George had restrained himself for four and a half days. Simon supposed that was more than he could have asked for.

"What makes you think I was doing anything with Isabelle Lightwood?"

"Oh, I don't know, maybe because last I saw you, you wouldn't shut up about her?" George affected an American accent—poorly. "What should I do on my date with Isabelle? What should I say on my date with Isabelle? What should I wear on my date with Isabelle? Oh, George, you bronze

Scottish love god, tell me what to do with Isabelle."

"I don't recall those words coming out of my mouth."

"I was paraphrasing your body language," George said. "Now spill."

Simon shrugged. "It didn't work out."

"Didn't work out?" George's eyebrows nearly rocketed off his forehead. *"Didn't work out?"*

"Didn't work out," Simon confirmed.

"You're telling me that your epic love story with the hottest Shadowhunter of her generation that spanned multiple dimensions and several incidences of saving the world is over with a shrug and a"—his voice flattened again to an American accent—"'didn't work out.'"

"Yeah. That's what I'm telling you." Simon tried to sound casual about it, but he must have failed, because George got up and gently slugged his roommate's shoulder.

"Sorry, mate," George said quietly.

Simon sighed again. "Yeah."

How I Spent My Summer Vacation
By Simon Lewis

I screwed up my chances with the most amazing girl in the world.

Not once, not twice, but three times.

She took me on a date to her favorite nightclub, where I stood around like an idiot clod all night and once literally tripped over my own two feet. Then I dropped her off at the Institute and shook her hand good night.

Yes, you read that right: Shook. Her. Hand.

Then I took her on date number two, to my favorite movie theater, where I made her sit through a Star

Wars: The Clone Wars marathon and didn't notice when she fell asleep, then I accidentally insulted her taste because how was I supposed to know she once dated some warlock with a tail and not that I wanted to know that anyway and then: Zoom in on yet another good-night handshake.

Date number three, another of my genius ideas: double date with Clary and Jace. Which maybe would have been fine, except for how Clary and Jace are more in love than any people in love in the history of love, and how I'm pretty sure they were playing footsie under the table, because there was that one time when Jace started rubbing his foot against my leg by accident. (I think by accident?) (It better have been by accident.) And then we got attacked by demons, because Clary and Jace are apparently some kind of demon magnet, and I got knocked down in about thirty seconds and just kind of lay around in a corner while the rest of them saved the day and Isabelle did her amazing warrior goddess thing. Because she's an amazing warrior goddess—and I'm a weenie.

After that they all went off on some super-awesome cross-country road trip to chase down the demons that sent the other demons after us, and they wouldn't let me come. (See above re: my weenie-ness.) Then when they came back, Isabelle didn't call me, probably because what kind of warrior goddess wants to date a cowering-in-the-corner weenie? And I didn't call her, for the same reason ... and also because I thought maybe she'd call me.

Which she didn't.

The End

Simon decided to ask his Chthonian teacher for an extension.

The second-year curriculum, it turned out, was much the same as the first—with one exception. This year, as the months ticked down toward Ascension day, the Shadowhunter Academy students were expected to learn current events. Although judging from what they'd learned so far, Simon thought, their current events class could just as easily be titled Why Faeries Suck.

Every day Shadowhunter and mundane second-years crowded into one of the classrooms that had been locked down the year before. (Something about a demonic beetle infestation.) Each squeezed into a rusty chair-desk combo that seemed designed for students half their size, and listened as Professor Freeman Mayhew explained the Cold Peace.

Freeman Mayhew was a scrawny, bald man with a graying Hitler mustache, and though he started most of his sentences with "Back when *I* was fighting demons..." it was difficult to imagine him fighting so much as a cold. Mayhew believed it was his responsibility to persuade his students that faeries were shrewd, untrustworthy, coldhearted, and—not that the "lily-livered politicians" running the Clave would admit it any time soon—worthy of extinction.

The students quickly realized that disagreeing—or even interrupting to ask a question—drove up Mayhew's blood pressure, an angry red blotch blooming across his skull as he snapped, "Were you there? I don't *think* so!"

This morning Mayhew ceded the classroom to a girl a few years older than Simon. Her white-blond hair fell in ringlets around her shoulders, her blue-green eyes sparkled, and her mouth was set in a grim line that suggested she'd rather be anywhere else. Professor Mayhew stood beside her, but Simon noticed the way he kept his distance and was careful not to turn his back on her. Mayhew was afraid.

"Go on," the professor said gruffly. "Tell them your name."

The girl kept her eyes on the floor and mumbled something.

"Louder," Mayhew snapped.

Now the girl lifted her head and faced the class full on, and when she spoke, her voice was loud and clear. "Helen Blackthorn," she said. "Daughter of Andrew and Eleanor Blackthorn."

Simon gave her a closer look. Helen Blackthorn was a name he knew well from the stories Clary told him about the Dark War. The Blackthorns had all lost quite a bit in that fight, but he thought Helen and her brother Mark had lost most of all.

"Liar!" Mayhew shouted. "Try again."

"If I can lie, shouldn't that prove something to you?" she asked, but it was clear she already knew the answer.

"You know the conditions of your presence here," he snapped. "Tell them the truth or go home."

"That's not my home," Helen said quietly but firmly.

After the Dark War, she had been exiled—not that anyone officially used that term—to Wrangel Island, an Arctic outpost that was the hub of the world's protective wards. It was also, Simon had heard, a desolate frozen wasteland. *Officially*, Helen and her girlfriend, Aline Penhallow, were studying the wards, which had to be rebuilt after the Dark War. Unofficially, Helen was being punished for the accident of her birth. The Clave had decided that despite her bravery in the Dark War, despite her impeccable history, despite the fact that her younger siblings were orphans and had no one to care for them but an uncle they barely knew, she couldn't be trusted in their midst. The Clave thought that even though her skin could bear the angelic runes, she wasn't a real Shadowhunter.

Simon thought they were all idiots.

It didn't matter that she had no weapons, was clad in a pale yellow shirt and jeans, and had no visible runes. It was clear, simply from her posture and the control she exerted over herself, transforming rage into dignity, that Helen Blackthorn *was* a Shadowhunter. A warrior.

"Last chance," Mayhew grumbled.

"Helen Blackthorn," the girl said again, and tucked her hair back, revealing delicate pale ears, each of which tapered to an elfin point. "Daughter of Andrew Blackthorn the Shadowhunter and the Lady Nerissa. Of the Seelie Court."

At that Julie Beauvale stood up and, without a word, walked out of the classroom.

Simon felt for her, or tried to. During the final hours of the Dark War, a faerie had murdered Julie's sister right in front of her. But that wasn't Helen's fault. Helen was only half-faerie, and it wasn't the half that counted.

Not that anyone in the Clave—or the classroom—seemed to believe it. The students buzzed, faerie slurs bouncing between them. At the front of the classroom, Helen stood very still, hands clasped behind her back.

"Oh, shut up," Mayhew said loudly. Simon wondered, not for the first time, why the man had become a teacher when it seemed the only thing he loathed more than young people was the obligation to teach them. "I don't expect any of you to respect this ... *person.* But she's here to offer you a cautionary tale. You will listen."

Helen cleared her throat. "My father and his brother were once students here, just like you." She spoke softly, with flat affect, as if she were talking about strangers. "And perhaps like you, they didn't realize how dangerous the Fair Folk could be. Which almost destroyed them."

It was my father, Andrew's, second year at the Academy—Helen continued—and Arthur's first. Normally, only second-years would be sent on a mission to the land of the fey, but everyone knew Arthur and Andrew fought best side by side. This was long before the Cold Peace, obviously, when the fey were bound by the Accords. But it didn't stop them from breaking the rules where they thought they could get away with it. A Shadowhunter child had been taken. Ten students from the Academy, accompanied by one of their teachers, were sent to get her back.

The mission was a success—or would have been, if a clever faerie hadn't snared my father's hand in a berry thornbush. Without thinking, he sucked the blood from a small wound—and, with it, took in a bit of the juice.

Drinking something in Faerie bound him to the Queen's whim, and the Queen bade him stay. Arthur insisted on staying with him—that's how much the brothers cared for each other.

The Academy teacher quickly made a bargain with the Queen: Their imprisonment would last only one day.

The Academy teachers have, of course, always been rather clever. But the fey were more so. What passed as one day in the world lasted much longer in Faerie.

It lasted for years.

My father and my uncle had always been quiet, bookish boys. They served bravely on the battlefield, but they preferred the library. They weren't prepared for what happened to them next.

What happened to them next was they encountered the Lady Nerissa, of the Seelie Court, the faerie who would become my mother, a faerie whose beauty was surpassed only by her cruelty.

My father never spoke to me of what happened to him at Nerissa's hands, nor did my uncle. But upon their return, they both made full reports to the Inquisitor. I've been ... *invited* to read these reports in full and relay the details to you.

The details are these: For seven long years Nerissa made of my father her plaything. She bound him to her, not with chains but with dark faerie magic. As her servants held him down, she latched a silver choker around his neck. It was enchanted. It made my father see her not as she was, a monster, but as a miracle. It deceived his eyes and his heart, and turned his hatred of his captor into love. Or, rather, the curdled faerie version of love. A claustrophobic worship. He would do anything for her. He did, over those seven years, do everything for her.

And then there was Arthur, his brother, younger than Andrew and young for his age. Kind, they say. Soft.

Lady Nerissa had no use for Arthur, except as a toy, a tool, something with which to torture my father and affirm his loyalty.

Nerissa forced my father to live all those years in love; she forced Arthur to live in pain.

Arthur was burned alive, many times over, as a faerie fire ate away his flesh and bone but would not kill.

Arthur was whipped, a chain of thorns slashing wounds in his back that would never heal.

Arthur was chained to the ground, cuffs binding his wrists and ankles as if he were a wild beast, and forced to watch his worst nightmares play out before his eyes, faerie glamours impersonating the people he loved most dying excruciating deaths before his eyes.

Arthur was left to believe his brother had abandoned him, had chosen faerie love over flesh and blood, and that was the worst torture of all.

Arthur was broken. It took only a year. The faeries spent the next six stomping and giggling over the rubble of his soul.

And yet.

Arthur was a Shadowhunter, and these should never be underestimated. One day, half-mad with pain and sorrow, he had a vision of his future, of thousands of days of agony, decades, centuries passing in Faerie as he aged into a wizened, broken creature, finally returned to his world to discover that only one day had passed. That everyone he knew was young and whole. That they would pray for his death, so they wouldn't have to live with what had become of him. Faerie was a land beyond time; they could steal his entire life here—they could give him *ten* lifetimes of torture and pain—and still stay true to their word.

The terror of this fate was more powerful than pain, and it gave him the strength he needed to break free of his bonds. He was forced to fight against his own brother, who'd been enchanted into believing he should protect Lady Nerissa at all costs. Arthur knocked my father to the ground and used Lady Nerissa's own dagger to slice her open from neck to sternum. With that same dagger, he cut the enchanted silver from my father's throat. And together, both of them finally free, they escaped Faerie and returned to the world. Both of them still bearing their scars.

After they made their report to the Inquisitor, they left Idris, and left each other. These brothers, once as close as *parabatai*, couldn't stand each other's sight. Each was a reminder of what the other had endured and lost. Neither could forgive the other for where they had failed, and where they had succeeded.

Perhaps they would have reconciled, eventually.

But Arthur went to London, while my father returned home to Los Angeles, where he quickly fell in love with one of the Shadowhunters training at the L.A. Institute. She loved him too and helped him forget those nightmare years. They married. They were happy—and then, one day, their doorbell rang. My mother would have been painting, or developing photographs in her darkroom. My father would have been buried in his books. One of them would have answered the door and discovered two baskets on their doorstep, each of them bearing a sleeping toddler. My brother Mark and me. My father, in his bewitched state, never realized the Lady Nerissa had borne two children.

My father and his wife, Eleanor, raised us like we were full-blooded Shadowhunters. Like we were their own. Like we weren't half-blooded monsters who'd been slipped into their midst by their enemy. Like we weren't constant reminders of destruction and torture, of the long nightmare my father had labored so long to forget. They did their best to love us. Maybe they even *did* love us, as much as anyone could. But I'm assured that Andrew and Eleanor Blackthorn were the best of Shadowhunters. So they would have been smart enough to know, deep down, that we could never truly be trusted.

Trust a faerie at your own risk, because they care for nothing but themselves. They sow nothing but destruction. And their preferred weapon is human love.

This is the lesson I've been asked to teach you. And so I have.

"What the hell was *that*?" Simon exploded as soon as they were dismissed from class.

"I know!" George sagged against the corridor's stone wall—then quickly reconsidered as something green and sluggish wriggled out from behind his shoulder. "I mean, I knew faeries were little bastards, but who knew they were *evil*?"

"I did," Julie said, her face paler than usual. She'd been waiting for them outside the classroom—or, rather, waiting for Jon Cartwright, with whom she now seemed to be somewhat of an item. Julie was even prettier than Jon and almost as big a snob, but still, Simon had thought she had slightly better taste.

Jon put his arm around her, and she curled herself against his muscled torso.

They make it look so easy, Simon thought in wonder. But then, that was the thing about Shadowhunters—they made everything look so easy.

It was slightly disgusting.

"I can't believe they tortured that poor guy for *seven* years," George said.

"And how about his brother!" Beatriz Mendoza exclaimed. "That's even worse."

George looked incredulous. "You think being forced to fall in love with a sexy faerie princess is *worse* than getting burned alive a couple hundred times?"

"I think—"

Simon cleared his throat. "Uh, I actually meant, what the hell was that with Helen Blackthorn, trotting her in here like some kind of circus freak, making her tell us that horrible story about her own mother?" As soon as Helen finished her story, Professor Mayhew had pretty much ordered her out of the room. She'd looked like she wanted to decapitate him—but instead, she'd lowered her head and obeyed. He'd never seen a Shadowhunter behave like that, like she was ... tamed. It felt sickeningly wrong.

"'Mother' is a bit of a technicality in this situation, don't you think?" George asked.

"You think that means this was *fun* for her?" Simon said, incredulous.

"I think a lot of things aren't fun," Julie said coldly. "I think watching your sister get sliced in half isn't so fun, either. So you'll excuse me if I don't care much about this halfling thing or her so-called feelings." Her voice shook on the last word, and very abruptly she slid out from under Jon's arm and raced off down the hallway.

Jon glared at Simon. "Nice, Lewis. Really nice." He took off after Julie, leaving Simon, Beatriz, and George to stand around awkwardly in their hushed wake.

After a tense moment George scratched his stubbled chin. "Mayhew *was* pretty harsh back there. Acting like she was some kind of criminal. You could tell he was just waiting for her to stab him with a piece of chalk or something."

"She's fey," Beatriz pointed out. "You can't just let your guard down with them."

"Half-fey," Simon said.

"But don't you think that's enough? The Clave must have thought so," Beatriz said. "Why else send her into exile?"

Simon snorted. "Yeah, because the Clave is always right."

"Her brother rides with the Wild Hunt," Beatriz argued. "How much more faerie can you get?"

"That's not his fault," Simon protested. Clary had told him the whole story of Mark Blackthorn's capture—the way the faeries had snatched him up during the massacre at the Los Angeles Institute. The way the Clave refused to bother trying to get him back. "He's there against his will."

Beatriz was starting to look somewhat cross. "You don't know that. No one can know that."

"Where is this even coming from?" Simon asked. "You've never bought into any of that anti-Downworlder crap." Simon might not have remembered his vampire days very well, but he made it his business not to befriend anyone inclined to stake first, ask questions later.

"I'm *not* anti-Downworlder," Beatriz insisted, full of self-righteousness. "I don't have any problem with werewolves or vampires. Or warlocks, obviously. But the fey are different. Whatever the Clave is doing with them, or to them, it's for *our* benefit. It's to protect us. Don't you think it's possible they know a little more about it than you do?"

Simon rolled his eyes. "Spoken like a true Shadowhunter."

Beatriz gave him an odd look. "Simon—do you realize that you almost always say 'Shadowhunter' like it's an insult?"

That stopped him. Beatriz rarely spoke to anyone sharply like that, especially not him. "I..."

"If you think it's so terrible, being a Shadowhunter, I don't know what you're doing here." She took off down the corridor toward her room—which was, like the rest of the second-year elite rooms, high up in one of the turrets with a nice southern exposure and a meadow view.

George and Simon turned the other way, toward the dungeons.

"Not making many friends today," George said cheerfully, softly slugging his roommate. It was George-speak for *don't worry, it'll blow over.*

They clomped down the corridor side by side. A summer cleaning had done nothing to address the dripping ceilings or puddles of suspicious-smelling slime that cluttered the path to the dungeons—or maybe the Academy's janitorial ministrations just didn't extend to dregs' quarters. Either way, by this point Simon and George could have made it down the hallway blindfolded; they sidestepped puddles and ducked spurting pipes by habit.

"I didn't mean to upset anyone," Simon said. "I just don't think it's right."

"Trust me, mate, you made that perfectly clear. And obviously I agree with you."

"You do?" Simon felt a rush of relief.

"Of course I do," George said. "You don't fence off a whole herd just because one sheep's nibbling at the wrong grass, right?"

"Er ... right."

"I just don't know why you're getting so worked up about it." George wasn't the type to get worked up about much of anything, or at least, not the type to admit it. He claimed apathy was a family credo. "Is it the vampire thing? You know no one thinks about you that way."

"No, it's not that," Simon said. He knew that these days, his friends barely gave a thought to his vampire past—they considered it irrelevant. Sometimes Simon wasn't so sure.

He'd been *dead* ... how could that be irrelevant?

But that had nothing to do with this.

This simply wasn't right, the way Professor Mayhew ordered Helen around like a trained dog, or the way the others talked about the Fair Folk—as if, because *some* faeries had betrayed the Shadowhunters, *all* Faeries were guilty, now and forevermore.

Maybe that was it: the question of guilt handed down through bloodlines, the sins of the fathers visited on not just their sons but their friends, neighbors, and random acquaintances who happened to have similarly shaped ears. You couldn't just indict an entire people—or in this case, Downworlder species—because you didn't like how a few of them behaved. He'd spent enough time in Hebrew school to know how that kind of thing ended. Fortunately, before he could formulate an explanation for George that didn't name-check Hitler, Professor Catarina Loss materialized before them.

Materialized, literally, in a rather theatrical puff of smoke. Warlock prerogative, Simon supposed, although showing off wasn't Catarina's style. Usually she blended in with the rest of the Academy faculty, making it easy to forget she was a warlock (at least, if you overlooked the blue skin). But he'd noticed that whenever another Downworlder was on campus, Catarina went out of her way to play up her warlockiness.

Not that Helen was a Downworlder, Simon reminded himself.

On the other hand, Simon wasn't a Downworlder either—or hadn't been for more than a year now—and Catarina still insisted on calling him Daylighter. According to her, once a Downworlder, always, in some tiny, subconscious, embedded-in-the-soul part, a Downworlder. She always sounded so certain of this, as if she knew something he didn't. After talking to her, Simon often found himself tonguing his canine teeth, just to make sure he hadn't sprouted fangs.

"Might I speak with you for a moment, Daylighter?" she said. "Privately?"

George, who'd been a bit nervous around Catarina ever since she had, very briefly, turned him into a sheep, had clearly been waiting for an excuse to run away. He took it.

Simon found himself surprisingly glad to be alone with Catarina; *she*, at least, was certain to be on his side. "Professor Loss, you won't believe what just happened in class with Professor Mayhew—"

"How was your summer, Daylighter?" She gave him a thin smile. "Pleasant, I trust? Not too much sun?"

In all the time he'd known Catarina Loss, she'd never bothered with small talk. It seemed an odd time to start. "You did know Helen Blackthorn was here, right?" Simon said.

She nodded. "I know most everything that goes on around here. I thought you'd figured that out."

"Then I'm guessing you know how Professor Mayhew was treating her."

"Like something less than human, I would imagine?"

"Exactly!" Simon exclaimed. "Like something scraped off the bottom of his shoe."

"In my experience, that's how Professor Mayhew treats most people."

Simon shook his head. "If you'd seen it ... this was worse. Maybe I should tell Dean Penhallow?" The idea seized him only as it was coming out of his mouth, but he liked the sound of it. "She can, I don't know..." It wasn't like she could give him a detention. "*Something.*"

Catarina pursed her lips. "You must do what you think is right, Daylighter. But I can tell you that Dean Penhallow has little authority on the subject of Helen Blackthorn's treatment here."

"But she's the dean. She should—oh." Slowly but surely, the pieces slotted into place. Dean Penhallow was cousin to *Aline* Penhallow. Helen's girlfriend. Aline's mother, Jia, the Consul, was supposedly biased on the subject of Helen, and had recused herself from determining her treatment. If even the Consul couldn't intercede on Helen's behalf, then presumably the dean had even less hope of doing so. It seemed hideously unfair to Simon, that the people who cared most for Helen were the ones least involved in deciding her fate. "Why would Helen even come here?" Simon wondered. "I know Wrangel Island must suck, but could it be any worse than getting paraded around here, where everyone seems to hate her?"

"You can ask her yourself," Catarina said. "That's why I wanted to speak with you. Helen asked me to send you over to her cabin after your classes end today. She has something for you."

"She does? What?"

"You'll have to ask that for yourself too. You'll find her lodgings at the edge of the western quad."

"She's staying on campus?" Simon said, surprised. He couldn't understand why Helen would come here in the first place, but it was even harder to imagine her wanting to stay. "She must have friends in Alicante she could stay with."

"I'm sure she does, even now," Catarina said, something kind and sad in her voice, as if she were, very, very gently, letting down a child. "But, Simon, you're presuming she had a choice."

* * *

Simon hesitated at the door of the cabin, willing himself to knock. It was his least favorite thing, meeting someone he'd known in his before life, as he'd come to think of it. There was always the fear they would expect something of him he couldn't deliver, or assume he knew something he'd forgotten. There was, too often, a gleam of hope in their eyes that was extinguished as soon as he opened his mouth.

At least, he told himself, he'd barely known Helen. She couldn't be expecting much from him. Unless there was something he didn't know.

And there must be *something* he didn't know... Why else would she have summoned him?

Only one way to find out, Simon thought, and knocked at the door.

Helen had changed into a bright polka-dotted sundress and looked much younger than she had in the classroom. Also much happier. Her smile widened substantially when she saw who was at the door.

"Simon! I'm so glad. Come on in, sit down, would you like something to eat or drink? Maybe a cup of coffee?"

Simon settled himself on the small living room's only couch. It was uncomfortable and threadbare, embroidered with a faded flower pattern that looked like something his grandmother might have owned. He wondered who usually lived here, or whether the Academy simply maintained the ramshackle cabin for visiting faculty. Though he couldn't imagine there were many visiting faculty members who wanted to live in a broken-down hut on the edge of the woods that looked like somewhere Hansel and Gretel's witch might have lived before she discovered candy-based architecture.

"No, thanks, I'm fine—" Simon stopped as her last word

registered with him. "Did you say *coffee?*"

Half a week into the new school year, Simon was already in serious caffeine withdrawal. Before he could tell her *yes, please, a bucketful*, Helen had already placed a steaming mug in his hands. "I thought so," she said.

Simon swallowed greedily, caffeine buzzing through his system. He didn't know how anyone was supposed to be human—much less, in the Shadowhunter case, superhuman—without a daily dose. "Where did you get this?"

"Magnus magicked me up a nonelectric coffeemaker," Helen said, grinning. "Kind of a parting gift before we left for Wrangel Island. Now I can't live without it."

"How is it there?" Simon asked. "On the island?"

Helen hesitated, and he wondered if he'd made a mistake. Was it rude to ask someone how they were enjoying their exile in a Siberian-like wilderness?

"Cold," she said finally. "Lonely."

"Oh." What could he say to that? "Sorry" didn't quite seem to cover it, and she didn't look like she wanted his pity.

"But we're together, at least. Aline and I. That's something. That's everything, I suppose. I still can't believe she agreed to marry me."

"You're getting married?" Simon exclaimed. "That's amazing!"

"It is, isn't it?" Helen smiled. "It's hard to believe how much light you can find in the darkness, when you have someone who loves you."

"Did she come with you?" Simon asked, looking around the small cabin. There was only one other room, the bedroom, he assumed, its door closed. He couldn't remember meeting Aline, but from everything Clary had told him, he was curious.

"No," Helen said sharply. "That wasn't part of the deal."

"What deal?"

Instead of answering, she abruptly changed the subject. "So, did you enjoy my lecture this morning?"

Now it was Simon who hesitated, unsure how to answer. He didn't want to suggest he'd found her lecture dull—but it seemed equally wrong to suggest he'd enjoyed hearing her terrible story or seeing Professor Mayhew humiliate her. "I was surprised you'd want to give the lecture," he said finally. "It can't be easy, telling that story."

Helen gave him a wry smile. "'Want' is a strong word." She got up to pour him another cup of coffee, then began bustling with a stack of dishes in the tiny kitchenette. Simon got the feeling she was just trying to keep her hands busy. And maybe avoid meeting his eye. "I made a deal with them. The Clave." She ran her hands nervously through her blond hair, and Simon caught a brief glimpse of her pointed ears. "They said if I came to the Academy for a couple days, let them parade me around like some kind of half-faerie show pony, then Aline and I could come back."

"For good?"

She laughed bitterly. "For one day and one night, to be married."

Simon thought, suddenly, of what Beatriz had asked him earlier that day. Why he was trying so hard to become a Shadowhunter.

Sometimes he couldn't quite remember.

"They didn't even want to let us come back at all," Helen said bitterly. "They wanted us to have the wedding on Wrangel Island. If you can even call that a wedding, in a frozen hellhole without anyone you love there with you. I guess I should feel lucky I got this much out of them."

Less lucky than disgusted, or maybe enraged, Simon thought, but it didn't seem like it would be helpful to say so out loud. "I'm surprised they care so much about one lecture," he said instead. "I mean, not that it wasn't educational, but Professor Mayhew could have just told us the story himself."

Helen turned away from her kitchen busywork and met Simon's gaze. "They don't care about the lecture. This isn't about your education. It's about humiliating me. That's all." She gave herself a little shake, then smiled too brightly, her eyes shining. "Forget about all that. You came here to get something from me—here it is." Helen slipped an envelope from her pocket and handed it to Simon.

Curious, he tore it open and pulled out a small piece of thick ivory stationery, inscribed with a familiar hand.

Simon stopped breathing.

Dear Simon, Izzy wrote.

I know I've developed a habit of ambushing you at school.

This was true. Isabelle had popped up more than once when he'd least expected her. Every time she showed up on campus, they fought; every time, he was sorry to see her go.

I promised myself I'm not going to do that anymore. But there's something I'd like to talk to you about. So this is me, giving you advance warning. If it's okay for me to come for a visit, you can let Helen know, and she'll get word to me. If it's not okay, you can tell her that, too. Whatever.—Isabelle

Simon read the brief note several times, trying to intuit the tone behind the words. Affectionate? Eager? Businesslike?

Until this week he'd been only an e-mail or a phone call away—why wait until he was back at the Academy to reach out? Why reach out at all?

Maybe because it would be easier to reject him for good when he was safely on another continent?

But in that case, why Portal all the way to Idris to do it face-to-face?

"Maybe you need some time to think about it?" Helen said finally.

He'd forgotten she was there. "No!" Simon blurted out. "I mean, no, I don't need time to think about it, but yes, yes, she can come visit. Of course. Please, tell her."

Stop babbling, he ordered himself. Bad enough he turned into a driveling fool every time Isabelle was in the room with him these days—was he now going to start doing so at the sound of her name?

Helen laughed. "See, I told you so," she said loudly.

"Er, you told me what?" Simon asked.

"You heard him, come out!" Helen called, even louder, and the bedroom door creaked open.

Isabelle Lightwood didn't have it in her to look sheepish. But her face was doing its best. "Surprise?"

When Simon had regained his power of speech, there was only one word available in his brain. "Isabelle."

Whatever crackled and sizzled between them was apparently so palpable that Helen could sense it too, because she swiftly slid past Isabelle into the bedroom and shut the door.

Leaving the two of them alone.

"Hi, Simon."

"Hi, Izzy."

"You're, uh, probably wondering what I'm doing here." It wasn't like her to sound so uncertain.

Simon nodded.

"You never called me," she said. "I saved you from

getting decapitated by an Eidolon demon, and you didn't even *call*."

"You never called me, either," Simon pointed out. "And … uh … also, I kind of felt like I should have been able to save myself."

Isabelle sighed. "I thought you might be thinking that."

"Because I *should* have, Izzy."

"Because you're an *idiot*, Simon." She brightened. "But this is your lucky day, because I've decided I'm not giving up yet. This is too important to give up just because of a bad date."

"Three bad dates," he pointed out. "Like, *really* bad dates."

"The worst," she agreed.

"The *worst*? Jace told me you once went out with a merman who made you have dinner in the river," Simon said. "Surely our dates weren't as bad as—"

"The *worst*," she confirmed, and broke into laughter. Simon thought his heart would burst at the sound of it—there was something so carefree, so joyous in the music of her laugh, it was almost like a promise. That if they could navigate a path through all the awkwardness and pain and burden of expectations, if they could find their way back to each other, something that pure and joyful awaited them.

"I don't want to give up either," Simon said, and the smile she rewarded him with was even better than the laughter.

Isabelle settled beside him on the small couch. Simon was suddenly extremely conscious of the inches separating their thighs. Was he supposed to make a move *right now?*

"I decided New York was too crowded," she said.

"With demons?"

"With memories," Isabelle clarified.

"Too many memories is not exactly my problem."

Isabelle elbowed him. Even that made a spark. "You know what I mean."

He elbowed her back.

To touch her like that, so casually, like it was no big deal...

To have her back, so close, so willing...

She wanted him.

He wanted her.

It should have been that easy.

Simon cleared his throat and, without knowing why, rose to his feet. Then, like that wasn't enough distance, retreated safely to the other side of the room. "So what do we do now?" he asked.

She looked thrown, but only for a moment. Then she barreled ahead. "We're going on another date," she said. Not a request; a command. "In Alicante. Neutral territory."

"When?"

"I was thinking ... now."

It wasn't what he expected—but then, why not? Classes were over for the day, and second-year students were allowed off campus. There was no reason *not* to go out with Isabelle immediately. Except that he'd had no time to prepare, no time to come up with a game plan, no time to obsess over his hair and his "casually rumpled" look, no time to brainstorm a list of discussion topics in case conversation flagged ... but then, none of those things had saved their previous three dates from disaster. Maybe it was time to experiment with spontaneity.

Especially since it didn't seem like Isabelle was giving him much of a choice.

"Now it is," Simon agreed. "Should we invite Helen?"

"On our *date?*"

Idiot. He gave himself a mental slap upside the head.

"Helen, you want to crash our romantic date?" Isabelle called.

Helen emerged from the bedroom. "Nothing I would love more than being an awkward third wheel," she said. "But I'm not actually allowed to leave."

"Excuse me?" Isabelle's fingers played at the electrum whip wrapped around her left wrist. Simon couldn't blame her for wanting to strike something. Or someone. "Please tell me you're kidding."

"Catarina laid a circle of protection around the cabin," Helen said. "It won't stop you from coming and going, but I'm told it will be rather effective if I try to leave before I'm summoned."

"Catarina wouldn't do that!" Simon protested, but Helen put out a hand to quiet him.

"They didn't give her much of a choice," Helen said, "and I asked her to just go along. It was part of the deal."

"That is *unacceptable*," Isabelle said with barely concealed fury. "Forget the date, we're staying here with you."

She was lit up with a beautiful glow of righteous rage, and Simon wanted suddenly, desperately, to sweep her in his arms and kiss her until the end of the world.

"You will most certainly *not* forget the date," Helen said. "You're not staying here a single second longer. No argument."

There was, in fact, plenty more argument, but Helen finally convinced them that being stuck there with them, knowing she'd ruined their day, would be even worse than being stuck there alone. "Now please, and I say this with love, get the hell out."

She gave Izzy a hug, and then embraced Simon in turn. “Don’t screw this up,” she whispered in his ear, then pushed them both out the door and closed it behind them.

There were two white horses neighing by the front path, as if they were waiting for Isabelle. Simon supposed they were; animals in Idris behaved differently from how they did back home, almost as if they could understand what their humans wanted and, if you asked nicely enough, were willing to deliver.

“So, where exactly are we going on this date?” Simon asked. It hadn’t occurred to him that they would ride into Alicante, but of course, this was Idris. No cars. No trains. Nothing but medieval or magical transportation, and he supposed a horse was better than a vampire motorcycle. Marginally.

Isabelle grinned and swung herself up onto the saddle as easily as if she were mounting a bike. Simon, on the other hand, clumsily heaved himself onto his horse with enough grunting and sweating that he was afraid she’d take one look and call the whole thing off.

“We’re going shopping,” Isabelle informed him. “It’s time you get yourself a sword.”

“It doesn’t actually have to be a sword,” Isabelle said as they stepped into Diana’s Arrow. The ride to Alicante had been like something out of a dream, or at least a cheesy romance novel. The two of them astride white stallions, galloping across the countryside, charging across emerald meadows and through a forest the color of flames. Isabelle’s hair streamed behind her like a river of ink, and Simon had even managed not to fall off his horse—never a foregone conclusion. Best of all, between the rush of wind and the thunder of hoofbeats, it had been too loud for conversation. In motion, things felt easy between them—natural. Simon could almost forget that this was one of the most important moments of his life and anything he said or did could screw it up forever. Now, back at ground level, the weight settled back on his shoulders. It was hard to think of anything clever to say with his brain echoing the same four words over and over again.

Don't. Screw. This. Up.

"They have everything here," Izzy continued, presumably trying to fill the dull silence Simon's nerves left in their wake. "Daggers, axes, throwing stars—oh, and bows, of course. All kinds of bows. It's awesome."

"Yeah," Simon said weakly. "Awesome."

He had, in his year at the Academy, learned to fight almost as well as any beginning Shadowhunter, and had a proficiency with every weapon she'd named. But he'd discovered that knowing how to use a weapon was very different from *wanting* to. In his pre-Shadowhunter life, Simon had delivered many passionate rants on the subject of gun control, and would have loved nothing more than for every weapon in the city to be dumped into the East River. Not that a gun was the same as a sword, and not that he didn't love the feel of unleashing an arrow from his bow and watching it fly swiftly and surely into the heart of his target. But the way Isabelle loved her whip, the way Clary talked about her sword, like it was a member of the family ... the Shadowhunter passion for deadly weapons still took some getting used to.

Diana's Arrow, a weapons shop on Flintlock Street at the heart of Alicante, was full of more deadly objects than Simon had ever seen in one place—and that included the Academy weapons room, which could have supplied an army. But while the Academy arsenal was more like a storage closet, swords and daggers and arrows piled in haphazard stacks and crowded onto dangerously rickety shelves, Diana's Arrow reminded Simon of a fancy jewelry store. The weapons were on proud display, shining blades fanned across velvet cases, the better to show off their metallic gleam.

"So, what kind of thing are you looking for?" The guy behind the counter had a spiky Mohawk and a faded Arcade Fire T-shirt and looked more suited to a comic-book counter than this one. Simon assumed this probably wasn't Diana.

"How about a bow?" Izzy said. "Something really spectacular. Fit for a champion."

"Maybe not *that* spectacular," Simon said quickly. "Maybe something a little more ... unobtrusive."

"People often underestimate the importance of good battle style," Isabelle said. "You want to intimidate the enemy before you even make a move."

"You don't think my intimidating wardrobe will do the job there?" Simon gestured at his own T-shirt, which featured an anime cat spewing green puke.

Isabelle gave him what sounded like a pity laugh, then turned back to not-Diana. "What have you got in daggers?" she asked. "Anything gold plated?"

"I'm not really a gold-plated kind of guy," Simon said. "Or, uh, a dagger kind of guy."

"We have some nice swords," the guy said.

"You do look hot with a sword," Isabelle said. "As I recall."

"Maybe?" Simon tried to sound encouraging, but she must have heard the skepticism in his voice.

She turned on him. "It's like you don't even *want* a weapon."

"Well..."

"So what are we doing here?" Isabelle snapped.

"You suggested it?"

Isabelle looked like she wanted to stomp her foot—or stomp his face. "Excuse me for trying to help you behave like a respectable Shadowhunter. Forget it. We can go."

"No!" he said quickly. "That's not what I meant."

With Isabelle, it was never what he meant. Simon had always considered himself a man of words, as opposed to a man of deeds. Or of swords, for that matter. His mother liked to say he could talk her into almost anything. All he could do with Isabelle, it seemed, was talk himself out of a girlfriend.

"I'll, ah, just give the two of you some space to look around," the shopkeeper said, backing quickly away from the awkward. He disappeared into the back.

"I'm sorry," Simon said. "Let's stay, please. Of course I want your help picking something out."

She sighed. "No, I'm sorry. Choosing your first weapon is a really personal thing. I get it. Take your time, look around. I'll shut up."

"I don't want you to shut up," he said.

But she shook her head and zipped her lips shut. Then raised three fingers in the air—Scout's honor. Which didn't seem like a Shadowhunter thing, and Simon wondered who had taught her to do that.

He wondered if it had been him.

Sometimes he hated before-Simon and all the things he'd shared with Isabelle, things today-Simon could never understand. It was weird and headache inducing, competing with yourself.

They browsed the store, taking in the options: pole-arms, athames, seraph blades, elaborately carved cross-bows, chakhrams, throwing knives, a full display case of golden whips, over which Isabelle nearly began to drool.

The silence was oppressive. Simon had never had a *good* date—at least not that he could recall—but he was pretty sure they tended to involve some talking.

"Poor Helen," he said, testing the heft and balance of a medieval-looking broadsword. At least this was one subject they were sure to agree on.

"I hate what they're doing to her," Isabelle said. She was stroking a deadly-looking silver *kindjal* as if it were a puppy. "How was it, in class? Was it as bad as I imagine?"

"Worse," Simon admitted. "The look on her face, when she was telling the story of her parents..."

Isabelle's grip tightened around the *kindjal*. "Why can't they see how hideous it is to treat her like this? She's *not a faerie.*"

"Well, that's not really the point, is it?"

Isabelle laid the *kindjal* down carefully in its velvet case. "What do you mean?"

"Whether or not she's a faerie. It's beside the point."

She fixed Simon with a fiery gaze. "Helen Blackthorn is a *Shadowhunter*," she spit out. "Mark Blackthorn is a *Shadowhunter*. If we can't agree on that, we have a problem."

"Of course we agree on that." It made him love her all the more, seeing how angry she got on behalf of her friends. Why couldn't he just *say* that to her? Why was everything so hard? "They're as much Shadowhunters as you are. I just mean that even if they weren't, if we were talking about some actual faerie, it still wouldn't be right to treat her like she's the enemy, because of what she was, right?"

"Well..."

Simon was astonished. "What do you mean, 'well...'?"

"I mean that maybe any faerie *is* potentially an enemy, Simon. Look what they did to us. Look how much misery they caused."

"They didn't *all* cause that misery—but they're all paying for it."

Isabelle sighed. "Look, I don't like the Cold Peace any more than you do. And you're right, not all faeries are the enemy. Obviously. Not all of them betrayed us, and it's not fair that they should all be punished for that. You think I don't know that?"

"Good," Simon said.

"But—"

"I really don't see how there can be a 'but,'" Simon cut in.

"*But* it's not as simple as you're trying to make it. The Seelie Queen *did* betray us. A legion of faeries *did* join Sebastian in the Dark War. A lot of good Shadowhunters got killed. You've got to see why that would leave people angry. And afraid."

Stop talking, Simon told himself. His mother had once told him you should never discuss religion or politics on a date. He was never quite sure which one of those categories Clave policies fell into, but either way, this was like trying to defend J. J. Abrams to a hard-core Trekkie: hopeless.

But inexplicably, and despite the sincere wishes of his brain, Simon's mouth kept moving. "I don't care how angry or scared you get, it's not right to punish all the faeries for a few faeries' mistakes. Or to discriminate against people—"

"I'm not saying anyone should discriminate—"

"Actually, that's exactly what you're saying."

"Oh, great, Simon. So the Seelie Queen and her minions screw us over and enable the death of hundreds of Shadowhunters, not to mention the ones they slaughtered themselves, and *I'm* the terrible person?"

"I didn't say you were a terrible person."

"You're thinking it," she said.

"Would you stop telling me what I think?" he barked, more harshly than he'd intended.

Her mouth snapped shut.

She took a deep breath.

He counted to ten.

Each waited the other out.

When Isabelle spoke again, she sounded calmer—but also, somehow, angrier. "I told you, Simon. I don't like the Cold Peace. I hate it, for your information. Not just for what it's doing to Helen and Aline. Because it's wrong. But ... it's not like I have a better idea. This isn't about who you or I want to trust; this is about who the *Clave* can trust. You can't sign accords with leaders who refuse to be bound by their promises. You simply can't. If the Clave wanted revenge"—Isabelle looked pointedly around the store, gaze resting on each weapons display in turn—"trust me, they could take it. The Cold Peace isn't just about the Fair Folk. It's about us. I may not like it, but I understand it. Better than you do, at least. If you'd been there, if you knew—"

"I was there," Simon said quietly. "Remember?"

"Of course I do. But you *don't*. So it's not the same. You're not..."

"The same," he finished for her.

"That's not what I meant, I just—"

"Trust me, Izzy. I get it. I'm not him. I'll never be him."

Isabelle made a noise halfway between a hiss and a

yowl. "Would you drop it already with this old Simon/new Simon inferiority complex? It's getting old. Why don't you get a little creative and find a new excuse?"

"New excuse for what?" he asked, genuinely confused.

"For you not to be with me!" she yelled. "Because you're obviously looking for one. Try harder."

She stomped out of the store, slamming the door shut behind her. It dinged as it closed and not-Diana emerged from the back. "Oh, it's still just you," he said, sounding distinctly disappointed. "Have you decided?"

Simon could give up right now; he could stop trying, stop fighting, just let her go. That would be the easiest of decisions. All he'd have to do would be to let it happen.

"I decided a long time ago," Simon said, and ran out of the shop.

He needed to find Isabelle.

It wasn't much of a challenge. She was sitting on a small bench across the street, head in her hands.

Simon sat down beside her. "I'm sorry," he said quietly.

She shook her head without lifting it from her hands. "I can't believe I was dumb enough to think this would work."

"It still can," he said with an embarrassing tinge of desperation. "I still want it to, if you—"

"No, not you and me, idiot." She finally looked up at him. Mercifully, her eyes were dry. In fact, she didn't look sad at all—she looked furious. "This stupid weapons-shopping idea. Last time I take dating advice from *Jace*."

"You let *Jace* plan our date?" Simon said, incredulous.

"Well, it's not like either of us was doing a very good job of it. He took Clary here to buy a sword, and it was this whole disgustingly sexy thing, and I just thought, maybe..."

Simon laughed in relief. "I hate to break it to you, but you're not dating Jace."

"Um, yeah. Disgusting."

"No, I mean, you're not dating a guy who's anything *like* Jace."

"I wasn't aware I was dating anyone at all," she said, frost in her voice. His heart caught in his throat like it was snagged on barbed wire. But then, ever so slightly, she melted. "Kidding. Mostly."

"Relieved," he said. "Mostly."

Isabelle sighed. "I'm sorry this was such a disaster."

"It's not all your fault."

"Well, obviously it's not all my fault," she said. "Not even mostly my fault."

"Uh ... I thought we'd moved into the apologies portion of the day."

"Right. Sorry."

He grinned. "See, now you're talking."

"So, what now? Back to the Academy?"

"Are you kidding?" Simon stood up and extended a hand to her. Miracle of miracles, she took it. "We're not giving up until we get this right. But we're not going to get there pretending to be Jace and Clary. That's our whole problem, isn't it? Trying to be people we're not? I can't be some kind of cool, hipster nightclub hopper."

"I don't think there's any such thing as a 'nightclub hopper,'" Isabelle said wryly.

"This proves my point. And you're never going to be some kind of gamer who wants to stay up all night debating Naruto plot points and battling D&D orcs."

"Now you're just making up words."

"And neither of us is ever going to be Jace and Clary—"

"Thank God," they said, in sync, then exchanged a grin.

"So what are you suggesting?" Izzy asked.

"Something new," Simon said, mind racing to come up with an actual concrete, useful idea. He knew he was onto something, he just wasn't sure what. "Not your world, not my world. A new world, for just the two of us."

"Please tell me you don't want us to Portal to some other dimension. Because that didn't work out so well the last time."

Simon grinned, an idea dawning. "Maybe we can find a spot slightly closer to home..."

As the sun dipped beneath the horizon, the clouds overhead blushed cotton-candy pink. Their reflections gleamed on the crystalline waters of Lake Lyn. The horses whinnied, the birds chirped, and Simon and Isabelle crunched their peanut brittle and popcorn. This, Simon thought, was the sound of happiness.

"You still haven't told me how you found this place," Isabelle said. "It's perfect."

Simon didn't want to admit that it was Jon Cartwright who'd told him about the isolated inlet on the edge of Lake Lyn, its hanging willows and rainbow of wildflowers making it the perfect spot for a romantic picnic. (Even when the picnic consisted of peanut brittle, popcorn, and the handful of other random teeth-decaying, artery-clogging snacks they'd grabbed on their way out of Alicante.) Simon, who had long ago grown tired of hearing about Jon's romantic exploits, had done his best to tune the jerk out. But apparently a few details had lodged in his subconscious. Enough, at least, to find the place.

Jon Cartwright was a blowhard and a buffoon—Simon would maintain this to his dying day.

But it turned out the guy had good taste in romantic date spots.

"Just stumbled on it," Simon mumbled. "Good luck, I guess."

Isabelle gazed out at the impossibly smooth water. "This place reminds me of Luke's farm," she said softly.

"Me too," he said. In that other life, the one he barely remembered, he and Clary had spent many long, happy days at Luke's summer house upstate, splashing in the lake, lying in the grass, naming the clouds.

Isabelle turned to him. Simon's jacket was spread out between them as an improvised picnic blanket. It was a small jacket—not very much distance for him to cross, if he wanted to reach her.

He'd never wanted anything more.

"I think about it a lot," Izzy said. "The farm, the lake."

"Why?"

Her voice softened. "Because that was where I almost lost you—where I was sure I would lose you. But I got you back."

Simon didn't know what to say.

"It doesn't even matter," she said, harder now. "Not like you even know what I'm talking about."

"I know what happened there." Namely, Simon had summoned the Angel Raziel—and the Angel had actually shown up.

He wished he could remember it; he would like to know how that felt, talking to an angel.

"Clary told you," she said flatly.

"Yeah." Isabelle was a little sensitive on the subject of Clary. She definitely didn't need to hear about all the time he'd had with Clary this summer, the long hours spent lying in Central Park, side by side, swapping stories of their past—Simon telling her what he remembered; Clary telling him what actually happened.

"But she wasn't even there," Isabelle said.

"She knows the important stuff."

Isabelle shook her head. She reached across the picnic blanket and rested a hand on Simon's knee. He worked very hard to hear her over the sudden buzzing in his ears. "If she wasn't there, she can't know how brave you were," Isabelle said. "She can't know how scared I was for you. *That's* the important stuff."

There was silence between them, then. But finally, it wasn't the awkward kind. It was the good kind, the kind where Simon could hear what Isabelle was saying without her having to say it, and where he could answer her in kind.

"What's it like?" she asked him. "Not remembering. Being a blank slate."

Her hand was still warm on his knee.

She'd never asked him that before. "It's not quite a blank slate," he explained, or tried to. "It's more like ... double vision. Like I'm remembering two different things at the same time. Sometimes one seems more real, sometimes the other does. Sometimes everything is blurry. That's when I usually take some Advil, and a nap."

"But you're starting to remember things."

"Some things," he allowed. "Jordan. I remember a lot about Jordan. Caring about him. Losing—" Simon swallowed hard. "Losing him. I remember my mom freaking out about me being a vampire. And some stuff before Clary's mom got kidnapped. The two of us being friends, before all of this started. Normal Brooklyn stuff." He stopped talking as he realized her face was clouding over.

"Of course you remember *Clary*."

"It's not like that," he said.

"Like what?"

Simon didn't think about it. He just did it.

He took her hand.

She let him.

He wasn't sure how to explain this—it was still all jumbled in his head—but he had to try. "It's not like the things I remember are more important than the things I can't remember. Sometimes it seems like it's random. But sometimes ... I don't know, sometimes it feels like the most important things are going to be the hardest to get back. Picture all these memories buried, like dinosaur bones, and me trying to dig them up. Some of them are just lying right beneath the surface, but the important ones, those are miles down."

"And you're saying that's where I am? Miles beneath the surface?"

He held on to her tightly. "You're basically down there at the molten center of the earth."

"You are *so weird*."

"I try my best."

She threaded her fingers through his. "I'm jealous, you know. Sometimes. That you can forget."

"Are you kidding?" Simon couldn't even begin to understand that one. "Everything you have, all the people in your life—no one would *want* that taken away."

Isabelle looked back out at the lake, blinking hard. "Sometimes people get taken away from you whether you want it or not. And sometimes that hurts so much, it might be easier to forget."

She didn't have to say his name. Simon said it for her. "Max."

"You remember him?"

Simon had never realized what a sad sound it was, hope.

He shook his head. "I wish I did, though."

"Clary told you about him," she said. Not a question. "And what happened to him."

He nodded, but her gaze was still fixed on the water.

"He died in Idris, you know. I like being here sometimes. I feel closer to him here. Other times I wish this place would evaporate. That no one could ever come here again."

"I'm sorry," Simon said, thinking they had to be the lamest, most useless words in the English language. "I wish I could say something that would help."

She faced him; she whispered, "You did."

"What?"

"After Max. You ... said something. You helped."

"Izzy..."

"Yes?"

This was it, this was The Moment—the moment talking gave way to gazing, which would inevitably give way to kissing. All he had to do was lean slightly forward and give himself over to it.

He leaned back. "Maybe we should start heading back to campus."

She made that angry cat noise again, then lobbed a chunk of peanut brittle at him. "What is *wrong* with you?" she exclaimed. "Because I know there's nothing wrong with me. You would be insane not to want to kiss me, and if this is some stupid playing-hard-to-get thing, you're wasting your time, because trust me, I know when a guy wants to kiss me. And you, Simon Lewis, want to kiss me. So what is happening here?"

"I don't know," he admitted, and ridiculous as this was, it was also wholly true.

"Is it the stupid memory thing? Are you seriously still afraid that you can't live up to some amazing forgotten version of yourself? Do you want me to tell you all the ways you weren't amazing? For one, you snored."

"Did not."

"Like a Drevak demon."

"This is slander," Simon said, outraged.

She snorted. "My point, Simon, is that you're supposed to be past all of this. I thought you figured out that no one is expecting you to be anyone other than who you are. That I just need you to be you. I only want you. This Simon. Isn't that why we're here? Because you finally got that through your thick head?"

"I guess."

"So what are you afraid of? It's obviously something."

"How do you know?" he asked, curious how she could be so certain, when he still had no clue himself.

She smiled, and it was the kind of smile you give to someone who can make you want to throttle them and kiss them all at the same time. "Because I know *you*."

He thought about gathering her up in his arms, about how it would feel—and that's when he realized what he was afraid of.

It was that feeling, the hugeness of it, like staring into the sun. Like *falling* into the sun.

"Losing myself," he said.

"What?"

"That's what I'm afraid of. Losing myself, in this. In you. I've spent this whole year trying to find myself, to figure out who I am, and now there's you, there's us, there's this all-consuming, terrifying black hole of a feeling, and if I give into it ... I feel like I'm standing on the edge of the Grand

Canyon, you know? Like, here's something bigger, deeper than the human mind is built to fathom. And I'm just supposed to ... jump in?"

He waited nervously for her reaction, suspecting that girls probably didn't like it much when you admitted you were afraid of them. Girls like Izzy probably didn't like it when you admitted you were afraid of anything. Nothing scared her; she deserved someone just as brave.

"Is that all?" Her face lit up. "Simon, don't you think I'm scared of that too? You're not the only one on that ledge. If we jump, we jump together. We fall *together*."

Simon had spent so long trying to gather together the pieces of himself, to fit the puzzle back together. But the final piece, the most important piece, had been right in front of him the whole time. Losing himself to Izzy—could it be that this was the only way to really find himself?

Could it be that this, here, was home?

Enough bad metaphors, he told himself. *Enough delaying. Enough being afraid.*

He stopped thinking about the person he used to be or the relationship they used to have; he stopped thinking about whether he was screwing things up or why he wanted to; he stopped thinking about demon amnesia and Shadowhunter Ascension and the Fair Folk and the Dark War and politics and homework and the unregulated traffic of deadly sharp objects.

He stopped thinking about what could happen, and what could go wrong.

He took her in his arms and kissed her—kissed her the way he'd been longing to kiss her since he first laid eyes on her, kissed her not like a romance novel hero or a Shadowhunter warrior or some imaginary character from the past, but like Simon Lewis kissing the girl he loved more than anything in the world. It *was* like falling into the sun, falling together, hearts blazing with pale fire, and Simon knew he would never stop falling, knew that now that he'd grabbed hold of her again, he would never let go.

The marriage of true minds admits no impediments—but the make-out sessions of teenagers all too often do. Especially when one of the teenagers was a student at Shadowhunter Academy, with both homework and a curfew. And when the other was a demon-fighting warrior with a stakeout in the morning.

If Simon had had his way, he would have spent the next week, or possibly the next eternity, entangled with Izzy on the grass, listening to the lake lap against the shore, losing himself in the touch of her fingers and the taste of her lips. Instead, he spent a memorable two hours doing so, then galloped at breakneck speed back to Shadowhunter Academy and spent another hour kissing her good-bye, before letting her leap into the Portal with a promise to return as soon as she could.

He had to wait until the next day to thank Helen Blackthorn for her help. He caught her just as she was packing up to leave.

"I see the date went well," she said as soon as she opened the door.

"How could you tell?"

Helen smiled. "You're practically radioactive."

Simon thanked her for relaying Izzy's message and handed her a small bag of cookies he'd cadged from the dining hall. They were the only thing at the Academy that actually tasted good. "Consider this a small down payment on what I owe you," he said.

"You don't owe me anything. But if you really want to pay me back, come to the wedding—you can be Izzy's plus one."

"I wouldn't miss it," Simon promised. "So when's the big day?"

"First of October," she said, but there was a quavering note in her voice. "Probably."

"Maybe sooner?"

"Maybe not at all," she admitted.

"What? You and Aline aren't breaking up!" Simon caught himself, remembering that he was talking to someone he barely knew. He couldn't exactly command her to have a happy ending just because he'd suddenly fallen in love with love. "I'm sorry, it's none of my business, but ... why would you come all this way and take all their crap if you didn't want to marry her?"

"Oh, I want to marry her. More than anything. It's just, being back here has made me wonder if I'm being selfish."

"How could marrying Aline be selfish?" Simon asked.

"Look at my life!" Helen exploded, the day's—or maybe the year's—worth of pent-up fury blasting out of her. "They look at me like I'm some kind of freak show—and those are the kind ones, the ones who don't look at me like I'm the enemy. Aline is already stuck on that godforsaken island because of me. Is she supposed to suffer like that for the rest of her life? Just because she made the mistake of falling in love with me? What kind of person does that make me?"

"You can't possibly think any of this is *your* fault." He didn't know her very well, but none of this sounded right to him. Not like something she would say or believe.

"Professor Mayhew told me that if I really loved her,

I would leave her," Helen admitted. "Instead of dragging her into this nightmare with me. That holding on to her is just proof I'm more faerie than I think."

"Professor Mayhew is a troll," Simon said, and wondered what it would take to get Catarina Loss to turn him into one for real. Or maybe a toad or a lizard. Something that would more befit the reptilian nature of his soul. "If you really loved Aline, you would do everything you can to hold on to her. Which is exactly what you're doing. Besides, you're assuming that if you tried to break up with her for her own good, she'd let you. From what I've heard about Aline, that's not likely."

"No," Helen said fondly. "She'd fight me tooth and nail."

"Then why not fast-forward to the inevitable? Accept that you're stuck with her. The love of your life. Poor you."

Helen sighed. "Isabelle told me what you said about the fey, Simon. About how you think it's wrong to discriminate against them. That faeries can be good, just as much as anyone else."

He didn't understand where she was going with this, but he wasn't sorry to have the chance to confirm it. "She was right, I do think that."

"Isabelle believes that too, you know," Helen said. "She's been doing her best to convince me."

"What do you mean?" Simon asked, confused. "Why would *you* need convincing?"

Helen kneaded her fingers together. "You know, I didn't want to come here to tell a bunch of kids the story of my mother and father—I didn't do that voluntarily. But I also didn't make it up. That's what happened. That's who my mother was, and that's what half of me is."

"No, Helen, that's not—"

"Do you know the poem 'La Belle Dame Sans Merci'?"

Simon shook his head. The only poetry he knew was by Dr. Seuss or Bob Dylan.

"It's Keats," she said, and recited a few stanzas for him by memory.

She took me to her elfin grot,
And there she wept, and sigh'd fill sore,
And there I shut her wild wild eyes
With kisses four.

And there she lullèd me asleep,
And there I dream'd—Ah! woe betide!
The latest dream I ever dream'd
On the cold hill's side.

I saw pale kings and princes too,
Pale warriors, death-pale were they all;
They cried—"La Belle Dame sans Merci
Hath thee in thrall!"

"Keats wrote about *faeries?*" Simon asked. If they'd covered this in English class, he might have paid closer attention.

"My father used to recite that poem all the time," Helen said. "It was his way of telling me and Mark the story of where we came from."

"He recited you a poem about an evil faerie queen luring men to their deaths as a way of telling you about your mother? Repeatedly?" Simon asked, incredulous. "No offense, but that's kind of … harsh."

"My father loved us despite where we came from," Helen said in the way of someone trying to convince herself. "But it always felt like he kept some part of himself in reserve. Like he was waiting to see her in me. It was different with Mark, because Mark was a boy. But girls take after their mothers, right?"

"I'm not really sure that's scientifically accurate logic," Simon said.

"That's what Mark said. He always told me the faeries had no claim on us or our nature. And I tried to believe him, but then, after he was taken … after the Inquisitor told me the story of my birth mother … I wonder…" Helen was looking past Simon, past the walls of her domestic prison cell, lost in her own fears. "What if I'm luring Aline to that cold hill's side? What if that need to destroy, to use love as a weapon, is just hibernating in me somewhere, and I don't even know it? A gift from my mother."

"Look, I don't know anything about faeries," Simon said. "Not really. I don't know what the deal was with your mother, or what it means for you to be half one thing and half another. But I know your blood doesn't define you. What defines you is the choices you make. If I've learned anything this year, it's that. And I also know that loving someone—even when it's scary, even when there are consequences—is never the wrong thing to do. Loving someone is the opposite of hurting her."

Helen smiled at him, her eyes brimming with unshed tears. "For both our sakes, Simon, I really hope that you're right."

* * *

In the Land under the Hill, in the Time Before...

Once upon a time, there was a beautiful lady of the Seelie Court who lost her heart to the son of an angel.

Once upon a time, there were two boys come to the land of Faerie, brothers noble and bold. One brother caught a glimpse of the fair lady and, thunderstruck by her beauty, pledged himself to her. Pledged himself to stay. This was the boy Andrew. His brother, the boy Arthur, would not leave his side.

And so the boys stayed beneath the hill, and Andrew loved the lady, and Arthur despised her.

And so the lady kept her boy close to her side, kept this beautiful creature who swore his fealty to her, and when her sister lay claim to the other, the lady let him be taken away, for he was nothing.

She gave Andrew a silver chain to wear around his neck, a token of her love, and she taught him the ways of the Fair Folk. She danced with him in revels beneath starry skies. She fed him moonshine and showed him how to give way to the wild.

Some nights they heard Arthur's screams, and she told him it was an animal in pain, and pain was in an animal's nature.

She did not lie, for she could not lie.

Humans are animals.

Pain is their nature.

For seven years they lived in joy. She owned his heart, and he hers, and somewhere, beyond, Arthur screamed and screamed. Andrew didn't know; the lady didn't care; and so they were happy.

Until the day one brother discovered the truth of the other.

The lady thought her lover would go mad with the grief of it and the guilt. And so, because she loved the boy, she wove him a story of deceitful truths, the story he would want to believe. That he had been ensorcelled to love her; that he had never betrayed his brother; that he was only a slave; that these seven years of love had been a lie.

The lady set the useless brother free and allowed him to believe he had freed himself.

The lady subjected herself to the useless brother's attack and allowed him to believe he had killed her.

The lady let her lover renounce her and run away.

And the lady beheld the secret fruits of their union and kissed them and tried to love them. But they were only a piece of her boy. She wanted all of him or none of him.

As she had given him his story, she gave him his children.

She had nothing left to live for, then, and so lived no longer.

This is the story she left behind, the story her lover will never know; this is the story her daughter will never know.

This is how a faerie loves: with her whole body and soul. This is how a faerie loves: with destruction.

I love you, she told him, night after night, for seven years. Faeries cannot lie, and he knew that.

I love you, he told her, night after night, for seven years. Humans can lie, and so she let him believe he lied to her, and she let his brother and his children believe it, and she died hoping they would believe it forever.

This is how a faerie loves: with a gift.

Bitter of Tongue

By Cassandra Clare and Sarah Rees Brennan

There were more horses joining the roan, more and more of the Wild Hunt. Simon saw Kieran, a white silent presence. The faerie on the roan turned his horse toward the place where Simon and Isabelle stood, and Simon saw the roan sniff the air like a dog.

—Bitter of Tongue

WHY DO I SPY SHADOWHUNTERS, THEN, IN OUR LAND AND ANSWERABLE TO US?
SHOULD I ASK THEM WHAT THEY ARE ABOUT?
I SEE NOTHING.
AND NOTHING SHOULD GO— NOW.

The sun was shining, the birds were singing, and it was a beautiful day at Shadowhunter Academy.

Well, Simon was pretty sure the sun was shining. There was a faint luminescence to the air in his and George's underground chamber, casting a pleasant glow upon the green slime that coated their walls.

And all right, he could not hear the birds from his subterranean room, but George did come back from the showers singing.

"Good morning, Si! I saw a rat in the bathroom, but he was taking a nice nap and we didn't bother each other."

"Or the rat was dead of a very infectious disease, which has now been introduced to our water system," Simon suggested. "We may be drinking plague-rat water for weeks."

"Nobody likes a Gloomy Gus," George scolded him.

"Nobody likes a Sullen Si. Nobody is here for a Moody Mildred. No one fancies—"

"I have gathered the general tenor of your discourse, George," said Simon. "I object strongly to being referred to as a Moody Mildred. Especially as I really feel like I'm a Mildly Good-Humored Mildred right now. I see you're looking forward to your big day?"

"Have a shower, Si," George urged. "Start the day refreshed. Maybe style your hair a little. It wouldn't kill you."

Simon shook his head. "There's a dead rat in the bathroom, George. I am not going in the bathroom, George."

"He's not dead," George said. "He's just sleeping. I'm certain of it."

"Senseless optimism is how plagues get started," Simon said. "Ask the medieval peasants of Europe. Oh, wait, you can't."

"Were they a jolly bunch?" George asked skeptically.

"I'm sure they were much jollier before all the plague," said Simon.

He felt he was making really good points, and that he was backed up by history. He pulled off the shirt he'd slept in, which read LET'S FIGHT! and below in tiny letters OUR ENEMY OFF WITH CUNNING ARGUMENTS. George whipped Simon's back with his wet towel, which made Simon yelp.

Simon grinned as he pulled his gear out of their wardrobe. They were getting started right after breakfast, so he might as well change into gear straight off. Plus, every day wearing gear made for men was a victory.

He and George went up to breakfast in good humor with all the world.

"You know, this porridge isn't at all bad," Simon said, digging in. George nodded enthusiastically, his mouth full.

Beatriz looked sad for them, and possibly sad that boys were so stupid in general. "This isn't porridge," she told them. "These are scrambled eggs."

"Oh no," George whispered faintly, his mouth still full, his voice terribly sad. "Oh no."

Simon dropped his spoon and stared into the depths of his bowl with horror.

"If they are scrambled eggs...?" he asked. "And I'm not arguing with you, Beatriz, I'm just asking what I feel is a very reasonable question ... if they are scrambled eggs, why are they gray?"

Beatriz shrugged and continued eating, carefully avoiding the lumps. "Who can say?"

That could be made into a sad song, Simon supposed. *If they are eggs, why are they gray? Who can say, who can say?* He found himself still thinking of song lyrics sometimes, even though he was out of the band.

Admittedly, "Why Are the Eggs So Gray?" might not be a big hit, even on the hipster circuit.

Julie plopped her bowl down on the table beside Beatriz.

"The eggs are gray," she announced. "I don't know how they do this. Surely at this point, it would actually make sense for them not to mess up the food sometimes. Every time, every day, for over a year? Is the Academy cursed?"

"I have been thinking it might be," George said earnestly. "I hear an eldritch rattling sometimes, like ghosts shaking their terrible chains. Honestly, I was hoping the Academy *was* cursed, since otherwise it's probably creatures in the pipes." George shuddered. "Creatures."

Julie sat down. George and Simon exchanged a private pleased look. They had been keeping track of how often Julie chose to sit with the three of them, rather than with Jon

Cartwright. Currently they were winning, sixty percent to forty.

Julie choosing to sit with them seemed like a good sign, since this was George's big day.

Now that they were Shadowhunter trainees in their second year, and in the words of Scarsbury "no longer totally hopeless and liable to cut off your own stupid heads," they were given their own slightly more important missions. Every mission had an appointed team leader, and the team leader got double points if the mission was a success. Julie, Beatriz, Simon, and Jon had already been team leaders, and they had killed it: everyone's mission accomplished, demons slain, people saved, Downworlders breaking the Law penalized severely but fairly. In some ways it was a pity that Jon's mission had gone so well, as he had bragged about it for weeks, but they couldn't help it. They were just too good, Simon thought, even as he slapped the wooden table so as not to jinx himself. There was no way for them to fail.

"Feeling nervous, team leader?" asked Julie. Simon had to admit she could sometimes be an unsettling companion.

"No," said George, and under Julie's gimlet eye: "Maybe. Yes. You know, an appropriate amount of nervous, but in a cool, collected, and good-under-pressure way."

"Don't go all to pieces," said Julie. "I want a perfect score."

An awkward silence followed. Simon comforted himself by looking over at Jon's table. When Julie abandoned him, Jon had to eat all alone. Unless Marisol decided she wanted to sit with him and torment him. Which, Simon noted, she was doing today. Little devil. Marisol was hilarious.

Jon made urgent gestures for help, but Julie had her back turned to him and did not see.

"I'm not saying this to scare you, George," she said. "That's a side benefit, obviously. This is an important mission. You know faeries are the worst kind of Downworlder. Faeries crossing over into the mundane realm and tricking the poor things into eating faerie fruit is no joke. Mundanes can wither away and die after eating that fruit, you know. It's murder, and it's murder we can hardly ever get them for, because by the time the mundanes die, the faeries are long gone. You're taking this seriously, right?"

"Yes, Julie," said George. "I actually do know murder is bad, Julie."

Julie's whole face pursed up in that alarming way it did sometimes. "Remember it was you who almost screwed up my mission."

"I hesitated slightly to tackle that vampire child," George admitted.

"Precisely," said Julie. "No more hesitation. As our team leader, you have to act on your own initiative. I'm not saying you're bad, George. I am saying you need to learn."

"I'm not sure anybody needs this kind of motivational speech," Beatriz said. "It would freak anyone out. And it's too easy to freak George out as it is."

George, who had been looking touched at Beatriz's gallant defense, stopped looking touched.

"I just think they should do a repeat team leader occasionally," Julie grumbled, letting them know where all this hostility was coming from. She stabbed her gray eggs wistfully. "I was so good."

Simon raised his eyebrows. "You had a horsewhip and threatened to beat me about the head and face if I didn't do what you said."

Julie pointed her spoon at him. "Exactly. And you did

what I said. That's leadership, that is. What's more, I *didn't* beat you about the head and face. Kind but firm, that's me."

Julie discussed her own greatness at some length. Simon got up to get another glass of juice.

"What kind of juice do you think this is?" Catarina Loss asked, joining him in the line.

"Fruit," said Simon. "Just fruit. That's all they would tell me. I found it suspicious as well."

"I like fruit," Catarina said, but she did not sound sure about that. "I know you're excused from my class this afternoon. What are you up to this morning?"

"A mission to stop faeries from slipping over their borders and engaging in illicit trade," Simon said. "George is team leader."

"George is team leader?" Catarina asked. "Hm."

"Why is everyone so down on George today?" Simon demanded. "What's wrong with George? There's nothing wrong with George. It is not possible to find fault with George. He's a perfect Scottish angel. He always shares the snacks that his mother sends him, and he's better-looking than Jace. There, I said it. I'm not taking it back."

"I see you're in a good mood," said Catarina. "All right then. Go on, have a good time. Take care of my favorite student."

"Right," said Simon. "Wait, who's that?"

Catarina gestured him away from her with her indeterminate juice. "Get lost, Daylighter."

Everyone else was excited to go on another mission. Simon was looking forward to it as well, and pleased for George's sake. But Simon was mostly excited because after the mission, he had somewhere else to be.

* * *

The Fair Folk had been seen last on a moor in Devon. Simon was a bit excited to Portal there and hoped there would be time to see red postboxes and drink lager at an English pub.

Instead, the moor turned out to be a huge stretch of uneven field, rocks, and hills in the distance, no red postboxes or quaint pubs in sight. They were immediately given horses by the contact with the Sight who was waiting for them.

Lots of fields, lots of horses. Simon was not sure why they had bothered to leave the Academy, because this was an identical experience.

The first words George said as they were riding on the moor were: "I think it would be a good idea to split up."

"Like in ... a horror movie?" Simon asked.

Julie, Beatriz, and Jon gave him looks of irritated incomprehension. Marisol's uncertain expression suggested she agreed with Simon, but she did not speak up and Simon didn't want to be the one mutinying against his friend's leadership. They would cover more moor if they split up. Maybe it was a great idea. More moor! How could it go wrong?

"I'll be partners with Jon," Marisol said instantly, a glint in her dark eyes. "I wish to continue our conversation from breakfast. I have many more things to say to him on the subject of video games."

"I don't want to hear any more about video games, Marisol!" snapped Jon, a Shadowhunter in a nightmare of torrential mundane information.

Marisol smiled. "I know."

Marisol had only just turned fifteen. Simon was not sure how she had worked out that telling Jon every detail about the mundane world would be such effective psychological terrorism. Her evil had only grown in the year and change Simon had known her. Simon had to respect that.

"And Si and I will be together," George said easily.

"Um," said Simon.

Neither he nor George was a Shadowhunter yet, and though Catarina helped them see through glamours, no mundane ... er, non-Shadowhunter ... was as securely protected from faerie glamour as one of the Nephilim. But Simon didn't want to question George's authority or suggest he didn't want to be partners. He was also scared of being partnered with Julie, and beaten about the head and face.

"Great," Simon finished weakly. "Maybe we can split up but also stay ... within hearing range of each other?"

"You want to split up but stay together?" Jon asked. "Do you not know what words mean?"

"Do you know what the words 'World of Warcraft' mean?" asked Marisol menacingly.

"Yes, I do," said Jon. "All put together in that way, no, I do not, and I do not wish to."

He urged his horse onward across the moor. Marisol followed in pursuit. Simon stared at the back of Jon's head and worried he would go too far.

Except that they were meant to be splitting up. This was all right.

George gazed around at the remaining members of the team and appeared to come to a decision. "We'll stay within hearing range of each other, and comb over the moors, and see if we can see the Fair Folk in any of the places they were reported lurking. Are you with me, team?"

"I'm with you to the end, if it doesn't take too long! You know I'm going to Helen Blackthorn and Aline Penhallow's wedding," said Simon.

"Ugh, hate weddings," said George sympathetically.

"You have to wear a monkey suit and go sit around for ages while everybody secretly hates each other over some fight about the flower arrangements. Plus, bagpipes. I mean, I don't know how Shadowhunter weddings go. Are there flowers? Are there bagpipes?"

"Can't talk right now," said Beatriz. "Picturing Jace Herondale in a tuxedo. In my head, he looks like a beautiful spy."

"James Bond," George contributed. "James Blond? I still don't like monkey suits. But it doesn't seem like you mind, Si."

Simon lifted a hand from the reins to point proudly to himself, a maneuver that would've had him falling off his horse a year ago. "This monkey is going as Isabelle Lightwood's date."

Just saying the words suffused Simon with a sense of well-being. In such a wonderful world, how could anything go wrong?

He looked around at his team: the whole lot of them, wearing long-sleeved gear against the autumn chill, figures in black with bows strapped to their backs and their breath white plumes in the cold air, riding fast horses through the moors on a mission to protect humankind. His three friends by his side, and Jon and Marisol in the distance. George, so proud to be team leader. Marisol, scornful city kid, riding her horse with easy grace. Even Beatriz and Julie, even Jon, born Shadowhunters all, looked a little different to Simon, now that they were well into their second year at the Academy. Scarsbury had honed them, Catarina had lectured them, and even their fellow Academy students had changed them. Now the born Shadowhunters rode with mundanes and performed missions with them as a unit, and the so-called dregs could keep up.

The moor was rolling fields, tree line to their left all quivering leaves as if the trees were dancing in the slight breeze. The sunlight was pale and clear, shining on their heads and their black clothes alike. Simon found himself thinking, with affection and pride, that they looked like they might make real Shadowhunters after all.

He noticed that by silent mutual agreement, Beatriz and Julie were coaxing their mounts on faster. Simon squinted up into the distance, where he could just about still make out Jon and Marisol, and then squinted at Beatriz's and Julie's backs. He felt again that pang of uneasiness.

"Why are they all racing ahead?" Simon asked. "Um, not to tell you your job, but, brave team leader, maybe command them not to go too far."

"Ah, give them a minute," George said. "You know she kind of likes you."

"What?" said Simon.

"Not that she's going to do anything about it," said George. "Nobody who likes you is going to do anything about it. On account of, nobody would enjoy having Isabelle Lightwood cut their head off."

"Likes me?" Simon echoed. "Something about the way you're talking suggests multiple people. Who like *me*."

George shrugged. "Apparently you're the type who grows on people. Don't ask me. I thought girls liked abs."

"I could have abs," Simon told him. "I watched in the mirror once and I think I found an ab. I'm telling you, all this training is doing my body good."

It wasn't like Simon thought he was a hideous creature or anything. He'd now seen several demons who had tentacles coming out of their eyes, and he was fairly sure it did not revolt people merely to look upon him.

But he wasn't Jace, who made girls' heads spin around as if they were possessed. It made no sense that out of all the students in the Academy, Beatriz might like *him*.

George rolled his eyes. George did not truly understand the slow development of actual physical fitness. He'd probably been born with abs. Some were born with abs, some achieved abs, and some—like Simon—had abs thrust upon them by cruel instructors.

"Yes, Si, you're a real killer."

"Feel this arm," said Simon. "Rock hard! I don't mean to brag, but it's all bone. All bone."

"Si," said George. "I don't need to feel it. I believe in you, because that's what bros do. And I'm happy for your mysterious popularity with the ladies, because that's how bros are. But seriously, watch out for Jon, because I think he's going to shank you one of these days. He does not get your indefinable but undeniable allure. He's got abs to the chin and he thought he had the ladies of the Academy locked down."

Simon rode on, somewhat dazed.

He'd been thinking that Isabelle's affection for him was a stunning and inexplicable occurrence, like a lightning strike. (Gorgeous and courageous lightning whom he was lucky to be struck by!) Given current evidence, however, he was starting to believe it was time to reevaluate.

He had been reliably informed that he'd dated Maia, the leader of the New York werewolf pack, though he'd received the impression that he had well and truly messed that one up. He'd heard rumors about a vampire queen who might have been interested. He'd even gathered, strange as it seemed, that there was a brief period of time when he and Clary had gone out. And now possibly Beatriz liked him.

"Seriously, George, tell me the truth," said Simon. "Am I beautiful?"

George burst out laughing, his horse wheeling back a few easy paces in the sunlight.

And Julie shouted: "Faerie!" and pointed. Simon looked toward a hooded and cloaked figure with a basket of fruit over one arm, emerging as if innocently from the mist behind a tree.

"After it!" roared George, and his horse charged for the figure, Simon plunging after him.

Marisol, far ahead, shouted: "Trap!" and then gave a scream of pain.

Simon looked desperately toward the trees. The faerie, he saw, had reinforcements. They had been warned the Fair Folk were all more wary and desperate in the aftermath of the Cold Peace. They should have listened better and thought harder. They should have planned for this.

Simon, George, Julie, and Beatriz were all riding hard, but they were too far from her. Marisol was swaying in her saddle, blood pouring down her arm: elfshot.

"Marisol!" Jon Cartwright shouted. "*Marisol*, to me!"

She pulled the horse toward his. Jon stood on his horse and leaped onto hers, bow already in hand and firing arrows into the trees, standing on the horse's back and thus shielding Marisol like a strange bow-shooting acrobat. Simon knew he'd never be able to do anything like that, ever, unless he Ascended.

Julie and Beatriz turned their horses toward the trees where the concealed faeries were firing.

"They have Marisol," George panted. "We can still get the fruit seller."

"No, George," Simon began, but George had already

wheeled his horse toward the hooded figure, now disappearing behind the tree and the mist.

There was a spear of sunlight shooting between the trunk and the branch of the tree, a dazzling white line between the crooked arc of tree limbs. It seemed to refract in Simon's eyes, becoming broad and fair, like the path of moonlight on the sea. The hooded figure was slipping away, half-disappeared into the dazzle, and George's horse was inches from danger, George's hand reaching for the edge of the figure's cloak, George heedless of the course he had placed himself upon.

"*No, George!*" Simon shouted. "We are not going to trespass into Faerie!"

He forced his own horse into George's path, making George pull up, but he was so hell-bent on stopping George that he did not take into consideration his mount, now terrified and fleeing and urged to speed.

Until the white dazzling light filled Simon's vision. He remembered suddenly the feeling of falling away into Faerie, soaked to the skin, in a pool filled with water: remembered Jace being kind to him, and how much he had resented that, how he'd thought: *Don't show me up any further*, and his chest had burned with resentment.

Now he was tumbling into Faerie with the scream of a terrified horse in his ears, leaves blinding him and twigs scraping at his face and his arms. He tried to shield his eyes and found himself thrown on rock and bones, with darkness rushing at him. He would have been very grateful if Jace had been there.

Simon woke in Faerieland. His whole skull was throbbing, in the way your thumb did when you hit it with a hammer.

He hoped nobody had hit his head with a hammer.

He woke in a gently swaying bed, slightly prickly under his cheek. He opened his eyes and saw that he was not exactly in a bed, but lying amid twigs and moss, scattered across a swaying surface constructed of wooden laths. There were strange stripes of darkness in front of his vision, obscuring his view of the vista beyond.

Faerieland almost looked like the moors in Devon, yet it was entirely different. The mists in the distance were faintly purple, like storm clouds clinging to the earth, and there was movement in the cloud suggesting odd and menacing shapes. The leaves on the trees were green and yellow and red like the trees of the mundane world, but they shone too brightly, like jewels, and when the wind rustled through them Simon could almost make out words, as if they were whispering together. This was nature run riot, alchemized into magic and strangeness.

And Simon was, he realized, in a cage. A big wooden cage. The stripes of darkness across his vision were his cage bars.

The thing that outraged him most was how familiar it felt. He remembered being trapped like this before. *More than once.*

"Shadowhunters, vampires, and now faeries, all longing to throw me in prison," Simon said aloud. "Why exactly was I so anxious to get back all these memories? Why is it always me? Why am I always the chump in the cage?"

His own voice made his aching head hurt.

"You are in my cage now," said a voice.

Simon sat up hastily, though it made his head throb fiercely and all of Faerieland reel drunkenly around him. He saw, on the other side of his cage, the hooded and cloaked figure whom George had tried so desperately to capture on the moors. Simon swallowed. He could not see the face beneath the hood.

There was a whirl in the air, like a shadow whipping over the sun. A new faerie dropped out of the clear blue sky, the leaves of the forest floor crunching under his bare feet. Sunlight washed his fair hair into radiance, and a long knife glittered in his hand.

The hooded and cloaked faerie dropped his hood and bowed his head in sudden deference. Unhooded, Simon saw, he had large ears, tinted purple, as if he had an eggplant stuck to each side of his face, and wisps of long white hair that curled over his eggplant ear like cloud.

"What has happened, and why are your tricks interfering with the work of your betters, Hefeydd? A horse from the mundane world ran into the path of the Wild Hunt," the new faerie said. "I do hope the steed was not of immense emotional significance, because the hounds have it now."

Simon's heart bled for that poor horse. He wondered if he, too, was about to be fed to the hounds.

"I am so sorry to have disturbed the Wild Hunt," the cloaked faerie said, bowing his white head even further.

"You should be," answered the faerie of the Wild Hunt. "Those who cross the path of the Hunt always regret it."

"This is a Shadowhunter," continued the other anxiously. "Or at least one of the children they hope to change. They were lying in wait for me in the mortal world, and this one pursued me even into Faerie, so he is my rightful prey. I had no wish to disturb the Wild Hunt and bear no fault!"

Simon felt this was an inaccurate and hurtful summary of the situation.

"Is it so? Come now, I am in a merry mood," said the

Wild Hunt faerie. "Give me your regrets and words with your captive—as you know, I have some little interest in Shadowhunters—and I will not bring back my lord Gwyn your tongue."

"Never was a fairer bargain made," said the cloaked faerie in some haste, and ran off as though afraid the Wild Hunt faerie might change his mind, almost tripping over his own cloak.

As far as Simon was concerned, this was out of the faerie frying pan and into the faerie fire.

The new faerie looked like a boy of sixteen, not much older than Marisol and younger than Simon, but Simon knew that how faeries looked was no indicator of their age. He had mismatched eyes, one amber as the beads found in the dark heart of trees, and one the vivid blue-green of sea shallows when sunlight strikes through. The jarring contrast of his eyes and the light of Faerie, filtered green through wickedly whispering leaves and touched with false gold, made his thin, dirt-streaked face wear a sinister aspect.

He looked like a threat. And he was coming closer.

"What does a faerie of the Wild Hunt want with me?" Simon croaked.

"I am no faerie," said the boy with eerie eyes, pointed ears, and leaves in his wild hair. "I am Mark Blackthorn of the Los Angeles Institute. It doesn't matter what they say or what they do to me. I still remember who I am. I am Mark Blackthorn."

He looked at Simon with wild hunger in his thin face. His thin fingers clutched the bars of the cage.

"Are you here to save me?" he demanded. "Have the Shadowhunters come for me at last?"

* * *

Oh no. This was Helen Blackthorn's brother, the one who was half-faerie like her, the one who had believed his family dead and been taken by the Wild Hunt and never returned. This was very awkward.

This was worse than that. This was horrific.

"No," said Simon, because hope seemed the cruelest blow he could deal Mark Blackthorn. "It's just like the other faerie said. I wandered here by accident and I was captured. I'm Simon Lewis. I … know your name, and I know what happened to you. I'm sorry."

"Do you know when the Shadowhunters are coming for me?" Mark asked with heartbreaking eagerness. "I—sent them a message, during the war. I understand the Cold Peace must make all dealings with faerie difficult, but they must know I am loyal and would be valuable to them. They must be coming, but it has been … it has been weeks and weeks. Tell me, when?"

Simon stared at Mark, dry-mouthed. It had not been weeks and weeks since the Shadowhunters had abandoned him here. It had been a year and more.

"They're not coming," he whispered. "I was not there, but my friends were. They told me what happened. The Clave took a vote. The Shadowhunters do not want you back."

"Oh," said Mark, a single soft sound that was familiar to Simon: It was the kind of sound creatures made when they died.

He turned away from Simon, his back arched in a spasm of pain that looked physical. Simon saw, on his bare lean arms, the old marks of a whip. Even though Simon could not see his face, Mark covered it for a moment, as if he could not even bear to look upon Faerieland.

Then he turned and snapped: "What about the children?"

"What?" Simon asked blankly.

"Helen, Julian, Livia, Tiberius, Drusilla, Octavian. And Emma," said Mark. "You see? I have not forgotten. Every night, no matter what has happened during the day, no matter if I am torn and bloodied or so bone-tired I wish I were dead, I look up at the stars and I give each star a brother's name or a sister's face. I will not sleep until I remember every one. The stars will burn out before I forget."

Mark's family, the Blackthorns. They were all younger than Mark but Helen; Simon knew that. And Emma Carstairs lived with the younger Blackthorn kids in the Los Angeles Institute, the little girl with blond hair who had been orphaned in the war and who wrote to Clary a lot.

Simon wished he knew more about them. Clary had talked about Emma. Magnus had spoken passionately this summer, several times, about the Cold Peace and had given the Blackthorns as an example of the horrors that the Clave's decision to punish faeries had visited on those of faerie blood. Simon had listened to Magnus and felt sorry for the Blackthorns, but they had seemed like just another tragedy of the war: something terrible but distant, and ultimately easy to forget. Simon had felt he had so much to remember himself. He had wanted to go to the Academy and become a Shadowhunter, to learn more about his own life and remember everything he had lost, to become someone stronger and better.

Except that you did not become someone stronger and better by only thinking about yourself.

He did not know what they were doing to Mark in Faerie, to make his family slip away from him.

"Helen's well," he said awkwardly. "I saw her recently. She came and lectured at the Academy. I'm sorry. I had a demon take—a lot of memories from me, not so long ago. I know what it's like, not to remember."

"Fortunate are the ones who know the name of their heart. They are the ones whose hearts are never truly lost. They can always call their heart back home," Mark said, his voice almost a chant. "Do you remember the name of your heart, Simon Lewis?"

"I think so," Simon whispered.

"How are they?" Mark asked in a low, worn voice. He sounded very tired.

"Helen's getting married," Simon offered. It was the only good thing, he felt, that he had to offer Mark. "To Aline Penhallow. I think—they really love each other."

He almost said he was going to their wedding, but even that felt cruel. Mark could not go to his own sister's wedding. He had not been invited. He had not even been told.

Mark did not seem angry or hurt. He smiled, softly as a child being told a bedtime story, and leaned his face against the bars of Simon's cage.

"Sweet Helen," he said. "My father used to tell stories about Helen of Troy. She was born out of an egg, and the most beautiful woman in the world. Being born out of an egg is very unusual for humans."

"I've heard that," said Simon.

"She was very unhappy in love," Mark continued. "Beauty can be like that. Beauty cannot be trusted. Beauty can slip through your fingers like water and burn on your tongue like poison. Beauty can be the shining wall that keeps you from all you love."

"Um," said Simon. "Totally."

"I am glad that my beautiful Helen will be happier than the last beautiful Helen," said Mark. "I am glad she will be given beauty for beauty, love for love, and no false coin. Tell her that her brother Mark sends her felicitations on her wedding day."

"If I make it there, I will."

"Aline will be able to help her with the children, too," Mark said.

He was paying very little attention to Simon, his face still wearing that fixed and faraway expression, as if he were listening to a story or recalling a memory. Simon feared that stories and memory were becoming much the same to Mark Blackthorn: longed-for, beautiful, and unreal.

"Ty needs special attention," Mark went on. "I remember my parents talking about it." His mouth twisted. "I mean my father and the woman who sang me to sleep every night though I was not of her blood, the Shadowhunter I am no longer allowed to call my mother. Songs are not blood. Blood is all that matters to Shadowhunters and faeries alike. The songs matter only to me."

Blood is all that matters to Shadowhunters.

Simon could not remember the context, but he could remember the constant refrain, from people he loved now but had not loved then. *Mundane, mundane, mundane.* And later, *vampire. Downworlder.*

He remembered that the first prison he had ever been inside was a Shadowhunter prison.

He wished he could tell Mark Blackthorn that anything he said was wrong.

"I'm so sorry," he said.

He was sorry for not listening, and sorry for not caring more. He'd thought he was the voice of reason in the

Academy, and had not realized how complacent he'd grown, how easy it was to hear his friends sneer at people who were—after all—not like him anymore, and let them get away with it.

He wished he knew how to say any of this to Mark Blackthorn, but he doubted Mark would care.

"If you are sorry, speak," said Mark. "How is Ty? There is nothing wrong with Ty, but he is different, and the Clave hates all that is different. They will try to punish him, for being who he is. They would punish a star for burning. My father was there to stand between him and our cruel world, but my father is gone and I am gone too. I might as well be dead, for all the good I am to my brothers and sisters. Livvy would walk over hot coals and hissing serpents for Ty, but she is as young as he is. She cannot do and be everything to him. Is Helen having difficulties with Tiberius? Is Tiberius happy?"

"I don't know," Simon said helplessly. "I think so."

All he knew was that there were a bunch of Blackthorn kids: faceless, nameless victims of the war.

"And there's Tavvy," said Mark.

His voice grew stronger as he kept talking, and he used nicknames for his brothers and sisters rather than the full names he had worked so laboriously to remember. Simon supposed Mark was not usually allowed even to speak of his mortal life or his Nephilim family. He didn't want to think about what the Wild Hunt might do to Mark, if he tried.

"He is so little," said Mark. "He won't remember Dad, or M—or his mother. He's the littlest thing. They let me hold him, the day he was born, and his head fit into the palm of my hand. I can still feel its weight there, even when I cannot grasp his name. I held him and I knew I had to support his head: that he was mine to support and protect. Forever. Oh, but forever lasts such a short time in the mortal world. He will not remember me either. Maybe Drusilla will forget as well." Mark shook his head. "I do not think so, though. Dru learns everything by heart, and she has the sweetest heart of us all. I hope her memories of me stay sweet."

Clary must have told Simon every one of the Blackthorns' names, and talked a little bit about how each of them was doing. She must have let fall some scrap of information, which Simon had discarded as useless and which would be better than treasure to Mark.

Simon stared at him helplessly.

"Just tell me if Aline is helping with the younger ones," said Mark, his voice growing sharper. "Helen cannot do it all by herself, and Julian will not be able to help her!" His voice softened again. "Julian," he said. "Jules. My artist, my dreamer. Hold him up to the light and he would shine a dozen different colors. All he cares about is his art and his Emma. He will try to help Helen, of course, but he is still so young. They are so young and so easily lost. I know what I am saying, Shadowhunter. In the land under the hill we prey on the tender and new-hearted. And they never grow old, with us. They never have the chance."

"Oh, Mark Blackthorn, what are they doing to you?" Simon whispered.

He could not keep the pity out of his voice, and he saw it sting Mark: the slow flush that rose to his thin cheeks, and the way he lifted his chin, holding his head high.

Mark said: "Nothing I cannot bear."

Simon was silent. He did not remember everything, but he remembered how much he had been changed. People could bear so much, but Simon did not know how much of the original you was left when the world had twisted you into a whole different shape.

"I remember you," Mark said suddenly. "We met when you were on your way to Hell. You were not human then."

"No," said Simon awkwardly. "I don't remember much about it."

"There was a boy with you," Mark continued. "Hair like a halo and eyes like hellfire, a Nephilim among Nephilim. I'd heard stories about him. I—admired him. He pressed a witchlight into my hand, and it meant—it meant a lot to me. Then."

Simon could not remember, but he knew who that must have been.

"Jace."

Mark nodded, almost absentmindedly. "He said, 'Show them what a Shadowhunter is made of; show them you aren't afraid.' I thought I was showing them, the Fair Folk and the Shadowhunters both. I could not do what he asked me. I was afraid, but I did not let it stop me. I got a message back to the Shadowhunters and I told them the Fair Folk were betraying them and allying with their enemy. I made sure they knew and could protect the City of Glass. I warned them, and the Hunters could have killed me for it, but I thought if I died I would die knowing my brothers and sisters were saved, and that everyone would know I was a true Shadowhunter."

"You did," said Simon. "You got the message back. Idris was protected, and your brothers and sisters were saved."

"What a hero I am," Mark murmured. "I proved my loyalty. And the Shadowhunters left me here to rot."

His face twisted. In the depths of Simon's heart, fear twined with pity.

"I tried to be a Shadowhunter, even in the depths of Faerie, and what good did it do me? 'Show them what a Shadowhunter is made of!' What is a Shadowhunter made of, if they desert their own, if they throw away a child's heart like rubbish left on the side of the road? Tell me, Simon Lewis, if that is what Shadowhunters are, why would I wish to be one?"

"Because that's not all they are," Simon said.

"And what are faeries made of? I hear Shadowhunters say they are all evil now, barely more than demons set upon the earth to do wicked mischief." Mark grinned, something wild and fey in the grin, like sunlight glittering through a spiderweb. "And we do love mischief, Simon Lewis, and sometimes wickedness. But it is not all bad, to ride the winds, run upon the waves, and dance upon the mountains, and it is all I have left. At least the Wild Hunt wants me. Maybe I should show Shadowhunters what a faerie is made of instead."

"Maybe," said Simon. "There's more to both sides than the worst."

Mark smiled, a faint terrible smile. "Where has the best gone? I try to remember my father's stories, about Jonathan Shadowhunter, about all the golden heroes who have served as shields for humanity. But my father is dead. His voice fades away with the north wind, and the Law he held sacred is something written in the sand by a child. We laugh and point, that anyone should be so foolish as to think it would last. All that is good, and true, is lost."

Simon had never thought there was much of a silver lining about his memory loss. It occurred to him now that he had been shown some small accidental mercy. All his memories had been stripped away at once.

While Mark's memories were being torn at and worn

away, sliding from him one by one, in the cold dark under the hill where nothing gold lasted.

"I wish I could remember," Simon said, "when we first met."

"You weren't human then," said Mark bitterly. "But you're human now. And you look like more of a Shadowhunter than I do."

Simon opened his mouth and found all words wanting. He did not know what to say: It was true, as everything Mark said was true. When he'd first seen Mark, he'd thought *faerie*, and felt instinctively uneasy. Shadowhunter Academy must have been rubbing off on him even more than he'd thought.

And the environment Mark was in had changed him, too, changed him already almost past reclaiming. There was an eerie quality to him that went beyond the fine bones and delicately pointed ears of faerie. Helen had possessed those too, but ultimately she had moved like a fighter, stood tall like a Shadowhunter, spoken as the Clave and the people of the Institutes spoke. Mark spoke like a poem and walked like a dance. Simon wondered, even if Mark found his way back, if he could possibly fit into the Shadowhunter world now.

He wondered if Mark had forgotten how to lie.

"What do you think I am, apprentice Shadowhunter?" Mark asked. "What do you think I should do?"

"Show them what Mark Blackthorn is made of," said Simon. "Show them all."

"Helen, Julian, Livia, Tiberius, Drusilla, Octavian. And Emma," Mark whispered, his voice low and reverent, one Simon recognized from the synagogue, from the voice of mothers calling their children, from all the times and places he had heard people call on what they held most sacred. "My brothers and sisters are Shadowhunters, and in their name I will help you. I will."

He turned and shouted: "Hefeydd!"

Hefeydd of the purple ears sidled back into view, back from among the trees.

"This Shadowhunter is my kinsman," said Mark, with some difficulty. "Do you dare to insist you have a claim on a kinsman of the Wild Hunt?"

That was ridiculous. Simon was not even a Shadowhunter yet, Hefeydd was never going to believe—Only here was Mark, Simon realized. A faerie, to all appearances, and a faerie somewhat to be feared. Even Simon had not known if he could lie.

"Of course I would not insist," Hefeydd said, bowing. "That is—"

Simon was watching the sky. He had not even realized he was doing so, that he had been scanning the skies since someone had dropped from them, until now.

Now that Simon was watching, he could see what was happening more clearly: not someone falling from the sky, but a wild sky-bound horse charging for the earth and letting fall its rider. This horse was white as a cloud or mist given proud and shining shape, and the rider who hurtled toward the ground was in dazzling white as well. He had cobalt hair, the dark blue of evening before it became the black of night, and one gleaming-jet and one gleaming-silver eye.

"The prince," whispered Hefeydd.

"Mark of the Hunt," said the new faerie. "Gwyn sent you to find out why the Hunt had been so disturbed. He did not suggest you delay the Hunt yourself by tarrying a year and a day. Are you running away?"

The question was asked with emotion behind it, though Simon could not tell if it was suspicion or something else. He could tell that the question was more serious, perhaps, than the asker had meant it to be.

Mark gestured to himself. "No, Kieran. As you see. Hefeydd has caught himself a Shadowhunter, and I was a little curious."

"Why?" asked Kieran. "The Nephilim are behind you, and looking behind causes nothing but broken spells and wasted pain. Look forward, to the wild wind and to the Hunt. And to my back, because I am like to be before you in any hunt."

Mark smiled, in the way you did with a friend you were used to teasing. "I can recall several hunts in which that has not been the case. But I see you hope for better luck in the future, while I rely on skill."

Kieran laughed. Simon felt a leap of hope—if this faerie was Mark's friend, then the rescue mission was still on. He had moved unconsciously closer to Mark, his hand closing on one of the bars of his cage. Kieran's eye was drawn to the movement, and for an instant he glared at Simon with eyes gone perfectly cold: shark-black, mirror-shard eyes.

Simon knew, with absolute bone-deep certainty and with no idea why, that Kieran did not like Shadowhunters and did not wish Simon any good.

"Leave Hefeydd with his toy," said Kieran. "Come away."

"He told me something interesting," Mark informed Kieran in a brittle voice. "He said the Clave voted against coming for me. My people, the people I was raised among and taught by and trusted, agreed to leave me here. Can you believe that?"

"Can you be surprised? His kind has always liked

cruelty full as much as justice. His kind have nothing to do with you any longer," Kieran said, voice caressing and persuasive, laying a hand on Mark's neck. "You are Mark of the Wild Hunt. You ride on the air, a hundred dizzy wheeling miles above them all. They will never hurt you again, save that you let them. Do not let them. Come away."

Mark hesitated, and Simon found himself doubting. Kieran was right, after all. Mark Blackthorn owed the Shadowhunters nothing.

"Mark," Kieran said, a thread of steel in his voice. "You know there are those in the Hunt who would seize any reason to punish you."

Simon could not tell if Kieran's words were a warning or a threat.

A smile crossed Mark's face, dark as a shadow. "Better than you," he said. "But I thank you for your care. I will go with you and explain myself to Gwyn." He turned to look at Simon, his bicolored eyes unreadable, sea glass and bronze. "I will come back. Do not harm him," he told Hefeydd. "Give him water."

He nodded toward Hefeydd, slight emphasis in the gesture, and nodded toward Simon. Simon nodded in return.

Kieran, whom Hefeydd had called a prince, kept his grip on Mark and turned him so that he was facing away from Simon. He whispered something to Mark that Simon could not hear, and Simon could not tell if the tight grasp of Kieran's hand was affection, anxiety, or a wish to imprison.

Simon had no doubt that if Kieran had his way, Mark would not come back.

Mark whistled, and Kieran made the same sound. On the wind, as a shadow and a cloud, came a dark and a light horse swooping down for their riders. Mark leaped into the air and was gone in a flicker of darkness, with a cry of joy and challenge.

Hefeydd chuckled, the low sound creeping through the undergrowth.

"Oh, I will give you water with pleasure," he said, and came over with a cup fashioned out of bark, filled to the brim with water that seemed to shine with light.

Simon reached out through the bars and accepted the drink, but fumbled it and spilled half the water. Hefeydd cursed and caught the cup, holding it to Simon's lips and smiling a darkly encouraging smile.

"There is still some left," he whispered. "You can drink. Drink."

Except Simon was Academy trained. He had no intention of accepting food or drink from faeries, and he was sure Mark had not meant him to. Mark had been nodding at the key dangling from one of the long sleeves of Hefeydd's cloak.

Simon pretended to drink as Hefeydd smiled. He slipped the key into his gear, and when Hefeydd trotted away he waited, and counted the minutes until he thought the coast was clear. He slid his hand through the bars, slipped the key into the lock, and swung the cage door slowly open.

Then he heard a sound, and froze.

Stepping out of the whispering green trees, wearing a red velvet jacket and a long black lace dress that turned into transparent cobwebs around the knees, in boots and red gloves that Simon thought he might remember, graceful as a gazelle and intent as a tiger, was Isabelle Lightwood.

"Simon!" she exclaimed. "What do you think you're doing?"

Simon drank her in with his eyes, better than water

from any land. She had come for him. The others must have fled back to the Academy and said that Simon was lost in Faerie, and Isabelle had gone charging into Faerieland to find him. First out of anybody, when she was meant to be getting ready to attend a wedding. But she was Isabelle, and that meant she was always ready to fight and defend.

Simon recalled feeling conflicted when she had rescued him from a vampire last year. Right now he could not imagine why.

He knew her better now, he thought, knew her all over again, and knew why she would always come.

"Er, I was escaping my terrible captivity," said Simon. Then he took a step back from the cage door, met Isabelle's eyes, and grinned. "But, you know ... not if you don't want me to."

Isabelle's eyes, which had been hard with worry and purpose, were suddenly glittering like jet.

"What are you saying, Simon?"

Simon spread his hands. "I'm just saying, if you came all the way here to rescue me, I don't wish to appear ungrateful."

"Oh no?"

"No, I'm the grateful type," Simon said firmly. "So here I am, humbly awaiting rescue. I hope you can see your way clear to saving me."

"I think I could possibly be persuaded," Isabelle said. "Given an incentive."

"Oh, please," Simon said. "I languished in prison, praying that someone brave and strong and babelicious would swoop in and save me. Save me!"

"Brave and strong *and* babelicious? You don't ask for much, Lewis."

"That's what I need," Simon said, with growing conviction. "I need a hero. I'm holding out for a hero, in fact, until the morning light. And she's gotta be sure, and it's gotta be soon—because I have been kidnapped by evil faeries—and she's gotta be larger than life."

Isabelle did look larger than life, like a girl on a big screen with her lip gloss glittering like starlight and music playing to accompany every swish of her hair.

She opened the cage door and stepped inside, twigs crackling under her boots, and crossed the floor of the cage to slide her arms around Simon's neck. Simon drew her face to his and kissed her lips. He felt the luxurious give of her ruby mouth, the slide of her tall strong beautiful body against his. Isabelle's kiss was like rich wine laid out for him alone, like a challenge offered and a promise kept.

He felt, curving against his mouth, her smile.

"Why, Lord Montgomery," Isabelle murmured. "It's been such a long time. I was worried I'd never see you again."

Simon wished he had braved the showers in the Academy this morning. What did dead rats matter, in the face of true love?

There was a rush of blood in his ears, and the sound of a tiny creak: the cage door swinging shut again.

Simon and Isabelle pulled abruptly apart. Isabelle looked ready to spring, like a tiger in lace. Hefeydd did not look particularly worried.

"Two Shadowhunters for the price of one, and a new bird for my cage," Hefeydd said. "And such a pretty bird."

"You think your cage can hold this bird?" Isabelle demanded. "You're dreaming. I got in, and I can get out."

"Not without your stele and your bag of tricks," Hefeydd said. "Throw them all through the bars of the cage, or I shoot your lover with elfshot and you watch him die before your eyes."

Isabelle looked at Simon and, stone-faced, began to strip off her weapons and shove them through the cage bars. Simon was now, perhaps unsettlingly, aware of the placement of many of Isabelle's weapons, and he noted that she had skipped the knife on the inside of her left boot. Oh, and the long knife in the sheath at her back.

Isabelle had many, many knives.

"It will not be so long until you need water to live, pretty bird," said Hefeydd. "I can wait."

He shimmered away. Isabelle collapsed at the bottom of the cage as if her strings had been cut.

Simon stared at her in horror. "Isabelle—"

"I am so humiliated," said Isabelle, her face in her hands. "I didn't even hear him coming. I have brought shame upon the Lightwood name. Utter shame. Total, total humiliation."

"I'm really flattered, if that helps."

"I got distracted making out with a boy, and then locked up by a goblin," Isabelle moaned. "You don't understand! You don't remember, but I was never like this before you. No boy ever meant anything to me. I had poise. I had purpose. I didn't get dumb crushes, because I was never dumb. I was pure battle skill in a bustier. Nobody could shatter my sheer demon-hunting sangfroid. I was cool before I met you! And now I spend my time chasing after a guy with demon amnesia and losing my head in enemy territory! Now I'm a chump."

Simon reached out for one of Isabelle's hands, and after a moment Isabelle let him peel the hand off her face and link her fingers with his. "We can be two chumps in a cage together."

"You're definitely a chump," Isabelle snapped. "Remember, you're still a mundane."

"How could I forget?"

"Did it never occur to you that I might be a faerie wearing a strong glamour, sent to deceive you?"

Do you remember the name of your heart?

"No," said Simon. "I'm a chump, but I'm not that much of a chump. I don't remember everything about our past, but I remember enough. I haven't learned everything about you now that we have another chance, but I have learned enough. I know you when I see you, Isabelle."

Isabelle looked at him for a long moment, and then smiled her lovely defiant smile.

"We're two chumps going to a wedding," she said. "I hope you noticed that I let him think I busted my way into this cage myself. Of course, I secured the key before I ever stepped into the cage." She pulled the key out of the front of her dress and held it up, glittering in the light of Faerie. "I may be a chump, but I'm not an idiot."

She leaped to her feet, her lace skirts swaying around her like a bell, and let them out of the cage. She picked up her weapons and stele from where they were lying in the dirt, and once her weapons were secured, she took Simon's hand.

They were only a few steps into the faerie forest when a shadow swooped down and upon them. Isabelle went for her knives, but it was only Mark.

"You have not escaped yet?" Mark demanded, looking harried. "And you stopped to acquire a paramour?"

Isabelle stopped dead. She, unlike Simon, recognized him right away. "Mark Blackthorn?" she asked.

"Isabelle Lightwood," Mark noted, mimicking her tone of voice.

"We met earlier," said Simon. "He helped me get that key."

"Oh now," said Mark, tilting his head in a birdlike movement. "It was no uneven bargain. You gave me some very interesting information about the Shadowhunters, and the great loyalty they have shown one of their own."

Isabelle's back straightened as it did at any challenge, black hair flying like a flag as she took a step toward him. "You have been done a terrible wrong," she said. "I know you are a true Shadowhunter."

Mark took a step back. "Do you?" he asked softly.

"For what it's worth, I disagree with the Clave's decision."

"That's the Clave, isn't it? I mean, I like Jia Penhallow okay, and it's not that I ... dislike your dad," Simon, who did not actually like Robert Lightwood, said awkwardly. "But the Clave, basically assholes, am I right? We all know that."

Isabelle held her hand out, palm down, and rocked it back and forth in a gesture that said *You've got a point but I refuse to agree with it out loud.*

Mark laughed. "Yeah," he said, and he sounded a little more sane, a little more human, as if the laugh had grounded him somehow. There was an accent to his words that made Simon think not *faerie* but: *L.A. boy*. "Basically assholes."

There was a rustle in the trees, a rising of the wind. Simon thought he could hear laughter and calling voices, hoofbeats upon the cloud and the currents of the air, the baying of hounds. The sounds of a hunt, the Hunt, the most remorseless hunt in this or any world. Faint, but not far enough away, and coming closer.

"Come with us," said Isabelle suddenly. "Whatever price there is to be paid, I will pay it."

Mark gave her a look that was equal parts admiring and disdainful. He shook his fair head, leaves quivering and light lancing through the bright locks.

"What do you think would happen if I did? I would go home ... home ... and the Wild Hunt would follow me there. Do you imagine I have not dreamed of running home a thousand times? Every time, I see gentle Julian pierced with the spears of the Wild Hunt. I see little Dru and baby Tavvy ridden down. I see my Ty, ripped apart by their hounds. I cannot go until there is some way to go to them without bringing destruction down on them. I will not go. You go, and go fast."

Simon pulled Isabelle backward, toward the trees. She resisted, her eyes still on Mark, but she let him draw her away into concealing leaves as more faerie horses hurtled down, lightning amid the trees, shadows against the sun.

"What trouble are you causing now, Shadowhunter?" asked a faerie on a roan horse, laughing as the steed whirled. "What is this word of more of your kind?"

"No word," said Mark.

There were more horses joining the roan, more and more of the Wild Hunt. Simon saw Kieran, a white silent presence. The faerie on the roan turned his horse toward the place where Simon and Isabelle stood, and Simon saw the roan sniff the air like a dog.

The rider pointed. "Why do I spy Shadowhunters, then, in our land and answerable to us? Should I ask them what they are about?"

He rode forward, but he did not make it far. He was wearing a cloak embroidered with silver, showing the constellations, the silver enchanted to move as though time were sped up and planets spun fast enough for the eye to see. His horse stopped short, its rider almost falling, when his beautiful silvery cloak was suddenly pinned to a tree by a well-placed arrow.

Mark lowered his bow. "I see nothing," he said, pronouncing the lie with a certain satisfaction. "And nothing should go—now."

"Oh, boy, you will pay for this," hissed the rider on the roan.

The horses and the riders shrieked like pterodactyls, circling him, but Mark Blackthorn of the Los Angeles Institute stood his ground.

"Run!" he shouted. "Get home safe! Tell the Clave that I have saved more Shadowhunter lives, that I will be a Shadowhunter and be damned to them, that I will be a faerie and curse them! And tell my family that I love them, I love them, and I will never forget. One day I will go home."

Simon and Isabelle ran.

George threw himself on Simon the instant he and Isabelle appeared in the grounds of the Academy, his arms strangling-tight. Beatriz and, to Simon's amazement, even Julie flew at him only a second behind George, and both of them mercilessly pummeled his arms.

"Ow," said Simon.

"We're so glad you're alive!" said Beatriz, punching him again.

"Why must you hurt me with your love?" asked Simon. "Ow."

He disentangled himself from their grip, touched but also mildly bruised, then looked around for another familiar face. He felt a cold touch of fear.

"Is Marisol all right?" he demanded.

Beatriz snorted. "Oh, she's better than all right. She's in the infirmary with Jon waiting on her hand and foot. Because you mundanes can't be healed with runes and she is milking that for all it's worth. I'm not sure which has Jon more terrified, the thought of how fragile mundanes are, or the fact that she keeps threatening to explain X-ray machines to him."

Simon was very impressed that even elfshot could not slow down Marisol and all her evil.

"We thought *you* might be dead," said Julie. "The Fair Folk will do anything to vent their spite against Shadowhunters, those evil, treacherous snakes. They could have done anything to you."

"And it would have been my fault," George said, pale-faced. "You were trying to stop me."

"It would have been the faeries' fault," said Julie. "But you were careless. You have to remember what they are, less human than sharks."

George was nodding humbly. Beatriz looked as if she was in full agreement.

"You know what?" said Simon. "I've had enough."

They all stared at him in blank incredulity. But Isabelle glanced at him and smiled. He thought he finally understood the fire that burned in Magnus, what made him keep talking when the Clave would not listen.

"I know you all think I'm always criticizing the Nephilim," Simon went on. "I know you believe I don't think enough of—the sacred traditions of the Angel, and the fact that you are ready to lay down your lives, any day, to protect humans. I know you think it doesn't matter to me, but it does matter. It means a lot. But I don't have the luxury of only seeing things from one perspective. You all notice when I put down Shadowhunters, but none of you check yourselves when you talk about Downworlders. I *was* a Downworlder. Today I was saved by someone the Clave decided to condemn as a Downworlder, even though he was brave as any Shadowhunter, even though he was loyal. It seems like you want me to just accept that the Nephilim are great and nothing needs to change, but I won't accept anything."

He took a deep breath. He felt as if all the comfort of the morning had been stripped away. But maybe that was for the best. Maybe he'd been getting too comfortable.

"I wouldn't want to be a Shadowhunter if I thought I was going to be a Shadowhunter like your father or your father's father before him. And I wouldn't like any of you as much as I do if I thought you were going to be Shadowhunters like all the Shadowhunters before you. I want all of us to be better. I haven't figured out how to change everything yet, but I want everything to change. And I'm sorry if it upsets you, but I'm going to keep complaining."

"Later," said Isabelle. "He's going to keep complaining later, because we're going to a wedding right now."

Everyone looked mildly stunned that their emotional reunion had turned into a speech on Downworlder rights. Simon thought Julie might beat him about the head and face, but instead she patted him on the back.

"All right," she said. "We'll listen to your tedious whining later. Please try to keep it brief."

She walked off with Beatriz. Simon squinted after her, and noticed that Isabelle was squinting after as well, a look of faint suspicion on her face.

Simon had a moment of doubt. George had meant Beatriz when he was talking about a girl liking Simon, right?

Surely not Julie. It couldn't be Julie.

No, surely not. Simon was pretty certain he was just getting a pass on account of the narrow escape in Faerie.

George hung back. "I really am so sorry, Si," he told Simon. "I lost my head. I—I maybe wasn't quite ready to lead a team. But I'm going to be ready one day. I'm going to do what you said. I'm going to become a better Shadowhunter than any Shadowhunters before us. You won't have to pay for my mistakes again."

"George," Simon said. "It's fine."

None of them was perfect. None of them could be.

George's sunny face still looked under a cloud, unhappy as he almost never did. "I'm not going to fail again."

"I believe in you," said Simon, and grinned at him, until finally George grinned back. "Because that's what bros do."

Once he arrived in Idris, Simon found himself plunged into a state of wedding chaos. Wedding chaos seemed to be very different from normal kinds of chaos. There were, in fact, many flowers. Simon had a sheaf of lilies shoved upon him and he stood holding it, afraid to move in case the flowers spilled and he was responsible for ruining the whole wedding.

Many wedding guests were running about, but there was only one group that was all kids and no adults. Simon clutched his lilies and focused his attention on the Blackthorns.

If he had not met Mark Blackthorn, he was pretty sure he would've thought of them as a riot of anonymous kids.

Now, though, he knew they were someone's family: someone's heart's desire.

Helen, Julian, Livia, Tiberius, Drusilla, Octavian. And Emma.

Willow-slim, silver-fair Helen, Simon already knew. She was in one of the many rooms he was forbidden to go into, having mysterious bridal things done to her.

Julian was the next oldest, and he was the calm center of a bustling Blackthorn crowd. He had a kid in his arms, who was a little big for Julian to carry but was clinging tenaciously to Julian's neck like an octopus in unfamiliar surroundings. The kid must be Tavvy.

All the Blackthorns were dressed up for the wedding, but already a little grubby around the edges, in that mysterious way kids got. Simon wasn't sure how. They were all, aside from Tavvy, a little too old to be playing in the dirt.

"I'll get Dru all cleaned up," volunteered Emma, who was tall for fourteen, with a crown of blond hair that made her stand out among the dark-haired Blackthorns like a daffodil in a bed of pansies.

"No, don't bother," said Julian. "I know you want to spend some quality time with Clary. You've only been talking about it for, oh, fifteen thousand years, give or take."

Emma shoved him playfully. She was taller than he was: Simon remembered being fourteen and shorter than all the girls too.

All the girls except one, he recalled slowly, the real picture of his fourteenth year sliding over the false one, where the most important person in his life had been clumsily photoshopped out. Clary had always been tiny. No matter how short or awkward Simon had felt, he had always towered over her and felt it was his right to protect her.

He wondered if Julian wished Emma were shorter than he was. From the look on Julian's face as he regarded Emma, there was not one thing about her he would change. *His art and his Emma,* Mark had said, as if they were the two essential facts about Julian. His love of beauty and his wish to create it, and his best friend in all the world. They were going to be *parabatai*, Simon was pretty sure. That was nice.

Emma sped away on a quest to find Clary, with one last grin for Julian.

Only, Mark had been wrong. Art and Emma were clearly not all that occupied Julian's thoughts. Simon watched as he held on to Tavvy and stooped over a small girl with a round beseeching face and a cloud of brown hair.

"I lost my flower crown and I can't find it," whispered the girl.

Julian smiled down at her. "That's what happens when you lose things, Dru."

"But if I'm not wearing a flower crown like Livvy, Helen will think I'm careless and I don't mind my things and I don't like her as much as Livvy does. Livvy still has her flower crown."

The other girl in the group, taller than Dru and in that coltish stage where her arms and legs were thin as sticks and too long for the rest of her body, was indeed wearing a flower crown on her light brown hair. She was sticking close to the side of a boy who had headphones on in the midst of the chaos of the wedding, and winter-gray eyes fixed on some distant private sight.

Livvy would walk over hot coals and hissing serpents for Ty, Mark had said. Simon remembered the infinite tenderness with which Mark had said: *my Ty*.

"Helen knows you better than that," Julian said.

"Yes, but..." Drusilla tugged at his sleeve so he would bend down and she could say, in an agonized whisper: "She's been gone such a long time. Maybe she doesn't remember ... everything about me."

Julian turned his face away, so none of his siblings could see his expression. Only Simon saw the flash of pain, and he knew he wasn't meant to. He knew he wouldn't have seen it, if he hadn't seen Mark Blackthorn, if he hadn't been paying attention.

"Dru, Helen has known you since you were born. She does remember everything."

"But just in case," said Drusilla. "She's going away again really soon. I want her to think I'm good."

"She knows you're good," Julian told her. "The best. But we'll find your flower crown, all right?"

The younger kids did not know Helen in the same way Julian did, as a sibling who was there all the time. They could not rely on someone who was so far away.

Julian was their father, Simon thought with a dawning of horror. There was nobody else.

Even though the Blackthorns had family who wanted to be there for them, wanted it desperately. The Clave had ripped a family apart, and Simon did not know what effects that would have in the future or how the wounds the Clave had inflicted would heal.

He thought, again, as if he were still speaking to his friends at the Academy: *We have to be better than this. Shadowhunters have to be better than this. We have to figure out what kind of Shadowhunters we want to be, and show them.*

Maybe Mark had not known Julian as well as he thought. Or maybe Mark's little brother, with no choice, had changed quietly and profoundly.

They all had to change. But Julian was so young.

"Hey," said Simon. "Can I help?"

The two brothers did not look much alike, but Julian flushed and lifted his chin in the same way Mark had: as if no matter what, he was too proud to admit he might be hurting.

"No," he said, and gave Simon a bright warm smile that was actually very convincing. "I'm fine. I have this."

It seemed true, until Julian Blackthorn had gone out of Simon's reach, and then Simon noticed again that Julian was carrying a kid who was too big for him to carry, with another kid holding on to his shirt. Simon could actually see how much there was on those thin young shoulders.

Simon did not fully understand the traditions of the Shadowhunter people.

There was a lot in the Law about whom you could and could not marry: If you married a mundane who did not Ascend, you got your Marks stripped and were out on your ear. You could marry a Downworlder in a mundane or a Downworlder ceremony, and you wouldn't be out on your ear but everyone would be embarrassed, some people would act like your marriage did not count, and your terribly traditional Nephilim great-aunt Nerinda would start referring to you as the shame of the family. Plus with the Cold Peace functioning as it was, any Shadowhunter wanting to marry a faerie was probably out of luck.

But Helen Blackthorn was a Shadowhunter, by their own Law, no matter how many people might despise or distrust her for her faerie blood. And Shadowhunters had not actually built it into their precious Law that Shadowhunters could not marry someone of the same sex. Possibly this was just because it hadn't occurred to anyone even as an option way back when.

So Helen and Aline actually could be married, in a full Shadowhunter ceremony, in the eyes of both their families and their world. Even if they were exiled again right afterward, they got this much.

In a Shadowhunter wedding, Simon had been told, you dressed in gold and placed the wedding rune over each other's hearts and arms. There was a tradition a little like giving away the bride, for both parties in a marriage. The bride and groom (or in this case, the bride and bride) would each choose the most significant person to them from their family—sometimes a father, but sometimes a mother, or a *parabatai* or a sibling or chosen friend, or their own child or an elder who symbolized the whole family—and the chosen one, or *suggenes*, would give the bride or groom to their beloved, and welcome the beloved to their own family.

This was not always possible in Shadowhunter weddings, on account of sometimes your whole family and all your friends had been eaten by snake demons. You never knew with Shadowhunters. But Simon thought it was kind of beautiful that Jia Penhallow, Consul and most important member of the Clave, was standing as *suggenes* to give her daughter Aline to the tainted, scandalous Blackthorns, and to receive Helen into the bosom of her family.

Aline'd had some nerve suggesting it. Jia'd had some nerve agreeing to it. But Simon supposed that the Clave had already effectively exiled Jia's daughter: What more could they do to her? And how better to politely spit in their eye than to say: Helen, the faerie girl you spat on and sent away, is now as good as the Consul's daughter.

What is a Shadowhunter made of, if they desert their own, if they throw away a child's heart like rubbish left on the side of the road?

Julian was the one standing to give Helen away. He stood in his gold-inscribed clothes, his sister on his arm, and his sea-in-the-sunlight eyes shone as if he was happy as any kid could be. As though he had not a care in the world.

Helen and Aline were both dressed in golden gowns, golden thread glittering like starlight in Aline's black hair. They were both so happy, their faces outshone their gowns. They stood at the center of the ceremony, twin suns, and for a moment all the world seemed to spin and turn on them.

Helen and Aline drew the marriage runes over each other's hearts with steady hands. When Aline drew Helen's bright head down to her own for a kiss, there was applause all throughout the hall.

"Thank you for letting us come," whispered Helen after the ceremony was over, embracing her new mother-in-law.

Jia Penhallow folded her daughter-in-law in her arms and said, in a voice considerably louder than a whisper: "I am sorry I must let you be sent away again."

Simon did not tell Julian Blackthorn about meeting Mark, any more than he had told Mark that Helen was not there to care for the Blackthorn children. It seemed hideous cruelty, to load another burden on shoulders already burdened almost past bearing. It seemed better to lie, as faeries could not.

But when he went to Helen and Aline to congratulate them, he stepped up and kissed Helen on the cheek, so he could whisper to her: "Your brother Mark sends you his love, and his happiness for your love."

Helen stared at him, sudden tears in her eyes but her smile even more radiant than before.

Everything is going to change for the Shadowhunters, Simon thought. *For all of us. It has to.*

Simon had special permission to stay the night in Idris, so he would not have to leave the wedding celebrations early.

There was going to be dancing later, but for now people

were standing about in groups talking. Helen and Aline were sitting on the floor, in the center of the Blackthorns, like two golden flowers who had sprung up from the ground and bloomed. Tiberius was describing to Helen, in a serious voice, how he and Julian had prepared for the wedding.

"We went through any potential scenario that might occur," he told her. "As if we were reconstructing a crime scene, but in reverse. So I know exactly what to do, no matter what happens."

"That must have been a lot of work," Helen said. Tiberius nodded. "Thanks, Ty. I really appreciate it."

Ty looked pleased. Dru, wearing her flower crown and beaming ear to ear, tugged at Helen's golden skirts for her attention. Simon thought he had rarely seen any group of people who all seemed so happy.

He tried not to think of what Mark would have given to be here.

"You want to go for a walk down the river with me and Izzy?" Clary asked, nudging him.

"What, no Jace?"

"Ah, I see him all the time," said Clary, with the comfort of familiar and trusted love. "Not like my best friend."

Jace—who was sitting talking with Alec, Alec who once again had not addressed a single word to Simon—made an obscene gesture to Simon as he left with Isabelle and Clary on either arm. Simon was not actually fooled that Jace was angry. Jace had hugged him when he saw him, and more and more Simon was coming to believe that he and Jace had not had a relationship in which they hugged before.

But apparently they were huggers now.

Simon, Isabelle, and Clary went walking down by the river. The waters looked like black crystal in the moonlight, and in the distance the demon towers gleamed like columns of moonlight itself. Simon walked a little more slowly than the girls, not used as they were to the strangeness and magic of this city, a city most of the world did not know existed, the shining heart of a secret and hidden land.

Simon was used to the Academy now. He would no doubt get used to all of Idris in time.

So much had changed, and Simon had changed too. But in the end, he had not lost what was most precious to him. He had been given back the name of his heart.

Isabelle and Clary looked back at him, walking so close that Isabelle's waterfall of raven hair mingled with Clary's fiery sunset of curls. Simon smiled and knew how lucky he was, lucky compared to Mark Blackthorn, who was locked away from what he loved best, lucky compared to a billion other people who did not know what it was they loved best of all.

"Are you coming, Simon?" Isabelle called out.

"Yes," Simon called back. "I'm coming."

He was lucky to know them, and lucky to know what they were to him, what he was to them: beloved, remembered, and not lost.

The Fiery Trial

By Cassandra Clare and Maureen Johnson

He turned his head back down to tell Clary to look at the statue, but Clary was gone. He spun around, a full rotation. She was nowhere in sight.

—The Fiery Trial

MAYBE MAGNUS DID MESS UP.
CLARY?

Simon was starting to wonder about the fires. The fires didn't like him. The fires moved around.

That seemed paranoid.

Outside, the trees were bare and the grass was brown. Inside, even the mold had retreated to its winter quarters between the stones in the basement walls. Shadowhunters didn't believe much in central heating. The Academy had fireplaces, never too close together, and never near enough to anyone. No matter where Simon sat, they were at the far end of the room, crackling away. The elites tended to get into rooms first, and they took the fireside seats. But even when they didn't—even when everyone entered at once—Simon ended up farthest from the fire. When you're cold, a crackling fire starts to sound like gentle, mocking laughter. Simon tried to dismiss this thought from his head, because clearly the fires were not laughing at him.

Because *that* was paranoid.

There were several fireplaces in the cafeteria, but George and Simon had stopped trying to get seats near them. Simon had enough to worry about. He was looking at his plate. He had also told himself to stop doing this. Stop thinking about the food. Just eat the food. But he couldn't help himself. Every night he teased it apart. Tonight looked to be some kind of stir-fry, but it appeared to have bread in it. There were peppers. There was something red.

It was pizza. Someone had stir-fried a pizza.

"No," he said out loud.

"What?"

His roommate, George Lovelace, was already shoveling down his dinner. Simon just shook his head. These things didn't bother George in the same way. Back home in Brooklyn, if Simon had heard that someone had stir-fried a pizza he would not have been upset. He would have assumed that some hipster restaurant had decided to deconstruct the pizza, because that is what hipster restaurants in Brooklyn do. Simon would have laughed, and maybe at some point it would have become popular, and then there would be trucks that sold stir-fried pizza, and then he would have eaten it. Because that is how Brooklyn works and because pizza. Best guess in this situation? Maybe someone dropped the pizza, or it broke up in the middle of cooking and for some reason the only conceivable solution was to put it in a pan and wing it.

The problem wasn't the pizza, not really. The problem was that the pizza made him think of home. Any New Yorker confronted with bad pizza will mentally return home for at least a few moments. Simon was born and raised a

New Yorker in the same way the elites were born and raised Shadowhunters. It was a part of him—the hum and the throb of the city. It could be as rough as the Academy. He knew to look down for rats on the subway tracks or near the edges of public squares. He was trained instinctively to swerve to avoid getting splashed with dirty snow slush by cabs. He didn't even need to look down to step over puddles left by dogs.

Obviously, there were better parts than that. He missed coming over the Brooklyn Bridge at night and seeing the sweep of it all—the city lit up for the night; the grand, man-made mountains; the river surging underneath. He missed the feeling of being around so many people doing and making amazing things. He missed the constant feeling of the whole thing being a magnificent show. And he missed his family and friends. It was the holiday season now, and he should have been at home. His mother would have already taken out the menorah that he had painted at the do-it-yourself clay workshop when he was a kid. It was bright, decorated in thick, messy strokes of blue, white, and silver paint. He and his sister were in charge of making potato pancakes together. They'd all sit on the sofa and exchange gifts. And everyone he cared about was just a short walk away, a subway stop at the most.

"You've got that look again," George said.

"Sorry," Simon said.

"Don't be sorry. It's okay to be miserable. It's the holidays, and we're here."

This was what was so great about George—he always got it, and he never judged. There were many downsides to Shadowhunter Academy, but George made up for most of them. Simon had had good friends before. George was like having a brother. They shared a room. They shared their misery and their small triumphs and their terrible meals. And in the competitive atmosphere of the Academy, George always had his back. He never reveled in doing something better than Simon (and being built like one of the lesser Greek gods, George often did excel at physical things). Simon felt his spirits buoy again. Just that George knew what he was thinking—just having his friend there—it was everything.

"What's she doing here?" George asked, nodding his head at someone behind Simon.

Dean Penhallow had appeared at the far end of the room (near the laughing fireplace). She didn't usually come to dinner in the cafeteria. She never came near the place.

"Your attention, please," she said. "We have some wonderful news to share with all students at the Academy. Julie Beauvale. Beatriz Mendoza. Please join me."

Julie and Beatriz stood at the same time and looked at each other with a smile. Simon had seen that kind of smile before, that kind of synchronized movement. That was Jace and Alec all over. The pair made their way through the room. Chairs scraped as people made way, and there was the lightest murmur. The fire laughed and laughed and popped and laughed. When they reached the end of the room, the dean put an arm around each, and they all faced the school body.

"I am pleased to announce that Julie and Beatriz have decided to become *parabatai*."

A sudden rush of applause. Several people stood, mostly in the elite track, and hooted and called out. This was allowed for a few moments, and then the dean raised her hand.

"As you all know, the *parabatai* ceremony is a serious commitment, a bond broken only by death. I know this news will cause many of you to consider whether you will find a *parabatai*. Not all Shadowhunters have a *parabatai*, or even want one. In fact, most of you will not. That is very important to remember. If you feel, as Julie and Beatriz do, that you have found your *parabatai*, or if you want to speak to someone about any part of the ceremony or what it means, you can speak to any of us. We are all here to help you make this most important of decisions. But again, congratulations to Julie and Beatriz. In their honor, there is a cake this evening."

As she spoke, the lurking evil that was the Academy cooks were bringing out a large, uneven cake.

"You may now resume your meal, and please do have some cake."

"Where did *that* come from?" George asked. "Those two? *Parabatai*?"

Simon shook his head. Shadowhunter families twined around each other like climbing vines. It was easier to find your lifetime partner when you started from birth. Many at the Academy were strangers. Julie and Beatriz, in the elite track, had more connections to each other, but Simon had never gotten the idea that they were that close.

"Well, that was a surprise," George said in a low voice. "You all right?"

It had hit Simon like a bit of a blow. He had thought of asking Clary to be his *parabatai*. But *parabatai* were like Alec and Jace, training together as Shadowhunters since they were kids. Sure, Simon and Clary had known each other that long, but not in the throwing-knives-and-killing-demons way (except in video games, which, unfortunately, did not count). Simon started to move the idea of *parabatai* into the mental category of things he probably would not have. He was training all the time. He hadn't seen her. He was ...

... very good at making up excuses.

He'd chickened out. He had seen his birthday coming, like a giant countdown clock. Every day he told himself it was too late. Clary had come the day before his birthday, bringing him a *Sandman Omnibus* as a gift. By then, he told himself, the countdown was over. The buzzer went off in his mind. He was nineteen.

He'd tried to put it out of his mind. But now, looking at these two newly announced *parabatai*, he delivered himself a mental kick.

"It's not for everyone, Si," George said. "Come on. Eat up, and we'll go back and you can tell me more about *Firefly*."

In the evenings, Simon had been expanding George's cultural education by explaining the plot of every episode of *Firefly*, one by one. This had become a pleasant ritual, but it, too, had a countdown. There was only one more episode to go.

Before they could do this, the dean made her way past their table and stopped.

"Simon Lewis, if you would please come with me for a moment?"

People from other tables glanced over. George looked down and poked at his pizza-fry.

"Sure?" Simon said. "Am I in trouble?"

"No," she said, her voice flat. "No trouble."

Simon pushed back his chair and stood.

"I'll see you back at the room, yeah?" George said. "I'll bring you some cake."

"Sure," Simon said.

Many people watched him go, because that is what happens when the dean gets you in the middle of dinner. Most of the elites, though, had clustered around Julie and Beatriz. There were laughs and squeals and everyone was talking very loudly. Simon worked his way around them to get to the dean.

"This way," she said.

Simon tried to pause by the fire just for a second, but the dean was already moving toward the door that teachers used to enter and leave the cafeteria. The teachers didn't eat with them all the time. There was clearly some other place, some other dining room somewhere in the Academy. Catarina Loss was the only one who came regularly, and Simon got the impression that she did so because she would rather brave the terrible student food than sit around with a bunch of Shadowhunters in a private room.

Simon had never been in the hall that the dean led him down. It was more dimly lit than the halls the students used. There were tapestries on the stone walls that were certainly as threadbare as the ones in the rest of the school, but they also looked more valuable. The colors were brighter and the gold threading had the glint of real gold. There were weapons along these walls. The student weapons were all in the weapons room, and those had some kind of safety to keep them in place. If you wanted a sword, you needed to undo several straps to get it down. These were placed in simple holders, making them easy to snatch at a second's notice.

The noise of the cafeteria shrank away within the first few steps, and then there was quiet all around. The hall was a series of closed doorways, and the silence crowded him in.

"Where are we going?" Simon asked.

"To the reception room," the dean said.

Simon looked out of the windows as they passed. Here, the glass was a quilt of tiny panes, held together by lead piping. Each diamond of glass was old and warped, and the overall effect was like a cheap kaleidoscope, one that showed only dark and a very lightly falling snow. It was the kind of snow that didn't amount to anything on the ground. It would just dust the dead grass. The technical term for that level, he decided, was an "annoyance" of snow.

They reached a turn in the hall. The dean opened the first door after the turn and revealed a small but grand room, with furnishings that were not in the slightest bit broken or threadbare. Every chair in the room had legs of the same length, and the sofas were long and comfortable-looking with no visible sags or stuffing. Everything was upholstered in a lush, grape-purple velvet. There was a low table made of cherrywood, and on it was a massive and elaborate silver tea set with china cups. And sitting around the table on the fine-quality chairs and sofas were Magnus Bane, Jem Carstairs, Catarina Loss, and Clary, her red hair bright against her light blue sweater. Magnus and Catarina were together at the end (near the fire—of course it was, as in all other rooms, at the far end). Clary looked up at Simon, and though she smiled as soon as she saw him, her expression suggested that her invitation to this little party had also been recent and not well explained.

"Simon," Jem said. "So good to see you. Please have a seat."

Simon had only had a few encounters with Jem Carstairs, who was apparently as old as his wife, Tessa Gray. They both looked amazingly fit for 150 years. Tessa even looked pretty hot. (Maybe Jem looked hot too? As Simon had thought once before, he probably wasn't the greatest judge of male attractiveness.) Was it weird to think people who were twice as old as your grandparents were good-looking?

"I'll leave you to it," the dean said, and again there was something missing in her tone. It was like she had just said, "I'll just give you this dead snake." She closed the door.

"We're having tea," Magnus said. He was measuring out spoonfuls of loose tea leaves into the strainer of a tiny teapot. "One for each cup. One for the pot."

He set the tiny tea canister aside and picked up one of the large silver pots and poured steaming water through the strainer into the teapot. Catarina was watching him do this with a strange fascination.

Jem looked at ease in a white sweater and dark jeans. His black hair had a single, dramatic streak of silver in it that stood out against his brown skin. "How are you finding the training?" he asked, leaning forward.

"I don't bruise as much anymore," Simon said, shrugging.

"That's excellent," Jem said. "It means you're finding your feet and deflecting more blows."

"Really?" Simon said. "I thought it was because I was dead inside."

Magnus dropped the lid back onto the tiny tea canister very suddenly, making a loud clanking noise.

"I'm very sorry to interrupt your dinner," Jem said. He had a formal way of speaking that was the only thing about him that really showed his age.

"Never be sorry about that," Simon muttered.

"I take it the food in the Academy isn't its best feature."

"I'm not sure it has a 'best' feature," Simon replied.

Jem smiled, his face lighting up. "We have cakes here, and scones. I think these are of a slightly higher quality than you are currently used to."

He indicated a china plate full of small cakes and scones that looked very edible. Simon didn't hesitate. He grabbed the closest scone and shoved it into his mouth. It was a bit dry, but it was better than anything he'd had in a while. He knew crumbs were falling out of his mouth and onto his dark T-shirt, but he found himself not caring.

"Okay, Magnus," Clary said. "You said you would explain why you brought me here when Simon got here. Not that I'm not happy to see you, but you're making me nervous."

Simon nodded and chewed to show he agreed and backed Clary up 100 percent, as best friends were supposed to do. At least he hoped he was communicating that.

Magnus pulled himself up. When a very tall warlock with cat eyes pulls himself up to attention, it changes the mood in the room. There was suddenly a real air of purpose, with an undercurrent of strange energy. Catarina sank back into the sofa, dropping into Magnus's shadow. It wasn't like Catarina to be so silent. Catarina was the blue-tinted voice of reason and minor rebellion in the hallowed halls of the Academy.

"I've been asked to bring you both a message," Magnus said, twisting one of the many rings that adorned his long fingers. "Emma Carstairs and Julian Blackthorn are to become *parabatai*. The ceremony requires two witnesses, and they have asked for you to be those witnesses."

Clary raised an eyebrow and looked over to Simon.

"Of course," she said. "Emma's a sweetheart. Definitely. I'm in."

Simon was midreach for another scone. He drew back his arm.

"Definitely," he said. "Me too. But why couldn't they just send us a letter?"

Magnus paused for a moment and looked at Catarina, then turned to Simon with a wink.

"Why send a letter when you can send something truly magnificent?"

It was a very Magnus thing to say, but it rang a little hollow. Something about Magnus seemed a little hollow. His voice, maybe.

"The ceremony will be performed in the Silent City tomorrow," Jem said. "We have already arranged permission for you to attend."

"Tomorrow?" Clary said. "And we're just being asked now?"

Magnus shrugged elegantly, indicating that sometimes things like this just happened.

"What do we have to do?" Simon asked. "Is it complicated?"

"Not at all," Jem said. "The position of the witness is largely symbolic, much like a wedding. You have nothing you have to say. It's just a matter of standing with them. Emma chose Clary—"

"I can understand that," Simon said. "But Julian wouldn't choose me. We hardly know each other. Why not Jace?"

"Because Julian isn't particularly close to him, either," said Jem, "and Emma made the suggestion that you and Clary, as best friends, would be meaningful witnesses for them. Julian agreed."

Simon nodded as if he understood, though he wasn't sure he did, really. He remembered having spoken to Julian at Helen and Aline's wedding, not long ago. He remembered thinking what a weight he had on his slight shoulders, and how much he seemed to hold contained, hidden and within.

Perhaps it was simply that there was no one else Julian cared for enough to stand as his witness? No one he looked up to? That was incredibly sad, if so.

"In any case," said Magnus, "you are to stand with them as they go through the Fiery Trial."

"The what?" Simon asked.

"That is the true name of the ceremony," Jem said. "The two *parabatai* stand inside rings of fire."

"Tea's ready," Magnus said suddenly. "Never let it sit for more than five minutes. Time to drink up."

He poured two cups from the small pot.

"There's only two cups," Clary said. "What about you?"

"The pot is small. I'll make another one. These are for the two of you. Drink up."

The two cups were presented. Clary shrugged and sipped. Simon did the same. It was, to be fair, exceptional tea. Maybe this was why English people got so excited about it. There was a wonderful clarity to the flavor. It warmed his body as it went down. The room was no longer cold.

"This really is good," Simon said. "I don't really do tea, but I like this. I mean, they give us tea here, but one time I had a cup that had a bone in it, and that was one of the best cups I had."

Clary laughed. "So what are we supposed to wear?" she said. "As witnesses, I mean."

"For the ceremony, formal gear. For the dinner afterward, regular clothing. Something nice."

"Wedding stuff," Catarina finally said. "It's a lot like a wedding but ..."

"... without the romance and flowers."

That was Jem.

Magnus was now eying them intently, his cat eyes

glistening in the dark. The room had gotten very dark indeed. Simon gave Clary a look that was supposed to mean: *This is weird.* She responded with a very clear look of response that said: *Superweird.*

Simon drank his tea down in a few large gulps and returned the cup to the table.

"It's funny," he said. "There was just another *parabatai* announcement at dinner. Two students from the elite track."

"That's not uncommon for this time of year," Jem said. "As the year draws to a close, people reflect, they make decisions."

The room suddenly got warmer. Had the fire gotten higher? Had it sneaked closer? It was definitely crackling loudly, but now it didn't sound like laughter—it sounded like breaking glass. The fire was speaking to them.

Simon caught himself. The fire was *speaking?* What was wrong with him? He looked around the room fuzzily, and heard Clary make an odd, surprised sound, as if she'd seen something she hadn't expected.

"I think it's time to begin," said Jem. "Magnus?"

Simon could hear Magnus sigh as he stood up. Magnus was *really* tall. This, Simon had always known. Now he looked like he might hit the ceiling. He opened a door that Simon hadn't noticed was there.

"Come through here," Magnus said. "There are some things you need to see."

Clary got up and went over to the door. Simon followed. Catarina caught his eye as he went. Everything was unsaid in this room. She didn't quite approve of what was happening. Neither did Magnus.

Whatever was on the other side of the doorway was utterly dark, and Clary hesitated for a second.

"It's fine," Magnus said. "It's just a bit cold in there. Sorry."

Clary went in, and Simon followed a step behind. They were in a shadowy space, definitely cold. He turned, but could no longer see the door. It was just him and Clary. Clary's hair shone bright red in the dark.

"We're outside," Clary said.

Sure enough. Simon blinked. His thoughts were a little slow and stretched. Of course they were outside.

"They maybe could have said we were going outside," Simon said, shivering. "No one here believes in coats."

"Turn around," Clary said.

Simon turned. The door they had just come through—in fact, the entire building they had just come from—was gone. They were simply outdoors, surrounded by just a few trees. The sky above was a purple-gray parchment that seemed to be lit by a low haze of lights on the horizon, just out of sight. There was a web of brick paths all around, dotted with fenced-off areas of trees and urns that probably contained flowers in better weather and now stood as reminders of the season.

It was familiar, and yet, it was like nowhere Simon had ever been.

"We're in Central Park," Clary said. "I think..."

"What? We..."

But as soon as he said it, it became clear. The low metal fences that marked off the brick paths. But there were no benches, no trash cans, no people. There was no view of the skyline in any direction.

"Okay...," said Simon. "This is weird. Did Magnus just completely screw up? Can that happen? You guys just came from New York. Did he just open up the same Portal?"

"Maybe?" Clary said.

Simon took a deep breath of the New York air. It was bitterly cold and burned the inside of his nose, waking him up.

"They'll realize in a second," Clary said, shivering in the cold. "Magnus doesn't make mistakes."

"So maybe it wasn't a mistake. Maybe we just got a free trip to New York. Or, I did. I'm going to assume that we go wherever we want until they come and get us. You know they have their ways. Might as well take advantage!"

This unexpected and utterly sudden trip home had completely reinvigorated Simon.

"Pizza," he said. "Oh my God. They stir-fried pizza tonight. It was the worst. Maybe coffee. Maybe there's time to get to Forbidden Planet? I just..."

He patted his pockets. Money. He had no money.

"You?" he asked.

Clary shook her head.

"In my bag. Back there."

That didn't matter. It was enough to be home. The suddenness of it only made it more wonderful. Now that he looked more carefully, Simon could see clearly the outlines of the skyscrapers that lined the south end of the park. They looked like the blocks he used to play with as a kid—just a series of rectangles of various sizes set side to side. Some had the faint glow of signs above them, but he couldn't read the writing. He could, however, see the colors of the signs with an unusual clarity. One sign was a pink rose, a bright bloom. The next was the color of electricity. It wasn't just the colors that were sharp. He could smell everything in the air. The metallic tang of the cold. The sea funk of the East River, blocks away. Even the jutting bits of bedrock that reached up and made the many tiny mountains of Central Park seemed to have an odor. There was no garbage, though, and no smells of food or traffic. This was elemental New York. This was the island itself.

"I feel a little weird," Simon said. "Maybe I should have finished dinner. And now that I've just said that, I know there must be something wrong with me."

"You need to eat," Clary said, giving him a light punch. "You're turning into a big muscle man."

"You noticed?"

"It's hard *not* to notice, Superman. You're like the after photo on some commercial for home workout equipment."

Simon blushed and looked away. It wasn't snowing anymore. It was just dark and open, with many trees around. There was a bright bitterness to the cold.

"Where do you think we are?" Clary said. "I'm guessing about ... midway?"

Simon knew it was possible to walk for some time in Central Park without really having a sense of where you are. The paths wind. The trees create a canopy. The land goes up and down in sharp inclines and declines.

"Over there," he said, pointing at a low pattern of shadows. "It opens up over there. It's the entrance to something. Let's go that way and look."

Clary rubbed her hands together and huddled against the cold. Simon wished he had a coat to offer her, almost more than he wished he had a coat to offer himself. Still, being cold in New York was better than being cold in the Academy. He had to admit, though, that Idris was more temperate. New York weather went to more extremes. This was the kind of cold that would give you frostbite if you stayed out in it too long. They probably needed to figure out where they were and get out of the park and into a building—any building. A store, a coffee shop, whatever they could find.

They walked toward the opening, which revealed itself to be a collection of elaborately carved stone plinths. There were several of these, in sets. Eventually they led to an equally elaborately carved staircase that bent on its way down to a wide terrace with a massive fountain. There was a lake just beyond, covered in ice.

"Bethesda Terrace," Simon said, nodding. "That's where we are. That's in the Seventies, right?"

"Seventy-Second," Clary said. "I've drawn it before."

The terrace was just a large, ornamental area inside of the park and not really somewhere to be on a cold night—but it seemed to be the only place to be. If they walked toward it, at least they would know where they were, as opposed to wandering around in the trees and looping paths. They walked down the stairs together. Strangely, the fountain was going tonight. It was often turned off in the winter, and certainly when it was freezing cold. But the water flowed freely, and there was no ice on the water in the fountain base. The lights were on and all focused on the statue of the angel that stood in the middle of the fountain on top of two layered tiers and four tiny cherubs.

"Maybe Magnus did mess up," she said.

Clary walked right up to the low edge of the fountain, sat down, and wrapped her arms around herself. Simon stared at the fountain. Funny, he thought, how they hadn't noticed any lights a few minutes ago as they approached. Maybe they'd just come on. The angel of the Bethesda Fountain was one of the most famous statues in all of Central Park—wings extended, water pouring off her outstretched hands.

He turned his head back down to tell Clary to look at the statue, but Clary was gone. He spun around, a full rotation. She was nowhere in sight.

"Clary?" he called.

There were no real places to conceal yourself on the terrace, and he'd looked away for only a moment. He walked halfway around the base of the fountain, calling her name several times. He looked up at the statue again. Same statue, looking down benevolently, water still dripping from her hands.

Except the statue was facing him. And he'd walked to the other side. He should have been looking at the back of it. He took a few more steps. While he never saw anything move, with every step the statue was still facing him directly, her stone expression soft and blank and angelic.

Something clicked in Simon's head.

"Pretty sure this isn't real," he said. "Pretty sure."

The evidence now seemed ridiculously obvious. The geography of the park was subtly wrong. For a moment he considered the bright, glowing sky, which was now filled with bleached-white clouds the size of entire states. They slid along the firmament, as if watching his progress in an embarrassed drive-by fashion. He was certain he could smell the Atlantic Ocean, and the rocks and stones.

"Magnus!" Simon screamed. "Are you kidding me? Magnus! Jem! Catarina!"

No Magnus. No Jem. No Catarina. No Clary.

"Okay," Simon said to himself. "You have been in worse situations than this. This is just weird. That's all. Just weird. Just very, very weird. Weird's okay. Weird's normal.

"I am in some kind of dream. Something has happened. And I'm going to figure this out. What would I do if this were D and D?"

It was as good a question as any, except the answer had to do with rolling a D20, so maybe it wasn't actually that helpful.

"Is this a trap? Why would they send us to a trap? It must be a game. It's a puzzle. If she was in trouble, I'd know."

That was interesting. He had the sudden and complete knowledge that if Clary were hurt, he would absolutely know it. He didn't feel any hurt. He did feel an absence, a pull to locate her.

As this thought occurred to him, a very unusual thing happened—namely, the great stone angel of Bethesda Fountain flapped her wings and flew straight up into the night sky. As she flew, the base of the fountain remained connected to her feet and pulled up the fountain like it was a plant. The massive reservoir of the fountain became unmoored and started to pull toward the sky. The bricks and mortar tore, and a root network of pipes was revealed, and a raw hole in the earth that rapidly filled with water. The ice on the lake cracked all at once, and the entire terrace started to flood. Simon backed up toward the steps as the water spilled out. He retreated slowly, step by step, until the water evened. The lake now incorporated the terrace, eight steps high. The fountain and the angel were gone.

"That," Simon said, "was weirder than normal."

As he spoke, a sound seemed to tear the night in two. It was a chord, a pure, thundering harmonic that rattled the tympanic bones in his head and physically shook him to his knees. The clouds scattered, as if in fear, and the moon shone clear and full above him. It was a bright yellow, so bright he could barely look at it. He had to shield his eyes and look down.

There was a rowboat. This was not so mysterious—it had come loose from the boathouse, not far away. All of the boats were floating freely, excited to be out on their own for the evening. But this boat had come all the way over and bumped up next to where he was standing.

Also, unlike all of the other rowboats, this one was shaped like a swan.

"I take it I'm supposed to get in," he said, flinching, in case the sky decided to make any more terrifying noises. There was no reply from the sky, so Simon grabbed the neck of the swan with both hands and carefully stepped inside and sat in the middle. The water couldn't be very deep. He would certainly be able to stand in it if the boat capsized. But still—freezing night, flying fountain, magic boat, and missing Clary. No reason to add "falling into cold water" to the mix.

As soon as he was in it, the little swan boat bobbed off, as if it knew it had somewhere to be. It drifted into the lake, avoiding the other loose boats. Simon huddled in, wrapping his arms around himself as he took his cold, gentle journey on the lake. The surface was utterly smooth, reflecting the moon and clouds. Simon hadn't ever done this before. The whole "boating in Central Park" thing seemed like it was meant for tourists. But in his recollection, the lake was fairly small and wide. He was surprised when it narrowed very suddenly and made itself into a channel under a thick canopy of trees. Once under the trees, there was absolutely no light at all for several minutes. Then everything lit up at once—rows of superbright bulbs lined the sides of the channel, and in front of him was a low tunnel with the words TUNNEL OF LOVE written around the arch in lights. Bright pink hearts bookended the word.

"You're joking," Simon said for what felt like the millionth time.

The air was now thick with the smell of popcorn and sea air, and there were sounds of fairground rides. The swan boat bumped, as if moving onto a track that would take it into the tunnel ride. Simon glided in. The light behind him faded, and the tunnel had a soft, blue glow. Some nondescript, classical-lite music played, full of violins. The boat settled into the track. The walls were painted in old-fashioned scenes of lovers—people sitting on porch swings kissing, women lounging on a depiction of a crescent moon, sweethearts leaning over an ice cream soda to kiss. The water was lit from underneath and glowed green, reflecting off the ceiling. Simon looked over the side of the boat to get a sense of how deep it was, or if there was something under him, but it looked shallow, like any normal water ride.

"This is a weird place to meet," said a voice.

Simon turned to see that he was now sharing his little swan with Jace. Jace was standing at the front of the boat, leaning against the swan's head. Being Jace, his balance was perfect, so the boat didn't rock to the side.

"Okay," Simon said, "this is really taking a turn I didn't expect."

Jace shrugged and looked around at the tunnel.

"I suppose these things had a use at one time," he said. "It was probably risqué to take this ride. You'd get a whole four minutes of unsupervised *necking*."

The word "necking" was bad. Hearing Jace say it was a new kind of bad.

"So," Jace said, "do you want to talk or should I?"

"Talk about what?"

Jace indicated the tunnel around them, as if this was very obvious.

"I'm not going to kiss you," Simon said. "Ever."

"I've never heard anyone say that before," Jace mused. "It was a unique experience."

"Sorry." Simon didn't feel even a little guilty. "If I *was* into guys, I don't think you'd make the top ten."

Jace released the swan's head and came to sit down by Simon's side. "I remember how we met. Do you?"

"You're playing a game of *what do you remember* with me?" Simon asked. "That's classy."

"It's not a game. I saw you. You didn't see me. But I saw. I saw it all."

"This is fun," Simon said. "You and me and the tunnel of what the hell are you talking about."

"You need to try to remember this," Jace said. "This is important. You need to remember how we met."

Whatever this was—a dream, some kind of altered state—it was veering in a very odd direction.

"How is it everything is about you?" Simon said.

"This isn't about me at all. This is about what I saw. This is about what you know. You can get there. You need to get this one back. You need this memory."

"You're asking me to remember somewhere I *didn't see you?*"

"Exactly. Why wouldn't you have seen me?"

"Because you were glamoured," Simon said.

"But someone did see me."

That had to be Clary. Obvious choice. But...

Now there was something rocking in the back of Simon's mind. He had been somewhere with Clary, and Jace was there ... except Jace wasn't there.

That was both in his memory and in the present. Jace was gone. The boat trundled on, turning a corner and plunging back into the dark. There was a short decline and a burst of fog, then the *ooOoOOOoOOoo* of a cartoon ghost and the mocked-up entryway of some kind of Gothic mansion. The ride had gone from lovers' lane to haunted mansion. Simon rode along, through tableaux of the mansion's rooms. In the library, ghosts dangled from wires and a skeleton popped out of a grandfather clock.

This fantasy, or whatever it was, seemed to be tapping into his memories of going to the Haunted Mansion at Disney World when he was a kid. And yet, as they moved from room to room, things looked more familiar—the cracking stone walls, the threadbare tapestries ... the Haunted Mansion was turning into the Academy. There was a ghostly version of the cafeteria and the classrooms.

"Over here, Simon."

It was Maia, waving from what looked like an elegant, wood-paneled office. There was a sign on the wall behind her, some kind of verse of poetry. Simon only caught a line of it: *"as old and as true as the sky."* Maia wore an elegant suit, her hair clipped back, and gold bangle bracelets on her wrists. She looked sadly at Simon. "Are you really going to leave us?" she said. "Leave being a Downworlder? Become one of them?"

"Maia," Simon said, a lump in his throat. He remembered only bits and pieces of his friendship with her—more than friendship, maybe? How brave she was, and how she'd been his friend when he'd desperately needed one.

"Please," she said. "Don't go."

The boat moved swiftly past, to another room, a completely standard apartment living room, with some cheap furniture. It was Jordan's apartment. Jordan stepped out of the bedroom doorway. There was a wound in his chest; his shirt was black with blood.

"Hey, roomie," he said.

Simon's heart felt like it stopped in his chest. He tried to speak, but before he could say a word, everything plunged into darkness. He felt the boat slide off its track with a soft bump, as if he had come to the end of the ride. Everything rushed forward. The tunnel opened out, and the boat lurched forward suddenly and began to speed up, as if carried on a current. Simon gripped the bench he sat on to hold himself steady.

He had been dumped out on a massive body of water, a river, very wide. Next to him the New York skyline was dark—the buildings eerily not illuminated—but he could make out their shapes. Not far up on the left side, he could see the silhouette of the Empire State Building. Ahead of him, maybe a mile or so up, there was a bridge spanning the river he was on. He could even make out the shadowy outline of an old-fashioned Pepsi-Cola sign on the right bank. That, he knew. That sign was near the base of the 59th Street Bridge to Queens.

"The East River," he said to himself, casting a glance around.

The East River was not somewhere to be at night, in the cold, in a small rowboat shaped like a swan. The East River was dangerous, fast, and deep.

He felt something bump the back of his tiny swan and turned, expecting a trash barge or a freighter. Instead it was another swan-shaped boat. This one contained a young girl, maybe thirteen or fourteen, in a tattered prom dress. She had long blond hair drawn up in uneven pigtails, giving the impression of constant lopsidedness. She pulled her swan to the side of Simon's and, seemingly without a care in the world, pulled up her skirt and stepped from one boat to the other. Simon instinctively reached one hand out to help her and one hand to steady himself. He was sure that the transfer would cause their little swan to topple, and while it did sway uncertainly as the weight distribution changed, somehow they stayed upright. The girl dropped herself next to Simon on the bench. The swan was designed for people to cozy up to each other, so she was pressed against his side.

"Hi!" she said happily. "You're back!"

"I ... am?"

There was something wrong with the girl's face. She was too pale. There were deep circles all the way around her eyes, and her lips were faintly gray. Simon wasn't sure who she was, but he got a very uneasy feeling.

"It's been forever!" she said. "But you're back. I knew you'd come back for me."

"Who are you?"

She fun-punched him in the arm, like he'd told a great joke.

"Shut up," she said. "You're so funny. That's why I love you."

"You love me?"

"Shut up!" she said again. "You know I love you. It's always been you and me. You and me forever."

"I'm sorry," Simon said. "I don't remember."

The girl looked around at the churning river and dark buildings as if this was all very wonderful and exactly where she wanted to be.

"It was all worth it," she said. "You're worth it."

"Thanks?"

"I mean, they killed me for you. They dumped me in a trash can. But I don't hold it against you."

The chill was now inside of Simon as well as out.

"But you're looking for her, aren't you? She's so annoying."

"Clary?" Simon asked.

The girl waved her hand as if blowing away a cloud of unwanted cigarette smoke.

"You could be with me. Be my king. Be with Queen Maureen. Queen Maureen, queen of death! Queen of the night! I ruled over all of this!"

She swept her hand toward the skyline. While it seemed unlikely that this very young girl could have ruled over New York, there was something about the story that rang true. He knew this. It was his fault. He didn't do anything exactly, but he could feel guilt—terrible, crushing guilt and responsibility.

"What if you could save me?" she asked, leaning into him. "Would you?"

"I..."

"What if you had to pick?" Maureen said, smiling at the thought. "We could play a game. You could pick. Me or her. I mean, you are the reason I died, so ... you should pick me. Save me."

The clouds, ever watchful when something interesting was going on, crowded back in. The wind kicked up and the river took on a heavy wake, rocking the boat from side to side.

"She's in the water, you know," Maureen said. "The water in the fountain that comes from the lake. The water in the lake that comes from the river. The water in the river that comes from the sea. She's in the water, in the water, in the water..."

There was a tremendous pang in Simon's chest, like someone had punched him right in the sternum. Just off to the side of the boat, something appeared, something like stone and seaweed. No. A face, and a crown of hair. It was Clary, floating on her back, eyes closed, hair leading the way. He reached out to her, but the water was going too fast and she was pulled upriver.

"You could make it all better!" Maureen shouted, jumping up. The boat rocked. "Who are you going to save, Daylighter?"

With that she dove off the other side of the boat. Simon grasped the long neck of the swan to hold his balance and scanned the waters. Clary had already floated twenty or more feet away, and Maureen was floating in the same manner, now quiet and seemingly asleep, at about half the distance.

There was not a lot of time to think. He wasn't the strongest swimmer, and the undertow of the river would probably pull him down. The cold would render him numb and probably kill him first.

And he had two people to save.

"This isn't real," he said to himself. But the pain in his chest said otherwise. The pain was calling to him. He was also sure that, real or not, when he jumped in the river, it was going to hurt as much or more as anything he'd ever felt. The river was real *enough*.

What was real? What did he have to do? Was he supposed to swim *past* a young girl and leave her? If he ever made it that far.

"Hard choices," said a voice behind him.

He didn't have to turn to know it was Jace, balanced elegantly on the tail of the wooden swan.

"That's what it's all about. Hard choices. They never get easier."

"You're not helping," Simon said, kicking off his shoes.

"So you're going in?" Jace looked at the water and cringed. "Even I'd think twice about that. And I'm amazing."

"Why do you have to get involved in everything?" Simon asked.

"I go where Clary goes."

The two bodies drifted on.

"So do I," Simon said. And he jumped off the right side of the boat, holding his nose. No diving. No need for theatrics. Jumping was enough, and at least it would keep him upright.

The pain of the water was even worse than he thought. It was like jumping through glass. The icy cold crackled all over his body, forcing all the air from his lungs. He reached for the boat but it drifted off, with Jace at the tail, waving. Simon's clothes were pulling him under, but he had to fight. Hard as it was to move his arms, he stretched out to try to swim. His muscles contracted, unable to function at this temperature.

None of them could survive this. And this did not feel like a dream. Being in this water, which was pulling harder now, pulling him down—this was as good as being dead. But something crackled into his mind, some knowledge that had been well, well pushed away. He had known what it was like to be dead. He had had to claw his way out of the ground. He'd had soil in his eyes and in his mouth. The girl, Maureen, she was dead. Clary was not. He knew this because his own heart was still beating—erratically, but still beating.

Clary.

He reached out again and struggled with the water. One stroke.

Clary.

Two strokes. Two strokes were ridiculous. The water was faster and stronger and his limbs were shaking and so heavy. He started to feel sleepy.

"You can't give up now," said Jace. The boat had circled around and was now on Simon's right side, just out of reach. "Tell me what you know."

Simon was not in the mood to be quizzed. The river and the earth itself were pulling him down.

"Tell me what you know," Jace insisted.

"I ... I..."

Simon couldn't make words.

"Tell me!"

"C ... C ... Clar..."

"Clary. And what do you know about her?"

Simon definitely couldn't speak anymore. But he knew the answer. He would go to her. Alive. Dead. Fighting the river. Even if his dead body drifted alongside hers, that would somehow have to be enough. The knowledge caused his body to warm, just a bit. He kicked against the water.

"There you go!" said Jace. "Now you're getting it. Now, you go."

Simon's entire body shuddered violently. His face dipped below the surface for a moment and he took on water, which burned him from the inside. He pushed out again, spat it out.

One stroke. Two. Three. It wasn't as futile now. He was swimming. Four. Five. He counted them off. Six. Seven.

"I know the feeling," Jace said, drifting alongside him. "It's hard to explain. They don't make greeting cards for it."

Eight. Nine.

The city began to light up. Starting at the ground level, the lights appeared, reaching up toward the sky.

"When you realize it," Jace said, "you know that you can do anything, because you have to. Because it's you. You're one."

Ten. Eleven.

No need to count now. Jace and the swan were lagging behind, and now he was alone, swimming on, his body pumping with adrenaline. He turned to look for Maureen, but she was gone. Clary, however, was still clearly visible, floating just ahead. Not floating.

Swimming. Toward him. She was doing exactly what he was doing, forcing her body on, shuddering, pushing through the water.

Simon powered through the last strokes and felt the touch of her hand. He would go—he would go with her. And she was smiling, her lips blue.

And then he felt the ground under him—some surface under the water, something just a foot or two down. Clary reacted at the same moment, and they both grabbed at each other and struggled to their feet. They were standing in the Bethesda Fountain, the angel statue looking down on them, pouring water on their heads.

"Y—you—" Clary said.

Simon didn't try to speak. He embraced her, and they shuddered together before stepping carefully out of the fountain and lying down on the bricks of the terrace, heaving for breath. The moon was wide—too wide and too close.

Mentally, Simon told the moon to stop being so close and bright and that it should just generally shut up with the mooniness. He reached out and took Clary's hand, which was already extended, waiting for his.

When he opened his eyes, he was not outside. He was on something fairly comfortable and plush. Simon reached around and felt a velvety surface under him. He sat up and realized he was on a sofa in the reception room. The tea set was there, in front of him. Magnus and Catarina were standing against the wall, conferring, and Jem sat in the chair between them and watched them both.

"Sit up slowly," he said. "Take a few deep breaths."

"What the hell?" Simon said.

"You drank water from Lake Lyn," Jem said quietly. "The waters produce hallucinations."

"You had us drink water from *Lake Lyn*? Where's Clary?"

"She is fine," Jem said quietly. "Drink some water. You must be thirsty."

A glass was already against Simon's lips. Catarina was holding it.

"Are you joking?" Simon said. "You want me to drink that? After what just happened?"

"It's fine," Catarina said. She took a long sip from the glass and held it back in front of Simon's mouth. He did have a crazy case of cottonmouth, actually. His tongue felt thick. He took the glass and drank it back in one go, then filled it again, and again from a pitcher on the table. Only after the third glass did he feel like he could speak again.

"Doesn't that drive people insane?" he said, not bothering to disguise his anger in any way.

Jem sat calmly, his hands resting on his knees. Simon could see his age now, not in his face but behind his eyes. They were dark mirrors that reflected the passage of uncounted years.

"Had something gone wrong, you would have been with the Silent Brothers within the hour. I may not be a Silent Brother anymore, but I have previously treated those who have consumed the waters. Magnus prepared the tea because he has worked with both of your minds. Catarina, of course, is a nurse. You were always safe. I am sorry. None of us wanted to deceive you. This was done for your benefit."

"Not an explanation," Simon said. "I want to see Clary. I want to know what's going on."

"She's fine," Catarina said. "I'll go check on how she's doing. Don't worry."

She left, and Jem leaned forward in his chair.

"Before Clary comes in, I need to know: What did you *see?*"

"When you drugged me?"

"Simon, this is important. What did you see?"

"I was in New York. I … thought I was in New York. Did we go to New York? Did you open a Portal?"

Jem shook his head.

"You were in this room the entire time. Please. Tell me."

"Clary and I were in Central Park, by the Bethesda Fountain. The angel in the fountain flew away and the fountain flooded, and Clary disappeared. Then some boat came and I was on a 'tunnel of love' ride with Jace, and he kept telling me to remember where we met, even though I didn't see him."

"Stop a moment," Jem said. "What does that mean to you?"

"I have no idea. I just know he was saying that I had to remember."

"*Do* you remember?"

"No," Simon snapped. "I barely remember anything. I know I was probably with Clary. Clary could see him."

"Go on," Jem said. "What happened then?"

"I saw Maia," he said. "And I saw Jordan. He was covered in blood. Then this ride dumped me out on the East River, and some kid named Maureen said she died because of me and jumped in. Clary was floating on the water and I..."

He shuddered again, and Jem immediately stood and produced a blanket, wrapping it around his shoulders.

"Move closer to the fire," Jem said, guiding him up and to a chair. When Simon had settled a bit and warmed, Jem encouraged him to continue.

"Maureen told me I had to decide which one of them to save. Jace showed up again and gave me some lecture about how all the choices were hard. I jumped in."

"Who did you decide to save?" Jem asked.

"I hadn't ... decided ... anything. I knew I had to jump. And I guess I knew Maureen was dead. She said she was dead. But Clary wasn't. I just had to get to Clary. I got all of this energy all of a sudden and I could swim to her. And when I swam to her, I looked up and she was swimming to me."

Jem sat back and tented his fingers together for a moment.

"I want to see Clary," Simon said through chattering teeth. His body was warm—it had probably never been cold, really—but the river water still felt so real.

Catarina reappeared a moment later with Clary, who was also wrapped in a blanket. Jem immediately got up and offered her his chair. Clary's eyes were wide and shining, and she looked to Simon in relief.

"Did it happen to you, too?" she said. "Whatever that was."

"I think we both got it," he replied. "Are you okay?"

"I'm fine. I'm just ... really cold. I thought I was in the river."

Simon stopped shivering.

"You thought you were in the river?"

"I was trying to swim to you," Clary said. "We were in Central Park, and you got sucked into the ground—like you were being buried alive. And Raphael came, and I was on his motorcycle, and we were flying over the river and I saw you. I jumped off..."

From behind Clary's chair, Catarina nodded.

"I saw something kind of like that," Simon said. "Not exactly, but ... enough. And I reached you. You were swimming to me. Then we were back ..."

"... in Central Park. By the fountain with the angel."

Magnus had joined the group as well and stretched himself out on a sofa. "Bethesda Fountain," he said. "Shadowhunters may have had something to do with building it. I'm just saying."

"What does this all mean?" Simon asked. "What was this about?"

"The two of you are different," Magnus said. "There are things in your backgrounds that mean that ... things have to be done differently. For a start, both of you have had blocks put on your memories. Clary has an unusual amount of angel blood. And you, Simon, used to be a vampire."

"We know that. But why did you have to drug us to do something symbolic?"

"It wasn't symbolic. The *parabatai* test is the test of fire," Catarina said. "You stand in rings of fire to make your bond. This ... this is the test of water. The nature of the test requires that you have no knowledge of the test. Mentally preparing for the test can affect the outcome. This test wasn't about Julian and Emma. It's about the two of you. Think about what you both saw, what you both learned. Think about what you felt. Think about when you were both able to swim to each other when you had nothing left, when you should have died."

Simon and Clary stared at each other. The fog began to lift.

"You took the water," Jem said. "And you joined in the same place in your minds. You were able to find each other. You were linked. 'And it came to pass that the soul of Jonathan was knit with the soul of David, and Jonathan loved him as his own soul.'"

"*Parabatai?*" Simon said. "Wait, wait, wait. Are you trying to tell me this is about being *parabatai?* I can't have a *parabatai.* I turned nineteen two months ago."

"Not exactly," Magnus said.

"What do you mean *not exactly?*"

"Simon," Magnus said plainly, "you died. You were dead for nearly half a year. You may have been walking around, but you were not alive, not as a human. That time does not count. By Shadowhunter standards, you are still eighteen. And you have the whole year until your nineteenth birthday to find a *parabatai.*" He looked toward Clary. "Clary, as you know, is still within the age limit. There should be time for you to Ascend and then for you two to become *parabatai* immediately—if that's what you want."

"Some people are uniquely suited to be *parabatai,*" said Magnus. "Born to it, you might say. People think it's about getting along, about always agreeing, being in sync. It's not. It's about being better together. Fighting better together. Alec and Jace haven't always agreed, but they've always been better together."

"It has been spoken of often to me," Jem said in his soft voice, "how much the two of you were dedicated to each other. The manner in which you have always stood up for each other and put the other first. When a *parabatai* bond is true, when the friendship runs deep and honest, it can be ... transcendent." There was sadness in his eyes, a sadness so profound it was almost frightening. "We needed to find out if what had been observed about the two of you was true for your sake. You're about to witness the ceremony. That can cause a powerful reaction in true *parabatai*. We had to know for sure that it was true and that you could withstand it. The test told us what we needed to know."

Clary's eyes had gone very wide. "Simon...," she whispered. Her voice was raspy.

"It's a bit of a technicality," Magnus added, "but Shadowhunters have no problems with technicalities. They love a technicality. Look at Jem. Jem is a technicality in the flesh. People don't come back from being Silent Brothers, either, and there he is."

Jem smiled at this, the sadness in his eyes receding.

"Parabatai," Clary said again.

And in that moment, something settled over Simon. Something like a blanket on a cold day. Something completely reassuring.

"Parabatai," he said.

A long moment settled between them, and in that moment, all was decided. There was no need to discuss it. You do not need to ask if your heart should beat, or if you should breathe. He and Clary were *parabatai*. All of Simon's anger was gone. Now he knew. He had Clary, and she would have him. Forever. Their souls knit.

"How did you know?" Simon asked.

"It's not that hard to see," Magnus replied, and finally some of the usual levity was in his voice. "I'm also literally magic."

"It's pretty obvious," Catarina added.

"Even I knew," said Jem. "And I don't know you very well. There's always something about true *parabatai*. They don't need to speak to communicate. I saw the two of you having entire conversations without saying a word. It was like that with my *parabatai*, Will. I never had to ask Will what he was thinking. In fact, it was usually *better* not to ask Will what he was thinking..."

That got a smile from Magnus and Catarina both.

"But I see it between you. True *parabatai* are linked long before the ceremony takes place."

"So we can ... we can do the ceremony?" Clary asked.

"You can," Jem said. "Not tonight. There will be some discussions in the Silent City about it, surely, as this is an unusual case."

"All right," Catarina said. "Now the nurse is taking over. That's enough for tonight. You two need sleep. That water packs a punch. You'll be fine in the morning, but you need to rest. Rest and hydrate. Come on."

Simon went to stand and found that his legs had left him and had been replaced with a wobbly, leg-shaped substance. Catarina caught him up under the shoulder and helped him. Magnus helped Clary to her feet.

"There's a room for you here tonight, Clary," Catarina said. "In the morning we'll have the dress gear brought to you both for Julian and Emma's ceremony."

"Wait," Simon said as he was being ushered out. "Jace kept saying something about how I had to remember how he and I met. What does that mean?"

"That's for you to figure out," Jem said. "The visions caused by Lake Lyn can stir very powerful feelings."

Simon nodded. His body was giving out. He allowed Catarina to help him back to his room.

"What happened to you?" George said as Catarina got him in the door.

"How long have I been gone?" Simon replied, dropping face-first onto his bed. It was a sign of his exhaustion that his terrible, sharp-springed bed felt good. It felt like a hundred down pillows heaped on the back of a bouncy castle.

"Maybe two hours," George said. "You look terrible. What was it?"

"The food," Simon mumbled. "It finally got me."

And then he was asleep.

He felt surprisingly okay when he woke up. He woke before George, even. He got out of bed quietly and picked up his towel and things to go down to the bathrooms. On the ground outside the door, in a black box, was a set of formal gear. Formal Shadowhunter gear looked much like regular gear—it was just lighter in weight, somehow more deeply black, and cleaner than most gear. No tears. No ichor. Fancy duds. He put the box on his bed and quietly continued to the bathroom. No one was awake yet, so he had the whole moldy place to himself. It turned out if you woke up first, you could actually get a tiny bit of hot water, so he stood under the spray, pretended that it didn't taste of rust, and let his body relax in the warmth. There was just enough light coming through the window high up on the wall that he could get what amounted to an almost even shave.

He walked through the empty halls of the Academy, which were softened by the early morning light. Nothing looked so severe this morning. It was almost cozy. He even found one of the hall fires burning, and he stood beside it to get warm before going outside for some air. He wasn't surprised to find Clary there, already dressed, sitting on the top step, looking out over the mist that floated over the grounds at dawn.

"You woke up early too, huh?" she said.

He sat down next to her.

"Yup. Get up before the kitchen starts cooking. That's the only way to escape it. I'm starving, though."

Clary rummaged around in her bag for a moment and produced a bagel wrapped in several small deli napkins.

"Is that...," Simon said.

"You think I would come from New York empty-handed? No cream cheese, but, you know, it's something. I know what you need."

Simon held the bagel for a moment.

"It makes sense," she said. "You and me. I feel like it's always been true. It's always what we were. You don't ... I know you don't remember it all, but it's always been you and me."

"I remember enough," he said. "I feel enough."

He wanted to say more, but the enormity of it all—much of this was best left unsaid. For now, anyway. It was still so fresh in his mind, this feeling. This feeling of *completeness*.

So he ate the bagel. Always eat the bagel.

"Emma and Julian," Simon said between bites. "They're only fourteen."

"Jace and Alec were fifteen."

"Still, it seems ... I mean, they've been through a lot. The attack on the L.A. Institute."

"I know," Clary said, nodding. "But bad stuff ... it brings people together sometimes. They've had to grow up fast."

A black horse-drawn carriage appeared on the edge of the road leading to the Academy. As it grew closer, Simon could see a figure in a plain, parchment-colored robe at the reins. When the carriage stopped and the figure turned to them, Simon could see the runes that sealed the man's mouth. When the man spoke, it was not through normal words, but in a voice that landed right inside of Simon's mind.

I am Brother Shadrach. I am here to take you to the ceremony. Please get inside.

"You know," said Simon quietly as they got into the carriage, "there was probably a time when we would have considered this creepy."

"I don't remember that time anymore," replied Clary.

"I guess we're finally even on something we don't remember."

The carriage was simply appointed in black silk, black curtains, black everything, really. But it was well sprung and comfortable, as far as speeding horse carriages go. Brother Shadrach had no fear of speed, and soon the Academy was in the distance and Simon and Clary were looking at each other from across the carriage as they bounced along. Simon tried to talk a few times, but his voice juddered from the impact, the constant *thud thud thud* of the carriage making its way across Brocelind Plain. The roads in Idris were not the smooth highways Simon was used to. They were paved in stone, and there were no rest stops with bathrooms and Starbucks. There was no heat, but each had been provided with a heavy fur blanket. As a vegetarian, Simon didn't really want to use it. As a person without much choice who was freezing, he did.

Simon also had no watch, no phone, nothing to tell the passing time except the rising of the late-autumn sun. He estimated that they rode an hour, maybe more. They entered the calming shade of the Brocelind Forest. The smell of the trees and leaves was almost intoxicating, and the sun came through in slashes and ribbons, illuminating Clary's face and hair, her smile.

His *parabatai.*

They stopped not too far into the forest. The door opened, and Brother Shadrach was there.

We have arrived.

Somehow, it was worse when it stopped. Simon's head and body still felt like they were shaking. Simon looked up and saw that they were near the base of a mountain. It stretched above the trees.

This way.

They followed Brother Shadrach down a barely marked track—a light trail where several feet had passed, leaving just the tiniest scar on the ground, a few inches wide. Through a thicket of trees against the mountainside, there was a doorway, about fifteen feet in height. It was wide at the base and narrower at the top. There was a bas-relief carving of an angel just above the lintel. Brother Shadrach took one of the rings on the door and knocked it hard, just once. The door opened, seemingly of its own accord.

They walked down a narrow passage with smooth marble walls, and descended a staircase made of stone. There were no rails, so he and Clary put their hands on either wall to keep from falling. Brother Shadrach, in his long robe, had no such fear of falling. He seemed to glide down. From there, they were in a larger space, which Simon at first thought was made of stones. After a moment he saw that the walls were mosaicked with bones—some chalky white, some gray, some ashy, and some a disturbing brownish color. Long bones formed arches and columns, and skulls, top side out, formed most of the walls. They were finally left in a room where the bone art was really ambitious—great circling patterns of skulls and bones gave the room shape. Above, smaller bones formed more delicate structures, such as chandeliers, which glowed with witchlights. It was like being shown the end of the world's worst home-decorating show.

You will wait here.

Brother Shadrach exited the chamber, and Simon and Clary were left alone. One thing about the Silent City: It really lived up to its name. Simon had never been anywhere so utterly devoid of sound. Simon worried that if he spoke, the walls of bones would come down on his head and bury them both. They probably wouldn't—that would be a major design flaw—but the sensation was strong.

After several moments the door opened again and Julian appeared alone. Julian Blackthorn may only have been fourteen, but he seemed older, even older than Simon. He had grown quite a bit, and now Simon could look him eye to eye. He had his family's characteristic thick, curling dark-brown hair, and his face had a look of quiet seriousness. It was a seriousness that reminded Simon of the way his mother had looked when his father died, and she'd spent nights awake worrying about how to pay the mortgage and feed her children, how to raise them all by herself. No one wore this kind of expression by choice. The only sign that Julian wasn't an adult was the way his dress gear fit a bit loose, and the way he was just a bit gangly.

"Julian!" Clary said, looking as if she was considering hugging him and then discarding the idea. He seemed too dignified to be squeezed. "Where's Emma?"

"Talking to Brother Zachariah," Julian said. "I mean Jem. She's talking to Jem."

Julian seemed deeply puzzled about this, but also didn't

look to be in the mood to be questioned further.

"So," Clary said, "how do you feel?"

Julian simply nodded and looked around.

He hesitated. "I just want to ... do it. I want to get it done."

This seemed like a slightly odd response. Now that Simon was thinking about his own ceremony with Clary, the prospect seemed amazing. Something to be looked forward to. But Julian had been through a lot. He'd lost his parents, his older brother and sister. It was probably hard to go through something this major without them there.

It was hard to look at Julian and not remember that he had seen Julian's brother Mark not that long ago—Mark, imprisoned and half-mad. That he had decided not to share this fact with Julian, because it would have been unbelievably cruel to do so. Simon still believed his decision had been the right one, but that didn't mean it didn't weigh like a stone in his soul.

"How's L.A.?" he said, and immediately regretted it. How's L.A.? How's that place you live in where you saw your father murdered and your brother taken hostage forever by faeries? How's that?

Julian's mouth curled up at the corner. As if he sensed that Simon was feeling uncomfortable, and he felt sympathetic, but also thought it was funny.

Simon was used to that.

"Hot," Julian said.

Which was fair enough.

"How's your family?" Clary asked.

Julian's face lit up, his eyes glowing like the surface of water. "Everyone is good. Ty's really into detective stuff, Dru's into horror—watching all sorts of mundane movies she's not supposed to. But then she scares herself and has to sleep with the witchlight on. Livvy's gotten really good with the sabre, and Tavvy—"

He broke off as Jem and Emma came down the stairs. Emma's step seemed lighter. There was something about Emma that made Simon think of eternal summers on a beach—her sunbleached hair, her graceful way of moving, her winter tan. Along the inside of one of her arms was a vicious long scar.

She looked at once to Julian, who nodded before starting to pace around the room. Emma immediately wrapped Simon in a hug. Her arms, though smaller than his, wound around him like steel cables. She smelled like sea spray.

"Thank you for being here," she said. "I wanted to write to you but they..." She looked at Jem for a moment. "They said they would tell you. Thank you, both of you."

Julian ran his hand along the smooth marble wall. He seemed to have trouble looking over at Emma. Emma went to him, and Jem followed, speaking to them both for a moment. Clary and Simon stood back and watched them. Something about the way Emma and Julian were acting wasn't quite what Simon expected. Sure, they would be nervous but...

No, it was something else.

Clary tugged on Simon's sleeve, indicating that he should lean down so she could whisper to him.

"They look so"—Clary broke off her sentence and cocked her head slightly to the side—"young."

There was a hint in her voice that this was not a completely satisfactory statement. Something about this was off. But Simon had no time to figure out what. Jem, Emma, and Julian joined them again.

"I will accompany you into the chamber," Jem said. "Clary will walk with Emma. Simon will walk with Julian. Do you feel ready to continue?"

Both Emma and Julian visibly swallowed hard and got very wide-eyed, but both managed to say yes.

"Then we will proceed. Please follow me."

More corridors, but the bone gave way to more white marble, and then marble that had the appearance of gold. They arrived at a great set of doors, which were opened by Brother Shadrach. The room they led to was the largest yet, with a towering, domed ceiling. There were marbles of all colors—white, black, pink, gold, silver. Every surface was utterly smooth. The room was occupied by a ring of Silent Brothers, maybe twenty in all, who parted to allow them in. The light in the room was dim and came from golden sconces and flickering candlelight. The air was thick with incense.

"Simon Lewis and Julian Blackthorn." Jem's voice resonated—for a moment Simon almost thought he heard it inside his mind, the way he had once heard Brother Zachariah's. It still held a depth to it that seemed richer than human. "Cross to the other side of the circle, where they have made a space for you. When you get there, remain there. You will be told what to do."

Simon looked to Julian, who had turned the color of copier paper. Despite looking like he might faint, Julian walked firmly across the room, and Simon followed. Clary and Emma took their places on the opposite side. Jem joined the circle of Silent Brothers, who all stepped back as one, widening the circle. Now the four of them were at the center.

Suddenly, two rings of white and gold fire appeared out of the floor, the flames rising just a few inches, but burning bright and hot.

Emma Carstairs. Step forward.

The voices rang in Simon's head—it was all of the Brothers speaking as one. Emma looked to Clary, then took a single step into one of the rings. She fixed her eyes on Julian and smiled widely.

Julian Blackthorn. Step forward.

Julian stepped into the other ring. His step was quicker, but he kept his head down.

Witnesses, you will stand on the wings of the angel.

This took Simon a moment to work out. He finally saw that at the top of the circle, carved roughly into the floor, was another figure of an angel with outstretched wings. He took his place on one, and Clary the other. This brought him a little closer to the ring of fire. He felt the heat of it creep pleasantly over his cold feet. From this vantage point, he could see Emma's and Julian's expressions.

What was he seeing? It was something he knew.

We begin the Fiery Trial. Emma Carstairs, Julian Blackthorn, enter the center ring. In this ring, you will be bound.

A central ring appeared, joining the two. A Venn diagram of fire. As soon as Emma and Julian were in it, the center ring burned higher, reaching waist height.

Something flickered between Julian and Emma at that moment. It was so quick that Simon couldn't tell which direction it had come from, but he'd seen it out of the corner of one of his eyes. Some look, something about the way one of them stood, something—but it was a look or a stance or *something* that he had seen before.

The fire flashed higher. It was up to their shoulders now.

You will now recite the oath.

Emma and Julian began speaking as one, their voices

both with a small tremble as they recited the ancient Biblical words.

"Whither thou goest, I will go..."

Simon was hit with a bolt of anxiety. What had he just seen? Why was it so familiar? Why did it put him on edge? He studied Emma and Julian again, as best as he could over the fire. They looked like two nervous kids about to do something very serious, while standing in a flaming circle.

There it was again. So quick. The direction was obscured by the flickering at the top of the ring. What the hell was it? Maybe this was precisely what witnesses were supposed to do. Maybe they were supposed to watch for this kind of thing. No. Jem said it was a formality. A formality. Maybe he should have asked this question before standing next to the giant ring of fire.

"Where thou diest, I will die, and there will I be buried..."

Shadowhunter rituals, always cheery.

"The Angel do so to me, and more also..."

Julian tripped on the words "do so to me." He cleared his throat and finished the statement a second after Emma.

Something clicked in Simon's mind. He remembered Jace, suddenly, in his hallucination, saying something about the first time they'd met. And then the memory flashed across his mind like one of those banners trailing off the back of the little planes that flew above the beach off Long Island...

He was sitting with Clary in Java Jones. They were watching Eric read poetry. Simon had decided this was the moment—he was going to tell her. He had to tell her. He had gotten them both coffees and the cups were hot. His fingers were burned. He had to blow on them, which was not a smooth move.

He could feel the burning. The feeling that he had to speak.

Eric was reading some poem that contained the words "nefarious loins." *Nefarious loins, nefarious loins* ... the words danced in his head. He had to speak.

"There's something I want to talk to you about," he said.

Clary made some remark about his band name, and he had to get her back on point.

"It's about what we were talking about before. About me not having a girlfriend."

"Oh, I don't know. Ask Jaida Jones out. She's nice, and she likes you."

"I don't want to ask Jaida Jones out."

"Why not? You don't like smart girls? Still seeking a *rockin' bod?*"

Was she blind? How could she not see? What exactly did he have to do? He had to keep it together. Also, "seeking a rockin' bod"?

But the more he tried, the more oblivious she seemed. And then she became fixated on a green sofa. It was like that sofa contained everything in the world. Here he was, trying to declare his lifelong love, and Clary had fallen for the furniture. But it was more than that. Something was wrong.

"What is it?" he asked. "What's wrong? Clary, what's wrong?"

"I'll be right back," she said. And with that, she put

down the coffee and ran away. He watched her through the window, and somehow he knew that this moment was over, forever. And then he saw...

The ring of fire had extinguished. It was over. The oath was made, and Emma and Julian stood before them all. Julian had a rune on his collarbone, and Emma on her upper arm.

Clary was tugging his arm. He looked over at her and blinked a few times.

You okay? her expression said.

His memory had chosen quite a moment to return.

After the ceremony, they returned to Alicante, where they were taken to the Blackthorn manor to change their clothes. Emma and Julian were taken by the staff to rooms on the main floor. Clary and Simon were led up the grand staircase.

"I don't know what I'm supposed to change into," Simon said. "I didn't get a lot of advance notice."

"I brought you a suit from home," Clary said. "I borrowed it."

"Not from Jace."

"From Eric."

"Eric has a suit? Do you promise it wasn't, like, his dead grandfather's?"

"I can't promise anything, but I do think it will fit."

Simon was shown to a small, fussy bedroom on the second floor, overstuffed with furniture and crowded in by flocked wallpaper and the penetrating stares of some long-deceased Blackthorns who had taken up residence in the form of severe portraits. The suit bag was on the bed. Eric did have a suit—a plain black one. A shirt had also been provided, along with a silver-blue tie and some dress shoes. The suit was an inch or two too short. The shirt was too tight—Simon's daily training had made him into one of these people who burst through a dress shirt. The shoes didn't fit at all, so he wore the soft black shoes that were part of the formal gear. The tie fit fine. Ties were good for this.

He sat on the bed for a moment and let himself think about all that had happened. He closed his eyes and fought the urge to sleep. He felt himself wobbling and dropping off when there was a soft knock on the door. He snorted as he came back from the microsleep.

"Sure," he said, which wasn't what he meant to say. "Yeah. I mean, come in."

Clary entered wearing a green dress that perfectly complemented her hair, her skin, every part of her. And Simon had a revelation. If he still felt romantic attraction toward Clary, seeing her at that moment might have caused him to start sweating and stammering. Now he saw someone he loved, who looked beautiful, and was his friend. And that was all.

"Listen," she said, shutting the door, "back at the ceremony, you looked ... weird. If you don't want to do it... The *parabatai* thing. It was a shock and I don't want you to be..."

"What? No. No."

Instinctively he reached for her hand. She squeezed it hard.

"Okay," she said. "But something happened in there. I saw it."

"In the hallucination I had, from the lake water, I saw Jace, and he kept telling me to remember how we met," he said. "So I was trying to remember. And then right in the middle of the ceremony, I got the memory back. It just kind of ... downloaded."

Clary frowned, her nose wrinkling in confusion. "The

memory of how you met Jace? Wasn't it at the Institute?"

"Yes and no. The memory was really about us, you and me. We were in the coffee shop, Java Jones. You were naming all of these girls I could date and I was ... I was trying to tell you that you were the one I liked."

"Yeah," Clary said, looking down.

"And then you ran out. Just like that."

"Jace was there. You couldn't see him."

"That's what I thought." Simon studied her face. "You ran out while I was telling you how I felt. Which is okay. We were never meant to be ... like that. I think that's what my subconscious, in the annoying form of Jace, wanted me to know. Because I think we are meant to be *together. Parabatai* can't like each other like that. That's why it was important for me to remember. I had to remember that I felt like that. I had to know it was different now. Not in a bad way. In the right way."

"Yes," Clary said. She had gotten a little teary-eyed. "In the right way."

Simon nodded once. It was too big to reply to in words. It was everything. It was all the love he saw in Jem's eyes when he talked about Will, and the love in Alec's face when he looked at Jace, even when Jace was being annoying, and a clear memory he had of Jace holding Alec while he was wounded and the desperation in Jace's eyes, that terror that comes only from thinking you might lose someone you can't live without.

It was Emma and Julian, looking at each other.

Someone was calling for them from downstairs. Clary brushed away a tear and got up and smoothed her already smooth dress.

"This *is* like a wedding," she said. "I feel like they're

going to tell us we have to go pose for the photographer in a minute."

Clary hooked her arm through his.

"One thing," he said, remembering Maia, and Jordan. "Even when I'm a Shadowhunter, I'm still going to be a little bit a Downworlder. I'm never going to turn my back on them. That's the kind of Nephilim I want to be."

"I wouldn't have expected anything else," Clary said.

Downstairs, the two new *parabatai* were examining each other from across the room. Emma stood on one side, wearing a brown dress covered in twining gold flowers. Julian stood on the other, twitching inside his gray suit.

"You look amazing," Clary said to them both, and they looked down shyly.

At the Accords Hall, Jace was waiting for them on the front step, looking like Jace in a suit. Jace in a suit was unbearable. He gave Clary a look up and down.

"That dress is..."

He had to clear his throat. Simon enjoyed his discomfiture. Not much ever threw Jace, but Clary had always been able to throw him like a Wiffle ball on a windy day. His eyes were practically cartoon hearts.

"It's very nice," he said. "So how was the ceremony? What did you think?"

"Definitely more fire than a bar mitzvah," Simon said. "More fire than a barbecue. I'm going to go with Formal Event with the Most Fire."

Jace nodded.

"They were amazing," Clary said. "And..."

She looked to Simon.

"We have news," she said.

Jace cocked his head in interest.

"Later," she said, smiling. "I think everyone is waiting for us to sit down."

"Then we need to get Emma and Julian over here."

Emma and Julian were lurking in the corner of the room, heads close, but with an awkward gap between their bodies.

"I'm going to go talk to them," Jace said, nodding at Julian and Emma. "Give them a few words of manly, thoughtful advice."

As soon as Jace walked away, Clary started to speak, but they were immediately joined by Magnus and Alec. Magnus was about to start guest teaching at the Academy, and they wanted to know how bad the food was. Julian's younger brothers and sisters—Ty, Livvy, Drusilla, and Octavian—were clustered together around the table with the appetizers. Simon glanced over his shoulder and saw Jace unloading Jacely advice onto the new *parabatai*. There was the delicious smell of roasting meat. Large platters of it were being placed on the tables now, along with vegetables and potatoes and breads and cheeses. The wine was being poured. It was time to celebrate. It was nice, Simon thought, in the midst of all the terrible things that could happen and sometimes did happen, there was also this. There was a lot of love.

As Simon turned back, he saw Julian hurrying out of the hall. Jace returned, his arm around Emma's shoulders.

"Everything okay?" Clary asked.

"Everything's fine. Julian needed air. This ceremony, it's intense. So many people. You need to eat."

This was to Emma, who smiled, but kept looking over at the door her *parabatai* had just gone through. Then she turned and saw Ty running across the Hall with a tray containing an entire wheel of cheese.

"Oh," she said, "yeah, that's bad. He can actually eat that entire cheese, but then he'll throw up. I'd better get that or this will end badly for Jules."

She ran after Ty.

"They have a lot on their hands," Jace said, watching her go. "Good thing they have each other. They always will. That's what being *parabatai* is about." He smiled at Alec, who grinned back at him in a way that lit up his whole face.

"About that *parabatai* business," Clary said. "We might as well tell you the news..."

Born to Endless Night

By Cassandra Clare and Sarah Rees Brennan

Magnus had left behind a sleeping child and his worn-out love, and he opened the door on a scene of absolute chaos. For a moment it seemed as if there were a thousand people in his rooms, and then Magnus realized the real situation was far worse.

—Born to Endless Night

CREAK
MURMUR
(...)

Every Night & every Morn
Some to Misery are Born
Every Morn and every Night
Some are Born to sweet delight
Some are Born to sweet delight
Some are Born to Endless Night
—"Auguries of Innocence," William Blake

Magnus believed that many old things were creations of enduring beauty. The pyramids. Michelangelo's *David.* Versailles. Magnus himself.

However, just because something was old and imbued with years of tradition did not *make* it a work of art. Not even if you were Nephilim and thought having the blood of the Angel meant your stuff was better than anybody else's.

Shadowhunter Academy was not a creation of enduring beauty. Shadowhunter Academy was a dump.

Magnus did not enjoy the countryside in early spring, before winter had truly ended. The whole landscape was as monochrome as an old movie, without the narrative energy. Dark gray fields rolled under a pale gray sky, and trees were stripped down to gray claws clutching for the rain clouds. The Academy matched its surroundings, squatting in the landscape like a great stone toad.

Magnus had been here a few times before, visiting friends. He had not liked it. He remembered walking long ago under the cold eyes of students who had been trained in the dark, narrow ways of Clave and Covenant, and who were too young to realize the world might be more complicated than that.

At least back then the place had not been falling down. Magnus stared at one of the slender towers that stood at each of the four corners of the Academy. It was not standing up straight; in fact, it looked like a poor relation of the Leaning Tower of Pisa.

Magnus stared at it, concentrated, and snapped his fingers. The tower leaped back into place as if it were a crouching person who had suddenly straightened up. There was a faint series of cries issuing from the tower windows. Magnus had not realized there were people inside. This struck him as unsafe.

Well, the inhabitants of the formerly leaning tower would soon realize he had done them a favor. Magnus eyed the angel in the stained-glass window set above the door. The angel stared down at him, sword blazing and face censorious, as if he disapproved of Magnus's dress sense and was going to ask him to change.

Magnus walked under the judgmental angel and into the stone hall, whistling softly. The hall was empty. It was still very early in the morning, which perhaps explained some of the grayness. Magnus hoped the day would brighten before Alec arrived.

He had left his boyfriend in Alicante, at his father's house. Alec's sister, Isabelle, was staying there too. Magnus had slept uneasily at the Inquisitor's house last night, and said he would leave them to have breakfast alone—just the family. For years he and Robert and Maryse Lightwood had arranged their lives so that they never saw each other unless duty called or large cash payments for Magnus beckoned.

Magnus was fairly sure Robert and Maryse missed those days and wished they would come back. Magnus knew they would never have chosen him for their son, and even if their son had to date a man, they would have preferred not a Downworlder, and certainly not a Downworlder who had been around during the days of Valentine's Circle and seen them at a time in their lives they were not proud of now.

For himself Magnus did not forget. He might love one Shadowhunter, but it was impossible to love them all. He expected many more years politely avoiding and, when necessary, politely tolerating Alec's parents. It was a very small price to pay to be with Alec.

Just now he had escaped Robert Lightwood and had a chance to inspect the rooms Magnus had requested the Academy prepare for them. From the state of the rest of the Academy, Magnus had dark forebodings about these rooms.

He ran lightly up the stairs in that silent, echoing place. He knew where he was going. He had agreed to come and give a series of guest lectures at the request of his old friend Catarina Loss, but he was, after all, the High Warlock of Brooklyn and he had certain standards. He had no intention of leaving his boyfriend for weeks. He had made it clear that he required a suite for himself and for Alec, and that the suite had to include a kitchen. He was not going to eat any of the meals Catarina had described in her letters. If possible, he intended to avoid even seeing any of the meals Catarina had described.

The map Catarina had drawn him was accurate: He found their rooms at the top of the building. The connected attic rooms could, Magnus guessed, possibly count as a suite. And there was a little kitchen, though Magnus feared it had not been updated since the 1950s. There was a dead mouse in the sink.

Maybe someone had left it there to welcome them. Maybe it was a festive gift.

Magnus wandered through the rooms, waving a hand that encouraged the windows and countertops to wash themselves. He snapped his fingers and sent the dead mouse as a present to his cat, Chairman Meow. Maia Roberts, the leader of the New York werewolf pack, was cat-sitting for them. Magnus hoped she would think Chairman Meow was a mighty hunter.

Then he opened the little refrigerator. The heavy door fell off, until Magnus gave it a stern look and it hopped back on. Magnus looked inside the refrigerator, waved his free hand, and saw to his satisfaction that it was now filled with many items from Whole Foods.

Alec would never have to know, and Magnus would send the money to Whole Foods later anyway. He swept through the rooms one more time, adding cushions to the bare, sad wooden chairs and heaping their multicolored blankets from home onto the lopsided canopy bed.

Emergency decorating mission accomplished and

feeling far more cheerful, Magnus descended into the main hall of the Academy, hoping to find Catarina or see Alec coming. There was no sign of activity, so despite his misgivings, Magnus went to check for Catarina in the dining hall.

She was not there, but there were a few scattered Nephilim students having breakfast. Magnus supposed the poor creatures had gotten up early to throw javelins or some other unsavory business.

There was a thin blond girl heaping a gray substance that could have been porridge or eggs onto her plate. Magnus watched with silent horror as she carried it toward a table, acting as if she actually intended to eat it.

Then she noticed Magnus.

"Oh, *hello*," said the blonde, stopping in her tracks as if she had been hit by a beautiful truck.

He gave her his most charming smile. Why not? "Hello."

Magnus had been around the block before blocks were invented. He was familiar with what this look meant. People had undressed him with their eyes before.

He was impressed with the intensity of this particular look. It was rarer for people to rip off his clothes and send them flying to various corners of the room with their eyes.

They were not even particularly exciting clothes. Magnus had decided to dress with quiet dignity, as befitted an educator, and was wearing a black shirt and tailored pants. He was also, for that stylish educator touch, wearing a short robe over the shirt, but the glittering gold thread running through the robe was very subtle.

"You must be Magnus Bane," the blonde said. "I've heard a lot about you from Simon."

"I can't blame him for bragging," said Magnus.

"We're so glad to have you here," continued the blonde. "I'm Julie. I'm practically Simon's best friend. I'm very cool with Downworlders."

"How nice for us Downworlders," Magnus murmured.

"I'm very excited for your lectures. And to spend time together. You, me, and Simon."

"Won't that be a party," said Magnus.

She was trying, at least, and not all Nephilim did. And she mentioned Simon every other breath, despite Simon being a mundane. Besides, the attention was flattering. Magnus turned the smile up another notch.

"I look forward to getting to know you better, Julie."

It was possible he misjudged the smile. Julie reached out a hand as if to take Magnus's, and dropped her tray. She and Magnus looked down at the broken bowl and the sad, gray contents.

"It's better this way," Magnus said with conviction.

He gestured, and the whole mess vanished. Then he gestured to Julie's outstretched hand, and a pot of blueberry yogurt with a small spoon appeared in it.

"Oh!" Julie exclaimed. "Oh, wow, thank you."

"Well, since the alternative was going back and getting more of the Academy food," said Magnus, "I think you owe me big. Possibly you owe me your firstborn. But don't worry, I'm not in the market for anybody's firstborn."

Julie giggled. "Do you want to sit down?"

"Thank you for the offer, but actually, I was looking for someone."

Magnus surveyed the room, which was slowly filling up. He still did not see Catarina, but at the door he saw Alec, with the air of someone newly arrived and talking to a mundane Indian boy who looked about sixteen.

He caught Alec's eye and smiled.

"There's my someone," he said. "Lovely to meet you, Julie."

"Likewise, Magnus," she assured him.

As Magnus approached Alec, the other boy shook Alec's hand. "I just wanted to say thanks," the boy said, and left, with a nod to Magnus.

"Do you know him?" Magnus asked.

Alec looked mildly dazed. "No," he said. "But he knew all about me. We were talking about—all the ways there are to be a Shadowhunter, you know?"

"Check you out," said Magnus. "My famous boyfriend, inspiration to the masses."

Alec smiled, a little embarrassed but mostly amused. "So, that girl was flirting with you."

"Really?" Magnus asked. "How could you tell?"

Alec gave him a skeptical look.

"Well, it has been known to happen. I've been around for a long time," said Magnus. "I've also been gorgeous for a long time."

"Is that so?" said Alec.

"I'm in high demand. What are you going to do about it?"

He could not, and would not, have teased Alec like this years ago. Alec had been new to love, stumbling through his own terror at who he was and how he felt, and Magnus had been as careful with him as he knew how to be, afraid to hurt Alec and afraid to shatter this feeling between them, new to Magnus as it was to Alec.

It was a recent joy to be able to tease Alec and know he would not hurt him, to see Alec standing in a different way than he used to, easy and casual and confident in his own skin, with none of his *parabatai*'s swagger but with a quiet assurance all his own.

The dimly lit stone dining room, the clatter of students eating and gossiping, faded away, nothing but background to Alec's smile.

"This," said Alec. He reached out and tugged Magnus to him by the front of his robe, leaning back against the door frame and drawing Magnus slowly in for a kiss.

Alec's mouth was soft and sure, the kiss slow, his strong hands holding Magnus close, pressed along the warm line of his body. Behind Magnus's closed eyelids, the morning turned from gray to gold.

Alec was here. Even a hell dimension, as Magnus recalled, had been greatly improved by Alec's presence. Shadowhunter Academy was going to be a snap.

Simon came up late to breakfast and found Julie capable of talking about nothing but Magnus Bane.

"Warlocks are sexy," she said in the tones of one who had had a revelation.

"Ms. Loss is our teacher, and I am trying to eat." Beatriz stared dispiritedly at her plate.

"Vampires are gross and dead, werewolves are gross and hairy, and faeries are treacherous and would sleep with your mom," said Julie. "Warlocks are the sexy Downworlders. Think about it. They *all* have daddy issues. And Magnus Bane is the sexiest of them all. He can be High Warlock of my pants."

"Uh, Magnus has a boyfriend," said Simon.

There was a frightening glint in Julie's eye. "There are some mountains you still want to climb, even though there are 'No Trespassing' signs up."

"I think that's gross," said Simon. "You know, the way you think vampires are."

Julie made a face at him. "You're so sensitive, Simon. Why must you always be so sensitive?"

"You're so terrible, Julie," said Simon. "Why must you always be so terrible?"

Alec had been with Magnus, Julie reported. Simon was thinking more about that than Julie's terribleness, which after all was not anything new. Alec was going to be staying at the Academy for weeks. He usually saw Alec in crowds of people, and it had never seemed the right time to talk to him. It was the right time now. It was time to talk it out, the problem between them that Jace had hinted at so darkly. He didn't want there to be something wrong between him and Alec, who seemed like a good guy from what Simon could remember. Alec was Isabelle's big brother, and Isabelle was—he was almost certain—Simon's girlfriend.

He wanted her to be.

"Should we try to get a little archery practice in before class?" George asked.

"That's jock talk, George," said Simon. "I've asked you not to do that. But sure."

They all got up, pushing their bowls aside, and walked to the front doors of the Academy, heading for the practice grounds.

That was the plan, but none of them made it to the practice grounds that day. None of them made it past the threshold of the Academy. They all stood on the front step, in a horrified cluster.

On the stone of the front step was a bundle, wrapped in a fuzzy yellow blanket. Simon's eyes failed him in a way that had nothing to do with his glasses and everything to do with panic, refusing to register what was actually before him. *It's a bundle of junk,* Simon told himself. Someone had left a parcel of garbage on their doorstep.

Except the bundle was moving, in small incremental movements. Simon watched the fretful stir beneath the blanket, looked at the gleaming eyes peering out from the cocoon of fuzzy yellows, and his mind accepted what he was seeing, even as another shock came. A tiny fist emerged from the blankets, waving as if in protest at everything that was occurring.

The fist was blue, the rich navy of the sea when it was deep and you were on a boat as evening fell. The blue of Captain America's suit.

"It's a baby," Beatriz breathed. "It's a warlock baby."

There was a note pinned to the baby's yellow blanket. Simon saw it at the precise moment that the wind caught it, snatching it off the blanket and whirling it away. Simon grabbed the paper out of the cold grip of the wind and looked at the writing, a hasty scribble on a torn scrap of paper.

The note read: *Who could ever love it?*

"Oh no, the baby's blue," said George. "What are we going to do?"

He frowned as if he had not meant that to rhyme. Then he knelt down, because George was the not-so-secret sweetheart of the group, and awkwardly took the yellow-wrapped bundle in his arms. He stood up, his face ashen, holding the baby.

"What are we going to do?" Beatriz warbled, echoing George. "What are we going to do?"

Julie was plastered up against the door. Simon had personally seen her cut off a very large demon's head with a very small knife, but she appeared as if she would expire with terror if someone asked her to hold the baby.

"I know what to do," said Simon.

He would go find Magnus, he thought. He knew Magnus and Alec had arrived and were awake. He needed to talk to Alec anyway. Magnus had fixed Simon's demon amnesia. Magnus had been around for centuries. He was the most adult adult that Simon knew. A warlock baby abandoned in this fortress of Shadowhunters was a problem Simon had no idea how to fix, and he felt he needed an adult. Simon was already turning to go.

"Should I give the baby mouth to mouth?" George asked.

Simon froze. "No, don't do that. The baby is breathing. The baby's breathing, right?"

They all stood and stared at the little bundle. The baby waved his fist again. If the baby was moving, Simon thought, the baby must be breathing. He was not even going to think about zombie babies at this time.

"Should I get the baby a hot water bottle?" George said.

Simon took a deep breath. "George, don't lose your head," he said. "This baby is not blue because he is cold or because he cannot breathe. Mundane babies are not blue in this way. This baby is blue because he is a warlock, just like Catarina."

"Not just like Ms. Loss," Beatriz said in a high voice. "Ms. Loss is more of a sky blue, whereas this baby is more of a navy blue."

"You seem very knowledgeable," George decided. "You should hold the baby."

"No!" Beatriz squawked.

She and Julie both threw up their hands in surrender.

As far as they were concerned, it was clear, George was holding a loaded baby and should not do anything rash.

"Everybody stay where you are," said Simon, trying to keep his voice calm.

Julie perked up. "Oooh, Simon," she said. "Good idea."

Simon fled across the hall and up the stairs, moving at a pace that would have amazed his evil Shadowhunter gym teacher. Scarsbury had never provided him with motivation like this.

He knew that Magnus and Alec had been put in a fancy suite up in the attics. Apparently there was even a separate kitchen. Simon just kept heading up, knowing he would hit the attics at some point.

He reached the attics, heard murmuring and movement behind the door, and flung the door wide open.

Then he stood, arrested on his second threshold of the day.

There was a sheet over Alec and Magnus, but Simon could see enough. He could see Alec's white, rune-scarred shoulders and Magnus's wild black hair spread on the pillow. He could see Alec freeze, then turn his head and give Simon a look of absolute horror.

Magnus's golden cat eyes gleamed from over Alec's pale shoulder. He sounded almost amused as he asked: "Can we help you?"

"Oh my God," Simon said. "Oh wow. Oh wow, I am really sorry."

"Please leave," said Alec in a tight, controlled voice.

"Right!" said Simon. "Of course!" He paused. "I can't leave."

"Believe me," said Alec. "You can."

"There is an abandoned baby on the front steps of the

Academy and I think it's a warlock!" Simon blurted out.

"Why do you think the baby is a warlock?" Magnus asked. He was the only one in the room who was composed.

"Um, because the baby is navy blue."

"That is fairly compelling evidence," Magnus admitted. "Could you give us a moment to get dressed?"

"Yes! Of course!" said Simon. "Again, I'm very sorry."

"Go now," Alec suggested.

Simon went.

After a short while Magnus emerged from the attic suite dressed in skintight black clothes and a shimmering gold robe. His hair was still wrecked, going every which way as if Magnus had been caught in a small personal tempest, but Simon was not going to quibble about the hair of his potential savior.

"Really sorry again," said Simon.

Magnus made a lazy gesture. "Seeing your face was not the best moment of my day, Simon, but these things happen. Admittedly, they have never happened to Alec before, and he needs a few more minutes. Show me where the child is."

"Follow me," said Simon.

He ran down the stairs as fast as he had run up them, taking two at a time. He found the tableau at the threshold just as he had left it, Beatriz and Julie the horrified audience to George's terrified and inexpert baby-holding. The bundle was now making a low, plaintive sound.

"What took you so long?" Beatriz hissed.

Julie still looked very shaken, but she managed to say: "Hello, Magnus."

"Hello again, Julie," said Magnus, once again the only calm person in a room. "Let me hold the baby."

"Oh, thank you," George breathed. "Not that I don't like

the baby. But I have no idea what to do with it."

George appeared to have bonded in the time it took Simon to run up and down a flight of stairs. He looked mushily down at the baby, clutching the bundle for a moment, and then as he handed the baby over to Magnus, he fumbled and almost dropped the baby on the stone floor.

"By the Angel!" Julie exclaimed, hand pressed to her breast.

Magnus arrested the fumble and caught the child, holding the blanket-wrapped bundle close against his gold-embroidered chest. He held the baby with more expertise than George did, which meant that he supported the baby's head and it appeared as if he might have held a baby once or twice in his life. George had not looked like he was going to win any baby-holding championships.

With a hand glimmering with rings, Magnus drew the blanket back a little, and Simon held his breath. Magnus's eyes traveled over the baby, his impossibly small hands and feet, the wide eyes in his small face, the curls on his head so dark a blue they were almost black. The baby's low constant sound of complaint rose a little, complaining harder, and Magnus smoothed the blanket back into place.

"He's a boy," said Magnus.

"Aw, a boy," said George.

"He's about eight months old, I would say," Magnus continued. "Someone raised him until they could not bear it anymore, and I suppose through the recruitment of mundanes to the Academy, someone thought they knew the place to bring a child they did not want."

"But someone wouldn't leave their child...," George began, and fell silent under Magnus's gaze.

"People would. People do. And the choices people make

are different, with warlock children," Magnus said. His voice was quiet.

"So there's no chance anyone is coming back for him," said Beatriz.

Simon took the note he had found folded on the child's blanket and gave it to Magnus. He did not feel, looking into Magnus's face, that he could give it to anyone else. Magnus looked at the note, nodded. *Who could ever love it?* flashed between his fingers, and then he tucked it away into his robe.

There were other students gathering around them, and a rising hubbub of noise and confusion. If Simon had been in New York, he figured people would have been taking pictures of the baby with their phones. He felt a little like an exhibition in a zoo, and he was so grateful Magnus was there.

"What is happening?" asked a voice from the top of the stairs.

Dean Penhallow was standing there, with her strawberry-blond hair loose over her shoulders, clutching around her a black silk robe etched with dragons. Catarina stood at her side, fully dressed in jeans and a white blouse.

"Seems like someone left a baby instead of the milk bottles," she said. "That was careless. Welcome, Magnus."

Magnus gave her a little wave with his free hand and a wry smile.

"What? Why? Why would anyone do such a thing? What are we supposed to do with it?" the dean asked.

Sometimes Simon forgot that Dean Penhallow was really young, young for a teacher, let alone a dean. Other times he was forcefully reminded of that fact. She looked as panicked as Beatriz and Julie had.

"He's much too young to be taught," said Scarsbury,

peering down from the crowded staircase. “Perhaps we should contact the Clave.”

“If the baby needs a bed,” George offered, “Simon and I could keep him in our sock drawer.”

Simon gave George an appalled glare. George looked distressed.

Alec Lightwood moved like a shadow through the crowds of students, head and shoulders above most of them but not shoving anyone aside. He moved quietly, persistently, until he was where he wanted to be: at Magnus’s side.

When Magnus saw Alec, his whole body relaxed. Simon had not even been aware of the tension running all through Magnus’s frame until he saw the moment when ease returned.

“This is the warlock child Simon was talking about,” Alec said in a low voice, and nodded toward the baby.

“As you see,” said Magnus, “the baby would not be able to pass for a mundane. His mother clearly does not want him. He is in a nest of the Nephilim, and I cannot think, among faeries or Shadowhunters or werewolves, where in the world he could possibly belong.”

Magnus’s calm and amusement had seemed infinite until a few minutes ago. Now Simon heard his voice fraying, a rope on which too much strain had been put, and which must soon snap.

Alec put a hand on Magnus’s upper arm, just above the elbow. He clasped Magnus’s arm firmly, almost absently providing silent support. He looked up at Magnus and then looked down, for a long, thoughtful moment, at the baby.

“Can I hold him?” Alec asked.

Surprise flew over Magnus’s face but did not linger. “Sure,” he said, and put the baby in Alec’s arms, held out to receive him.

Maybe it was that Alec had held a baby more recently than Magnus had, and certainly more often than George. Maybe it was that Alec was wearing what seemed to be an incredibly ancient sweater, worn soft with years and faded from dark green to gray, with only traces remaining of the original color.

Whatever the reason, as soon as Alec took the baby, the continuous soft whimpering noise ceased. There was still the buzzing of urgent whispers, up and down the hall, but the small group surrounding the child suddenly found themselves in a pocket of hushed silence.

The baby gazed up at Alec with grave eyes only a shade darker than Alec's own. Alec gazed back at the baby. He looked as surprised as anyone else by the baby's sudden hush.

"So," said Delaney Scarsbury. "Should we contact the Clave and put this matter before them, or what?"

Magnus turned in a whirl of gold and fixed Scarsbury with a look that made him shrink back against the wall.

"I do not intend to leave a warlock child to the tender mercies of the Clave," Magnus declared, his voice extremely cold. "We have this, don't we, Alec?"

Alec was still looking down at the baby. He glanced up when Magnus addressed him, his face briefly dazed, as a man woken from a dream, but his expression set as with a sudden resolve.

"Yeah," he answered. "We do."

Magnus mirrored the move Alec had made before, clasping Alec's upper arm in silent thanks, or a show of support. Alec returned to looking down at the baby.

It felt as if a huge weight had been lifted off Simon's chest. It was not that he had been truly worried that he and

George would have to raise the baby in their sock drawer—well, possibly a little worried—but the specter of a huge responsibility had loomed before him. This was a helpless, abandoned little child. Simon knew, all too well, how Downworlders were viewed by Shadowhunters. Simon had had no idea what to do. Magnus had taken the responsibility. He had taken the baby from them, both metaphorically and in actuality. He had not turned a hair as he did it. He had not acted as if it were a big deal at all.

Magnus was a really cool guy.

Simon knew Isabelle had slept over in Alicante, so she and Alec would both be with her father for one night. She was going down to the house where Ragnor Fell had once lived, where there was a working telephone. Catarina had set up another telephone in the Academy she said he could use this once. They had a telephone date. Simon was planning to tell her how cool Magnus and her brother had been.

Magnus thought he might become the first recorded warlock in history to have a heart attack.

He was walking around the practice grounds of Shadowhunter Academy at night because he could not stay in there and breathe stifling air with hundreds of Nephilim any longer.

That poor child. Magnus had hardly been able to look at him, he was so small and so entirely helpless. He could not do anything but think of how vulnerable the child was, and how deep the misery and pain of his mother must have been. He knew what kind of darkness warlocks were conceived under and born into. Catarina had been brought up by a loving family who had known what she was, and raised her to be who she was. Magnus had been able to pass for human, until he was not.

Magnus knew what happened to warlock children who were born visibly not human, who their mothers and the whole world could not bring themselves to accept. He could not calculate how many children there might have been down all the dark ages of the world, who could have been magical, who could have been immortal, but had never gotten the chance to live at all. Children abandoned as this one had been, or drowned as Magnus himself had almost been, children who never left a bright magical mark in history, who never received or gave love, who were never anything but a whisper fading on the wind, a memory of pain and despair fading into the dark. Nothing else was left of those lost children, not a spell, not a laugh, not a kiss.

Without luck, Magnus would have been among the lost. Without love, Catarina and Ragnor would have been among the lost.

Magnus had no idea what to do with this latest lost child.

He thanked, not for the first time, whatever strange, beautiful fortune had sent him Alec. Alec had been the one who carried the warlock baby up the stairs to the attic, and when Magnus had conjured up a crib, Alec had been the one to place the baby tenderly in it.

Then when the baby had started to scream his little blue head off, Alec had taken the baby out of the crib and walked the floor with him, patting his back and murmuring to him. Magnus called up supplies and tried to make formula milk. He'd read somewhere that you tested how hot the milk was on yourself, and ended up burning his own wrist.

The baby had cried for hours and hours and hours. Magnus supposed he could not blame the small lost soul.

The baby was finally sleeping now that the sun had set

through the tiny attic windows, and the whole day was gone. Alec was half sleeping, leaning against the baby's crib, and Magnus had felt he had to get out. Alec had simply nodded when Magnus said he was stepping out for a breath of air. Possibly Alec had been too exhausted to care what Magnus did.

The moon shone, round as a pearl, turning the stained-glass angel's hair to silver and the bare winter fields into expanses of light. Magnus was tempted to howl at the moon like a werewolf.

He could not think of anywhere he could take the child, anyone he could entrust the child to who would want it, who might love it. He could scarcely think of anywhere in this hostile world where the child might be safe.

He heard the sound of raised voices and rushing footsteps, this late, out in front of the Academy. *Another emergency*, Magnus thought. *It's been one day, and at this rate the Academy is going to kill me.* He went running from the practice grounds to the front of the door, where he saw the very last person he had ever expected to see here in Idris: Lily Chen, the head of the New York vampire clan, with blue streaks in her hair that matched her blue waistcoat and her high heels leaving deep indentations in the dirt.

"Bane," she said. "I need help. Where is he?"

Magnus was too tired to argue with her.

"Follow me," said Magnus, and led the way back up the stairs. Even as he went, he thought to himself that all the noise he had heard outside the Academy could not possibly have been Lily alone.

He thought that, but he did not suspect what was to come.

Magnus had left behind a sleeping child and his worn-out

love, and he opened the door on a scene of absolute chaos. For a moment it seemed as if there were a thousand people in his rooms, and then Magnus realized the real situation was far worse.

Every single one of the Lightwood family was there, each one causing enough noise for ten. Robert Lightwood was there, saying something in his booming voice. Maryse Lightwood was holding a bottle and appeared to be waving it around, giving a speech. Isabelle Lightwood was standing on top of a stool for no reason in the world Magnus could see. Jace Herondale was, even more mysteriously, lying flat out on the stone floor, and apparently he'd brought Clary, who looked at Magnus as if she were puzzled by her presence here as well.

Alec was standing in the middle of the room, in the middle of the human storm that was his family, holding the baby protectively to his chest. Magnus could not believe it was possible for his heart to sink further, but it somehow struck him as the greatest disaster in the world that the baby was awake.

Magnus stopped on the threshold, staring at the chaos, feeling entirely uncertain about what to do next.

Lily had no such hesitation.

"LIGHTWOOD!" Lily bellowed, charging in.

"Ah yes, Lily Chen, I believe?" said Robert Lightwood, turning to her with the dignity of the Inquisitor and no sign of surprise. "I remember you were interim representative for the vampires on the Council for a time. Glad to see you again. What can I do for you?"

Robert was obviously doing his best to show every courtesy to an important vampire leader. Magnus appreciated that, a little.

Lily did not care. "Not you!" she snapped. "Who even are you?"

Thick black brows shot up to the sky.

"I'm the Inquisitor?" said Robert. "I was the head of the New York Institute for over a decade?"

Lily rolled her dark eyes. "Oh, congratulations, do you want a medal? I need *Alexander* Lightwood, obviously," said Lily, and swanned past a staring Robert and Maryse to their son. "Alec! You know that faerie dealer, Mordecai? He's been selling fruit to mundanes at the edge of Central Park. Again! He's at it again! And then Elliott bit a mundane who had partaken."

"Did he reveal his vampire nature to anyone while intoxicated?" Robert asked sharply.

Lily gave him a withering look, as if wondering why he was still here, then returned her attention to Alec. "Elliott performed a dance called the Dance of the Twenty-Eight Veils in Times Square. It is on YouTube. Many commenters described it as the most boring erotic dance ever performed in the history of the world. I have never been so embarrassed in my unlife. I'm thinking of quitting being leader of the clan and becoming a vampire nun."

Magnus noticed Maryse and Robert, who did not have the best relationship and hardly ever spoke to each other, having a brief whispered consultation about what YouTube might be.

"As the current head of the New York Institute," Maryse said, with an attempt at firmness, "if there is illegal Downworlder activity happening, it should be reported to me."

"I do not *talk* to *Nephilim* about *Downworlder business*," Lily said severely.

The Lightwood parents stared at her, and then swung

their heads in sync to stare at their son.

Lily waved a dismissive hand in their direction. "Except for Alec, he's a special case. The rest of you Shadowhunters just come in, lay down your precious Law, and chop off people's heads. We Downworlders can handle our business ourselves. You Nephilim can stick to chopping off demons' heads and I will consult with you as soon as the next great evil occurs, instead of the next great annoyance, which will occur probably on Tuesday, and which I, Maia, and Alec will deal with. Thank you. Please stop interrupting me. Alec, can these people even be trusted?"

"They're my parents," said Alec. "I know about the faerie fruit. The fey have been taking more and more chances lately. I already sent a message to Maia. She's got Bat and some other boys prowling the precincts of the park. Bat's friends with Mordecai; he can reason with him. And you keep Elliott away from the park. You know how he is with faerie fruit. You know he bit that mundie on purpose."

"It could have been an accident," Lily muttered.

Alec gave Lily a deeply skeptical look. "Oh, it could have been his seventeenth accident? He has to stop or he's going to lose control under the influence and kill somebody. He didn't kill the man, did he?"

"No," Lily said sullenly. "I stopped Elliott in time. I knew you'd kill him, and then I knew you'd give me your disappointed look." She paused. "You're sure the werewolves have this in hand?"

"Yes," said Alec. "You didn't need to charge to Idris and spill Downworlder business in front of my whole family."

"If they're your family, they know you can handle a little thing like this," Lily said dismissively. She ran two hands through her sleek black hair, fluffing it up. "This is such a relief. Oh," she added, as if she had just noticed. "You're holding a baby."

Lily tended to have laser focus.

After the war with Sebastian, the Shadowhunters had been left dealing with the betrayal of the faeries and the crisis of how many Institutes had fallen and how many Nephilim had been Endarkened and lost in the war, their second war in a year.

They were in no shape to keep a close eye on the Downworlders, but the Downworlders had lost a great deal as well. Old structures that had held their society in place for centuries, like the Praetor Lupus, had been destroyed in the war. The faeries were waiting to revolt. And the werewolf and vampire clans of New York both had brand-new leaders. Both Lily and Maia were young to be leaders, and had succeeded entirely unexpectedly to leadership. Both of them had found themselves, due to inexperience and not lack of trying, in trouble.

Maia had called Magnus and asked if she could come and visit him, to ask his advice on a few things. When she showed up, she'd dragged Lily along with her.

Lily, Maia, and Magnus then sat around Magnus's coffee table shouting at each other for hours.

"You can't just kill someone, Lily!" Maia kept saying.

Lily kept saying: "Explain why."

Alec had been cranky that day, having wrenched his arm almost out of its socket during a fight with a dragon demon. He'd been leaning against the kitchen counter, listening, nursing his arm, and texting Jace messages like Y DO U SAY THINGS R XTINCT WHEN THINGS R NOT XTINCT and Y R U THE WAY THAT U R.

Until he ran out of patience.

"Do you know, Lily," he said in a cold voice, putting down his phone, "that you spend more than half the time you are speaking baiting Magnus and Maia, instead of offering suggestions? And you make them spend about the same amount of time arguing you down. So you're making everything last twice as long. Which means you're wasting everyone's time. That's not a really efficient way for a leader to behave."

Lily was so startled she looked almost blank for a moment, almost truly young, before she hissed: "Nobody asked you, Shadowhunter."

"I am a Shadowhunter," said Alec, still calm. "The issue you're having with the mermaids. The Rio de Janeiro Institute was having the same problem a couple of years ago. I know all about it. Do you want me to tell you? Or do you want to end up with half a dozen tourists on a boat to Staten Island drowned, at least that many Shadowhunters asking you embarrassing questions, and a little voice in your head saying, 'Wow, I wish I'd listened to Alec Lightwood when I had the chance'?"

There was a silence. Maia had put an entire cookie into her mouth as they waited. Lily kept her arms crossed and looked sulky.

"Don't waste my time, Lily," Alec said. "What do you want?"

"I want you to sit down and help me, I suppose," Lily grumbled.

Alec had sat down.

Magnus had not expected the meetings to happen more than a few times, let alone to see a rapport spring up between Alec and Lily. Alec had not been entirely comfortable with vampires, once. But Alec always responded to being relied on, being turned to. Whenever Lily came to him with a problem, at first haughtily and with an air of reluctance and later with demanding confidence, Alec did not rest until he had solved it.

One Thursday evening Magnus had heard the doorbell and walked in from the bedroom to find Alec laying out glasses, and realized that the occasional emergency gatherings had become regular meetings. That Maia and Lily and Alec would unroll a map of New York to pinpoint problem areas and have heated debates in which Lily made very nasty werewolf jokes, and each of them would call the other when they had a problem they did not know how to solve. That Downworlders and Shadowhunters alike would come to New York knowing there was a group with Downworlders and Shadowhunters who had power and would cooperate to solve problems. They would come to consult and find out if the group could help them, too.

On the occasions when Alec had served as acting head of the New York Institute, it had been obvious that he didn't enjoy it very much. Alec had less patience with bureaucracy now than he had before the war. He'd accidentally found his calling, working with Downworlders rather than the Clave. Magnus realized that this was his life now, and he would not have it different.

"I like Alec so much," Lily told Magnus at a party months later, slightly drunk and with glitter in her hair. "Especially when he gets snippy with me. He reminds me of Raphael."

"How dare you," Magnus had replied. "You are speaking of the man I love."

He was bartending. His tuxedo had a glow-in-the-dark waistcoat, which made bartending in the artful gloom of the party somewhat easier. He'd spoken without thinking, casually, and then stopped, glass in his hand winking turquoise in the party lights. He'd been talking about Raphael easily, casually insulting, as if Raphael were still alive.

Lily had been Raphael's ally and backup for decades. She had been utterly loyal to him.

"Well, I loved Raphael," said Lily. "And Raphael never loved anyone, I know that much. But he was my leader. If I compare anybody to Raphael, it's a compliment. I like Alec. And I like Maia." She regarded Magnus with wide eyes, pupils dilated until they were almost black. "I've never been terribly fond of you. Except Raphael always said you were an idiot, but you could be trusted."

Raphael had loved many people, Magnus knew. He had loved his mortal family. Maybe Lily didn't know about them: Raphael had been so careful about them. Magnus thought Raphael might have loved Lily, though not in the way she had wanted.

He knew Raphael had trusted her. And Raphael had trusted Magnus. They stood together, these two Raphael had trusted, in one of those quietly terrible moments remembering the dead and knowing you would never see them again.

"Do you want another drink?" Magnus asked. "I can be trusted to make you another drink."

"Bring on the party O neg, I'm feeling frisky," Lily told him. She stared off into the distance as Magnus made her drink, her eyes fixed on showers of glitter that fell from the ceiling at intervals, but not seeing them. "I never thought I'd have to lead the clan. I thought Raphael would always be there. If I didn't have the sessions with Alec and Maia, I wouldn't know what to do half the time. A werewolf and a

Shadowhunter. Do you think Raphael would be ashamed?"

Magnus slid Lily's drink across the bar to her. "I don't," he told her.

Lily had smiled, a flash of fang beneath her plum-colored lipstick, and, clutching her drink, wandered over to Alec.

Now Lily stood next to Alec, having followed him to Idris, and looked at the baby in his arms.

"Hello, baby," Lily whispered, hovering over the child. She snapped her fangs in the baby's direction.

Jace rolled lightly, off the floor and to his feet. Robert, Maryse, and Isabelle put their hands on their weapons. Lily snapped her teeth again, entirely unaware the Lightwood family was clearly ready to mobilize and tear her into pieces. Alec looked at his family over Lily's head and shook his own head in a small, firm gesture. The baby looked up at Lily's glinting fangs and laughed. Lily clicked her teeth for him again and he laughed again.

"What?" Lily asked, looking up at Alec and sounding shy suddenly. "I always liked children, when I was alive. People said I was good with them." She laughed, a little self-consciously. "It's been a while."

"That's great," said Alec. "You'll be willing to babysit occasionally, then."

"Ha-ha, I'm the head of the New York vampire clan and I'm much too important," Lily told him. "But I'll see him when I drop by your place."

Magnus wondered how long Alec was envisioning it would be until they found the baby a home. Alec must think that it would take a while, and Magnus feared Alec was right.

He watched Alec, his head bowed over the baby in his

arms, leaning toward Lily as they murmured to the baby together. Alec did not seem too upset, he thought. It was Lily who, after a space of baby-whispering, began to look a little uneasy.

"It occurs to me that I might be intruding," Lily said.

"Oh really?" asked Isabelle, her arms crossed. "Do you think?"

"Sorry, Alec," said Lily, pointedly not apologizing to anyone else. "See you in New York. Come back quick or some fool will burn the place down. Good-bye, Magnus, random other Lightwoods. Bye, baby. Good-bye, little baby."

She stood on her tiptoes in high-heeled boots, kissed Alec on the cheek, and sashayed out.

"I do not like that vampire's attitude," said Robert in the silence following Lily's departure.

"Lily's all right," said Alec mildly.

Robert did not say another word against Lily. He was careful with his son, Magnus had observed, painfully careful, but Robert was the one who had made the pain necessary. Robert had been thoughtless with his son in the past. It would be a long time of pain and care until things were right between them.

Both Robert and Alec were trying. That was why Alec had stayed to have breakfast with his father this morning.

Though Magnus was not at all sure what Robert Lightwood was doing here at the Shadowhunter Academy in the dark of night.

Let alone Maryse, who should be running the New York Institute. Let alone Isabelle and Jace.

Magnus was always pleased to see Clary.

"Hello, biscuit," he said.

Clary sidled over to the doorway and grinned up at him,

a thousand gallons of trouble in a pint-size body. "Hi."

"What's—"

Magnus intended to discreetly ask what the hell was going on, but he was interrupted by Jace lying down full length on the floor again. Magnus looked down, somewhat distracted.

"What are you doing?"

"I'm stuffing crevices with bits of material," said Jace. "It was Isabelle's idea."

"I ripped up one of your shirts to do it," Isabelle told him. "Not one of your nice shirts, obviously. One of the shirts that don't suit you and which you shouldn't wear again."

The world blurred briefly in front of Magnus's eyes. "You did what?"

Isabelle stared down at him from the stool where she was standing, her hands on her hips.

"We're childproofing the whole suite. If you could call this a suite. This whole Academy is a baby death trap. After we get finished here, we're going to childproof your loft."

"You're not allowed in our apartment," Magnus told her.

"Alec gave me a set of keys that says different," Isabelle told him.

"I did do that," Alec said. "I did give her keys. Forgive me, Magnus, I love you, I did not know she was going to be like this."

Usually Robert looked slightly uneasy whenever Alec expressed affection to Magnus. This time, however, he was staring fixedly at the warlock baby and did not even seem to hear.

Magnus was starting to feel ever more disturbed by the turns this night was taking.

"Why are you being like this?" Magnus asked Isabelle. "*Why?*"

"Think about it," said Isabelle. "We had to deal with the crevices. The baby could crawl around and get his hand or his foot stuck in a crevice! He could be hurt. You don't want the baby to get hurt, do you?"

"No," said Magnus. "Nor do I intend to tear my whole life into strips and rearrange it because of a baby."

What he said sounded eminently reasonable to him. He was stunned when Robert and Maryse both laughed.

"Oh, I remember thinking that way," Maryse said. "You'll learn, Magnus."

There was something strange in the way Maryse was speaking to him. She sounded fond. Usually she was carefully polite or businesslike. She had never been fond before.

"I expected this," declared Isabelle. "Simon told me all about the baby on the phone. I knew you guys would be stunned and overwhelmed. So I got hold of Mom, and she contacted Jace, and Jace was with Clary, and we all came right away to pitch in."

"It's really good of you," Alec said.

There was an air of surprise about him, which Magnus fully understood, but he seemed touched, which Magnus did not understand at all.

"Oh, it's our pleasure," Maryse told her son. She advanced on Alec, her hands out. She reminded Magnus of a bird of prey, talons outstretched, overcome by hunger. "What do you say," she said in an alarmingly sweet voice, "you let me hold the baby? I'm the one in the room with the most experience with babies, after all."

"That's not true, Alec," said Robert. "That is not true!

I was very involved with all of you when you were young. I'm excellent with babies."

Alec blinked at his father, who had appeared by Alec's side with Shadowhunter speed.

"As I recall," Maryse said, "you *bounce* them."

"Babies love that," Robert claimed. "Babies love bouncing."

"Bouncing will make the baby spit up."

"Bouncing will make the baby spit up *with joy*," said Robert.

Magnus had, for several moments, believed that the only possible explanation was that the whole family was drunk. Now he was coming to a much worse conclusion.

Isabelle had come, in an organizing whirlwind, to childproof the whole suite. She had been able to persuade Jace and Clary to come and childproof too. And Maryse had spoken to her son's partner with affection she had never shown before, and now she wanted to hold the baby.

Maryse was experiencing full-on grandma fever.

The Lightwoods thought he and Alec were keeping the baby.

"I need to sit down," said Magnus in a hollow voice. He held on to the door frame so he did not fall down.

Alec glanced over at him, startled and concerned. His parents took their chance to pounce, hands outstretched for the baby, and Alec retreated a step. Jace sprang up from the floor, having his *parabatai*'s back, and Alec visibly came to a decision and put the baby into his *parabatai*'s arms so he had his hands free to ward his parents off.

"Mom and Dad, maybe don't crowd him," Magnus heard Alec suggesting.

Magnus found, for some reason, that his own focus had

slipped to the baby. It was natural concern, he told himself. Anybody would be concerned. Jace, as far as Magnus knew, was not accustomed to children. It was not like the Shadowhunters were always babysitting for the kids down the block.

Jace was holding the baby somewhat awkwardly. His golden head, his hair full of fluff and dirt from lying down on the floor dealing with crevices, was bowed over the baby, staring down into the baby's solemn little face.

The baby was dressed, Magnus saw. He was wearing an orange onesie, and the feet of the onesie were shaped to look like little fox paws. Jace rubbed one of the fox paws with a brown hand, fingers scarred like a warrior's and slim as a musician's, and the baby gave a sudden, vigorous wriggle.

Magnus rushed forward, realizing he had moved only when he was halfway across the room. He also realized that everyone else had lunged forward to catch the baby too.

Except Jace had kept hold of the baby despite the wriggle.

Jace looked flat-out terrified for a minute, then relaxed and looked around at everyone with his usual air of mild superiority.

"He's fine," Jace told them. "He's tough."

He looked toward Robert, clearly remembering Robert's early words, and bounced the baby gingerly. The baby flailed, one small fist bouncing off Jace's cheek.

"That's good," Jace encouraged. "That's right. Maybe a little harder next time. We'll have you punching demons in the face in no time. Do you want to punch demons in the face with me and Alec? Do you? Yes, you do."

"Jace, honey," Maryse cooed. "Give me the baby."

"Want to hold the baby, Clary?" asked Jace in the tone

of one offering an enormous treat to his lady love.

"I'm good," said Clary.

The Lightwoods, including Jace, all stared at her with a kind of sad wonder, as if she had just proven herself tragically insane.

Isabelle had leaped down from the stool at the same time they had all rushed forward, ready to catch him. She looked at Magnus now.

"Are you going to kneecap your parents so you can hold the baby?" Magnus asked.

Isabelle laughed lightly. "No, of course not. Soon his formula will be ready. Then..." Isabelle's face changed, set with terrifying determination. "*I* am going to feed the baby. Until then, I can wait, and help you guys come up with the perfect name for him."

"We were talking about that a little as we came in from Alicante," said Maryse, her voice eager.

Robert made another of his lightning-swift, cat-footed, and unsettling moves, this time to Magnus's side. He put a heavy hand on Magnus's shoulder. Magnus eyed Robert's hand and felt deep unease.

"Of course, it's up to you and Alec," Robert assured him.

"Of course," said Maryse, who never agreed with Robert on anything. "And we don't want you to do anything you're not comfortable with. I would never want the little darling to have a name associated with—sadness rather than joy, or for either of you to feel like you have to do this. But we thought since ... well, warlocks pick their own surnames a little later, so 'Bane' is not part of a family tradition... We thought you might consider, in memory but not as a burden..."

Isabelle said, her voice clear: "Max Lightwood."

Magnus found himself blinking, partly in perplexity,

but partly because of another feeling he found much less easy to define. His vision had blurred again and something in his chest had twisted.

The mistake the Lightwoods had made was ridiculous, and yet Magnus could not help but be stunned by their offer, and how genuine and sincere it had been.

This was a warlock child, and they were all Shadowhunters. Lightwood was an old, proud Shadowhunter name. Max Lightwood had been the Lightwoods' youngest son. It was a name for one of their own.

"Or if you don't like that ... Michael. Michael's a nice name," Robert offered into the long silence. He cleared his throat after he spoke, and looked out of the attic windows, into the woods surrounding the Academy.

"Or you could hyphenate," Isabelle said, her voice a little too bright. "Lightwood-Bane or Bane-Lightwood?"

Alec moved, reaching out not to take the baby but to touch him. The baby flung a hand up, tiny fingers curling around Alec's finger, as if reaching back. Alec's face, stricken since the mention of his brother's name, was warmed by a sudden faint smile.

"Magnus and I haven't talked about it yet, and we need to," he said quietly. His voice had authority, even when it was quiet. Magnus saw Robert and Maryse nodding along to it, almost unconsciously. "But I was thinking maybe Max as well."

That was when Magnus realized the magnitude of the situation. It was not just a wild conclusion Isabelle had leaped to and improbably convinced everyone else of. It was not just the Lightwoods.

Alec thought that he and Magnus were keeping the baby as well.

Magnus did go and sit down then, on one of the rickety chairs with a cushion from home placed on it. He could not feel his fingers. He thought he might be in shock.

Robert Lightwood followed him.

"I couldn't help but notice that the baby is blue," Robert said. "Alec's eyes are blue. And when you do the"—he made a strange and disturbing gesture, and then made the sound *whoosh, whoosh*—"magic, sometimes there's a blue light."

Magnus stared at him. "I'm failing to see your point."

"If you made the baby for yourself and Alec, you can tell me," said Robert. "I'm a very broad-minded man. Or—I'm trying to be. I'd like to be. I would understand."

"If I made ... the ... baby...?" Magnus repeated.

He was not certain where to start. He had imagined Robert Lightwood knew how babies were made.

"Magically," Robert whispered.

"I am going to pretend you never said that to me," said Magnus. "I am going to pretend we never had this conversation."

Robert winked, as if they understood each other. Magnus was speechless.

The Lightwoods continued on their quest to child-proof the suite, feed the baby, and all hold the baby at once. Witchlight on every side, filling the whole small space of the attic, blazed and burned in Magnus's vision.

Alec thought they were keeping the baby. He wanted to name him Max.

"I saw Magnus Bane and a sexy vampire lady in the hall," Marisol announced as she passed Simon's table.

Jon Cartwright was carrying her tray, and he almost dropped it. "A vampire," he repeated. "In the *Academy*?"

Marisol looked up into his scandalized face and nodded. "A sexy one."

"They're the worst kind," Jon breathed.

"So you weren't too bad, then, Simon," Julie remarked as Marisol walked on, spinning her tale of an alluring vampiress.

"You know," Simon said, "sometimes I think Marisol goes too far. I know she likes jerking Jon's chain, but nobody is dumb enough to believe in a warlock baby and a vampire on the same day. It's too much. It makes no sense. Jon is going to catch on."

He poked a mysterious lump in his stew. Dinner was very late tonight, and very congealed. Marisol fibbing about vampires must have put the idea in his head: Simon looked back on drinking blood and thought that it could not have been as bad as this.

"You would think she'd had enough excitement for one day," George agreed. "I wonder how the poor little baby is doing. I was thinking, do you think he might change colors like a chameleon? How cool would that be?"

Simon brightened. "So cool."

"Nerds," said Julie.

Simon took that as praise. He did feel that George had really come along under his tutelage. He had even voluntarily bought graphic novels when he was in Scotland over Christmas. Maybe someday the student would become the master.

"This is hard luck for you, Simon," said George. "I know you wanted to talk to Alec."

Simon's brief moment of cheer faded, and he collapsed with his face on the table. "Forget about talking to Alec. When I went to tell them about the baby, I walked in on

Alec and Magnus. If Alec didn't like me before, he *definitely* hates me now."

Another old memory flashed in Simon's mind, absolutely unwelcome: Alec's pale, furious face as he looked down at Clary. Maybe Alec hated Clary, too. Maybe once someone crossed him, he never forgot and never forgave, and would always hate them both.

His hideous imaginings were interrupted by a sensation around their dinner table.

"What? Where? When? How? Did Magnus seem like an athletic yet tender lover?" Julie demanded.

"Julie!" said Beatriz.

"Thank you, Beatriz," said Simon.

"Don't say a word, Simon," said Beatriz. "Not until I have acquired a pen and paper so I can write down everything you say. I'm sorry, Simon, but they are famous, and celebrities have to bear with this interest in their love lives. They're like Brangelina."

Beatriz rummaged through her bag until she found a notebook, and then opened it and gazed at Simon with an expectant air.

Julie, Idris born and bred, made a face. "What is Brangelina? It sounds like a demon."

"It does not!" George protested. "I believe in their love."

"They are not like Brangelina," Simon said. "What would you even call them? Algnus? That sounds like a foot disease."

"Obviously you would call them Malec," said Beatriz. "Are you stupid, Simon?"

"I will not be distracted!" said Julie. "Does Magnus have piercings? Of course he does; when would he miss an opportunity to shine?"

"I didn't notice, and even if I had noticed, I wouldn't discuss it," said Simon.

"Oh, because people in the mundane world never obsess about celebrities and their love lives," Beatriz said. "See also, Brangelina. And that boy band George is obsessed with. He has all kinds of theories about their romances."

"What ... boy band ... George is obsessed with?" Simon asked slowly.

George looked shifty. "I don't want to talk about it. The band's going through some hard times lately, and it makes me too sad."

Far too many disturbing and upsetting things had happened to Simon today. He decided to stop thinking about George and the boy band.

"I'm the one who grew up a subway ride from Broadway, I know people get too interested in celebrities," he said. "But it's weird for me when you girls obsess over Jace or Magnus. It's weird when Jon trails after Isabelle with his tongue hanging out."

"Is George's crush on Clary weird too?" asked Beatriz.

"Is this Betray George Day, Beatriz?" George demanded. "Si, I may have had certain thoughts about certain pocket-size vixens, but I would never tell you about them! I don't want to make it weird!"

"Pocket-size vixens?" Simon stared. "Congratulations, you made it weird."

George hung his head in shame.

"It's weird for me because everybody acts as if they know famous people, but I really do know these people. They're not images, like posters to hang on the wall. They're not anything like you think they are. They have a right to privacy. It's weird because I see everyone acting like they know who my friends are, when they only know a tiny bit of them, and it's weird to see anyone acting as if they have some sort of claim on my friends and their lives."

Beatriz hesitated, then put her pen down. "Okay," she said. "I can see it's weird for you, but—it does come from everyone admiring what they've done. People act like they know them because they want to know them. And being admired means they have a lot of influence over other people. They can do a lot of good with that. Alec Lightwood is Sunil's inspiration to be a Shadowhunter. And you, Simon. A lot of people follow you because they admire you. There might be some weirdness mixed in with being admired like that, but I think there's more good."

"Oh, it's not the same for me," Simon mumbled. "I mean, I don't even remember. I meant my friends. Including Alec, who is ... my friend who doesn't like me. They're the special ones."

He couldn't be cool and assured like Magnus or Jace. He didn't know what Beatriz was talking about. Also he felt suddenly paranoid over whether people were wondering if he had piercings.

Simon had no piercings. He used to be a musician in Brooklyn. He probably should have piercings.

Beatriz hesitated another instant, then tore off the page she'd written on and rolled it into a ball. "You're special too, Simon," she said, and blushed. "Everybody knows that."

Simon looked at her red face and remembered George mentioning someone had a crush on him. He'd thought for a moment it might be Julie, and though it would be both bizarre and bizarrely flattering to have changed the heart of a Shadowhunter ice princess with his manly charms, he supposed Beatriz made more sense. He and Beatriz were really good friends. Beatriz had the best smile in the Academy. Simon would've been thrilled to have an attractive girl he was friends with get a crush on him, back in Brooklyn.

He felt mainly awkward now. He wondered if he was supposed to let Beatriz down easily.

Julie cleared her throat. "And just so you know...," she said, "there have been invasive questions asked about you. Also there was an incident where someone tried to steal one of your used socks and keep it as a trophy."

"Who was the sock person?" Simon demanded. "That's just nasty."

"We never tell them anything," Julie said. "And they may ask once, but they never ask again." Her lip curled back from her teeth. She looked like a snarling blond tiger. "Because you're a real person to us, Simon. And you're our friend."

She reached across the table and touched Simon's hand, then drew it back as if she had been burned. Beatriz snatched Julie's hand as soon as she'd drawn it back and pulled her out of her chair and toward the corner of the room where the food was laid out.

Neither of them needed more food. They had barely touched their stew. Simon watched as they went, and then stood talking to each other in fraught whispers.

"Well, they both seem strangely upset."

George rolled his eyes. "Come on, Si, don't be dense."

"You can't mean...," began Simon. "They can't both—like me?"

There was a long silence.

"Neither of them like you?" Simon said. "You work out. And! You have a Scottish accent."

"Don't rub it in. Maybe girls fear me, because my keen

eyes see too deeply into their souls," George said. "Or maybe they're intimidated by my good looks. Or maybe... Please don't make me talk about what a lonely bugger I am anymore."

He looked after Julie and Beatriz a little wistfully. Simon could not tell if George was wistful about Julie or Beatriz, or simply wistful about love in general. He'd had no idea his friends were involved in such an emotional tangle.

He was surprised. He felt awkward. And he didn't feel anything else.

He liked Beatriz a lot. Julie was terrible, but Simon thought of Julie telling him about her sister, and he had to admit: Julie was terrible, but he liked her, too. Both of them were beautiful and badass and did not come with a burden of lost memories and tangled emotions.

He wasn't even pleased they liked him. He wasn't even slightly tempted.

He wished, with single-minded intensity, that Isabelle was here—not a letter, not a voice on the phone, but here.

He looked at George's sad face and offered: "Want to talk about when Magnus and Alec go, and we steal their suite and make our own meals in our own little kitchen?"

George sighed. "Could we really, Simon, or is that too beautiful a dream? Every day would be a song. All I want is to make a sandwich, Simon. Just a humble sandwich, with ham, cheese, maybe a little dab of ... oh my God."

Simon wondered what a dab of "oh my God" would taste like. George had frozen, spoon to his lips, eyes fixed on a point over Simon's shoulder.

Simon turned around in his seat and saw Isabelle framed in the doorway of the Academy dining hall. She was wearing a long dress the color of irises and her arms were spread wide, bracelets gleaming. Time seemed to slow, like a movie, like magic, like she was a genie who could appear in a puff of glittering smoke to grant wishes, and every wish would be her.

"Surprise," said Isabelle. "Miss me?"

Simon jumped to his feet. He might have knocked his bowl clear across the table and into George's lap. He was sorry, but he would make it up to him later.

"Isabelle," he said. "What are you doing here?"

"Congratulations, Simon, that's a very romantic question," Isabelle told him. "Am I meant to take it as 'No, I didn't miss you, and I'm seeing other girls'? If so, don't worry about it. Why worry, when life is short? Specifically, your life, because I am going to cut off your head."

"I'm confused by what you're saying," Simon told her.

Isabelle raised her eyebrows and opened her lips, but before she could speak Simon caught her by the waist and drew her in against him, kissing her surprised mouth. Isabelle's mouth relaxed, curving under his. She flung her arms around his neck and kissed him back, sultry and exuberant at once, a femme fatale and a warrior princess, all the dream girls of all his nerdy fantasies in one. Simon pulled back for a moment to look into Isabelle's night-dark eyes.

"I wasn't aware," said Simon, "that there are any other girls in the world but you."

He was embarrassed as soon as he said it. It was in no way a smooth line. It was pathetically honest, trying to tell Isabelle what he had only just realized himself. But he saw Isabelle's eyes shine like new stars waking in the night, felt her arm around his neck pulling him down for another kiss, and he thought to himself that the line might be a little smooth. After all, it had gotten him a girl, *the* girl. The only girl Simon wanted.

* * *

It was midnight before Magnus got all of the Lightwoods out of their suite. Isabelle had left to see Simon some time before, and Clary and Jace could usually be persuaded to go off together, but for a while he thought he was actually going to have to use magic on Maryse and Robert. He shoved them out of the door while they were still giving him helpful baby tips.

As soon as they were gone, Alec stumbled over to the bed and lay flat on his face, instantly asleep. Magnus was left with the baby.

It was possible the baby was stunned by the Lightwoods too. He lay in his crib staring up at the world with wide eyes. The crib was under a window, and he was in a small pool of light, moonshine shimmering on his crumpled blanket and his little fat legs. Magnus crouched down by the crib and watched him, waiting for the next eruption of screaming that meant he needed to be changed and fed. Instead he fell asleep too, his mouth open, a tiny blue rosebud.

Who could ever love it? the baby's mother had written, but the baby did not know that yet. He slept, innocent and serene as any child secure of love. Magnus's mother might have thought the same despairing words.

Alec thought they were keeping him.

Keeping him had not even occurred to Magnus. He had thought he lived life believing a thousand possibilities were open to him, but he had not thought of this possibility as being open to him: family life like mundanes and Nephilim had, love so secure that it could be shared with someone brand-new to the world and helpless.

He tried out the thought now.

Keeping him. Keeping the baby. Having a baby, with Alec.

Hours passed. Magnus hardly noticed, time went by so quietly, as if someone had laid out the carpet of the night to muffle time's footsteps. He did not register anything but that small face, until he felt a soft touch on his shoulder.

Magnus did not get up, but he turned to see Alec looking down at him. The moonlight turned Alec's skin silver and his eyes a darker, deeper blue, infinitely tender.

"If you thought I was asking you to keep the baby," Magnus said, "I wasn't."

Alec's eyes widened. He absorbed this in silence.

"You're ... still really young," Magnus said. "I'm sorry if sometimes it seems as if I do not remember that. It's strange to me—being immortal means both being young and being old are strange to me. I know I must seem strange to you sometimes."

Alec nodded, thoughtful and not hurt. "You do," he said, and leaned down with one hand gripping the side of the crib, touched Magnus's hair, and gave him a moonlight-soft kiss. "And I never want anything but this. I never want a less strange love."

"But you don't have to be scared I would ever leave you," said Magnus. "You don't have to be scared of what will happen to the baby or that I will be hurt because the baby—is a warlock, and was not wanted. You do not have to feel trapped. You do not have to be scared, and you do not have to do this."

Alec knelt down in the shadows and on the bare, dusty boards of the attic, next to the crib and facing Magnus.

"What if I want to?" he asked. "I'm a Shadowhunter. We marry young, and we have children young, because we might die young, because we want to do our duty to the world and have all the love in the world we can. I used to ...

I used to think I could never do that, never have that. I used to feel trapped. I don't feel trapped now. I could never ask you to live in an Institute, and I don't want to. I want to stay in New York, with you, and with Lily and Maia. I want to keep doing what we're doing. I want Jace to run the Institute after my mother, and I want to work with him. I want to be part of the connection between the Institute and Downworlders. For so long I thought I could never have any of the things I wanted, except that I could maybe keep Jace and Isabelle safe. I thought I could have their backs in a fight. Now I have more and more people I care about, and ... I want everyone I care about—I want people I don't even know, I want all of us—to know we have each other's backs so we do not have to fight alone. I am not trapped. I'm happy. I am exactly where I want to be. I know what I want, and I have the life I want. I'm not scared of any of the things you said."

Magnus took a deep breath. It was better to ask Alec than to keep imagining the wrong thing. "What are you scared of, then?"

"Do you remember Mom suggesting calling the baby Max?"

Magnus nodded, carefully quiet.

He had never even met Alec's little brother, Max. Robert and Maryse Lightwood had always tried to keep their children away from Downworlders, and Max had been too young to disobey.

Alec's voice was soft, both for the baby and with memory. "I was never the cool brother. I remember when Mom used to leave Max with me, when he was really little, just learning how to walk, and I was always scared he would fall down and it would be my fault. I'd constantly try to get him to obey the rules and do what Mom said. Isabelle was so great with him, always making him laugh, and by the Angel, Max wanted to be *just* like Jace. He thought Jace was the coolest, the best Shadowhunter who ever lived, that the sun rose and set on him. Jace gave him a little toy soldier and Max used to take it to bed with him. I was jealous of how much Max loved that toy. I used to give him other things, toys that I thought were better, but he always loved that soldier best. He died holding that toy for comfort. I'm so glad he had it, that he had something he loved to comfort him. It was stupid and petty to be jealous."

Magnus shook his head. Alec gave him a rueful smile, and then bowed his black head, looking at the floor.

"I always thought there would be more time," said Alec. "I thought Max would get older, and he'd train with us more, and I'd help him train. I thought he would come on missions with us, and I'd have his back, the way I always try to have Jace's and Isabelle's backs. He'd know his boring big brother was good for something then. He'd know he could count on me, no matter what. He should have been able to count on me."

"He was able to count on you," Magnus said. "I know that. He knew that. Nobody who has ever met you could doubt it."

"He never even knew that I'm gay," said Alec. "Or that I love you. I wish he could have met you."

"I wish I could have met him," said Magnus. "But he knew you. He loved you. You know that, don't you?"

"I do know that," said Alec. "I just ... I always wished I could be more for him."

"You always try to be more, for everyone you love," Magnus said. "You don't see how your whole family turns to you, how they rely on you. I rely on you. Even *Lily* relies on you, for God's sake. You love the people you love so much that you want to be an impossible ideal for them. You don't realize that you are more than enough."

Alec shrugged, a little helplessly.

"You asked me what I was scared of. I'm scared he won't like me," Alec said. "I'm scared I'll let him down. But I want to try to be there for him. I want him. Do you?"

"I didn't expect him," said Magnus. "I didn't expect anything like this to come, for me. Even if I thought sometimes about what it might be like if you and I did have a family, I thought it would not be for years. But yes. Yes, I want to try as well."

Alec smiled, his smile so brilliant that Magnus realized how relieved he was, and realized belatedly how worried Alec had been that Magnus would say no.

"It is quick," Alec admitted. "I thought about having a family, but I guess I always thought... Well, I guess I never expected anything like this to happen before we got married."

"What?" said Magnus.

Alec just stared up at him. One long, strong archer's hand was dangling into the baby's crib, but Alec was intent on Magnus, his dark blue eyes darker than ever in the shadows, one look from Alec more important than a kiss from anyone else. Magnus saw he meant it.

"Alec," he said. "My Alec. You have to know that's impossible."

Alec looked stunned and horror-struck. Magnus began to speak, the words tumbling out of his mouth faster and faster, trying to get Alec to see.

"Shadowhunters can marry Downworlders, in Downworlder or mundane ceremonies. I've seen it happen. I've seen other Shadowhunters dismiss those marriages as meaning nothing, and I've seen some Shadowhunters bow under pressure and break the vows they made. I know you would never bow or break. I know that type of marriage would mean just as much to you. I know that any promises you made me, you would keep. But I was alive before the Accords. I sat and ate and talked with Shadowhunters about peace between our people, and then those same Shadowhunters threw away the plates I ate off because they thought I irredeemably tainted whatever I touched. I will not have a ceremony that anyone looks down on as lesser. I do not want you to have any less than the ceremony you could have had, to honor your vows to a Shadowhunter. I have had enough of making compromises in the name of trying to make peace. I want the Law to change. I do not want to get married until we can get married in gold."

Alec was quiet, his head bowed.

"Do you understand?" Magnus demanded, feeling almost desperate. "It's not that I don't want to. It's not that I don't love you."

"I understand," said Alec. He took a deep breath and looked up. "Changing the Law might take a while," he said simply.

"It might," said Magnus.

They were both quiet for a little while.

"Can I tell you something?" Magnus asked. "Nobody ever wanted me to marry them before."

He'd had other loves, but none of them had ever asked, and he had known—had sensed with a cold, sinking feeling that it would be useless—not to ask them. Whether it was because they did not feel they could promise until death did them part when Magnus would not die, because they took Magnus lightly or thought, being immortal, that he took them lightly. He had never known the reasons they did not want to marry him, but there it was: There had been lovers willing to die with him, but nobody had ever been willing to swear to live with him every day for as long as they both had to live.

Nobody until this Shadowhunter.

"I never asked anyone to marry me before," said Alec. "So that's a no, then?"

He laughed as he asked, a soft laugh, worn but happy. Alec always tried to give those he loved a path or an open door; he tried to give those he loved anything they wanted. They sat there, leaning against their baby's crib together.

Magnus lifted his hand, and Alec caught it in midair, their fingers linking. Magnus's rings flashed and Alec's scars glowed in the moonlight. Both of them held on.

"It's yes, one day," Magnus said. "For you, Alec, it's always yes."

After classes the next day Simon sat in his dank dungeon room, resisted the almost irresistible temptation to go find Isabelle, and mustered up his courage.

He marched up the many flights of stairs and knocked on the door of Alec and Magnus's rooms.

Magnus answered the door. He was wearing jeans and a loose, frayed T-shirt, holding the baby, and he looked very tired.

"How did you know he'd just woken up from a nap?" Magnus asked as he opened the door.

"Uh, I didn't," said Simon.

Magnus blinked at him, in the slow way that tired people did, as if they had to think deeply about blinking. "Oh, my apologies," he said. "I thought you were Maryse."

"Isabelle's mother is here?" Simon exclaimed.

"Shhhh!" said Magnus. "She might hear you."

The baby was grizzling, not quite crying but making a sound like a small, unhappy tractor. He wiped his damp face against Magnus's shoulder.

"I'm really sorry to interrupt," said Simon. "I was wondering if I could have a word alone with Alec."

"Alec's sleeping," Magnus said flatly, and began to close the door.

Alec's voice rang out before the door was quite closed. He sounded as if he was midyawn. "No, I'm not. I'm awake. I can talk to Simon." He appeared in the doorway, pulling the door back open. "Go out and take a long walk. Get some fresh air. It'll wake you up."

"I'm great," said Magnus. "I don't need sleeping. Or waking. I feel great."

The baby waved his fat hands in Alec's direction, the gestures loose and uncoordinated but unmistakable. Alec looked startled but smiled, a sudden, unexpectedly nice smile, and reached out to take the baby in his arms. As soon as he did, the baby stopped grizzling.

Magnus waved his finger in the baby's face. "I find your attitude insulting," he informed him. He kissed Alec briefly. "I won't be gone long."

"Take as long as you need," said Alec. "I have this feeling my parents might be coming to help very shortly."

Magnus left, and Alec stepped away from the door, going to stand at the window with the baby.

"So," said Alec. His shirt was rumpled, clearly slept in, and he was bouncing a baby. Simon felt bad even bothering him. "What did you want to talk to me about?"

"I'm really sorry again about yesterday," Simon told him.

Then he wondered if it was terrible that he had referenced sex in front of Alec's baby. Maybe Simon was just doomed to mortally offend Alec, over and over again. Forever.

"It's okay," said Alec. "I once walked in on you and Isabelle. I guess turnabout's fair play." He frowned. "Although you two were in my room at the time, so actually I think you still owe me."

Simon was alarmed. "You walked in on me and Isabelle? But we haven't... I mean, we didn't... Did we?"

It would be typical of Simon's life, he thought. Of all things in the world, he would forget that.

Alec looked upset to be having this discussion, but Simon fixed him with a pleading stare and Alec apparently took pity on Simon's great patheticness.

"I don't know," Alec said at last. "You were in the process of taking your clothes off, as I remember. And I try not to remember. And you seemed to be engaging in some sort of role-play."

"Oh. Whoa. Like advanced role-play? Were there costumes? Were there props? What is Isabelle going to be expecting here, exactly?"

"I won't discuss this," said Alec.

"But if you could just give me a tiny hint..."

"Get out of here, Simon," said Alec.

Simon yanked himself back from the edge of role-playing panic, and pulled himself together.

This was more words than he had spoken to Alec in years.

Though Alec had just ordered him out of the room, so Simon had to admit things were not exactly going well.

"I'm sorry," said Simon. "I mean, I'm sorry for the inappropriate questions. And I'm sorry for walking in on you, er, yesterday morning. I'm sorry for everything. I'm sorry for whatever it is that went wrong between us. Whatever you're angry about. I honestly don't remember, but I do remember how you are when you're angry, and I don't want things to be like that between us. I remember you don't like Clary."

Alec looked at Simon as if he was crazy.

"I like Clary. Clary's one of my best friends."

"Oh," said Simon. "I'm sorry. I thought I remembered... I must have gotten it wrong."

Alec took a deep breath and admitted: "No, you didn't get it wrong. I didn't like Clary at first. I got—rough with her once. I slammed her up against a wall. She hit her head. I was a trained warrior and she didn't have any training at all, back then. I'm twice her size."

Simon had come here to conciliate Alec, so he was unprepared for the strong urge to take a swing at him. He couldn't do it. Alec was holding a baby.

All he could do was stare at him in furious silence, at the very idea someone would touch his best friend.

"It's no excuse," Alec continued. "But I was afraid. She knew about me being gay, and she told me that she knew. She wasn't telling me anything I didn't already know, but I was scared of her because I didn't know her. She wasn't my friend then. She was just some mundane invading my family, and I knew Shadowhunters, I was friends with Shadowhunters, who if they'd ever guessed—they would have gone running to tell my parents, so my parents could talk sense into me. They would have told everybody. They would have thought they were doing the right thing."

"It wouldn't have been the right thing," said Simon, still furious but shaken. "Clary would *never* do that. She never even told me."

"I didn't know her then," said Alec. "You're right. She never told anyone, about any of it. She had every right to say that I'd gotten rough with her. Jace would have punched me in the face if he'd known. I was terrified she would tell Jace that I was gay, because I wasn't ready for Jace to know about me. But you're right. She would never, and she didn't." He looked out of the window, patting the baby on the back. "I like Clary," he said simply. "She always tries to do what's right, and she never lets anyone else tell her what right is. She reminds my *parabatai* that he wants to live. Occasionally I wish she'd take fewer mad risks, but if I hated reckless crazy-brave people, I'd hate..."

"Let me guess," said Simon. "His name rhymes with Face Herringfail."

Alec laughed and Simon mentally congratulated himself.

"So you like Clary," said Simon. "I'm the only one you don't like. What did I do? I know you have a lot on your plate, but if you could just tell me what I did so I can apologize for it and so we can maybe be okay, I'd really appreciate it."

Alec stared at him, then turned and walked toward one of the chairs in the attic. There were two rickety wooden chairs, both of which held cushions with peacocks embroidered on them, and there was a sofa. The sofa was a little slanted. Alec took one of the chairs, and Simon decided not to risk the sofa and took the other.

Alec put the baby on his knee, one arm carefully around his small, round body. With his free hand he played with the baby's tiny hands, tapping them with his fingertips, as if he were teaching the baby how to play patty-cake. He was clearly getting ready for a confession.

Simon drew in a deep breath, preparing for whatever

it was. He knew it might be really bad. He had to be ready.

"What did you do?" Alec asked. "You saved Magnus's life."

Simon was at a loss. An apology seemed inappropriate.

"Magnus was kidnapped, and I went into a hell dimension to save him. That was my whole plan. All I wanted to do was rescue him. On the way, Isabelle was badly hurt. My whole life, I always wanted to protect the people I loved, to make sure they were safe. I should have been able to do it. But I couldn't. I wasn't able to help either of them. You did. You saved Isabelle's life. When Magnus's father was intent on taking him and there was nothing I could do about it, nothing at all, you stepped in. I'd undervalued you, in the past, and you did everything I ever wanted to do, and then you were gone. Isabelle was a wreck. Clary was worse. Jace was so upset. Magnus felt guilty. Everyone was so hurt, and I wanted to help them, and you came back but you didn't remember what you had done. I'm not really good with strangers, and you were a really complicated stranger. I couldn't talk to you. It wasn't that you did anything wrong. It was that there was nothing I could do to make it even between us. I owed you more than I could ever repay, and I didn't even know how to thank you. It wouldn't have meant anything. You didn't even remember."

"Oh," said Simon. "Wow."

It was weird to think of faceless strangers thinking of Simon as a hero. It was even weirder to have Alec Lightwood, who he'd thought did not even like him, talk about him as if he was a hero.

"So you don't hate me, and you don't hate Clary. You don't hate anyone."

"I hate people forcing me to talk about my feelings," said Alec.

Simon stared at him for a moment, an apology on his lips, but he did not speak it. Instead he grinned, and Alec grinned shyly back.

"I've been doing it way too much since I got to the Academy."

"I can imagine," said Simon.

He had not been sure what would happen with the baby Alec and Magnus were taking care of, but from everything Isabelle had said, she was sure they were keeping him. That must have required a conversation.

"I would like," Alec said, "not to talk about feelings again for about a year. Also maybe to sleep for a year. Do babies ever sleep?"

"I used to babysit sometimes," Simon said. "As I recall, babies do sleep a lot, but when you least expect it. Babies: more like the Spanish Inquisition than you think."

Alec nodded, though he seemed confused. Simon made a mental note that it was his duty now, as Alec's established friend, to introduce Alec to Monty Python as soon as possible. The baby crowed as if he were pleased by the comparison.

"Hey," said Alec. "I'm sorry that I made you think I was mad at you, just because I didn't know what to say."

"Well," Simon said. "Here's the thing. I was helped along in my assumption."

Alec stopped playing patty-cake with the baby. He went still all over. "What do you mean?"

"You didn't talk to me a lot, and I was a little worried about it," Simon explained. "So I asked my friend, between us guys, if you had a problem with me. I asked my good friend Jace."

There was a pause as Alec absorbed this news. "You did."

"And Jace," said Simon. "Jace told me that there was a big, dark secret issue between us. He said it wasn't his place to talk about it."

The baby looked at Simon, then back at Alec. His small face looked thoughtful, as if he might shake his head and go: *That Jace, what will he do next?*

"Leave this to me," Alec said calmly. "He's my *parabatai* and we have a sacred bond and everything, but now he has gone too far."

"That's cool," said Simon. "Please exact awful vengeance for both of us, because I'm pretty sure he could take me in a fight."

Alec nodded, admitting this very true fact. Simon could not believe he had been so worried about Alec Lightwood. Alec was great.

"Well," Alec said. "Like I said ... I do owe you."

Simon waved a hand. "Nah. Call it even."

Magnus was so tired, he stumbled into the Shadowhunter Academy dining room and thought about eating there.

Then he actually looked at the food and came to his senses.

It was not quite dinnertime, but there were a few students gathered early, even though Magnus did not anticipate there would be a rush on the slime lasagna. Magnus saw Julie and her friends at one table. Julie looked him up and down, taking in the wrecked hair and Alec's T-shirt, and he read deep disillusionment on her face.

So a young girl's dreams died. Magnus admitted, after a sleepless night and wearing one of Alec's shirts because Isabelle had destroyed several of his own and the baby had been sick on several others, he might not be at his most glamorous.

It was probably good for Julie to face reality, though Magnus was determined to, at some point, take a shower, wear a better shirt, and dazzle the baby with his resplendence.

Magnus had visited Ragnor at the Academy, and he knew how the meals there worked. He squinted, trying to figure out which tables belonged to the elites and which to the dregs, the humans who aspired to be Nephilim but were not accepted by the Nephilim as good enough until they Ascended. Magnus had always thought the dregs showed enormous self-restraint by not rising up against Shadowhunter arrogance, burning down the Academy, and fleeing into the night.

It was possible that the Clave was right when they called Magnus an insurgent.

He could not work out, however, which tables belonged to whom. It had been very clear, years ago, but he was certain the blonde and the brunette Simon knew were Nephilim, and almost sure the gorgeous idiot who wanted to raise a baby with Simon in a sock drawer was not.

Magnus's attention was attracted by the sound of a throaty, imperious voice coming from a Latina girl who looked all of fifteen. She was a mundane, Magnus knew at a glance. Something else he could tell at a glance: In a couple of years, whether she Ascended or not, she would be a holy terror.

"Jon," she was saying to the boy across the table from her. "I am in so much pain from stubbing my toe! I need aspirin."

"What's aspirin?" asked the boy, sounding panicked.

He was obviously Nephilim, through and through and through. Magnus could tell without seeing his runes. In fact, he was prepared to bet the boy was a Cartwright. Magnus had known several Cartwrights through the centuries. The Cartwrights all had such distressingly thick necks.

"You buy it in a pharmacy," said the girl. "No, don't tell me, you don't know what a pharmacy is either. Have you ever left Idris in your whole life?"

"Yes!" said Jon, possibly Cartwright. "On many demon-hunting missions. And once Mama and Papa took me to the beach in France!"

"Amazing," said the girl. "I mean that. I'm going to explain all of modern medicine to you."

"Please don't do that, Marisol," said Jon. "I did not feel good after you explained appendectomies. I couldn't eat."

Marisol made a face at her plate. "So what you're saying is, I did you a huge favor."

"I like to eat," said Jon sadly.

"Right," said Marisol. "So, I don't explain modern medicine to you, and then a medical emergency occurs to me. It could be solved with the application of a little first aid, but you don't know that, and so I die. I die at your feet. Is that what you want, Jon?"

"No," said Jon. "What's first aid? Is there a ... second aid?"

"I can't believe you're going to let me die when my death could so easily be avoided, if you had just listened," Marisol went on mercilessly.

"Okay, okay! I'll listen."

"Great. Get me some juice, because I'll be talking for a while. I'm still very hurt that you even considered letting me die," Marisol added as Jon scrambled up and made for the side of the room where the unappetizing food and potentially poisonous drinks were laid out. "I thought

Shadowhunters had a mandate to protect mundanes!" Marisol shouted after him. "Not orange juice. I want apple juice!"

"Would you believe," said Catarina, appearing at Magnus's elbow, "that the Cartwright kid was the biggest bully in the Academy?"

"Seems like he met a bigger bully," Magnus murmured.

He congratulated himself on the correct Cartwright guess. It was hard to be sure, with Shadowhunter families. Certain traits did seem to run in their family lines, inbred as they were, but there were always exceptions.

For instance, Magnus had always found the Lightwoods rather forgettable. He'd liked some of them—Anna Lightwood and her parade of brokenhearted young ladies, Christopher Lightwood and his explosions, and now Isabelle—but there had never been a Lightwood who touched his heart, as some Shadowhunters had: Will Herondale or Henry Branwell or Clary Fray.

Until the Lightwood who was unforgettable; until the Lightwood who had not only touched but taken his heart.

"Why are you smiling to yourself?" Catarina asked, her voice suspicious.

"I was just thinking that life is full of surprises," said Magnus. "What happened to this Academy?"

The mundane girl could not bully the Cartwright boy unless the boy cared about what happened to her—unless he saw her as a person, and did not dismiss her the way Magnus had seen countless Nephilim dismiss mundanes and Downworlders, too.

Catarina hesitated. "Come with me," she said. "There's something I want to show you."

She took his hand and led him out of the Academy

cafeteria, her blue fingers intertwined with his blue-ringed hands. Magnus thought of the baby and found himself smiling again. He had always thought blue was the loveliest color.

"I've been sleeping in Ragnor's old room," Catarina said.

She mentioned their old friend briskly and practically, with no hint of feeling. Magnus held her hand a little tighter as they went up two flights of stairs and down through stone corridors. The walls bore tapestries illustrating Shadowhunters' great deeds. There were holes in several of the tapestries, including one that left the Angel Raziel headless. Magnus feared sacrilegious mice had been at the tapestries.

Catarina opened a large, dark oak wood door and led him into a vaulted stone room where there were a few pictures on the walls Magnus recognized as Ragnor's: a sketch of a monkey, a seascape with a pirate ship on it. The carved oak bed was covered in Catarina's severe white hospital sheets, but the moth-eaten curtains were green velvet, and there was a green leather inlay on a desk placed under the room's single large window.

There was a coin on it, a circle of copper turned dark with age, and two yellowed pieces of paper, turning up at the edges.

"I was going through the papers in Ragnor's desk when I found this letter," Catarina said. "It was the only really personal thing in the room. I thought you might like to read it."

"I would," said Magnus, and she put it into his hands.

Magnus unfolded the letter and looked at the spiky black writing set deep into the yellow surface, as if the writer had been annoyed by the page itself. He felt as if he were listening to a voice he had thought silenced forever.

To Ragnor Fell, preeminent educator at Shadowhunter Academy, and former High Warlock of London:

I am sorry but not surprised to hear the latest crop of Shadowhunter brats are just as unpromising as the last lot. The Nephilim, lacking imagination and intellectual curiosity? You astonish me.

I enclose a coin etched with a wreath, a symbol of education in the ancient world. I was told a faerie placed good luck on it, and you are certainly going to need luck reforming the Shadowhunters.

I am as ever impressed by your patience and dedication to your job, and your continuing optimism that your students can be taught. I wish I could have your bright outlook on life, but unfortunately I cannot help looking around at the world and noticing that we are surrounded by idiots. If I were teaching Nephilim children, I imagine I would sometimes feel forced to speak to them sharply and occasionally feel forced to drain them entirely of blood.

(Note to any Nephilim illegally reading Mr. Fell's letters and invading his privacy: I am, naturally, joking. I have a very droll personality.)

You ask how life in New York is and I can only report the usual: smelly, crowded, and populated almost entirely by maniacs. I was almost knocked over by a party of warlocks and werewolves on Bowery Street. One particular warlock was in the front, waving a glittering purple ladies' feather boa over his head like a flag. I am so embarrassed to know him. Sometimes I pretend to other Downworlders that I do not. I hope they believe me.

The main reason I am writing to you is, of course, so

that we may continue your Spanish lessons. I enclose a fresh list of vocabulary words, and assure you that you are coming along very well. If you should ever make the terrible decision to accompany a certain badly dressed warlock of our acquaintance to Peru again, this time you will be prepared.

Yours most sincerely,
Raphael Santiago

"Ragnor would not have known the Academy was going to be shut down after Valentine's Circle attacked the Clave," Catarina said. "He kept the letter so he could learn the Spanish, and then he was never able to come back for it. From the letter, though, it seems like they wrote to each other quite frequently. Ragnor must have burned the others, since they contained comments that would have gotten Raphael Santiago into trouble. I know Ragnor was fond of that sharp-tongued little vampire." She leaned her cheek against Magnus's shoulder. "I know you were, as well."

Magnus shut his eyes for a moment and remembered Raphael, who he had once done a favor; Raphael, who had died for him in return. He had known him when he was first turned, a snippy child with a will of iron, and known him through the years as Raphael led a vampire clan in all but name.

Magnus had never known Ragnor when Ragnor was young. Ragnor had been older than Magnus and, by the time Magnus met him, had become perpetually cranky. Ragnor had been yelling at kids to get off his lawn before lawns were invented. He had always been kind to Magnus, willing to fall in with any of Magnus's schemes as long as he could complain throughout while they did it.

Still, in spite of Ragnor's dark outlook on life in general and Shadowhunters in particular, Ragnor had been the one who came to Idris to teach Shadowhunters. Even after the Academy was closed, he had stayed in his little house outside the City of Glass and tried to teach the Nephilim who were willing to learn. He had always hoped, even when he refused to admit it.

Ragnor and Raphael. They were both supposed to be immortal. Magnus had thought they would last forever, as he did, down the centuries, that there would always be another meeting and another chance. But they were gone, and the mortals Magnus loved lived on. It was a lesson, Magnus thought, to love while you could, love what was fragile and beautiful and imperiled. Nobody was guaranteed forever.

Ragnor and Magnus had not gone to Peru again, and never would now. Of course, Magnus was banned from Peru, so he could not go anyway.

"You came to the Academy for Ragnor," Magnus said to Catarina. "For the sake of Ragnor's dreams, to see if you could teach the Shadowhunters to change. It seems a pretty different place, this time around. Do you think you succeeded?"

"I never thought I would," said Catarina. "This was always Ragnor's dream. I did it for him, and not the Shadowhunters. I always thought Ragnor teaching was foolish. You cannot teach people anything if they do not want to learn."

"What changed your mind?"

"I didn't change my mind," said Catarina. "This time, they did want to learn. I could not have done this alone."

"Who helped you?" asked Magnus.

Catarina smiled. "Our former Daylighter, Simon Lewis. He's a sweet boy. He could have skated by on being a hero of the war, but he declared himself a member of the dregs, and he kept speaking up even though he had nothing to gain from it. I tried to help him along, but that was all I could do, and I could only hope it would be enough. One by one, the students followed his lead and started to fall from strictly Nephilim ways, like a set of rebellious dominoes. George Lovelace moved to the dregs dormitory with Simon. Beatriz Velez Mendoza and Julie Beauvale sat with them at mealtimes. Marisol Rojas Garza and Sunil Sadasivan started fighting with the elite kids at every opportunity. The two streams became a group, became a team—even Jonathan Cartwright. It was not all Simon. These are children who know Shadowhunters fought side by side with Downworlders when Valentine attacked Alicante. These are children who saw Dean Penhallow welcome me to their Academy. They are the children of a changing world. But I think they needed Simon here, to be their catalyst."

"And you here, to be their teacher," said Magnus. "Do you think you have found a new vocation in teaching?"

He gazed down at her, slim and sky blue in their friend's old stone-and-green room. She made a terrible face.

"Hell no," said Catarina Loss. "The only thing more terrible than the food is all the horrible, whiny teenagers. I'll see Simon safely Ascended and then I am out of here, back to my hospital, where there are easy problems to deal with like gangrene. Ragnor must have been crazy."

Magnus lifted Catarina's hand, which he was still holding, to his lips. "Ragnor would have been proud."

"Oh, stop it," said Catarina, shoving him. "You're so mushy since you fell in love. And now you're going to be even worse, because you have a *baby*. I remember what it was like. They're so small, and you put so much hope into them."

Magnus glanced at her, startled. She almost never mentioned the child she had raised, Tobias Herondale's child. Partly because it was not safe: It was not a secret the Nephilim could ever know, not a sin they would ever forgive. Partly, Magnus had always suspected, Catarina did not speak of him because it hurt too much.

Catarina caught the glance. "I told Simon about him," she said. "My boy."

"You must really trust Simon," Magnus said slowly.

"Do you know?" said Catarina. "I really do. Here, take these. I want you to have them. I'm done with them."

She picked up the old coin on the desk and put it in Magnus's palm, in the hand that already held Raphael's letter to Ragnor. Magnus looked at the coin and the letter.

"Are you sure?"

"I'm sure," said Catarina. "I read the letter a lot during my first year in the Academy, to remind myself what I was doing here and what Ragnor would have wanted. I've honored my friend. I've almost completed my task. You take them."

Magnus tucked away the letter and the good-luck charm, sent by one of his dead friends to another.

He and Catarina walked out of Ragnor's room together. Catarina said she was going to eat dinner, which Magnus thought was extremely reckless of her.

"Can't you do something safe and soothing, like bungee jumping?" he asked, but she insisted. He dropped a kiss on her cheek. "Come by the attics later. The Lightwoods will be there, so I need protection. We'll have a party."

He turned and left her, unwilling to enter the dining hall and behold the slime lasagna again. As he made his way up the stairs, he met Simon on his way down.

Magnus looked at Simon consideringly. Simon seemed alarmed by this.

"Come with me, Simon Lewis," Magnus commanded. "Let's have a chat."

Simon stood at the top of one of the towers in Shadowhunter Academy with Magnus Bane, looking out at the gathering twilight and feeling vaguely uneasy.

"I could swear this tower used to be crooked."

"Huh," said Magnus. "Perception's a funny thing."

Simon was just not sure what Magnus wanted. He liked Magnus. He'd just never had a heart-to-heart with Magnus, and now Magnus was giving him a look that said *what is your deal, Simon Lewis?* Magnus even made the tatty gray shirt he was wearing look faintly stylish. He was fairly certain Magnus was too cool to care about his deal.

He glanced over at Magnus, who was standing at one of the large, glassless windows in the tower, the night wind blowing his hair back.

"I said to you once," Magnus offered, "that one day, of all the people we know, the two of us might be the only ones left."

"I don't remember," said Simon.

"Why should you?" Magnus asked. "Barring some freak tornado that sweeps away everyone we love, that is no longer true. You're mortal now. And even the immortal can be killed. Maybe this tower will collapse and leave everyone to mourn us."

The view from the tower, the stars over the woods, was

beautiful. Simon wanted to get down.

Magnus reached into his pocket and took out an old, carved coin. Simon could not see the inscription on it in the dark, but he could see that there was one.

"This belonged to Raphael once. Do you remember Raphael?" Magnus asked. "The vampire who turned you."

"Only in bits and pieces," Simon said. "I remember him telling me Isabelle was out of my league."

Magnus turned his face away, not quite successfully hiding a smile. "That sounds like Raphael."

"I remember—feeling him die," said Simon, his voice sticking in his throat. That was the worst of his stolen memories, that the weight of the memory remained when all else was gone, that he felt loss without knowing what he had lost. "He meant something to me, but I don't know if he liked me. I don't know if I liked him."

"He felt responsible for you," Magnus said. "It occurred to me today that maybe I should have felt responsible for you in the same way. I was the one who performed the spell that brought you back your memories; I was the one who set you on the path to Shadowhunter Academy. Raphael was the first one to place you in another world, but I placed you in another world as well."

"I made my own choices," Simon said. "You gave me the chance to do that. I'm not sorry you did. Are you sorry you restored my memories?"

Magnus smiled. "No, I'm not sorry. Catarina filled me in on a little of what's been going on at the Academy. It seems like you have been doing just fine making your choices without me."

"I've been trying," said Simon.

He had been shocked by Alec praising him, and it was

not as if he had expected Magnus to do it. But he felt warmed by Magnus's words, suddenly warm all over, despite the wind sweeping in from the crystalline coldness of the sky. Magnus was not talking about the bits and pieces of his half-forgotten past but about what he was now and what he had done with his time since then.

It wasn't anything remarkable, but he had been trying.

"I also heard you had a little adventure in Faerieland," said Magnus. "We've been having trouble in New York with faerie fruit sellers as well. Part of the faeries running wild is the Cold Peace itself. People who are not trusted become untrustworthy. But there is something else wrong as well. Faerie is not a land without rules, without rulers. The Queen who was Sebastian's ally has vanished, and there are many dark rumors as to why. None of which I would repeat to the Clave, because they would only impose harsher punishments on the faeries. They become harsher, and the fey wilder, and the hate between both sides grows day by day. There are storms behind you, Simon. But there is another and a greater storm coming. All the old rules are falling away. Are you ready for another storm?"

Simon was silent. He didn't know how to answer that.

"I've seen you with Clary, and with Isabelle," Magnus continued. "I know you are on the path to Ascension, to having a *parabatai* and a Shadowhunter love. Are you happy with it? Are you certain?"

"I don't know about being certain," Simon said. "I don't know about being ready, either. I can't say I haven't had doubts, that I haven't thought about turning back and being a kid in a band in Brooklyn. I think sometimes it's too hard to believe in yourself. You just do the things you're not sure you can do. You just act, in spite of not being certain.

I don't believe I can change the world—it sounds stupid to even talk about it—but I'm going to try."

"We all change the world, with every day of living in it," Magnus said. "You just have to decide *how* you want to change the world. I brought you into this world, the second time around, and though your choices are your own I do take some responsibility. Even if you are committed, you have other choices. I could arrange for you to be a vampire again, or a werewolf. Both are risky, but none as risky as Ascension."

"Yes. I want to try changing the world as a Shadowhunter," said Simon. "I really do. I want to try and change the Clave from the inside. I want that particular power to help people. It's worth the risk."

Magnus nodded.

He had meant it, Simon thought, when he said that Simon's choices were his own. He had left it up to Simon, that day in Brooklyn when he and Isabelle had approached Simon outside his school. He did not question Simon now, even though Simon was afraid that choosing to be a Shadowhunter and not a Downworlder might have offended him. He didn't want to be like the Shadowhunters who acted as if they were better than Downworlders. He wanted to be an entirely different kind of Shadowhunter.

Magnus did not look offended. He stood on the tower top, on stone in starlight, turning the coin that had belonged to the dead over and over in his fingers. He looked thoughtful.

"Have you thought about your Shadowhunter name?"

"Um...," Simon said shyly. "A little bit. I was wondering, actually—what's your real name?"

Magnus sent him a sidelong glance. Nobody gave

side-eye like someone with cat's eyes. "Magnus Bane," he said. "I know you've forgotten a lot, Smedley, but *really*."

Simon accepted the subtle reproof. He understood why Magnus would object to the implication that the name he had chosen to define himself by, kept over long years and made both infamous and illustrious, was not real.

"I'm sorry," he said. "It's just that my mind does keep coming back to names. If I survive Ascension, I'll have to pick a Shadowhunter name. I don't know how to pick the right one—I don't know how to pick one that will mean something, mean more than any other name would."

Magnus frowned.

"I'm not sure I'm cut out for this wise-advice business. Maybe I should wear a fake white beard to convince myself I am a sage. Pick the one that feels right, and don't worry too much," Magnus said eventually. "It's going to be your name. You're going to live with it. You're going to give it meaning, not the other way around."

"I'm going to try," said Simon. "Is there any reason why 'Magnus Bane' was the one that felt right?"

"Magnus Bane felt right for a lot of reasons," Magnus said, which was not really an answer. He seemed to sense Simon's disappointment and take pity on him, because he added: "Here's one."

Magnus flipped the coin over and under his fingers, the circle of metal moving faster and faster. Blue lines of magic seemed to spring from his rings, a tiny storm rising in Magnus's palm and catching the coin in a net of lightning.

Then Magnus threw the coin off the tower, into the night wind. Simon could see the falling coin, still touched with blue fire, going beyond the limits of the Academy grounds.

"There's a scientific phenomenon to describe something that happens when an object is in motion. You think you know exactly what path it will take and where it will end up. Then suddenly, for no reason you can see ... the arc changes. It goes somewhere you would never have expected."

Magnus snapped his fingers, and the coin zigzagged in the air and returned to them as Simon stared, feeling like he was seeing magic for the first time. He dropped the coin in Simon's hand and smiled, a blazing rebel's smile, his eyes as gold as newly discovered treasure.

"It's called the Magnus effect," he said.

"Fzzzz," Clary said, her bright red head hovering over the baby's small dark-blue one. She pressed little kisses onto the baby's cheeks, buzzing like a bee as she did so, and the baby chuckled and grasped at her curls. "Fzzzz, fzzz, fzzzz. I don't know what I'm doing. I have never had a close relationship with any babies. For sixteen years I thought I was an only child, baby. And after that, baby, you don't want to know what I thought. Please forgive me if I'm doing this wrong, baby. Do you like me, baby? I like you."

"Give me the baby," Maryse said jealously. "You've had him for four whole minutes, Clarissa."

It *was* a party in Magnus and Alec's suite, and the game of choice was Pass the Baby. Everyone wanted to hold him. Simon had shamelessly tried to curry favor with Isabelle's father by teaching Robert Lightwood how to use Simon's digital watch as a timer. Robert was now holding the watch in a death grip and studying it carefully. It would be Robert's turn with the baby again in sixteen minutes, and he had clasped Simon's shoulder and said, "Thanks, son," which Simon took as a blessing to date Robert's daughter. He did not regret the loss of his watch.

Clary surrendered the baby, and leaned back against the sofa between Simon and Jace. The sofa creaked dangerously as she settled back. Simon might have been safer in the formerly crooked tower, but he was willing to be in danger if he could stay next to Clary.

"He's so sweet," Clary whispered to Jace and Simon. "It's strange to think he's Alec and Magnus's, though. I mean, can you imagine?"

"It's not that strange," Jace said. "I mean, I can *imagine*."

A flush rose on his high cheekbones. He edged into the corner of the sofa as Simon and Clary both turned and stared at him.

Clary and Simon continued to stare judgmentally. It made Simon very happy. Judging people together was an essential part of best friendship.

Then Clary leaned forward and kissed Jace.

"Let's pick up this conversation in about ten years," she said. "Maybe longer! I'm going to dance with the girls."

She went to join Isabelle, who was already dancing to the soft music in the midst of a circle of admirers who had come because they heard she was back. Foremost among them was Marisol, who Simon was pretty sure had determined to be Isabelle when she grew up.

The Lightwood baby celebration was in full swing. Simon smiled, watching Clary. He could remember a couple of times she had been wary around other girls, and they had stuck together instead. It was nice to see Isabelle hold out her hands to Clary, and Clary grasp them without hesitation.

"Jace," said Simon as Jace watched Clary and smiled. Jace glanced at him and looked annoyed. "Remember when you told me that you wished I could remember?"

"Why are you asking me if I remember things?" Jace asked, sounding definitely annoyed. "I'm not the one who has problems with remembering. Remember?"

"I just wondered what you meant by that."

Simon waited, giving Jace a chance to take advantage of his demon amnesia and tell him another fake secret. Instead, Jace looked incredibly uncomfortable.

"Nothing," he said. "What would I mean? Nothing."

"Did you just mean you wanted me to remember the past generally?" Simon asked. "So I'd remember all the adventures we had and the manly bonds we formed together?"

Jace continued to make an uncomfortable face. Simon remembered Alec saying Jace was so upset.

"Wait, was that actually it?" Simon asked incredulously. "Did you *miss* me?"

"Obviously not!" snapped Jace. "I would never miss you. I, um, was talking about something specific."

"Okay. So, what specific thing did you want me to recall?" Simon asked. He eyed Jace suspiciously. "Was it the biting?"

"No!" said Jace.

"Was that a special moment for you?" Simon asked. "One that you wanted me to remember that we shared?"

"Remember this moment," said Jace. "At the very next opportunity that offers, I am going to leave you to die at the bottom of an evil boat. I want you to remember why."

Simon smiled to himself. "No, you won't. You would never leave me to die at the bottom of an evil boat," he muttered as Alec strolled over to the slanted sofa and Jace looked outraged by what he was hearing.

"Simon, normally it's a pleasure to talk to you," Alec

said. "But could I have a word with Jace?"

"Oh, right," Simon said. "Jace, I'd forgotten what I was trying to talk to you about. But now I remember very clearly. Alec and I had a little talk about his problem with me. You know, the one you told me he had. The terrible secret."

Jace's golden eyes went blank. "Ah," he said.

"You think you're hilarious, don't you?"

"Though I realize that you are both a little annoyed with me, and this might not be the time to shower myself with praise," Jace said slowly, "honesty compels me to tell you: Yes. Yes, I do think I am hilarious. 'There goes Jace Herondale,' people say. 'Cutting wit, and also totally cut. It's a burden Simon could never understand.'"

"Alec's going to kill you," Simon informed him, and patted Jace on the shoulder. "And I think that's fair. For what it's worth, I'll miss you, buddy."

He got up from the sofa. Alec advanced on Jace.

Simon trusted Alec to exact terrible vengeance for both of them. He had wasted enough time on Jace's dumb joke.

George was dancing with Julie and Beatriz, clowning around to try and get them to laugh. Beatriz was already laughing, and Simon thought Julie would soon.

"Come on, dancing with me isn't so bad," George told Julie. "I may be no Magnus Bane…" He paused and looked over at Magnus, who had changed into a black gauze shirt with blue sequins twinkling underneath. "I definitely could not pull that off," he added. "But I do work out! And I have a Scottish accent."

"You know that's right," said Simon. He high-fived George and smiled at the girls, but he was already moving past them, on his way to the center of the dancers.

On his way to Isabelle.

He came up behind her and slid his arm around her waist. She leaned back against him. She was wearing the dress she'd worn the day he'd first met her for the second time, reminding him of the starry night over Shadowhunter Academy.

"Hey," he whispered. "I want to tell you something."

"What is it?" Isabelle whispered back.

Simon turned her toward him, and she let him. He thought they should have this conversation face-to-face.

Behind her, he could see Jace and Alec. They were hugging, and Alec was laughing. Jace was patting him on the back in a congratulatory way. So much for terrible vengeance, though Simon couldn't really say he minded.

"I wanted to tell you before I try to Ascend," he said.

The smile dropped off Isabelle's face. "If this is an in-case-I-die speech, I don't want to hear it," she said fiercely. "You're not going to do that to me. You're not going to even consider dying. You're going to be fine."

"No," Simon said. "You've got it all wrong. I wanted to say this now, because if I Ascend, I get my memories back."

Isabelle looked confused instead of angry, which was an improvement. "What is it, then?"

"It doesn't matter if I get my memories back or not," Simon said. "It doesn't matter if another demon gives me amnesia tomorrow. I know you: You'll come find me again, you'll come rescue me no matter what happens. You'll come for me, and I'll discover you all over again. I love you. I love you without the memories. I love you right now."

There was a pause, broken by irrelevancies like the music and the murmur of the people all around them. He could not quite read the look on Isabelle's face.

Isabelle said in a calm voice: "I know."

Simon stared at her. "Was that...," he said slowly. "Was

that a *Star Wars* reference? Because if it was, I would like to declare my love all over again."

"Go on, then," said Isabelle. "I mean it. Say it again. I've been waiting awhile."

"I love you," said Simon.

Isabelle was laughing. Simon would have thought he would be appalled to say those words to a girl and have her laugh at him. But Isabelle was always surprising him. He could not stop looking at her. "Really?" she asked, and her eyes were shining. "Really?"

"Really," said Simon.

He drew her to him, and they danced together, on the top floor of the Academy, in the heart of her family. Since she'd been waiting awhile, he told her again and again.

Magnus kept misplacing his baby. This did not seem a good sign for the future. Magnus was sure you were meant to keep a firm grip on their location.

He eventually located the baby with Maryse, who had seized him in triumph and run away to coo over her treasure in the kitchen.

"Oh, hello," said Maryse, looking a little guilty.

"Hello, you," said Magnus, and curved a hand around the small blue head, feeling the crisp curls. "And hello, you."

The baby let out a fretful little wail. Magnus thought he was learning to distinguish between the different wails, and he magicked up a bottle of formula, ready-made. He held out his arms and Maryse visibly summoned up the willpower to surrender the baby.

"You're good with him," Maryse offered as Magnus tucked him into the corner of his arm and popped the bottle into his small mouth.

"Alec's better," Magnus said.

Maryse smiled and looked proud. "He's very mature for his age," she said fondly, and hesitated. "I ... wasn't, at his age, when I was a young mother. I didn't ... behave in a way I would want any of my children to see. Not that it's an excuse."

Magnus looked down at Maryse's face. He remembered facing off on opposite sides against her once, long ago, when she had been one of Valentine's disciples and he had felt as if he would hate her and everyone to do with her forever.

He also remembered choosing to forgive another woman who had been on Valentine's side, and who had come to him holding a child in her arms and wanting to make things right. That woman had been Jocelyn, and that baby had become Clary, the first and only child Magnus had ever seen grow up.

He had never thought he would have his own child, to watch grow up.

Maryse looked back at him, standing very tall and straight. Perhaps his assumption about how she had felt for all these years was wrong; perhaps she had never decided to ignore the past, and thought with Nephilim pride that he had to follow her lead. Perhaps she had always wanted to apologize and always been too proud.

"Oh, Maryse," Magnus said. "Forget it. I'm serious, don't mention it again. In one of those turns I never expected, we're family. All the beautiful surprises of life are what make life worth living."

"You still get surprised?"

"Every day," said Magnus. "Especially since I met your son."

He walked out of the kitchen with his son in his arms and Maryse behind him, back to the party.

His beloved Alec, paragon of maturity, appeared to be hitting his *parabatai* repeatedly around the head. Last time Magnus had seen them, they had been hugging, so he presumed Jace had made one of his many unfortunate jokes.

"What is wrong with you?" Alec demanded. He laughed and kept raining down blows as Jace flailed on the sofa, sending cushions flying, a vision of Shadowhunter grace. "Seriously, Jace, what is wrong with you?"

This seemed a reasonable question to Magnus.

He looked around the room. Simon was dancing with Isabelle, very badly. Isabelle did not seem to mind. Clary was jumping up and down with Marisol, barely taller than the younger girl. Catarina appeared to be fleecing Jon Cartwright at cards, over by the window.

Robert Lightwood was standing right beside Magnus. Robert had to stop creeping up on people like this. Someone was going to have a heart attack.

"Hello, little man," said Robert. "Where did you go off to?"

He shot a suspicious look at Maryse, who rolled her eyes.

"Magnus and I were having a talk," she said, touching Magnus's arm.

Her behavior made perfect sense to Magnus: win over the son-in-law, gain more access to the grandchild. He had seen these kind of family interactions before, but he had never, never thought he would be part of them.

"Oh?" Robert said eagerly. "Have you decided on his name?"

The latest song stopped playing just as Robert asked the question. His booming voice rang out in the hush.

Alec leaped off Jace and over the back of the sofa, to

stand beside Magnus. The sofa collapsed, gently, with Jace still trapped in the cushions.

Magnus looked at Alec, who looked back at him, hope shining in his face. That was one thing that had not changed about Alec in the time they had been together: He had no guile, used no tricks to hide how he really felt. Magnus never wanted him to lose that.

"We did talk about it, actually," Magnus said. "And we thought that you had the right idea."

"You mean...," Maryse said.

Magnus inclined his head, as close as he could come to a sweeping bow while holding the baby. "I am delighted to introduce you all," he said, "to Max Lightwood."

Magnus felt Alec's hand rest, warm as gratitude and sure as love, against his back. He looked down at the baby's face. The baby seemed much more interested in his bottle than his name.

The time might come when the child, being a warlock, would want to choose his own name to bear through the centuries. Until the time came when he was old enough to choose who he wanted to be, Magnus thought he could do a lot worse than this name, this sign of love and acceptance, grief and hope.

Max Lightwood.

One of the beautiful surprises of life.

There was a humming, delighted hush, with murmurs of pleasure and approval. Then Maryse and Robert began to fight about middle names.

"Michael," Robert repeated, a stubborn man.

Catarina strolled up, tucking a roll of money into her bra and thus not looking like the most appropriate teacher in the history of time. "How about Ragnor?" she asked.

"Clary," said Jace from the fallen sofa. "Help me. It's gone all dark."

Magnus wandered away from the debate, because Max's bottle was almost empty and Max was starting to cry.

"Don't magic a bottle, make a real one," Alec said. "If he gets used to you being faster at feeding him, you have to feed him all the time."

"That is blackmail! Don't cry," Magnus urged his son, going back into the kitchen so he could make up a bottle by hand.

It was not so difficult, getting the formula ready. Magnus had watched Alec do it several times now, and he found that he was able to follow along by doing what Alec had done.

"Don't cry," he coaxed Max again as the milk heated up. "Don't cry, and don't spit up on my shirt. If you do either of those things, I will forgive you, but I will be upset. I want us to get along."

Max cried on. Magnus wiggled the fingers of his free hand over the baby's face, wishing there was a magic spell to make babies hush that would not be wrong to cast.

To his surprise Max ceased crying, in the same way he had in the hall yesterday when transferred to Alec's arms. He stared with a liquid, interested gaze at the sparkles cast on his face by Magnus's rings.

"See?" Magnus said, and restored Max's bottle to him, full again. "I knew we were going to get along."

He went and stood in the kitchen doorway, cradling Max in his arms, so he could watch the party. Three years ago, he would not have thought any of this was possible. There were so many people he felt connected to, in this one room. So much had changed, and there was so much potential for change. It was terrifying, to think of all that might be lost, and exhilarating to think of all he had gained.

He looked to Alec, who was standing between his parents, his stance confident and relaxed, his mouth curved in a smile at something one of them had said.

"Maybe one day it will be just you and me, my little blueberry," Magnus said conversationally. "But not for a long, long time. We'll take care of him, you and I. Won't we?"

Max Lightwood made a happy burbling sound that Magnus took as agreement.

This warm, bright room was no bad starting place for his child's path to knowing there was more to life than many people ever learned, that there was limitless love to be found, and time to discover it. Magnus had to trust that for himself, for his son, for his beloved, for all of the shining, fading mortals and enduring, struggling immortals that he knew, there would be time enough.

He put the bottle down to one side and pressed his lips to the fuzzy curls covering his son's head. He heard Max make a small murmuring sound in his ear. "Don't worry," Magnus murmured back. "We're all in this together."

Angels Twice Descending

By Cassandra Clare and Robin Wasserman

Simon knew if he looked up he could meet Isabelle's eyes, or Clary's, and draw strength from them. He could silently ask them if this was the right path, and they would reassure him.

But this choice couldn't belong to them. It had to be his, and his alone.

—Angels Twice Descending

WILL YOU TAKE INTO YOURSELF THE BLOOD OF THE ANGEL RAZIEL AND HONOR THAT BLOOD?
DO YOU SWEAR TO SERVE THE CLAVE, TO FOLLOW THE LAW AS SET FORTH BY THE COVENANT, AND TO OBEY THE WORD OF THE COUNCIL?
WILL YOU DEFEND THAT WHICH IS HUMAN AND MORTAL, KNOWING THAT FOR YOUR SERVICE, THERE WILL BE NO RECOMPENSE AND NO THANKS BUT HONOR?

"I think we should have a funeral," George Lovelace said, voice trembling on the last word. "A proper one."

Simon Lewis paused in his labors and peered up at his roommate. George was the kind of guy Simon had once loathed on sight, assuming anyone with that bronze glow, those six-pack abs, that maddeningly sexy (at least, according to every girl and more than a few of the guys Simon had checked with) Scottish brogue, must have a brain the size of a rat turd and a personality about as appealing. But George turned Simon's assumptions on their head on a daily basis. As he was doing right at this moment, wiping away something that looked suspiciously like a tear.

"Are you ... *crying*?" Simon asked, incredulous.

"Of course not." George gave his eyes another furious wipe. "Well, in my defense," he added, sounding only slightly abashed, "death is a terrible thing."

"It's a dead rat," Simon pointed out. "A dead rat in *your shoe*, I might add." Simon and George had discovered that the key to a happy roommate relationship was clear division of labor. So George was in charge of disposing of all creatures—rats, lizards, cockroaches, the occasional odd-shaped mishmash of the three whose ancestor had, presumably, once insulted a warlock—found in the closets or beneath the beds. Simon handled all those that had crawled inside items of clothing and—he shuddered to remember the moment they realized this labor needed assigning—under pillows. "Also, for the record, only one of us has actually *been* a rat—and you'll note he's not the one crying."

"It could be the last dead rat we ever find!" George sniffled. "Think about it, Si. *This* could be the last shared dead rat of our entire lives."

Simon sighed. As Ascension Day approached, the day they would officially stop being students and start being Shadowhunters, George had been mournfully noting every last time they did anything. Now, as the moon rose over their last night at the Academy, he'd apparently lost his mind. A little nostalgia made sense to Simon: That morning, at their last-ever calisthenics session, Delaney Scarsbury had called him a spaghetti-armed, four-eyed, bow-legged demon-snack-in-waiting for the last time, and Simon had almost said *thank you*. And that night's final bowl of "meat-flavored" custard had admittedly gotten them all a little choked up.

But losing it over a rat with stiffening limbs and athlete's foot? That was taking things too far.

Using the torn-off cover from his old demonology textbook, Simon managed to scoop the rat out of the shoe without touching it. He dropped it into one of the plastic bags he'd had Isabelle bring him specifically for this purpose, tied the bag tightly, then—humming taps—dropped it into the trash.

"RIP, Jon Cartwright the Thirty-Fourth," George said solemnly.

They named all their rats Jon Cartwright—a fact that drove the original Jon Cartwright nuts. Simon smiled at the thought of it, their gallingly cocky classmate's forehead flush with anger, that vein in his disgustingly muscled neck starting to throb. Maybe George was right.

Maybe, someday, they would even miss the rats.

Simon had never put much effort into imagining his graduation day, much less the night before. Like prom and homecoming, these seemed like rituals meant for a very different kind of teenager—the school-spirited, letter-jacketed jocks and cheerleaders he knew mostly from bad movies. No keg parties for him, no weepy farewells or ill-advised hookups fueled by nostalgia and cheap beer. Two years ago, if he'd bothered to think about it at all, Simon would have assumed he'd spend that night like he'd spent most of his nights in Brooklyn, hanging with Eric and the guys in Java Jones, guzzling coffee and brainstorming names for the band. (*Dead Sneaker Rat*, Simon mused out of habit. *Or maybe Rodent Funeral.*)

Of course, that was back when he'd assumed high school would lead to college, which would lead to rock stardom ... or at least a moderately cool job at a moderately cool record label. Before he knew there was such a thing as demons, before he knew there was a race of superpowered, angel-blooded warriors eternally pledged to battle them—and definitely before he'd volunteered himself up to be one of them.

So instead of Java Jones, he was in the Academy's student lounge, squinting through candlelight, sneezing from two centuries' worth of dust, and dodging the intimidating glares of noble Shadowhunters past whose portraits lined the room, their expressions seeming to say, *How could you possibly imagine* you *could be one of* us? Instead of Eric, Matt, and Kirk, who he'd known since kindergarten, he was with friends he'd met only a couple of years before, one of whom nurtured an intense affection for rats and another who shared his name with them. Instead of speculating about their futures in rock and roll, they were readying themselves for a life battling multidimensional evils. Assuming, that is, they survived graduation.

Which wasn't exactly a safe assumption to make.

"What do you think it will be like?" Marisol Garza asked now, nestled beneath Jon Cartwright's beefy arm and looking like she was almost happy to be there. "The ceremony, I mean. What do you think we'll have to do?"

Jon, like Julie Beauvale and Beatriz Mendoza, descended from a long line of Shadowhunters. For them, tomorrow was just another day, their official farewell to student life. Time to stop training and start battling.

But for George, Marisol, Simon, Sunil Sadasivan, and a handful of other mundane students, tomorrow loomed as the day they Ascended.

No one was quite sure what it meant: Ascension. Much less what it entailed. They'd been told very little: That they would drink from the Mortal Cup. That they would, like the first of the warrior race, Jonathan Shadowhunter, sip the blood of an angel. That they would, if they were lucky, be transformed on the spot into real, full-blooded Shadowhunters. That they would say good-bye to their mundane lives forever and pledge themselves to a fearless life of service to humanity.

Or if they were very unlucky, they would die an immediate and presumably gruesome death.

It didn't exactly make for a festive evening.

"I'm just wondering what's in the Cup," Simon said. "You don't think it's actual blood, do you?"

"Isn't that your specialty, Lewis?" Jon sneered.

George sighed wistfully. "The last time Jon makes a stupid vampire joke."

"I wouldn't count on it," Simon muttered.

Marisol whacked Jon's shoulder. "Shut up, idiot," she said. But she said it rather too lovingly for Simon's taste.

"I bet it's water," Beatriz said, always the peacemaker. "Water that you're supposed to pretend is blood, or that the Cup turns into blood, or something like that."

"It doesn't matter what's in the Cup," Julie said in her best obnoxiously knowing way, even though she clearly didn't know any better than the rest of them. "The Cup's magic. You could probably drink ketchup out of it and it would still work."

"I hope it's coffee, then," Simon said with a wistful sigh of his own. The Academy was a caffeine-free zone. "I would be a much better Shadowhunter if I got to Ascend well-caffeinated."

"Sunil said he heard that it's water from Lake Lyn," Beatriz said skeptically. Simon hoped she was right to be skeptical; his last encounter with Lake Lyn's water had been unsettling, to say the least. And given that some unknown percentage of mundanes died upon Ascending, it seemed to him like the Cup didn't need any additional help on the occasionally fatal front.

"Where is Sunil, anyway?" Simon asked. They hadn't exactly made a plan to meet up tonight, but the Academy offered limited recreational options—at least if you didn't enjoy spending your free time accidentally getting locked in the dungeons or stalking the giant magical slug rumored to slither through the corridors in the predawn hours. Most nights for the last couple of months, Simon and his friends had ended up here, talking about their futures, and he'd expected they would spend this last night the same way.

Marisol, who knew Sunil the best, shrugged. "Maybe he's 'considering his options.'" She curled her fingers around the phrase. This was how Dean Penhallow had advised students on the mundane track to spend their final evening, assuring them there was no shame in backing out at the last moment.

"Humiliation. Lifelong embarrassment over your mundie cowardice and guilt for wasting all of our very valuable time," Scarsbury had growled at them, and then, when the dean shot him a disapproving look, "But yeah, sure, no shame."

"Well, shouldn't he be 'considering'?" Julie asked. "Shouldn't you all be? It's not like going to doctor school and taking the Hypocritical oath or something. You don't get to change your mind."

"First of all, it's the Hippocratic oath," Marisol said.

"And it's called *medical* school," Jon put in, looking rather proud of himself. Marisol had been schooling him on mundane life. Against his will, or so Jon had led them to believe.

"Second of all," Marisol added, "why would you think any

of us would be likely to change our minds? Are *you* planning to change your mind about being a Shadowhunter?"

Julie looked affronted by the idea. "I *am* a Shadowhunter. You might as well have asked if I'm planning to change my mind about being alive."

"So what makes you think it's any different for us?" Marisol said fiercely. She was the youngest of them by two years and the smallest by several inches, but Simon sometimes thought that she was the bravest. She was certainly the one he'd bet on in a fight. (Marisol fought well—she also, when necessary, fought dirty.)

"She didn't mean anything by it," Beatriz said gently.

"I really didn't," Julie said quickly.

Simon knew it was true. Julie couldn't help sounding like a mundane-hating snob sometimes, any more than Jon could help sounding like—well, like an asshole sometimes. That's who they were, and Simon realized that, inexplicably, he wouldn't have it any other way. For better or worse, these were his friends. In two years they'd faced so much together: demons, faeries, Delaney Scarsbury, the dining hall "food." It was almost like a family, Simon reflected. You didn't necessarily like them all the time, but you knew, push come to shove, you'd defend them to the death.

Though he very much hoped it wouldn't come to that.

"Come on, aren't you a little nervous?" Jon asked. "Who can remember the last time anyone Ascended? It sounds utterly ridiculous when you think about it: One drink from a cup and—poof—*Lewis* is a Shadowhunter?"

"It doesn't sound ridiculous to me," Julie said softly, and they all fell silent. Julie's mother had been Turned during the Dark War. One drink from Sebastian's Infernal Cup, and she'd become Endarkened. A shell of a person, nothing more than a hollow vessel for Sebastian's evil commands.

They all knew what one drink from a cup could do.

George cleared his throat. He couldn't stand a somber mood for more than thirty seconds—it was one of the things Simon would miss most about living with him. "Well, I for one am entirely ready to claim my birthright," he said cheerfully. "Do you think I'll become unbearably arrogant on first sip, or will it take a little time to catch up with Jon?"

"It's not arrogance if it's accurate," Jon said, grinning, and just like that, the night righted itself again.

Simon tried to pay attention to his friends' banter and did his best not to think about Jon's question, about whether or not he was nervous—whether he should be spending this night in sober consideration of his "options."

What options? How, after two years at the Academy, after all his training and study, after he'd sworn over and over again that he wanted to be a Shadowhunter, could he just walk away? How could he disappoint Clary and Isabelle like that ... and if he did, how could they ever love him again?

He tried not to think about how it would be even harder for them to love him—or at least for him to appreciate it—if something went wrong in the ceremony, and he ended up dead.

He tried not to think about all the *other* people who loved him, the ones who, according to Shadowhunter Law, he was supposed to pledge never to see again. His mother. His sister.

Marisol and Sunil didn't have anyone waiting for them back home, something that had always seemed unbearably sad to Simon. But maybe it was easier, walking away when you were leaving nothing behind. Then there was George, the lucky one—his adopted parents were Shadowhunters themselves, even if they'd never picked up a sword. He would still be able to go home for regular Sunday dinners; he wouldn't even have to pick a new name.

George had been teasing him lately, saying that Simon shouldn't have much trouble picking a new name, either. "'Lightwood' has quite a ring to it, don't you think?" he liked to say. Simon was getting very good at feigning deafness.

Secretly, though, a blush rising to his cheeks, he would think: *Lightwood ... maybe*. Someday. If he dared let himself hope.

In the meantime, though, he had to come up with a new name of his own, a name for his new Shadowhunter self—which was approximately as unfathomable as everything else about this process.

"Um, can I come in?" A scrawny, spectacled girl of around thirteen stood in the doorway. Simon thought her name was Milla, but he wasn't sure—the Academy's new class was so large, and so inclined to goggle at Simon from a distance, that he hadn't gotten to know many of them. This one had the eager but confused look of a mundane, one who, even after all these months, couldn't quite believe she was really here.

"It's public property," Julie said, a haughty—or rather, even-haughtier-than-usual—note entering her voice. Julie loved lording it over the new kids.

The girl crept toward them skittishly. Simon found himself wondering how someone like her had ended up at the Academy—then caught himself. He knew better than to judge by appearances. Especially given how he'd looked when he showed up two years before, so skinny he could only fit into girl-size gear. *You're thinking like a Shadowhunter,* he chided himself.

Funny how that almost never sounded like a good thing.

"He told me to give this to you," the girl whispered, handing a folded paper to Marisol, and then quickly backing away. Marisol, Simon gathered, was somewhat of a hero to the younger mundanes.

"Who did?" Marisol asked, but the girl was already gone. Marisol shrugged and opened the note, her face falling as she read the message.

"What?" Simon asked, concerned.

Marisol shook her head.

Jon took her hand, and Simon expected her to slap him, but instead she squeezed tight. "It's from Sunil," she said in a tight, angry voice. She passed the note to Simon. "I guess he 'considered his options.'"

I can't do it, the note read. *I know it probably makes me a coward, but I can't drink from that Cup. I don't want to die. I'm sorry. Say good-bye to everyone for me? And good luck.*

They passed the note around one by one, as if needing to see the words in black and white before they could really believe it. Sunil had run away.

"We can't blame him," Beatriz said finally. "Everyone has to make his own choice."

"I can blame him," Marisol said, scowling. "He's making us all look bad."

Simon didn't think that was why she was really angry, not exactly. He was angry too—not because he thought Sunil was a coward, or had betrayed them. Simon was angry because he'd put so much effort into trying not to think about what could happen, or how this was his last chance to walk away, and now Sunil had made that impossible.

Simon stood up. "Think I need to get some air."

"Want company, mate?" George asked.

Simon shook his head, knowing George wouldn't be offended. It was another thing that made them such good roommates—each knew when to leave the other alone.

"See you guys in the morning," Simon said. Julie and Beatriz smiled and waved good night, and even Jon gave him a sardonic salute. But Marisol wouldn't even look at him, and Simon wondered whether she thought he'd be the next to run.

He wanted to reassure her there was no chance of that. He wanted to swear that, in the morning, he'd be there beside the rest of them in the Council Hall, ready to take the Cup to his lips without reservation. But swearing was a serious thing for Shadowhunters. You never promised unless you were absolutely sure.

So Simon just said a final good night and left his friends behind.

Simon wondered whether, in the history of time, anyone had ever said, "I need to get some air," and actually meant it. Surely it was only ever used as code for "I need to be somewhere else." Which Simon did. The problem was, nowhere felt like the right place to be—so, for lack of a better idea, he decided his dorm room would have to do. At least there he could be alone.

This, at least, was the plan.

But when he stepped into the room, he found a girl sitting on his bed. A petite, redheaded girl whose face lit up at the sight of him.

Of all the strange things that had happened to Simon in the last couple of years, the strangest had to be that this—beautiful girls eagerly awaiting him in his bedroom—no longer seemed particularly strange at all.

"Clary," he said as he encompassed her in a fierce hug. It was all he needed to say, because that's the thing about a best friend. She knew exactly when he most needed to see her and how grateful and relieved he was—without his having to say a thing.

Clary grinned at him and slipped her stele back into her pocket. The Portal she'd created was still shimmering in the decrepit stone wall, by far the brightest thing in the room. "Surprised?"

"Wanted to get one last look at me before I go all buff and demon-fightery?" Simon teased.

"Simon, you do know that Ascending isn't going to be like getting bitten by a radioactive spider or something, right?"

"So you're saying I won't be able to leap tall buildings in a single bound? And I don't get my own Batmobile? I want my money back."

"Seriously, though, Simon—"

"Seriously, Clary. I know what Ascension means."

The words sat heavily between them, and as always, Clary heard what he didn't say: That this was too big to talk about seriously. That joking was, for the moment, the best he could do.

"Besides, Lewis, I'd say you're buff enough already." She poked his biceps, which, he couldn't help but notice, were very close to bulging. "Any more and you'll have to buy new clothes."

"Never!" he said indignantly, and smoothed out his T-shirt, which had a baker's dozen holes in the soft cotton and read I'M COSPLAYING AS MYSELF in letters nearly too faded to read. "Did you, uh, did you happen to bring Isabelle with you?" He tried to keep the hope out of his voice.

Hard to believe that two years ago, he'd come to the Academy in part to escape Clary and Isabelle, the way they'd looked at him like they loved him more than anyone else in the world—but also like he'd drowned their puppy in a bathtub. They'd loved some other version of him, the one he could no longer remember, and that version had loved them, too. He didn't doubt it; he just couldn't feel it. They'd been strangers to him. Terrifyingly beautiful strangers who wanted him to be someone he wasn't.

It felt like another life. Simon didn't know if he'd ever get all of his memories back—but somehow, despite that, he'd found his way back to Clary and Isabelle. He'd found a best friend who felt like his other half, who would someday soon be his *parabatai*. And he'd found Isabelle Lightwood, a miracle in human form, who said "I love you" whenever she saw him and, incomprehensibly, seemed to mean it.

"She wanted to come," Clary said, "but she had to go deal with this rogue faerie thing in Chinatown, something about soup dumplings and a guy with a goat head. I didn't ask too many questions and—" She smiled knowingly at Simon. "I lost you at 'soup dumplings,' didn't I?"

Simon's stomach growled loudly enough to answer for him.

"Well, maybe we can grab you some on the way," Clary said. "Or at least a couple slices of pizza and a latte."

"Don't toy with me, Fray." Simon was very touchy these days on the subject of pizza, or the lack thereof. He suspected that any day now his stomach might resign in protest. "On the way where?"

"Oh, I forgot to explain—that's why I'm here, Simon." Clary took his hand. "I've come to take you home."

* * *

Simon stood on the sidewalk staring up at his mother's brownstone, his stomach churning. Traveling by way of Portal always made him feel a bit like puking up his lower intestine, but this time he didn't think he could blame the interdimensional magic. Not entirely, at least.

"You sure this is a good idea?" he said. "It's late."

"It's eleven p.m., Simon," Clary said. "You know she's still awake. And even if she's not, you know—"

"I know." His mother would want to see him. So would his sister, who, according to Clary, was home for the weekend because *someone*—presumably a well-meaning, redheaded someone with his sister's cell number—had told her Simon was stopping in for a visit.

He sagged against Clary for a moment, and, small as she was, she bore his weight. "I don't know how to do it," he said. "I don't know how to say good-bye to them."

Simon's mother thought he was away at military school. He'd felt guilty lying to her, but he'd known there wasn't any other choice; he knew, all too well, what happened when he risked telling his mother too much truth. But this—this was something else. He was forbidden by Shadowhunter Law to tell her about his Ascension, about his new life. The Law also forbade him from contacting her after he became a Shadowhunter, and though there was nothing saying he couldn't be here in Brooklyn to say good-bye to her forever, the Law forbade him from explaining why.

Sed lex, dura lex.

The Law is hard, but it is the Law.

Lex sucks, Simon thought.

"You want me to go in with you?" Clary asked.

He did, more than anything—but something told him

this was one of those things he needed to do on his own.

Simon shook his head. "But thanks. For bringing me here, for knowing I needed it, for—well, for everything."

"Simon..."

Clary looked hesitant, and Clary never looked hesitant.

"What is it?"

She sighed. "Everything that's happened to you, Simon, everything..." She paused, just long enough for him to think through how much that everything encompassed: getting turned into a rat and then a vampire; finding Isabelle; saving the world a handful of times, at least so he'd been told; getting locked in a cage and tormented by all manner of supernatural creatures; killing demons; facing an angel; losing his memories; and now standing at the threshold of the only home he'd ever known, preparing himself to leave it behind forever. "I can't help thinking it's all because of me," Clary said softly. "That I'm the reason. And..."

He stopped her before she could get any further, because he couldn't stand for her to think she needed to apologize. "You're right," he said. "You are the reason. For everything." Simon gave her a gentle kiss on the forehead. "That's why I'm saying thank you."

"Are you sure you don't want me to heat that up for you?" Simon's mother asked as he shoveled another heaping spoonful of cold ziti into his mouth.

"Mmff? What? No, it's fine."

It was more than fine. It was tangy tomato and fresh garlic and hot pepper and gooey cheese, and better than leftover pasta from the corner pizza place had any right to be. It tasted like actual *food*, which already put it head and shoulders above what he'd been eating for the last several months. But it wasn't just that. Takeout from Giuseppi's was a tradition for Simon and his mother—after his father died and his sister went away to school, after it was just the two of them knocking around an apartment that felt cavernous with just the two of them left in it, they'd lost the habit of having daily meals with each other. It was easier to just grab food whenever they thought of it, on the way in or out of the apartment, his mother heating up TV dinners after work, Simon picking up some pho or a sandwich on his way to band practice. It was, maybe, easier not to face the empty chairs at the table every night. But they made it a rule to eat together at least one night each week, slurping down Giuseppi's spaghetti and drenching garlic knots in spicy sauce.

These cold leftovers tasted like home, like family, and Simon hated to think of his mother sitting in the empty apartment, week after week, eating them on her own.

Children are supposed to grow up and leave, he told himself. He wasn't doing anything wrong; he wasn't doing anything he wasn't meant to do.

But there was a part of him that wondered. Children were supposed to leave home, maybe. But not forever. Not like this.

"Your sister tried to wait up for you," his mother said, "but apparently she's been up for a week straight studying for exams. She was passed out on the couch by nine."

"Maybe we should wake her up," Simon suggested.

She shook her head. "Let the poor girl sleep. She'll see you in the morning."

He hadn't *exactly* told his mother he was staying over. But he had let her believe it, which he supposed amounted to about the same thing: yet another lie.

She settled into the chair beside him and stabbed a ziti onto her fork. "Don't tell my diet," she stage-whispered, then popped it into her mouth.

"Mom, the reason I'm here ... I wanted to talk to you about something."

"That's funny, I've actually—I've been wanting to talk to you about something too."

"Oh? Great! Uh, you go first."

His mother sighed. "You remember Ellen Klein? Your Hebrew school teacher?"

"How could I forget?" Simon said wryly. Mrs. Klein had been the bane of his existence from second grade through fifth. Every Tuesday after school, they'd fought a silent war, all because, in an unfortunate playground incident, Simon had accidentally dislodged her wig and sent it flying into a pigeon's nest. She'd spent the next three years determined to ruin his life.

"You know she was just a nice old lady trying to get you to pay attention," his mother said now with a knowing smile.

"Nice old ladies don't throw your Pokémon cards in the trash," Simon pointed out.

"They do when you're trading them for kiddish wine at the back of the sanctuary," she said.

"I would never!"

"A mother always knows, Simon."

"Okay. Fine. But that was a very rare Mew. The only Pokémon that—"

"*Anyway*. Ellen Klein's daughter just got married to her girlfriend, a lovely woman, you'd like her—we all like her. But..."

Simon rolled his eyes. "But let me guess: Mrs. Klein is a raging homophobe."

"No, it's not that—the girlfriend's Catholic. Ellen had a fit, wouldn't go to the wedding, and now she's wearing mourning clothes and telling everyone that her daughter might as well be dead."

Simon opened his mouth to crow about how he'd been right all along, that Mrs. Klein was indeed a horrible shrew, but his mother held up a finger to stop him.

A mother, apparently, always knows.

"Yes, yes, it's horrible, but I'm not telling you so you can feel vindicated. I'm telling you..." She knitted her fingers together, looking suddenly nervous. "I had the strangest feeling when I heard the story, Simon, like I knew she would regret it—because *I* regretted it. Isn't that strange?" She let out a nervous little giggle, but there was no humor in it. "Feeling guilty for something you haven't even done? I can't say why, Simon, but I feel like I've betrayed you in some terrible way I can't remember."

"Of course you haven't, Mom. That's ridiculous."

"Of course it's ridiculous. I would *never*. A parent should have unconditional love for her child." Her eyes were glossy with unshed tears. "You know that's how I love you, Simon, don't you? Unconditionally?"

"Of course I know that."

He said it like he meant it—he did mean it. But, of course, it was just another lie. Because in that other life, the one that had been wiped clean from both their minds, she *had* betrayed him. He'd told her the truth, that he'd been turned into a vampire, and she had thrown him out of the house. She had told him he was no longer her son. That her son was dead. She'd proven, to both of them, the conditions of her love.

He couldn't remember it happening, but on some level

deeper than conscious thought, he remembered the feeling of it—the pain, the betrayal, the loss. It had never occurred to him she might remember too.

"This is silly." She brushed away a tear, gave herself a little shake. "I don't know why I'm getting so emotional over this. I just ... I just had this *feeling* that I needed to tell you that, and then you showed up here like it was meant to be, and..."

"Mom." Simon pulled his mother out of her chair and into a tight hug. She seemed so small to him suddenly, and he thought how hard she'd worked all these years to protect him, and how he would do anything to protect her in return. He was a different person now than he'd been two years before, a different Simon than the one who'd confessed to his mother and been turned out of the house—maybe his mother was different too. Maybe making that choice once was enough to ensure she would never make it again; maybe it was time to stop holding it against her, this betrayal neither of them could quite remember. "Mom, I know. And I love you, too."

She pulled away then, just far enough to meet his gaze. "What about you? What did you have to tell me?"

Oh, nothing much, I'm just joining a supernatural cult of demon-fighters who've forbidden me to ever see you again, love ya.

It didn't have quite the right ring to it.

"I'll tell you in the morning," he said. "You look exhausted."

She smiled, exhaustion painted across her face. "In the morning," she echoed. "Welcome home, Simon."

"Thanks, Mom," he said, and miraculously managed to do so without getting choked up. He waited for her to disappear behind her bedroom door, waited for her soft snores to begin. Then he scribbled a note apologizing for having to leave so abruptly. Without saying good-bye.

His sister snored too—though, like their mother, she denied it. He could, if he stayed very silent, hear her all the way in the kitchen. He could wake her up, if he wanted, and he could probably even tell her the truth, or some version of it. Rebecca could be trusted—not just to keep his secrets, but to understand them. He could do what he'd come here to do, what he was *supposed* to do, say good-bye to her and tell her to love and protect their mother enough for both of them.

"No." He'd spoken softly, but the word seemed to echo in the empty kitchen.

The Law was hard, but it was also riven with loopholes. Hadn't Clary taught him that? There were Shadowhunters who found a way to keep their mundane loved ones in their lives—Simon himself was proof. Maybe that was why Clary had brought him here tonight—not to say good-bye, but to realize that he couldn't. Wouldn't.

This isn't forever, Simon promised his mother and sister as he slipped out the door. He promised himself it wasn't cowardly, leaving without saying anything. It was a silent promise—that this wasn't the end. That he'd find a way. And despite the fact that there was no one to appreciate his flawless Schwarzenegger accent, he swore his oath aloud: "I'll be back."

Clary had said to give her a call when he was ready to head back to the Academy, but he wasn't ready yet. It was strange: In another day, there'd be nothing keeping him from returning to New York for good. After his Ascension, he'd be a Shadowhunter for real. No more school, no more training missions, no more long days and nights in Idris missing his morning coffee. He hadn't given much thought to what would happen next, but he knew he'd come home to the city and stay in the Institute, at least temporarily. There was no reason to feel so homesick for New York when he was *this close* to being back for good.

Except he wasn't quite sure who he'd be when he came back. When he Ascended. *If* he Ascended, if nothing terrible happened when he took his drink from the Mortal Cup.

What would it mean to become a Shadowhunter, really? He'd be stronger and swifter, he knew that much. He'd be able to bear runes on his skin, see through glamours without a warlock's help. He knew plenty about what he'd be able to do—but he didn't know anything about how it would feel. About who he'd be when he was a Shadowhunter. It's not that he thought one drink from a magic cup would instantly turn him into an egomaniacal, preternaturally handsome, wildly reckless snob like ... well, like almost all the Shadowhunters he knew and loved. Nor did he expect that turning into a Shadowhunter would make him automatically disdain D&D, *Star Trek*, and all technology and pop culture invented after the nineteenth century. But who could know for sure?

And it wasn't just the confusing transformation from human to angel-warrior. He'd been assured that, in all likelihood, if he survived Ascension, he would get back all his memories. All those memories of the original Simon, the "real" Simon, the one he'd worked so hard to persuade people would be gone forever, would come flooding back into his brain. He supposed this should make him happy, but Simon found he felt rather territorial of his brain as it was now. What if that Simon—the Simon who'd saved the world, the

Simon whom Isabelle had first fallen in love with—didn't much like this Simon that he'd become? What if he drank from the Cup and lost himself all over again?

It gave him a headache, thinking of himself as so many different people.

He wanted one last night in the city as just this one: Simon Lewis, myopic, manga-loving mundane.

Also, he still wanted some of those soup dumplings.

Simon wandered down Flatbush, soaking in the familiar noises of New York at night, sirens and construction drills and road-rage honking, along with the slightly less familiar sounds of glamoured faerie hounds barking at the pigeons. He crossed the Manhattan Bridge, metal rattling beneath his feet as the subway roared past, the lights of the Financial District glittering through the fog. Even before he'd known anything about demons and Downworlders, Simon thought, he had always known New York was full of magic. Maybe that was why it had been so easy for him to accept the truth about the Shadow World: In his city, anything was possible.

Conveniently, the bridge dumped him off in the heart of Chinatown. As he popped into his favorite hole-in-the-wall and scarfed a to-go order of dumplings, Simon's mind strayed to Isabelle, wondering if she was close by, slashing evildoers with her electrum whip. It boggled his mind—if you thought about it, he was basically dating a superhero.

Of course, the thing about dating a superhero was that you couldn't exactly ask them to take a break from saving the world just because you were in the mood for a last-minute date. So Simon kept walking, soaking in the rhythm of the midnight city, letting his mind wander as aimlessly as his feet. At least, he thought he was wandering aimlessly, until he found himself on a familiar block of Avenue D, passing a bodega where the milk was always sour but the guy behind the counter would give you free coffee with your morning doughnut, if you knew enough to ask.

Wait, how did I know that? Simon thought. The answer came to him on the heels of the question. He knew that because, in some other forgotten life, he had lived here. He and Jordan Kyle had shared an apartment in the crumbling redbrick building on the corner. A vampire and a werewolf living together—it sounded like the beginning of a bad joke, but the only bad joke was that Simon had practically forgotten it ever happened.

And Jordan was dead.

It hit him now almost as hard as it had when he first heard: Jordan was dead. And not just Jordan. Raphael was dead. Isabelle's brother Max, dead. Clary's brother Sebastian, dead. Julie's sister. Beatriz's grandfather and father and brother, Julian Blackthorn's father, Emma Carstairs's parents—all of them dead, and those were only the ones Simon had been told about. How many other people he had cared about, or people the people he loved had cared about, had been lost to one Shadowhunter war or another? He was still a teenager—he wasn't supposed to know this many people who had died.

And me, he thought suddenly. *Don't forget that one.*

Because it was true, wasn't it? Before life as a vampire, there'd been death. Cold and bloodless and underground.

Then, later, there'd been the forgetting, and that was a kind of death too.

Simon wasn't even a Shadowhunter yet, and already, this life had taken so much from him.

"Simon. I thought you'd be here."

Simon turned around and was reminded that for all the losses, there'd also been some very significant gains. "Isabelle," he breathed, and then, for quite a while, his lips were too occupied to speak.

They went back to Magnus and Alec's apartment. The couple had taken their new baby on vacation to Bali, which meant Simon and Isabelle could have the place to themselves.

"You sure it's okay for us to be here?" Simon asked, looking nervously around the apartment. The last time he'd seen it, the decorating ethos had been part–Studio 54, part-bordello: lots of disco balls, velvet curtains, and some appallingly placed mirrors. Now the living room looked like something puked up by a Babies"R"Us—blankets and diapers and mobiles and stuffed bunnies everywhere you looked.

He still couldn't believe *Magnus Bane* was someone's dad.

"I'm sure," Isabelle said, stripping off her dress in one smooth motion to reveal the unending stretches of smooth, pale skin that lay beneath. "But if you want to leave..."

"No," Simon said, struggling for enough breath to speak. "Definitely. No. Here's good. Very good."

"Well, then." Isabelle swept a family of stuffed kittens off the couch, then stretched across like a very satisfied and very dangerous cat. She looked pointedly at Simon's shirt, which was still on his body.

"Well. Then." Simon stood above her, unsure what to do next.

"Simon."

"Yes?"

"I'm looking pointedly at your shirt."

"Uh-huh."

"Which is still on your body."

"Oh. Right." He took care of that. Dropped down beside her on the couch.

"Simon."

"Yes? Oh. Right." Simon leaned toward her and pulled her close for a kiss, which she indulged for about thirty seconds before extricating herself.

"What's wrong?" he asked.

"You tell me," she said. "I, your incredibly sexy girlfriend that you never get to see, am prostrating myself before you half-naked, and you seem like you'd rather be watching a baseball game."

"I hate baseball."

"Exactly." Isabelle sat up—though, mercifully, she didn't put any clothes back on. Not yet. "You know you can talk to me about anything, right?"

Simon nodded.

"So if, hypothetically, you were feeling a little nervous about this whole Ascension thing tomorrow, and wondering whether you still wanted to go through with it, you could talk to me about that."

"Hypothetically," Simon said.

"Just picking a topic at random," Isabelle said. "We could also talk about *Avatar: The Last Airplane*, if you want."

"It's the Air*bender*," Simon said, suppressing a grin, "and I love you even if you are nerd-clueless."

"And I love you, even if you are a mundane," she said. "Even if you stay a mundane. You know that, right?"

"I..." It was easy for her to say, and he thought she probably even meant it. But that didn't make it true. "You think you would? *Really*?"

Isabelle let out her breath in an irritated puff. "Simon

Lewis, are you forgetting that you were a mundane when I first kissed you? A rather scrawny mundane with terrible fashion sense, I should point out. And then you were a *vampire*, and I started dating you. Then you were a mundane again, but this time with freaking amnesia. And still, inexplicably, I fell in love with you all over again. What could possibly make you think I have any standards left when it comes to you?"

"Uh, thank you, I think?"

"'Thank you' is the correct response. And also 'I love you, too, Isabelle, and I would love you even if you lost your memory or grew a mustache or something.'"

"Well, obviously." Simon tugged at her chin. "Though I'd draw the line at a beard."

"Goes without saying." Then she looked serious again. "You do believe me, right? You can't be doing this for me."

"I'm not doing it for you," Simon said, and that was true. He may have gone to the Academy, in part, because of Isabelle—but he'd stayed for himself. When he Ascended, it wouldn't be because he needed to prove something to her. "But ... if I did back out, which I would never do, but if I did, wouldn't that make me a coward? You'd date a mundane, maybe. But I know you, Izzy. You couldn't date a coward."

"And you, Simon Lewis, couldn't *be* a coward. Not if you tried. It's not cowardly to make a choice about what you want your life to be. Choosing what's right for you, maybe that's the bravest thing you can do. If you choose to be a Shadowhunter, I will love you for it. But if you choose to stay a mundane, I'll love you for that, too."

"What if I just choose not to drink from the Mortal Cup because I'm afraid it will kill me?" Simon asked. It was a relief to finally say it out loud. "What if it had nothing to do with how I want to spend the rest of my life? What if it's just being scared?"

"Well, then, you're an idiot. Because the Mortal Cup could never hurt you. It will know what I do, which is that you'd make an amazing Shadowhunter. The blood of the Angel could *never* hurt you," she said, intensity blazing in her eyes. "It's not possible."

"You really believe that?"

"I really do."

"So the fact that we're here, and you're, you know—"

"Partially disrobed and wondering why we're still making small talk?"

"—has nothing to do with the fact that you think this might be our last night together?"

This earned him another exasperated sigh. "Simon, do you know how many times I've been almost certain one of us wouldn't survive the next twenty-four hours?"

"Um, several?"

"Several," she confirmed. "And on not one of those occasions have we ever had any sort of desperate, angsty farewell sex."

"Wait—we haven't?"

Over the last several months, Simon and Isabelle had gotten very close. Closer, he thought, than they'd ever been before, not that he could quite remember. At least conversationally. As for the other kind of close—talking on the phone and writing each other letters wasn't exactly conducive to losing your virginity.

Then there was the excruciating fact that Simon wasn't certain he still had a virginity to lose.

All this time he'd been too embarrassed to ask.

"Are you kidding me?" Isabelle asked.

Simon could feel his cheeks burning.

"You're *not* kidding me!"

"Please don't be mad," Simon said.

Isabelle laughed. "I'm not mad. If we'd had sex, and you'd *forgotten*—which, by the way, I assure you would not be possible, demon amnesia or no demon amnesia—maybe I'd be mad."

"So we really never...?"

"We really never," Isabelle confirmed. "I know you don't remember, but things were a little hectic around here, what with the war and all the people trying to kill us and such. And like I said, I don't believe in 'farewell sex.'"

Simon felt like the whole night—possibly the most important night of his young and sorrowfully inexperienced life—was hanging in the balance, and he was very afraid of saying the wrong thing. "So, uh, what kind of sex do you believe in?"

"I think it should be a beginning of something," Isabelle said. "Like, say, hypothetically, if your entire life were going to change tomorrow, if it were going to be the first day of the rest of your life, I'd want to be a part of that."

"The rest of my life."

"Yep."

"Hypothetically."

"Hypothetically." She took off his glasses then and kissed him hard on the lips, then very softly on the neck. Exactly where a vampire would sink its fangs in, some part of him thought. Most of him, though, was thinking, *This is actually going to happen.*

This is going to happen tonight.

"Also, most of all, I believe in doing it because I want to

do it," Isabelle said plainly. "Just like anything else. And I want to. Assuming you do."

"You have no idea how much," Simon said honestly, and thanked God that Shadowhunting blood didn't bestow telepathy. "I should just warn you, I don't, I mean, I haven't, I mean, this would be the first time I, so—"

"You'll be a natural." She kissed his neck again, then his throat. Then his chest. "I promise."

Simon thought about all the opportunities here for humiliation, how he had absolutely no idea what he was doing, and how usually when he had no idea what he was doing, he screwed things up. Riding a horse, wielding a sword, leaping from a tree—all these things people kept saying would come naturally to him usually came with bumps, bruises, and, more than once, a face full of manure.

But he had tried none of those things with Isabelle by his side. Or in his arms.

As it turned out, that made all the difference.

"Good morning!" Simon sang, stepping out of the Portal and into his bedroom at the Academy—just in time to catch Julie slipping out the door.

"Er, good morning," George mumbled, tucked beneath the covers. "Wasn't sure you'd be back."

"Did I just see—?"

"A gentleman doesn't kiss and tell." George grinned. "Speaking of which, should I ask where you've been all night?"

"You should not," Simon said firmly. As he crossed the room to his closet to find something clean to wear, he tried his best to keep a silly, moony, heartsick smile off his face.

"You're *skipping*," George said accusingly.

"Am not."

"And you were *humming*," George added.

"I most definitely was not."

"Would this be a good time to tell you that Jon Cartwright the Thirty-Fifth seems to have done his business in your T-shirt drawer?"

But this morning nothing could dampen Simon's mood. Not when he could still feel the ghost of Isabelle's touch. His skin buzzed with it. His lips felt swollen. His heart felt swollen. "I can always get new T-shirts," Simon said cheerfully. He thought that from this point forward, he might say everything cheerfully.

"I think this place has officially driven you round the bend." George sighed then, sounding a bit heartsick himself. "You know, I'm really going to miss it here."

"You're not going to cry again, are you? I think there may be another sentient slime mold growing in the back of my sock drawer, if you want to get really choked up."

"Does one wear socks to get transformed into a half-angel superhuman fighting machine?" George mused.

"Not with sandals," Simon said promptly. He hadn't dated Isabelle all these months without learning something about proper footwear. "Never with sandals."

They got dressed for the ceremony—choosing, after some deliberation, their most Simon-like and George-like outfits. Which meant, for George, jeans and a rugby shirt; for Simon, a faded tee that he'd had made back when the band was called Guinea Pig Death Posse. (This, fortunately, had been lying on the floor for a week, so was rat crap free.) Then, without much talking, they started packing up their belongings. The Academy wasn't much for big celebrations—probably a good thing, Simon mused, since at the last all-school party, one of the first-years had misfired his flaming crossbow and accidentally set the roof on fire. There would be no graduation ceremony, no mugging for cameras with proud parents, no yearbook signings or tossing of mortarboard caps. Just the Ascension ritual, whatever that meant, and that would be it. The end of the Academy; the beginning of the rest of their lives.

"It's not like we'll never see each other again," George said suddenly, in a tone that suggested he'd been worrying about exactly that.

Simon was going back to New York, and George was going to the London Institute, where, they said, a Lovelace was always welcome. But what was an ocean of distance when you could Portal? Or at least e-mail?

"Of course not," Simon said.

"But it won't be the same," George pointed out.

"No, I guess it won't."

George busied himself with neatly tucking his socks into a suitcase compartment, which Simon found alarming, since it was the first time in two years George had done anything neatly. "You're my best friend, you know," George said without looking up. Then, quickly, as if to forestall argument, "Don't worry, I know I'm not *your* best friend, Si. You've got Clary. And Isabelle. And your bandmate mate. I get it. I just thought you should know."

On some level, Simon had already known this. He'd never bothered to think much about it—he didn't think much about George, period, because that was the beauty of George. Simon never had to *think* about him, to puzzle out what he would do or how he would react. He was just steady, dependable George, always there, always full of cheer and eager to spread it around. Now Simon did think about him, about how well George knew him, and vice versa—not just in the big ways: their dead-of-night fears about washing out of the Academy, Simon's hapless pining for Isabelle, George's even more hapless, if more halfhearted, pining for most girls who crossed his path. They knew each other in the little ways—that George was allergic to cashews, that Simon was allergic to Latin homework, that George had a paralyzing fear of large birds—and somehow, that seemed to matter even more. Over the past two years, they'd developed a roommate shorthand, almost a silent language. Not exactly like a *parabatai*, Simon thought, and not exactly like a best friend. But not something *less than*. Not something he ever wanted to leave behind for good.

"You're right, George. I do have more than enough best friends."

George's face fell, so slightly that only someone who knew him as well as Simon would have noticed.

"But there's something else I've never had," Simon added. "At least until now."

"What's that?"

"A brother." The word felt right. Not someone you chose—someone the fates assigned you, someone who, under any other circumstances, might never have given you a second look, nor you him. Someone you would die for and kill for without a second thought, because he was family. Judging from George's radiant smile, the word sounded right to him, too.

"Are we going to have to hug now or something?" George said.

"I think that may be inescapable."

The Council Hall was intimidatingly beautiful, morning light streaming in through a window in its high domed ceiling. It reminded Simon of pictures he'd seen of the Pantheon, but this place felt more ancient than even ancient Rome. This felt timeless.

The Academy students huddled together in small clumps, all of them looking too nervous and distracted to do much more than comment blandly on the weather. (Which was, as the inhabitants always agreed, perfect.) Marisol gave Simon a bright smile and a sharp nod when she saw him enter the chamber, as if to say, *I never doubted you ... almost.*

Simon and George were the last to arrive, and shortly after they did, everyone took their places for the ceremony. The seven mundanes were arranged in alphabetical order in the front of the chamber. There were meant to be ten of them, but apparently Sunil wasn't the only one who'd reconsidered at the last moment. Leilana Jay, a very tall, very pale girl from Memphis, and Boris Kashkoff, an Eastern European with ropy muscles and ruddy cheeks, had both slipped away sometime in the night. No one spoke of them, not the teachers, not the students. It was like they never existed, Simon thought—and then imagined Sunil, Leilana, and Boris out there in the world somewhere, living alone with their knowledge of the Shadow World, aware of evil but without the will or ability to fight it.

There's more than one way to fight evil in this world, Simon thought, and it was Clary's voice in his head, and it was Isabelle's, and his mother's, and his own. *Don't do this because you think you have to. Do it because you want to.*

Only *if you want to.*

The Academy's Shadowhunter students—Simon never thought of them as the "elites" anymore, just as he no longer thought of himself and the other mundanes as the "dregs"—sat in the first two rows of the audience. The students weren't two tiers anymore; they were one body. One unit. Even Jon Cartwright looked proud of, and a little nervous for, the mundanes at the front of the chamber—and when Simon caught him locking eyes with Marisol and pressing two fingers to his lips and then his chest, it seemed almost right. (Or, at least, not a total crime against nature, which was a start.) There were no family members in the audience—those mundanes with living relatives (and there were depressingly few of them) had, of course, already severed ties. George's parents, who were Shadowhunters by blood if not by choice, could have attended, but he'd asked them not to. "Just in case I explode, mate," he'd confided to Simon. "Don't get me wrong, the Lovelaces are hardy folk, but I don't think they'd enjoy a faceful of liquefied George."

Nonetheless, the room was almost full. This was the first class of Academy mundanes to Ascend in decades, and more than a few Shadowhunters had wanted to see it for themselves. Most of them were strangers to Simon, but not all. Crowded in behind the rows of students were Clary, Jace, and Isabelle, and Magnus and Alec—who had made a surprise return from Bali for the occasion—tag-teaming their squirming blue baby. All of them—even the baby—were intensely fixed on Simon, as if they could get him through the Ascension with sheer force of will.

This, Simon realized, was what Ascending meant. This was what being a Shadowhunter meant. Not just risking his life, not just carving runes and fighting demons and occasionally saving the world. Not just joining the Clave and agreeing to follow its draconian rules. It meant joining his *friends*. It meant being a part of something bigger than himself, something as wonderful as it was terrifying. Yes, his life was much less safe than it had been two years ago—but it was also much more full. Like the Council Hall, it was crowded with all the people he loved, people who loved him.

You might almost call them a family.

And then it began.

One by one the mundanes were summoned to the dais, where their professors stood in a somber line, waiting to shake their hands and wish them luck.

One by one the mundanes approached the double circles traced on the dais and knelt in their center, surrounded by runes. Two Silent Brothers stood by just in case something went wrong. Each time a mundane took position, they bent over the runes and scratched in a new one to symbolize that student's name. Then they returned to the edges of the dais again, statue-still in parchment robes, watching. Waiting.

Simon waited too as one by one his friends brought their lips to the Mortal Cup. As a blinding flare of blue light encompassed them, then faded away.

One by one.

Gen Almodovar. Thomas Daltrey. Marisol Garza.

Each student drank.

Each student survived.

The wait was interminable.

Except that when the Consul called his name, it felt much too soon.

Simon's feet were cement blocks. He forced himself toward the dais, one step at a time, his heartbeat pulsing like a subwoofer, making his whole body tremble. The professors shook his hand, even Delaney Scarsbury, who murmured, "Always knew you had it in you, Lewis." A blatant lie. Catarina Loss gripped his hand tightly and pulled him close, her brilliant white hair sweeping his shoulder as her lips brushed his ear. "Finish what you started, Daylighter. You have the power to change these people for the better. Don't waste it."

Like most things Catarina said to him, it didn't quite make sense, but some part of him still understood it completely.

Simon knelt at the center of the circles and reminded himself to breathe.

The Consul stood over him, her traditional red robe brushing the floor. He kept his eyes on the runes, but he could sense Clary out there rooting for him; he could hear the echo of George's laughter; he could feel the ghost of Izzy's warm touch on his skin. At the center of these circles, surrounded by runes, waiting for the blood of the divine to run through his veins and change him in some unfathomable way, Simon felt profoundly alone—and yet, at the same time, less alone than he'd ever been in his life.

His family was here, holding him up.

They would not let him fall.

"Do you swear, Simon Lewis, to forsake the mundane world and follow the path of the Shadowhunter?" Consul Penhallow asked. Simon had met the Consul before, when she'd delivered a lecture at the Academy, and again at her daughter's wedding to Helen Blackthorn. On both occasions she had seemed like your basic mom: brisk, efficient, nice enough, and none too surprising. But now she seemed fearsome and powerful, less an individual than the walking repository of millennia of Shadowhunter tradition. "Will you take into yourself the blood of the Angel Raziel and honor that blood? Do you swear to serve the Clave, to follow the Law as set forth by the Covenant, and to obey the word of the Council? Will you defend that which is human and mortal, knowing that for your service, there will be no recompense and no thanks but honor?"

For Shadowhunters, swearing was a matter of life and death. If he made this promise, there was no turning back to the life he'd once had, to Simon Lewis, mundane nerd, aspiring rock star. There were no more options to consider. There was only his oath, and a lifetime's effort to fulfill it.

Simon knew if he looked up he could meet Isabelle's eyes, or Clary's, and draw strength from them. He could silently ask them if this was the right path, and they would reassure him.

But this choice couldn't belong to them. It had to be his, and his alone.

He closed his eyes.

"I swear." His voice did not shake.

"Can you be a shield for the weak, a light in the dark, a truth among falsehoods, a tower in the flood, an eye to see when all others are blind?"

Simon imagined all the history behind these words, all the Consuls before Jia Penhallow stretching back for decades and centuries, holding this same Cup before one mundane after another. So many mortals, volunteering to join the fight. They had always seemed so brave to Simon, risking their lives—sacrificing their futures to a greater cause—not because they'd been *born* into a great battle between good and evil, but because they had *chosen* not to live on the sidelines, letting others fight for them.

It occurred to him, if they were brave for making the choice, maybe he was too.

But it didn't feel like bravery, not now.

It simply felt like taking the next step forward. That simple.

That inevitable.

"I can," Simon answered.

"And when you are dead, will you give up your body to the Nephilim to be burned, that your ashes may be used to build the City of Bones?"

Even the thought of this didn't frighten him. It seemed suddenly like an honor, that his body would live on in usefulness after death, that from this time forward, the Shadowhunter world would have a claim on him, for eternity.

"I will," Simon said.

"Then drink."

Simon took the Cup into his hands. It was even heavier than it looked and curiously warm to the touch. Whatever was inside it didn't look much like blood, fortunately, but it didn't look like anything else he recognized either. If he didn't know better, Simon would have said the Cup was full of light. As he peered down at it, the strange liquid almost seemed to pulse with a soft glow, as if to say, *Go ahead, drink me.*

He couldn't remember the first time he'd seen the Mortal Cup—that was one of the memories still lost to him—but he knew the role it had played in his life, knew that if it weren't for the Cup, he and Clary might never have discovered the existence of Shadowhunters in the first place. It had all begun with the Mortal Cup; it seemed fitting that it should all end here too.

Not *end*, Simon thought quickly. Hopefully not *end*.

It was said that the younger you were, the less likely drinking from the Cup was to kill you. Simon was, subjectively, nineteen, but he'd recently learned that by

Shadowhunter rules, he was only eighteen. The months he'd spent as a vampire apparently didn't count. He could only hope the Cup understood that.

"Drink," the Consul repeated quietly, a note of humanity creeping into her voice.

Simon raised the Cup to his lips.

He drank.

He is tangled in Isabelle's arms, he is curtained by Isabelle's hair, he is touching Isabelle's body, he is lost in Isabelle, in her smell and her taste and the silk of her skin.

He is onstage, the music pounding, the floor shaking, the audience cheering, his heart beating beating beating in time with the drumbeat.

He is laughing with Clary, dancing with Clary, eating with Clary, running through the streets of Brooklyn with Clary, they are children together, they are one half of a whole, they hold hands and squeeze tight and pledge never to let go.

He is going cold, stiff, the life draining out of him, he is below, in the dark, clawing his way to the light, fingernails scraping dirt, mouth filled with dirt, eyes clogged with dirt, he is straining, reaching, dragging himself up toward the sky, and when he reaches it, he opens his mouth wide but does not breathe, for he no longer needs to breathe, only to feed. And he is so very hungry.

He is sinking his teeth into the neck of an angel's child, he is drinking the light.

He is bearing a Mark, and it burns.

He is raising his face to meet the gaze of an angel, he is flayed by the fury of angel fire, and yet still, impudent and bloodless, he lives.

He is in a cage.

He is in hell.

He is bent over the broken body of a beautiful girl, he is praying to whatever god that will listen, please let her live, anything to let her live.

He is giving away that which is most precious to him, and he is doing so willingly, so that his friends will survive.

He is, again, with Isabelle, always with Isabelle, the holy flame of their love encompassing them both, and there is pain, and there is exquisite joy, and his veins burn with angel fire and he is the Simon he once was and the Simon he then became and the Simon he now will be, he endures and he is reborn, he is blood and flesh and a spark of the divine.

He is Nephilim.

Simon didn't see the flash of light he'd expected—he saw only the flood of memories, a tidal wave that threatened to drown him in the past. It wasn't simply a lifetime that passed before his eyes; it was an eternity, all the versions of himself that ever could have been, that ever would be. And then it was over. His mind stilled. His soul quieted. And his memories—the parts of himself he'd feared were lost forever—had come home.

He'd spent two years trying to convince himself that it was okay if he never remembered, that he could live with piecing together the fragments of his past, relying on others to tell him about the person he'd once been. But it had never felt right. The empty hole in his memory was like a missing limb; he'd learned to compensate, but he'd never stopped feeling the absence or its pain.

Now, finally, he was whole again.

He was more than whole, he realized, as the Consul said proudly, "You are Nephilim now. I name you Simon Shadowhunter, of the blood of Jonathan Shadowhunter, child of the Nephilim." It was a placeholder name, until he chose a new one for himself. Moments before, that had seemed unthinkable, but now it simply felt true. He was the same person he'd always been ... and yet. He wasn't Simon Lewis anymore. He was someone new.

"Arise."

He felt ... he didn't know how he felt, except stunned. Filled with joy and confusion and what felt like a flickering light, growing brighter by the second.

He felt strong.

He felt ready.

He felt like his abs were still pretty much only a two-pack, but he supposed even a magic cup could get you only so far.

The Consul cleared her throat. "Arise," she said again. Then she lowered her voice to a whisper. "That means you stand up and give someone else a turn."

Simon was still trying to shake off his joyous daze as he made his way back to the others. George was next, and as they passed each other, he gave Simon a surreptitious high five.

Simon wondered what George would see inside the light, if it would be as wondrous. He wondered whether, after the ceremony was over, they would compare notes—or if this was the kind of thing you were supposed to keep to yourself. He supposed there was probably some kind of Shadowhunter protocol to follow—the Shadowhunters had a protocol for everything.

We, he corrected himself wryly. *We have a protocol for everything.*

This would take some getting used to.

George was on his knees inside the circles, the Mortal

Cup in his hands. It was strange, being a Shadowhunter while George was still a mundane, as if there was now an invisible divide between them. *This is the farthest apart we'll ever be*, Simon thought, and silently urged his roommate to hurry up and drink.

The Consul said the traditional words. George swore his oath of loyalty to the Shadowhunters without hesitation, drew in a deep breath, then jauntily raised the Mortal Cup as if giving a toast. "*Slàinte!*" he shouted, and as his friends broke into indulgent laughter, he took a slug.

Simon was still laughing when the screaming began.

The room fell dead silent, but inside Simon's mind, there was a siren of pain. An inhuman, unearthly scream.

George's scream.

On the dais, George and the Consul were engulfed in an impossible flash of blinding darkness. When it faded away, the Consul was on her feet, the Silent Brothers already by her side, all of them peering down at something horrible, something with the shape of a person, but not its face and not its skin. Something with black veins bulging through cracking flesh, something with the Mortal Cup still clenched in its rigid fist, some withered, writhing, crumbling creature with George's hair and George's sneakers, but in place of George's smile, a tortured, toothless rictus leaking something too black to be blood. *Not George*, Simon thought furiously as the thing stopped jerking and trembling and fell still. And somehow, in Simon's head, George screamed and screamed.

The chamber was a storm of motion—responsible adults hustling students out of the room, gasps and cries and shrieks—but Simon barely registered any of it. He was moving forward, toward the thing that couldn't be George, pressing toward the dais with Shadowhunter strength and Shadowhunter speed. Simon was going to save his roommate, because he was a Shadowhunter now, and that's what Shadowhunters do.

He didn't notice Catarina Loss come up behind him, not until her hands were on his shoulders, her grip light enough that he should have been able to break free—but he couldn't move.

"Let go of me!" Simon raged. The Silent Brothers were kneeling by the thing now, the body, but they weren't *doing* anything for it. They weren't helping. They were just staring fixedly at the spiderweb of inky veins spreading across flesh. "I have to help him!"

"No." Catarina's hand feathered across his forehead and the screaming in his mind fell silent. She was still holding on; he still couldn't move. He was a Shadowhunter, but she was a warlock. He was helpless. "It's too late."

Simon couldn't watch the black veins eat up skin or the hollow eyes melt into the skull. He focused on the sneakers. George's sneakers. One was untied, as it often was. Just that morning George had tripped over the laces, and Simon had caught him from falling. "The last time you'll save me," George had said with another of his wistful sighs, and Simon had shot back, "Not likely."

The veins were popping, with a sound like Rice Krispies in milk. The body was starting to ooze.

Now Simon was holding on to Catarina too. He held tight.

"What's the point?" he said in despair, because what was the point of dying like this, not in battle, not for a good cause, not to save a fellow warrior or the world, but for *nothing*? And what was the point of living as a Shadowhunter, what was the point of skill and bravery and superhuman powers, when you couldn't do anything but stand by and *watch?*

"Sometimes there is no point," Catarina said gently. "There only is what is."

What is, Simon thought, the wave of rage and frustration and horror nearly consuming him. He would not let himself be consumed; he would not waste this moment, if this was all he had. He'd spent two years making himself strong—he would be strong for George, now, in the only way left to him. He would bear witness.

Simon summoned his will. *What is.*

He forced himself not to look away.

What is: George. Brave and kind and *good*. George, dead. George, gone.

And though he didn't know what the Law had to say about dying by the Mortal Cup, whether the Clave would consider George one of their own and give him Shadowhunter burial rights, he didn't care. He knew what George was, what he was meant to be, and what he deserved.

"*Ave atque vale*, George Lovelace, child of Nephilim," he whispered. "Forever and ever, my brother, hail and farewell."

Simon grazed a finger over the small stone plaque, tracing the engraved letters: GEORGE LOVELACE.

"It's pretty, isn't it?" Isabelle said from behind him.

"Simple," Clary added. "He would have liked that, don't you think?"

Simon thought that George would have preferred to be interred in the City of Bones, like the Shadowhunter he was. (More to the point, he would have preferred not to be dead at all.) The Clave had refused him. He died in the act of Ascension, which in their eyes marked him as unworthy. Simon was trying very hard not to be angry about this.

He spent a lot of time these days trying not to be angry.

"It was nice of the London Institute to offer a place for him, don't you think?" Isabelle said. Simon could hear in her voice how hard she was trying, how worried she was for him.

They told me a Lovelace is always welcome at the London Institute, George had said when he heard about his placement.

After his death the Institute made good on their word.

There had been a funeral, which Simon had endured. There had been a variety of reunions, big and small, with his friends from the Academy, Simon and the others telling stories and trading memories and trying not to think about that last day. Jon almost always cried.

Then there had been everything else: Life as a Shadowhunter, mercifully busy with training and experimenting with his newfound physical grace and energy, along with fighting off the occasional demon or rogue vampire. There had been long days with Clary, reveling in the fact that he could now remember every second of their friendship, preparing for their *parabatai* ceremony, which was only days away. There had been numerous training bouts with Jace, usually ending with Simon flat on his back while Jace stood over him, gloating about his superior skill, because that was Jace's way of showing affection. There had been evenings babysitting Magnus and Alec's son, snuggling the little blue boy to his chest and singing him to sleep, and feeling, for a few precious minutes, almost at peace.

There had been Isabelle, who loved him, which made every day glow.

There had been so much to make life worth living, and so Simon had lived, and time had passed—and George was still dead.

He'd asked Clary to Portal him here, to London, for reasons he didn't quite understand. He'd said good-bye to George so many times now, but somehow none of it felt quite final—it didn't feel right.

"I'll take you there," Clary had said. "But I'm coming with you."

Isabelle had insisted too, and Simon was glad of it.

A soft breeze blew through the Institute's garden, rustling the leaves and carrying the faint scent of orchids. Simon thought that George would be glad, at least, to spend eternity in a place where there was no threat of sheep.

Simon rose to his feet, flanked by Clary and Isabelle. Each of them slipped her hand into his, and they stood silently, bound together. Now that Simon had regained his past, he could remember all the times he'd almost lost one of them—as he could remember now, vividly, all the people he *had* lost. To battle, to murder, to sickness. Being a Shadowhunter, he knew, meant being on an intimate basis with death.

But then, so did being human.

Someday he would lose Clary and Isabelle, or they would lose him. Nothing could stop that. So what was the point? he'd asked Catarina, but he knew better than that. The point wasn't that you tried to live forever; the point was that you *lived*, and did everything you could to live well. The point was the choices you made and the people you loved.

Simon gasped.

"Simon?" Clary said in alarm. "What is it?"

But Simon couldn't speak; he could only gape at the gravestone, where the air was shimmering, and translucent light was shaping itself into two figures. One was a girl about his age; she had long blond hair, brown eyes, and the old-timey petticoats of a BBC duchess. The other was George, and he was smiling at Simon. The girl's hand was on his shoulder, and there was something kind about the gesture, something warm and familiar.

"George," Simon whispered. Then he blinked, and the figures were gone.

"Simon, *what* are you staring at?" Isabelle asked in the tight, irritated tone she used only when she was trying not to be afraid.

"Nothing." What was he supposed to say? That he'd seen George's ghost rise from the mist? That he'd seen not just George, which would have almost made sense, but some beautiful old-fashioned stranger? He knew Shadowhunters could see ghosts when those ghosts wanted to be seen, but he also knew that grieving people often saw what they wanted to see.

Simon didn't know what to think. But he knew what he *wanted* to think.

He wanted a beautiful Shadowhunter spirit from the past, maybe even a long-dead Lovelace, to take George away with her, to wherever it was spirits went. He wanted to believe that George had been welcomed into the arms of his ancestors, where some part of him would live on.

Not likely, Simon reminded himself. George was adopted, not a Lovelace by blood. And for Shadowhunters—presumably even the dead ones who haunted British gardens—everything came down to blood.

"Simon—" Isabelle pressed her lips to his cheek. "I know how much you ... I know he was like your brother. I wish I could have known him better."

Clary squeezed his hand. "Me too."

Both of them, Simon was reminded, had also lost a brother.

And both of them cared about more than just bloodlines. Both understood that family could be a matter of choice—a matter of love. So did Alec and Magnus, who'd taken someone else's child into their home and their hearts. So did the Lightwoods, who'd adopted Jace when he had no one else.

And so did Simon, who was now a Shadowhunter himself. Who could change what it meant to be a Shadowhunter just by making new choices. Better choices.

He understood now why he'd felt the need to come here, almost as if he'd been summoned. Not to say goodbye to George but to find a way to hold on to a piece of him.

"I think I know what I want my Shadowhunter name to be," he said.

"Simon Lovelace," Clary said, as always, knowing his mind as well as he did. "It has a certain ring to it."

Isabelle's lips quirked. "A sexy ring."

Simon laughed and blinked away a tear. For one blurry-eyed moment, he thought he saw George grinning through the mist again, and then he was gone. George Lovelace was gone.

But Simon Lovelace was still here, and it was time to make that count.

"I'm ready," he told Clary and Isabelle, the two wonders who had changed his life, the two warriors who would risk anything and everything for those they loved, the two girls who had become his heroes and his family. "Let's go home."

READ ALL THE BOOKS IN THE BREATHTAKING

THE MORTAL INSTRUMENTS

Clary Fray is seeing things: vampires in Brooklyn and werewolves in Manhattan. Irresistibly drawn to the Shadowhunters, a secret group of warriors dedicated to ridding the earth of demons, Clary encounters the dark side of New York City – and the dangers of forbidden love...

www.ukshadowhunters.com

eBook
available

GHOSTS OF THE SHADOW MARKET

Also by Cassandra Clare

THE MORTAL INSTRUMENTS

City of Bones
City of Ashes
City of Glass
City of Fallen Angels
City of Lost Souls
City of Heavenly Fire

THE INFERNAL DEVICES

Clockwork Angel
Clockwork Prince
Clockwork Princess

THE DARK ARTIFICES

Lady Midnight
Lord of Shadows
Queen of Air and Darkness

THE ELDEST CURSES
With Wesley Chu

The Red Scrolls of Magic

The Shadowhunter's Codex
With Joshua Lewis

The Bane Chronicles
With Sarah Rees Brennan and Maureen Johnson

Tales from the Shadowhunter Academy
With Sarah Rees Brennan, Maureen Johnson,
and Robin Wasserman

Ghosts of the Shadow Market

CASSANDRA CLARE

SARAH REES BRENNAN

MAUREEN JOHNSON

KELLY LINK

ROBIN WASSERMAN

This is a work of fiction. Names, characters, places and incidents are either the product of the author's imagination or, if real, used fictitiously. All statements, activities, stunts, descriptions, information and material of any other kind contained herein are included for entertainment purposes only and should not be relied on for accuracy or replicated as they may result in injury.

First published 2019 by Walker Books Ltd
87 Vauxhall Walk, London SE11 5HJ

This edition published 2020

2 4 6 8 10 9 7 5 3 1

"Cast Long Shadows," "Every Exquisite Thing," "Learn About Loss," "A Deeper Love," "The Wicked Ones," "Son of the Dawn," "The Land I Lost," and "Through Blood, Through Fire" were previously published in other media.

Interior illustrations by Davood Diba

This book has been typeset in Dolly

Printed and bound by CPI Group (UK) Ltd, Croydon CR0 4YY

British Library Cataloguing in Publication Data:
a catalogue record for this book is available from the British Library

ISBN 978-1-4063-8538-0

www.walker.co.uk

MIX
Paper from responsible sources
FSC® C020471
FSC www.fsc.org

For our wonderful readers

Whatever you are physically, male or female, strong or weak, ill or healthy—all those things matter less than what your heart contains. If you have the soul of a warrior, you are a warrior. Whatever the color, the shape, the design of the shade that conceals it, the flame inside the lamp remains the same. *You* are that flame.

GHOSTS OF THE SHADOW MARKET

CONTENTS

Cast Long Shadows

By Cassandra Clare and Sarah Rees Brennan

Old sins cast long shadows.
—English proverb

The Shadow Market, London, 1901

The railway viaduct passed only a hairsbreadth away from St. Saviour's Church. There had been discussion among the mundanes about the possibility of demolishing the church to make way for the railroad, but it had met with unexpectedly fierce opposition. Instead the railway took a slightly more circuitous route, and the spire of the church still remained, a silver dagger against the night sky.

Beneath the arches, crosses, and rattling rails, a mundane market was held by day, the largest association of grocers in the city. By night, the market belonged to Downworld.

Vampires and werewolves, warlocks and fey, met under the stars and under glamour that human eyes could not pierce. They had their magic stalls set up in the same pattern as the humans' stalls, under the bridges and through tiny streets, but the Shadow Market stalls did not hold apples or turnips. Under the dark arches the stalls shone, laden with bells and ribbons, gaudy with color: snake green, fever red, and the startling orange of flames. Brother Zachariah smelled incense burning and heard the songs of werewolves for the distant beauty of the moon, and faeries calling for children to *come away, come away.*

It was the first Shadow Market of the New Year by English standards, though it was still the old year in China. Brother Zachariah had left Shanghai when he was a child, and London when he was seventeen, to go to the Silent City, where there was no acknowledgment of time passing save that the ashes of more warriors were laid down. Still he remembered the celebrations of the New Year in his human life, from eggnog and fortune-telling in London to the setting off of fireworks and nibbling of moon dumplings in Shanghai.

Now snow was falling on London. The air was crisp and cold as a fresh apple, and felt good against his face. The voices of his Brothers were a low hum in his head, affording Brother Zachariah a little distance.

Zachariah was here on a mission, but he took a brief time to be glad he was in London, in the Shadow Market, to breathe air clear of the dust of the departed. It felt something like freedom, like being young again.

He rejoiced, but that did not mean the people of the Shadow Market rejoiced with him. He observed many Downworlders, and even mundanes with the Sight, casting him looks that were the opposite of welcoming. As he moved, a dark murmur threaded through the hum of conversation all around him.

The denizens of Downworld considered this Market time as space snatched away from angels. They clearly did not relish his presence among them. Brother Zachariah was one of the Silent Brothers, a voiceless fraternity that lived long amid old bones, sworn to seclusion with hearts dedicated to the dust of their City and their dead. Nobody could be expected to embrace a Silent Brother, and these people would not be likely to take pleasure in the appearance of any Shadowhunter at all.

Even as he doubted, he saw a stranger sight than any he had expected in the Market.

There was a Shadowhunter boy dancing a cancan with three faeries. He was Charlotte and Henry Fairchild's younger son, Matthew Fairchild. His head was thrown back, his fair hair bright by firelight, and he was laughing.

Brother Zachariah had an instant to wonder if Matthew was spellbound before Matthew caught sight of him and sprang forward, leaving the faeries behind him looking discomfited. The Fair Folk were not accustomed to having mortals skip out on their dances.

Matthew did not appear to notice. He ran up to Brother Zachariah, threw an exuberant arm about his neck, and ducked his head under the hood of the Silent Brother to give him a kiss on the cheek.

"Uncle Jem!" Matthew exclaimed joyfully. "What are you doing here?"

Shadowhunter Academy, Idris, 1899

Matthew Fairchild hardly ever lost his temper. When he did, he tried to make the occasion memorable.

The last time had been two years ago, during Matthew's short-lived stint at Shadowhunter Academy, a school intended to mass-produce perfect demon-fighting bores. It began with half the school crowded on a tower top, watching the parents arrive after an incident in the woods with a demon.

Matthew's usual good humor had already been sorely tried. His best friend, James, was being blamed for the incident, simply because James happened to have a tiny, insignificant amount of demon blood and the—Matthew thought prodigiously lucky—ability to transform into a shadow. James was being expelled. The actual people to blame, unmitigated wart Alastair Carstairs and his rotten friends, were not being expelled. Life in general, and the Academy in particular, was a positive parade of injustice.

Matthew had not even had the chance to ask James if he wanted to be *parabatai* yet. He had been planning to ask him to be sworn warrior partners in a very elaborate and stylish fashion so Jamie would be too impressed to decline.

Mr. Herondale, James's father, was among the first of the parents to arrive. They saw him stride in the doors with his black hair turbulent from wind and rage. Mr. Herondale undeniably had an air.

The few girls permitted to come to the Academy were casting James speculative glances. James shuffled about the place with his head in a book and had an unfortunate haircut and an unassuming demeanor, but he bore a very marked resemblance to his father.

James, Angel bless his oblivious soul, failed to notice anyone's attention. He slunk away to be expelled, sunk in despair.

"Gosh," said Eustace Larkspear. "It would be *something* to have a father like that."

"I heard he was mad," said Alastair, and let out a bark of laughter. "You'd have to be mad, to marry a creature with infernal blood and have children who were—"

"Don't," said little Thomas quietly. To everyone's surprise, Alastair rolled his eyes and desisted.

Matthew wanted to be the one who had made Alastair stop,

but Thomas had already done it and Matthew could not think of any way to stop Alastair permanently short of challenging him to a duel. He was not even sure that would work. Alastair was not a coward, and would probably accept the challenge and then talk twice as much. Besides which, getting into fights was not precisely Matthew's style. He could fight, but he did not think violence solved many problems.

Aside from the problem of demons laying waste to the world, that was.

Matthew left the tower top abruptly and wandered the halls of the Academy in a foul mood. Despite his commitment to dark brooding, he knew he was duty bound not to lose track of Christopher and Thomas Lightwood for long.

When he was six, Matthew's older brother, Charles Buford, and their mama had left the house for a meeting at the London Institute. Charlotte Fairchild was the Consul, the most important person of all the Shadowhunters, and Charles had always been interested in her work instead of resenting the bothersome Nephilim for taking up her time. As they prepared to go, Matthew had stood in the hall crying and refusing to let go of his mother's dress.

Mama had knelt down and asked that Matthew please take care of Papa for her while she and Charles were gone.

Matthew took this responsibility seriously. Papa was a genius and what most people considered an invalid, because he could not walk. Unless he was carefully watched, he would forget to eat in the excitement of invention. Papa could not get on without Matthew, which was why it was absurd that Matthew had been sent to the Academy in the first place.

Matthew liked to take care of people, and he was good at it.

When they were eight, Christopher Lightwood had been discovered in Papa's laboratory performing what Papa described as a very intriguing experiment. Matthew had noticed that there was now a wall missing in the laboratory, and he took Christopher under his wing.

Christopher and Thomas were real cousins, their fathers brothers. Matthew was not a real cousin: he only called Christopher's and Thomas's parents Aunt Cecily and Uncle Gabriel, and Aunt Sophie and Uncle Gideon, respectively, out of courtesy. Their parents were only friends. Mama had no close family and Papa's family did not approve of Mama being Consul.

James was Christopher's blood cousin. Aunt Cecily was Mr. Herondale's sister. Mr. Herondale ran the London Institute, and the Herondales tended to keep to themselves. Unkind people said it was because they were snobbish or thought themselves superior, but Charlotte said those people were ignorant. She told Matthew the Herondales tended to keep to themselves as they had experienced unkindness due to Mrs. Herondale being a warlock.

Still, when you ran an Institute, you couldn't be completely invisible. Matthew had seen James at various parties before and tried to acquire him as a friend, only Matthew was impeded because he felt he should contribute to parties being a success and James tended to be in a corner, reading.

It was usually a simple matter for Matthew to make friends, but he did not see the point unless it was a challenge. Friends who were easy to get might be easy to lose, and Matthew wanted to keep people.

It had been rather shattering when James seemed to actively

dislike Matthew, but Matthew had won him over. He still was not entirely sure how, which made him uneasy, but James had recently referred to himself, Matthew, Christopher, and Thomas as the three Musketeers and D'Artagnan, from a book he liked. Everything had been going splendidly aside from missing Papa, but now James was expelled and everything was ruined. Still, Matthew could not forget his responsibilities.

Christopher had a tempestuous relationship with science, and Professor Fell had commanded Matthew not to let Christopher come into contact with any flammable materials after the last time. Thomas was so quiet and small they were always losing him, rather like a human marble, and if left to his own devices he would inevitably roll toward Alastair Carstairs.

This was a hideous situation with only one bright side. It was a simple matter to locate Thomas when he was lost. Matthew only had to follow the sound of Alastair's irritating voice.

Unfortunately, this meant being forced to behold Alastair's irritating face.

He found Alastair soon enough, gazing out a window, with Thomas shyly standing at his elbow.

Thomas's hero worship was inexplicable. The only things Matthew could find to like about Alastair were his extraordinarily expressive eyebrows, and eyebrows did not make the man.

"Are you very sad, Alastair?" Matthew heard Thomas ask as he approached, bent on retrieval.

"Stop bothering me, pip-squeak," said Alastair, though his voice was tolerant. Even he could not strongly object to being adored.

"You heard the low, snaky serpent," said Matthew. "Come away, Tom."

"Ah, Mother Hen Fairchild," sneered Alastair. "What a lovely wife you will make for somebody one of these fine days."

Matthew was outraged to see Thomas's tiny smile, though Thomas quickly concealed it out of respect for Matthew's feelings. Thomas was meek and much afflicted by sisters. He seemed to think Alastair being rude to everyone was daring.

"I wish I could say the same for you," said Matthew. "Has no kind soul thought to inform you that your hairstyle is, to use the gentlest words available to me, ill-advised? A friend? Your papa? Does nobody care enough to prevent you from making a spectacle of yourself? Or are you simply too busy perpetrating acts of evil upon the innocent to bother about your unfortunate appearance?"

"Matthew!" said Thomas. "His friend *died*."

Matthew strongly desired to point out that Alastair and his friends had been the ones to unleash a demon upon James, and their nasty prank going wrong was no more than their just deserts. He could see, however, that would distress Thomas extremely.

"Oh, very well. Let us go," he said. "Though I cannot help but wonder whose idea their nasty little trick was."

"Wait a moment, Fairchild," snapped Alastair. "You can go ahead, Lightwood."

Thomas looked deeply worried as he went, but Matthew could see he was loath to disobey his idol. When Thomas's worried hazel eyes flicked to Matthew, Matthew nodded, and Thomas reluctantly departed.

When he was gone, Matthew and Alastair squared off. Matthew understood that Alastair had sent Thomas away for a purpose. He bit his lip, resigned to a scuffle.

Instead Alastair said, "Who are *you* to play the moralist, talking about tricks and papas, considering the circumstances of your birth?"

Matthew frowned. "What on earth are you driveling about, Carstairs?"

"Everyone talks about your mama and her unwomanly pursuits," said awful, unthinkable worm Alastair Carstairs. Matthew scoffed but Alastair raised his voice, persisting. "A woman cannot be a good Consul. Nevertheless your mother can continue her career, of course, since she has such strong support from the powerful Lightwoods."

"Certainly our families are friends," said Matthew. "Are you unfamiliar with the concept of friendship, Carstairs? How tragic for you, though understandable on the part of everyone else in the universe."

Alastair raised his eyebrows. "Oh, great friends, no doubt. Your mama must require friends, since your papa is unable to play a man's part."

"I beg your pardon?" said Matthew.

"Odd that you were born so long after your papa's terrible accident," Alastair said, all but twirling an imaginary mustache. "Strange that your papa's family will have nothing to do with you, to the extent of demanding that your mother renounce her married name. Remarkable that you bear no resemblance to your papa, and your coloring is so like Gideon Lightwood's."

Gideon Lightwood was Thomas's papa. No wonder Alastair had sent Thomas away before making a ridiculous accusation like that.

It was absurd. Perhaps it was true that Matthew had fair hair, while his mama's was brown and his father's and Charles

Buford's was red. Matthew's mama was tiny, but Cook said she thought Matthew would be taller than Charles Buford. Uncle Gideon was often with Mama. Matthew knew he had spoken for her when she was at odds with the Clave. Mama had once called him her good and faithful friend. Matthew had never thought much about it before.

His mama said his papa had such a dear, friendly, freckled face. Matthew had always wished he looked like him.

But he didn't.

Matthew said, his voice strange in his own ears, "I do not understand what you mean."

"Henry Fairchild is not your father," spat Alastair. "You are Gideon Lightwood's bastard. Everybody knows it but you."

In a white and blinding rage, Matthew struck him in the face. Then he went to find Christopher, cleared the area, and gave him matches.

A short but eventful time passed before Matthew left school, never to return. In that interval, a wing of the Academy blew up.

Matthew realized it had been rather a shocking thing to do, but while he was deranged, he also demanded James be his *parabatai*, and by some miracle James agreed. Matthew and his papa arranged to spend more time at the Fairchilds' London home so that Matthew could be with both his papa and his *parabatai*. It had all, Matthew considered, worked out rather well.

If only he could forget.

The Shadow Market, London, 1901

Jem halted in the midst of the dancing flames and black iron arches of the London Market, startled by the appearance of a familiar face in an unexpected context, and even more so by the warmth of Matthew's greeting.

He knew Charlotte's son, of course. Her other boy, Charles, was always very cool and distant when he encountered Brother Zachariah on official business. Brother Zachariah knew that the Silent Brothers were meant to be detached from the world. His uncle Elias's son, Alastair, had made that very clear when Brother Zachariah reached out to him.

This is how it should be, said his Brothers in his mind. He could not always tell one of their voices from the others. They were a quiet chorus, a silent, ever-present song.

Jem would not have held it against Matthew if he felt the same way as many others, but he didn't seem to. His bright, delicate face showed dismay all too clearly. "Am I being too familiar?" he asked anxiously. "I only supposed since I was James's *parabatai* and that is what he calls you, I might do so as well."

Of course you may, said Brother Zachariah.

James did, and James's sister, Lucie, and Alastair's sister, Cordelia, had taken to doing so as well. Zachariah considered that they were the three sweetest children in the world. He knew he might be a little partial, but faith created truth.

Matthew glowed. Zachariah was reminded of Matthew's mother, and the kindness that had taken in three orphans when she was hardly more than a child herself.

"They all talk about you all the time in the London Institute," Matthew confided. "James and Lucie and Uncle Will and Aunt Tessa too. I feel as if I know you a great deal better than I actually do, so I beg pardon if I trespass on your kindness."

There can be no trespass when you are always welcome, said Jem.

Matthew's smile spread. It was an extraordinarily engaging expression. His warmth was closer to the surface than Charlotte's, Jem thought. He had never been taught to close himself off, to do anything but delight and trust in the world.

"I would like to hear all about your and Uncle Will's and Aunt Tessa's adventures from your point of view," Matthew proposed. "You must have had a very exciting time! Nothing exciting ever happens to us. The way everyone talks about it, one might think you had a dramatic star-crossed passion with Aunt Tessa before you became a Silent Brother." Matthew stopped himself. "Sorry! My tongue ran away with me. I am heedless and excited to talk to you properly. I'm sure it is strange to think of your past life. I hope I did not upset or offend you. I cry peace."

Peace, echoed Brother Zachariah, amused.

"I am certain you could have had a torrid affair with any person you wanted, of course," said Matthew. "Anyone can see that. Oh Lord, that was a heedless thing to say too, wasn't it?"

It is very kind of you to say so, said Brother Zachariah. *Is it not a fine night?*

"I can see you are a very tactful fellow," said Matthew, and clapped Brother Zachariah on the back.

They wandered through the stalls of the Shadow Market. Brother Zachariah was searching for one warlock in particular, who had agreed to help him.

"Does Uncle Will know you are in London?" asked Matthew. "Are you going to see him? If Uncle Will finds out you were in London and did *not* come to call, and I knew about it, that will be curtains for me! Young life cut off in its prime. A bright flower of manhood withered untimely. You might think of me and my doom, Uncle Jem, you really might."

Might I? asked Brother Zachariah.

It was fairly obvious what Matthew was angling to know.

"It would also be very kind of you if you refrained from mentioning that you saw me at the Shadow Market," Matthew wheedled, with his engaging smile and a distinct air of apprehension.

Silent Brothers are terrible gossips as a rule, said Brother Zachariah. *For you, though, Matthew, I will make an exception.*

"Thanks, Uncle Jem!" Matthew linked his arm with Jem's. "I can see we are going to be great friends."

It must be a horrible contrast for the Market to behold, Jem thought, seeing this bright child hanging so carelessly off the arm of a Silent Brother, hooded and cloaked and shrouded in darkness. Matthew seemed blissfully unaware of the incongruity.

I believe we will be, said Jem.

"My cousin Anna says the Shadow Market is tremendous fun," said Matthew happily. "Of course, you know Anna. She's always tremendous fun herself and has the best taste in waistcoats in London. I met some very agreeable faeries who invited me, and I thought I would come see."

The faeries Matthew had been dancing with previously whisked past, streaks of light in flower crowns. One faerie boy, lips stained with the juice of strange fruit, paused and winked at Matthew. He appeared not to resent being deserted in their dance, though appearances were seldom reliable with faeries. Matthew hesitated, casting a wary eye upon Brother Zachariah, then winked back.

Brother Zachariah felt he had to warn: *Your friends may mean mischief. Faeries often do.*

Matthew smiled, the lovely expression turning wicked. "I mean mischief frequently myself."

That is not exactly what I mean. Nor do I intend to insult any Downworlders. There are as many trustworthy Downworlders as there are Shadowhunters, which means the opposite is also true. It might be wise to remember that not all those at the Shadow Market look with favor on the Nephilim.

"Who can blame them?" said Matthew airily. "Stuffy lot. Present company excepted, Uncle Jem! My papa has a warlock friend he talks of frequently. They invented Portals together, did you know? I would like to have an intimate Downworlder friend too."

Magnus Bane would be a good friend for anyone to have, Brother Zachariah agreed.

It would have seemed disrespectful to Magnus, who had been such a good friend to Jem's *parabatai*, to press the issue with Matthew any further. Perhaps he was being too cautious. Many of the Downworlders were sure to be taken with Matthew's ready charm.

Will had made it clear his Institute was there to help Downworlders who sought aid, as surely as it was for mundanes and Shadowhunters. Maybe this new generation could grow up in more charity with Downworlders than any before them.

"Anna is not here tonight," Matthew added. "But you are, so all's well. What are we going to do together? Are you looking for something special? I rather thought I might buy Jamie and Luce a book. Any book would do. They love 'em all."

It made Jem warm to him even more to hear him speak of James and Lucie with such obvious affection.

If we see a suitable book, he said, *let us buy it for them. I would rather not buy them a tome of dangerous enchantment.*

"By the Angel, no," said Matthew. "Luce would read it for sure. Bit of a daredevil in a quiet way, Lu."

As for me, said Jem, *I have a commission from someone else whom I hold in high regard. Out of respect for them, I can say nothing more.*

"I completely understand," said Matthew, looking pleased to be this far in Jem's confidence. "I won't ask, but is there anything I can do to help? You could rely on me, if you would. We love all the same people, don't we?"

Thank you most sincerely for the offer.

There was no way for this child to help him, not in this current search, but his presence made Zachariah feel as if he could borrow some of Matthew's delighted wonder as he looked around the Market, and they strolled around taking in its sounds and sights together.

There was a stall selling faerie fruit, though there was also a werewolf outside the stall making dark remarks about being cheated and not making deals with goblin men. There were stalls with red-and-white-striped awnings selling cinder toffee, though Brother Zachariah had doubts about its provenance. Matthew stopped and laughed for sheer joy at a warlock woman with blue skin who was juggling toy unicorns, mermaids' shells, and small wheels on fire, and he flirted until she told him her name was Catarina. She added that he certainly might not call on her, but when he smiled, she smiled back. Brother Zachariah imagined people usually did.

The Shadow Market as a whole seemed rather bemused by Matthew. They were accustomed to Shadowhunters arriving on the hunt for witnesses or culprits, not demonstrating huge enthusiasm.

Matthew applauded when another stall sidled up to him, walking on chicken feet. A faerie woman with dandelion-fluff hair peered out among vials of many-colored lights and liquids.

"Hello, pretty," she said, her voice rasping like bark.

"Which one of us are you talking to?" asked Matthew, laughing and leaning his elbow against Brother Zachariah's shoulder.

The faerie woman regarded Zachariah with suspicion. "Oooh, a Silent Brother at our humble market. The Nephilim would consider that we were being honored."

Do you feel honored? asked Zachariah, shifting his stance slightly to stand protectively in front of Matthew.

Oblivious, Matthew sauntered past Zachariah to examine the vials laid out before him.

"Jolly nice potions," he said, flashing his smile on the woman. "Did you make them yourself? Good show. That makes you something of an inventor, does it not? My papa is an inventor."

"I am happy to have anyone at the Market who has an interest in my wares," said the woman. "I see you have a honey tongue to match your hair. How old are you?"

"Fifteen," Matthew replied promptly.

He began to sort among the vials, his rings clinking against the glass and their wood-and-gold or wood-and-silver stoppers, chattering about his father and faerie potions he had read about.

"Ah, fifteen summers, and by the look of you it has been all summer. Some would say only a shallow river could flash so bright," said the faerie woman, and Matthew looked up at her, an unguarded child surprised by any hurt dealt him. His smile flickered for an instant.

Before Jem could intervene, the smile resumed.

"Ah well. 'He has nothing, but he looks everything. What more can one desire?'" Matthew quoted. "Oscar Wilde. Do you know his work? I heard faeries like to steal poets. You should definitely have tried to steal him."

The woman laughed. "Perchance we did. Do you wish to be stolen, honey-sweet boy?"

"I do not think my mama the Consul would like that at all, no."

Matthew continued to beam radiantly on her. The faerie looked discomfited for a moment, then smiled back. Faeries could prick like thorns because it was their very nature, not because they meant harm.

"This is a love charm," said the faerie woman, nodding to a vial filled with a delicately sparkling pink substance. "No use to you, fairest child of the Nephilim. Now this would blind your opponents in a battle."

I imagine it would, said Brother Zachariah, studying the vial full of charcoal-colored sand.

Matthew was transparently pleased to hear about the potions. Zachariah was sure Henry's boy had been regaled with tales of the elements over dinner time and time again.

"What's this one?" Matthew asked, pointing to a purple vial.

"Oh, another one that would be of no interest to the Nephilim," said the woman dismissively. "What need would you have of a potion that would make the one who took it tell you all the truth? You Shadowhunters have no secrets among each other, I hear. Besides which, you have that Mortal Sword to prove one of you is telling the truth. Though I call that a brutal business."

"It *is* brutal," Matthew agreed vehemently.

The faerie woman looked almost sad. "You come of a brutal people, sweet child."

"Not me," said Matthew. "I believe in art and beauty."

"You might be pitiless one day, for all that."

"No, never," Matthew insisted. "I don't care for Shadowhunter customs at all. I like Downworlder ways much more."

"Ah, you flatter an old woman," said the faerie, waving a hand, but her face wrinkled up like a pleased apple as she smiled once more. "Now come, since you are a darling boy, let me show you something very special. What would you say to a vial of distilled stars, guaranteeing the one who carried it long life?"

Enough, said the voices in Zachariah's head.

Shadowhunters do not make bargains for their own lives, said Brother Zachariah, and towed Matthew away by his sleeve.

Matthew flailed and squawked a protest.

The woman's potions were in all likelihood colored water and sand, said Zachariah. *Do not waste your money or make any bargains with the fey. You must be careful at the Market. They sell heartbreak as well as dreams.*

"Oh, very well," said Matthew. "Look, Uncle Jem! That werewolf is running a book stall. Werewolves are surprisingly ardent readers, you know."

He dashed over and began to ask artless questions of a lady werewolf in a prim dress, who was soon patting her hair and laughing at his nonsense. Brother Zachariah's attention was suddenly arrested by the warlock he had been searching for.

Wait for me here, he told Matthew, and went to meet Ragnor Fell by the side of a fire built under one of the railway arches.

As the fire leaped, it birthed green sparks that matched the clever face of the warlock and lit his snowy white hair, curling around the sterner curl of his horns.

"Brother Zachariah," he said, nodding. "A pleasure, but I wish I had better news for you. Ah well. Bad news comes like rain and good news like lightning, barely seen before a crash."

A cheerful thought, said Brother Zachariah, his heart sinking.

"I went to several sources about the information you asked for," said Ragnor. "I have a lead, but I have to tell you—I was warned that this quest might prove fatal: that it has already proved fatal to more than one person. Do you truly want me to follow up on the lead?"

I do, said Brother Zachariah.

He had hoped for more. When he had met Tessa on the bridge that year, she had seemed concerned as she talked to him. It had been a gray day. The wind had blown her brown hair back from the face that trouble could touch as time could not. Sometimes it seemed like her face was all the heart he had left. He could not do much for her, but he had once promised to spend his life guarding her from the very wind from heaven.

He intended to keep his word in that at least.

Ragnor Fell nodded. "I will keep searching."

So will I, said Brother Zachariah.

Ragnor's face changed to a look of deep alarm. Brother Zachariah turned and beheld Matthew, who had wandered back to the faerie woman's stall of potions.

Matthew! Brother Zachariah called. *Come here.*

Matthew nodded and came reluctantly forward, smoothing his waistcoat.

The look of alarm on Ragnor's face deepened. "Why is he coming over? Why would you do this to me? I had always considered you one of the more sensible Shadowhunters, not that this is saying much!"

Brother Zachariah studied Ragnor. It was unusual to see the warlock rattled, and he was usually very discreet and professional.

I thought you had a long and cherished history of mutual esteem with the Fairchilds, said Brother Zachariah.

"Oh, certainly," said Ragnor. "And I have a long and cherished history of not getting blown up."

What? asked Zachariah.

The mystery was explained when Matthew caught sight of Ragnor and beamed.

"Oh, hello, Professor Fell." He glanced in Jem's direction. "Professor Fell taught me at the Academy before I was expelled. Very expelled."

Jem had been aware that James had been expelled, but he had not known Matthew was too. He had thought Matthew had simply chosen to follow his *parabatai*, as anyone would if they could.

"Is your friend with you?" asked Ragnor Fell, and twitched. "Is Christopher Lightwood on the premises? Is our Market shortly to be engulfed in flames?"

"No," Matthew said, sounding amused. "Christopher is at home."

"At home in Idris?"

"In the Lightwoods' London home, but it is far away."

"Not far enough!" decided Ragnor Fell. "I shall decamp to Paris forthwith."

He nodded at Brother Zachariah, visibly shuddered at Matthew, and turned away. Matthew waved forlornly after him.

"Good-bye, Professor Fell!" he called. He looked up at Brother Zachariah. "Christopher did not *mean* to cause any of the accidents, and the large explosion was entirely my fault."

I see, said Brother Zachariah.

Brother Zachariah was not sure he did see.

"You must know Gideon quite well," Matthew remarked, his quicksilver mind flashing onto another topic.

I do, said Brother Zachariah. *He is the best of good fellows.*

Matthew shrugged. "If you say so. I like my uncle Gabriel better. Not as much as Uncle Will, of course."

Will has always been my favorite too, Jem agreed solemnly.

Matthew chewed on his lower lip, clearly considering something. "Would you care to accept a wager, Uncle Jem, that I can clear that fire with a foot to spare?"

I would not, said Brother Zachariah with conviction. *Matthew, wait—*

Matthew charged at the flames sparkling with jade light, and leaped. He twisted in midair, slim black-clad body like a dagger thrown by an expert hand, and landed on his feet in the shadow of the church spire. After a moment, several members of the Shadow Market began to clap. Matthew mimed taking off an imaginary hat and bowed with a flourish.

His hair was gold even by strange flames, his face bright even in shadow. Brother Zachariah watched him laugh, and foreboding crept into his heart. He experienced sudden fear for Matthew, for all the shining, beloved children belonging to his dear friends. By the time he was Matthew's age, he and Will had been through fire and burning silver. His generation had suffered so they could bring the next one forth into a better world, but now it occurred to Jem that those children, taught to expect love and walk fearless through shadows, would be shocked and betrayed by disaster. Some of them might be broken.

Pray disaster never came.

Fairchild Residence, London, 1901

Matthew was still thinking about his visit to the Shadow Market the next day. In some ways it had been rotten luck, coming upon Uncle Jem like that, though he had been glad for the chance to become better acquainted. Perhaps Uncle Jem would think Jamie had not made a bad choice in his *parabatai*.

He rose early to help Cook with the baking. Cook had arthritis, and Matthew's mama had asked if she was not getting along in years and wishing to retire, but Cook did not wish to retire and nobody had to know if Matthew lent a hand in the early morning. Besides, Matthew liked to see his papa and mama and even Charles eating breakfast he had prepared. His mother always worked too hard, lines of worry etched between her brows and around her mouth that never disappeared even if Matthew managed to make her laugh. She liked scones with cranberries baked in, so he tried to make them for her whenever he might. Matthew could not do anything else for her. He was not a strong support for her like Charles.

"Charles Buford is so serious-minded and reliable," one of his mother's friends had said when they were taking tea together in Idris. She had bit into one of Mother's special scones. "And Matthew, well, he is . . . charming."

That morning at breakfast Charles Buford reached for the plate of Mama's scones. Matthew gave him a smile and a very decided shake of his head, moving the plate to his mother's elbow. Charles Buford grimaced in Matthew's direction.

Charlotte gave him a distracted smile, then returned to contemplating the tablecloth. She was in a brown study. Matthew wished he could say that was an unusual occurrence these days, but it was not. For months there had been something wrong in the atmosphere of home, with not only his mother but his father and even Charles Buford looking abstracted and occasionally snapping at Matthew. Sometimes Matthew dreaded the thought of what he might be told: that it was time he knew the truth, that his mother was going away forever. Sometimes Matthew thought if he only knew, he could bear it.

"My dear," said Papa. "Are you feeling well?"

"Perfectly, Henry," said Mama.

Matthew loved his father beyond reason, but he knew him. He was well aware that there were times when the entire family could have had their heads replaced with parakeet heads and Papa would simply tell the parakeet heads all about his latest experiment.

Now his father was watching his mother with worried eyes. Matthew could picture him saying, *Please, Charlotte. Do not leave me.*

His heart lurched in his chest. Matthew folded his napkin three times over in his hands and said: "Could somebody tell me—"

Then the door opened, and Gideon Lightwood came in. Mr. Lightwood. Matthew refused to think or speak of him as Uncle Gideon any longer.

"What are you doing here?" said Matthew.

"Sir!" Mama said sharply. "Really, Matthew, call him sir."

"What are you doing here?" said Matthew. "Sir."

Mr. Gideon Lightwood had the cheek to give Matthew a brief smile before he walked over and put his hand on Mama's shoulder. In front of Matthew's papa.

"Always a pleasure to see you, sir," said Charles Buford, that wretch. "May I serve you some kippers?"

"No, no, not at all, I already ate breakfast," said Mr. Lightwood. "I merely thought to accompany Charlotte through the Portal to Idris."

Mama smiled properly for Mr. Lightwood, as she had not for Matthew. "That's very kind, Gideon, though not necessary."

"It is most necessary," said Mr. Lightwood. "A lady should always have the escort of a gentleman."

His voice was teasing. Matthew usually waited until after breakfast to take his father down in his chair to his laboratory, but he could not bear this.

"I must see James at once upon urgent business!" he declared, bolting upright.

He slammed the door of the breakfast parlor shut behind him, but not before he heard Mama apologize for him, and Mr. Lightwood say: "Oh, that is all right. The age he is at is a difficult one. Believe me, I remember it well."

Before Matthew left, he ran up to his bedroom mirror to adjust his hair and cuffs and smooth his new green waistcoat. He stared at his face in the glass, framed in gold. A pretty face, but not a clever one like everyone else's in his family. He remembered the faerie woman saying, *Some would say only a shallow river could flash so bright.*

He tilted his head as he looked into the glass. Many people thought his eyes were dark like his mama's, but they were not. They were such a dark green that they fooled people, except when light struck the dark a certain way and the depths flashed emerald. Like the rest of him, his eyes were a trick.

He drew the vial of truth potion from his sleeve. Uncle Jem had not seen him buy it. Even if he suspected Matthew had it, Uncle Jem would not peach on him. When Uncle Jem said something, you believed it: he was that kind of person.

Matthew had refrained from ever mentioning his thoughts about Gideon to James, because Matthew was the soul of discretion and Jamie had an awful temper on him sometimes. Last summer a perfectly amiable Shadowhunter named Augustus Pounceby had come to the London Institute on his tour abroad, and Matthew had left Pounceby in James's sole company for less than half an hour. When Matthew returned, he found Jamie had thrown Pounceby into the Thames. All James would say was that Pounceby had insulted him. It was quite a feat, since Pounceby was a Shadowhunter fully grown and Jamie was fourteen at the time. Still, however impressive, it could not be considered good manners.

Neither James nor Uncle Jem would buy potions like a sneak, or consider administering them. Only, what harm would it do to finally learn the truth? Matthew had considered adding a drop from the vial to breakfast this morning; then Father and Mother would *have* to tell them all what was happening. Now that Mr. Gideon Lightwood had started popping in of a morning, he wished he had.

Matthew shook his head at his reflection and determined to banish melancholy and dull care.

"Do I look dapper?" he asked Mr. Oscar Wilde. "Do I look dashing and debonair?"

Mr. Oscar Wilde gave him a lick on the nose, because Mr.

Oscar Wilde was a puppy Jamie had given Matthew on his birthday. Matthew took this as approval.

He pointed to his reflection.

"You may be a waste of space in a waistcoat," he told Matthew Fairchild, "but at least your waistcoat is fantastic."

He checked his pocket watch, then tucked the pocket watch and vial into his waistcoat. Matthew could not linger. He had an important appointment at a most exclusive club.

First Matthew had to breeze into the London Institute to collect a parcel known as James Herondale. He had a shrewd idea of where James was likely to be, so he told Oscar to stay and guard a lamppost. Oscar obeyed: he was very well behaved for a puppy, and people said Matthew must have trained him well, but Matthew only loved him. Matthew threw a grappling hook up to the library window, climbed up while being careful of his trousers, and tapped on the glass.

James was in the window seat, his black head bent over—what a surprise!—a book. He looked up at the tap and smiled.

James had never really needed Matthew. James had been so shy, and Matthew had wanted to take care of him, but now that James was growing into his angular features and accustomed to having the certain company of three good friends, he was far more collected during social gatherings. Even when Jamie was shy, he never seemed to doubt or wish to alter himself. He never looked to Matthew for rescue. There was a quiet, deep certainty to James that Matthew wished he had himself. From the start, there was something between them that was more equal than between him and Thomas or him and Christopher. Something that made Matthew want to prove himself to James. He was not sure he ever truly had.

James never looked relieved to see Matthew, or expectant. He only looked pleased. He opened the window and Matthew crawled in, upsetting both James and the book from the window seat.

"Hello, Matthew," said James from the floor, in slightly sardonic tones.

"Hello, Matthew!" chimed Lucie from her writing desk.

She was a picture of dainty disarray, clearly in the throes of composition. Her light brown curls were half pulled out of a blue ribbon, one shoe dangling precariously from her stockinged toes. Uncle Will frequently gave dramatic readings from the book he was writing on the demon pox, which were very droll. Lucie did not show her writing around. Matthew had often considered asking her if she might read him a page, but he could think of no reason why Lucie would make a special exception for him.

"Bless you, my Herondales," said Matthew grandly, scrambling up from the floor and making Lucie his bow. "I come upon an urgent errand. Tell me—be honest!—what do you think of my waistcoat?"

Lucie dimpled. "Devastating."

"What Lucie said," James agreed peacefully.

"Not fantastic?" Matthew asked. "Not positively stunning?"

"I suppose I am stunned," said James. "But am I positively stunned?"

"Refrain from playing cruel word games with your one and only *parabatai*," Matthew requested. "Attend to your own attire, if you please. Heave that beastly book away. The Misters Lightwood await us. We must hook it."

"Can't I go as I am?" asked James.

He looked up at Matthew with wide gold eyes from his position on the floor. His pitch-black hair was askew, his linen shirt rumpled, and he was not even wearing a waistcoat. Matthew nobly repressed a convulsive shudder.

"Surely you jest," said Matthew. "I know you only say these things to hurt me. Off with you. Brush your hair!"

"The hairbrush mutiny is coming," warned James, making for the door.

"Come back victorious or on the hairbrushes of your soldiers!" Matthew called after him.

When Jamie had flown, Matthew turned to Lucie, who was scribbling intently but who looked up as if sensing his glance and smiled. Matthew wondered how it would be, to be self-sufficient and welcoming with it, like a house with sturdy walls and a beacon light always burning.

"Should I brush my hair?" Lucie teased.

"You are, as always, perfect," said Matthew.

He wished he could fix the ribbon in her hair, but that would be taking a liberty.

"Do you wish to attend our secret club meeting?" asked Matthew.

"I cannot, I am doing lessons with my mother. Mam and I are teaching ourselves Persian," said Lucie. "I should be able to speak the languages my *parabatai* speaks, shouldn't I?"

James had recently started calling his mother and father Mam and Da rather than Mama and Papa, since it sounded more grown-up. Lucie had instantly copied him in this matter. Matthew rather liked hearing the Welsh lilt in their voices when they called their parents, their voices soft as songs and always loving.

"Of a certainty," said Matthew, coughing and making a private resolution to return to his Welsh lessons.

There had been no question of Lucie attending Shadowhunter Academy. She had never demonstrated any abilities like James's, but the world was cruel enough to women who were even suspected of being the least bit different.

"Lucie Herondale is a sweet child, but with her disadvantages, who would marry her?" Lavinia Whitelaw had asked Matthew's mama once over tea.

"I would be happy if either of my sons wished to," said Charlotte, in her most Consul-like manner.

Matthew thought James was very lucky to have Lucie. He had always wanted a little sister.

Not that he wanted Lucie to be his sister.

"Are you writing your book, Luce?" Matthew asked tentatively.

"No, a letter to Cordelia," Lucie answered, shattering Matthew's fragile plot. "I hope Cordelia will come to visit, *very* soon," she added with earnest eagerness. "You will like her so much, Matthew. I know you will."

"Hmm," said Matthew.

Matthew had his doubts about Cordelia Carstairs. Lucie was going to be *parabatai* with Cordelia one day, when the Clave decided they were grown-up ladies who knew their own minds. Lucie and James were acquainted with Cordelia from childhood adventures that Matthew had not been part of, and which Matthew felt a bit jealous about. Cordelia must have some redeeming qualities, or Lucie would not want her for a *parabatai*, but she was Alastair Loathly Worm Carstairs's sister, so it would be strange if she was entirely amiable.

"She sent me a picture of herself in her latest. This is Cordelia," Lucie continued in tones of pride. "Is she not the prettiest girl you ever saw?"

"Oh, well," said Matthew. "Perhaps."

He was privately surprised by the picture. He would have thought Alastair's sister might share Alastair's unpleasant look, as if he were eating lemons he looked down on. She did not. Instead Matthew was reminded of a line in a poem James had read to him once, about an unrequited love. "That child of shower and gleam" described the vivid face laughing up at him from the frame exactly.

"All I know is," Matthew continued, "*you* have every other girl in London beat to flinders."

Lucie colored faint pink. "You are always teasing, Matthew."

"Did Cordelia ask you to be *parabatai*," Matthew said casually, "or did you ask her?"

Lucie and Cordelia had wanted to be made *parabatai* before they were parted, but they were warned that sometimes you regret a bond made young, and sometimes one partner or other would change their mind. Particularly, Laurence Ashdown had remarked, since ladies could be so flighty.

Lucie was not flighty. She and Cordelia wrote to each other faithfully, every day. Lucie had even once told Matthew she was writing a long story to keep Cordelia amused since Cordelia was always so far away. Matthew did not really wonder why someone like Lucie found it difficult to take someone like him seriously.

"I asked *her*, of course," Lucie said promptly. "I did not wish to miss my chance."

Matthew nodded, confirmed in his new belief that Cordelia Carstairs must be something special.

He was sure that if he had not asked James to be *parabatai*, James would never have thought of asking him.

James returned to the room. "Satisfied?" he asked.

"That is a strong word, Jamie," said Matthew. "Consider my waistcoat wrath somewhat appeased."

James still had his book tucked under his arm, but Matthew knew better than to fight doomed battles. James told him about the book as they walked the London streets. Matthew enjoyed the modern and humorous, such as the works of Oscar Wilde or the music of Gilbert and Sullivan, but Greek history was not so bad when it was Jamie telling him. Matthew had taken to reading more and more literature of old, stories of doomed love and noble battles. He could not find himself in them, but he saw James in them, and that was enough.

They walked unglamoured, as Matthew always insisted they do in his quest to make Jamie feel less self-conscious after the disasters of the Academy. A young lady, arrested by Jamie's bone structure, stopped in the path of an omnibus. Matthew seized her waist and whirled her to safety, giving her a tip of his hat and a smile.

Jamie seemed to miss the whole incident entirely, fiddling with something beneath his shirt cuff.

There were crowds protesting the mundane war outside the Houses of Parliament.

"The Bore War?" asked Matthew. "That cannot be right."

"The Boer War," said James. "*B-o-e-r*. Honestly, Matthew."

"That makes more sense," Matthew admitted.

A lady in a shapeless hat caught hold of Matthew's sleeve.

"May I be of any assistance, madam?" asked Matthew.

"They are committing unspeakable atrocities," said the lady.

"They have children penned up in camps. Think of the children."

James fastened his hand on Matthew's sleeve and towed him away, with an apologetic hat tip to the lady. Matthew looked over his shoulder.

"I do hope affairs go right for the children," he called.

James appeared pensive as they went. Matthew knew James wished Shadowhunters could solve problems like mundane war, though Matthew felt they were rather overstretched as it was with all the demons.

In order to cheer Jamie up, he stole his hat. Jamie burst into startled laughter and pursued Matthew, both of them racing and jumping high enough to amaze the mundanes, under the shadow of St. Stephen's Tower. Matthew's puppy lost his head, forgot his training, and dashed under their feet, yapping with the sheer joy of being alive. Their rushing footsteps outpaced the steady tick of the Great Clock, under which was written in James's beloved Latin, *O Lord, keep safe our Queen Victoria the First*, and their laughter mingled with the gleeful chime and roar of the bells.

Later Matthew would look back and remember it as his last happy day.

"Do I sleep, do I dream, or are these visions I see?" demanded Matthew. "Why are Aunt Sophie and *both of Thomas's sisters* taking tea in the same establishment as our private and exclusive club room?"

"They followed me," said Thomas in beleaguered tones. "Mama was understanding, or they would have followed us directly into the club room."

Aunt Sophie was a good sport, but that did not make

Matthew feel any less uneasy about the advent of Thomas's sisters. They were not kindred spirits, and they were liable to consider all the doings of their little brother both their business and very silly.

Matthew loved their club room and would brook no interference. He had chosen the materials for the curtains himself, made certain that James put the works of Oscar Wilde in their extensive book collection, and reinforced the corner that was Christopher's laboratory with steel sheets on the walls.

Which led Matthew to another grievance. He regarded Christopher with a steely gaze.

"Did you sleep in those clothes, Christopher? I know Aunt Cecily, Uncle Gabriel, and Cousin Anna would never let you inflict these horrors on the populace. What are those peculiar lavender stains upon your shirtfront? Did you set your sleeves on fire?"

Christopher regarded his sleeves as if he had never beheld them before. "A bit," he said guiltily.

"Ah well," said Matthew. "At least the purple stains match your eyes."

Christopher blinked said eyes, the improbable shade of violets in summer, and smiled his slow-blossoming smile. He clearly did not understand Matthew's objections, but was vaguely pleased they had been overcome.

It was not like with James, who actually presented a very fine appearance to the world. Christopher was incorrigible. He could rumple leather boots.

He could certainly set fire to anything. Matthew had not meant for Christopher to be asked to leave Shadowhunter Academy, but as it emerged, they did not let you remain in school if you blew up any portion of it. Besides which, Professor Fell had threatened to leave the Academy forever if Christopher remained.

Thomas had stayed out the full year, but found no reason to return with his friends gone and Alastair God-Help-Us Carstairs graduated.

So by luck, the closeness between their families, and an irresponsible attitude to flammable materials, more often than not all Matthew's bosom friends could live near each other in London. They trained together at the London Institute and took lessons together in various schoolrooms, and Lavinia Whitelaw had referred to them as "that notorious bunch of hooligan boys." Matthew and James had called themselves Shadowhooligans for some time after that remark. They had decided it was long past time to have a room of their own, inviolate from parents—however well-meaning—and preserved from siblings; though Cousin Anna and Luce were always welcome, due to being kindred spirits. So they had rented a room from the proprietor of the Devil Tavern, who owed the Herondales some sort of favor. They paid a monthly fee and had it all to themselves.

Matthew regarded their room with deep satisfaction. It looked very well, he thought, and best with all four of them sitting in it. In honor of Ben Jonson's Apollo Club, which had once held its meetings in this very tavern, a bust of the god hung over the fireplace with words cut into the marble beneath the head and shoulders:

Welcome all, who lead or follow,
To the Oracle of Apollo

All his answers are divine,
Truth itself doth flow in wine.

There was, of course, a window seat for Jamie, and Jamie was already installed with his book upon his lap. Christopher sat in his laboratory, adding an alarming orange liquid to a bubbling purple liquid, his face a picture of contentment. Thomas was seated cross-legged upon the sofa and earnestly practicing his blade work. Thomas was very conscientious and worried about not being a good enough Shadowhunter due to being undersized.

Thomas's sisters were a good deal taller than he was. So was everybody. Aunt Sophie, Tom's mama, said that Thomas would shoot up someday. She said she believed one of her grandpapas had been a blacksmith and a giant of a man, small as a pea until he was seventeen.

Aunt Sophie was a kind lady, very beautiful and most interesting with her tales of mundanes. Matthew did not know how Mr. Gideon Lightwood could live with himself.

He turned over the vial of truth potion in his waistcoat.

"Friends, now we are all gathered together, shall we share secrets?"

Jamie fiddled with his shirt cuff again, which he always did upon certain occasions, and pretended not to hear. Matthew suspected he had a secret love. He sometimes wondered whether James would have confided in him if he had been a different sort of person, more serious-minded and dependable.

Matthew laughed. "Come now. Any deadly hatreds you harbor in your bosom? Any ladies of your heart?"

Thomas flushed a deep red and dropped his knife. "No."

Oscar bounded over to fetch the knife for Thomas, and Thomas stroked his floppy ears.

Matthew sauntered closer to the laboratory corner, though he knew it was rash.

“Is there anyone who has caught your eye?” he asked Christopher.

Christopher eyed Matthew with alarm. Matthew sighed and prepared himself to explain further.

“Is there a lady you find yourself thinking of more often than other ladies?” he asked. “Or a fellow,” he added tentatively.

Christopher’s face cleared. “Oh! Oh yes, I see. Yes, there is a lady.”

“Christopher!” Matthew exclaimed, delighted. “You sly dog! Do I know her?”

“No, I cannot think so,” said Christopher. “She is a mundane.”

“Christopher, you dark horse,” said Matthew. “What is her name?”

“Mrs.—”

“A married lady!” Matthew said, overwhelmed. “No, no. I beg your pardon. Please go on.”

“Mrs. Marie Curie,” said Christopher. “I believe her to be one of the preeminent scientists of the age. If you read her papers, Matthew, I believe you would be most interest—”

“Have you ever met this lady?” said Matthew in dangerous tones.

“No?” said Christopher, heedless of danger as he often was around irate teachers and naked flames.

Christopher had the audacity to look surprised when Matthew began to belabor him mightily about the head and face.

"Watch the test tubes!" cried Thomas. "There is a hole in the floor at the Academy that Professor Fell calls the Christopher Lightwood Chasm."

"I suppose I hate some people," offered James. "Augustus Pounceby. Lavinia Whitelaw. Alastair Carstairs."

Matthew regarded his very own *parabatai* with deep approval.

"This is why we are chosen warrior partners, because we share such a perfect bond of sympathy. Come to me, Jamie, that we might share a manly embrace."

He made incursions upon Jamie's person. James thwacked him over the head with his book. It was a large book.

"Betrayed," said Matthew, writhing prone upon the floor. "Is that why you insist on carrying about enormous tomes everywhere you go, that you might visit violence upon innocent persons? Done to death by my best friend—my heart's brother—my own dear *parabatai*—"

He snagged James around the waist and brought him crashing to the floor for the second time that day. James hit Matthew with the book again, then subsided, leaning his shoulder against Matthew's. They were both thoroughly rumpled, but Matthew did not mind being rumpled for a good cause.

Matthew jostled James, very thankful that he had brought up Alastair and provided Matthew an opening to tell his secret.

"Alastair is not so bad," said Thomas unexpectedly from the sofa.

They all looked at him, and Tom curled up like an earwig under their scrutiny but persisted.

"I know what Alastair did to James was wrong," Thomas

said. "Alastair knows that very well too. That was why he was prickly whenever it was mentioned."

"How is that different from his usual ghastly demeanor?" Matthew demanded. "Besides him being particularly noxious the day everybody else's parents came to the Academy."

He paused to consider how to tell them, but that gave Thomas a chance to speak.

"Yes, exactly. Everybody's papa came but Alastair's," Thomas said quietly. "Alastair was jealous. Mr. Herondale came rushing to Jamie's defense, and nobody came for Alastair."

"Can one truly blame the man?" asked Matthew. "Had I such an insufferable toad of a son, and were he blessedly to be sent away to school, I am not sure I could bring myself to blast my sight with his visage until the accursed holidays carried him back to me again."

Thomas did not look convinced by Matthew's sound argument. Matthew took a deep breath.

"You do not know what he said to me the day we were expelled."

Tom shrugged. "Some nonsense, I expect. He always speaks the most shocking nonsense when he is overset. You shouldn't listen to him."

James's shoulder was tense against Matthew's. James had been the chief object of Alastair's malice. Thomas clearly intended to defend Alastair stoutly. This line of argument was bound to upset either James or Thomas. Matthew was not about to soothe his own feelings at the expense of Jamie's or Tom's.

Matthew gave up. "I cannot imagine why anyone would listen to him."

"Oh well," said Tom. "I like his nonsense." He looked wistful. "I think Alastair masks his pain with cleverly turned phrases."

"What absolute bosh," said Matthew.

Thomas was too nice, that was his problem. Really, people would let you get away with being the worst sort of scoundrel if you simply had a secret sorrow or did not rub along terribly well with your father.

It was definitely something to look into.

His papa was the best papa in the world, so Matthew had no opportunity to be cruelly oppressed or sadly neglected. Perhaps he should spend his time brooding over a forbidden passion like James was currently doing.

Matthew decided to give unrequited love a try. He stared out the window with all the pensive force he could muster. He was preparing to pass a hand across his fevered brow and murmur, "Alas, my lost love," or some other such rot when he was abruptly rapped upon the head with a book.

Honestly, Jamie was lethal with that thing.

"Are you quite well, Matthew?" Jamie inquired. "Your face suggests you are suffering from an ague."

Matthew nodded, but he ducked his head down against Jamie's coat and stayed there for a moment. It had never occurred to Matthew that Alastair might be jealous of James's father. He could not imagine being jealous of anybody's papa. Having the best papa in the world, Matthew would be perfectly satisfied with him.

If only he could be certain that Henry *was* his papa.

Early in the morning, Matthew unstoppered the faerie's vial and tipped a drop in among the cranberries for his mama's scones. The scones came out of the oven plump, golden, and smelling delicious.

"You are the best boy in London," said Cook, giving Matthew a kiss.

"I am entirely selfish," declared Matthew. "For I love you, Cook. When shall we be married?"

"Get along with you," said Cook, waving her wooden spoon in a menacing fashion.

When Jamie was a little boy, he had his own beloved special spoon. The family always reminisced about this. It embarrassed Jamie to death, especially when Uncle Gabriel presented him with a spoon at family gatherings. Uncles thought all sorts of sorry jests were a fine idea.

Jamie kept the spoons Uncle Gabriel gave him. When asked why, he said it was because he loved his uncle Gabriel. James was able to say such things with a sincerity that would shame anyone else.

After James said that, Uncle Will loudly asked what was the point in even having a son, but Uncle Gabriel looked touched. Uncle Gabriel loved Anna and Christopher, but Matthew was not sure he entirely understood his children. James greatly resembled his aunt Cecily, and tried very hard at being a Shadowhunter, while Christopher might not be aware any of them even *were* Shadowhunters. Uncle Gabriel was especially fond of James. Of course, who would not be?

Matthew stole Cook's spoon to give to James.

"I suppose that is for some absurd jest," said Charles Buford when he saw the spoon at breakfast. "I wish you would grow up, Matthew."

Matthew considered this, then stuck his tongue out at

Charles. His puppy was not allowed in the breakfast parlor, because Charles Buford said Oscar was not hygienic.

"If you would simply make an effort to be sensible," said Charles.

"I shan't," said Matthew. "I might sustain a strain from which I would never recover."

His mother did not smile at his theatrics. She was staring at her teacup, to all appearances lost in thought. His father was watching her.

"Is Mr. Gideon Lightwood coming to conduct you to Idris this morning?" Matthew asked, and pushed the plate of scones toward his mother.

Mama picked up a scone, buttered it liberally, and took a bite.

"Yes," she said. "I would thank you to be civil to him this time. You can have no idea, Matthew, how much I—"

Mama stopped speaking. Her small hand flew to her mouth. She sprang to her feet as if trying to take action in an emergency, in the manner she always did. Under Matthew's horrified gaze, tears shimmered in her eyes and abruptly spilled in two long, bright tracks down her face. In the morning light, Matthew discerned a faint tinge of violet in her tears.

Then she collapsed, her hair falling out of its tidy coil, her gray skirts a sudden riot on the floor.

"Charlotte!" cried Father.

Henry Fairchild used all kinds of ingenious contraptions to get about, but at family breakfasts he had only an ordinary chair. Not that it mattered. He simply launched himself from the chair in his haste to get to Charlotte, and fell heavily on the ground. He hardly seemed to notice he had fallen. Instead he crawled on his elbows toward the inert heap that was Mama, dragging his body painfully across the carpet as Matthew watched, frozen in horror.

He reached Mama and clasped her in his arms. She was always so small, but now she looked small as a child. Her face was still and white as the face of the marble busts in mundane tombs.

"Charlotte," murmured Papa, as if he was praying. "Dearest. Please."

"Mama," Matthew whispered. "Papa. Charlie!"

He turned to his brother the way he had when he was small, when he had followed Charlie around everywhere and believed his brother could do anything in the world.

Charles had bolted out of his chair and was shouting for help. He turned back in the doorway, staring at his parents with a wretched expression that was very unlike him. "I knew how it would be, Portaling back and forth from London to Idris so that Matthew could be near his precious *parabatai*—"

"What?" asked Matthew. "I didn't know. I swear I didn't know. . . ."

Cook had appeared in the doorway in response to Charles's shouts. She gasped. "Mrs. Fairchild!"

Matthew's voice shook. "We need Brother Zachariah—"

Brother Zachariah would know what he had given Mama and what to do. Matthew began to explain the evil thing he had done, but then there was a noise from Charlotte, and the room went still.

"Oh yes," faltered Mama, her voice terrifyingly weak. "Oh, please. Fetch Jem."

Charles and Cook raced from the room. Matthew did not

dare approach his mother and father. Finally, after some long and terrible time, Brother Zachariah came, parchment-colored cloak swirling about him like the robes of a fell presence come to deliver judgment and punishment.

Matthew knew Brother Zachariah's always closed eyes still saw. He could see Matthew, through to his sinful heart.

Brother Zachariah bent and scooped Matthew's mother up in his arms. He carried her away.

All day Matthew heard the sounds of comings and goings. He saw the carriage from the London Institute rattle up to the door and Aunt Tessa emerge with a basket of medicine. She had been learning some warlock magic.

Matthew understood that they needed a Silent Brother *and* a warlock, and they still might not save his mother.

Charles did not return. Matthew had helped his father back to his chair. They sat together in the breakfast parlor as the light turned from the glow of morning to the blaze of day, then faded into the shadows of evening.

Papa's face looked carved out of old stone. When he spoke at last, he sounded as if he were dying inside. "You should know, Matthew," he said. "Your mama and I, we were . . ."

Separating. Ending our marriage. She loved another. Matthew braced himself for the horror, but when it came, it was greater than anything he could have imagined.

"We were in anticipation of—of a happy event," said Papa, his voice catching in his throat.

Matthew stared at him with blank incomprehension. He simply could not understand. It would hurt too much.

"Your mama and I had to wait some time for Charles Buford, and for you, and we thought you were both worth the wait," said Father, and even in the midst of that awful moment he tried to smile for Matthew. "This time Charlotte was hoping for—for a daughter."

Matthew choked on his horror. He thought he might never speak another word or eat another bite. He would be choking on horror for years.

We thought. We were in anticipation. It was entirely clear that Father was certain, and had reason to believe, his children were his.

"We were concerned since you and Charles are both now quite grown up," said Henry. "Gideon, good fellow, has been dancing attendance on Charlotte during Clave meetings. He has always stood as your mother's friend, lending her the Lightwood name and consequence whenever she needed support, and advising her when she wished for good counsel. I am afraid I have never truly understood the workings of an Institute, let alone the Clave. Your mama is a wonder."

Gideon had been helping his mother. Matthew was the one who had attacked her.

"I had thought we might name her Matilda," Father said in a slow, sad voice. "I had a Great-Aunt Matilda. She was very old when I was still a young rip, and the other boys used to tease me. She would give me books and tell me that I was smarter than any of them. She had splendid buttery-white wavy hair, but it was gold when she was a girl. When you were born, you already had the dearest fair lovelocks. I called her Aunt Matty. I never told you, because I thought you might not like to be named for a lady. You already have a great deal to endure with your foolish father, and those who cavil at your mother and your *parabatai*. You bear it all so gracefully."

Matthew's father touched his hair with a gentle, loving hand. Matthew wished he would pick up a blade and cut Matthew's throat.

"I wish you could have known your great-great-aunt. She was very like you. She was the sweetest woman God ever made," said Father. "Save your mother."

Brother Zachariah glided in then, a shadow amid all the other shadows crowding that room, to summon Matthew's father to his mother's bedside.

Matthew was left alone.

He stared in the gathering darkness at his mother's overturned chair, the dropped scone and its trail of crumbs going nowhere, the greasy remnants of breakfast over the disarranged table. He, Matthew, was always dragging his friends and family to art galleries, always anxious to dance through life, always prattling of truth and beauty like a fool. He had run headlong into a Shadow Market and blithely trusted a Downworlder, because Downworlders seemed exciting, because she had called Shadowhunters brutal and Matthew had agreed, believing he knew better than they. It was not the faerie woman's fault, or Alastair's, or the fault of any other soul. He was the one who had chosen to distrust his mother. He had fed his mother poison with his own hands. He was not a fool. He was a villain.

Matthew bowed the fair head that had been passed to him through his father, from his father's best-loved relative. He sat in that dark room and wept.

Brother Zachariah descended the stairs after a long battle with death, to tell Matthew Fairchild that his mother would live.

James and Lucie had come with Tessa and waited in the

hall all this long day. Lucie's hands were chilled when she clung to Jem.

She asked, "Aunt Charlotte, is she safe?"

Yes, my darlings, said Jem. *Yes.*

"Thank the Angel," breathed James. "Matthew's heart would break. All our hearts would."

Brother Zachariah was not so sure of Matthew's heart, after the mischief Matthew had wrought, but he wanted to offer James and Lucie what comfort he could.

Go to the library. There is a fire lit. I will send Matthew to you.

When he went into the breakfast room, he found Matthew, who had been all gold and laughter, cowering in his chair as if he could not bear what was to come.

"My mother," he whispered at once, his voice brittle and dry as old bones.

She will live, said Jem, and softened seeing the boy's pain.

James had known his *parabatai*'s heart better than Jem. There had been a time when Will was a boy everybody assumed the worst of, with good reason. Everybody except for Jem. He did not want to learn harsh judgment from the Silent Brothers, or a less forgiving heart.

Matthew lifted his head to face Brother Zachariah. His eyes told of agony, but he held his voice steady.

"And the child?"

Brother Zachariah said, *The child did not live.*

Matthew's hands closed on the edge of his chair. His knuckles were white. He looked older than he had a mere two nights ago.

Matthew, said Brother Zachariah, and walled off his Brothers in his head as well as he might.

"Yes?"

Rely upon a Silent Brother for silence, said Jem. *I will not tell anybody about the Shadow Market or any bargains you may have made there.*

Matthew swallowed. Jem thought he might be about to be thanked, but Jem had not done this for thanks.

I will not tell anybody, he said, *but you should. A secret too long kept can kill a soul by inches. I watched a secret almost destroy a man once, the finest man ever made. Such a secret is like keeping treasure in a tomb. Little by little, poison eats away at the gold. By the time the door is opened, there may be nothing left but dust.*

Brother Zachariah stared into the young face that had been so bright. He waited and hoped to see that face lit again.

"All this about the Shadow Market," Matthew faltered.

Yes? said Jem.

The boy flung back his golden head.

"I'm sorry," said Matthew coldly. "I do not know what you are talking about."

Zachariah's heart fell.

So be it, he said. *James and Lucie are waiting for you in the library. Let them give you whatever comfort they can.*

Matthew stood from his chair, moving as if he had grown suddenly old over the course of a day. Sometimes the distance Silent Brothers possessed moved them to dispassionate observation and too far from pity.

It would be a long time, Brother Zachariah knew, before there could be any comfort for Matthew Fairchild.

The library in Matthew's house was a far smaller and less loved and lived-in room than the library in the London Institute, but tonight there was a fire burning and Herondales waiting within. Matthew stumbled into the room as if he were walking in from midwinter cold, his limbs too chilled to move.

As one, as if they had only been waiting for his coming, James and Lucie looked up at him. They were pressed together on a sofa at the hearth. By firelight, Lucie's eyes were as eerie as James's, a paler and more fiercely burning blue than her father's. It was as though James's gold were the corona of a flame and Lucie's blue its burning heart.

They were a strange pair, these two Herondales, thorned mysterious plants in the hothouse of the Nephilim. Matthew could not have loved either of them more dearly.

Lucie leaped to her feet and ran to him with her hands outstretched. Matthew shuddered away. He realized, with dull pain, that he did not feel worthy of being touched by her.

Lucie glanced at him sharply, then nodded. She always saw a lot, their Luce.

"I will leave you two together," she said decisively. "Take as long as ever you may."

She reached out her hand to touch his, and Matthew shrank away from her again. This time he saw that it hurt, but Lucie only murmured his name and withdrew.

He could not tell Lucie this, and see her disgust of him, but he and James were bound. Perhaps James would try to understand.

Matthew advanced, every step a terrible effort, toward the fire. Once he was near enough, James reached out and clasped Matthew's wrist, drawing him close to the sofa. He laid Matthew's hand over James's heart, and covered it with his own. Matthew looked down into James's fire-gold eyes.

"*Mathew*," said Jamie, pronouncing his name in the Welsh way and with the Welsh lilt that let Matthew know he meant it as an endearment. "I am so sorry. What can I do?"

He felt he could not live on with this massive stone of a secret crushing his chest. If he was ever going to tell anyone, he should tell his *parabatai*.

"Listen to me," he said. "I was talking about Alastair Carstairs yesterday. What I meant to tell you was that he insulted my mother. He said—"

"I understand," said James. "You do not have to tell me."

Matthew drew in a small shaky breath. He wondered if James really could understand.

"I know the kind of thing they say about Aunt Charlotte," said James with quiet fierceness. "They say similar things about my mother. You remember that man Augustus Pounceby, last year? He waited until we were alone to cast slurs upon my mother's good name." A small grim smile curved James's mouth. "So I threw him in the river."

Aunt Tessa had been so glad to have a Shadowhunter visitor, Matthew remembered numbly. She displayed Shadowhunter family coats of arms on her walls to welcome any traveler to the London Institute.

"You never told me," said Matthew.

Jamie was telling him now. Tom had told him that whatever Alastair said was nonsense. If Matthew had asked his father about what Alastair had said, his father could have told him about Great-Aunt Matty, and they might even have laughed about how absurd it was to think some stupid malicious boy could ever make them doubt their family.

Jamie's mouth crooked down a little. "Oh well. I know you

have to hear a lot about me and my unfortunate antecedents already. I do not want you to think I am an unbearable nuisance and you got a bad bargain with your *parabatai*."

"Jamie," Matthew said on a wounded breath, as if he had been hit.

"I know it must feel wretched to remember anything hurtful that worm Carstairs said about your mother," James plunged on. "Especially when she is—she is unwell. The very next time we see him, we will punch him in the head. What do you say to that, Mathew? Let's do it together."

Matthew's father and his mother and his brother and his *parabatai* had all been trying not to burden him, while Matthew pranced on thinking he was no end of a fine fellow and dealing remarkably by himself. James would not have done what Matthew had. Nor would Christopher or Thomas. They were loyal. They were honorable. When someone had insulted Jamie's mother, Jamie had thrown him in the river.

Matthew pressed his palm against James's linen shirt, over the steady beat of his loyal heart. Then Matthew clenched his hand into a fist.

He could not tell him. He could never do it.

"All right, old chap," said Matthew. "We will do it together. Do you think I could have a moment alone, though?"

James hesitated, then drew back.

"Is that what you want?"

"It is," said Matthew, who had never wanted to be alone in his life, and never wanted to be alone less than in this moment.

James hesitated again, but he respected Matthew's wishes. He bowed his head and went out, Matthew assumed to rejoin his sister. They were both good and pure. They should be together and comfort each other. They deserved comfort as he did not.

After James was gone, Matthew could not keep standing. He fell to his hands and knees in front of the fire.

There was a statue above the fire showing Jonathan Shadowhunter, the first Shadowhunter, praying for the world to be washed clean of evil. Behind him was the Angel Raziel flying to gift him with strength to defeat the forces of darkness. The first Shadowhunter could not see him yet, but he was standing firm, because he had faith.

Matthew turned his face away from the light. He crawled, as his father had crawled across another floor at the beginning of this endless day, until he was in the darkest and farthest corner of the room. He had not believed. He laid his cheek against the cold floor and refused to let himself weep again. He knew he could not be forgiven.

It was long past time for Brother Zachariah to return to the City of Bones. Tessa stood with him in the hall and touched his hand before he went.

The sweetest woman God ever made, he had heard Henry say earlier. Jem loved Charlotte, but he had his own image of the sweetest this world could offer.

She was always his anchor in cold seas, her warm hand, her steadfast eyes, and it was as if a flame leaped between them and a mad hope. For a moment Jem was as he had been. It seemed possible to be together in sorrow, united as family and friends were, to sleep under the Institute roof and go down in the morning to breakfast, sad but safe in the warmth of a shared hearth and human hearts.

He thought, *Yes, ask me to stay.*

He could not. They both knew he could not.

Good-bye, Tessa, he said.

She swallowed, her long lashes screening the shine of her eyes. Tessa was always brave. She would not let him take a memory of her tears back to the Silent City, but she called him by the name she was always careful not to call him when anybody but they could hear. "Good-bye, Jem."

Brother Zachariah bowed his head, his hood falling about his face, and went out into the winter cold of London.

Finally you leave, said Brother Enoch in his mind.

All the Silent Brothers hushed when Brother Zachariah was with Tessa, like small animals in the trees hearing the approach of that which they did not understand. In a way, they were all in love with her, and some resented her for that. Brother Enoch had made it clear he was tired of two names ceaselessly echoing in their minds.

Brother Zachariah was halfway down the street where the Fairchilds lived when a tall shadow struck his across the pale streets.

He looked up from the shadows and saw Will Herondale, head of the London Institute. He carried a walking stick that had once been Zachariah's, before Zachariah took a staff into his hands.

Charlotte will live, said Brother Zachariah. *The child never had a chance to.*

"I know," said Will. "I already knew. I did not come to you for those tidings."

Brother Zachariah should really have learned better by now. Of course Tessa would have sent word to Will, and while Will often traded upon Brother Zachariah's position as a Silent

Brother to command his services and thus his presence, he very seldom spoke to Zachariah of his duties as a Silent Brother, as if he could make Zachariah not what he was by dint of sheer determination.

If anyone could have done it, Will would have been that one.

Will threw him the walking stick, which he must have stolen from James's room, and confiscated Brother Zachariah's staff. Jem had asked them to give James his room at the Institute, fill it with their son's bright presence, and not keep it as some dreary shrine. He was not dead. He had felt when they made him a Silent Brother as if he had been cut open and all things inside him ripped out.

Only, there was that which they could not take away.

"Carry it awhile," said Will. "It lightens my heart to see you with it. We could all do with lighter hearts tonight."

He traced a carving upon the staff, the Herondale ring winking by moonlight.

Where shall I carry it?

"Wherever you please. I thought I would walk with you a little way, my *parabatai*."

How far? asked Jem.

Will smiled. "Need you ask? I will go with you as far as I possibly may."

Jem smiled back. Perhaps there was more hope and less sorrow in store for Matthew Fairchild than he feared. None knew better than Jem that someone could be not fully known yet still entirely loved. Forgiven all sins, and dearest in darkness. James would not let his *parabatai* travel any shadowy paths alone. No matter what catastrophe came, Jem believed the son had as great a heart as his father.

New streetlights showed Will's and Jem's silhouettes, walking together through their city, as they had of old. Even though both knew they must part.

Across London the bells rang all together in a sudden terrifying clamor. Frightened birds in mad wheeling flight cast deeper shadows across the city at night, and Jem knew the queen was dead.

A new age was beginning.

Every Exquisite Thing

By Cassandra Clare and Maureen Johnson

J

London, 1901

This one was stained with something purple.

This one had a hole in the sleeve.

This one was missing a . . . back. An entire *back*. It was just a front of a shirt and two sleeves clinging on for dear life.

"Christopher," Anna said, turning the garment over in her hands, "how do you do these things?"

Everyone had their small wonderland. For her brother Christopher and Uncle Henry, it was the laboratory. For Cousin James and Uncle Will, the library. For Lucie, her writing desk, where she wrote her long adventures for Cordelia Carstairs. For Matthew Fairchild, it was any troublesome corner of London.

For Anna Lightwood, it was her brother's wardrobe.

In many ways, it was very good to have a brother who was largely oblivious about his clothes. Anna could have taken Christopher's coat right off his back and he would hardly have noticed. The only downside was that Christopher's clothes had suffered fates no clothes should suffer. They were dipped in acids, brushed by fire, poked with sharp objects, left out in the rain. . . . His wardrobe was like a museum of experiment and disaster, tattered, stained, charred, and stinking of sulfur.

To Anna, though, the clothes were still precious.

Christopher was over visiting the Institute and Uncle Henry, so he would be gone for hours. Her mother and father were both out in the park with her baby brother, Alexander. This was her golden hour, and there was no time to waste. Christopher was taller than her now and growing all the time. This meant that his older trousers suited her frame. She chose a pair and found the least-damaged shirt and a satisfactory gray-striped waistcoat. She dug through the pile of ties, scarves, kerchiefs, cuffs, and collars that lay on the bottom of Christopher's wardrobe and selected the most passable items. On his dressing stand she found a hat that had a sandwich in it. It was ham, Anna noted, as she tipped it out and dusted away the crumbs. Once she had everything she needed, she bundled it all under her arm and slipped out into the hall, shutting his door quietly.

Anna's room was so different from her brother's. Her walls were papered in a dusty rose. There was a white lace coverlet, a pink vase with lilacs next to her bed. Her cousin Lucie thought her bedroom quite charming. Anna had different tastes. Given her choice, the paper would be a rich, deep green, her decor black and gold. She would have a deep chaise longue on which she could read and smoke.

Still, she had a long dressing mirror, and that was all that mattered right now. (Christopher's mirror had met its fate in an experiment in which he attempted to magnify the effect of glamours. It had not been replaced.) She drew the curtains against the warm summer sun and began to change. Anna had long forsworn wearing a corset—she had no interest in squeezing her internal organs into a lump or pushing her small bosom up. She slipped out of her tea gown, letting it drop to the floor. She kicked it away. Off went the stockings, down came the hair. The trousers were tucked in at the ankle to adjust for height. A few adjustments of the waistcoat hid the damage to the shirt. She put one of Christopher's black ascots around her slender neck and tied it expertly. Then she took the derby that had been hosting the ham sandwich and placed it on her head, tucking her black hair carefully up under it and arranging it until it appeared that her hair was shorn short.

Anna stood before the mirror, examining the effect. The waistcoat flattened her chest a bit. She tugged it up and adjusted it until the fit was right. She rolled the legs of the trousers and knocked the hat down over her eye.

There. Even in these clothes—stains and ham sandwiches and all—her confidence swelled. She was no longer a gangly girl who looked awkward in ribbons and flounces. Instead she looked elegant, her lean body complemented by more severe tailoring, the waistcoat nipping in her slim waist and flaring over her narrow hips.

Imagine what she could do with Matthew Fairchild's wardrobe! He was a real peacock, with his colorful waistcoats and ties, and the beautiful suits. She walked back and forth a bit, tipping her hat to imaginary ladies. She bowed, pretending to be taking the hand of a fair maiden, keeping her eyes turned up. Always keep the fair maiden's eye as you press your lips to her hand.

"Enchanted," she said to her imaginary lady. "Would you care for a dance?"

The lady would be delighted to dance.

Anna crooked her arm around the waist of her phantom beauty; she had danced with her many times. Though Anna could not see her face, she swore she could feel the fabric of her lover's dress, the soft swooshing noise it made as it brushed the floor. The lady's heart was fluttering as Anna pressed her hand. Her lady would wear a delicate scent. Orange blossom, perhaps. Anna would press her face closer to the lady's ear and whisper.

"You are quite the most beautiful girl here," Anna would say.

The lady would blush and press closer.

"How is it you look more lovely in every light?" Anna would go on. "The way the velvet of your dress crushes against your skin. The way your—"

"Anna!"

She dropped her airy companion to the floor in her surprise.

"Anna!" her mother called again. "Where are you?"

Anna hurried to her door and opened it just a crack.

"Here!" she said in a panic.

"Can you come down, please?"

"Of course," Anna replied, already pulling at the ascot around her neck. "Coming!"

Anna had to step right through her fallen dancing partner in her haste. Off with the waistcoat, the trousers. Everything off, off, off. She shoved the clothes into the bottom of her wardrobe. The discarded dress was hastily put back on, her fingers fumbling on the buttons. Everything about girls' clothing was fussy and complicated.

Several minutes later, she hurried downstairs, attempting to look composed. Her mother, Cecily Lightwood, was sifting through a stack of letters at her desk in the sitting room.

"We ran into Inquisitor Bridgestock while we were walking," she said. "The Bridgestocks have just arrived from Idris. They've asked us to dine with them this evening."

"Dinner with the Inquisitor," Anna said. "What a thrilling way to spend an evening."

"It is necessary," her mother said simply. "We must go. Can you keep an eye on Christopher while we are talking? Make sure he doesn't set anything on fire. Or anyone."

"Yes," Anna said automatically, "of course."

It would be a dreadful affair. Clave business accompanied by overcooked beef. There were so many other things she could be doing on a fine summer night in London. What if she could walk the streets, finely dressed, a beautiful girl on her arm?

Someday, the lady would not be imaginary. The clothes would not be borrowed and ill-fitting. Someday she would stride down the street and women would fall at her feet (not failing to notice her perfectly polished brogues) and men would tip their hats to a lady-killer more accomplished than they.

Just not tonight.

It was still sunny when the Lightwood family got into their carriage that evening. There were costermongers out and flower sellers and bootblacks . . . and so many lovely girls, walking in their light summer dresses. Did they know how lovely they were? Did they look at Anna and see the way she looked at them?

Her brother Christopher bumped gently against her as they rode.

"This seems like a long route to the Institute," he noted.

"We're not going to the Institute," Anna said.

"Aren't we?"

"We're having dinner with the Inquisitor," her father said.

"Oh," Christopher said. And with that, he was off in his own thoughts, as ever—inventing something in his mind, working out a calculation. In this, Anna felt close to her brother. They were both somewhere else in their minds at all times.

The Bridgestocks lived in Fitzrovia, just off Cavendish Square. Theirs was a fine three-across town house. The paint on the shiny black door looked like it could have still been wet, and there were electric lights outside. A servant showed them into a dark and close reception room where the Inquisitor and his wife greeted them. They took little notice of Anna except to say what a charming young lady she was. She and Christopher sat politely on stiff chairs and added a decorative element to a dreary occasion.

The dinner gong finally sounded, and everyone shuffled through to the dining room. Anna and Christopher were seated at the far end of the table, and there was an empty place set across from her. Anna ate her asparagus soup and stared at a painting of a ship on the wall. The ship was in the throes of a storm, the masts on fire, and on the verge of disintegrating into the sea.

"Did you hear they are building a Portal in the Gard?" the Inquisitor asked Anna's parents.

"Oh dear," Mrs. Bridgestock said, shaking her head, "is that a good idea? What if it were to let demons through?"

Anna envied the ship in the painting and all who sank in her.

"Of course," the Inquisitor droned on, "there's also the

matter of money. The Consul has rejected the proposal to create an official currency of Idris. A wise decision. Very wise. As I was saying earlier—"

"I'm so sorry for my lateness," said a voice.

In the doorway of the dining room stood a girl, probably Anna's age, in a midnight-blue dress. Her hair was jet-black, like Anna's, but fuller, more luxurious, deep as night sky against her soft brown skin. But what captured Anna were her eyes—eyes the color of topaz—large, the lashes thick.

"Ah," the Inquisitor said. "This is our daughter, Ariadne. These are the Lightwoods."

"I was meeting my tutor," Ariadne said as a servant pulled out her chair. "We were delayed. I do apologize. It sounds like I came in just as you were debating the new currency. Shadowhunters are an international group. We must blend seamlessly with many international economies. Having our own currency would be a disaster."

On that, she plucked up her napkin and turned to Anna and Christopher and smiled.

"We have not met," she said.

Anna had to force herself to swallow, then to breathe. Ariadne was something beyond the realm of humanity or Shadowhunter. The Angel himself must have made her.

"Anna Lightwood," Anna said.

Christopher was pushing peas onto the back of his fork, unaware that a goddess had seated herself across from him.

"And this is my brother Christopher. He can be a bit distracted."

She gave him a nudge.

"Oh," he said, noticing Ariadne. "I'm Christopher."

Even Christopher, now that he had seen Ariadne, could not help but be mesmerized by her. He blinked, taking in the sight.

"You're . . . you're not English, are you?"

Anna died several deaths inside, but Ariadne simply laughed.

"I was born in Bombay," she said. "My parents ran the Bombay Institute until they were killed. I was adopted by the Bridgestocks in Idris."

She spoke very plainly, in the tone of someone who has long accepted a set of facts.

"What killed your parents?" Christopher asked conversationally.

"A group of Vetis demons," Ariadne said.

"Oh! I knew someone at the Academy that was killed by a Vetis demon!"

"Christopher," Anna said.

"You go to the Academy?" Ariadne asked.

"Not anymore. I caused one of the wings to explode." Christopher took a bread roll from a plate and happily began buttering it.

Anna looked at the painting of the ship again, trying to will herself onto the deck and then into the black, pitiless waters. The most lovely girl in the world had just walked into her life and in thirty seconds her dear brother had managed to bring up the death of her family, a death at school, and the fact that he had blown up part of the Academy.

But Ariadne was not looking at Christopher, even as he inadvertently placed his elbow into the butter dish.

"Have *you* caused any explosions?" she asked Anna.

"Not yet," Anna replied. "But the evening is young."

Ariadne laughed, and Anna's soul sang. She reached over and lifted her brother's elbow from the butter, never taking her gaze from Ariadne. Did she know how beautiful she was? Did she know her eyes were the color of liquid gold, and that songs could be written about the way she turned out her wrist to reach for her glass?

Anna had seen beautiful girls before. She had even seen a few beautiful girls who looked at her the way she looked at them. But that was always in passing. They went by on the street, or their gaze lingered a bit long in a shop. Anna had practiced the art of the prolonged stare, the one that invited them: *Come. Tell me of yourself. You are lovely.*

There was something in the way Ariadne was looking at Anna that suggested . . .

No. Anna had to be imagining it. Ariadne was being polite and attentive. She was not eyeing Anna romantically over the dinner table, over the roasted potatoes and the duck. Ariadne's perfection had caused Anna to hallucinate.

Ariadne continued to contribute to the conversation at the other end of the table. Anna had never been so interested in the economic policies of Idris. She would study them night and day if she could join Ariadne in discussing them.

Every once in a while, Ariadne would turn back to Anna and look at her knowingly, her mouth twisting in a smile like a bow. And each time this happened, Anna would wonder again what was happening, and why that particular look made the room spin. Maybe she was ill. Maybe she had developed a fever from looking at Ariadne.

The pudding came and went, and Anna vaguely remembered eating it. As the dishes were cleared and the women stood to leave the table, Ariadne came and hooked her arm through Anna's.

"We have quite a good library," she said to Anna. "Perhaps I could show it to you?"

Anna, with a show of supreme self-control, did not immediately fall to the floor. She managed to say yes, the library, yes, she would love to see it, yes, library, yes, yes . . .

She told herself to stop saying she wanted to see the library and looked over at her mother. Cecily smiled. "Go on, Anna. Christopher, would you mind accompanying us to the greenhouse? Mrs. Bridgestock has a collection of poisonous plants that I think you will quite enjoy."

Anna cast Cecily a grateful look as Ariadne led her from the room. Her head was full of Ariadne's orange-blossom perfume and the way her tumble of dark hair was pinned up in a gold comb.

"It's this way," Ariadne said, leading Anna to a set of double doors toward the back of the house. The library was dark and had a chill. Ariadne released Anna's arm and illuminated one of the electric lights.

"You use electricity?" Anna said. She had to say something, and that was as good a thing as any.

"I convinced Father," Ariadne said. "I am modern and possessed of all sorts of advanced notions."

The room was full of crates, and only some of the books had been unpacked and shelved. The furniture, however, had been placed. There was an ample desk, and many comfortable reading chairs.

"We're still settling in here," Ariadne said, sitting herself prettily (she had no other way) on a deep red chair. Anna was too nervous to sit, and paced along the opposite side of the room. It was almost too much to look at Ariadne here in this dark, private place.

"I understand your family has a very interesting history," Ariadne said.

Anna had to speak. She had to figure out a way to *be* around Ariadne. In her mind she donned her real clothing—the trousers, the shirt (the mental one had no stains), the fitted waistcoat. She slipped her arms through the sleeves. Thus attired, she felt confident. She managed to sit opposite Ariadne and meet her gaze.

"My grandfather was a worm, if that's what you mean," Anna said.

Ariadne laughed aloud. "You didn't like him?"

"I didn't know him," Anna said. "He was, quite literally, a worm."

Clearly, Ariadne didn't know that much about the Lightwoods. Usually, when one's demon-loving relative develops a serious case of demon pox and turns into a giant worm with massive teeth, word gets around. People will talk.

"It's true," Anna said, now examining the gilded edge of a writing desk. "He ate one of my uncles."

"You *are* funny," Ariadne said to Anna.

"I'm glad you think so," Anna replied.

"Your brother's eyes are quite extraordinary," Ariadne noted.

Anna heard this a good deal. Christopher's eyes were lavender in color.

"Yes," Anna said. "He's the good-looking one in the family."

"I quite disagree!" Ariadne exclaimed, looking surprised.

"Gentlemen must compliment you all the time on the shade of your eyes."

Then Ariadne blushed and looked down, and Anna's heart skipped a beat. It wasn't possible, she told herself. There was simply no chance that the Inquisitor's beautiful daughter was . . . like her. That she would look at another girl's eyes and note their color as lovely instead of simply asking her what fabrics she wore to bring out their shade best.

"I'm afraid I am quite behind on my training," Ariadne said. "Perhaps we could . . . train together?"

"Yes," Anna said, maybe too quickly. "Yes . . . of course. If you . . ."

"You may find me clumsy." Ariadne twisted her hands together.

"I'm sure I won't," Anna said. "But that is the point of training, in any case. It is a delicate thing, training, despite the obvious violence, of course."

"You will have to be delicate with me, then," Ariadne said very softly.

Just as Anna thought she might faint, the doors opened and Inquisitor Bridgestock came in, with Cecily, Gabriel, and Christopher in tow. The Lightwoods looked vaguely exhausted. Anna was conscious of her mother's eyes on her—a sharp and thoughtful look.

". . . and we have our map collection . . . ah. Ariadne. Still in here, of course. Ariadne is a fiendish reader."

"Absolutely *fiendish*." Ariadne smiled. "Anna and I were just discussing my training. I thought it would be sensible to partner with another girl."

"Very sensible," Bridgestock said. "Yes. A very good idea.

You shall be partners. Anyway, Lightwood, we'll look at the maps at some point. Now, Ariadne, come into the parlor. I'd like you to play the piano for our guests."

Ariadne looked up at Anna.

"Partners," she said.

"Partners," Anna replied.

It was only on the way home that Anna realized that Ariadne had asked her to the library and not shown her a single book.

"Did you like young Ariadne Bridgestock?" said Cecily as the Lightwoods' carriage rumbled home through the dark streets of the city.

"I thought her very amiable," said Anna, looking out the window at London sparkling in the vast night. She longed to be out there among the earthbound stars, walking in the streets of Soho, living a life of music and adventure and dancing. "Very pretty, too."

Cecily tucked a stray lock of hair back behind her daughter's ear. In surprise, Anna looked at her mother for a moment—there was a little sadness in Cecily's eyes, though she couldn't have guessed why. Perhaps she was simply tired after being bored by the Inquisitor all night. Papa, for instance, was quite asleep in the other corner of the carriage, and Christopher was leaning against him, blinking drowsily. "She isn't nearly as pretty as you."

"*Mother,*" Anna said in exasperation, and turned back to the carriage window.

Under the arches of the railway viaduct, near the south end of London Bridge, a large gathering was taking place.

It was midsummer, so the sun set over London at nearly ten

o'clock. This meant the time to sell at the Shadow Market was reduced, and the whole place had a bit of a frenzied air. There was steam and smoke and flapping silks. Hands reached out, shoving wares under shoppers' noses—gems and trinkets, books, pendants, powders, oils, games and toys for Downworlder children, and items that could not be classified. There was a hum of smells. The tang of the river and the smoke from the trains overhead mixed with the remains of the day's produce from the mundane market—squashed produce, bits of meat, the odor wafting from oyster barrels. Vendors burned incense, which tangled with spices and perfumes. The miasma could be overpowering.

Brother Zachariah moved through the crush of stalls, immune to the smells and the crowding. Many Downworlders drew back at the approach of the Silent Brother. He had been coming here for weeks now to meet Ragnor Fell. Tonight, he also glanced around to see if he spotted the vendor he had seen on one of his previous visits. The stall he was looking for could move on its own; it had feet like a chicken. The woman behind it was an elderly faerie woman with a wild mass of hair. She sold colorful potions, and Matthew Fairchild had purchased one and given it to his mother. It had taken all of Jem's efforts to bring Charlotte back from death's door. She had not been the same since, nor had Matthew.

The stall was not present tonight; neither, it seemed, was Ragnor. He was about to take a final turn around the Market before departing when he saw someone he knew bent over a stall of books. The man had a shock of white hair and striking purple eyes. It was Malcolm Fade.

"Is that you, James Carstairs?" he said.

How are you, my friend?

Malcolm simply smiled. There was always something a little sad about Malcolm: Jem had heard gossip about a tragic love affair with a Shadowhunter who had chosen to be an Iron Sister rather than be with the one she loved. Jem knew that for some, the Law was more important than love. Even as he was now, he could not understand it. He would have given anything to be with the one he loved.

Anything except that which was more sacred than Jem's own life: Tessa's life, or Will's.

"How goes your quest?" said Malcolm. "Has Ragnor turned up any information for you about a certain demon you've been seeking?"

Jem gave Malcolm a quelling look; he preferred that not too many people knew of the quest he had undertaken.

"Malcolm! I have the book you wanted!" A warlock woman carrying a book bound in yellow velvet strode up to Malcolm.

"Thank you, Leopolda," said Malcolm.

The woman stared at Jem's face. Jem was used to this. Though he was a Silent Brother, his lips and eyes had not been sewn shut. He did not see or speak as humans did, but the fact that without runes he could have done so seemed to distress some people more than the sight of a Silent Brother who had bound himself less reluctantly to the quiet dark.

We have not met.

"No," the woman replied. "We have not. My name is Leopolda Stain. I make a visit here from Vienna."

She had a German accent and a soft, purring voice.

"This is Brother Zachariah," Malcolm said.

She nodded. There was no hand extended, but she continued to stare.

"You must forgive me," she said. "We do not often see Silent Brothers in our Market. London is a strange place to me. The Market in Vienna is not so bustling. It is in the Wienerwald, under the trees. Here, you are under this railway. It is quite a different experience."

"Zachariah is not quite like other Silent Brothers," said Malcolm.

Leopolda seemed to conclude the study she was making of Jem's face and smiled.

"I must bid you a good night," she said. "It is good to see you, Malcolm. It has been too long, *mein Liebling*. Too long. And it has been most interesting to meet you, James Carstairs. Auf Wiedersehen."

She slipped away through the crowd. Jem watched her go. She had decided to call him James Carstairs, not Brother Zachariah, and the choice seemed deliberate. There were certainly many denizens of Downworld who knew his Shadowhunter name—it was no secret—but suddenly Jem felt like a butterfly under a pin, caught in the gaze of the lepidopterist.

Can you tell me about her? he asked Malcolm, who had returned to examining the book in his hand.

"Leopolda is a bit of an odd one," Malcolm said. "I met her while I was traveling in Vienna. I don't think she leaves her city often. She seems to get around with some famous mundanes. She is . . ."

He hesitated.

Yes?

". . . more connected, I suppose, to her demon side than her human side than most of us are. More than me, certainly. She makes me feel uneasy. I'm glad that you came over. I was looking for a way to politely escape."

Jem looked in the direction that Leopolda had gone. Someone more connected to the demon side. . . .

That was someone he might need to speak with. Or watch.

Anna lay in her bed, eyes closed, trying to will herself to slumber. In her mind, she was dancing again. She wore her imaginary finest evening wear—a suit of deep gray, a waistcoat of sunny yellow with matching gloves. On her arm was Ariadne, as she had been tonight, in the blue dress.

Sleep was not coming. She pushed herself out of bed and went to the window. The night was warm and close. She had to do something with herself. Her brother's clothes were still in her wardrobe. She picked them out and smoothed them on the bed. She had planned on returning them, but . . .

Who would miss them? Not Christopher. Their laundress might, but no one would question that Christopher might simply *lose* his trousers, possibly in the middle of a crowded dance floor. And the older clothes—he wouldn't need them, not at the rate he was growing. The trousers were too long, but they could be hemmed. The shirt could be nipped in at the back. A few simple stitches were all it would take.

Anna was not a natural seamstress, but like all Shadowhunters, she possessed the basic skills to repair gear. She couldn't have made lace or done precise tailoring, but she could get this job done. She tacked his shirt and waistcoat in the back to make them fit and flatter her torso. The jacket was a bit more complex, requiring tucks on the back and the side. The shoulders were a bit wrong, and the effect a bit triangular, but all in all it was a passable effort. She practiced her walk in the fitted trousers, now that they no longer scraped the ground.

She had always loved gear as a child, its easy maneuverability, the way it allowed her to move unfettered. She had always been surprised that other girls, unlike her, didn't resent being pressed back into dresses and skirts when training was over. That they didn't resent the loss of freedom.

But it was more than the comfort of the clothes. In silks and ruffles Anna felt silly, as if she were pretending to be someone she was not. When she wore dresses out on the street, she was ignored as a gawky girl, or stared at by men in a way she did not like. She had been out in her brother's clothes only twice, both times late at night—but oh, women looked at her then, smiling women, conspiratorial women, women who knew that in donning the clothes of men, Anna walked in their power and their privilege. They looked at her soft lips, her long eyelashes, her blue eyes; they looked at her hips in tight trousers, the curve of her breasts under a man's cotton shirt, and their eyes spoke to her in the secret language of women: *You have taken their power for your own. You have stolen fire from the gods. Now come and make love to me, as Zeus made love to Danaë, in a shower of gold.*

In her mind's eye, Anna bent to take Ariadne's hand in hers, and the hand seemed real.

"You are so beautiful tonight," she said to Ariadne. "You are the most beautiful girl I have ever seen."

"And you," Ariadne answered in her mind, "are the most handsome person I have ever known."

The next day, Anna spent two hours writing a note to Ariadne that ended up reading:

Dear Ariadne,

It was very nice to meet you. I hope we can train together sometime. Please do pay a call.

Regards,

Anna Lightwood

Two entire hours for that, and a pile of drafts. Time no longer had meaning, and might never have meaning again.

In the afternoon, she had plans to meet her cousins James, Lucie, and Thomas, along with Matthew Fairchild. James, Matthew, Thomas, and Christopher were inseparable, and always meeting at a house or a hideout. They were invading her aunt Sophie and uncle Gideon's home today. Anna attended their little gatherings only on occasion, as did Lucie—the girls had many occupations to amuse themselves with; today, she desperately needed something to do, something to moor her mind in place, to keep her from fighting and pacing her room.

She walked with Christopher, who was excitedly talking of some kind of device that would fly through the air by means of four rotating blades. It sounded like he was describing a mechanical insect. Anna made noises that indicated she was listening although she was most assuredly not.

It was not far to their cousins' house. Her cousins Barbara and Eugenia were in the morning room. Barbara was stretched out on a sofa, while Eugenia was furiously working at a bit of needlepoint as if she truly hated it and the only way she could express her hatred was by stabbing the stretched cloth with the needle as vigorously as she could.

Anna and Christopher went up to the rooms that had been set aside for the use of Sophie and Gideon's children. James was there, sitting on his window seat, reading. Lucie was sitting at the desk, scribbling away. Tom was throwing a knife at the opposite wall.

Christopher greeted everyone and immediately sat down in the corner with a book. Anna dropped down next to Lucie.

"How's Cordelia?" she asked.

"Oh, she's wonderful! I was just writing to her quickly before Thomas helps me go over my Persian lesson." Lucie was always writing to her future *parabatai*, Cordelia Carstairs. Lucie was always writing. Lucie could write in a room full of people talking, screaming, singing. Anna was sure that Lucie could probably write in the middle of battle. Anna approved of this highly—it was very good to see two girls so devoted to each other, even platonically. Women should value other women, even if society often did not.

Ariadne came into her mind again.

"What's wrong, Anna?" James said.

He was looking at her curiously. Anna loved all her cousins, but she had a very soft spot for James. He had been a somewhat awkward young boy, gentle and quiet and bookish. He had grown up into a young man Anna could see was extraordinarily handsome, like his father. He had a soft fall of the Herondale black hair; from his mother, he had inherited his demonic trait—his inhuman golden eyes. Anna had always thought they were rather pretty, though Christopher had told her that James had been teased relentlessly at the Academy because of them. It was the teasing that prompted Matthew to get the explosives and Christopher to arrange for a wing of the building to blow up.

It was honorable to defend your friends, your *parabatai*. Anna was proud of them for doing it. She would have done the same. James had been such a shy, delightful little boy—it made Anna furious to think that he had been mocked. He was older now, given a bit more to brooding and staring into the distance, but still kind under it all.

"Nothing," she said. "I just . . . need a new book to read."

"A most sensible request," James said, swinging his long legs off his reading perch. "What sort of book? Fortunately, Aunt Sophie and Uncle Gideon have a respectable collection. Adventure? History? Romance? Poetry?"

All the younger set were fearfully bookish. Anna put it down to Uncle Will and Aunt Tessa's influence. They seldom let one leave the Institute without a book they felt one simply must read.

Now that they were talking about this, perhaps this would be useful in talking to Ariadne. She was a fiendish reader, after all.

"I'm training with someone new," Anna said. "Her name is Ariadne. She does quite a lot of reading, so—"

"Ah! Ariadne. That's a name from mythology. We could start you on a course of that. Would you like to begin with *The Golden Bough*, by Frazer? There's a new edition of three volumes. Unless you want to start with the basics. There's always Lemprière's *Bibliotheca Classica*. . . ."

James flipped gracefully through the books on the wall. He was an accomplished fighter and excellent dancer. Perhaps it was these traits, combined with the fact that he was growing into his looks, that explained why he seemed to suddenly be so popular with girls. He couldn't walk through a room of them without them sighing and giggling. Anna supposed she was pleased for him, or would be if he ever noticed it was happening.

He had soon plucked a dozen books from the shelf, passing one to Christopher almost as an afterthought. A silver bracelet flashed upon his wrist as he held his arm out—a love gift? Anna wondered. Perhaps one of the sighing gigglers had attracted his interest after all. Anna supposed she ought to be more charitable toward them—she felt herself on the verge of sighing and giggling over Ariadne at any moment.

The door flew open, and Matthew Fairchild entered the room and draped himself dramatically over the back of a chair. "Good afternoon, you wonderful bunch of villains. James, why are you clearing the shelves?"

"Anna asked me for something to read," James said, surveying a table of contents with a furious eye. He set the book aside.

"Anna? Reading? What dark magic is this?"

"I am hardly an illiterate," Anna said, throwing an apple at him. He caught it easily and smiled. Matthew was normally very fastidious. He and Anna often spoke of gentlemen's fashion together, but today Anna noticed that his hair was a bit wild and one of the buttons on his waistcoat was undone. These were small things, to be sure, but on Matthew, they spoke of something larger.

"What is your interest?" Matthew asked.

"Is it a crime to want to become more literate?"

"Not at all," Matthew said. "I love literature. In fact, I've found a marvelous place. It's a salon, full of writers and poets. But it is a bit . . . disreputable."

Anna cocked her head in interest.

"Here we go," James said, bringing over a pile of a dozen or so books and setting it down with a heavy thump. "Do any of these appeal? Have a look and see. Of course, I can recommend others. Wait. No. Not these. Not these."

He scooped the books away and returned to the shelves. James was clearly absorbed in his task. Christopher was happily reading his book, which had a horribly scientific title. Lucie and Thomas were at the desk, Thomas helping Lucie go over some phrases: Lucie was learning for Cordelia, and Tom liked languages, since he spoke Spanish with Uncle Gideon and Welsh with his cousins. Angel bless their sweet studious souls, none of them seemed likely to hear Anna and Matthew hatching a dark plot. Nevertheless, Matthew pitched his voice very low.

"Why don't I come and get you at midnight," Matthew said. "We can go together. I could use a companion who knows how to have a bit of fun. You might need a disguise, though. No reputable young lady walks the streets of London at midnight."

"Oh," Anna said. "I think I can manage something."

Just before midnight, as promised, Anna heard a tapping at her bedroom window. Matthew Fairchild was there, dancing along the edge. Anna threw it open.

"My my!" he said approvingly. "Are those Christopher's?"

Anna had dressed herself in her brother's clothes. The sewing had helped a good deal.

"A disguise," she said simply.

He laughed, spinning carelessly on the sill. She could see he had been drinking—his reflexes were slow, and he only caught himself a half second before tumbling back out to the ground.

"They suit you better than they suit him, but still . . . we need to get you something nicer than that. Here."

He pulled the ascot from his neck and handed it to her.

"I insist," he said. "I could never let a lady go out in inferior menswear."

Anna felt herself exhaling slowly and smiling as she put on the tie. The two of them jumped from her window, landing noiselessly on the courtyard in front of the house.

"Where is this place?" Anna said.

"A nefarious corner of Soho," he said with a smile.

"Soho!" Anna was delighted. "How did you find out about it?"

"Oh, just through my wanderings."

"You do a lot of those."

"I have a periphrastic soul."

Matthew was more drunk than he had first appeared. He rolled back on his heels and spun around the occasional lamppost as they walked. He had been like this a lot in recent weeks—what was fun and light about Matthew had taken on an edge. On some level, she felt a bit of worry rising. But this was Matthew, and he did not do well under confinement. Perhaps the summer night had just gotten his spirits particularly high.

The house Matthew took Anna to was deep in the warren of Soho, off Brewer Street. It was painted black, with a green door.

"You'll like it here," Matthew said, smiling at Anna.

The door was opened by a tall, pale man in a maroon frock coat.

"Fairchild," he said, looking at Matthew. "And . . ."

"Fairchild's good friend," Matthew replied.

Anna could feel the intelligence of the vampire's gaze, as he took her in for a long time. He seemed intrigued, both by her and by Matthew, though his expression was unreadable.

At last he stepped aside and allowed them in.

"You see?" Matthew said. "No one can resist our company."

The hall was utterly dark—the fanlight had been covered in a velvet drape. The only light came from candles. The house was decorated in a style that Anna thoroughly approved of—heavy green paper run through with gold, velvet curtains and furniture. It smelled of cigars and strange, tiny, rose-colored cigarettes and gin. The room was crowded with a mix of Downworlders and mundanes, all elaborately dressed.

Anna noticed many people taking in the sight of her in her men's clothing and nodding appreciatively. The men seemed pleased or amused, the women either admiring or—interested. Quite a few raked Anna boldly with their eyes, their gazes clinging to the feminine body revealed by her fitted clothes. It was as if in casting off dresses she had cast off society's expectation of a woman's modesty and could allow herself to be admired, desired. Her soul soared with new confidence: she felt herself a gorgeous creature, neither a gentleman nor a lady. A gentlewoman, she thought, and winked at one of the only people she recognized: the werewolf Woolsey Scott, head of the Praetor Lupus. He wore a bottle-green smoking jacket and was puffing away on a hookah pipe while holding court for a cluster of fascinated mundanes.

"Of course," Anna heard him say, "they had a difficult time getting my bathtub into one of the tree houses, but I would hardly leave it behind. One must always bring one's own bathtub."

"That's Somebody Somebody Yeats over there," Matthew said, indicating a tall, bespectacled man. "He read a new work the last time I was here."

"And it was wonderful," said a voice. It came from a woman sitting near where Matthew and Anna stood. She was a stunning warlock with the scaled skin of a snake, colored silver, almost opalescent. Her long green hair tumbled over her shoulders and was strung through with a fine gold mesh. She wore a red gown that clung to her frame. She tipped her head up elegantly toward Matthew and Anna.

"Are all London Shadowhunters so handsome as you?" she asked. She had a German accent.

"No," Anna said simply.

"Definitely not," Matthew agreed.

The warlock smiled.

"Your London Shadowhunters are more interesting than ours," she said. "Ours are very tedious. Yours are beautiful and amusing."

Someone grumbled something at this, but the rest of the group laughed appreciatively.

"Do sit and join us," the woman said. "I am Leopolda Stain."

Most of the people around Leopolda seemed to be fawning mundanes, like the group around Woolsey Scott. One man wore a black robe covered in symbols Anna did not recognize. Matthew and Anna sat down on the rug, against a pile of tasseled pillows that served as a sofa. Next to them was a woman wearing a gold turban scarf pinned with a sapphire.

"Are you two of the Chosen?" she asked Matthew and Anna.

"Certainly," Matthew said.

"Ah. I could tell from the way Leopolda reacted to you. She is quite wonderful, is she not? She is from Vienna and knows simply *everyone*—Freud, Mahler, Klimt, Schiele. . . ."

"Marvelous," Matthew said. He probably did think it was marvelous—Matthew adored art and artists.

"She's going to help us," the woman said. "Obviously, we've had such troubles here. Why, Crowley wasn't even recognized here in London! He had to go to the Ahathoor Temple in Paris to be initiated to the grade of Adeptus Minor, which I'm sure you heard about."

"The moment it happened," Matthew lied.

Anna bit her lip and looked down to keep herself from laughing. It was always amusing to meet mundanes who had fantastical notions of how magic worked. Leopolda, she noticed, was smiling indulgently at the entire group, like they were adorable but somewhat dim-witted children.

"Well," the woman continued, "I was an Adept of the Isis-Urania temple, and I can assure you that I was adamant that—"

This was interrupted by a man standing in the middle of the room and raising a glass of something green.

"My friends!" he said. "I demand that we remember Oscar. You must raise your glasses!"

There was a general noise of agreement, and glasses were raised. The man began to recite Oscar Wilde's "The Ballad of Reading Gaol." Anna was struck by one of the stanzas:

Some love too little, some too long,
Some sell, and others buy;
Some do the deed with many tears,
And some without a sigh:
For each man kills the thing he loves,
Yet each man does not die.

She didn't quite know what it meant, but the spirit of it haunted her. It seemed to have an even more pointed effect on Matthew, who slumped down.

"It is a rotten world that would allow a man like Wilde to die," Matthew said. There was a hardness in his voice that was new and a bit alarming.

"You're sounding a bit dire," Anna said.

"It's true," he replied. "Our greatest poet, and he died in

poverty and obscurity, not so long ago. They threw him in jail because he loved another man. I do not think love can be wrong."

"No," Anna said. She had always known that she loved women the way she was expected to love men. That she found women beautiful and desirable, while men were good friends, brothers-in-arms, but nothing more. She had never pretended otherwise, and her close friends all seemed to accept this about her as a known fact.

But it was true that though Matthew and the others often joked with her about slaying the hearts of pretty girls, it was not something she and her mother had ever talked about. She recalled her mother touching her hair fondly in the carriage. What did Cecily truly think of her odd daughter?

Not now, she told herself. She turned to the woman in the turban, who had been trying to get her attention. "Yes?"

"My dear," the woman said. "You must be sure to be here in a week's time. The faithful will be rewarded, I promise you. The ancient ones, so long hidden from us, shall be revealed."

"Of course," Anna said, blinking. "Yes. Wouldn't miss it for the world."

While she was simply making conversation, Anna found that she would like to return to this place. She had come here dressed as she was, and she had received only approbation. In fact, she was sure that one of the vampire girls was examining her with a look that was not entirely wholesome. And Leopolda, the beautiful warlock, had not taken her eyes from Anna. Had Anna's mind and soul not been full of Ariadne . . .

Well, it could only be left to the imagination.

* * *

As Matthew and Anna left the house that night, they did not notice a figure across the street, standing in the shadows.

Jem recognized Matthew at once but was confused at first as to who was with him. The person resembled his *parabatai*, Will Herondale—not Will as he was now, but Will at seventeen, with his confident swagger and upturned chin. But that could not be. And the person was obviously not James, Will's son.

It took him several minutes to realize that the young man was not a young man at all. It was Anna Lightwood, Will's niece. She had inherited the dark hair and the profile from the Herondale side of her family, and clearly, she had inherited her uncle's swagger. For a moment Jem felt a pang in his heart. It was like seeing his friend as a young man again, as the two of them had been when they lived at the Institute together and fought side by side, as they had been when Tessa Gray first arrived at their door.

Was it really so long ago?

Jem shook the thought loose and focused on the present. Anna was in some sort of disguise, and she and Matthew had just been at a Downworlder gathering with a warlock he had come to observe. He had no idea what they were doing there.

A full week passed. A full week of Anna running for the post, looking from the window, walking partway to Cavendish Square before turning back. A lifetime. It was agony, and just as it was turning to acceptance, Anna was called downstairs early Friday morning to find Ariadne waiting for her in a yellow dress and a white hat.

"Good morning," Ariadne said. "Why aren't you ready?"

"Ready?" Anna said, her throat gone dry at the sudden appearance of Ariadne.

"To train!"

"I—"

"Good morning, Ariadne!" Cecily Lightwood said, coming in with Alexander.

"Oh!" Ariadne's eyes lit up when she saw the baby. "Oh, I must hold him—I simply adore babies."

The appearance of Alexander bought Anna enough time to scramble upstairs, catch her breath, splash water on her face, and collect her gear. Five minutes later, Anna was seated next to Ariadne in the Bridgestock carriage, rumbling toward the Institute. They were alone now, close to each other in the warm carriage. The smell of Ariadne's orange-blossom perfume wafted up and wrapped around Anna.

"Did I disturb you?" Ariadne said. "I had simply hoped . . . that you might be free to train with me. . . ." She looked worried. "I hope I did not presume. Are you angry?"

"No," Anna replied. "I could never be angry with you."

Anna tried to make it sound light, but a husky note of truth rang through.

"Good." Ariadne looked radiantly pleased at that and crossed her hands on her lap. "I would hate to displease you."

When they arrived at the Institute, Anna changed much more quickly than Ariadne. She waited in the training room, nervously pacing, taking knives from the walls and throwing them to steady her nerves.

Just training. Simple training.

"You have a good arm," Ariadne said.

Ariadne was stunning in her dresses; the gear revealed something else. She was still feminine, with her long hair and lush curves, but unencumbered by pounds of fabric, she moved with grace and speed.

"How would you like to begin?" Anna said. "Do you have a preferred weapon? Or should we do some climbing? Work on the beam?"

"Whatever you think is best," Ariadne replied.

"Shall we start with blades?" Anna said, taking one from the wall.

Whatever Ariadne had been doing in Idris, it did not involve much training. She had been accurate in that. When she threw, her arm was weak. Anna came up and guided her, forcing herself to maintain her composure as she took Ariadne's hand in hers and guided the toss. Ariadne was surprisingly good at climbing, but once on the ceiling beam, she took a bad tumble. Anna jumped underneath and caught her neatly.

"Oh, very impressive!" Ariadne said, smiling.

Anna stood there for a moment, Ariadne in her arms, unsure of what to do. There was something in Ariadne's gaze, in the way she was looking at Anna . . . as if mesmerized. . . .

How did she ask? How did this happen with someone like Ariadne?

It was too much.

"A very good attempt," Anna said, gently setting Ariadne on her feet. "Just . . . watch your footing."

"I think I've had enough of that for today," Ariadne said. "How does one have fun in London?"

Oh, so many ways.

"Well," Anna said. "There is the theater, and the zoo is—"

"No." Ariadne took hold of one of the pillars and gently spun around it. "*Fun.* Surely you know a place."

"Well," Anna said, searching her mind frantically, "I know

a place full of writers and poets. It is quite louche. It is in Soho and starts after midnight."

"Then I assume you will be taking me," Ariadne said, eyes sparkling. "I will wait for you by my window at midnight tonight."

The wait that evening was excruciating.

Anna picked at her dinner and watched the clock across the room. Christopher was forming his carrots into a pyramid and working something out in his head. Her mother was feeding Alexander. Anna was counting her heartbeats. She had to try not to appear conspicuous. She spent some time in the family room with her baby brother; she picked up a book and cast an eye blankly over the pages. By nine she was able to stretch and say she was going to have a bath and retire.

Back in her room, Anna waited until she heard the other members of the household go to bed before changing her clothes. She had taken the time to clean her outfit and mend it as best she could. When she dressed, she looked dapper and dangerous. She had decided now that this was how she would dress if she slipped out on adventures, even to meet Ariadne.

She climbed from her window at eleven, sliding down a rope, which she tossed back inside. She could have jumped, but it had taken her some time to arrange her hair under the hat correctly. She walked to Fitzrovia, and this time she did not bother to avoid the pools of streetlight. She wanted to be seen. She straightened her back and widened her step. The more she walked, the more she felt herself slipping into the gait, the attitude. She tipped her hat to a lady passing in a carriage; the lady smiled and looked away shyly.

Anna knew now that she was never going to go back to wearing dresses. She had always loved the theater, always loved the idea of a performance. The first time she had worn her brother's clothes it had been a performance, but with each time she did it again, it became more her reality. She was not a man and did not want to be—but why should men get to keep all the good pieces of masculinity for themselves because of an accident of birth? Why should she, Anna, not wear their clothes, and their power and confidence too?

You have stolen fire from the gods.

Anna's swagger faded a bit as she turned the corner onto Cavendish Square. Would Ariadne accept her like this? It had felt so right a moment before, but now . . .

She almost turned back, but then she forced herself on.

The Bridgestock house was dark. Anna looked up, fearing that Ariadne had been teasing. But then she saw a flick of a curtain, and the sash window opened. Ariadne looked down at her.

And she smiled.

A rope sailed out of the window, and Ariadne slid down it, more gracefully than she had in training. She wore a light blue dress, which fluttered as she dropped.

"Oh my," she said, walking up to Anna. "You look . . . quite devastating."

Anna would not have traded the way Ariadne looked at her in that moment for a thousand pounds.

They took a carriage to Soho. Though she and Ariadne were both glamoured to hide their Marks from mundanes, Anna enjoyed the look she got from the driver when he realized the handsome young gent in his cab was a handsome young lady. He doffed his cap as she and Ariadne alighted from the cab, muttering something about "young people these days."

They arrived at the house, but this time, when Anna knocked on the door, the person answering was less accommodating. He looked at Anna, then at Ariadne.

"No Shadowhunters," he said.

"That was not your previous policy," Anna said. She noticed that the windows were now covered by the heavy velvet curtains.

"Go home, Shadowhunters," he said. "I have made myself clear."

The door was slammed in their faces.

"Now I am curious," Ariadne said. "We must go in, don't you think?"

Ariadne certainly had a wicked streak in her that complemented her bubbly cheerfulness, a love of things that were just a bit . . . naughty. Anna felt she should encourage this impulse.

There was no clear point of access on the flat front of the house, so they moved down to the end of the street and found a narrow alley backing the houses. This was bricked up to the third floor. There was, however, a drainpipe. Anna got a hold on this and made the climb. She could not reach the third-story windows from there, but she could get onto the roof. She looked down to see Ariadne climbing up after her, again showing more skill than she had in the training room. They managed to pry open an attic window. From there they crept down the winding stairs, Anna first, with Ariadne behind. Ariadne kept a hand on Anna's waist, possibly for guidance as they walked, or . . .

Anna would not think about it.

They were burning a great deal of incense in the house tonight. It hummed through the hall and up the stairs, almost causing Anna to cough. It was not a pleasant smell—it was acrid and hard. She detected wormwood, mugwort, and something else—something with a metallic edge, like blood. The group was unusually quiet. There was only one voice, speaking low. A female voice with the Germanic accent. She heard the incantations.

Anna knew a summoning when she heard one. She turned to Ariadne, who had a look of concern on her face.

Anna reached for her seraph blade and murmured, "*Adriel,*" indicating to Ariadne that she would go ahead and look. Ariadne nodded. Anna crept down the hall. She pushed back a bit of the velvet curtain that closed off the main sitting room. Everyone there was turned toward the center of the room, so mostly she saw backs and the faint flicker of candlelight.

Anna could make out the form of a circle drawn on the floor. The woman in the turban was just on the edge of it, her face tilted up in ecstasy. She wore a long black robe and held a book with a pentagram over her head. The book was bound in something odd. It looked like skin.

Towering above all was the warlock Leopolda, her eyes closed and her arms raised. She held a curved dagger in her hands. She was chanting in a demonic language. Then she looked to the woman in the turban and nodded. The woman took a long step into the circle. Green flame flashed all around, making the mundanes murmur and back away. There were not, Anna noticed, many Downworlders present.

"Come forth!" cried the woman. "Come forth, beautiful death. Come forth, creature, that we may worship you! Come forth!"

There was a terrible smell, and the room filled with darkness. Anna knew she could no longer stand still.

"Get out!" she yelled, pushing her way into the room. "All of you!"

The group had no time to be surprised. A massive Ravener demon burst forth out of the darkness. The woman in the turban went down on her knees before it.

"My lord," she said. "My dark—"

The Ravener whipped its tail around and easily severed the woman's turbaned head from her neck. The assembled let up a collective scream, and there was a rush for the door. Anna had to fight her way toward the demon. The Ravener was making short work of the woman's remains.

Leopolda Stain simply looked on the scene with gentle amusement.

It was hard to fight a demon in such close quarters without killing all the people as well. Anna shoved several mundanes aside and launched herself at the demon, her seraph blade raised. The demon made an angry screeching noise. This was because something had just struck out one of its eyes. Ariadne was next to her, holding an electrum whip and smiling.

"Very good aim," Anna said as the angry demon wheeled around. It made a leap and broke through one of the front windows. Anna and Ariadne went right after it, Anna making the jump easily in her new clothes. Ariadne went through the door, but she was fast on her feet, snapping her whip in the air. Between them, they quickly made short work of the beast.

There was a strange crackling noise. They turned to see that the demon had not come alone—a cluster of smaller Raveners poured through the broken window, their jaws dripping green liquid. Anna and Ariadne turned to face them, weapons drawn. A small Ravener jumped forward first. Ariadne sliced through it with her whip. Another sprang out, but as soon as it appeared, a staff swung through the air next to Anna, bashing its head in. She turned as it disappeared, to find herself looking at Brother Zachariah. She was well acquainted with her uncle's former *parabatai*, though she had no idea what he was doing here.

How many? he asked.

"I don't know," she said as another demon came forth from the house. "They're coming from a circle inside the house. There are people hurt."

He nodded and indicated that he would proceed inside, while Anna and Ariadne fought outside. One of the creatures was about to descend on one of the fleeing mundanes. Anna jumped on its back, dodging its angrily swinging tail, and plunged her seraph blade into the back of its neck. The stunned mundane crab-crawled backward as the Ravener fell dead to the ground. She turned to look for Ariadne, who was laying waste to one of the Raveners, slicing her electrum whip through the air and then right through the demon's legs. Anna was surprised—the only other electrum whip she had ever seen was owned by the Consul, Charlotte Fairchild.

Ariadne and Anna stood back-to-back, fighting like *parabatai* might, their movements in sync. Though they were certainly not *parabatai*. It would be very wrong to feel about a *parabatai* the way Anna felt about Ariadne. There was no mistaking it, Anna thought, though it was an awkward revelation to have in the middle of a demon fight.

She was definitely in love with Ariadne Bridgestock.

* * *

Jem entered the house through the open door, his staff at the ready. The room was quiet. There was a tremendous amount of blood on the floor, and the torn remains of a human.

"Herein!" said a voice. "I was hoping you would come."

Jem turned. Leopolda Stain was sitting on a large brocade chair, holding the head of a woman in her lap. Jem raised his staff.

You have murdered innocent mundanes, Jem said.

"They slew themselves," Leopolda said. "They were playing with fire. They were burned. You know of such creatures. They believe they understand magic. They must come to understand its true nature. I do them a service. They will not call another demon. If I wanted to teach them a lesson, where's the harm? There is hellfire in me, but I do not think I am your chief concern."

Jem was torn. His instinct was to strike her down for what she had done, and yet . . .

"You hesitate, James Carstairs," she said with a smile.

My name is Brother Zachariah.

"You were James Carstairs, the Shadowhunter who was addicted to *yin fen.* You were acquainted with Axel Mortmain, the one they called the Magister, I think?"

At the sound of Mortmain's name, Jem lowered his staff.

"Ah," Leopolda said with a smile. "You remember dear Axel."

You knew him?

"Quite well," she said. "I know many things. I know a warlock helps run the Institute here, yes? Named Tessa Herondale. She is a Shadowhunter, and she can bear no Marks. She is married to your *parabatai.*"

Why are you asking me about Tessa? Jem said. It was as if cold fingers were touching his spine. He did not like this warlock. He did not like her interest in Tessa and Will.

"Because you have been in the Shadow Market, asking many questions about her. About her father. Her *demonic* father."

She let the head roll from her lap.

"As I said, I knew Mortmain," she said. "Since you have been asking about him and how Tessa was created, news has trickled back to me—one of his only remaining friends. I believe you are curious about how Mortmain created Tessa. You seek the demon he summoned to be her father. If you put your weapon away, perhaps we can have a conversation."

Jem did not set down his staff.

"She might not have been too curious about her demon father before"—Leopolda played with the gold netting in her hair—"but now that she has *children* . . . and those children show signs of their demon heritage . . . I imagine things are very different?"

Jem stood coldly stricken. It was as if she had reached into his mind and touched his memory. Standing on Blackfriars Bridge with Tessa on a cold January day. The fear on her face. *I do not want to trouble Will . . . but I worry so over Jamie and Lucie. . . . James despairs of his eyes, calls them doorways into Hell, as if he hates his own face, his own bloodline. If I but knew who my demon father was, perhaps I could know, prepare them and myself . . . and Will.* Jem had feared even then that it was a dangerous errand, that knowledge would gift them only further worries and doubts. But it was something Tessa had wanted for Will and the children, and he loved them all too much to say no.

"Your friend Ragnor's queries have finally borne fruit," said

Leopolda. "I know who Tessa's father was." She narrowed her eyes. "In exchange I only need something small. Just the smallest amount of blood from a living Shadowhunter. You will not even feel it. I was going to get it from the girl, the one who dresses as a boy. I like her very much. I would like to collect her, if I could."

You will stay away from her.

"Of course I will," Leopolda said. "I will help you as well. Just the smallest amount of blood, and I can tell you of Tessa Herondale's true father."

"Brother Zachariah!" he heard Anna yell.

Jem turned for one moment, and Leopolda moved toward him. He flung up his staff, knocking her backward. She let out a hiss and darted away faster than seemed possible. She lifted her curved blade.

"Do not toy with me, James Carstairs. Do you not want to know of your Tessa?"

There was another cry from outside. Jem had no choice. He ran in the direction of Anna's voice.

Outside, Anna and the other girl were in a fierce fight with at least six Raveners. They were pressed to the wall, fighting back-to-back. Jem swung out with his staff and brought it down on the back of the closest one. He continued swinging until Anna and the girl were able to regain some ground. Jem took down another, while Anna destroyed two at once with a long swing of her blade. There was but one Ravener left. It extended its spiked tail and pointed it at the other girl's chest. In a second, Anna was diving through the air, knocking the other girl out of the way. They rolled together, Anna's arms around the girl, shielding her. Jem struck out at this last demon, landing a blow on its head.

The street fell quiet. Anna was in the girl's arms, very still.

Anna. Jem raced over. The Shadowhunter girl was already tearing away Anna's sleeve to get to the wound. Anna hissed as the poison stung the surface of her skin.

Behind them, Leopolda stepped out of the house and began to simply walk away.

"I'm fine," Anna said. "Go after her, Ariadne."

The other girl, Ariadne, exhaled and sat back. "The poison did not enter your system. But it did get on your skin. We must wash the site with herbs, immediately. And your wound is deep. You will need several *iratzes.*"

The girl looked up at Jem.

"I'll take care of her," she said. "I am well trained in healing. I was taught by Silent Brothers while I lived in Idris. Anna's right. Go after the warlock."

You are sure? Anna will need an amissio, *a blood-replacement rune—*

"Quite sure," the girl said, easing Anna to her feet. "Believe me when I say Anna would rather lose a bit of blood than have her parents find out what we did tonight."

"Hear, hear," agreed Anna.

Take care of her, said Jem.

"I will." Ariadne spoke with a firm confidence, and from the way she was handling the wound, her words appeared true.

"Come," Ariadne said to Anna. "My house is not far. Can you walk?"

"With you," Anna said, "I can go anywhere."

Thus assured, Jem turned in the direction of Leopolda Stain.

* * *

They walked back to Ariadne's house, Anna occasionally leaning on her friend for support. The poison on her skin was starting to have an effect, which was a bit like having too much wine, too fast. She tried to keep herself steady. They were glamoured now, walking unseen through the street.

When they arrived, Ariadne let them in quietly through the front door. They took the stairs gently, so as not to wake anyone. Luckily, Ariadne's room was on the opposite side of the house from her parents' room. Ariadne led Anna in and shut the door.

Ariadne's room was like the person who inhabited it—perfumed, perfect, delicate. There were lace curtains on the large windows. The walls were papered in silver and rose, and there were fresh-cut lilacs and roses in vases around the room.

"Come," Ariadne said, leading Anna to her bureau, where there was a water basin. She removed Anna's jacket and pushed up her sleeve. Having mixed a few herbs into the basin, she poured the mixture over the wound, which stung.

"It is a nasty injury," Ariadne said, "but I am a good nurse."

She moistened a cloth and gently cleaned the wound with soft strokes, careful to wipe away any poison that had splashed on Anna's skin. Then she got her stele and drew an *amissio* rune to speed blood replacement and an *iratze* to encourage healing. The wound began to close.

Throughout all of this, Anna was silent, breathless. She did not feel pain. She felt only Ariadne's careful hands on her.

"Thank you," she finally said.

Ariadne set her stele down. "It is nothing. You sustained this wound while saving me. You stepped in front of me. You protected me."

"I would protect you always," Anna said.

Ariadne looked at Anna for a long moment. The only light came in through the pattern in the lace.

"My dress," Ariadne said softly. "I think it is quite ruined. I look a fright."

"Nonsense," Anna replied. Then, after a beat, she added, "You have never looked more beautiful."

"It has blood on it, and ichor. Help me remove it, please."

With trembling fingers, Anna undid the many buttons on the front of the dress, and it slid to the ground in a pile. Ariadne turned so that Anna could undo the stays of her corset. Ariadne wore a cotton chemise underneath, trimmed in delicate lace. Her chemise and bloomers were stark white against her brown skin. Her eyes glowed.

"You must rest a bit, Anna," Ariadne said. "You cannot leave right now. Come."

She took Anna by the hand and led her to the bed. Anna realized as she sank into it how exhausted she was from the fight, and also that she had never been so awake and alive.

"Lean back," Ariadne said, stroking Anna's hair.

Anna put her head down on the pillow. Her boots were gone. Her hair had come down, and she pushed it back impatiently.

"I would like to kiss you," Ariadne said. Her voice shook with a fear Anna understood all too well. Ariadne was afraid Anna was going to push her away, reject her, run screaming. But how could Ariadne not know how she felt? "Please, Anna, may I kiss you?"

Unable to speak, Anna nodded.

Ariadne leaned forward and pressed her lips to Anna's.

Anna had lived this moment in her mind a hundred times

or more. She did not know her body would grow so warm, that Ariadne would taste so sweet. She returned the kiss, then kissed Ariadne along her cheek, her chin, down her neck. Ariadne made a low sound of delight. She brought her lips up to Anna's again, and they fell back against the pillows. They were tangled together, laughing and warm, intent on only each other. The pain was gone, replaced by rapture.

During the day, the streets and alleys of Soho could be hard to navigate. At night, they became a dangerous and confusing warren. Jem kept his staff aloft. At this late hour, the only people about were drunkards and ladies of the night. The alleys smelled of refuse, and there was broken glass and the assorted detritus of a London day.

Jem made his way to a storefront on Wardour Street. He knocked, and the door was opened by two young werewolves, neither of whom seemed surprised to see him.

Woolsey Scott is expecting me.

They nodded and guided him through a dark and empty shop that sold buttons and ribbons and through a door. On the other side was a dimly lit but tastefully furnished room. Woolsey Scott was stretched out on a low divan. Sitting opposite him was Leopolda Stain, surrounded by a half a dozen more werewolves. She seemed calm and composed, and was even sipping from a cup of tea.

"Ah, Carstairs," Scott said. "Finally. I thought we'd be here all night."

Thank you, said Jem, *for looking after her for me.*

"It was no trouble," said Scott. He tipped his chin at Leopolda. "As you know, this one arrived a few weeks ago. We've been keeping an eye on her ever since. I didn't think she would go as far as she did tonight. Can't have her egging on idiot mundanes to raise demons. It's the sort of thing that inspires anti-Downworlder sentiment."

Leopolda seemed to take no offense at the way he spoke.

Woolsey rose to his feet. "You had said you wanted to speak with her," he said. "Shall I leave the matter with you?"

Yes, Jem said.

"Good. I have an appointment with a rather staggering bottle of red. I'm sure she won't cause any further fuss, will you, Leopolda?"

"Of course not," Leopolda said.

Scott nodded, and the werewolves left the room as one. Leopolda looked up at Jem and smiled.

"It is good to see you again," she said. "We were so rudely interrupted earlier."

You will tell me what you know of Tessa.

Leopolda reached over to a teapot on a low table and refilled her cup.

"These terrible beasts," she said, nodding at the door. "They handled me quite roughly. I would like to leave this place now."

You will not be leaving until you tell me what I want to know.

"Oh, I will. Your Tessa . . . and she was yours, wasn't she? I may not be able to see your eyes, but I can see it in your face."

Jem stiffened. He was no longer that boy, the young man who had planned a wedding to Tessa, who had loved her as much as his heart could bear. He loved her still, but he survived it by having put that young man away, by putting away his human loves as he had put away the violin. Instruments for another time, another life.

Still, there was no joy in being so cruelly reminded.

"I imagine her powers are great," Leopolda said, stirring her tea. "I envy her. Axel was . . . so very proud."

There was nothing but the sound of the spoon hitting the sides of the china cup. In the depths of his mind, Jem heard the murmuring of the other Silent Brothers. He ignored it. This was his mission alone.

Tell me of Tessa's father.

"The blood," she said. "You will give me the blood first. It is a very small amount."

That will never happen.

"No?" she said. "You know, I am merely the humble daughter of a Vetis demon, but your Tessa . . ."

She waited to see the effect on Jem.

"Yes," she said. "I know all. You will put out your arm. I will take the blood, I will tell you what you so wish to know, and I will leave. We will both be satisfied. I assure you, what I give you is so much more than I ask. It is a bargain of the highest order."

You do not have the advantages you think you have, Leopolda Stain, he said. *I have known you were here since you set foot on these shores. I knew you were a friend of Mortmain's. I know you want this blood to continue his works, and I will never allow that.*

Her lip curled. "But you are kind," she said. "You are famous for it. You will not hurt me."

Jem took his staff, spinning it between his hands, and held it balanced lightly between himself and Leopolda. He knew a hundred different ways to kill her with it. He could break her neck.

That was my Shadowhunter self, he said. *I have killed with this staff, though I prefer not to. Either you tell me what I wish to know, or you die. It is your choice.*

He saw, from the look in her eyes, that she believed him.

Tell me what I want to know, and I will let you go with your life.

Leopolda swallowed. "First, swear upon your Angel that you will allow me to leave tonight."

I swear upon the Angel.

Leopolda smiled a long, vulpine smile.

"The ritual that created your Tessa was magnificent," she said. "Such glory. I never thought such a thing could be done, mating a Shadowhunter with a demon. . . ."

Do not delay. Tell me.

"Your Tessa's father is a prince, the greatest of Eidolon demons. The most beautiful creature in any hell, for he has a thousand shapes."

A Prince of Hell? Jem had feared it. No wonder James could turn himself to smoke and Tessa herself could take any form, even that of an angel. A line of Nephilim whose blood was mixed with demonic royalty? There was no history of such impossible beings. Even now, he could not think of Tessa and her children as new and strange creations with incredible powers. They were simply people he loved beyond measure. *You are saying Tessa's father is a Prince of Hell?*

The Clave could never know. He could not tell them. His heart lurched. Could he tell Tessa? Would it be better for her to know or not?

"Indeed a prince," Leopolda said, "brother to Asmodeus and Sammael. What an honor to be born of him. Sooner or later, Jem Carstairs, blood will out, and such a beautiful power will blaze through this city."

She rose to her feet.

The greatest of Eidolons? I need more than that. What is his name?

She shook her head. "The price for the name is blood, James Carstairs, and if you will not pay it, another will."

She brought her hand out from behind her back and flung a handful of powder at Jem. Had his eyes not been protected by magic, it would likely have blinded him. As it was, he staggered back long enough for her to run past him to the door. She reached it in seconds and threw it open.

On the other side of it were two huge werewolves, flanking Woolsey Scott.

"As expected," Woolsey said, looking at Leopolda with contempt. "Kill her, boys. Let her be an example to others who would freely spill blood in our city."

Leopolda screamed and whirled on Jem, wide-eyed. "You said you would let me leave! You swore!"

Jem felt very weary. *I am not the one who is stopping you.*

She cried out as the werewolves, already half-transformed, flung themselves on her. Jem turned away while the sounds of ripping flesh and shrieks tore through the room.

The summer dawn came early. Ariadne was sleeping gently, and Anna heard the maid stirring downstairs. She had not slept yet, even after Ariadne had dropped off. Anna did not want to move from this warm spot. She played with the lace edges of the pillow and watched Ariadne's eyelashes flicker as if she were in the depths of a dream.

But the sky was turning from black to the soft peach color of sunrise. Soon there would be a maid at the door with a tray. Soon, life would intrude.

It would only hurt Ariadne if she were found here. It was her duty to leave this place.

She kissed Ariadne softly, so as not to wake her. Then she dressed and slipped out the sash window. The dark did not quite obscure her now as she walked through the misty London morning in her men's clothes. A few people turned their heads to get a second look at her, and she was fairly sure that some of those looks were admiring, even if she was mostly missing one of her sleeves and had lost her hat. She decided to take a circuitous route home, along Regent's Park. The colors were soft in the sunrise, the waters of the boating lake still. She felt friendship toward the ducks and the pigeons. She smiled at strangers.

This was what love was. It was total. It brought her together with everything. Anna barely cared if she made it home before someone would notice her missing. She wanted to feel like this forever—exactly this, this soft and fragrant and friendly morning, with the feel of Ariadne still on her skin. Her future, so confused before, was clear. She would be with Ariadne forever. They would travel the world, fight side by side.

Eventually, she had to walk toward her home, where she climbed up to her window with ease. She removed her brother's clothing and slipped into bed. Within seconds, she dropped into the easy embrace of sleep and felt herself back in Ariadne's arms.

She woke just before noon. Someone had brought her a tea tray and left it next to her bed. She drank the now-cold tea. She took a cool bath and examined the wound on her arm. The healing runes Ariadne had drawn had done their work. The area was still red and angry, but she could cover it with a shawl. She dressed in her plainest, most severely cut gown—so funny now, to be dressed as a girl—and put a silk shawl over her shoulders, winding it carefully over the damaged arm. She went downstairs. Her mother sat in a sunny corner of the sitting room, little Alexander on her lap.

"There you are," her mother said. "Are you ill?"

"No," Anna said. "I was foolish. I stayed up quite late reading a book."

"Now I know you are ill," her mother said with a smile, which Anna returned.

"I need to take a walk in the sunshine. It is such a lovely day. I shall go see Lucie and James, I think, and discuss my book with them."

Her mother gave her a curious look, but agreed.

Anna did not walk to the Herondale house. She turned instead toward Fitzrovia, stopping to buy a bunch of violets from an old woman selling them in the street. Her steps were light. The world was perfectly arranged, and all things and beings in it were worthy of love. Anna could have done anything in that moment—fought off a hundred demons at once, lifted a carriage over her head, danced on a wire. She passed along the pavements she had been on only hours before, back to her love.

At the house off Cavendish Square, Anna knocked once, then stood nervously on the step, looking up. Was Ariadne in her room? Would she look down?

The door was opened by the Bridgestocks' unsmiling servant.

"The family is receiving guests at the moment, Miss Lightwood. Perhaps you would like to wait in the—"

At that moment, the reception-room door opened, and

the Inquisitor walked out with a young man who had familiar features and red hair—Charles Fairchild, Matthew's brother. Anna rarely saw Charles. He was always somewhere, usually Idris. He and the Inquisitor were mid-conversation.

"Oh," Inquisitor Bridgestock said, seeing Anna. "Miss Lightwood. How fortuitous. Do you know Charles Fairchild?"

"Anna!" Charles said with a warm smile. "Yes, of course."

"Charles will be the interim head of the Paris Institute," the Inquisitor said.

"Oh," Anna said. "Congratulations. Matthew didn't tell me."

Charles rolled his eyes. "I imagine he thinks of such things as political aspirations as crass and bourgeois. What are you doing here, anyway?"

"Anna and Ariadne have been training together," the Inquisitor explained.

"Ah," Charles said. "Excellent. You must visit us in Paris sometime, Anna."

"Oh," Anna said, not knowing what "us" Charles was talking about. "Yes. Thank you. I shall."

Ariadne stepped out of the morning room. She wore a dress of fresh peony pink, and her hair was coiled on her head. On seeing Anna, her cheeks flushed. Charles Fairchild stepped ahead with Inquisitor Bridgestock, and Ariadne stepped up to her.

"I did not expect to see you so soon," she said to Anna in a low voice.

"How could I keep away?" Anna replied. Ariadne was wearing her perfume again, and it wafted lightly through the air. Orange blossom was Anna's favorite scent now.

"Perhaps we can meet later," Ariadne said. "We are—"

"I will be back again in a year's time," Charles said, concluding whatever conversation he was having with Inquisitor Bridgestock. He returned to them, bowed, took Ariadne's hand, and kissed it formally.

"I hope to see more of you when I next return," he said. "It should not be more than a year."

"Yes," Ariadne replied. "I would like that very much."

"Anna!" Mrs. Bridgestock said. "We have a parrot. You must see it. Come."

Suddenly, Anna found that Mrs. Bridgestock had hooked her by the arm and was gently leading her into one of the other rooms, where there was a large multicolored parrot in a massive gold cage. The bird cawed loudly on their approach.

"It is a very nice bird," Anna said, confused, as Mrs. Bridgestock shut the door behind them.

"I do apologize, Anna," she said. "I just needed to give the two of them the chance to properly say their farewells. These things can be so delicate. I am sure you understand."

Anna did not understand, but there was a creeping numbness coming over her.

"It is our hope that they might wed in a few years' time," Mrs. Bridgestock went on. "Nothing has been settled, but it is such a good match."

The parrot screeched and Mrs. Bridgestock went on talking, but Anna heard only a ringing in her ears. She could still taste Ariadne's kiss on her lips; she saw Ariadne's dark hair spread out on the pillow. Those things had happened just hours before, and yet it was like a hundred years had passed and the world had grown cold and unfamiliar.

The door opened again, and a quiet Ariadne joined them.

"Has mother introduced you to Winston?" she said, looking at the parrot. "She dotes on him. Aren't you a nasty beast, Winston?"

She said it warmly, and Winston the parrot danced along his rail and extended a foot to Ariadne.

"Did you have a fruitful discussion?" her mother asked.

"Mother!" Ariadne protested. She was a little pale, but her mother seemed not to notice. "Please, may I speak to Anna?"

"Yes, of course," Mrs. Bridgestock said. "You girls have a good chat. I'll have the cook make up some nice strawberry lemonade and some biscuits."

When she left, Anna stared blankly at Ariadne.

"You are to be married?" she said, her voice gone dry. "You cannot *marry him*."

"Charles is quite a good match," Ariadne said as if she were discussing the quality of a piece of cloth. "Nothing has been settled, but we should reach an agreement soon. But come, Anna, come. Sit."

Ariadne took Anna's hand and led her over to one of the sofas.

"That won't be for at least another year or more," Ariadne said. "You heard Charles. It's a year before I even see him again. All that time, I will spend with you."

She drew a small circle on the back of Anna's hand with her finger, a gentle motion that took Anna's breath away. Ariadne was so beautiful, so warm. Anna felt like she was being torn to pieces.

"Surely you cannot wish to marry Charles," said Anna. "There is nothing wrong with him, but he is . . . Do you *love* him?"

"No," Ariadne said, clutching Anna's hand tighter. "I do not love him that way, or any man that way. All my life, I have looked at women and known only they could pierce my heart. As you have pierced it, Anna."

"Then why?" Anna said. "Why marry him? Because of your parents?"

"Because that is the way the world *is*," Ariadne said, her voice shaking, the way it had when she had first asked Anna if she might kiss her. "If I were to tell my parents the truth about myself, if I were to reveal who I really am, they would despise me. I would be friendless, cast out, alone."

Anna shook her head.

"They would not," she said. "They would love you. You are their daughter."

Ariadne drew her hand back from Anna's. "I am adopted, Anna. My father is the Inquisitor. I do not have parents who are as understanding as yours must be."

"But love is what matters," said Anna. "I would have no one but you. You are all to me, Ariadne. I will not marry a man. I only want you."

"And I want children," Ariadne said, lowering her voice in case her mother was returning. "Anna, I have always wanted to be a mother, more than anything else in the world. If I had to bear Charles's touch, it would be worth it for that." She shuddered. "I shall never, never love him as I love you. I thought you understood—that this would be a bit of happiness we could snatch for ourselves before the world forced us apart. We can love each other for the next year, before Charles returns—we could have that time and always remember it, hold it close to ourselves—"

"But when Charles returned, it would be over," Anna said coldly. "He would claim you. That is what you are saying."

"I would not be unfaithful to him, no," Ariadne said quietly. "I am not a liar."

Anna stood up. "I think you are lying to yourself."

Ariadne raised her lovely face. Tears poured down her cheeks; she wiped them away with shaking hands. "Oh, Anna, won't you kiss me?" she said. "Oh, please, Anna. Do not leave me. Please kiss me."

She looked at Anna pleadingly. Anna's breaths were short, and her heart beat a wailing tattoo in her chest. The perfect world she had dreamed of was shattered into a million pieces, turned to dust, and blown away. What replaced it was something cruel and strange. There was not enough air to breathe. Hot tears stung her eyes.

"Good-bye, Ariadne," she managed, and staggered from the room.

Anna sat on the edge of her bed and cried for a very long time. She cried until no tears came and her body heaved reflexively.

There was a soft knock on her door, and her brother peeked his head in.

"Anna?" he said, blinking his lavender eyes. "Are you all right? I thought I heard something."

Oh, Christopher. Sweet Christopher. Anna roughly wiped her face.

"I'm fine, Christopher," she said, clearing her throat.

"Are you sure?" Christopher asked. "Is there nothing I can do to help you? I could perform a saving act of science."

"Christopher, get along with you." It was Anna's mother,

appearing silently as a cat in the corridor behind her son. "Go and do something else. Something without explosives," she added, shooing her second-born off down the hall.

Anna hastily scrubbed the last traces of tears from her eyes as her mother came into her room, carrying a long, beribboned box. She sat down on the bed and looked at her daughter placidly.

As always, Cecily was perfectly dressed and perfectly calm-looking, her dark hair in a smooth chignon at the back of her neck, her dress a becoming blue. Anna couldn't help but think how ghastly she must look in her nightshirt with her face blotchy and red.

"Do you know why I named you Anna?" Cecily said.

Anna shook her head, puzzled.

"I was awfully ill during my pregnancy," said Cecily. Anna blinked—she hadn't known that. "I was worried all the time that you wouldn't live to be born, or you would be sickly and ill. And then you were born, and you were the most beautiful, healthy, perfect child." She smiled. "Anna means 'favor,' as in 'God has favored me.' I thought the Angel had favored me with you, and I would make sure you were always happy, always content." She reached out to gently touch Anna's cheek. "She broke your heart, didn't she? Ariadne?"

Anna was speechless. So her mother did know. She had always thought her mother knew that she loved women, and that her father did as well . . . but they had never spoken of it until now.

"I am so sorry." Cecily kissed Anna's forehead. "My darling lovely one. I know it does not help to be told it, but someone else will come, and she will treat your heart as the precious gift it is."

"Mama," she said. "You do not mind—that I might not get married or have children?"

"There are many Shadowhunter children orphaned, as Ariadne was, seeking loving homes, and I see no reason why you might not provide one someday. As for marriage . . ." Cecily shrugged. "They said your uncle Will could not be with your aunt Tessa, that your aunt Sophie and uncle Gideon could not be together. And yet, I think you will find that they were wrong, and they would have been wrong even if marriage had been forbidden. Even where laws are unjust, hearts can find a way to be together. If you love someone, I have no doubt you will find a way to spend your life with them, Anna. You are the most determined child I know."

"I am not a child," Anna said, but she smiled, in some amazement. Ariadne might have disappointed her, but her mother was astonishing her in quite the opposite way.

"Still," her mother said. "You cannot keep wearing your brother's clothes."

Anna's heart fell. Here it was. Her mother's understanding could go only so far.

"I thought you didn't know," she said in a small voice.

"Of course I knew. I am your mother," Cecily said as if she were announcing that she were the queen of England. She tapped the long, ribboned box. "Here is a new outfit for you. Hopefully you will find it suitable for accompanying your family in the park today."

Before Anna could protest, a loud and demanding cry sounded through the house. Exclaiming, "Alexander!" Cecily swept out the door, instructing Anna to meet her downstairs in the sitting room when she was dressed.

Glumly, Anna untied the ribbons holding the box closed. She had received many clothes from her mother in the past. Another pastel silk? Another cunningly constructed dress, meant to make the most of her slight curves?

The ribbons and paper fell away, and Anna gasped.

Inside the box was the most gorgeous suit she had ever seen. Charcoal tweed with a thin blue stripe, the jacket was neatly tailored. A gorgeous silk waistcoat in radiant shades of blue complemented a crisp white shirt. Shoes, braces—nothing had been forgotten.

In a daze, Anna dressed herself and gazed into the mirror. The clothes fit perfectly—her mother must have given her measurements to the tailor. And yet there was still one thing not right.

She tightened her jaw, then crossed the room to get the pair of scissors. Standing before the mirror, she grabbed a thick fistful of hair.

She hesitated for only a moment, Ariadne's soft voice in her ears.

I thought you understood—that this would be a bit of happiness we could snatch for ourselves before the world forced us apart.

The hair made a satisfying sound as she cut through it. It rained down on the carpet. She took another fistful, then another, until her hair was to her chin. The cut brought her features into sharp relief. She trimmed more in the front, clipped away at the back, until there was just enough to sweep into a gentlemanly wave.

And now it was perfect. Her reflection gazed back at her, lips curved in an incredulous smile. The waistcoat brought out her eyes; the trousers, the slimness of her legs. She felt she could breathe, even with the ache of Ariadne's loss in her chest. She might have lost the girl, but she had gained herself. A new Anna, confident, dapper, powerful.

Hearts were broken across London every day. Perhaps Anna might break a heart or two herself. There would be others—lovely girls would come and go, and she would remain in control of her heart. She would never be torn like this again.

She was a Shadowhunter. She would take the blow. She would harden herself and laugh in the face of pain.

Anna descended the stairs soon after. It was late afternoon now, though the sun was still shining brightly through the windows. This day would last forever.

Her mother was in the sitting room with a tea tray, baby Alex in a basket by her side. Her father sat opposite, engaged in reading the newspaper.

Anna stepped into the room.

Both her parents looked up. She saw them take in her new clothes, as well as her short hair. She stood in the doorway, bracing herself for whatever response was coming.

A long moment passed.

"I told you the blue waistcoat was the one," Gabriel said to Cecily. "It brings out her eyes."

"I did not disagree," said Cecily, rocking the baby. "I just said she would also look very well in red."

Anna began to smile.

"Much better than your brother's clothes," Gabriel said. "He does dreadful things to them with sulfur and acids."

Cecily examined Anna's shorn locks.

"Very sensible," she said. "Hair can be cumbersome in battle. I like it very much." She rose to her feet. "Come sit," she added. “Stay with your brother and father a moment. There is something I meant to fetch for you.”

As her mother left the room, Anna felt her limbs go tingly as she sat down on the settee. She reached down to Alex. He was looking all around the room, taking in all the wonders anew in the way that babies do whenever they awake and find that the world is still there, to be understood in all its myriad complexities.

“I understand how you feel,” she said to her brother.

He smiled a toothless smile at her and reached up a chubby hand. She extended her own, and he grabbed her finger.

Her mother returned only a few minutes later with a small blue box.

“You know,” Cecily said, sitting down and refilling her teacup, “my parents did not want me to be a Shadowhunter. They had fled the Clave. And your uncle Will . . .”

“I know,” Anna said. Gabriel gazed fondly at his wife.

“But I was a Shadowhunter. I knew it then, when I was fifteen. I knew it was in my blood. Foolish people say so many things. But we know who we are, inside.”

She set the blue box on the table and pushed it toward Anna.

“If you will accept it,” her mother said.

Inside the box was a necklace with a glimmering red gem. Latin words were etched onto the back.

“For your protection,” she said. “You know what it does.”

“It senses demons,” Anna said, astonished. Her mother wore it nearly every time she went out to fight, though that was rarer now that Alexander had come along.

“It cannot protect your heart, but it can protect the rest of you,” Cecily said. “It is an heirloom. It should be yours.”

Anna fought back the tears that sought to fill her eyes.

She took up the necklace and clasped it about her throat. She stood up and gazed at herself in the mirror over the fireplace. A handsome reflection gazed back at her. The necklace felt right, just as her short hair did. *I do not have to be only one thing,* Anna thought. *I can choose what suits me when it suits me. The trousers and jacket do not make me a man, and the necklace does not make me a woman. They are only what makes me feel beautiful and powerful in this moment. I am exactly as I choose to be. I am a Shadowhunter who wears gorgeous suits and a legendary pendant.*

She looked at her mother's reflection in the glass. "You were right," she said. "The red does suit me."

Gabriel chuckled softly, but Cecily only smiled.

"I have always known you, my love," Cecily said. "You are the gem of my heart. My firstborn. My Anna."

Anna thought of all the pain of the day again—the wound that had ripped her chest open and exposed her heart. But now it was as if her mother had drawn a rune over it and closed it. The scar was there, but she was whole.

It was like being Marked all over again, defining who she was. This was Anna Lightwood.

Learn About Loss

By Cassandra Clare and Kelly Link

J

Chattanooga, 1936

On the morning of October 23, the inhabitants of Chattanooga, Tennessee, woke up to discover posters tacked up on the sides of buildings on every street. FOR A LIMITED TIME ONLY, the posters declared, MAGIC & MUSIC & MOST MYSTERIOUS MERCHANTS' BAZAAR. PAY ONLY WHAT YOU CAN AFFORD & ENTER FAIRYLAND. SEE WHAT YOU MOST DESIRE. ALL WELCOME.

Some men and women passed these posters, shaking their heads. It was the height of the Great Depression, and even if the president, Franklin Delano Roosevelt, was promising more work on projects like the tunnel and trails and campgrounds underway in the Great Smoky Mountains National Park, jobs were scarce and times were hard and most people didn't have money to spare on fripperies or fun. And who wanted to travel all the way up Lookout Mountain only to be turned away because what you could afford was nothing? Besides, no one ever gave you something for nothing.

But plenty of other Chattanoogans saw the posters and thought that maybe better times really were just around the corner. There was a New Deal, and maybe there would be new fun, too. And there was not a single child who caught sight of the posters and didn't yearn with their entire heart for what the posters promised. The twenty-third of October was a Friday. On Saturday, at least half the city of Chattanooga lit out for the carnival. Some of them packed bedrolls or tarps to sleep under. If there was music and festivity, maybe they would stay longer than a day. The churches of Chattanooga were poorly attended on Sunday morning. But the carnival in the Fairyland neighborhood of Lookout Mountain was busier than a beehive.

Up on top of Lookout Mountain, a local boy named Garnet Carter had quite recently established the community of Fairyland, which included Tom Thumb Golf, the first miniature golf course in the United States. There was the eerie natural landscape of Rock City, where his wife, Frieda Carter, had laid out paths between towering, mossy rock formations, planting wildflowers and importing German statuary so that the trails were watched over by gnomes and characters from fairy-tale stories like "Little Red Riding Hood" and the "Three Little Pigs."

Rich people came on vacations and rode the funicular, which also happened to be the world's steepest passenger railway, the mile up from Chattanooga to the Lookout Mountain Hotel. The hotel was also known as the Castle In the Clouds, and if all the rooms were taken, well, there was also the Fairyland Inn. For the wealthy, there was golf and ballroom dancing and hunting. For the civic-minded, there was the site of the Battle Above the Clouds, where the Union Army had, in living memory, driven off at great cost the Confederates. You could still find minié bullets and other traces of the dead all down the slopes of the mountain, along with flint arrowheads used by the Cherokee. But the Cherokee had all been driven off, and the Civil War was over too. There had been a greater war in recent memory, and many a family in Chattanooga had lost sons or fathers to it. Human beings did terrible things to each other, and the traces of those terrible things were everywhere if you looked.

If your taste ran more to corn whiskey than history, well, there were plenty of moonshine stills up on Lookout Mountain too. And who knew what other illegal or immoral delights might be found at a Mysterious Merchants' Bazaar?

There were men and women of money and taste at the carnival on that first Saturday, rubbing alongside the thin-faced children and wives of farmers. The rides were free to all. There were games with prizes, and a petting zoo with a three-headed dog and a winged snake so large that it was able to swallow a full-grown steer each day at noon. There were strolling fiddle players who drew such melancholy and lovely songs out on their instruments that tears came to the eyes of all who heard them. There was a woman who said that she could speak with the dead, and asked no coin. There was a magician, too, Roland the Astonishing, who grew a dogwood tree from a seed on his stage and then caused it to flower, drop its leaves, and grow bare again as if all the seasons were passing in the blink of an eye. He was a handsome man in his sixties, with bright blue eyes, a luxuriant white mustache, and snowy white hair with a black streak running through it as if some devil had touched it with a sooty hand.

There were delicious things to eat at such a negligible cost, or freely given as samples, that every child ate himself or herself sick. As promised, the bazaar was full of remarkable objects on display, tended by even more remarkable people. Some of the customers, too, drew curious glances. Were there people in faraway lands who had curly tails or flames in their pupils? One of the most popular stalls had on offer a local product: a clear, potent liquor rumored to give dreams of a moonlit forest full of running wolves to those who drank it. The men at that booth were taciturn and did not smile often. But when they did, their teeth were unsettlingly white. They lived up in the mountains and mostly kept to themselves, but here at the bazaar they seemed quite at home.

One tent was staffed by nurses so very lovely it wasn't a chore at all to let them draw your blood. They took a cup or two, "for research purposes," they said. And to those who donated, they gave away tokens that could be used elsewhere in the bazaar, just like money.

Just beyond the tents of the bazaar was a sign that led to the Maze of Mirrors. It said SEE FOR YOURSELF. THE TRUE WORLD AND THE FALSE LIE NEXT DOOR TO ONE ANOTHER. Those who went through the Maze of Mirrors came out looking a little dazed. Some of them had found their way to the very center, in which they had been made an offer by an entity that each described differently. To some, the person in the room had appeared as a small child, or an old woman in an elegant gown, or even in the shape of a loved one long dead. The person in the room had a mask, and if you confessed a thing that you desired, the mask was put on you and, well, you should really go and see for yourself. If, that is, you could find your way through the maze and to the place where that person and the mask were waiting.

By the end of the first weekend, most of Chattanooga had come up to see for themselves the strange charms of the carnival. And many came back to the carnival in the following days, although by then rumors were beginning to spread of troubling behavior exhibited by some who had returned. A woman claimed that the man she was married to was an impostor who had killed her real husband: this claim would have been easier to dismiss if a body had not been discovered in the river, in all ways a double of the man she was married to. A young man stood up in church and said that he saw and knew the secrets of all the congregation by looking at them. When he began to say these secrets out loud, the pastor tried to shout him down until the man began to declaim the things he knew about the pastor. At this, the pastor fell silent, then left his church and went home and slit his throat.

Another man won again and again at a weekly game of poker, until, drunk, he confessed, sounding astonished, that he could see the cards every man there held as if they were his very own hand. He proved this by calling out each card in order, and after that was beaten soundly and left unconscious and bloody in the street by men who had been his friends since childhood.

A boy of seventeen, newly engaged to be married, came home from the carnival and that night woke up everyone in his household screaming. He had put out his own eyes with two hot coals, but refused to say why. In fact, he never spoke again, and his poor fiancée at last broke off the engagement and went to live with an aunt in Baltimore.

A beautiful girl turned up at the Fairyland Inn at dusk one evening, claiming that she was Mrs. Dalgrey, when the staff of the inn knew very well Mrs. Dalgrey was a bucket-faced dowager in her late seventies. She stayed at the inn every fall, and never tipped anyone no matter how good the service.

Other terrible incidents were reported in the neighborhoods of Chattanooga, and by the middle of the week after the carnival had put up its signs, word of these happenings had made its way to those whose business it was to prevent the human world from being troubled and tormented by the malicious whims of Downworlders and demons.

It is only to be expected that some amount of trouble will arrive with a carnival. Pleasure and trouble are brother and sister to each other. But there were indications that this particular carnival was more than it seemed. For one thing, the Bazaar of the Bizarre was not just trinkets and gaudy junk. The bazaar was a full-on Shadow Market where there had never been one before, and humans were strolling its aisles and freely handling its wares. And there were indications, too, that there was an artifact made out of *adamas* in the hands of one who should not have had it. For this reason, at sunset on Thursday, the twenty-ninth of October, a Portal opened at Lookout Point, and two individuals who had only just met stepped through it unnoticed by any of the human sightseers gathered there.

One was a young woman not yet fully invested as an Iron Sister, although already her hands showed the scars and calluses of one who worked *adamas*. Her name was Emilia, and this was the last task her Sisters had set her before she joined their company: to recover the *adamas* and bring it back to the Adamant Citadel. She had a smiling, watchful face, as if she liked the world but did not quite trust that it would be on its best behavior.

Her companion was a Silent Brother who bore the runic marks on his face, although neither his eyes nor his mouth had been sewn shut. Instead, they were merely closed, as if he had voluntarily chosen to withdraw inside the citadel of his own self. He was handsome enough that if any of the women at Lookout Point had seen his face, one or two might have thought of fairy tales where a kiss is sufficient to wake one who is under an enchantment. Sister Emilia, who could see Brother Zachariah quite plainly, thought he was one of the handsomest men she had ever seen. Certainly he was one of the first men she had seen in quite some time. And if their errands were successful and she returned to the Adamant Citadel with the *adamas* in her possession, well, it wouldn't be the worst thing if handsome Brother Zachariah was the last man she ever laid eyes on. There was no harm in appreciating beauty when you chanced upon it.

She said, "Nice view, isn't it?" Because from the place they stood you could see Georgia, Tennessee, Alabama, both North and South Carolina, and, on the horizon, Virginia and Kentucky too, all spread out and rumpled like a tapestry quilt haphazardly embroidered in green and blue, little pricks of red and gold and orange where, in places, the trees were already beginning to turn.

Inside her head, Brother Zachariah said, *It's extraordinary. Though, I confess, I had imagined America to look somewhat different. Someone I . . . knew . . . told me about New York City. That was where she grew up. We talked one day of going together to see the things and places that she loved. But we talked of many things that I knew, even then, would likely never happen. And this is a very large country.*

Sister Emilia was not at all sure that she liked having someone else talking inside her head. She had encountered Silent Brothers before, but this was the first time one had spoken directly into her mind. It was like having company show up when you hadn't had the inclination to do the dishes or straighten up your living quarters in a while. What if they could see all the untidy thoughts you sometimes just shoved under the carpet?

Her mentor, Sister Lora, had assured Emilia that although Silent Brothers could ordinarily read the minds of those around them, their Sisterhood was exempt. But on the other hand, what if this was part of the test she had been set? What if Brother Zachariah's task was also to look inside her brain, to be sure that she was a deserving candidate? She thought, as loudly as she could, *Excuse me! Can you hear me thinking?*

When Brother Zachariah didn't respond, she said, relieved, "Your first time in the States, then?"

Yes, Brother Zachariah said. Then, as if to be polite, he said, *And you?*

"Born and bred in California," Sister Emilia said. "I grew up in the San Francisco Conclave."

Is San Francisco very like this? Brother Zachariah said.

She almost choked. "Indeed," she said, "it is not. Not even the trees are the same. And the ground there is like as not to give you a little shake now and then. Sometimes just enough to move your bed a few inches while you're trying to sleep. Other times, it knocks buildings down without so much as a warning. Oh, but the fruits on the trees are the best thing you've ever tasted. And the sun shines every single day."

Her oldest brother had been an infant in their mother's

arms during the earthquake of 1906. Half the city had burned, and Emilia's father said that even demons had stayed away during the destruction. Their mother, who had been pregnant, had had a miscarriage. If that baby had lived, Emilia would have had seven siblings, all brothers. Her first night in the Adamant Citadel, she had woken up every hour because it was all so quiet and peaceful.

You sound as if you miss it, Brother Zachariah said.

Sister Emilia said, "I do miss it. But it was never home. Now. I believe the carnival is thataways, and here we stand jawing when we have work to do."

Although his eyes and ears and mouth had all been closed by the magic of the Silent City, Brother Zachariah could still smell and hear the carnival much better than any mortal—here was the scent of sugar and hot metal and, yes, blood as well, and the sounds of barkers and calliope music and excited shrieks. Soon enough he could see it too.

The carnival stood on mostly level ground where once there must have been quite a battle. Brother Zachariah could feel the presence of the human dead. Now their forgotten remains lay buried under a grassy field where a kind of stockade fence had been erected around all manner of brightly colored tents and fanciful structures. A Ferris wheel stood above these, carriages dangling from the central wheel, full of laughing people. Two great gates stood flung wide open, with a broad avenue between them welcoming all who approached.

Sweethearts in their Sunday clothes strolled through the gates, arms around each other's waists. Two boys pelted past, one with tousled black hair. They looked about the age that

Will and Jem had been, a very long time ago, when they'd first met. But Will's hair was white now, and Jem was no longer Jem. He was Brother Zachariah. A few nights ago, he had sat at Will Herondale's bedside and watched his old friend struggle to draw a breath. Jem's hand on the coverlet was the hand of a young man still, and Tessa, of course, would never grow old. How must it seem to Will, who loved them both, that he must go on so far ahead of them? But then, Jem had left Will first, and Will had had to let him go. It would only be fair when, soon, Jem would be the one left behind.

Inside his head, Brother Enoch said, *It will be hard. But you will be able to bear it. We will help you bear it.*

I will endure it because I must, Brother Zachariah said.

Sister Emilia had stopped, and he caught up with her. She was taking in the carnival, her hands on her hips. "What a thing!" she said. "Did you ever read *Pinocchio?*"

"I don't believe so," Brother Zachariah told her. Though he thought that once, when he'd been in the London Institute, he might have heard Tessa reading it to a young James.

"A wooden puppet yearns to be a real boy," Sister Emilia said. "And so a fairy gives him his wish, more or less, and he gets into all sorts of trouble at a place that I always thought would look rather like this."

Brother Zachariah said, almost against his will, *And does he?*

"Does he what?" Sister Emilia said.

Does he become real?

"Well, of course," Sister Emilia said. Then, saucily, "What kind of story would it be if he only ever got to be a puppet? His father loves him, and that's how he starts to become real, I guess. I always liked those stories the best, the ones where people could make things or carve things and make them come to life. Like Pygmalion."

In his head, Brother Enoch said, *She's quite lively, for an Iron Sister.* He didn't sound exactly disapproving, but neither was it a compliment.

"Of course," Sister Emilia said, "you're something of a story yourself, Brother Zachariah."

What do you know of me? Brother Zachariah said.

She said pertly, "That you fought Mortmain. That you once had a *parabatai* and he became the head of the London Institute. That his wife, the warlock Tessa Herondale, wears a pendant that you gave her. But I know something of you that perhaps you do not know yourself."

That seems unlikely, Brother Zachariah said. *But go on. Tell me what I do not know about myself.*

"Give me your staff," Sister Emilia said.

He gave it to her, and she examined it carefully. "Yes," she said. "I thought so. This was made by Sister Dayo, whose weapons were so exquisitely wrought that it was rumored an angel had touched her forge. Look. Her mark."

It has served me well enough, Brother Zachariah said. *Perhaps one day you too will find renown for the things that you make.*

"One day," said Sister Emilia. She handed him back the staff. "Perhaps." There was a formidable glint in her eyes. Brother Zachariah thought it made her look very young. The world was its own sort of crucible, and in it all dreams were tempered and tested. Many crumbled away entirely, and then you went on without them. In his head his Brothers murmured in agreement. After nearly sixty years, Brother Zachariah was almost used to this. Instead of music, he had this stern brotherly chorus. Once upon a time, he had imagined each of the Silent Brothers as a musical instrument. Brother Enoch, he'd thought, would be a bassoon heard through the high-up window of a desolate lighthouse, the waves crashing down at the base. *Yes, yes,* Brother Enoch had said. *Very poetic. And what are you, Brother Zachariah?*

Brother Zachariah had tried not to think of his violin. But you couldn't keep secrets from your Brothers. And that violin had lain silent and neglected for a very long time.

He said, attempting to think of other things as they walked, *Can you tell me if you know anything of an Annabel Blackthorn? An Iron Sister? She and a friend of mine, the warlock Malcom Fade, fell in love and made plans to run away together, but when her family discovered this, they forced her to join the Iron Sisterhood. It would ease his mind to know something of what her life had been in the Adamant Citadel.*

Sister Emilia said, "It's clear that you know very little about the Iron Sisters! No one is ever forced to join against their will. Indeed, it is a great honor, and many who attempt the path are turned away. If this Annabel became an Iron Sister, she chose that for herself. I know nothing of her, although it's true that most of us change our names when we are consecrated."

Brother Zachariah said, *If you come to know anything of her, my friend would be most grateful. He does not speak of her much, but I believe that she is always in his thoughts.*

When Brother Zachariah and Sister Emilia passed through the gates of the carnival, the first strange thing they saw was a werewolf eating cotton candy out of a paper cone. Sticky pink strands were caught in his beard.

"Full moon tonight," Sister Emilia said. "The Praetor Lupus

has sent down some of their people, but it's said the werewolves here are a law to themselves. They run moonshine and ride roughshod in the mountains. These boys should be steering clear of mundanes this time of the month, not eating cotton candy and peddling rotgut."

The werewolf stuck out its tongue at them and sauntered away. "Sauce!" Sister Emilia said, and would have pursued the werewolf.

Brother Zachariah said, *Hold. There are worse things here than Downworlders with terrible manners and a sweet tooth. Can you smell that?*

Sister Emilia wrinkled her nose. "Demon," she said.

They followed the smell through the winding alleys of the carnival, through the strangest iteration of the Shadow Market that Brother Zachariah had ever seen. The Market was, of course, much bigger than you would have expected a carnival, even one of this size, to encompass. Some of the vendors he recognized. Some watched warily as he and Sister Emilia passed. One or two, with looks of resignation, began to pack up their wares. The rules by which Shadow Markets existed were more the rules of long custom than those written down and codified, but everything about this Shadow Market felt wrong to Brother Zachariah, and the Silent Brothers in his head were all debating how it might have come to be. Even if a Shadow Market had been right and proper in this place, there should not have been mundanes browsing and exclaiming over the strange goods on offer. Here went a man, looking pale and dreamy-eyed, blood still trickling from two neat punctures in his neck.

"I've never actually been to a Shadow Market," Sister Emilia said, slowing down. "My mother always said it was no place for

Shadowhunters and insisted that my brothers and I stay away from it." She seemed particularly interested in a booth that sold knives and weapons.

Souvenirs later, Brother Zachariah said, pushing on. *Business first.*

They were suddenly out of the Shadow Market and in front of a stage where a magician was telling jokes as he turned a small shaggy dog into a green melon and then cut the melon in half with a playing card. Inside was a fiery sphere that rose up and hung in the air like a miniature sun. The magician (the sign above his head proclaimed him to be Roland the Astonishing) poured water out of his hat onto it, and the sphere became a mouse and ran off the stage into an audience that gasped and shrieked and then applauded.

Sister Emilia had stopped to watch, and Brother Zachariah stopped too.

She said, "Real magic?"

Real illusions at least, Brother Zachariah said. He gestured at the woman who stood at the side of the stage watching the magician perform his tricks.

The magician looked to be in his sixties, but his companion could have been any age at all. She was clearly of high fey lineage, and there was a baby in her arms. The way that she watched the magician on the stage made Brother Zachariah's chest grow tight. He had seen Tessa look at Will the same way, with that rapt attention and love mingled with the knowledge of future sorrow that must, one day, be endured.

Brother Enoch said, again, *When the day comes, we will bear it with you.*

A thought came to Brother Zachariah like an arrow, that

when that day came and Will left the world, he did not wish to share his grief with his Brothers. That others would be there with him when Will was not. And, too, there was Tessa. Who would stay to help her endure when Brother Zachariah took the body that Will had left behind back to the Silent City?

The faerie woman looked out over the crowd and then drew back suddenly behind a velvet curtain. When Brother Zachariah tried to see what she had seen, he saw a goblin perched on a flag above the top of a nearby tent. It appeared to be sniffing the wind as if it smelled something particularly delicious. Mostly what Brother Zachariah smelled now was demon.

Sister Emilia craned her neck to see where Brother Zachariah was looking and said, "Another faerie! It's nice to be out in the world again. I'll have such a lot to write about in my diary when I'm back in the Adamant Citadel."

Do Iron Sisters keep diaries? Brother Zachariah asked politely.

"That was a joke," Sister Emilia said. She actually looked disappointed in him. "Do Silent Brothers have any kind of a sense of humor, or do they stitch that up too?"

We collect knock-knock jokes, Brother Zachariah said.

She perked up. "Really? Do you have any favorites?"

No, Brother Zachariah said. *That was a joke.* He smiled. Sister Emilia was so very human that he found it was waking up some of the humanity he'd put aside so long ago. That too must have been why he was thinking of Will and Tessa and the person he'd been before. His heart would ache slightly less, he was sure, once he and Sister Emilia had completed their mission and been dispatched back to the places where they belonged. She had some of the same spark that Will had had, back when he and Jem had chosen to be *parabatai*. Jem had been drawn to that fire in Will, and Brother Zachariah thought that he and Sister Emilia could have been friends too, under other circumstances.

He was thinking this when a small boy tugged at his sleeve. "Are you part of the carnival?" the boy said. "Is that why you're dressed like that? Is that why your face looks like that?"

Brother Zachariah looked down at the boy and then at the runes on his arms to make sure they hadn't somehow rubbed off.

"You can see us?" Sister Emilia said to the boy.

"'Course I can," the boy said. "Nothing wrong with my eyes. Although I think there must have been something wrong with them before. Because now I see all sorts of things that I never used to see."

How? Brother Zachariah said, bending over to peer into the boy's eyes. *What's your name? When did you start seeing things that you never used to see?*

"My name's Bill," the boy said. "I'm eight. Why are your eyes closed like that? And how can you talk when your mouth isn't open?"

"He's a man of special talents," said Sister Emilia. "You should taste his chicken potpie. Where are your people, Bill?"

The boy said, "I live down in St. Elmo, and I came up here on the Incline Railway with my mother and today I ate a whole bag of saltwater taffy and didn't have to share a piece with anyone else."

"Maybe the taffy had magical properties," Sister Emilia said softly to Brother Zachariah.

"My mother said not to wander off," the boy said, "but I never pay any attention to her unless she's het up like a kettle. I went through the Maze of Mirrors all by myself, and I got all the way to the middle where the fancy lady is, and she said as a prize I could ask her for anything I wanted."

What did you ask her for? Brother Zachariah said.

"I thought about asking for a battle with real knights and real horses and real swords, like in King Arthur, but the lady said if what I wanted was real adventures, I should ask to see the world as it really was, and so I did. And after that she put a mask on me, and now everything's strange, and also she wasn't a lady at all. She was something that I didn't want to be around anymore, and so I ran away. I've seen all kinds of strange people, but I haven't seen my mother. Have you seen her? She's little but she's ferocious. She has red hair like me, and she's got an awful temper when she's worried."

"I know all about that kind of mother," Sister Emilia said. "She must be looking everywhere for you."

Bill said, "I am a constant trial to her. Or so she says."

Over there, Brother Zachariah said. *Is that her?*

A small woman standing by a tent advertising MYSTERIES OF THE WORM DEMONSTRATED THRICE DAILY was looking over in their direction. "Bill Doyle!" she said, advancing. "You are in a heap of trouble, my little man!"

She had a carrying voice.

"I see my fate is upon me," Bill said in grave tones. "You should flee before you become a casualty of battle."

"Don't worry for us, Bill," Sister Emilia said. "Your mother can't see us. And I wouldn't mention us to her either. She'll think you're making it all up."

"It appears I have gotten myself into a real predicament," Bill said. "Fortunately I am as good at getting out of tight spots as I am at getting into them. I've had lots of practice. A pleasure to have met both of you."

Then Mrs. Doyle was upon him. She seized her son's arm and began to pull him back toward the exit of the carnival, scolding him as they went.

Brother Zachariah and Sister Emilia turned to watch them go in silence.

Finally Sister Emilia said, "The Maze of Mirrors, then."

And even if they hadn't encountered young Bill Doyle, they would have known they'd found the place they were looking for when they came to the Maze of Mirrors at last. It was a pointy structure, painted all over in glossy forbidding black, fissures of red running through the black paint, the red paint looking so fresh and wet that the building appeared to be seeping blood. Through the entrance, mirrors and lights dazzled. THE TRUE WORLD AND THE FALSE, said the sign. YOU SHALL KNOW EVEN AS YOU ARE KNOWN. THOSE WHO SEEK ME WILL FIND THEMSELVES.

The reek of demon malignance here was so strong that even Brother Zachariah and Sister Emilia, wearing runes to keep from being overpowered by the stench, flinched.

Be careful, the voices in Brother Zachariah's head warned. *This is no ordinary Eidolon demon.*

Sister Emilia had drawn her sword.

Brother Zachariah said, *We should be careful. There may be dangers here that we are not prepared for.*

Sister Emilia said, "I think we can be at least as brave as little Bill Doyle was, facing danger."

He didn't know he was dealing with a demon, Brother Zachariah said.

"I meant his mother," Sister Emilia said. "Come on."

And so Brother Zachariah followed her into the Maze of Mirrors.

* * *

They found themselves in a long, glittering corridor with many companions. Here was another Sister Emilia and another Brother Zachariah, stretched out monstrously thin and wavy. Here they were again, squashed and hideous. There they were, their reflections' backs turned to them. In one mirror, they lay on the shores of a shallow purple sea, dead and bloated and yet looking utterly content to be so, as if they had died of some great happiness. In another, they began to age rapidly and then to crumble away to bare bones, the bones to dust.

Sister Emilia had never been fond of mirrors. But she had a craftswoman's interest in these. When a mirror is made, it must be coated in some reflective metal. Silver could be used, though vampires were not fond of this kind. The mirrors in the Maze of Mirrors, she thought, must have been treated with some kind of demonic metal. You could smell it. Every breath she took in here coated her mouth, her tongue, her throat with a kind of greasy residue of despair and horror.

She walked forward slowly, her sword held in front of her, and stumbled into a mirror where she had thought there was an open space.

Careful, Brother Zachariah said.

"You don't come to the carnival to be careful," she said. This was bluster, and perhaps he knew it. But bluster is a kind of armor too, as much as taking care is. Sister Emilia had appreciation for both.

"If it's a maze, then how are we to know which way to go?" she said. "I could shatter the mirrors with my sword. If I broke them all, we would find the center."

Hold your sword, Brother Zachariah said.

He had paused in front of a mirror in which Sister Emilia was not present. Instead, there was a slender white-haired boy holding the hand of a tall girl with a solemn, beautiful face. They were on a city avenue.

"That's New York," Sister Emilia said. "I thought you hadn't been there!"

Brother Zachariah advanced through the mirror, which allowed passage as if it had never been there at all. The image was gone like a popped soap bubble. *Go toward the reflections that show you whatever thing you most long to see*, Brother Zachariah said. *But that you know to be impossible.*

"Oh," Sister Emilia said involuntarily. "Over there!"

Over there was a mirror where a Sister much like her, but with silvery hair, held a glowing blade between tongs. She plunged it into a bath of cold water, and steam shot up in the shape of a dragon, writhing and splendid. All her brothers were there too, watching in admiration.

They passed through that mirror too. They made their way through mirror after mirror, and Sister Emilia felt her chest grow tight with longing. Her cheeks burned red too, that Brother Zachariah could see the vainest and most frivolous longings of her heart. But she saw the things that he longed for too. A man and a woman she thought must have been his parents, listening to their son play his violin in a great concert hall. A black-haired man with blue eyes and laugh lines around his mouth, building up a fire in a drawing room while the solemn girl, smiling now, perched on the lap of Brother Zachariah, no longer a Brother but a husband and a *parabatai* in the company of the ones he loved most.

They came to a mirror where the black-haired man, now

old and frail, lay in a bed. The girl sat curled up beside him, stroking his forehead. Suddenly Brother Zachariah came into the room, but when he threw back his hood, he had open, clear eyes and a smiling mouth. At this sight, the old man in the bed sat up and grew younger and younger, as if joy had renewed his youth. He sprang out of bed and embraced his *parabatai*.

"It is horrible," Sister Emilia said. "We should not see inside each other's hearts like this!"

They passed through that mirror and now came face-to-face with one that showed Sister Emilia's mother, sitting before a window, holding a letter from her daughter. There was the most desolate look in her eyes, but then the mother in the reflection began, slowly, to compose a fire-message to her daughter. *I am so very proud of you, my darling. I am so happy you have found your life's work.*

I see nothing shameful in you, Brother Zachariah said in his tranquil voice. He held out his hand, and after a moment Sister Emilia looked away from the reflection of her mother writing all the things she had never said. She took the offered hand gratefully.

"It is shameful to be vulnerable," she admitted. "Or so I have always thought."

They passed through the mirror, and someone said, "And that is exactly what a weapon maker and armorer *would* think. Don't you agree?"

They had found their way to the heart of the maze, and a demon was there with them—a handsome man in a well-cut suit that was the worst thing that Sister Emilia had ever seen.

Belial, Brother Zachariah said.

"Old friend!" Belial said. "I was so hoping it would be you they sent sniffing after me."

This was Sister Emilia's first time encountering a Greater Demon. She held the sword she had forged herself in one hand, and Brother Zachariah's warm hand in the other. If it had not been for those two things, she knew she would have turned and fled.

"Is that human skin?" she asked, her voice wavering.

Whatever the suit was made of, it had the glazed, slightly cracked appearance of poorly tanned leather. It had a pink, blistered look to it. And yes, she could now see that what she had thought was an odd flower poking out of the boutonniere hole was actually a mouth pursed in agony, a cartilaginous lump of nose sagging over it.

Belial looked down at the stained cuff sticking out past the sleeve. He flicked a speck off. "You have an eye, my dear," he said.

"Whose skin is it?" Sister Emilia said. Her voice was steadier now, she found to her great relief. It was not so much that she wanted to know the answers, as that she had found quite early on in her training in the Adamant Citadel that asking questions was a way to discipline your fear. Taking in new information meant you had something to focus on besides how terrifying your teachers or your environment were.

"A tailor I employed," Belial said. "He was a very bad tailor, you see, but in the end he has made a very good suit after all." He gave her and Brother Zachariah the most charming smile. But in the mirrors all around them, his reflections gnashed their teeth and raged.

Brother Zachariah gave every appearance of calm, but

Sister Emilia could feel how tight his grip had grown. She said, "You're friends with him?"

We have met before, Brother Zachariah said. *Silent Brothers do not choose the company they keep. Though I will confess I find yours more to my taste than his.*

"Hurtful!" said Belial, leering. "And, I fear, honest. And I only enjoy one of those things."

What is your business here? Brother Zachariah said.

"No business at all," Belial said. "This is purely fun. You see, they turned up some *adamas* in the caverns underneath Ruby Falls. A small vein of it in the limestone. Do you know that people come from all over the country to gawk at Ruby Falls? A subterranean waterfall! I haven't seen it myself, but I hear it's spectacular. I did play a few rounds of Tom Thumb Golf, though. And then gorged myself sick on the famous saltwater taffy. Had to eat the taffy seller afterward to get the taste out of my mouth. I think there's still a little stuck in my teeth. Chattanooga, Tennessee! The slogan should be 'Come for the *Adamas*, Stay for the Saltwater Taffy!' They could paint it on barns.

"Did you know there's a whole city underneath the city of Chattanooga? They had such terrible floods over the last century that finally they built over the original buildings. The old buildings are still there, underground, hollowed out like rotten teeth. And sure, everything is on higher ground now, but the floods still come. They wash away all the limestone, and what happens eventually? The foundations will crumble, and everything will be washed away in a deluge. There's a metaphor there somewhere, little Shadowhunters. You build and you struggle and you fight, but the darkness and the abyss will come one day in a great tide and sweep away everything that you love."

We didn't have time to tour Chattanooga, Brother Zachariah said. *We're here for the* adamas.

"The *adamas*! Of course!" Belial said. "You people kept such a tight grasp on the stuff."

"You have it?" Sister Emilia said. "I thought it was death to demons, just the touch."

"Your ordinary sort will just explode, yes," Belial said. "But I am a Prince of Hell. Made of sterner stuff."

Greater Demons can handle adamas, Brother Zachariah said. *Though my understanding is that it is agonizing to them.*

"To-may-to of agony, to-mah-to of ah-gony," Belial said. His reflections in the various mirrors wept tears of blood. "Do you know what causes us pain? The one who made us has turned his face from us. We are not allowed before the throne. But *adamas*, that's angelic stuff. When we touch it, the pain of our absence from the divine is indescribable. And yet it's the closest we ever get to being in its presence. So we touch *adamas*, and we feel the absence of our creator, and in that absence we feel the smallest spark of what we once were. Oh, it's the most wonderful thing you can imagine, that pain."

Brother Zachariah said, *And God said, "I shall not retain Belial within my heart."*

A sly, wounded look came over Belial's face. "Of course you, too, my dear Brother Zachariah, have been cut off from the ones you love. We understand each other." And then he said something in a language that Sister Emilia did not recognize, almost spitting out the awful, hissing syllables.

"What is he saying?" she said. She thought that the room seemed to be growing hotter. The mirrors were blazing brighter.

He's speaking Abyssal, Brother Zachariah said calmly. *Nothing of any interest.*

"He's doing something," Sister Emilia hissed. "We have to stop him. Something is happening."

In all the mirrors, Belial was swelling up, the suit of skin bursting like the skin of a sausage. The mirror versions of Sister Emilia and Brother Zachariah were dwindling, shrinking and blackening as if scorched by the heat of Belial.

Knock, knock, Brother Zachariah said.

"What?" Sister Emilia said.

He said again, *Don't pay any attention to Belial. He thrives on it. It's not real. It's illusions. Nothing more. Demons won't kill those they owe a debt to. Knock, knock.*

"Who's there?" she said.

Spell.

Sister Emilia's throat was so dry she could barely speak at all. The pommel of her sword was blazingly hot, as if she had her hand in the heart of a forge. "Spell who?"

If you insist, Brother Zachariah said. *W-H-O.*

And when Sister Emilia understood the joke, it was so very ridiculous that she laughed in spite of herself. "That's terrible!" she said.

Brother Zachariah looked at her with his sealed-off face. He said, *You didn't ask me if Silent Brothers had a* good *sense of humor.*

Belial had stopped speaking Abyssal. He looked incredibly disappointed in them both. "This is no fun," he said.

What did you do with the adamas*?* Brother Zachariah said.

Belial reached down into the neck of his shirt and drew up a chain. Dangling on the end of it was an *adamas* half mask. Sister Emilia could see his skin go red and then grow raw and festering and yellow with pus where the mask touched him. And where he touched the mask, the metal flared up in coruscating ripples of turquoise, scarlet, viridian. But Belial's expression of proud indifference never changed. "I've been using it on behalf of your precious mundane folk," he said. "It strengthens my power as I strengthen its. Some of them want to be people other than themselves, and so I give them the illusion of that. Strong enough that they can fool others. Other people want to see something that they want, or that they've lost, or that they can't have, and I can do that, too. There was a young man the other day—a boy, really—he was to be married. But he was afraid. He wanted to know the worst things that might happen to him and the girl he loved, so that he could prepare for them and go on bravely. I hear he wasn't that brave after all."

"He put out his eyes," Sister Emilia said. "And what about Bill Doyle?"

"That one, I think, will have a remarkable life," Belial said. "Or else end up in a lunatic asylum. Care to wager which?"

There shouldn't be a Shadow Market here, Brother Zachariah said.

"There are many things that shouldn't be that are," Belial said. "And many things that aren't that might still be if you only want them enough. I'll admit, I hoped that the Shadow Market would provide better cover. Or at least a warning to me, when your kind showed up to spoil my fun. But you weren't distracted at all."

Sister Emilia will take the adamas, *Brother Zachariah said. And once you've given it to her, you will send the Market away because I ask it of you.*

"If I do so, will that cancel out the favor I owe you?" Belial said.

"He owes you a favor?" Sister Emilia said. She thought, *No wonder they stitch up the Silent Brothers' mouths. They have so many secrets.*

It will not, Brother Zachariah said to Belial. To Emilia, he said, *Yes, and that is why you need not be afraid of him. A demon cannot kill one it is indebted to.*

"I could kill her, though," Belial said. He took a step toward Sister Emilia, and she raised her sword, determined to make her death count.

But you won't, Brother Zachariah said calmly.

Belial raised an eyebrow. "I won't? Why not?"

Brother Zachariah said, *Because you find her interesting. I certainly find her so.*

Belial was silent. Then he nodded. "Here." He threw the mask at Sister Emilia, who let go of Brother Zachariah's hand to catch it. It was lighter than she would have expected. "I imagine they won't let you work it, though. Too worried I might have corrupted it in some way. And who is to say that I didn't?"

We're done, Brother Zachariah said. *Go from here and do not return.*

"Absolutely!" Belial said. "Only, about that favor. It pains me so to be in debt to you when I might be of some service. I wonder if there isn't a thing that I could offer you. For example, the *yin fen* in your blood. Do the Silent Brothers still not know what the cure might be?"

Brother Zachariah said nothing, but Sister Emilia could see how his knuckles grew white where his fist was clenched. At last he said, *Go on.*

"I might know a cure," Belial said. "Yes, I think I know a sure cure. You could be who you once were. You could be Jem again. Or."

Brother Zachariah said, *Or?*

Belial's long tongue flicked out, as if he was tasting the air and found it delicious. "Or I could tell you a thing you don't know. There are Herondales, not the ones you know, but of the same bloodline as your *parabatai*. They are in great danger, their lives hang by a thread, and they are closer to us as we stand here than you can imagine. I can tell you something of them and set you on the path to find them if that is what you choose. But you must choose. To aid them or else to be who you once were. To once more be the one who left behind those who loved him best. The one they still yearn for. You could be him again if that is what you choose. Choose, Brother Zachariah."

Brother Zachariah hesitated for a long moment.

In the mirrors around them, Emilia saw visions of what Belial was promising, of all that his cure would mean. The woman Brother Zachariah adored would not be alone. He would be with her, able to share her pain and to love her wholly once more. He could rush to the side of the friend he loved, see his friend's blue eyes shine like stars on a midsummer night as he beheld Brother Zachariah transformed. They could clasp hands with no shadow of grief or pain upon them, just once. They had been waiting all their lives for that moment, and feared it would never come.

In a hundred reflections, Brother Zachariah's eyes flew open, blind and silver with agony. His face twisted as if he were being forced to endure the most terrible pain or, worse, forced to turn from the most perfect bliss.

The real Brother Zachariah's eyes stayed closed. His face remained serene.

At last he said, *The Carstairs owe a life debt to the Herondales. That is my choice.*

Belial said, "Then here is what I will tell you about these lost Herondales. There is power in their blood, and there is great danger, too. They are in hiding from an enemy who is neither mortal nor demon. These pursuers are resourceful, and close on their heels, and they will kill them if they find them."

"But where are they?" Sister Emilia said.

Belial said, "The debt is not that great, my dear. And now it is paid."

Sister Emilia looked at Brother Zachariah, who shook his head. *Belial is what he is,* he said. *A fornicator, a miser, and a polluter of sanctuaries. A creator of illusions. If I had made the other choice, do you really think I would be better off?*

"How well we know each other!" Belial said. "We all play a role, and it would astonish you, I think, to know how helpful I am being. You think I have offered you only tricks and sleights, but truly I have extended the hand of friendship. Or do you think that I can simply draw these Herondales out of a hat like so many rabbits? As for you, Sister Emilia, I owe you no debt, but would do you a good turn. Unlike our acquaintance here, you have chosen the path that you are set on."

"I have," Sister Emilia said. All she had ever wanted was to make things. To shape seraph blades and be known as a master of the forge. Shadowhunters, it seemed to her, gloried in destruction. What she longed for was to be permitted to create.

"I could make it so that you were the greatest *adamas* worker the Adamant Citadel has ever seen. Your name would be spoken for generations."

In the mirrors, Sister Emilia saw the blades she could make. She saw how they were used in battle, how the ones who wielded them thanked the one who had made them. They blessed the name of Sister Emilia, and acolytes came to study with her, and they, too, blessed her name.

"No!" Sister Emilia said to her reflections. "I will be the greatest *adamas* worker the Adamant Citadel has ever seen, but it will not be because I accepted aid from you. It will be because of the work that I do with the aid of my sisters."

"Nuts!" Belial said. "I don't even know why I bother."

Brother Zachariah said, *Roland the Astonishing!*

And before Sister Emilia could ask him what he meant by that, he was running out of the maze. She could hear him knocking over mirror after mirror with his staff, in too much of a hurry to find his way out as they had found their way in. Or maybe he knew that all the magic was bound up to make the center hard to find, and that smashing things on the way out would work just fine.

"A little slow on the draw, that one," Belial said to Sister Emilia. "Anyhow, I ought to make tracks. See you around, girlie."

"Wait!" Sister Emilia said. "I have an offer to make you."

Because she could not stop thinking of what she had seen in Brother Zachariah's mirrors. How much he longed to be with his *parabatai* and with the girl who must have been the warlock Tessa Herondale.

"Go on," Belial said. "I'm listening."

"I know that the things you offer us aren't real," Sister Emilia said. "But perhaps the illusion of a thing that we can't have is better than nothing at all. I want you to give Brother Zachariah a vision. A few hours with the one he misses most."

"He loves the warlock girl," Belial said. "I could give her to him."

"No!" Sister Emilia said. "Warlocks endure. I believe one day he will have his hours with Tessa Herondale even if he does not dare to hope for it. But his *parabatai*, Will Herondale, is old and frail and drawing near the end of his life. I want you to give them both a span of time. Both of them in a time and place where they can be young and happy and together."

"And what will you give me in return?" Belial said.

"If I had agreed to your previous offer," Sister Emilia said, "I think that my name would have lived on in infamy. And even if I was one day celebrated for my work, still every blade that I made would have been tainted by the idea that you had had some part in my successes. Every victory would have been poisoned."

"You're not as stupid as most Shadowhunters," Belial said.

"Oh, stop trying to flatter me!" Sister Emilia said. "You're wearing a suit made of human skin. No one of any sense should care what you have to say. But you should care very much about what I say to you. And that is this. I promise you if you do not give Brother Zachariah and Will Herondale the thing that I am asking for them, my life's work will be to forge a blade that is capable of killing you. And I will go on making blades until one day I accomplish my goal. And I warn you, I am not only talented, I am single-minded. Feel free to ask my mother if you don't believe me."

Belial met her gaze. He blinked twice and then looked away. Sister Emilia could see, now, the way he saw her reflected in the remaining mirrors, and she quite liked, for once, how she looked.

"You are interesting," he said. "As Brother Zachariah said. But perhaps you are also dangerous. You're too small to make a suit. But a hat. You would make a fine trilby. And perhaps a pair of spats. Why shouldn't I kill you now?"

Sister Emilia stuck her chin out. She said, "Because you are bored. You are curious whether or not I will be good at my work. And if my swords fail those who wield them, you will find it good entertainment."

Belial said, "True. I will."

Emilia said, "Then our deal?"

"Done," Belial said. And was gone, leaving Sister Emilia in a room walled in mirrors, holding an *adamas* mask in one hand and in her other a sword that was quite remarkable and yet in no way the equal of the blades that she would make one day.

When she emerged onto the carnival thoroughfare, already many of the tents were gone or else simply abandoned. There were few people about, and those she saw looked dazed and dreamy, as if they had just woken up. The Mysterious Merchants' Bazaar was gone entirely, and there was not a single werewolf to be seen, although the cotton-candy machine was still spinning slowly, filaments of sugar floating in the air.

Brother Zachariah was standing in front of the empty stage where they had seen the magician and his faerie wife. "*We all play a role, and it would astonish you, I think, to know how helpful I am being,*" he said.

She realized he was quoting Belial. "I have no idea what that means," she said.

He waved his hand at the sign above the stage. ROLAND THE ASTONISHING.

"Role and," she said slowly. "It would astonish you."

Tricks and sleights. He offered me the hand of friendship. Sleight of hand. Magic tricks. I should have known sooner. I thought the magician had the look of my friend Will. But he and his wife have fled.

"You'll find them again," Sister Emilia said. "I feel quite sure."

They are Herondales, and they are in trouble, said Brother Zachariah. *So I will find them, because I must. And Belial did say something that has proved of some interest to my Brothers.*

"Go on," Sister Emilia said.

I am as I am, Brother Zachariah said. *A Silent Brother but not entirely of the Brotherhood, because for so long I was unwillingly dependent on* yin fen. *And now I am, not entirely wholeheartedly, a Silent Brother, so that I might remain alive in spite of the* yin fen *in my blood that should have killed me years ago. Brother Enoch and the others have long searched for a cure and found nothing. We had begun to think perhaps there was no cure. But Brother Enoch was extremely interested in the choice Belial offered me. He said he's already researching demonic cures associated with Belial.*

"Then if you were cured," Sister Emilia said, "you would choose not to be what you are?"

Brother Zachariah said, *Without hesitation. Though not without gratitude for what my Brothers in the Silent City have done for me. And you? Will you regret choosing a life in the Adamant Citadel?*

Sister Emilia said, "How can I know that? But no. I am being given an opportunity to become what I have always known I was meant to be. Come on. We've done what we were sent to do."

Not quite, Brother Zachariah said. *Tonight is a full moon, and we don't know whether or not the werewolves have gone back into the mountains. As long as there are mundanes here, we must wait and watch. The Praetor Lupus take a hard-line Prohibitionist stance, not to mention they crack down hard on eating mundanes, but they may still need assistance.*

"Seems a little harsh," Sister Emilia said. "The Prohibitionist stance. I get that eating people is wrong, generally."

Werewolves live by a harsh code, Brother Zachariah said. She could not tell, by looking at his face, whether or not he was joking. But she was fairly sure that he was.

He said, *Though now that you have passed your test, I know you must be anxious to return to the Adamant Citadel. I'm sorry to keep you here.*

He wasn't wrong. She longed with all her heart to go to the only place that had ever truly felt like home to her. And she knew, too, that some part of Brother Zachariah must dread returning to the Silent City. She had seen enough in the mirrors to know where his home and his heart was.

She said, "I'm not sorry to tarry here a little longer with you, Brother Zachariah. And I'm not sorry that I met you. If we never meet again, I will hope that one day a weapon made by my hand may yet prove useful to you in some way." Then she yawned. Iron Sisters, unlike Silent Brothers, required things like sleep and food.

Brother Zachariah hoisted himself up onto the edge of the stage and then patted the space beside him. *I'll keep watch. If you grow weary, sleep. No harm will come while I keep vigil.*

Sister Emilia said, "Brother Zachariah? If something strange happens tonight, if you should see something that you thought you would not see again, don't be alarmed. No harm will come of it."

What do you mean? Brother Zachariah said. *What did you and Belial discuss when I had gone?*

In the back of his mind, his Brothers murmured: *Be careful, be careful, be careful. Oh, be careful.*

Sister Emilia said, "Nothing of any great importance. But I think he is a little afraid of me now, and he should be. He offered me something so that I would not become his nemesis."

Tell me what you mean, Brother Zachariah said.

"I'll tell you later," Sister Emilia said firmly. "Right now I'm so tired I can barely talk at all."

Sister Emilia was hungry as well as tired, but she was so very tired she couldn't be bothered to eat. She would sleep first. She climbed up on the stage beside Brother Zachariah and took off her cloak and made it into a pillow. The evening was still warm, and if she grew cold, well, then she would wake up, and she and Brother Zachariah could keep watch together companionably.

She hoped that her brothers, now grown men all, were as kind and stouthearted as this man was. She fell asleep remembering how she and they had played at fighting before they were old enough to train, laughing and tumbling and vowing to be great heroes. Her dreams were very sweet, though she did not remember them in the morning when she woke.

Silent Brothers do not sleep as mortals do, but nevertheless Brother Zachariah, as he sat and watched and listened in the deserted carnival, felt as the night drew on that he was in a dream. Silent Brothers do not dream, and yet slowly the voices of Brother Enoch and the others in his head dissipated and blew away and were replaced by music. Not carnival music, but the sound of a *qinqin*. There should not have been a *qinqin* anywhere on the mountain above Chattanooga, and yet he heard it. Listening to the sound of it, he discovered that he was no longer Brother Zachariah at all. He was only Jem. He did not sit on a stage. Instead, he was perched on a tiled roof, and the sounds and smells and sights around him were all familiar ones. Not the Silent City. Not London. He was Jem again, and he was in the city where he had been born. Shanghai. Someone said, "Jem? Am I dreaming?"

Even before he turned his head, Jem knew who would be sitting there beside him. "Will?" he said.

And it was Will. Not Will old and tired and wasted as Jem had last seen him, and not even Will as he had been when they'd first met Tessa Gray. No, this was Will as he had been in the first few years when they had lived and trained together in the London Institute. As he had been when they made their oath and became *parabatai*. Thinking this, Jem looked at his shoulder, where his *parabatai* rune had been inscribed. The flesh there was unmarked. He saw that Will was doing the same thing, looking under his collar for the rune on his chest.

Jem said, "How is this possible?"

Will said, "This is the time between when we had pledged to become *parabatai* and when we went through the ritual. Look. See the scar here?" He showed Jem a distinctive mark on his wrist.

"You got that from an Iblis demon," Jem said. "I remember. It was two nights after we had decided. It was the first fight we had once we'd made up our minds."

"So that is *when* we are," Will said. "But what I don't know is *where* we are. Or how this is happening."

"I think," Jem said, "that a friend has made a bargain for me. I think that we are here together because the demon Belial is afraid of her, and she asked this for me. Because I would not ask for myself."

"Belial!" Will said. "Well, if he's afraid of this friend of yours, I hope I never meet her."

"I wish you could," Jem said. "But let's not waste whatever time we have talking about people you don't have any interest in. You may not know where we are, but I do. And I am afraid that the span of time we have together may not be long."

"That has always been the case with us," Will said. "But let us be grateful to your terrifying friend, because however long we have, here we are together and I see no sign of *yin fen* on you, and we are in possession of the knowledge that there was never any curse on me. For however long, there is no shadow on us."

"There is no shadow," Jem agreed. "And we are in a place that I long wished to go with you. This is Shanghai, where I was born. Remember when we used to talk about traveling here together? There were so many places I wanted to show you."

"I remember you thought very highly of a temple or two," Will said. "You promised me gardens, although why you think I care for gardens, I don't know. And there were some vistas or famous rock formations or things."

"Forget the rock formations," Jem said. "There's a dumpling place down the street, and I haven't eaten human food in half a century. Let's go see who can eat the most dumplings in the shortest amount of time. And duck! You really ought to try pressed duck! It's a great delicacy."

Jem looked at Will, suppressing a smile. His friend glared back, but at last neither of them could hold back their laughter. Will said, "There is nothing so sweet as feasting upon the bones of my enemies. Especially with you at my side."

There was a lightness in Jem's chest that he realized, finally, was joy. He saw that joy mirrored in his *parabatai*'s face. The face of the one you love is the best mirror of all. It shows you your own happiness and your own pain and it helps you to bear both, because to bear either alone is to be overwhelmed by the flood.

Jem stood up and held out his hand to Will. Without realizing it, he held his breath. Perhaps this was a dream after all, and when Jem touched him Will would vanish away again. But Will's hand was warm and solid and strong, and Jem drew him up easily. Together they began to run lightly over the tiles of the roof.

The night was very beautiful and warm, and they were both young.

A Deeper Love

By Cassandra Clare and Maureen Johnson

London, December 29, 1940

"I think first," Catarina said, "lemon cake. Oh, lemons. I think I miss them most."

Catarina Loss and Tessa Gray were walking down Ludgate Hill, just passing the Old Bailey. This was a game they sometimes played: What will you eat first when this war is over? Of all the terrible things that were going on, sometimes the most ordinary ran the deepest. Food was rationed, and the rations were small—an ounce of cheese, four thin pieces of bacon, and one egg a week. Everything came in tiny amounts. Some things simply went away, like lemons. There were oranges sometimes—Tessa saw them at the fruit-and-veg market—but they were only for children, who could have one each. The nurses were fed at the hospital, but the portions were always tiny, and never enough to keep up with all the work they performed. Tessa was lucky to have the strength she did. It was not all the physical strength of a Shadowhunter, but some trace of angelic endurance lingered within her and sustained her; she had no idea how the mundane nurses kept up.

"Or a banana," Catarina said. "I never liked them much

before, but now that they are gone, I find myself craving them. That's always the way, isn't it?"

Catarina Loss did not care about food. She barely ate at all. But she was making conversation as they walked down the street. This was what you did—you pretended life was normal, even as death rained from above. It was the London spirit. You kept to your routines as much as you could, even if you slept in a Tube station at night for shelter, or you returned home to find the neighbor's house or yours was no longer there. Businesses tried to stay open, even if all the glass blew out of the windows or a bomb went through the roof. Some would put out signs that said, MORE OPEN THAN USUAL.

You carried on. You talked about bananas and lemons.

At this point in December, London was at its darkest. The sun started going down just after three in the afternoon. Because of the air raids, London was under blackout orders every night. Blackout curtains blocked light from every window. Streetlamps were turned off. Cars dimmed their lights. People walked the streets carrying torches to find their way through the velvety darkness. All of London was shade and corner and nook, every alley blind, every wall a dark blank. It made the city mysterious and mournful.

To Tessa, it felt like London itself grieved for her Will, felt his loss, turned out every light.

Tessa Gray had not particularly enjoyed Christmas this year. It was difficult to enjoy things with the Germans raining bombs overhead whenever the whim suited them. The Blitz, as it was called, was designed to bring terror to London, to force the city to its knees. There were deadly bombs that could crush a home, leaving a pile of smoking rubble where children once slept and families laughed together. In the mornings, you would see walls missing and the inner workings of houses, exposed like a doll's house, scraps of cloth flapping against broken brick, toys and books scattered in piles of rubble. More than once she saw a bathtub hanging off the side of what remained of a house. Extraordinary things would happen, like the house where the chimney fell, smashing through the kitchen table where a family ate, shattering it but harming no one. Buses would be upturned. Rubble would fall, instantly killing one family member, leaving the other stunned and unscathed. It was a matter of chance, of inches.

There was nothing worse than being left alone, the one you loved ripped from you.

"Did you have a good visit this afternoon?" Catarina asked.

"The younger generation are still trying to talk me into leaving," Tessa replied, stepping around a hole in the pavement where part of it had been blown away. "They think I should go to New York."

"They're your children," Catarina said gently. "They want what's best for you. They don't understand."

When Will died, Tessa had known there could be no place for her among the Shadowhunters. For a time it had seemed as if there was no place for her in all the world, with so much of her heart in the cold ground. Then Magnus Bane had taken Tessa into his home when she was almost mad with grief, and when she slowly emerged, Magnus's friends Catarina Loss and Ragnor Fell encircled her.

No one understood the pain of being immortal save another immortal. She could only be grateful they had taken her in.

It was Catarina who introduced Tessa to nursing when the

war broke out. Catarina had always been a healer: of Nephilim, of Downworlders, of humans. Wherever she was needed, she went. She had nursed in the last Great War, only twenty years before, the war that was never supposed to happen again. The two of them had taken a small flat off Farringdon Street, close to the London Institute and to St. Bart's Hospital. It was not as luxurious as her previous homes—just a small, second-story walk-up with a shared bath in the hall. It was easier this way, and cozier. Tessa and Catarina shared one small bedroom, hanging a sheet down the middle for privacy. They often worked at night and slept during the day. At least the raids were only at night now—no more sirens and planes and bombs and antiaircraft guns at noon.

The war had caused increased demonic activity—as all wars did, demons taking advantage of chaos caused by battle—which was almost overwhelming the Shadowhunters. Though it was a terrible thought to have, Tessa regarded the war as a kind of personal blessing. Here, she could be useful. One of the good things about being a nurse was that there was always something that needed doing. Always. Constant activity kept grief at bay because there was no time to think. Going to New York, sitting in safety, would be hellish. There would be nothing to do but think about her family. She did not know how to do this, how to go on agelessly as her descendants grew older than her.

She looked up at the great dome of St. Paul's Cathedral, lording over the city exactly as it had done for hundreds of years. How did it feel, seeing its city below, its sprawling child, blown to pieces?

"Tessa?" Catarina said.

"I'm fine," Tessa replied.

At that moment, a scream broke out all over the city—the air-raid siren. Moments later came the humming noise. It sounded like the approach of an army of angry bees. The Luftwaffe was overhead. The bombs would be falling soon.

"I thought we might be spared for a few more days," Catarina said grimly. "It was so nice to only have two air raids this week. I suppose even the Luftwaffe wants to celebrate the holiday."

The two quickened their steps. Then it came—that uncanny sound. As the bombs fell, they whistled. Tessa and Catarina stopped. The whistling was just above them, all around. The whistling was not the problem—the problem was when it stopped. The silence meant the bombs were less than a hundred feet overhead. That was when you waited. Were you going to be next? Where could you go when death was silent and came from the sky?

There was a clanking and a hissing sound up ahead, and the street was suddenly illuminated with spitting, phosphorescent light.

"Incendiaries," Catarina said.

Tessa and Catarina rushed forward. The incendiary bombs were canisters that looked harmless enough up close, similar to a long thermal flask. When they hit the ground, they spread fire. They were being scattered all up and down the street by the planes, highlighting the road and spitting flames at the buildings. The fire wardens began running from all directions, dampening the incendiaries as quickly as possible. Catarina bent down to one. Tessa saw a blue flash; then the bomb extinguished. Tessa ran up to another and stamped at the sparks until a fire warden poured a bucket of water over it. But now there were hundreds all over the road.

"Must get on," Catarina said. "It looks to be a long one tonight."

Passing Londoners tipped their hats. They saw what Tessa and Catarina wanted them to see—just two brave young nurses headed to the hospital, not two immortal beings trying to stem an endless tide of suffering.

On the other side of the Thames, a figure was making its way through the dark beneath the viaduct, past where the normally flourishing Borough Market was held by day. Usually, this place was heaving with activity and scraps of the day's market. Tonight, everything was muted and there was barely anything remaining on the ground. Every old cabbage and bruised piece of fruit had been plucked up by hungry people. The blackout curtains, lack of streetlights, and absence of mundanes on the streets made this corner of London foreboding. But the cloaked figure walked without hesitation, even as the air-raid siren ripped through the night. His destination was just around the corner.

Even with the war, the Shadow Market went on, though it was fragmentary. Like the mundanes with their ration cards, their limited supplies of food, of clothing, and even of bathwater, things here were in short supply. The old-book stalls had been picked through. Instead of hundreds of potions and powders, only a dozen or so graced the vendors' tables. The sparkle and the fire were nothing compared to the flames that raged on the opposite bank or the machines that dropped death from the sky, so there seemed little point in putting on light shows. The children still ran about—the young werewolves, the street children and orphans who had been Turned in the dark corners of the blackout and now roamed, seeking nourishment and parental guidance. A small vampire, Turned far too young, trailed alongside Brother Zachariah, pulling on his cloak for fun. Zachariah did not disturb him. The child looked lonely and dirty, and if it pleased him to trail a Silent Brother, then Zachariah would allow it.

"What are you?" said the little boy.

A kind of Shadowhunter, Brother Zachariah replied.

"Did you come to kill us? I heard 'at's what they do."

No. That is not what we do. Where is your family?

"Gone," the little boy said. "A bomb dropped on us, and my master came and got me."

It had been all too easy to pluck these little ones out of the wreckage of a home, take them by the hand to some pitch-black alley, and Turn them. Demon activity too was at an all-time high. After all, who could tell whether that torn limb was from someone killed by a bomb or someone ripped apart by a demon? Did it make a difference? Mundanes had their own demonic ways.

A crowd of other vampire children ran past, and the little boy ran off with them. The sky roared, thick with the sound of planes. Brother Zachariah listened to the noise of the bombing with a musician's ear. The bombs whistled when they dropped, but there was that strange punctuating silence as they neared the earth. Silences in music were as important as sound. In this case, the silences told so much of the story to come. Tonight, the bombs were falling on the other side of the river like rain—a thundering symphony with too many notes. Those bombs would be falling near the Institute, near St. Bart's Hospital, where Tessa worked. Fear for her ran through Zachariah, cold as the river cutting across the city. In these empty days since

Will's death, emotion was a rare visitor for him, but when it came to Tessa, feeling always bloomed.

"Bad one tonight," said a faerie woman with silver scaled skin who sold enchanted toy toads. They leaped about on her table, with protruding golden tongues. "Like a toad?"

She pointed at one of the toy toads. It turned blue, then red, then green, then flipped on its back and spun, before turning into a stone. Then it burst forth into toad form again and the cycle continued.

No, thank you, Zachariah said.

He turned to keep moving, but the woman spoke again.

"He's waiting for you," she said.

Who is he?

"The one you have come to meet."

For months now, he had been slowly trailing a series of contacts through the faerie world, trying to find out about the lost Herondales he had learned of at the Shadow Market and carnival in Tennessee. He had not come specifically to meet anyone tonight—he had a number of contacts who provided information as they came by it. But someone had come to meet him.

Thank you, he said politely. *Where am I to go?*

"The King's Head Yard," she said, smiling widely. Her teeth were small and pointed.

Brother Zachariah nodded. The King's Head Yard was a nearby alley—a horseshoe-shaped offshoot of Borough High Street. It was accessed through an arch between the buildings. As he approached it, he heard the sound of planes overhead, then the whistling of a payload being dropped.

Nothing to do but keep going. Zachariah crossed under the archway partway, then stopped.

I am here, he said to the darkness.

"Shadowhunter," a voice said.

From the bend at the end of the yard, a figure emerged. It was a faerie, and clearly one of the Court. He was extremely tall and almost human in appearance but for his wings, which were brown and white and spread wide, almost touching the opposite walls.

I understand you wish to speak to me, Brother Zachariah said politely.

The faerie stepped closer, and Zachariah could see a copper mask in the form of a hawk covering the top half of his face.

"You have been interfering," the faerie said.

In what, precisely? Zachariah inquired. He did not move back, but he tightened his grip on his staff.

"Things that do not concern you."

I have been making inquiries about a lost Shadowhunter family. That is very much something that concerns me.

"You come to my brethren. You ask the fey."

This was true. Since his encounter with Belial at the carnival in Tennessee, Brother Zachariah had been pursuing many leads in Faerie. He had seen, after all, a Herondale descendant with a faerie wife and child. They had fled, but it had not been him they feared. Whatever danger threatened the lost Herondale, Zachariah had learned it came from Faerie.

"What is it you know?" the faerie asked, stepping forward.

I would advise you not to come closer.

"You have no idea of the danger of what you seek. This is Faerie business. Cease your meddling in that which affects our Lands and our Lands alone."

I repeat, Zachariah said calmly, though his grip on the staff was firm now, *I ask of Shadowhunters. That is very much my business.*

"Then you do so at your peril."

A blade flashed in the faerie's hand. He swung at Zachariah, who moved at once, rolling to the ground and coming up next to the faerie, striking his arm and knocking the sword free.

The whistling of the bombs had stopped. That meant they were right overhead.

Then, they fell. Three of them clanked down on the stones at the opening of the archway and began spitting their phosphorescent flames. This distracted the faerie for just a moment, and Zachariah took the opportunity to dash around the horseshoe and out the other side. He had no desire to continue this fight, to cause problems between the Silent Brothers and the fey. Zachariah had no idea why the faerie had become so violent. Hopefully he would simply return from whence he came. Zachariah slipped onto the Borough High Street, dodging the falling cylinders. But he had barely begun his flight when the faerie was behind him. Zachariah spun, his staff ready.

I have no quarrel with you. Let us go our separate ways.

Below the hawk mask, the faerie's teeth were gritted. He sliced out with his sword, ripping the air in front of Brother Zachariah, slashing his cloak. Zachariah leaped and spun, his staff wheeling through the air to slam against the sword. As they fought, the canisters landed closer and closer, coughing fire. Neither flinched.

Brother Zachariah took care not to injure the faerie, only to block the attack. His purpose must remain secret, but the faerie was coming with increasing force. He slashed upward with his sword, meaning to cut Zachariah's throat—and Zachariah smashed it from his hands, sending it flying across the road.

Let us finish with this. Call it a fair fight ended. Walk away.

The faerie was out of breath. Blood trickled from a wound at his temple.

"As you wish," he said. "But take my warning."

He turned to go. Brother Zachariah loosened his grip on his staff for just a moment. The faerie turned back, a short blade in his hand, aimed at Zachariah's heart. With the speed of the Silent Brothers he whirled away, but he could not move fast enough. The blade sank deep into his shoulder and came out the other side.

The pain. The wound immediately began to hiss as if acid was dissolving Zachariah's flesh. Pain and numbness ran down his arm, causing him to drop his staff. He staggered back, and the faerie retrieved his sword and advanced toward him.

"You have interfered with the fey for the last time, Gregori," he said. "Our people are our people, and our enemies, our enemies. They will never be yours!"

The incendiaries landed around them now, clanking loudly against pavement and cobblestone, flashing light and licking flames at the buildings. Zachariah tried to get away, but his strength was fading. He could not run—he could only stagger drunkenly. This was no normal wound. There was poison flooding his body. The faerie was coming at him, and he would not get away.

No. Not without seeing Tessa one more time.

He looked down and saw one of the incendiaries that had fallen from the sky. This one had not detonated.

Brother Zachariah used the last of his strength to spin around, swinging out with the canister. Small bombs were still falling. Several more dropped nearby. The canister flew through the air and struck the faerie in the chest. It cracked apart, and the faerie shrieked as the iron inside was released. Zachariah fell to his knees as the iron flame burned.

The hospital was rumbling.

At St. Bart's, the upper floors of the hospital were considered too unsafe to use. The activity was all on the lower level and in the basement, where doctors and nurses ran to attend the injured and sick. The fire wardens were being brought in, their skin covered in soot, gasping for air. There were injuries from the attacks—the burns, the crushings, the people cut through with exploding glass or struck by debris. Plus all the normal business of London went on—people still had babies and became ill and had normal accidents. But the war multiplied incidents. People fell or crashed in the dark. There were heart attacks as bombs came down. There were so many people who needed help.

From the moment they arrived, Catarina and Tessa ran from one end of the hospital to the other, tending to the injured as they came in, fetching supplies, carrying bloodied bowls of water, wrapping and removing bandages. Being a Shadowhunter, Tessa could easily cope with some of the grislier aspects of the job, like the fact that no matter how hard you tried to keep your apron clean, you would be covered in blood and grime within minutes. No amount of washing got it out. No sooner would you scrub it off your arms than another patient would come in and your skin would be covered again. Through it all, the nurses strove to maintain an air of calm competence. You moved quickly but not hastily. You spoke loudly when you needed assistance, but you never screamed.

Tessa was stationed by the door, directing the orderlies as they brought in a dozen new patients. They were bringing in groups of fire wardens now, some walking wounded, others on stretchers.

"Over there," Tessa said as the orderlies carried in burn victims. "To Sister Loss."

"I've got one asking for you, Sister," said the orderly, setting down a stretcher with a figure on it wrapped tight in a gray blanket.

"Coming," Tessa said. She hurried to the stretcher and bent down. The blanket was pulled partway over the man's face.

"You're all right," Tessa said, pulling back the blanket. "You're all right now. You're at hospital. You're here at St. Bart's. . . ."

It took her a moment to realize what she was seeing. The marks on his skin were not all wounds. And his face, though covered in soot and streaked with blood, was more familiar to her than her own.

Tessa, Jem said, the echo deep inside her head like the memory of a bell ringing.

Then he went limp.

"Jem!" It couldn't be. She seized his hand, hoping she was dreaming—that the war had addled her sense of reality completely. But the slim, scarred hand in hers was familiar, even limp and without strength. This was Jem, her Jem, dressed in the bone-colored robes of a Silent Brother, the marks on his neck pulsing as his heart pumped furiously. His skin burned under her touch.

"He's in a bad way," the orderly said. "I'll fetch the doctor."

"No," Tessa said quickly. "Leave him with me."

Jem was glamoured, but he could not be examined. No mundane doctor could do anything about his injuries, and they would be shocked at his runes, his scars, even his blood.

She tore away the parchment robes. It took her only a

moment to find the source of the trauma—a massive wound in his shoulder that went clean through. The wound was black with a silvery edge, and his tunic was saturated with blood all the way down to his waist. Tessa scanned the hallway. There were so many people, she could not immediately see Catarina. She could not scream.

"Jem," she said into his ear. "I am here. I am getting help."

She stood up, as calmly as she could, and hastily made her way through the chaos of the hall, her heart beating so fast she felt like it might come up her throat and through her mouth. She found Catarina working on a burned man, her hands on his wounds. Only Tessa could see the snow-white glow emanating from under the blanket as she worked.

"Sister Loss," she said, trying to control her voice. "I need you at once."

"Just a moment," Catarina said.

"It cannot wait."

Catarina looked over her shoulder. Then the glow stopped. "You should feel better in a moment," she said to the man. "One of the other sisters will be over very soon."

"I feel better already," the man said, touching his arm in wonder.

Tessa hurried Catarina back to Jem. Catarina, seeing Tessa's taut expression, asked no questions; she only bent down and peeled the blanket back.

She looked up at Tessa. "A Shadowhunter?" Catarina said in a low voice. "Here?"

"Quickly," Tessa said. "Help me move him."

Tessa took one end of the stretcher and Catarina the other, and they moved Jem down the hallway. There was another explosion, closer. The building pulsed from the impact. The lights swung and went out for a moment, causing cries of alarm and confusion. Tessa froze in place, assuring herself that the ceiling wasn't about to come down and bury them all. After a moment, the lights came back on, and movement continued.

"Come on," Tessa said.

There was a small room at the end of the hall that was used for the nurses' tea breaks and naps, or when they could not return home because of bombings. They set Jem's stretcher gently on the empty cot on the side of the room. Jem was lying quietly, his features still, his breathing jagged. The color was draining from his skin.

"Hold the light," Catarina said. "I need to examine this."

Tessa pulled a witchlight from her pocket. It was safer and more reliable than the electric lights, but she could only use it in private. Catarina grabbed a pair of shears and cut away the cloth around the tunic to expose the wound. The veins on Jem's chest and his arm had turned black.

"What is that?" Tessa said, her voice shaking. "It looks very bad."

"I haven't seen this in a long time," Catarina said. "I think it's a cataplasm."

"What is that?"

"Nothing good," Catarina said. "Be patient."

She must be mad, Tessa thought. Be patient? How could she be patient? This was Jem, not some nameless patient under a gray blanket.

But every nameless patient was precious to someone. She forced herself to breathe more deeply.

"Take his hand," Catarina said. "It will work better if you

do it. Think of him, who he is to you. Give him your strength."

Tessa had practiced a small amount of warlock magic before, though she was not advanced. As Catarina watched, Tessa took Jem's slender hand in her own. She curled her fingers around his, his violinist's fingers, remembering the care with which he had played. The time he had composed for her. His voice echoed in her heart.

People still use the expression "zhi yin" *to mean "close friends" or "soul mates," but what it really means is "understanding music." When I played, you saw what I saw. You understand my music.*

Tessa smelled burned sugar. She felt Jem's lips hot against hers, the carpet underneath them, his arms holding her against his heart. *Oh, my Jem.*

His body surged against the stretcher, his back arching. He gasped, and the sound sent a shock through Tessa. Jem had been silent so long.

"Can you hear us?" Catarina asked.

I—can, came the halting reply in Tessa's mind.

"You need the Silent Brothers," Catarina said.

I cannot go to my Brothers with this.

"If you do not go to them, you will die," Catarina said.

The words hit Tessa like a blow.

It is not possible for me to go to the Bone City like this. I came here hoping you might be able to help.

"This is no time for pride," Catarina said sternly.

It is not pride, Jem said. Tessa knew this was the truth; he was the least proud person she had ever known.

"Jem!" Tessa begged. "You must go!"

Catarina started. "This is James Carstairs?" she asked.

Of course Catarina knew the name of Will Herondale's

parabatai, though she had never met him. She did not understand all that had passed between Tessa and Jem. She did not know that they had been engaged to be married. That before there was a Tessa and Will, there had been a Tessa and Jem. Tessa did not speak of these things because of Will, and then because of the absence of Will.

I have come here because it is the only place I can go, Jem said. *To speak the truth to the Brothers would be to endanger another life than mine. I will not do it.*

Tessa looked to Catarina in desperation. "He means it," she said. "He will never seek help if it means someone else will be hurt. Catarina—he cannot die. He *cannot die*."

Catarina inhaled sharply and opened the door a crack to peer into the hall.

"We will need to get him back to the flat," she said. "I can't work on him here. I don't have what I need. We will need to move quickly."

Tessa seized hold of Jem's stretcher. She understood the complications involved. They were nurses, in charge of many sick people who would be pouring in during the attack. The city was being bombed. It was on fire. Getting home was not a simple matter.

But it was what they were going to do.

The city they stepped back out into was not the same one that it had been only an hour before. The air was so hot that breathing burned the lungs. A high wall of orange jumped out of the buildings around them, and the silhouette of St. Paul's stood out in intense relief. The scene was at once terrifying and almost beautiful, like a dream image from Blake, a poet her son

James had always loved. *On what wings dare he aspire? What the hand dare seize the fire?*

But there was no time to think of things like London burning. There were two ambulances right outside on the street. Next to one, a driver was having a cigarette and talking to a fire warden.

"Charlie!" Catarina called.

The man tossed his cigarette aside and came running over.

"We need your help," she said. "This man has an infection. We can't keep him in the ward here."

"You need me to take him to St. Thomas', Sister? The going will be rough. We've got fires in almost every street."

"We can't make it that far," Catarina said. "We've got to move him quickly. Our flat is just on Farringdon Street. That will have to do for now."

"All right, Sister. Let's get him in the ambulance."

He opened the back and assisted them in getting Jem inside.

"I'll be back in one moment," Catarina said to them. "I just need to get a few supplies."

She dashed back into the hospital. Tessa climbed into the back with Jem, and Charlie got into the driver's seat.

"Don't usually take patients to nurses' flats," Charlie said, "but needs must when the devil drives. Sister Loss always looks after them. When my Mabel was having our second, she had a terrible spell. I thought we was going to lose them both. Sister Loss, bless her. She saved them both. I wouldn't have Mabel or my Eddie without them. Whatever she needs."

Tessa had heard many stories like this. Catarina was both a warlock and a mundane nurse with over a hundred years of experience. She had nursed in the last Great War. Old soldiers were always coming up to her and saying how she was "the spitting image of that nurse who saved me in the last one." But, of course, she couldn't be. That was twenty years ago, and Catarina was still so young. Catarina stood out to them because of her dark skin. They did not see a blue woman with white hair—they saw a nurse from the West Indies. She had faced considerable prejudice, but it was clear that not only was Catarina a good nurse, she was the *best* nurse in all of London. Anyone who got Catarina as a nurse was considered lucky. Even the most miserable bigot desired to live, and Catarina nursed all who came to her with equanimity. She could not save them all, but there were always a few, at least one a day, who survived something unsurvivable because Sister Loss was the one at their side. Some called her the Angel of St. Bart's.

Jem stirred and groaned lightly.

"Don't you worry, mate," Charlie called back to him. "Best nurses in the city, this lot. You couldn't be in safer hands."

Jem tried to smile—but instead he shuddered, and blood trickled from the side of his mouth. Tessa immediately wiped it away with the edge of her cloak and leaned close to him.

"You hold on, James Carstairs," she said, trying to sound brave. She gripped his hand in hers. She had forgotten how wonderful it was to hold Jem's hands—his long, graceful hands, the ones that could produce such beautiful music from the violin.

"Jem," she whispered, leaning low, "you must hold on. You must. Will needs you to. I need you to."

Jem's hand tightened on hers.

Catarina came running out of the hospital carrying a small canvas bag. She leaped into the back of the ambulance, slamming the doors behind her and snapping Tessa back to the present.

"Go, Charlie," she said.

Charlie shifted the ambulance into gear, and they started forward. Overhead, the drone of the Luftwaffe was back, like the hum of an army of bees. Catarina immediately scooted next to Jem and passed Tessa a bandage to unwind.

The ambulance juddered, and Jem was jolted on his stretcher. Tessa tented herself over him to keep him in place.

"Catarina," Tessa said, "you said this was a cataplasm. What does that mean?"

"It's a rare belladonna concentrate with demon poison added in to it," Catarina said quietly. "Until I can get the antidote, we need to try to keep it from spreading in his bloodstream, or at least slow it down. We're going to tie some tourniquets, start cutting off blood flow."

This sounded incredibly dangerous. By tying off the limbs, they could be risking their loss. But Catarina knew what she was doing.

"This will not be comfortable," Catarina said, unwinding a bandage, "but it will help. Hold him."

Tessa pressed her body down on Jem a bit more as Catarina looped the bandage around the injured arm and shoulder. She made a knot, then grabbed the ends of the bandages and pulled tight. Jem arched against Tessa's chest.

"You're all right, Jem," she said. "You're all right. We're here. I'm here. It's me. Tessa. It's me."

Tessa, he said. The word came out like a question. He writhed as Catarina wound the bandage tightly around the shoulder and arm. A mundane would not have been able to withstand it; Jem was barely able to. Sweat broke out all over his face.

"It's going to be rough going, Sisters," Charlie called back.

"They're trying to burn down St. Paul's, the bastards. I'm going to have to go around the long way. It's fires everywhere."

Charlie did not exaggerate. In front of them was a view of solid orange against the black silhouettes of burning buildings. The fires were so high that it was like there was a sun rising up from the earth, dragging day out of the ground. As they drove on, it was like they were pressing into a solid wall of heat. The wind had quickened, and now fire was meeting fire, creating walls instead of pockets. The air shimmered and cooked. Several times they turned down streets that no longer seemed to be there anymore.

"It's no good this way either," Charlie said, turning the ambulance again. "I'll have to try another way."

Then came the sharp whistling in the air. This time the pitch was different. These were not the incendiary bombs—these were the large explosives. After the fires, the idea was to kill. Charlie stopped the ambulance and craned his head to look up to see where the bomb was likely to land. They all froze, listening to the whistle go quiet.

It was a long moment. Then it came. The impact was at the other end of the street, sending the shock wave down the road and a spray of rubble into the air. Charlie started on again.

"Bastards," he said under his breath. "Bloody bastards. You all right there, Sisters?"

"We're fine," Catarina said. She had both hands on Jem's shoulder, and there was a low blue glow around the bandages. She was holding it back, whatever it was that was going through Jem's body.

They had just made another turn when there was another whistle and another silence. They stopped again. The impact was to their right this time, down at the next intersection. The ambulance rocked as the corner of a building was blown away. The ground shook. Charlie turned the ambulance away from it.

"Not going to get through this way," he said. "I'll try down Shoe Lane."

The ambulance turned once more. On the stretcher, Jem had stopped moving. Tessa could not tell if the pulsing heat was coming from the air or from Jem's body. There was fire on both sides of the street here, but the path looked almost clear to get through. There were fire wardens in the road, shooting water into a burning warehouse. Suddenly there was a creaking sound. The fire began to arc over the road.

"Blimey," Charlie said. "Hang on tight, Sisters."

The ambulance ground into reverse and started speeding backward down the alley. Tessa heard a crackling noise—uncanny, almost merry—a great tinkling. Then, all at once, the bricks of the building exploded and the building tumbled down into a mass of fire and rubble, the flames blowing up in a mighty roar. The men with the hose vanished.

"God almighty," Charlie said, grinding the ambulance to a halt. He jumped out of the driver's seat and started running for the men, two of whom were stumbling out of the flames. Catarina looked up and out the windscreen.

"Those men," she said. "The building's come down on them."

You must help them, Jem said.

Catarina looked between Jem and Tessa for a moment. Tessa felt herself full of an unbearable anxiety. She had to get Jem to safety, and yet, in front of them, men were being consumed in flame.

"I will be quick," Catarina said, and Tessa nodded.

Alone in the ambulance, Tessa looked down at Jem.

If they need you, then you must go, Jem said.

"They need Catarina," Tessa said. "You need me, and I need you. I do not leave you. No matter what happens, I do not leave you."

The ambulance was heating up like an oven, trapped as it was between multiple fires. There was no water to cool Jem's brow, so Tessa mopped it and fanned it with her hand.

After a minute, Catarina opened the back of the ambulance. She was covered in soot and water.

"I have done what I can," she said. "They will live now, as long as they reach the hospital. Charlie will have to take the ambulance."

Her eyes reflected her pain.

Yes, Jem said. Somehow he had found enough strength to rise on his elbows. *You must get them to safety. I am a Shadowhunter. I am stronger than those men.*

He had always been strong. It was not because he was a Shadowhunter. It was because he had a will fierce as starlight, burning in darkness and refusing to be put out.

Charlie brought the wounded fire wardens over, carrying one over his shoulder.

"You'll be all right, Sisters?" he said. "You can ride back with me?"

"No," Catarina said, climbing inside to help Tessa get Jem to his feet. Tessa placed herself under Jem's wounded shoulder. He winced from the movement. It was clear Jem couldn't really walk but had decided that he would do it anyway. He got his body into a standing position through sheer will. Catarina hurried to prop him up on the other side, and Tessa used her full strength to support him completely. It was strange, feeling Jem's body against hers after so long. They got out of the lane and back onto the road.

Lovely night for a walk, Jem said, clearly trying to cheer her. He was sweating all over and could no longer hold up his head. His legs had gone limp. He was like a marionette with the strings gone slack.

The buildings all around were on fire as well, but the fire was still contained inside. Tessa was covered in sweat, and the temperature was cooking them. The air was swollen with heat, and every mouthful of air scorched its way down her throat. It felt like when she first learned to change herself: the exquisite, strange pain.

The street was narrowing now to the point where they could barely walk three abreast. Catarina's and Tessa's sides scraped the hot walls. Jem's feet dragged along the ground, no longer able to take any steps. When they emerged onto Fleet Street, Tessa gasped in the relatively cool air. The sweat on her face was chilled for a moment.

"Come," Catarina said, leading them toward a bench. "Let's get him down for a moment."

They gingerly rested Jem on the empty bench. His skin was slick with sweat. Catarina pulled his shirt open to expose his chest and cool him, and Tessa could see the runes of the Silent Brothers on his skin and his veins throbbing in his throat.

"I don't know how much farther we can get him in this state," Catarina said. "The effort is too much."

Once on the bench, Jem's limbs began to jerk and twitch as the poison moved through his body once more. Catarina set to work on him again, putting her hands on the wound. Tessa scanned the road. She made out a large shadow coming in their direction, with two dimmed lights like heavily lidded eyes.

A bus. A great red double-decker London bus was making its way through the night, because nothing stopped the London buses, not even a war. They were not at a stop, but Tessa jumped into the road and waved it down. The driver opened the door and called out.

"You sisters all right?" he said. "Your friend, 'e doesn't look so good."

"He's injured," Catarina said.

"Then you get yourselves inside, Sisters," the driver said, shutting the door after they had done so, dragging Jem between them. "You've got London's best private ambulance at your service. Do you want to go to St. Bart's?"

"We've come from there. It's full. We're taking him home to care for him, and we need to go quickly."

"Then give me the address, and that's where we'll go."

Catarina shouted their address over the sound of another, slightly more distant explosion, and they got Jem over to a seat. It was instantly clear that he would not be able to hold himself sitting up, as he was too exhausted from the effort of trying to walk. They rested him on the ample floor of the bus and sat next to him on either side.

Only in London, Jem said, smiling weakly, *would a bus keep making its rounds during a massive bombing.*

"Keep calm and carry on," Catarina said, feeling Jem's pulse. "There now. We'll be at the flat in no time."

Tessa could tell from the way Catarina was becoming more and more chipper in tone that things were getting worse quickly.

The bus could not go at a high speed—it was still a London

bus on a dark night during an air raid—but it was going faster than any bus she had ever encountered. Tessa had no illusions about the safety of the bus. She had seen one of these flipped over completely after a hit, lying in the road like an elephant on its back. But they were moving, and Jem was resting on the floor. Tessa looked at the advertisements on the walls—happy images of people using Bisto gravy next to posters telling people to get their children out of London for safety.

London would not give up, and neither would Tessa.

They had another piece of good luck back at the flat. Tessa and Catarina lived in the upstairs of a small house. Their neighbors, it seemed, had gone to the shelters, so there was no one else in the house to see them dragging a bleeding man up the steps.

"The bathroom," Catarina said as they set Jem down on the dark landing. "Fill the tub with water. Lots of it. Cold. I'll get my supplies."

Tessa ran to the bathroom in the hall, praying that the water had not been disrupted by the bombing. Relief washed over her as water flowed from the tap. They were allowed to have only five inches in the bath, which was enforced by a line painted around the inside of the tub. Tessa ignored this. She opened the window wide. There was some cool air coming from the direction away from the fires. She hurried down the hall. Catarina had removed Jem's tunic, leaving his chest bare. She had taken off the bandages, and the wound was exposed and angry, the black marks tracing along his veins once again.

"Get his other side," Catarina said. Together they lifted Jem up. He was dead weight as they maneuvered him down the hall and carefully put him into the tub. Catarina positioned him so that his wounded arm and shoulder hung over the side, then reached into her apron pocket and removed two vials. She poured the contents of one into the water, turning it a light blue. Tessa knew better than to ask if Catarina thought he was going to survive. He was going to survive, because they would make sure of it. Also, you didn't ask those sorts of questions if you were concerned about the answers.

"Keep sponging him," Catarina said. "We need to keep him cool."

Tessa got down on her knees and drenched the sponge, then ran the blue-tinted water over Jem's head and chest. It smelled of a strange combination of sulfur and jasmine, and it seemed to lower his temperature. Catarina rubbed the contents of the other vial on her hands and began working at the wound and his arm and chest, massaging the spreading darkness back toward the opening. Jem's head lolled back, his breathing rough. Tessa swabbed his forehead, reassuring him all the while.

They did this for an hour. Tessa soon forgot the sound of the bombs outside, or the smoke or burning debris that drifted in. Everything was the motion of the water and the sponge, Jem's skin, his ordinarily calm face twisted in pain, then going still and slack. Both Catarina and Tessa were drenched, and there was water pooling on the floor around them.

Will, Jem said, and the voice in Tessa's head was lost but seeking. *Will, is that you?*

Tessa fought back the lump in her throat as Jem smiled at nothing. If he saw Will, let him see Will. Maybe Will was here, after all, come to help his *parabatai*.

Will, Tessa thought to herself, *if you are here, you must help. I cannot lose him too, Will. Together we will save him.*

Perhaps she imagined it, but Tessa felt something guiding her arm as she worked. She was stronger now.

Jem suddenly lurched in the water and came halfway out of the tub, his back arching into a shape that should not have been possible and sending his head under.

"Grab him," Catarina said. "Don't let him hurt himself! This is the worst of it!"

Together, and with whatever force was aiding Tessa, they grabbed Jem as he writhed, his strange, inward screams filling their heads. Because he was wet, they had to wrap themselves around his limbs to try to prevent him from flailing, from bashing his head against the tiles. He knocked Catarina loose, and she fell to the floor and smashed her head into the wall, but she came back and got her arms around his chest again. Jem's screams blended with the chaos of the night—the water splashed and the smoke blew in. Jem begged for *yin fen*. He kicked so hard that Tessa was thrown back against the sink.

Then, all at once, he stopped moving completely and fell back into the tub. He looked lifeless. Tessa crawled back across the wet floor and reached for him.

"Jem? Catarina . . ."

"He's alive," Catarina said, her chest heaving as she caught her breath. She had her fingers on his wrist. "We've done all we can do here. Let's get him into bed. We'll know soon."

The all clear rang out across London just after eleven, but there was nothing clear or safe. The Luftwaffe may have returned home, and the bombs may have stopped falling for a few hours, but the fires only increased. The wind fueled and propelled them. The air was rank with burning soot and flying scraps of debris, and London glowed.

They had moved Jem into the little bedroom. The rest of his wet clothing had to be removed. Tessa had dressed and undressed countless men at this point, and Jem was a Silent Brother, for whom intimacy was impossible. Perhaps she should have been able to do it with calm professionalism, but she could not be a nurse with Jem. She had thought once that she would see him, that they would see each other, naked on their wedding night. This was too intimate and strange—this was not how Jem would want Tessa to see him, like that, for the first time. So she left the task to Catarina, the nurse, who managed it quickly and dried Jem off. They put him in the bed and wrapped him with all the blankets in the flat. The clothes were easy enough to dry—they hung them from the window for the baking hot air of the fires. Then Catarina went into the sitting room, leaving Tessa to stay with Jem and hold his hand. It was so strange to be again in this position of standing by the bed of the man she loved, waiting, hoping. Jem was—Jem. Exactly as he had been all those years ago, except for the marks of the Silent Brothers. He was Jem, the boy with the violin. Her Jem. Age had not consumed him, as it had her Will, but he might be taken from her all the same.

Tessa reached up to her jade pendant, hidden beneath her collar. She sat and waited and listened to the roar and the wail outside as she held his hand.

I am here, James, she said in her mind. *I am here, and I will always be here.*

Tessa let go of Jem's hand only to occasionally go to the window to make sure the fires did not come too close. There was a halo of orange all around. The fires were only a few streets away. It was strangely beautiful, this terrible blaze. The city was burning; hundreds of years of history, ancient beams and books were alight.

"They mean to burn us out this time," Catarina said, coming up behind her friend. Tessa had not heard her enter. "This ring of fire, it goes around St. Paul's. They want the cathedral to burn. They want to break our spirits."

"Well," Tessa said, pulling the curtain closed, "they won't succeed."

"Why don't we go and make a cup of tea?" Catarina said. "He'll be sleeping for some time."

"No. I need to be here when he wakes."

Catarina looked at her friend's face.

"He means a great deal to you," she said.

"Jem—Brother Zachariah—and I have always been close."

"You love him," Catarina said. It was not a question.

Tessa squeezed a handful of curtain in her fist. They stood in silence for a moment. Catarina rubbed her friend's arm consolingly.

"I'll make the tea," she said. "I'll even let you have the last biscuits in the tin."

Biscuits?

Tessa whirled around. Jem was sitting up. She and Catarina hurried to him. Catarina began checking his pulse, his skin. Tessa looked at his face, his dear and familiar face. Jem was back; he was here.

Her Jem.

"It is healing," Catarina said. "You'll need to rest, but you will live. It was a narrow escape, though."

Which is why I came to the best nurses in London, Jem said.

"Perhaps you can explain that wound you have?" Catarina said. "I know where it comes from. Why were you attacked with a faerie weapon?"

I was looking for information, Jem said, shifting himself painfully to sit up a bit higher. *My inquiries were not appreciated.*

"Clearly, if you were attacked with a cataplasm. That is intended to kill. It does not wound. It is usually not survivable. Your Silent Brother markings gave you some protection, but . . ."

Catarina felt his pulse again.

But? Jem said curiously.

"I did not believe you would make it through the night," she said simply.

Tessa blinked. She'd known it was serious, but the way Catarina said it hit her physically.

"You should perhaps avoid making those inquiries again," Catarina said, putting the blankets back over Jem. "I'll go and make the tea."

She left the room quietly, closing the door behind her, leaving Tessa and Jem together in the darkness.

The raid seems worse than any before tonight, Jem finally said. *Sometimes I think the mundanes will do more harm to each other than any demon could ever do to them.*

Tessa felt a wave of emotion go through her—everything from the night burst to the surface, and she sank her head into the side of Jem's bed and wept. Jem sat up and pulled her close, and she rested her head on his chest, now warm, his heart beating strong.

"You might have died," Tessa said. "I might have lost you, too."

Tessa, he said. *Tessa, it's me. I am here. I am not gone.*

"Jem," she finally said. "Where have you been? It's been so long since . . ."

She pulled herself up and rubbed the tears from her cheeks. She still couldn't say the words "since Will died." Since that day she sat next to him on the bed and he drifted gently to sleep and never woke again. Jem had been there then, of course, but over the last three years she saw him less and less. They still met at Blackfriars Bridge, but otherwise he stayed away.

I thought it best to keep away from you. I am a Silent Brother, he said, and his voice in her head was quiet. *I am no use to you.*

"What do you mean?" Tessa asked helplessly. "It is always better for me to be with you."

Being what I am, how can I comfort you? asked Jem.

"If you cannot," said Tessa, "there is nobody in this world who can."

She had known that always. Magnus and Catarina had both tried to speak to her tactfully of immortal lives and other loves, but if she lived until the sun died, there would never be any other for her besides Will and Jem, those two twin souls, the only souls she had ever loved.

I do not know what comfort a creature like me could bring, said Jem. *If I could die to bring him back, I would, but he is gone, and with his loss the world seems even more lost to me. I fight for every drop of emotion I have, but at the same time, Tessa, I cannot see you lonely and not wish to be with you. I am not what I was. I did not want to cause you more pain.*

"The whole world seems to have gone mad," she said, tears burning in her eyes. "Will is gone from me, and you are gone from me, or so I have long thought. And yet tonight, I realized—I could still lose you, Jem. I could lose the hope, the slim hope of the possibility that someday . . ."

The words hung in the air. They were words they never spoke to each other aloud, not before Will died and not after. She had taken the part of her heart that loved Jem wildly, violently, and locked it up in a box: she had loved Will, and Jem had been her best friend, and they had never, ever spoken of what might happen if he were no longer a Silent Brother. If somehow the curse of that cold fate could be lifted. If his silence were gone, and he became human again, able to live and breathe and feel. Then what? What would they do?

I know what you are thinking. His voice in her mind was soft. His skin under her hands was so warm. She knew it was fever, but she told herself it was not. She lifted her face and looked into his, the cruel runes shutting his beloved eyes forever, the unchanged planes of his countenance. *I think of it too. What if it ended? What if it were possible for us? A future? What would we do?*

"I would seize that future," she said. "I would go with you anywhere. Even if the world was burning, if the Silent Brothers hunted us to the ends of the earth, I would be happy, if I was with you."

She could not quite hear him in her head, but she could feel him: the edge of a jumble of emotions, his longing now as desperate as it had been when they had fallen together onto the carpet of the music room, the night she had begged him to marry her as soon as possible.

He caught her in his arms. He was a Silent Brother, a Gregori, a Watcher, barely human. And yet he felt human enough—his lean chest hot against her skin as she tilted her face up. His lips met hers, soft and so sweet it made her ache. It had been so many, many years, but this was still the same.

Almost the same. *I am not what I was.*

Almost the fire of lost nights, the sound of his passionate music in her ears. She put her arms around his slim shoulders and clung to him fiercely. She could love enough for both of them. Any part of Jem was better than all of any other man alive.

His musician's hands drew over her face, over her hair, over her shoulders, as though he was seizing a last chance to memorize what he could never touch again. Even as she kissed him and insisted desperately to herself that it was possible, she knew it was not.

Tessa, he said. *Even when I cannot see, you are so beautiful.*

Then he grasped her shoulders in his beautiful hands and gently put her away from him.

I am sorry, my darling, he told her. *That was not fair of me, or well done. When I am with you, I want to forget what I am, but I cannot change it. A Silent Brother can have no wife, no love.*

Tessa's heart was pounding, her skin blazing like the fires all over London. She had not felt desire like this since Will. She knew she would never feel it for anyone else; only Will or Jem. "Don't go away from me," she whispered. "Don't stop talking to me. Don't retreat into silence. Will you tell me how you were injured?" she asked, grasping his hand. He drew it against his heart. She could feel it hammering through his rib cage. "Please. Jem, what were you doing?"

Jem sighed.

I was looking for lost Herondales, he said.

"Lost Herondales?"

This was from Catarina, who stood in the bedroom

doorway, holding a tray with two cups of tea. The tray rattled in her hands, as shaken as Tessa felt. She had not even thought of Catarina's presence.

Catarina steadied her grip and quickly set the tray down on the dresser. Jem's eyebrow quirked up.

Yes, Jem said. *Do you know something about them?*

Catarina was still visibly shaken. She didn't answer.

"Catarina?" Tessa asked.

"You have heard of Tobias Herondale," she said.

Of course, Jem replied. *His story is infamous. He ran from a battle and his fellow Shadowhunters were killed.*

"That is the story," Catarina said. "The reality was that Tobias was under a spell, made to believe that his wife and unborn child were in danger. He ran to help them. His fear was for their safety, but nevertheless, he broke the Law. When he could not be found, the Clave punished Tobias's wife in his stead. They killed her, but not before I helped her birth the child. I enchanted her so that it appeared she was still with child when she was executed. In reality, she had a son. His name was Ephraim."

She sighed and leaned against the wall, knotting her hands together.

"I took Ephraim to America and raised him there. He never knew what he was or who he was. He was a happy boy, a good boy. He was *my* boy."

"You had a son?' Tessa asked.

"I never told you," Catarina replied, looking down. "I should have. It's just . . . it was so long ago now. But it was a wonderful period in my life. For a time, there was no chaos. There was no fighting. We were a family. I did only one thing to connect him to his secret heritage—I gave him a necklace in the shape of a heron. I couldn't allow his Shadowhunter lineage to be blotted out completely. But, of course, he grew up. He had a family of his own. And his family had their own families. I stayed the same and gradually faded out of their lives. It is what we immortals must do. One of his descendants was a boy named Roland. He became a magician, and he was famous in Downworld. I tried to warn him away from using magic, but he wouldn't listen. We had a terrible fight and parted badly. I tried to find him, but he was gone. I've never been able to find any trace of him. I drove him away when I tried to save him."

No, Jem said. *That is not why he ran away. He married a woman who was a fugitive. Roland went into hiding to protect her.*

Catarina looked up at him.

"What?" she said.

I was in America a short while ago with an Iron Sister, he said, *to retrieve some* adamas. *While there, we encountered a Shadow Market connected to a carnival. It was run by a Greater Demon. We confronted him, and he told us that there were Herondales lost in the world and that they were in danger and that they were very close by. He said that they were hiding from an enemy neither mortal nor demon. Also at this market, I saw a faerie woman with a mortal man. They had a child. The man was called Roland.*

Tessa was stunned by the rush of information coming from all sides, but she was caught by the thought of a man throwing away his whole life to run with the woman he loved, giving everything he had to shield her and counting it as nothing. That sounded like a Herondale.

"He was alive?" Catarina said. "Roland? At a carnival?"

When I realized what was happening, I tried to track him down, but I was unable to find him. Please know that it was not you he was running from. The Greater Demon told me that they were being chased and that they were in great danger. Now I know that to be true. The faerie who came to me tonight—he meant to kill me. The forces looking for the Herondales are neither mortal nor demon—they are fey, and the fey mean to keep something secret.

"So . . . I did not chase him away?" Catarina said. "All this time . . . Roland . . ."

Catarina shook herself and regained her composure. She picked up the tea tray and brought it over to the bed, setting it on the edge.

"Drink your tea," she said. "I used the last of our ration of milk and the biscuits."

You know that Silent Brothers do not drink, Jem said.

Catarina gave him a sad smile. "I thought you might still find comfort in holding the warm cup."

She wiped her eyes covertly and turned and left the room.

You did not know of this? Jem said.

"She never said," Tessa replied. "So many problems are caused by unnecessary secrets."

Jem turned his face away and ran his finger along the edge of the teacup. She caught at his hand. If that was all she could have, she would hold on to it.

"Why have you kept so far away?" Tessa said. "We have both been grieving Will. Why do so separately?"

I am a Silent Brother, and Silent Brothers cannot—

Jem cut himself off. Tessa clasped his hand to the point where she might have broken it.

"You are Jem—my Jem. Always my Jem."

I am Brother Zachariah, Jem returned.

"So be it!" said Tessa. "You are Brother Zachariah, and my

Jem. You are a Silent Brother. That does not mean you are not dear to me as you always were, and you always will be. Do you think anything could separate us? Are either of us so weak as that? After all we have seen and all we have done? I spend every day grateful that you exist and are in the world. And as long as you live, we keep Will alive."

She saw the impact these words had on Jem. Being a Silent Brother meant destroying some parts of you that were human, burning them away, but Jem was still there.

"We have so much time, Jem. You must promise me that we will not spend it apart. Do not keep away from me. Make me a part of this quest as well. I can help. You must be more careful."

I would not put you in danger, he said.

At this Tessa laughed—a true, ringing laugh.

"Danger?" she said. "Jem, I am immortal. And look outside. Look at the city burning. The only thing I am frightened of is being without those I love."

At last she felt the pressure of his fingers, holding her hand back.

Outside, London burned. Inside, in this moment, all was well.

The morning came, cold and gray, with the smell of the still-burning fires in the air. London woke, shook itself off, picked up its brooms and buckets, and began the daily act of repair. The blackout curtains were opened to the morning air. People went to work. The buses ran, and the kettles boiled; the shops opened. Fear had not won. Death and fire and war had not won.

Tessa had fallen asleep around dawn, sitting by Jem's side, holding his hand, her head leaning on the wall. When she stirred awake, she found that the bed was empty. The blankets had been neatly pulled back up and the clothes were gone from the sill.

"Jem," Tessa said, frantic.

Catarina was asleep in their little sitting room, her head basketed in her arms and resting on their kitchen table.

"He is gone," Tessa said. "Did you see him go?"

"No," Catarina said, rubbing her eyes.

Tessa returned to the bedroom and looked around. Had it all been a dream? Had the war driven her mad? As she turned, she saw a folded note on the dresser that said *TESSA*. She opened it:

> *My Tessa,*
> *There will be no separation between us.*
> *Where you are, I am. Where we are, Will is.*
> *Whatever else I may be, I remain always,*
> *Your Jem*

Brother Zachariah walked through London. The city was gray with night, its buildings reduced to broken remnants of what they had once been, until it seemed a city made of ash and bone. Perhaps all cities would become the Silent City, one day.

He was able to conceal some things from his Brothers, even though they had ready access to his mind. They did not know all his secrets, but they knew enough. Tonight every voice in his mind was hushed, overwhelmed by what he had felt and what he had almost done.

He was bitterly ashamed of what he had said this night. Tessa was still grieving Will. They shared that grief, and they loved each other. She did still love him. He believed that. But she could not feel what she had felt for him once. She had not, thank the Angel, lived as he had lived, in bones and silence and on memories of love. She'd had Will, and loved him so long, and now Will was lost. He worried that he had taken advantage of her misery. She might well cling to what was familiar in a world gone mad and strange.

But she was so brave, his Tessa, carving out a new life now the old life was lost. She'd done it once already, as a girl coming from America. He had felt it as a bond between them long ago, that they had both come across the seas to find a new home. He had thought they could find a new home with each other.

He knew now that had been a dream, but what had been dreams for him could be real for Tessa. She was immortal and valiant. She would live again in this new world, and build a whole new life. Perhaps she would love again, if she could find a man who would measure up to Will, though in almost a hundred years Zachariah had not known any who could. Tessa deserved the richest life and the greatest love imaginable.

Tessa deserved more than a being who could never truly be a man again, who could not love her with a whole heart. Even though he loved her with all the broken fragments of heart he had left, it was not enough. She deserved more than he had to offer.

He should never have reached for her that way.

Nevertheless, there was a selfish joy within him, a warmth that he could carry even into the deathlike coldness of the City of Bones. She had kissed him and clung to him. For one shining night, he had held her in his arms again.

Tessa, Tessa, Tessa, he thought. She could never be his again, but he was hers forever. That was enough to live on.

* * *

That evening, Catarina and Tessa walked in the direction of St. Bart's.

"A bacon sandwich," Catarina said. "Piled so high you can barely hold it. And thick with so much butter the bacon slides off the bread. That's what I'm having first. How about you?"

Tessa smiled and shone her torch down the pavement, stepping over a bit of rubble. Around them, there were shells of buildings. Everything around had been reduced to charred brick and ash. But already London was picking up, pushing the debris back. The dark was like an embrace. All of London was under a blanket together, holding each other close.

"An ice cream," Tessa said. "With strawberries. Loads and loads of strawberries."

"Oh, I like that," Catarina said. "I'm changing mine."

A man walking toward them tipped his hat.

"Evening, Sisters," he said. "You see that?"

He gestured up at St. Paul's Cathedral, the great building that had sat guarding over London for hundreds of years.

"They wanted to take it down last night, but they didn't, did they?" The man smiled. "No, they didn't. They can't break us. You have a good evening, Sisters. You keep well."

The man walked on, and Tessa looked up at the cathedral. Everything around it was gone, but it had been saved—impossibly, improbably saved from thousands of bombs. London would not let it die, and it had lived.

She touched the jade pendant around her neck.

The Wicked Ones

By Cassandra Clare and Robin Wasserman

J

Paris, 1989

It was said among the Shadowhunters that one could not know true beauty until one had seen the gleaming towers of Alicante. It was said that no city on earth could rival its wonders. It was said that no Shadowhunter could feel truly at home anywhere else.

If anyone had asked Céline Montclaire her opinion on the subject, she would have said: obviously these Shadowhunters had never been to Paris.

She would have rhapsodized about gothic spires spearing the clouds, cobblestone streets shimmering with rain, sunlight dancing on the Seine, and, *bien sûr*, the infinite varieties of cheese. She would have pointed out that Paris had been home to Baudelaire and Rimbaud, Monet and Gauguin, Descartes and Voltaire, that this was the city that had birthed a new way of speaking, seeing, thinking, *being*—drawing even the most mundane of mundanes a little closer to the angels.

In every way, Paris was *la ville lumière*. The City of Light. *If you ask me,* Céline would have said, *nothing could be more beautiful than that.*

But no one ever asked. As a general rule, no one asked Céline Montclaire's opinion on anything.

Until now.

"You sure there's not some kind of rune to keep these foul beasts away?" Stephen Herondale said as a thunderous flutter of wings descended. He ducked, whacked blindly at his feathered foe.

The flock of pigeons quickly passed, without dealing any mortal blows. Céline waved off a couple of stragglers, and Stephen breathed a sigh of relief.

"My hero," he said.

Céline felt her cheeks warm alarmingly. She had a terrible blushing problem. Especially when she was in the presence of Stephen Herondale. "The great Herondale warrior afraid of pigeons?" she teased, hoping he wouldn't hear the quaver in her voice.

"Not afraid. Simply exhibiting a prudent amount of caution in the face of a potentially demonic creature."

"Demon pigeons?"

"I look upon them with great suspicion," Stephen said with as much dignity as a pigeon-phobe could muster. He tapped the longsword hanging by his hip. "And this great warrior stands at the ready to do what needs be done."

As he spoke, another flock of pigeons took flight from the cobblestones, and for a moment all was wings and feathers and Stephen's rather high-pitched squeal.

Céline laughed. "Yes, I can see you're fearless in the face of danger. If not in the beak of danger."

Stephen glared fiercely at her. Her pulse quickened. Had she overstepped? Then he winked.

Sometimes she wanted him so much she felt like her heart might explode.

"You sure we're still going in the right direction?" he said. "I feel like we're walking in circles."

"Trust me," she said.

Stephen clapped a hand to his heart. "*Bien sûr*, mademoiselle."

Unless you counted the starring role he played in her daydreams, Céline hadn't seen Stephen since he'd graduated from the Academy four years before. Back then, he'd barely noticed her. He was too busy with his training, his girlfriend, and his friends in the Circle to give much thought to the slip of a girl whose eyes tracked his every move. But now, Céline thought, her cheeks burning again, they were practically equals. Yes, she was seventeen, still a student, while he was twenty-two, not just a full-fledged adult but Valentine Morgenstern's most trusted lieutenant in the Circle—the elite group of young Shadowhunters sworn to reform the Clave and return it to its pure and ancient glory. But Céline was finally a member of the Circle too, handpicked by Valentine himself.

Valentine had been a student at the Academy alongside Stephen and the other founding members of the Circle—but unlike the rest of them, he'd never seemed quite young. Most of the students and teachers at the Academy had thought of Valentine's crowd as nothing but a harmless clique, odd only in that it preferred late-night policy debates to partying. Even then, Céline understood that this was exactly how Valentine wanted to appear: harmless. Those who paid attention knew better. He was a fierce warrior, with an even fiercer mind—once he fixed his inky black gaze on a goal, nothing would stop him from achieving it. He'd composed his Circle of young

Shadowhunters he knew to be as capable as they were loyal. Only the best of them, he'd told her that day he'd approached her at a particularly boring lecture on Downworlder history. "Every member of the Circle is *exceptional*," he'd said. "Including, if you accept my offer, you." No one had ever called her exceptional before.

Ever since then, she'd felt different. Strong. *Special*. And it must have been true, because even though she still had one more year at the Academy, here she was, spending her summer vacation on an official mission with Stephen Herondale. Stephen was one of the greatest fighters of his generation, and now—owing to Lucian Graymark's unfortunate werewolf situation—Valentine's most trusted deputy. But Céline was the one who knew Paris, its streets and its secrets. It was the perfect moment to show Stephen that she'd changed, that she was exceptional. That he couldn't do this without her.

Those had, in fact, been his exact words. *I couldn't do this without you, Céline.*

She loved the way her name sounded on his tongue. She loved every detail of him: the blue eyes that sparkled like the sea of the Côte d'Azur. The white-blond hair that glowed like the golden rotunda of the Palais Garnier. The curve of his neck, the tautness of his muscles, the smooth lines of his body like something carved by Rodin, a model of human perfection. Somehow he'd gotten even more handsome since she saw him last.

He'd also gotten married.

She tried not to think about that.

"Can we pick up the pace?" Robert Lightwood grumbled. "The sooner we get this done, the sooner we can get back to civilization. And air-conditioning."

Robert was something else she tried not to think about. His grouchy presence made it substantially more difficult to pretend she and Stephen were taking a romantic stroll through the moonlight.

"The faster we go, the more you'll sweat," Stephen pointed out. "And trust me, no one wants that." Paris in August was approximately ten degrees hotter than Hell. Even after dark, the air felt like a blanket soaked in hot soup. For the sake of discretion, they'd traded their Shadowhunter gear for mundane fashion, choosing long sleeves to cover up their runes. The white T-shirt Céline had selected for Stephen was already soaked through. This was not exactly unfortunate.

Robert just grunted. He was different than Céline remembered him from the Academy. Back then, he'd been a little stiff and curt, but never deliberately cruel. Now, though, there was something in his eyes she didn't like. Something icy. It reminded her too much of her father.

According to Stephen, Robert had had some kind of falling-out with his *parabatai* and was understandably cranky. *It's just Robert being Robert*, Stephen had said. *Great fighter but a bit of a drama queen. Nothing to worry about.*

Céline always worried.

They trudged up the final hill of Rue Mouffetard. By day, this was one of Paris's most bustling market streets, bursting with fresh produce, colorful scarves, falafel vendors and gelato stands, and obnoxious tourists. At night, its storefronts were shuttered and silent. Paris was a market town, but all of its markets went to sleep after dark—all except one.

Céline hurried them around a corner, down another narrow, winding road. "We're almost there." She tried to keep the anticipation out of her voice. Robert and Stephen had made it very clear that the Circle did not approve of Shadow Markets. Downworlders mingling with mundanes, illicit goods changing hands, secrets swapped and sold? According to Valentine, this was all the unseemly consequence of the laxness and corruption of the Clave. When the Circle took power, Stephen had assured her eagerly, the Shadow Markets would be shut down for good.

Céline had been in the Circle for only a few months, but she'd already learned this lesson: if Valentine hated something, it was her duty to hate it too.

She was trying her best.

There was no Law that a Shadow Market had to be located on a site rich with dark energy, marinated in the blood of a violent past—but it helped.

Paris had no shortage of possibilities. It was a city of ghosts, most of them angry. Revolution after revolution, blood-spattered barricades and heads rolling from the guillotine, the September Massacres, the Bloody Week, the burning of the Tuileries, the Terror . . . As a child, Céline had spent many sleepless nights wandering the city, summoning visions of its greatest cruelties. She liked to imagine she could hear screams echoing through the centuries. They made her feel less alone.

This, she knew, was not a normal childhood hobby.

Céline's had not been a normal childhood. She discovered this only when she arrived at the Academy, where for the first time she'd met Shadowhunters her own age. That first day, the other students had chattered about their idyllic lives in Idris, galloping horses across the Brocelind Plain; their idyllic lives in London, New York, Tokyo, training under the kind eye of loving parents and Institute tutors; their idyllic lives anywhere and everywhere. After a while Céline stopped listening and drifted out unnoticed, too bitterly jealous to stay. Too embarrassed by the prospect that someone might make her tell her own story. After all, she'd grown up on her parents' Provence estate, surrounded by apple orchards, vineyards, rolling fields of lavender: by all appearances, *la belle epoque*.

Céline knew her parents loved her, because they told her so repeatedly.

We're only doing this because we love you, her mother would say before locking her in the basement.

We're only doing this because we love you, her father would say before lashing her with the whip.

We're only doing this because we love you, when they set the Dragonidae demon on her; when they dumped her for the night, eight years old and weaponless, in a werewolf-ridden wood; when they taught her the bloody consequences of weakness or clumsiness or fear.

The first time she ran away to Paris, she was eight years old. Young enough to think she could escape for good. She'd found her way to the Arènes de Lutèce, the remains of a Roman amphitheater from the first century AD. It was, perhaps, the city's oldest blood-soaked ruin. Two thousand years before, gladiators had warred to the death before a cheering, bloodthirsty crowd, until the arena—and its crowd—were overtaken by an equally bloodthirsty barbarian horde. For a time, it had been a cemetery; now it was a tourist trap, yet another heap of stones for bored schoolchildren to ignore. By day, at least. Under the midnight moon, it came alive with Downworlders, a bacchanalia of faerie fruits and wines, gargoyles enchanted by warlock magic, waltzing werewolves, vampires in berets painting portraits in blood, an ifrit accordionist who could make you weep yourself to death. It was the Paris Shadow Market, and from the moment Céline first saw it, she felt herself finally home.

That first trip, she'd spent two nights there, haunting the booths, befriending a shy werewolf cub, sating her gnawing hunger with the Nutella crepe that a Silent Brother had purchased for her, no questions asked. She'd napped beneath the tablecloth of a vampire's jewelry stand; she'd whirled with horned children in an improvised faerie revel; she'd finally discovered what it meant to be happy. On the third night, the Shadowhunters of the Paris Institute tracked her down and returned her home.

That was when she learned—not for the last time—the consequences of running away.

We love you too much to lose you.

That night, Céline had curled fetal in the corner of the basement, back still bloody, and thought, *So this is how it feels to be loved too much.*

Their mission was straightforward. First, track down the warlock Dominique du Froid's booth at the Paris Shadow Market. Second, find some evidence of her shady business dealings with two rogue Shadowhunters.

"I have reason to believe they've been trading Downworlder blood and parts to her in return for illegal services," Valentine had told them. He needed proof. It was up to Céline, Stephen, and Robert to find some.

"*Quietly,*" Valentine had cautioned. "I don't want her

tipping off her associates." Valentine made the word "associates" sound like a vulgarity. For him, it was: Downworlders were bad enough, but Shadowhunters allowing themselves to be corrupted by a Downworlder? That was unforgivable.

Step one proved simple. Dominique du Froid was easy to find. She'd conjured her name in neon lights, right out of thin air. Literally—the letters glowed brightly, three feet above her booth, with a neon arrow pointing down. DOMINIQUE DU FROID, LES SOLDES, TOUJOURS!

"Just like a warlock," Robert said sourly. "Always for sale."

"Always *on* sale," Céline corrected, too quietly for him to hear.

The booth turned out to be an elaborate tent with display tables and a curtained-off area in the back. It was crammed with tacky jewelry and colorful potions—none quite as tacky or as colorful as Dominique herself. Her hair was dyed in platinum-blond and hot-pink stripes, half of it scooped into a side ponytail. The other half was crimped and hair-sprayed to a hard sheen. She wore a ripped lace shirt, a black leather miniskirt, purple fingerless gloves, and what looked like a significant portion of her jewelry inventory around her neck. Her warlock mark, a long, feathered pink tail, was slung over her shoulders like a boa.

"It's like an Eidolon demon tried turning into Cyndi Lauper and accidentally got stuck midway through," Céline joked.

"Huh?" Robert said. "Is that another warlock?"

Stephen smirked. "Yeah, Robert. Another warlock. The Clave executed her 'cause she just wanted to have fun."

Céline and Stephen laughed together, and Robert's obvious fury at being mocked only made them laugh harder. Like most Shadowhunters, Céline had grown up entirely ignorant of mundane pop culture. But Stephen showed up at the Academy full of arcane knowledge about bands, books, songs, movies that no one had ever heard of. Once he'd joined the Circle, he'd dropped his love of the Sex Pistols just as quickly as he'd traded his leather jacket and frayed denim for the dull black uniform that Valentine favored. Still, Céline had spent the last couple of years studying mundane TV, just in case.

I can be whatever you want me to be, she thought, wishing she had the nerve to *say* it.

Céline knew Amatis, Stephen's wife. At least, she knew enough. Amatis was sharp-tongued and stuck-up. She was opinionated, argumentative, stubborn, and not even that pretty. There were also rumors that she still secretly associated with her werewolf brother. Céline didn't much care about that—she had nothing against Downworlders. But she had plenty against Amatis, who obviously didn't appreciate what she had. Stephen needed someone who would admire him, agree with him, support him. Someone like Céline. If only she could make him see that for himself.

They surveilled the warlock for a couple of hours. Dominique du Froid was constantly leaving her booth unattended, scurrying off to gossip or trade with other sellers. It was almost like she wanted someone to rifle through her belongings.

Stephen yawned theatrically. "I was hoping for slightly more of a challenge. But let's get this done and get out of here. This place stinks of Downworlders. I already feel like I need a shower."

"Ouais, c'est terrible," Céline lied.

The next time Dominique left her booth, Stephen tailed her. Robert slipped into the booth's curtained-off area to poke around for evidence of dirty dealings. Céline was left to play lookout, browsing the booth next to Dominique's, where she could signal Robert if Dominique unexpectedly came back.

Of course they'd assigned her the most boring job, the one that required nothing but shopping for jewelry. They thought she was useless.

Céline did as she was told, feigning interest in the hideous display of enchanted rings, chunky gold chains, charm bracelets jangling with Greater Demons carved in brass and pewter. Then she spotted something that actually did interest her: a Silent Brother, gliding toward the booth in that disconcertingly inhuman way they all had of moving. She watched out of the corner of her eye as the robed Shadowhunter studied the jewelry display with great care. What could someone like him possibly be looking for in a place like this?

The scruffy preteen werewolf manning the booth had barely acknowledged Céline's presence. But he scurried straight over to the Silent Brother, eyes wide with fear. "You can't be poking around here," he said. "My boss doesn't like doing business with your kind."

Aren't you a bit young to have a boss?

The words reverberated in Céline's mind, and she wondered for a moment whether the Silent Brother wanted her to overhear. But that seemed unlikely—she was standing several feet away, and there was no reason for him to have noticed her.

"Parents threw me out when I got bitten, so it's either work or go hungry," the kid said. He shrugged. "And I like food. Which is why you got to get out of here before the boss comes back and thinks I'm selling to a Shadowhunter."

I am in search of a piece of jewelry.

"Look, man, there's nothing here you can't get somewhere

else, better and cheaper. This stuff is all junk."

Yes, that I can see. But I am looking for something particular, something I've been told I can find here only. A silver necklace, with a pendant in the shape of a heron.

The word "heron" pricked Céline's ear. It was such a specific request. And it was something so suited to a Herondale.

"Uh, yeah, I don't know how you heard about that, but it's possible we've got one of those back here. I told you, though, I can't sell to—"

What if I doubled the price?

"You don't even know what the price is."

No, I do not. And I imagine you won't get a better offer, given that the necklace is not on display for customers.

"Yeah, I pointed that out myself, but . . ." He leaned forward and lowered his voice. Céline tried not to make it too obvious she was straining to hear. "Boss doesn't want his wife to know he's selling it. Said he just needs to put the word out, and a buyer will find us."

And now a buyer has. Imagine how pleased your employer will be when you tell him it sold for more than his asking price.

"I guess he never needs to know who bought it. . . ."

He will not hear it from me.

The kid considered this for a moment, then ducked beneath the counter for a moment and reappeared dangling a silver pendant. Céline suppressed a gasp. It was a delicately shaped heron, sparkling in the moonlight, the perfect gift for a young Herondale proud of his heritage. She closed her eyes, letting herself drift into an alternate reality, one in which she was allowed to give Stephen gifts. Imagining fastening the pendant around his neck, nuzzling his soft skin, breathing him in.

Imagining him saying, *I love it. Almost as much as I love you.*

It is beautiful, is it not?

Céline flinched at the voice of the Silent Brother in her head. Of course he couldn't know what she'd been thinking. But nonetheless, her cheeks burned with shame. The kid had retreated to the back of the booth to count his money. The Silent Brother had now fixed his blind gaze on her.

He was different from the other Silent Brothers she'd seen, his face young—even handsome. His jet-black hair was marked with a streak of white, and his eyes and mouth were sealed but not sewn shut. Runes sliced viciously across each cheek. Céline was reminded how envious she had once been of the Silent Brotherhood. They had scars like she had scars; they endured great pain like she endured great pain. But their scars gave them power; their pain felt like nothing, because they had no feeling. You could not be a Silent Brother if you were a girl. This had never seemed very fair to Céline. Women were, however, allowed to join the Iron Sisters. Céline had liked the idea when she was younger, but now she felt no desire to live cloistered on a volcanic plain, with nothing to do but craft weapons of *adamas*. The very thought of it made her claustrophobic.

I am sorry to startle you. But I noted your interest in the pendant.

"It's . . . it just, it reminded me of someone."

Someone you care about a great deal, I sense.

"Yeah. I guess."

Is that someone perhaps a Herondale?

"Yes, and he's wonderful." The words slipped out accidentally, but there was an unexpected joy in saying them out loud. She'd never let herself do so before—not in front of someone else. Not even alone.

That was the thing about Silent Brothers. Being with them wasn't quite like being with someone else *or* like being alone. Confiding in a Silent Brother was like confiding in no one, she thought, because who was he going to tell?

"Stephen Herondale," she said, softly but firmly. "I'm in love with Stephen Herondale."

There was a jolt of power in saying the words, almost as if speaking her claim aloud made it a little more real.

The love of a Herondale can be a great gift.

"Yeah, it's awesome," she said, bitterly enough that even the Silent Brother noticed her tone.

I have upset you.

"No, it's just . . . I said *I* love *him*. He barely knows I'm alive."

Ah.

It was stupid, hoping for sympathy from a Silent Brother. Like hoping for sympathy from a rock. His face remained completely impassive. But the voice that spoke in her head was gentle. She let herself believe it was even a little kind.

That must be difficult.

If Céline had been another type of girl, the type with friends or sisters or a mother who spoke to her with anything but icy disdain, she might have told someone else about Stephen. She might have spent hours dissecting his tone, the way he sometimes seemed to flirt with her, the way he'd once touched her on the shoulder in gratitude when she lent him a dagger. Maybe talking about it would have blunted the pain of loving him; maybe she even would have talked herself *out* of loving him. Talking about Stephen might have become commonplace, like talking about the weather. Background noise.

But Céline had no one to talk to. All she had were her secrets, and the longer she kept them, the more they hurt.

"He's never going to love me," she said. "All I've ever wanted was to be near him, but now he's right here, and I can't have him, and in a way that's even worse. I'm just . . . I just . . . it just hurts so much."

I sometimes think there is nothing more painful than love denied. To love someone you cannot have, to stand beside your heart's desire and be unable to take them in your arms. A love that cannot be requited. I can think of nothing more painful than that.

It was impossible that a Silent Brother could understand how she felt. And yet . . .

He sounded as if he understood exactly how she felt.

"I wish I could be more like you," she admitted.

In what sense?

"You know, just shut off my feelings? Feel nothing. For anybody."

There was a long pause, and she wondered if she'd offended him. Was that even possible? Finally, his cool, steady voice spoke again.

This is a wish you should dispense with. Feeling is what makes us human. Even the most difficult feelings. Perhaps especially those. Love, loss, longing—this is what it means to be truly alive.

"But . . . you're a Silent Brother. You're not supposed to feel any of those things, right?"

I . . . There was another long pause. *I remember feeling them. That is sometimes as close as I can get.*

"And you're still alive, as far as I can tell."

Sometimes that, too, is difficult to remember.

If she didn't know any better, she would think he had sighed.

The Silent Brother she met on her first trip to the Shadow

Market had been kind like this. When he bought her the crepe, he hadn't asked her where her parents were or why she was wandering the crowds alone or why her eyes were red from crying. He only knelt and pinned his blind eyes on hers. *The world is a hard thing to face alone,* he said inside her mind. *You do not have to.*

Then he did what Silent Brothers did best and fell silent. She knew, even as a child, that he was waiting for her to tell him what she needed. That if she asked for help, he might even offer it.

No one could help her. Even as a child, she knew that, too. The Montclaires were a respected, powerful Shadowhunter family. Her parents had the ear of the Consul. If she told the Brother who she was, he would only bring her home. If she told him what waited for her there, what her parents were *really* like, he probably wouldn't believe her. He might even tell her parents she was spreading lies about them. And there would be consequences.

She'd thanked him for the crepe and skittered away.

She'd endured so many years since then. After this summer, she would return to the Academy for her final year, and graduate; she would never have to live in her parents' house again. She was almost free. She didn't need anyone's help.

But the world was still a hard thing to face alone.

And she was so, so lonely.

"Maybe the pain of loving someone is a fact of life and all, but do you really think that, like, *all* pain is? You don't think it would be better if you could just stop hurting?"

Is something hurting you?

"I . . ." She summoned her nerve. She could do it. She almost believed that. She could tell this stranger about the cold house. About the parents who seemed to notice her only when she did something wrong. About the consequences, when she did. "The thing is—"

She broke off abruptly as the Silent Brother turned away. His closed eyes seemed to be tracking a man in a black trench coat hurrying toward him. The man stopped short when he caught sight of the Silent Brother. His face abruptly drained of color. Then he spun on his heel and hustled away. Most Downworlders were skittish around Shadowhunters these days—news of the Circle's exploits had gotten around. But this looked almost personal.

"Do you *know* that guy?"

I apologize, I must attend to this.

Silent Brothers did not display emotion, and, as far as Céline knew, they didn't feel it. But if she didn't know any better, she would say this Silent Brother was feeling something very deeply. Fear, maybe, or excitement—or that strange combination of the two that descended just before a fight.

"Okay, I just—"

But the Silent Brother was already gone. She was alone again. And thank the Angel for that, she thought. It had been careless, even toying with the idea of dredging her dark truths into the light. How foolish, how weak, wanting to be heard. Wanting to be truly *seen* by anyone, much less a man with his eyes fused shut. Her parents always said she was stupid and weak. Maybe they were right.

Brother Zachariah wove through the crowded Shadow Market, careful to keep a few feet of distance between him and his target. It was a strange game they were playing. The man, who went by the name of Jack Crow, certainly knew that Zachariah was following him. And Brother Zachariah could have picked up his speed and overtaken the man at any point. But for whatever reason, Crow didn't want to stop, and Brother Zachariah didn't want to make him. So Crow strode across the arena and into the dense warren of streets just beyond its gates.

Brother Zachariah followed.

He was sorry to have left the girl so abruptly. He felt a certain kinship with her. They'd both given a piece of their hearts to a Herondale. And they both loved someone they could not have.

Of course, Brother Zachariah's love was a pale imitation of the real, raw, human thing. He loved through a scrim, and every year it got harder to remember what lay beyond. To remember how it had felt to *long* for Tessa the way a living, breathing human longed. How it had felt to *need* her. Zachariah no longer truly needed anything. Not food, not sleep, not even, much as he sometimes tried to summon it in himself, Tessa. His love persisted, but it was blunted. The girl's love had a jagged edge, and talking to her had helped him remember.

She had wanted his help too, he could tell. The most human part of him was tempted to stay by her side. She'd seemed so fragile—and so determined to seem otherwise. It touched his heart. But Brother Zachariah's heart was encased in stone.

He tried to tell himself otherwise. After all, the very fact of his presence here was evidence of his still-human heart. He'd been hunting for decades—because of Will, because of Tessa, because a part of him was still Jem, the Shadowhunter boy who had loved them both.

Still loves them both, Brother Zachariah reminded himself. Present tense.

The heron pendant had confirmed his suspicions. This was definitely the man he'd been seeking. Zachariah couldn't let him get away.

Crow ducked into a narrow cobblestone alley. Brother Zachariah followed, tense and alert. He sensed their slow-motion chase was nearing its end. And indeed, the alley was a dead end. Crow whirled around to face Zachariah, a knife in his hand. He was still young, barely into his twenties, with a proud face and a shock of blond hair.

Brother Zachariah had a weapon and was quite good at using it. But he made no move to draw his staff. This man could never be a threat to him.

"Okay, Shadowhunter, you wanted me, you got me," Crow said, feet braced and knife ready, clearly expecting an attack.

Brother Zachariah studied his face, searching for something familiar. But there was nothing. Nothing but the pretense of brash courage. With his closed eyes, Zachariah could see beneath such facades. He could see fear.

There was a rustling behind him. Then a woman's voice.

"You know what they say, Shadowhunter. Be careful what you wish for."

Brother Zachariah turned, slowly. Here was a surprise. A young woman—even younger than Crow—stood in the mouth of the alley. She was almost ethereally beautiful, with shining blond hair and the kind of ruby lips and cobalt eyes that had inspired millennia of bad poetry. She was smiling sweetly. She was aiming a crossbow directly at Brother Zachariah's heart.

He felt a jolt of fear. Not because of the knife or the crossbow; he had nothing to fear from these two. He would prefer not to fight at all, but if necessary he could disarm them harmlessly.

They weren't equipped to protect themselves. That was the problem.

The fear stemmed from the realization that he had achieved his goal. This search was the one thing that still bound him to Tessa, to Will, to his former self. What if today he lost his only remaining tie to Jem Carstairs? What if this, today, was his last truly human act?

"Come on, Shadowhunter," the woman said, coming closer but keeping the crossbow steady. "Spit it out. If you're very lucky, maybe we'll let you live."

I don't want to fight you. From their reaction, he could tell they hadn't expected the voice in their head. These two knew enough to recognize a Shadowhunter—but apparently they didn't know as much as they thought. *I have been looking for you, Jack Crow.*

"Yeah, so I heard. Someone should have warned you, people who come looking for me tend to regret it."

I mean you no harm. I only want to deliver a message. It is about who you are and where you came from. You might find this difficult to believe, but—

"Yeah, yeah, I'm a Shadowhunter too." Crow shrugged. "Now tell me something I don't know."

"You here to buy or to shoplift?"

Céline dropped the potion bottle. It shattered on the ground, releasing a puff of noxious blue smoke.

After the Silent Brother had ditched her for the hot guy in the trench coat, the werewolf kid had shut down the booth. He glared at Céline until she accepted it was time to move on. So she'd meandered over to Dominique du Froid's booth, trying to look innocuous. Which worked fine, until the warlock herself appeared, seemingly out of nowhere.

"Or just here to cause havoc?" Dominique said in French.

Céline cursed silently. She'd had *one* job, a humiliatingly easy one at that, and she'd still managed to fail. Stephen was nowhere in sight, and Robert was still rummaging through the warlock's tent.

"I was waiting for you to come back," Céline said loudly and in English, so Robert would be sure to hear. "Thank goodness you finally did. *I'm melting in this heat*." She said that last part even louder. It was a prearranged signal, just in case. Translation: get out, *now*. Hopefully she could keep the warlock distracted long enough that he could slip out unseen.

Where was Stephen?

"*Bien sûr.*" The warlock had a terrible accent, French by way of Southern California. Céline wondered if warlocks could surf. "And what is it you're looking for, mademoiselle?"

"A love potion." It was the first thing that popped into her head. Maybe because she'd just spotted Stephen, hurrying toward them—while trying very much to look like he wasn't hurrying. Céline wondered how Dominique had managed to give him the slip in the first place, and if she'd done so on purpose.

"A love potion, eh?" The warlock followed her gaze and made an approving noise. "Not bad, though a little beefy for my taste. The better the body, the worse the mind, I always find. But maybe you prefer dumb and pretty. *Chacun à son goût*, eh?"

"Um, *oui*, dumb and pretty, sure. So—" What was Robert *doing* back there, anyway? Céline hoped he'd managed to slip out without her seeing him, but she couldn't take the risk. "Can you help me?"

"Love is a little beyond my pay grade, *chérie*. Anyone around here who tells you different is lying. But I can offer you . . ."

She fell silent as Stephen arrived, looking slightly harried. "Everything okay here?"

He shot Céline a concerned look. Her heart pounded; he was worried about her. She nodded. "Totally fine. We were just—"

"Your friend here wanted me to sell her a potion to make you fall in love with her," the warlock said. Céline thought she might drop dead on the spot. "I was about to tell her I could only offer her the next best thing." She pulled what looked like a can of hair spray from beneath the booth and sprayed a puff of it in Stephen's face. His expression went slack.

"What did you do?" Céline cried. "And why did you *say* that?"

"Oh, relax. Trust me, in this state, he won't care what anyone says. Watch."

Stephen was staring at Céline like he'd never seen her before. He reached out a hand and touched her cheek, gently, his expression wondering. He looked at her like he was thinking, *Could you be* real?

"Turns out your little blond friend here has a nasty case of demon pox," Dominique told Stephen. Céline decided she was not, in fact, going to drop dead; she was going to murder the warlock.

"Demon pox is so sexy," Stephen said. "Will there be warts?" He batted his eyes at Céline. "You would look beautiful with warts."

"See?" the warlock said. "I fixed him for you."

"What did you *do*?"

"It's not obvious? I did what you asked for. Well, it's a cheap approximation of what you asked for, but what else is the Shadow Market for?"

Céline didn't know what to say. She was furious on Stephen's behalf.

On her own behalf, she was . . . something else. Something she should not have been.

"Did anyone ever tell you that you're beautiful when you're confused?" Stephen gushed. He gave her a moony grin. "Of course, you're also beautiful when you're angry, and when you're sad, and when you're happy, and when you're laughing, and when you're . . ."

"What?"

"When you're kissing me," he said. "But that one's just a theory. Do you want to test it out?"

"Stephen, I'm not sure you really know—"

Then he was kissing her.

Stephen Herondale was kissing her.

Stephen Herondale's lips were on her lips, his hands were on her waist, caressing her back, cupping her cheeks. Stephen Herondale's fingers were threading through her hair.

Stephen Herondale was holding her tight, tighter, as if he wanted more of her than he could have, as if he wanted all of her.

She tried to hold herself at a distance. This was not real, she reminded herself. This was not him. But it felt real. It felt like Stephen Herondale, warm in her arms, wanting her, and her resistance gave way.

For one eternal moment, she was lost to bliss.

"Enjoy it while you can. It'll wear off in an hour or so."

Dominique du Froid's voice yanked her back to reality—the reality in which Stephen was married to someone else. Céline forced herself to pull away. He let out a tiny whimper and looked like he was going to cry.

"First taste is free. You want permanent, you have to pay," the warlock said. "But I suppose I could give you the Shadowhunter discount."

Céline froze. "How did you know I was a Shadowhunter?"

"With your grace and beauty, how could you be anything else?" Stephen said. Céline ignored him. Something was very wrong here. Her runes were covered; her clothing was convincingly mundane; her weapons were hidden. There was nothing to mark her true identity.

"Or perhaps you'd like to buy two doses," the warlock said. "One for this schmuck, and one for the schmuck behind the curtain. Not quite as handsome, of course, but those uptight ones can be a lot of fun once they let loose. . . ."

Céline's hand crept toward her hidden dagger.

"You look surprised, Céline," the warlock said. "Did you honestly think I didn't know you three stooges were watching me? Did you think I would just leave my booth without a security system? I guess lover boy's not the only thing dumb but pretty around here."

"How do you know my name?"

The warlock threw back her head and laughed. Her molars gleamed with gold. "Every Downworlder in Paris knows about poor Céline Montclaire, wandering the city like a murderous little Éponine. We all feel a little sorry for you."

Céline lived with a steady, secret simmer of rage, but now she felt it boiling over.

"I mean, I can't afford to have Shadowhunters poking around in my business, so I'm still going to have to take care of you, but I'll feel sorry for you as you die."

Céline drew her dagger just as a flock of Halphas demons exploded from the tent. The winged beasts swooped toward her and Stephen, razor-sharp talons extended, beaks open to unleash an unearthly screech.

"Demon pigeons!" Stephen shouted in disgust, his longsword in his hand. The blade flashed silver in the starlight as he sliced and slashed through thick, scaly wings.

Céline danced and dodged two birdlike demons, fending them off with her dagger as she pulled out two seraph blades with her free hand. *"Zuphlas,"* she whispered. *"Jophiel."* As the blades began to glow, she flung them in opposite directions. Each flew true, straight into a demon's throat. Both Halphas demons exploded in a cloud of bloody feathers and ichor. Céline was already in motion, leaping through the warlock's curtain. "Robert!" she cried.

He was locked inside what looked like a gigantic antique birdcage, its floor coated with Halphas feathers—as was he. He looked unharmed. And *very* unhappy.

Céline broke through the lock as quickly as she could, and the two of them rejoined Stephen, who had managed to dispatch several of the demons, though a handful of them swooped off the ground to safety, looping and diving through the night sky. Dominique had opened a Portal and was about to leap through it. Robert seized her by the throat, then slammed the blunt end of his sword down on her head with a resounding thud. She dropped to the ground, out cold.

"So much for stealth," he said.

"Céline, you're wounded!" Stephen said, sounding horrified.

Céline realized a demonic beak had torn a chunk out of her

calf. The blood was seeping through her jeans. She had barely felt it, but as the adrenaline of battle faded away, a sharp, stabbing pain took its place.

Stephen already had his stele in his hand, eager to apply an *iratze*. "You're even more beautiful when you're bleeding," he said.

Céline shook her head and backed away. "I can do it myself."

"But it would be my honor to heal your perfect skin," Stephen protested.

"Did he get hit on the head?" Robert asked.

Céline was too embarrassed to explain. Fortunately, the cawing of Halphas demons echoed in the distance, followed by a woman's scream. "You two watch the warlock," she said. "I'll deal with the rest of the demons before they eat anyone." She took off before Robert could ask any more questions.

"I'll miss you!" Stephen called after her. "You're so cute when you're bloodthirsty!"

More than a hundred and fifty years before, the Shadowhunter Tobias Herondale had been convicted of cowardice, a crime punishable by death. The Law, in those days, was not just hard, it was merciless. Tobias went mad and took flight, so he could not be tried and executed for his crimes, so in his absence, the Clave meted his punishment out on his wife, Eva. Death to her. Death to the Herondale child she carried.

This, at least, was the story.

Many decades ago, Zachariah had learned the truth behind this tale. He had met the warlock who saved Eva's child—and then, after the mother's death, raised that child as her own.

That child had sired a child, who had sired a child, and so

forth: a secret line of Herondales, lost to the Shadowhunter world. Until now.

The surviving member of this line was in grave danger. For a long time, that was all Brother Zachariah knew. For Tessa, for Will, he had dedicated himself to learning more. He had followed bread crumbs, run headlong into dead ends, and nearly died at the hand of a faerie who wanted the lost Herondale to stay that way. Or worse, Zachariah feared.

The lost descendant of Tobias Herondale had fallen in love with a faerie. Their child—and all their child's children—were part Shadowhunter, part fey.

Which meant Zachariah wasn't the only one seeking. He strongly suspected, however, he was the only seeker who meant no harm. If an emissary of Faerie was willing to attack not just a Shadowhunter but a Silent Brother—willing to break the Accords in the most egregious of ways—simply to stop his search, then surely the search was imperative. Surely the danger was mortal.

Decades of quiet inquiries had led here, to the Paris Shadow Market, to a booth run by the man rumored to have in his possession a precious heron-shaped pendant, a Herondale heirloom. The man named Crow, who most assumed to be a mundane with the Sight, known as savvy but untrustworthy, a man all too satisfied by life in the shadows.

Zachariah had learned the whereabouts of the pendant first—it was a Parisian warlock who'd heard about his search and contacted him with confirmation. She told him his suspicions were correct: the owner of the pendant, whatever he wanted to call himself, was a Herondale.

Which, apparently, was old news to everyone but Zachariah himself.

You've known about your heritage all this time? And yet you never revealed yourself?

"Sweetheart, I think you can put down the crossbow," Crow told the woman. "The psychic monk doesn't seem like he means us any harm."

She lowered the weapon, though she didn't look very happy about it.

Thank you.

"And maybe you should leave us alone to talk," Crow added.

"I don't think that's a good idea—"

"Rosemary, trust me. I got this."

The woman, who must have been his wife, sighed. It was the sound of someone who understood stubbornness and had long ago given up trying to fight it. "Fine. But you . . ." She poked Brother Zachariah with the crossbow, hard enough he could feel it through his thick robes. "Anything happens to him, and I will hunt you down and make you pay."

I have no intention of letting anything happen to either of you. That's why I've come.

"Yeah, whatever." She took Crow in her arms. The two embraced for a long moment. Zachariah had often heard the expression "holding on for dear life," but rarely had he seen it enacted. The couple clung to each other like it was the only way to survive.

He remembered loving someone like that. He remembered the impossibility of saying good-bye. The woman whispered something to Crow, then hoisted her crossbow and disappeared into the Paris night.

"We're newlyweds, and she's a little overprotective," Crow said. "You know how it is."

I'm afraid I do not.

Crow looked him up and down, and Brother Zachariah wondered what this man saw. Whatever it was, he seemed unimpressed. "Yeah, I guess you wouldn't."

I have been looking for you for a long time, longer than you can imagine.

"Look, I'm sorry you wasted your time, but I don't want anything to do with you people."

I fear you don't realize the danger you're in. I am not the only one looking for you—

"But you're the only one who can protect me, right? 'Come with me if you want to live,' and all that? Yeah, I've seen that movie. Not interested in living it."

He was plenty sure of himself, Brother Zachariah thought, and felt the strange urge to smile. Maybe there was a trace of the familiar here after all.

"A man like me, he makes his fair share of enemies. I've been looking out for myself my whole life, and I don't see any reason I—"

Whatever he said next was drowned out by an unholy screeching. A giant birdlike demon swooped down, speared Crow's coat with its razor-sharp beak, and lifted him into the air.

Brother Zachariah seized one of the seraph blades he had brought along, just in case. *Mebahiah*, he named it, and flung it at the birdlike demon. The blade embedded itself in the feathered sternum, and the demon exploded midair. Crow tumbled several feet to the ground, landing in a noisy heap of feathers and ichor. Zachariah rushed over to help the man to his feet, but these efforts were rebuffed.

Crow examined the large, ragged hole in his trench coat

with disgust. "That was brand-new!"

It is indeed a very nice coat. Or . . . it was. Zachariah refrained from pointing out the good fortune that the Halphas demon hadn't ripped a hole through anything more valuable. Like his rib cage.

"So is that the danger you came to warn me about? Saving my new coat from a demon seagull?"

It struck me as more of a demon pigeon.

Crow brushed himself off. He darted several suspicious looks at the sky, as if expecting another attack. "Listen, Mr. . . ."

Brother. Brother Zachariah.

"Right, okay, bro, I can see that a guy like you could come in handy in a fight. And if you're that determined to protect me from some big, scary danger, I guess I won't fight you on it."

Brother Zachariah was surprised by the sudden change of heart. Perhaps nearly getting pecked to death by a demon pigeon had that effect on people.

I'd like to take you somewhere safe.

"Sure. Fine. Give me a few hours to tie up some loose ends, and Rosemary and I will meet you on the Pont des Arts at dawn. We'll do whatever you want. Promise."

I can accompany you, as you tie these ends.

"Listen, *brother*, the kinds of ends I'm talking about, they don't take kindly to Shadowhunters poking around in their business. If you catch my drift."

Your drift sounds mildly criminal.

"You want to make a citizen's arrest?"

I am concerned only with your safety.

"I made it twenty-two years without your help. I think I can make it another six hours, don't you?"

Brother Zachariah had invested decades into this search.

It seemed wildly unwise to let this man slip away, with only a promise that he would return. Especially given what he'd learned about the man's reputation. It didn't exactly inspire confidence in his word.

"Look, I know what you're thinking, and I know I can't stop you from following me. So I'm just asking you flat out: You want me to trust you? Then you try trusting me. And I'm swearing, on whatever you need me to, that your precious lost Shadowhunter will be on that bridge waiting for you at dawn."

Against his better judgment, Brother Zachariah nodded.

Go.

Céline had no taste for torture. Not that this was what they would call it, whatever they did to the warlock to get her to talk. Valentine had taught his Circle to be careful with their words. Robert and Stephen would "interrogate" Dominique du Froid, using whatever methods they deemed requisite. When they got the answers they needed—names of her Shadowhunter contacts, details of crimes committed—they would deliver her and an inventory of her sins to Valentine.

The warlock was bound to a folding chair in the cheap flat they were using as a home base.

The warlock was unconscious, blood trickling from the shallow wound on her forehead.

This was how Robert and Stephen referred to her, not by name but as "the warlock," as if she were more thing than person.

Valentine had wanted them to conduct this investigation without alerting the warlock to their presence. It was only midnight on their first day in Paris, and they'd already screwed everything up. "If we bring him some answers, he can't be too mad," Stephen said. It sounded more like wish than prediction.

Stephen had stopped commenting on the gamine beauty of Céline's legs and the addictive qualities of her porcelain skin. He claimed not to remember the effects of the warlock's potion, but his glance strayed to Céline every time he thought she wasn't looking. She couldn't help wondering.

What if he did remember?

What if, having finally touched her, held her, kissed her, he'd discovered a new desire in himself?

He was still married to Amatis, of course; even if he desired Céline—maybe even, a little bit, loved Céline—there was nothing to be done about it.

But what if?

"Is anyone else hungry?" Céline said.

"Am I ever not hungry?" Stephen said. He slapped the warlock sharply. She stirred but did not wake.

Céline backed toward the door. "Why don't I go find us something to eat, while you're . . . taking care of this?"

Robert yanked the warlock's hair back, hard. She yelped, and her eyes flew open. "Shouldn't take long."

"Great." Céline hoped they couldn't tell how desperate she was to get out of the apartment. She didn't have the stomach for this kind of thing, but she couldn't have them report that back to Valentine. She'd worked too hard to gain his respect.

"Hey, you're limping," Stephen said. "You need another *iratze?*"

He was worried about her. She told herself not to read anything into it. "It doesn't even hurt anymore," she lied. "I'm fine."

She'd applied the healing rune half-heartedly, and it had

not completely closed her wound. She preferred, sometimes, to feel the pain.

When she was a child, her parents had often refused her *iratzes* after training sessions, especially when her injuries were caused by her own mistakes. *Let the pain remind you to do better next time*, they told her. All these years later, she was still making so many mistakes.

Céline was halfway down the precarious staircase when she realized she'd forgotten her wallet. She tromped painfully back up, then hesitated outside the door, stopped by the sound of her name.

"Me and Céline?" she heard Stephen say.

Feeling slightly ridiculous, Céline withdrew her stele and drew a careful rune on the door. Their amplified voices came through loud and clear.

Stephen laughed. "You've got to be kidding me."

"It sounded like a pretty good kiss. . . ."

"I was under the influence!"

"Still. She's pretty, don't you think?"

There was an excruciating pause. "I don't know, I never really thought about it."

"You do realize that marriage doesn't mean you're never allowed to *look* at another woman, right?"

"It's not that," Stephen said. "It's . . ."

"The way she follows you around like a drooling puppy?"

"That doesn't help," Stephen acknowledged. "She's just such a *child*. Like, no matter how old she gets, she's always going to need someone else telling her what to do."

"I'll give you that," Robert said. "But Valentine seems convinced there's something more to her."

"Nobody's right all the time," Stephen said, and now they were both laughing. "Not even him."

"Don't let him hear you say that!"

Céline didn't realize she was in motion until she felt the rain on her face. She collapsed against the cool stone of the building's facade, wishing she could melt into it. To turn herself to stone; to shut down her nerves, her senses, her heart; to feel *nothing* . . . if only.

Their laughter echoed in her ears.

She was a joke.

She was pathetic.

She was someone Stephen had never thought about, never cared about, never wanted. Would never want, under any circumstances.

She was a pathetic creature. A child. A mistake.

The sidewalks were empty. The streets shimmered with rain. The searchlight beacon atop the Eiffel Tower had gone to sleep, along with the rest of the city. Céline felt utterly alone. Her leg throbbed. Her tears would not stop. Her heart screamed. She had nowhere to go but could not go back upstairs, back to that room, to that laughter. She set off blindly into the Paris night.

Céline was at home in the dark, slumbering streets. She wandered for hours. Through the Marais and past the hulking Pompidou, crossing from the Right Bank to the Left and back again. She visited with the gargoyles of Notre Dame, those hideous stone demons clinging to Gothic spires, awaiting their chance to devour the faithful. It seemed unfair that the city was so full of stone creatures who could feel nothing, and here she was, feeling so unbearably much.

She was in the Tuileries—more bloody ghosts, more creatures carved of stone—when she spotted the trail of ichor. She was still a Shadowhunter, and she was a Shadowhunter in desperate need of distraction, so she followed it. She caught up with the Shax demon in the Opera district but stayed in the shadows, wanting to see what it was up to. Shax demons were trackers, used to hunt people who didn't want to be found. And this demon was definitely tracking something.

Céline tracked it in turn.

She tracked it through the slumbering courtyards of the Louvre. It was oozing ichor from a wound, but it wasn't moving like a creature slinking off to nurse its wounds. Its giant pincers skittered at the cobblestones as it hesitated at corners, deciding which way to turn. This was a predator, tracking its prey.

The demon paused in the archway of the Louvre, at the foot of the Pont des Arts. The small pedestrian bridge stretched across the Seine, its railings crowded with lovers' locks. It was said that if a couple attached a lock to the Pont des Arts, their love would last forever. The bridge was almost deserted at this hour, except for one young couple, locked in an embrace. Completely oblivious to the Shax demon slithering out of the shadows, pincers clicking together in eager anticipation.

Céline always carried a misericord blade. Its narrow point was exactly what she needed to penetrate the insectoid demon's carapace.

She hoped.

"*Gadreel*," Céline whispered, naming a seraph blade. She crept behind the Shax demon, as steady and silent as it was. She, too, could be a predator. In one smooth, sure motion, she stabbed the misericord straight through the carapace, then slid the seraph blade into the wound she'd opened.

The demon dissolved.

It had all happened so swiftly, so quietly, that the couple on the bridge didn't even break from their embrace. They were too intent on each other to realize how close they'd come to being a demon's late-night snack. Céline lingered, trying to imagine it: standing on the bridge with someone who loved her, a man gazing so intently into her eyes that he wouldn't have noticed the world ending.

But Céline's imagination gave out. Reality had caged her in. As long as she thought Stephen hadn't noticed her, she could fantasize about what might happen if he ever did.

Now she knew. She could not unknow.

Céline wiped and sheathed her blades, then crept closer to the couple, close enough to hear what they were saying. She was glamoured, so there was no danger in doing a little eavesdropping, but she tried to keep herself hidden in case more demons appeared. What words did a man say to the woman he loved, when he thought no one else could hear? She might never find out, if she waited for someone to say them to her.

"I hate to say I told you so," the woman said, "but . . ."

"Who knew he'd be so willing to trust a warlock?"

"Who knew anyone would believe *you* were the long-lost descendant of some noble Shadowhunter line?" she said, then laughed. "Oh wait, I knew. Admit it, deep down, you knew it would work. You just didn't want it to."

"Of course I didn't want it to." He touched her cheek, impossibly gently. "I hate this. I hate leaving you here." Céline realized with a slight shock that she recognized him. This was the man the Silent Brother had chased after at the Market.

"It's not for long. And it's for the best, Jack, I promise."

"You'll come find me in L.A. as soon as it's taken care of? You swear?"

"In the Shadow Market. At our old place. I swear. As soon as I can be sure the trail's gone cold." She kissed him, long and hard. When she pressed her hand to his cheek, Céline spotted the glint of a wedding band.

"Rosemary—"

"I don't want you anywhere near these people. It's not safe."

"But it's safe for you?"

"You know I'm right," she said.

The man hung his head and tucked his hands into the pockets of his trench coat. It looked expensive, except for the giant gaping hole torn through the left side. "Yeah."

"You ready?"

He nodded, and she pulled a small bottle from her bag. "This better work the way it's supposed to." She handed it to her husband, who uncorked it, swallowed its contents, and tossed it into the river.

A moment later, he clutched his hands to his face and began to scream.

Céline panicked. It wasn't her place to interfere, but she couldn't just stand here and watch as this woman murdered her—

"Jack, Jack, it's okay, you're okay."

She clung to him as the man moaned and shuddered, and, finally, slumped quietly into her arms. "I think it worked," he said.

When they backed away from each other, Céline gasped. Even in the dim light of the streetlights, she could see that his face had transformed. He had been a blond with sparkling green eyes and sharp, chiseled features, around the age of Stephen and nearly as handsome. Now he looked ten years older, his face carved with worry lines, his hair mud colored, his smile crooked.

"Hideous," the woman named Rosemary said approvingly. Then she kissed him again, just as desperately as before, as if nothing had changed. "Now go."

"You sure?"

"As sure as I am that I love you."

The man fled into the night, his coat melting into the darkness.

"And ditch the trench!" Rosemary called after him. "It's too obvious!"

"Never!" he shouted back, and then he was gone.

Rosemary sagged against the bridge and buried her face in her hands. So she didn't see the gargoyle behind her blink its eyes and swivel its stone snout in her direction.

Céline suddenly remembered: the Pont des Arts *had* no gargoyles. This was a flesh-and-blood Achaieral demon, and it looked hungry.

With a furious roar, the monstrous shadow peeled itself off the bridge and unfolded a set of huge, batlike wings that blotted out the night. It opened its jaw wide and bared razor-like teeth, then lunged straight for Rosemary's throat. With shocking speed, Rosemary hefted a sword and slashed. The demon screeched in pain, raking its talons against the metal blade with enough force to knock it from the woman's hands. Rosemary stumbled to the ground, and the demon seized its moment. It leaped onto her chest, immobilizing her beneath its massive wings, and hissed. Teeth neared flesh.

"Sariel," Céline whispered, and stabbed a seraph blade through the demon's neck. It yowled with pain and whirled

toward her, its innards bursting through its hide even as it tried, in its last remaining moments, to attack.

Rosemary heaved her sword and sliced off the creature's head, seconds before head and torso exploded into a cloud of dust. Satisfied, she collapsed backward, the wound in her shoulder bleeding freely.

Céline could tell how much it hurt—and how determined the woman was to reveal no pain. She knelt by her side. Rosemary flinched away. "Let me see—I can help."

"I would never ask for help from a Shadowhunter," the woman said bitterly.

"You didn't exactly ask. And you're welcome."

The woman sighed, then examined her bloody wound. She touched it gingerly, winced. "As long as you're here, you want to give me an *iratze*?"

It was obvious the woman was no mundane. Even a mundane with the Sight couldn't have fought the way she did. But that didn't mean she could withstand an *iratze*. No one but a Shadowhunter could.

"Look, I don't really have the time to explain it, and I can't exactly go to the hospital and tell them I got gnawed on by a demon, can I?"

"If you know about *iratzes*, you know that only a Shadowhunter can bear a rune," Céline said.

"I know." Rosemary met her gaze steadily.

She didn't bear the Voyance rune. But the way she had moved, the way she had fought . . .

"Have you borne a rune before?" Céline asked hesitantly.

Rosemary smirked. "What do you think?"

"Who *are* you?"

"No one you need to worry about. You going to help or not?"

Céline drew her stele. Applying a rune to anyone who wasn't a Shadowhunter meant probable death, certain agony. She took a deep breath, then carefully applied stele to skin.

Rosemary let out a relieved sigh.

"Are you going to tell me who sent a Shax demon after you?" Céline said. "And whether it was the same person who made sure an Achaieral demon was here to finish the job?"

"No. You going to tell me why you're wandering around in the middle of the night looking like someone just drowned your pet rock in the Seine?"

"No."

"Okay, then. And thank you."

"That guy who was here with you before . . ."

"You mean the one you didn't see and won't say anything about, ever, if you know what's good for you?"

"You love him, and he loves you, right?" Céline asked.

"I guess he must, because there are some dangerous people out there looking for me," Rosemary said. "And he's done his best to make sure they think they're looking for him instead."

"I don't understand."

"And you don't have to. But yeah. He loves me. I love him. Why?"

"I just . . ." She wanted to ask what that was like, how it felt. She wanted, also, to extend the conversation. She was afraid to be alone again, stranded on this bridge between the endless black of river and sky. "I just want to make sure you have someone to take care of you."

"We take care of each other. That's how it works. Speaking of which . . ." She gave Céline an appraising look. "I'm in your debt now, for helping me out with the demon. And for keeping my secret."

"I didn't say I would—"

"You will. And I don't believe in debts, so let me do you a favor."

"I don't need anything," Céline said, meaning, *I don't need anything anyone can give me.*

"I keep my eyes open, and I see what's happening in the Shadowhunter world. You need more than you think you do. Most of all, you need to stay away from Valentine Morgenstern."

Céline stiffened. "What do you know about Valentine?"

"I know that you're just his type, young and impressionable, and I know that he can't be trusted. I pay attention. You should too. He's not telling you everything. I know that." She looked over Céline's shoulder, and her eyes widened. "Someone's coming. You should get out of here."

Céline turned around. A Silent Brother was gliding along the Left Bank, nearing the edge of the bridge. There was no way of knowing if it was the same one she'd met in the Shadow Market, but she couldn't risk running into him again. Not after what she'd told him. It was too humiliating.

"Remember," Rosemary said. "Valentine is not to be trusted."

"And why should I trust *you?*"

"No reason at all," Rosemary said. Without another word, she strode down the bridge toward the Silent Brother.

The sky was pinking. The endless night had finally given way to dawn.

I had expected to find your husband on this bridge. But even as he formed the words, Brother Zachariah sensed their untruth.

He had trusted a man he knew could not be trusted. He had let his sympathies for the Herondale line, his desire to believe there remained some bond between the Carstairs and the Herondales—even though this man was barely a Herondale and Zachariah was barely a Carstairs—cloud his judgment. And now it was Jack Crow who might bear the consequences.

"He's not coming. And you're never going to see him again, Shadowhunter, so I suggest you not bother to look."

I understand that the Shadowhunters have given your family every reason not to trust us, but—

"Don't take it personally. I don't trust anyone," she said. "It's how I've managed to stay alive."

She was stubborn and rude, and Brother Zachariah couldn't help but like her.

"I mean, if I *was* going to trust someone, it wouldn't be a cult of violent fundamentalists who get a kick out of executing their own . . . but like I said, I don't trust anyone."

Except Jack Crow.

"That's not his name anymore."

Whatever name he chooses, he will always be a Herondale.

She laughed, and when she did, her face took on a strangely familiar cast. Familiar in the way that Jack Crow's had never been. "You don't know nearly as much as you think you do, Shadowhunter."

Brother Zachariah reached into his robe and pulled out the heron necklace he'd bought from the Shadow Market. The necklace, he remembered, that Crow had sold without his wife's permission or knowledge. As a man might do if it were not truly his to sell. The pendant glittered in the dawn light. Zachariah marked her surprise and offered the chain.

She opened her palm and allowed him to place the pendant gently in her possession. Something deep in her seemed to settle as her hand wrapped around the heron charm—as if she had lost some essential piece of her soul, and now it was returned to her.

"A pigeon?" She raised her eyebrows.

A heron. Perhaps you recognize it?

"Why would I?"

Because I purchased it from your husband.

Her lips were pressed together in a thin, tight line. Her hand had formed a fist around the chain. It was clear the child at the booth had spoken the truth: she didn't know the pendant had been for sale.

"Then why give it to me?"

She could pretend a lack of interest, but Zachariah wondered what she would say if he asked for it back. He suspected he would have a fight on his hands.

Because I have a feeling it belongs to you—and to your family.

She stiffened, and Brother Zachariah marked the minute twitch of her hand, as if instinctively reaching for a weapon. She had sharp instincts, but also self-control—and arrogance, grace, and loyalty, and the capacity for great love, and a laugh that could light up the sky.

He had come to Paris looking for the lost Herondale.

And he had found her.

"I don't know what you're talking about."

You are the Herondale. Not your husband. You. The lost heir to a noble line of warriors.

"I'm nobody," she snapped. "Nobody of interest to you, at least."

I could reach into your mind and confirm the truth.

She flinched. Zachariah didn't have to read her mind to understand her panic, or her welling self-doubt as she scrambled to figure out how he had seen through the ruse.

But I would not trespass on your secrets. I want only to help you.

"My parents told me everything I need to know about the Shadowhunters," she said, and Brother Zachariah understood this was as close to an admission as he was going to get. "Your precious little Clave. Your *Law*." She spit out that last word like it was poison.

I am not here as a representative of the Clave. They have no idea I've come to you—or even that you exist. I have my own reasons for finding you, for wanting to protect you.

"And they are?"

I would not trespass on your secrets, and I would ask that you not trespass on mine. Know only that I owe a great debt to your family. The bonds holding me to the Herondales run deeper than blood.

"Well, that's nice of you and all, but no one asked you to pay any debts," Rosemary said. "Jack and I are doing just fine, taking care of each other, and that's what we'll keep doing."

It was clever of you to make it seem as if your husband was the one I sought, but—

"It was clever of *Jack*. People underestimate him. And they pay for it."

—but, if I could penetrate your ruse, others who seek you may as well. And they are more dangerous than you know.

"These 'others' you talk about butchered my parents." Rosemary's face betrayed no expression. "Jack and I have been on the run for years. Trust me, I know exactly how dangerous this is. And I know exactly how dangerous it is to trust a stranger, even a stranger with psychic ninja powers and a deeply weird fashion sense."

One of the things Brother Zachariah had learned in the Silent Brotherhood was the power of acceptance. Sometimes it was stronger to recognize an unwinnable fight and accept defeat—the better to begin laying groundwork for the next battle.

Though this was not a battle, he reminded himself. You could not war for a person's trust; you could only earn it.

Your heron necklace now has an enchantment on it. If you encounter trouble you cannot face on your own, you need only summon me, and I will come.

"If you think you can track us through this thing—"

Your husband suggested that the only way to earn trust is by offering it. I will not try to find you if you prefer not to be found. But with this pendant, you can always find me. I trust you will summon me for help, if and when you need it. Please trust that I will always answer.

"And who are you, exactly?"

You may call me Brother Zachariah.

"I could, but if I end up in this hypothetical situation where I need my life saved by some bloodthirsty monk, I'd rather know his actual name."

I was once . . . It had been so long. He almost didn't feel entitled to the name. But there was a deep, nearly human pleasure in allowing himself to claim it. *I was once known as James Carstairs. Jem.*

"So who will *you* summon when you encounter trouble you can't face on your own, Jem?" She fastened the pendant around her neck, and Zachariah felt a sliver of relief. At least he'd accomplished that much.

I don't anticipate that.

"Then you're not paying attention."

She touched him on the shoulder then, unexpectedly, and with unexpected gentleness.

"Thank you for trying," she said. "It's a start."

Then he was watching her walk away.

Brother Zachariah watched the water stream beneath the bridge. He thought about that other bridge, in another city, where once a year he returned to remember the man he'd once been and the dreams that man had once had.

At the far end of the Pont des Arts, a young street musician opened a violin case and raised the instrument to his chin. For a moment, Zachariah thought he was imagining it—that he had conjured up a fantasy of his former self. But as he drew closer—because he could not stay away—he realized the musician was a girl. She was young, no more than fourteen or fifteen, her hair swept up beneath a newsboy cap, a neat, old-fashioned bow tie at the collar of her white blouse.

She bowed the strings and began to play a haunting melody. Brother Zachariah recognized it: a Bartók violin concerto that had been written well after Jem Carstairs had put down his violin.

Silent Brothers played no music. They didn't listen to music either, not in the ordinary way. But even with their senses sealed off to mortal pleasures, they still heard.

Jem heard.

He was glamoured; the musician must have assumed she was alone. There was no audience for her music, no possibility of payment. She wasn't playing for spare change but for her own pleasure. She faced the water, the sky. This was a song to welcome the sun.

Distantly, he remembered the soft pressure of the chin rest. He remembered his fingertips capering across the strings. He remembered the dance of the bow.

He remembered how, sometimes, it had felt like the music was playing him.

There was no music in the Silent City; there was no sun, no dawn. There was only dark. There was only quiet.

Paris was a city that luxuriated in the senses—food, wine, art, romance. Everywhere was a reminder of what he'd lost, the pleasures of a world no longer his. He had learned to live with the loss. It was harder, when he immersed himself in the world like this, but it was bearable.

This was something else, though.

The nothing he felt, as he listened to the melody, watched the bow waltz up and down the strings—the great hollow it opened inside him, echoing only with the past? That made him feel utterly, dismally inhuman.

The longing he felt, to truly hear, to want, to *feel*? That made him feel almost alive.

Come home, the Brothers whispered in his mind. *It is time.*

Over the years, as he'd gained more control, Brother Zachariah had learned how to isolate himself from the voices of his Brothers when need be. It was a strange thing, the Brotherhood. Most assumed it was a lonely, solitary life—and it was, indeed, solitary. But he was never truly alone. The Brotherhood was always there, on the edge of his awareness, watching, waiting. Brother Zachariah needed only extend a hand, and the Brotherhood would reclaim him.

Soon, he promised them. *But not yet. I have more business here.*

He was more Silent Brother than not. But he was still less

Silent Brother than the others. It was a strange, liminal space, one that allowed him a modicum of privacy—and a desire for it that his Brothers had long since abandoned. Zachariah shut himself off from them for the moment. He felt a deep regret over his failure here, but it was good, it was *human*, to feel regret, and he wanted to savor it, all on his own.

Or maybe not all on his own.

There was, in fact, one more piece of business before he could return to the Silent City. He needed to explain himself to the one person who cared as much about the Herondales as he did.

He needed Tessa.

Céline didn't go to Valentine's apartment intending to break in. That would have been madness. And anyway, after a night and day of blindly wandering the city, she was too sleep deprived to form clear intentions of anything. She simply followed a whim. She wanted the certainty that settled over her in Valentine's presence, the power he had to make her believe. Not just in him but in herself.

After her strange encounter on the bridge, she'd considered going back to the flat in the Marais. She knew Stephen and Robert should be apprised of the unexpected demon activity, the possibility of a rogue Shadowhunter causing trouble and spreading suspicion about the Circle.

She couldn't face them. Let them worry about what had become of her. Or not worry. She no longer cared.

At least, she was trying very hard not to care.

She'd spent the day in the Louvre, haunting galleries that none of the tourists cared to see, old Etruscan masks and

Mesopotamian coins. She'd spent hours there when she was younger, blending in with the hordes of schoolchildren. It was easy, when you were a child, to go unseen.

The challenge, Céline understood now, was to be seen—and once seen, to endure judgment.

She couldn't stop thinking about the couple on the bridge, the way they'd gazed at each other. The way they'd touched each other, with so much care and so much need. Nor could she stop thinking about the woman's warning about Valentine. Céline was certain she could trust Valentine with her life.

But if she'd been so wrong about Stephen, how could she know for sure she was right about anything?

Valentine was staying in opulent quarters in the sixth arrondissement, down the street from a famous chocolatier and a *mercerie* where the custom hats cost more than most people spent on rent. She knocked loudly. When no one answered, it was easy enough to pick the lock.

I am breaking into Valentine Morgenstern's apartment, she thought, bewildered by herself. It didn't seem quite real.

The apartment was elegant, almost regal, walls draped with gold fleurs-de-lis, furniture covered with velvet. Plush rugs dotted the gleaming hardwood floors. Heavy golden curtains dimmed the light. The room's only anachronism was a large glass case in the center, inside of which lay Dominique du Froid, bound, beaten, and unconscious.

Before she could decide what to do, there was the sound of a key rattling in the lock. The doorknob turned. Without thinking, Céline dove behind the thick curtains. She held herself very, very still.

From her hiding spot, she couldn't see Valentine pacing

back and forth across the living room. But she could hear everything she needed to.

"Wake up," he snapped.

There was a pause, a rustling, and then a woman's yelp of pain.

"Halphas demons?" he said, sounding halfway between amused and enraged. "Really?"

"You told me to make it look real," Dominique whined.

"Yes, I told you to make it *look* real—not endanger them."

"You also told me you'd pay, but here I am, in some kind of cage. With an empty wallet. And a couple unseemly lumps on my head."

Valentine sighed heavily, as if this were all an irritating imposition on his time. "You told them exactly what we agreed upon, yes? And signed the confession?"

"Isn't that what the little brats told you when they dumped me here? So how about you pay me for my services, and we can forget this ever happened."

"Gladly."

There was a strange sound, one that Céline couldn't place. Then a smell, one that she could: burnt flesh.

Valentine cleared his throat. "You can come out now, Céline."

She froze. Didn't so much catch her breath as lose the ability to breathe.

"Not very good at subterfuge lately, are we? Come on now, show yourself." He clapped his hands together sharply, as if summoning a pet. "No more games."

Céline stepped out from behind the curtains, feeling like a fool.

"You knew I was here? The whole time?"

"You would be surprised what all I know, Céline." Valentine smiled coldly. As always, he was dressed in all black, which made his white-blond hair seem to glow with pale fire. Céline supposed that by objective standards, Valentine was just as handsome as Stephen, but it was impossible to think of him that way. He was handsome the way a statue was handsome: perfectly sculpted, unyielding as stone. Sometimes at the Academy, Céline would watch him with Jocelyn, wondering at the way a single touch from her could melt his ice. Once Céline had come upon them in an embrace and had watched from the shadows as they lost themselves in each other. When they broke from the kiss, Valentine had raised a hand to Jocelyn's cheek in an impossibly tender touch, and his expression, as he gazed at his first and only love, was almost human.

There was no trace of that in him now. He opened his arms wide, as if welcoming her to make herself at home in the opulent living room. The cage at the center was empty, except for a smoldering pile of black lace and leather. Dominique du Froid was gone.

Valentine followed her gaze.

"She was a criminal," he said. "I simply expedited the inevitable sentence."

There were rumors about Valentine, about the change that had come over him when his father was killed. Dark whispers about the cruelties he carried out not just on trespassing Downworlders but on anyone who crossed him. Anyone who *questioned* him.

"You look worried, Céline. Even . . . afraid."

"No," she said quickly.

"It's almost as if you think breaking into my apartment to spy on me might draw some kind of nasty consequence."

"I wasn't spying, I was just—"

He favored her with a smile then, so warm, so sunny, that she felt ridiculous for having been so afraid. "Would you settle for tea? And maybe some biscuits. You look like you haven't eaten in a year."

He set out a bounty: not just tea and biscuits but a sliced baguette, fresh chèvre and a small pot of honey, and a bowl of blueberries that tasted like they'd just been plucked from the branch. Céline hadn't known she was hungry until the taste of honey hit her tongue. She realized she was ravenous.

They made polite Paris small talk: their favorite cafés, their preferred picnic spots, the best crepe stand, the relative merits of the Orsay and the Pompidou. Then Valentine took a hearty bite of cheese-smeared baguette and said, almost cheerfully, "You know, of course, that the others think you're weak and not particularly bright."

Céline almost choked on a blueberry.

"If it were up to most of the Circle, you wouldn't be in it. Fortunately, this isn't a democracy. They think they know you, Céline, but they don't know the half of it, do they?"

Slowly, she shook her head. No one knew her, not really.

"I, on the other hand, believed in you. I trusted you. And you repay this trust with suspicion?"

"I really didn't—"

"Of course you had no suspicions. You just thought you'd pay a social call. Behind my curtains. While I was out."

"Okay. *Oui.* I was suspicious."

"See? You are smart." That smile again, warm and

approving, like she'd fulfilled his intentions. "And what is it you've discovered about me, with your intrepid investigation?"

There was no point in pretense. And Céline was almost as curious as she was terrified. So she told the truth, as she'd surmised it. "Dominique du Froid wasn't in business with two Shadowhunters. She was in business with you. You're trying to set someone up, and you're using us to do it."

"Us?"

"Me. Robert. Stephen."

"Robert and Stephen, yes. I'm indeed using them. But you? You're here, aren't you? You're getting the full story."

"I am?"

"If you want it . . ."

Céline had not had the kind of parents who read her fairy tales. But she'd read enough of them herself to know the cardinal rule of these stories: be careful what you wish for.

And like every Shadowhunter, she knew: all the stories are true.

"I want to know," she said.

He told her she was right. He was framing two Shadowhunters, innocent of these crimes but guilty of a much larger one—standing in the Circle's way. "They're bogged down in tradition, they're beholden to the Clave's corruption. And they're dead set on destroying me. So I acted first." He'd used the warlock to plant evidence, he admitted. Now he would use Stephen and Robert as witnesses to her confession. "Since she is, unfortunately, no longer able to testify."

"What about the Mortal Sword?" Céline asked. "Aren't you worried what will happen when the accused Shadowhunters are interrogated?"

Valentine tsked, as if disappointed that she hadn't jumped to the correct conclusion. "It's very unfortunate, they'll never make it that far. I happen to know these two Shadowhunters will make an escape attempt during their transport to the Silent City. They'll be killed in the ensuing chaos. Tragic."

The words sat heavy between them. Céline tried to process it. Valentine wasn't just setting up two Shadowhunters, two *innocent* Shadowhunters. He was planning to murder them in cold blood. This was an unthinkable crime, for which the Law would demand death.

"Why are you telling me this?" she said, trying to keep her voice from trembling. "What makes you think I won't turn you in? Unless . . ."

Unless he had no intention of letting her leave this apartment alive.

A man who could kill two Shadowhunters in cold blood could presumably kill a third. Everything in her said that she should leap to her feet, draw her weapon, fight her way out of here, run straight to the Paris Institute, tell them everything. Stop this—stop *him*—before he went any further. Valentine watched her calmly, palms up on the table, as if to say, *Your move.*

She didn't move.

The Verlac family, who ran the Paris Institute, were friends with her parents. More than once, a Verlac had sought out her hiding place and dumped her back home. That first time, she'd pleaded for asylum at the Institute, where all Shadowhunters were supposedly guaranteed a safe home. Céline was told she was too young to make such requests, too young to know what "safe" meant. She was told her parents loved her and she should stop causing them so much trouble.

She owed these people nothing.

Valentine, on the other hand, had singled her out. Given her a mission, a family. She owed him everything.

He leaned toward her, reached out his hand. She willed herself not to flinch. He touched her neck, lightly, where the Achaieral demon had scratched her. "You're hurt."

"It's nothing," she said.

"And you were limping."

"I'm fine."

"If you need another *iratze*—"

"I'm *fine*."

He nodded, like she'd confirmed a suspicion. "Yes. You prefer it this way, don't you."

"What way?"

"In pain."

Now Céline flinched. "I do not," she insisted. "That would be sick."

"But do you know *why* you prefer it? Why you chase the pain?"

She had never understood this about herself. Only knew it, in the deep, wordless way you knew your most essential truth.

There was something about pain that made her feel more solid, more real. More in control. Sometimes the pain felt like the only thing she *could* control.

"You covet pain, because you know it makes you strong," Valentine said. It felt like he had given name to her nameless soul. "You know why I understand you better than the rest of them? Because we're the same. We learned early, didn't we? Cruelty, harshness, pain: no one shielded us from the realities of life, and that made us strong. Most people, they're ruled by fear. They flee the specter of pain, and that makes them weak. You and I, Céline, we know the only way through is to *face* pain. To invite the cruelty of the world—and master it."

Céline had never thought of herself this way, hard and strong. She'd certainly never dared think of herself as anything like Valentine.

"That's why I wanted you in the Circle. Robert, Stephen, the others? They're still just boys. Children playing at adult games. They haven't yet been tested—they will be, but not yet. You and I, though? We're special. We haven't been children for a long time."

No one had ever called her strong. No one had called her special.

"Things are accelerating," Valentine said. "I need to know who's with me and who's not. So you can see why I told you the truth about this"—he gestured to the singed heap of warlock clothes—"situation."

"It's a test," she guessed. "A loyalty test."

"It's an opportunity," he corrected her. "To invite you into my confidence, and reward you for yours. My proposal: you stay silent about what you've learned here and allow events to proceed as I intend, and I will deliver you Stephen Herondale on a silver platter."

"What? I—I don't—I—"

"I told you, Céline. I know things. I know you. And I can give you what you want, if you really want it."

Be careful what you wish for, she thought again. But oh, she wished for Stephen. Even knowing what he thought of her, even with his mocking laughter ringing in her ears, even believing what Valentine said, that she was strong and Stephen was weak, even knowing what she knew to be true, that Stephen did not love her and never would, she wished for him. Always and forever.

"Or you can leave this apartment, run to the Clave, tell them whatever story you like. Save these two 'innocent' Shadowhunters—and lose the only family who's ever truly cared about you," Valentine said. "The choice is yours."

Tessa Gray breathed in the city that had once, briefly but indelibly, been her home. How many nights had she stood on this same bridge, gazing at the hulking shadow of Notre Dame, the rippling waters of the Seine, the proud scaffolding of the Eiffel Tower—all of it, Paris's heartbreaking beauty, blurred by her ceaseless tears. How many nights had she searched the river for her ageless reflection, imagining the seconds, days, years, centuries she might live, and every one of them in a world without Will.

No, not imagining.

Because it had been unimaginable.

Unimaginable, but here she was, more than fifty years later, still living. Still without him. Heart forever broken yet still beating, still strong.

Still capable of love.

She'd fled to Paris after he died, stayed until she was strong enough to face her future, and hadn't been back since. On the face of things, the city hadn't changed. But then, on the face of things, neither had she. You couldn't trust the face of things to show you their truth. You didn't have to be a shape-shifter to know that.

I'm so sorry, Tessa. I had her, and I let her go.

Even after all these years, she wasn't used to it, this cold version of Jem's voice speaking inside her mind, at once so intimate and so far away. His hand rested on the railing bare inches from hers. She could have touched him. He wouldn't pull away, not from her. But his skin would be so cold, so dry, like stone.

Everything about him like stone.

"You found her—that's what we set out to do, right? This was never about bringing the lost Herondale back to the Shadowhunter world or choosing a path for her."

There was comfort in the familiar weight of the jade pendant around her neck, warm against her chest. She still wore it, every day, as she had since the day Jem gave it to her, more than a century before. He didn't know.

What you say is true, but still . . . it does not seem right for a Herondale to be in danger while we do nothing. I fear I failed you, Tessa. That I have failed him.

Between her and Jem, there was only ever one *him*.

"We found her, for Will. And you know Will would want her to choose for herself. Just like he did."

If he had still been wholly Jem, she would have put her arms around him. She would have let him feel, in her embrace, her breath, her heartbeat, how impossible it was for him to fail either her or Will.

But he was both Jem and not Jem. Both himself and unfathomably other, and she could only stand beside him, assure him with useless words that he had done enough.

He'd warned her once what would happen, as he became less himself, more Silent Brother—promised her that the transformation would never be complete. *When I no longer see the world with my human eyes, I will still be in some part the Jem you knew*, he had said. *I will see you with the eyes of my heart.*

When she looked at him now, his sealed eyes and lips, his cold face, when she breathed in his inhuman smell, like paper, like stone, like nothing that had ever lived or loved, she tried to remember this. She tried to believe that some part of him was still in there, seeing her, and longing to be seen.

It got harder every year. There had been moments, over the decades, when the Jem she remembered truly broke through. Once, during one of the mundane world's innumerable wars, they had even stolen a kiss—and almost more. Jem had pushed her away before things could go too far. After that, he'd held himself more distant from Tessa, almost as if afraid of what might happen if he let himself near the brink. That embrace, which she thought about almost every day, was more than forty years ago now—and every year, he seemed a little less Jem, a little less human. She feared he was forgetting himself, piece by piece.

She could not lose him. Not him, too.

She would be his memory.

I met a girl here, he said, *in love with a Herondale.*

She imagined she could hear a faint smile in his voice.

"Did she remind you of anyone?" Tessa teased.

Her love seemed to cause her great pain. I would have liked to help her.

It was one of the things she loved about him, his abiding desire to help anyone in need. This was something the Silent Brotherhood could not strip away.

"I used to come to this bridge all the time, you know, when I lived in Paris. After Will."

It is very peaceful here. And very beautiful.

She wanted to tell him that wasn't it. She hadn't come

for the peace or the beauty—she'd come because this bridge reminded her of Blackfriars Bridge, the bridge that belonged to her and Jem. She'd come because standing here, suspended between land and water, her hands tight on the iron railing, her face raised to the sky, reminded her of Jem. The bridge reminded her that there was still someone in the world that she loved. That even if half of her heart was gone forever, the other half was still here. Unreachable, maybe, but *here*.

She wanted to tell him, but she couldn't. It wouldn't be fair. It would be asking something of Jem that he couldn't deliver, and the world had already asked far too much of him.

"He would have hated it, the idea of a Herondale out there somewhere who thinks she can't trust the Shadowhunters. Who thinks *we're* the villains."

He might well have understood.

It was true. Will himself had been raised to distrust the Shadowhunters. He knew, better than most, how harshly the Clave treated those who turned their backs on it. He would have been enraged to learn about this lost branch of his family, at the thought of the Clave attempting to execute a mother and child for a father's sins. Tessa feared for the safety of this lost Herondale, but just as much, she longed to persuade her that some Shadowhunters could be trusted. She wanted to make this young woman understand that they weren't all hard and unfeeling: that some of them were like Will.

"I get so angry at them sometimes, the Shadowhunters who came before us, the mistakes they made. Think how many lives have been ruined by the choices of an earlier generation." She was thinking of Tobias Herondale, but also Axel Mortmain, whose parents had been murdered in front of him, and Aloysius Starkweather, who'd paid for that sin with his granddaughter's life. She was thinking, even, of her own brother, whose mother had refused to claim him as her own. Who might have found his way to being a better man had he been better loved.

It would be unjust to blame the past for choices made in the present. Nor can we justify present choices by invoking the sins of the past. You and I know that, better than most.

Jem, too, had seen his parents murdered in front of him. Jem had endured a life of pain, but he'd never let himself be warped by it—never turned to revenge or vindictiveness. And Tessa had been conceived as a demonic tool, literally. She could have chosen to accept this fate; she could have chosen to flee the Shadow World altogether, return to the mundane life she'd once known and pretend she did not see the darkness. Or she could have claimed that darkness as her own.

She'd chosen a different path. They both had.

We always have a choice, Jem said, and for once, the voice in her mind sounded like him, warm and close. *It's not always the choice we would want, but it's a choice nonetheless. The past happens to us. But we choose our future. We can only hope that our lost Herondale ultimately chooses to save herself.*

"That's the best hope for any of us, I suppose."

Jem slid his hand across the railing and rested it atop hers. It was, as she knew it would be, cold. Inhuman.

But it was also Jem: flesh and blood, undeniably alive. And where there was life, there was hope. Maybe not now, not yet, but someday, they could still have their future. She chose to believe it.

* * *

The Saint-Germain-des-Prés Church was founded in 558 AD. The original abbey was built on the ruins of an ancient Roman temple, then destroyed two centuries later in a Norman siege. Rebuilt in the tenth century AD, the church has now endured, in one form or another, for a millennium. The Merovingian kings are buried in its tombs, as is the torn-out heart of John II Casimir Vasa and the headless body of René Descartes.

Most mornings the abbey saw a steady trickle of tourists and observant locals wandering through its apse, lighting candles, bowing heads, whispering prayers to whoever might be listening. But this particular drizzly August morning, a sign on the door indicated the church was closed to the public. Inside, the Paris Conclave had assembled. Shadowhunters from all across France listened solemnly to charges lodged against two of their own.

Jules and Lisette Montclaire stood silently, heads bowed, as Robert Lightwood and Stephen Herondale testified to their crimes.

Their daughter, Céline Montclaire, was not called on to speak. She had, of course, not been present for the warlock's revelation of her parents' crimes.

The scene played out as if Valentine had scripted it himself, and like everyone else present, Céline did exactly as Valentine intended: nothing.

Inside, she was at war with herself. Furious at Valentine for making her complicit in her parents' destruction; furious with herself for sitting silently as their fates were sealed; more furious at her own instinct for mercy. After all, her parents had never shown any to her. Her parents had done their best to teach her that mercy was weakness, and cruelty was strength. So she steeled herself to be strong. Told herself this wasn't personal; this was about protecting the Circle. If Valentine believed this was the righteous way forward, then this was the only way forward.

She watched her parents quaver with fear under the steely eye of the Inquisitor, and she remembered the two of them backing away from her, ignoring her cries, closing her into darkness—and she said nothing. She sat very still, head lowered, and endured. They had taught her that, too.

The Shadowhunters of France all knew Céline, or thought they did: that sweet and obedient daughter of the Provençal countryside. They knew how devoted she was to her parents. Such a dutiful daughter. She would, of course, inherit their estate.

Céline bore the weight of the stares with dignity. She did not acknowledge the pitying looks. She kept her eyes on the floor when the judgment was issued and so did not see the horror on her parents' faces. She did not watch them placed in the custody of the Silent Brothers, to be transported to the Silent City. She did not expect them to survive long enough to face the Mortal Sword.

She did not speak to Robert or Stephen, and let them believe this was because they had just consigned her parents to death.

Valentine caught up with Céline just outside the church. He offered her a Nutella crepe. "From the stand across from Les Deux Magots," he said. "Your favorite, right?"

She shrugged but took what he had to offer. The first bite—warm chocolate hazelnut, sweet pastry—was as perfect as ever and made her feel like a child again.

Sometimes it was difficult to believe she had ever been young.

"You could have told me," she said.

"And ruin the surprise?"

"Those are my parents."

"Indeed."

"And you've killed them."

"They're still alive, last I checked," Valentine said. "They could probably stay that way, with a word from you. But I didn't hear it."

"You took a pretty big risk, not telling me the whole story. Expecting me to let you . . . to let them go."

"Did I?" he said. "Or did I simply know you well enough to know exactly what you would choose? To know I was doing you a favor."

He met her eyes. She could not look away. For the first time, she didn't want to.

"You don't have to admit it, Céline. Just know that I know. You're not alone in that."

He *saw* her; he understood. It was as if a muscle she'd been clenching her entire life finally released.

"A deal's a deal, though," he said. "Even if you got more than you bargained for. Stephen is all yours—assuming that's still what you want?"

"How exactly would you make that happen?" she asked, clear now on what Valentine was capable of. "You wouldn't . . . you wouldn't hurt him, would you?"

Valentine looked disappointed in her. "Stephen is my closest friend, my most trusted lieutenant. The fact that you could even ask that makes me question your loyalty, Céline. Do you want me questioning your loyalty?"

She shook her head.

Then that warm, buttery smile broke over his face again. She couldn't tell whether this was the real Valentine breaking through or the mask dropping back over his face. "On the other hand, it would be foolish of you not to ask. And as we've discussed, there's nothing foolish in you. No matter what people might think. So, your answer: no. I swear to you, on the Angel, I will cause Stephen no harm in the enactment of this agreement."

"And no threat of harm?"

"Do you think so little of yourself that you assume a man would need to be threatened with harm before he could love you?"

She didn't answer. She didn't need to: he could surely read it all over her face.

"Stephen is with the wrong woman," Valentine told her, almost gently. "Deep down, he knows that. I'll simply make this as clear to him as it is to us, and the rest will be as easy as falling off a cliff. You need only relax and let gravity do its work. Don't be afraid to reach for the things you really want, Céline. It's beneath you."

What she really wanted . . .

It wasn't too late to speak up, to save her parents.

Or she could keep her word and keep his secret. She could let her parents pay for what they'd done to her. For the lattice of scars on her skin and her heart. For the ice in her blood. If she was the kind of daughter who could consign her parents to death, then they had no one to blame but themselves.

But that didn't mean she had to accept the entire bargain. Even if she stayed silent, she could walk away: away from Valentine, now that she knew what he was capable of. Away from Stephen, now that she knew what he thought of her. She could close the door on the past, start again. She could choose a life without pain, without suffering or fear.

But who would she be without pain?

What was strength, if not the endurance of suffering?

There is nothing more painful than love denied, the strange Silent Brother had told her. *A love that cannot be requited. I can think of nothing more painful than that.*

If Valentine said he could give her Stephen Herondale, he meant it. Céline did not doubt this. He could do anything, and that included finding a way to force Stephen Herondale into her life and her arms. But even Valentine could not make Stephen love her.

To have Stephen would mean *not* having him—it would mean knowing in every moment, every embrace, that he wanted someone else. It would mean a lifetime of longing for the one thing she could not have. The Silent Brother was wise and spoke the truth. There could be no greater pain than that.

"Take your time," Valentine said. "It's a big choice."

"I don't need time," she told Valentine. "I want it. I want Stephen."

It didn't feel like choosing, because it was the only choice she had.

Son of the Dawn

By Cassandra Clare and Sarah Rees Brennan

New York City, 2000

Every world contains other worlds within it. People wander through all the worlds they can find, searching for their homes.

Some humans thought their world was the only world there was. Little did they know of other worlds as close to their own as the next room, or of the demons trying to find a door through to them, and the Shadowhunters who barred those doors.

Still less did they know of Downworld, the community of magical creatures who shared their world and carved out their own little space therein.

Every community needs a heart. There had to be a common area where everyone could gather, to trade for goods and secrets, to find love and riches. There were Shadow Markets, where Downworlders and those with the Sight met, all over the world. Usually they were held outside.

Even magic was a little different in New York.

The abandoned theater on Canal Street had stood since the 1920s, silent witness to but not part of the blaze of activity that was the city. Humans who did not have the Sight passed by its terra-cotta facade in a hurry about their own affairs. If they spared the theater a look, they thought it as dark and still as ever.

They could not see the haze of faerie light that turned the gutted amphitheater and bare concrete halls to gold. Brother Zachariah could.

He walked, a creature of silence and darkness, through halls with sunshine-yellow tiles, panels of gold and red blazing on the ceiling above him. There were busts grimy with age set in alcoves along the walls, but for tonight faeries had coaxed flowers and ivy to twine around them. Werewolves had set little twinkling charms depicting the moon and stars in the boarded windows, lending brightness to the decayed red curtains still hanging in the arched frames. There were lamps with casements that reminded Brother Zachariah of a time long ago, when he and all the world had been different. In one vast echoing theater room there hung a chandelier that had not worked in years, but tonight warlock magic had suffused each bulb with a different-colored flame. Like burning jewels, amethyst and ruby, sapphire and opal, their light created a private world that seemed both new and old, and restored the theater to all its former glory. Some worlds lasted only one night.

If the Market had the power to lend him warmth and illumination for only a night, Brother Zachariah would have taken it.

A persistent faerie woman had tried to sell him a love charm four times. Zachariah wished such a charm would work on him. Creatures as inhuman as he did not sleep, but sometimes he lay down and rested, hoping for something like peace. It never came. He spent his long nights feeling love slip through his fingers, more a memory by now than a feeling.

Brother Zachariah did not belong to Downworld. He was a Shadowhunter, and not only a Shadowhunter but one of the cloaked and hooded Brotherhood dedicated to arcane secrets and the dead, sworn and runed to silence and withdrawal from any world. Even his own kind often feared the Silent Brothers, and Downworlders usually avoided any Shadowhunter, but the Downworlders were used to the presence of this particular Shadowhunter at Markets now. Brother Zachariah had been coming to Shadow Markets for a hundred years, on a long quest that even he had begun to believe would be fruitless. Yet he continued searching. Brother Zachariah had little enough, but one thing he did have was time, and he had always tried to be patient.

Tonight, though, he had already been disappointed. The warlock Ragnor Fell had no word for him. None of his few other contacts, painstakingly gathered over the decades, had attended this Market. He was lingering not because he was enjoying this Shadow Market but because he remembered enjoying Markets once.

They had felt like an escape, but Brother Zachariah hardly remembered the wish to escape from the City of Bones, where he belonged. Always in the back of his mind, cold as a tide waiting to wash all other things away, were the voices of his Brothers.

They were urging him home.

Brother Zachariah turned under the glitter of diamond-paned windows. He was leaving the Market, making his way through the laughing, bargaining crowd, when he heard a woman's voice saying his name.

"Tell me again why we want this Brother Zachariah. The normal Nephilim are bad enough. Angel in the veins, stick up the butts, and I bet with Silent Brothers it's a whole staff. We definitely can't take him out for karaoke."

The woman was speaking in English, but a boy's voice

replied to her in Spanish: "Quiet. I see him."

It was a pair of vampires, and as he turned, the boy lifted a hand to attract Zachariah's attention. The vampire with his hand up looked fifteen years old at most, and the other like a young woman about nineteen, but that told Zachariah nothing. Zachariah still looked young too.

It was unusual for a strange Downworlder to want his attention.

"Brother Zachariah?" asked the boy. "I came here to meet you."

The woman whistled. "Now I see why we might want him. Helloooo, Brother *Mack*ariah."

Did you? Brother Zachariah asked the boy. He felt what would once have been surprise and now was at least intrigue. *Can I be of any use to you?*

"I certainly hope so," said the vampire. "I am Raphael Santiago, second in command of the New York clan, and I dislike useless people."

The woman waved her hand. "I'm Lily Chen. He's always this way."

Brother Zachariah studied the pair with new interest. The woman had hair streaked neon yellow and wore a scarlet qipao that suited her, and despite her own remark she was smiling at her companion's words. The boy's hair was curly, his face sweet, and his air disdainful. There was a burn scar at the base of his throat, where a cross might lie.

I believe we have a mutual friend, said Brother Zachariah.

"I don't think so," said Raphael Santiago. "I don't have friends."

"Oh, thank you very much," said the woman at his side.

"You, Lily," said Raphael coldly, "are my subordinate." He turned back to Brother Zachariah. "I assume you refer to the warlock Magnus Bane. He is a colleague who always has more dealings with Shadowhunters than I approve of."

Zachariah wondered if Lily spoke Mandarin. The Silent Brothers, speaking mind to mind, had no need for language, but sometimes Zachariah missed his. There had been nights—in the Silent City it was always night—when he could not remember his own name, but he could remember the sound of his mother or his father or his betrothed speaking Mandarin. His betrothed had learned some of the language for him, in the time when he had thought he would live to marry her. He would not have minded talking with Lily longer, but he did not particularly like her companion's attitude.

Since you do not appear to care for Shadowhunters, and you have little interest in our mutual connection, Brother Zachariah observed, *why approach me?*

"I wished to talk to a Shadowhunter," said Raphael.

Why not go to your Institute?

Raphael's lips curled back from his fangs in a sneer. Nobody sneered like a vampire, and this vampire was particularly adept. "My Institute, as you call it, belongs to people who are . . . how do I put this tactfully . . . bigots and murderers."

A faerie selling ribbons with glamour twined in them passed by, trailing blue and purple banners.

The way you put that was not particularly tactful, Brother Zachariah felt bound to point out.

"No," said Raphael thoughtfully. "I am not gifted in that arena. New York has always been a place of heightened Downworlder activity. The lights of this city work on people as if we are all werewolves howling for an electric moon. A warlock tried to destroy the world here once, before my time. The leader of my clan made a disastrous experiment with drugs here, *against* my advice, and made the city her slaughter ground. The werewolves' fatal struggles for leadership are far more frequent in New York than anywhere else. The Whitelaws of the New York Institute understood us, and we them. The Whitelaws died defending Downworlders from the people who now occupy their Institute. Of course the Clave did not consult us when they made us the punishment of the Lightwoods. We do not have any dealings with the New York Institute now."

Raphael's voice was uncompromising, and Brother Zachariah thought he should be concerned. Zachariah had fought in the Uprising, when a band of renegade youths rose up against their own leaders and against peace with Downworld. He had been told the story of Valentine's Circle hunting werewolves in New York City, and the Whitelaws getting in their way, resulting in a tragedy that even that group of angry Downworlder-hating youths had not intended. He had not approved of the Lightwoods and Hodge Starkweather being banished to the New York Institute, but the word was that the Lightwoods had settled down with their three children and were truly remorseful for their past actions.

The pain and power struggles of the world seemed very far away, in the Silent City.

It had not occurred to Zachariah that the Downworlders would resent the Lightwoods so much they might decline their aid even when Shadowhunter help was truly needed. Perhaps it should have.

Downworlders and Shadowhunters have a long, complicated history full of pain, and much of the pain has been the fault of the Nephilim, Brother Zachariah admitted. *Yet through the ages, they have found a way to work together. I know that when they followed Valentine Morgenstern, the Lightwoods did terrible things, but if they are truly repentant, could you not forgive them?*

"Being a damned soul, I have no moral objection to the Lightwoods," said Raphael in deeply moralistic tones. "I do have strong objections to my head being cut off. Given the least excuse, the Lightwoods would lay waste to my clan."

The only woman Zachariah had ever loved was a warlock. He had seen her weep over the Circle and its effects. Brother Zachariah had no reason to support the Lightwoods, but everyone deserved a second chance if they wanted that chance enough.

And one of Robert Lightwood's ancestors had been a woman called Cecily Herondale.

Say they would not, suggested Brother Zachariah. *Would it not be preferable to reestablish relations with the Institute rather than hope to catch a Silent Brother at the Shadow Market?*

"Of course it would," said Raphael. "I fully recognize this is not an ideal situation. This is not the first stratagem I have been forced to employ when I required an audience with Shadowhunters. Five years ago I had coffee with a visiting Ashdown."

He and his companion shared a shudder of distaste.

"I absolutely hate the Ashdowns," remarked Lily. "They are so tedious. I believe that if I fed on one of them I would nod off halfway through."

Raphael gave her a warning look.

"Not that I would ever dream of nonconsensually drinking the blood of any Shadowhunter, because it would violate the Accords!" Lily informed Brother Zachariah in a loud voice. "The Accords are deeply important to me."

Raphael shut his eyes, a briefly pained expression crossing his face, but after an instant he opened them and nodded.

"So how about it, Brother Lipsmackariah, will you help us out?" Lily asked brightly.

A cold weight of disapproval made itself known from his silent brethren, like stones being pressed against his mind. Zachariah was allowed a great deal of latitude for a Silent Brother, but his frequent visits to the Shadow Markets and his annual meeting with a lady on Blackfriars Bridge were already testing the limits of what could be allowed.

If he began consorting with Downworlders on issues that could be handled perfectly well by an Institute, Brother Zachariah's privileges were in danger of being suspended.

He could not risk missing that meeting. Anything but that.

The Silent Brothers are forbidden to interfere with the affairs of the outside world. Whatever your problem is, said Brother Zachariah, *I strongly urge you to consult with your Institute.*

He bowed his head and began to turn away.

"My problem is werewolves smuggling *yin fen* into New York," Raphael called after him. "Ever heard of *yin fen?*"

The bells and songs of the Shadow Market seemed to go quiet.

Brother Zachariah turned sharply back to the two vampires. Raphael Santiago stared at him with glittering eyes, which left Zachariah in no doubt that Raphael knew a good deal about the Silent Brother's own history.

"Ah," said the vampire. "I see you have."

Zachariah usually tried to preserve memories of his mortal life, but now he had to make an effort to banish the intruding horror of waking up as a child with all he loved dead, and silver fire burning in his veins.

Where did you hear about the yin fen?

"I don't intend to tell you," said Raphael. "Nor do I intend to let that stuff be freely available in my city. A large quantity of *yin fen* is on its way to the city, on board a ship carrying cargo from Shanghai, Ho Chi Minh, Vienna, and Idris itself. The ship unloads at the New York Passenger Ship Terminal. Will you help me or not?"

Raphael had already mentioned the leader of his clan performing disastrous experiments with drugs. Zachariah's guess was that many potential customers in Downworld were talking about the shipment of *yin fen* at the Market. The fact that a Downworlder with conservative views had heard about it was sheer luck.

I will help you, said Brother Zachariah. *But we must consult with the New York Institute. If you wish, I can go with you to the Institute and explain matters. The Lightwoods will appreciate the information, and you offering it. This is an opportunity to improve relations between the Institute and all the Downworlders in New York.*

Raphael did not look convinced, but after a moment he nodded.

"You will go with me?" he asked. "You will not fail? They would not listen to a vampire, but I suppose it is possible they will listen to a Silent Brother."

I will do whatever I can, said Brother Zachariah.

Cunning crept into Raphael's voice. "And if they don't help me, if they or even the Clave refuse to believe me, then what will you do?"

Then I will still help you, said Brother Zachariah, ignoring the chill howl of his brethren in his mind and thinking of Tessa's clear eyes.

He dreaded being forbidden to meet with Tessa this year, but when he did meet her, he wanted to face her with no stain upon him. He could not let any child suffer what he had suffered, not if he could prevent it.

Zachariah was not able to feel all he had felt when he was mortal, but Tessa could still feel. He could not let her be disappointed in him. She was the last star he had to steer by.

"I'll come to the Institute with you," Lily volunteered.

"You will do no such thing," snapped Raphael. "It is not safe. Remember, the Circle attacked Magnus Bane."

The ice in Raphael's voice could have laid the whole of New York City under frost for a week in midsummer. He eyed Brother Zachariah with disfavor.

"Magnus invented your Portals, not that he receives any credit for it from Shadowhunters. He is one of the most powerful warlocks in the world, and so tenderhearted he rushes to the aid of vicious killers. He is the best Downworld has to offer. If the Circle targeted him, they would cut down any one of us."

"Would've been a damn shame," Lily confirmed. "Magnus throws an amazing rager, too."

"I wouldn't know," said Raphael, casting a look of distaste on the joyful riot of the Market. "I do not enjoy people. Or gatherings."

A werewolf wearing an enchanted papier-mâché full-moon head shoved past Raphael, shouting, "Awoooo!" Raphael turned to look at him, and the werewolf backed away with his hands up, mumbling, "Uh, sorry. My mistake."

Despite slight fellow feeling with the werewolf, Brother Zachariah unbent a little at the vampire's words regarding Magnus, evidence that he was not entirely awful.

I understand that you value Magnus highly. So do I. Once he aided someone very dear to—

"No, I don't!" Raphael interrupted. "And I don't care about your story. Don't tell him I said any of that. I can have opinions on my colleagues. It does not mean I have personal feelings about them."

"Hey, my man, great to see you," said Ragnor Fell, passing by.

Raphael paused to fist-bump the green warlock before Ragnor disappeared among the stalls and sounds and many-colored lights of the Market. Lily and Brother Zachariah regarded him.

"He's another colleague!" Raphael protested.

I like Ragnor, said Brother Zachariah.

"Good for you," snapped Raphael. "Revel in your hobby of liking and trusting everyone. It sounds as appealing to me as sunbathing."

Zachariah felt he had become acquainted with another reason, besides Magnus's evil vampire ex, why Magnus always seemed to develop a migraine when people mentioned the vampire clan of New York in his presence. Brother Zachariah, Lily, and Raphael strolled through the Market.

"Love charm for the handsomest Silent Brother?" asked the faerie woman for the fifth time, leering through her dandelion-clock hair. Sometimes one could wish the Shadow Market had not become quite so comfortable with him.

He remembered this woman, he thought, dimly recollecting her hurting a golden-haired child. It had been so long ago. He had cared very much at the time.

Lily snorted. "I hardly think Brother Beast-with-two-backs-ariah needs a love charm."

Thank you, but no, Brother Zachariah told the faerie woman. *I'm very flattered, though Brother Enoch is a fine figure of a man.*

In Zachariah's head, Brother Enoch was annoyed at being the subject of a joke.

"Or perhaps you and the lady would enjoy some phoenix tears for a night of burning pass—" She went suddenly silent, and the whole stall scuttled away across the bare concrete floor on little chicken feet. "Oops, never mind! Didn't see you there, Raphael."

Raphael's thin eyebrows went up and down like a guillotine.

"More of a buzzkill than the Silent Brother," murmured Lily. "Oh, the shame."

Raphael looked smug. The gleam and whirl of the Shadow Market shone with pale radiance in Brother Zachariah's eyes. He did not like the thought of *yin fen* spreading like silver wildfire in another city, killing fast as flame or slowly as choking smoke. If it was coming, he had to stop it. This trip to the Market had been useful after all. If he could not feel, he could act.

Perhaps tomorrow night the Lightwoods will earn your trust, said Brother Zachariah as he and the vampires stepped out into the mundane bustle of Canal Street.

Raphael said, "Unlikely."

I have found it always better to hope than despair, said Brother Zachariah mildly. *I will wait for you outside the Institute.*

Behind them, enchanted lights shimmered and the sound of faerie music rang through the halls of the theater. A mundane woman turned to face the building. Glittering blue light fell in a strange beam across her unseeing eyes.

The two vampires were heading east, but partway up the

street, Raphael turned back to where Brother Zachariah stood. In the night, away from Market lights, the vampire's scar was white and his eyes were black. His eyes saw too much.

"Hope is for fools. I will meet you tomorrow night, but remember this, Silent Brother," he said. "Hate like that does not fade. The work of the Circle is not done yet. The Morgenstern legacy will claim more victims. I do not intend to be one of them."

Wait, said Brother Zachariah. *Do you happen to know why the ship is unloading its cargo at the Passenger Ship Terminal?*

Raphael shrugged. "I told you the ship was carrying cargo from Idris. I believe some Shadowhunter brat is on board."

Brother Zachariah walked away from the Market alone, thinking of a child on a ship with deadly cargo, and the potential of more victims.

Isabelle Lightwood was not accustomed to feeling nervous about anything, but anyone might be apprehensive when faced with the prospect of a new addition to the family.

This was not like before Max was born, when Isabelle and Alec had laid bets on whether it would be a boy or a girl, and afterward Mom and Dad trusted them enough to let them take turns holding him, the smallest and tenderest bundle imaginable.

A boy older than Isabelle was being dumped on their doorstep and was supposed to live with them. Jonathan Wayland, the son of Dad's *parabatai*, Michael Wayland. Far away in Idris, Michael Wayland had died, and Jonathan needed a home.

For herself, Isabelle was a little excited. She liked adventure and company. If Jonathan Wayland was as much fun and as good a fighter as Aline Penhallow, who came to visit sometimes with her mother, Isabelle would be glad to have him.

Except there was not just Isabelle to consider.

Her parents had been fighting over Jonathan Wayland ever since the news of Michael's death came. Isabelle gathered Mom had not liked Michael Wayland. She was not sure Dad had liked him much either. Isabelle herself had never met Michael Wayland. She had never even known that Dad had a *parabatai*. Neither Mom nor Dad ever talked about when they were young, except that Mom had once said they made many mistakes. Isabelle sometimes wondered whether they had been mixed up in the same trouble as their tutor, Hodge. Her friend Aline said Hodge was a criminal.

Whatever her parents had or had not done, Isabelle did not think her mother wanted Jonathan Wayland to be a reminder of her mistakes in her own home.

Dad did not seem happy when he talked about his *parabatai*, but he did seem determined that Jonathan would come to live with them. Jonathan had nowhere else to go, Dad insisted, and he belonged with them. That was what being *parabatai* meant. Once when she was eavesdropping on them shouting, Isabelle heard Dad say, "I owe Michael this."

Mom agreed to let Jonathan come for a trial period, but now that the shouting had died down, she was not really speaking to Dad. Isabelle was worried about both her parents, and especially her mom.

Isabelle also had to consider her brother.

Alec did not like new people. Whenever new Shadowhunters arrived from Idris, Alec would mysteriously slope off. Once Isabelle had found him lurking behind a large vase, claiming he got lost trying to find the training room.

Jonathan Wayland was taking a ship to New York. He should be in the Institute by the morning after next.

Isabelle was in the training room, practicing with a whip and pondering the problem of Jonathan Wayland, when she heard rushing footsteps, and Alec poked his head around the door. His blue eyes were sparkling.

"Isabelle!" he said. "Come quickly! There's a Silent Brother meeting with Mom and Dad in the Sanctuary. And a *vampire*!"

Isabelle ran to her room to get out of her gear and into a dress. The Silent Brothers were fancy company, almost as if the Consul had come to visit.

By the time she got downstairs, Alec was already in the Sanctuary observing the proceedings, and her parents were deep in conversation with the Silent Brother. Isabelle heard her mom say something to the Silent Brother that sounded like "Yogurt! Unbelievable!"

Maybe not "yogurt." Maybe it was a different word.

"On the ship with Michael's son!" Dad said.

It couldn't be "yogurt," unless Jonathan Wayland had a very serious allergy to dairy.

The Silent Brother was a lot less scary than Isabelle had been expecting. His mouth and eyes weren't stitched shut like they were on other Silent Brothers, only closed in a peaceful way that made it look like he was sleeping. In fact, from what Isabelle could see beneath the hood, he resembled one of the mundie singers she had seen in posters around the city. From the way Robert was nodding at him and Maryse was leaning toward him in her chair, Isabelle could see they were getting along.

The vampire was not conversing with their parents. He was

leaning against one of the walls, arms crossed, and glaring at the floor. He did not seem as if he was interested in getting along with anyone. He looked like a kid, hardly older than they were, and he would have been almost as handsome as the Silent Brother if not for his sour expression. He was wearing a black leather jacket to go with his scowl. Isabelle wished she could see the fangs.

"Can I offer you a coffee?" Maryse said to the vampire in a cool, stilted tone.

"I do not drink . . . coffee," said the vampire.

"Odd," said Maryse. "I heard you had a delightful coffee with Catherine Ashdown."

The vampire shrugged. Isabelle knew vampires were dead and soulless and all, but she did not see why they had to be rude.

She nudged Alec in the ribs. "Get a load of the vampire. Can you believe that?"

"I know!" Alec whispered back. "Isn't he *amazing*?"

"What?" Isabelle said, grabbing Alec's elbow.

Alec did not glance at her. He was studying the vampire. Isabelle started to get the same uneasy feeling that she got whenever she noticed Alec looking at the same posters of mundie singers that she did. Alec always got red and angry when she saw him looking. Isabelle sometimes thought it would be nice to talk about the singers, the way she'd heard mundie girls doing, but she knew Alec wouldn't want to. Once Mom had asked them what they were looking at, and Alec had looked afraid.

"Don't go near him," Isabelle urged. "I think vampires are gross."

Isabelle was used to being able to whisper to her brother in a crowd. The vampire turned his head slightly, and Isabelle remembered vampires did not have pathetic hearing like mundanes. The vampire could definitely hear her.

This nasty realization caused Isabelle to relax her hold on Alec. She watched in horror as he pulled away from her and advanced with nervous determination toward the vampire. Not wanting to be left out, Isabelle trailed a few steps behind him.

"Hello," said Alec. "It's, um, very nice to meet you."

The vampire boy gave him a thousand-yard stare that suggested a thousand yards was too close up and the vampire wished he were enjoying blissful solitude in the far reaches of space. "Hello."

"I'm Alexander Lightwood," said Alec.

Grimacing as if the introduction were vital information being tortured out of him, the vampire said: "I am Raphael."

When he made that face, Isabelle did see the fangs. They were not as cool as she had hoped.

"I'm basically twelve," continued Alec, who was totally eleven. "You don't look a lot older than me. But I know it's different with vampires. I guess you kind of stay the same age you stop at, though, right? Like you're fifteen, but you've been fifteen for a hundred years. How long have you been fifteen?"

Raphael said flatly, "I'm sixty-three."

"Oh," said Alec. "Oh. Oh, that's cool."

He advanced several steps toward the vampire. Raphael did not take a step back, but he looked like he wanted to.

"Also," Alec added shyly, "your jacket is cool."

"Why are you talking to my *children*?" Mom asked sharply.

She was already up from her chair opposite the Silent

Brother, and as she spoke she seized hold of Alec and Isabelle. Her fingers pinched, she was holding them so hard, and fear seemed to travel to Isabelle through her mother's touch, even though she had not been afraid before.

The vampire had not been looking at them as if he thought they would be delicious at all. Maybe that was how he lured you in, though, Isabelle considered. Maybe Alec was just ensorcelled by vampire wiles. It would be nice to be able to blame the Downworlder for making Isabelle worry.

The Silent Brother rose from his chair and glided to join them. Isabelle heard the vampire whisper to the Silent Brother, and she was pretty sure he said, "This is my nightmare."

Isabelle stuck her tongue out at him. Raphael's lip curled the tiniest fraction farther from his fangs. Alec did glance at Isabelle then, to make sure she was not scared. Isabelle wasn't scared of much, but Alec was always fussing.

Raphael came here out of concern for a Shadowhunter child, said the Silent Brother.

"No, I didn't," Raphael sneered. "Better watch your children. I once killed a whole gang of boys not much older than your boy here. Shall I take this as a refusal to help with the shipment? I am deeply shocked. Well, we tried. Time to go, Brother Zachariah."

"Wait," said Robert. "Of course we will help. I will meet you at the drop-off point in New Jersey."

Naturally her dad would help, Isabelle thought indignantly. This vampire was an idiot. Whatever mistakes they might have made when they were really young, her parents ran this whole Institute and had killed lots and lots of evil demons. Anyone sensible would know you could always count on her dad.

"You can consult with us on other Shadowhunter matters

at any time," her mom added, but she did not let go of Alec and Isabelle until the vampire and Brother Zachariah had left the Institute.

Isabelle had thought the visit would be exciting, but she had ended up feeling more apprehensive than ever. She wished that Jonathan Wayland was not coming.

Guests were terrible, and Isabelle never wanted any more.

The plan was to stow away aboard ship undetected, apprehend the smugglers, and dispose of the *yin fen*. The child would never have to know about any of it.

It was almost nice to be in one of the sleek Shadowhunter boats again. Brother Zachariah had been in the multihulled trimarans as a child on lakes in Idris, and once his *parabatai* had stolen one and they had rowed it down the Thames. Now he, an edgy Robert Lightwood, and two vampires had used one to navigate the black nighttime waters of the Delaware River, coming down from the port of Camden. Lily kept complaining that they were practically in Philadelphia, until the boat drew close to the tall cargo ship. DAWN TRADER was painted in dark blue letters against its gray side. They waited for their moment, then Robert threw a grappling hook.

Brother Zachariah, Raphael, Lily, and Robert Lightwood made it onto the boat and into a deserted cabin. This journey, short and stealthy though it was, left them with the impression that there was no mundane crew on board at all. Hiding there, they counted the voices of the smugglers and realized there were far more than had been reported.

"Oh no, Brother Hop-in-the-sack-ariah," Lily whispered. "I think we're going to have to fight them."

She looked very cheerful about the prospect. As she spoke, she winked and pulled her feathered flapper's headband from her yellow-streaked hair.

"It's actually from the 1920s, so I don't want to damage it," she explained, and nodded to Raphael. "I've had it longer than I've had him. He's from the 1950s. Jazz baby and greaser teen take on the world."

Raphael rolled his eyes. "Desist with the nicknames. They are getting worse."

Lily laughed. "I will not. Once you go Zachariah, you never go backariah."

Raphael and Robert Lightwood both looked appalled, but Zachariah did not mind the nicknames. He did not hear laughter often.

What worried him was the child.

We cannot allow Jonathan to be scared or hurt, he said.

Robert was nodding and the vampires looking supremely unconcerned, when a boy's voice came from outside the door.

"I'm not frightened of anything," he said.

Jonathan Wayland, Zachariah presumed.

"Then why are you asking about the Lightwoods?" asked a woman's voice. She sounded irritated. "They're taking you in. They won't be unkind to you."

"I was only curious," said Jonathan.

He was clearly doing his best to sound airy and aloof, and his best was not bad. His voice almost swaggered. Brother Zachariah thought it would have convinced most people.

"Robert Lightwood's got some influence in the Clave," remarked the woman. "Solid man. I'm sure he's ready to be a father to you."

"I had a father," said Jonathan, cold as the night wind.

The woman was silent. Across the cabin, Robert Lightwood's head was bowed.

"But the mother," said Jonathan, a touch tentative. "What's Mrs. Lightwood like?"

"Maryse? I barely know her," the woman replied. "She's already got three kids. Four's a lot to handle."

"I'm not a kid," said Jonathan. "I won't bother her." He paused and observed, "There are a lot of werewolves aboard this ship."

"Ugh, kids raised in Idris are exhausting," said the woman. "Werewolves are a fact of life, unfortunately. Creatures are everywhere. Go to bed, Jonathan."

They listened as another cabin door shut and a lock was shot home.

"Now," said Robert Lightwood. "Vampires, starboard. Brother Zachariah and I, port. Contain the werewolves by any means necessary, then locate the *yin fen*."

They spilled out onto the deck. It was a rough night, the wind pulling Zachariah's hood down farther, the deck jerking beneath their feet. Zachariah could not open his lips to taste the salt in the air.

New York was a glimmer on the horizon, shining like the lights of the Shadow Market in the dark. They could not allow the *yin fen* to hit the city.

There were a couple of werewolves on the deck. One was in wolf form, and Zachariah could see a tinge of silver in his fur. The other had lost color in his fingertips. Zachariah wondered if they knew that they were dying. He remembered, too vividly, how it had felt when the *yin fen* was killing him.

Sometimes it was good to be without feeling. Sometimes being human hurt too much, and Zachariah could not afford pity now.

Brother Zachariah slammed his staff against one of their heads, and when he turned, Robert Lightwood had already dealt with the other. They stood braced, listening to the howl of the wind and the surge of the sea, waiting for the others to come from belowdecks. Then Zachariah heard the sounds from the other side of the ship.

Stay where you are, he told Robert. *I will go to the vampires.*

Brother Zachariah had to fight his way to them. There were even more werewolves than he had guessed. Across their heads, he could see Raphael and Lily, leaping as if they were insubstantial as shadows, teeth shining in the moonlight.

He could see the werewolves' teeth too. Zachariah shoved one werewolf over the side of the ship and knocked out another one's teeth in the same swing, then had to dodge a swipe of claws that almost sent Zachariah over himself. There were so many of them.

It was with vague surprise that Zachariah thought this could be the end. There should have been something more than surprise to the idea, but all he knew was the hollowness he had felt walking through the Market and the sound of his Brothers' voices, colder than the sea. He did not care about these vampires. He did not care about himself.

The roar of a werewolf sounded in his ear, and behind it came the crash of a wave. Brother Zachariah's arms ached from wielding the staff. It should all have ended a long time ago, anyway. He could scarcely remember a reason why he fought.

Across the deck a werewolf, almost fully shifted, whirled a

clawed fist directly at Lily's heart. She already had her hands locked around another werewolf's neck. She did not have a chance to defend herself.

A door swung open, and a Shadowhunter woman ran out into the path of the werewolves. She was not ready. A wolf tore her throat out, and as Zachariah tried to get to her, a werewolf slammed against his back. The staff fell from his nerveless fingers. A second werewolf piled onto him, claws digging into his shoulders, bearing him down to his knees. Another climbed on, and Zachariah's head slammed onto the wood. The dark rose before him. His Brothers' voices could be gone, along with the crash of the sea and all the light of the world that no longer touched him.

The dead woman's eyes stared into his face, a last empty gleam before the dark consumed all. It seemed as if he were as empty as she. Why had he ever fought?

Only he remembered. He would not allow himself to forget.

Tessa, he thought. *Will.*

Despair was never stronger than the thought of them. He could not betray them by giving up.

They are Will and Tessa, and you were Ke Jian Ming. You were James Carstairs. You were Jem.

Brother Zachariah drew a dagger from his belt. He fought to his feet, sending two of the werewolves sprawling and backhanding the third through the open cabin door. He looked to Lily.

Raphael was standing in front of her. His arm was flung out to shield her, his blood a macabre scarlet splash across the deck. Human blood was black at night, but vampire blood never looked anything but red. Lily screamed his name.

Brother Zachariah needed his staff. It was rolling across the wood of the deck, silver in the moonlight and rattling like bones. Its carving leaped out, shadow dark against the silver, as the staff rolled to the feet of a boy who had just stepped out into this space of chaos and blood.

The boy who must be Jonathan Wayland stared around him, at Brother Zachariah, at the wolves, at the woman with her throat ripped out. A werewolf woman was bearing down on him. The boy was too young to even bear warriors' runes.

Brother Zachariah knew he was not going to be fast enough.

The boy turned his head, hair bright gold in the silver moonshine, and picked up Zachariah's staff. Small and slim, the most fragile of barriers possible against darkness, he charged at the snarling teeth and bared claws. He struck her down.

Two more went for the boy, but Zachariah killed one, and the boy spun and struck the other. When he twisted in the air, Zachariah thought not of shadows, as he had with the vampires, but of light.

When the boy landed on the deck, feet spread wide and staff twirling between his hands, he was laughing. It was not a child's sweet laugh, but a wild exuberant sound that rang out stronger than sea or sky or silent voices. He sounded young, and defiant, and joyful, and a little mad.

Brother Zachariah had thought earlier in the night that he did not hear laughter often. It had been an achingly long time since he had heard a laugh like that.

He stabbed another werewolf running for the boy, and another, throwing his body between the boy and the wolves. One got past his guard and swiped at the boy, and Zachariah heard him make a small sound between his locked teeth.

Are you all right? he asked.

"Yes!" the boy shouted. Brother Zachariah could hear him panting at his back.

Never fear, said Brother Zachariah. *I am fighting with you.*

Zachariah's blood ran colder than the sea, and his heart hammered until he heard Robert Lightwood and Lily coming to their aid.

Once the remaining werewolves were subdued, Robert took Jonathan with him to the bridge. Zachariah turned his attention to the vampires. Raphael had taken off his leather jacket. Lily had ripped part of her shirt off and was tying the material around his arm. She was crying.

"Raphael," she said. "Raphael, you shouldn't have done it."

"Sustained a wound that will heal in a night in preference to losing a valuable member of the clan?" Raphael asked. "I acted to benefit myself. I generally do."

"You'd better," Lily muttered, wiping tears savagely with the back of her hand. "What would I do if something happened to you?"

"Something practical, I hope," said Raphael. "Please salvage material from one of the many dead werewolves next time. And stop embarrassing the clan in front of Shadowhunters."

Lily followed Raphael's line of vision, over her shoulder to Brother Zachariah. There was blood smudged and mixed with her blurred eyeliner, but she gave him a cheeky fanged smile.

"Maybe I wanted to rip my shirt for Brother Let-him-see-my-rack-ariah."

Raphael lifted his eyes to heaven. Since he was not looking at her, Lily could look at him. She did. Brother Zachariah saw her lift a hand, her fingernails painted red and gold, and almost touch his curly hair. Her hand moved as if she might stroke the shadows over his head, then curled into a fist. She did not permit herself the luxury.

Raphael motioned her away and got to his feet.

"Let's go find the *yin fen*."

It was not difficult to locate. It was in a large box in a cabin belowdecks. Lily and Brother Zachariah carried the box up between them, Lily clearly ready to make a scene if Raphael tried to help.

Zachariah pried open the lid of the box. Even after all these years, seeing the glimmer of *yin fen* in the moonlight made his stomach lurch and turn, as if the sight pitched him onto a boat on a different sea, one in which he could never keep his balance.

Lily moved to tip the box over the side and let it be swallowed by the hungry waters.

"No, Lily!" said Raphael. "I will not have drug-addled mermaids infesting the rivers of my city. What if we end up with glowing silver alligators in the sewers? Nobody will be surprised, but I will know it is your fault, and I will be extremely disappointed in you."

"You never let me have any fun," Lily grumbled.

"I never let anyone have any fun," said Raphael, and looked smug.

Brother Zachariah stared into the box full of silver powder. It had meant the difference between quick and slow death to him once. He set the fire using a rune known only to the Silent Brothers, a rune meant to burn away harmful magic. Life and death were nothing but ashes in the air.

Thank you for telling me about the yin fen, he told Raphael.

"From my perspective, I took advantage of your weakness over the stuff," said Raphael. "You used to take it to keep yourself alive once, as I understand it. Didn't work, I see. Anyway, your emotional state is no concern of mine, and my city is safe. Mission accomplished."

He wiped his hands, gleaming with blood, over the lapping waves.

Does your leader know anything about this mission? Zachariah asked Lily.

She was watching Raphael.

"Of course," she said. "My leader told you all about it. Didn't he?"

"Lily! That is stupidity and treason." Raphael's voice was chill as the sea breeze. "If I was ordered to execute you for it, make no mistake, I would do so. I would not hesitate."

Lily bit her lip and tried to pass off how hurt she clearly was. "Oh, but I have a good feeling about Brother Zacharide-him-like-a-bad-pony. He won't tell."

"Is there a place here for a vampire to be stowed away safely from the sunrise?" Raphael asked.

Brother Zachariah had not considered that the protracted fight with the werewolves meant the sun was close to rising. Raphael glanced at him sharply when he did not answer.

"Is there only room for one? Lily needs to be secured. I am responsible for her."

Lily turned her face away so Raphael did not see her expression, but Zachariah saw it. He recognized her expression from a time when he had been able to feel that way himself. She looked sick with love.

There was room for both vampires in the cargo hold. On their way to examine the hold, Lily almost tripped over the dead Shadowhunter woman.

"Oooh, Raphael!" she exclaimed brightly. "It's Catherine Ashdown!"

It was like the faint cold spray of seawater, to see how utterly indifferent she was to human life. Brother Zachariah saw her belatedly recall his presence.

"Oh no," she added in not terribly convincing tones. "What a senseless tragedy."

"Go to the hold, Lily," Raphael commanded.

Will you not both go? asked Brother Zachariah.

"I prefer to wait as long as I can before dawn to test myself," said Raphael.

Lily sighed. "He's Catholic. So very, very Catholic."

Her hand moved restlessly by her side, as if she wanted to reach out and pull Raphael along with her. Instead, she used it to give Zachariah another little wave, the same one she had given when they first met.

"Brother Sixpackariah," she said. "It's been a pleasure."

And for me, said Brother Zachariah, and listened to her skip lightly down the stairs.

She had, at least, given him the woman's name. Brother Zachariah could take her back to her family and the City of Bones, where she could rest and he could not.

He knelt down by the dead woman's side and closed her staring eyes.

Ave atque vale, *Catherine Ashdown,* he murmured.

He rose to find Raphael still by his side, though not looking at him or the dead woman. Raphael's eyes rested on the black sea touched with moonlight, the black sky edged with the faintest line of silver.

I am glad to have met you both, Zachariah added.

"I can't imagine why," said Raphael. "Those names Lily came up with were very bad."

People do not joke with the Silent Brothers often.

The prospect of not being joked around with made Raphael look wistful. "It must be nice to be a Silent Brother. Aside from the fact that Shadowhunters are annoying and pathetic. And I don't know that she was joking. I'd watch yourself next time you're in New York."

Of course she was joking, said Brother Zachariah. *She is in love with you.*

Raphael's face twisted. "Why do Shadowhunters always want to talk about feelings? Why can nobody ever be a professional? For your information, I do not have any interest in romance of any kind and never will. Now can you drop this revolting subject?"

I can, said Brother Zachariah. *Perhaps you would like to talk about the gang of boys you claim to have killed?*

"I've killed many people," said Raphael distantly.

A group of children? said Zachariah. *In your city? Did this happen in the 1950s?*

Maryse Lightwood might have been fooled. Brother Zachariah was familiar with what it looked like when someone blamed and hated themselves for what had happened to those they loved.

"There was a vampire hunting children on the streets where my brothers played," Raphael said, his voice still distant. "I led my gang to his lair to stop him. None of us survived."

Brother Zachariah tried to be gentle.

When a vampire is newborn, they cannot control themselves.

"I was the leader," said Raphael, his steely voice brooking no argument. "I was responsible. Well. We did stop the vampire, and my family lived to grow up."

All but one, Brother Zachariah thought.

"I generally do accomplish what I set my mind on," said Raphael.

That is extremely clear, said Brother Zachariah.

He listened to the sound of the waves hitting the side of the boat, carrying them to the city. On the night of the Market he had been detached from the city and everyone in it, and certainly he had felt nothing for a vampire determined to feel nothing himself.

But then had come a laugh, and the sound had woken things inside him that he had feared dead. Once woken to the world, Zachariah did not want to be blind to any of it.

You saved people today. The Shadowhunters saved people, even though they did not save you when you were a child trying to fight monsters.

Raphael twitched as if this implication of why he disliked Shadowhunters was a fly landing on him.

"Few are saved," said Raphael. "Nobody is spared. Somebody tried to save me once, and I will pay him back one day. I don't choose to owe another debt, or for anyone to owe me. We all got what we wanted. The Shadowhunters and I are done."

There might always be another time for help or cooperation, said Brother Zachariah. *The Lightwoods are trying. Consider letting the other Downworlders know you survived dealing with them.*

Raphael made a noncommittal sound.

There are more kinds of love than stars, said Brother Zachariah. *If you do not feel one, there are many others. You know what it is to care for family and friends. What we keep sacred keeps us safe. Consider that by trying to cut yourself off from the possibility of being hurt, you shut the door on love and live in darkness.*

Raphael staggered over to the rail and pretended to vomit. Then he straightened up.

"Oh wait, I'm a vampire and we don't get seasick," he said. "I got nauseous for a second. Can't think why. I heard Silent Brothers were withdrawn. I was looking forward to withdrawn!"

I am not a typical Silent Brother, observed Brother Zachariah.

"Just my luck I got the touchy-feely Silent Brother. Can I request a different one in the future?"

So you think there might be a time when your path crosses with Shadowhunters again?

Raphael made a disgusted noise and turned away from the sea. His face was pallid as moonlight, ice white as the cheek of a child long dead.

"I am going belowdecks. Unless, of course, you have any other brilliant suggestions?"

Brother Zachariah nodded. The shadow of his hood fell across the scar of a cross on the vampire's throat.

Have faith, Raphael. I know you remember how.

With the vampires safely hidden below and Robert Lightwood steering the ship toward Manhattan, Brother Zachariah took on the task of cleaning up the deck, moving the bodies out of sight. He'd call on his Brothers to help him attend to them, and to the survivors, who were currently secured in one of the cabins. Enoch and the others might not approve of his decision to help Raphael, but they would still fulfill their mandate to keep the Shadow World hidden and safe.

Once Brother Zachariah had finished, all there was to do was wait for the ship to carry them to the city. Then he would have to return to his own city. He took a seat and waited, enjoying the sensation of the light of a new day on his face.

It had been a long time since he felt the light, and longer since he could truly enjoy the simple pleasure of it.

He sat near the bridge, where he could see Robert and young Jonathan Wayland in the morning light.

"You're sure you're all right?" Robert said.

"Yes," said Jonathan.

"You don't look much like Michael," Robert added awkwardly.

"No," said Jonathan. "I always wished I did."

Zachariah could see the boy's thin back. He seemed braced to be a disappointment.

Robert said, "I am sure you're a good boy."

Jonathan did not look sure. Robert saved himself from awkwardness by conspicuously examining the controls.

The boy left the bridge, graceful despite the lurch of the boat and how weary he must be. Zachariah was startled when young Jonathan advanced across the deck to where Zachariah himself sat.

Brother Zachariah pulled his hood close around his face. Some Shadowhunters were disquieted by a Silent Brother who did not appear exactly as the rest did, though the Silent Brothers looked fearsome enough. He did not want to distress the boy, either way.

Jonathan carried Brother Zachariah's staff back to him, balanced flat as a tightrope along his palms, and laid the staff with a respectful bow on Zachariah's knees. The boy moved with military discipline unusual in one so young, even among Shadowhunters. Brother Zachariah had not known Michael Wayland, but he guessed he must have been a harsh man.

"Brother Enoch?" the boy guessed.

No, said Brother Zachariah. He knew Enoch's memories as his own. Enoch had given the boy his first Mark, though his memories were gray with lack of interest. Brother Zachariah briefly wished he could have been the Silent Brother who oversaw the rite of passage for this child.

"No," the boy repeated slowly. "I should've known. You moved differently. I just thought it might be, since you rolled your staff to me."

He bowed his head. It struck Zachariah as a sorry thing, that the child would not have expected even the smallest mercy from a stranger.

"Thank you for letting me use it," Jonathan added.

I am glad it was useful, returned Brother Zachariah.

The boy's glance up at his face was shocking, the flare of twin suns in what was still almost night. They were not the eyes of a soldier but a warrior. Brother Zachariah had known both, and he knew the difference.

The boy took a step back, nervous and agile, but stopped with his chin high. Apparently he had a question.

Zachariah was not expecting the one he asked.

"What do the initials mean? On your staff. Do all Silent Brothers have them?"

They looked together at the staff. The letters were worn by time and Zachariah's own flesh, but they had been struck deep into the wood in the precise places where Zachariah would put his hands on them when he fought. So, in a way, they would always be fighting together.

The letters were *W* and *H*.

No, said Brother Zachariah. *I am the only one. I carved them into the staff on my first night in the City of Bones.*

"Were they your initials?" the boy asked, his voice low and a little timid. "Back when you were a Shadowhunter, like me?"

Brother Zachariah still considered himself a Shadowhunter, but Jonathan clearly did not mean any offense.

No, said Jem, because he was always James Carstairs when he spoke of what was dearest to him. *Not mine. My* parabatai*'s.*

W and *H*. William Herondale. Will.

The boy looked struck yet wary at the same time. There was a certain guardedness about him, as if he was suspicious of whatever Jem might say before he even had the chance to say it.

"My father says—said—a *parabatai* can be a great weakness."

Jonathan said the word "weakness" with horror. Jem wondered what a man who had drilled a boy to fight like that might have considered weakness.

Jem did not choose to insult an orphan boy's dead father, so he arranged his thoughts carefully. This boy was so alone. He remembered how precious that new link could be, especially when you had no other. It could be the last bridge that connected you to a lost life.

He remembered traveling across the sea, having lost his family, not knowing that he was going to his best friend.

I suppose they can be a weakness, he answered. *It depends on who your* parabatai *is. I carved his initials here because I always fought best with him.*

Jonathan Wayland, the child who fought like a warrior angel, looked intrigued.

"I think—my father was sorry he had a *parabatai*," he said. "Now I have to go and live with the man my father was sorry about. I don't want to be weak, and I don't want to be sorry. I want to be the best."

If you pretend to feel nothing, the pretense may become true, said Jem. *That would be a pity.*

His *parabatai* had tried to feel nothing, for a time. Except what he felt for Jem. It had almost destroyed Will. And every day, Jem pretended to feel something, to be kind, to fix what was broken, to remember names and voices almost forgotten, and hoped that would become truth.

The boy frowned. "Why would it be a pity?"

We battle hardest when that which is dearer to us than our own lives is at stake, said Jem. A parabatai *is both blade and shield. You belong together and to each other not because you are the same but because your different shapes fit together to be a greater whole, a greater warrior for a higher purpose. I always believed we were not merely at our best together but beyond the best either of us could be apart.*

A slow smile broke across the boy's face, like sunrise bursting as a bright surprise upon the water.

"I'd like that," said Jonathan Wayland, adding quickly, "To be a great warrior."

He flung his head back in a sudden, hasty assumption of arrogance, as if he and Jem might both have imagined he meant that he would like to belong to someone.

This boy, hell-bent on fighting rather than finding a family. The Lightwoods guarding against a vampire, when they could have extended some trust. The vampire, holding every friend at bay. All of them had their wounds, but Jem could not help resenting them, for even the privilege of feeling hurt.

All these people were struggling not to feel, trying to freeze their hearts inside their chests until the cold fractured and broke them. While Jem would have given every cold tomorrow he had for one more day with a warm heart, to love them as he once had.

Except Jonathan was a child, still trying to make a distant father proud even when death had made the distance between them impossible. Jem should be kind.

He thought of the boy's speed, his fearless strike with an unfamiliar weapon on a strange and bloody night.

I'm sure you will be a great warrior, said Jem.

Jonathan Wayland ducked his shaggy golden head to hide the faint color in his cheeks.

The boy's forlornness made Jem recall too vividly the night he had carved those initials into his staff, a long, cold night with all the icy strangeness of the Silent Brothers new in his head. He had not wanted to die, but he would have chosen death rather than the awful severing from love and warmth. If only he could have had a death in Tessa's arms, holding Will's hand. He had been robbed of his death.

It seemed impossible to stay anything like human, in among the bones and endless dark.

When the alien cacophony of the Silent Brothers threatened to engulf all that he had been, Jem held fast to his lifelines. There had been none stronger than that one, and only one other so strong. His *parabatai*'s name had been a shout into the abyss, a cry that always received an answer. Even in the Silent City, even with the silent howl insisting that Jem's life was no longer his own but a shared life. No longer my thoughts, but our thoughts. No longer my will, but our will.

He would not accept that parting. *My Will.* Those words meant something different to Jem than to anyone else, meant: my defiance against encroaching dark. My rebellion. Mine, forever.

Jonathan scuffed his shoe against the deck and peered up at Jem, and Jem realized he was trying to see his face beneath the hood. Jem drew the hood, and the shadows, close. Even though he had been rebuffed, Jonathan Wayland offered him a small smile.

Jem had not looked for any kindness from this hurt child. It made Jem think that Jonathan Wayland might grow up to be more than a great warrior.

Maybe Jonathan would have a *parabatai* one day, to teach him the kind of man he wanted to be.

This is the link stronger than any magic, Jem had told himself that night, knife in hand, cutting deep. *This is the bond I chose.*

He had made his mark. He had taken the name Zachariah, which meant "remember." *Remember him,* Jem had willed himself. *Remember them. Remember why. Remember the only answer to the only question. Do not forget.*

When he looked again, Jonathan Wayland was gone. He wished he could thank the child, for helping him remember.

Isabelle had never been to the New York Passenger Ship Terminal before. She was not very impressed. The terminal was like a glass-and-metal snake, and they had to sit in its belly and wait. The ships were like warehouses on the water, when Isabelle had been picturing a boat from Idris as like a pirate ship.

It had been dark when they woke, and it was barely dawn now, and freezing. Alec was huddled in his hoodie against the wind blowing off the blue water, and Max was fussing at their mother, cranky about being up so early. Basically both her brothers were cranky, and Isabelle did not know what to expect.

She saw her father walk down the gangway with a boy beside him. The dawn drew a line of thin gold over the water. The wind made little white capelets for every wave in the river and played with the gold locks of the boy's hair. The boy's back was straight and slim as a rapier. He was wearing dark, close clothes that looked almost like gear. And there was blood on them. He had actually been part of the fighting. Dad and Mom had not let her or Alec fight even one tiny demon yet!

Isabelle turned to Alec, confident he would share her sense of deep betrayal at this unfairness, and found him staring at the new arrival with wide eyes as though beholding a revelation with the morning.

"Wow," Alec breathed.

"What about that vampire?" Isabelle demanded, outraged.

Alec said, "What vampire?"

Mom hushed them.

Jonathan Wayland had gold hair and gold eyes, and those eyes had no depths but only shiny reflective surface, showing as little as if they were metal doors slammed down on a temple. He did not even smile as he came to a stop in front of them.

Bring back that Silent Brother, was Isabelle's feeling.

She looked to her mother, but Mom was staring at this new boy with an odd expression on her face.

The boy was looking back at her. "I'm Jonathan," he told her intently.

"Hello, Jonathan," said Isabelle's mother. "I am Maryse. It's nice to meet you."

She reached out and touched the boy's hair. Jonathan flinched but held himself still, and Maryse smoothed back the shining gold waves the wind had ruffled.

"I think we need to get you a haircut," Mom said.

It was such a Mom thing to say, it made Isabelle smile at the same time as she rolled her eyes. Actually, the boy Jonathan did need a haircut. The ends of his hair were spilling over his collar, untidy as if whoever had cut it last—too long ago—had not cared enough to do a good job. He had the faint air of a stray animal, fur rough and one breath away from a snarl, though that did not make sense for a kid.

Mom winked. "Then you will be even more handsome."

"Is that even possible?" Jonathan asked dryly.

Alec laughed. Jonathan looked surprised, as if he had not noticed Alec before then. Isabelle did not think he had paid attention to any of them except her mother.

"Say hello to Jonathan, kids," said Isabelle's dad.

Max stared up at Jonathan in awe. He dropped his stuffed rabbit on the cement floor, shuffled forward, and hugged Jonathan's leg. Jonathan flinched again, though this time it was more of an instinctive rear back, until the genius figured out he was not being attacked by a two-year-old.

"Hello, Jonathing," said Max, muffled in the material of Jonathan's trousers.

Jonathan patted Max on the back, very tentatively.

Isabelle's brothers were *so* not showing sibling solidarity on the issue of Jonathan Wayland. It was worse when they got home and made awkward small talk even though everybody really wanted to go back to bed.

"Jonathing can sleep in my room because we love each other," Max proposed.

"Jonathan has his own room. Say 'Sleep well, Jonathan,'" said Maryse. "You can see Jonathan after we've all had a little more rest."

Isabelle went to her own room, but she was still buzzing with excitement and could not sleep. She was painting her toenails when she heard the tiny creak of a door down the hall.

Isabelle leaped up, the toenails of one foot painted sparkly black and the other foot still encased in a fuzzy pink sock, and ran to the door. She edged it open a fraction and poked her head out, and caught Alec doing the same thing from his own room. They both watched the silhouette of Jonathan Wayland creeping down the corridor. Isabelle made a complicated series of gestures to determine whether Alec wanted to follow him together.

Alec stared at her in total bafflement. Isabelle loved her big brother, but sometimes she despaired about their future demon-hunting endeavors. He was so bad at remembering her cool military-style signals.

She gave up and they both hurried after Jonathan, who did not know the layout of the Institute and could only retrace his steps to the kitchen.

Which was where they found him. Jonathan had his shirt pulled up, and he was dabbing a wet dish towel along the red cut running up his side.

"By the Angel," said Alec. "You're hurt. Why didn't you say?"

Isabelle hit Alec in the arm for not being stealthy.

Jonathan stared at them, guilt written across his face as if he had been stealing from the cookie jar rather than injured.

"Don't tell your parents," he said.

Alec left Isabelle's side and ran to Jonathan. He examined the cut, then shepherded Jonathan toward a stool, making him sit down. Isabelle was unsurprised. Alec always fussed when she or Max fell down.

"It's shallow," Alec said after a moment, "but our parents really would want to know. Mom could put an *iratze* on—or something—"

"No! It's better for your parents not to know it happened at all. It was just bad luck one of them got me. I'm a good fighter," Jonathan protested sharply.

He was so vehement it was almost alarming. If he hadn't been ten years old, Isabelle would have thought he was worried they might send him away for being an inadequate soldier.

"You're obviously great," said Alec. "You just need someone to have your back."

He put his hand lightly on Jonathan's shoulder as he spoke. It was a small gesture Isabelle would not even have noted, except for the fact that she had never seen Alec reach out like that to anyone who was not family and that Jonathan Wayland went perfectly still at his touch, as if he was afraid the tiniest movement would scare Alec away.

"Does it hurt a lot?" Alec added sympathetically.

"No," Jonathan Wayland whispered.

Isabelle thought it was perfectly clear Jonathan Wayland would claim having his leg cut off did not hurt, but Alec was an honest soul.

"Okay," said her brother. "Let me grab a few things from the infirmary. Let's deal with this together."

Alec nodded in an encouraging fashion and went to fetch supplies from the infirmary, leaving Isabelle and this weird bleeding boy alone together.

"So you and your brother seem . . . really close," Jonathan said.

Isabelle blinked. "Sure."

What a concept, being close to your family. Isabelle refrained from being sarcastic, as Jonathan was both unwell and a guest.

"So . . . I guess you're going to be *parabatai*," Jonathan ventured.

"Oh, no, I don't think so," said Isabelle. "Being *parabatai* is a little old-fashioned, isn't it? Besides, I don't like the idea of giving up my independence. Before I am my parents' daughter or my brothers' sister, I am my own. I'm already a lot of people's something. I don't need to be anyone else's anything, not for a long time. You know?"

Jonathan smiled. He had a chipped tooth. Isabelle wondered how that had happened, and hoped it had been chipped in an awesome fight. "I don't know. I'm not really anyone's anything."

Isabelle bit her lip. She had never realized before that she took feeling secure for granted.

Jonathan had glanced at Isabelle as he spoke, but immediately after he returned to watching the door through which Alec had disappeared.

Isabelle could not help observing that Jonathan Wayland had lived in their home for less than three hours, and he was already trying to lock down a *parabatai*.

Then he slouched further into his chair, resuming his too-cool-for-the-Institute attitude, and she forgot the thought in annoyance that Jonathan was such a show-off. She, Isabelle, was the only show-off this Institute needed.

She and Jonathan stared each other down until Alec returned.

"Oh—would you rather I put on the bandages or do you want to do it yourself?"

Jonathan's face was opaque. "I can do it myself. I don't need anything."

"Oh," Alec said unhappily.

Isabelle could not tell if Jonathan's expressionless face was to ward them off or protect himself, but he was hurt. Alec was still shy with strangers, and Jonathan was a closed-off human being, so they were going to be awkward even though Isabelle could tell they both really liked each other. Isabelle sighed. Boys were hopeless, and she had to take charge of this situation.

"Hold still, idiot," she ordered Jonathan, seized ointment from Alec's hands, and began to smear it over Jonathan's cut. "I am going to be a ministering angel."

"Um," said Alec. "That's a lot of ointment."

It did look a little like when you squeezed the center of the tube of toothpaste too hard, but Isabelle felt you did not get results without being willing to make a mess.

"It's fine," said Jonathan quickly. "It's great. Thank you, Isabelle."

Isabelle glanced up and grinned at him. Alec efficiently unwound a bandage. Having gotten them started, Isabelle stepped back. Her parents would object if she accidentally turned their guest into a mummy.

"What's going on?" said Robert Lightwood's voice from the door. "Jonathan! You said you were not hurt."

When Isabelle looked, she saw both her mom and dad standing at the threshold of the kitchen, arms folded and eyes narrowed. She imagined they would have objections to her and Alec playing doctor with the new kid. Strong objections.

"We were just patching Jonathan up," Alec announced anxiously, ranging himself in front of Jonathan's stool. "No big deal."

"It was my fault I got hurt," said Jonathan. "I know excuses are for incompetents. It won't happen again."

"It won't?" asked her mother. "All warriors get wounded sometimes. Planning to run away and become a Silent Brother?"

Jonathan Wayland shrugged. "I applied to the Iron Sisters, but they sent me a hurtful and sexist refusal."

Everyone laughed. Jonathan looked briefly startled again, then pleased, before he shut away his expressions as if slamming a lid down on a treasure chest. Isabelle's mother was the one who went and gave Jonathan an *iratze*, while her father stayed by the door.

"Jonathan?" Maryse remarked. "Does anyone ever call you anything else?"

"No," said Jonathan. "My father used to tell a joke about having another Jonathan, if I wasn't good enough."

Isabelle did not think that was much of a joke.

"I always think that naming one of our kids Jonathan is like the mundanes calling kids Jebediah," said Isabelle's mother.

"John," said her father. "Mundanes often call their kids John."

"Do they?" asked Maryse, and shrugged. "I could have sworn it was Jebediah."

"My middle name is Christopher," said Jonathan. "You can—you can call me Christopher if you like."

Maryse and Isabelle exchanged a speaking look. She and her mother had always been able to communicate like this. Isabelle thought it was because they were the only girls, and special to each other. She could not imagine her mother telling her anything she would not want to hear.

"We're not going to *rename* you," said Maryse sadly.

Isabelle was not sure if her mother was sad that Jonathan thought they would do that, give him a different name as if he were a pet, or sad that he would have let them.

What Isabelle was sure about was that her mother was watching Jonathan in the same way she had watched Max when he was still learning to walk, and there would be no more discussion of a trial period. Jonathan was obviously here to stay.

"Maybe a nickname," Maryse proposed. "What would you think of Jace?"

He was silent for a moment, observing Isabelle's mother carefully from the corner of his eye. At last he offered her a smile, faint and cool as the light in early morning, but growing warm with hope.

Jonathan Wayland said, "I think Jace will work."

As a boy was introduced to a family, and vampires slept cold but curled together in the hold of a ship, Brother Zachariah walked through a city not his own. The people hurrying by could not see him, but he saw the light in their eyes as if it had been made new. The blare of car horns and scream of tires from yellow cabs and the chatter of many voices in many tongues formed a long, living song. Brother Zachariah could not sing the song, but he could listen.

This was not the first time this had happened to him, seeing a trace of what had been in what was. The coloring was entirely different. The boy did not really have anything to do with Will. Jem knew that. Jem—for in the moments he remembered Will, he was always Jem—was used to seeing his lost and dearest Shadowhunter in a thousand Shadowhunter faces and gestures, the turn of a head or the note of a voice. Never the beloved head, never the long-silent voice, but sometimes, more and more rarely, something close.

Jem's hand was firmly clasped around his staff. He had not paid attention to the carving beneath his palm like this for many a long, cold day.

This is a reminder of my faith. If there is any part of him that can be with me, and I believe there is, then he is at hand. Nothing can part us. He allowed himself a smile. His mouth could not open, but he could still smile. He could still speak to Will, though he could no longer hear any answer.

Life is not a boat, bearing us far away on a cruel, relentless tide from all we love. You are not lost to me on some forever distant shore. Life is a wheel.

From the river, he could hear mermaids. All the sparks of the city by morning were kindling a new fire. A new day was born.

If life is a wheel, it will bring you back to me. All I must do is keep faith.

Even when having a heart seemed hard past bearing, it was

better than the alternative. Even when Brother Zachariah felt he was losing the struggle, losing everything he had been, there was hope.

Sometimes you seem very far away from me, my parabatai.

Light on water had not rivaled the boy's blazing contradiction of a smile, somehow both indomitable and too easily hurt. He was a child going to a new home, as Will and the boy Zachariah had been had once traveled in lonely sorrow to the place where they would find each other. Jem hoped Jonathan would find happiness.

Jem smiled back at a boy long gone.

Sometimes, Will, he said, *you seem very close.*

The Land I Lost

By Cassandra Clare and Sarah Rees Brennan

J

New York, 2012

The sky was soft gray with evening, stars not yet out. Alec Lightwood was napping because he and his *parabatai* had been out fighting Croucher demons all last night, and Jace Herondale, famed among the Nephilim as a master strategist, apparently thought "about a dozen demons" was a fair estimate for "definitely thirty-seven demons." Alec had gone around counting them out of spite.

"Give yourself a break, Should-Be-Sleeping Beauty," Magnus had told him. "I need to make a potion, and Max is scheduled for his evening temptation."

Alec woke in a nest of lavender-and-green silk sheets. Under the door of the bedroom, eerie silver lights played. There was a smell of sulfur, and the hiss of a demon, and the sound of beloved voices. Alec smiled against his pillow.

Just as he was about to roll out of bed, letters of fire appeared on the wall.

> *Alec, we need your help. For years we have searched for a family in peril and the truth behind why they are in danger.*

We believe we have found a lead in the Shadow Market of Buenos Aires.

But there is unrest between the Shadowhunters and Downworlders of this city. This Shadow Market is guarded like a throne room, run by a werewolf known as the Queen of the Market. She says her doors are closed to every soul associated with the Nephilim. Every soul, except for Alexander Lightwood, who she says she has need of. We need to enter the Shadow Market. Lives are at stake.

Will you open the doors for us? Will you come?

—Jem and Tessa

Alec stared at the letter for a long moment. Then he sighed, fished a sweater up from the floor, and weaved his way out of their bedroom, still half-asleep.

In their main room, Magnus stood with one elbow casually propped against their mantel, decanting a vial of turquoise liquid into a jar of black powder. His green-gold eyes were narrowed with focus. The dark worn floorboards and the woven silk rug alike were littered with their son Max's toys. Max himself was sitting on the rug, wearing a sailor suit with elaborate navy ribbons to match his hair, tightly embracing Chairman Meow.

"You are my meow friend," he told the Chairman solemnly, squeezing him.

"Meow," Chairman Meow protested. He'd lived a life of torment since Max learned to walk.

The pentagram had been drawn a safe distance away from the rug. Silvery light and mist rose from within the pentagram, shrouding its inhabitant in shimmering fog. The demon's long, writhing shadow fell dark against their green wallpaper and family pictures.

Magnus raised an eyebrow. “Ease up,” he suggested to the pentagram. “It’s like someone loaned overly enthusiastic kids a dry-ice machine for their high-school production of *Demon Oklahoma!* in here.”

Alec grinned. The silvery mist dissipated enough to see the demon Elyaas in the pentagram, his tentacles drooping in a sulky fashion.

“Child,” he hissed to Max. “You know not of what dark lineage you come. You are naturally inclined to evil. Join me, infernal foundling, in my revels—”

“My *bapa* is Ultra Magnus,” Max announced proudly. “And Daddy is a Shadowhunter.”

Alec thought Max had gotten the name Ultra Magnus from one of his toys. Magnus seemed to like it.

“Don’t interrupt me when I’m promising you dark demonic delights,” the demon Elyaas said fussily. “Why are you always interrupting me?”

Max brightened at the word “demonic.”

“Uncle Jace says we will kill all the demins,” he reported with joy. “All the demins!”

“Well, have you considered that your uncle Jace is a hurtful person?” said the demon. “Always rudely stabbing everyone, and sarcastic.”

Max scowled. “Love Uncle Jace. Hate demins.”

With his free hand, Magnus picked up a marker and drew another blueberry on the whiteboard to show Max had successfully resisted today’s demonic wiles. Ten blueberries, and Max got a reward of his choosing.

Alec crossed the floor to where Magnus stood considering the whiteboard. Carefully, since Magnus was still holding a bubbling jar, he slid his arms around Magnus's waist, linking his hands together over the embossed buckle of Magnus's belt. The T-shirt Magnus was wearing had a dramatic scoop neckline, so Alec put his face down in the smooth bare expanse of skin and breathed in the smell of sandalwood and spell ingredients.

"Hi," he mumbled.

Magnus reached back with his free hand, and Alec felt the slight sweet pull of rings in his hair. "Hi, yourself. Couldn't sleep?"

"I slept," Alec protested. "Listen, I have some news."

He filled Magnus in on the message Jem Carstairs and Tessa Gray had sent: the family they were searching for, the Shadow Market they could not enter without his help. As Alec spoke, Magnus gave a little sigh and leaned against him, one of the small unconscious gestures that meant the most to Alec. It reminded him of the first day he'd ever touched Magnus, drawn close to and kissed another man, someone even taller than he was, his body lean and lithe and right against Alec's. At the time, he'd thought he felt dizzy with relief and joy because he was finally touching someone he wanted to be touched by, when he'd thought he might never have that. Now he thought he'd felt that way because it was Magnus: that even then, he'd known. Now the gesture spoke of all the days since the first.

When he felt Magnus relax against him, he felt like he could relax too.

Whatever this strange task Jem and Tessa needed him for, he could do it. Then he would come home.

As Alec fell silent, Chairman Meow made a break for

freedom from Max's loving stranglehold, streaking across the floor, through the door Alec had left open, and into Alec and Magnus's bedroom, where Alec suspected he would be hiding under the bed for the rest of the night. Max stared sadly after the cat, then looked up and grinned, his teeth tiny pearls. He launched himself at Alec as if he had not seen him for several weeks. Alec always got the same enthusiastic greeting, whether he was back from a trip, back from patrolling, or had simply been in the other room for five minutes.

"Hey, Daddy!"

Alec took a knee and opened his arms to scoop Max up. "Hey, my baby."

He stood with Max curled against his chest, a warm soft bundle of ribbons and round limbs, Max's gurgling laughter in his ears. When Max was tiny, Alec used to marvel at how neatly his little body fit into the crook of Alec's arm. He'd scarcely been able to imagine Max getting bigger. He needn't have worried. Whatever size his kid was, he was always a perfect fit for Alec to hold.

Alec tugged at the front of Max's sailor suit. "That's a lot of ribbons there, buddy."

Max nodded sadly. "Too much ribbons."

"What happened to your sweater?"

"That's a fine question, Alexander. Allow me to unfold to you the tale. Max rolled his sweater in the cat litter," Magnus related. "So he could 'look like Daddy.' Thus he must wear the sailor suit of shame. I don't make the rules. Oh wait, yes, I do."

He waved a reproving finger at Max, who laughed again and tried to grab for the glitter of rings.

"It's really inspiring to see you crazy kids making it work," chipped in Elyaas the tentacle demon. "I don't have much luck with romance. Everyone I meet is treacherous and heartless. Well, we are demons. Comes with the territory."

Magnus had insisted warlocks needed to know what summoning demons entailed. He said that the more comfortable Max was with them, the less likely he was to be tricked or terrified when he summoned his first. Hence the temptation lessons. Elyaas was not so bad, as demons went, which meant he was still terrible. As Max had passed the pentagram, Alec had seen the wicked silver curve of one tentacle moving hungrily close to the edge lest Max make a false move.

Alec looked at Elyaas with narrowed eyes.

"Don't imagine I ever forget what you are," Alec said grimly. "I'm watching you."

Elyaas held up all his tentacles in surrender, scooting to the other side of the pentagram. "It was a reflex! I didn't mean anything by it."

"Demins," said Max darkly.

Magnus banished Elyaas with a snap of his fingers and a murmur, then turned back to Alec.

"So, they're asking for you in Buenos Aires," said Magnus.

"Yeah," said Alec. "I don't know why anyone at the Market wants me specifically, as opposed to any other Shadowhunter."

Magnus laughed. "I can see why someone might."

"Okay, other than that." Alec grinned. "I don't speak Spanish."

Magnus could speak Spanish. Alec wished that Magnus could go with him, but one of them always tried to stay home with Max. Once, when Max was still a baby, there had been a terrible time when they were both forced to leave him. Neither of them wanted to repeat it.

Alec was trying to learn Spanish, as well as several other

languages. The Speak in Tongues rune didn't last and seemed like cheating. Downworlders from all over the world came to New York to consult with them these days, and Alec wanted to be able to talk with them properly. First on the list of languages he was trying to learn was Indonesian, for Magnus.

Unfortunately, Alec wasn't great at languages. He was able to read them, but when he was talking he found words difficult, no matter the tongue. Max had picked up more words in various languages than Alec.

"It's fine," Magnus had commented once. "I never knew any Lightwood but one who was good at languages."

"Which one?" Alec had asked.

"His name was Thomas," Magnus said. "Tall as a tree. Very shy."

"Not a green-eyed monster like the other Lightwoods you've mentioned?"

"Oh," said Magnus. "There was a bit of the monster in him."

Magnus had elbowed him and laughed. Alec remembered a time when Magnus never talked about the past, when Alec thought it meant he was doing something wrong or Magnus didn't care. Now he understood it was only that Magnus had been hurt before and was afraid Alec would hurt him too.

"I thought I might bring Lily," he told Magnus. "She can speak Spanish. And I thought it might cheer her up. She likes Jem."

Nobody at any Market would question Lily's presence. Everybody had heard of the Downworlder-Shadowhunter Alliance by now, and it was well known that members of the Alliance helped each other out.

Magnus raised his eyebrows. "Oh, I know Lily likes Jem. I've heard the nicknames."

Max looked back and forth at their expressions, his face bright.

"Bring back brother orra sister?" Max hoped.

They had talked with Max about the idea of another kid, as they had talked to each other. Neither of them had expected Max would take to the idea so much. Max asked about the brother or the sister every time one of them left the house: last Tuesday Magnus had forestalled the question by yelling, "Not getting a baby, going to Sephora. There are no babies at Sephora!" and bolting. One day at the park, Max had seized a pram with a mundane baby in it. Luckily, he'd been glamoured at the time, and the mundane mother thought it was a rogue gust of wind rather than Alec's little rogue.

It would be nice for Max to have someone to grow up with. It would be nice to have another baby, with Magnus. Still, Alec remembered when he'd first held Max, how the world and Alec's heart had gone quiet and certain. Alec was waiting to be sure again.

Alec's pause left Max obviously thinking there was room for negotiation here.

"Bring back brother anna sister anna dinosaur?" asked Max. Alec blamed Max's attitude on his aunt Isabelle, who kept telling him his bedtime was never.

They were saved by Jace's signal, a faerie-leaf folded plane striking the glass of the window.

Alec gave Max a little kiss, in the midst of his curls but avoiding his horns. "No, I'm going on a mission."

"I come with you," Max proposed. "I be a Shadowhunter."

Max said that a lot too, for which Alec blamed Max's uncle Jace. Alec looked appealingly at Magnus over Max's head.

"Come to Papa, bluebottle," said Magnus, and Max went unsuspectingly to his open arms.

"Go get Lily," said Magnus. "I'll have a Portal set up for you."

Max shrieked his outrage. "Down!"

Magnus put him down gently. Alec paused at the door to catch one last glimpse of them. Magnus glanced up at him, touched his own heart with his ringed hand, and made a little flicking gesture. Alec grinned and opened his own hand to see the tiny blue spark of magic burning briefly there.

"Hate you, Daddy," Max said, and sulked.

"That's a shame," said Alec. "I love you both," he added quickly, and closed the door on his own embarrassment.

The words were seldom easy for him to say, but he tried to say them whenever he was going on a mission. Just in case they were the last words.

Jace was waiting for him on the sidewalk, leaning against a sad-looking city tree, flipping a knife from palm to palm.

As Alec reached the sidewalk, there was a sound from above. Alec looked up to see Magnus, but instead he saw Max's round face. Alec assumed Max wanted to get a glimpse of his magnificent uncle Jace. Then he saw Max was looking at him, big blue eyes mournful. He put his hand on the front of his sailor suit, then gestured to Alec the same way Magnus had, as if Max could do magic already.

Alec pretended to see a magic spark in his hand and put the magic kiss in his pocket. Then he gave Max a last wave as he and Jace headed down the street.

"What was that about?" Jace asked.

"He wanted to come patrolling."

Jace's face softened. "My good boy! He should—"

"No!" said Alec. "And nobody will let you have your own kid until you stop putting other people's kids in bags meant for axes and trying to smuggle them out on patrol."

"I almost got away with it, due to my supernatural speed and unmatched cunning," Jace claimed.

"No, you didn't," said Alec. "That bag was wriggling."

Jace shrugged philosophically. "Ready for another round of heroically defending the world from evil? Or if it's a slow night, pranking Simon?"

"Actually, I can't," said Alec, and explained the message from Jem and Tessa.

"I'll come with you," Jace offered instantly.

"And leave Clary to run the Institute alone?" asked Alec. "A week before her exhibition?"

Jace looked shaken by the force of this argument.

"You're not letting Clary down. Lily and I can deal with whatever's going on," said Alec. "Besides, it's not like Jem and Tessa can't handle themselves. We'll be a team."

"Fine," said Jace reluctantly. "I guess three other fighters are an acceptable substitute for me."

Alec thumped him swiftly on the shoulder with a fist, and Jace smiled.

"Well," he said. "To the Hotel Dumort."

From the outside the hotel's facade was grimy, the graffitied sign the dark brown of old blood.

Since Lily Chen had become the leader of the vampires of New York, she'd redecorated on the inside. Alec and Jace opened splintered double doors on a shining hall. The flight of stairs and the balcony above them had a glittering rail, gilt-painted iron fretwork depicting snakes and roses. Lily liked things to look like the 1920s, which she said was the best decade. The decor wasn't the only thing that had changed; now there were hipsters in the know, and though Alec didn't understand the allure himself, there was a waiting list to be a party victim.

A pair of legs was sticking out from under the curving flight of stairs. Alec strode over and peered into the shadowy alcove, seeing a man wearing suspenders, a blood-smudged shirt, and a grin.

"Hi," Alec said. "Just checking. Is this a voluntary situation?"

The man blinked. "Oh yes. I signed the consent form!"

"There's a consent form now?" Jace murmured.

"I told them they didn't have to do that," Alec murmured back.

"My fabulous fanged lady friend said I should sign it, otherwise the Clave would get stern with her. Are *you* the Clave?"

"No," said Alec.

"But Hetty said that if I didn't sign the consent form, the Clave would look at her with those disappointed blue eyes. Your eyes are very blue."

"And very disappointed," said Alec sternly.

"Are you bothering Alec?" demanded a vampire girl, running out of the double doors that led to the parlor. "Don't bother Alec."

"Oh dear," said the man in delighted tones. "Is my mortal soul doomed? Are you about to visit your undead wrath upon me?"

Hetty snarled, and dived under the stairs with a giggle. Alec averted his eyes and headed for the parlor, Jace falling in behind him. Jace let Alec take point when it came to the vampires. As head of the New York Institute, Jace reprimanding a vampire might sound like a threat. Jace and Alec had talked over how to make the city welcoming to all Downworlders, now that New

York was a refuge in the times of the Cold Peace.

Through the parlor doors came the sound of music: not Lily's usual jazz but a pounding mix that sounded like rap and jazz combined. Inside the parlor were tufted chairs, a gleaming piano, and an elaborate set of turntables and wires. Bat Velasquez the werewolf DJ was sitting cross-legged on a plush velvet sofa, fiddling with dials.

In other cities, vampires and werewolves didn't get along. Things were different in New York.

Elliott, second in command of the vampire clan, was dancing around in a happy circle by himself. His arms and dreadlocks waved to the beat like plants underwater.

"Is Lily up?" asked Alec.

Elliott suddenly looked hunted. "Not yet. We had a bit of a late morning yesterday. There was an incident. Well, more a disaster."

"What caused this disaster?"

"Well," Elliott said. "Me, like usual. But this time it really wasn't my fault! It was a total and complete accident that could have happened to anyone. You see, I have this regular selkie Thursday-night booty call."

Selkies were water faeries who shed their sealskins to assume human form. They were fairly rare.

Alec subjected him to a judgmental stare. "So this disaster could have happened to anyone with a regular selkie booty call."

"Yeah, exactly," said Elliott. "Or, like, regular booty calls with two different selkies. One of them found the other's sealskin in my wardrobe. There was a scene. You know how it is with selkies."

Alec, Jace, and Bat shook their heads.

"Only one tiny wall fell down, but now Lily's all mad."

Lily had made Elliott her second in command because they were friends, not because Elliott had any aptitude for leadership. Sometimes Alec worried about the New York vampire clan.

Bat said, "This guy. Why do you have to suggest threesomes to everybody? Why are vampires like this?"

Elliott shrugged. "Vampires love threesomes. Live long, get decadent. We aren't all the same, of course." His face brightened with a pleasant memory. "The boss used to get very cross about decadence. But really, I'm ready to settle down. I think you and I and Maia—"

"My *abuela* wouldn't like you," Bat said firmly. "My *abuela* loves Maia. Maia's learning Spanish for her."

Bat's slightly raspy voice went low and warm whenever he talked about Maia, the leader of the werewolves, and his girlfriend. Alec couldn't blame him. Alec never worried about the werewolves. Maia always had everything under control.

"Speaking of Spanish," Alec said, "I'm going to Buenos Aires, and I'm asking Lily to come with me, since she's fluent. By the time Lily gets back, she'll have cooled off."

Elliott nodded. "A trip would be good for her," he said, his voice unusually serious. "She hasn't been doing well lately. She misses the boss. Well, we all do, but it's different for Lily. It takes us like this sometimes." He glanced at Alec and clarified: "Immortals. We're used to seeing each other off and on through the centuries. Years go by, then someone's back, and it's just the way it was before. Because we stay the same, though the world doesn't. When someone dies, it takes us a while to process. You think to yourself: I wonder when I'll see him again. Then you remember, and it's a shock every time. You have to keep reminding yourself, until you believe it: I'll never see him again."

There was an achingly sad note in Elliott's voice. Alec nodded. He knew how it would be, one day, when Magnus had to think "never again" about him.

He knew how strong someone had to be, to withstand the loneliness of immortality.

"Also, honestly, Lily could use some help with the clan."

"You could help her," said Alec. "If you were just a bit more responsible . . ."

Elliott shook his head. "Not gonna happen. Hey, Mr. Head of the Institute, you're a leader! How about it? I make you a vampire, you help lead the clan, you stay gorgeous forever."

"That would be a gift to future generations," Jace remarked thoughtfully. "But no."

"Elliott!" Alec snapped. "Stop offering to make people immortal! We have spoken about this!"

Elliott nodded, looking abashed but smiling a tiny smile. From outside and above, a voice drifted down.

"I hear someone bossing people around! Alec?"

One of the most worrying things about the vampire clan was that speaking to them reasonably didn't work at all, but they were delighted to be told off. Raphael Santiago had really left a mark on these people.

Alec walked over and peered out the open doors. Lily was standing on the balcony, wearing rumpled pink pajamas with drawings of snakes and the words RISE AND STRIKE on them. She looked tired.

"Yeah," he said. "Hey. Jem asked me to come to Buenos Aires and help him out. Do you want to come with?"

Lily lit up. "Do I want to come on a bro road trip with you, rushing to the aid of gorgeous damsel-in-distress Jem I'd-love-to-climb-'em Carstairs?"

"So, yes."

Lily's smile was wide enough to show fangs. "Hell yes."

She darted away from the balcony. Alec noted the door she went through, and climbed the stairs. He waited a bit, leaning against the rail, then tapped on the door.

"Come in!"

He didn't come in, but he opened the door. The room inside was narrow as a cell, with stripped floorboards and walls bare except for a cross on a hook. This was the only room in the Hotel Dumort Lily hadn't redecorated. She was sleeping in Raphael's room again.

Lily was wearing a leather jacket that had been Raphael's too. Alec watched as she fluffed her hot-pink-streaked hair, then kissed the cross for luck and headed out. Christian vampires were burned by a cross, but Lily was a Buddhist. The cross meant nothing to her, except that it had been Raphael's.

"Do you . . ." Alec coughed. "Do you want to talk?"

Lily tipped her head back to stare all the way up at him. "About feelings? Do we do that?"

"Preferably not," said Alec, which made her smile. "But we could."

"Nah," Lily answered. "Let's go on a road trip and see hotties instead! Where's that idiot Elliott?"

She ran lightly down the stairs to the parlor, and Alec followed her.

"Elliott, I'm leaving you in charge of the clan!" said Lily. "Bat, I'm stealing your girl!"

Bat shook his head. "Why are vampires like this?" he murmured again.

Lily grinned. "For administrative purposes. Maia's running the Downworlder-Shadowhunter Alliance until we get back."

"I don't want to be in charge of the clan," Elliott wailed. "Please be a vampire and lead us, Jace! Please!"

"I used to walk in here and have to fight for my life as the place fell down around me," Jace mused. "Now it's all velvet cushions and insistent offers of immortal beauty."

"It's just one tiny bite," Elliott coaxed him. "You'll like it."

"Nobody likes getting all their blood sucked out, Elliott," Alec said severely.

Both the vampires in the room smiled because he was telling them off, then looked upset because of what he was saying.

"You only think that because Simon did it wrong," Lily argued. "I've pointed out to him many times that he messed up everything for all of us."

"Simon did fine," Jace muttered.

"I didn't like it," said Alec. "I won't talk about this again. Let's get going."

"Ah yes." Lily brightened. "I'm very curious to see how the hottest Shadowhunter in the world is doing."

"I'm great," said Jace.

Lily tapped her foot. "Nobody's talking about you, Jason. Have you heard the phrase 'tall, dark, and handsome'?"

"Sounds like an old-fashioned saying," said Jace. "Sounds like something people used to say before I was born."

He grinned at Lily, who grinned back at him. Jace didn't just pull the pigtails of people he had crushes on. He pulled the pigtails of everyone in the world he liked. This was something

Simon still had not figured out over the years.

"There are a lot of hot Shadowhunters," said Elliott. "That's the point of them, isn't it?"

"No," said Alec. "We fight demons."

"Oh," said Elliott. "Right."

"I don't mean to brag. I'm just saying that if they made a book of hot Shadowhunters, my illustration would be on every page," Jace said serenely.

"Nope," said Lily. "It would be filled with pictures of the Carstairs family."

Alec said, "Are you talking about Emma?"

Lily frowned. "Who's Emma?"

"Emma Carstairs," said Jace helpfully. "She's Clary's pen pal who lives in L.A. Sometimes I write postscripts to Clary's letters and tell Emma handy knife tricks. Emma's very good."

Emma was a single-minded force of destruction, which of course Jace liked. Jace fished out his phone and showed Lily a recent picture of Emma that Emma had sent Clary. Emma was holding her sword on a beach and laughing.

Lily breathed, "Cortana."

Alec glanced at her sharply.

"I don't know Emma," Lily said. "But I'd like to. I don't normally go for blonds, but she's hot. Bless the Come-and-Stare family. They never fail me. On that note, I'm off to admire the views in Buenos Aires."

"Jem is *married*, you know," said Alec.

"Don't leave me in charge!" Elliott begged. "You can't trust me! It's a terrible mistake!"

Lily ignored them both, but she caught Alec studying her as they left the hotel.

"Don't look so worried," she said. "Elliott probably won't burn the city down. When I get back, everybody will be so grateful that they'll do everything I say. Leaving that fool in charge is part of my leadership strategy."

Alec nodded and didn't say that he was worried about her.

There had been a time when Alec was unsettled by vampires, but Lily had always so clearly needed someone, and Alec had wanted to be there for her. They'd been teammates running the Alliance with Maia for long enough now that Lily felt like Aline Penhallow, a friend close enough to be family.

The thought of Aline sent a familiar pang through Alec. Aline had gone into exile on Wrangel Island to be with her wife, Helen. They had lived in that stony wasteland for years, just because Helen had faerie blood.

Whenever Alec thought of Helen and Aline, he wanted to change everything about the way the Clave worked and bring them home.

It wasn't only Aline and Helen. He felt that way about all the warlocks and vampires and werewolves and faeries who streamed to New York to talk to the Alliance because they couldn't go to their Institutes. Every day, he felt the same urge he'd felt on his first mission, when he saw Jace and Isabelle charge into a fight. *Protect them,* he'd thought desperately, and lunged for his bow.

Alec squared his shoulders. Worrying wouldn't help anyone. He couldn't save everybody, but he could help people, and now he intended to help Jem and Tessa.

Brother Zachariah walked through the Silent City, down corridors lined with bones. The ground was marked with the relentless passage of the Silent Brothers' feet, of his own feet, moving in their accustomed path day after silent day, year after dark, endless year. He could not get out. Soon he would forget how it had ever been to live and love in the light. Every skull grinning at him from the wall was a thing more human than he.

Until the darkness he'd thought inescapable was obliterated by consuming fire. The silver fire of *yin fen* had burned in him once, the worst burning the world had to offer, but this golden fire was remorseless as heaven. He felt as if he were being torn apart, every burning atom of him weighed in the balance by a cruel god, and every piece found wanting.

Even in the midst of agony, there was some small measure of relief. This was the end, he told himself desperately, and was desperately thankful. At last this was the end, after all that misery and darkness. He would die before his humanity was entirely crushed out. Finally, there might be rest. He might see his *parabatai* again.

Except with the thought of Will came the thought of another. He thought of soft cool air drifting from the river, and her sweet serious face, unchanging as his own heart. With the thought of Will, he knew what Will would say. He could hear him, as if even the veil of death were burning between them and Will was shouting in his ear. *Jem, Jem. James Carstairs. You can't leave Tessa on her own. I know you better than you know yourself. I always did. I know you would never give up. Jem, hold on.*

He would not dishonor love by letting go. In the end, he chose to endure any pain rather than do that. Through the fire, as through the darkness, he held on.

And impossibly, through fire and darkness and time, he survived.

Jem woke gasping. He was in a warm bed, with his wife in his arms.

Tessa was still sleeping, on white sheets in the small white-washed room they were renting in the small lodging house. She murmured as Jem watched her, a soft string of incomprehensible words. She talked in her sleep, and every sound was a comfort. More than a century ago, he'd wondered how it would be to wake up with Tessa. He'd dreamed of it.

Now he knew.

Jem listened to her sweet sleepy murmurs, and watched the rise and fall of the white sheet with her breathing, and his body eased.

Tessa's curling lashes stirred on her cheeks.

"Jem?" she asked, and her hand found his arm, palm sliding down his skin.

"I'm sorry," Jem said. "I didn't mean to disturb you."

"Don't be sorry." Tessa smiled sleepily.

Jem leaned over to the pillow beside his and kissed his wife's eyes closed, then watched them open again, clear and cool as river water. He kissed her cheek, the eloquent curve of her mouth, her chin, and trailed his open mouth hungrily down the line of her throat.

"Tessa, Tessa," he murmured. "*Wǒ yào nǐ.*"

I want you.

Tessa said, "Yes."

Jem lifted the sheet and kissed the line of her collarbone, loving the taste of her soft sleep-warm skin, loving every atom of her. He laid a trail of kisses for himself to follow all the way down her body. When he drew his mouth down the tender skin of her stomach, her hands slipped into his hair and fastened tightly there, anchoring him, encouraging him on. Her voice, no longer soft, made the walls ring with his name.

She was all around him. All horror and pain was washed away.

Jem and Tessa lay facing one another on the bed, their hands entwined, their voices hushed. They could whisper and laugh all night together, and often had: it was one of Jem's great joys, just to lie with Tessa and talk for hours.

But that required quiet and peace, which was not to be had tonight. Light exploded through their dim room, and Jem bolted upright, shielding Tessa from any possible threat.

Words of shimmering blue and silver had appeared on the wall. Tessa sat up, tucking the sheet around her. "Message from Magnus," she said, twisting her hair up into a knot at the back of her head.

The message said that Alec and Lily Chen were on their way to help. Once they had stowed their belongings at the Buenos Aires Institute, they would meet Tessa and Jem outside the walls of the Shadow Market.

Jem met Tessa's gaze and read his own alarm in her eyes.

"Oh no," said Tessa. Jem was already scrambling off the bed, searching for their clothes. "We have to find them. We have to stop them. They *can't* go to the Institute."

The Buenos Aires Institute was located in the town of San Andrés de Giles. To mundane eyes, the Institute looked like a large crypt standing in an abandoned cemetery, in a profusion of ghost-pale wildflowers.

To Alec's eyes, it looked worse. It was a tall edifice, painted a dull rust color, but one wing of the building was a charred ruin. Alec had known the Institute was damaged during the Dark War, but he'd thought it would have been repaired long before.

Lily sniffed the air. "They mixed blood in the paint."

The Institute looked abandoned, except for the fact there was a guard at the door. Even that made Alec's eyes narrow. Shadowhunters didn't typically keep watch on their own Institutes, unless it was a time of war.

He nodded to Lily, and they moved forward to meet the Shadowhunters of Buenos Aires. The guard at the door looked a few years younger than Alec. His face was hard, his black eyebrows drawn sharply together, and he was squinting at them suspiciously.

"Um," said Alec. "*Bonjour?* Wait, that's French."

Lily smiled a sunny fanged smile at the guard. "Let me handle this."

"I can speak English," the guard told Alec hastily.

"Great," said Alec. "I'm from the New York Institute. My name is—"

The guard's dark eyes went wide. "You're Alexander Lightwood!"

Alec blinked. "That's me."

"I was in the Inquisitor's office once," the guard confided shyly. "He has a tapestry of you hanging up in there."

"Yeah," said Alec. "I know."

"That's how I know what you look like. I'm so thrilled to meet you. I mean, it's such an honor. Oh no, what am I doing? I'm Joaquín Acosta Romero. It's a pleasure."

Joaquín held out his hand for Alec to shake. When Alec shook it, he felt the younger man vibrating slightly with excitement. He cast a panicked glance toward Lily, who grinned and mouthed "cute" at him.

"This is Lily, who is no help," said Alec.

"Oh yes, oh, pleased to meet you, too," said Joaquín. "Wow, come in."

Lily smiled sweetly, showing her fangs. "I can't."

"Oh, right! I'm sorry. I'll show you around to the back entrance. There's a door to the Sanctuary there."

Magnus had enchanted the New York Institute so Downworlders could walk in certain places there, but most Institutes still kept them out of all but the Sanctuary rooms. Alec was pleased to see Joaquín flash a smile at Lily that seemed genuine and welcoming.

"Thanks," said Alec. "We're meeting friends on a mission, but I hoped we could stow our bags now so we can come back to sleep later. We can set up cots in the Sanctuary."

Joaquín led them down a dark cobwebbed alley. Alec thought of the wing that was rubble. Possibly this Institute wouldn't have cots.

"Um, will your friend—will she need a coffin?" asked Joaquín. "I don't think we have coffins. I mean, I'm sure I could find one somewhere! The head of our Institute is, um, very careful about visitors, but I'm certain he can't object to a guest who is coming with Alec Lightwood."

"I don't need a coffin," said Lily. "Just a windowless room. It's no problem."

"You can address her when you're talking about her," said Alec mildly.

Joaquín cast an anxious look at Alec, then an even more anxious look at Lily. "Of course! I'm sorry. I don't have much experience talking to—"

"Vampires?" asked Lily sweetly.

"Women," said Joaquín.

"It's true I'm five fabulous feet of pure woman," Lily mused.

Joaquín coughed. "Well, I don't know any vampires, either. My mother died in the Dark War. A lot of us did. And afterward, most of the women left. Mr. Breakspear says that women aren't suited to the rigor of a tightly run Institute."

He peered anxiously at Alec, as if checking in on Alec's opinion on this.

"Clary Fairchild is one of the heads of my Institute," said Alec curtly. "Jia Penhallow is the leader of all Shadowhunters. Anyone who says women are weak is afraid they're too strong."

Joaquín nodded several times in rapid succession, though Alec wasn't sure if it was agreement or pure nerves.

"I haven't been to any other Institutes. I was born in the Institute when it was located in the city of Buenos Aires, near the Casa Rosada."

"I was wondering why the Buenos Aires Institute was here, and not in the city," said Alec.

"Our old Institute was leveled in the Dark War," Joaquín explained. "Not many of us got out, and we took refuge in the nearest remaining Institute. Together, we were able to defend this place, though you can see the building was damaged by the Endarkened. I still remember the old Institute, and its red arched roof against the blue sky, how beautiful it was, when my parents were alive and the world was different. Now this is the only Institute Buenos Aires has. We used to talk about going back, but . . . we don't anymore. The head of our Institute says we're not ready and corruption is everywhere, but I still want to try. When I turned eighteen, I was hoping I could go to another Institute on my travel year and see how other Institutes worked, maybe even meet a girl, but the head of our Institute said I couldn't be spared. Not when the Downworlders in our Shadow Market are so dangerous."

Joaquín hung his head. Alec was trying to phrase a question that wouldn't shock the boy further, about why this was such a harsh posting. About what exactly was going on with the Buenos Aires Institute. But before he could, they reached the end of the alley and passed through the battered door to the Sanctuary of the Institute. Inside it looked like a church that had suffered a blast, the long windows boarded up, the floor blackened.

There was a man in the center of the charred floor, holding forth to a group of silent Shadowhunter men. He looked about forty, his fair hair already turning silver, and he was the only one in the room wearing gear that was not patched or worn.

"That's Clive Breakspear, the head of our Institute," said Joaquín. "Sir, we have a visitor. It's Alexander Lightwood."

He said something in Spanish, which judging by the repetition of Alec's name, Alec thought was the same thing, then glanced around as if expecting an enthusiastic response. He didn't receive one. Several of the men in the circle seemed immediately wary.

Clive Breakspear did not look wary at all.

"So you're Alec Lightwood," said the head of the Buenos Aires Institute slowly. "Then this must be your Downworlder whore."

There was a terrible silence.

It was broken by Lily, who blinked and said, "Excuse me? Have you been living in a hole? Are you not aware Alec is dating famous warlock Magnus Bane and is not interested in ladies of any persuasion?"

There was a rush of whispers. Alec didn't think everyone was stunned by this information. They were stunned that Lily would say it, as if they expected him to be ashamed.

"Let's be clear on this matter. This is my friend Lily, the head of the New York vampire clan." Alec put his hand on his seraph blade, and the whispers hushed. "Think very carefully," said Alec, "about how you wish to speak of her. Or of Magnus Bane."

He almost said "my fiancé," but it was an awkward word. Once he'd said "my betrothed" and felt like a total idiot. He longed sometimes, with an almost physical ache, just to say "my husband" and have it be true.

"I'm here on a mission," Alec continued. "I thought I could rely on the hospitality of the Institute and my fellow Shadowhunters. I see I was wrong."

He cast a look around the room. Several of the men could not meet his eyes.

"What mission?" demanded Clive Breakspear.

"One that requires discretion."

Alec regarded him steadily, until Clive Breakspear flushed and looked away.

"You can stay here," he agreed grudgingly. "The Downworlder cannot."

"Like I want to," Lily sneered. "I don't stay in places where the decor isn't ten out of ten, and this place is a minus fourteen thousand. Okay, Alec, let's make a plan for where we will meet up after I find a nice windowless hotel room. Do you want to—"

"What are you talking about?" Alec demanded. "If they won't have you, I won't stay here. To hell with this place. I'm going with you."

Lily's face went soft, for the space of time it took to blink. Then she patted his arm and said, "Of course you are."

She sniffed disdainfully and spun on her heel. Clive Breakspear barreled toward her.

"I have some questions for you, Downworlder."

Alec caught his arm and stepped in front of Lily. "Are you sure about that?"

They were outnumbered, but Alec was the Inquisitor's son, Jace Herondale's *parabatai*. He was protected in a way many others were not. That meant he had to use whatever he had, for those who had no protection.

After a long moment, Breakspear stepped back.

Alec wished he could've thought of a really scathing exit line, but those weren't his specialty. He and Lily just left, Joaquín chasing after them.

"By the Angel," Joaquín said. "I didn't expect that—I didn't think—I'm so sorry."

"It's not the first Institute I haven't been welcome in," said Alec.

Especially if he was with Magnus. It didn't happen often, but a couple of Institutes before now had tried to separate them or suggested that they shouldn't have come together. Alec always made clear what he thought of that.

"I'm so sorry," Joaquín repeated helplessly.

Alec nodded to him; then Alec and Lily went out into the night. Alec stood with the blasted building at their backs and breathed in one long, deep breath.

"Shadowhunters are trash," Lily announced.

Alec gave her a look.

"Present company excepted. And Jem," said Lily. "I'm having a terrible time in Buenos Aires, and I don't eat, but I'm in the mood for a delicious bowl of Jembalaya."

"He's married!" Alec pointed out once again.

"Please stop reminding me. She smells like books. I may be immortal, but life is too short to spend reading." Lily paused for an instant, then added quietly, "Raphael liked her. She and Ragnor Fell and Raphael used to have little meetings and tell each other secrets."

Alec understood the tension in her voice now. Lily was slightly wary of Magnus too, of anyone not in her clan whom she thought Raphael Santiago might have loved.

"I told Jem we'd meet him outside the Shadow Market," said Alec, effectively distracting Lily. "We can just carry our bags until we find a place to stay. For now let's see about this place that has the Buenos Aires Institute running scared, where only I can go."

Alec went to the New York Shadow Market on Canal Street with Magnus and Max often, but the first time at a new Shadow Market as a Shadowhunter could be tricky.

The Buenos Aires Shadow Market looked more than tricky. Barbed wire was hung on every plank. The smooth sun-bleached wood and snarled loops of barbed wire were an impenetrable stretch of silver. There was a large metal door in front of them, more suited to a prison than a market, and a werewolf's eyes shone behind a metal grille. He snapped something at them.

"He said 'No Shadowhunters,'" Lily interpreted cheerfully.

There was a line of Downworlders behind them, staring and murmuring. Alec felt a shadow of the old discomfort at being the focus of attention, and a sudden doubt about the information Jem had provided.

"I'm Alec Lightwood," he said. "I hear that I'm allowed in."

There was a stir behind his back, a brief silence, and then a rush of different-sounding whispers, like listening to a tide turn.

"You could just be another lying Nephilim," the werewolf snarled, switching to English. "Can you *prove* you're Alec Lightwood?"

Alec said, "I can."

He took his hands out of his pockets and held up the right one to the grille so the werewolf could see it plainly: scarred skin, calluses from his bow, the dark lines of his Voyance rune, and moonlight striking and holding on the bright band of his family ring with its etched pattern of flames.

Another set of eyes appeared at the grille, this pair a faerie's, pupil-less and green as woodland lakes fathoms deep. She said something soft in Spanish.

"She says the magic in your ring is very strong," Lily reported at his shoulder. "Too strong. She says that kind of power comes from the very heart of Hell."

Alec knew that was true. There was not only one charm in this ring but spell after spell: magic for protection and deflection, magic to guide his arrows and blades, all the power at Magnus's command poured into the metal. There was everything Magnus had been able to think of, to act as Alec's armor and ensure Alec would return home safe to him. Most important, there was the look on Magnus's face when he returned the ring, now symbolizing Alec's family in two ways, to Alec. That was when Magnus had assured him that he believed they would be married one day.

"I know where this kind of power comes from." Alec raised his voice so that the whole murmuring crowd could hear. "I'm

Alec Lightwood. Magnus Bane wove this enchantment for me."

The werewolf guard held open the door to the Shadow Market.

Alec and Lily walked into a barbed-wire tunnel. Alec could hear the sounds and glimpse the lights of a Market, but the tunnel split off in two directions. The guard took them to the left, away from light and sound, into a shed lined with wards and metal. The room was lit by a single lantern that hung from the ceiling. Broken weapons were fixed on the walls, and there was a roughly hewn circular platform in the center of the room, and on that platform a huge chair. There were crossed axes on the back of that chair, and a row of glittering spikes ran along the top. A slender faerie girl, with a crown of thorns and a wistful face, was sitting cross-legged at the foot of the throne.

Upon the throne was a young woman who looked about Alec's age. She was wearing jeans and a flannel shirt, her legs swung carelessly over the throne's arm, the row of spikes glinting above her light hair. This must be the woman Jem had written about, the werewolf Queen of the Market.

She saw Alec and her face went blank. Then she started to smile and said in English but with a distinct French accent, "Alec! It's really you. I can't believe it!"

This was very awkward.

"Sorry," said Alec. "Have we met?"

The werewolf swung her legs to the floor, leaning forward. "I'm Juliette."

"I'm not Romeo," said Lily. "But you are cute, so tell us more about yourself in your sexy accent."

"Um, who are you?" asked Juliette.

"Lily Chen," said Lily.

"Head of the New York vampire clan," added Alec.

"Oh, of course," said Juliette. "From the Alliance! Thank you for coming with Alec to help us. It's a real privilege to meet you."

Lily beamed. "I know, right?"

Juliette's eyes went back to Alec. The way she was looking at him, wide-eyed and startled, did ring a faint bell.

"And this is my daughter Rose," said Juliette the werewolf, her hands firm on the young faerie's shoulders.

Alec didn't recognize the woman, but he recognized that tone of voice. He knew how it was to lay claim to what you loved, all the more insistently because people doubted the love that belonged to you. Alec wasn't sure what to say, so he did one of his favorite things. He produced his phone and found a really good picture, walked up to the dais, and showed it to them both.

"This is my son, Max."

Juliette and Rose leaned forward. Alec saw the werewolf's eyes flicker, saw the moment where it registered with Juliette that Max was a warlock.

"Oh." Juliette's voice was soft. "He's beautiful."

"I think so," said Alec shyly, and showed them a few more pictures. Alec found it difficult to select the best pictures. So many of them were great. It was hard to take a bad picture of Max.

Juliette gave the adolescent faerie a push between the shoulder blades.

"Go get your brother and sister," she urged. "Quick."

Rose sprang to her feet, faerie light, cast a shy sidelong glance at Alec, and ran out.

"You know me," said Alec. "How?"

"You saved my life," Juliette said. "Five years ago, when

demons attacked the Orient Express."

"Oh," said Alec.

His and Magnus's first vacation. He tried not to think of the less pleasant aspects of that trip, but he remembered the train, the warm falling water and the shine of demons' eyes, the screaming wind and the abyss below. He'd been terrified for Magnus that night.

"You fought demons on the Orient Express?" Lily asked with interest.

"I fight demons in lots of places," said Alec. "It was all very normal."

"I'd never seen anything like it in my life," Juliette told Lily enthusiastically. "There were so many demons! They broke the windows. I thought I was about to be killed. Then Alec took out every demon he saw. He was soaking wet, and he wasn't wearing a shirt."

Alec didn't see how that was relevant.

"Very normal," he repeated. "Except normally I wear a shirt."

Lily's eyes were dancing with glee. "What a wild time you seem to have on holiday, Alec."

"I had a totally standard and boring time," Alec told her.

"Sounds like it."

"And I was at that party in Venice," Juliette continued. "When the mansion collapsed."

"I was there too!" said Lily. "Raphael was super sad to be at a party; it was hilarious. I made out with so many people, it was a personal record. I think one of them was a hot blonde! Was it you?"

Juliette blinked. "Er, no. I don't really . . . make out with girls."

Lily shrugged. "Sorry you're wasting your life."

"I don't either," Alec commented mildly.

Juliette nodded. "I remember Magnus at that party too. He was trying to help."

Alec heard his own voice go low and tender, entirely out of his control. "He always does."

There was a clatter of feet behind them. Rose the faerie girl had returned. There were two more kids hand in hand with her now, another faerie girl with the sturdy build of a goblin and a dark-skinned warlock boy with a fox tail. They ran up to the chair and clustered about Juliette. The girl looked about ten, and the boy no more than six.

"Kids," said Juliette, "this is Alec Lightwood, whom I've told you about. Alec, these are my kids."

"Hi," said Alec.

The kids stared.

"When you saved me on the Orient Express," said Juliette, "I asked how I could repay you, and you said you'd seen a faerie child alone in the Paris Shadow Market. You asked me if I could look out for her. I'd never spoken to a Shadowhunter before. I didn't think they were like you. I was—surprised you asked me that. So when I got back to Paris, I went looking for her. My Rosey and I have been together ever since."

She ruffled Rose's wispy hair around her crown of thorns. Rose flushed green.

"*Maman*. Do not embarrass me in front of Alec Lightwood!"

The Paris Shadow Market Alec and Magnus had visited on their first vacation together had been Alec's first Market ever. The Downworlders hadn't been used to him then, and he hadn't been used to them. He did recall the faerie child he'd seen there:

how skinny she'd been, and how sorry he'd been for her.

She'd been about the same age as his baby brother, whom Max was named for. Unlike his brother, she had lived to be older.

"Rose," Alec said. "How grown up you are now."

Rose beamed.

"We were happy together in Paris, you and I, weren't we, *ma petite?*" Juliette asked Rose, sounding wistful. "I thought the end of the war with Valentine would be an end to all wars. But then there was another war, and so many Shadowhunters died, and so many faeries, too. And the Cold Peace began."

She fixed her eyes on Alec. The light from the lantern above the throne caught her eyes, like headlights catching the eyes of a wolf.

"I heard about you and Magnus, and the Downworlder-Shadowhunter Alliance you set up. You were both helping people. I wanted to do that too. I heard about people hunting faeries in Belgium, and I got my youngest girl out."

Rose's hands closed on the goblin girl's shoulders. Alec recognized that gesture too: the constant worry of the oldest in the family, the knowledge that you were responsible for the younger ones.

"Then I heard about Buenos Aires," said Juliette. "The Institute in the city was crushed in the Dark War. Most of the Downworlders fled the city before the Institute fell. The Downworlders of the Shadow Market ran here, and for a time cooperated with the surviving Shadowhunters, but then the Clave sent a new leader to the Institute. Breakspear was supposed to help, but Shadow Markets in Europe began to hear dark rumors. I came to see if there was anything I could do. At the time, I thought we could work with the Shadowhunters, rebuild the Institute in the city of Buenos Aires, and make sure the Shadow Market could return safely. It didn't work out that way. I've lost all hope for the Shadowhunters of this Institute."

The little boy lifted his arms to her, and Juliette picked him up, cuddling him on her knee. The boy watched Alec, sucking thoughtfully on the tip of his fox tail.

"There were a lot of children orphaned in the war," said Juliette. "The Shadow Market here became a refuge for unwanted children. A haphazard kind of orphanage, among the stalls and lights and magic. The Market became a community, because we needed one, a Market that never ceased. People live inside these walls. My baby was left here, because he manifested his warlock mark so young."

"So did Max," said Alec.

"There are so many kids." Juliette closed her eyes.

"What's wrong with this Institute?" Alec asked. "Why hasn't someone reached out to the Clave?"

"We did," Juliette returned. "It was useless. Breakspear has powerful friends. He made sure the message went right to a man called Horace Dearborn. Do you know him?"

Alec's eyes narrowed. "I know him."

The aftereffects of too many wars and the constant pressure of the Cold Peace provided opportunities for a certain kind of person. Horace Dearborn was one of the type who flourished on unrest and fear.

"After the Institute was destroyed by the Endarkened," said Juliette, "Clive Breakspear arrived here with that man Dearborn's name behind him, like a vulture glutting himself on the remains. The word is, his Shadowhunters take missions for money. Like—if someone wanted a rival dead, Breakspear's

Shadowhunters would see it done. They don't hunt demons. They don't hunt Downworlders who break the Law. They hunt us all."

Alec's stomach turned. "They're mercenaries."

"The decent Shadowhunters left, when they couldn't make any difference to the way things were done," said Juliette. "I don't think they talked. I think they were ashamed. This Market, with all the kids in it—the Market wasn't safe. It seemed like the leaders were being picked off, so people would be more vulnerable. They didn't try for me. I've got friends in Paris and in Brussels who would raise a howl if I disappeared. So I ordered wards and fences put up. I let people call me a queen. I tried to seem as strong as I could, so they wouldn't come at us. But things are getting worse, not better. Female werewolves are disappearing."

"Killed?" asked Alec.

"I don't know," said Juliette. "We thought they were running at first, but there are too many. Mothers who wouldn't have left their families. Girls as young as my Rosey. Some people say they've seen a strange warlock about. I have no idea what's happening to those women, but I knew I couldn't trust anyone at the Institute to find out. I won't risk trusting any Shadowhunter. Except you. I put out the word I wanted you. I wasn't sure you would come, but here you are."

She lifted her face imploringly to Alec's. The Queen of the Shadow Market looked, in that moment, as young as the kids clustered around her.

"Will you help me? One more time?"

"As many times as you need me," said Alec. "I'll find those women. I'll find out who's doing this. I'll stop them. You have my word."

He hesitated, remembering Jem and Tessa's mission.

"I have friends here, besides Lily. A warlock woman and a man who used to be a Silent Brother, with a white streak in his hair. Can they enter the Market? I swear to you they can be trusted."

"I think I know who you mean," Juliette said. "They were asking for admittance a few nights back, weren't they? I heard the man was handsome."

"Boy, did you hear right," said Lily.

Juliette's smile spread. "There really are some very handsome Nephilim around."

"Uh, I guess," said Alec. "I don't really think about Jem that way."

"How can you be good at archery, when you're so blind?" Lily demanded.

Alec rolled his eyes. "Thanks, Juliette. I'll let you know as soon as I find something out."

Juliette said softly, "I'm glad you're here."

"I won't leave until I've helped you," said Alec, then glanced at the kids, who were still staring. "Um. Bye, kids. It was very nice to meet you."

He nodded to them awkwardly, then made his way back toward the lights and music of the Market.

"Okay," he told Lily as they walked. "Let's take a quick look around the Market, ask some questions before we meet Jem and Tessa."

"Let's drop by the faerie fruit gin stall!" Lily suggested.

Alec said, "No."

"We can't be all business all the time," said Lily, who was seldom all business for five minutes. "So, who do you think is hot?" When Alec stared at her, she said, "We're on a bro road trip! We're meant to share secrets. You said not Jem. So who?"

Alec shook his head at a faerie trying to sell them charmed bracelets, though she insisted they were real charms and really charming. When Alec asked about the disappearances, the faerie's eyes widened, but she didn't know any more than Juliette.

"Magnus is hot," Alec said finally, as they went on their way.

Lily rolled her eyes. "Wow, you and Monogamous Bane make me tired. He's even dumber than you are."

"He's not dumb."

"An immortal who sets his soft heart on one person?" Lily bit her lip, fangs pressing down too hard. "That's dumb."

"Lily," said Alec, but Lily was shaking her head and proceeding, her voice firmly light.

"Leaving aside your destined honey lamb and all, I know there was Jace. Is it just guys with golden eyes?" asked Lily. "That is a very particular taste you have there, friend. It really narrows the playing field. So no other crushes besides Jace? Even a teeny tiny one when you were young?"

"Why are you leering like you know something I don't?" Alec asked warily.

Lily giggled.

There was a lot of noise happening behind one of the stalls. Alec turned his head toward it automatically, but also because he didn't know how to explain that specific crushes hadn't been the problem. It had been a relief, in a way, to pretend even to himself that a crush on Jace was the thing that was making him miserable.

Even when he was a kid, he'd found his attention caught by posters of mundane men in the streets of New York, or found himself drawn to guys visiting the Institute, listening from behind his vase to their stories of demon-hunting and thinking they were cool. He'd had unfocused childish daydreams, created hazy bright dreamlands featuring boys, and then he'd lost the dream with his childhood. He'd been too young to understand himself, and then he hadn't been. He heard the way Shadowhunter visitors sneered, how his dad hinted at the subject as if it were too awful even to be said outright, when saying things outright was the only way Alec knew how to say them. Alec felt guilty every time he had to pull his eyes off another boy, even just a curious look, and then there had been Magnus, and he hadn't been able to look away from him at all.

The noise from behind the stall was growing closer.

A lot of noise, very close to the ground.

The orphans of the Buenos Aires Shadow Market exploded from behind a stall where a werewolf was selling stew. There were kids everywhere, Downworlders of every kind, and all of them seemed to be trying to get his attention, shouting out names, requests, jokes. The main language was Spanish, but Alec heard a few others, and was immediately confused about which words belonged to which language. Multicolored lights swung on dozens of faces. He turned his head, overwhelmed, not able to make out any face or voice in the chaos.

"Hey," he said, stooping over the kids and pulling food out of his duffel bag. "Hey, is anybody hungry? Take these."

"Gross, are those energy bars?" Lily demanded. "Way to pile misery on orphans!"

Alec took out his wallet and began to give the kids money. Magnus was always magically making cash appear there, in case of emergencies. Alec wouldn't spend it on himself.

Lily was laughing. She liked kids, though sometimes she

pretended she didn't. Then she froze. For a moment her bright black eyes went flat and dead. Alec stood up straight.

"You, kid." Lily's voice was trembling. "What did you say your name was?"

She shook her head and repeated the question in Spanish. Alec followed her line of sight to one particular child in the crowd.

The other children were jostling each other, pressed up against each other and the stalls, but there was a small circle of space around this boy. Now that he had their attention, he wasn't shouting. His curly head was tipped back so he could study them, and he was doing so with narrowed, very dark eyes. His extremely critical air had to be Alec's imagination. The kid looked about six years old.

The boy answered Lily, his voice calm: "Rafael."

"Rafael," Lily whispered. "Right."

Rafael's face was one of the youngest in that crowd of heartbreakingly young faces, but there was a chilling air of self-possession about him. He advanced, and Alec wasn't surprised to see the other kids move out of his path. He carried distance with him.

Alec's own eyes narrowed. He couldn't tell what kind of Downworlder this kid was, but there was something about the way he moved.

Rafael said something else in Spanish. From the imperious tilt at the end of the sentence, it was a question or a demand. Alec looked helplessly at Lily. She nodded, visibly gathering her composure.

"The kid said . . ." She cleared her throat. "He says: 'Are you a Shadowhunter? Not like the ones at the Institute. Are you a *real* Shadowhunter?'"

Alec blinked. Rafael's eyes were fixed on his face.

Alec knelt on the ground amid the bright riot of the Shadow Market, so he could look into those dark intent eyes.

"Yes," said Alec. "I'm a Shadowhunter. Tell me how I can help you."

Lily translated. Rafael shook his curly head, expression even cooler, as if Alec had failed some sort of test. He snapped out several more lines of Spanish.

"He says he doesn't want help," said Lily. "He says he overheard you ask about the women who vanished."

"So the kid can understand some English?" asked Alec, hopeful.

Rafael rolled his eyes and said something else in Spanish.

Lily grinned. "He says no, not at all. He has information, but he doesn't want to talk here."

Alec frowned. *"Boludo,"* he repeated. "He said that. What does that word mean?"

Lily grinned. "It means he thinks you're a nice man!"

It hadn't sounded nice. Alec squinted at Rafael. Rafael gave him a blank stare back.

"All right," Alec said slowly. "Who's taking care of you? Let's go to them, and we can talk together."

The night was dark, especially under the awning of a stall, but Alec was pretty sure Rafael rolled his eyes. He transferred his attention from Alec, whom he clearly found to be hopeless, and looked to Lily.

"He says that he takes care of himself," said Lily.

"But he can't be more than six!" said Alec.

"He says he's five," Lily said, her brows knitted as she listened and translated slowly. "His parents died in the Dark War, when the Institute fell, and then there was a werewolf woman who looked after a bunch of kids. But she's gone now. He says nobody else wants him."

She must be one of the women who disappeared, Alec thought grimly. That thought was lost in the rush of horror when he realized what Lily was saying.

"His parents died when the Institute fell?" Alec repeated. Every cell in his body sparked with shock. *"Is this boy a Shadowhunter?"*

"Would it be worse to find a Shadowhunter child like this?" Lily asked, her voice cold.

"*Yes,*" Alec snarled back. "Not because Downworlder kids deserve this. My kid's a Downworlder. No kid deserves this. But you heard Juliette. Everybody's doing the best they can. Shadowhunters fall in battle every day, and homes are found for orphans. There is a system in place for Shadowhunter children. The Shadowhunters should be doing better than this. The Law is meant to protect the most helpless among us. What is *wrong* with this Institute?"

"As you're using your stern voice, I guess we're going to find out," Lily remarked, sounding chipper again.

Alec was still looking at Rafael with dismay so profound it felt almost like despair. He saw now that Rafael looked dirtier, and less cared for, than any other child in the crowd. Alec had learned the Law at his mother's knee, at his father's, from his tutor and every book in the library at the Institute back home. It had made sense to him when he was young, when very little made sense to him. The Shadowhunters' sacred duty, for all time: to stand unseen against the darkness, to defend at any cost.

Now he was older, and he knew how complicated the world could be. It still hurt like an unexpected blow when he saw that shining ideal tarnished. If he were in charge of it all—

But they didn't live in that world.

"Come with me for now," Alec told the Nephilim child. "I'll take care of you."

If Rafael really was alone, Alec could take Rafael to the New York Institute or to Alicante. He wasn't going to leave him here where he looked so friendless and neglected. He reached out, arms open, to pick Rafael up and carry him away.

Rafael bolted backward with the speed of a wild animal. He gave Alec a filthy look, as if he might bite if Alec tried that again.

Alec drew his arms back and lifted his hands in a gesture of surrender. "All right," he said. "Sorry. But will you come with us? We want to hear your information. We want to help."

Lily translated. Rafael, still watching Alec warily, nodded. Alec rose and offered Rafael his hand. Rafael eyed the hand with disbelief, shaking his head and muttering something. Alec was almost sure it was that word again. He looked Rafael over. The kid's clothes were stained and torn, he was much too thin, and he was barefoot. There were dark circles of exhaustion under his eyes. Alec didn't even know where they were going to sleep.

"Okay," he said at last. "We have to buy him some shoes."

He walked out of the throng of kids, with Lily at his side and Rafael orbiting them like a wary moon.

"Maybe I can help you, Shadowhunter," called out a faerie woman with dandelion hair from a stall.

Alec started forward, then stopped. Lily had caught his arm in a grip like iron.

"Don't go near that woman," she whispered. "I'll explain later."

Alec nodded and went on, despite the call of the faerie

woman to come buy. Juliette had been right: this Market was a community, with huts and wagons surrounding the stalls. It was the biggest Market Alec had ever seen.

Alec found a faerie cobbler who seemed nice enough, though even the smallest pair of boots he had were too big. Alec took them anyway. He asked the cobbler, who spoke English, if anyone was taking care of Rafael. Surely, no matter what the kid said, someone must care.

After a moment the cobbler shook his head. "When the werewolf woman who looked after the orphans vanished, the other kids were given homes by my people. But, no offense meant, faeries won't take in a Shadowhunter."

Not with the Cold Peace breeding hatred between Shadowhunters and faeries. The laws were all wrong, and children were paying the price.

"Also, that child hates everybody," said the faerie cobbler. "Watch out. He bites."

They were almost at the wire tunnel leading to the exit of the Shadow Market now. This far out from the center of the Market there were fallen walls, more signs of a place crushed by war and then left to decay.

"Hey," Alec told Rafael. "Come here a second. *Mach dir keine Sorgen*—"

"You're telling him not to worry in German," Lily reported gleefully.

Alec sighed and knelt in the gray dust, among the rubble, gesturing for Rafael to sit on a piece of the fallen wall. The child eyed Alec and the boots in his hand with an air of extreme mistrust. Then he plunked himself down and let Alec slip his feet into the too-large boots.

The kid's feet were small, his soles black with filth. Alec swallowed, and drew the laces on the boots as tight as he could, so they would stay on and Rafael could walk properly.

Rafael stood as soon as Alec was done tying his laces. Alec stood as well.

"Come on," he said.

Rafael's dark, measuring gaze was on Alec again. He stood perfectly still, for a long moment.

Then he lifted both his arms in a commanding gesture. Alec was so used to that gesture from Max that he moved without even thinking and scooped Rafael up in his arms.

It was nothing like carrying Max, small and plump, always laughing and cuddling. Rafael was much too thin. Alec could feel the knobbly bones of his back. Rafael held himself very stiffly, as though he was undergoing an unpleasant ordeal. It was like holding a small statue, if you felt desperately sorry for the statue and unsure what to do.

"Carrying you means the boots are pointless," murmured Alec. "But that's all right. I'm glad you're coming with us. You're safe now. I have you."

"No te entiendo," said Rafael's small clear voice in his ear, then after a thoughtful pause: *"Boludo."*

Alec was sure of two things: that word was not a nice word, and this kid didn't like him at all.

Jem and Tessa were standing at the gates of the Shadow Market when they saw him. They'd hoped to catch Alec and Lily before they reached the Buenos Aires Institute. Finding no sign of them, they'd worried Breakspear had detained them, but a warlock acquaintance of Tessa's had sent word that a

Shadowhunter had been let into the Market.

Now they were worried the Queen of the Market had detained them. Jem was conferring with Tessa when the gates opened. Against barbed wire and starlight they saw a tall man, his black head bowed and his tender blue eyes fixed on the child in his arms. *Will*, thought Jem, and grasped Tessa's hand tight. Whatever he felt, it was worse for her.

Alec looked up and said, sounding relieved, "Tessa."

"What a handsome end to a long night," Lily said delightedly. "If it isn't the former Brother Snackariah."

"Lily!" Alec exclaimed.

But Tessa, still holding Jem's hand, gave Jem a highly amused look and smiled her gradual, beautiful smile. "It's Raphael's Lily," she said. "How nice to see you. Forgive me, I feel like I know you better than I do. He talked about you often."

Lily's grin fractured as if someone had dropped a mirror.

"What did he say about me?" she asked in a small voice.

"He said you were more efficient and intelligent than most of the clan, who were morons."

It sounded very cold to Jem, but that had been Raphael's way. Lily's smile returned, warm as a flame held between cupped hands. It reminded Jem of the way she'd looked when they first met. He had not known then that Tessa had sent Raphael to him for help. He'd done his best then, and now Lily was a friend.

"Thank you both for coming to help us," said Jem. "Who is the child?"

Alec explained the events of the night—being turned away from the Buenos Aires Institute, learning of the disappearances, and the discovery of Rafael, the child the Institute had abandoned.

"I'm sorry you went to the Institute at all," Jem said. "We should have warned you, but I haven't been a Shadowhunter in a long time. I didn't realize that your first instinct would be to go there. Our lodging house has rooms available, and at least one of them is windowless. Come with us."

Alec carried the child with the ease of long habit. One hand remained free to grab a weapon, and he walked easily through the streets with the small precious weight. Jem, long out of practice, wouldn't have been able to do it himself. He'd held Tessa's children, James and Lucie, when they were little, but that had been more than a century ago. Not many people wanted a Silent Brother close to their child, unless that child was near death.

They walked through the streets, past houses painted in flamboyant hues—flame scarlet, sea blue, crocodile green—the streets lined with jacaranda and olive trees. At last they reached their lodgings, the low whitewashed building turned blue by the first signs of dawn. Jem pushed open the circular red door and requested more rooms from their landlady, one without a window.

Jem and Tessa had already secured the use of the little courtyard at the center of the lodging house, a group of small stone pillars open to the sky, circled with the soft violet-blue of bougainvillea. They gathered there, Alec placing Rafael carefully down on the stone bench beside him. Rafael scooted to the other edge of the bench. He hung his head and was silent when Tessa spoke to him softly in Spanish, asking him for any information about the missing women. Jem hadn't heard about them before, but now that he knew, it was clear they had to help. Rosemary Herondale might be in danger, but so were these werewolf women. Jem wanted to do whatever he could for them.

Returning to speech had been strange for Jem, but Tessa had learned many languages and taught him everything she could. Jem tried asking Rafael too, but Rafael shook his head sullenly.

Lily was sitting cross-legged on the ground, one elbow propped on Alec's knee, to be near the child. She tilted her head toward Rafael and asked him if he would please get on with it, because the sun was rising and she'd have to go to bed soon.

Rafael reached out and patted the bright pink streak in Lily's hair.

"Bonita," he said, face still solemn.

The poor child didn't smile much, Jem thought. Of course, neither did Alec, who was looking miserable and determined about the missing women.

Lily, who smiled very easily, did so now. "Aw, cute baby," she said in Spanish. "Do you want to call me Aunt Lily?"

Rafael shook his head. Lily looked undaunted.

"I have a trick," she offered, and snapped her fangs in Rafael's direction.

Rafael looked absolutely appalled.

"What are you guys saying?" asked Alec worriedly. "Why is he looking like that? Why did you do that?"

"Max loves it when I do that!" said Lily, and added in Spanish, "I didn't mean to scare you."

"Wasn't scared," Rafael responded in Spanish. "That was stupid."

"What did he say?" Alec asked.

"He said that was an awesome trick and he really enjoyed it," Lily reported.

Alec raised a skeptical eyebrow in her direction. Rafael pressed close to Alec. Tessa joined Lily on the ground. Tessa talked to Rafael gently, and Lily teased him, and together they got the full story, Lily translating for Alec as they went. Alec's face went more and more grim as he heard the story.

"Rafael knows he's a Shadowhunter, and he's trying to learn—"

Rafael, who Jem thought understood more English than he was letting on, interrupted to correct Lily.

"Excuse me," Lily said. "He's trying to train. He spies on the other Shadowhunters, so he knows what to do. He's small, and he makes sure they don't see him. While he was spying on them, he saw a Shadowhunter creeping off down a lane. He met a warlock at the door of a big house. Rafael got as close as he could, and he heard women inside."

"Can you describe the Shadowhunter you saw?" asked Alec, and Jem translated for him.

"I think you can do it," Jem added to the child encouragingly. "You see so much."

Rafael gave Jem a dark look, as though he disliked praise. He spent a few more moments in furious thought, kicking his too-big boots over the edge of the stone bench, then reached into the pocket of his tattered trousers and placed a slim wallet in Alec's hands.

"Oh." Alec looked startled. "You stole this from the Shadowhunter you saw?"

Rafael nodded.

"That's great. I mean . . ." Alec paused. "It's good that you're helping us, but it's very bad to steal wallets generally. Don't do it again."

"No te entiendo," Rafael announced firmly.

He said that he didn't understand Alec, and his tone suggested that he wasn't planning to understand Alec on this topic anytime soon.

"Don't say the other word," Alec said quickly.

"What other word?" Jem asked.

"Don't ask," said Alec, and opened the wallet.

Shadowhunters did not carry mundane forms of identification like passports or ID cards, but they carried other things. Alec took out a weapons requisition document marked with the Breakspear family symbol.

"Clive Breakspear," Alec said slowly. "The head of the Institute. Juliette said that these Shadowhunters act as mercenaries. What if this warlock hired them?"

"We have to find out what's happening," said Jem. "And stop it."

Alec set his jaw. "Rafael can show us the house after he gets some rest," he said. "Tomorrow night we'll go back to the Shadow Market. We'll try to find the information you're looking for and tell the Queen of the Market what, if anything, we've discovered."

Rafael nodded, then held his hand out for the wallet. Alec shook his head.

"What is this secret you want to know about?" Lily asked Jem.

"Lily, it's a secret," Alec said reprovingly.

There were crickets chirping in an odd beautiful melody beyond the walls.

"I trust you both," Jem said slowly. "You came here to help

us. I trust this will go no further. I'm looking for someone who needs my help. There's a hidden line of Shadowhunters I became aware of in the 1930s."

Lily shook her head. "The 1930s were such a disappointment. Every year, they insisted on not being the 1920s."

Will had died in the 1930s, and Tessa had been in agony. Jem had not liked the 1930s much either.

"This family has been hunted for decades," said Jem. "I don't know why. I learned how they split off from the Nephilim, but I still didn't know why faeries are hunting them. I met one of them, but she refused my help and ran away. Since then, I have looked for them, and friends I trust have asked discreetly around the Shadow Markets. The year I met you there, Lily, I was searching for Ragnor Fell, to find out what he could tell me. I want to know why they are being hunted, so that I can help them. Whoever their enemies are, they are mine, too."

Because the Carstairs owe the Herondales.

"I asked in the Spiral Labyrinth as well," said Tessa. "There was never any word. Until suddenly we heard that someone was telling stories to the children of this Market, stories of love and revenge and misery. We heard a whisper of the name Herondale."

She said the name that had once been hers very softly. Alec jumped as if someone had shouted it in his ear.

Neither Jem nor Tessa mentioned Catarina Loss, who had carried the first lost Herondale child over the seas and raised him on strange shores. That wasn't their secret to tell. Jem trusted Alec, but he was still a Shadowhunter, and his father was the Inquisitor. Jem and Tessa were both well aware of the sentence the Law would pass on Catarina for her act of love and mercy.

"I'll ask Juliette," said Alec. "I'll find out whatever I can. I won't go home until I've helped you."

"Thank you," Jem said.

"Now Rafael has to go to bed," said Alec.

"We have a nice little room for you," Tessa told Rafael in Spanish, her voice soft and encouraging. Rafael shook his head. "Do you not want to be alone?" Tessa asked. "That's fine too. You can sleep with me and Jem."

When Tessa reached out her hands, Rafael turned his face into Alec's bicep and screamed. Tessa drew back at the long mutinous howl. Alec automatically put his arm around the child.

"Lily's vulnerable during the day," he said. "I'd rather stay with her. Will you be all right in the windowless room, Rafael?"

Lily translated. Rafael nodded emphatically.

Jem showed them the way. At the door, he caught Alec's arm before he could follow Lily and Rafael.

"I appreciate this," said Jem. "I truly do. Please don't tell Jace yet."

Jem still thought about Jace, that fierce helpless child he'd met on a dark sea, and the young man burning with heavenly fire. He'd imagined a hundred scenarios where he did better by Jace. If he'd been the Silent Brother who cared for Jace after his father left him, if he'd spent more time with Jace, if Jace had been just slightly older, the age Will had been when Jem first met him . . . maybe Jem would have known.

But what could he have done for Jace, even if he had known?

"I don't want Jace to think he has family somewhere he won't get to know," said Jem. "Blood is not love, but it offers a chance for love. He never had the chance to know Céline Montclaire or Stephen Herondale. I don't want him to feel he is missing another chance."

Jace was happy in New York, though Jem had not helped him be so. He had his love and his *parabatai* and his Institute. If Jem couldn't help him, at least he did not want to hurt him.

Jem still thought about Céline Montclaire, too. If he hadn't been a Silent Brother, with his heart turning to stone in his breast, perhaps he would have understood how much trouble she was in. Perhaps he could have found a way to help her.

He didn't call Céline Jace's mother, because Jem had seen how Jace looked at Maryse Lightwood. Maryse was Jace's mother.

Many years ago, when Jem was still a child, his uncle Elias had come to the London Institute and offered to take him away. "After all," he'd said, "we are family."

"You should go," Will had said stormily to Jem. "I don't care."

Will had slammed the door on his way out, declaring he was off on a wild adventure. After Elias departed, Jem had found Will sitting in the dark in the music room, staring at Jem's violin. He'd sat down on the floor beside Will.

"Entreat me not to leave thee, idiot," Jem had said, and Will had put his head down on Jem's shoulder. Jem had felt him trembling with the effort not to laugh or cry, and known Will wanted to do both.

Blood was not love.

But Jem didn't forget that Céline had never had the chance to be Jace's mother. Life was full of broken hearts and missed chances, but Jem could try to redress some of the wrong done Céline by the world. He could do his best for Jace.

Alec was studying Jem intently.

"I won't tell Jace," he said. "Not yet. Not if you tell him soon."

"I hope I will," said Jem.

"Can I ask you something?" said Alec abruptly. "The Buenos Aires Institute is corrupted, and the Cold Peace is fraying our bonds with Downworlders. You could do a lot of good, if you were with us. Why did you stop being a Shadowhunter?"

"I am with you," said Jem. "Do I have to be a Shadowhunter to be that?"

"No," said Alec. "But I don't understand—why you don't want to be one anymore."

"Don't you?" Jem asked. "You have a *parabatai*. Once, so did I. Can you imagine fighting without him?"

Alec was holding on to the doorframe, and as Jem watched, his knuckles went white.

"I have Tessa, so I have more joy every day than some do in their whole lives. Far more than I deserve. I have seen the world with my wife by my side, and we have our tasks to make life meaningful. We all have different ways to serve. She has the secrets from the Spiral Labyrinth, and I those of the Silent Brothers, and we have combined our knowledge and saved lives that I believe couldn't have been saved by any other means. I do want to help, and I will. But not as a Shadowhunter. I will never be that again."

Alec looked at Jem, those blue eyes wide and sorrowful. He looked like Will, but he wasn't Will, any more than Jace was. None of them could ever be Will.

"When you fight, you should fight with your whole heart," said Jem softly. "I don't have the heart for life among the Nephilim, for that particular fight, not any longer. Too much of my heart is in a grave."

"I'm sorry," Alec said awkwardly. "I do understand."

"There's nothing to be sorry for," Jem told him.

He went back to his room, where Tessa was waiting, a book open in her lap. She looked up when he came in, and she smiled. There was no smile like hers in the world.

"Everything all right?" she asked.

He looked down at her and said, "Yes."

Tessa shut her book and reached up to him. She was kneeling on the bed and he was standing beside it, and the world was filled with missed chances and heartbreak, but then there was Tessa.

Tessa kissed him, and he felt her grin against his mouth. "Brother Snackariah," she murmured. "Come here."

The room might be windowless, but there was a brown jar crowded with red flowers on the table, and two white single beds. Lily had tossed her leather jacket onto the bed closest to the wall.

Rafael was sitting on the other bed, turning over a metallic object thoughtfully in his hands. Alec suddenly understood why he had agreed to be carried.

"What's that you have there, sweetie?" Lily asked as Alec came in.

"What he has is my phone," said Alec. "Which he *stole*."

In Rafael's hands, Alec's phone buzzed. Alec reached for it, but Rafael moved casually out of reach. He didn't seem terribly concerned that Alec had grabbed for him. He was staring at the phone.

Alec reached for the phone again, then stopped, caught off guard. As Rafael studied the phone, the sullen line of his mouth twitched, then slowly curved into a smile. The smile, slow and warm and sweet, altered his whole face.

Alec's hand dropped. Rafael turned a suddenly bright countenance up to him and chirped a question. Even his voice sounded different when he was happy.

"I don't understand you," Alec said helplessly.

Rafael waved the phone in Alec's face to illustrate his point. Alec looked at the screen and kept looking. He'd had a sick unsteady feeling in his chest since he realized what the Shadowhunters might be doing here, but the world felt steady again now.

Magnus had sent a photo with the caption BLUEBIRD AND I HOME FROM A WILD AND DANGEROUS MISSION WITH A SWING SET.

Magnus was leaning against their front door. Max was laughing, all dimples, the way he did whenever Magnus did magic to amuse him. There were blue and golden lights streaming all around them, and huge iridescent bubbles that seemed made of light too. Magnus was smiling a small fond smile, the black spikes of his hair wreathed with radiant ribbons of magic.

Alec had asked Magnus to send him pictures whenever he was away, after their first mission when Max was a baby. To remind Alec what he was fighting for.

Lily cleared her throat. "The kid asked: 'Who is that cool man?'"

"Oh," said Alec, kneeling by the bed. "Oh, that's—that's Magnus. His name is Magnus Bane. He's my—I'm his—he and I are going to get married."

One day they would.

Alec wasn't sure why it felt important to tell this child.

Lily translated. Rafael looked from the phone to Alec's face, then back again, his brow furrowed in clear surprise. Alec waited, and listened apprehensively as Rafael said something Alec couldn't understand. He'd heard kids say terrible things before now. Adults poured poison in their minds, and then it came out of their mouths.

Lily laughed.

"He said," she reported with unholy joy, "'What is that cool man doing with you?'"

Alec said, "Rafael, give me back my phone."

"Let him have it for a bit while he goes to sleep," said Lily, who was one of the reasons Max was spoiled.

Alec glanced over and found Lily wearing an unusually serious look.

"Come here to me a minute," she said. "I promised to tell you why I didn't want you to go near that faerie woman at the Shadow Market. I have a story I want you to hear, that I think might help Jem. I don't want to tell anybody but you."

Alec let Rafael keep the phone. In return, Rafael let Alec tuck him into bed. Alec took the chair by the door and placed it by Lily's bed. They waited until Rafael's eyes fell shut, with Alec's phone on the pillow beside him.

Lily studied the striped pillow on her bed as if it were fascinating.

"Are you hungry?" Alec asked at last. "If you—need blood, you can take mine."

Lily glanced up, her face startled. "No. I don't want that. You're not for that."

Alec tried not to show how relieved he was. Lily looked back down at the pillow and squared her shoulders.

"Remember when you asked me if I was a jazz baby, and I said to call me *the* jazz baby?"

"I'm still not going to do that."

"I still think you should," Lily argued. "But that's . . . not what I meant. The 1920s were my favorite decade, but . . . I may have been misleading you about my age." She grinned. "It's a lady's prerogative."

"Okay," Alec said, not sure where this was going. "So—how old are you, then?"

"I was born in 1885," said Lily. "I think. My mother was a Japanese peasant girl, and she was—sold to my father, a rich Chinese merchant."

"Sold!" said Alec. "That's not—"

"It wasn't legal," Lily said in a tight voice. "But it happened. They lived together for a few years, in Hong Kong, where he worked. I was born there. My mother thought my father would take us back home with him. She taught me to speak the way he would want and dress the way he would want, like a Chinese lady. She loved him. He got tired of her. He left, and before he left, he sold us off. I grew up in a place called the House of Eternal Pearl."

She looked up from the pillow.

"I don't have to tell you, do I?" she asked. "What kind of place it was, where women were sold, and men came and went?"

"Lily," Alec breathed, in horror.

Lily shook her black-and-pink head defiantly. "They called it the House of Eternal Pearl because—some men want women to be young and beautiful forever. Pearls are created from a center of dirt that can't be washed away. In the cellar without windows, in the heart of that house, were chained women.

Those women were cold and lovely forever. They would never age and would do anything for blood. They were for the richest men, they fetched the highest prices, and they had to be fed. My mother grew too old, so they fed her to the vampires. And that night, I crept down and I made a deal with one of them. I promised if she Turned me, I'd free us all. She kept her side of the bargain, but I didn't keep mine." Lily studied the toes of her pointed boots. "I woke up and killed a lot of people. I don't mean that I drank from somebody, though I did that, too. I burned the place to the ground. Nobody got out, not the men, not the women. Nobody but me. I didn't care about anybody but myself."

Alec moved his chair closer to her, but Lily drew her legs up onto the bed, making herself as small as possible.

"Nobody knows all that," she said. "A few people know a little. Magnus knows I wasn't made in the 1920s, but he could tell that I didn't want to say. He never asked for any of my secrets."

"No," said Alec. "He wouldn't."

Magnus knew all about painful secrets. Alec had learned.

"Raphael bribed somebody to find out," said Lily. "I don't know who, or how much he paid. He could have asked me, but he wasn't like that. I only knew that he knew because he was sweet to me for a few nights. In his way. We never talked about it. I've never told anybody. Not until you."

"I won't tell anybody," Alec promised.

The corner of Lily's mouth lifted. "I know you won't, Alec."

Some of the tension went out of her thin shoulders.

"I told you so you'd understand what happened next," she said. "I couldn't stay in Hong Kong. I came to London, I think it was 1903, and I met Shadowhunters for the first time."

"Shadowhunters!" said Alec.

He understood why Downworlders said the word with fear sometimes. Already he couldn't bear what had happened to Lily. He didn't want to hear about Shadowhunters doing anything worse to his friend.

But Lily was smiling now, just a little. "I noticed one in particular, a girl with hair the color of blood in shadows. I barely knew what Shadowhunters were, but she was brave and kind. She protected people. Her name was Cordelia Carstairs. I asked around about Shadowhunters. I heard about a faerie woman with a grudge against all Shadowhunters, particularly against one family. We saw her at the Shadow Market tonight. Tell Jem to ask the woman with dandelion hair about the Herondales. She knows something."

Lily fell silent. Alec knew he had to say something, but he didn't know how. "Thanks, Lily," he said at last. "Not for the information. Thanks for telling me."

Lily smiled, as though she didn't think what Alec had said was too dumb. "After London I traveled on and met Camille Belcourt in Russia. Camille was fun. She was bright and heartless and hard to hurt. I wanted to be like her. When Camille traveled to New York and became head of the vampire clan there, I went with her."

Lily bowed her head. After a long moment sunk in memory, she looked up.

"Want to know something dumb? When Camille and I reached New York after the Great War," she said brightly, "I looked around for Shadowhunters. Wasn't that stupid? Most Shadowhunters are not like you or Jem or Cordelia. I encountered Nephilim who made it very clear the angelic warriors were not sent to shield a creature like me. I didn't care about anybody, and nobody cared about me, and that was how it was, for decades and decades. It was really fun."

"Was it?" Alec asked.

He kept his voice noncommittal. She sounded so brittle.

"The twenties in New York were the brightest time for both of us, when the whole world seemed as frenzied as we were. Decades later Camille was still trying to replicate them, and so was I, but even I thought Camille went too far sometimes. There was an emptiness in her she was always trying to fill. She'd permit her vampires to do anything. Once, in the 1950s, she let a very old vampire called Louis Karnstein stay at the hotel. He preyed on children. I thought he was disgusting, but I didn't care much. I was very good at not caring by then."

Lily shrugged and laughed. The sound was not convincing.

"Maybe I hoped the Shadowhunters would come, but they didn't. Someone else came instead. A pack of scruffy mundane boys who wanted to defend their streets from the monster. They all died, except one. He always did what he set out to do. He killed the monster. He was my Raphael."

Lily stroked the leather jacket where it lay in a heap on her bed.

"Before he killed the monster, Raphael was made into a vampire himself. Your Magnus came to Raphael's aid, but I didn't. Raphael could have died then, and I would never have even known. I met Raphael later. He came upon a bunch of us feeding in an alley and gave us a terrible lecture. He was so solemn, I thought he was funny. I didn't take him seriously at all. But when he came to live at the hotel, I was pleased. Because hey, it seemed like more fun. Who doesn't want more fun? There was nothing else in the world."

Magnus had told Alec this story, though Magnus had never painted himself as anyone's savior. It was strange to hear it from Lily, and stranger to hear knowing how the story ended.

"Raphael asked for better security at the hotel on his second day of living there. He argued that a pack of mundane kids had been able to break in and kill one of our own. Camille laughed at him. Then we were attacked by a rogue band of werewolves, and Raphael's security measures were put in place. Guards were posted, and Raphael always took his turn guarding the hotel, even once he was second in command and didn't have to. He took the first watch, on the first day and night. I remember him showing me plans of the hotel, every weak point, the ways he'd figured out how to best defend ourselves. He had it all worked out, though he'd been with us less than a week. He left to take up his post, and as he went he said, 'Sleep, Lily. I'll watch the doors.' I never slept peacefully before then. I didn't know how to rest and trust I was safe. I slept that day as I'd never slept before."

Lily stared at the vase of flowers, bright red as vampire blood. Alec didn't think she was seeing them.

"Later it turned out that Raphael hired the werewolves to attack us so that we would implement the safety precautions he wanted," Lily added in pragmatic tones. "He was extremely set on having his own way. Also, he was a total asshat."

"That is clear to me," said Alec.

Lily laughed again. She got up from the bed, gripping Alec's shoulder for a moment as she passed, then she began to pace the little room as if it were a cage.

"Raphael was always there, from then on. Camille would demote him from being second in command now and then, to annoy him. It didn't matter. He never wavered, no matter what anyone else did. I thought he'd be there forever. Then he was taken. I told myself I had to hold it together, form an alliance with the werewolves, hold the line against madness. Just until Raphael came back. Only Raphael never came back."

Lily drew a hand over her eyes. She went to Rafael's bedside, passing her tearstained hand lightly over his curly hair.

"Well," she said. "I was happy for fifty-four years. That's more than most people get. Now there's the clan to look after, like Raphael would've wanted. The night we knew he was gone, and every night since, I watch my vampires in the home he guarded. I watch the mundanes in the streets he loved. Every one of them looks like a child I should help, a possibility for a future I wasn't able to imagine. Every one of them seems precious, worth defending, worth the world. Every one of them is Raphael."

The child stirred, as if he were being called. Lily pulled her hand away.

It was day, after a long night.

Alec rose and guided her, a hand on her trembling shoulder, to the bed. He pulled a sheet over her as if she were Rafael. Then he positioned the chair between Lily and Rafael and the entrance, and took his place there.

"Sleep, Lily," Alec said gently. "I'll watch the doors."

Alec didn't rest well. His mind was churning with thoughts of Lily's story, the Buenos Aires Institute's corruption, lost Herondales and werewolves, and Jem and Tessa's quest.

He was used to waking up in dark silk sheets and strong arms. He missed home.

Rafael slept in, not stirring until afternoon. Alec suspected that the orphans of the Shadow Market had all developed nocturnal tendencies. When Rafael woke, Alec took him out to the courtyard, where he sat on the stone bench moodily eating an energy bar. Alec thought he was sulking because Alec had taken back his phone.

"Has anyone ever given you a nickname?" he asked Rafael. "Do people ever call you Rafe?"

Rafael gave him a blank look. Alec worried he hadn't conveyed his meaning.

"Rafa," Rafael said finally.

He finished one energy bar and held his hand out for another. Alec gave it to him.

"Rafa?" Alec tried. "Do you want me to call you that? Are you getting any of this? I'm sorry I can't speak Spanish."

Rafael made a face, as if to say what he thought of being called Rafa.

"Okay," said Alec. "I won't call you that. Just Rafael, then?"

The boy gave Alec a massively unimpressed look. *Here this fool goes again,* his air suggested, *talking to me when I cannot understand him.*

Jem and Tessa joined them in the courtyard, ready for Rafael to lead them to the house he'd seen.

"I'll stay and guard Lily," said Tessa, reading Alec's mind. "Don't worry about her. I have wards up, and even if somebody came, I've got it covered."

She made a tiny gesture. Gray glowing magic, like the shine of light on river water or the sheen of pearls in shadow, twined about her fingers. Alec smiled his gratitude at Tessa. Until he was sure about what was happening with this warlock and these Shadowhunters, he didn't want anybody undefended.

"Don't you worry about me, either," Tessa told Jem, settling her magic-bright fingers into his black-and-white hair, drawing him down for a good-bye kiss.

"I won't," Jem told her. "I know my wife can take care of herself."

My wife, Jem said, his voice sounding casual and delighted in that mutual possession: the bargain made between them in the sight of everyone they loved.

Alec had heard a poem read at weddings: *My true love has my heart, and I have his. Never was a fairer bargain made.* Love that was permanent in the eyes of all the world, demanding respect, blazoning the certain knowledge Alec had when he woke every morning. Nobody else for me, until the day I die: having everyone else know that. Jem and Tessa had that, as Helen and Aline had it. But a Shadowhunter couldn't marry a Downworlder in gold. A Shadowhunter was forbidden to wear the wedding rune for a Downworlder, and he wouldn't insult Magnus with a ceremony the Nephilim saw as lesser. He and Magnus had agreed to wait until the Law was changed.

Alec couldn't help the tiny sting of jealousy.

His phone buzzed in his pocket, and Rafael perked up. Magnus had sent Alec a picture of Max sleeping, using Chairman Meow as his pillow. Rafael glared, obviously disappointed Magnus was not in the picture.

Alec was slightly disappointed about that himself.

The afternoon was hot, the streets mostly deserted. The house where the warlock lived was down several winding streets, some cobbled and some dirt. Most of the houses on the curving roads were small, painted bright yellow or brick red or snowy white, but the warlock's house that Rafael pointed out was a huge gray building on the end of a street. A figure was approaching the door—a Shadowhunter. Alec and Jem exchanged a grim look. Alec recognized him as one of Breakspear's men from the Institute. He pulled Jem and Rafael into an alleyway.

"Stay with Jem a minute," he told Rafael, and tossed a grappling hook to the roof of a neighboring house.

Alec climbed up and made his way across the sloping terracotta tile until he was across from the gray building. There were bars on the windows, and the enchantments Magnus had put on his ring allowed him to sense wards with enormous accuracy. The place was heavily warded. Alec crouched down behind a chimney and swiftly drew runes for Clarity and Awareness on his arms.

With increased ability, he could hear noises from behind those walls. There were a lot of people in that house. Shuffling feet, muffled conversation. Alec was able to pick out a few distinct words.

". . . next delivery from Breakspear will be at midnight tonight . . ."

He heard another noise, much closer up, and twisted to see Rafael and Jem coming toward him across the roof.

Jem offered a small rueful smile. "He slipped away from me and climbed a drainpipe."

Jem was hovering at Rafael's back, obviously nervous about touching him. Alec saw how Rafael had managed to slip away.

"Can you sense those wards?" Alec asked, and Jem nodded. Alec knew Tessa had taught him ways to use and discern magic, even though Jem no longer had all the power of a Silent Brother or a Shadowhunter. "Can Tessa handle them?"

"Tessa can handle anything," Jem said proudly.

"I said to stay down there with Jem," Alec told Rafael.

Rafael gave him a look that was at once uncomprehending and insulting, and then his big boots slipped on the ridged terra-cotta tiles. Jem caught him before he hit the tile, and set him upright. If Rafael kept walking like this, he was going to skin his knees.

"You have to walk differently on roofs," Alec told him. He took Rafael's hands in his, showing him how. "Like this, because they slope. Do it like me."

It was oddly nice, to teach a child these things. He'd had all sorts of plans to teach his little brother, when he got older, but his baby brother hadn't lived to be older.

"When will you give your parents a real grandchild?" he'd heard Irina Cartwright ask Isabelle after a Clave meeting.

"By the Angel," said Isabelle. "Is Max imaginary?"

Irina paused, then laughed. "A Shadowhunter child, to teach our ways. Nobody would give those people a Shadowhunter child. Imagine a warlock around one of our little ones! And that kind of behavior. Children are so impressionable. It wouldn't be right."

Isabelle went for her whip. Alec dragged his sister back.

"You Lightwood kids are out of control and out of your minds," muttered Irina.

Jace had appeared beside Alec and Isabelle, and given Irina a radiant smile. "Yes, we are."

Alec had told himself that it was all right. It was a comfort, sometimes, when he was most worried about his friends, to consider that both Magnus and Max were warlocks. They didn't have to fight demons.

Rafael mimicked how Alec was walking with careful precision. He was going to be good one day, Alec thought. Whoever got to raise him would be proud.

"Well done, Rafe," he said. He hadn't meant the nickname to come out: it just had, but Rafael glanced at him and smiled. They fell silent, crouching down as the Shadowhunter departed the warlock's house. Jem raised his eyebrows at Alec, who shook his head.

Once the man was gone, they helped Rafe down from the roof.

"I wonder how far the corruption goes in this Institute," Jem said soberly.

"We'll know soon enough," Alec said. "I heard that mercenary say 'the next delivery from Breakspear will be at midnight tonight.' If he's delivering women, we need to save them and stop the Shadowhunters as well as the warlock. We need to catch them all at once, and there are a lot of people inside. We don't know how many might be prisoners and how many are guards. We need reinforcements, and there's someone I want to talk to about that before we go back to Tessa and Lily. I have to believe not all the Shadowhunters in this city are traitors."

Jem nodded. As they left the alley, Alec described the faerie woman he and Lily had seen, her withered-apple face and dandelion hair. "Lily said she might have information about the family you're searching for."

Jem's expression darkened. "I've encountered her before. I'll know who she is when I see her at the Market. And I will make sure she talks." His face was cold and grim for a moment. Then he glanced toward Alec. "How is Lily?"

"Um." Alec tried to work out if he'd let something slip.

"You're worried for your friend," Jem said. "Perhaps you are more worried for her, because how she feels makes you think of how Magnus will feel, one day." Jem's eyes were as dark as the Silent City, and as sad. "I know."

Alec wouldn't have been able to put any of that into words himself. There was only the nameless shadow on Magnus's face sometimes, the echo of old loneliness, and Alec's yearning to protect him always and knowledge he could not.

"You were nearly immortal. Is there any way to make it—easier?"

"I lived a long time," said Jem, "but I lived in a cage of bones and silence, feeling my heart turn to ashes. I can't explain what it was like."

Alec thought of growing up in the Institute, crushed under the weight of his father's expectations as if they were stones, trying to teach himself not to look, not to speak, not to dare try and be happy.

"Maybe I know," he said. "Not—entirely. Not for a hundred years, obviously. But—maybe a little."

He worried he was presuming, but Jem smiled as if he understood.

"It's different, for my Tessa and your Magnus. They were born what they are, and we love them for it. They live forever in a changing world, and still have the courage to find it beautiful. We all want to shield our best beloved from whatever danger or sorrow comes," he said. "But we have to trust them too. We have to believe that they will have the strength to live on and laugh again. We fear for them, but we should believe in them past fear."

Alec bowed his head and said, "I do."

A block from the Buenos Aires Institute, Alec's phone

buzzed again. Clary had sent him a message.

A few months ago, they'd left Max with Maryse and gone out on the town. Simon's old band was playing at Pandemonium and Simon had agreed to sub in for their missing bass player, as he occasionally did. Alec, Magnus, Jace, Clary, and Isabelle had all gone to listen. Simon's friend Eric had written a song called "My Heart Is an Overripe Melon Bursting for You," and that song was the worst.

Alec didn't like to dance, unless it was with Magnus. Even then, he preferred the music not be terrible. Magnus, Jace, and Isabelle went to dance, the brightest points in the crowd. Alec enjoyed watching Magnus for a while, his chin propped on his hands. Then he grew tired of the assault on his ears. He caught Clary's eye. She was sitting bolt upright in her chair, only wincing occasionally.

"This is fine," Clary told him, nodding bravely.

"This is terrible," said Alec. "Let's go for tacos."

Simon was only just offstage by the time they got back, drinking from a bottle of water and asking everybody what they'd thought of the set.

"You were very sexy up there," Isabelle was saying, sparkling up at Simon, as Alec and Clary arrived.

Simon smiled a crooked smile. "Really?"

Jace said, "No."

"You were so great!" Clary exclaimed, dashing up to Simon. "Wow, I don't know what other word there could be. You were great. The band was great."

Clary was a true and noble *parabatai*, but Simon was a sharp guy and had known her a long time. His eyes traveled from Clary's guilty face to Alec's.

"You went for tacos *again*?" Simon lamented.

Alec grinned. "They were great."

He went over to Magnus, sliding an arm around his waist. Since they were going to a club, Magnus had swept silver glitter under his golden eyes, and he looked like starshine and moonlight.

"I know you were dancing," Alec said in his ear. "But that band was terrible, right?"

"I can dance to anything," Magnus murmured back, "but I have personally heard Mozart play. Also the Sex Pistols in their best days. I can confirm Simon's band is beyond terrible."

Alec's friends were gathered all around him, and his family, and it was one of those moments when he remembered the desperate loneliness of when he was younger, hopelessly torn between fearing for what he might never have and what he might lose. Alec secured his hold on Magnus's waist and felt a small incredulous starburst of happiness in his chest: that he could have all this.

"Tacos again next time?" Alec had whispered as they left, and Clary nodded behind Simon's back.

That was how Alec had come to love her, after resenting her so much at first: in the greatest or smallest of ways, Clary never failed.

She hadn't failed him now. She'd sent a picture saying WE HAVE BEEN IMPRISONED BY THE DREAD PIRATE MAX! Alec suspected this was a joke he didn't understand.

Clary was at an odd angle taking the selfie, but he could see Magnus and Max well enough. Magnus had dashed brilliant blue color through the front of his hair. Max was holding on to Magnus's spiky blue locks and Clary's red curls with one hand each and looking supremely self-satisfied. Magnus was laughing.

"Oh, look," said Alec softly, and showed Rafael the picture.

Rafael snatched the phone, then skipped away to contemplate the photo further.

Alec let him keep it for now. He and Jem stopped at the door of the Buenos Aires Institute. As Alec had hoped, Joaquín was guarding the door again. He greeted Alec happily, then gave the faint scars on Jem's face a startled glance.

"Are you the Silent Brother whom the heavenly fire changed?" he asked eagerly. "The one who—"

"Ran off and married a warlock, yes," said Jem. Somewhere in his quiet voice and his smile, there was an edge of shining defiance.

"I'm sure she's very nice," said Joaquín hastily.

"She is," Alec confirmed.

"I don't know many Downworlders," Joaquín said apologetically. "Though I met Alec's friend yesterday! She also seemed . . . nice. There are a lot of nice Downworlders, I'm sure! Just not in our city. They say the Queen of the Shadow Market is a terrifying tyrant."

Alec thought of Juliette with her kids gathered around her. "I didn't think so."

Joaquín looked at him with wide eyes. "I bet you're not afraid of anything, though."

"Some things," said Alec. "Failing. You know there's something wrong with your Institute, don't you? I want to believe you're not part of it, but you have to know something is very wrong."

Joaquín avoided Alec's gaze, and as he did he caught sight of Rafael for the first time. Rafael was hanging back, clutching Alec's phone.

"That's little Rafael," said Joaquín.

Rafael blinked up at him and corrected, in his small stern voice: "Rafe."

"You know him?" asked Alec. "Then you knew there was a Shadowhunter child living in the Shadow Market. It's the duty of Nephilim to care for war orphans."

"I—" Joaquín faltered. "I tried. But he won't let anyone near him. It was like he didn't want to be helped."

"Everyone wants to be helped," said Alec.

Joaquín was already kneeling down, offering Rafael a brightly wrapped piece of candy. Rafe eyed him, then came cautiously forward, snatched the candy, and retreated behind Alec's legs.

Alec understood being young and scared, but there came a time where you had to choose to be brave.

"Here's an address," he said, offering a scrap of paper. "If you want to find out what's really happening at your Institute, meet me there tonight. Bring reinforcements—only the people you trust."

Joaquín didn't meet Alec's eyes, but he accepted the piece of paper. Alec walked away, with Jem and Rafael on either side of him.

"Do you think he will come?" Jem asked.

"I hope so," said Alec. "We have to trust people, right? Like you were saying. Not just people we love. We have to believe in people, and we have to defend them. As many people as possible, so we can be stronger." He swallowed. "I have a confession to make. I'm—jealous of you."

Jem's face was genuinely startled. Then he smiled.

"I'm a little jealous of you, too."

"Of me?" Alec asked, startled.

Jem nodded toward Rafael and the picture of Magnus and Max in Rafael's hands. "I have Tessa, so I have the world. And I have loved going all through the world with her. But there are times I think about—a place that could be home. My *parabatai*. A child."

All the things Alec had. Alec felt as he had last night, putting on Rafael's boots over his battered feet: stricken, but knowing this was not his pain.

He hesitated. "Couldn't you and Tessa have a child?"

"I could never ask her," said Jem. "She had children once. They were beautiful, and they are gone. Children are meant to be our immortality, but what if you live forever and your child does not? I saw how she had to rip herself away from them. I saw what it cost her. I will not ask her to suffer like that again."

Rafe held up his hands to be carried. Alec swung him up in his arms. Warlock hearts beat differently, and Alec was used to feeling the sound of Magnus's and Max's hearts, infinitely steady and reassuring. It was odd, holding a child with a mortal heartbeat, but Alec was getting used to the new rhythm.

The evening sun was scorching on whitewashed walls of the street they were heading down. Their shadows were long behind them, but the town was still bright, and Alec saw for the first time that it could be lovely.

Occasionally he despaired: that the world couldn't be changed, or even that it wouldn't change fast enough. He was not immortal, and didn't want to be, but there were times he was afraid he wouldn't live long enough, that he'd never have the chance to take Magnus's hands in front of everyone they loved and make a sacred promise.

At those times, there was an image Alec held against

exhaustion or surrender, a reminder to always keep fighting.

When he was gone, when he was dust and ashes, Magnus would still be walking through this world. If the world was changed for the better, then that unknowable future would be better for Magnus. Alec could imagine that on some scorching-hot day like this, on a strange street in a strange land, Magnus might see something good that reminded him of Alec, some way that the world was changed because Alec had lived. Alec couldn't imagine what the world would be like then.

But he could imagine, in some faraway future, the face he loved best.

Jem filled Tessa in on what they had seen and who they were searching for in the Shadow Market.

Lily caught Jem's glance at her as he explained. "What are you looking at, you delicious peanut-butter-and-Jem sandwich?"

Tessa snorted behind Jem.

"I've got more names," Lily told her, encouraged. "They just come to me. Want to hear them?"

"Not really," said Jem.

"Definitely not!" snapped Alec.

"Yes," said Tessa. "Yes, I really do."

Lily regaled her with many names on their way to the Shadow Market. Tessa's laughter was like a song to Jem, but he was glad when they reached the Shadow Market, though the place was a barbed-wire fortress and the door had been barred against them last time.

The door was not barred against them tonight.

Jem was accustomed to Shadow Markets by now, after years searching through them for answers about demons and

Herondales. He was also used to being somewhat conspicuous among the people of the Market.

Tonight, though, everyone was looking at Alec and Lily. The Queen of the Shadow Market, a rather lovely and dignified young woman, came out among the stalls to greet them personally. Alec drew her aside to tell her of their plans for the evening and to ask for her help. The Queen smiled and agreed.

"They're from the *Alliance*," he heard one teenage werewolf whisper to another, in awed tones.

Alec bowed his head and fussed over Rafe. Alec seemed slightly abashed by the attention.

Jem met Tessa's eyes and smiled. They had seen other generations pass, shining bright and hopeful, but Alec's was something new.

Alec paused to talk to a faerie girl in her teens. "Rose, have you seen a fey woman with dandelion hair at the Market tonight?"

"You must mean Mother Hawthorn," said Rose. "She's always here. She tells stories to the children. Loves children. Hates everybody else. If you're looking for her, stick around the kids. She's sure to come."

So they headed toward a campfire where most of the children were congregated. A faerie was playing the bandonion at this fire. Jem smiled to hear the music.

Rafe clung to Alec's shirt and glared jealously around. The other kids seemed intimidated by his scowl.

A teenage warlock girl was doing magic tricks, creating shadow puppets in the smoke of the fire. Tessa whispered helpful hints in the girl's ear. Even Rafe laughed, all the sullenness gone from his face. He was only a child, leaning into

Alec's side, learning to be happy.

"He says she is very good," Lily translated for Alec. "He likes magic, but most of the powerful warlocks left ages ago. He wants to know if the cool man can do that."

Alec took out his phone to show Rafael a video of Magnus and a witchlight.

"Look, it turns red," Alec said, and Rafe instantly seized the phone. "No, we don't grab! We stop stealing. I have to text Magnus back sometime, and I can't if you keep stealing my phone."

Alec glanced through the leaping iridescent flames at Jem.

"I was actually wondering if you could give me some advice," he said. "I mean, you were saying all that stuff earlier. Like—romantic stuff. You always know what to say."

"Me?" Jem asked, startled. "No, I've never thought of myself as very good with words. I like music. It's easier to express what you feel with music."

"Alec is right," said Tessa.

Jem blinked. "He is?"

"At some of the worst and darkest times in my life, you have always known what to say to comfort me," said Tessa. "I had one of my darkest moments when we were young, and we had only known each other a little while. You came to me and said words that I carried with me like a light. That was one of the moments that made me fall in love with you."

She lifted her hand to his face, her fingers tracing the scars there. Jem dropped a kiss on her wrist.

"If my words comforted you, we are even," he said. "Your voice is the music I love best in all the world."

"You see," Alec muttered darkly to Lily.

"We do love an eloquent babe," said Lily.

Tessa leaned close to Jem and whispered in the language she'd learned for him: "*Wǒ ài nǐ.*"

And at that moment, looking into her eyes, Jem caught a flash of movement and then stillness in the dark. The faerie woman with the dandelion hair had been coming toward the children, pushing her little cart full of poisons. She stopped at the sight of Jem. She recognized him, as he did her.

"Mother Hawthorn," said the warlock girl Tessa had talked to. "Have you come to tell us a story?"

"Yes," said Jem. He rose to his feet and advanced on her. "We want to hear a story. We want to hear why you hate the Herondales."

Mother Hawthorn's eyes widened. Her eyes were colorless and pupil-less, as if her eye sockets were filled with water. For a moment Jem thought she would run, and he tensed to spring after her. Tessa and Alec were ready to come for her as well. Jem had waited too long to wait another moment.

Then Mother Hawthorn looked around at the children and shrugged her thin shoulders.

"Ah well," she said. "I have waited more than a century to boast of a trick. I suppose it doesn't matter now. Let me tell you the story of the First Heir."

They found a solitary campfire, with no children to hear a dark tale save Rafael, solemn faced and silent in the protective curve of Alec's arm. Jem sat down with his friends and his best beloved to listen. Light and shadows danced a long dance together, and by the strange fireside of the Shadow Market, an old woman wove a tale of Faerie.

"The Seelie Court and the Unseelie have always been at war, but there are times in war that wear the mask of peace. There was even a time that the King of the Unseelie Court and the Queen of the Seelie Court made a secret truce and had a union to seal it. They conceived a child together and agreed that one day that child would inherit both the Seelie and Unseelie thrones, and unite all Faerie. The King wished all his sons to be raised as pitiless warriors, and he believed this First Heir would be the greatest of them all. Since the child would have no mother in the Unseelie Court, he engaged my services, and I thought myself honored. I have always been fond of children. Once they called me the great faerie midwife.

"The King of the Unseelie Court had not expected a daughter, but when the child was born, a daughter she was. She was given into my hands in the Unseelie Court on the day she came into the world, and from that day to this day, the light of her eyes was the only light I wished for.

"The Unseelie King was displeased with his daughter, and the Seelie Queen was enraged that he would not, being displeased, give her back. There came a prophecy from our soothsayers that the day the First Heir reached for their full power, all of Faerie would fall under shadow. The King was murderously angry, and the Queen was terrified, and all the shades and shadows and rushing waters in my land seemed to threaten the girl that I loved. The war between Seelie and Unseelie raged all the more fiercely for the brief peace, and the faerie folk whispered that the First Heir was cursed. And so she fled, fearing for her life.

"I did not call her the First Heir. Her name was Auraline, and she was the loveliest thing that ever walked.

"She took refuge in the mortal world, and she found it

beautiful. She was always searching for the beauty in life, and it always made her sad to find ugliness instead. She liked to go to the Shadow Market and mingle with the Downworlders and mundanes who did not know of her birth and would not call her cursed.

"After visiting the Shadow Market for many decades, she met a magician there who made her laugh.

"He called himself Roland the Astonishing, Roland the Extraordinary, Roland the Incredible, as if he were something special, when she was the unique one. I hated that insolent boy from the moment I laid eyes on him.

"When he was not calling himself one of his foolish magician's names, he called himself Roland Loss, but that was another lie."

"No," Tessa said very softly. "It wasn't."

Nobody heard her but Jem.

"There was a warlock woman he said he loved as a mother, but Roland was no warlock, nor a mundane with the Sight. He was something far more deadly than that. I learned this warlock's secret. She took a Shadowhunter child across the seas to America and raised him, pretending he was not Nephilim. Roland was descended from that child: Roland was drawn to our world because his blood called him to it. That boy's true name was Roland Herondale.

"Roland suspected enough of his heritage, and he paid to learn more at the Market. He told Auraline all his secrets. He said he couldn't go to the Nephilim and be one of them, lest it endanger the warlock woman he loved like a second mother. He said instead he would become the greatest magician in the world.

"Auraline lost all caution. She told him of the prophecy and the danger attached to it.

"Roland said they were both lost children, and they could be lost together. He said he didn't mind being lost, if he could be lost with her. She swore the same. He lured her away from my side. He told her to come live with him in the mortal world. He doomed her and called it love.

"They ran away together, and the King's fury was a fire that would have consumed a forest. He wanted the prophecy kept secret, which meant he needed Auraline back under his thumb or killed. He sent his trusted messengers to every corner of the world hunting her, even the bloodthirsty Riders of Mannan. He had all the worst eyes of Faerie looking for her. I kept watch for her myself, and love made my eyes the sharpest. I found her a dozen times, though I never told the King where she was. I will never forgive him for turning against her. I followed them and watched them together, my shining First Heir and that awful boy. Oh, how she loved him, and oh, how I hated him.

"I was at a Shadow Market not long after Roland and Auraline went away together, and there I saw another angel boy, proud as God. He told me of his high position among the Nephilim, and I knew that his *parabatai* was another Herondale. I played a cruel trick on him. I hope he paid for his arrogance in blood."

"Matthew," whispered Tessa, the name sounding unfamiliar in her mouth, spoken for the first time in years.

Matthew Fairchild had been *parabatai* to Tessa's son, James Herondale. Jem had known that this faerie had tricked Matthew to do a terrible deed, but he had thought it was only spite, not revenge.

Even this faerie woman's voice sounded tired. Jem remembered feeling that way, near the end of his days as a Silent Brother. He remembered being that hollow.

"But what does that matter now?" asked the woman, as if speaking to herself. "What did it matter then? Long years passed. Auraline spent decade after decade with her magician in the filth of the mundane world, my girl born to a golden throne. They were together all the days of his life. Auraline shared what she could of her faerie power with Roland, and he stayed young longer, and lived longer, than most of their filthy kind could. She wasted her magic, like someone prolonging the life of a flower: they can only make the flower last for a little more time, before it withers. At last Roland grew old, and older, in the way of mortals, until he reached an end, and Auraline met the end with him. A faerie can choose the season of their own death. I knew how it would be, when I first beheld them together. I saw her death in his laughing eyes.

"My Auraline. When Roland Herondale died, she laid down her golden head on the pillow next to her mortal love and never rose again. Their child wept for them both and threw flowers on their grave. Auraline could have lived for century after century, but she was hunted to the point of desperation, and she threw her life away for a foolish mortal love.

"Their child wept, but I never wept. My eyes stayed dry as the dust and dead flowers on their grave. I hated Roland from the day he took her from me. I hate all Nephilim for *her* sake, and the Herondales most of their kind. Whatever the Shadowhunters touch is brought to destruction. Auraline's child had a child. There is still a First Heir in the world. When the First Heir rises, in all the awful glory bought by the blood of Seelie and Unseelie and Nephilim, I hope destruction comes to the Shadowhunters as well as Faerie. I hope the whole world is lost."

Jem thought of Roland and Auraline's descendant Rosemary and the man she'd loved. They might have a child by now. The curse the faeries had talked about had already claimed lives. This danger was far greater than he had ever suspected. Jem had to protect Rosemary from the Unseelie King and the Riders who brought death. If there was a child, Jem had to save that child. Jem had already failed to save so many.

Jem rose and left Mother Hawthorn. He went to the barbed-wire edge of the Market, moving desperately fast, as if he could race back into the past and save those he had lost there.

When he stopped, Tessa caught him. She held him in her arms, and when he stopped trembling, she drew his head down to hers.

"Jem, my Jem. It's all right. I thought it was a very beautiful story," she said.

"What?"

"Not her story," said Tessa. "Not the story of her warped sight and terrible choices. I can see the story behind hers. The story of Auraline and Roland."

"But all the people who were hurt," Jem murmured. "The children we loved."

"My James knew the power of a love story, as well as I do," said Tessa. "No matter how dark and hopeless the world seemed, Lucie could always find beauty in a story. I know what they would have thought."

"I'm sorry," said Jem instantly.

He hadn't meant to make Tessa speak of her children. He knew how much losing them had hurt her. Every time he dreamed of a child, he remembered the pain she had endured, and knew he could never ask her to lose more. She was enough for him: she always would be.

"Auraline grew up in horror. She felt cursed. And he was lost and wandering. They seemed destined for misery. Only they found each other, Jem. They were together and happy, all the days of their lives. Her story is just like mine, because I found you."

Tessa's smile lit the night. She always brought hope when he was in despair, as she had brought words when everything within him was silence. Jem put his arms around her and held on tightly.

"I hope you learned what you needed to learn tonight," Alec told Jem and Tessa when they reached their rooms.

Jem had looked upset when he bolted from the fireside, but he and Tessa had seemed different when they returned.

"I hope they're all right," Alec said quietly to Lily when Jem and Tessa went off to prepare for their midnight visit to the warlock's house.

"Of course Tessa's fine," said Lily. "You do realize she gets to go to the Jem-nasium anytime she wants?"

"I'm never talking to you again if those names don't stop," Alec told her, gathering his arrows and tucking daggers and seraph blades into his weapons belt. He found himself thinking of the heartbroken way Jem said *parabatai*. It made him remember the shadow that hung over his father, the wound where a *parabatai* should be. It made him think of Jace. Ever since he could remember, Alec had loved and felt responsible for his family. There had never been any choice, but with Jace it was different. Jace, his *parabatai*, the first person who'd ever chosen him. The first time Alec had decided to choose someone back, to take on another responsibility. The first choice, opening the door to all the others.

Alec took a deep breath and tapped out MISS U into his phone.

He immediately received back MISS U TOO and let himself take a breath, the ache in his chest easier now. Jace was there, waiting for him in New York with the rest of his family. Talking about feelings wasn't so bad.

Then he received another text.

R U OK?

In rapid succession, Alec received several more texts.

R U IN SOME KIND OF TROUBLE?

DID U GET HIT IN UR HEAD!

Then he got a text from Clary.

WHY DID JACE GET A TEXT FROM YOU AND LOOK VERY PLEASED BUT THEN SUDDENLY VERY WORRIED? IS SOMETHING GOING ON?

Talking about feelings was the worst. Once you did it, everybody immediately wanted you to do it more.

Alec typed out a grouchy I'M FINE and then called out cautiously, "Rafe?"

Rafael popped immediately up from his bed.

"Would you like the phone back?" asked Alec. "Here it is. Take it. Don't worry if any more texts arrive. Just show me if there are any more pictures."

He didn't know how much Rafael understood of what he said. He suspected not much, but Rafe certainly understood the gesture of Alec offering his phone. He held out his hands eagerly.

"You're a good kid, Rafe," said Alec. "Take that phone away."

* * *

"Are we going to smuggle our way into the house in laundry carts?" Lily asked Alec excitedly.

Alec blinked at her. "No, we're not. What laundry carts? I'm a straightforward person. I'm going to knock on the door."

He stood with Lily on the cobbled street before that great gray house. Jem and Tessa were waiting on the roof. Alec had literally used rope to tie Rafe to Jem's wrist.

"I know Rafe stole your phone," said Lily, "but who stole your sense of adventure?"

Alec waited, and the door opened. A warlock blinked up at him. He looked as if he was in his early thirties, a businessman with close-cropped blond hair and no visible warlock mark until he opened his mouth and Alec saw his forked tongue.

"Oh, hello," he said. "Are you another of Clive Breakspear's men?"

Alec said, "I'm Alec Lightwood."

The warlock's face cleared. "I see! I've heard of you." He winked. "Fond of warlocks, aren't you?"

"Some of them," said Alec.

"Want your cut, I expect?"

"That's right."

"No problem," the warlock told him. "You and your vampire friend should come in, and I'll explain what I'll want in return. I think the vampire will be very amused. They don't like werewolves, do they?"

"I don't like most people," Lily said helpfully. "But I do love murder!"

The warlock waved his hand to let them through the wards, and led them through a hexagonal hall with a ceiling carved in a shape like a plaster jelly mold. The green quartz of the floor shone like jade. There were no signs of ruin or decay here. The warlock obviously had money.

There were several doors, all painted white, set in the many walls. The warlock chose one and led Alec and Lily down rough-hewn stone steps into the dark. The smell hit Alec before the sight did.

There was a long stone passage, with flaming torches on the walls and with grooves on either side for filth and blood. Along the passageway were rows of cages. Eyes shone from behind the bars, catching the firelight in the same way Juliette's eyes had shone from her throne in the Shadow Market. Some cages were empty. In others were huddled shapes that were not moving.

"So you've been taking werewolf women, and hiring the Shadowhunters to help you," said Alec.

The warlock nodded with a cheery smile.

"Why werewolves?" Alec asked grimly.

"Well, warlocks and vampires can't bear children, and faeries find it difficult," said the warlock in a practical tone. "But the werewolves whelp more easily, and there's a great deal of animal strength. Everybody says that Downworlders can't bear warlock children, that their bodies always reject them, but I thought of putting a little magic in the mix. People whisper about a warlock born from a Shadowhunter woman, and that's probably a myth, but it got me thinking. Imagine the power a warlock might have, with a werewolf mother and a demon father." He shrugged. "Seems worth trying. Of course, you do use up the werewolf women at a terrible rate."

"How many have died?" Lily asked casually. Her expression was unreadable.

"Oh, a few," the warlock admitted genially. "I'm always in need of a fresh supply, so I'm happy to pay you to snatch more. But these experiments haven't been going as well as I'd like. Nothing has worked yet. You're, uh, close to Magnus Bane, aren't you? I'm probably the most powerful warlock you'll ever meet, but I hear he's pretty good too. If you can get him to come on in an assisting capacity, you'll be very well rewarded. So will he. I think you'll both be very happy."

Alec said, "Yeah, I hope so."

It wasn't the first time someone had assumed Magnus was for sale. It wasn't the first time someone had assumed that because Alec was connected to Magnus, Alec was sullied.

That used to make Alec angry. It still did, but he'd learned to use it.

The warlock turned his back to Alec, surveying the cages as if selecting a product from a market stall. "So, what do you say?" he asked idly. "Do we have a deal?"

"I don't know yet," said Alec. "You don't know my price."

The warlock laughed. "What is it?"

Alec scythed the warlock's feet out from under him, so he fell to his knees. He drew his seraph blade and held it to the man's throat.

"All the women go free," he said. "And you are under arrest."

Alec realized why the warlock was burning torches, and not using witchlight or electricity, when a torch tumbled out of the wall and onto the straw. Lily, who was kneeling to speak to someone behind the bars, rolled hastily away from the flames. She came up to her feet with fangs out. Alec had to leap to stamp out the fire.

The warlock was good, Alec thought, as the world went orange with not just fire but magic, crisscrossing from the bars, blinding Alec with its light.

Then another light sliced through the orange wires of magic, pearly gray, cutting through all darkness. Tessa Gray, daughter of a Prince of Hell, stood at the foot of the stairs with her hands glowing.

Tessa's magic was all around him. Alec had learned how to sense magic over the years, learned to move with it and fight with it as another weapon on his side. This wasn't the singing power he was used to, well-known and well-beloved as his bow, but it felt friendly. He let Tessa's magic wrap around him, cooling and protecting, as he ducked through the fiery sparks of power back to the warlock.

"The most powerful warlock I've ever seen?" Alec snarled. "She cut through your wards like tissue paper. And my man would eat you for *breakfast*."

He made a mistake, because he was overconfident. He didn't hear Tessa's stifled sound, and he didn't see the shadow moving as he swept his blade toward the warlock.

Clive Breakspear's seraph blade met his. Alec met Breakspear's furious eyes. He looked to Tessa, struggling with three Shadowhunters with Jem coming to help her, Lily with another Shadowhunter prowling toward her, and he glanced toward the warlock, who was making every torch fall. Alec was used to being able to see the whole battle, fighting at a distance.

Too late, he saw the blade in Clive Breakspear's free hand, aimed for his heart.

Rafael barreled out of the shadows and sank his teeth deep into Breakspear's wrist. The blade dropped to the stone.

The man roared, and with all the Nephilim strength that should be used to shield the defenseless, he hurled Rafael's body into the cage bars. There was a sickening crack.

Alec shouted: *"No!"*

He backhanded Clive Breakspear in the face. The warlock dashed a torch at his feet, and Alec stepped over the flames and seized him by the throat, then lifted him like a doll and smashed the warlock's skull against Breakspear's forehead. The warlock's eyes rolled back, but Breakspear screamed in outrage and charged at Alec. There was still a seraph blade shining in his hand, so Alec broke that hand, then used his hold on it to force the corrupt Shadowhunter to his knees. Alec stood over them, panting so hard his chest felt as if it would split apart. He wanted to kill them both.

Only Rafael was here. Magnus and Max were at home, waiting for him. Tessa, Jem, and Lily had made short work of the Shadowhunters attacking them. Alec turned to Tessa now.

"Will you enchant ropes to hold them?" he asked. "They have to stand trial."

Tessa moved forward. So did Lily. Alec knew the situation was desperate because Lily didn't make a joke about murdering them. Alec was too close to the edge. He was afraid he would have taken her up on it.

He went to the place where Rafael lay, his body a small wretched shape thrown into the dirt. Alec pulled Rafe into his arms, feeling his throat close up. He understood now what he had found here in Buenos Aires. He understood now that it might be too late.

Rafael's grubby face was still. He was barely breathing. Jem came to kneel beside them.

"I'm so sorry. He slipped the rope, and I came in for him, but—but—"

"It isn't your fault," Alec said numbly.

Jem said, "Give him to me."

Alec stared at Jem, then bundled Rafe into his arms.

"Take care of him," he said. "Please."

Jem took Rafe and ran toward Tessa, and together they rushed up the stone steps. There was still orange magic in the air, and the flames had caught in earnest. Smoke was rising fast, in a thick choking cloud.

One of the werewolf women reached out a thin hand and clutched the bars.

"Help us!"

Alec took an axe with an electrum head from his belt and struck open the lock on her cage. "That's what I'm here to do." He paused. "Um, Lily, are there keys on that warlock?"

"Yep," said Lily. "Just grabbed them. I'll open the doors with the keys, and you can keep doing your cool dramatic axe thing."

"Fine," said Alec.

The werewolf woman who had spoken to him bolted out the door as soon as she was free. The woman in the next cage was unconscious. Alec walked into the cage and knelt beside her, and that was when he heard the sounds of a fight breaking out at the top of the stairs.

He picked the woman up and ran for the stairs.

Tessa and Jem were in the hall, almost at the doors. The burning house was crawling with Shadowhunters. Jem couldn't fight, because he was holding Rafael. Tessa was doing her best to clear a way for them, but Rafael needed Tessa's help too.

One man shouted, "Where's our leader?"

"You call *that* a leader?" Alec shouted back. He looked at the woman in his arms, then held her out so the Shadowhunters of the Buenos Aires Institute could see. "He helped a warlock do this. He crushed a child's body against a wall. Is that what you want to lead you? Is that what you want to *be*?"

Several Shadowhunters turned to him in total puzzlement. Lily quickly shouted out a translation.

Joaquín stepped forward.

Lily said quietly, "He told them to stand down."

The man who'd shouted for his leader hit Joaquín across the mouth. Another Shadowhunter shouted in startled fury and produced a whip, defending Joaquín.

Alec ran his eyes over the crowd. Some of the Shadowhunters looked uncertain, but Shadowhunters were soldiers. Too many of them were intent on following whatever orders they had been given, fighting Joaquín and Alec and whoever else stood in their way, to get to an unworthy leader. They were blocking Jem and Tessa's way. They were keeping Rafe from help.

The doors of the burning house burst open. The Queen of the Shadow Market stood outlined against the smoke.

"Get to Alec!" Juliette shouted, and a dozen Downworlders sprang.

Juliette cleared a path. Jem and Tessa slipped out the door. Rafe was out of this place of filth and smoke. Alec fought toward Juliette.

"Mon Dieu," she breathed when she saw the woman in Alec's arms.

She made a gesture, and a warlock jumped to take the unconscious werewolf out into the night.

"There are more women down there," Alec said. "I'll get them. Some of the Shadowhunters are on our side."

Juliette nodded. "Which ones?"

Alec turned to see Joaquín, fighting two Shadowhunters at once. The man with the whip who'd come to help him was down.

"That one," said Alec. "And whoever else he tells you."

Juliette set her jaw and began to transform to her wolf shape, striding across the green-quartz floor to Joaquín's side. She tapped one of the men fighting him on the shoulder. When he turned, she ripped out his throat with one clawed hand.

"Maybe take them alive!" said Alec. "Not that guy, obviously."

Joaquín was staring at Juliette with eyes gone enormous. Alec remembered that Joaquín had heard tales of horror about the Queen of the Shadow Market. Juliette, with blood on her hands and firelight in her snarled hair, might not be doing a lot to dispel that image.

"Don't hurt her!" Alec cried. "She's with us."

"Oh good," said Joaquín.

Juliette squinted at him suspiciously through the smoke. "You're not evil?"

"Trying not to be," said Joaquín.

"Bien," said Juliette. "Show me who to kill. I mean . . . take alive if possible."

Alec left them to it. He spun around and raced back down the stairs, Lily at his heels. The smoke was thick in the passage below by now. Alec saw there were Shadowhunters there already, getting Clive Breakspear and his warlock confederate out. Alec's lip curled. "If your loyalty is to the Clave, put a watch on them. They're going to stand trial."

He and Lily opened the remaining doors. The women who

could move on their own did. Too many could not. Alec picked up one woman after another and carried them out. Lily helped women who needed support to walk. Alec gave the women to the Downworlders of the Shadow Market whenever he could, so he was able to get back to the basement faster. He reached the top of the stairs with another woman and saw the hall was deserted, taken over by smoke and falling masonry. Everyone had fled the death trap this building had become.

Alec bundled the woman into Lily's arms. Lily was small enough that it was difficult, but she was strong enough to bear her weight.

"Take her. I have to get the others."

"I don't want to go!" Lily shouted over the crackling fire. "I don't ever want to abandon anybody again!"

"You won't. Lily, go."

Lily stumbled for the door under her heavy burden, sobbing. Alec turned back. The smoke had turned the whole world into a gray hell. He couldn't see or breathe.

A hand caught his shoulder. Joaquín stood behind him.

"You can't go down there!" he panted. "I'm so sorry about those women, but they're—"

Alec said icily, "Downworlders?"

"It's too dangerous. And you—you have a lot to go back to."

Magnus and Max. If Alec closed his eyes, he could see them with absolute clarity. But he knew he had to be worthy of going back to them.

Joaquín was still holding on to him. Alec shrugged him off, and not gently.

"I will not leave one woman down there, abused and forgotten," he said. "Not *one*. No real Shadowhunter would."

He looked over his shoulder at Joaquín as he was going down the steps into hell.

"You can leave," said Alec. "If you do, you can still call yourself a Shadowhunter. But will you be one?"

Rafael lay on the cobbled street as Jem and Tessa hovered over him. Jem used every silent enchantment he had learned among the Silent Brothers. Tessa whispered every healing spell she had learned in the Spiral Labyrinth. Jem could tell, from long, bitter experience, that there was too much broken and bruised within that small body.

There was a fire burning and a battle raging. Jem could not pay attention to any of it, could not bring himself to care about anything but the child under his hands.

"Dittany, Jem," Tessa whispered desperately. "I need dittany."

Jem climbed to his feet, searching the crowd. There were so many from the Shadow Market here, there was surely one who could help. His gaze fell on Mother Hawthorn, with starlight on her dandelion hair.

She met his eyes and made to run. Jem was fast as a Shadowhunter still, when he had to be. He was at her side in a moment, catching her wrist.

"Do you have dittany?"

"If I do," snarled Mother Hawthorn, "why should I give it to you?"

"I know what you did, more than a century ago," he said. "I know better than you do. The trick you played, causing one Shadowhunter to poison another? It poisoned an unborn child. Does that amuse you?"

The faerie's mouth went slack.

"That child died, because of you," said Jem. "Now there is another child who needs help. I could take the herb from you. I will if I have to. But I'm giving you the chance to make another choice."

"It's too late!" said Mother Hawthorn, and Jem knew she was thinking of Auraline.

"Yes," said Jem, merciless. "It's too late to save the ones we lost. But this child is not lost yet. This choice is not lost yet. Choose."

Mother Hawthorn turned her face away, her mouth set in bitter lines. But she reached inside the worn pouch at her belt and put the herb into his hand.

Jem took it and raced back to Tessa. Rafael's body was arching under her hands. The dittany flared to life at her touch, and Jem joined his hands with Tessa's, joined his voice with hers as they spoke in all the languages they had ever taught each other. Their words were a song, their linked hands magic, and they poured everything they knew, together, into the child.

Rafael's eyes opened. There was a flash of Tessa's pearlescent magic in his dark irises, then it was lost. The child sat up, looking perfectly all right, well and whole and somewhat annoyed. He gazed into their distraught faces and asked, in clipped Spanish, "Where is he?"

"He's in there," Lily answered.

The narrow cobbled street was full of members of the Shadow Market seeing to the werewolf victims or herding Shadowhunters, with some different, deeply nervous-looking Shadowhunters tentatively assisting or trying to put out the flames. Lily was not doing any of that. She stared at the house with her arms crossed and her eyes dark with tears.

As they watched, part of the roof collapsed. Rafe started

forward. Tessa lunged and seized him, holding him as he strained against her grip. Jem stood.

"No, Jem," said Tessa. "Take the child. Let me go in."

Jem tried to take Rafe, but he was fighting them both. Then Rafe went still. Jem twisted around to see what the child was looking at.

What everybody was looking at. There was a ripple in the crowd, then a hush. Jem did not think any of the Shadow Market or the Institute would forget what had happened here tonight.

From the swirling smoke, out of the collapsing building, came two Shadowhunters with werewolves in their arms. They walked tall, their faces grim, and people parted to let them pass.

The women had been saved, and the child. Jem felt new resolution rise in him. Tessa was right. If Rosemary could be saved, he would save her. If there was a child, he and Tessa would stand between that child and the Riders and the King.

Alec carried the werewolf he bore to Tessa, who immediately began enchanting the smoke from her lungs. Then he dropped to his knees in front of Rafe.

"Hey, my baby," said Alec. "Are you all right?"

Rafael might not have entirely understood the language, but anyone could have understood the message of Alec on his knees in the rubble, the love and concern on his face. Rafael nodded, dust drifting from his curly hair, and walked into Alec's open arms. Alec folded the little boy against his chest.

"Thank you both," Alec said to Tessa and Jem. "You're heroes."

"You're welcome," said Jem.

"You're a moron," said Lily, and put her face in her hands.

Alec rose and patted her awkwardly on the back, Rafe

held in the circle of his other arm. He turned to Juliette, who had called one of her warlocks over to see to the werewolf in Joaquín's arms.

"You got them all out." Juliette smiled at them both, her expression wondering, as if she were as young as Rafe and seeing magic for the first time. "You did it."

"The werewolf woman who was looking after Rafe," said Alec. "Is she . . . here?"

Juliette looked at the ashes drifting on the cobbled streets. The fire was dying, now that Tessa could spare magic to cool the flames, but the house was a ruin.

"No," said Juliette. "My girls tell me she was one of the first to die."

"I'm sorry," Alec told her, then his voice changed as he addressed Rafe. "Rafe, I have to ask you something," he said. "*Solomillo*—"

"Steak?" Lily smirked.

"Dammit," said Alec. "Sorry, Rafe. But will you come back with me to New York? You can—I have to talk to—if you don't like it there, you don't have to—"

Rafe watched him stumble over his words.

"I can't understand you, fool," he said sweetly in Spanish, and tucked his head down under Alec's chin, his arms going around Alec's neck.

"Okay," said Alec. "Good. I think."

Tessa walked away from the burned-out building. There were several warlocks in the crowd watching her with awe, Jem noted proudly. She strode over to the bound warlock and the head of the Buenos Aires Institute.

"Shall we ask Magnus to open a Portal for them?" she asked.

"Not just yet," said Alec.

There was a change in his demeanor, his shoulders going back, his face stern. If it weren't for the child in his arms, he might have been fearsome.

Alec Lightwood, leader of the Alliance, said, "First, I want a word."

Alec looked around at the assembled faces. His breathing felt as if it were tearing his throat and his eyes were still stinging, but he was holding Rafe, so everything was perfectly all right.

Except for the fact that he had no idea what to say. He couldn't know how many of the Shadowhunters had cooperated with the capture and torture of these women. He suspected most of them had gone along with their leader's orders, but he didn't know how responsible that made them. If he arrested everybody, then the Institute would be left an empty ruin. The people here were owed protection.

"Clive Breakspear, the head of the Buenos Aires Institute, broke the Accords and will pay for it," he said at last, and paused. "Lily, can you translate for me?"

"Absolutely, yes," Lily said promptly, and began to do so.

Alec listened to her talk, watched the faces of the people listening, and saw a few smirks. Alec listened more intently and picked up a word.

"*Boludo*," Alec said to Jem. "What does that mean?"

Jem coughed. "It's not . . . a polite word."

"I knew it," Alec said. "Lily, stop translating! Sorry, Jem, could you translate instead?"

Jem nodded. "I'll do my best."

"The head of your Institute has brought shame on us all,"

Alec told the Shadowhunters. "I could bring everybody here to Alicante. I could have every one of you put to the trial of the Sword. I know you were left after the war, to rebuild as best you could, and instead of leading you, this man brought more ruin. But the Law says that I should make each of you pay."

Alec thought of Helen and Mark Blackthorn, cut off from their family by the Cold Peace. He thought of the way Magnus had sunk his face into his hands, despairing, when the Cold Peace was passed. Alec never wanted to see that despair again. Every day since that day, he'd tried to work out ways that they could all live united.

"What happened in that house should sicken any Shadowhunter," said Alec. "We have to earn back the trust of everyone we have wronged. Joaquín, you will know the names of every man who was in Breakspear's inner circle. They will go with their leader to stand trial. For the rest, it is time for a new leader and a new chance to live as Nephilim should."

He glanced at Joaquín, who was wiping tears from his eyes. Alec frowned at him and mouthed, "What?"

"Oh, it's j-just the way Jem is translating," Joaquín explained. "I mean, your speech is good too, very stern, it makes me want to do everything you say. And Jem is basically repeating it, but it's the way he puts things, you know? It's beautiful."

"Uh-huh," Alec said.

Joaquín grabbed his free hand. "You be the new head of the Institute."

"No, I will not," Alec snapped.

People were always trying to make him head of Institutes, and it made Alec tired. He couldn't change enough, if he took that kind of position. He had more important things to do.

"No," repeated Alec, less grouchily but no less firmly. "I'm not Clive Breakspear. I'm here to help you, not to take over. When you saw what was happening, you told your men to stand down. You should act as the head of your own Institute until the Consul can consider your case."

Joaquín stood amazed. Alec nodded at him.

"You can work with the Shadow Market to rebuild," he said. "I can provide you with resources."

"So can I," said Juliette.

Joaquín stared at her, then swung his head back to Alec.

"The Queen of the Shadow Market," said Alec. "Do you think you will be able to cooperate with her?"

Juliette gave Joaquín a hostile look. There was still a suggestion of wolfish teeth in her mouth. Joaquín reached out, as if to point to the blood on Juliette's hands, and Alec wondered for a nasty moment if the hatred between the Nephilim and the Downworlders in this place ran too deep.

Joaquín lifted Juliette's hand to his lips and kissed it.

"I did not know," he breathed, "that the Queen of the Shadow Market was so beautiful."

Alec realized abruptly that he'd gotten everything wrong. Juliette mouthed several shocked demands for explanation, and several more French expletives, at Alec over Joaquín's bowed head.

"Shadowhunters go *so hard*." Lily cackled.

"Okay, fine, glad we're entering into the spirit of cooperation," said Alec, and turned back to the crowd. "This Nephilim child is now under the protection of the New York Institute," he said. "Let's say this was a very standard and normal adoption.

Let's say that though the head of your Institute was corrupt, you survived under a bad leader and kept your honor. You hold Breakspear here until he can be tried. I will, of course, be returning here often to finalize details of the adoption, and I'll see what is happening. I want to believe in my fellow Shadowhunters. Don't let me down."

He had no doubt Jem would make that sound better in Spanish. He turned back to Juliette, who had succeeded with difficulty in freeing her hand and was retreating several steps under Joaquín's rapt gaze.

"I should be getting back to my kids!" she said, gesturing to the three kids. Rosey gave Alec a little wave.

"Oh," said Joaquín, a world of devastation in the syllable, then he seemed to notice the lack of anyone else with the kids. "Has it been very difficult, ruling the Shadow Market as a single mother?" he asked with sudden transparent hope.

"Well, none of this has exactly been easy!" said Juliette.

Joaquín beamed at her. "That's wonderful."

"What?" said Juliette.

Joaquín was already heading toward the kids, on an obvious mission to endear himself to them. Alec hoped he had a lot of candies.

Juliette demanded, "Did he inhale a lot of smoke in there?"

"Probably," said Alec.

"Shadowhunters get very set on things," said Lily. "Very set. Do you enjoy intensely serious romantic commitment?"

"I don't know his name," Juliette pointed out. She sneaked a self-conscious look over at Joaquín, whose endearing of himself seemed to be going very well. He had Juliette's warlock boy up on his shoulders.

"His name's Joaquín," Alec said helpfully.

Juliette smiled. "I suppose I do like some Shadowhunters. It's always a pleasure, Alec Lightwood. Thanks for everything."

"It was nothing," said Alec.

Juliette strolled over to her kids, calling out to them to stop bothering the head of the Institute.

Alec looked around at the smoke drifting up to the stars and the people in the streets all talking to each other without barriers. His eyes fell on Tessa and Jem.

"Is it time to go home?" Tessa asked.

Alec bit his lip, then nodded. "I'll text Magnus and ask him to open a Portal."

There was an official protocol for adopting Shadowhunter children. He knew that he and Rafael would have to go back and forth from Buenos Aires several times, but this trip home would be worth it, even if it did not last long. Alec wanted to take Rafael home as soon as he could.

He was tired, and he wanted to sleep in his own bed.

"I don't suppose you have any ideas for how I can explain all this to Magnus?" he asked Jem.

"I think you'll find all the words you need, Alec," said Jem.

"Thanks, that's very helpful."

Jem smiled. "You even found a way to make the boy who doesn't like anybody like you. Thanks for all your help, Alec."

Alec wished he could help more, but he knew that at least for now he had done his part. They all had to trust each other, and he did trust his friends. If there was a Herondale in danger, they could not ask for better protection than Jem and Tessa.

"I didn't do much, but it was good to see you both. Good luck with the Herondale."

Jem nodded. "Thank you. I think we might need it."

The Portal was open, and shimmering.

"Bye, Jem," said Lily.

"Oh, no nickname?" Jem sounded pleased. "Bye, Lily."

Alec studied Rafe's face. "*Do* you like me?" he asked.

Rafe beamed and shook his head, then secured his arms more tightly around Alec's neck.

"Oh, fine, *that* you understand," Alec grumbled. "Come on. Let's go home."

They stepped out of the Portal into the electric starriness of a New York night. Alec could see his apartment down the street, the shimmer of a witchlight behind pale blue curtains. He checked his watch: it was past Max's bedtime. Max fought bedtime like it was a demon, so Magnus was probably reading him a fifth story or singing him a third song.

Every brown-and-white facade, every tree surrounded by wire on the cracked sidewalk, was dear to him. Alec used to think, when he was younger and felt as if he might die amid the crushing expectations and stone walls of the Institute, that he might feel better if he could live among the glass towers of Alicante. He hadn't known home was across the city, waiting for him.

He set Rafe on the steps of their building and hopped him up one step, then swung him up another, for sheer joy. He opened the door to home.

"Alec," boomed a voice behind him.

Alec jumped. Lily swiftly thrust Rafael behind the protection of Alec's front door and spun, lip curling from her needle-sharp teeth.

Alec turned as well, very slowly. He wasn't scared. He knew that voice.

"Alec," said Robert Lightwood. "We need to talk."

"Okay, Dad," said Alec. "Lily, I need to explain everything to Magnus, so could you watch Rafe for a second?"

Lily nodded, still giving Robert the evil eye. There was a pause.

"Hello, Lily," Robert added gruffly.

"Who the hell are you?" asked Lily.

"My dad," said Alec. "The Inquisitor. The second most important person in the Clave. Someone you have met at least twenty-six times."

"I don't recall," said Lily.

Alec's incredulous look was mirrored on his father's face.

"Lily," said Robert. "I know you know me."

"Never gonna, don't wanna." Lily shut the door of Alec's apartment building in his father's face.

There was an awkward silence.

"Sorry about that," said Alec finally, jogging down the steps to join his father on the sidewalk.

"All your other vampires like me," muttered Robert.

Alec blinked. "My other vampires?"

"Your friend Elliott reaches out whenever Lily leaves him in charge," explained Robert. "He says he feels in need of Lightwood guidance. I visited the Hotel Dumort while you were away, and the vampires had a little dinner just for me, and they all talked to me about you. Elliott gave me his phone number, I presume so I can call him in case of emergencies. Elliott's always charming to me."

Alec didn't know how to break it to his dad that Elliott was shamelessly hitting on him.

"Huh," said Alec.

"How is Magnus? Doing well? Dressing, uh, uniquely?"

"Still gorgeous," said Alec defiantly. "Yeah."

His father looked abashed. Alec wasn't comfortable talking about how he felt, but he wasn't ashamed, and nobody was going to make him be ashamed ever again. He didn't know why his father never stopped poking at him, with the obsessive curiosity of a child poking at a scab.

When he was younger, his dad used to joke insistently about Alec and girls. It was too painful to respond to those comments. Alec talked less and less.

He remembered the day he'd walked out of the Institute to find Magnus. He'd met Magnus twice and couldn't forget him. The Institute lay behind him, its stark outlines cutting the sky. He'd been breathless and terrified, with one thought very clear in his mind.

Is this how you want to live your whole life?

Then he'd gone to Magnus's place and asked him out.

Alec couldn't bear the idea of one of his kids ever feeling trapped in their own home. He knew his dad hadn't meant to do that. But he had.

"How's my little M&M?" asked Robert.

Max's middle name was Michael, after Robert's long-dead *parabatai*.

Usually that was Alec's cue to take out his phone and show his dad all the new pictures of Max he possessed, but he was in a hurry today.

"He's the best," Alec said. "Is there something you need, Dad?"

"I heard some rumors about the Buenos Aires Institute," said Robert. "I heard you were there."

"Right," said Alec. "Clive Breakspear, the head of the Institute, had his Shadowhunters acting as mercenaries. They'll need to stand trial. But I encouraged a change in leadership. The Buenos Aires Institute is going to be all right."

"This is why I needed to talk to you, Alec," said Robert.

Alec studied the cracks in the sidewalk and tried to think of a way to explain everything that would implicate nobody else.

"Do you know, the positions of Consul and Inquisitor often stay within the same families? I've been thinking about what happens when the time comes for me to retire."

Alec stared at a weed growing through the cracks in the sidewalk. "I don't think Jace wants to be Inquisitor, Dad."

"Alec," said Robert. "I'm not talking to Jace. I'm talking to you."

Alec jolted. *"What?"*

He looked up from the sidewalk. His father was smiling at him as if he meant it.

Alec remembered his own words. *The Inquisitor. The second most important person in the Clave.*

Alec allowed himself a moment to dream. Being Inquisitor, and having a hand in the making of the Law itself. Being able to get Aline and Helen back. Being able to put some sort of dent in the Cold Peace. Being able, Alec thought with slow-dawning hope, to get married.

Having his dad believe that Alec could do it. Alec knew his dad loved him, but that wasn't the same as his dad believing in him. He hadn't known that before.

"I'm not saying it would be easy," said Robert. "But several members of the Clave have mentioned it as a possibility. You know how popular you are with Downworlders."

"Not really," mumbled Alec.

"A few more people in the Clave are coming around," said Robert. "I have that tapestry up of you, and I take care to mention your name often."

"Here I thought it was up because you love me."

Robert blinked at him, as if he was wounded by the joke. "Alec. It—it is. But I want this for you too. That's what I came here to ask. Do you want it for yourself?"

Alec thought of the power to change the Law from a sword that hurt people into a shield to defend them.

"Yeah," said Alec. "But you have to be sure you want me to have it, Dad. People won't be happy with me taking it, and once I have it, I'm going to split the Clave apart."

"You are?" Robert asked, his voice faint.

"Because I have to," said Alec. "Because everything has to change. For everybody's sake. And for Magnus and our kids."

Robert blinked. "Your what?"

"Oh, by the Angel," said Alec. "Please don't ask me any questions! I have to go! I have to talk to Magnus right away."

Robert said, "I am very confused."

"I really have to go," said Alec. "Thanks, Dad. I mean it. Come for dinner again soon, all right? We'll talk more about the Inquisitor thing then."

"All right," said Robert. "I'd like that. When I had dinner with you three a few weeks ago? I don't remember the last time I had such a happy day."

Alec remembered how difficult it had been during Robert's visit to keep the conversation going, how only Max prattling at his grandpa's knee had broken the frequent silences. It broke Alec's heart to think Robert had thought of that strained awkward dinner as happiness.

"Come over anytime," said Alec. "Max loves seeing his grandpa. And—thank you, Dad. Thanks for believing in me. Sorry if I caused you a lot of paperwork tonight."

"You saved lives tonight, Alec," said Robert.

He took an awkward step toward Alec, and his hand lifted, as if he was going to pat Alec on the shoulder. Then his hand dropped. He looked into Alec's face, and his eyes were so sad.

"You're a good man, Alec," he said at last. "You're a better man than I am."

Alec loved his father and would never be cruel to him. So he didn't say: *I had to be.* Instead he reached out and pulled his father into an awkward hug, patting him on the shoulder before he stepped back.

"We'll talk later."

"Whenever you like," said Robert. "I've got all the time in the world."

Alec waved to his dad, then ran up the steps of his building. He opened the door and bounded up his stairs to find Lily alone. The door of his loft was open a crack, light filtering through, but Lily was standing in the shadows and appeared to be filing her nails.

"Lily," Alec said dangerously, "where is Rafael?"

"Oh, him." Lily shrugged. "He heard Magnus singing some Indonesian lullaby, and he bolted inside. Nothing I could do. Shadowhunters. They're speedy."

Neither of them mentioned Magnus's wards, which couldn't be forced by any magic or any strength Alec knew of. Magnus didn't have wards up for anyone defenseless, anyone who might need his help. Of course a child could go through.

Alec fixed her with a reproachful glare but was distracted

by the deep, lovely murmur of Magnus's voice through the open door. His tone was warm and, as it often was, amused. Alec thought of Jem telling Tessa, *Your voice is the music I love best in all the world.*

"Ah, there's that smile," said Lily. "It's been two days, and I missed it."

Alec stopped smiling and made a face at her, but when he looked at her properly, she was fiddling with the zipper of her leather jacket. There was something about the set of her mouth, as if she'd set it determinedly so it wouldn't tremble.

"Thanks for coming with me," Alec said. "Also, you're the worst."

That made her smile. Lily wiggled her fingers in farewell. "Don't you forget it."

She slipped away like a shadow, and Alec opened the door and stepped inside his apartment at last. His coffee machine was on the counter; his cat was sleeping on the sofa.

There was a door standing open to a room he'd never seen before, which happened sometimes at his place. The room inside had golden-brown floorboards and whitewashed walls. Magnus was standing in the room, with Rafe beside him. Magnus was wearing a red-and-gold silk robe, and Rafe's face was tipped up to watch him as he produced a low, soothing stream of Spanish. It was a beautiful room.

Alec realized Magnus knew he was there because Magnus started translating what he was saying into rapid English, switching between languages with fluid ease so everybody knew what was going on.

"Let's put away the cross for now, and talk about organized religion later," said Magnus, snapping his fingers at the crucifix on the wall. "And let's have a window and let the light in. Do you like this one?"

He gestured easily to the wall, and a circular window opened up onto their street, showing a tree catching the moon. Then he gestured again and the window was red-and-gold stained glass.

"Or this one?" Magnus waved a third time and the window was arched and tall as a church window. "Or this one?"

Rafe was nodding and nodding, his face wreathed in eager smiles.

Magnus smiled down at him. "Want me to just keep doing magic?"

Rafe nodded again, even more vehemently. Magnus laughed and set a hand on Rafe's curly head: Alec was about to warn that Rafael was shy at first and would duck away, but Rafe didn't. He let Magnus stroke his hair, the rings on Magnus's hand catching the light through their new window. Magnus's smile went from gleaming to glowing. He met Alec's eyes over Rafe's head.

"I've been getting to know Rafe," said Magnus. "He told me that was what he liked to be called. We've been doing up a bedroom for him. See?"

"I do," said Alec.

"Rafe," said Magnus. "Rafael. Do you have a last name?"

Rafe shook his head.

"That's all right. We have two. How would you feel about a middle name? Would you like one?"

Rafe broke into a stream of Spanish. From all the nodding, Alec was fairly sure he was agreeing.

"Um," Alec said. "We probably need to talk."

Magnus laughed. "Oh, do you think so? Excuse us for a minute, Rafe." He moved toward Alec, then stopped short.

Rafe's hands were clenched hard on the edge of Magnus's robe. Magnus looked startled.

Rafe burst out crying. Magnus cast Alec a wild glance, then ran his hands distractedly through his own hair. Between torrential sobs, Rafael began to eke out words.

Alec couldn't speak Rafael's language, but he understood nonetheless. *Don't let me see you, and then have to go away into the loneliness that is the world without you. Please, please, keep me. I'll be good, if you would just keep me.*

Alec started forward, but before he was even in the room, Magnus dropped to his knees and touched the child's face with tender hands. All trace of tears disappeared with a shimmer of magic.

"Hush," said Magnus. "Don't cry. Yes, of course we will, my darling."

Rafe put his face down onto Magnus's shoulder and sobbed his heart out. Magnus patted his shaking back until he was quiet.

"I'm sorry," Magnus said at last, and rocked Rafe in the curve of one red-silk arm. "I really do need to talk to Alec. I'll be right back. I promise you."

He stood and tried to move forward, then cast a rueful glance downward. Rafe was still holding on to his robe.

"He's very determined," Alec explained.

"So, completely unlike any other Shadowhunters of my acquaintance, then," said Magnus, and swept off his robe.

Underneath he was wearing a tunic shirt shimmering with gold thread, and loose ratty gray sweatpants.

"Are those sweatpants mine?"

"Yes," said Magnus. "I missed you."

"Oh," said Alec.

Magnus settled the robe around Rafe's shoulders, wrapping him up so he was a red silk cocoon with a startled face on top. Then he knelt down by Rafe again and lifted Rafael's hands in his, holding them together. Inside Rafe's cupped palms, a tiny fountain of glitter leaped in a shining loop. Rafe gave a hiccuping laugh, full of surprised delight.

"There, you like magic, don't you? Keep your hands together and it will keep going," Magnus murmured, then made his escape while Rafe was watching the fountain.

Alec took Magnus's hand, pulling him out of the new room into the main loft and through into their bedroom. He shut the door and said, "I can explain."

"I think I might understand already, Alexander," said Magnus. "You were away a day and half and you adopted us another kid. What happens if you go away for a week?"

"I didn't mean to," said Alec. "I wasn't going to do anything without asking you. Only he was there, and he's a Shadowhunter, and nobody was looking after him, so I thought I could take him to the Institute here. Or to Alicante."

Magnus had been smiling, but now he stopped. Alec felt even more alarmed.

"We're not adopting him?" Magnus asked. "But . . . can't we?"

Alec blinked.

"I thought we were," Magnus said. "Alec, I promised him. Do you not want to?"

Alec stared at him for another instant. Magnus's face was tense, intent but confused at the same time, as if he was baffled by his own vehemence. Suddenly Alec was laughing. He'd thought he was waiting to be sure, yet this was better, as all the best things in his life were better than any dream that had come before. Not Alec knowing right away, but seeing *Magnus* know right away. It was so sweet, and so obvious that this was exactly the way things should be: seeing Magnus experience the instant instinctive love as Alec had with Max, as Alec learned with Rafael the slow, sweet, and conscious way of love that Magnus had learned with Max. Opening a new door in their familiar beloved home, as if it had always been there.

"Yes," Alec said, breathless with laughter and love. "Yes, I want to."

Magnus's smile returned. Alec pulled him into his arms, then turned so Magnus had his back to the wall. Alec cupped Magnus's face in both hands.

"Give me a minute," Alec said. "Let me look at you. God, I missed home."

Magnus's fascinating eyes were narrowed slightly, watching Alec back, and his smiling mouth was a little startled, as it often was, though what surprised him Alec didn't know. Alec couldn't just look at him. He kissed him, and that mouth was against his own, the kiss making every tired muscle in Alec's body turn to liquid sweetness. To Alec, love always meant this: his shining city of eternal light. The land of lost dreams reclaimed, his first kiss and his last.

Magnus's arms went around him.

"My Alec," Magnus murmured. "Welcome home."

Now when Alec asked himself *Is this how you want to live your whole life?* he could answer yes, and yes, and yes. Every kiss was the answer yes, and the question he would get to ask Magnus someday. They kissed up against the bedroom wall for long bright moments, then both stepped away from the other with a wrench.

"The—" Alec began.

"—kids," Magnus finished. "Later."

"Wait, the kids plural?" asked Alec, and became aware of what Magnus had heard: the stealthy sound of tiny feet exiting Max's room.

"That hellborn brat," Magnus muttered. "I read him eight stories."

"Magnus!"

"What, I can call him that. It's you who can't call him that, because it's infernally insensitive." Magnus grinned, then squinted at his own stained hand. "Alec, I know you don't really care about your clothes, but you don't usually come home covered in soot."

"Better see to the kids," said Alec, ducking out of the bedroom and the conversation.

In the main room was Max, in his triceratops footie pajamas and dragging his fuzzy blankie, regarding Rafe with wide eyes. Rafe stood on the woven rug before the fireplace, wrapped in Magnus's red silk robe. His eyes narrowed into the death stare that had frightened the other kids at the Shadow Market.

Max, who had never felt threatened by anything in his life, smiled guilelessly up at him. Rafe's scowl faltered.

Max turned at the opening of the door. He padded swiftly over to Alec, and Alec knelt down to embrace him.

"Daddy, Daddy!" Max caroled. "This the brother orra sister?"

Rafael's eyebrows went up. He said something quickly in Spanish.

"Not a sister," Magnus translated from the door. "Max, this is Rafe. Say hi."

Max clearly took this as confirmation. He patted Alec's

shoulder as if to say: *great job, Dad, finally you deliver the goods.* Then he turned back to Rafe.

"What are you? Werewolf?" Max guessed.

Rafe glanced at Magnus, who translated. "He says he's a Shadowhunter."

Max beamed. "Daddy's a Shadowhunter. I'm a Shadowhunter too!"

Rafe regarded Max's horns with an air suggesting: *Can you believe this guy?* He shook his head firmly and attempted to explain the situation.

"He says you're a warlock," Magnus translated faithfully. "And that this is a very good thing to be, because it means you can do magic, and magic is cool and pretty." Magnus paused. "Which is so true."

Max's face screwed up in rage. "I'm a Shadowhunter!"

Rafe waved a hand, his attitude one of deep impatience.

"All right, my blue-ringed octopus," Magnus interposed hastily. "Let's continue this debate tomorrow, shall we? Everybody needs sleep. Rafe has had a long day, and it is incredibly past your bedtime."

"I'll read you a story," Alec promised.

Max dropped his fury as swiftly as he'd assumed it. His blue brows knit. He seemed to be thinking deeply. "No bed!" he argued. "Stay up. Be with Rafe." He sidled up to a stunned-looking Rafael and gave him a big hug. "I'm love him."

Rafe hesitated, then hugged Max shyly back. The sight of them made Alec's chest hurt.

He cast a glance back at Magnus, who had an equally smitten expression.

"It's a special occasion," Alec pointed out.

"I was never very good at discipline anyway," said Magnus, and threw himself down beside the kids on the rug. Rafe edged closer, and Magnus looped an arm around him. Rafe cuddled up. "How about you tell us all a bedtime story about what happened in Buenos Aires?"

"It wasn't that exciting," Alec said. "Other than: I found Rafe. I missed you. I came home. That's it. We'll have to go back and forth to Buenos Aires a few times to finalize the adoption, before we can make it official and tell everyone. Maybe we can all go together sometime."

Rafe said several swift sentences in Spanish.

"Is that so?" asked Magnus. "How extremely interesting."

"What are you saying?" Alec asked Rafe anxiously.

"You aren't getting away with this one, Alec Lightwood." Magnus pointed at him. "Not this time. I have a spy!"

Alec went over to the rug, knelt down, and made earnest eye contact with Rafe.

"Rafe," he said. "Please don't be a spy."

Rafe gave Alec a look of firm incomprehension and burst into a torrent of Spanish for Magnus. Alec was certain at least some of it was Rafe promising to be a spy anytime Magnus wanted.

"Sounds like you did some pretty impressive things in Buenos Aires," said Magnus at last. "A lot of people would have given up. What were you thinking?"

Alec picked Max up, tipped him upside down, then sideways, then returned him to the rug, grinning when Max crowed with laughter.

"All I did was think about being worthy of coming home to you," said Alec. "It was nothing much."

There was a silence. Alec turned, a little concerned, to find Magnus staring at him. That surprised look was on his face again, and there was a softness along with it that was rare for Magnus.

"What?" said Alec.

"Nothing, you stealth romance attacker," Magnus said. "How do you always know what to say?"

He leaned forward easily, keeping Rafe held comfortably against him, to give Alec a kiss on the jaw. Alec smiled.

Rafe was studying Max, who seemed gratified Rafe was taking an interest.

"If you want to be a Shadowhunter," said Rafael, in careful English, "you have to train."

"No, Rafe," said Alec. "Max doesn't need to train."

"I train!" said Max.

Alec shook his head. His baby was a warlock. Alec would train Rafe, but Max didn't need to learn any of that. He looked to Magnus for backup, but Magnus was hesitating, his lip caught between his teeth.

"Magnus!"

"Max wants to be just like you," Magnus said. "I can understand that. Are we going to tell him he can't be whatever he wants to be?"

"He's not—" Alec began, and stopped.

"There's nothing to say a warlock couldn't physically fight," said Magnus. "Using magic to substitute for Shadowhunter attributes. It might keep him safe, because people don't expect a warlock to be trained that way. It wouldn't hurt to try. Besides . . . we found Max on the steps of Shadowhunter Academy. Someone might have wanted him to have Shadowhunter training."

Alec hated the idea. But he'd thought, hadn't he, that he

wished he could train a kid? He'd promised himself that he would never be the kind of father who made the walls of home feel like a trap.

If you loved somebody, you trusted them.

"All right," said Alec. "I guess it wouldn't hurt to show them a few ways to stand and fall. Might get them tired enough for bedtime."

Magnus grinned and snapped his fingers. Practice mats suddenly covered the floor. Max scrambled to his feet. Rafe, head pillowed against Magnus's chest, seemed uninterested until Magnus nudged him gently, but then he got up willingly enough.

"Maybe I can teach Rafe a few magic tricks as well," Magnus mused. "He can't be a warlock any more than Max can be a Shadowhunter, but there are magicians around. He might be a very good one."

Alec recalled a story about a magician with Shadowhunter blood, known as Roland the Astonishing, who had lived a long, happy life with his best beloved. He thought of the Market and the Institute mingling in the streets of Buenos Aires, of Jem and Tessa, of love and trust in a changing world, and showing his sons they could be anything they wanted, including happy. He rose and walked to the center of the room.

"Boys? Follow the moves I make," said Alec. "Stand with me, now. All together."

Through Blood, Through Fire

By Cassandra Clare and Robin Wasserman

J

2012

Once upon a time, in a land not so far away, there was a child who should not have been born. A child of disgraced warriors—his blood the blood of the angels, his birthright forfeit while he slept, unknowing, in his mother's womb. A child sentenced to death for the sins of his ancestors, a child spirited away from the Law that condemned and the family that couldn't yet know how much they might someday need him and his progeny.

Once upon a time, a child was lost—or, at least, such is the story as told by those foolish enough to lose him. No one is ever lost to himself.

The child was simply hiding. As his child, and his child's child, learned to hide, and on through the generations, evading those who hunted them—some seeking forgiveness, some seeking annihilation—until, inevitably, that which had been hidden was revealed. The lost child was found.

And that was the end.

Later, when Jem Carstairs tried to remember how the end began, he would remember the tickle of Tessa's hair on his face as he bent close, breathed deep the scent of her, which that day carried a hint of lavender. They were in Provence—so, of course, everything smelled like lavender. But Tessa was alive with it; breathing her in was like breathing in a sunlit meadow, a sea of purpling blossoms, springtime itself. That was what Jem would remember, later. The desire that time stop, freeze the two of them inside this perfect moment; he would remember thinking, with wonder, that this was how it felt to be perfectly satisfied.

When Tessa Gray returned to that moment, the moment before, she remembered the taste of honey, which Jem had drizzled onto a sliver of baguette, then popped into her mouth. The honey, fresh from the hive behind the estate, was almost painfully sweet. Her fingers were sticky with it, and when she pressed them to Jem's soft cheek, they didn't want to let go. She couldn't blame them.

Memory has a tendency to fog the mundane. What Jem and Tessa were actually doing: bickering about whether the cheese they'd acquired that morning was goat or cow, and which of them was responsible for eating so much of it that a second trip to the fromagerie was required. It was a lazy, loving bickering, as befitted their sun-dappled afternoon. They'd come to this retreat in the French countryside to strategize about the lost Herondale—who, they had recently discovered, was also heir to the Seelie and Unseelie Courts, and so in more danger than anyone had ever imagined. This estate, the use of which had been offered by Magnus Bane, was a safe, quiet place to plan where to go from here. The lost Herondale had made it very clear to Jem that she didn't want to be found, but Jem worried this was because she didn't know the depths of danger she was in. They needed to find her. Warn her. Now more than ever.

The urgency was real, but so was their inability to *do* anything about it, which left many hours to fill, gazing out at the sunlit hillside—and at each other.

Tessa had nearly decided to give in and admit that Jem was right about the provenance (goat), if wrong about who'd eaten the most (Tessa), when a light sparked between them, like a tiny falling star. Except it didn't fall; it froze in midair, getting brighter and brighter, blindingly bright, and forming itself into a familiar shape. Tessa sucked in a sharp breath. "Is that . . . ?"

"A heron," Jem confirmed.

Years before, Jem had enchanted a silver pendant in the shape of a heron and pressed it into the palm of a young woman with Herondale blood. A young woman in danger, who steadfastly refused his help.

With this pendant, you can always find me, he had promised, in the silent voice with which he had once spoken. Jem had been Brother Zachariah then, still bearing the robes and duties of the Silent Brotherhood, but this mission—and this promise—had nothing to do with the Brotherhood. Jem was still bound by it, would always be bound by it. *I trust you will summon me for help, if and when you need. Please trust that I will always answer.*

The woman he'd given that pendant to was a Herondale, the last heir of the lost Herondale, and the silver heron meant that after all these years, she needed him. As Jem and Tessa watched, the bird traced letters of fire on the air.

I turned away from you once, but please help me now. I thought I could do this on my own, but the Riders are closing in. If you will not come for me, come for my boy. I thought I could buy his life with my suffering. I thought if I left him, he would be safe. He is not. Please come. I beg you. Save me. Save my child.

—Rosemary Herondale

The light winked out. Jem and Tessa were already in motion. In the century and a half they'd known each other, much had changed, but this truth endured: when a Herondale called, they would answer.

L.A. traffic wasn't as bad as everyone said. It was exponentially worse. Six lanes, all of them nearly at a standstill. As Tessa inched forward, shifting lanes every time a space opened up, Jem felt like he was going to crawl out of his skin. They'd Portaled from France to Los Angeles, but the closest location that was familiar enough to them for the Portal to work was halfway across the city from the source of the distress call. Magnus had reached out to his network of West Coast acolytes and secured them transport to get the rest of the way. The turquoise convertible didn't exactly scream "incognito," but it was enough to carry them the handful of miles from Echo Park to Rosemary Herondale's house in the Hollywood Hills. The ride should only have taken a few minutes. It felt like it had been a year.

I turned away from you once, but please help me now.

The words echoed in Jem's mind. He'd spent decades searching for the lost Herondale—finding her, finally, only to lose her again. But after she'd refused his offer of protection, he'd made her a promise. He would come when she called. He would save her when she needed saving.

I thought I could do this on my own.

James Carstairs would always come to the aid of a Herondale. He would never stop repaying the debts of love.

She had summoned him, using the necklace, and he would do everything in his power to honor his promise, but—

Please come, I beg you. Save me.

There was more than just one life at stake now.

Save my child.

What if they were too late?

Tessa put her hand on Jem's. "This isn't your fault," she said.

Of course she knew what he was thinking. She always did.

"I had her, and I let her walk away." Jem couldn't stop picturing it, that morning on the bridge in Paris, when he'd begged Rosemary Herondale to accept his protection. He had asked a Herondale to trust him and been judged unworthy.

"You didn't *let* her do anything," Tessa pointed out. "She made her own choice."

"The Herondale way," Jem said wryly.

"You let her know you would always be there if she needed you, and now that she does—"

"I'm twiddling my thumbs five miles away, useless."

"Enough." Tessa abruptly swerved onto the shoulder of the road and sped past the clogged lanes, then careened onto the first exit ramp they came to. Instead of slowing down, she picked up speed as they hit the surface streets, weaving wildly from lane to lane to sidewalk. Soon, finally, they found their way into the hills, the road narrowing to a single lane of hairpin turns bounded by a vertiginous drop. Tessa didn't slow down.

"I know you have superhuman reflexes, but—"

"Trust me," she said.

"Infinitely."

He couldn't tell Tessa the other reason he felt guilty—it wasn't simply that he'd let Rosemary slip through his fingers all those years ago. It was what he'd done for her since, which suddenly seemed like next to nothing. Ever since he'd sloughed off his life as Brother Zachariah and fought his way back to James Carstairs—and back to Tessa Gray, the other half of his soul, his heart, his self—he'd given himself permission to be happy. They'd visited Shadow Markets all over the world, keeping watch for Rosemary, always searching for ways they might be able to assist her from a distance. They'd even visited the Market here in L.A. several times, but they had found no trace of her there. What if, despite his best intentions, Jem had missed something, some opportunity to find and help Rosemary before it was too late? What if, lost in his own happiness with Tessa, he'd enabled her suffering?

The car screeched to a stop in front of a small Spanish-style bungalow. The yard was a riot of color: monkeyflowers, hummingbird sage, desert mallow, jacaranda blossoms. A gauntlet of sunflowers watched over the path to the door, nodding in the breeze, as if to welcome them.

"It's like a house from a storybook," Tessa marveled, and Jem agreed. The sky was an impossible blue, dotted with cotton-candy clouds, and the mountains on the horizon made it feel like they were in an Alpine village, rather than the middle of a sprawling metropolis. "It's so peaceful," she added. "Like nothing bad could ever happen here—"

She was interrupted by a piercing scream.

They erupted into motion. Jem shouldered the front door open, readying his sword to face whatever lay beyond. Tessa followed close behind, her hands sparking with angry light. Inside, they found a nightmare: Rosemary lying still in a pool of blood. Looming over her, a massive faerie, his body covered in thick bronze armor, a longsword raised overhead. Its point aimed straight at Rosemary's heart.

In many ways, Jem Carstairs was no longer a Shadowhunter. But in the most important ways, he would always be a Shadowhunter.

He launched himself forward, a whirl of deadly motion, sword stick a silver blur as he hacked at the faerie with the full, righteous force of Shadowhunter rage. His blows glanced off the creature's body without leaving a single mark. Tessa raised her hands and dispatched a blinding white wave of energy at the faerie—he absorbed it without flinching, then, almost carelessly, grabbed Tessa in one massive hand and flung her across the room. She slammed into the wall with a thud that caused Jem physical pain. Jem threw himself in the faerie's path, kicked, spun, swung the sword down sharp and sure in what should have been a mortal blow. Any ordinary faerie—any ordinary Downworlder—would have been felled. This one only laughed, shoved Jem to the floor, and pinned him there beneath a massive foot. Leaving Jem helpless to do anything but watch as the longsword found its mark and stabbed Rosemary through the chest.

The faerie stepped back, freeing Jem to rush to her side—too late. He tore off his shirt, pressed it desperately to Rosemary's gushing wound, determined to keep her life from draining away. Too late.

"I have no quarrel with you, Shadowhunter," the faerie said, then gave a sharp whistle. An enormous bronze steed crashed through the bungalow's front windows in a hail of glass. The faerie hoisted himself onto the horse. "I suggest you refrain from quarreling with me." The horse reared and leaped into the air.

And just like that, horse and Rider were gone.

Rosemary's face was deathly pale, her eyes closed. She was still breathing, if barely. Jem put pressure on the wound, willing her to hold on. Tessa knelt beside him.

He let out a sharp breath, his heart clenching. "Are you hurt?"

"I'm fine. But Rosemary . . ." Tessa gripped Rosemary's hands and closed her eyes in concentration. Seconds passed as she summoned the will to heal. He could see the effort written on her face, the torment. Finally, Tessa turned to Jem, a hollow look in her eyes. He knew what she would say before she said it.

"It's a mortal wound," she murmured. "There's nothing to be done."

Tessa had volunteered as a nurse during one of the mundane world wars—she knew a mortal wound when she saw one. And Jem, during his decades in the Silent Brotherhood, had seen too many Shadowhunters beyond help. Far too many in the Dark War. He too could recognize death in all its guises.

Rosemary's eyes flickered open. Her lips parted, as if she was trying to speak, but she managed only a rasping breath.

There was still one Herondale they could save. "Your child," Jem said. "Where is he?"

Rosemary shook her head, the effort of motion causing her obvious pain.

"Please," she whispered. There was so much blood. Everywhere, blood, her life streaming away. "Please, protect my son."

"Just tell us where to find him," Jem said. "And on my life, I will protect him, I swear—" He stopped, realizing there was no one to receive his promise. The shuddering breath had given way to stillness.

She was gone.

"We'll find him," Tessa promised Jem. "We'll find him before anyone can hurt him. *We will.*"

Jem hadn't moved from Rosemary's body. He held her cool hand in his own, as if he couldn't bring himself to let go. She knew what he was feeling, and it hurt. This was the joy and punishment of loving someone the way she loved Jem—she felt with him. His guilt, his regret, his powerlessness and fury: as they consumed him, they consumed her, too.

Of course, it wasn't just Jem's guilt, Jem's fury. She had plenty of her own. Every Herondale was a part of Will, and so a part of her. That was what it meant to be family. And she had knelt by the cold body of too many Herondales. She could not stomach another meaningless death.

They would find Rosemary's son. They *would* protect him. They would ensure this death was not in vain. Whatever it took.

"It's not just that she's dead," Jem said quietly. His head was lowered, his hair a curtain over his face. But she'd memorized his face, his every expression. She'd spent so many hours, since his return, gazing at him, unable to believe he was really here, restored to life—restored to her. "It's that she died alone."

"She wasn't alone. She's not alone." This was not the first time she and Jem had helped a Herondale into eternity. Once, she had sat on one side of Will, Jem on the other, both of them longing to hold on to him, both summoning the strength to let him go. Jem had been Brother Zachariah then, or that was what the world had seen: runed face, sealed eyes, cold skin, closed heart. She had only ever seen her Jem. It still seemed a miracle that he could open his eyes and see her back.

"Wasn't she?" Very gently, Jem unclasped Rosemary's necklace. He dangled the long silver chain, letting the heron charm spin slowly, gleaming in the afternoon light. "I thought this would be enough—a way to reach out if she needed me. But I *knew* she was in danger from the fey. I shouldn't have underestimated that!"

"I recognized that faerie, Jem," Tessa said. "The bronze braid, the designs on his armor—all those etchings of the sea—that was Fal of Mannan." She'd studied the Riders of Mannan during her time in the Spiral Labyrinth, part of her efforts to better understand the Faerie world. They were very old—ancient, even, from an age of monsters and gods—and they served at the pleasure of the Unseelie King. These were no ordinary faeries. They were more powerful; they were made of wild magic. Perhaps most terrifyingly, they could lie. "Seraph blades are useless against the Riders of Mannan, Jem. They're born assassins—a walking death sentence. Once he found her, no power on earth could have stopped him."

"So then what hope is there for the boy?"

"There's always hope." She risked putting her arms around him then, and very softly extricated Rosemary's hand from his grip. "We find the boy first. Then we make sure the fey never do."

"Not until we're ready for them, at least," Jem said, a note of steel entering his voice.

There were those who believed that because Jem was so kind, so capable of gentleness and generosity, because Jem loved so selflessly, that Jem was weak. There were those who suspected he was not capable of violence or vengeance, who assumed they could hurt Jem and the ones he loved with impunity, because he did not have it in him to strike back.

Those who believed this were wrong.

Those who acted on it would be sorry.

Tessa squeezed the heron charm tightly, its beak pricking sharply against the soft meat of her palm. She could feel Rosemary's essence simmering in the silver, and reached for it with her mind, opening herself to the traces of the woman left behind. It was second nature to her now, Changing into someone else. Usually she needed only to close her eyes and let it wash over her.

This was different. Something felt—not wrong, exactly, but *sticky*. Like she had to yank herself out of her own form and forcibly shove it into another. The transformation felt difficult, almost painful, as it had in her earliest days in London, her bones and muscles and flesh tearing and distorting themselves into alien form, body rebelling against mind, while mind fought its own battle, defending its territory against the colonizing force of an *other*. Tessa forced herself to stay calm, focused. Reminded herself that it was always more difficult to embody the dead. She felt herself shrinking, fading, firm limbs narrowing to Rosemary's delicate, bony frame, and as she did so, the horror flooded in, those final moments. The flash of the longsword. The hot breath of the faerie Rider. The unthinkable pain and pain and pain of the blade thrust once, twice, and finally, fatally. The terror, the despair, and beneath it, the fierce, loving rage on behalf of the boy who must, somewhere out there, survive, he must, he must, he—

"Tessa!"

Then Jem was there, steady, his arms on her shoulders, his gaze firm and kind, his love a tether to keep her from floating away. Jem, always, bringing her home to herself.

"Tessa, you were screaming."

She breathed. She focused. She was Rosemary and she was Tessa, she was the Change itself, the possibility of transformation, the inevitability of flux, and then, mercifully, she was clear.

"I'm okay. It's okay." Even now, after more than a century of Changing, it was strange to hear herself speak with another woman's voice, to look down and see another woman's body as her own.

"Do you know where he is? The boy?"

My boy. Tessa could hear the wonder in Rosemary's voice, could feel the other woman's ongoing surprise that it was possible to love like this. *They won't have him. I won't allow it.*

There was fear, but mostly rage, and Tessa realized that "they" were not the fey. "They" were the Shadowhunters. This was one secret she would keep for herself. Jem didn't need to know that Rosemary had died as she'd lived: convinced they were the enemy.

"Let me go deeper," Tessa said. "She's spent years burying what she knows about him, but it's there. I can feel it."

Rosemary's being was in battle with itself. She'd been entirely consumed with her son, with the fierce need to protect him, but had also spent these years trying with all her might to forget him, to force all thought of him from her consciousness, for his own safety. "She knew the greatest danger in his life was *her*," Tessa said, horrified by the sacrifice this woman had made. "She knew the only way to keep him alive was to let him go."

Tessa let herself sink into the memory—she let go of *Tessa* and gave herself wholly over to *Rosemary*. Focused on the boy, on the strongest memories of him and what had become of him, and let them possess her.

She remembered.

"I don't understand," her husband is saying, but the desperation in his eyes, the grip of his hands on hers as if he knows what will happen when he lets go? That says different. That says he does understand, that this has to be the end, that their son's safety is more important than anything. More important, even, than the two of them, which Rosemary used to think was everything.

Things were different, before she was a mother.

Christopher is three. He looks like and unlike his mother, like and unlike his father. He is their love come to life, their two hearts intertwined and given shape and breath and cherubic cheeks and golden hair and a nose to kiss and a forehead to stroke and a perfect, perfect body that has never known pain or horror and never should. Must never.

"It's about him now. That's all that matters."

"But we're already so careful. . . ."

For one year, they have forced themselves to live apart. In one small apartment, seedy blocks from the Vegas strip: her son and her husband—who now calls himself Elvis, but who has been Barton and Gilbert and Preston and Jack and Jonathan, who has changed not just his name but his face, over and over again, all for her. In an even smaller, much lonelier apartment in a sad stretch of desert behind the airport: Rosemary, feeling their absence with every breath. She haunts their shadows, watches Christopher on the playground, at the zoo, in the pool, never letting him see her. Her son will grow up unable to recognize his mother's face.

She allows herself monthly encounters with her husband—an

hour of stolen kisses and all the details of a childhood passing without her—but that was selfish. She sees that now. Bad enough that the Shadowhunters were able to get as close as they did. Now the fey have sniffed her out. She's set up charms around the apartment, a warning system—she knows their emissaries have been there; her position has been compromised. And she knows what will happen if they find her. If they find him.

"You have to go deeper underground," she tells her husband. "You have to change your identities again, but this time, I can't know what they are. If they find me . . . you can't let me lead them to you."

And he is shaking his head, he is saying no, he can't do this, he can't raise Christopher alone, he can't let her go knowing he can never have her back, he can't risk her facing danger without him, he can't, he won't.

"I have the heron," she reminds him. "I have a way to summon help if I need it."

"But not my help," he says. He hates the necklace, he always has, even before it was tainted with the Shadowhunter's enchantment. He tried to sell it once, without telling her, because he knows her heritage only brings her pain; she forgave him. She always forgives him. "What if you need me*?"*

She knows he hates it, the idea that she would call on a stranger over him. He doesn't understand: this is because a stranger's life means nothing to her. She would let the world burn if it meant keeping Jack and Christopher safe.

"What I need is for you to keep him alive."

The world believes Jack—for that is how she first loved him and how she always thinks of him—is a crook. Untrustworthy, venal, without capacity for trust or love. Rosemary knows better. Most people are spendthrift with their care, spreading it around without discretion.

Jack loves only two things in this world: his wife and his son.

She wishes, sometimes, that he would include himself on that list. She would worry less for him if she thought he allowed any worry for himself.

"Okay, but what if we win?" he says.

"What do you mean?"

"Let's say you defeat the evil faeries and you convince the Shadowhunters you're of no use to them. What if everyone just stops looking for you, and for Christopher, and it's finally safe to be together. How will you find us?"

She laughs, even in her despair. He has always been able to make her laugh. This time, though, he doesn't see the joke. "That's never going to happen," she says gently. "You can't even risk hoping for that to happen."

"Then let's go to the Clave, all of us. Let's throw ourselves on their mercy, ask for their protection. You know they'd give it to you."

This cuts her laughter off abruptly. The Shadowhunters are without mercy. Who knows that better than she? She squeezes his hands, tight enough to hurt. She is very strong. "Never," she says. "Never forget that the Shadowhunters are as grave a threat to Christopher as anyone else. Never forget what they were willing to do to my ancestor—to one of their own. They will not *get their hands on him. Promise me."*

"I swear. But only if you promise too."

There is no other way. He won't do what she asks, won't disappear forever, unless she leaves one thin thread between them. One hope.

"The place you first told me who you really are," he says. "The first place you trusted me with yourself. If you need help, you go there. Help will find you. I will find you."

"It's too dangerous—"

"You don't need to know where we are. You don't need to find us. I'll never go looking for you, I promise. And Christopher will be safe. But you, Rosemary—" His voice catches on her name, as if he knows how rarely he will allow himself to voice it again. "If you need me, I will find you."

They don't say good-bye. Between them, there can be no such thing as good-bye. Only a kiss that should last forever. Only a closed door, a silence, a void. Rosemary sinks to the ground, hugs her knees, prays to a god she does not believe in that she will have enough strength never to let herself be found.

"I know how to find him," Tessa said, already pulling herself out of the Change. It was, again, harder than it should have been. An unfamiliar friction holding the Rosemary shape in place.

Except it wasn't entirely unfamiliar, was it? Something tickled the back of her mind, a memory just out of grasp. Tessa reached, almost had it—but it skittered away, gone.

It felt wrong to be in Los Angeles without checking in on Emma Carstairs. But Jem reminded himself that involving her in this could bring danger to her door, and the girl had faced enough. She reminded him of himself sometimes—both of them orphans, both of them taken in by an Institute, adopted into someone else's family but harboring, always, the secret pain of losing their own. They had both found salvation in a *parabatai*, and Jem could only hope that Emma had found in Julian what he'd always found in Will: not just a partner but a refuge. A home. No one, not even a *parabatai*, could replace what had been lost. Even now, there was a hole in Jem's heart, a raw wound where his parents had been ripped away. This was a limb that could not be replaced, only compensated for. As it had been when he lost Will. As it would be if he ever lost Tessa.

Loss was an inevitability of love, pain the inescapable price of joy. Everyone had to learn this someday—maybe this was what it meant to grow up. He wished, for Emma, that her childhood could have lasted just a little longer. And he wished that he could have been there for her when it ended. But this was always the cold calculus when it came to Emma Carstairs: balancing his desire to be part of her life with the consequences. When he was a Silent Brother, he would have been taunting her with something she couldn't have—her only remaining family, who could, nevertheless, not be her family. Now, as Jem Carstairs, he would have happily taken her into his care, but he was no longer a Shadowhunter—and choosing him would mean Emma would have to give up her entire world. The Law was hard—it was also, so often, lonely.

He kept telling himself: soon. Soon, when he and Tessa had gotten their bearings again. Soon, when he had helped Tessa find the lost Herondale, that piece of Will lost to Will's world. Soon, when the danger had passed.

He worried, sometimes, that these were all flimsy excuses. He'd been alive, one way or another, for over a hundred and fifty years. He should know by now that danger never passed. It only paused, and then only if you were lucky.

"You sure this is the place?" Jem asked Tessa. She'd Changed into Rosemary again, and he could barely look at her. Sometimes Jem missed the cool distance the Silent Brotherhood had forced on him, the way no emotion, however powerful, could penetrate his stony heart. Life was easier without feeling. It wasn't life, he knew. But it was easier.

"Unfortunately, this is definitely the place."

Every city had a Shadow Market, and in a way, they were all the same Market, branches of a single tree—but that didn't stop each Market from taking on the character of its environs. From what Jem could tell, Los Angeles's environs were: tanned, health conscious, and obsessed with automobiles. The Shadow Market was located on a tony corner of Pasadena, and everything there was shiny, including its occupants: vampires with bleach-white fangs, bodybuilding faeries whose bulging muscles sheened with gold-spangled sweat, witches with neon hair and self-writing screenplays for sale, ifrits hawking glittering "star maps" that, on closer examination, had nothing to do with astronomy but were in fact self-updating maps of Los Angeles with a tiny photograph of Magnus Bane marking each location the infamous warlock had caused some infamous chaos. (Tessa bought three of them.)

They threaded through the crowds as quickly as they could. Jem was relieved to no longer bear the robes of the Silent Brotherhood, the ineradicable mark of his creed. There was a taste of the frontier to the Shadow Market, a sense that the rules applied here only as far as anyone was willing to enforce them. Faeries cavorted openly with their fellow Downworlders; warlocks did business with mundanes that should never be done; Shadowhunters were, for obvious reasons, unwelcome.

Their destination lay just beyond the buoyant chaos. In the liminal space between the Shadow Market and the shadows, there stood a ramshackle structure with no sign and no windows. There was nothing to suggest it was anything but a ruin, certainly nothing to mark it as a seedy Downworlder bar, home away from home for down-on-their-luck Downworlders for whom even the Shadow Market wasn't quite shadowy enough. The last thing Jem wanted to do was let Tessa set foot inside, especially wearing the face of someone the Unseelie Court intended to assassinate—but since he'd met her, no one had *let* Tessa do anything.

According to Tessa, Rosemary and her husband had a deal. If Rosemary ever needed him, she would come to this place and somehow make it known that she needed him, and he would appear. It was that middle part of the plan that seemed a little too vague for comfort, but there was no way out but through, Tessa had said cheerfully, then kissed him. Even in someone else's body, even with someone else's lips, her kiss was all Tessa.

They went inside. Tessa went first, Jem following a few minutes later. It seemed prudent to appear they were not together. The bar wasn't much of one. It was just as ramshackle inside as it was out. The large werewolf bouncer at the door sniffed him once, warily, grunted something that sounded very much like "behave," then waved him inside. The crumbling walls were blackened by scorch marks, the floor spattered with beer and, by the smell of it, ichor. Jem surreptitiously clocked the other denizens for potential threat: One bikinied faerie slow dancing with herself, despite the silence, teetering drunkenly on her sky-high heels. One werewolf wrapped in a tattered silk cape, slumped facedown on a table, his scent suggesting he'd been there for days. Jem watched just long enough to make sure he was still breathing, then took a seat at the bar. The bartender, a wizened, balding vampire who looked like he'd been hiding from the sun since long before he Turned, looked Jem up and down, then slid him a drink. The glass was spotted, its contents a filmy pale green. Whatever floated in the center looked like it might once have been alive. Jem decided it was probably safer to stay thirsty.

Three stools away, Tessa hunched over a glass of her own. Jem pretended not to notice.

The faerie sidled between them, her forked tail caressing the rim of Jem's glass. "What's a guy like you, et cetera?"

"Excuse me?"

"You know, all tall, dark, and handsome and"—she shot a glance at the guy in the corner, now snoring with such force that his table rattled beneath him with each exhale—"upright. You don't look like the kind of guy who would hang out around here."

"You know what they say about books and covers," Jem said.

"So you're not as lonely as you look, then?"

Jem realized Tessa, pretending not to listen, was suppressing a smile—and only then understood that the faerie was flirting with him.

"I could help you with that, you know," she said.

"I came here to be alone, actually," Jem said, as politely as he could. The faerie's tail slipped from his glass to his hand, tracing up and down his fingers. Jem pulled away. "And, uh, I'm married."

"Pity." She leaned in, too close, her lips brushing his ear. "See you around, Nephilim." She strutted out of the bar, freeing Jem to concentrate fully on the conversation Tessa was having with the bartender.

"Do I know you?" the bartender asked. Jem stiffened.

"I don't know," Tessa said, "do you?"

"You look familiar around the edges. A little like a girl who used to come in here all the time, with her boyfriend. Bad news, that guy, but she wouldn't hear it. Head over heels, like only a kid can be."

Out of the corner of his eye, Jem caught Tessa's slight smile. "Oh, I don't know that I'd put an age limit on 'head over heels.'"

The bartender gave her an appraising look. "If you say so. Not this girl, though. She grew up to be the flaky kind. Ran off on him and their kid, I heard."

"Terrible," Tessa said dryly. "And Mr. Bad News?"

"Maybe not such bad news. Loyal enough that he's still coming back here after all these years. The kind of guy a certain type can lean on when they need help, if you get me."

"And how would a certain type go about finding him?" Tessa asked. Jem could tell she was trying very hard to keep the eagerness out of her voice.

The bartender cleared his throat, began halfheartedly wiping down the bar. "The right kind of woman, I'm told, would know exactly how to find him," he said, without looking at her. "Because he's exactly the same bird he used to be, just a little less of a crook." He put special emphasis on the words, and Jem could tell by Tessa's expression that they meant something to her. His heart leaped.

Tessa jumped to her feet and tossed a few dollars on the bar. "Thank you."

"Anything for the girl as pretty as a rose. Good luck to—" The dagger seemed to materialize in the center of his forehead. He was dead before he hit the ground. Jem and Tessa whirled around to find Fal of Mannan and his bronze horse thundering through the doorway, bearing down on them with inhuman speed, Fal's longsword falling, Jem's body reacting before his mind had time to process, every second of a lifetime of Shadowhunter training poured into a storm of slashing kicking leaping fighting—all this in under a second, all this ineffectual, because the blade was already falling, was dropping Tessa to the floor in a limp pile of blood and flesh, and Fal of Mannan, impervious, had already taken flight by the time Jem dropped to his knees beside her pale form.

"I suggest you stay dead this time," the faerie advised, and was gone.

She was so pale.

Her features were melting back into her own. The Change always released when she lost consciousness, but something was wrong this time, almost as unsettling as the wound. Her features had nearly returned to Tessa's when, like a taut rubber band suddenly released, they snapped back to Rosemary's. And back again, and again, as if her body couldn't decide whom it wanted to be. Jem pressed the wound, tried to hold in the blood, didn't care whom she looked like, just wanted her body to choose life over death. *The faerie in the bikini.* The thought cut through his haze of panic. Maybe she'd been planted there to spy for the Riders, knowing this place had special meaning for Rosemary and her family; maybe she'd simply recognized "Rosemary" as a woman with a target on her back, a woman who was supposed to be dead, and done her faerie duty. It didn't matter how it had happened. What mattered was that Jem had overlooked her as a threat, which made this his fault, and if Tessa didn't—

But he stopped the thought before it could continue. The wound would have killed a mundane. Maybe even a Shadowhunter. But Tessa's body had shaped itself to Rosemary's form at the time of the attack, the form of a woman who was not just Shadowhunter but heir to the faerie throne—who knew what magic the body might be working on itself in its struggle to survive? Maybe that was why the Change wouldn't let her go—maybe that was her body's way of staving off death until she could heal. Tessa moaned. Jem scooped her into his arms, begging her to hold on.

He had learned much about healing in the Silent Brotherhood, and he did what he could. He thought about how she'd sat by what they all thought was his deathbed, his supply of *yin fen* finally exhausted, the demonic poison overtaking his system, and remembered telling her that she had to let him go. He remembered, too, sitting with the dying Will, giving him permission to leave. He didn't know whether it was strength or selfishness now, but he refused to do the same for Tessa. Not yet: they had waited so long for a life together. They had only just begun.

"Stay," he begged her. "Fight." She was so cold. So light in his arms. Like something essential had already fled. "Whatever it takes, you stay here. I need you, Tessa. I have always needed you."

She wasn't dead. A full day had passed, and she wasn't dead. But she wasn't awake, either, and she hadn't stopped Changing, from Tessa to Rosemary and back again. Sometimes she lasted minutes, once even an hour, in a single form. Sometimes the Change whipped back and forth so quickly that she seemed to have no form at all. Her skin was slick with sweat. At first it was cold to the touch. Then, as fever tore through her, it burned. She had been given medicines—to staunch the blood loss, to give her strength, endurance—remedies that Jem, no longer a

Silent Brother, couldn't treat her with himself. The moment he had gotten her to safety, he'd summoned help.

Or rather, because he and Tessa weren't part of the Clave and had no claim over the Silent Brotherhood, no power with which to summon, he'd *asked* for help. Begged for it. Now Brother Enoch was here, mixing tonics, enacting the complicated, secret rituals that Jem had once been able to do himself. Never before had he regretted leaving the Silent Brotherhood, returning to the land of mortals and mortal peril, but to save Tessa he would have happily pledged the rest of his eternity to those parchment robes, that heart of stone. Instead he could only stand beside Enoch, helpless. Useless. Sometimes, Brother Enoch even made him leave the room.

He understood; he had done the same himself, many a time, secreting himself with the patient, never giving much thought to the torture their loved one might feel on the other side of the wall. In his first life, Jem himself had been the patient, Tessa and Charlotte and Will hovering anxiously around his bed, reading to him, murmuring in comforting voices as he swam between darkness and waking, waiting for him to get stronger, and for the day he would not.

Exiled to the hallway of the small apartment that Magnus—via his ever-expanding and ever-ambiguous network of "friends"—had secured for them, Jem sagged against the wall. *I'm sorry, Will,* he thought. *I never knew.*

To watch the person you loved most fight for every breath. To watch them slipping away, powerless to hold on. To see the face you loved contort with pain, the body you would die to protect trembling, shuddering, broken. It wasn't that Jem had never endured this before. But always before, there had been an intercessor between him and the raw horror of absence. When he was growing up as a Shadowhunter, Jem had always, in the back of his mind, been conscious of the fact that he would die young. He had known he would die long before Will or Tessa, most likely, and even when Tessa or Will flung themselves at danger—as they did so often—there was a part of Jem that had understood he would not be forced to stay very long in a world without them. There had been moments too, in the Silent Brotherhood, when he had stood by Will or Tessa's side, uncertain if they would live or die—but the pain of that had always been mitigated by the same icy distance that mitigated everything else. Now, though, there was nothing in his way, nothing to distract his gaze from the terrifying truth of it. Tessa could die, and he would live on without her, and there was nothing to be done but wait and see. To endure this took all the strength Jem had.

Will had never flinched from Jem's suffering—over and over again, he had endured. He had sat by Jem's bed, held Jem's hand, seen Jem through the darkest of hours. *You were the strongest man I knew,* Jem said silently to his lost friend, *and I never even knew the half of it.*

The door creaked open, and Brother Enoch emerged. Jem still marveled at how alien the Silent Brothers seemed to him now that he was no longer among them. It had taken him some time to get used to the silence in his mind, the chorus of voices that had accompanied his every moment for decades suddenly gone. But now he couldn't imagine it. It felt like trying to remember a dream.

"How is she?"

The wound is no longer a mortal threat. Her shape-shifting abilities seem to have prevented it from having the expected effect.

Jem nearly collapsed with relief. "Can I see her? Is she awake?"

The Silent Brother's runed face was immobile, his eyes and mouth sewn shut, and yet Jem could still sense his concern.

"What is it?" he said. "What aren't you telling me?"

The wound is healing. Her Changing has saved her, but I fear now it is the Changing that poses the greatest threat. Her body, her mind are trapped within it. She seems unable to find her way back to herself—the Change will not let her go. It is as if she has lost her hold on what makes her, essentially, Tessa Gray.

"How do we help her?"

There was true silence then.

"No." Jem refused to accept this. "There's always something. You have a *millennium* of knowledge to draw on. There must be *something*."

In all those years, there has never been a being like Tessa. She is a strong woman, and a powerful one. You must have faith she will find her own way home.

"And what if she doesn't? She just stays like this, in limbo, forever?"

The Changing takes its toll, James. Every transformation requires energy, and no body can sustain this level of energy indefinitely. Not even hers.

The voice in Jem's head was so cool, so measured, it was easy to imagine he didn't care at all. Jem knew better. It was simply that caring, for a Silent Brother, took a different, alien form. This much, Jem could remember: the icy distance from life. The inhuman calm with which events were processed. Words like "care," "need," "fear," "love": they had meaning; it was just a meaning unrecognizable to anyone who could sleep and eat and speak, who lived a life of animal passions. He remembered how grateful he was for the rare moment—almost always, a moment with Tessa—in which he felt a spark of true emotion. How he'd longed for the fires of human passion, for the privilege of *feeling* again, even fear, even sorrow.

Now he almost envied Brother Enoch the ice. This fear, this sorrow; it was too great to bear. "How long, then?"

You should go to her now. Stay with her, until . . .

Until it was over, one way or another.

Tessa knows and does not know that this is a dream.

She knows that Jem is alive and so this must be a dream, this corpse in her lap wearing Jem's face, this body decaying in her arms, skin sloughing from muscle, muscle flaying from bone, bone dissolving to dust. He belonged to her, so briefly, and now he is dust, and she is alone.

He is cold, he is lifeless, he is meat, her Jem, meat for maggots, and they swarm his flesh, and somehow she can hear them, chittering and gobbling, millions of mouths nibbling to nothing, and she screams his name but there is no one to hear but the wriggling death worms, and she knows it to be impossible, but still, she can hear them laugh.

Jem is alive, his eyes bright with laughter, his violin raised to his chin, his music the music he wrote for her, the song of her soul, and the arrow that sails toward him is swift and sure and coated with poison, and when it pierces his heart, the music stops. The violin breaks. All is silence forever.

He flings himself between her and the Mantid demon and she is saved but he is speared in half, and by the time she can catch her breath enough to scream, he is gone.

The Dragonidae demon breathes a cloud of fire and the flames consume him, a blinding blue-and-white fire that burns him from the inside out, and she watches the flames shoot from his mouth, watches his eyes melt with the heat and run down his smoldering cheeks, and his skin crackles like bacon, until, almost mercifully, the light is too bright, all-consuming, and she turns away, only for a single moment of weakness, but when she turns back, there is only a pile of ash; everything that was Jem is gone.

A flash of sword, and he is gone.

A wailing beast swooping out of the sky, a talon raked across pale skin, and he is gone.

And he is gone.

She is alive, and she is alone, and he is gone.

When she can no longer bear it, when she has watched love die ten times, a hundred times, felt her own heart die with him, when there is nothing left but an ocean of blood and a fire that's burned away all but the excruciating pain of loss after loss after loss, she flees to the only place she can, the only safe harbor from horror.

She flees into Rosemary.

The night air is thick and sweet with jacaranda. The hot rush of the Santa Ana winds feels like a hair dryer aimed at her face. Her hands are scratched and bloody from the trellis thorns, but Rosemary barely notices. She drops from the trellis, excitement surging through her the moment her feet touch cement. She made it. The mansion glows pearly in the moonlight, a hulking monument to privilege and privacy. Inside, protected by their alarms and their security patrols, her parents sleep soundly, or at least as soundly as two paranoiacs ever can. But Rosemary is, for the night, free.

Around the block, a jet-black Corvette idles by the curb, its driver in shadow. Rosemary leaps in and favors him with a deep, long kiss.

Since when do you have a Corvette?

Since I found this little guy idling behind the In-N-Out, just begging for a new owner. Like a lost puppy, *Jack says.* I couldn't exactly say no, could I?

He hits the gas. They speed away, screech of the wheels tearing through the hushed silence of Beverly Hills.

He's lying about how he got the car, probably. He lies about everything, her Jack Crow. He's probably even lying about his name. She doesn't care. She's sixteen, she doesn't need to care, she just needs to see the world, the real *world, the* Downworld, *the world her parents are so obnoxiously determined to keep her away from, and he's happy to show her. He's only one year older than she, so he says, but he's already lived enough for twenty lives.*

They met at the beach. She was cutting school—she was, always, cutting school—looking for trouble, not realizing she was looking for him. He aimed her at a strolling couple, all golden hair and glowing tans like they'd stepped out of a catalog for L.A. living, had her ask them for directions, distract them while he lifted the purse. Not that he told her this was his plan. He told her nothing ahead of time, other than trust me, *and so she waited until they were alone, sharing a burrito bought with stolen coin, to ask why he wasn't more worried about stealing from the fey. It had not occurred to him that she had the Sight, that she could see truth beneath their glamour. She said,* What did you think, I was just some bored little rich girl? *He did. She informed him she* was *a bored little rich girl: bored because she could see how much more interesting the world could be. He said,* What do you think of me, that I'm just some cute bad boy you can use to piss off Mommy and Daddy? *She said,* If Mommy and Daddy knew you existed, they'd have you murdered. And no one said you were cute. *One truth and one lie: he is very, very cute, swoop of dark hair over hooded brown eyes, knowing smile saved only for her, face like a stone, sharp in all the right places. It's true, if her parents knew about him, they would want him dead. Which was usually all it took. That first day, he took her to a Downworlder café in Venice. She has always had the Sight, and her father has it too, of course. But her parents have fought so hard to keep her away from Downworld, to stop her from knowing its delights and terrors. This is her first taste—literally, a sundae that, whatever the faeries had infused it with, tasted like summer sunlight. When she kissed him, he tasted like chocolate fudge.*

Tonight he will finally, after weeks of pleading, bring her to the Shadow Market. She lives for these nights with him—not just because of him but because of the world he's opened to her.

He's right, though—also because she knows how much it would piss off her parents.

He makes her wait with the mergirls selling seaweed bracelets while he conducts his business, so she waits and watches and wonders at the magical chaos swirling around her. She's not so awestruck that she doesn't notice the hooded figure shadowing Jack, the werewolf with the handlebar mustache perking up as he passes by, the djinn who tenses at his approach and throws a glance to someone behind her, and she may not know Downworld but she has been taught since childhood to recognize danger, to sense the signs of enemies lying in wait. She has been schooled only in the hypotheticals of battle, learned to gauge, fight, strategize, flee, all in the cosseted comfort of her own home, and has always wondered whether practice could ever prepare her for reality, whether her training would evaporate in the face of terror. Now she has her answer: she knows an ambush when she sees one, and there is no hesitation about what to do next.

She screams. Drops to the ground. Clutches her ankle. Screams,

Jack, Jack, Jack, something bit me, I need you, *and like lightning he is at her side, a tenderness on his face she never knew was possible. He scoops her into his arms, murmurs assurances, until she whispers her warning in his ear,* ambush, *and they run.*

The Corvette is flanked by three werewolves. Jack shouts at her to run, save herself, as he launches himself into the fight, but she hasn't put in all those hours and years of training simply to run. It's different, fighting a real enemy—but not that different. She whirls and leaps, slips the dagger from her ankle holster, slashes and stabs, and she can feel the burn in her cheeks, the fire in her heart as the werewolves flee in defeat and she and Jack fling themselves into the Corvette, screech away, speed wildly into the hills and around the hairpin turns of Mulholland Drive, without speaking, without looking at each other, until he swerves hard onto a lookout point and the car squeals to a stop. Then he's staring at her. Let me guess, *she says,* I've never looked more beautiful. *She knows her cheeks are flushed, her face shining, her eyes sparkling. He says who cares how she looks.* It's the way you fought! The way you think! *He asks where she learned how to do what she did. She can't tell him why her parents have made certain that she knows how to defend herself, that she hasn't left the house without a weapon since she was five years old. She simply says there's a lot he doesn't know about her. He says he knows enough. He says,* I think I'm in love. *She whacks him, hard, tells him it's rude to say that as a joke, even to a girl like her, hard as* adamas. *He says,* What makes you think I'm joking?

Her parents want to move again.

She refuses. Not this time, not again.

They want to know if it's because of him, that guy, the one you sneak out with, *and she can't believe they know. They're having her followed. They are not sorry. They tell her she doesn't understand how dangerous the world is,* that *world, the Downworld, and she says that's because they won't let her. Sixteen years old and she's never lived anywhere longer than a year, because they never stop moving. When she was a child, she accepted their explanations, believed the nightmarish fairy tale of the monster lurking in the dark, longing to destroy them. But the monster has never shown itself, the danger has never manifested, and she has begun to wonder whether her parents are simply paranoid, whether running and hiding has become easier for them than staying still.*

It's not easy for her. She's never had a real friend, because she's forbidden from telling anyone who she actually is.

She is alone.

She has one thing: him. She will not let them take that away.

Her mother says, You're sixteen, you have plenty of time to fill your life with love, but only if we keep you alive long enough to do so. *She says she's already filled her life with love, she loves him, she's staying. Her father says,* You're too young to know what love is, *and she thinks about Jack, about the touch of his hand, the silent laughter in his crooked smile. She thinks about him holding an umbrella over her head to protect her from the rain, about him asking her to teach him to fight, so he can protect himself. She thinks about training him, how he loves that she's stronger, faster, better, and thinks about sitting with him, still and silent, watching the waves.*

She is young, but she knows. She loves him.

Her father says they are leaving in the morning, all of them, a family. He says no more sneaking out.

So she runs out the door in plain sight, openly defies her parents for the first time, and they are too slow, their warnings too familiar, to stop her. She leaves, with nowhere to go—Jack is taking care of some typically vague business somewhere vaguely downtown, and so she walks the deserted streets, skirting freeways, melting into the shadows of underpasses, murders the minutes until she can be sure her parents have gone to sleep. She knows exactly how to slip into the house without waking them, but there's no need.

The doors are flung wide open.

Her mother's body is in the grass, in pieces.

Her father's blood is pooling across the marble entryway. He is holding on for her. He says, They found us. *He says,* Promise me you'll disappear, *and she promises and promises and promises but there's only his corpse to hear.*

She flees without ID or credit card, nothing that could be used to trace her, not that the enemy uses technology to trace, but these things can never be counted on, and her parents are dead.

Her parents are dead.

Her parents are dead because she slowed them down, because they knew it was time to go and she insisted they stay, she fought, she complained, she sulked, they loved her and she held it against them and now they are dead.

She waits at Jack's favorite bar, the one by the Shadow Market that tries its best to look like it doesn't exist. She waits for him there, because he always comes back eventually, and when he does, alarmed to see her, and to see her covered with blood, she collapses in his arms.

Then she tells him the truth.

She tells him she is a Shadowhunter, by line if not by choice. She is fey, by spirit and blood if not by choice. She tells him she is hunted, she is dangerous to all those who love her, she is leaving forever. She tells him this is good-bye.

He doesn't understand. He wants to come with her. She tries again.

Tells him the Unseelie Court wants her dead, has sent an ancient group of faerie assassins with godlike powers to murder her. To let him stay with her would mean signing his death warrant. She tells him staying with her would mean giving up his identity, his city, his whole life. He says, You're supposed to be smart, but you don't get it. You are my life. You are my identity. I will not give you up. As for everything else? *He shrugs.* Who needs it?

*She laughs. She shakes with laughter. Cannot believe she's laughing. Then feels the wet on her cheek, feels him press her face to his chest, wrap his arms around her, realizes: she's not laughing, she's weeping. He promises he will always protect her. She says—out loud, for the first time in her life—*I am a Herondale. I'll protect you. *He says it's a deal.*

It doesn't feel like living on the run. It feels like stones skipping across a lake. They dip into a life, wherever they feel like it—Berlin, Tokyo, Rio, Reykjavik—they establish identities, connections to Downworld, and when Jack burns one too many bridges or Rosemary sniffs out a faerie or, that one time in Paris, they discover a Shadowhunter on their trail, they slough off their identities, change their names and faces, resurface elsewhere. They consider, sometimes, going underground, living as mundanes, but this was her parents' choice, and it proved a fatal one. They will be smarter, safer, and when they build new identities for themselves, they build a network of contacts to call on if the need comes. Contacts, but never allies, never friends, never anyone who would ask too many questions when they appear or disappear. No obligations, no ties, no roots. They need only each other—and then they have Christopher, and everything changes.

She insists on having the baby in secret. No one can know there's another link in this cursed chain. Even when she was pregnant, she realizes later, she understood at some level what she would have to do.

Once she has Christopher, she finally understands her parents, their lives consumed by fear. Not for themselves but for her. She refuses to impose that on her son. She wants a better life for him, something more than barbed wire and security alarms. She wants him to have a home. She wants him to know trust, to know love. She wants to save him from hiding.

Jack hates it. So you want to protect him from having to keep his secret by keeping it for him? You want to keep him from knowing he *has* a secret? *And she says yes, exactly, and then he will grow up unafraid of the world.*

Jack says growing up unafraid of the world is a good way to get destroyed by it.

She waits until the baby is old enough to eat solid food, old enough to survive without her, or—more to the point—that she can persuade herself he can survive without her. She doesn't know if she can survive without him, without either of them, but it's time.

She sends them away.

She is lying on the floor. She is dying. There are strangers here, but she is alone. She is hiding in the secret place in her mind where she keeps her memories of Jack and Christopher. She thinks, maybe she knew this was inevitable, why else return to L.A., where it would be so easy to find her?

She is so tired of being alone. She is tired of missing her son and her husband, tired of forcing herself not to look for them. At least in L.A., she can feel close to the past, to the family she's lost. This is the only city that's ever felt like home, because this was where she found her home in Jack's arms, and in her weakest moments, this is where she imagined a home for them, Rosemary and Jack and

Christopher, a family again, a fairy-tale life in the bungalow. She planted a garden she thought Christopher might like. She filled her days imagining them with her, and now, dying, she imagines them with her still.

Maybe she has won. Maybe Fal will believe the line has died with her, and Christopher can be safe. This is the relief in dying. This, and knowing that if she's wrong, if she's failed, she will be saved having to watch him suffer. She will never watch him die because of who his mother is. This is her last thought, as the pain carries her into darkness. She will never have to know a world without Christopher—

And then she is Tessa again, and she is at Will's side, and Jem is there, and Will is slipping away, and she is trying to fathom how she will face a world without him.

And then Tessa is on a bridge, the Thames beneath her, a miracle beside her. Love reawakened, love returned. Jem, her own true, real, flesh-and-blood James Carstairs, returned to her from silence and stone, and Tessa, whose heart has remained so full through the years and years of empty days, is finally no longer alone.

And then she is standing by a great sea, mountains looming against a crystalline sky. The waves crash loud and sure against the beach, and Jem is beside her, his face as beautiful as the sea. She knows this moment has never been, yet here they are, together. I can't believe this is real, *she says,* that you're here with me.

Come back to me, *Jem says.*

But she is right here, with him.

Stay with me, *Jem says.* Please.

But where would she go?

He's aging, right in front of her, skin sagging, hair graying, flesh withering from the bones, and she knows, she's losing him, she will watch him die as she watches everyone die, she will have to learn all over again to survive in a world without love.

He says, Please, Tessa, I love you.

He is crumbling before her eyes, and she thinks of Rosemary, enduring so many years without the ones she loved most—knowing that her family lived, but could not be with her—and she is grateful, because Jem is here. Now. That's enough, *she says to Jem.* We have right now. We have each other.

Jem says, Please, Tessa, stay with me, I love you, *and she holds on to him, will keep holding, for as long as she can, unafraid of—*

—Tessa woke to find Jem by her side, his hand warm in hers, his eyes closed, his voice low, urgent, chanting, "Stay with me, I love you, stay with me—"

"Where would I go?" she said weakly, and, as his gaze met hers, his face broke into the most beautiful smile she'd ever seen.

Everything hurt, but the pain was a welcome reminder of life. Jem's lips were impossibly soft against hers, as if he was afraid she would break. Tessa didn't recognize the room she was lying in, but she recognized the hooded figure who glided into the room upon Jem's frantic call. "Brother Enoch," she said warmly. "It's been some time."

He has been very worried about you, the Silent Brother said in her mind.

Tessa's fever dreams were already fading, but she felt like she was vibrating with love—and despair. She understood the panicked relief in Jem's eyes, because she had lived inside her own terror, watched him die again and again, and even now, awake, the dreams felt too solid, too much like memory.

She felt the traces of Rosemary in her mind, those last desperate seconds of life giving way to death, almost willingly, and understood: it was easier to die protecting the people you loved than to watch them die in your stead. What horrific choices mortality had to offer.

That was the devil's bargain of Jem's return, the truth she had tried to escape. He could live for centuries, but never truly live—never love—or she could have him back, fully alive and fully *mortal*, inevitably to lose him for good. It hadn't been her choice to make, of course. But Jem had chosen her. She could never regret this.

The Silent Brother asked Jem to step outside and leave them in privacy for a moment, and Jem, laying a final kiss on her forehead, took his leave. Tessa propped herself up in bed, her strength already returning.

Do you remember what happened? Brother Enoch asked.

"I remember that Fal attacked, and then . . . there were so many dreams, and they were so vivid. And . . ." Tessa closed her eyes, trying to retrieve the details of the strange lives she'd lived in her head. "They weren't all mine."

You were trapped for several days inside the Change, Brother Enoch said.

"How could that happen?" Tessa asked in alarm. When she'd first experimented with her powers, there was always fear attached to the transformation. To let herself sink so fully into another person's body and mind was to risk losing herself. It had taken much time and will to make herself trust the Change, trust that no matter how many forms she forced herself into, she remained, indelibly, Tessa Gray. If that faith was misplaced, then how could she ever risk Changing again? "Was it something about the weapon?"

It was not the weapon that caused this.

The cause is in you.

"You sure you're up to this?" Jem asked as he and Tessa approached the L.A. Shadow Market.

"For the hundredth time, yes." She spun around in a very un-Tessa-like pirouette, and Jem smiled, doing his best to disguise his worry. Brother Enoch had given her a clean bill of health, but she was trying too hard to seem like everything was well. And the harder she tried, the more Jem suspected that it was not.

He trusted Tessa, to the ends of the earth. If there was something wrong, she would tell him when she was ready. In the meantime, though, he would worry.

"We've wasted enough time," Tessa said. "Rosemary's counting on us to find her son."

It turned out Jem had been right that something the bartender said tipped off Tessa about how to find Christopher Herondale's father, the man once known as Jack Crow. *He's exactly the same bird he used to be, just a little less of a crook.*

"It's a riddle," Tessa had explained, once she shook off the haze of her fever dreams. "And not even a particularly good one. What's another word for 'crow' . . . that's just a *little less* than a crook?"

"A *rook*," Jem had realized quickly. It gave them, at least, a question to ask—and, given Jack Crow's proclivity for shady Downworlders and small-time crime, the L.A. Shadow Market seemed the obvious place to ask it. Even in the middle of the night and miles in from the coast, the Market smelled like sunshine and ocean. It was crowded, that night, with suntanned witches selling enchanted hemp bracelets, werewolves peddling elaborate wrought-iron mounting equipment that attached weapons to luxury cars, and booth after booth of artisanal, organic juices, all of which seemed to feature some combination of ancient mystical potion and banana.

"Guaranteed to boost muscles, manhood, and personal magnetism by two hundred percent?" Tessa read skeptically as they walked past a warlock juicer.

"Also an excellent source of vitamin C," Jem noted, laughing.

They were both trying so hard to seem normal.

It didn't take very long to find someone who'd heard of a petty criminal by the name of Rook.

"You looking for *Johnny* Rook?" a grizzled werewolf asked, then spit on the ground. Rook apparently had his own booth in the Market but hadn't been seen that night. "You tell him Cassius says hello, and that if he ever tries to scam me again, I'll happily rip his face off with my teeth."

"We'll do that," Tessa said.

They got a similar answer from everyone they spoke to—"Johnny Rook," it seemed, had torn a swath of bad will through the entire L.A. Downworlder community. "It's amazing he still *has* a face to rip off," Tessa observed, after a pretty, young witch explained in great detail the way she would go about disfiguring him if she ever got her long-awaited chance.

"He's not very good at this hiding-out thing, is he?" Jem said.

"I don't think he wants to be very good," Tessa said, with the faraway look she sometimes got when she was hearing someone else's inner voice. "After all this time, all these identities, he comes back home, makes a name for himself at the Shadow

Market—a name painfully close to the one Rosemary knew him by? He wanted her to come find him."

"She came back to L.A. too. Maybe she wanted the same thing."

Tessa sighed, and neither of them said the obvious, that if they'd only loved each other a little less, Rosemary might still be alive, and her son might have a better chance of staying that way.

They roamed the Market—no one knew where to find Johnny Rook that night, and most seemed delighted by the prospect that he might have disappeared forever. Tessa and Jem heard about Johnny's bad attitude, bad business practices, badly fitting trench coat, bad habit of feeding information to whoever asked for it, including—the vampire complaining about this had paused here to aim a murderous look at Jem—filthy Shadowhunters. Until finally, as the sun was rising and the last vendors were departing, they heard something they could use: an address.

Once again, the traffic was terrible. Tessa and Jem finally arrived at the right neighborhood, only to find themselves circling the shady streets for an alarmingly long period of time, unable to locate Rook's house. Tessa eventually realized this was due to unraveling misdirection spells that surrounded their destination, the magic flickering through a few last bursts of power as it faded. *Why unraveling?* Tessa wondered with a sense of dread. At least the deterioration of the spell meant they'd be able to find Rosemary's husband and son.

But they were not the only ones looking. They arrived, again, too late. The house was a ruin of blood and ichor, Mantid demons wreaking bloody destruction in desperate battle with—Tessa's eyes widened—*Emma Carstairs?* There was no time to ask questions, not with the insectoid demons swarming angrily in search of warm-blooded prey. The Riders of Mannan would never have sent demons to do this job, but after what Tessa had learned about Rook, she supposed it was no surprise he had more than one enemy to worry about. Though perhaps his worries were at an end: the ruined body lying in a pool of blood was surely Johnny Rook's. As she launched into action, slicing a razored foreleg, spearing a bulging eyestalk—she spared a moment of sorrow for Rosemary, who had died so desperately hoping that her husband would live.

But all was not lost. Because there, miraculously alive despite the swarm of ravening Mantids, was the treasure Rosemary had sacrificed everything to protect: her son. He was crouched against the wall. As Emma and Jem waged fierce battle against the remaining demons, Tessa approached the boy. She thought she would have recognized him anywhere—not just from Rosemary's memories of her child as a toddler, but from Tessa's own memories of her children and grandchildren, her memories of Will. The determination in his blue eyes, the fierce, graceful way he held himself in the face of danger—there was no doubt, this was a Herondale.

She introduced herself. He said nothing. He was so young, and trying so hard to look brave. She honored this effort, speaking to him as a man, rather than a child needing her care. "Get up, Christopher."

He didn't move, his gaze straying toward—then quickly away from—the body. The boy's jeans were coated in blood, and Tessa wondered if it belonged to his father.

"My father. He . . ." His voice trembled.

"You must grieve later," Tessa told him. He was, by blood if not by training, a warrior. She knew his strength better than he knew it himself. "Right now you are in great danger. More of those things may come, and worse things as well."

"Are you a Shadowhunter?"

She flinched at the disgust in his voice.

"I am not," she said. "But—" Rosemary had tried so hard to keep this from him. Had sacrificed everything so he could live in ignorance of the darkness surrounding him. That life was over now, that lie was dead, and Tessa would be the one to deal it the final, fatal blow. "But you are."

The boy's eyes widened. She extended a hand. "Come now. On your feet, Christopher Herondale. We've been looking for you a long time."

Jem gazed out at a picture-perfect landscape—white crests on a sun-dappled sea, the peaks of the palisades poking at a storybook blue sky, and beside him, Tessa Gray, the love of his many lifetimes—and tried to ascertain why he felt so uneasy. Christopher Herondale, or Kit, as he preferred to be called, was safely under the protection of the L.A. Institute. Jem and Tessa hadn't failed Rosemary, not entirely—they'd lost her but saved her son. Returned a lost Herondale to the Shadowhunter world, where, hopefully, he would find a new home. He and Tessa would soon part—she'd been summoned to the Spiral Labyrinth to look into some troubling reports of illness in the warlock community, while Jem went in search of Malcolm Fade's body and the Black Volume of the Dead. He had a feeling that what Fade had begun here in Los Angeles was only the beginning of a graver danger. All of these were ample reasons to feel uneasy, but that wasn't it.

It was Tessa, who was still holding herself at some remove from him, as if there was something she couldn't bear for him to know.

"This place," Tessa said, sounding troubled. Jem put an arm around her shoulders, held her close. These felt like stolen moments together, before they turned to their respective missions. He breathed her in, trying to memorize the feel of her, already preparing for her absence. "There's something so familiar about it," Tessa said.

"But you've never been here before?" he asked.

She shook her head. "No, it's . . . it's more like something I saw in a dream."

"Was I there with you?"

Tess's smile had an unmistakable trace of sorrow. "You're always in my dreams."

"What's wrong?" Jem said. "Is it Rosemary? I can't help but feel her death is on my shoulders."

"No!" Tessa insisted. "We did everything we could for her. We're still doing everything we can—Kit is safe, for the moment, and hopefully the Riders of Mannan still have no idea he exists. Maybe the Unseelie Court will consider their job done."

"Maybe," Jem said dubiously. They both knew it was unlikely to end here, but at least they'd bought Kit some time. "I wish we could do more for him. No child should have to see his father murdered."

Tessa took his hand. She knew exactly what Jem was thinking about—not just all the orphans scattered through the Shadowhunter world who'd watched their parents cut down in the Dark War, but his own parents, tortured and killed before his eyes. Jem had told no one but Tessa and Will the full horror he'd endured at the hands of that demon, and telling the story even once was almost more than he could stand.

"He's in good hands," Tessa assured him. "He's got a Carstairs by his side. Emma will help him find a new family, as we did with Charlotte, Henry, and Will."

"And each other," Jem said.

"And each other."

"It won't be a replacement for what he's lost, though."

"No. But you can never replace what you've lost, can you?" Tessa said. "You can only find new love to fill the void left behind."

As always, the memory of Will sat between them, his absence a presence.

"We both learned that lesson too young," Jem said, "but I suppose everyone learns it eventually. Loss is what it means to be human."

Tessa started to say something—then burst into tears. Jem wrapped his arms around her, holding her tight against the racking sobs. Smoothed her hair, rubbed her back, waited for the storm to pass. Her pain was his pain, even when he didn't understand its source. "I'm here," he whispered. "I'm with you."

Tessa took a deep, shuddering breath, then met his gaze.

"What is it?" he asked. "You can tell me anything."

"It's . . . it's you." She touched his face gently. "You're with me now, but you won't always be. That's what it means to be human, like you said. Eventually I'll lose you. Because you're mortal, and I'm . . . me."

"Tessa . . ." There were no words to say what he needed to

say, that his love for her stretched beyond time, beyond death, that he had spent too much time these last few days imagining his own world without her, that even unfathomable loss could be survived, that they would love each other for as long as they could—so instead, he held her tight, let her feel his arms sturdy and sure around her, physical evidence: *I am here.*

"Why now?" he asked gently. "Is it something Brother Enoch said?"

"Maybe I didn't realize how much I'd shut myself away from humanity all those years in the Spiral Labyrinth," she admitted. "You fought in the War, you saw so much violence, so much death, but I was hiding—"

"You were fighting," Jem corrected her. "In your way, which was as essential as mine."

"I was fighting. But I was also hiding. I didn't want to be fully in the world until you could be there too. And now, I suppose, I'm waking up to being fully human again. Which is terrifying, especially now."

"Tessa, why *now*?" he said again, alarm growing. What could Brother Enoch have told her to send her into this kind of spiraling panic?

Tessa took his palm and pressed it flat against her stomach. "The reason I had so much trouble Changing back to myself is that I'm not *only* myself right now."

"You mean . . . ?" He was almost afraid to hope.

"I'm pregnant."

"Really?" He felt like a live wire, the idea of it, a *baby*, lighting his synapses on fire. He had never let himself hope for this, because he knew better than anyone how difficult it had been for Tessa, watching her children age as she did not. She had been a wonderful mother, she had loved being a mother, but he knew what it had cost her. He'd always assumed she would never want to endure that again.

"Really. Diapers, strollers, playdates with Magnus and Alec, assuming we can persuade Magnus to wait a few years before he starts training our child to blow things up, the whole nine yards. So . . . what do you think?"

Jem felt like his heart would burst. "I'm happy. I'm—'happy' doesn't even begin to cover it. But you . . ." He examined her expression carefully. He knew her face better than his own, could read it like one of Tessa's beloved books, and he read now: terror, longing, sorrow, and most of all, joy. "You're happy too?"

"I didn't think I could ever feel this way again," Tessa said. "There was a time when I thought there was no more joy left to me. And now . . ." Her smile blazed like the sun. "Why do you look so surprised?"

He didn't know how to say it without hurting her, making the pain fresh again by reminding her of her loss—but of course, she could read his face just as well as he could read hers.

"Yes," said Tessa. "I might lose them someday. As I'll lose you. I can't bear the thought of it."

"Tessa—"

"But we bear so much that seems unthinkable. The only truly unbearable burden is living without love. You taught me that." She laced her fingers through his, squeezed tight. She was so unimaginably strong. "You and Will."

Jem cupped her face in his hands, felt her skin warm against his palms, and felt grateful all over again for the life that had been returned to him. "We're having a child?"

Tessa's eyes shone. The tears had stopped, and in their wake was a look of fierce determination. Jem knew what it had cost her to lose Will, then to lose the family she'd built with him. Jem had lost a piece of himself when his *parabatai* died; Will's absence had left behind a void that nothing could fill. There was, all these years later, still pain. But the pain was evidence of love, was a reminder of Will.

It was easier not to feel. It was safer not to love. It was possible to make oneself silent and still as stone, to wall oneself off from the world and its losses, to empty one's heart. It was possible, but it was not human.

It was not worth losing the chance to love. He had learned this from the Silent Brotherhood and, before that, from Tessa. And before that, of course, from Will. They had both tried so hard to hide from the pain of future loss, to stay solitary, safe from the dangers of connection. They had failed so beautifully.

"We're having a child," Tessa echoed him. "I hope you're ready to give up sleep for a few years."

"Fortunately, I've got plenty of practice at that," he reminded her. "Less so when it comes to diapers."

"I hear they're much improved since the last time I needed them," Tessa said. "We'll have to figure it out together. All of it."

"You're sure?" Jem said. "You want to take all this on yourself again?"

She smiled like Raphael's Madonna. "The nappies, the sleepless nights, the endless crying, the love like you've never imagined was possible, like your heart is living on the outside of your body? The chaos and the fear and the pride and the chance to tuck someone in and read them to sleep? To do all of that with you? I couldn't be more sure."

He took her in his arms then, imagining the life growing

inside of her and the future they would have together, a family, more love to fill the absences left by those they'd lost, more love than either of them had ever imagined still possible. The future was so precarious, shadowed by a looming danger neither of them fully understood, and Jem wondered what kind of world his child would be born into. He thought of all the blood that had been shed these last few years, the growing sense among the Shadowhunters he knew that something dark was rising, that this Cold Peace after the war might be only the eerie calm at the eye of the hurricane, those still, silent moments in which it was possible to deceive yourself into imagining the worst was over.

He and Tessa had been alive too long to deceive themselves, and he thought about what might happen to a child born at the eye of such a storm. He thought about Tessa, her will and her strength, her refusal to let loss after loss harden her against love, her refusal to hide any longer from the brutality of the mortal world, her determination to fight, to hold on.

She too had been a child born of storms, he thought, as had he, as had Will. All three had risen in love through their struggles to find happiness—and without the struggle, would the happiness have been so great?

He closed his eyes and pressed a kiss to Tessa's hair. Behind his lids, he did not see darkness but the light of a London morning and Will there, smiling at him. *A new soul made of you and Tessa,* Will said. *I can hardly wait to meet such a paragon.*

"Do you see him too?" Tessa whispered.

"I see him," Jem said, and he held her even more tightly against him, the new life they had created together between them.

The Lost World

By Cassandra Clare and Kelly Link

The world and everything in it had changed . . . people passed me as I sat—people who laughed and joked and gossiped. It seemed to me that I watched them almost as a dead man might watch the living.

—Arthur Conan Doyle, *The Fate of the Evangelion*

2013

"So you didn't sense any kind of demonic energy or other kind of supernatural emanation from the tarn?" Ty asked.

It was March, and outside the Scholomance the world was wintry white, as if all the Carpathian Mountains were in mourning. Ty was writing at his desk, in the black notebook where for six months he had been keeping a record of the side effects, benefits, and discoverable qualities of Livvy's resurrected state.

Early entries ran along the lines of *Incorporeal. Invisible to all with some exceptions. Some animals appear to sense her. Most cats, for example, though cannot entirely be sure since cats do not talk. Can, with some effort, make herself invisible to me. Have asked her not to do this. Find it worrying. Does not sleep. Does not need food. Says she believes it is possible she can taste things that I (Ty) eat. Will test this—Livvy wait in other room while I taste various foods—but not the most pressing of experiments, and there is the question of whether or not this is entirely related to Livvy's current state or whether it is due to being twins or the undeniable fact that I have made all of this happen. Magnus says there is very little reliable information. Sense of smell unimpaired. Tested her on clean and dirty socks as well as various herbs. Insensible to extremes of heat or cold. Says that she is happy to be here with me. Says that she loves me and wishes to stay with me. Proof, can we assume, that some things (some emotions or relationships) survive the grave?*

"No?" Livvy said. Often, while Ty wrote, she hovered at his shoulder, to see what he wrote down and to qualify his notes with her own observations. But at the moment, she was more interested in something she had discovered carved into the wall just below the headboard of Ty's bed. If she made an effort, she could push herself through the wooden headboard, just like a ghost in one of Dru's movies, who could walk through walls. How she would have liked to show off this ability to her sister—but she and Ty had agreed that she should not manifest in front of the rest of their family.

Behind the headboard of Ty's dorm-issue bed, the tops of letters just faintly visible, someone had gouged a rough sentence into the wall, and a date. "'I did not choose this life,'" Livvy said out loud.

"What?" Ty said, sounding startled.

"Oh," Livvy said hastily. "That's not an observation, Ty. It's something that someone carved here on the wall. There's a year, too. '1904.' But no name."

Ty had been at the Scholomance for four months now. And where Ty went, Livvy went too. Four months at the Scholomance, and six months since Livvy had come back as a ghost when the catalyst Ty was using in his attempt to resurrect her had failed him, and the spell from the Black Volume of the Dead had gone awry. At first Livvy had not been entirely herself. There were pages in Ty's notebook about the gaps in her memory, the ways in which she did not seem to be the same person. But, gradually, she had come back to herself. Ty had written in his notebook: *Jet lag, when one travels between coasts or countries and experiences a change in time zones, is part of the human condition. It is possible that Livvy is experiencing some version of this. A writer once called Death "that unknown country." Presumably Livvy had to travel, at least psychically, quite far to come back to me.*

All in all, the last few months had been a time of great and alarming changes—Livvy's ghostly return from the dead had been neither the greatest nor the most alarming. The Cohort and their supporters were now shut off in Idris, while supporters of the Clave had been exiled to all the corners of the globe. No one could get into Idris and none could get out. "What do you think they're eating?" Ty had asked Livvy. "Each other, hopefully," Livvy replied. "Or zucchini. Lots of zucchini." She felt sure that no one honestly enjoyed zucchini.

The Scholomance, too, had changed. Historically it was the institution where Centurions were trained, and Livvy had heard the Centurions who descended on the L.A. Institute speak of the place. It had become a recruiting ground for the Cohort, and it had sounded thoroughly horrible. Those Cohort sympathizers were now in Idris, and that was no great loss as far as Livvy could see. Every member of the Cohort she had ever met had been a bully, a bigot, or a petty-minded bootlicker. The zucchini of the Shadowhunter world. Who missed them? The real problem now was not that they were gone but that they were not gone enough. There they were, lurking inside the wards of Idris, planning and plotting only the Angel knew what.

Some of the Scholomance's instructors had gone to Idris with the Centurions, and now Jia Penhallow, the former Consul, was in charge here. She'd decided to step down as Consul so that she could have time to rest, but once her health improved, she wanted something useful to do. Her husband, Patrick, was with her, and Ragnor Fell had stepped in too, to teach and offer guidance. Catarina Loss was a frequent presence as well. She spent more time at the new Academy on Luke Garroway's farm in upstate New York, but she would stop by the Scholomance now and then to restock the infirmary or heal unusual magical maladies.

There were other changes. Kit had gone off to live with Jem and Tessa, while Helen and Aline were now ensconced at the Los Angeles Institute. Livvy wished with all of her ghostly heart that she and Ty could have stayed in Los Angeles, but Ty had been adamant. Going off to the Scholomance was the penance he must endure for his great crime—the great crime of attempting to bring Livvy back. Not very flattering, Livvy thought, to now be the ghostly albatross that Ty wore around his neck, but better a ghostly albatross than simply a dead sister.

Ty said, "No one chooses this life." He had put down his pen.

He sounded as if he were somewhere far away. Livvy didn't think he was talking about the Scholomance.

She said hastily, "I saw animal tracks around Dimmet Tarn. It isn't fully iced over—I heard some of the other students say that this year is warmer than any on record. Can you imagine more snow than we've had? It looks as if animals come down to drink from Dimmet Tarn. I wonder what they are."

"A Carpathian lynx, perhaps," Ty said. "They are supposed to haunt the area."

"Same," Livvy said. But Ty didn't laugh at her joke.

He said, "You were away for nearly three hours. I noted it

in the book. I felt as if some part of me was falling asleep. Pins and needles."

Livvy said, "I felt it too. Like a rubber band being stretched."

The past week, when Ty was not in classes, they had been experimenting with timed intervals in which Livvy moved progressively farther and farther away from Ty. Dimmet Tarn was only just past the Scholomance, less than a quarter of a mile away from Ty's room, but it was the farthest Livvy had ventured. She'd hovered over the surface of the water for so long she had almost begun to feel hypnotized by the unmoving black stillness beneath her. She had been able to see the reflection of leafless trees on the tarn, but no matter how close she pressed her face to the flat inky surface of the water, she had not been able to see herself. She could see her hand if she held it out, but not the reflection of her hand, and that had made her feel very strange. So instead she looked only at the water and tried to let go of all her unhappinesses and worries. The only thing to hold on to was Ty.

So eventually she had withdrawn her attention from Dimmet Tarn and she had come back to him. She said, "I would have liked to see a Carpathian lynx."

"They're endangered," Ty said. "And very shy."

"And I am very invisible," Livvy said. "So I feel my chances are quite good. But please mark down that Dimmet Tarn is quite an ordinary tarn. Those old stories, I think, must be only that. Stories."

"Further investigation required, let us say," Ty said. "I will continue to do research in the library."

They had picked Dimmet Tarn as a destination for Livvy not only because the distance was a useful measure but because there were lots of interesting stories about Dimmet Tarn among the other students at the Scholomance. It had once been a place of great uncanniness, supposedly, but none of the stories were in agreement as to the nature of its uncanniness. Some stories said that it was once a place beloved of the faeries. Others said that there was a great clutch of demonic eggs far down at the bottom of the tarn, so deep down that no sounding rope could give a true measure. Another story said that an unhappy warlock had enchanted the water so that to swim in it would curse the swimmer with a toe fungus that eventually hatched miniature blue and green toadstools, which sounded improbable, but then warlocks were often improbably petty. It was one of the potential side effects of immortality. You got very bad at letting go of things.

"Did you try to submerge yourself?" Ty asked.

"Yes," Livvy said. Much like pushing through a headboard, she had been able to push herself down into the water. It had been nothing like swimming had been back in Los Angeles, where the water was green or blue or gray, depending on the time of day and whether the sun was shining, and all the waves wore a cap of white froth and came rushing up noisily on the wet sand. Dimmet Tarn was black, utterly black, as black as night but without stars or moon or the promise that dawn would ever come. Black as tar, black as—nothingness.

Livvy had not felt the water of Dimmet Tarn, but she had sunk into it all the same, slowly, until her head was beneath the surface, darkness below her, the suggestion of the winter sky above shrinking until it was gone altogether and she saw and felt nothing. She had sunk down and down into that void, that blackness, that nothingness, until it was not clear to her whether she was still sinking at all. Nothingness was all around her. Only that strand that connected her to Ty remained, as thin as it could be and yet stronger than the strongest metal.

She and Ty had theorized that perhaps since she was now, as a ghost, uncanny herself, she might be able to discover the secret of Dimmet Tarn. Livvy had liked the idea she might have a superpower of some kind, be useful in some way, and Ty liked the idea that there might be a local mystery that they could solve. But if Dimmet Tarn was keeping an occult secret, Livvy had not discovered it.

"They're going to ring the bell for dinner soon," Livvy said.

"I hope it's not olive loaf," Ty said.

"It is," Livvy said. "Can't you smell it?"

"Ugh," Ty said. He put down the black notebook and picked up the red one in which he kept his timetables. He flipped back a page and said, "That's three times in four weeks."

Livvy had worried about what it would be like for her brother, to be so far away from home, but Ty had adapted surprisingly well. He'd drawn up a schedule for himself on the first night, and he followed it faithfully. He laid out his clothes each night for the following morning, and before he fell asleep he checked his alarm clock against the watch he wore around his wrist. Ty kept one of Julian's old empty lighters in the pocket of his jeans, for when he needed to keep his fingers busy, and he wore his headphones around his neck during classes like a kind of talisman.

After he'd failed to resurrect Livvy from the dead, Ty had thrown his phone into the Pacific Ocean so he wouldn't be tempted to try other spells from the Black Volume. He had a new phone now, but he hadn't uploaded his photos. More penance, Livvy thought, although Ty hadn't said so. Instead, he had a triptych of paintings by Julian on the wall above his desk: one of their parents, one of all the Blackthorn siblings and Diana and Emma, with the ocean behind them. The third painting was of Livvy, and Livvy often found herself staring at it so that she wouldn't forget her own face. Not being able to see yourself in a mirror was not a big deal, compared to other parts of being dead, but all the same it was not very pleasant.

Ty wrote a letter to Julian every week, and he wrote Dru and Mark and Diana and Tavvy and Helen postcards, but Livvy couldn't help but notice that he never wrote Kit at all. She knew Kit had been angry at Ty for trying the resurrection spell, but surely Kit had gotten over that by now? If she brought up Kit, though, Ty shrugged and put his headphones on.

In general, though, Ty seemed to be fitting in just fine at the Scholomance. Better than Livvy would have imagined, before her death, had she imagined such a thing. Ty hadn't made any friends, but he managed everything that the instructors asked of him, and if he was mostly quiet or withdrawn otherwise, no one seemed to think that was strange. There were a lot of Shadowhunter kids at the Scholomance now who were worried or afraid or occasionally went off to cry in a corner. Ty was keeping his head down. No one except for Livvy, and maybe Julian, would have known there was something wrong.

But there was something wrong. And Livvy had no idea how to fix it, especially since she had no idea what was wrong. All she could do was be there. She had promised him that she would always be there. He had saved her from death, and she loved him.

Anyway, she didn't have anywhere else to be.

Sometimes, while Ty was studying or sleeping, she went exploring. To the library, where the great silvery tree grew through the broken ceiling like a promise that no wall or hardship (or promise) endured forever.

Sometimes she lingered by a student reading by themselves in the library, or perched on a window ledge, looking out at Dimmet Tarn. She would press all her attention upon them, testing them, to see if she could make herself known. "Can you see me? Can you see me?"

But no one saw her. Once, late at night, Livvy came across two girls kissing in an alcove, one with curly black hair and the other fair. They were only a year or two older than she, and Livvy wondered if this was their first kiss. The fair-headed one drew back at last and said, "It's late. I should get back to my room. Books aren't going to read themselves."

The curly-haired girl sighed but said, "Okay, but that's true of kisses, too. I'm not going to make out with myself."

The other said, "Good point."

But this time the curly-haired girl was the one who broke away from the embrace, laughing. She said, "Okay, okay. It's late and you've got the kissing thing down. Top marks. And there'll be time for more kissing later. So much time for so much kissing. Go read your books. See you at practice tomorrow?"

"Sure," the fair-haired girl said, and ducked her head, blushing. Livvy trailed her all the way back to her room. "Can you see me? Can't you see?" she demanded. "Life is short! Oh, can't you see? There's less time than you think, and then it's gone."

Sometimes Livvy wondered if she was going crazy. But it was easier in the day, when Ty was awake. Then she wasn't so alone.

After dinner, which was indeed olive loaf, while he was getting ready for bed, Ty said, "Everyone keeps talking about Idris. About what might be going on in there."

"Jerks being jerks is what's going on there," Livvy said.

"No one can get in because of the wards," Ty said. "But I was listening to them and I had an idea. No one can get in, but what if *you* could get in?"

"Me?" Livvy said.

"You," Ty said. "Why not? You can pass through all sorts of things. Walls. Doors. We could at least test it."

"Well," Livvy began, and then was silent. A feeling came over her, and she realized that the feeling was excitement.

She grinned back at her twin. "You're right," she said. "We should at least test it."

"Tomorrow, after Volcanoes and the Demons that Dwell in Them," Ty said. He made a note in his schedule.

But that night, while Ty was sleeping, Livvy found herself pulled toward Dimmet Tarn again, toward the nothingness of its depths. Every time she thought of Idris, and the experiment that she and Ty would try tomorrow, she thought of her own death, of the blow that Annabel had struck. That moment of pain and dislocation. The stricken look on Julian's face as she fled her body.

Of course Annabel wasn't in Idris now. Annabel was dead. And of course, even if Annabel had still been alive, Livvy shouldn't be afraid of her murderer. A Shadowhunter shouldn't be afraid. But the thought of her own body on the cold stone of the Accords Hall, the thought of her body burnt upon a pyre, the thought of Lake Lyn, where she had returned, all of these pursued her as she sank into the blackness of Dimmet Tarn and let its nothingness hide her.

It was almost morning when at last she rose up, pearly light already sliding over the crust of snow around the tarn. And there, too, on the lip of the tarn was a small crumpled heap as if someone had dropped their hat or scarf.

Livvy drew near and saw that it was a kitten, starved and motionless. Its paws were torn by the ice, and there were marks of bright blood in the snow. Its ears were long, tipped in black, and its coat was spotted with black as well. "You poor thing," Livvy said, and the kitten opened its eyes. It looked right at Livvy and snarled noiselessly. Then its eyes closed again.

Livvy fled back to the Scholomance, to Ty.

"Wake up, Ty!" she said. "Hurry, wake up, wake up!"

Ty sat bolt upright. "What is it? What's wrong?"

"There's a Carpathian lynx down by Dimmet Tarn," Livvy said. "A kitten. I think it's dying. Hurry, Ty."

He threw a coat over his pajamas and pulled on his boots. He bundled up a blanket in his arms. "Show me," he said.

The kitten was still alive when they got back to Dimmet Tarn, Ty's boots breaking through the snow with each step. He sank, sometimes, to his knees. But Livvy, of course, floated above the snow. There were advantages, sometimes, to being dead. Livvy could admit that.

You could see the small rise and fall of the lynx's chest. Small wisps of breath rose from its black nose.

"Is it going to be okay?" Livvy asked. "Will it live?"

Ty knelt down in the bank of snow beside the lynx. He began to wrap it in the blanket. "I don't know," he said. "But if it lives, it will be because you saved it, Livvy."

"No," Livvy said. "I found it. But I can't save it. You'll have to be the one who saves it."

"Then we'll both have saved it," Ty said, and smiled at her. If Livvy had had a notebook, she would have written it down. It had been a long time since she'd seen her brother smile.

Ty found a box and put an old sweater in it. From the kitchen he got a plate of chicken casserole and a bowl to fill with water. When the lynx wouldn't eat or drink, he went to the infirmary and asked Catarina Loss what to do.

"She says to moisten a piece of cloth—a T-shirt, maybe? Or a hand towel?—and then drip water into its mouth."

"Then do it," Livvy said anxiously. How useless she felt!

"Catarina gave me a hot water bottle too," Ty said. He reached into the box and unwrapped the bundle of blanket enough to put the hot water bottle in as well. Then he began to drip water onto the lynx's mouth until the fur was wet all around its face.

Ty was more patient than Livvy thought she could have been. He dipped the smallest section of T-shirt sleeve into a bowl of water and then wrung it out gently, until the animal's mouth opened and a pink tongue poked out. Ty dripped water onto the tongue, and when the lynx swallowed it, he picked up the bowl and tipped it slowly so that the lynx could drink without moving its head. After that, he tore the chicken into small pieces and fed the pieces to it. The lynx ate ravenously, making small, angry noises.

At last the chicken was gone. "Go get more," Livvy said.

Ty said, "No. Catarina said not to let it eat too much at first." He tucked a towel in around the lynx, and then covered over the box with a jacket. "We'll let it sleep now. I'll give it more later."

"What about a name? Are you going to give it a name?"

Ty scratched his head. Livvy saw, with a pang, that he had the faintest beginnings of a beard on his face. But he, of course, would continue to grow older. One day he would be a man, but she would always be a child. Ty said, gaze fixed on one black-tipped ear, all that was visible of the lynx, "But we don't know if it's a boy or a girl."

"Then we can give it a gender-neutral name," Livvy said. "Like Stripes or Hero or Commander Kitty."

"Let's see if it lives first," Ty said. By mutual agreement, they put off the plan to test Livvy's capabilities to bypass the boundaries of Idris until the next day. Ty attended his classes, and Livvy watched over the lynx, and in between Ty's classes he supplied their ever more lively captive with scraps of food and bowls of milk. By the time the dinner bells were ringing, they had ascertained the lynx's gender and Ty's arms were bloody with scratches. But the lynx was asleep and purring in his lap.

There was a makeshift litter box in the closet, and as it turned out, Ty's fidget toys also made excellent cat toys.

"Irene," Ty said. Once again, Livvy saw, he was smiling. "Let's call her Irene."

In the end, he skipped dinner altogether. And that night, Livvy did not go back to Dimmet Tarn. Instead she watched over her brother, Irene curled around his head on the pillow, her glowing eyes closing and opening, always fixed on Livvy.

There was a new note in Ty's book. It said, *Lynx sees her. Is this because the Lynx (have given her a name, Irene) was close to death? Or because she is a cat, though larger than house cats? Inconclusive. More research needed, though large cats may be hard to come by.*

* * *

If it hadn't been for the matter of Idris, Livvy could have spent the whole next day playing with Irene. She and Ty had discovered that if Livvy drew her foot along the ground, back and forth, Irene would try to pounce, over and over. She could not understand why she couldn't catch Livvy. "Like a laser pointer," Ty said. "You're the red dot that always escapes."

"That's me," Livvy said. "The elusive red dot. So, Idris. How do we do this?"

Shadowhunters used Portals to go to Idris. Only now, Idris was warded and Portals wouldn't work. Livvy, being dead, didn't need Portals. When Ty had come to the Scholomance, he had stepped through a Portal and Livvy had willed herself to go with Ty. To be in the place where Ty was.

Ty said, "It should be the same as Dimmet Tarn. Or when I'm in class and suddenly you just show up. Hold Idris in your mind, like a picture. Let yourself go there."

"You make it sound easy," Livvy said.

"Something ought to be easy," Ty said. "Everything can't be hard all the time."

"Fine," Livvy said. "Here we go."

She thought of Idris, of Lake Lyn. Of the moment she was no longer dead. Saw it in her mind and held it there. And then she was no longer in the room with Ty and Irene. Instead she was floating above the great stillness of Dimmet Tarn.

"Great job, Livvy," she told herself. But she didn't go back to Ty. Instead she thought of Idris once more, and imagined, this time, that she was alive again. She thought of how once, when she'd been very young, she had Portaled with her family from the beach outside the L.A. Institute into Idris. Had that been the first time she'd gone to Idris?

She closed her eyes, opened them, and found herself beside the ocean in L.A. The sun was just coming up, turning the foam atop the waves to fiery lace. And there was the Institute where her family would be waking up soon. Making breakfast. Did they think of her? Dream of her and then wake and think of her again?

"This isn't where I want to be," she said, and knew it wasn't true. She tried again. "This isn't where I'm *supposed* to be."

The sun was rising, and she tried to feel its warmth—something other than its brightness. To warm herself. What she would have given to feel that wet velvet crust of the top layer of sand under her feet, to feel the cold grittiness of the sand underneath change in temperature as the warmth of her human feet soaked away. To scream herself hoarse, knowing that no one would hear over the roar of the surf. She squatted and tried with every particle of herself to pick up a piece of beach glass. But it was a useless endeavor. She had no more effect on the world than a fragment of dream. It seemed to her, in fact, that she was shrinking, growing smaller and smaller until she no longer stood on the sand, but was instead slipping between the icy grains, now large as boulders around her.

"No!" she said. And was no longer on the beach in Los Angeles. Instead she was back at Dimmet Tarn, her bare feet skimming the deep black.

"Get a grip on yourself," she told herself sternly. "And try again. What's the worst that could happen?"

This time, instead of thinking of Idris, Livvy thought of the way in which it was bounded. She thought of the wards that kept out everyone who was not welcome. She imagined Idris, picturing the terrible dessert they served at least once a month at the Scholomance, in which unidentifiable pieces of fruit were embedded in a vast Jell-O dome. There were certain advantages to being dead: you were not expected to be enthusiastic about terrible desserts simply because they were desserts. But nevertheless, even dead, she remembered the consistency of Jell-O, and she imagined Idris as if it had been encased in gelatin instead of magic. She imagined traveling to Idris, to the shore of Lake Lyn, as if she were pressing up against a Jell-O mold. Doing this, she could almost feel the wards of Idris resisting her: tingling, slippery, and only the slightest bit yielding. Still she persisted, imagining pressing all of her incorporeal self against their magic.

Livvy closed her eyes, and when she opened them, she was in a green meadow where she had never been before. There were sugar-white mountains against the horizon, and insects, buzzing languorously like secrets, in among the blades of grass. She was not in Idris. What was even the point of being a ghost if you didn't get to infiltrate the bad guys' lair in order to haunt jerks like the Cohort?

"This would prove that you fail at life, Livvy, except, you know," she said to herself. And then was surprised, because it seemed that someone had heard and was answering her.

"If they failed, would it really matter?" the voice said. A male voice with a strong Spanish accent. Livvy could see no one, but she could hear the voice as if the speaker stood beside her. "Then we could fight. I'm tired of this. We've been sitting around on our asses for months now, eating basic rations and arguing about the pettiest of goals."

"Shut up, Manuel," said a voice that Livvy knew. Zara. And now she recognized Manuel's voice as well. "We have been told to check the wards, and so we will check the wards. Obedience is a virtue in a Shadowhunter. So is patience."

"Patience!" Manuel said. "Like you've ever practiced patience in your life, Zara."

Livvy could see nothing but the meadow around her, the far white peaks of the mountain range. But she found that she could feel Idris, warded against her, pressing against her consciousness. Though she couldn't penetrate the wards, apparently she could eavesdrop through them. They must be standing right there, Livvy on one side of the wards and Zara and Manuel on the other.

"I am practicing enormous patience right now in not killing you," Zara retorted.

"I wish you would," Manuel said. "Then I wouldn't have to suffer through another dinner of dandelion greens and half a parsnip garnished with unseasoned pigeon while your father's cronies bicker about whether we mark the start of this new age by naming ourselves Raziel's Chosen Angels or the Birthright or the Glorious Front. Why not just call ourselves Super Amazing People Who Did the Right Thing but Now Have Run Out of Coffee and Staples?"

"You think with your stomach," Zara said.

Manuel ignored this. "Meanwhile, out there, there are Downworlders having baguettes slathered with Brie, and chocolate chip cookies, and vats and vats of coffee. Do you know how awful it is to spy on people who are eating delicious things like chocolate croissants when you don't even have a cube of sugar? By the Angel, I never thought I would say this, but I miss the food at the Scholomance. What I would give for olive loaf. Olive loaf!"

Livvy thought, *I'm dead and I wouldn't eat olive loaf. But then, I wouldn't hang out with Zara, either.* She could still see nothing of Idris inside the wards, but as she tried to push through again, glittering symbols she did not recognize appeared, hanging in the air.

"This will be a brief chapter in the history of the Imperishable Order," Zara said. "Or whatever historians end up calling us. Anyway, the point is, when we see that the time is right to leave Idris and we have the whole world to set to rights, no one is going to bother recording that you missed olive loaf. They're going to write about all the battles that we won, and how good we looked winning them, and how all our enemies like Emma Carstairs died pitifully choking on their own pleas for mercy."

"Last time I looked, she was partying on a beach," Manuel said. "As if she wasn't thinking about us at all."

"Good," Zara said. "Let them not think about us. And then let us be the last thing they ever see. Come on. The wards are holding. Let's get back before there's nothing left for lunch."

And like that, the voices were gone. Livvy was alone in the green meadow, Idris as inaccessible as ever. But she had succeeded, sort of, hadn't she? She hadn't gotten past the wards, but she had gathered information. She'd learned, what? That the Cohort was low on food, and just as unpleasant as ever. They had some sort of plan to emerge at some unknown date from Idris, in some kind of surprise attack. Most important, they seemed to be able to spy, somehow, on the outside world. She should go back to Ty and report what she had learned. All she had to do was tug on that strand of necromantical magic that connected her to Ty, and she would go flying back. This was the farthest she had ever gone from her twin, and it was not entirely a comfortable sensation. And yet it *was* a sensation and Livvy found herself savoring it. There was so little left to feel. For months now she had been less than a shadow at Ty's heels. Now, stretched so far away from him, she felt both more and less solid than she had been.

She sank into the grassy meadow, feeling herself growing smaller and smaller until the blades of grass towered around her. The noise of the insects changed—where before it had been shrill, now it slowed and grew thunderous. Why could she hear and see but not touch anything? She stretched out her hand toward a towering stalk of grass and then drew it back with a gasp. There was a bead of blood on her palm as if she had cut herself on the green edge. And when she raised her hand to her mouth, her blood was the most delicious thing she had ever tasted. She closed her eyes, savoring the taste, and when she opened them again, she was floating above the placid black nothing of Dimmet Tarn.

There was something she was supposed to do. There was someone who knew her, who knew what she should be doing. She could feel them tugging at her, as if she were a balloon on a tenuous string. They were pulling her away from the black reflective surface in which she could see no face, hard as she looked, and she let herself be reeled in.

Then she was in a room with a tall, rather thin boy with messy hair who was pacing up and down, fiddling with an empty lighter, a small creature stalking after him, pouncing at his heels. "Livvy!" the boy said.

As he said this, she recognized both herself and him. He was quite tall now. Hardly a boy now at all. It wasn't that she was growing smaller. It was just that he was growing, would continue to grow, and she was dead. That was all.

"Ty," she said.

"You've been gone all day," he said. "It's three in the morning. I stayed up because I got worried. It felt like you were . . . well, far away. It felt like something was . . . wrong."

"Nothing was wrong," Livvy said. "I just couldn't get into Idris. But I think I was just outside of it, somehow. Just outside the wards. I overheard people talking. Zara and Manuel. They were checking the wards and talking."

"Talking about what?" Ty said. He sat down at his desk and flipped open his notebook.

"Mostly about how hungry they were. But I think they have a way to spy on us. Well, not us, but you know. They can spy on everyone out here outside Idris. And they're planning some kind of surprise attack."

"When?" Ty said, busily writing.

"They didn't say. And 'surprise attack' is overstating it. They mentioned in a vague kind of way that when they did attack us, we were going to be really surprised and then really dead. Because they think they're super awesome and all we do is sit around and eat delicious croissants. And then they finished testing the wards and went away, and I couldn't hear anything else."

"Still," Ty said. "Those are two pieces of information. We should go tell someone. I could tell Ragnor. Or Catarina."

"No," Livvy said. "I'm the one who figured it out. I want to be the one who gets to tell. I'll go find Magnus and tell him. Didn't Helen say in her last letter that Magnus was spending time at the Los Angeles Institute?"

Ty didn't look at her. "Yes," he said at last. "That seems fair. You should go. Only, Livvy?"

"What," she said.

"While you were gone," he said, "did you feel different? Did you feel anything strange?"

Livvy considered his question. "No," she said. "Write that down in the book. That I didn't feel anything strange at all. You don't need to worry about me, Ty. I'm dead. Nothing bad can happen to me now."

Irene was curled up on Ty's bed now, leg extended as she fastidiously groomed one haunch. Her unblinking golden eyes stayed fixed on Livvy. They said, *I belong here. Do you?*

"You and Irene take care of each other while I'm gone, okay?" Livvy said.

"You're going now?" Ty said. He grimaced as if the thought was causing him physical discomfort.

"Don't wait up," Livvy said, and then the room around her was gone, and she was once again standing on the beach beside the Los Angeles Institute, the sun slipping down below the darkening waves of the Pacific Ocean. The rush of the water down the sand was wrong somehow.

She could see lights blazing in the windows of the Institute. She wasn't sure, but most likely they had already had dinner. Someone, probably Helen or Aline, would be doing the dishes. Tavvy would be getting ready for bed. Someone would read a book to him. Mark and Cristina would be in New York, most likely. Was Mark more settled in the human world now? It had always seemed so strange to her, how he had been taken from them and then restored. How alien he had seemed when he came back. And yet now she had become something even stranger.

She wished to be inside the Institute suddenly, away from the blackness of the water so like the blackness of Dimmet Tarn. And so she was inside. She found herself in the kitchen. Helen was sitting at the table, the dishes still waiting to be washed. Aline's head rested against her shoulder. Her arm was around Helen's shoulders. They looked utterly at home, as if they had always lived there. As if they had never been exiled to a small frozen island far away from their family.

"It's nice to have Mark home for a few days," Helen said.

Aline turned her face into Helen's neck. "Mmm," she said. "Do you think we could trust him to hold down the Institute for a few hours? I was thinking I could book a spa day for the two of us."

"No," Helen said. "Probably not. But let's do it anyway."

It was wonderful to see how settled in Helen and Aline were, but it was also all extremely unfair, Livvy felt. Everyone else got to come home. Mark. Helen. Even Ty would come home someday. But she would never truly be home again. A shudder of envy and despair and longing went through her, and as if she had any material effect on the world at all, the pile of dishes beside the sink suddenly toppled over, sending shards and bits of food all over the counter and floor.

"What was that?" Aline said, standing up.

Helen groaned. "A tremor, I think. You know, welcome to California."

Livvy fled the kitchen, up to Dru's room, where her sister sat on her bed, watching one of her horror movies on the Institute's battered television.

"Hey!" Livvy said. "You like scary movies so much? Well, here I am! The real deal. Boo!"

She got right into Dru's face, being as loud as she could. "Here I am! Can you see me? Dru? Why can't you see me! I'm right here!"

But Dru went on watching her stupid movie, and Livvy felt herself shrinking, growing smaller and smaller until she could have slipped right into the still, black calm of her sister's pupil as if it were a pool of water and lodged herself there. She could be safe there. A secret from everyone, even Dru. And then Ty wouldn't have to worry about her anymore. He would be safe too.

"Safe from what, Livvy?" she asked herself.

The screen of the television went dark then, and the witch-light sconces over Dru's bed flickered and went out. "What the hell," Dru said, and got up. She went over to the wall and touched the sconce. The room filled with light again.

There was a knock on the door, and when Dru opened it, Helen and Aline were there. Helen said, "Did you feel anything just now?"

"We were in the kitchen and then a bunch of dishes fell," Aline said eagerly. "Helen says it might have been an earthquake! My first one!"

"No," Dru said. "I don't think so? But the TV went off a second ago. So, maybe?"

In the doorway behind Helen and Aline, Mark appeared.

Helen said, "Did you feel it too?"

"Feel what?" Mark said.

"A tiny earthquake!" Aline said, grinning.

"No," Mark said. "No, but Magnus just got a message from Jem. He says Tessa's in labor. So he's gone to them."

"Of course," Helen said dryly. "Because Magnus is exactly the person I want to keep me company when I'm about to give birth."

"I bet he gives amazing baby presents, though," Aline said. "And to be fair, I think that he feels he should have been there when Tessa and Will had their children, considering. Where are Julian and Emma right now? We should let them know."

"Paris," Helen said. "They like it so much there they keep extending their stay. Or do you think Magnus has let them know too?"

Magnus! Livvy realized that she had entirely forgotten why she had come. She had information for him. Well. In one moment she was in Dru's room, ignored and forgotten by a good number of the people she had loved most in the whole world. In the next, all the doors of the Los Angeles Institute flung themselves open and all the windows of the Institute shattered outward and Livvy did not even notice because she was suddenly beneath a full moon above a black pond carpeted in lily pads, fat velvet pads of the softest gray in the moonlight. Frogs, invisible in the shadows, were singing.

She knew, without knowing how she knew this, that she was now in the countryside, somewhere outside London. This was Cirenworth Hall, the estate where Jem and Tessa lived with Kit Herondale. Julian had visited there, and described it in a letter to Ty. There were horses and cows and apple trees. Tessa had an herb garden, and there was a glass conservatory that Jem had converted into a kind of music studio. How nice life was for the living! Jem, too, had gone away from the world for whole lifetimes and been allowed to return. Oh, why couldn't Livvy do the same? Why was she the only one who could not return and take up her life again?

It must be very late at night here, or else very early in the morning, but as with the Institute, lights were blazing in all the windows of the house. She drifted toward it, and then was inside. She was in another kitchen, this one very different from the cheery contemporary kitchen of the Institute. The walls were white plaster, hung with bundles of herbs and copper pots. Enormous beams dark with age ran across the whitewashed ceiling. Sitting at a long, scarred oaken table was Kit, playing solitaire and sipping from a mug. It might have been tea, but Livvy suspected from the face that he made as he sipped that it was something alcoholic instead.

"Boo!" she said, and Kit fumbled the mug, spilling liquid all down his pants.

"Livvy?" he said.

"That's right," she said, pleased. "You can see me. It gets really, really boring being invisible to everyone."

"What are you doing here?" Kit said. Then, "Is he okay? Ty?"

"What?" Livvy said. "No, he's fine. I'm looking for Magnus, actually. There's something that I need to ask him. Or tell him. I think I'm supposed to tell him something."

"Are *you* okay?" Kit said.

"What, aside from being dead?" Livvy said.

"Just, um, you seem a little off," Kit said. "Or something."

"Yeah, well, dead," Livvy said. "But other than that."

"Magnus is in the old conservatory with Jem and Tessa. Tessa's in labor, but, like, they seem like it's not a big deal or anything. They're just sitting around and talking about stuff. But, you know, it was kind of freaking me out. Like, she's going to have a baby, you know? Which is cool! But I thought I should give them some space."

"Okay, thanks," Livvy said. "Great to see you, Kit. Sorry I scared you. Sort of."

And then she was in the conservatory, which had been completely outfitted for a musician. There was a grand piano in one corner, and various instruments hanging on a beautiful wooden cabinet. Jem was playing a cello, his long hands drawing the bow across the strings as if he were coaxing out those low, beautiful, belling notes. Tessa was pacing, slowly, along a glass wall, one hand on her great belly and the other on her back. Magnus was nowhere to be seen.

Livvy wasn't really thinking about Magnus, though. Not anymore. All of her attention was focused on Tessa. On the hand that rested on the pregnant belly. She could not take her eyes away.

There was a voice in Livvy's head, way below the song that Jem was playing, below the sounds of the living hearts that beat in the conservatory: Jem, Tessa, and the unborn baby. She almost recognized the voice. It belonged to someone who had once been very dear to her. "Livvy," it was saying. "Something's wrong. I think that something's wrong."

Livvy did her best to ignore the voice. She thought, *If I make myself very small, I bet that I could do the thing I am thinking of. I could make myself so very small that I could slip into that baby. I wouldn't take up much room at all. A baby is hardly a person at all, really. If I took the place of whoever the baby is going to be, if I wanted a do-over, it wouldn't hurt Tessa and Jem at all. They would be good parents to me. And I would be a good daughter. I was good when I was alive! I could be good again. And it isn't fair. I shouldn't have died. I ought to get another chance. Why shouldn't I have another chance?*

She drew closer to Tessa. Tessa groaned.

"What is it?" Jem said, putting down his bow. "Is it my rank, terrible playing? Magnus may have magically transformed this space to be hospitable to instruments, but I am still an amateur when it comes to the cello." His face changed. "Or is it time? Shall we go back to the house?"

Tessa shook her head. "Not yet," she said. "But drawing nearer. Keep playing. It helps me."

"Magnus will be back soon with the herbs you wanted," Jem said.

"There's still time," Tessa said. "There's still time too if you don't want to be the one to deliver this baby. Magnus could fetch someone."

"What, and miss my chance at the big time?" Jem said. "I'd like to think that all my years as a Silent Brother weren't totally pointless."

Livvy was shrinking, shrinking, shrinking down almost to nothingness. All the darkness outside the glass walls of the conservatory was pressing in as if they were all submerged beneath Dimmet Tarn, but she could still escape. She could be a living girl again.

Jem got up and went over to Tessa. He knelt down in front of her and laid his head against her belly. "Hello there, Wilhelmina Yiqiang Ke Carstairs. Little Mina. You are welcome, little Mina, my heart. We are waiting for you in joy and hope and love."

Tessa rested her hand on Jem's head. "I think she heard you," she said. "I think she's hurrying now."

"Livvy!" said the other voice. The one that Livvy didn't want to hear right now, the one that tugged at her as if it were a leash. "Livvy, what are you doing? Something's wrong, Livvy."

And oh, the voice was right. Livvy came back to herself. What had she been thinking of doing? She had been going to—and as she realized what she had been about to do, all the walls of the conservatory exploded outward into the night in a great cloud of glass shards.

Jem and Tessa both cried out, crouching down. And then Magnus was there in green silk pajamas beautifully embroidered with Pokémon. "What in the world?" he said, bending over to help Jem and Tessa up.

"I don't know," Jem said wildly. "Demons? A sonic boom?"

Magnus looked around the conservatory. A strange expression came over his face when he saw Livvy.

"I'm sorry!" she said. "I didn't mean to, Magnus!"

Looking hard at her, Magnus said to Jem and Tessa, "Not a demon, I think. There's nothing dangerous here now. Come on. Let's get you back to the house. I have your herbs, Tessa. Kit's brewing you a nice cup of tea."

"Oh good," Tessa said faintly. "The intervals between contractions are getting shorter. I thought there would be more time. Are you sure we shouldn't be more concerned about whatever broke all the windows?"

"Everyone always thinks they'll have more time," Magnus said. He was still looking right at Livvy as he said it. "And no. I don't think you have to be concerned at all. I would never let anything happen to you. Think of it as part of the christening! You know that when they christen a ship, they break a bottle of champagne against the forward bow. Your baby just gets the deluxe version. Imagine her voyage! Her life, I predict, will be full of wonders."

"Come on," Jem said. "Let's get inside the house. Magnus, will you bring my cello?" He took down his violin from the cabinet, and with his other hand, he took Tessa's arm and began to walk her toward the house, over the dark ground strewn with broken glass.

Magnus said, "Oh, Livvy."

"I almost—" she said.

"I know," he said. "But you didn't. Go find Kit and stay with him. I'll come to you in a little while to fetch Tessa's tonic."

Kit seemed relieved, actually, to have company, even if company was only a ghost. "What happened out there?" he said. "What happened to the conservatory?"

"I think that was me," Livvy said. "I didn't mean to, though."

"Is this the kind of thing that you've been getting up to at the Scholomance?" Kit said. "Is that why you came to find Magnus?"

"No!" Livvy said. "I haven't done anything like this. Well, not until today. I think I smashed some plates at the Los Angeles Institute. And I made the lights go out in Dru's room while she was watching a scary movie."

"Nice," Kit said. "So, like, basic poltergeist stuff."

"I didn't mean to do any of it!" Livvy said. "It just sort of happened. I'm sorry I wrecked the conservatory."

"Maybe you could try not to do anything like that again," Kit said.

"Sure," Livvy said. "Of course. I don't *want* to do anything like that again."

There was a glint off something Kit wore on a chain around his neck. "Oh," Livvy said, looking closer. It was a heron made of silver.

"It belonged to my mother," Kit said. "Jem and Tessa gave it to me a while ago. I found it again this morning. I'd forgotten about it."

"It's so pretty," Livvy said.

Kit said, "I'd give it to you if I could. She used it to summon Jem and Tessa to her side when she was attacked. In the end, it didn't save her. So I guess I have a grudge against it."

Livvy said, "I'm sorry."

"Why?" Kit said. "You didn't kill them. Anyway, everything's okay?" He was looking at his hands very intently, as if he thought there might be something wrong with them.

"What?" Livvy said. "Yes. Everything's fine. Oh. You mean Ty."

Kit didn't say anything, but he nodded. He looked as if he wished he hadn't asked at all, and also as if he were listening with all of his being.

It was ridiculous, Livvy thought. You could tell how much he missed Ty. As much as Ty missed him. She didn't understand boys at all. Why couldn't they just say what they felt? Why did they have to be so stupid?

"He's okay," Livvy said. "He's doing well at the Scholomance. He has a Carpathian lynx in his room! He doesn't really have any friends, though. He misses you, but he won't talk about it. But other than that, he's fine."

As she said it, though, she realized that she wasn't sure at all that Ty was fine. The strand that bound her to Ty—that filament of magic—felt wrong, somehow, as if it were slackening. She could feel Ty reaching for her, but weakly.

"Livvy?" Kit said.

"Oh no," she said. "No, I think I have to go back. I think I shouldn't be here."

Now Kit looked truly alarmed. "What's wrong?" he said.

"Ty," she said. "It's hurting him that I'm here. Tell Magnus

I'm sorry, but I have to go. Tell him to come find me. I have information for him about Idris."

"About Idris?" Kit said. "Never mind. I'll tell him. Go!"

And Livvy went.

She must have been back at the Scholomance in the space of a breath, although to be fair, since she didn't breathe anymore, she was only guessing that was how long it took. She was in Ty's room, but Ty wasn't there. Only Irene, looking accusingly at her from the door, which she appeared to be attempting to chew open.

"Sorry," Livvy said, and then felt ridiculous. This time she let her awareness of Ty, where he was, pull her toward him, and yet that was not where she found herself. She found herself, instead, hovering once more over Dimmet Tarn.

"No!" she said. And, feeling as if she were fighting her way to him through some impenetrable and gloomy dark chasm, she came at last to her brother.

He was lying in a bed in the infirmary, looking very pale. Catarina Loss was by his side, and a boy that Livvy recognized from Ty's classes. Anush.

"He just collapsed," Anush was saying. "Is it food poisoning?"

"I don't think so," Catarina Loss said. "I don't know."

Ty opened his eyes. "Livvy," he said, so softly that her name was barely a sound at all.

"What did he say?" Anush asked.

"Livvy," Catarina said, laying her hand on Ty's head. "His sister. The one who was slain by Annabel Blackthorn."

"Oh," Anush said. "Oh, how sad."

Catarina Loss said, "His color is improving a little, I think.

Are you good friends?"

"Uh, not really?" Anush said. "I don't know who his friends are. If he has friends. I mean, he seems like a good guy. Smart. Super focused. But he kind of keeps to himself."

"I'm going to keep him in the infirmary overnight," Catarina Loss said. "But if it occurs to you to come back to visit him, it wouldn't be the worst thing in the world. Everyone needs friends."

"Yeah, sure," Anush said. "I'll come back later. See if he needs anything."

Catarina Loss poured a glass of water for Ty and helped him sit up to take a drink. "You fainted," she said in a neutral voice. "Sometimes new students take their course of study too seriously and forget about things like getting enough sleep or eating."

"I don't forget things like that," Ty said. "I have a schedule so that I don't forget."

"You came to me the other day about the lynx," Catarina Loss said. "How is she doing? I see there are scratches on your arm."

"She's great!" Ty said. "She eats everything I bring her and she's drinking fine too. How long have I been here? I should go make sure that she's okay."

"You've only been here a little while," Catarina Loss said. "When Anush comes back, you can tell him to look after her for tonight. I think he'd be happy to do that. Do you think you could eat something?"

Ty nodded, and Catarina Loss said, "I'll see what delights the kitchen can supply. Stay in bed. I'll be right back."

When she was gone, Livvy said, "Ty!"

Ty frowned at her. He said, "I could feel you getting farther and farther away. It hurt, Livvy. And you were getting stranger and stranger, the farther away you got. I could *feel* you. But you didn't feel like you anymore. You felt—"

Livvy said, "I know. I felt it too. It was scary, Ty. *I* was scary. You're going to have to write that down in your notebook. I don't think it's good when I'm away too long. I think the farther away from you that I get, the more dangerous it is for both of us. The longer I stayed away, the more I forgot things. Like who I was. Like you. Why I should come back."

Ty said, "But you did come back."

"I came back," Livvy said. "Almost too late. But I'm here now. And just in time. Irene is gnawing her way through your door."

She grinned at Ty reassuringly, and Ty smiled back. Then his eyes closed again.

"Ty?" she said.

"I'm fine," he said. "Just really tired. Going to sleep for a little while, Livvy. Will you stay with me while I fall asleep?"

"Sure," she said. "Of course I will."

He was asleep when Catarina Loss returned with a tray of food, and still asleep when Magnus Bane came through the door several hours later in a puffy scarlet down parka trimmed in black fake fur that came all the way down to his ankles. He looked as if he had been mostly swallowed by a very fat eider-down dragon.

Catarina Loss was with him. "A girl!" she said. "I've been knitting a blanket for her, but it isn't done yet. Wilhelmina Yiqiang Ke Carstairs. That's quite a big name for a very small baby."

"Mina for short," Magnus said. "Oh, she's lovely, Catarina. She has Jem's fingers. A musician's fingers. And Tessa's chin. So how's our patient?"

"He'll be fine," Catarina Loss said. Then, "Though what was wrong with him in the first place isn't quite apparent to me. He seems perfectly healthy. I'm due to teach a class. Will you still be here in an hour or so?"

"I'll be here or somewhere close at hand," Magnus said. "Come and find me when you're done."

When Catarina Loss was gone, Magnus said to Livvy, "Well. There is apparently something that you must say to me. And then there is something that I must say to you."

Livvy said, "I know. I think I know what you must say to me. But first let me tell you about Idris." And she told him everything she had heard Zara and Manuel say.

"We knew that sooner or later they plan to attack us," Magnus said at last. "But now that we know they are spying on us, we will have to find out how. And perhaps if it is possible for them, then it is also possible for us to spy on Idris. But I don't think we can risk you doing it again."

"No," Livvy said. "Because every time I get too far away from Ty, things start to go wrong. I start to change. I get stronger, I think. I can do things! Like I did with the conservatory. I broke dishes, too, and I think I almost hurt Tessa's baby somehow. And Ty, it's bad for him, too, when we're apart. That's why he ended up in the infirmary. Because I was gone too long."

"Yes," Magnus said. "Smart girl."

"If I had stayed away longer," Livvy said, "would he have died?"

"I don't know," Magnus said. "But the magic he tried to use to bring you back from the dead was dark magic, Livvy. Necromancy. A spell from the Black Volume of the Dead! And a failed spell, at that. When the spell failed, the thing that kept you here, that bound you, was Ty. Your twin. That's not normal for ghosts. Most of them are bound to an object. Things like a ring or a key or a house. But you're bound to a person. It makes sense that you need to stay close to Ty now. And that he has to stay close to you. I think that when you are away from him for too long, you become less yourself. More powerful. Less human. More a hungry ghost. Something dangerous to the living."

"When I was in the conservatory," Livvy said, forcing the words out, "I felt as if I could swap places with Tessa's baby. That I could be alive again, if I were willing to take her baby's life. Her baby's place."

Magnus said, "Necromancy is a very dark art. Yes. Perhaps you could have. Or perhaps you might have killed the baby or Tessa, and ended up with nothing at all. Magic can have a high price, Livvy."

"I don't want to hurt anybody," Livvy said. "That's what Annabel did. I don't want to be like Annabel, Magnus. I don't! But I don't want to be dead, either! It isn't fair!"

"No," Magnus said. "It isn't fair. But life isn't fair. And you died bravely, Livvy."

"Stupidly," Livvy said. "I died stupidly."

"Bravely," Magnus said. "Though I admit that sometimes I wish Shadowhunters were a little less brave and used their heads a little more."

Livvy sniffed. "Well," she said. "Ty is good at that. Using his head."

"Ty is exceptional," Magnus said. "I expect great things from him. And from you, too, Livvy. Because if you do not do great things, then I fear you may do terrible things. The two of you have remarkable potential."

"Me?" she said. "But I'm dead."

"Nevertheless," Magnus said. He reached into his pocket and said, "And I have a present for you. Well, it's from Kit, too. It's for you and Ty." He held out a silver chain from which hung the figure of a bird. A heron, Livvy realized.

"You're bound to Ty," Magnus said, "but it's a necromantical bond. I was poking around for something to use that might work to bear a little of the weight that bond must be on you and Ty, and Kit asked what I was doing. He gave me this, and I have altered it a little. Given it some potency. If Ty wears it, it should shield him a little from any side effects of being bound to the dead. And it should sustain you a little. It should ease some of the strangeness of being in the living world. You can touch it. And, too, should you or he feel in need of help, you can use it to call on me. Or Ty can. Once it belonged to Kit's mother. It was given to her by Jem, so that when she was in danger she could summon him. Now it will serve you and your brother."

Livvy stretched out a finger. Stroked the silver heron. "Oh," she said. "I can! I can feel it!"

Magnus said, "Yes. Well. Good."

"Like one of Ty's fidget toys," Livvy said. "Like Julian's lighter." She was running her fingers along the chain now. "Is the baby okay? Mina?"

"Yes," Magnus said. "She's fine. Everyone is fine. The conservatory, on the other hand . . ."

Livvy thought, suddenly, of Dimmet Tarn. She said, "You've been here before, to the Scholomance?"

"Yes," Magnus said. "Many times, over the years."

"Have you ever been to Dimmet Tarn?" Livvy said.

"Yes," Magnus said. "A most unimpressive body of water. You must find it a sad change from the Pacific Ocean."

"Yeah, well, there are stories that it's supernatural in some way," Livvy said. "But nobody knows how. Ty and I were trying to see if we could find out anything about it."

Magnus said, "Let me see. There were stories about it, but I never paid much attention to them. What was it?"

He sat in silence for a minute, and Livvy sat companionably with him. Ty stirred as if he were dreaming in a way that made Livvy think that he would wake up soon.

"Yes!" Magnus said. "Of course. The story was this. That if you went to Dimmet Tarn and looked into the water for long enough, you would see something of your future. That was the enchantment placed on it by some warlock or other. Funnily enough, I believe he was from Devon, actually. Dimmet is a Welsh word. Why? Did you go there? Livvy? Did you see something there?"

"No," Livvy said at last. She tried to think of what it had been like, sinking into that vast dark nothingness. "I didn't see anything. It was nothing at all."

"I see," Magnus said in a tone that suggested he saw everything she wasn't saying. "But let us say that there was someone who happened to look into dismal Dimmet Tarn and let's say they saw something they didn't like. Something that suggested a future they didn't want. And let's say that this someone came and talked to me. Do you know what I would tell them?"

"What?" Livvy said.

Magnus said, "I would tell them this. That the future isn't fixed. If we see a path in front of us that we would not choose, then we can choose another path. Another future. Dimmet

Tarn be damned. Would you agree with that, Livvy?"

He stared hard at Livvy and Livvy stared right back. She couldn't think of anything to say at all, but finally she set her mouth and nodded.

From the bed, Ty said, "Livvy!" His eyes opened and found her, and he said, "Livvy," again. This time he didn't sound despairing. He hadn't noticed yet that Magnus was there at all.

A terrible wailing came from the doorway as Ty spoke. It was Irene, her whiskery jaws stretched open and all of her fur standing on end. Livvy would not have thought that such a tiny animal could have produced such a large noise. Still wailing, Irene leaped onto the bed and butted Ty in the chin. The noise she was making changed to smaller, angry inquiring trills like a hot teakettle who had a lot of questions but suspected she wasn't going to like any of the answers.

"What on earth is that?" Magnus said.

"This is Irene," Ty said. "She's a Carpathian lynx."

"Of course!" said Magnus. "A Carpathian lynx. How silly of me." His eyes met Livvy's. "A boy, a Carpathian lynx, and a ghost. Truly I expect great things from you and your brother, Livvy. Here, Ty. This is for you." He dropped the Herondale necklace into Ty's palm. "Livvy will explain its purpose. Suffice it to say that if you need me for any reason at all, you can use it to summon me. Livvy's been telling me about Idris, about what she overheard. But I have been up all night long, and I need some strong tea. I'm going to go find Ragnor Fell and make him find me some strong tea."

He made as grand an exit as anyone can make when they are wearing an oversize down coat, and as he exited, Anush entered, his arms bloody with scratches.

Anush gazed after Magnus in astonishment. "That was Magnus Bane," he said to Ty. "Was he here to see you?"

"Yes. He's our friend," Ty said.

Anush said, "I knew that you know him, but I didn't realize you had a just-dropping-by-the-Scholomance-to-see-you type of relationship! Sorry about that animal. I went to your room to see if I could bring you back a book or some clothes or something, and she got away from me. She's so pretty. But she's so mean."

"Her name is Irene," Ty said, looking fondly at the lynx curled up beside him.

Anush said, "Again, rhymes with 'mean.' Do you want me to go get some scraps from the kitchen for her?"

When Anush was gone, Livvy told Ty everything that had happened while she had been in Los Angeles and in the conservatory in England. Ty said, "I'm so sorry, Livvy."

"For what?" she said.

"For doing this to you," he said.

"Oh, Ty," she said. "I would have done it for you. It isn't a thing that should be done, but I would have done it anyway. And so we would be in just the same mess we're in now. Besides, I think I'm getting the hang of this ghost thing."

Ty nodded. He turned the necklace over and over in his hand, then held it out, dangling the heron over the bed so that the sunlight caught the silver, and Irene batted it with her paw. Livvy thought of Kit sitting at the table in the kitchen, so carefully not asking her anything about Ty.

She reached over and caught the chain in her hand. Gently untangled it from Irene's sharp claws. Holding the necklace still, Livvy said, "This belonged to Kit. You'll have to write him.

To say thank you. You'll write him and give the letter to Magnus to take back when he goes."

"Okay," Ty said at last. "But he won't write back."

"Then you'll keep on writing until he does," Livvy said. "Necromancy is bad. We're all agreed on that. But postcards are pretty harmless. You know. Something scenic on the front." Dimmet Tarn flashed in front of her. That black nothingness. "Wish you were here. That kind of thing."

She held the chain tighter. Rubbed the small links between her fingers. Maybe that was her future. Black nothingness. But right now she had Ty. She could choose the path that led away from Dimmet Tarn for as long as she could. She had an anchor. She would hold on as tightly as she could.

Forever Fallen

By Cassandra Clare and Sarah Rees Brennan

Awake, arise! Or be forever fallen.
—Milton

J

New York, 2013

Jem Carstairs and Kit Herondale came through the Portal together, from the black midnight velvet of the English woods into the orange-starred deep blue of a New York street in the evening. Kit eyed the silver stream of honking cars with the same expression he'd worn since Jem suggested going: a mixture of excitement and nerves.

"They didn't, uh, exactly welcome me at the L.A. Shadow Market the last few times I went," Kit said. "You're sure this will be okay?"

"I am," Jem assured him.

The yellow and red lights of cars played over the intricate scrollwork and arched windows of the abandoned theater. The Shadow Market on Canal Street was much like he remembered it from a decade ago and more, though Jem himself was so different. To a mundane, steel shutters and boards covered the entrance. To Jem and Kit, they were silver and wood beads, a curtain that chimed a song as they passed through.

A warlock woman paused when she saw them.

"Hello, Hypatia," said Jem. "I think you know Kit?"

"I know that two Shadowhunters make even more trouble than one," said Hypatia.

She rolled her starry eyes and passed on, but a werewolf Jem knew from the Paris Shadow Market stopped and chatted with them for a moment. He said it was a pleasure to meet Kit, and always a pleasure to see Jem.

"Congratulations, by the way," he added.

Jem glowed. "Thank you."

Jem had been surprised to find that he was welcome in most Shadow Markets now. He had been to many, over the years, and quite a few of the vendors and attendants were immortal. People remembered him, and after a time, they had stopped fearing him. He hadn't even realized it, but he had become a familiar sight, his visits marking a Market night as lucky: he was the only Silent Brother most of them had ever seen. The first time he'd gone to a Shadow Market once he was no longer a Silent Brother, hand in hand with a warlock woman, seemed to confirm the Shadow Market people's opinion that he was close to being one of their own. Showing up with Kit, who had basically grown up in the Shadow Market in Los Angeles, pretty much cemented that.

"You see?" Jem murmured. "No problem."

Kit's shoulders were relaxing and his blue eyes beginning to shine with a familiar wicked gleam. He pointed out several interesting features of the Market that Jem was already aware of, a Market boy showing off, and Jem smiled and encouraged him to keep talking.

"They do it with magic mirrors," Kit whispered in Jem's ear when they stopped to see two mermaids doing tricks in a tank.

The mermaid glared at Kit, and Kit laughed. They stopped at a stall to buy candied moonflowers, since Kit had a fiendish sweet tooth.

"I know you," said the faerie vendor. "Aren't you Johnny Rook's boy?"

Kit's smile died a swift death. "Not anymore."

"Whose are you now?"

"Nobody's," Kit answered quietly.

The faerie vendor blinked, a second eyelid sliding in sideways and making the blink rather impressive. Jem reached out to touch Kit's shoulder, but Kit was already moving on, browsing the sweets as if he found them deeply fascinating.

Jem cleared his throat. "I hear there is a special stall run by warlocks and faeries, offering potions and illusions? My friend Shade told me of it."

She nodded understanding and leaned down to whisper in his ear.

The stall devoted to the faerie-and-warlock joint venture was a carved wooden caravan parked in an antechamber of the Canal Street building. The caravan was painted bright blue and adorned with paintings that moved: as Jem and Kit approached, birds took flight from several gilded cages and soared free over the bright-blue painted sky.

The faerie woman had mushrooms growing in her hair, and ribbons looped around them. She seemed very young, and enthusiastic about selling Jem the medicine he asked for. Jem lifted the porcelain lid to examine its contents carefully and apologized for doing so.

She waved this off. "Perfectly understandable, considering what it's for. Lovely to meet you properly at last. Any friend of

Shade's. Such a distinguished gentleman. Perhaps it's the Irish in me, but I do love a fellow in green."

Kit became overwhelmed by a fit of coughing. Jem smiled discreetly and patted him on the back.

"Also . . . ," the faerie said in a rush. "I saw you once, about eight years ago, when you were still . . . I only got one glimpse, but you seemed so hauntingly sad. And so hauntingly attractive."

"Thank you," said Jem. "I'm very happy now. Your cough seems to be getting worse, Kit. Do you need medicine as well?"

Kit straightened up. "Nope, I'm good. Come on, Brother Hauntingly Attractive."

"There's no need to mention this to Tessa."

"And yet," said Kit, "I'm gonna."

"Congratulations!" the faerie woman yelled after Jem.

All of his knowledge as a Silent Brother told him the potion was harmless and would do its work. Jem offered another smile over his shoulder to the woman and let Kit pull him toward the row of stalls in the next room across the way. The Market was growing more crowded, so crowded that all the faeries who could take wing were flying overhead. One was being pursued by a werewolf, who was yelling that the faerie had unfairly snatched the last hat in her size. The fleeing faerie's winged shadow darkened a golden head and broad shoulders that struck Jem as familiar.

"Isn't that Jace? I think that's—" Jem began, turning to Kit. Then he saw Kit's face was white.

Kit was staring over at a tall boy with dark hair and headphones, browsing through a stall and running his fingers through the dried herbs. Jem laid his hand on Kit's shoulder. Kit seemed oblivious, rooted to the spot, until the boy turned around and had blue eyes and a crooked nose, and was not Ty Blackthorn.

"I have what we came for," Jem said. He spoke with his usual, and carefully cultivated, calm. "Shall we go, or do you want to look around? We can do whatever you want."

Kit's jaw was still set. Jem knew that look. Herondales were always flames, he thought. They loved and suffered as if they would burn away with the sheer force of their own fire.

"Let's go home," Kit mumbled.

In spite of his slight disappointment, Jem found himself smiling. It was the first time Kit had called their house that.

The man, who had never had the chance to be Jace Herondale and who was no longer Jace at all, was starting to think that coming here had been a bad idea.

The Seelie Queen had been the one to insist he should have a new name, when he made his way to Faerie wanting protection for Ash and help with his plans. The Queen had answered all his questions about Clary, but her help hadn't come free. Royalty tended to make demands.

"I'm accustomed to the other Jace," she said with a regal sneer. "Though I admit, not overly fond. What else can we call you?"

Jonathan, he'd thought first, and flinched at even the thought of that name, which had surprised him. He hadn't done much flinching in Thule.

"Janus," he'd told the Queen. "The god with two faces. The god of endings and beginnings, and passages between strange doorways."

"The god?" the Queen repeated.

"My father gave me a classical education," Janus told her. "To go with my classical good looks."

That had made the Queen laugh. "I see some things do not change, no matter the world."

She saw nothing. Nobody in this world could know what he had been forced to become.

It was in Faerie that Janus had heard of the faerie-and-warlock stall and the magic it could do, and he hadn't been able to resist. He knew Shadowhunters were not welcome at Shadow Markets. He'd thought that if he wore a hood and cloak, the risk would be minimal.

Unfortunately, several people were looking at him as if they recognized him. Well, let them think that the Jace of this world made a regular practice of haunting the Shadow Market. He had nothing invested in protecting that Jace's reputation.

Janus turned. A werewolf slammed into him and cursed.

"Hey, Shadowhunter, watch where you're going!"

Janus had his hand on his dagger when another werewolf came by and slapped the first werewolf upside the head.

"Do you know who you're talking to?" he demanded. "That's Jace Herondale, the head of the Institute."

The werewolf paled. "Oh my God. I'm so sorry. I didn't know."

"Please forgive him. He's from a horrible desert wasteland and he doesn't know what's going on," said the other werewolf.

"I'm from Ohio!"

"That's what I said."

The two werewolves gazed at Janus in apologetic misery. Janus was very confused, but he slowly let go of the hilt of his dagger. This pair might be more useful alive.

"*So* sorry," the second werewolf stressed.

"It's . . ." Janus cleared his throat. "It's fine."

"He's also the Consul's *parabatai*," said the werewolf. "You know, Alec Lightwood."

Janus felt something twist deep in his gut. The sensation surprised him. He was used to feeling nothing at all.

He held the thought of Alec being Consul in front of his mental eye, like a peculiar stone he was studying. He'd heard from the Queen that in this new strange world everything was different and everyone was alive, but when he had imagined those he'd known once alive again, he'd imagined them unchanged. Alec as Consul. He couldn't imagine it.

"I'm actually here on . . . a secret mission," he said. "I'd appreciate it if you kept quiet about seeing me."

"I thought so," said the second werewolf. "Cloak. Hood. 'Secret mission,' I said to myself."

Janus's smile became less real and far more easy. "I can tell you're perceptive. Perhaps in the future, if I needed your help—"

"Anything we can do!" the werewolves rushed to assure him. "Absolutely anything."

Janus kept smiling. "Oh good."

It *was* good to make allies—especially those who were stupid and eager to please.

Janus headed to what he had come for, the bright blue caravan where he had been assured that faeries and warlocks together could produce impenetrable glamours.

In Thule, there was no more warlock magic. There were no more warlocks at all. But there were demons crawling everywhere across the surface of that world, thick as flies on spoiled meat, and Sebastian could make the demons create illusions. Very occasionally, when Janus had pleased Sebastian, he would give him such a gift. Only sometimes, and it was never enough.

A faerie with mushrooms in her hair let him into the caravan. She seemed young, and she quailed when his eyes fell on her, but he paid the price she and the warlock demanded. It was exorbitant. He would have paid more.

The inside of the caravan was a wooden shell that had a jewel hidden within. The faeries had not been wrong when they said the combined magic could produce an extraordinary result. She was the most convincing illusion he had ever seen.

She was small, always so small. Her hair fell in red loops and swirls around her face and her shoulders. He had wanted to follow every loop with his finger, work out the precise shape of each curl, as he'd wanted to trace connections between every golden freckle. He'd wanted to know her completely.

"Clary," he said.

Her name sounded foreign in his mouth. He hadn't said it often, even in Thule, where whatever he felt had been buried under layers and layers of a weight like cement.

"Come here," he said. He was surprised by the roughness in his own voice. His hands were shaking. It felt like a distant, even despicable weakness.

She moved toward him. He caught her by the wrists and pulled her roughly against his chest.

Holding her was a mistake. That was where the illusion began to collapse. He could feel her trembling, and Clary would not have done that. Clary was the bravest person he knew.

The illusions were never convincing enough. No illusion could love you back. No illusion would ever look at him the way Clary had once looked at him. And though he didn't know why he needed that, he did. He had needed it before, and the severing of his bond with Sebastian had made it a thousand times worse.

Clary. Clary. Clary.

He fooled himself for another moment, pressing his lips against her forehead, then her cheek, then burying his face in the cloud of her bright hair.

"Oh, my darling," he murmured, reaching for his knife as her eyes widened in realization and fear. "My darling. Why did you have to die?"

Kit ran up the stone steps to his room, slamming the door behind him, as soon as they retured to Cirenworth Hall. Jem thought it might be best to give him privacy, for a little while.

He was still slightly worried as he climbed the steps himself, following the sound of a song echoing off the slate walls.

"Black for hunting through the night
For death and mourning the color's white
Gold for a bride in her wedding gown
And red to call enchantment down.

Saffron lights the victory march,
Green will mend our broken hearts.
Silver for the demon towers,
And bronze to summon wicked powers."

It was a variation on an ancient Shadowhunter song; Jem could not have guessed how old. His father had sung it to him when he was a child.

When he pushed open the door, the world narrowed down for a moment to a single room, and that room was full of soft light. There was a cluster of shining witchlights arranged in the old-fashioned iron grate, and pearlescent rays caught in Tessa's brown curls as she bent over the cradle, rocking it gently. The cradle had been carved more than a hundred years ago from an oak felled in these woods. Jem had seen it made, with careful hands and patient love. The cradle rocked just as smoothly now as it had then.

Plaintive grizzling drifted from the cradle, and Jem leaned over to see its occupant. She lay on soft white bedding, piles on piles of fleeciness so it seemed she slept on a cloud. Her shock of hair was very black against the sheets and her small face was screwed up in outraged distress.

Wilhelmina Yiqiang Ke Carstairs. For their lost Will, the first and only possible name, and *wild rose*, because all those who Jem loved best grew in beautiful rebellion. He'd wanted a Chinese name for his darling, and wanted to commemorate lost Rosemary, who had trusted Jem and Tessa with what was infinitely precious to her and was now infinitely precious to him: Rosemary had trusted him with Kit. Rosemary was the herb meant for remembrance, and Zachariah meant *remember*. The longer Jem lived, the more surely he believed that life was a wheel, coming full circle, and bringing you to those you were meant to love. She had an imposing name, their little one, and it might have been longer had they included Gray, but Tessa said that warlocks chose their own name, if she chose to be a warlock. Mina might choose to be a Shadowhunter. She might be anything she pleased. She was everything already.

Jem was often lost in admiring her, but he did not let himself do so for long tonight. Instead he lifted her in his arms. Her hands flew out like startled starfish and came to rest, the smallest tenderest weights, against his collarbone. Mina's dark eyes popped open all the way, and she went quiet.

"Oh, I see how it is," Jem's wife whispered, laughing softly. "Daddy's girl."

"She knows I brought her something from the Market," said Jem, and gently rubbed the faerie salve on Mina's soft pink gums.

Mina wriggled and fussed as he did so, kicking her legs as if she were swimming in a race, but when Jem was finished the salve seemed to do its work quickly. Then she settled, her small face bewildered but happy, as if Jem had performed some peculiar and marvelous feat.

Tessa said it was early for a baby to start teething. Mina was remarkable and advanced in all sorts of ways, Jem considered proudly.

"*Qiān jīn,*" Jem murmured to her. "You are more like your mother every day."

She was very like Tessa. Whenever he pointed this out, Tessa and Kit seemed skeptical.

"I mean, she's a baby, so she mostly looks like a kind of screwed-up turnip," said Kit. "In . . . uh, a good way. But if she looks like anyone . . ."

Kit had shrugged. Tessa had the same expression on her face now as Kit had worn then.

"Still no," Tessa informed him. "She looks just like you."

Jem lifted Mina up and toward the witchlights, one hand cupped protectively around the fragile curve of her head. Happiness came easily to Mina. She crowed with delight, witchlight radiant around her ruffled cap of black hair and her round waving arms, and he was dazzled and overwhelmed by the sheer immensity of his good fortune.

"But—she's so beautiful," Jem said helplessly.

"And where might she get that from? I love you forever, James Carstairs," said Tessa, leaning her dear head against his shoulder. "But you are a fool."

Jem drew Mina back in and held her close, and she nuzzled her dimpled cheek against his, burbling to him joyfully. From the day she was born, Mina had gurgled at ceilings and walls and into the tiny caves of her cupped hands. Her gurgling grew higher pitched and more excited when she was in Tessa's or Jem's arms, trying to attract their attention. She talked in her sleep as her mother did. She was always talking, and Jem was always listening, and soon he would understand every word.

Their daughter was so like Tessa. Jem knew what he knew.

Janus zipped his jacket up to hide the blood as he passed a faerie stall. He'd decided he'd risked his luck long enough and he should make his way home.

"Yo, Jason," called a black-haired vampire girl in a blue minidress. She was looking at him expectantly, but from what she'd called him, she couldn't know him that well.

"Actually, it's Jace," said Janus casually, still moving for the exits.

He didn't understand what he'd said wrong, but he understood it had been something. Instant alarm flashed across her face, and she darted away through the crowd, making it out of the Market, but even a vampire wasn't faster than Janus. Nobody was.

He cornered her in an alleyway, backhanding her when she fought, pinning her thrashing limbs. He got his dagger to her throat, but she didn't stop struggling.

"You're *not* Jace," said the vampire girl. "What are you? Eidolon? Shape-shifter? Herondale cosplayer?" She squinted at him.

He was going to have to break her neck, he realized. Tedious. Vampires were hard to kill, but he was still stronger than they were. "I am Jace Herondale," he told her. It was a relief to say it to someone, even someone who was going to die. "A stronger, better Jace Herondale than you have in this world. Not that you'll understand a word I say."

He reached for her throat, but she was staring at him with a look of realization. "You're from Thule," she said. "Alec told me about this freaky other world where Clary died and everything was screwed literally to hell. And Jace was bound to Sebastian Morgenstern. You're *that* Jace."

She glared up at him defiantly, and something about her face rang a dull, funereal bell.

"I know who you are too," Janus said slowly. "You're Lily Chen. In my world, Sebastian killed you."

"He did?" Lily looked outraged. "To hell with that guy. Irony intended."

"You're the girl Raphael Santiago started a war for."

Lily abruptly and entirely ceased fighting. It was startling enough that Janus almost let go, but his father had trained him to be remorseless.

"What?" Her voice trembled. "Raphael?"

"When Sebastian was taking over," Janus said slowly, lost to memory, to the time when Clary fell and the world broke, "the warlocks were gone. The faeries were with us. Sebastian asked the vampires and the werewolves to join him. Most of the vampires left were rounded up by Raphael Santiago, the head of the New York vampire clan, and Sebastian was in talks with him. Raphael was not pleased by what had happened to the warlocks, but he said he was the practical type. He wanted protection for his vampires. We thought we might be able to come to an arrangement. Only Sebastian found out you were sending secret information to a werewolf girl. He asked if you wanted to have fun with him, and you said you did."

Janus was surprised he even remembered that time. He'd been blind with pain back then, before Sebastian made him stop thinking of Clary so often. Sebastian had said he was pathetic and useless and *feeling*. So he'd made it stop.

"I wish I could resist killer parties," said Lily, "but I can't. This is a fully plausible scenario."

Her voice was almost absentminded. Her eyes were searching Janus's face.

"Sebastian killed you and showed Raphael what was left. Raphael said you were stupid, and it served you right. Six hours later he led every vampire he could, and some of the werewolves, out of the talks. He set the building on fire as he went. I had to pull Sebastian out from the burning rubble. Next we heard, Raphael was with Livia Blackthorn and the resistance."

"He's alive?" Lily's voice was sharp. "In your stupid, messed-up world. Raphael's alive?"

The words burst out of her mouth. "Take me to him."

Even though Janus had been expecting it, the words were shocking, so shocking that the truth fell from his own mouth without him meaning to say it. "There isn't any hope for that world. Even the sun has been blotted out."

His head ached as soon as he spoke. The pain felt like Sebastian being displeased with him, even now.

"Then bring him here," said Lily. "Please. Go back and bring him here."

Her hands were no longer shoving at him, but clinging to him, almost pleading.

"If I did," Janus ground out, "what would you do for me?"

He saw her mind working, behind her watchful black eyes. She wasn't stupid, this vampire girl.

"Depends," she snapped. "What are you going to ask me for?"

"Let's be clear," Janus said. "You'd do anything for this."

The vampire girl's sharp face softened. She liked Jace, Janus realized. She trusted him. Some part of her still thought Janus was her friend. She was underestimating him, not on guard as she should be. She didn't really think he would hurt her.

"I guess so," she said. "I guess I would." She leaned back against the alley wall. "Would it help if I told you that you were still hot?"

"Probably not," Janus said.

"Don't repeat that to the other Jace," said Lily. "He shouldn't be encouraged. You know, I think some people might find you *more* hot. Little less of a pretty boy, little more rugged thing going on. It's a trade-off."

"Most things are," Janus agreed.

"I'm not hitting on you, by the way, I'm just making observations here."

Janus shrugged. "Wouldn't do any good if you were."

"Still a one-woman man, huh?"

"Still," Janus said very quietly.

Lily was gazing at him as if she was sorry for him. As if she could know how he felt. He wanted to put out her eyes, to stop her looking at him like that, but she might be useful.

"Let's make a bargain," Janus suggested. "You do me one favor, when the time comes, without asking questions, and I will do what I can to bring Raphael to your world. It isn't going to be easy, and it will take time. You don't tell anyone you've seen me. If you do, I can always send a message back to Thule telling them to kill Raphael."

She winced.

"Do we have a deal?" Janus said.

There was a long silence. Janus could still hear the songs and bells of the Shadow Market flowing on, past this dark alley with the undead.

Then Lily said, "We have a deal."

He let Lily leave, and followed her quietly. He saw her take out her phone, as if she might call somebody and warn them. But she didn't. She put her phone back in her pocket.

It was almost funny. Janus knew no way back into that other world, but it didn't matter if this girl was smart or if she wanted to be good, because she was wild and clawing and frantic to believe him. Hope made everybody a fool.

To make people obey, all you had to do was first make sure they were desperate. Janus should know that well enough. He'd been desperate for years. *Don't repeat that to the other Jace,* Lily had said. As if Janus was planning to have any conversations with the other Jace, the one from this world, the one who'd gotten lucky. Janus didn't need to talk to him. Janus would learn everything he had to know about this world, so he could pass himself off as the other Jace.

Then he would kill this world's version of himself and take his place. Beside Clary.

It was near dawn when Mina woke crying. Tessa stirred, but Jem dropped a kiss on her bare shoulder and murmured, "I'll go, love."

Tessa had suffered pains that Jem could not, bringing Mina into the world. His wife would never lose sleep with the baby while Jem was in the house. That was Jem's privilege.

Jem crept up to Mina's room, quiet so as not to wake Kit and to let Tessa go back to sleep.

When he reached her room, though, he saw Kit was awake. Kit was already in the baby's room, with Mina in his arms.

"Hey," Kit said to the baby, speaking seriously as if to a teammate. "C'mon, do me a solid, will you, Min? You've been waking them up all week. I bet they're tired."

Mina's small face was tearstained, but she had clearly forgotten her tears before they were dry. She was smiling a gummy smile, apparently enchanted by this new experience.

"Jem always talks about how advanced you are, so how about advancing to the part where you sleep through the night?" Kit said. "I wonder if having a mom who is an immortal warlock means that you've been maturing faster than other babies."

Mina had no response for this. Kit didn't hold Mina often, though he would bend over the cradle or someone else's arms and awkwardly offer her attention when he came into a room where she was. He did give her his forefinger to hold frequently, and now that Mina could focus better, she would hold her hands out imperiously when Kit came near. Jem was sure she knew Min-Min was Kit's name for her, and Kit was the boy who held her hand.

Now she was bundled inelegantly in Kit's arms, the long white woolen blanket Catarina Loss had knitted for her trailing. Kit tripped over it as he walked the floor and stumbled. Jem tensed to lunge across the room and catch them. But Kit caught himself against the wall, though he let out a curse as he did so and promptly looked horrified and belatedly tried to cover one of Mina's ears.

"Please don't tell Jem and Tessa I said that word in front of you!" Kit exclaimed.

Mina, who clearly thought Kit was playing a game with her, gave him another sleepy smile that split her small face, then yawned like a kitten. Kit bit his lip and hummed a broken line of a song to her, several times over. Soon she was drooling against Kit's T-shirt, which had a design on it that Kit had informed Jem meant superheroes. Kit patted her on the back.

"There we go," Kit murmured, sounding proud of himself. "It's our secret."

Jem watched Kit and Mina for a little while longer, then crept back to his room, letting Kit return to his own bed believing he'd helped Jem and Tessa to rest.

Janus kept thinking of that word, "Consul," and Alec, and he decided he should survey the situation for himself. He couldn't pass himself off as Alec's *parabatai* if he didn't know about Alec's life. His father had always said that knowledge was power to be used in battle.

It was too dangerous to go to the Institute and risk someone seeing him, but Janus remembered where Magnus's loft had been. He concealed himself and watched the door until Alec emerged. It was one of the sunny spring days in New York that was better than summer, the sky full of clear light and soft breezes.

Alec was where Alec had always wanted to be: walking easily by Magnus's side. There were two children with them. One had very dark, short, crisply curling hair, and even though he was too young to bear Marks, there was still a suggestion of grace about him that said *Shadowhunter*. His small fingers were curled securely within one of Magnus's ringed hands. Magnus's other hand was tucked, with Alec's, in the pocket of Alec's ratty, unzipped hoodie. The other kid was glamoured to look like a mundane, but Janus saw beneath it to blue skin and horns. The warlock boy was up on Alec's shoulders, laughing and kicking his feet against Alec's chest.

It took Janus a moment to realize the strangest thing. Alec's chest and shoulders were broader than they had been in his world. Alec had died when he was still a boy always a little afraid to be in love.

Consul, thought Janus. *You must be so proud.*

Janus followed as they made their way to the Brooklyn Botanic Garden, where the cherry trees were blooming. Alec and Magnus seemed to be taking these kids to the cherry blossom festival.

The kids were excited. The pink clusters of flowers formed a soft avenue around them, a pink marble arch come alive, petals falling like bright confetti into their hair. The little boy on Alec's shoulders caught the petals in his hands. The trees provided plenty of cover so that Janus would not be seen.

There were *taiko* drummers under a bandstand, and people

dancing in the grass. Alec set the warlock child down, and he immediately ran into the crowd of dancers and began to strike dramatic poses. Magnus went and danced with the little kid, though Magnus's dancing did not involve any falling on his butt.

The Shadowhunter boy copied Alec, leaning against a tree with his arms folded in the same way Alec's were, until Magnus beckoned and said, "Rafe," and the boy's small surly face lit up and he ran to him. Then he held Magnus's hands and let Magnus pirouette him about, his shoes lighting up as he twirled in the dust.

Alec watched them for a while, fondly, then wandered away to buy ice creams. A couple of Downworlder teens, a young werewolf girl and a faerie boy, were waiting in the line and watched him come with nervous delight.

"It's our Consul!" said the werewolf girl.

"He's not technically ours," said the faerie boy. "He belongs to the Shadowhunters who aren't assholes. Maia is your leader and King Kieran is mine."

"I can have a Consul as well as a pack leader if I want," muttered the werewolf. "He's coming right over! What do we say?"

"I cannot lie, Michelle!" said the faerie. "You know this! You have to pretend to be cool for both of us."

Alec nodded to them, a little strained with strangers still, but trying to be friendly in a way the Alec Janus had known might not have.

Alec smiled crookedly into their silence and offered, "Hey, here for the festival?"

The faerie boy gasped out, "Yes!"

"Me too," said Alec. "Family outing. Those are my kids over there, with my husband. Over there. That's my husband."

Alec said "my husband" so proudly, as if the word was a new

and dearly prized acquisition with the shine still on it, something he wanted to show everybody.

My boyfriend, Clary had called Janus, a few times, and it had made him so happy to finally be hers, to think she might be proud he was hers. He'd been embarrassed to show how happy he was. He remembered the emotions now and they prickled like pins and needles, like dead limbs starved of blood finally beginning to wake up. And like pins and needles, they hurt.

"Oh, congratulations," Michelle the werewolf said to Alec, looking as if she might cry. "Your husband. That's so nice."

The boy nodded vigorously.

"Um, thanks," said Alec. "Nice to meet you. Enjoy the festival."

He went back to his family, where the kids hailed the ice creams with great joy. Alec slid his arms around Magnus, and they danced a little together, Alec slightly clumsy in a dance as he never was in battle, but smiling, with his eyes shut and his cheek laid against Magnus's.

The young couple wandered off with their ice creams, which were decorated with rose petals and which the faerie seemed to enjoy more than his girlfriend, chattering excitedly about the amazing experience they had just had.

Janus watched them, and when they wandered off among the trees for privacy, he let them see him.

"You're Jace Herondale," breathed the werewolf girl, obviously thrilled. "Jace Herondale *and* Alec Lightwood. This is literally the best day of my life. I can't wait to tell Mom."

"Actually," said Janus, "I'd appreciate it if you didn't tell anybody. You two are about the same age my friends and I were when we saved the world. I think I can trust you two. I think you could do great things. I'd love your help."

They looked at each other with awkward, surprised enthusiasm. "Help with what?" said the werewolf.

Janus told them. It seemed to go well at first. Their eyes were shining. They wanted so badly to be heroes. He'd wanted to be one himself, once.

The werewolf girl, who seemed to know more of Alec and Jace in this world, was nodding eagerly. The faerie boy nodded less and said very little. Janus wasn't certain of him. After he was done talking and pretended to leave, Janus swung around and quietly followed them. He could feel his Soundless rune sparking against his skin: a novel sensation after so long.

"I don't care who he is," said the faerie boy. "I don't trust him. I'm going to tell the King."

Well, win some, lose some. The important thing was knowing when to cut your losses.

Janus cut their throats and buried the two young lovers side by side under the green leaves of the springtime trees. He made sure to close their eyes and clasp the girl's hand safe in the boy's before he smoothed the soil over them, so they were sleeping peacefully together. He gave them the death he would have wanted for himself.

Mina woke early in the morning. This time Jem got to her first, before Kit or Tessa had a chance to stir. Mina smiled with surprised delight when she saw Jem's face over the side of the crib, as if she'd worried that this time he wouldn't come.

"There is never any need to worry, Mina mine," said Jem. "Silly melon."

He dressed her in the red romper with a blue rabbit on the front that Magnus had sent them, then put her in his front pack. Mina cooed excitedly as he did so. She loved an outing.

They walked together through the woods to the village. The village was very small, and there was a great bakery they often patronized. The two ladies who ran the bakery were very welcoming.

"Aw, look," he heard one of the ladies whisper to the other, quietly enough so he wouldn't have heard them if he did not still have Shadowhunter hearing. "He brought the baby again!"

Jem bought *pain au chocolat* for Kit, because he liked it, and apple-and-raisin pastries for Tessa.

"My wife doesn't like chocolate," he explained. "But my—but Kit does."

"Right, your wife's . . . nephew?" The woman's tone was friendly as well as curious.

"Nephew, cousin." Jem shrugged. "Same family. We were very glad when he agreed to come live with us."

The woman winked. "My little sister says he's a total beast."

Jem didn't think that was a very nice thing to say about Kit.

"You guys seem like such a happy couple," the woman continued, which *was* nice. "Have you been together long?"

"We've only been married a few years," said Jem. "But we had a very long engagement." He accepted the paper bag of pastries with a smile and waved Mina's dimpled hand at them. "Say bye to the kind ladies, Mina."

"So cute!" he heard the woman whisper as the door of the bakery closed behind them. "I'm dying."

"Hear that, Mina mine?" Jem murmured. "They think you're cute. They're right, of course."

Mina waved at the trees in loose uncoordinated movements, like a tiny queen accepting tribute. He took the long way through the woods, past the thatched pub where they had afternoon tea sometimes, and across the bridge so Mina could babble to the brook.

Through the shifting green leaves and radiant splashes of sunlight, Jem saw the slate roof and uneven white plaster of the small manor house that was their home.

This house, nestled on the edge of Dartmoor, had been in the Carstairs family for a long time. Jem's uncle Elias Carstairs had owned it once and lived there with his family. Out of concern for Kit, Jem and Tessa had enlisted Magnus to put up wards around the house that prevented those with ill intentions from crossing onto the property.

At the side of the house, blue-shuttered French doors hung open, showing a white-painted kitchen splashed with sunlight. Jem's family was having breakfast at a massive farmer's table. Tessa was in a white robe, and Kit was still in his superhero pajamas, and they hailed the coming of pastries with acclaim.

"Mina and I journeyed far, and have returned bearing love and baked goods."

"My adventurous Mina," said Tessa, kissing Mina's silky hair, then tipping up her face for Jem's kiss. "Are you ready to defeat evil vampires using your knowledge of technology and the train timetables, like in *Dracula*?"

"Saw that movie," said Kit.

"Read that book," Tessa shot back.

"I have no idea what you two are talking about," Jem said, on cue. "But Mina was much admired in town."

Tessa raised an eyebrow. "I'm sure she was."

"But one of the lady's sisters was unkind about Kit. Don't

make friends with her, Kit. She called you a beast."

Kit beamed. "Really? Did someone really say that? Who said that?"

"Oh, is that good?" asked Jem.

"I *have* been working out," said Kit happily to himself.

"I didn't know that was good either," Tessa confided to Jem. "Language changes so often through the years, it's hard to keep track of. Especially slang. It's fascinating, but sometimes I liked the earlier meanings of the words best."

"Yeah, well, Min has to know how people speak in this day and age," Kit said sternly.

Mina cooed and reached out her hands to him, and Kit surrendered his forefinger to her grasp. He continued to eat *pain au chocolat* with his free hand.

"You want the other kids to think you're cool, right, Min?" he asked her as she burbled agreement. "You're lucky I'm here."

Tessa swooped on Kit from behind, ruffling his golden hair with the hand not holding her pastry, on her way to get Jem coffee from the stove.

"We're all lucky you're here," she told him.

Kit bowed his head, but not before Jem saw his face flush, pleased and shy.

Once he buried the kids, Janus went back and found that Magnus and Alec had wandered in the opposite direction, farther afield from the music. Alec and the kids were playing soccer with a fluorescent pink ball. Alec, being Alec, was half playing, half patiently teaching them. Janus remembered when they were kids, how whenever he or Isabelle wasn't as good as Alec was, Alec would practice with them endlessly until they were better than Alec was himself. Every time, he would do that. Janus had forgotten, until now.

The Shadowhunter boy was good at soccer when he was concentrating, but he was constantly abandoning the game and zigzagging back to Magnus, hovering by his side like an adoring bumblebee.

Janus envisioned what Magnus had become in his world, the pitiful thing his body had been. It was odd to see Magnus whole and well, sitting under a cherry blossom tree. He was wearing buckled purple boots, skinny jeans, and a tank top that had BABE WITH THE POWER scrawled on it in pixie dust. He was leaning against the tree, cat's eyes slitted lazily, but he smiled whenever the Shadowhunter boy returned to him, and after the fifth time he made a small gesture, and the falling cherry blossoms began to circle around the boy's head, winding intricate patterns like bracelets around his arms, brushing against his plump cheeks and making him giggle.

The warlock boy was very intense about soccer, short legs pumping furiously over the grass. Eventually he seemed to become concerned Alec might win, and he picked up the ball and ran away with it, back to Magnus and the other kid.

"I won!" announced the warlock boy. "I always win."

Magnus kissed the boy on the cheek and laughed, and the sound of his laugh made a smile light on Alec's face as he jogged up to them. Janus had forgotten how much more Alec had begun to smile, once Magnus was in his life.

"I heard you lost your soccer game?" teased Magnus. "I heard the Consul is a big loser?"

Alec shrugged. "No kiss for me, I guess."

He was flirting, Janus realized. Alec hadn't lived long enough to learn how to do that, not in the confident way he was now.

"Oh, there just might be," said Magnus.

The Shadowhunter kid was still playing with the floating blossoms. The warlock kid put his ball on the ground and trotted after it as it glided gently away.

Alec leaned down, taking Magnus's pixie dust shirt in both hands to pull Magnus up toward him. Magnus's spiky head tipped back, and one of Alec's arms went around Magnus's waist.

Janus remembered another world. Alec had still been clinging to what Magnus had become, at the very last. Those strong scarred archer's hands, always swift to protect and defend, held him fast. Even in death, there seemed no way to break Alec's grip.

Janus hadn't had the chance to take Clary in his arms one last time, as Alec had with Magnus. Janus understood the choice his *parabatai* had made, the only choice he could've made with evil on his threshold and all he loved in ruins.

When Janus and Sebastian found them lying together in the rubble, Sebastian had been furious. He had wanted to capture Alec alive. Alec knew secrets about the resistance, about small pockets of hidden free humans: information Sebastian craved and that Alec had died to hide.

With a howl, Sebastian had kicked at Alec's body. The desolate lack where the *parabatai* bond had been screamed. It was one of the few times Janus was able to think, *Kill him.*

Now, in the sunlight of the park, the undergrowth crackled. Janus spun around to face the enemy, cursing himself for being distracted, for being sentimental, as Sebastian and Valentine always said he was.

"What're you doing, Uncle Jace?" asked the warlock boy, clutching his ball and clearly pleased at making a much greater discovery. His round face was smiling and curious.

Janus went still.

"Are you playing hide-and-seek?" the boy continued.

Slowly, Janus's hand moved toward his dagger.

He whispered, "Yes."

The boy darted into the bushes and put his arms around Janus's leg. Janus's hand tightened on his knife.

"I love you, Uncle Jace," the boy whispered, with a conspiratorial grin, and Janus shuddered. "Don't be sad. I won't tell where you're hiding."

Janus drew his knife. Warlocks were not safe to be around. It would be a quick, clean kill, and better for Alec, in the end.

"Max!" Alec shouted. He didn't sound concerned now, but if there was no response, he would be.

Max, thought Janus. Long ago, the youngest Lightwood. In this world Magnus was alive, so Alec was alive. Alec was the Consul, and they had children. Alec had named his son for that lost Max.

Janus let go of his knife. He let go of the boy. His hands were shaking too much to hold on to either.

Little Max darted out of the bushes with his arms outstretched, making a zooming sound as if he were an airplane, and ran back to his family. When they went home from the park, Max was still holding on to his ball, trotting at Magnus's side as Magnus sang a soft Spanish lullaby, while the Shadowhunter boy slept, drooling on Alec's shoulder.

Janus did not follow them out of the park. He stayed by the gates and watched them go.

The words of Janus's *parabatai* oath echoed in his head, worse than a death sentence. *Where thou diest, will I die, and there will I be buried.* He had not kept his oath, but he'd wanted to. Death would have been welcome. Death would have meant being with Clary.

Long ago in the other world, when Sebastian was sleeping, Janus had gone back for Alec, but the bodies had vanished. Janus hoped now that they had not been eaten by the roving, starving demons. He hoped Maryse had burned Alec and Magnus both. He wished that a kind wind had carried their ashes away, and let them stay together.

When they first moved into Cirenworth Hall, the house in England that they intended to be their family's home, Jem and Tessa had noticed how often Kit's eyes fell on the valuables they had decorated the house with.

One evening they collected up everything they could think of and placed all their most prized possessions in Kit's room, lining them up on tables and windowsills.

When Kit went into his room next, he stayed in there for some time and was absolutely quiet. Eventually Jem and Tessa tapped on his door. At his assenting mumble, they pushed open the door and looked inside. They found Kit standing in the middle of the room. He hadn't touched anything.

"What does all this mean?" Kit asked. "Do you think I'd take them and—do you want me to—?"

He sounded lost. His blue eyes fell on Tessa's first editions, on Jem's Stradivarius violin, as though they were signposts and he was trying to find his way in a terribly strange land.

Jem said, "We want you to stay, and to know that the choice

is entirely yours, and we wanted to show you something. We want you to know there is nothing in this house more precious to us than you."

Kit had stayed.

The home the Seelie Queen had given them stood on a hollow hill near bone-white sea cliffs, a hundred leagues from either Seelie or Unseelie Court, and far from any prying eye that might spy the Queen's long-lost and long-sought-for son.

Within the house, the walls flickered with shadows. As Janus came through the doorway into the dark, the shadows trembled in the wind that crept in with him.

Ash was draped over a sofa, long legs stretched out, dressed in the faerie clothes the Queen had provided. Black silk, green velvet. Nothing but the finest for her boy. Ash hadn't aged much since they had come from Thule. He still looked sixteen, which was the age Janus believed him to be. He was holding up a piece of paper to the light, studying it intently.

When he heard the door close, Ash turned his head, the white-gold gossamer-fine hair he had inherited from his father falling around his curved faerie ears, and hastily tucked the bloodstained piece of paper away into his pocket.

"What's that?" Janus asked.

"Nothing important," said Ash with a slow blink of his grass-green eyes. "You're back."

"Do you think I would have had eyes that color," Sebastian had said once, late at night when he was in one of his most melancholy moods, "if our father had not . . . done what he did, and made me what I am?"

Janus had not been able to reply. He couldn't imagine

Sebastian or his flat shark's eyes, dead as the sun and black as the eternal night in their world, as anything other than they were. When he looked in Ash's eyes, green as springtime, green as new beginning, he thought of someone else entirely.

It was hard to keep secrets from Sebastian. He always took them away. But Janus had kept that one.

"It's good to be back," Janus told Ash slowly.

He didn't like it much in Faerie, but Ash was here. He'd needed a secure place for Ash. Ash was going to change everything. Ash was the key. Nothing bad could happen to him.

Janus knew Ash wanted him to like it here more than he did. When they came here, Ash had asked the Queen, his mother, for a piano. Now the piano stood near the doors, sleek and shining darkly, reflected by all the mirrors. Janus tried not to look at it.

"You said you used to play once," Ash offered when the piano came.

Ash seemed disappointed when Janus said he no longer remembered how.

Janus had imagined Ash would be happy and safe, back with his mother, but the Queen said Ash couldn't stay at Court.

"I lost a daughter who will never return," she'd told them, thorns in her voice. "I lost a son who returned past hope. I will never risk him again. He must be kept secret and secure."

So Ash lived in this isolated house, this cliff-top palace, and Janus lived here with him. For now.

Janus didn't like the idea of abandoning Ash to live in the New York Institute. But that was where Clary was.

Wherever you are is where I want to be.

Janus needed water to wash away the bitter taste in his mouth. He went to get it, and Ash followed him. Ash's step was faerie soft and Shadowhunter trained, entirely noiseless, like having a pale shadow.

When Ash first came to Thule, Sebastian had been pleased. Sebastian had always liked the idea of blood binding someone to him. He'd seen it as a sign that he was doing everything right, that another world had delivered an heir to him, since in Thule, the Seelie Queen had died before she had ever given birth.

It pleased Sebastian's vanity that Ash resembled him. Sebastian had thought that finally here was what he had always wanted: someone like him. Sebastian embraced Ash and allowed Janus to do the same. For a while Sebastian played with Ash, tried to teach him, but Sebastian grew tired of his toys quickly and broke them.

Sebastian had not been patient with Ash for some time before the end.

Once Sebastian had been training Ash, and Ash had made a mistake. Sebastian had gone for Ash with a whip.

Sebastian's face was startled and offended when Janus moved between them and caught the lash between his hands. The whip split Janus's palms open, and blood dappled the ground.

"Why not whip him? Father did it to *me*." Sebastian's voice was the whip now. "And I'm strong. He didn't do it to you, and you were weak until I got my hands on you. I should do the best thing for my boy, shouldn't I?"

Janus was already convinced. He should drop the whip and let Sebastian hurt Ash.

But his words were racing ahead of his thoughts, as if he couldn't control them. "Of course. It's just that there are so many things for you to do. Training a boy should be the general's work, not the ruler's. You are higher than this. You know I want only to serve you and never to fail you. Let me train him, and if he isn't satisfactory, then the lash can be his guide."

He could feel Sebastian was bored with training anyway. After a moment Sebastian cast whip and boy aside and strode off. Ash watched Sebastian walk away.

"Hell of a father," Ash murmured.

"Don't talk like that," Janus ordered.

Ash's face changed when he transferred his gaze from Sebastian to Janus, lingering on Janus's bloody hands. When Ash's eyes were not so hard and guarded, he reminded Janus of Clary. It made him think of how Clary had once looked at Simon or at Luke, before Clary and Luke died and Simon disappeared. When Sebastian came for Clary's mother, Luke had tried to stand in Sebastian's way.

"I will do as you tell me," Ash offered suddenly. "Since you're going to be my teacher. You'll see. I'll make you proud."

After that, Janus trained Ash, but Janus should never have stepped in. Sebastian noted how many hours Janus spent with Ash and decided he wanted to see results from all this training.

Sebastian kept a pit of demons under the floor of Psychopomp, his favorite nightclub. It made for a nice showpiece and a convenient method of disposing of those disloyal to the Star. Sebastian ordered that Ash be given a sword and dropped into it.

Ash did not protest or struggle. He let Janus lead him forward, to the very edge of the pit. Then he stepped out into the empty air and fell.

A dark wave of demons closed over him.

Sebastian and Janus both leaned forward, Janus sick with a pain he did not understand and Sebastian smiling like a guardian angel. They watched as Ash's head broke through the wave of demons, a swimmer fighting his way to the surface in a dark sea. He rose—and rose, and rose again. He soared into the air, black wings spreading from his back.

"Ah." Sebastian sounded delighted. "So it has come to pass."

"What is it?" Janus had demanded. "What's happening to him?"

"He is becoming more," said Sebastian. "The Unseelie King worked magic upon him, and he has the blood of Lilith in him. Those are the wings of an angel—one of the fallen sort. They were always in his blood, but Thule has drawn them out of him."

Sebastian was applauding, laughing as Ash spun and flew low, slashing with his silver sword, slicing through the necks of a dozen demons at once. Ichor splashed the walls of the pit.

Janus's hands itched.

He had beaten Sebastian once, long ago, when he was someone else.

We were both trained by Valentine. But I tried harder, because I loved my father and I wanted to please him so badly. Then there was Robert and Maryse and Isabelle and Alec, always Alec, every one of them teaching me whatever they knew, so I could protect myself. Because they loved me. I was better than Sebastian. I was better.

He'd trained with Clary, too, a few times. He'd meant to teach her everything he knew, so she could always protect herself. So they could fight together. Ash was as fearless and determined as she was. Janus could teach him everything, so

Ash would always be safe. He did not know why, but it was important that Ash always be safe.

When Janus watched Ash fight, he thought that when Ash was grown, he might beat Sebastian too. He crushed the treacherous idea down, but he couldn't help smiling a small smile down at Ash.

Ash's lip curled back from his teeth. It was his father's sneer, his father's scorn, aimed at Sebastian himself. Then his green eyes passed with total withering indifference over Sebastian, and caught on Janus. Ash smiled up at him.

Janus went cold.

So did Sebastian's voice. "My father," he mused. "My sister."

"Please," Janus begged. He couldn't talk about Clary. "No. Please."

Sebastian never did have any mercy. "My father, my sister, my son. They were all mine. And yet they all wanted *you* more. Valentine's sweet boy. Clary's golden prince. Ash's guardian angel."

Nobody else ever dared speak Clary's name aloud.

"You might as well know," Sebastian said. "Nothing you feel for Ash is real. The Unseelie King gifted him with many gifts. The wings are but an outward expression of that. He also has the power to command perfect love and perfect loyalty. You have no choice but to want to protect him."

Janus froze. His heart beat slowly, thickly in his chest. It never occurred to him to doubt Sebastian. He had seen the way Annabel was with Ash. How she would have laid down on broken glass so he could walk on her.

This was why. *This* was why. Nothing Janus felt for Ash was real.

Sebastian ordered that the pit be closed. Ash flew up, straight and dark as an arrow, and knelt at the pit's edge, his sword gleaming. His wings beat softly in the still air of Thule.

"Are you angry, Jace?" Sebastian said. "That I told you the truth?"

Janus had shaken his head. "No. I exist to serve you."

It was true. Sebastian was stronger. Whatever Janus had done once, Sebastian had beaten him in the end.

"Yes." Sebastian sounded thoughtful. "You're mine. And so is the world. But the world's hollow these days, isn't it?"

The world had been hollow since Clary died. Janus had never expected to find meaning again. He thought of that later, when he bound Ash's wounds, and when they trained. If Ash had power over him, Janus thought, he didn't use it. He never ordered Janus to do anything he didn't want to do.

Ash listened to him. He was careful. He didn't defy Sebastian. He kept training. Ash was very good, but it didn't please Sebastian any longer.

Sometimes Janus caught Sebastian looking at Ash in a way Janus recognized. There was an edge and steel to that look, as if it were a dissecting knife.

One day, when Sebastian was sleeping—it was a little easier to do certain things when Sebastian was sleeping—Janus took Ash outside and talked about traveling, about going somewhere, about not upsetting his father.

Janus tried to explain, tried to work out how he could possibly explain. He couldn't say: *He wants to hurt you, and I don't.* That would be impossible. Janus and Sebastian only wanted the same things.

Janus ended up on his knees in the ashes, trying to choke

out the words. Ash did what his father had never done, and went on his knees too. He'd put his arms around Janus.

"Come with me," he said.

"I can't," Janus gasped through waves of agony. "You know I can't."

He screamed then. It felt right, doing what Sebastian wanted, it was right. He didn't know how to do anything else, and when he tried, it went wrong. It hurt too much. He kept screaming.

"Don't," Ash said. "Don't."

"Do you understand what I am trying to tell you?" Janus asked, his voice blurred. His head rang with pain and his mouth was full of blood from biting his tongue, but he was used to blood.

"Yes," Ash had whispered. "I understand. You can stop."

The next time Ash and Sebastian were together, Ash pretended indifference as usual. But Janus caught a covert look in those green eyes, as cold as any in Sebastian's. *Ash hates Sebastian now,* Janus realized, and he knew that he'd made everything worse.

He'd known Ash was doomed. But Sebastian had died instead, and now Janus and Ash were in another world. It had not been easy to get here. But it was worth it. Everything could be different here.

Janus finished his glass of water, and tried to breathe, and glanced over to where Ash stood. Ash was watching him, and Janus swept the pale hair off Ash's brow. He tried to be gentle. It always made him feel steadier, in this world and the other, to look at Ash. Sebastian's son, with Clary's green eyes. The only thing besides Sebastian Janus was allowed to love. Ash, who was beloved and still not safe, Ash, who was all Janus had.

For now.

"There's blood on your hands," Ash murmured.

Janus shrugged. "That's nothing new."

He sat at the carven oak table, where the last acorn that had ever fallen from the dead tree was set in the table's center. He laid his weary head in his arms. Once Sebastian had told Janus that Sebastian was always burning, but it was better when he had Janus, when they were burning together. Now Sebastian was dead, and Janus was still burning. Ash laid a cool hand on Janus's shoulder.

"I thought you would get better here," Ash said, his voice low. "But you're not. Are you?"

Janus lifted his head, for Ash's sake. "I will be," he promised. "Soon."

"Oh yes. I'd almost forgotten," Ash remarked, withdrawing. "When you go away and leave me."

Janus looked at him in surprise. "Why would I leave you?"

"Because you only love me because you have to," said Ash. "It's the spell. Perfect loyalty. Did you think I didn't know?"

Ash's eyes were green ice. They didn't look anything like Clary's then.

Janus went back to Magnus's, hardly knowing why he did so. He was aware it would be madness to go near the Institute, but surely this was safe. He wore all black, like the Shadowhunter he used to be. He stood concealed by the shadow of a wall near Magnus's loft, waiting for someone he knew to come out, but instead he saw light and movement behind the windows. Perhaps they were staying in this evening. It was a foggy, misty night, after all.

Then a voice coming from the other direction said, "I'll kill you, Jace Herondale."

The last time Janus had seen Simon in his world, Simon had said something similar.

Simon's face had been moon pale and sixteen years old, always sixteen years old. He'd looked like a lost child, but in that world so many were lost children.

Now Simon was walking down a street in New York. He was taller and older, his skin tanned and runed, and he was carrying groceries.

Simon wasn't a vampire, Janus realized. He was—he was a *Shadowhunter*. What had *happened* in this world?

"Yeah?" Simon said, his voice amused. "Yeah, yeah, yeah. Keep bragging, it's what you're best at. Prepare to be decimated. You are not as good at video games as you think."

He shifted his brown paper shopping bag to the crook of his elbow, his phone pressed between shoulder and ear.

"Yes, I got the cupcakes," he added. "And you're doing your job, right? Keep all the Lightwoods out of the kitchen! You can't let them touch anything."

There was a pause.

"Isabelle is the love of my life, but her seven-layer dip is like the nine circles of Hell," said Simon. "Don't tell her I said that! Are you telling her I said that literally while you are on the phone with me? You are so dead."

Simon hung up and dropped his phone in the pocket of his jeans, shaking his head. Then he let himself in through the door. He seemed to have a key. Janus sidled around to the fire escape and clambered up to the second floor. Kneeling, he peered in through the window.

Through the rain-wet glass he saw someone dancing, laughing, long black hair swirling around her shoulders. After a dazed moment, Janus realized who it was. Isabelle, alive. Isabelle, striking poses and laughing. Alec went to the window and gave her a hug, one-armed, as she showered the squirming child tucked under Alec's other arm with kisses.

Janus had been with Valentine, and then with Sebastian, longer than he had been with these, his family. Sometimes it had seemed like a sentimental dream—*more of your weakness, Jace*—that he'd ever had the Lightwoods at all. Alec, Isabelle, Max, Maryse, Robert. His family.

But what had he done to Maryse?

What he'd had to do, Janus reminded himself, clenching his hand around his sword hilt. The best thing, the right thing. He couldn't be weak.

There was brightness at the edge of Janus's vision, as there often was, taunting and tormenting, never coalescing into anything real. Except this time, it did. So many times since Clary died, Janus had swung around thinking he would see her, hoping desperately for a ghost, for a whisper, for anything but this endless darkness without her. He had to stop wishing for her, stop hoping for her, stop searching for her. He had to burn his heart out until there was nothing left but ash. No matter where he looked, she was never there.

Until now.

Now he understood why Isabelle had been striking poses.

Clary was drawing her.

She had wedged herself into a window seat opposite Isabelle, her sketchbook balanced between them, her profile outlined against the glass. This time, she did not fade away or go wrong. This time, she was real.

She'd died in his world when she was a girl, but here she was a woman. She had scars from runes on her arms, her skin was a little darker and her freckles a little lighter, and her eyes were the color of the grass that no longer grew in Thule. Her hair was twisted up into a bun at the back of her head, a few fiery tendrils escaping. She glowed like a light. She was everything.

Wherever you are is where I want to be.

He was dizzy with the yearning to hold her, overwhelmed by the urge. *Why not*, he thought for a reckless moment, though he knew he was not allowed to be reckless. He had been once. He could see himself doing it: going to her, going to them. Telling Clary everything, and resting at last, with his head on her knee.

Then *he* came into the room, and the world went black and red with furious despair.

He was all in black, as Janus was, but he was smiling: looking around easily, casually, with an absolute air of belonging. Alec smiled at him. Isabelle leaned over and poked him in the side with a painted fingernail. And Clary, Clary, his Clary—she lifted her beautiful face up to his and gave him a kiss.

He was there, the Jace from this world, and Janus hated him. Janus wanted to kill him, and he could do it. Why should he have everything, when Janus had nothing? He should have been the one to remain in this dimension. Not Jace.

The rain hit the windows and blurred those within from his sight. He strained to see a glimpse of Clary's bright hair, and could not. She was lost to him again. He was bitterly tired of her being lost. He couldn't breathe with the pain of it. He clambered down the fire escape and stumbled to the nearest alley, where it was dark, where he would be hidden, where he could scream out all the agony in his soul. He tried, but as in a nightmare, no sound came out.

Janus wanted to remember Clary's face at the window. But he could not see hers without seeing Jace's. That smooth young face, the bright head held arrogantly high, the clear golden eyes that had never seen his *parabatai* dead, the hands that had never killed Maryse and countless others. That face had never known a world blackened and ruined after the loss of Clary. That was the boy who fought on the side of the angels, all grown up. *Valentine's sweet boy. Clary's golden prince.* Janus understood the wretched, murderous jealousy in Sebastian's voice now, the jealousy of all you could never be.

Janus could never be that boy again or the man he had become.

His shuddering breaths sounded almost like sobs, but he stopped breathing when he heard her voice. Clary's. As if she was standing only a few feet away.

"How can *all* the vampires be drunk?" said Clary. "No, I mean, I understand how, Maia, I just don't know why anybody thought that would be a good idea."

There was a pause. Janus crept to the mouth of the alleyway. It still seemed impossible to believe, but she was there. Clary was standing outside, a phone pressed between her shoulder and her ear as she paced back and forth, a slim vivid shape against the darkness. She was fighting her way into a coat and trying to keep hold of an umbrella. In doing so, her stele fell to the sidewalk, unnoticed, rolling until it came to a stop against a trash can.

". . . Well, I assumed we both blamed Elliott," Clary said.

"Say no more! Simon the former Downworlder and his trusty *parabatai* are on their way to keep the peace." Clary half turned toward him. Streetlights made the raindrops caught in her hair glimmer like a radiant veil.

This was another world. There were still angels here. Janus crept from the alleyway, picking up her stele.

". . . *Who* invited a stripper called Faerie Buns?" Clary demanded into the phone.

She stepped closer to him. His hand tightened on the stele. He knew that to approach her in his current state was madness, but she was so close. . . .

"I don't even know what to say about the stripper. Bye, Maia," said Clary, shaking her head as she ended the call.

Janus took a few steps and was beside her, just outside the pool of the streetlights.

"Hey," Clary said, still distracted by her phone. "I thought you were staying behind."

She wasn't looking up at him. He swallowed and held out the stele. "I chased after you," he said, his voice sounding strange to his own ears. "You left this inside. You should have it with you."

"Oh," Clary said, taking it from him and slipping it into her coat. "Thanks. I thought it was in my pocket."

She lifted the umbrella so it sheltered him, too, and leaned slightly against him. No more fantasies, no more dreams. He knew then that none of the illusions he'd tried to fool himself with had ever even come close. Every detail had been wrong, everything in the world had been wrong, and everything about himself.

He'd been crawling across the scorching sand of the desert

where her dead body lay for years, but now there was a shimmering oasis before him. She was here. She was alive again. She was with him, and he would have suffered through every long day of every hopeless year again to touch her for a moment more.

Clary was warm, and breathing. She was staying that way, no matter what he had to do or who he had to kill to keep her safe, to keep her with him. She leaned against him with perfect trust.

A rain-bright curl brushed against Janus's shoulder, and he felt blessed, saved, though he'd failed to save her. It could all be different here.

"The vampire-and-werewolf meet 'n' greet has descended into total chaos," Clary reported, her voice indescribably sweet in his ears. "But Simon and I will get things under control. You go have a good time."

He wanted her to go on talking, to let him hold her and drink up every word, but she was waiting for him to say something. He had to say something. He knew he was being stiff and strange, and he knew from the tension in her body that she could tell something was not right, but he had no idea how to fix it, how to relax, how to be the person he once was.

His voice cracked. "I—I missed you."

She had to believe him. He had never meant any words so much.

"Aw," said Clary, her cheek against his shoulder. "Nobody but me would ever believe you're as sweet as you are."

His whisper was hoarse. "Nobody but you would ever believe I'm sweet at all."

She laughed. He'd made her laugh. It had been so many silent years since he last heard that sound. "This shouldn't take long. I told Maia that Simon and I would drop in and maybe escort a couple of the worst offenders back to the Hotel Dumort. Normally Lily would keep a handle on things, but Maia says Lily's really drunk too."

"I'll come with you." Janus breathed in the scent of her hair. "I'll keep you safe."

"No need," Clary told him. She began to draw away.

Janus held on, crushing her against him. He would not let her leave him. Not again.

She lifted her head. He glimpsed her beautiful face in a flash of moonlight followed by shadow, saw her eyes narrow. "What's wrong with you, Jace? You're acting really weird—"

No. No. You believe it's me, you know it's me, you know I'm the one who really belongs with you.

The words stuttered through Janus's mind. He wanted to quiet the unease in her voice. He wanted her to lean against him again. Her touch made the world right.

There was the sound of a van's wheels, squealing to a stop on the street outside. "That's Simon," Clary said. "Don't worry. I'll come back soon."

You will come back. But not to me.

He let her go. It took all his strength. She smiled when he did, clearly puzzled by the way he was acting. *She knows,* he thought in terror, but then he had his reward.

She stood on tiptoe and kissed him on his starving mouth. The memory of a thousand years ago came to him, kissing Clary in an alley full of rain, the feel of her wet skin, the scent of her sweat and perfume and the taste of her mouth. Her arms were around him; her body was curvier now, fuller, and the roundness of her hips under his hands and the feel of her breasts through her jacket overwhelmed his reeling senses, making him dizzy. He could scarcely breathe, but he would rather have her than air. The kiss painted every shadow gold.

She drew away, and now the expression on her face was more confused than ever. She pressed her fingers to her lips. Her eyes searched his face, even as his heart beat unevenly in his chest. He stepped back, into the deeper shadows. She was starting to guess, he thought.

"I love you," he told her. "So much. Someday you'll know how much."

"Jace," she said, and then Simon honked the horn of the van.

Clary exhaled, her breath condensing to mist. "Go have fun. You've been working too hard," she said, smiled a swift uncertain smile, and dashed away to Simon's van.

Janus crumpled as the van peeled away, falling to his knees on the drenched and dirty cement. He kissed the ground where Clary had stood. He huddled there, face pressed against the stone, shuddering on his knees.

He wouldn't be able to kill Jace easily and take his place by Clary's side. They would all know. He knew none of their jokes, the way they interacted. He had barely been able to fool Clary for a few stolen moments in the dark. Even now, she suspected him, and later on, she might ask Jace why he'd been acting so strange. . . . Janus couldn't bear to think of it. He could never fool them all in the light. Not yet.

He did not realize for some time that he was soaked to the skin, shaking with cold and rage. He hated them all. He hated Alec and Isabelle and Magnus and Simon. He hated and loved

Clary in equal measure and it was like poison in his throat. For all these years he had been tortured and they had not noticed or cared or missed him.

He would show them what that darkness could be like, one day.

The woods and the gardens were full of memories, but so was their home. Jem and Tessa had put up pictures on the stone walls, black-and-white photographs carefully preserved: of Will, of James and Lucie, who were Mina's half brother and half sister separated by a more than a century. Someday they could point out each face to Mina and tell her their names and that they would have loved her.

Memories were like love: wound and cure, both at once.

That night, they were all together in the nursery, reading Mina her bedtime story. Mina was in Tessa's lap, gumming avidly at the edge of her rubber book. Tessa finished the story and looked down at Kit, who was lying on the carpet, propped up on his elbows.

"I transformed into your mother once," Tessa told him in a low voice. "I know you never knew her."

Kit stiffened but tried to pass it off casually, as he did most things.

"Yeah, I'm still absorbing the fact that I'm literally Rosemary's baby," he remarked.

"Read that book," Tessa said with a faint smile.

"Saw that movie," returned Kit.

"I have no idea what you two are talking about," said Jem, as he usually did when they played Read that book/Saw that movie.

Later Tessa would give him the book, or Kit would cue up the movie on his laptop.

"I don't want to hurt you," Tessa said. "I know I can't replace her or make up for the loss of her. But I wanted to tell you that your mother, the lost Herondale, the descendant of the First Heir—she loved you. She never wanted to leave you. She spent her life running because she thought that was the best way to protect you. She'd always been running: it was the only way she knew. But the happiest time for her was the time when she returned to your father, and they lived together in hiding for a few years, and she had you. I don't get memories as clearly as I once did, but I can remember being her, remember holding you when you were as small as my Mina is now. I know the song she used to sing to you."

Kit scrambled up now. He sat at Tessa's feet with his head bowed as she began to sing. Jem reached for his violin. He played a tune of love and loss, of searching and finding, a melody that ran like a river beneath the bridge of his wife's voice, the melody he loved best in all the world.

"I gave my love a story that had no end. I gave my love a baby with no crying."

She sang the song of Rosemary Herondale, and Jem thought of how impossibly lucky he had been. It could all have been darkness for him, and silence, forever, until he lost hope even for what came after death. If there had been no Tessa, if he had lost her, too, if she had not been immortal—but then she would not have been who she was. That might have been part of what drew him to her first, when he was a dying boy a century and more ago, and she was the loveliest girl he'd ever seen: a girl who had traveled to him across the sea, impossible and magical and beautiful beyond stories or music, a girl who would live forever.

At last, he was no longer doomed, and she was still so lovely.

Jem played a song for Will, for all those he loved on the farthest shore, and for his wife and his baby and the boy who was safe in his keeping, here together in this warm small room at home. One day they might be parted, but they could remember this moment and this melody.

"The story that I love you," Tessa sang. *"It has no end."*

Jem believed her.

Janus visited the Seelie Queen before he went back to Ash.

"You knew my plans had no chance of succeeding," he said to her, his voice flat. "You knew that I could not pretend to be that—that arrogant fool."

"He has the arrogance of luck and being loved," said the Queen. "But would you really want all of them to love you and believe you were him? Or would you rather be loved as your own self?"

"You know what I would want," he said.

Her smile was the curve of a cat's tail. "And you can have it. Let us make new plans."

The Queen had always wanted him to stay in the house of mirrors by the sea, he realized that now. She wanted him to be Ash's guardian, Ash's guard who nobody could pass.

Janus could do that. He wanted to do that. He would help her to her heart's desire, if she would give him his. They talked for a long time. The Queen seemed pleased by the idea that they had someone in New York who would do Janus a favor. She said she could slip Lily a forgetting potion, until the time came for

Janus to collect his favor. The Queen suggested several more ideas, and then said that Ash was waiting.

The Queen was right.

This time Janus did not catch Ash by surprise. Ash met him as Janus made his way up the winding road to home.

Ash had been out flying. Janus watched as Ash landed, alighting in the long grass of the cliff by the sea. His black wings folded down against his narrow back and his broadening shoulders, and there was a bright expectancy on Ash's face that was almost like hope.

Ash had looked at his father, Sebastian, that way long ago, but it hadn't lasted. He looked at his mother, the Queen, that way, but the brightness was beginning to fade now, as Ash learned how different his mother was from his childish memories and yearnings.

Ash only had Janus, but Janus would not fail him as his parents had.

"You're back. I was watching out for you," said Ash.

"How did you know I was coming?" Janus asked.

"I didn't. I just sometimes look out to see if you might come. That's all."

Ash shrugged, but Janus didn't think his shrug was as indifferent as Ash made it seem.

"I saw Clary," Janus said quietly. "She'll be with us, one day."

"I thought . . ." Ash looked puzzled. "I thought you were going to live with her in the New York Institute."

"Plans change," said Janus.

"What's the new plan?" Ash said. "Will you stay?"

My last hope, Janus wanted to say. *I will always love you and never leave you. I knew this world must be better than ours, because you come from this one.*

"What if I did?" Janus asked Ash. "What would you say if I said I would stay with you and train you?"

Ash kicked at a pebble. "I would say that I didn't understand why," he said. "I know you know you don't have real feelings for me. You want to stay and protect me because the Dark Artifices make it so. You *have* to love me and be loyal to me. But distance makes that feeling fade. I know my mother actually loves me, in her way, because she still missed me when I was gone. But I thought that you—once you started traveling to the human world so often—"

"I didn't know that," said Janus, thinking back to Sebastian's long-ago words about Ash's power to inspire love. "That distance makes it fade."

"It does," Ash said. "So if you want to go now—"

"I don't," said Janus, a swell of warmth, like a small tide, lifting his heart. "I never felt any differently about you in the mundane world than I do when you're right next to me. You're mine."

Ash smiled. "Who else's?"

The Queen's son and Sebastian's. Lilith's blood and Valentine's and Clary's. *He was well named,* Sebastian had said once. *He was born to rule over a land turned to ash.*

Janus had seen what Sebastian had done to a world. Time to see what Ash did to this one. When Janus's plans were complete—when the world became chaos and death—Janus and Ash could both belong.

This was a second chance. When the darkness came, Janus could protect Clary. He could keep his family safe. Everybody he loved, starting with Ash.

"If I teach you to be a Shadowhunter, if I teach you to bear runes, it will hurt."

"That's okay," Ash replied. "The old Unseelie King hurt me. My father hurt me. I'm used to it."

"I don't want to hurt you," murmured Janus.

"I know," said Ash. "That's why it's okay."

Valentine had taught Janus through discipline that sometimes seemed harsh, and it had been right to teach Janus that way, but Ash was different. He was strong and smart and quick, and he would learn fast. Janus would never have to kill Ash or stand by and watch him be killed. Sebastian was dead, and Janus still breathed. Sebastian was dead, and Janus and Ash were free.

Ash hesitated. "What did you see out there? In the mundane world?"

His voice was fascinated and almost yearning. Ash had been a captive most of his life, a winged thing in a golden cage. Even now he could not go far from their home. There were too many dangers for the son of the Queen, and Ash had such a bright future ahead of him: so bright it was like the sun, impossible to contemplate. Janus shouldn't have left Ash alone, but he'd make it up to him.

Janus would do better than tell Ash hollow words. Ash must be defended. If he had to, Janus would deal with anyone who posed a threat to Ash or his plans for Ash. This new Unseelie King might be a problem. Far worse, there were rumors about a danger the Queen would not speak of, but that Janus had heard about nonetheless: the descendant of someone called the First Heir. Whoever it was, if they dared threaten Ash, if anyone ever dared threaten Ash again, Janus would hunt them down and present Ash with their heads.

The blue waves crashed against the stones, miles down from the cliff at their feet. It made Janus recall a poem about the ocean in Faerieland.

For whatsoever from one place doth fall,
Is with the tide unto an other brought:
For there is nothing lost, that may be found, if sought.

"It's a beautiful world out there," Janus answered. "I was thinking I'd wrap a bow around it and give it to you."

Soon Janus would have Clary, and Ash would have the world. They only had to wait.

Ash smiled. Behind his green eyes, a predator lurked, like a tiger half-obscured by leaves. "I'd like that," he said.

Tessa was putting Mina down for her nap. Jem lay in the long grass beneath the oak tree, with his cat curled against his chest, almost napping himself. Church pressed his flat, fuzzy face on the place where he could feel Jem's heartbeat. Jem could feel the cat's purr reverberating through his chest, as if his heart and the cat's contentment were combining to form the same song.

"It took us a long, long time to be happy," said Jem. "But here we are. I think it was worth it, don't you?"

Church purred agreement.

They were waiting, as the sun dipped lower in the sky, for Kit to stop feinting and parrying, fighting intently with nothing but air, and notice they were there.

"Oh, hey, Jem," said Kit at last, lowering his broadsword and wiping the sweat from his brow with one suntanned forearm. "Hey, bad cat."

"He's a sweet cat, really," said Jem. "You have to learn how he likes to be petted."

"I know how he likes to be petted," said Kit. "By you and no one else. That cat is waiting for the chance to literally pee in my Cheerios." He pointed the sword accusingly at Church. "I'm watching you."

Church seemed unimpressed.

They'd cleared a training ground for Kit at the bottom of the garden. It had been the first request he made, hesitantly and with many assurances that it was fine if it wasn't convenient, and Tessa had used magic and Jem a scythe to clear a space at once. Kit trained there every day.

"I saw you running laps at dawn," Jem observed.

"Wow, that's a horrible thing to say about anybody." Kit shrugged uncomfortably, as if trying to shift the weight of a burden. "I'm not . . . very naturally gifted at this Shadowhunter thing. The Blackth—other people, they were born in Institutes, raised to it, but mostly my dad taught me card tricks. I don't think demons will be impressed by my card tricks. Though they are pretty excellent."

"You don't have to be a Shadowhunter," said Jem. "I'm not one. But I was. It was what I wanted, once. I know what it looks like, when you want something so much it almost breaks you."

To fight. To be *parabatai* with Will. To kill demons and protect the innocent, to live the kind of life his parents would be proud of, when he saw them again. And the thought that carried Jem through the worst nights as he grew to manhood, to find love like his parents' love, transforming and sanctifying. He had to last, until love came.

Love had been worth the wait.

"If you're asking whether I'm working out my emotional pain through a punishing physical regimen," said Kit, "my answer is obviously a manly yes. But I was hoping time would speed up when I did, and a rock soundtrack would start up, and I would get buff via a montage like in the movies. All the superhero movies and that one boxing movie have lied to me."

"You're getting better," said Jem.

Kit grimaced. "I still get winded easily."

"When I learned to fight, I was dying from slow poison," said Jem. ". . . And I was, yes, still faster than you."

Kit laughed. His eyes were Herondale eyes, but his laugh was all his own, mischievous and cynical and a little innocent, despite that.

"Train with me," said Kit.

Jem smiled.

"What?" Kit asked anxiously. "Do you . . . not want to?"

"I said that to somebody once," said Jem. "A long time ago. He did train with me. And now I'll train you."

Kit hesitated, then said, "Will?" and Jem nodded. "Do you . . ." Kit bit his lip. "Do you still think about him a lot?"

"I loved him better than I love myself," said Jem. "I still do. I think about him every day."

Kit blinked quickly. There was pain behind his eyes, the hidden kind, the sort Will had carried along with his secrets for so many years. Jem did not know its exact meaning or shape, but he could guess.

"Whoever you have loved, and however you loved them," said Jem, "anyone you loved would be lucky."

Kit was staring at the ground again, at the dust of the training ground. *We are dust and shadows,* Will used to say.

"Yeah, well, that's a minority opinion," Kit mumbled. Then he lifted his chin, blue eyes defiant, throwing a challenge at pain. "Tessa says my mom loved me, but I never knew her. She didn't know me. My dad knew me, and he didn't care. Don't say he did. I know he didn't. But he loved my mom, apparently, so it wasn't that he couldn't love anyone. It was that he couldn't love me. And—and the—and—nobody else has, either. I wasn't enough, to stop—I wasn't enough. I've never been enough, not for anyone, and I'm trying, but I don't know if I ever will be."

Jem didn't know exactly what had happened at the Los Angeles Institute, where he and Tessa had left Kit believing he would be safe. It was clear Kit had been badly hurt, there with Emma and the Blackthorns. Jem believed the Blackthorns all had good and open hearts, but they had suffered great losses while Kit was with them, and sometimes when people were wounded they hurt others. They were all very young, and Kit had not been with them long.

Jem did know enough to see Johnny Rook must have done something truly wrong, if he'd had all Kit's life to show him that he was loved and never convinced him.

"I loved my parents," said Jem. "And they loved me."

Kit blinked. "Um, good for you."

"I had a happy childhood with them in Shanghai, the kind of childhood you should have had, the kind of childhood everyone should have. Then they were tortured and murdered in front of me, and I was tortured too, and the Shadowhunters told me I would die. I knew I would die. I could feel the poison coursing in my veins. And I remember lying curled in a cabin at the bottom of a boat, on my way to England, feeling utterly small, hollow and hopeless and miserable. I thought I might die that way, that I couldn't bear the torture of loving and losing someone, not ever again. But then . . . there was Will, and I loved him, and he loved me. If your father's heart was too little and wretched to love someone else after losing your mother, then I pity him, but I know it was his fault. None of yours."

The wind went sighing through the leaves, but it was only a soft sigh. Summer was coming, and winter would not be for a while yet.

Kit laid his sword down and walked over to the tree where Jem was sitting. He came and sat in the grass in front of Jem, as he'd sat at Tessa's feet while she told him about his mother.

"All this 'being the descendant of the First Heir' stuff," said Kit. "I don't know what to do about it, but I know I have to be ready. I think about evil faeries, and Herondales, and my dad, and I don't know how to be anything but a big mess."

Jem did not know what would come either, but he was sure of one thing. Kit would not run when danger called. Kit would stand and fight. The search for the lost Herondale, Jem refusing the Greater Demon Belial's temptations, Jem being turned away and then called back by Rosemary Herondale, had all led to this. Rosemary's child was Jem's now. It was Jem's job to teach Kit how to fight as well as he could.

"Think of the people you love," said Jem, and Kit startled. "It doesn't matter if they didn't love you back, or if they did. You keep them here."

Jem reached out and laid his hand against Kit's chest, felt it beating too swiftly beneath his palm.

"Do you want to keep them somewhere small and mean, with the walls closing in?"

Kit shook his head silently, lips pressed tight together.

"No," Jem said softly. "You won't. You choose to be yourself, your best self. You can be descended from gods and monsters. You can take the light they left you and be a lamp shining out all their light made new. You can battle the darkness. You can choose always to fight and hope. That is what it means to have a great heart. Don't be afraid of being yourself."

"But . . ." Kit fumbled for words. "I know that you and Tessa took me in because of Will. And I'm—I'm grateful, I want to—I can be like—"

His shoulders shook and Jem reached out, putting his arms around Kit. He felt Kit's muscles lock, almost straining away, then felt the moment when Kit chose to lean in and lay his head down on Jem's shoulder.

"No," Jem told him fiercely. "Don't be grateful. Where there is love, Kit," he murmured into the wild gold of his hair, "there is no need for gratitude. And I love you."

Kit shook, and nodded, once.

"Okay," Kit whispered.

Jem felt tears drop hot into the curve of his neck. He held Kit safe in his arms, until his tears were dry and they could both pretend he had not wept. He held Kit until Church growled jealously and tried to squirm in between them.

"Dumb cat," Kit muttered.

Church hissed and swiped at him. Jem gave Church a disappointed look, then stood and offered Kit a hand.

"Come inside where it's warm," Jem said. "Tomorrow, we'll start you on weights so you can learn the right balance to strike with that sword. For now I can hear Tessa and Mina. Let's go be with our family."

The doors were already standing invitingly open. As they came closer Jem could see Tessa, in a gown the same gray as her eyes, gray as the river under the bridge where she had met him year after year after year. She was laughing.

"I couldn't get Mina to sleep," she called. "She thinks you might go on an adventure without her."

Kit said, "Not today."

He went in ahead of Jem, and Mina wriggled in her mother's arms, eagerly reaching out toward them.

Jem smiled at the sight of his daughter, and paused long enough to think, *Will, my Will. You would be so proud.*

Jem went inside to his wife and his baby and his boy, to his long-awaited home. Above the low slate roof, sunset had dyed the clouds a color darker than gold. This evening the whole sky was bronze, as though to summon wicked powers.

Acknowledgments

Thank you to Cathrin Langner for fact checking, Gavin J. Grant and Emily Houk for keeping us organized, and Holly Black and Steve Berman for their cheerleading and support. Thank you also to Melissa Scott for her assistance with "Every Exquisite Thing," and to Cindy and Margaret Pon for their translation help. Our everlasting love and thanks to our friends and families.

About the Authors

CASSANDRA CLARE was born to American parents in Tehran, Iran, and spent much of her childhood traveling the world with her family. She lived in France, England, and Switzerland before she was ten years old. Since her family moved around so much, she found familiarity in books and went everywhere with a book under her arm. She spent her high school years in Los Angeles, where she used to write stories to amuse her classmates, including an epic novel called *The Beautiful Cassandra* based on the eponymous Jane Austen short story (and from which she later took her current pen name).

After college, Cassie lived in Los Angeles and New York, where she worked at various entertainment magazines and even some rather suspect tabloids. She started working on her YA novel *City of Bones* in 2004, inspired by the urban landscape of Manhattan, her favorite city.

In 2007, the first book in the Mortal Instruments series, *City of Bones*, introduced the world to Shadowhunters. The Mortal Instruments concluded in 2014 and includes *City of Ashes*, *City of Glass*, *City of Fallen Angels*, *City of Lost Souls*, and *City of Heavenly Fire*. She also created a prequel series, inspired by *A Tale of Two Cities* and set in Victorian London. This series, the Infernal Devices, follows bookworm Tessa Gray as she discovers the London Institute in *Clockwork Angel*, *Clockwork Prince*, and *Clockwork Princess*.

The sequel series to the Mortal Instruments, the Dark Artifices, where the Shadowhunters take on Los Angeles, began with *Lady Midnight*, continues with *Lord of Shadows*, and concludes with *Queen of Air and Darkness.*

Other books in the Shadowhunters series include *The Bane Chronicles*, *Tales from the Shadowhunter Academy*, *The Red Scrolls of Magic*, and *The Shadowhunter's Codex.*

Her books have more than fifty million copies in print worldwide and have been translated into more than thirty-five languages. Visit her at CassandraClare.com.

SARAH REES BRENNAN was born and raised in Ireland by the sea, where her teachers valiantly tried to make her fluent in Irish (she wants you to know it's not called Gaelic) but she chose to read books under her desk in class instead. The books most often found under her desk were Jane Austen, Margaret Mahy, Anthony Trollope, Robin McKinley, and Diana Wynne Jones, and she still loves them all today. After college she lived briefly in New York and somehow survived in spite of her habit of hitching lifts in fire engines. She began working on *The Demon's Lexicon* while doing a creative writing MA and library work in Surrey, England. Since then she has returned to Ireland to write and use as a home base for future adventures. Her Irish is still woeful, but she feels the books under the desk were worth it. Sarah is also the author of the Lynburn Legacy series and the novels *Tell the Wind and Fire* and *In Other Lands*. Follow her on Twitter at @sarahreesbrenna or visit her at sarahreesbrennan.com.

MAUREEN JOHNSON is the *New York Times* and *USA Today* bestselling author of several YA novels, including *13 Little Blue Envelopes*, *Suite Scarlett*, and *The Name of the Star.* She has also done collaborative works, such as *Let It Snow* (with

John Green and Lauren Myracle), and *The Bane Chronicles* (with Cassandra Clare and Sarah Rees Brennan). Maureen has an MFA in writing from Columbia University. She has been nominated for an Edgar Award and the Andre Norton Award, and her books appear frequently on YALSA and state awards lists. *Time* magazine has named her one of the top 140 people to follow on Twitter (@maureenjohnson). Maureen lives in New York, and online on Twitter (or at maureenjohnsonbooks.com).

KELLY LINK is the author of the collections *Stranger Things Happen*, *Magic for Beginners*, *Pretty Monsters*, and Pulitzer Prize finalist *Get in Trouble*. Her short stories have been published in *The Magazine of Fantasy & Science Fiction*, *The Best American Short Stories*, and *The O. Henry Prize Stories*. She has received a grant from the National Endowment for the Arts. She and Gavin J. Grant have coedited a number of anthologies, including multiple volumes of *The Year's Best Fantasy and Horror* and, for young adults, *Steampunk!* and *Monstrous Affections*. She is the cofounder of Small Beer Press and coedits the occasional zine *Lady Churchill's Rosebud Wristlet*.

Link (kellylink.net/@haszombiesinit) was born in Miami, Florida. She currently lives with her husband and daughter in Northampton, Massachusetts.

ROBIN WASSERMAN is a graduate of Harvard University and the author of several successful novels for young adults including the Seven Deadly Sins series, *Hacking Harvard*, the Skinned trilogy, and *The Book of Blood and Shadow*, as well as *Girls on Fire*, her first novel for adults. A recent recipient of a MacDowell fellowship, she lives in Los Angeles.